THE

BOY ROVER;

OR,

THE SMUGGLER OF THE SOUTH SEAS.

———

LONDON :

HENRY LEA, ALDINE CHAMBERS, 13, PATERNOSTER ROW.

THE BOY ROVER;

OR,

THE SMUGGLER OF THE SOUTH SEAS.

THE MAIDEN ON THE ROCK.

CHAPTER I.

THE STORM—THE WATCHER—THE FALSE LIGHT— THE DOOMED SHIP.

IT was night—night upon the ocean—and dark clouds hung like a funeral pall upon all around.

The day had been fair and bright, but the coming darkness had given unmistakeable tokens of approaching storm.

Dark clouds were rising and gathering, and the atmosphere was sultry and oppressive.

In the distance the low rumbling thunder was breaking through the clouds, and echoing from wave to cliff.

The sea was rising, and the waves were crested with a white sparkling foam.

The lightning played in the heavens, and ever and anon cast its lurid glare across the reeking waters.

It was a terrible night, and ashore the prayers of the inhabitants of the coast were offered for the souls of the poor mariners at sea.

On a steep cliff, overhanging the shingly beach, on which the waves were now breaking with mad fury and throwing their foam-bespangled crests, sat a lad of some seventeen summers, peering out into the far-off darkness of the ocean.

Motionless as a corpse, his hand shading his eyes, and his thin lips compressed tightly together, there he sat gazing steadfastly over the waters.

An hour had passed since he had first taken up his present position, but not for one moment had he taken his gaze from the spot on which he looked.

Still the storm-clouds gathered, and higher and higher dashed the waves upon the beach.

The lightning became more vivid, and the thunder louder in its intensity: large drops of rain fell; yet still motionless as a statue sat the eager watcher.

Suddenly a bright flash of forked-lightning lit up the foaming ocean, and the boy started to his feet.

"At last," he exclaimed, "my patience has been rewarded!"

With one bound he leaped from the cliff, and disappeared in the darkness.

The storm now burst forth with redoubled fury. Flash followed flash—lighting up the foam-crested billows with a phosphorescent glare—and the thunder rolled away in the distance like salvos of artillery.

It was a fearful night, and woe to the vessel that should lose her course, and approach those dangerous rocks.

For the waves dashed upon them in mad fury; and strength and skill would prove of no avail in contest with their powers.

A bright light now shone forth over the waves, and in the far off distance the white sails of a vessel were plainly discernible.

Her course was set fair for the rock-bound shore.

They had seen the beacon, and now steered their course direct for their expected haven of refuge.

But all is not gold that glitters; and the hand extended in welcome oft hides the dagger in the sleeve.

On came the fated bark, ploughing the angry waves like a thing of life.

But the storm was fast gathering in fury, and the captain saw with the eye of an experienced mariner the danger that threatened them.

It was, therefore, with a gladdened heart that he saw the bright light shining over the sea.

And the passengers hearts beat in unison with his own.

On steered the tight little craft towards the now brilliant beacon; and on, fiercer and fiercer, raged the storm.

Every sail was reefed close—not a stitch of canvas was left exposed for the wind to lay hold of—and, with anxious mien, the captain paced the deck, giving his orders in a cool collected manner.

"Breakers ahead!" suddenly rang out from the mast-head.

"Where?—away!" shouted the captain.

"On the larboard-bow," was the response.

"Helm a port!" shouted the captain.

There was a breathless suspense for a moment; and then the voice of the helmsman rang out, clear and loud—

"She will not answer her helm."

"Breakers ahead!" rang out again, clear and loud, from the mast-head. "Helm a port!—helm a port!—or we are lost!"

For a moment—and a moment only—the captain stood irresolute; then, grasping his glass and springing into the rigging, he surveyed the surrounding coast.

Long and anxious was his gaze; his face paled, and his limbs trembled, but not a word or act betrayed his fears. Leaping to her deck, he exclaimed: "Stand by with the hatchets to clear her! Men, to your duty!"

There was an awful suspense as the brave ship rushed madly on to her doom.

"Lighten her," exclaimed the captain; "throw everything overboard that can ease her."

"Aye, aye, sir," was the immediate response.

"Now she rides more easy," said the captain, as one by one the casks and bales fell over her side.

"'Bout ship!" again commanded Captain Walters. "More hands at the tiller."

Three or four men rushed up to assist the helmsman; but all in vain were their endeavours to ease her off the coast.

The first mate now approached to where the captain stood, and, placing his hand to his cap, remarked—

"Captain, I fear yon light has deceived us."

"How, sir?" asked his superior.

"I cannot help thinking that is a wrecker's beacon, luring us to destruction."

"By heaven, such a suspicion but now crossed my mind, as I perceived, by the lightning's flash, the long line of breakers on our larboard bow."

"And we are drifting towards them, sir, with a speed which threatens the destruction of our brave little craft, and every soul on board her."

"We will place our faith in Providence, Mr Murray. The wind may yet change, and bear us out seaward."

"It may!" was the laconic reply.

But Mr. Murray was too old a sailor to believe it; and Captain Walters had dared the dangerous waves too long not to doubt even his own remark.

Too well he knew the danger to which his vessel was exposed, and the fate which awaited his crew and passengers, when once within that line of foaming breakers.

Still on she went, her bows pointed direct to the seething foam; and the cheeks of the brave seamen paled as each succeeding flash showed the white line of breakers nearer and nearer to their devoted vessel.

And the passengers clung to each other in terror, and murmured a prayer to heaven for their safety.

"Hold on, for your lives!" exclaimed the captain, as a bright flash of lightning lit up the sea for a moment and revealed the dreadful breakers close under her bows.

"Hold on, and stand firm," echoed the mate, "or, by heavens, we are food for fishes!"

Scarce had the words passed his lips than the fated bark was lifted, as it were, by giant hands, high up on the crested waves, and then hurled wildly down into the vortex of the foaming water.

Every plank of the gallant little bark creaked

and groaned, as though in agony at the fearful strain upon her timbers, and every joint started and gaped.

Up again she rose, and down again, with mad fury, she plunged, whilst her beams creaked, and her joints gaped wider and wider.

The foaming waves dashed madly over her decks, and, with a thundering sound, swept back into the angry sea, carrying with them every article in their course.

Frantically did the crew and passengers of that doomed ship hold on to the rigging; for so fearful was the violence of the waves that they literally tore portions of the clothing from their persons as they rushed back into the surging waste.

Up again she rose, and for a moment steadied herself on the bosom of the waves.

"Get all ready," exclaimed the captain, "to lower the boats. Though heaven knows," he added, in a low tone, to his inferior officer, "nothing can live in such a sea as this."

"Aye, aye, sir," said an old salt, and several of the seamen instantly set about the work.

But scarce had they commenced their task when a high wave swept her decks, and carried three of the men over her sides.

A loud cry for help rose above the howling of the storm; but all on board that craft were powerless to aid them.

The angry waves dashed them forward towards the beach, and the thunder roared the requiem of three as brave fellows as ever sailed the salt waters.

On drifted the ship, into the line of foam. Up high on the crested waves she rose—then down into the valley of waters—creaking, groaning, careering, rolling, like a thing of life in agony—whilst the now pale-faced trembling crew clung to every available rope in horror and dismay.

All chance of saving her was now lost. Not a soul on board that fated ship but now saw plainly that she must be dashed to pieces; and, in the frenzy of despair, they cast their eyes eagerly around for any article that would serve to support them in the water.

The waves tore over her decks, and the water poured through her joints. Again she was lifted high up; and then, with the speed of an arrow, down she went.

There was a fearful crash—a wild piercing shriek from the women, a cry of horror from the men—and the main-mast fell, carrying with it many of its living freight over the side.

"Cut away! exclaimed Captain Walters—"strike for your lives, men—strike!"

The sailors brought their hatchets down with fearful force upon the cordage, and in a few moments the mast went over her sides.

The vessel shivered and shook; then righted herself for a moment. But it was for a moment only: for down again she went upon the rocks, crushing in her timbers, with a fearful shock, and she careened over on her side.

The waves swept over her decks, and, as one long, agonised, piercing shriek rose from that ill-fated craft, with a gurgling sound, she parted amidships, and sunk in the wild foaming waters that lashed that rock-bound shore.

Down she went, whilst the lightning flashed, as though in mockery at her fate; and the foam-crested waves leaped and sported around her, forming a winding-sheet for those who a few short hours before were full of life and hopes.

CHAPTER II.

THE SECRET CAVERN—THE MURDER ON THE ROCKS—THE CURSE.

WHEN the young watcher whom we saw seated on the cliff had disappeared from the rocks, he hurried on a distance of some hundred yards, when, taking a small tube from his pocket, he placed it to his lips, and blew a shrill sharp whistle.

In a moment another whistle answered his own, and a form, which seemed to arise from the ground, suddenly stood by his side.

"There is work to-night for the boys," he said, addressing the new comer. "The beacon must be lighted, and all hands turn out."

"All right, captain," remarked the other; "it will put them in good spirits."

And, as he spoke, he disappeared, as mysteriously as he came, in the darkness.

For a moment the other stood gazing around him, and appeared to listen eagerly; then he muttered to himself—

"Another ship doomed; more souls to perish; more homes to be made desolate! Psha!—away with all qualms of conscience! Let them die. There is music in their groans. My oath is registered, and it shall be kept. My hand shall be at the throat of all. I have sworn it, and I will keep my oath."

A bright flash of lightning at this moment lit up the spot on which he stood, and revealed an opening at his feet.

This he descended into, and, stooping low, passed through a dark passage, some twenty feet in length; and from thence into a large cave, which was dimly lighted by an oil lamp that swung from the roof.

In this cavern, which Nature herself had formed in the rocks, and which was only known to its present occupants, were several persons—all young—not one exceeding the age of twenty years; but a more determined-looking set of fellows could seldom or ever be met with at a time.

Their costume was principally that of fishermen, or persons engaged about the coast; but their occupation, we shall see, was anything but that which is known by the word "honourable."

He who had watched upon the cliff approached to the centre of the cave, and, as the light of the lamp fell upon his features, revealed a face deathly pale, a forehead high, and smoothed as polished marble. But there was an expression about the eyes and mouth that denoted a firm resolve and an unflinching courage. He was tall and well-built, and his limbs bore that sinewy development seldom seen among those to whom fresh air and healthy exercise are things to be coveted but rarely possessed.

There was something, too, commanding in his tones, as he addressed those assembled in that out-of-the-world place.

"Throw open the port-hole," he exclaimed, "and fire the beacon."

In an instant several stout boards, rudely but firmly joined together, and bedaubed so as to resemble as much as possible the stone, were drawn aside, and revealed an opening in the cavern.

Before this opening several busy hands placed a quantity of wood, and then poured over it some oil.

"Light up?" said one, addressing him we have described.

"At once," was the reply: "and to your different stations."

"Aye, aye," was the only remark to this.

In another moment the fire was burning brightly, and throwing a lurid glare over the waves, which could be seen rolling in their fury on the beach.

One by one the occupants of that subterranean retreat passed through the passage, and out into the open air.

Not a word was spoken, and each took his way in a different direction.

He who had been called "captain" was left alone.

When the echoes of the last footstep had died away, he approached the opening, and looked forth upon the sea.

For some moments he gazed intently upon the rolling billows, as they danced and leaped in the glare of the fire-light. Then he muttered—

"How wild and furious is this scene—wild as my own heart! There is music, too, in those foaming waters, that sends the life-blood coursing through my veins. It was such a night as this when he left us—when his cruel hand struck her to the earth! But she shall be avenged—aye, though seas divide us, and a life-time is spent in its consummation!"

Still far over the waters his gaze was fixed, as though there he would find the subject that lay at his heart, when a loud crash of thunder seemed to break the reverie into which he had fallen, for he started suddenly round, and walked hastily towards the passage.

Then as suddenly he halted, and taking a long Spanish clasp-knife from his pocket, opened the blade, and placed the weapon in his belt.

Once more casting his eyes around the apartment, he strode from the cave, and again made for the rock where he had been so intently watching a short time before.

The vessel was now rapidly nearing the breakers, and, seating himself on the same position he had before occupied, he watched intently the doomed ship.

Not a muscle of his face moved—not a word of hope or fear for its safety escaped him—as he saw her nearing those dangerous rocks.

But when she struck, his eye brightened, and he leaped to his feet.

But not with the intention of rendering aid—no, his mission there was not mercy.

For the passions of hell were in his heart, and his soul was filled with blood.

So young—so noble in his mien—so base, so hellish in his thoughts!

The generous qualities of manhood were eradicated from his breast, and he was actuated but by one thought—revenge.

On whom, and for what, time will show.

Scarce had the echoes of those fearful shrieks died away in the storm, when he perceived, by the light of the false beacon, several forms being hurled towards the rock on which he stood.

Plainly he could distinguish a man bearing on one arm the form of a young female, whilst with the other he buffetted the fierce waves.

Vainly he strove to save her from being dashed to pieces. A huge wave rolled in, and carried them some distance up the rock.

As it receded, the stout swimmer caught hold of a projection of the stone, and succeeded, at the sacrifice of lacerated hands, in preventing himself and companion from being carried back into the surging waters.

But here he seemed powerless to move, and, with his insensible burden, sank exhausted.

The watcher now descended from his position to the ledge of the rock on which the shipwrecked beings lay.

Intently he gazed upon them for a moment, and then, stooping down, placed his hand upon the breast of the exhausted man.

Did he seek to know if he still lived? No; his hand strayed not to ascertain the pulsation of the heart: but to discover if wealth were concealed there.

He thrust his hand into the bosom of the man's shirt, and drew forth a small canvas bag.

The shipwrecked man started to his feet as the other was about to secrete his booty about his own person.

"Villain!" he exclaimed, as he grasped the throat of the young captain. "Is your heart so callous that you can rob a man in my position?"

So sudden was the attack that for a moment the youth was staggered; but the next instant the long Spanish knife was raised above his head, and then buried up to its handle in the bosom of the shipwrecked mariner.

The hot blood spurted up over his hand, and the grasp on his throat relaxed.

"The curse of a dying man," exclaimed the sailor, "pursue you through life! Sleeping and waking may you never more know peace! May you live in misery, and die in despair!"

His head fell back. He was dead; and the young murderer thrust him over the rock into the foaming billows.

CHAPTER III.

THE LOVERS—THE ROPE.

WHEN the ill-fated ship went to pieces amid the breakers, the most fearful confusion prevailed among the panic-stricken souls who so short a time before had looked forward with fond hope and expectation to the meeting of friends so dear to them; and the thought of the kind words and cheerful smiles which would greet them after their long absence from their native land had cheered the dreary voyage and made their hearts light and buoyant.

But, alas! how oft are we doomed to disappointment when our fond desires are about to be realised; how oft the black clouds of adversity throw their dark shadow across the sunshine of joy!

Many a heart that beat high with pleasure now lie still and cold, never more to throb; and many an eye that gazed anxiously across the sea to catch the first glimpse of the white cliffs of Old Albion now was glazed and stony in the embrace of death!

To them the joys and sorrows of this world were nought; their souls had winged their flight to eternity.

Out of forty-four souls, who a short time before were full of life and health, but three had escaped Death's keen scythe.

Dashed to pieces upon the rocks, or washed out to sea by the receding waves, they had sunk beneath the billows, never more to rise.

We have seen how the brave sailor, after buffetting the furious waves, succeeded in landing his fair burden on the rock; but we have yet to follow the fortunes of another, who, when the ship struck, was carried overboard by the shock, and succeeded in grasping a portion of the wreck, which buoyed him up upon the bosom of those furious waters.

Ere the shades of evening had closed in, he had stood upon the deck, gazing towards the shore, with hope and love in his breast; his arm was encircling the waist of a fair girl, whom he was conducting to that home where the sunlight of her smile, and her innocent and loving nature, were to shed a halo of love and peace.

But the clouds gathered, and the storm burst forth, and the first shadow was cast upon their happiness.

He had stood by her side during those fearful moments, and she had clung to his bosom for help and safety.

But the fearful crash, when the keel struck upon the rocks, had severed their frantic embrace, and, as the vessel lurched over, they were precipitated at the same moment into the boiling waves.

Each, in their horror, uttered the other's name; but the angry winds carried their tones far away, and the roaring waters hissed their voices to scorn.

And the cruel waters bore them rapidly from each other. The poor girl closed her eyes, and breathed a prayer to heaven. She was fast sinking under the waves, and insensibility was stealing over her soul; but a strong arm grasped her fragile form, and she was hurried away, as the waters faded from her sight.

But he, bearing upon his frail support, breasted the raging billows with a strength and determination that showed he would struggle on whilst he had life.

It was not the frenzy of despair; but the determination to live for himself and for her.

"While there is life there is hope," he thought, as he strained his eyes to penetrate the darkness, in the hope of seeing that loved form.

But it was hope against hope.

The shadows were too dense; he could see nothing but the white-crested waves, and the now fast-fading beacon that had lured them to their doom.

With a groan of agony he struck out manfully for that light, and, with a prayer to heaven for the safety of her he sought in vain, he laid his breast upon the friendly timber, and swam with long and rapid strokes.

The spray dashed in his face and half-blinded him, and the force of the waves nearly deprived him of his breath. But still he battled on.

The light drew nearer and nearer, though fainter and fainter in its brilliancy.

He found that he was upon the rocks, and he drew himself up to save being dashed to pieces on them.

A huge wave rolled in, and threw him forward.

He stretched forth his hand to save his skull from being split by the mass of stone before him.

As he did so, his friendly raft slipped from beneath him, and his hand came in contact with a rope.

This he grasped firmly, and the receding wave left him dangling by his hand in the air.

So close was he to the fire-beacon that its warmth almost scorched his face.

But the rope! The thought instantly took possession of his mind that it had been thrown by some friendly hand.

He found that his exertions in the water had almost exhausted his strength, for his arms would scarce bear the weight of his body.

But to hang there was to enhance his weakness; to drop might cause him to fracture his limbs; or he might be carried out by the next wave: he therefore determined to climb the rope.

But this was a task of some difficulty, so weak had he become.

He put forth all the strength he could muster, and ascended. When he had got some few yards up, he placed his foot upon the rock to take breath, and, to his surprise, found the ledge sufficiently wide to stand upon. He looked round, gazed intently at the fire, and saw that it was at the mouth of an opening in the rock.

With a thankful heart, he once more grasped the rope firmly in his hands, and drew himself upwards to a level with the opening. Then, swinging himself forward, landed himself in the opening, beside the burning embers.

He saw there was a large open space beyond, and he rushed forward; but here his strength gave way, and he sank exhausted upon the floor of the cavern.

And there he lay for several minutes, scarcely able to realise his situation—his hair matted on his temples, his clothes clinging tightly to his limbs, and striking a chilling numbness to his weary frame.

His mind, too, was paralysed, and his brain bewildered; and it was not till a loud clap of thunder reverberated through the cave that he aroused himself from the lethargic stupor into which he had fallen, and started hurriedly to his feet.

With surprise and astonishment he gazed around him.

"Where am I?" he wondered. "What place can this be?"

Then he looked again and again at the various things the cave contained.

And it was filled indeed with a heterogenous mass. Barrels, chests, cordage, and articles of all descriptions, met his sight.

He walked from one end of the cavern to the other. Yet, go which way he would, still he saw nothing but piles of goods. It resembled the warehouse of a ship-chandler; for most every article that he saw was appertaining to furnishing of ships.

He looked in vain for some one to solve the mystery.

But not a living being encountered his sight. Yet there was unmistakeable evidence of human life about the place.

On a huge board, which was placed across several barrels, in the centre of the cave, were cans, drinking-horns, pipes, and all the evidences of several persons having but recently been regaling themselves. But where were they now?

He once more approached the opening where the fire, now but a few smouldering ashes, had lured the fated ship to her doom. He looked out upon the tossing waves for a moment; then turned again, with a heavy heart, to the cave.

As he did so, his eye caught the glare of a polished sheet of metal, which was placed in a slanting direction above his head. It was placed there as a reflector, and it had reflected the light of those treacherous embers over the waves.

Then he started, and a cold shiver ran through his frame.

"Heavens! I see it all now," he exclaimed aloud. "This fire is a wrecker's light, and this a wrecker's cave. They have lured us upon this treacherous coast; they have sacrificed us to their accursed longing for plunder. Oh! I see it all now. I see it all!"

He paused, irresolute, for a moment; and then,

dashing the wet locks from his forehead, he almost hissed between his teeth, in agonized tones—

"Curse them for their hellish work! Oh! that earth can produce such wretches to sacrifice innocent lives to their fiendish lust for gain. And Ellen—my poor loved Ellen—to meet such a fate through the instrumentality of these fiends!"

He buried his face in his hands, in an agony of grief and despair.

But not long thus did he remain, for, raising his head, he muttered—

"But I know their haunt! Providence has made me the instrument of their detection, and Justice shall meet them out their reward. Yes, I know their haunt—the means by which they lure so many souls to destruction! Though the waves roll mountains high, I will again breast them, that I may bring the blood-hounds of the law upon their track! Oh! Ellen, you shall be avenged—terribly avenged."

He turned again to the opening, and stretched forth his hand to clutch the rope by which he ascended, with the firm resolve of again daring the waves, and endeavouring to swim to some portion of the coast where he might obtain assistance to secure those whom he believed had been the cause of his present misery. But the rope was gone!

'Twas well for him that it was so: for, in his desperate mood, he would have rushed upon his destruction.

He gazed down upon the dashing spray; he saw that the leap would be madness, and, with clenched hands and firm-set teeth, he strode to the centre of the cave.

He listened intently; not a human sound broke the silence.

"I have escaped a watery grave," he thought, "perhaps to meet a worse fate; for, should I be discovered, they will doubtless slay me, for I know their secret haunt, and would betray them. Aye, they would slay me; for well they know that dead men tell no tales. They may shortly return with anything they may pick up from the wreck; I must endeavour to conceal myself, and wait some opportunity to escape from here. Oh! would that I had some weapon with which to defend myself; and I would sell my life dearly."

He looked anxiously around, in the hope of possessing himself with some means of defence; but nothing caught his eye.

Against the side of the cavern was a large seaman's chest: he walked towards it, and raised the lid.

He started with joy, for it contained a pair of pistols, a powder-flask, and several articles of clothing.

To possess himself of the weapons and flask was the work of a moment; and, as he was about to examine them, he heard the voices of men in conversation.

To close the lid of the box, and seek some place of concealment, rushed across his mind; but where, where to hide?

He could see no place where he was not likely to be discovered. A pleased expression broke over his face.

Advancing to the rude table, he raised one end of the board; the casks upon which it stood were empty, and minus their tops.

"This is my only chance," he muttered; "but any port in a storm."

And, as the voices sounded louder and nearer, he lifted the board high enough to give him a passage, and drew himself over the edge of the cask, and

lowered himself into its interior. Then, easing the board steadily down again into its place, he crouched into a painful attitude, and listened intently.

Scarce had he done so, when two men, staggering under a couple of heavy bales, entered the cavern.

"I'm blowed, Bill, if it ain't nearly broke my back!" exclaimed one, addressing his companion. "No little weight, and I'm cursed glad to get rid of it!"

And so saving it, let it drop from his shoulders on to the table.

"That makes two," exclaimed the other, with a grin, as he placed another bale beside its companion on the table. "This will be a good night's work, for the shore is covered with them. So come on; no skulking!"

And, with an oath, they left the cavern.

The hidden youth heard all that passed, and the blood almost stagnated at his heart as he heard the bales fall upon the board above his head. His heart sunk within him. He put forth all his strength to raise it, but was powerless to move it one inch; he felt that he was indeed doomed, and he leant back against the side of the cask in an agony of despair.

CHAPTER IV.

THE MURDERER AND HIS CAPTIVE—THE ATTEMPTED OUTRAGE—AN UNLOOKED-FOR DELIVERANCE.

LET us now return to the youthful murderer on the rock, and the poor girl who lay insensible at his feet.

When Mr. Murray, the mate of the vessel which had gone to pieces on the rocks (for he it was whose strong arms had borne the fair girl through the waves), had disappeared over the cliff into the boiling surf, the young man coolly wiped the bloody knife upon his sleeve, and replaced it in his belt; then, stooping down, he lifted the head of Ellen upon his knee, and peered into her face.

The flashes of lightning, which still continued in quick succession, revealed to his gaze the features of a damsel of some eighteen years of age, and of surpassing beauty, though the pallor of death was now upon her face, and her long glossy black curls hung wildly and matted over a neck and bosom of voluptuous symmetry.

There was a fiendish gleam in the eyes of the youth as his ravished gaze feasted upon the inanimate form of that poor girl.

And there was a demon in his heart, urging on his base passions to more unholy deeds.

He raised her, and, grasping her firmly in his strong arms, ascended to his former position.

But, powerful as he was, this was no easy task. He accomplished it, however; and, after resting a moment, commenced descending on the other side, and made his way towards the cavern.

So still did she lie in his arms, that but for the gentle rise and fall of her bosom he would have thought she was dead.

Having arrived at the entrance of the cave, he gently lowered his burden down, descended himself, then half carried and half drew her along the passage and into the cave.

Here he placed her upon the large chest out of which her lover, a few minutes before, had abstracted the pistols to defend himself in case of need. Then, seating himself on a cask which stood in close proximity to the chest, he awaited anxiously her recovery.

But her late horrible adventure had so prostrated her faculties, that it seemed she would never recover them.

After a few moments, he descended from his seat and approached the board. He selected a small flask from among the various articles, and, returning to the side of the insensible girl, placed it to her lips, and poured a portion of its contents into her mouth. He watched eagerly its effects; but still there were no signs of returning animation.

Again he applied the flask; but still the same effect.

"She had better sleep, perhaps," he muttered to himself; she will recover soon enough to know her doom."

And walking to another part of the cavern, he drew another chest to the side of the one on which Ellen reclined; then, selecting some portions of sailcloth, he rolled one piece up, into a kind of pillow, and, lifting the girl from her seat, threw them over the boxes, and laid her down upon them, placing the piece he had rolled up under her head. This business accomplished, he took a deep draught from the flask, and walked towards the opening which looked out upon the sea.

Kicking the remains of the fire out of the opening into the beach, he seized the wooden partition and drew it back into its place; and the cave now presented no appearance of having the least outlet.

"It won't do her much good," he thought, "sleeping in her wet clothes in such a place as this; but she shall have dry ones ere long; aye, and a softer bed, too; that couch is too hard for her tender flesh."

And seating himself at the table, he waited impatiently the return of his followers.

It was not long before two came in, each bearing some article washed ashore from the wreck.

Their eyes immediately rested upon the form of Ellen as she lie motionless upon her rude couch, and a smile lit up their rude features as they turned enquiringly towards their leader."

"My eye, captain, she's a spanker!" exclaimed a broad-shouldered bull-headed fellow of twenty years of age. "Enough to make a fellow's mouth water to look at."

"Yer'd better mind what you're a saying," remarked the other, "or, maybe, the captain will make your eyes water, if you make any remark till your turn comes."

"Well, that won't be long, Jim, I reckon, for the captain soon gets over his lot. Then comes Black Bill's, then Tom's, then mine."

"Silence!" exclaimed the captain, in a commanding tone. "No more of this foolery. Your turns will come in good time; but till then remember our compact. Ned Wilton, any news from the schooner?"

"None captain."

"All's right on board then? No cutter attempted to overhaul her, I suppose?"

"No; but Black Bill says he fancies there's one on the look-out."

"I've heard as much; and, as all her cargo's landed safely, I'll go aboard to-morrow, and we'll have another run."

"Well, if we can only keep it up for a year or two," said Jim—"that and the wrecker business together—we shall all be able to retire and live like gentlemen for the rest of our lives. Happy and glorious!"

"Happy!" echoed the captain.

But the word seemed to die on his lips, and his brow contracted.

Several more of the wreckers now entered, all loaded like their predecessors. Each cast a furtive glance at the poor girl, and then at the captain; but the frowns that greeted their looks warned them to hazard no remark; so, divesting themselves of their various burdens, they sat about the cave in different attitudes.

When all had returned, the captain rose from his seat, and, after commanding attention, said:

"Now, lads, I have to tell you that I think it will be wiser to put to sea. I have heard enough to-day to convince me that the cutters are on the alert. We have hitherto succeeded in cheating the revenue of its due; I hope we shall be able to do so for some time to come. Our retreat is not likely to be discovered if we are not seen in the vicinity; and I do not think there is a traitor amongst us who would tell the secret. Nay, I am sure there is not; for it would not be worth while, as there is not one of us but is a branded felon. There lies our greatest security; for each has a hold upon his fellow, and the law has a hold upon us all. Besides, I have a another motive than business in once more putting to sea. Therefore, you will all at once take your departure for the schooner, except Jim and Ned, who will remain here on guard, and they, together with myself and yon maiden, will embark in the morning. Tell Black Bill to have everything in readiness for a cruise, and that nothing will remain but to weigh anchor and bid farewell for a time to the shores of Old England; and likewise tell him to see that Wild Madge has the cabin prepared for a lady-passenger. That is all I have to say till I rejoin you in the morning."

Without a word, all there assembled, save Ned and Jim, left the cave, and started for their mission. These two worthies stood awaiting any further orders of their leaders

"You, Ned," said the captain, "after a time, will see that all is secure before our departure, lest any curious person should pry into our warehouse; but, for the present, one of you will keep guard at the entrance to the passage, the other at the coast. Should I need your presence, you will know the signals. To your posts!"

"Aye, aye, captain," replied both the men, as they departed—Jim poking his tongue in his cheek, and twisting his eye round at his companion with a comical leer.

Ned dug his elbow into the ribs of his mate, as a sort of acknowledgment that he perfectly understood the other's meaning.

When the last echo of their footsteps had died away, the youthful captain again rose from his seat, and approached the side of the insensible girl.

He leant over the rigid form, and gazed intently, yet anxiously, at those still rigid features, and a bitter smile of triumph curled his lip, while the hot passionate blood mounted to his hitherto pale cheeks, as his lustful loving gaze dwelt upon that swan-like neck and exquisitely moulded bust.

Sleep on, fair Ellen! Better that thy sleep be that of death, than awake to the terrible reality of thy position! Better, far better, indeed, had it been for thee had thy graceful form have sunk beneath the heaving billows, than that the arms of the brave sailor had borne thee to that rock!

For the serpent hath thee in her coils, and her sting is death.

Thus, for the space of an hour, did the poor girl remain in her lethargic stupor, and her companion sat eagerly watching for the first signs of recovery.

They came at last.

A sigh broke from the hitherto silent form, and

her lips breathed the words, "Charles, dear Charles!"

The eyes of the eager watcher glistened, and he bent his head low down, till his face almost touched her cheeks.

Gradually her eyelids unclosed; the death-like pallor of her face gave place to a hectic flush; she stared wildly for a moment, then started from her rude couch with a loud shriek.

For a moment she gazed abstractedly around her; then, placing her hand to her head, staggered, and would have fallen had not the young captain caught her in his arms.

With bewildered and half-affrighted looks she gazed upon his features; then, struggling to release herself from the arms which encircled her form, she almost shrieked, "Where am I? Oh! where am I? You are not Charles; no, no, you are not him! This place! Oh, God! I recollect all now: the storm, the ship on the rocks, the wreck, the foaming waters, and Charles! Charles, where are you?"

And, in an agony of horror, she buried her face in her hands, while scalding tears paced each other rapidly down her cheeks.

If that poor girl's beauty had charmed the heart of the young captain when her cheeks were pale, and her form rigid in insensibility, now that the crimson blood had mounted to her temples, and her bosom rose and fell with the violence of her emotions, that passion was enhanced threefold in his breast, and he impulsively strained the weeping girl to his heart, as the hot blood coursed like molten lead through his veins.

But grief so violent must have an end, and the heart-breaking sobs of the poor girl were succeeded by long-drawn sighs.

"Where am I?" she again asked. "What place is this? How came I here?"

"Give not way so," exclaimed the young captain; "you are safe. I discovered you on the rocks, and brought you hither."

As the tones of his voice fell upon her ears, a slight shiver ran through her frame. Not that his tones were harsh or grating; but an instinctive feeling of dread took possession of her soul.

Involuntarily, she endeavoured to free herself from his embrace; but the arms of the young man grasped her far more tightly, while she could feel his hot breath upon her cheek, and his heart throb violently against her bosom.

That undefined feeling of dread for which it is almost impossible to account seized upon her heart; and, as the deep flush of maiden modesty suffused her neck and shoulders, a tremor of horror ran through her frame, and a cold perspiration broke out upon her temples.

She struggled to free herself from the arms that encircled her; but in vain; his grasp, at each fresh endeavour, only became the more tenacious.

Turning her tearful eyes full upon his face, she exclaimed, in imploring accents:

"Why have you brought me to this strange place?"

"Because it was the nearest to that where you were cast ashore."

"Oh! pardon me," she said, "if I do you wrong; but this wild place frightens me. You have not saved me from death to add to my sufferings? Oh! release me; let me depart from hence to some more genial place."

"Where would you go?" he asked.

"I know not," she replied. "Anywhere from here; anywhere to seek for one dearer to me than mine own existence."

The young captain gave a slight start as she said this. The thought flashed upon his mind that the man he had slain upon the rock was perhaps him she would seek; and, in a moment, he replied:

"Your search would be useless; 'tis seldom that the sea gives up its dead."

"Oh, heaven! has he not escaped?" she cried, in agony. "Have the cruel waves torn him from me, and left me to mourn in sorrow and anguish his untimely end?"

"'Tis useless to mourn for that which is irretrievably lost," was the cool reply. "Better be grateful that you yourself are safe, when all besides have perished."

The young girl looked steadfastly at him, and asked:

"Have you never mourned for a loved one?--- never grieved when the cruel hand of fate has struck some dear friend from your side?"

There was a pause for a moment, and then he replied·

"Never."

"Then you have never known sorrow," said Ellen, as a sigh rose to her lips, and the tears again started to her eyes.

In a moment his brow became black as midnight.

"Never know sorrow!" he exclaimed, in passionate tones. "It has made me what I am; it has sapped up the well-springs of my heart, and planted in my bosom a hatred to mankind which nothing can eradicate. It has turned the stream of every generous impulse awry, and has grafted in the heart of a generous youth the passions of a fiend!"

Ellen listened with affrighted soul to these words, and again endeavoured to free herself from his grasp.

Scarce knowing what to say, she exclaimed, "Pray release me; I am stronger now, and need not your kind support."

A sarcastic smile played around the mouth of the youth as she spoke, and, pressing her tighter to his breast, he said:

"Doubtless; but I prefer to hold you in these arms; to feel the beating of your heart against my breast; to gaze into those eyes; to press the velvet softness of those cheeks with my own unhallowed lips; to bask in the sunshine of that beauty which nature has given you; to revel in thy charms, and to live in the happiness of thy caresses!"

Ellen trembled as the words smote her ears, and frantically she struggled to release herself from him.

"O! God," she exclaimed, "why am I doomed to these insults? Oh! if you have one spark of mercy in your heart, release me, and let me hence. Oh! why was I saved from the terrible fate that assailed me to be thus outraged? Why did the waves give me up to be thus tortured? Let go your hold; have mercy, as you hope for it hereafter!"

"Ha, ha!" he laughed, coarsely; "mercy is dead in this heart for ever. I have sued for mercy, but it was denied me. As well might you ask this rock to turn to gold as sue this black and seried heart of mine to feel one spark of mercy. That feeling is dead for ever in this breast; it is callous to every feeling of humanity; lost to every impulse of kindness; dead to every hope. I live but for revenge; my hand is at the throat of all; and heaven's curses are upon my soul!"

"Oh! heaven, help me---save me!"

"You plead in vain! I have saved you but for my own desires. This hand would have thrust you back into the boiling surf, but that I had motives more fierce to urge me to save you. This I have done; and now I claim my reward."

ELLEN PROTECTING CHARLES FROM THE ROVER'S VENGEANCE.

"Oh, heavens!" she exclaimed, still struggling to release herself. "If your heart is so callous to my sufferings, will not the memory of a sister, a mother —"

"Hold!' he almost shrieked, whilst his hand grasped her wrist as in a vice. "If there is one word could urge me on to greater crimes, it is that word, "mother." I would spare woman the misery I would inflict upon you but for the recollection of a mother's wrongs. Had there been one soft spot in my breast, that word had hardened it to stone; it is the watchword to your ruin, and your own lips have confirmed your doom."

Pale, breathless, and exhausted with her vain struggles to free herself, she gasped forth again:

"Mercy, mercy!"

"Ha, ha!" he laughed, scornfully, whilst the veins upon his forehead stood out prominently, like blue cords upon a polished marble. "You plead in vain; you plead in vain."

And, as he spoke, he forced her towards the rude couch on which she had been reclining.

Again she renewed her frantic struggles to release herself; and, as she seized his hand in her endeavours, she shrieked out:

"Away, away!" See, there is blood upon your hands, as well as on your soul!"

"Ha!" he exclaimed in brutal tones, "it is your lover's."

Wild and piercing was the shriek that echoed

2

through the cavern, as, with almost superhuman strength, she grasped him by the throat.

"Villain! murderer! man or devil! who art thou?"

"Hear and tremble! I am the BOY ROVER, THE SMUGGLER OF THE SOUTH SEAS, captain of the "Venomed Snake," whose trail is blood, and whose sting is death. Aye, I am he---the terror of the main, the dread of everyone, and the fear of mankind."

"And a coward," was the bold reply, "whose base heart can degrade his brute strength, and debase the man, by outraging a defenceless woman. Shame upon your boasted power! I despise it. In heaven do I place my trust. Back, villain! There is poison in the very air you breathe; contamination in your touch. Back! I say; for I scorn, contemn, and loathe thee."

Stung to madness by her taunts, he seized her roughly in his arms, and bore her to the couch. Vain and frantic were her endeavours to release herself.

Down upon that rude couch he forced her; and it required all his brute strength to accomplish this, so fearfully did she struggle. Her hands were lacerated, and her strength was deserting her; she was fast losing consciousness, and in another minute the villain would triumph. She felt his hot breath upon her cheek, and she shrieked in horror. There was a loud report; a fearful crash; a cry of pain! The ruffian's grip relaxed; and her head sank back as the Boy Rover fell heavily to the ground.

CHAPTER V.

THE CONCEALED LOVER—THE MYSTERY— WOMAN'S FAITH.

WHEN Charles Lawson (for such was the name of the young sailor whom we last saw ensconce himself in one of the casks which formed the supports of the rude table of the cave) found that all attempts were unavailing to raise the heavy weight placed above his head, he almost gave way to despair. He felt that escape from the cave without discovery was now impossible; and bitterly did he regret that he had not trusted to his own courage to meet the men whose voices he had heard in conversation, and stand his chance of escape.

But, after a few moments' calm reflection, he came to the decision that all regrets were useless, and he must now endeavour to devise some means by which he could liberate himself from his confinement.

Certain it is, he thought, that there were other means of entering this cave than by the opening through which he had gained admittance; and, therefore, he felt that if he could release himself from his present uncomfortable situation, he would soon be able to find his way from the cave, and to liberty.

He tried to think calmly, but his mind would wander to the fair girl who had been parted from him by the waves, and the anxiety as to her fate kept his brain in such a whirl of excitement that he could not conjure up to his mind any means by which he could accomplish his purpose.

Thus, bewildered by anxiety for her and liberty for himself, it was with feelings of horror and joy combined that he heard the conversation between the Boy Rover and his followers.

With ears glued, as it were, to the side of that barrel, did he listen to every word that passed, and his heart beat against his breast as though it would force itself from its tenement, as he breathlessly listened for one sound of that fair girl's voice.

But, after the men had left the cave, not a sound broke the stillness, and he would have believed the cave to have been deserted by all but himself had he not plainly heard the last words of the captain.

Painful, indeed, was that silence to him; for it conjured up to his mind the most dismal forebodings. He could plainly understand the significant words he had heard, and his imagination pictured vividly to his mind the fair and lovely Ellen outraged within his very presence, and himself powerless to aid her.

For, although he had no means of telling that it was the fond idol of his heart who had fallen into the hands of those ruthless wreckers, still that inward voice assured him that it was her, and not all the arguments he could bring forward could convince him to the contrary.

What, then, must have been the misery of those anxious moments as he listened for the first sound of her voice?

And it came at last—came upon his ears in tones of agony—which struck deep into his soul, with the poignancy of a barbed arrow.

His generous heart bounded with joy at the knowledge that she had been saved from a watery grave; but it almost died within him when he recollected to what a fearful fate she was now consigned.

Better that she should lie a corpse at the bottom of the boundless ocean than live to endure the horrible tortures and meet the degrading fate intended for her by that ruthless band of ruffians, to whom woman's sufferings were sport, and woman's virtue a thing to be violated at pleasure.

Who, then, can imagine the fearful horror of that imprisoned lad as he listened to the interview between the Boy Rover and his lovely captive? Who can describe the fearful agony of his mind when he heard the cruel words of the young smuggler? And who can pourtray the feelings of his breast at the determined struggles of that girl in defence of her honour?"

Worked up to a desperation maddening in its intensity, he endeavoured to force the staves of the cask; but too firmly were they bound by their iron girders. Cold drops of perspiration broke out upon his brow, and his brain whirled with the intensity of his sufferings. Then his heart would sink within him, and he would give way to despair; but only to arouse himself to redoubled energy as he heard the Rover's words, and could judge, by the struggles going on, of the critical moment which had arrived.

Summoning all his strength for a final effort, he forced his knees against the side of the cask, and, pressing his head and hands against the board, strove, with almost superhuman strength, to raise it.

It yielded but an inch; but, through the opening thus made, he saw all that was going on: he saw that fair girl struggling and battling in defence of her honour; he saw that powerful lad, with brutal violence, thrusting her back upon the couch; and he saw the look of mingled misery, horror, and despair upon the features of the woman he so fondly loved.

He thrust the barrel of one of the pistols into the opening between the board and the cask; and, as Ellen shrieked aloud in her agony, he pulled the trigger. He heard the report as it rang, like a clap of thunder, around that stone apartment; he saw the villain's hold on that fair girl's form relax, and, as the Boy Rover fell to the earth, with a burst of gratitude, he exclaimed:

"Thank God, I have saved her!"

And, with this burst of gratitude to heaven, he sank backwards into his small prison, faint and almost powerless from his almost superhuman exertions.

He left the barrel of the pistol firmly wedged between the cask and the board, and thereby left himself an opening through which he could observe all that took place. Besides, he thought it would not be politic to give himself the chance of having again to lift the heavy weight which had so fearfully tried his strength.

He did not doubt but that the report of the weapon would be heard by either one or other of the men who were on the watch, and, with a beating heart, he awaited their coming.

He had before dreaded discovery in that cave; but now he felt that his chance of life was of little value; for, had they been inclined to show him mercy, he could not expect that now at their hands, since he had attempted the life of their captain.

It was not long ere Ned and Jim entered, which they did hurriedly.

They had heard the report of the pistol, and imagined that their captain had taken summary vengeance on the poor girl, for some reason or another.

But when they saw the Boy Rover lying prostrate upon the ground, they turned an enquiring look upon each other. Surprise seemed absolutely to deprive them of speech.

Ned was the first to break the silence, which he did by saying:

"Well, I'm blowed!"

"So am I," returned Jim.

And then they looked at each other; then at the captain; then at the girl; and then at each other again.

It was evident that there was a mystery, which neither could solve; and so they gazed from those prostrate forms into each other's face, till they both exclaimed again, simultaneously:

"Well, I'm blowed!"

There was another pause—a few moments' duration: and then Ned, stooping down, raised the head of the Boy Rover on his knee, and peered into his face.

There was a thin streak of blood on his left cheek; and his face was otherwise deathly pale.

"Shot, by Davy!" he exclaimed.

"Then that gal's done it," said Jim; "and yet she don't seem to have come to yet. But where's the pistol?"

Don't know," was the answer.

"Then why don't you look for it? It couldn't have been done with a pop-gun."

"Well, I don't suppose it was. But here—just pour some of this down his throat, and see if that won't wake him up."

Jim took the flask, which still contained some brandy, from the table, and gave it to Ned, who immediately commenced to pour some of the spirit down the throat of the insensible boy.

"There's one thing to say," said Ned, "if it don't bring him up again, it won't do him much harm. But I'm blowed if I think that ere gal did it; I don't believe she's got strength enough in her to pull a trigger."

"It's a rum go, that's all I knows; and I don't think he's such a fool as to shoot himself."

"Don't 'now," replied Ned; "he's such a rum chap at times."

"Well, he is," said the other, looking about in the hopes of discovering the weapon; "but, if that gal did it, she's swallowed the pistol, so as there should be no evidence against her—that's all I got to say."

And so saying, he approached the couch, and thrust his hand down by the side of Ellen to feel for the weapons.

Slowly the Boy Rover's eyelids opened, and he gazed in bewilderment from the face of one to the face of the other.

"How are you now, captain?" asked Ned. "Here, take another pull at this; it will revive you."

And again he placed the flask to his mouth.

"Take it away!" exclaimed the Boy Rover, as with one bound he leapt to his feet.

"What's been the matter, captain?" asked Jim.

The youth gazed from one to the other, with a half-surprised, half-doubting look; then placing his hand to his head, and withdrawing it, he perceived it was covered with blood.

"Well, captain," remarked Ned, "I rather think you've had a narrow squeak; but it ain't done for you, that's certain."

"How did it happen, captain?" asked Jim.

Still the Boy Rover gazed intently into their eyes, with a look of doubt upon his face.

"Look you," he said, at length, "if either of you want to get rid of me, say so, and strike before my face."

It was Ned and Jim who now looked doubtfully at the captain.

"You ain't quite right yet," said Ned. "Here, take another pull; it'll do you good."

And again he proffered the flask.

But the Boy Rover struck it fiercely from his hand.

"What!" he exclaimed, savagely—"finding that the bullet has failed in its mission, you would now finish your work by poison? Speak—is it so?"

If Ned and Jim were surprised before, they were doubly so now; and, after exchanging glances with each other, and ominously shaking their heads, Ned exclaimed:

"Quite off his chump—quite!"

To this opinion Jim nodded his thorough conviction.

"Which of you," demanded the captain, "fired that shot?"

"Which of us?" echoed Ned.

"Yes."

"Why, neither," said Jim.

"Who did it, then?"

"That's just what we want to know," said Jim. "It wasn't the gal—was it?"

"The girl!" said the captain. "No."

"Then it must have been yourself," said Jim, "a trying to commit fellow-de-sea."

The eyes of the boy captain were fixed piercingly upon the features of his two followers: he was trying to read there the mystery of that shot which had so nearly deprived him of life, and sent to account for those sins for which he would surely have to answer.

But he could trace nothing in the looks and manners of these men, and he seated himself on the edge of the couch, surprised and puzzled in the extreme.

"Which of you," he said, after a pause, "was on watch at the mouth of the cave?"

"I was," said Ned.

"Who passed you?"

"Nobody."

"Did you desert your post for a moment? Speak the truth; and, if you did, I'll forgive you."

"I wish I may die, captain, if I did!" exclaimed the man, in the most emphatic tones.

"It is strange," said the Boy Rover, musingly. "That I have been shot at, there is the proof," he added, as he placed his hand to his face, and withdrew it covered with blood.

"There ain't no mistake about that," remarked Jim, "because we heard the report; and that's how we came to leave our posts."

"Have you searched the cave?"

"Well, we can see there's nobody here but ourselves and the gal; and if she didn't do it, and you didn't do it, then I'm blowed if it mustn't have been a ghost!" said Ned.

"Fool!" exclaimed the Boy Rover, "that pistol was fired by human hands. Some one must have gained admittance. But how—how?"

"I know a mouse couldn't have passed me," said Ned, without my seeing it; so, if anybody got in here, they must have come by some other way than the passage."

"There is but one other," said the captain— "the opening to the sea—and that I closed myself. There is a mystery in this I am determined to fathom; and when I have fathomed it, woe to him who fired that shot!"

Ellen now gave signs of recovery; and, perceiving this, the Boy Rover ordered the two men once more to their posts.

He was at a loss to understand the events of the last half hour, but he felt convinced in his own mind that both Ned and Jim were innocent of the attempt upon his life.

Could that girl, unseen by him, have perpetrated the deed? That could not be; for was she not firmly pinioned by his arms?"

He could not fathom it, and he therefore gave it up for the present, at all events, and turned to the now recovering girl.

His wound was not a dangerous one; the bullet had glanced along his cheek, and grazed the side of his temple; but it had stunned him for the time, as we have seen, and the only evil effect was a violent headache. Had the position of his head been once further, either way, the career of the Boy Rover would have been ended.

With returning consciousness came returning misery; and no sooner did the glance of poor Ellen rest upon the form of the Boy Rover than with one bound she sprang from the couch, and stood in the centre of the cave.

She feared that he would again endeavour to effect his purpose; and once more she summoned both her wits and her strength to her aid.

She resolved to meet death rather than dishonour, and she prepared herself for any emergency that might happen.

And thus she stood, like a beautiful tiger at bay, awaiting the first movement of the hunter.

Oh! had she but known that her lover was concealed beneath that rude table, and that two shining barrels were ready to belch forth their deadly fire (for he had placed the still charged pistol in that small crevice, reloaded the one which he had fired, and returned it to its former position), how her heart would have leaped for joy, and, instead of awaiting the assault, would have almost felt inclined to become the assailant.

With a woman's spirit, she would have avenged a woman's wrongs.

But the boy captain had no further intention of molesting her that night. He had resolved that she should fall a victim to his unholy passions; but for the present she was safe.

His first assault had ended in defeat; but in the second he resolved to win the victory.

"You need have no fear of me," he exclaimed: "for the present you are safe. To-night you may rest in peace; but I have resolved you shall yet fall. Your fiery spirit, and bold resistance, has strengthened the resolve. Think to-night how vain is that resistance, and prepare to-morrow to meet your doom."

"Villain!—there is a God above us, who never turns a deaf ear to the oppressed. He will shield the weak against the strong, and protect the defenceless in the hour of need."

"Ha, ha, ha!" laughed the boy captain, scornfully. "Put your trust in heaven; but, spite of all, you shall fall."

"Scoffer!" she exclaimed, "already has it sent me aid, and when needed will do so again."

The Boy Rover started at these words. He was not superstitious, but the mystery of the bullet which grazed his cheek, and the words of the young girl, uttered in that firm self-convinced tone, set the mind of that blood-stained youth wondering whether heaven did send aid to the virtuous and oppressed.

Sure it is that Providence, in its own good time, punishes the guilty. Vice may triumph for awhile; but, in the end, innocence and virtue will rise upon its downfall.

Finding that Ellen did not attempt to move, and still watched his every movement with suspicion, he said:

"I have promised not to molest you again to-night, and I will keep my word. This rude cave is ill-suited to your company; but to-morrow's sun shall see you better provided for. In the cabin of the 'Venomed Snake' you will meet with every luxury that you can hope for. There you will find your every wish supplied—your every command obeyed. There you shall remain mistress of all; and the only return I ask is your love."

Ellen listened patiently till he had done; and then her tall handsome form was drawn up to its full height, and, with flashing eyes and scornfully curled lip, she replied:

"I have listened to your insults, and if I have not interrupted your speech, it was because contempt held me powerless to speak. Is it possible that one can be so lost to all respect for the feelings of a poor unhappy girl as to insult her misery, and enhance her sufferings, by the offer of such a honour? Do you think that the comforts and luxuries, as you term them, of a rover's cabin, can compensate me for the loss of friends and honour? No, though you were to lay the wealth of the world at my feet, still would I scorn you! Here I stand, a poor weak and defenceless girl, without a friend to aid me in my sufferings; but, with my trust in Him who helps the widow and the fatherless, I will resist to the last your infamous designs: while one spark of life remains in this weak frame I will battle in defence of that jewel dearer to woman than her very existence. Rather would I dash my brains out at your feet than that you should triumph over my virtue.

hold my honour dearer than life; therefore will I freely, freely sacrifice my life in its defence."

Proud and defiant was the demeanour of that fair girl as she gave utterance to those words; and the tones of her voice carried to the ears of the Boy Rover the conviction of her determination to resist him to the last.

Little did he dream of the heroic courage to be found in woman when driven to despair; little did he know how fixed and unflinching is woman's resolve!

He had imagined that, perhaps, the prospect of meeting with every luxury on board his bark would have tempted her to look more favourably upon him. But he was undeceived. He could now see that her abhorrence of him was equally as great as before he spoke of his vessel and its comforts; and, with ill-suppressed rage, he returned:

"I will humble your proud spirit yet. I have marked you out for my own, and you shall yet submit. You have braved me, but as yet you know not my power. You shall fall—aye, fall at my feet in shame—and that virtue you so much prize shall remain but a memory of the past."

"Liar!" she almost shrieked.

"And no power on earth shall save you," he exclaimed, as his face reddened with passion. "You have scorned me, but you shall yet find that the Boy Rover will triumph—aye, triumph."

And, casting a look upon her full of hate, he turned and rapidly left the cavern, leaving Ellen standing in its centre, her bosom heaving violently, with feelings of scorn and indignation.

And thus she stood, till the last echoes of his footsteps died away; then, approaching the couch, she sank down on her knees beside it, and, burying her face in her hands, burst into tears.

CHAPTER VI.

WITH feelings better to be imagined than described Charles Lawson had heard and seen all that had passed; and often, indeed, did his fingers stray to the trigger of one or the other of the pistols, and as often did he withdraw his hand as he thought that the second shot might prove more fatal to himself than the first had done.

True it was that he might succeed in depriving the world of the presence of a ruffian who was a disgrace to humanity; but then, should he be discovered and slain, who would protect that poor girl.

Better, he thought, deprive himself of the pleasure of shooting the villain so long as he attempted no further violence to Ellen, and trust to something to turn up to release him from his present confinement and giving him a chance of effecting the escape of both.

It was with a feeling of joy, therefore, that he saw the Boy Rover stride from the cave.

He listened intently for a few moments and then finding that he did not return, he placed his hands to his mouth so as to guide his voice towards the couch and called out in a loud whisper:

"Ellen!"

But the poor girl was so overwhelmed with grief that she did not hear him.

Again he repeated her name, but still she heard him not.

Once more he essayed to speak, and this time in a louder tone.

"Ellen—dear Ellen!"

The young girl raised her head and looked around in bewildered amazement, then heaving a heavy sigh, once more buried her face in her hands.

In an agony of feeling, he once more called out:

"Ellen, Ellen, fear not! It is me—Charles."

With a suppressed scream she started up, and gazed, half-frightened, around the cave.

"That voice!" she gasped. "Merciful heavens! —there is no one there; and yet I thought I heard his voice."

"Ellen, Ellen!" was again repeated.

She clasped her forehead, and staggered towards the rude table, as she muttered:

"Oh God! is this madness that is seizing upon me? Have the sufferings that I have endured turned my brain?"

"No, dear Ellen, you are not mad," exclaimed the young man. "'Tis me—Charles—myself. Fear not; I am near you; but I cannot come to your side—I am imprisoned."

"Where,—where?" she almost shrieked.

"Hush, hush!" was the reply. "Here, beneath this rude table. Speak low; here, here!"

With a cry of joy she stooped and looked beneath the board.

"Where?" she again asked; but this time in a low tone of voice.

"In this cask, dear Ellen, powerless to move from the weight above me."

"Oh! Heaven, I thank thee," she murmured; "for thou hast not deserted me in this the hour of misery."

"Ellen," said the young man, "look around the cave, and see if you can find anything which you can insert between the board and this cask, and thus assist me to move the great weight. Be silent; let not a sound reach the ears of those cruel wretches, or we are lost."

Oh! with what anxiety did she look for something to assist in moving that board. For some moments she was unsuccessful; but at the farther end of the cave was a piece of plank, about four feet in length. This she seized eagerly, and returned to the table.

The eyes of the imprisoned youth watched her every movement, with the utmost anxiety.

"Stoop down," he said.

She did so.

"Look," he added, "the board is raised about an inch from the top of the cask. Place the end of that plank in the crevice; then bear all your strength upon the other end."

She forced one end of the plank into the crevice, and leant her whole weight on the other end, as Charles had bidden her; whilst he, at the same time, exerted all his strength to assist in raising the board.

Their united exertions were successful, and the board moved slowly along the top of the cask till it left about one-third of its circumference bare.

With a cry of joy she bent over it; and in a moment the arms of the young man were encircled around her neck.

"Ellen," he exclaimed, "dear, dear Ellen, I have heard all that passed between you and that heartless wretch; and the agony that I endured almost drove me to distraction. But fear not; I will protect you against his villanous designs; whilst one drop of blood remains in this frame, it shall be sacrificed for you. Here Ellen," he added, as he held up the pistols, "take these weapons while I extricate my cramped body from this cask. Be careful; they are loaded; already one of them has struck your friend, and shall again, Ellen, if necessity requires."

"Ah!" returned the now delighted girl, "I see now how timely aid came to my rescue when power and strength were leaving me. Oh! Charles, how can this poor heart feel sufficiently grateful for this preservation; and how can my tongue find words to express that gratitude?"

"It was the will of Providence," returned the youth, "and to that providence our prayers are due."

As he spoke he squeezed his body out of the cask, but it was with considerable difficulty that he did so, for his limbs had become stiff and cramped in his small hiding place, and his wet garments added in no small degree to impede his progress.

But he thought not of his own uncomfortable position, it was that fair girl's safety only that he cared for, and her release from that place where she had been submitted to such cruelty.

"Ellen," he exclaimed, as he once more threw his arms around the form of the maiden; "your sufferings have indeed been fearful. It was cruel destiny to be wrecked so near at home, but it was worse to fall into the hands of these monsters. But we must escape them, dear one: never shall you be again subjected to the agony you have but now endured. Those pistols will perhaps save us. I will shoot these wretches and gain our freedom.

"Charles," returned Ellen, trembling with emotion, "vengeance is not for us; they would slay you, but shall we take that life which it is not in our power to return. No, leave them to the laws of their country and their God!"

"Noble-minded girl," he exclaimed, as he imprinted an impassioned kiss upon her lips; "your generous heart would extend mercy to those who have so deeply wronged you; but he has forfeited all right to it. Ruthlessly would he have sacrificed you to his unholy lust; unfeelingly would he have trampled upon your peace of mind—savagely would he have destroyed your happiness for ever! Mercy for him—mercy for the wanton wretch who cannot grant it even to a woman—mercy for the base reptile who has not one spark of feeling in his soul?—No! he has violated every principle of honour and feeling—he has set alike the laws of God and man at defiance—he has forfeited every right to mercy, and he shall die!"

And the brave youth took one of the pistols in his hand, and, with clenched teeth and darkened brow, strode towards the passage.

Trembling with fear for his safety, she seized his arm, and, gazing tenderly in his face, while the tears filled her lustrous eyes, she said:

"Charles, if I can forgive the wrongs he has done me, can you wish to stain your soul with the blood of him who is as base as you are noble? Oh! let us endeavour to escape from hence without bloodshed; let us not have upon our conscience the crime of murder."

The soft sweet tones of her voice, the appealing look she fixed upon him, and the gentle, yet firm, pressure of the hand upon his arm, to stay his progress, caused him to pause, and, fixing on her a look full of love and tenderness, he replied:

"Ellen, you are an angel, and your woman's heart does honour to your sex. Let him live, then, to answer to those laws he has outraged. For your sake this hand of mine shall not be raised against his life, unless by any act of his own he rush upon his destruction."

"Knows he aught of your being here?" asked Ellen, suddenly.

"No," replied the youth; "I entered this cave during the absence of himself and his hellish band—not by the way you were brought here, but from the sea."

"His band?" said Ellen, in a tone of surprise.

"Yes, dear one; from what I overheard, he is evidently the captain of as desperate a set of ruffians as ever lived. He is a wrecker and a smuggler; and the light which we saw shining so brightly over the waves was in this cave—a false beacon, which was contrived to lure us to destruction."

"And well indeed has it played its part. Perhaps you and I are the only survivors of this cruel night's work."

"Indeed, I fear it is so," replied the youth, with a sigh. "Few indeed could survive amid those fearful breakers. I succeeded in grasping a portion of the wreck, and was carried on to this rock; and, by the aid of a rope, succeeded in landing myself in this cavern. But how did you succeed in reaching the shore?"

"I know not," replied Ellen. "I felt myself being drawn under the waves, and sense was fast leaving me, when some one grasped me in their arms. I recollect no more till I recovered from my swoon, and found myself in this place.

"And to the villanous treatment you have received at the hands of that lawless youth?"

"Yes. But is there more than one outlet to this place? I can can see none but the one yonder, through which my persecutor has gone."

"That is the one by which you were brought here. There is another, which is evidently used for the landing of their spoil. 'Tis here, and looks out upon the sea."

The youth walked to the spot where the fire had been burning, and examined the covering to the opening. Then, pushing the rude doorway aside, disclosed to the gaze of Ellen the open sea beneath them.

The fair girl laid her hand upon his shoulder, and, pointing out, exclaimed:

"Charles, there lies the road to liberty, should all other means fail."

The young man gazed at her, as though he could not understand her meaning,

"How?" he asked.

"Should all other means fail, we will leap from the place into the waves, and trust to Heaven to guide us to safety."

"But we should be dashed to pieces ere we reached the water," he answered. "It would be madness; nay, almost certain death."

"Better meet that, Charles, than dishonour. Better, far better, that we should meet in heaven, in purity and peace, than that I should live a thing broken in spirit, and loathsome to myself."

"Ellen," exclaimed the youth, while his tones trembled with emotion, "I care not for myself. If I can but succeed in releasing you from the power of these wretches—if I could but feel that you were in safety—I would submit to all the misery they could inflict upon me; for willingly would I sacrifice my life to preserve yours.

"Well, dear Charles," she answered, "do I know your generous nature; but you must not endanger yourself for me alone. If I die—for never till death has claimed me will I yield to the unholy passions of this daring smuggler—I shall leave but few to mourn me and suffer by my loss. But you, Charles, have much to live for. Life is but just opening upon you; 'tis now but the dawn of a future, bright and prosperous, upon which that existence must set. You have a mother, whose gray hairs would be bowed with sorrow to the grave should aught ill befall you. I have no right to expect you to sacrifice yourself for my sake. You may singly make your escape from the place; but trammelled by me, you may perish; and I should have the sad reflection, to enhance my misery, that I had been instrumental in your destruction.

A look of pain and sorrow crossed the features of the brave lad as Ellen gave utterance to these words; and, in a voice half choked by the violence of his feelings, he exclaimed, in a wounded tone:

"Oh! Ellen, do you no longer love me?"

"Love you, Charles?" she exclaimed, as she pressed his hand between her soft fingers. "It is that undying love for you that prompts me to urge you to seek your own safety; that love which cannot, will not, be selfish enough to lead you into further danger. Should you fall, nothing but the memory of that love would remain, like a bright star shining from a dark cloud—an oasis in the arid desert—but one happy thought to dwell upon when all is misery, despair, and wretchedness."

The head of the poor girl sank upon the bosom of the youth, as he fondly pressed her to his heart. A proud look overspread his features, and, drawing himself up to his full height, in a tone of pride, he exclaimed:

"By that love do I stand or fall! Look," he added, drawing her towards the opening, and pointing out upon the sea—"on those dancing billows I have met danger in many forms; but never once have feared to meet my fate, whatever it may have been. I have stood upon the deck of my gallant bark when the storm has raged in furious wrath, and has every instant threatened us with destruction. The heavens have belched forth their fires upon the bark, and struck my comrades down by my side. Still have I not quailed; for I have put my trust in Him who commands the winds and the waves. Ellen, within this breast, beats the heart of a British seaman, and may Heaven desert me if ever I degrade my profession, and disgrace the proud flag under which I have sailed, by refusing to succour a woman in distress, or shielding, to the last drop of blood, the girl I love!"

The heart of Ellen swelled within her bosom as she listened to these words, and she encircled her smooth, white, rounded arms about his neck, and imprinted a kiss of passionate fervour upon his brow.

If she had loved that brave youth before, how much more ardently did she love him now! The words he uttered had sent the warm blood coursing through her veins, and suffusing her face with a blush of pride. They seemed to imbue her limbs with a firmness and strength hitherto unknown, and to engraft in her bosom a feeling of courage to meet any danger by his side that might present itself.

"Generous Charles, my heart must indeed be cold," she murmured, "did it not bound with joy at your words. Proudly you claim it, and nobly you would defend it. By our loves we will stand or fall, live or die. Come weal or woe, we will live or die together!"

"Bravely spoken, Ellen!" he exclaimed. "With the knowledge that we battle in a righteous cause, and with a firm trust in Heaven's aid, we shall yet triumph over our enemies, and escape from this accursed place."

"Or perish in the attempt!" exclaimed a voice close behind them.

The lovers started round as these words fell upon their ears; and Ellen with difficulty suppressed the scream of fear which rose to her lips.

The Boy Rover, and his two followers, stood glaring upon them. The young smuggler had a short cutlass in his hand, which he held menacingly towards Charles.

But the brave boy quailed not at the sight of these reckless young men; but, casting a hurried look around the cave, darted towards the rude table, to repossess himself of the pistols, which he placed there when he drew the partition from the opening to the sea.

But as he stretched forth his hand to reach them his foot caught in a coil of rope which lay on the floor of the cave, and he fell heavily to the ground.

With a cry of horror Ellen clasped her hands in despair. The Boy Rover sprang forward and placed his foot upon the body of the prostrate youth.

"Fool," he hissed, "you then it was who attempted my life, and now would rob me of my mistress. Fool! you have rushed upon your doom."

He raised the cutlass above his head to strike, but ere it could descend Ellen stood before him with a pistol in each hand presented at his head. She had bounded forward and obtained possession of the weapons, and now stood ready to protect his life or avenge his death.

The Boy Rover recoiled a few paces as that brave girl stood over the prostrate body of her lover.

"Advance one step," she exclaimed in a determined tone—"lower that weapon but an inch to do him harm, and a woman's hand shall protect a brave boy's life, and avenge her outraged honour!"

The Boy Rover, whose daring spirit had never quailed before the greatest danger, now stood irresolute. He saw the proud form of that beautiful girl standing majestically before him, with her fingers pressed upon the triggers and the shining barrels pointing at his head, and for the time he was cowed.

But his was not a nature to give way for any length of time to fear; and in a few moments he had revolved in his mind a stratagem by which to disarm her.

Calling out to his followers, he exclaimed:

"Touch the spring; she is standing on the trap, and she will fall through and be dashed to pieces!"

At these words Ellen, with a start, lowered her gaze from the Rover's face and looked down upon the ground. That moment was fatal to her; with one bound the young smuggler threw his arms around her and pinioned her so firmly that she was powerless to move her hands.

"Secure the boy," he roared. "Ha, ha, ha! my pretty one, you see the Boy Rover is one too many for you this time."

Ned and Jim rushed upon the brave youth, as he was rising to his feet, and held him in their strong arms.

In vain were his struggles to free himself from their grasp. The exertions he had undergone had so weakened him, that he seemed, as it were, but a child in the hands of those rough strong men; and, in a few moments, he was bound by a strong cord.

With a countenance overspread with an agonising expression, poor Ellen watched the operation; and, when it was completed, and she saw her brave young lover and protector rendered powerless to help her, she burst into tears, and became almost insensible.

CHAPTER VII.

THE BOY ROVER AND HIS CAPTIVES.

"THERE'S many a slip 'twixt the cup and the lip," is an old proverb; and in this instance, perhaps, it was as truly proved as it was possible it could have been.

But a few moments before, both Ellen and her lover had felt almost assured of obtaining their release from the power of the Boy Rover; hope had dawned in their breasts; but, alas! to be dashed aside, to give place to despair.

It was but the bright sunshine for an instant through the dark cloud, to be overspread by one denser and blacker than before.

They both felt that their position was now more desperate than it had hitherto been; and they feared more for the safety of each other than they did for themselves.

In her agony, poor Ellen saw in imagination the form of her lover sacrificed to the brutal passions of those ruthless men; whilst Charles Lawson trembled for the fate of the poor girl, and bitterly cursed his own helplessness.

The Boy Rover guessed the thoughts that were preying upon the minds of both his prisoners, and, with a demoniac smile, he watched the countenances of his victims, and gloated in their misery.

He was the first to speak, and, in measured and determined tones, he said:

"I have been a listener to all that has passed between you, and have discovered the mystery of the shot aimed at my life; and, likewise, the means by which you gained access to this secret cave. You will find your escape from my power somewhat doubtful, as well as difficult. You have attempted my life, and, as mine is a revengeful nature, you can rest assured that I shall not forgive the deed—though doubtless you, and society in general, would have considered it one of the most justifiable. Had you even not attempted my destruction, still I should look upon you as a dangerous enemy; for you know our retreat, and would bring down upon us the officers of justice. So that you perceive that your freedom is that which we least desire, and your death most necessary to our existence. I have spoken thus much, so that you may entertain no hope of mercy at our hands."

There was a proud look in the eye of the young sailor as the Boy Rover waited to hear his reply.

He had not to wait long, for, in a firm tone, he said:

"Cowardly ruffian! I have heard you to the end because I am powerless to stay you. I scorn to sue for mercy to one so base and degraded as yourself. For myself I care nothing; but if there be one spark of humanity in your bosom—if every sense of feeling is not obliterated in that callous heart—have mercy on the fair being you hold in your arms. Stain not your soul with a crime so black that humanity must shudder in horror at the bare thought of. Have mercy on her! I am a British seaman, and have sailed under the colours that never struck to slave or dastard; and I scorn to bemean myself by asking quarter at your hands. But I beg, plead, pray of you to have mercy on her! Villain your actions prove you to be; but if one drop of English

blood runs in your veins, taint it not by the base and degrading name of coward: for a mean and despicable coward must he indeed be who can outrage a defenceless woman. 'Tis the act of a brute, who possesses not one spark of humanity; 'tis the crime of the cur, who forfeits all right to mercy at the hands of his fellow-men; a deed which would render you the despised of man, the accursed of heaven, and the abhorred of hell!"

Jim and Ned having seen that Charles was now powerless to do any harm walked to the end of the passage, and the Boy Rover having possessed himself of the pistols which Ellen had threatened his life with a few moments before, led her to the rude couch, and then advancing to the opening through which herself and lover had gazed forth upon the sea, he closed the partition, and once more confronted the bound youth.

"Fine sentiments," he exclaimed, sarcastically; "your friends have mistaken your forte: they should have made you a parson instead of a sailor; in that line you would have made a fortune, and doubtless have earned a destination which few in your hazardous calling obtain. On my ears your words fall needlessly. I have taken a fancy to this girl and resistance to my wishes but add fuel to my passions. I look upon her as my lawful prize; I have saved her from destruction——"

"But to inflict upon her a misery worse than a thousand deaths," interrupted the young sailor. "Ah, coward—coward!"

"As you will, my brave fellow," exclaimed the Rover, as he bit his lip with vexation at the emphasis Charles laid upon the word; "as you will, but nevertheless I tell you she shall succumb."

"Never, liar!" exclaimed the youth, "she is too pure, too good. Rather will she meet death a thousand times than yield to such a wretch as you!"

The Boy Rover clenched his fist, and bit his lips to suppress his rising passion.

"There is a limit," he exclaimed, "to every one's forbearance, so beware!"

Proudly the young sailor drew himself up, and casting a scornful, withering glance upon the Rover, he exclaimed:

"I fear not your menaces. I repeat it—coward and liar!"

With the yell of a tiger the Boy Rover drew back his arm, and was about to launch a heavy blow at the face of the young sailor, when Ellen started forward, and stood between them.

"Coward!" she exclaimed—aye, despicable coward!—would you strike one who is powerless to protect himself? Shame on you—shame! Strike if you will, but with my body do I shield him; strike, and let thy dastard hand fall upon a woman's breast!"

The Boy Rover's arm dropped to his side, and, villain that he was, he stood abashed before the scornful look of that young fair girl, as, throwing her arms around her lover's neck, she shielded him with her body.

"Let him do his worst," said Charles, with a look of tenderness at his fair preserver. "Still do I scorn him and his threats. With my arms free, singly would he fly like a craven cur from my presence."

"Oh, waste not words upon him," said Ellen, as her bosom rose and fell with the violence of her emotion; "he is alike worthless and contemptible. His base nature triumphs now in our

CHARLES AND ELLEN ESCAPING FROM THE CAVERN.

misery, but a day of retribution will come when he will not go scatheless. Heed him not, Providence will yet send us aid to thwart his hellish designs."

"Dear Ellen," murmured the youth, "I could bear all the misery, all the insults, he could inflict upon me; but you, you—"

"Fear not for me," interrupted the young girl. "I am strong in my resolve never to submit to him. He may kill me, but never dishonour me. No, no! —welcome death!—but never shall you blush for the girl who has bestowed on you her love."

"I know it, Ellen; I feel it.

"Heed him not, then, and let him do his worst."

The Boy Rover listened to the conversation with

feelings of rage and mortification. He clenched his hands, and bit his lips with passion; but the calm scornful glance of the young girl's eye cowed his brutal nature, and he feared to strike.

He grasped the arm of the young girl in his iron grip, and he hissed between his teeth, as he scowled revengefully upon her:

"You defy and scorn me; but you shall feel my power. You have called me liar and coward; and you shall find that I am one, but not the other. I will break the haughty spirits of yourself and him you call your love. I will make you that which is loathsome to yourself; and he shall be the instrument I will use for your destruction. Nay, frown if you will, I heed not your scornful looks. I will bring the blush of shame to your cheeks, plant the canker-worm of misery in your heart, and make your life a very hell of horror and despair."

"Fiend! devil! I despise your threats, and laugh to scorn your boasting lies."

And, with an indignant and scornful laugh, she flung his rude grasp from her arm.

Foaming with rage the Boy Rover strode towards the passage where his companions stood; then, turning, he exclaimed:

"Remember my words. You have defied me; you have scorned the Boy Rover—the dreaded smuggler of the South Seas—one who never forgets or forgives. Though I wade through rivers of blood to encompass your ruin, you shall yet be mine. The 'Venomed Snake' is making every preparation to sail; once on board, you shall both feel the power I possess. There shall be no torture too fearful for your lover that I will not invent; and his sufferings shall be the stepping stones to my success. So beware of him whose love you have scorned—of the Boy Rover, who is now your bitterest foe."

And, motioning to Ned and Jim to follow him, he hastily darted down the passage, and was lost to sight.

CHAPTER VIII.

THE BOY ROVER AND HIS COMPANIONS IN CRIME— THE SUSPICION.

CHAFING with rage, the Boy Rover strode on, followed by his two companions, Ned and Jim, till he had reached the open air. His savage nature had been partly cowed by the calm determination and bearing of the young lovers; and, like the brute who is only tamed by the steady gaze of the unflinching eye, he feared to make the spring, and for the time his brutal nature became dormant.

But his determination to possess the young girl was not for one moment shaken: resistance but added fuel to the flames that were consuming him, and he now sat himself to think of some diabolical means by which he could drag down the young and virtuous maiden to his wishes.

He saw plainly that she dearly loved the youth who had so mysteriously found his way into the secret cave; and he felt that in him lie the instrument of his success. He could see that no torture, however hellish, inflicted upon herself, would cause her to become a willing victim; but he thought, "to save him she loves, she may sacrifice herself." He resolved, then, to bear them both on board the "Venomed Snake," and let her witness the indignities and cruelties he would inflict upon her lover, and make her consent the only means by which she could save his life.

As these thoughts passed through his brain, a sardonic smile played around his mouth, and he felt sure in his own mind that he would yet conquer.

Gradually the fury of his passions wore themselves out, and he almost laughed outright at the imagination of his success.

Alas! for the immutability of human hopes—success is not always certain. 'Tis a phantom, that often vanishes at the touch. We stretch forth our hand to grasp the substance, but find, to our chagrin and disappointment, we clutch but at a shadow.

But to the young mind the certainty of ultimate success most always presents itself, whether it be for good or evil. Nor is it till disappointment falls upon them with its overwhelming crushing weight,

that they realise the truth that the substance is sometimes lost by grasping at the shadow.

The Boy Rover felt that the substance was indeed in his grasp; and firm was the hold he meant to keep upon it, to prevent its eluding his clutch.

With that youth firmly bound, and powerless to aid her, he thought now how easy would be his triumph over the poor girl, and how exquisitely demoniac should be the means employed on that youth whom she so fondly loved, to assure that consummation.

The man that grasps at a sunbeam to save himself from falling, strikes his head against the substance he is endeavouring to escape; and then it is he discovers how futile have been his exertions, how vain and absurd his endeavours.

Whether it be for weal or woe, certainty of success is not always realised. We dwell on it till we could sacrifice our life upon the cast; but yet it will disappoint us.

The greater our certainty, the greater our disappointment; and the more we cherish the hope, the more crushing is the failure.

Certainty only—positive certainty of success—reigned in the breast of the Boy Rover, and, with feelings of triumph swelling his unmanly breast, he paced thoughtfully up and down before the entrance to the passage of the cave.

The storm had ceased, and the bright chaste lamp of night sailed proudly in a sea of ethereal blue, high up above his head, and cast its mellow rays of refulgent splendour over the dancing waves, lining their crested tops with a sparkling lustre, and shedding a halo of glory aslant the grave of the brave crew of the doomed bark.

The raging elements had given place to a calm so peaceful and serene, that only the hum of the sea, and the monotonous plash of the waves upon the rocks, broke the now almost painful silence. The warring elements had expended their mad fury, and calm serenity now reigned around.

But still the black passions in that young Rover's heart were as deadly as before. The calm of nature found no response in his blackened soul.

Suddenly he stopped before his companions, and, addressing them, said:

"The moon will go down in an hour: we must then get these prisoners on board, and at once set sail."

"Do you mean taking the lad?" asked Ned, in a tone of surprise.

"I do," answered the captain.

"Why, you don't think he'll join us—do you?" asked Jim, inquiringly.

"He is necessary to the furtherance of my views," said the youth.

"Better drop him over the rocks," remarked Ned; "he'll only be in the way aboard. Besides, captain, I should say you owed him something for that shot."

"And doubt not I will pay him," returned the Boy Rover, as he ground his teeth at the thought of the defiance of the young man.

"Then," said Jim, "I shouldn't have any unnecessary trouble with him. He's bound tight enough now, and won't be able to take a stroke to save himself. Drop him over, I say, and there'll be an end of all trouble about him. Besides, while the girl knows he's all right and safe, she'll never give in."

"And there'll be an end of all fear of his betraying the secret entrance from the sea," remarked Ned.

The Boy Rover seemed thoughtful.

"No," he said, after a pause, "not yet. For the present he must live; but with the fear of death ever hovering over his head. He must live to be the instrument of bringing that girl to reason."

"Well," said Ned, shrugging his shoulders, "I suppose you know best; but I'm blowed if I think it will answer."

"I will try," said the captain, as he turned away, and continued pacing thoughtfully up and down.

"He's got his match in that gal," said Jim to his companion, in a low tone, as the Boy Rover walked from them; "and it wouldn't surprise me if she don't beat him yet."

"Then she'll be the first as has," exclaimed the other.

"That may be," said Jim; "but then you see she's got more pluck in her than most of her sort; and I'm blessed if I won't bet you my grog for a week that he don't succeed in doing as he likes with that ere gal.'

"Hush!" remarked Ned—"if he hears you he may think we intend to prevent him. He's as suspicious as he's daring, and as passionate as the devil. Speak lower."

"Is it a bet?" asked the other, in a low tone.

"No," replied Ned, after a pause; "for I'm blowed if I don't so too.

"And it strikes me she will," continued Jim; "she's a plucky gal, and if it wasn't that she'd blow the gaff, demme if I shouldn't like to see her get scot free."

"Hush!" said Ned, grasping his companion's arm in a vice-like grip. "Are you mad? If the captain had heard that, there would have been no escape for you.

Jim looked hard in his companion's face, as he replied, in a whisper:

"The words slipped out before I thought."

"Be careful, then, if you value your life," said Ned.

"Well, only you heard them. Would you split?"

And the rough sailor's hand fastened on the knife he carried in his belt.

"No," said Ned, "we have been pals too long to betray each other. But your tongue will endanger your head if you don't keep your thoughts to yourself. We must abide by our oath; and if he wants that gal we must do our best to help him to his wishes."

"Well, that's true; so let our thoughts go no further. We must stick to him through thick and thin, and where he leads we must follow, even though the gallows is our destination."

This conversation was interrupted by the Boy Rover, who once more approached his followers.

"Let us return to the cavern," he said, hurriedly. "We have been mad fools; we have secured the boy, but left the girl the free liberty of her hands."

"Blowed if we ain't, captain," said Ned. "Well, I never thought of that."

"We must repair the error at once, or, by all that's devilish, that girl will set him free," said the Boy Rover, as he entered the passage.

"Shouldn't be surprised, captain," remarked Jim, "if she hasn't been more wide awake than us, and done it afore now. Let a woman alone for having her wits about her."

"Curse her, if she has!" muttered the youthful captain; "for, in that case, we may have some tough work with him."

"Daresay we shall," remarked Ned, nudging his companion Jim in the ribs with his elbow, and leering round, as much as to intimate that he derived some slight pleasure at his captain's discomfort.

"At all events, he will not be able to do much damage," said the Rover, "as I have deprived him of his weapons; and there are none, I believe, in the cave that we need care much for."

"That was a rum go, that he should manage to lay hold of them," said Jim.

"Yes," remarked the other; "and confounded fortunate that he couldn't fire straight when he got them."

"Straight enough," said the Boy Rover, as he placed his hand to his grazed temple. "That shot was well meant, and nicely aimed. I have had a few escapes; but this was the most narrow one of all."

"Your time ain't come yet, captain," said Jim.

"No," he answered, in a somewhat thoughtful tone; "but the life we lead is so full of danger, that it may come at any moment. But, come when it will, it shall find the Boy Rover unflinching to the last."

It was the brutal courage of the boy captain that enabled him to hold with so firm a hand his crew of desperate ruffians in such admirable discipline, as we shall see anon; and his fearless disposition was held in the highest admiration by both Ned and Jim. In their ignorant natures, they mistook the desperate passions of the boy captain for the noble deeds of a hero; and the unflinching determination with which he followed out any pursuit, as the powerful force of the master's mind.

They feared him, for he inspired them with awe; they obeyed his every command, for they felt that any resistance to his orders would ensure their instant destruction; but not one of his desperate crew entertained for him the least respect. They would fight by his side, or shield him from harm at the sacrifice of their own lives; but yet they hated the man, or boy—for such he was in years—hated him with an undying hatred: but still they dared not show it, for he possessed indeed the master mind of that hellish band; he was the greatest villain in that assembly of villains, and his fall would have been their irreparable ruin.

Had his course of life been different, still he would have been superior to his fellows. His was a mind that would have soared above the ordinary difficulties of life, and he would have gained position and success in any other channel.

Had the Boy Rover been started in life in an honourable path, the qualities of his mind would have raised him to a proud eminence, and he would have commanded the respect and admiration of honourable men as much as he now awed and enslaved his ruffianly crew.

It was, then, with blind obedience to his orders that Ned and Jim followed the Boy Rover along the passage to the cave.

It was with a light step the youthful captain entered the cavern; but scarce had he done so than, with a yell of rage, he bounded forward, like a wounded tiger, followed by his two companions.

CHAPTER VIII.

THE LOVERS—THE ROPE—THE ESCAPE FROM THE CAVE—A MOMENT OF HORROR.

WHEN the Boy Rover, accompanied by his myrmidons, Ned and Jem, left the cave, Ellen gave a sigh of relief, and allowed her head to fall on the shoulder of Charles Lawson, in which position she relieved her overburdened heart by a flood of tears.

The youth did not attempt to interrupt her; he felt that it would be far better to let her grief have full sway.

And in this he was wise; for, after the lapse of a few moments, she once more became calm.

Then she raised her head from the shoulder of her lover, and, fixing her large lustrous eyes upon his face, with a gaze half melancholy, half fearful, she said:

"Charles, it would seem that Heaven had deserted us in this our terrible hour of need."

"Do not despair, Ellen," said the brave youth. "Hope for the best; hope on. If once we give way to despair we are lost."

"We are lost now, Charles—lost indeed!"

"Not so, Ellen. True, I am powerless, in my present position, either to aid you or to protect myself; but that villain, in the blindness of his passion, has forgotten that you are free to aid me."

"Would to heaven that I could!" replied Ellen.

"You can, dear one," said her lover.

"Oh! speak, Charles—now."

"Your hands are free, if mine are imprisoned. You can release me from these bonds," replied the young man.

"Oh! yes, yes," she exclaimed, eagerly. "Surely my poor brain must be turned, or I should have seen that before."

"She seized the rope which bound the hands of the youthful lover, and essayed to untie the fastenings.

"There," she exclaimed, as she cast the cord upon the ground, "you are free! But," she added, as a look of pain overspread her beauteous countenance, "we are still prisoners."

"For a time," he replied, with a sickly smile. "I will not be taken by surprise again. We will escape from here, Ellen, if escape by any means be possible."

"Would to heaven that we could; but much I fear that even now the eyes of that fiend is upon us, watching our every movement, and waiting ready to spring upon us from yonder passage."

"Let him come," said Charles, as he cast his eyes around, in the hope of discovering some weapon wherewith to defend himself and his companion in misery from any attack—"let him come; he shall not gain so easy a victory this time. Can I but once get his throat in this grasp, he should feel that a British sailor can hold tight, whether his grip be to save his body from the foaming waves or a villain's power."

"But, Charles, his companions would avenge him. Surely we are sorely placed."

"In truth we are, Ellen," he replied. "But he fears not to dare the winds and the waves, but not despair, when the whirlwind of misfortune encircles him. Fear not, Ellen; I will go to the passage, and listen if I can hear anything of them."

"Oh! be careful," she said, imploringly.

"For your sake, dear Ellen, I will seek no unnecessary danger."

He stooped, and raised from the floor a small piece of wood which had laid there. It was the only thing he could see which he might be able to turn into a weapon of defence; and he resolved to use it, if need be.

He advanced to the passage listening intently.

Not a sound broke the stillness, and he was about to return to Ellen's side, and bid her follow him, when the voice of Ned fell upon his ears.

He strained his eyes in the endeavour to catch a glimpse of the smuggler; but in this he was not successful. So he advanced silently a few paces into the passage, and again strained every nerve to overhear their conversation.

And in this he was successful.

Their words had little interest for him; but they proved to him that the passage was guarded, and that any attempt to escape by that direction was sure to lead to discovery.

He turned and entered the cave, where he found Ellen had followed him to the end of the passage, and was tremblingly awaiting his return.

He placed his finger on his lip to enjoin silence; then, taking her by the hand, led her back to the rude couch, and, seating himself beside her, said:

"Ellen, that passage is guarded. If we attempt to escape by that, we are sure to be discovered; yet we may succeed. We should have to contend with three desperate wretches, and the chances are we should again be overpowered; still I am willing for your sake to run the risk."

"It would be useless," replied the poor girl "We should but fail; and then our sufferings, if possible, would be made more terrible. Oh! Charles, cannot there be some other means of flight?"

The youth paused ere he replied.

"I can see but one," he said, at length.

"What is it?" she inquired eagerly.

"By the opening to the sea," he replied, pointing, as he spoke, to the partition through which they had looked upon the waves when the entrance of the Boy Rover surprised them.

The poor girl looked despairingly in his face.

"Then we are lost," she said.

Charles Lawson rose from her side as he exclaimed:

"Ellen, I am not unused to danger; but you have never had to encounter it till now. You saw the waves leaping and foaming upon these rocks through yonder opening; you saw the depth from this accursed place to those billows; you saw the fearful danger that must attend any attempt to reach the water from here. I ascended to this place by means of a rope; but that rope was gone when I again looked for it. Still, if you have the courage to try it, I will secure some of these cords, and descend with you in my arms to the waves beneath. There lies our only hope of escape; and a poor one indeed it is. The waves may dash upon the rocks, and leave our mutilated bodies upon their rugged sides; or may carry us out into the wide expanse to perish. Will you escape by this means? Will you risk your life to the mercy of the waves, or wait, and trust to chance to release us from this horrible place, and the power of these ruthless monsters."

Ellen rose, and, throwing her arms around his neck, exclaimed:

"The waves will be more merciful to us, dear Charles, than the fiends into whose power we have fallen; for they but follow the dictates of the Almighty. To them, then, will I trust my body, and, with my faith in Heaven, dare the dangers that will beset us."

"Nobly and heroically spoken, Ellen. This base-hearted Rover shall find that there is a woman who dares meet death rather than dishonour; and a British sailor who will brave every peril to save the woman he loves."

He imprinted a kiss upon her lips, and, bidding her listen intently for any sound which should denote the return of the smugglers to the cave, he walked round the rude place, and selecting some pieces of rope from among the immense quantity strewed about, placed them on the board which had served as a table.

Then he gathered together, as silently as possible, several planks. These he secured together by the ropes, till they formed, as it were, one piece. Then, fastening the end of a long rope, which he had laid aside from the rest, to the centre cord which bound the planks, he advanced to the partition, and drew it aside.

The bright moon shone full upon him, and revealed to his gaze the dancing waters beneath, and the rugged sides of the rock on which he stood.

He beckoned to Ellen, and in a moment she was at his side.

"Look forth," he exclaimed. "Does your courage fail you?"

"No," exclaimed the brave girl; "with you I will meet death in any form."

"'Tis well," he replied; and, returning to the rude table, he took the end of the rope in his hand, and returned to the opening."

"I must find some place to fasten this to," he said, as he cast his eyes about. "Ah! he added, suddenly placing his hand upon an uneven piece of the rock, at the side of the opening - "this will do; it would bear the weight of twenty."

Quickly he secured the rope to this; and then, laying his hand upon the arm of Ellen, he drew her back to the table.

"Help me," he whispered, "to get this timber to the mouth of this accursed place.'

Silently they bore the planks to the opening; and then grasping the rope firmly in his hands, he pushed it out over the rock with his foot, and gradually let the rope run through his hands till the planks floated on the heaving billows.

Poor Ellen watched him with a heart beating between hope and fear.

"On that frail support, Ellen," he said, "we must trust ourselves. Are you still resolved?"

"I am," she answered.

"Come, then," he exclaimed — "place your arms around my neck. Cling to me firmly, and fear not.''

She threw her arms around his neck, and placed her beating heart against his manly breast. The young sailor grasped the rope firmly.

"Are you ready?" he asked.

"Yes," she replied, firmly.

"Come, then," he exclaimed, as he flung himself from the opening. "Come, Ellen; this rope leads us to liberty or death."

Down, down they went, over the side of the fearful rock. Below them the waves were rolling in the bright moonlight, and curling their foam-crested heads upwards towards the lovers, as they dangled in mid-air, as though they wooed them to their embrace. Down, down that slender cord, her arms encircling her lover's neck, and her head nestling upon his manly breast; down, down, till the waves almost threw their silvery spray upon their forms! They had but a short distance now before they would reach the frail raft upon which they were to entrust themselves to the mercy of the boundless deep; a few yards more, and they have escaped from the power of the Boy Rover. Charles Lawson gazed upwards at the opening in the rock, and quickened his speed down the rope. A cry of horror would have escaped him, but he feared to alarm the poor girl, who reposed so confidently on his bosom. But a cold perspiration broke out upon his brow. In that glance upwards he had seen in the bright moonlight the demoniac features of the Boy Rover, gazing down upon him and his fair burden. He saw him draw his cutlass across the rope; he felt it twisting in his hand; and he allowed it to run through his fingers till they were almost torn to the bone. There was a sudden jerk, and he knew the rope was breaking. He let go his hold with one hand, and threw his arm around her form; and the next moment they were plunged violently upon the raft, which sank with them under the waves.

———

CHAPTER IX.

THE CAVE DESERTED FOR THE SHIP—THE FRUITLESS SEARCH FOR THE ESCAPE.

BOUNDING forward, followed closely by Ned and Jim, the Boy Rover stood in the centre of the cave.

He cast one rapid glance around, and his eye rested upon the opening. In a moment he perceived that it was by this that his captives had escaped him.

He rushed to the opening, and his quick eye instantly detected the rope. Casting his eyes downward the bright moonlight revealed to his gaze the young lovers suspended half-way down the rock.

Maddened with rage, he grasped the rope with one hand, and drew the keen edge of his cutlass across it.

"Curse them!" he exclaimed, his cheeks livid with passion—"curse them!" but they shall not escape. I will foil them yet. Never shall they escape to betray the secret of this cave. Ha, ha! down they go—to death, to death."

He watched the effect of his hellish work with foaming lips and blood-shot eyes; and his base cruel nature gloried in the act.

He saw those two young forms fall; he saw the waves close over them, and a fiendish smile wreathed his lips.

"There's an end to them both—curse them!" he exclaimed, turning to his followers, whose eyes had followed the young lovers till the waters shut them out from their sight, and who now turned their face to their captain, with a half-pitying look upon their countenances.

"Hard lines that, captain," said Jim. "They might just as well have never come ashore from the wreck of that ere craft."

"What a fool I must have been not to have known that the girl would release him if she got a chance! And you," he added, savagely, "even you had neither of you the sense to see it."

"Well," said Ned, in a nettled tone of voice, "if you didn't think of it, you couldn't expect us."

"It's no use being wild with us," remarked Jim. "If, instead of cutting the rope, we had all three caught hold of it, and hauled it up, why we should have got 'em back, safe and sound.

"Confusion!" said the captain, stamping his feet with rage. "My mad passion has foiled me. Why the devil couldn't you say so before I cut the rope?"

"Because you wouldn't give me time," was the reply. "But even now you may again get them in your power. They may float out to sea. The waves do not roll in so heavily now; and depend upon it the lad won't desert her while he can take a stroke."

"That fall has dashed them to pieces," said the captain, as he again looked out from the opening into the waves beneath.

"Don't think they fell very far," said Ned. "The rope went through his hands like lightning just before you severed it."

"Had we a boat at hand," said the Boy Rover, impatiently, "we might pick them up. But, curse it, not one is here because it is wanted. I can see nothing of them," he continued, "for that cloud that is now crossing the moon throws a gloom upon the waters. But they shall not escape me, if death has not already claimed them. Secure this opening, and we will away to the ship, and send off the boats to look for them. Curse them!—to be thus foiled; and at a time, too, when I felt so secure of the prey. Come!"

Ned and Jim closed and secured the wooden covering to the opening, which was used for the landing of the contraband goods from the boats, and followed the Boy Rover from the cave.

Emerging from the passage up into the open air, they lowered a large flat stone over the mouth of the entry, which effectually shut out all appearance of a cavity, and hurried away, along the rocks, in a southerly direction.

Chafing with rage and disappointment, the Boy Rover strode moodily on, followed by his two companions, for the distance of nearly a quarter of a mile. Then, turning the angle of a rock, the tall masts of a vessel were revealed to their view.

She was anchored in a narrow channel, between two high rocks, which effectually hid her from sight, either by land or sea.

This was the harbour of the "Venomed Snake," when gorged by contraband goods, or when it was found necessary to seek refuge from the revenue cutters, who were always on the look out for her.

They would oft chase her over the waves, and, when almost assured of seeing her, would suddenly find she had disappeared; but where she had gone to no one could tell.

Had they examined the coast more minutely they might have discovered her place of refuge; but from any distance the opening between the rocks was almost imperceptible; and, when once within it, she was so effectually hidden, that those who eagerly sought to capture her believed it to be a phantom ship, and would turn the heads of their vessels seaward again, under the belief that they had been lured on by a mirage to a fruitless chase.

She was a plain fore and aft schooner, and a most mischievous-looking craft. There was not a line of rope in her beautiful tracery of rigging, spars, or hull that could possibly have been found fault with. Even the most inexperienced observer could not have failed to observe a peculiar beauty and mystery in her appearance. The heavy sails, and long narrow hull that upheld them, proved that she had been built more for speed than aught else.

A gleam of pride sparkled for a moment in the eyes of the Boy Rover, as they rested with the glance of an experienced sailor upon the fine graceful proportions of the noble craft.

Taking the small whistle from his breast, which he had used to summon the smuggler from the cave a short time previously, he blew a long shrill note.

In a moment a sound similar to that which he himself produced floated from the vessel over the water, and echoed round the rocks.

Another minute, and a boat put off from the ship, and rapidly neared the spot on which the Boy Rover and his two companions stood.

Swiftly it glided over the waters that intervened between that gallant craft and the shore, and was suddenly and skilfully brought to a stand-still at the smugglers' feet.

The Boy Rover entered it, followed by his companions; and, waving his hand, the men bent to their oars, and the boat glided steadily from the rocks to the vessel's side.

Seizing a rope which hung from her bulwarks, the Boy Rover, with the agility of a cat, sprang from her side, and stood upon the deck.

In an instant he was followed by the others, and the boat secured to her stern.

A dark-featured young man appeared, and respectfully saluted him. This was Black Bill, lieutenant of the "Venomed Snake." He was a thick-set broad-shouldered fellow, with muscles of iron, and a cast of countenance that bespoke a cruel and determined disposition."

"Have the boats manned," said the Boy Rover, addressing his lieutenant. "A girl, together with her lover, a young sailor, have but now escaped from the cave, by the opening to the sea. They may not have perished. See that every search is made, and every means adopted to secure them, if they have not paid for their daring courage with their life."

Black Bill made no reply, but, saluting his captain, instantly gave the order to man the boats.

In a minute more the three boats belonging to the vessel were manned, and put off from the ship.

The Boy Rover leaned over the bulwarks, and gazed after them for some minutes. Then, turning to his lieutenant, he said:

"Have you made all preparations for sea?"

"Your orders have been implicitly obeyed, captain," returned Black Bill," and we but wait the command to weigh anchor."

"'Tis well," said the young captain. "As soon as the boats return, we will set sail."

"Whether they are successful or not?" asked his lieutenant.

"Yes," was the reply. "You will give me notice of their return."

So saying, the Boy Rover turned and strode to his cabin.

One by one the boats returned to the ships, after the lapse of about half an hour; but neither of them could discover anything of the escaped lovers.

Black Bill reported to the Boy Rover the failure of the expedition; and, with a bitter imprecation at his disappointment, the youthful captain gave the order to weigh anchor, and stand out to sea.

As the first gray streaks of morning were breaking through the eastern clouds, the "Venomed Snake" stole silently from out the narrow channel between the rocks, and glided majestically over the dancing waves.

———

CHAPTER X.

AFLOAT ON THE OCEAN — THE BOY ROVER AND WILD MADGE.

OVER the waves, like a thing of life and joy, glided the "Venomed Snake," bearing upon the bosom of those boundless waters a crew of the most reckless ruffians that ever congregated together at one time.

Perhaps no vessel ever set sail with so young a complement of hands; for there was not on board this craft one whose age exceeded two-and-twenty years; and yet better sailors or braver men could not often be met with.

But there was not the cool heroic courage of the

noble sailor, who steers his vessel amid the dangers of the ocean, or spills his blood like water for the honour of the flag under which he fights, or the security of the homes and happiness of his native land. Theirs was the bravery of the savage, and the daring of the brute, whose untamed passions know no bounds.

While the handsome little craft swept majestically on her course, her white sail glimmering in the morning sun, the Boy Rover. wearied by the excitement of the night's adventure, had sought his cot; and when the sun was high up in the heavens, and the land was almost receded from sight, he again made his appearance on deck.

But his whole demeanour and appearance had undergone a change. He had thrown off the garb of a fisherman, in which we have hitherto seen him, and was now attired as an officer of the navy.

A gold band encircled his cap; and attached to his belt was a sword, the handle of which was richly chased and studded. A pair of small pistols, also, were fixed at his waist; and from a small opening in the breast of his blue frock-coat the richly chased handle of a small dagger protruded.

An air of stern command now sat upon his brow, as silently he paced the deck, or moodily gazed across the ocean.

Black Bill anxiously followed every look and action of his superior; and when at last he leant over the taffrail, and, seeming lost in abstraction, gazed down upon the crested waves, as they broke upon the vessel's side, he remarked:

"The weather is cheerful, captain, after such a storm as last night. It was fortunate that we were anchored in our little harbour; for the gale would have tried her timbers severely."

The Boy Rover looked up at the face of his companion as he replied:

"She has stood worse gales than that; but, as you say, 'twas fortunate. But I had rather every plank in the hull had gaped wide enough to ship a hundred seas than that she should now dance over foam without that girl on board."

"Cursed unfortunate." remarked Bill; "but, captain, that young fellow must have had more pluck in him than a good many to have risked life and limb to save her in the way he did. By Jove! if he should succeed in carrying her safe into port, he will earn her gratitude, and deserve her love."

The Boy Rover bit his lips in vexation as he replied:

"Fury seize him!—but for the carelessness of leaving that confounded rope dangling from the rock. he would never have found his way into the cave, and the girl now would have been securely in my power. They must not escape; they know the secret of the cave, and can bring destruction upon us. If they did not both meet their deaths when I cut the rope, they must have been carried out to sea."

"And, if they were," said Bill, "that fellow would hold on to her while a gasp of breath remained in his body."

"Aye," said the boy captain, "and a passing vessel might have rescued them both. Have you made out a sail?"

"Not a speck on the ocean, captain."

"And her course has been kept as I ordered?" asked the Boy Rover.

"To a point," replied the lieutenant.

"Then they must have perished," muttered the young man, thoughtfully.

"I can scarcely entertain a thought otherwise," replied Bill, "or we must, under ordinary circumstances, have run foul of them."

The Boy Rover remained abstractedly gazing over the wide expanse of waters for a few moments; then, suddenly raising his head, and addressing his lieutenant, he said:

"We will make a longer run this time. It would not be safe to return to the cave too soon; for if, by any chance in the world, they should fall in with a vessel, the cave would be in the hands of the Philistines, and there would doubtless be not a few to welcome us home."

"True," said Bill; "and as I, for one, have no wish to fall into their hands, a long voyage will be preferable; and even then it will be desirable to feel the coast a little before we land either ourselves or our cargo."

"See that the helmsman keeps her on her present course for some time," said the young Rover, after a pause; and then, casting another look over the undulating ocean, he turned away from his lieutenant, and descended below.

There were two cabins; one devoted to the use of the Boy Rover; the other to that of a woman some forty years of age, and known on board the "Venomed Snake" by the name of Wild Madge.

Many and vain were the surmises of the smuggler crew as to who and what she was; and fruitless had hitherto been all their endeavours to discover what relation she bore to their captain.

To the rough crew of that schooner she was morose and silent, and seemed to inspire them with a kind of dread; and it would have been to many of them a feeling of relief had the boy captain not allowed her to sail with them. Still not one would have hazarded a remark to that effect to him.

Certain it was that there was some mysterious relation between them; for he, so rough and austere to them, was to her as gentle and kind as a child.

It was to the cabin occupied by this being that the Boy Rover now bent his steps.

Placing his hand upon the handle of the door, he entered without ceremony, and, advancing to the centre of the apartment, stood face to face with Wild Madge, who rose from her seat at the table when he entered.

She was a woman of commanding stature, and had at one time been handsome; but now her features presented a bloated and besotted appearance. The once lustrous eye was dimmed by dissipation; and the once majestic carriage was now bent with over-indulgence to that most fatal of all vices—drink.

At the moment of the Boy Rover's entrance she held the glass containing brandy to her lips, and set it down upon the table as he advanced into the cabin.

"Well, Richard," she said, "you have not brought the bird on board which they told me you had trapped. Why did you trouble me to get everything in readiness for her had you intended to come alone?"

"I did not intend to come alone, mother;" he answered; "but the bird has escaped."

"Ha!—escaped, has she?" replied the woman, in harsh vexed tones.

"Yes, for the present, at any rate."

"I am sorry for that," said Wild Madge, as she seated herself in the chair from which she rose at his entrance—"very sorry."

The Boy Rover fixed his eyes intently upon her countenance, as she gave utterance to these words, as though he would read there whether she truly meant them.

"Sorry," he iterated, "why should you be sorry?"

"Because," replied the woman, as her dim eyes lighted up with a momentary fire; "these would have then been one as wretched as myself on board this bark."

"But that one," said the Rover, "would have been a woman—one of your own sex."

"Aye, and there would have been the joy," she replied.

"Mother," said the young man, as he gazed almost sternly into the bloated countenance of his companion, "are you sober, or are you mad, that you should feel a pleasure in the misery of one of your own sex?"

"Boy," she exclaimed, as she rose from her seat and grasped his wrist, "it may seem strange to you, that I—a woman—should exult in a woman's misery; but I tell you that your disappointment at the escape of this girl does not equal mine."

"Strange," said the youth, half-aloud, half to himself, "that a mother should feel a delight at her son's triumph over an innocent girl."

"Aye," said the woman, "strange to you, but not to me. Richard, look upon me. I was once fair and innocent, with a nature full of love and kindness; what am I now?—a foul blot on the name of woman. But who made me what I am? Woman!—therefore do I hate my sex. I was once happy, but a woman blighted that happiness. I loved with all a woman's gentle nature, but a woman's wiles turned that love to bitter hate. Woman has been the serpent in my path, whose venomed sting has pierced my soul and poisoned every better feeling—woman's arts have curdled the milk of human kindness in my breast, have blasted my every hope, destroyed my every happiness, blighted my existence and made my life a living hell. This has woman done to me, and now a woman's wrongs and sufferings call for vengeance on a woman's head, and gloat in woman's misery!"

"Bad and dishonourable as was the nature of that youth he could scarcely help giving utterance to a feeling of disgust at these words.

For a moment or two he stood silently thinking. What wrongs must that woman whom he had called mother have endured, he thought, to embitter her so fearfully against her sex. There could be no slight cause for this expression of ill-feeling towards those who could have never wronged her; for surely the young girl whom he had intended to have brought on board his schooner could have never done her harm. Yet to that unfeeling woman it would have been a source of joy to have triumphed in her misery.

Suddenly he was aroused from the reverie into which he had fallen by Wild Madge thrusting a glass filled with brandy into his hand.

"Drink, Richard," she said; "it will to some extent allay the pain of your disappointment. 'Tis the elixir of life. It will smooth your ruffled spirit, as it drowns the bitter memory of the past. I should go mad, Richard, but for this. When the wrongs I have suffered force themselves upon me with their overwhelming weight, I fly to this, and forget in its soothing influence the blighted hopes, the sufferings of years, the promised happiness, destined never to be fulfilled."

The Boy Rover dashed the glass aside, and its contents fell upon the floor of the cabin.

"I want not that," he said, "to fire my blood. 'Tis heated sufficiently by my natural passions, and requires not artificial aid."

"Wait till you know misery such as mine has been," was the answer she made, as she refilled the glass, and poured its burning contents down her throat. "Ha, ha! it gives new life, as it sets the blood coursing through my veins. When my brain is fired by the fumes of this nerving liquor I feel equal to anything that may come."

"Would you but drink it less," said her companion, in a tone of disgust, "you would become more a woman, and less a fiend."

"Oh, oh!" she laughed, derisively—"has the Boy Rover foresworn his calling? Has the oath he swore been forgotten? Has his once bold heart become nerveless?"

"Hold!" he exclaimed, savagely. "I am what I am—an outcast from society, a smuggler, and—"

"A murderer!" said the woman, with marked emphasis.

"Aye," said the Boy Rover, "a murderer."

A smile played round the lips of the woman as she emptied the glass again.

"And now you shrink from your own crimes?"

"No," he replied, "I am what fate has destined me to be, and what your teaching has engendered."

"Would you shrink now," she asked, "from avenging a mother's wrongs?"

"No," he exclaimed—"I have sworn to track to the death the villain who destroyed your happiness; for he has made me what I am."

"Aye, Richard, he has made us what we are—outcasts in the wide, wide world; the scorn and loathing of all the right-minded portion of humanity. Long ere this had death folded me in its icy embrace, but that I have sworn to live for vengeance; live to triumph in the misery of one who could feel no pity for me; live to make you, my boy, the instrument to insatiate vengeance. Oh! how my brain whirls when I think of the time when I shall gloat in his anguish; for it will come—aye, it will come!"

And again did she refill and empty the glass.

"Drink, boy," she said—"drink! Some there are who deny that brandy gives vigour to the frame. Ha, ha! did they but know how its fumes cheer my heart and fire my brain—how it gives strength to my determined resolves—they would say different. Were it not for this I should go mad. It drowns my sorrows, the bitter recollections of my past life, and urges me on to the gratification of my revenge. It will come, boy—it will come; and then this weak frame shall be made strong by his agony; these dim eyes sparkle with joy at his sufferings—this withered heart bound with exultation at the misery that I will inflict upon him! Oh! how I long for the hour when he shall feel the vengeance of her whose love he scorned, whose life he embittered, whose honour he stole, and in whose misery he exulted. Drink!"

The Boy Rover took the proffered glass, and drank off its contents.

"There, mother," he said, as he handed the glass back to her—"are you satisfied?"

"Yes," she answered. "You will send me some more of this; for it is my greatest support. It is the only God that now I worship; for it stifles the bitter thoughts that at times rise to my heart, and is now the only medicine that will administer to this diseased heart."

There was a loud knock at the door of the cabin at this moment, and the Boy Rover placed his hand upon the latch and opened it.

Black Bill stood on the threshold.

"Captain," he said, "there's a sail coming up hard over hand."

THE PARTING OF THE RAFT.

"What do you make her out?" asked the Boy Rover.

"Looks all a cutter by the glass," was the reply.

"I will come on deck," said the young captain, "and see what I can make of her."

And, turning to Wild Madge, he remarked:

"I will be with you again;" then left the cabin, and returned to the deck with his lieutenant.

When the door of the cabin had closed behind him, Wild Madge sank back in her chair, and a smile stole over her blear countenance as she muttered to herself:

"It works! My teachings have not been in vain. I have instilled into his heart all the passions of a demon, and his soul is blackened in crime. But I must not rest here. No, no; he must become more hellish yet; his crimes must be greater, deeper, blacker! Would that I could induce him to drink more; then, under its fiery influence, he'd stop at nothing. Ha, ha! I shall yet mould him to my will; weave round him the web of crime so closely that escape will be impossible; ensnare him on to deeds so black that humanity shall stand appalled at the bare contemplation of them; and, when the time arrives, I, Wild Madge—mother as he calls me—will show myself to him in a form he has never dreamed of. But not yet; the time has not yet arrived. But it will come; and, when it does, I shall triumph; aye, triumph!"

4

And again did she swallow more of the fiery spirit; and then, leaning her arms upon the table, she buried her head upon them.

There was a hurried tramp of feet to and fro upon the deck; and the sound of hurried orders came upon her ears: but the fumes of the brandy were fast causing a drowsiness to steal over her senses; and in a few moments the deep heavy breathing showed that she slept.

But it was not the calm peaceful slumber of the mind, oppressed by the fatigue of honest toil. The brain still worked, and carried that diseased mind back to years gone by—back to the time when she was fair and happy, when the bright sunshine of peace shed a halo of love and joy around her; but, too soon, alas! to be dimmed by the murky haze of misery and crime.

CHAPTER XI.

THE FISHERMAN'S DAUGHTER—THE LIBERTINE AND HIS VICTIM—THE DOUBLE BIRTH—THE CHILDREN ON THE BEACH.

LET us, for a short time, go back eighteen years prior to the events related in the preceding chapters. Eighteen years! To the aged, as they look back, this space of time seems nothing. To the youth, as he looks forward to it, it seems an age. What thoughts, what aspiration, will not that space conjure up in his mind? What airy castles will he not build in his imagination? What joys will he not hope to realise in that time? Yet, when the days, weeks, and years have passed by, he looks back upon them with a sigh and finds that all his fond imaginings have vanished, and left not a wrack behind, save the marks on Time's hour-glass, to tell him that lifes's sands are running swiftly out.

Eighteen years! The child becomes a man; the strong man sinks to the sear and yellow age: thousands have been ushered into the world, and thousands have taken their flight to eternity.

Still the sands run out. History records their passage; but all alike are powerless to stay their progress. Still they run—grain by grain; and so they will continue, till chaos comes again, and all things cease.

But what a change had passed over the life of Wild Madge in eighteen years. Then she was a happy laughing girl, of twenty years of age, with scarce a care upon her mind—hardly one dark shadow in her path. She was happy; for she loved—loved with all a woman's fond devotion, and trusted with all a woman's faith.

But, alas! that faith was too soon to be shaken; that happiness to be blighted; that joy to be turned to sorrow.

She trusted, and was deceived; and her fond devoted love was turned to bitter hatred.

She was the daughter of a poor, but honest, fisherman. Her mother had been lost to her when but an infant; and she had none to advise and guide her in her girlhood but her father. True, he strove to do all that would render her happy; for he loved his beautiful child with all a parent's love. But she needed a mother's guidance: and that, unfortunately for her after peace, Providence had denied her.

She knew that she was beautiful; and the homage paid to that beauty had made her vain and haughty: and those of her own sex, in the little fishing village in which herself and father resided, pained by her contemptuous bearing, held aloof from her; and thus she was left with none to whom she could confide, or seek council.

A short distance from the village was a noble old mansion, the proprietor and occupier of which was also the owner of the property on which she resided.

He was a gay dashing young man, of a warm-hearted generous disposition; but he had the misfortune to inherit a considerable amount of property before he well knew how to take care of it; and his youth and inexperience soon caused him to make acquaintances, and consider those his friends who might have been much better described as enemies.

But their flattery won upon his heart, and ere long they had moulded him to their desires. Naturally free, he became reckless, and soon he was the gayest libertine among them.

He saw Madge Lovegrove, the fisherman's pretty daughter, and, as he fastened his glance upon her features, he saw the blood mount to her temples, and the smile of pleasure beam in her eye.

With a libertine's quick perception, he saw that she was pleased at his notice of her, and he felt that it would be no difficult task to win her.

He resolved to try, and often, as if by accident, he threw himself in her path.

Madge was pleased at his condescention, and her vanity became the more unbearable.

She thought that she was weaving a web round the heart of the gay young gentleman that would draw his love to her, and she fancied that one day she would be the mistress of the broad lands that surrouded her humble dwelling.

Poor fool! Like the moth she was hovering around the flame that at last would consume her.

She knew that she was beautiful, even if she was poor; and she imagined that that beauty would make her the mistress of his affections.

The young libertine saw that he had but to praise her beauty and feed her pride. He poured the honied words into her ears, and she dwelt enraptured upon his tones.

He promised to make her his bride; to take her from her humble cottage to a home of splendour; to administer to her every wish; to live for her, and her only.

She listened, she believed, and she fell!

Fell, as many have fallen before, at the shrine of ambition, vanity, and pride.

The love that had warmed the heart of Joseph Hanfield now cooled, and the fond girl whose love he had so striven to gain was now thrown heedlessly aside.

Months rolled on, and the too confiding girl found when too late that all is not gold that glitters.

But she found, too, that she was about to become a mother; and her soul was wrung with anguish.

She begged, prayed of him to fulfil his promise of marrying her; implored him to save her from shame: but in vain.

He offered the means of leaving her native village, and hiding her shame some distance from those who knew her: but he quietly, yet firmly, told her that he could not, nay, would not, make her his wife.

He said their stations in life were too distant, and ridiculed the idea of marrying a poor fisherman's daughter.

His pride was too great to make that humble girl his equal; but his soul had not been clean enough to hold her purity unsullied.

In vain were all her prayers and entreaties; he was firm, cold, and determined.

And, with tearful eyes and aching heart, she returned to that home where peace and happiness had reigned for so many years; to that father whose kindly smile had always greeted her, and welcomed her with a loving kiss.

And there, in misery and despair, she prayed for God's curses on the head of him who had blighted her happiness.

It was but a few days after her interview with her seducer, that one young girl of the village, whom, in her haughty pride, she had disdained to hold converse with, but whose keen perception had seen through the intentions of the young libertine, with a true woman's nature, hoping to warn her of her danger, ere it was too late, told Madge that her lover was married; that he had been married some few weeks prior, in London; and that his young bride would arrive at that place in a few days.

Had a thunderbolt fallen upon her head, it could not have rendered her more paralysed than did these words.

At first she would not believe it; but when she reflected that he had been absent some time, and, likewise, that she had observed many alterations being undergone in the old mansion, she felt that it was too true; and, in an agony of mind almost bordering upon distraction, she flung herself upon the floor of the cottage, and gave vent to her feelings in agonized sobs.

She cursed her pride, her beauty, which had lured her to her ruin; she cursed the hour she was born, and her betrayer: and, in feelings of bitter jealousy, she cursed the woman who had won his love, and usurped her place, and swore a bitter oath never to rest till she had encompassed the destruction of them both.

So fondly had she loved; so fiercely now did she hate—with that bitter hatred that never slumbers! She felt that her peace of mind was gone for ever, and she resolved to embitter the happiness of him who had wronged her, and of her whom her jealous madness made her firmly believe had robbed her of his love.

She had sank upon that floor in the overwhelming anguish of a broken-hearted woman; but she arose from it with the cool, determined, undying hatred of a fiend.

She had resolved to prove that

"Earth hath no pang like love to hatred turned:—
Nor hell a fury like a woman scorned."

From that day Madge Lovegrove went about her ordinary duties as usual; was cheerful in her conversation with her father; was affable and sociable with the other village maidens.

But beneath this calm exterior raged a volcano ready to burst forth when the moment should arrive to fan its slumbering fires into furious flame.

No one, not even her father, suspected her fearful secret, and thus months flew by.

The new mistress had arrived at the hall, as the residence of Joseph Hanfield was styled, and her presence there had kept away from her husband his libertine companions.

He who had once been all life and gaiety, now became the quiet unassuming gentleman, attending to the requirements and comforts of his tenants, and superintending the renovating of his estate which of late had gone somewhat to rack.

One evening about seven months after his marriage he had accompanied his young wife to the beach, and was walking with her upon the sands, when he was accosted by the person who was attending to several of the improvements on his estate, and leaving his wife to enjoy the cool evening breeze, he accompanied the man to some portion of the place where he wished to have his advice before proceeding with the alteration.

The sun was sinking into the west and tinting the clouds with a golden hue, and throwing across the sea a stream of golden splendour: the air was soft and balmy, and the hum of the sea came musically entrancing to the ears of Mrs. Hanfield as she gazed upon the lovely scene lost in wonder and admiration.

Suddenly she returned to retrace her steps up the beach, when she was confronted by Madge.

There was a look upon the young girl's face of mingled pain and sorrow.

The kind heart of Mrs. Hanfield was touched, for, with a woman's quick perception, she saw that Madge was like herself soon to become a mother.

Kindly she spoke to her, and inquired if she was not well.

The soft tones of the kind-hearted woman fell upon the ears of Madge with a poisoned sound, for they brought to her heart all the slumbering and bitter hatred she felt for her who she believed had stolen from her the man to whom she had sacrificed herself.

She saw the state of the poor lady, and she felt the pain it would inflict upon her heart to tell her all.

She resolved to tell her, that she might gloat in the misery that revelation would inflict; she determined to poison her happiness, and make her as wretched as herself.

And she spoke.

With flushed cheek and heaving bosom, the young wife listened to the tale of wrong; and, with the gratification of a demon grasping his prey, Madge told her all.

And those two women separated on that sandy beach, with feelings in the heart of each better imagined than described.

Madge returned to her humble cot with feelings gratified at the misery she had planted in the young wife's breast; and Mrs. Hanfield walked slowly towards the hall, her heart a prey to bitter feelings of anguish, and her mind dwelling upon the thought of how she had been deceived in him to whom she had given her pure and holy love.

That night, lights flashed hither and thither in that large house, and servants were astir; whilst Mr. Hanfield sat listening intently in a room adjoining the wife's chamber for the sound that should proclaim the birth of his firstborn.

And on that same night, in the humble fisherman's dwelling, a small weak voice and a mother's sobs alone broke the stillness that reigned around.

As the gray mists of early dawn were rising from the earth, a figure, slowly and painfully, dragged itself from the fisherman's cot towards the beach. It bore in its arms a young infant; and, painfully and sadly, it dragged itself along the sands, till close to the water's edge.

The sea was rolling in as Madge (for she it was), after kissing the infant she carried in her arms, laid it on the sands at her feet.

Then, slowly and painfully, she returned by the

way she came towards the cottage, ever and anon pausing and looking behind at the poor babe within a few feet of the rolling billows.

She gained the door of her cottage, opened it, and entered; closed it after her, and sought her couch.

The next day, when the old fisherman returned to shore, he found his daughter too ill to leave her bed. He tried everything in his power to give her ease and restore her health; but the case was beyond his skill—it was beyond his power to minister to a mind diseased.

Never, for a moment, had he dreamed of the state of his daughter; therefore, all thoughts of the truth were far from his mind.

Madge had successfully concealed her secret from all, save that poor broken-hearted lady who had just given birth to a daughter at the hall, and the father of that child, and her son.

On a bed of down, and nestled warmly to its mother's breast, lay one; on the sandy beach, with the silvery spray of the rolling waves splashing over its tender form, lie the other: the offspring of one father, but two mothers.

Both had loved fondly, faithfully. One was bowed with grief; the other torn with revenge.

A fortnight passed, and health and strength was fast returning to those two beings who on the same night, and at the same hour, had given birth to their firstborn.

One sat, supported by pillows, in a gorgeously furnished chamber; the other stood gazing fixedly and revengefully upon that mansion which contained those she had sworn to doom to misery and despair.

The firmness of resolve was stamped upon her features, and the passions of hell were loosened in her breast.

She was there to strike the first blow in her fight of vengeance.

Stealthily she approached one of the windows, and laid her hand upon the sash. It yielded to her touch; she opened it, and entered. Noiselessly she strode across the room, out at its door, along the hall, and up the staircase, till she arrived at the room next to that in which Mrs. Hanfield was sitting.

This she entered. A small lamp shed its feeble rays around the apartment, and, by its light, she perceived on one side of the room a child's cot. Silently she stole towards it, and gazed at the calm peaceful face of a slumbering infant.

A hellish smile played around her mouth as she raised the babe from its resting place, and nestled it to her breast; then, as noiselessly as she entered, departed from the room, descended the stairs, passed out at the low window, and stood once more in the front of the house, with the still sleeping babe pressed to her bosom.

"Now," she muttered, between her clenched teeth —"now shall the serpent-sting of misery fester in your hearts; now will I be avenged!"

In another moment she had gone; and years elapsed ere she again visited the place of her happiness and her misery.

Nine years passed away, and her existence had almost been forgotten by the inhabitants of that little fishing village, when one fearful night whilst a storm was raging, and the wild waves lashed the beach, and the heavens belched forth their electric fires, she stood close to her once happy home gazing upon the warring elements, and watching the eager throng of villagers who deserted their firesides to render any assistance that might be needed on the coast.

Suddenly her eye rested upon one who stood some distance from the villagers, and she strode silently and stealthily towards him and stood by his side. As a bright flash of lightning illumined the earth and sea he turned; their glances met; they recognized each other, and spell-bound the seducer stood face to face with his victim.

A gleam of triumph lit up the face of Madge as her grasp fastened on his wrist, and she hissed into his ears threats of so fearful a nature towards himself and his wife, that the blood ran back cold to his heart.

He strove to tear himself from her presence, but she clung to him with a demon's clutch; and, goaded to madness by her taunts, he raised his arm and struck her to the earth, then darted hurriedly from the spot.

In a short time the storm abated, and one by one the villagers returned to their homes, and the beach was once more deserted by all save that prostrate woman and a little boy, who with tearful eyes endeavoured to arouse her by sobbing out the words —"mother—mother!"

She recovered, and, leaning on that boy's shoulder, she swore to track to the death that man who but now had struck her down and all connected with him, and implored that child to assist in her revenge; and down upon that sandy beach they knelt together, and swore never to rest in peace till they had hurled destruction, misery and shame upon her seducer!

Ere the sun rose in golden splendour over the earth, that woman leading the child by the hand departed from the spot, and went none knew whither.

CHAPTER XII.

ON THE RAFT—THE OPEN SEA—THE SEPARATION. ALONE ON THE DEEP.

BREATHLESS, exhausted, and nearly senseless, our hero and heroine, together with the hastily and rudely-constructed raft, rose to the surface of the waves.

Never for one instant had the brave youth released his hold either of that fair girl or the rope by which he had descended from the rock.

Fortunately it was that he had not done so, for it brought the raft to their rescue; as, doubtless, had he once sacrificed his grasp on the cord, the raft would have floated away, and left them alone in their now almost powerless condition to the tender mercy of the waves.

In his descent, so suddenly accelerated by the cutlass of the Boy Rover, he had struck his head against a projection of the rock, and it was only the sense of poor Ellen's danger that saved him from sinking into insensibility.

It was with no inconsiderable difficulty that he succeeded in obtaining a safe footing on the raft for himself and his beauteous companion, for the waves threatened every moment to dash it to pieces against the side of the rock.

They succeeded at last in placing themselves firmly upon the frail support, and drawing the rope which he had fastened to the raft from out of the water and coiling it at his feet, he clasped Ellen firmly with one arm, so as to prevent her being thrown into the sea by any obstacle which they might encounter, and which, as the moon's disc was now obscured by black clouds, they might dash against ere they were aware of its proximity.

A huge wave rolled in and bore them close upon the rocks, then rushing back with a hissing, roaring sound, carried them far out into the waste of waters.

And thus they sat upon those three or four pieces of timber, rudely spliced together, clinging to each other, and dreading lest every wave as it broke against the raft should sweep them from it and separate them again.

And thus, fearing for each other's safety, hoping with the morning's light to find help and succour, they sat with their arms entwined around each other's form, till morning broke over that wide expanse of waters, and they saw that they had left the land far, far away, in the distance.

The sun rose in all its gorgeous splendour, lighting up the dancing waves, and tinting their crested tops with the hues of burnished gold, and thowing their refulgent beams upon those two wretched beings who had trusted their lives to the mercy of the waves, which rolled and tossed on the bosom of that boundless and unfathomable waste of waters.

Poor Charles, in his descent from the rock, he had struck his head so violently, as we have before stated, that the faintness caused thereby, together with the fearful exertions and trials he had undergone during the last few hours, were fast luring him to insensibility.

Higher and higher rose the refulgent orb in the blue vault of heaven; warmer and warmer became the slanting beams, until its bright rays poured down with an almost intolerable heat upon the devoted heads of the lovers.

Their misery was now added to by the almost intolerable pangs of thirst which assailed them; and down into the cool depths of those waters did they gaze, with longing eyes. Their lips were parched, and their tongues clave to the dry roofs of their mouths; and, though nothing but water was to be seen around them, yet they dared not attempt to quench their thirst from the clear blue fluid, for well they knew that to drink of it was but to accellerate the pangs with which they were assailed.

Fearful was the intentness with which Charles Lawson strained his now bloodshot eyes over that waste of waters, in the hopes of seeing the white sails of some vessel that might come to their rescue. But not a speck was to be seen on the ocean; nothing but the white crested waves met his sight on every side, and the blue expanse of sky above.

He gazed into the face of the fair being who sat silently by his side, and a heavy sigh rose to his breast as he saw there the misery she was suffering in silence and resignation.

On they went, carried by the winds and waves over the broad ocean, while the sun streamed upon their fevered brow, and burnt into their very flesh.

Still, silently and uncomplainingly, they gazed across the ocean for succour.

It was about mid-day, and when the sun was high in the heavens, and its fierce beams pierced their brains like molten lead, that Charles descried a small object in the sea drifting towards them.

He leant over the side of the raft, and watched it as it came nearer. He soon perceived it to be a small cask, and his heart beat with renewed hope as he thought it might perhaps contain something wherewith they might quench the thirst which consumed them.

Earnestly did he pray that it might drift within his reach; and that prayer was answered, for a

wave bore the cask close up to the side of the raft; and, stretching forth his hand, Charles grasped it firmly, and drew it on to the raft: but, to their disappointment, they discovered it was empty.

The hopes that had risen in their breasts now sunk lower and deeper in their hearts; and, with pale cheeks and fevered brows, they again turned their anxious gaze upon the ocean.

A long branch of some huge tree drifted alongside their raft, and Charles instantly secured it.

"Ellen," he said, "have you a handkerchief?"

"Yes," replied the poor girl, as, placing her hand in the pocket of her dress, she drew it forth, and held it towards him.

"I will secure this branch to our raft," he said; "and your handkerchief, fluttering in the breeze, may be seen by some vessel."

"Heaven grant it may," she exclaimed; for, if we are not rescued soon, I fear I shall die of thirst."

"God forbid!" exclaimed the noble-hearted youth, as he pressed her hand, and gazed tenderly and pityingly in her face. Surely Heaven will send us succour soon."

Tying the handkerchief to one end of the branch, he secured it to the raft, in the hope that it might be instrumental in bringing some passing vessel to their rescue; and they once more resigned themselves to their fate.

The burning rays of the sun now streamed down upon them with an intensity that scorched the flesh, and almost penetrated the brain; for, having no coverings for their heads, they could in no way shield them from its fierce power.

The exertions and trials he had undergone, together with the oppressive heat, the intolerable thirst, and the sickening pain from the blow on his temples, was fast drawing to a state of insensibility the brave young sailor who had so nobly struggled for the sake of his fair companion.

Gradually his head sunk upon his breast, in spite of all his efforts to shake off the drowsiness that was now stealing over him: his eyes closed, his limbs became rigid, and he fell forward upon the raft, insensible.

With a cry of despair, Ellen knelt down by his side, and endeavoured to restore him to consciousness—but in vain; and, burying her face in her hands, the scalding tears chased each other rapidly down her cheeks, while heavy sobs shook her frame, and her bosom swelled with the powerful emotions that heaved within her breast.

And thus the time flew by, till, raising her head to gaze once more across the ocean, she uttered a wild piercing shriek, and started to her feet.

The rope that had bound together the boards which formed the raft had become loose, and the planks were fast parting asunder.

She seized the rope, and strained every nerve and muscle to draw them together again, and secure them as before; but all in vain. The waves dashed up between the separating planks, and forced them further and further apart, till they left a huge gap between the portion on which her lover lay and that on which she herself stood.

In an agony of despair, she exerted all her strength to keep them from parting. Frantically, she strained every nerve upon that rope; but the waves dashed in between the planks, and forced them wider and wider asunder; and the spray splashed up in her face, and almost blinded her, whilst the waters swept over the planks, threatening every moment to carry the insensible youth from his frail support, down into their clear blue depths.

Who can pourtray the agony of that poor girl, as she perceived the planks parting wider and wider from each other, and found that all the strength she could bring to bear upon the rope was insufficient to keep them together!

Fiercely, madly, did she strain every nerve; but all to no avail. Further and further they parted—greater became the gap between them every instant—and higher and stronger dashed the water through the opening; and, the planks slipping from the only fastening which held them together at one end, the rope suddenly slackened, and she fell backwards, as though struck by some sudden agency.

So fierce was the shock caused by her bearing her whole strength upon the rope, that, for a few moments, she was rendered powerless, and almost insensible; but the fearful danger with which she was surrounded, the horror of the situation, and the despair which assailed her heart for the fate of her noble-minded lover, roused her to consciousness, and, half-bewildered, she gazed around her.

That portion of the raft on which her lover lay insensible had drifted some distance from the planks on which she sat, and every moment the space between them became greater and greater.

She saw the waves curling their crested tops over its sides; and every fresh billow, as it rolled towards it, threatened to hurl him from the frail support on which his body was borne over the dancing waters.

Not one thought for herself—not one care for her own perilous position—her whole mind was centred on him, and on him alone.

Never for a moment did her eyes wander from that loved form as it rose and fell upon the waves, and was carried hither and thither across the bosom of the boundless deep.

She was saturated by the salt spray as it dashed high up over her fair form, but she heeded it not; felt not the briny waves as they beat over her, and leapt and danced and sported in the bright sunlight, as if revelling in her misery, and in mad glee mocking her sufferings.

Further and further became the distance between them, and the sight of the poor girl became weaker and weaker as she strained her eyes through the bright sunbeams over the waves towards that loved object whom she now believed was lost to her for ever.

The waters danced and curled as though they strove to hide him from her view: a mist stole over her eyes and giddiness seized upon her brain; she closed her eyes for a moment, and when she opened them again, she could discern nothing but the sparkling waters as they rolled around her, and curled their crested tops over each other.

Now, and now only, did she fully realize the horror of her own situation. She felt that she was alone—alone upon that wild waste of waters—alone upon the deep and boundless sea, without one near her on whom she could gaze, without one hand to aid her, without food or water to moisten her parched lips—alone, with a single plank only between her and eternity, with the bright blue heavens above her head, and the dark green sea beneath her feet, and bounded on every side by the foaming ocean—alone in her agony and wretchedness—alone, to die in madness and despair!

She clasped her hands and raised her eyes to the clear blue vault of heaven; but, as though to enhance her sufferings, the burning rays of the noon-day sun streamed fiercely upon her upturned features, and scorched the lovely face that pleadingly gazed upwards for aid.

Gradually the heavens and the sea faded from her sight; the sound of the rolling waters died away in a low melancholy moan; her head sank upon her breast; her arms fell powerless by her side, and she became unconscious to all her misery, while the planks on which she lay glided over the bosom of the boundless deep.

CHAPTER XIII.

THE REVENUE CUTTER—THE DEJECTED OFFICER—AN OLD SAILOR'S COURTSHIP—LOVE AND DISAPPOINTMENT—THE SPECK ON THE SEA—THE RESCUE OF ELLEN—RECOGNITION AND DESPAIR.

OVER the sea, her white sail glistening in the bright sunlight, with every stitch of canvas that she could carry stretched to its utmost tension by the breeze, and with the proud union jack fluttering from her mast, sped the noble little revenue cutter, the "Flying Dart."

She was a well-built and well-armed little craft, and carried five-and-twenty as brave British sailors as ever trod the deck of an English vessel.

She had been for some time past on the lookout for the smuggler, and though her crew had several times sighted the sails of the "Venomed Snake," yet they had never been able to come up with her ere she had mysteriously disappeared.

But from information her captain had received he believed he was now upon the track of that daring smuggler, and he sincerely hoped that ere the sun went down himself and his crew might have a chance of overhauling the smuggler's vessel, and carrying him and his unprincipled crew into port as prisoners.

The crew of the "Flying Dart" were also in high spirits at the prospect of a brush with the Boy Rover, and the prize money which would fall to their share should they succeed in making him strike his flag.

But they knew not the desperate natures of that youthful band of marauders, nor their numbers, or means of defence: had they been acquainted with this they would not have been so sanguine of success.

But hope ever comes uppermost in the mind of the British seaman. With the utmost faith in the skill of his commanders, with the certainty of his messmates' bravery, and the knowledge of his own unflinching courage, together with the influence that the unstained flag under which he fights throws over all, he always looks for victory, never for defeat.

Captain Waters, a noble specimen of a British officer, stood upon the quarter-deck, ever and anon raising his glass to his eye, and scanning with a seaman's glance the surrounding ocean.

Leaning over the tafrail, and gazing abstractedly upon the waves, as they leaped and sported around the vessel, was a young man, in the garb of an officer. He was the second in command on board the cutter, and was much beloved by his crew, and esteemed by his captain.

He had stood thus lost in thought for some time, and several times had the eyes of Captain Waters been fixed almost pityingly upon him.

After a long survey through his glass, in the hopes of discovering some sign of the smuggler vessel, Captain Waters approached the side of his lieutenant, and laid his hand upon his shoulder.

The young man started, and looked up in his commander's face.

"Mr. Chambers," said the captain, in a half bantering tone, "you do not expect to see the smuggler sail along under our bows, that you so intently fix your gaze there? Or," he added, as he saw the blood rush to the young man's temples, "is it the face of your lady love you imagine reflected on the waters beneath us?"

"I beg your pardon, sir," stammered out the young lieutenant, in a confused tone—"my mind was wandering, and for the moment duty was forgotten."

A smile stole over the face of the captain, as he remarked:

"By Neptune! Mr. Chambers, this must be the swiftest sailer afloat; for she has run eight or ten knots in the moment."

Lieutenant Chambers looked hard in the face of Captain Waters, as though he could not understand the meaning of his words; but the next moment a smile broke over his face, and he knew that the reverie into which he had fallen had been of some duration.

"I have been somewhat inattentive," he said, after a pause; "but I trust my temporary abstraction has in no way interfered with the calls of duty?"

"In this instance—no," replied Captain Waters, good naturedly. But so deeply were you lost in thought, that I verily believe a gun fired over our bows would have failed to rouse you."

"Then I must have been abstracted indeed, sir."

"And indeed you were," said the captain. "In fact, Mr. Chambers, I have perceived that of late you are subject to these moody fits. I trust that you are not unwell."

"No, sir, thank heaven, my health is good."

"Yes," interrupted Captain Waters, "but this may be no disease of the body, but of the mind."

And his glance rested upon the countenance of the young man as though he would read in his features the answer to his surmise.

A crimson flush overspread the temples of the young officer as he replied:

"I know of no ill that can assail my mind, sir."

"Humph!" exclaimed the other; "are you sure it is not the eyes and cheeks of that pretty girl we met at Mr. Hanfield's when we went ashore at Gibraltar, six months ago. By my faith, I think Cupid planted his dart in your bosom there, for ever since you have been as dull as a girl in the sulks."

The young man looked confused, and seemed lost how to make any reply. At length he stammered out—

"Miss Hanfield is very beautiful, certainly, and I—"

"Like a true British sailor, fell over head and ears in love with her," interrupted Captain Waters. "Is it not so."

"I—I, certainly——" stammered out the lieutenant.

"There, there," again interrupted the captain, as he saw the young man was both pained and confused by his badinage; "never mind," he added, extending his hand to the young sailor good naturedly; "if my remarks have pained you I am sorry for it. Why, you are not the first man that has nearly lost his senses through a woman. Why, Mr. Chambers, when I was your age, I nearly went stark-staring raving mad;

got myself into innumerable scrapes, and stood a very fair chance of making a too intimate acquaintance with an ounce of lead, and all through a pretty girl to whom I set sail and gave chase."

"And did you succeed in capturing her?" said the lieutenant, smiling, and pleased at the turn the conversation had taken.

"Not till after a smart chase," replied the captain; "you see, Mr. Chambers, there was another craft alongside, and so I had to manœuvre a bit, I can tell you to cut him out; and I found it no easy work, for so sooner did I make a little headway than down he bears broadside abeam of me, and tries to get on the weather gage, and then in disgust at both of us, the prize we both wished to take would make all sail on another course, and leave us to shew our teeth to each other."

"But how did it all end, sir, at last?" asked the young lieutenant, smiling at the captain's odd way of comparing a woman with a ship.

"Why, I chased her into a channel at last, where she could not easily escape; and there I succeeded in capturing and bringing her to anchor in the port of matrimony."

"But how about your rival, sir?" asked the other.

"Why, he had to strike his colours, to be sure. But, like a brave foe, when he found that I had fairly won the prize, he gave in with a good grace, and has been ever since one of my warmest friends. So you see, Mr. Chambers, I have been in love—happy and miserable at the same time: but it all turned out right at last."

"But you, sir, were the favoured suitor," said the lieutenant, and a sigh rose to his lips.

"And so may you be," returned the other, as he heard the sigh—"so may you be, sir; for it would puzzle Old Nick himself to know which way a woman's mind steers when she takes it into her head to be obstinate. Believe me, its no use being miserable about a woman because she won't confess that you, and you only, hold possession of her heart. They will play with a man as a cat does with a mouse, before they kill it. But, then, with woman, it generally ends by your being torn to pieces by love and kindness; and that will be your fate at last."

"I fear not," murmured the young man.

"Then it is as I thought, eh?" said the good-natured captain, smiling.

The young lieutenant started, as he discovered that he had involuntarily betrayed his secret.

But, having gone thus far, he determined to make his captain his confident, and he said:

"Well, sir, in truth, I was thinking of Miss Hanfield, when you placed your hand upon my shoulder and roused me from the reverie into which I had fallen."

"I thought so!" exclaimed Captain Waters.

"But why my mind should dwell upon her I can scarcely imagine," said the young man, "since she can never be to me more than an esteemed and valued friend."

"Then you are not in love with her?" queried the captain of the cutter.

"She loves another," said the young man, and again a sigh forced its way from his bosom.

"How do you know that?" asked the other. "Do you fancy, because after an acquaintance of a few months she does not fall into your arms, that you are indifferent to her?"

"No, sir; nor should I esteem much the love so lightly bought. But she loves another; thus much have I learned from her own lips."

"Whew! that's how the cat jumps. Then endeavour to forget her."

"That is impossible," returned the young lieutenant. "I saw, and I loved her; and, though the love can never be returned, yet I shall ever cherish the image in my heart."

The brave captain looked almost pityingly upon the youth at his side. He saw how deep that love had sunk in his breast; and he dreaded lest the disappointment should blight and embitter the existence of one who bid so fair to become one of the bravest and most daring officers that ever trod the planks of a ship that floated under the Union Jack.

He almost regretted that he had spoken to the youth on the subject: but, having done so, he resolved to leave no means untried to soothe his disappointment, and instil into his mind a conviction that it was unworthy a brave man to be so cast down because he had failed in winning the love of one on whom he had centred all his affections.

"I must keep him to his duty," he thought to himself; "leave him no time to think; keep his mind always employed on one thing or another; and then time will do the rest. He is brave as a lion, and strong as a fortress, and yet a woman's smile has broken him. 'Tis sad, very sad!"

And the good-natured captain paced the quarter-deck of his little craft in deep thought; and Henry Chambers once more leant over the tafrail and gazed into the sea.

It was at this moment that the look-out at the mast-head fancied he could discern some object floating on the top of the waves, a long distance from the ship, on her larboard bow.

Shading his eyes with his hand, he gazed intently, and endeavoured to make out what it could possibly be.

But in this he was unsuccessful. He could see something; but what that something was he could not tell. It might be a portion of a wreck—something thrown overboard to lighten a vessel in the last night's storm—or even a human being. So, hailing the deck, he called the attention of those below to it.

The captain raised his glass, and gazed in the direction indicated by the look-out; but failed to make out what it was.

"Take my glass, Mr. Chambers," he said, turning to the lieutenant, and handing him the telescope, "and see what you can make it out to be."

The young man took the glass, and gazed long and anxiously: then, suddenly lowering it, he said:

"It appears like the dead body of a woman floating on the waves."

Again the captain took the glass and centred his gaze upon the spot.

"I fear you are right, Mr. Chambers," he said, as he lowered the glass. "Have the ship laid-to, a boat lowered, and take the command of her. Heaven knows life may yet be not extinct, and doubtless it is some poor wretch who was wrecked in the storm of last night."

The order to lower a boat was instantly and cheerfully complied with, and in a very short time it was manned and gliding over the waves, with Lieut. Chambers setting in its stern sheets.

Willing hands plied the oars, and leapt through the waters like a thing of life.

Captain Waters stood leaning over the bulwarks watching the receding boat, and wondering what had been the misery endured by that form floating in the sea, ere it had been cast upon the pitiless mercy of the waves.

And as he gazed after the small boat, a mere speck on that waste of waters, strange thoughts took possession of his mind.

"What might be his fate and the fate of his gallant crew? A storm might rise at any moment and his gallant little ship be dashed to pieces; she might strike upon some hidden rock, or a thousand other fates befall her; he might be cast to the mercy of those waves or buried beneath their rolling bosom, without one kind friend to sooth the last agonies of death—without one prayer to accompany his soul to eternity."

And as he thought his heart grew sad, and involuntarily he murmured a prayer to heaven for the safety of himself and crew; for though the bright sunlight of heaven now shown with all its sparkling glory upon the peaceful ocean, dark storms ere long might rise, and that world of waters lashed to fury by the howling winds, might engulph his devoted ship and crew in one fell vortex of destruction and death.

Eagerly, almost impatiently, did he watch the course of the boat, as it dashed over the waves on its mission of mercy.

And the crew, standing in knots of twos and threes, shading their eyes with their hands from the sun's rays, followed the boat's course, and speculated upon the object it would encounter.

With willing hands and willing hearts, the rowers pulled the little bark over the waters, cheered on by their much-loved lieutenant.

A heavy load seemed to have settled at the breast of the young officer—a load which he could not shake off, and for which he could not account.

He had been dull, nay, almost miserable, on board the ship; but now he was oppressed with some dismal foreboding for which he could not account.

He endeavoured to shake it off, but he could not succeed in doing so. There it sat, like some huge nightmare on his heart, and held him under its powerful influence.

Sailors are proverbially superstitious, and superstition reigned predominant in the breast of Henry Chambers.

He felt that he was going after something which was connected with his own destiny, and he believed that the object he was now so rapidly nearing would influence his life for good or for evil. Why, he knew not; but he felt it was so; and that feeling was rooted deeply in his heart.

"Pull, men — pull!" he said, addressing the rowers: "bend to your oars with a will!"

"Aye, aye, sir," responded the seamen, as they bent forward; and thus, bending themselves back, the boat shot through the water like an arrow.

"That's right," he exclaimed, as the long steady strokes of the oars brought them nearer and nearer every moment to the object they had descried from the ship. "Well done, lads! Now she glides through the water like a dolphin. Now, all together!"

And thus, urging on his men to renewed exertion, and ever and anon sinking into a train of thought, only to raise his eyes and find himself much nearer the object they had in view, they had placed a very considerable distance between themselve and their cutter.

The sea was now comparatively calm. The mad waves, which, a few hours before, had rolled so furiously, had now lost much of their vigour, and rolled more gently.

Had it been otherwise, Henry Chambers had not been sent on his errand of mercy, and one, at least, of our principal characters had met with an untimely fate.

THE DISCOVERY OF ELLEN.

But man proposes, and Heaven disposes; and providence works out its own ends in its own good time.

He that bids the winds and waves to ise, stills them likewise at his bidding.

The sailors, therefore, found their task one of no very great difficulty, and the boat glided easily and swiftly onwards—nearer and nearer to the object of their errand—closer and closer to their work of salvation.

A few more strokes, and they would gain the side of that prostrate and inanimate form.

Intently, the eyes of the young officer were fixed upon it.

He could now plainly see that it was a female form, supported in the waters by a couple of planks, with only a few feet of timber between her and destruction.

Never for an instant now did he take his eyes from off of it, lest, when he again raised them, he should find the body had disappeared from off it into the waves.

Eagerly and anxiously he panted for the moment when the boat would be alongside, so that he might stretch forth his hand and grasp her.

For every wave, as it rolled towards that frail raft, threatened to wash its occupant from off it.

And he could scarcely repress a cry of fear as each succeeding wave rolled towards it.

Again he urged the crew to greater exertions.

5

Again they struggled to pull the boat through the water with redoubled speed.

She literally darted forward; but, though quick as was her motion, it could not keep pace with their wishes.

And thus a few minutes of agonising suspense passed away, and the boat neared the raft, while the oars shivered like aspen leaves with the fury of the strokes.

She was alongside the raft, and the young officer leapt to his feet.

He stretched forth his arm, but the raft receded from his grasp.

The sailors once more pulled alongside.

Again he stretched forth his arm, and seized the edge of the plank in his hand.

He drew it close up to the side of the boat.

Five or six hands were thrust forward to seize its inanimate burden.

Henry Chambers clasped the fainting form of the young girl in his arms, and lifted her into the boat.

The raft, released of the weight of its occupant, floated swiftly away over the waves.

The young officer lay the senseless form of the poor girl in the bottom of the boat, and parted the matted and saturated hair from her temples.

Then he placed his hand upon her heart, to feel if life was yet extinct.

A strange thrill ran through his frame as he did so. There was a magnetism in that touch which sent the blood curdling round his heart.

"Give way, lads," he exclaimed—"give way with a will!"

"Aye, aye, sir," rang out, clear and joyously, from the throats of those brave British tars, as they once more bent to their oars.

In another moment the little boat was making rapid strides towards the cutter.

The young lieutenant found that there still existed a slight pulsation of the heart, and a feeling of joy rose to his bosom that she might yet be saved.

He raised her head upon his knee, and chafed her hands in his own.

He parted the matted locks on her brow, and gazed into her face.

A look of terror overspread his countenance, and a spasm shook his frame.

A cry of anguish and despair rose to his lips, and his limbs shook as though he had been seized with an ague.

He drew the head of the senseless girl to his breast, and pressed her cold pale face to his bosom.

And, in tones of heart-breaking piercing agony, he shrieked out:

"Oh, my God!—my Ellen, my Ellen!"

His face became pale and bloodless as that of the poor girl he held in his arms, and, with an agonised sob, his head dropped forward, and, sliding from his seat, he fell with his insensible burden to the bottom of the boat.

CHAPTER XIV.

THE LIEUTENANT AND ELLEN — THE VOW OF VENGEANCE — THE SMUGGLER IN SIGHT.

SWIFTLY the boat glided over the sea.

Propelled by the strong arms of eight hardy seamen, she rode over the waters like a thing of life.

Anxious and piteous looks were on the faces of the sailors, and one and all were eager to regain the cutter, with their now prostrate and much loved lieutenant, and his insensible companion.

Various and conflicting were the surmises of the men as to what could have caused the lieutenant to become so suddenly unmanned at the sight of the features of poor Ellen.

But not one was correct in the conclusion to which he had arrived in his own mind.

They were not long in regaining the side of the cutter, over which its captain was gazing intently upon the boat.

The young officer and his female companion were soon placed safely on board, and the boat made secure to her fastenings.

Captain Waters was surprised and pained to see the position of his young lieutenant, and he gazed anxiously at the seamen who had manned the boat for an explanation.

A merry-looking young tar stepped forward, and, pulling a lock which hung over his forehead, said:

"You see, captain, the lieutenant was somewhat turned keel upwards when he seed as how the poor cretur was all but dead."

"Mr. Chambers," replied the captain, "must have experienced a shock indeed to have been so completely unmanned; but he will, doubtless, give his own explanation in good time."

The young sailor gave another tug at the piece of hair, and moved from the spot.

The voice of Captain Waters, however, brought him to a sudden halt.

"Convey Mr. Chambers to his berth," said the commander. "He will soon recover, doubtless."

"Bear a hand," said the young seaman, calling to his mates, as he placed his arm around the shoulders of the lieutenant, who had been seated on a bulk-head by two of the men who had raised him from the boat.

In a moment two or three seamen strode by his side. The young officer was lifted in their arms as tenderly as though he were a child, and carried to his berth, on which they laid him, and then returned to their duties.

In the meantime Captain Waters had raised Ellen in his arms, and bore her to his cabin.

"Poor thing!" he muttered, as he laid her upon the bed—"her sufferings must have been indeed terrible. So young too," he added, as he looked earnestly into that rigid countenance, "and beautiful! What cruel destiny can have brought her to this? Wrecked, no doubt, in the storm last night, and perhaps the only survivor of an ill-fated crew. Poor thing! but she is safe now, and with those who will care for her, though they are ill-fitted to become nurses to a delicate woman."

And the good old captain strove by every means he could devise to restore the insensible girl to sensibility.

But, after exhausting all his efforts in fruitless endeavours to accomplish this feat, he stood looking upon her with a puzzled brow.

"Confound it!" he exclaimed, after a long pause, "I can think of no means to bring her round; and I doubt whether there is one among the crew doctor enough to accomplish it. Chambers is the best doctor, and now he wants a leech himself. How provoking! There, we must not let her lie in this state, if anything can be done for her, poor girl! And she's just about the age of my child, too. Well, well, I pity her, poor thing—from my heart I do! I'll go and see if I can't rouse the lieutenant, and then he can bring her round. Yes, yes, he'll do it, I've no doubt. Poor thing, poor thing!"

And the good-hearted officer left the cabin for the side of the lieutenant.

Arriving at the couch of Henry Chambers, he saw that the young man had recovered from the stupor into which he had fallen when he recognised the features of Ellen.

With that warm-hearted nature which was inherent in the brave old sailor, Captain Waters extended his hand to the lieutenant.

The young man grasped it in his own palm, with a fervent grip; for he looked up to Captain Waters more as a father than aught else.

"Well, lieutenant," said the old man, "I'm glad to see you all right again. Why, what in heaven could have thrown you into such a state?"

The young man paid no heed to the other's question, but asked, in a quick hurried tone:

"Is she safe; is she safe?"

"Yes," replied his commander.

"Thank God!" exclaimed Henry.

"Aye," said the captain; "God be praised that we have been instrumental in saving her from a watery grave. But, Mr. Chambers, from your manner, I should judge you to take more than an ordinary interest in the fate of this poor girl."

"Oh! sir," exclaimed the young man, "little did I think when upon the quarter-deck you rallied me upon my absence of mind, caused by my thoughts of Ellen Hanfield, that we should so soon meet again, and under such painful circumstances."

Captain Waters gazed into the face of the young man, with a long and earnest look.

"Whew!" came from the lips of the old sailor, and his grasp tightened upon the hand of Henry. "By heavens!" he muttered to himself, "his love for that young girl has turned his brain; and now he cannot see a petticoat but it drives him out of his senses."

He could perceive that the captain, by his manner, had not recognised Ellen, and he said:

"You have not recognised her, sir; you have—"

"Lie down a little while, Mr. Chambers," interrupted the captain; "you will be better soon."

And the old sailor forced him towards his cot.

"Sir," said the young man, "you think I am bereft of my senses, doubtless; but listen for one moment."

"Take my advice, lieutenant; lay down awhile, and I will pay the greatest attention to you by and bye."

"Captain Waters, listen for one moment. You think I am mad; but I assure you I am not. The poor girl whom I took from the raft is none other than the daughter of him who extended to us so friendly a welcome at Gibraltar. 'Tis Ellen, the girl on whom my thoughts have dwelt ever since the first moment I saw her. You appear incredulous; but, sir, that face once seen was by me never to be forgotten. When I raised her from her frail support on the waves, and recognised her loved features, a pang so sharp in its intensity pierced my heart at her sufferings that it rendered me powerless and insensible."

The captain still gazed incredulously upon him.

The young man saw the lingering doubt still upon his features, and he continued:

"Mr. Waters, if you will look upon that poor shattered frame you will see the truth of my words."

So persistent was the manner of the young lieutenant, that Captain Waters thought there must at least be some very powerful resemblance between the poor girl picked up by the boat's crew upon the ocean, and the young girl who had so infatuated his brave young lieutenant.

So, turning to Henry, after a pause, he said:

"Well, come with me to my cabin. She lies there insensible, poor thing. If it be indeed her, I ought to recognise her. But come, and you will doubtless then be convinced of your error."

On turning, he left the cabin for his own, followed by the young lieutenant.

They entered the captain's cabin, and stood by the side of the cot on which the insensible form of the young girl lay.

The rigidity of her form, and the deathly pallor of her features, struck a cold chill to the heart of the young lieutenant as he stood gazing upon her.

He leant over her inanimate form, and parted her hair from her forehead; then turned, with an inquiring glance, to the captain.

That officer bent forward, and gazed intently upon her pale cold face. Then, starting back a pace, he exclaimed:

"By heavens! the likeness is wonderful."

"'Tis the same," replied the young man; "'tis her, and none other. That inward voice told me that it was her, long ere the boat reached the side."

The captain looked, bewildered, from the face of his lieutenant to that of the inanimate Ellen.

"You are somewhat skilled in leechcraft," he said, at length. "Exert yourself to rouse her to animation, and let us hear from her lips the means by which she came in so fearful a position. In the meanwhile I will take a turn on deck; for, though we are men, and possess hearts that can feel for another's sufferings, we must not forget that we are officers in the service of his Britannic Majesty, and permit our feelings to lead us from our duty to our king and our country."

With these words, the brave and noble-hearted seaman turned and left the cabin.

Henry Chambers and the fair, yet senseless, girl were left alone.

Intently he gazed upon her inanimate features, whilst thoughts of a varied and conflicting nature passed through his mind.

Intense was the love he bore her, and he imagined, in the fondness of his hopes, that the service he had but now just rendered her would merit a return of those fond affections. Little did he know the heart of woman; that love, once centred upon a fond object, was not to be torn so suddenly away from its support.

But love is blind; it cannot perceive the obstacles that beset its path; and it is only when stopped in its mad and thoughtless career that it realises the thorough hopelessness of ever possessing the object upon which its selfish desires have placed its fondest hopes.

He bent over the loved form of Ellen, and imprinted a kiss on her pallid cheeks.

A deep sigh escaped the bosom of the poor girl.

"She lives," exclaimed the young officer, "and will soon awake to the knowledge of her situation; awake to the reality that she has been saved from the fearful death which awaited her upon those planks which bore her over the waves; awake to the conviction of my undying love for her whose image can never be obliterated from my breast."

Henry Chambers leant over the side of that couch, and watched intently every breath that escaped her body.

Long and anxiously did he gaze for the first sign of returning life; and fervent was the pressure of his hand upon her wrist as he looked into that face.

Slowly the eyelids of that inanimate girl were raised. Surprised and bewildered, she gazed round the little cabin; and then her eyes closed again, as though she could not realise the situation in which she found herself.

Henry suppressed his breathing; for he feared to break the silence of that cabin.

Yet he prayed for the first sound of her voice —that voice which was to wake him to hope, or plunge him to despair.

At last it came—came upon his senses like a death knell.

"Charles, Charles!" she said, in tones of agony.

A deathly pallor overspread the face of the young lieutenant. That name had struck a chill to his heart, which the roar of a broadside would have failed to have done.

It told that her thoughts and love were placed on another : and the heart which had beat with hope now throbbed with despair, and he sank down on a chair at the side of the couch.

In a short time he was aroused by one voice of Ellen, as, again looking vacantly around the cabin, she exclaimed:

"Where am I?"

The young man started to his feet.

"With those who will protect you," he said, in tremulous tones; "with those, dear Ellen, who will minister to your every wish."

The poor girl raised herself upon her elbow, and gazed earnestly into the face of the speaker.

"That voice," she gasped out at length, "those tones—good heavens! how came I here?"

"Compose yourself, dear one," said Henry. "I found you drifting over the waves on a few planks; but you are safe now, and with those who will care for you."

"Oh! I remember all now," she muttered, as the tears gushed to her eyes, and relieved her overburdened heart. "The wreck, the raft, and Charles! Oh! heaven, what of him? Tell me," she added, seizing the hand of Henry, and gazing wildly in his face—"have you saved him; or is he left to the mercy of the waves, left to meet the doom which I have escaped?"

A pang shot through the heart of the young officer, as he perceived that her whole thoughts were centred in his rival; and he felt pained that she had not one word for him.

"Oh! Mr. Chambers," she said, after a pause, during which time she had thoroughly realised the position in which she found herself, and recognised the person of the young man who stood beside her couch—"the sufferings of the last few hours had almost rendered me forgetful of those feelings of gratitude which I must ever entertain towards you. It has been Heaven's will that you should be instrumental in rescuing me from my perilous position; and if I have not tendered you those thanks which are due to you, it is not that I am ungrateful, but that my misery has made me forgetful of all but my own sufferings, and the fate of him to whom my destiny is linked."

As she spoke, she extended her hand to the young man, who, taking it in his own, raised it to his lips.

"Ellen," he murmured, "what cruel destiny can have placed you in the position in which you were found?"

And the young girl told him all; told him how, in company with her lover, she had sailed for England; how the vessel was lured upon the rocks in the storm, and went to pieces; the insults and indignities she had been subjected to at the hands of the Boy Rover; the escape of herself and Charles Lawson from the cavern by the rope; the parting of the raft, and the agony of her mind as she saw the form of her lover drifting away from her: and then all had become dark, and insensibility had thrown a veil over her sufferings, and steeped her senses in forgetfulness, to awake only to her present position.

Henry listened to the sad recital, and his bosom heaved with indignation at the indignities she had been subjected to by the young smuggler; but, for a moment, he almost wished that Charles Lawson might perish in the waves, and thus remove the obstacle that barred his way to the heart of that young girl: but this ungenerous feeling was but for a moment's duration, and his noble nature hurled it from his breast, as unworthy alike the man and the lover.

"Heaven help him!" he said, after a pause; "but give not way to despair, Ellen. Some passing vessel may see him, as we saw you from the deck of this craft. Hope for the best; despair will but add to your present weakness."

"Alas!" she murmured, "I fear to hope. Too well do I know the fearful dangers by which he is beset. Each wave, as it rolls onwards in its course, threatens to bear him from his raft, and he is too exhausted and powerless to struggle against them."

And Ellen buried her face in her hands, as if to shut from her mind's eye the picture so vividly presented to her soul.

"Besides," she added, "he may fall again into the hands of the fiendish smuggler; and, should this be, a fearful doom but too surely awaits him. Never shall I forget the threats of that unprincipled lad; never shall I be able to drive from my mind the terrible-meaning glances he fixed upon us when he swore to consign us to misery and despair."

"Let not such thoughts distress you, Ellen. A day of reckoning will come for that bold bad youth. We are now seeking to find him and his hellish crew; and the eyes of the look-out scan the ocean in the hope of seeing the sails of his vessel. Too long has he escaped the clutches of the law, and too often has he escaped from the cutters; but now the captain has every reason to believe that we are on his track; and I pray Heaven that our wishes to overtake him may be crowned with success; and, should we once come up with him, he shall find that honest British sailors have strong arms and stout hearts, and that there is one among the crew of the "Flying Dart" who will strike not only for the honour of his flag, but to revenge the insults he has dared to offer to one so fondly, though hopelessly, loved."

And Henry Chambers placed his hand upon his heart, as though he would force back the sigh that escaped his breast.

He fixed his eyes upon the poor girl with a halfpitiful, half appealing glance.

The eyes of the young maiden fell from before that glance, and the blood rushed to her face, and suffused her cheeks in a purple glow.

She knew well the meaning of his words, and she was grieved when she saw how her inability to return his love had plunged him into sadness. But her heart was already in another's keeping; her love was no longer her own to bestow.

She grasped the hand of the young man with a fervent pressure, and, looking into his face, she exclaimed, in tones of deep commiseration:

"Henry, dear brother—for such I would call you —you know not the pang your looks and words strike to my heart; you know not the grief I feel that you should so sadly take to heart my rejection of your suit; but it was not in my power to accept it. Already, when you sought my love, had I plighted my troth. Henry, I respect you as a dear and valued friend, made doubly so by the service you have this day rendered me; but love I cannot bestow, save the love of a sister for a much esteemed brother. Henry, if you love me, as you profess to do, speak not of it again. It can but cause useless regret, and inflict unnecessary pain."

The young man bowed his head as she concluded.

He saw how useless it would be to hope ever to win her love, save as a brother.

But a brother's love, pure and holy as it is, was not what he sighed for. He had met her in the home of her father, and the bright glance of her dark eye, the gentle sweetness of her smile, and the winning tones of her silvery voice, had called up feelings in his breast which neither time nor distance could eradicate

In a word, he loved that gentle being from the moment of their first meeting; loved her with a passion as fierce as it was genuine and noble.

He had thrown himself at her feet, and poured out his heart's devotion; but, alas! for his peace and happiness, she had firmly, but kindly, rejected his suit. Already was she the affianced bride of Charles Lawson; and he only could possess her affections.

From that time Henry Chambers became a sad and thoughtful man.

At times he would curse the ill-fortune that seemed to beset him in this epoch of his existence; at others, the better feelings of his nature would point out to him how inconsistent it was that he should be agrieved at that which thousands have experienced – unrequited love.

Long and earnest was the gaze which he fixed upon that poor girl as she reclined upon the couch in the cabin of Captain Waters; but the look of pain which had overspread his features at the words she had uttered, soon gave way to one of pity and admiration.

"Ellen," he said, "I feel—I know that I am selfish in my love, but I cannot help it. Would to Heaven we had met earlier, then, perhaps, I might not have pleaded in vain. But there," he added, as though ashamed of his weakness, "let it pass. Proud, indeed, would have been the time that I might call you my own, but fate has decreed it otherwise. Still I cannot forget that I am a man and a sailor, and one who would scorn to feel the smallest grain of animosity to the girl who could not, in honour, return his love. No, no, Ellen; mine is nature that can never truly love but once. On thy gentle form is all my adoration; I would make you my wife, but you say that cannot be: then will I be to you a brother, a friend, a protector!"

A smile broke over the features of Helen.

"Kind, generous friend," she exclaimed, with a sudden burst of fervent emotion; "your words do honour to the noble qualities of your soul. The heart of a British seaman beats within your breast, and a sailor's heart is laid bare by those words."

"And when the time comes, Ellen," exclaimed the young man, with an impulsive burst of passion, "you shall see that a sailor's arm will protect a woman's honour, and mark his sense of a villain's perfidy."

Scarce had the words escaped his lips ere the sound of a drum rang through the cabin.

Henry started: that drum was beating to quarters.

"Ellen," said the young man, hastily, "I must leave you; 'tis the call of duty, and that duty must be obeyed!"

He pressed her hand, and turned to leave the cabin; but, as he placed his fingers upon the handle of the door, the loud boom of a gun echoed through the apartment. The door of the cabin was thrust open, and a young sailor stood on the threshold.

"Lieutenant," he exclaimed, "the captain commands your presence on deck. The smuggler is in sight, and the gun has been fired to bring him to."

The young man simply inclined his head, as an intimation that he would obey his captain's orders at once.

Turning to Ellen, as the young sailor ascended the stairs to the deck, he exclaimed:

"Ellen, this bold smuggler is almost within our grasp, and, with Heaven's aid, we will sweep from the seas this daring marauder. He has insulted and outraged the woman I love beyond all else in the world, and, come weal or woe, I now stand forth her champion. There," he added, drawing his sword from its scabbard, and holding its shining blade aloft, I bear it at the command of my king and country; but I am actuated by that nearer and dearer to me at the present moment than the honour of the flag under which I sail. I have drawn it to avenge the insults offered to her who holds my heart in thraldom; and thus I throw aside its case. Never shall its bright surface be hidden again till it has found a sheath in that daring smuggler's breast."

And, as he spoke, he threw the scabbard on the floor of the cabin, and rushed from the apartment on to the deck.

Scarcely had his form disappeared through the doorway than the loud report of the gun again boomed through the cabin, and died away in the distance.

CHAPTER XV.

THE CHASE — THE STRATAGEM — THE FIGHT.

WHEN Lieutenant Chambers reached the deck of the revenue cutter, he found all the crew at their respective quarters, and Captain Waters pacing the quarter-deck with a glass in his hand; while, right a-head of them, the white sails of a rakish-looking schooner shone in the rays of the sun.

In a moment Henry stood by his commander's side.

"How fares the young girl you brought on board, sir?" asked the old captain, as he raised the glass to his eye.

"She has recovered her senses," replied the young man, "but is evidently very weak from her past sufferings."

"And she is—"

"None other than Ellen Hanfield, as I before asserted."

"I thought so," remarked the captain, "when I gazed upon her pale face a few minutes since. But how came she in the position in which you found her?"

The young man explained, not even omitting the indignities she met with at the hands of the Boy Rover.

The captain made no remark, but continued to look through his glass at the smuggler's vessel.

"We are fast gaining upon her," he said, after a pause. "She sails well, but there are few ships indeed can outstrip the 'Flying Dart.'"

"That is true, sir," replied the other. "In another hour we shall be alongside of her."

"I trust so," was the reply.

"And woe be to him who commands yonder bark," said the youth; "for he will have to meet one whose arm is nerved by a woman's sufferings."

Under a heavy press of canvas the two vessels kept on; the smuggler evidently wishing to give the cutter the slip, if possible; whilst Captain Waters determined not to let him slip through his hands this time.

They were both splendid sailers, for both had been built alike for speed; but slowly, yet surely, the cutter gained upon the Rover's craft.

"Give her another shot," said Captain Waters, addressing the man who had charge of a long heavy gun placed amidships.

"Aye, aye, sir," replied the man.

"And look you, Rowen, just depress your piece a little, and send our card right amidship of him. Touch him in the waist; then, perhaps, he may heave to, when he finds that we do not feel inclined to waste any more powder in harmless signals."

Tom Rowen, the gunner, depressed his piece, so as to bring it to bear directly upon the spot indicated, and stood awaiting the order to fire.

This was given, and the next moment the splinters flew from the bulwarks of the schooner.

"That will teach her to respect our orders, I should think, Mr. Chambers," said the captain, with a smile at the success of the shot.

"I am not too sanguine of that," replied the young lieutenant. "Depend upon it, sir, we shall yet have hard work with him and his rascally crew."

But, as if to give the denial to his words, the smuggler commenced to shorten, which allowed the cutter to come up with him in a very short time.

When they were within hailing distance, Captain Waters called through his trumpet:

"What ship?"

But the old captain, although he asked the question, expected a false reply. He was only too sure that she was the "Venomed Snake." He had not long to wait for an answer, for the next moment the voice of the Boy Rover called out:

"The Dolphin! Why do you stay our course?"

"Because your course is run," answered the captain, "and you will do well to surrender with a good grace. We know you to be the 'Venomed Snake,' spite of the colours under which you sail. So lay to, or I'll sink you, if you don't instantly lower your flag?"

The colours at the mast head of the smuggler were instantly lowered.

"As I expected, sir," said the commander of the cutter, addressing his lieutenant.

"I did not expect we should make so easy a prize of her," replied the youth. "I felt sure this desperate ruffian would have made some resistance; and I sincerely regret that he has not done so, for then I could have met him face to face, and proved to that dear girl how willingly I would endanger my life to avenge the insults offered to her."

And the young man bit his lips in mortification at the apparent surrender of the Boy Rover.

But neither the officers or crew of the cutter knew the boy they almost scorned now for his cowardice.

Thrown off their guard by the promptitude with which the smuggler obeyed the order to lower his flag, those on board the cutter paid no heed to the fact that the two vessels were nearing each other, till their close proximity was dangerous almost to each other's side.

Captain Waters was about to order his lieutenant aboard the smuggler, to take possession of her, and make her captain and crew prisoners, when, casting his eyes towards her, he saw the halyards run up

to the rover's peak a dark-blue flag, and, as the breeze spread it out to its full extent, revealed in its centre a snake, with protruded sting.

At the same moment blind portholes were opened in her sides, and half a dozen hitherto masked guns poured a deadly volley into the cutter's bows. Then she bore down upon them, and, ere the brave little crew of the government ship had recovered from the surprise into which this sudden attack had thrown them, the rover's hull grated against her sides, and grapnels thrown from the smuggler's deck locked them in deadly embrace.

The Boy Rover had manœuvred well. He knew that his best play was in close quarters—hand to hand. He, therefore, when he found that he could not escape from the cutter, hit upon the plan to lower the colours under which she was sailing, as a peaceful trader, and thus, disarming them of any suspicion they might entertain of his offering resistance, bear down upon them, and take them by surprise.

Captain Waters saw the trap into which he had fallen in a moment, and he called out, in a loud clear voice:

"Repel boarders on the larboard bow!"

Henry Chambers, too, recovered the surprise into which he had been thrown by the cunningly contrived ruse of the Boy Rover; and, knowing that it was the intention of the smugglers to board the cutter, he called on the men to follow him, and endeavoured to board the "Venomed Snake."

The Boy Rover, alive to the intentions of the young lieutenant, gave the order to his crew to repel boarders on the starboard quarter.

Both the crews of the smuggler and the cutter had endeavoured to board each other at the same time; and each strove to fight the battle on the other's deck.

For some few minutes neither were successful in gaining a footing upon the planks of his adversary's vessel; but, at length, Henry Chambers sprang on to the bulwarks of the smuggler, and called upon his men to follow him, which they did with a loud and ringing cheer.

The sword of the young lieutenant literally cut a passage through the smugglers for himself and followers to the deck of the rover; but every inch was fiercely contested; for, from every part of the vessel the rovers came: they doubled the number of the cutter's crew, and the brave young lieutenant was forced back again, with his sturdy followers.

Again and again did the sword of the brave young officer glisten in the sun only to fall on the head of one or another of that disreputable band, and once more he gained the deck of the smuggler ship.

His eye wandered round that fiendish crew in search of the Boy Rover.

He saw him, and his eye flashed fire, and his hand tightened on the hilt of his cutlass.

He flourished his now blood-stained steel with a giant's strength, and cut his way through his foes to the side of the youthful captain.

But by this act he lost the greater part of his followers.

The Boy Rover saw that he was the object of his furious onslaught, and he prepared to meet the shock.

Both seemed intent upon a personal conflict between themselves—hand to hand, foot to foot, steel to steel.

For a moment they paused, and eyed each other; and a look of deadly malice passed between them. They stood opposite to each other, with glaring eyes and firm-set teeth; and the next moment their reeking swords were crossed.

Then, as if by mutual consent, they paused.

"Villain," said Henry Chambers, "never have we met before; but there is that in my heart which tells me you are the wretch I seek. My duty to the government I serve makes me your foe; but there is a bitter and remorseless hatred between us, which nothing but your death can satiate. You have wounded and insulted one dearer to me than mine own existence. You drove her, to seek release from your hated power and unholy passions, to trust her lovely form, on a single plank, upon the foaming waves. You would have embittered her existence—made her that which would have rendered her loathsome to herself; and for that crime shall you answer; and may Heaven help me to cut thy black and craven heart from out thy coward breast!"

The Boy Rover smiled sarcastically, as he said:

"Fool! your words but nerve my arms with iron strength, for they tell that the girl who last night escaped my power is in yonder vessel—not long to wait the caresses of her smuggler lover! Even as I have scorned the flag under which you fight, so do I despise your steel!"

"Defend yourself, villain," said Henry, with a burst of passion.

The clang of the swords was terrible as they parried each other's furious strokes. Swelling with indignant rage, the young lieutenant fought with the fury of a tiger, but the Boy Rover was cool and wary, and he warded off the strokes of his adversary with an ease that showed him to be a proficient in the use of the weapon which he wielded.

A cynical smile wreathed his lips, as he sneeringly remarked:

"Your interest in this maiden is somewhat strong, doubtless you wish to purchase her love at the price of my blood, but your conquest will be less easy than you think for.

"Liar!" exclaimed the young lieutenant, goaded to fury by the sneering tones of the Boy Rover.

And, swinging his cutlass around, he brought it down with such fearful violence, that had not the smuggler have parried the blow with his own weapon, that moment had been his last.

As it was, so fearful was the shock, that the sword of the Boy Rover was shivered to the hilt, and he reeled backwards with the force of the blow.

Henry again raised his weapon to strike, and for ever rid the world of one so base; but, ere his arm descended, he received a blow on the back of his head, which laid him prostrate on the deck.

In an instant the Boy Rover sprang forward, and possessed himself of the sword of his fallen foe, and was about to plunge it into his heart, when his arm was arrested, and, raising his head, he stood face to face with Captain Waters.

The brave old man had followed his lieutenant to the smuggler's deck, and had fought his way to the side of his inferior just in time to avert the intended blow.

The Boy Rover raised the weapon to strike the brave old captain, but a ringing cheer, which burst at that moment from the lips of the smugglers, stayed his hand, and he cast a hurried glance around.

In that one hurried look he saw that his crew were victorious.

The brave British tars who had so gallantly followed their leader to the smuggler's deck, and played such desperate havoc with its crew, when they saw their brave young officer fall, lost heart, and, overwhelmed by such superior numbers, were cut down, or forced into the sea.

But two now remained out of that gallant band —Captain Waters, who had received a sabre cut in the shoulder; and his brave young lieutenant, Henry Chambers, who now lie senseless on the deck of the "Venomed Snake."

The former saw that further resistance was useless, and tears of mortification almost filled the eyes of the defeated, but not dishonoured, commander of the "Flying Dart."

The Boy Rover was the first to speak.

"Captain," he said, in his sarcastic tone, "you thought to bear me ashore a prisoner; but the tables are turned—you are now my prisoner. You will please to deliver up your sword to the safe keeping of the smuggler whom you would not have hesitated to have handed over to the tender mercies of the law."

"Never!" said Captain Waters. "Its bright blade has never been sullied by an outlaw's touch, and never shall it grace the side of a worse than pirate. I have worn it with pride, and wielded it in honour; and now that I have no further use for it, do I consign it to an honourable doom."

And, as Captain Waters said these words, he grasped its point between his fingers, and snapped the bright blade across his knee; and then, throwing the broken sword far out over the side of the vessel into the sea, he remarked:

"Never shall it be said that Captain Waters surrendered his sword to an outlaw, or that he struck his colours to a smuggler crew."

The Boy Rover quailed before the calm piercing glance of the old man, as he fixed his eyes upon his face. The smuggler saw that the brave commander, if defeated, was not humbled; and he ground his teeth, at he hissed:

"Captain Waters, the sword you so dearly prized shall not be long parted from you; for soon shall you follow it to its resting place at the bottom of the sea; and the colours you would scorn to strike shall form your winding-sheet, in your colossal grave, the boundless deep."

CHAPTER XVI.

THE PARLEY OF WATERS AND HENRY—ELLEN AGAIN IN THE HANDS OF THE SMUGGLER.

EXHAUSTED by the fearful exertions they had undergone, the smugglers had thrown themselves about the deck to repose their aching limbs, and recruit their wearied frames.

Those of their companions who had been wounded, and many indeed they were, had been carried below to have their maimed limbs attended to, whilst those who had paid the last debt of nature were hurled without ceremony over the sides into the billows.

No funeral service was read over their remains— no prayer was spoken for their departed souls. To the captain and crew of the "Venomed Snake" such rites were considered useless and unrequired.

Those who scorn to respect the laws of man have little respect for the laws of God. The laws of humanity being founded on those of divinity, he who despises the one must of necessity scorn the other.

But weary and exhausted as were the unprincipled crew of the smuggler ship, yet a perfect Babel of sounds rose from the throats of the victorious sailors, as some recounted their valorous deeds; others praised the heroism of some fallen messmate or derided his cowardice, and praises and curses, oaths and ribaldry reigned supreme.

For the time discipline was entirely set at defiance, and the evil-minded crew did just as they pleased.

Captain Waters leant against the bulwarks, and, with folded arms, gazed with looks of pity and contempt upon them.

The Boy Rover leant against the mast, with the cutlass grasped firmly in his hand, and a look of demoniac triumph upon his features.

He was thinking of the prize he would retake in the shape of the young and lovely Ellen, and the revenge he would have on the brave old captain of the revenue cutter, for the loss of so many of his daring and dissolute crew.

Poor Henry still lay insensible upon the deck—for the time uncared for, and almost unheeded.

The blow on his head, which had laid him prostrate at the very moment when his steel was raised to slay the Boy Rover, had been inflicted by the butt-end of a huge pistol, wielded by no other hand than that of Wild Madge, who, aroused from her drunken sleep by the noise of the affray on deck, had hurried up just in time to see the weapon struck from the hand of the youthful smuggler into shivers, and rendered powerless to further defend himself from the attack of the young lieutenant.

With the speed of lightning, Madge lifted a pistol from the deck, which lie by the side of a wounded smuggler, rushed forward, and inflicted the blow which had saved the Boy Rover from a well-merited doom.

Having rendered him this service, she instantly retreated to the cabin; and, as she entered it, she muttered:

"Not yet; he must not fall yet. The measure of his crimes is not yet full. Had he fallen, I should have been baulked of half my revenge."

She had seen, in the hurried glance she had cast around the scene of action, that the smugglers had the best of the encounter, and she felt assured of their ultimate success.

So, throwing herself into the seat she had previously occupied, she awaited patiently the issue of the contest, and the entrance of the Boy Rover.

She had not to wait long.

In a short time all sounds of strife ceased, and nothing but the victorious shouts of the smugglers rang in her ears.

A pleased expression played around her features, and she almost laughed aloud at the pleasure she felt in the blood that had been shed, and the hatred it would engender in the minds of honest men towards the youth around whom she was slowly, but surely, winding a fearful web of guilt.

And, in the exuberance of her joy, she filled a glass to its brim, and swallowed its contents.

There was a soft tap at the door, and the Boy Rover entered.

He advanced to the side of Madge, and placed his hand upon her shoulder.

"Thanks, mother," he said; "you saved my life."

"I did," replied Wild Madge. "Your time had not arrived."

And she looked, leering up from beneath her over-hanging brows, into the face of her youthful companion.

There was a momentary pause, and then the Boy Rover said:

"I am about to leave you for a short time, during which you will see that everything is placed in readiness for the reception of the young girl who escaped from my power at the cave last night."

Madge looked at him in surprise.

"How?" she asked.

"She is within my grasp," replied her companion.

"Where?" asked Madge, still more puzzled.

"On board the cutter," he answered.

"Ah!" exclaimed Madge, in tones of pleased surprise—"is it possible that fate has so soon placed her again in your power?"

"It is even so," replied the Boy Rover; "and now I must leave you, to escort her to her future home.

"Go," she said, exultingly; "lose not a moment. Listen not to her pleadings; pay no heed to her prayers for mercy; let no qualms of conscience soften your heart; but go determined to make her your own, in spite of man or heaven."

The Boy Rover left the cabin of the virago, and ascended to the deck.

Here he found that Henry Chambers had partially recovered from the stupor into which the blow on his head had thrown him, and was now in the grasp of two stout smugglers.

Captain Waters was also surrounded by several of the villanous crew. He had endeavoured to reach the deck of his own vessel; but being detected in the attempt, had been surrounded, and was now held firmly, though tenderly, a prisoner, till the captain should once more arrive on deck, and order what was to be done with him.

Turning to those who held the two revenue officers, he said:

"Convey the young one below, and place him in irons. I will deal with him anon. And, hark ye—see that you leave him no means of escape, or it will be the worse for you. Away with him!"

The sailors that held him bore the youth towards the hold.

Henry did not attempt to offer any resistance; he saw it was useless, but, bending himself up proudly to his full height, he exclaimed:

"Smuggler, beware! you triumph, but 'tis only for awhile."

"Down with him!" exclaimed the Boy Rover, in brutal tones; "put a speedy end to his croaking."

A contemptuous curl of the lip was the only evidence that Henry had heard his words.

"Captain Waters," he added, addressing his old commander, "we may never meet again; but we part now with the conviction that we have done our duty to our country, and the firm assurance that that country will avenge our fall. Kind generous commander, farewell!"

He extended his hand towards his old captain, but the brutal smuggler held him back.

"Bless you, Harry," exclaimed the old seaman, "I know not what fate this fiend has destined me to, but the hour of retribution will come when he will have to answer to the laws he has outraged. Justice holds the sword and scales, and his crimes will be weighed in the balance. She will yet tear the bandage from her eyes to judge him, and her keen blade will fall upon his head in overwhelming force. "Boy," he continued, turning to the Rover, "your hour will come, and your body yet dangle from the gibbet's beam."

"But you, at least, shall never see the day," replied the Boy Rover, "unless the sea gives up its dead."

"Farewell, Harry," exclaimed Captain Waters, "I feel that we are never destined to meet again, but in Heaven; and there, my dear boy, we shall meet with the clear consciousness of having done our duty to humanity and to God!—Farewell!"

THE MEETING OF THE RIVALS.

In another moment Henry was hurried from his sight, and as his head disappeared through the hatchway, a deep heavy sigh broke from the breast of the old captain, as an inward voice whispered to him that he would never gaze upon the features of that youth again in this world

When Henry had disappeared, the Boy Rover said—

"Now, then, bring him on board the cutter; there we will let him take his farewell of us and the world. We have many brave companions to avenge, and, by hell! they shall be terribly avenged."

So saying, the Boy Rover took his departure on board the cutter, followed by Black Bill, Ned,

Jem, and four or five of the smugglers, bearing with them Captain Waters.

When they had all reached the deck of the government ship, the Boy Rover gave the order for Captain Waters to be lashed to the mast.

This was soon done by the smugglers, who bound him firmly to the mizen-mast.

"Now," said the Boy Rover, "have everything shipped on board the 'Snake' that can possibly be of service to us; but take no useless lumber. The guns will add to our armament, and the powder replenish our magazine. In the meantime I have business in the cabin. Bill, see that all bear a hand, and have her cleared speedily. The captain will do very well as he is for the present."

And the Boy Rover descended to the cabin.

The eyes of Captain Waters followed him, and a paleness overspread his features.

He almost groaned in agony when he thought of the fate of the poor girl who had been rescued but a short time before.

Too well he could imagine what her sufferings would be in the hands of that daring crew; and, in his anxiety for her, he almost forgot his own position, and the indignities to which he was subjected.

The smugglers, under the command of Black Bill, now commenced their work of plunder and devastation.

The Boy Rover descended to the cabin, and entered it without ceremony.

At the furthest end he perceived the form of poor Ellen, trembling with fear, and almost ready to swoon at the sight of his hated presence.

She had undergone an agony of suspense during the short time of the conflict, and her features were blanched with horror as she felt that the brave crew of the cutter had fallen victims at the shrine of justice and right.

The Boy Rover advanced, and Ellen retreated, till she could go no further; and then she stood and faced her persecutor, like a tigress at bay.

A smile of demoniac triumph was on the face of the Boy Rover as he once more gazed upon that powerless and exhausted girl.

The dangers and sufferings she had passed through during the last two days had played fearful havoc with her tender frame.

The Boy Rover saw all this, and imagined that weakened in body she must of necessity be so in spirit, and would offer now but a feeble resistance to his wishes.

But he judged her nature by a mean standard; he dreamed not of the strength of virtue.

He saw only the poor trembling girl—not the woman resolved to sacrifice life for honour.

The smuggler was the first to break the silence that reigned in that cabin.

"Once more we meet," he said: "again are you in my power."

"Villain!" was all the reply Ellen made.

"As you will," said the Rover; "but still the fact remains that you have fallen once more into my hands; and flatter not yourself that I shall again let you escape so easily."

"Monster!" she exclaimed, "is there no limit to your unfeeling nature?"

"None," was the short reply of the smuggler captain.

"No feeling in your heart for the sufferings of one who has endured so much misery?"

"None," he again replied.

"Oh! heaven," she gasped—"there must be one spark of mercy in your breast. You cannot be all iron; you cannot see me worn down by my sufferings, and not feel one grain of pity!"

"I can," he said, coldly.

"Oh! mercy," she pleaded, while her frame shook with emotion.

"It is dead within this breast for ever," he replied.

In the agony of her feelings poor Ellen buried her face in her hands and sobbed aloud.

The Boy Rover watched her every movement with the utmost coolness.

Her sufferings would have melted the heart of the most callous, but he remained unmoved.

"Come," he said, stretching his hand towards her, "to your future home."

And he laid his hand upon her arm.

Had an adder stung her, she could not have started more violently.

There was contamination in his touch.

With one bound she darted half across the cabin.

"Away!" she shrieked. "Touch me not. Oh, heaven! where—where are my friends?"

"Dead!" he replied, with a demoniac smile, "and buried in the waters their rash hands have made their grave."

"All gone," she mummured; "then Heaven protect me!"

"It has made me your guardian," said the Boy Rover, sarcastically, "and as such I claim your obedience to my will."

"Scoffer!" she replied, "that heaven you affect to despise, will yet encompass your ruin."

"In the meantime I will assert my authority. All is prepared on board my bark for your reception," said the youth, in cold jeering tones.

"Leave me," said Ellen, "leave me here alone to die!"

"You have much to live for ere that time arrives," said the smuggler, as he fixed his ardent glance on her face.

"Live for—what have I to live for when all is misery and despair?"

"To enjoy the caresses of one who loves you,' was the answer.

"Loves! ah, monster! monster!——"

"A truce to this fooling," said the Boy Rover. "I am here to bear you to the cabin which is prepared for your reception on board my bark. Come, there are none to stand in my way, none to raise a hand in your defence. The crew of this ship have all perished in their fruitless efforts to capture the Boy Rover: like you, they despised my power and they fell. I have sworn that you should succumb, and I will keep that vow. Have you forgotten the words in the cavern? You despised and braved me, and I vowed to encompass your ruin. You are mine—mine! and all the powers of earth and hell combined shall not turn me from my purpose."

The villain grasped the hand of the poor weak trembling girl in his own rude grasp and forced her towards the door.

"Oh, horror! horror!" she almost shrieked, as she struggled in vain to release herself from his grasp. "Heaven aid me, and save me from the hands of this villain."

"You are mine now," he laughed; "mine till death!"

"Death claim then thy victim," she cried, in heartrending agony; "take me from this life to the side of him whom thy scythe has cut down in his youth."

"Ha! ha! ha!" he laughed. "Now proud and scornful beauty, the Boy Rover whom you scorned has you at his mercy. You defied me, for a time you triumphed; that time is passed: you are mine—mine!"

And he grasped her frail form roughly in his strong arms, and bore her to the door of the cabin.

With wild piercing shrieks she struggled to free herself from his embrace. In this she partially succeeded, and sinking on her knees at the foot of the ladder which led to the deck, she exclaimed:

"If you cannot feel mercy for a poor defenceless woman, have mercy on your own soul. Hurry it not to perdition. Sooner or later the day must come when you will have to answer for your crimes at the throne of God. Oh! man, man, condemn not your soul to eternal misery; forfeit not all hope of pardon from him. Human life is but of short duration; but after life is eternal. Stop, ere it is too late; or the vengeance of a just God will overtake you. Spare me, and save your soul. Think, think what you do; hold, ere it is too late. Have mercy, and that act will blot from the registry of heaven the crimes that lay heavily on your soul!"

"As you have defied me, so do I defy heaven; as you have scorned my power, so do I defy its. I live but for the gratification of my will; and you must minister to my wishes. I have chosen a life which, if short, shall be a round of pleasure: for the rest, I care not. I live for this, and this alone. Speak not—I am resolved. You cannot change my purpose; 'tis fixed irrevocably. As well might you strive to stay the rolling waves, as they beat on the rock-bound shore, as move me from my will; or stem the boiling lava of the burning mount, as turn me from my purpose. Girl, your doom is irrevocable!"

So fierce and determined were the tones of the Boy Rover, as he gave utterance to the words, that the heart of poor Ellen almost ceased to beat as she listened in horror to them.

She perceived that nothing would turn him from the gratification of his desires; that her prayers and tears were alike unavailing; that hopes of mercy in this world, and the world to come, could not move his heart to pity: and she breathed forth a silent prayer to heaven to stretch forth its hand to save her.

Again the Boy Rover endeavoured to bear her from the spot, and again she struggled with her villanous captor.

"Heaven forgive me," she shrieked; "but better die by my own act than live dishonoured and shamed! Thus do I escape the troubles of this world, and hurry my soul to the realms of bliss and eternity."

And madly, frantically, she strove to dash her head against the pannelling of the cabin, and thus yield up her life at the shrine of purity and honour.

Powerful as he was, the Boy Rover found it no easy task to prevent her accomplishing the fearful deed.

Long and fierce was the struggle between them; but the villain triumphed at last; and poor Ellen, faint and powerless, lie extended in the arms of the Boy Rover.

He bore her up the stairs to the deck, where he was met by Black Bill, and two or three of his followers.

Captain Waters saw the poor girl prostrate in the arms of the smuggler, and he appealed to him for mercy on her.

But the Boy Rover turned heedlessly away, and made for the deck of his own vessel.

He bore her to the cabin occupied by Wild Madge, and gave his fainting burden to her care.

A smile of hellish triumph played over the face of the woman as she received her charge.

The Boy Rover motioned to her to administer to the wants of his captive, and left the cabin, to return to the deck, and carry out his intentions towards Captain Waters.

Wild Madge placed the insensible form of Ellen on the couch, as she muttered, "I shall be avenged—deeply avenged!"

CHAPTER XVII.

THE DOOM OF CAPTAIN WATERS.

THE sun was fast sinking behind the world of waters into his western bed, and throwing fantastic streaks of molten gold across the horizon, and tinting the blue waste with a phosphorescent glow, when the Boy Rover once more stood upon the deck of the ill-fated "Flying Dart."

Every article which could be turned to service had been removed on board his own vessel, and that daring crew now only waited their captain's orders to cast off the grapnells which held the vessels together, and consign that brave and devoted man to a fate which none but the mind of a fiend could conjure up, and none but demon's execute.

They had not to wait long.

Turning to his followers, the Boy Rover asked: "Is everything on board that will prove useful to us?"

"Aye, aye, captain," answered Black Bill.

"Where's the carpenter?" he inquired.

"Here, captain," replied a heavy-browed young man, stepping forward and confronting his chief.

"Drill a dozen holes in her bottom," said the Boy Rover; "scuttle her, and let her go to the bottom with her flag flying."

The carpenter beckoned to two of the smugglers, and, followed by them, descended to the hold.

A look of demoniac exultation overspread the features of the Boy Rover as he turned to the bound captain of the brave little cutter.

"Captain," he said, sarcastically, "you would scorn to strike your colours to a smuggler?"

"I would," was the calm reply.

"And you scorn to sue for quarter?"

"I do," said the brave old man. "I expect no quarter at the hands of those whose hearts are dead to pity; and I scorn to sue for it from such a reptile as the leader of this hellish band."

"I admire your courage," was the mocking rejoinder; "and as, unfortunately for us, his Majesty claims the service of many like you, I deem it a duty I owe to myself and companions to get rid at least of one ship and one officer who seeks the extermination of myself and crew."

Captain Waters made no reply, but cast his eyes anxiously around the ocean.

The Boy Rover observed this movement, and he said:

"You would look for succour, but there is not a sail in sight: none near to know the fate of the 'Flying Dart,' and herald to your government the vengeance of the Boy Rover."

Captain Waters felt that he was indeed lost, and a dead weight settled at his heart.

He feared not for himself; his life had been so pure and honourable, that he feared not to die: but his mind wandered to his pretty little cottage, that overlooked the sea, and the fair girl and lovely matron that would look in vain for his return.

In imagination, he saw them bowed with grief —stricken down by the awful weight of their sorrows; and a tear started to the eye of the brave old sailor, and trickled slowly down his noble weather-beaten countenance.

And still the Boy Rover watched his every look, and gloated in the misery he was inflicting.

In a short time the carpenter and his companions returned to the deck.

"All ready?" asked the Boy Rover.

"All ready," was the reply; "she'll go down like a swallow."

"All hands on board!" he exclaimed; "and stand ready to throw off the grapnells."

"Aye, aye," rang out from the throats of the smugglers.

In a few moments there was no one on board the cutter but Captain Waters and the Boy Rover.

It would have pleased the heart of that bold bad youth could he have wrung from the breast of the brave old captain one cry for mercy. But no; firm as a rock he stood, his eyes fixed upon the sinking sun, and his lips moving in prayer to that supreme being into whose presence he was now being hurried.

"Captain," said the young smuggler, "have you any request to make—any wish to express?"

Captain Waters turned his eyes full upon the face of his murderer, as he said in low solemn tones:

"Assassin! I have but one wish—one prayer. Heaven grant that it may be heard. May the vengeance of heaven fall upon your soul; may the thunder-bolt of justice overtake you and your hellish crew; and may your doom be sure, speedy and terrible!'

"Ha, ha!" laughed the youth.

"Scoffer; that power you defy will overtake you sooner or later: the guilty may triumph for a time, but it will fall, and when it does, it is swift, fearful and overwhelming."

"Enough," said the Boy Rover, as he winced under the penetrating glance of the doomed officer. "'Till then I will reign the terror of the seas; my name shall be feared on the ocean and accursed on the shore; and when at last I can battle no longer with the overwhelming forces brought against me, I will die as I have lived, bold, firm, unflinching, and remorseless; with my foot on the deck and the ensign of my calling floating proudly above my head."

A look of pity stole over the old man's face, and the Boy Rover turned away and crossed to the deck of his own vessel.

Then he gave the order to cast off the grapnells.

In a moment this was done, and the vessels parted.

The Boy Rover leaned over the bulwarks and watched intently the doomed ship.

She was fast filling, by the waters rushing through the holes bored in her hull.

The brave old captain had fixed his eyes upon the blue vault of heaven, and was praying to the giver of all things to extend his mercy to those whom his cruel fate would render desolate. How beautiful to him appeared that gorgeous sunset; never, he thought, had he gazed upon a scene so lovely and so fair. He was taking his last gaze upon the world, and his soul was slowly drifting to those realms of bliss where the weary are at rest.

Lower and lower into that boundless waste sank the hull of the noble little revenue cutter—deeper and deeper into the western hemisphere glided the refulgent orb of day—and nearer and nearer to heaven's portals floated the soul of that brave and noble-minded man.

The waters were opening to receive his body—the gates of eternity were thrown apart to give entrance to his spirit.

Down, down into the vortex she went—the waters closed over her deck and engulphed him as he stood bound to the mast; and, as he disappeared beneath the foaming billows, the proud flag which floated triumphantly from the mast spread her folds majestically to the breeze, and fluttered over the head of the doomed mariner, entwining as it were a wreath of honour around his brow—and then was lost for ever in the deep, blue sea!

————

CHAPTER XVIII.

THE CONDEMNATION—THE ESCAPE—THE THREATENED MUTINY—NED DEFEATED AND MADE PRISONER.

SEATED in the darkness of the hold of the "Venomed Snake," with his head buried in his hands, and a prey to the most agonising thoughts, Henry Chambers passed the time away in which the noble little vessel was being hurried with her brave captain to its watery grave.

He was aroused from his painful reverie by Black Bill, who, descending the hold, informed him that the Boy Rover had commanded his presence on deck.

The young man merely bowed his head. He thought that his time had come, and that he was about to meet some terrible fate at the hands of the remorseless wretches who held him in their power.

Bitterly did he curse the hand that struck him down at the very moment when the Boy Rover was at his mercy; but it was vain to regret.

Drawing himself up to his full height, with a proud and defiant look upon his face, he resolved to brave the lion in his lair, and meet his fate, whatever it might be, as a man and a sailor.

When he arrived on deck, he cast his eyes anxiously around in search of the Boy Rover.

He saw him standing aft, surrounded by several of the smugglers.

All traces of the affray had been obliterated, and the utmost neatness and discipline now reigned on board the bark.

With head erect, and unflinching mien, Henry strode along the deck, till he stood face to face with the Boy Rover.

Then the young smuggler spoke:

"Pass the order—all hands aft," he said, addressing his lieutenant.

"All hands aft!" rang out over the vessel.

In a few moments all were assembled around their captain and their prisoner.

"I have summoned you all," began the Boy Rover, "to hear the answer of this officer, whose courage nearly deprived me of life, and lost you a captain. By the rules of our band we must not spare one who will not join us, should we deem him worthy to be a companion. Several of our brave messmates have fallen; and thus we are rendered somewhat short-handed. More than one met his death at the hands of him who stands before you. Did I ask you what shall be his fate, I know you will reply death. But in this case I shall reserve to myself the right of pardoning or condemning him."

The captain ceased speaking, and looked around the assembled smugglers to see if there was any dissentient; but he discovered none.

"You are all willing," he continued, "that I shall do as I think fit in this instance?"

"Aye, aye," said the smugglers.

"Lieutenant," he continued, turning to the young

officer, " by our laws your fate is death. You are young and brave, and cannot surely wish to die. I will waive the sentence on one condition."

And the Boy Rover paused for a reply.

"Name it," said Henry.

"That you will take the oath, and become one of us."

The young seaman paused ere he answered:

"Smuggler, I have trod the deck of a vessel at whose mast-head the proudest ensign in the world has floated. Beneath its folds I have learned to honour and reverence that flag, for it is the symbol of freedom and justice : and will you ask me, who have fought for its honour, to sully its purity by such an act? I respect my country, I honour its laws, and when I turn renegade let a traitor's doom overtake me."

"Is this your answer?" inquired the Boy Rover.

"It is," said Henry.

"Think again ere you condemn yourself to death."

"I shall but come to the same decision," returned the youth, in a firm tone.

"Is this your final resolve."

"It is," replied Henry; "firm, fixed, and irrevocable."

"Then you must die!" exclaimed the Boy Rover; "I have offered you the only means——"

"And I despise them," said the youth—"treat them with the scorn alone they merit."

The Boy Rover gazed upon the proud youth with a look of admiration; he could not disguise from himself the fact that the noble qualities of that young officer's soul made him the superior of any of that lawless crew.

Would the laws of their confederacy have permitted it he would have almost felt inclined to have let him go scatheless, but it was necessary for the safety of that lawless band that none should know their secrets and live unless they took the oath which bound them to each other.

"Run him up to the mast-head!" said the captain, as he turned away.

The youth heard this command with a scarcely perceptible quiver of the lip.

The sailors commenced to get every thing in readiness for the launch of that brave youth into eternity.

The eyes of the young sailor followed every movement, and a cold perspiration broke out upon his brow as he saw the noose made in the rope which was to consign him to death.

He gazed along the ocean over which the shades of evening were fast sinking; then upwards at the yard-arm from which the rope dangled.

"Oh, would that I could release my arms from this accursed cord," he muttered, as he strained the hempen bandage which held him so securely.

The word was now passed that all was in readiness, and Ned advanced to the side of the young officer to lead him to his doom.

He placed his hand upon his arm, and said:

"Your time has come."

"I am ready," replied the youth, drawing himself up. As he did so, the cord which bound him was loosened, and the ends fell by his side.

A rapid glance passed between Ned and the young officer.

Ned had cut the rope, and, with the rapidity of lightning, hid the knife up his sleeve.

Henry could have almost hugged him to his heart; but a look enjoining silence, warned him not to speak.

Another significant glance passed between them, and, with a sudden bound, the youth broke from Ned's grasp, and sprang over the bulwarks into the sea.

"Escaped, by God!" exclaimed Ned, as he rushed to the side, and gazed upon the form of the youth, as he disappeared under the waves.

"Escaped!" was echoed from several mouths, and, simultaneously, a rush was made to the side of the ship, and anxious glances were cast upon the waters in that spot where the young officer had disappeared.

The Boy Rover drew a pistol from his breast, and cocked it, and, with one bound, sprang to the side of Ned.

"Traitor!" he yelled—"traitor!"

"Captain, it's no use blaming me," said Ned, endeavouring to put on a look of injured innocence; "I couldn't help it."

"Liar!" roared the smuggler captain.

"Captain!"

"Another word, and I'll shoot you like a dog!"

And, as he gave utterance to these words, he seized Ned's throat in his left hand, with a vice-like grip, while his right hand tightened on the pistol, which he now presented at the head of his follower.

"Damn your treacherous soul!" he continued. "You thought the trick clean done; but my eye was on you, and saw your every movement."

"But, captain—" interrupted Ned, with some difficulty, for the fingers of the Boy Rover compressed his windpipe so firmly, that he could scarcely breathe.

"Silence!" roared the other, "or I'll send your soul to hell ere you can mutter three words of a prayer."

Ned was about to gasp out something, but the scowling look of determination on the captain's face warned him that a still tongue would show a wise head in this instance; so the half-uttered words died away in his throat, and, with flushed face and heaving breast, he stood glaring upon the smuggler chief.

He saw plainly that his act of mercy had been detected by the Boy Rover, in spite of the rapidity and precaution which he had used.

But the deed was done now, and he knew he would have to bear the consequences of his act; therefore, he endeavoured to conjure up in his mind some plan by which he might evade the vengeance of his chief and save the life he had risked for that of a fellow creature.

Ned was a lawless man, but, perhaps among that hellish crew, he was the only one whose heart was not entirely powerless to feel for the sufferings of another.

Hand to hand, and foot to foot, he would have neither given nor accepted quarter; but that still small voice which men call conscience, whispered to him that there was something more than a fiendish love of blood in consigning a brave youth whose only crime was fighting for honour and justice, to such a fate.

It was with a feeling of remorse that he had beheld and assisted in the bloody-minded work which had consigned the brave Captain Waters to so diabolical a doom, and he had resolved to ease his mind of so foul an act by stretching forth his hand to save the young lieutenant.

But he intended to do so secretly, and imagined he had succeeded in giving the youth a chance of life, without betraying that he had any hand in his escape.

But the eagle eye of the Boy Rover had detected the quick gleam of the knife as Ned secreted it up his sleeve, and all the passions of his nature burst forth as he sprang upon his better-minded follower.

The smuggler-captain had offered life to the youth, but the terms by which that existence was to be purchased had been rejected with scorn; and, chagrined and humbled by the proud bearing of the captive, he had resolved he should die at the yard-arm.

But Ned had stepped forward to prevent the execution of his command; and now all the fury of the Boy Rover was centred upon his luckless head.

Ned saw that nothing but a bold stroke would save him from the vengeance of his pitiless commander; and grasping the handle of the secreted knife in one hand, with the other he clutched the arm that extended the pistol at his head.

The attention of the smugglers had been called away from the object which had so bravely leaped over the bulwarks into the sea, and was now centred upon the two young men, who stood eyeing each other like enraged tigers, with all the bloody passions of their natures gleaming in their eyes.

Thunderstruck, as it were, by the defiant bearing and hostile determination of Ned towards their captain, the smugglers stood irresolute how to act, and turned their eyes ever and anon to Black Bill, as if to read there the part they were to take.

But that worthy merely stood with folded arms, looking on with as much surprise as did themselves.

The Boy Rover pulled the trigger of his pistol, but the bullet was turned from its course by the hand of Ned, who jerking up the captain's arm, the bullet flew harmlessly over his head.

At that moment Ned could have buried his knife in the heart of the youth who would have so remorselessly sent him to his last account; but he seemed to lack the spirit to do the deed.

Foaming with rage, and blind with passion, the grasp of the Boy Rover tightened upon the throat of his daring adversary, as he yelled out:

"Mutiny!—mutiny!"

These words aroused the smugglers from the surprise into which they had fallen, and they drew nearer to the enraged men.

"Send a bullet through his skull," roared out the captain, in enraged tones.

In an instant a dozen pistols were drawn from the belts of the smugglers, but not one raised his weapon to a level with Ned's head.

Then their eyes wandered again to the face of Black Bill, as though they considered he should be the one to fire the shot, or else that they deemed it necessary his command should endorse that of the captain's.

The Boy Rover observed the hesitation to obey his order, and his flushed face became livid, for he read in their unwillingness to kill his opponent the fact, that it but required the opposition of two or three of those bold spirits to render the power he held on board that vessel but a name; and his keen eye read in the countenances of those rough undisciplined men, that the slightest failing on his part and the authority he had so long wielded over that bold, bad crew, would be set at once and for ever at defiance.

But his was not a mind to quail when danger threatened, and in a moment he had resolved how to act.

Too well he knew that the brute natures of those around him were not to be bought by kindness; as well might he try, he thought, to tame the hungry tiger by caresses. No; the un-

flinching eye, the firm resolve, the merciless stroke alone would keep him what he had hitherto been—the captain of that lawless band.

"Drop that knife," he exclaimed after a pause.

"Take your hand from my throat," said Ned.

"Down with the knife," he iterated, "or it will be the worse for you."

"Let go your hold," exclaimed Ned, who was fast getting black in the face from the suffocating sensation engendered by the captain's grasp on the windpipe; "take your paw from my throat, or by hell! I'll drive it to the handle in your breast!"

And there was a determination in the tones of the smuggler that assured the Boy Rover he would keep his word if he were not released.

"Will you drop the knife?" he again said.

"If you will take your hand from my throat," replied the other.

"I make no conditions," said the Boy Rover, resolutely. "'Tis my province to command; yours to obey. I am captain here, and, while I tread the decks, I alone will make conditions here. Drop the knife!"

And the eyes of the captain fastened on those of his adversary with the glance of a basilisk.

Ned hesitated for a moment how to act. That indecision was fatal to him. The hand of the Boy Rover grasped the wrist of Ned, and gave it a sudden twist. So acute was the pain, that Ned opened his fingers, and the knife fell to the deck, at his feet.

With a smile of triumph the Rover held him at arms length, and said, addressing those around:

"Take him below; place him in irons. To-morrow he shall know his fate."

The smugglers, who had hitherto stood looking on, now that they saw Ned was rendered powerless to inflict any harm on the captain, advanced and laid hold of him.

Like all base natures, they would go with the strongest side. Had Ned conquered the Rover, he might have commanded them. In that assembly of ruffians, brute strength and brute courage alone were worshipped.

Black Bill now advanced to the side of his captain, and waited any further orders he might feel pleased to give.

But there was a look of savage disappointment in his face.

Who knows? Had the Boy Rover fallen by the hand of Ned, there was none other but himself in the ship who understood navigation; and it might have made things better for him. Ned could not have navigated the "Venomed Snake" over the seas. He could. And, besides, he was second in command to the Boy Rover; and strange things come to pass at times. The crew might have discovered that he was necessary to their welfare, and have offered him the post of captain.

As these thoughts ran through his mind, he almost regretted that Ned was now a prisoner. However, for the present he was subservient to the Boy Rover; and, therefore, he must obey his commands.

"See that my orders are strictly obeyed," said the Boy Rover, turning to the lieutenant. "Have a care that he does not find means to escape, or you may suffer for it. I will make him an example to those who would mutiny."

Black Bill bowed his head, and accompanied by Jem, and several of the smugglers, who now had Ned firmly secured, descended to the hold with their prisoner, there to place the irons upon his limbs, and leave him a prey to the bitter misery of his thoughts.

The shades of night had now fallen upon the ocean; and, one by one, the bright stars peeped forth from the blue canopy of heaven, and reflected their glistening rays in the white-topped rays, as they danced and sported around the hull of the smuggler vessel, as she glided, like a sea-bird, over the bosom of the deep and fathomless ocean, throwing the blue waters high up from her bows, and leaving behind her a trail stained with crime and blood.

CHAPTER XIX.

THE STRUGGLE IN THE WAVES—THE SPECK ON THE OCEAN—THE MEETING OF THE RIVALS.

WITH the confused hum of many noises in his ear, with eyelids heavy and drooping from the pressure of the water, and with limbs cramped and stiffened from their confinement, Henry Chambers rose again to the surface of the waves.

The shades of evening were fast gathering, and night's sable mantle was encircling the sea and enwrapping the world in its sombre pall.

The brave youth whose honourable nature had prompted him to meet death rather than dishonour the flag under which he had sailed, by accepting the alternative of joining that unprincipled band of smugglers, gazed anxiously around him to see where the 'Venomed Snake' rode upon the billows.

He discovered that he had risen to the surface some little distance from the vessel and astern of her, and then fearing that the Boy Rover would order out his boats to again make him his prisoner, he struck out manfully from the vessel.

But he needed not have entertained any fear of recapture, for the Boy Rover was at this time engaged with his mutinous follower, and the smugglers had almost forgotten the escaped youth, in their interest of the melee which was going on on board the ship.

But Henry struck out from the vessel with long and rapid strokes. He hoped that the fast-coming darkness would enable him to evade falling again into the hands of the hellish crew.

Better he thought to sink to rest for ever beneath the rolling waters, than dangle from the yard-arm of the smuggler.

So on he went—every moment placing greater space between himself and the bark—and every instant the darkness became deeper and denser.

Thus he continued to swim for about half an hour, when he found that he was gradually becoming more and more exhausted.

He slackened his speed and resolved (now that there had been no pursuit of him) to husband his failing strength to the utmost, and only to use such exertion as was necessary to keep him above the water.

But every minute now told upon him; and his garments clinging to his limbs almost rendered him powerless to save himself from sinking.

After considerable difficulty he succeeded in drawing his legs upwards and ridding himself of his boots, and thus freed he felt himself swim with greater ease.

And, so on he kept, the waves ever and anon dashing in his face, and the spray rising in showers above his head, at times literally depriving him of breath from the force with which they overwhelmed him.

But now it was that, worn out and exhausted by the adventures of the day, and his exertions to place himself out of reach of those on board the smuggler ship, he floated along, only using such action as was necessary to prevent him from sinking, and sad and bitter thoughts crept into his mind, and added to the agony he was enduring.

To all the horrors of his situation was combined the anxiety he felt for the fate of the poor helpless girl whom, only a few short hours before, he had borne insensible from her perilous position on the frail raft which had been observed from the deck of the revenue cutter while in pursuit of the smuggler.

Would that she had been borne away from their course, rather than that he should have been instrumental in her rescue from the fate that threatened her, to consign her to another, perhaps, worse than death!

He envied the brave young sailor on whom her affections were centred that love which she had bestowed upon him, and which he himself so madly covetted; but the thought that she had again fallen into the hands of the base-hearted miscreant from whose power she had but just escaped, and whose foul designs upon her honour she had told him of in the cabin of the cutter, caused him an agony of mind almost too great to be endured.

Then the fate of the noble captain, and the devoted little bark, rose to his thoughts; and although he had been spared the pain of witnessing that fearful deed, yet in his mind's eye was pictured vividly the agony of the brave old sailor, as, bound to the mast, he sank, together with the gallant craft he had so honourably and nobly commanded, into that grave where Heaven only knows how many have found a resting place for ever.

And the young lieutenant raised his bloodshot eyes to the star-spangled canopy above, and, murmuring a prayer for the repose of the soul of him he had alike loved and obeyed, vowed that should Providence permit him to escape the danger with which he was now encompassed, never to rest till he had tracked the author of that foul and bloody-minded deed to vengeance and the gibbet.

And thus, a prey to the agonising thoughts which floated through his mind, and ever and anon straining his eyes through the darkness across the sea, in hopes of perceiving one ray of hope to light up his dark path, he still kept on.

Alas! he hoped against hope. Nothing met his sight but the wide expanse of waters upon whose bosom he arose and fell by the undulating action of the waves, and the dark blue firmament above his head, dotted with the glorious lustre of myriads of stars.

Still on, on, with stiffening limbs and failing strength—still on through the crested waves, which ever and anon threw their foaming tops over his head, and almost deprived him of breath—still on, with the sea-gull's flapping wings above his head, and the loud screech of the sea-bird ringing in his ears—still on, with the waves dancing and splashing around him—on, with sinking frame and tottering brain—on, on!

One by one the lamps of heaven died out and darkness reigned upon the ocean, and darkness was fast enshrouding the senses of the young lieutenant.

Once more he was a little prattling child at his mother's knee, lifting his pouting lips for the kiss of love—he felt the glossy auburn ringlets of that loved being falling over his face and shoulders, and the warm press of affection as he nestled on the breast of her who gave him being.

He heard the sweet tones of her voice ringing in his ears—he heard her pronounce his name—and as he raised his eyes again to greet her, the rude waves threw their spray upon his brow and awoke him to the true misery of his situation.

Still on through the darkness—still on through the waste of waters.

He treads the deck of a proud ship for the first time—he hears the merry "ye-o-o" of the sailors as they heave up the anchor, and he sees the white sails filling by the wind as she glides from the shore. He sees the anxious forms watching him as he starts upon his first voyage, and breathe their prayers to heaven for his safety—he sees the loved forms gradually fading from sight as the vessel glides out to the ocean—he sees the fluttering of the handkerchief in the breeze which bids him farewell; he feels the tear rise to his eye, and a choaking sensation at the throat, as his native land fast fades from his sight; he stretches forth his arms as though he would once more enfold those loved friends of his childhood to his breast, and again the rude spray dashes over his brow, and the first grey streak of early dawn meets his upturned gaze.

How cold, how desolate and drear! and his heart sinks with despair as, half unconscious, he struggles with the waters which every moment threaten to engulph him. Again his eyes close and a dreaminess steals over his soul!

Once more he is on the deck of the cutter, gazing through the glass at a speck upon the sea. It comes nearer—nearer. It takes form and shape. He stretches forth his hand to grasp it; but another form intervenes, and tears it from him. 'Tis the Boy Rover; and exultingly he holds to his breast the form of the loved Ellen. He struggles to regain possession of her, but is held back by the smugglers, who laugh in triumph at his misery. He sees the brave form of Captain Waters rushing to his rescue; he hears the clash of steel, as he cleaves his way to his side.

Then the scene suddenly changes, and he sees the noble captain bound to the mast, and the gallant little cutter fast sinking beneath the waves.

He rushes forward to save him; but is powerless to move. He hears his call for help, as he goes down, down into the waters—sees the dying agony upon his face as he stretches his hands towards him. He sees the proud flag at the mast-head stretch wide to the breeze, as if to summon him to a sense of duty, and the rescue of the doomed man. He struggles to break the spell which holds him; he throws off the lethargy which bound him in thraldom; he rushes forward; he gains his side; he stretches forth his hand to save him: but too late! The waters rush over her deck, and he frantically clasps the side of the doomed ship, to stay her downward course; he holds madly to her timbers: but the waves dash him against the bulwarks, and, with a cry of pain, he releases his hold, and it fades for ever from his sight!

Once more he is alive to the horrors of his situation—once more he is awake to the truth that he is alone upon the heaving sea.

Poor wretched youth! cast thine eye around the ocean. What seest thou? One whose hand thou shalt grasp in friendship, and by whose side thou shalt yet fight for her whom ye both devotedly love!

Henry gazed around. The glorious orb of day was just rising from the sea and throwing across the cold grey clouds its warm red rays, and cheering that desolate waste with its golden tints.

Night had passed away, and day, bright and glorious, was stealing upon the world, and awaking slumbering nature to hope and joy.

How intently did the young lieutenant gaze over that expanse of waters, in the hope of seeing the white sails of some vessel.

But, alas! there was no sail in sight.

With a heavy sigh he withdrew his gaze from the distant horizon.

As he did so, a cry of surprise and joy escaped his lips.

And the sea-birds, frightened at the cry, rose, with louder screech, higher into the air.

Close to him was a raft, which his gaze, fixed upon distance, had not lighted upon till now.

He summoned all the strength he could muster to his aid, and swam towards it.

He saw there was a form lying upon it, with one leg hanging over its side, and either asleep or insensible.

He gained its side—he clasped it with both his hands, and drew his body higher up out of the water.

The rays of the rising sun were thrown across the insensible form.

Henry gazed into the pale and death-like features of the insensible being who lay so inanimate there.

His heart throbbed violently against his side, as, with a loud cry of surprise, he exclaimed:

"Heaven's! 'tis he—'tis Charles!"

Yes, the prostrate and insensible form upon the raft was that of the brave youth who had descended with Ellen from the cave; and who, overcome by the exhaustion of his arduous efforts and the effect of the blow upon his temples, had been unable to prevent the separation of himself and Ellen.

Only for a few seconds had a gleam of consciousness returned, in which he had discovered the loss of Ellen; and half mad with despair he threw aside his jacket and was about to breast the waves in search of her, when exhausted nature once more gave way, and he sank backwards on the raft insensible.

And thus he lay, drifting over the ocean, till the rising sun revealed his cold inanimate form to the gaze of his rival, who now clung to the planks on which he lie to support his exhausted frame.

What were the thoughts that now took possession of the mind of the young lieutenant?

He fondly, madly, loved Ellen, and he who possessed that love now lay insensible before him.

There was not a speck on the ocean—not a soul to see the deed.

He who had usurped the love of that fond being for which he sighed lay helpless before him.

One tilt of that raft, and its insensible occupant was lost for ever,

There was a demon voice whispering in his ear. Should he obey its dictates?

Long and earnestly he thought, as he clung to that raft.

He recollected his interview with Ellen, and the words she had uttered.

Those words had led him to think that if the brave young midshipman, Charles Lawson, had not forestalled him, there had yet been hope.

Where he dead, what then?

Could he possess the love of Ellen Hatfield? Aye, there he was puzzled.

True it was that she viewed him with favourable eyes, but who would convey to her the sad news of his death?

WILD MADGE REVEALS THE SECRET TO ELLEN.

Could he be the messenger to lacerate her heart with the sad tidings?

No.

Then who else could assure her that her lover was no more?

The young lieutenant paused to think.

And in that pause the better feelings of his nature rose uppermost.

He hesitated to do a deed which would brand him with the curse of Cain.

Yet the lovely form of Ellen dazzled his imagination, and the demon still kept tearing at his heart-strings.

And thus undecided he looked across the ocean.

Far—far out in the distance glistened the white sails of a noble vessel in the rising sun.

As Henry watched her rise and fall upon the bosom of the heaving waters, his heated brain became cooler, and the wild passions that assailed his heart gradually subsided.

And as the ship came nearer and nearer, the better nature of the young lieutenant rose triumphant over the demon that assailed his breast: and, with beating heart and throbbing brow, he anxiously awaited the approach of the stately vessel which was now bearing down upon them. And as the sun rose higher and higher in the heavens, larger and larger loomed the hull of the approaching ship.

And the white spreading canvas which bore her rapidly towards them appeared to the eyes of the exhausted mariner like angel's wings extended to enfold them.

Clinging tightly to the planks which supported the inanimate form of the brave and devoted Charles Lawson, the young lieutenant strove to guide the raft towards the ship, which he felt sure would rescue them from their perilous position.

CHAPTER XX.

HOPE—A SAIL IN SIGHT—SAVED.

It would seem that Providence in its all-wise dealings has implanted in the breast of every thinking human being the cheerful feeling—hope.

Hope on. Hope ever is an old axiom ; and but for hope how dreary would existence become.

It is the silver lining to the black cloud—the green spot in the arid desert—the cool drop to the fevered lips—the balm to the seried heart.

From the cradle to the grave hope is our companion and friend—it lights up the hours of our existence, and cheers the path to the grave.

It makes happy and joyous the hours of childhood—it is the bright beacon of youth and manhood—it is the cheerful lamp which lights the road to eternity.

Hope on, then—hope ever. Once the feeling dies in the breast all is black despair.

Cling to hope, hold on to it with a tenacity which nothing can shake off. Forsake it and you are lost, but cling to it and you are saved.

It will bring you safely up among the vicissitudes of life—it will smooth the bed of death.

Hope on—make it the guiding star of existence, the light of thy destiny.

With what feelings of hope and joy did the young officer watch every movement of the vessel which loomed a beacon of hope in the distance.

Hope now usurped every other feeling—hope for the rescue of himself and the insensible youth by whose side he now swam with renewed energy.

Nor did he hope in vain.

With every sail set, the bark made towards them.

They had been discovered by the look-out; and the glass of the captain, who happened thus early to be on deck, had set all doubt at rest as to the fact of it being necessary that he should steer towards the object discovered by the man at the mast-head.

And, surging through the waters at a fine speed, she made for the unfortunate young men.

But the anxiety and impatience of the young lieutenant was almost insupportable.

Exhausted and worn out with fatigue, moments seemed to him as hours, and he almost cursed the vessel, which was now coursing on to save him, for her tardy speed.

Still on it came—nearer and nearer to their frail support.

Henry could now see the figures of the seamen on her deck and in her rigging, and his heart throbbed violently with joy.

A gun boomed over the waves; it had been fired as a signal that they had been seen, and to bid them hope for rescue and succour.

The brave young lieutenant, now no longer sinking into unconsciousness, but thoroughly alive to the situation of himself and companion, struck out manfully with one hand in the direction of the ship. With the other he supported his body in the water, and guided the raft, which the waves beat hither and thither at their will.

Higher and higher the sun rose in the heavens, and brighter and nearer loomed the ship which had altered her course to save them.

A boat was now lowered and manned, and soon it was dancing over the waves to their rescue.

Henry now considered it but a waste of that strength which, in fact, was almost expended, to swim more; so, resting himself upon the raft, he awaited the approach of the boat.

Slowly the moments flew, but quickly and bravely did the crew of that boat ply their oars.

It was propelled by the willing hands of British sailors—urged forward by those whose hearts are ever open to the sufferings of their fellow creatures, whether on shore or afloat, and the generous impulses of whose natures will lead them into any danger, however great, to succour and save the weak or the oppressed.

From east to west, from north to south, in every clime where England's flag, that proud ensign of liberty, has floated in the passing breeze, the noble-minded and disinterested character of the British seaman is praised and admired: for peer and peasant, freeman and slave, alike acknowledge the fact that no hand is ever more ready to do an act of justice—no heart so soon prompted to feel for the sufferings of another—no breast that swells with prouder indignation and disgust at tyranny and oppression—no arm so soon ready to strike in the defence of honour or virtue.

Rough and uncouth as is sometimes the manner and appearance of the British sailor, beneath the shirt that covers his weather-beaten breast beats a heart as soft as woman's to the helpless and needy, and true as steel to justice and honour.

Such were the men who now, with strong arms and willing hearts, bent to the oars that sent the little bark leaping through the waters, like a thing of life, to the rescue of those two ill-fated youths.

With the perspiration standing in large beads upon their bronzed foreheads, the gallant little crew rowed to the side of the raft.

To stretch forth their arms and grasp the two young men in horny hands was but the work of a moment; and, with a look of gratitude and a sigh of relief, Henry felt himself lifted from the water into the boat, and laid, tenderly as a child, at its bottom, with his head supported on the knees of of a noble-looking old sailor.

The insensible form of poor Charles Lawson was likewise placed in the boat; and then, with a look of pity, the officer in command gave the order to pull back to the vessel, and once more over the dancing spray, now lit up by the bright morning sun, glided the little craft, with their rescued burden.

The ship had surged somewhat ahead, but now she had taken in sail to allow the boat to come up with her, and they were not long in reaching her side.

Henry, now that he found himself rescued from the doom which had threatened, became utterly powerless. His bruised and exhausted frame relaxed, and he sank by the side of his unfortunate rival, unconscious of all that was passing around him.

Tenderly were they carried on board the vessel; and as tenderly were they carried below, and placed in berths, side by side.

The ship which had so fortunately passed near enough to see and rescue these two youthful sailors from the fate which they appeared destined to meet, was the "Blue Bell"—a fine built square rigged merchantman, well armed, and equipped with as fine a complement of seamen as ever guided over the boundless deep the wealth of our merchant princes.

She carried a surgeon, and now his services were called into play to revive the young men, who now lie, in their death-like stupor, so close to each other.

He was a man well-skilled in his profession, and possessed a kind and generous heart.

He administered such remedies as the ship afforded and his skill dictated, and was not long in discovering that both his patients were in a fair way of recovery.

Then he ordered them to be left to that repose which was so necessary for their exhausted frames. And thus, for a time, we will leave these two youths, whom fate had destined to meet so many troubles, and undergo so many sufferings—whose love it had centred in one object—who were rivals in the affection of one fair girl—but who would soon become the firmest of friends, fighting side by side for the honour and virtue of her whose smile would gladden the hearts of both, but whose love could only repay the affection of one.

CHAPTER XXI.

RECOVERY OF ELLEN—WILD MADGE AND THE CAPTIVE.

THE sun was high in the heavens when poor Ellen, with throbbing brow and aching heart, unclosed her eyelids and gazed around the cabin of the "Venomed Snake."

Poor girl, too soon had she awoke to a true sense of her misery—too soon had the bitter recollections of the past once more placed themselves before her.

In an instant she remembered all, and with a burst of agony she placed her thin white hand to her temples as though she would stay their throbbing.

So weak and ill did she feel from the fearful struggles she had undergone since the vessel went to pieces amidst the breakers, that she began to think she was dying.

She almost wished that her spirit was passing away, for that would end her troubles for ever.

But then she thought of the poor youth she had seen float away from her side when the raft parted, and she prayer to live for his sake, or at least till she could learn his fate.

Then the fate of Henry flashed across her mind. Was he dead, or did he still live? She scarcely dared to hope so, the chances were too great against that.

The Boy Rover had said that he was dead—that none was left to protect her, and she felt that she was indeed a poor unhappy girl, around whom the web of cruel destiny was woven, and from out of whose meshes there was but one means of escape, and that was death.

And with closed eyes and heaving bosom she lay upon the couch in that cabin, a prey for some time to the agonizing thoughts that hurried through her mind.

At length she opened her eyes, and once more gazed around her.

The cabin was deserted, and not a sound but the plashing of the waters, as they dashed upon the bows of the smuggler, met her ears; and, ever and anon, the footstep of some one, as he paced the deck, or executed some order.

She lay listening for some few moments, and then raised herself upon her elbow, to take a more minute survey of the cabin. It was a well-furnished apartment, and an air of quiet and comfort pervaded it.

But, alas! too well she knew that comfort was not for her; and she almost groaned in agony of soul as she thought for what purpose she had been forced there.

Every moment she dreaded the appearance of the Boy Rover, and trembled at the insults she would receive at his hands.

Insults that bring the blush of shame to the face of the innocent and virtuous.

And her cheeks blanched with horror, and her lips quivered, as the agonising thoughts rushed with overwhelming power through her mind.

The light of her bright eye was becoming dimmed, and her brain, she felt, was fast whirling on to madness.

"Oh! Heaven," she prayed, "give me strength to battle with this demon, who now holds me in his power, in the defence of my honour. Save me from the fearful doom that now awaits me! Hold forth thy protecting arm, to shield the innocent and oppressed, and release me from the hands of him whose base purposes are fast driving reason from her seat! Oh! God, help me—save me; let me not go mad, lest my senses, tottering from their throne, leave me a powerless and resistless victim in the hands of the spoiler. Rather let my eyes take their last look of the world, and my soul wing its flight to the undiscovered bourne, than that mine existence be blighted by the deed, and my soul rendered desolate by the foul blot of dishonour that now threatens to stain the honour and purity of an innocent girl!"

And those eyes which had gazed with such loving tenderness upon the face of Charles Lawson, and whose bright beams had so often summoned the warm flush of honourable love to overspread his open and generous countenance, now, with appealing glance, were turned upward to Him who hath the power to save the innocent and punish the guilty.

At length, becoming somewhat more composed, she arose from the couch on which she had been placed by Wild Madge, and tottered, rather that walked, to the door of the cabin.

She laid her hand upon the handle of the door.

It was securely fastened.

She returned to the centre of the cabin, and sank into a chair at the side of the small table, and, letting her head fall upon her hands, her mind once more became a prey to the most agonising thoughts and conjectures.

And thus she remained for some little time; then she arose, and, approaching the window of the cabin, gazed out upon the sea.

The bright morning sun was throwing its golden rays across the white-crested waves, as they danced, and leaped, and rolled, in their sportive gambols, around the hull of her prison; and the wild sea-bird skimmed along the tops of the billows, as they rose and fell, curling their white heads to the rising sun; or flew shrieking upwards, in mad glee, towards the bright blue sky.

Ellen sighed as she gazed. Beyond that little cabin window brightness and freedom reigned supreme; but within that apartment, captivity and black despair!

She turned from the bright scene beyond with a heavy and beating heart, and once more gazed around her prison.

"When all means fail," she murmured to herself, "life must be sacrificed at the shrine of honour. But the means whereby to send the soul, in all its purity, to the shades of death—where, where shall I find it?"

The poor heart-broken girl searched every nook and corner of the cabin for some weapon by which she might defend her honour when again assailed, or sacrifice her life when she became powerless to protect it.

But her search was fruitless. Wild Madge had taken the precaution to remove everything which the poor girl might fly to either to protect or slay herself.

So, disappointed and dispirited, Ellen again sank into the chair, and buried her face in her hands, whilst her graceful slender form rocked to and fro with the powerful emotions that preyed upon her frame.

In this agonised state of mind she remained for some time, when suddenly she was aroused by hearing a key inserted in the lock of the cabin door.

With a bound she sprang to her feet.

Her temples throbbed more violently, and her heart beat against her side as though it would force a passage from its encasement, and her limbs trembled violently, as she stood, with glaring eyes and body bent forward, ready for the spring that was to place her beyond the polluted touch of her assailant.

She expected to see the form of the Boy Rover stand beside her; but she stepped back a pace in surprise as the door opened and revealed the red and bloated features of Wild Madge, standing upon the threshold of the doorway, bearing in her hand a bottle of her favourite beverage—brandy.

A heavy load was raised from the heart of the poor girl when she perceived that her visitor was not the one she had expected. She had thought to meet the gaze of none but the Boy Rover; but now that she saw standing before her a woman, instead of that unprincipled youth, her heart almost leaped for joy.

Besotted and repulsive as was the countenance of Wild Madge, poor Ellen could almost have pressed her to her heart, for she was one of her own sex, and she thought, with a woman's heart, she would feel for a woman's wrongs, and pity a woman's sufferings.

Alas! poor girl, thy kind and generous nature prompts you to believe all thy sex as good and holy as yourself!

In her noble loving nature the poor girl saw only a woman before her; and, with a woman's heart, she believed in a woman's nature—her mission on earth, peace and love.

But, alas! poor child, the well-springs of human kindness were dried up within that withered breast, and the rank weeds of desolation and misery had choked the pure sweet-scented flowers of happiness and love.

Better, far better, the arms of the Boy Rover encircled thy neck, than the breath of that drunken wretch assail thy nostrils!

For she will breathe into thy ears the poison of her soul, and wound thy breast with her venomed sting.

Madge placed the bottle she carried on the small table; then turned, closed, and fastened the door of the cabin.

Ellen watched her every look and movement with intense anxiety.

"So you've come to, at last?" said Madge, addressing Ellen, as she seated herself on the chair which had been occupied by the poor heart-broken girl previous to her entrance.

There was a harsh grating sound in the tones of her voice, that struck discordantly upon the ears of the young girl; and, with a sigh, she merely inclined her head.

"Well, all you have got to do now is to make yourself as happy and comfortable as you please in this your future home."

And a gleam of pleasure shot from the eyes of the fury as she fixed their glance, so full of meaning, on the face of Ellen.

"Oh! woman," exclaimed our heroine, in piteous tones, "sport not with my misery; add not to my sufferings by words like these; but pity and help me!"

"Pity!" replied Madge, as she raised her brows, and opened wider her bloodshot eyes—"pity! said you?"

"Yes, pity," returned Ellen; "for you, at least, must have a heart that can feel for the sufferings and misery endured by one of your own sex. You, at least, are human; you, at least, can be merciful, for you are a woman!"

"I was once," said Madge, bitterly, half-rising from her chair, and stretching out her arm for the bottle she had placed on the table; "aye, girl, I once was."

"And are now," returned Ellen.

"No," replied Madge, raising the glass she had filled to her lips; "no, not now."

"No?" iterated the trembling girl in surprise.

"No, girl!" she answered, vehemently; "that name is lost to me for ever; not one womanly feeling springs from this heart—demon passions alone reign within this breast!"

As she spoke she placed her hand upon her bosom.

With tottering steps Ellen approached close to her side and seized the hand of Wild Madge within her own, and looking imploringly into her face, said:

"Oh, you cannot wilfully sport with my sufferings. Heaven knows what may have rendered you thus callous to my misery; but you are still human; you are a woman, and with woman's heart must feel for a woman's wrongs, and stretch forth your hand to protect a woman's honour!"

With the spring of a tigress Wild Madge leapt to her feet and threw off the grasp of Ellen. Her bloodshot eyes gleamed demoniacly upon the pale face of the poor weak girl, and with clenched hands and harsh discordant tones, she exclaimed:

"Girl, you know not what you say, nor to whom you would plead; you sue to me for mercy and protection—to me whose heart is dead to every human feeling: you appeal in woman's name to woman's love, but better far had you appealed to the hellish passions which alone reside within my breast; for woman's love has embittered my existence, and now woman's misery alone gives joy to my soul!"

In fear and horror the poor despairing girl fell back a few paces from the now furious Madge. But the woman advanced, and grasping her tender wrist, fixed her bleared eyes upon her pale and tearful face as she said:

"Girl, look upon me. What do you see? A drunken half-demented wretch, whose besotted countenance bespeaks the indulgence in a vice whose infatuation dries up the noble qualities of the heart, engenders every crime, and gives birth to deeds of blood and horror. Turn from me in disgust, if you will; but, girl, I tell you there was a time when I was beautiful as you—happy and joyous as the young kid on the mountain's brow—trusting, loving as the angels. Life to me was then one bright happy day. But the spoiler crossed my path, his shadow fell upon my soul, and the first dark cloud overspread the sunshine of my life. But it would have drifted away, and revealed the silver lining behind its black surface, and all again been peace, but that woman crossed the path of woman's happiness, and blighted for ever all my fond aspiring hopes. She now usurped the love of him to whom I had surrendered all that woman holds dear—love, innocence, honour. For her smiles he discarded me—me, who had placed my trust in the noble qualities of his soul—my honour in his keeping; deserted me, whom he had ruined, and left me a thing loathsome to myself, the scorn of the virtuous, the jest of the pure!"

"Oh! Heaven," said Ellen, as the warm feeling tears of pity gushed to her eyes, "you have indeed suffered—"

"Interrupt me not!" exclaimed Wild Madge, vehemently; "hear me to the end." "Happiness," she continued, bitterly, "then deserted me for ever. I became a mother; and the first cry of my infant child, which should have made my heart bound with joy and happiness, plunged me deeper into despair. In imagination, I pictured the agony my poor old father would endure when he discovered my dishonour. I could not blight his peace of mind; I would not bow his gray hairs with sorrow to the grave. He believed me pure and innocent: should he know me guilty and debased? No! In my hours of travail none were near to see my sufferings, and know my wrongs; and, as the waves washed the shingly beach, at early dawn, a mother's hand consigned to the mercy of the billows the offspring of her guilt; and, ere the sun had cast its warm rays across the ocean's bed, I, once as pure, innocent, lovely as thou, stood the accursed of mankind, the abhorred of heaven—a MURDERESS!"

"Oh! horror, horror," exclaimed Ellen, almost forgetting her own sufferings in those of her companion's: "Heaven forgive you! Yours—"

"Silence!" passionately interrupted Wild Madge. "Speak not! I have not yet told you all. From that hour I have never known peace. In that humble cottage on the sea-shore, and whilst hovering between life and death, I swore a bitter oath of vengeance against him who had so basely wronged, and then deserted me, and her whose wiles had won him from my arms. That oath is registered in heaven and hell, and never shall it be forgotten; never shall my revenge slumber. O'er land and sea, day and night, sleeping or waking, do I track the authors of my misery to vengeance and a fearful doom!"

And, as Wild Madge gave utterance to these words, she released her hold of Ellen's arm, and pouring a glass of brandy from the bottle instantly drank it off.

"Girl," she continued, "never since that fearful morn have I known peace; never has the recollection of that deed been obliterated one moment from my mind. In the darkness of the night I see the form of my infant as the waves rush on to bear it to destruction. In the garish light of day, as I gaze across the ocean, I see its little form riding on the crested waves, and its arms extended, as though it pleaded to me for mercy. I hear its small infant cry; and I fly to this to quench the burning agony of my soul, and drown for a moment my misery and despair."

With trembling hand, Wild Madge refilled the glass, and poured the burning liquid down her throat. As its fumes rose to her brain, her eyes glared more wildly, and more revengeful became the look that overspread her features.

Ellen gazed with looks of pity and horror upon her companion. She pitied the sufferings she must have endured, but she was horrified at the fearful vindictive and revengeful feelings that possessed her.

Could this woman, half mad with drink and suffering, feel pity for her misery; could she be made an instrument to her salvation, Ellen thought, as she looked upon the woman, who had now gone to the window, and was gazing over the sea.

She would try: the wrongs Madge had endured might soften her heart to the sufferings of another.

Ellen crossed the cabin, and stood by her side, and, laying her hand gently upon her shoulder, she said:

"From my soul I pity you, and weep for your sufferings, for they have indeed been great—too great to bear. You, who have thus felt the weight of affliction, will surely feel pity for me. Oh! let me pray of you, by the memory of your past happiness, have pity on me. I know not if you have the power, but you may have the will: have pity then, and aid me to escape from the doom which threatens me!"

Wild Madge turned her gaze upon the face that now looked so pleadingly into her own; but no responsive expression rose to her countenance. On the contrary, a look of triumph overspread her features.

"It cannot be," she said.

"Why?" imploringly asked the young girl.

"Because I would not forego the pleasure of knowing that there was one as wretched as myself. Girl, I hate and despise the whole human race; and the cries of outraged woman is now the sweetest music to my soul."

"Oh! God," exclaimed the poor girl, with a burst of agony, and, burying her face in her hands, sobbed in despair.

All hope of mercy or escape was dying in her breast, and she felt that she must either fall or die.

But yet she resolved to die rather than fall dishonoured. Wild Madge meantime watched, with gloating eyes, the misery of the fair captive.

Ellen raised her tearful eyes to the face of her gaoler; and, as she did so, a strange wild expression passed over the features of Wild Madge, and she muttered:

"How like *her* face, when I told her all upon the beach! Ah! how that look joyed my agonised soul. How like; how very like! Curse her!" she added, aloud; "curse her! May her agony be greater than mine; aye, than mine!"

And, as though the thoughts that had taken possession of her mind could only be drowned in the accursed intoxicating cup, Wild Madge again seized the bottle in her grasp.

Ellen, trembling and fearful, advanced towards her, and placing her hand upon the arm of the woman, said:

"Oh, drink not this fiery liquid, 'tis this that dries up all the kindness of the heart; 'tis this which robs you of all the feelings of humanity, and——"

"Drowns my misery in its soothing fumes," said Madge, roughly hurling the hand of Ellen from her arm.

Ellen sighed. She could perceive that as the woman gave way to excess so all the worser passions of her nature rose in proportion.

Could she but prevail on her not to drink, she

imagined that she could soften her heart to pity her; she resolved, therefore, to try again to induce Wild Madge to forsake the brandy, and, again placing her thin white hand on the drunkard's arm, looked imploringly into her face, saying:

"Oh, do not—in mercy do not longer encourage this fearful vice. I am sure, did you but forsake this draught, that your mind would be less a prey to your sufferings—your better feelings would ride triumphantly over the lesser passions of your soul; and the true woman, shining forth in all the holiness of her nature, would throw a woman's protection around a woman's honour and save her from a fearful doom."

"Away!" said Madge, in infuriate tones, as she perceived the tenacity with which Ellen clung to her arm. "Let go your hold; I tell you, girl, that drunk or sober, sane or mad, not one grain of pity for your sufferings can ever enter my breast. I have suffered too deeply ever to feel aught but pleasure in the sufferings of others: a doom awaits you on board this bark—a doom which you cannot escape; therefore, let go your hold, for I must drink—drink."

"No, no!" pleaded the fair girl. "Give not way thus to this fearful vice; you believe it soothes your sorrows and deadens the recollections of your sufferings. Ah! be not deceived, it but adds to the poignancy of the agony you must endure; it but kindles anew the slumbering passion; it but stifles every generous impulse that rises to the heart; but deadens every kindly feeling that the Almightly has implanted in woman's breast; degrades her beneath the level of the beast, and makes her a thing loathsome in feature, in heart, in soul! Oh, woman, woman, have mercy on thyself!"

"Away! release your hold, or by——"

"Stay, stay!" continued Ellen, "ere it is too late. Think what you do by following this sin. Oh! if you cannot respect yourself, respect your maker; insult Him not, by changing the proud resemblance of angel which he has given unto woman into that of a devil! Pause, I beseech you, and have mercy on yourself."

And Ellen paused; but all the fury of her demon nature was pictured in the face of Wild Madge.

Her bloodshot eyes glared like living coals upon the fair girl who had thus abjured her to forsake the sin to which she was addicted: her bosom rose and fell with the wild infuriate passions that consumed her, and she foamed at the mouth like a worried beast.

Wild Madge felt the truth of Ellen's words; saw how contemptible her vice appeared to that young suffering girl—how her kindly feelings had prompted her to stretch forth hand and voice to prevent the indulgence in the vice that had brought her so low in the scale of humanity: but her base nature led to hate that girl the more, since she would prove her friend. Her's was a mind which could brook no catechising, and she resolved to reward the kindly feelings of poor Ellen by inflicting every misery she could upon her.

Like most base natures, she would bite the hand extended to save her—sear the heart that beat in kindliness for her sufferings.

With a fearful imprecation on her lips, she tore her arm rudely from Ellen's grasp; then, pushing her weak frame roughly from her, she raised the bottle to her lips.

Poor Ellen gave vent to a burst of emotion as she thought, "What mercy can I expect at the hands of one who can have none for herself?"

Poor girl! she had hoped to win that woman's heart to her protection; but now, alas! she felt that she had made Wild Madge her greatest foe.

The little bright speck of hope that glistened for a short time in her heart now died out, and despair alone held possession there.

"What can I do to be saved?" she thought. "My only hope is gone!"

And thus, dejected and heart-broken, that fair girl, but a few days before so full of life and joy, fell into a seat, and, covering her face with her hands, gave vent to the scalding tears of misery and despair.

And in this manner she remained for a few moments, when she was suddenly aroused by the hand of Wild Madge on her shoulder.

She started up, and looked into the woman's face.

"Come, girl," said Madge, "'tis useless thus to despair. You are here to meet a fate from which nothing can save you: therefore, give not way like this."

"How can I do otherwise, with a fearful doom hanging over my head? How can I be otherwise than wretched when not even one of my own sex can pity my sufferings? Oh! woman, woman, spare me—save me!"

The hellish and triumphant look that played upon the features of Wild Madge but too plainly bespoke the pleasure she felt in that poor girl's misery.

Another triumph was to be added to her soul; another victim to her oath of vengeance!

Pouring out a glass of brandy from the bottle, she held it towards Ellen.

"Look you, girl," she said: "from the doom which awaits you there is no escape. You must and shall fall a victim to the lust of the Boy Rover! But this," she added, forcing the glass almost into her hand, "will deaden the feelings of repugnance which you now exhibit, smooth the sharp edge of misery, and, if it will not make you a willing victim, at least kill somewhat the agony you endure at the prospect of your fate. Drink, girl, drink!—and then prepare yourself to meet your lover. Come, drink!"

With a look of horror and wounded pride, the poor girl shrunk back from before the lawless woman who thus addressed her.

Wild Madge followed, still forcing the glass towards her. Ellen put forth her hands to dash it to the ground; but this she was prevented doing, by Madge, every time she made the movement, withdrawing it from her reach.

"Oh! woman, woman," exclaimed Ellen, with a burst of agony, "how lost, how fallen, must you be to insult mine ears by such words as these."

"Drink!" exclaimed Wild Madge, rendered furious by the words and actions of her prisoner. "Drink, and drown your sorrows!"

And, forcing the glass into the hand of Ellen, she endeavoured to force the arm of the young girl upward to her lips, still holding the glass, to prevent it being dashed to the floor. So infuriate had the half-drunken woman now become, that she resolved, if the girl did not drink of her own free will, to force the liquor down her throat; and, finding that nothing could induce her to swallow the burning spirit, she essayed to carry out her intentions.

Resistance but added fuel to the fury which assailed the breast of Madge; and, grasping the fair girl by her throat, she hurled her from her.

As she did so, a small gold chain, which encircled the neck of Ellen, snapped in the rude grasp of the fury; and, as the young girl fell back by the violence of the shock, Wild Madge drew from her bosom a miniature.

The infuriated woman was about to throw it back to its owner, when a deathly pallor overspread her deathly countenance, and a white foam rose to her lips. Then, again, the hot passionate blood of the half-weird Madge suffused her face and neck, and she gazed intently upon the small portrait, with starting eyes and compressed lips.

Poor Ellen watched the workings of her countenance in wonder, pity, and disgust.

"Girl," at length shrieked out Madge, in tones tremulous with suppressed passion, "where did you obtain this portrait?"

"It was the gift of my father to his then happy child," answered Ellen, surprised at the question, and, likewise, the interest which Madge took in the picture.

"Know you," continued the fury, "whose features these are—whose lineaments are here so truthfully pourtrayed? Speak, girl! Know you this man?"

"Yes," replied Ellen, with a heavy sigh, "it is the faithful representation of him who, did he now know the misery his child is suffering, would be broken down with grief and horror."

With one bound Madge sprang to the side of the young girl, and grasped her wrist, as though in a vice; and, while her hot breath fanned the cheek of Ellen, she hissed into her ear:

"Speak, girl, speak! This man is——"

"My father," replied Ellen, frightened at the fearful workings of that woman's countenance.

"Thy father?" shrieked Wild Madge, whilst her frame shook with some powerful emotion.

"'Tis indeed the portrait of my revered parent."

"Oh, heaven! I thank thee," shrieked Madge, as her eyes wandered from the miniature to the pale trembling girl who stood surprised and pained, watching every movement of that bleared eye and bloated face. "At last, at last, my hours of triumph draw near, and the revenge for which I have prayed will yet be mine—mine. Oh, how my heart bounds as I gaze upon these once-loved but now hated features; how my breast swells at the recollection of what I have suffered through thy accursed wiles; but I shall be avenged—bitterly, avenged!"

And holding the small miniature out at arms length, she gazed upon it with a triumphant smile, whilst her bloodshot eyes wandered even and anon to the face of that poor girl who, pale and trembling, stood watching her every movement in horror and disgust.

"Yes, yes," continued Wild Madge, "I see it all now, the likeness of the mother; yes, yes, it must be, it is, and at last my prayer for vengeance has been answered. Girl," she shrieked, turning fiercely upon Ellen, who shrank from before her like a frightened fawn; "girl, this heart of mine has been steeled to the cries of mercy for years, but there might have been one spot within its beating pulse yet remaining green —one impulse within this breast which might have prompted me to save you. If there was, it has withered for ever, and not one grain of pity— one feeling of remorse—one pang of conscience, can ever again enter here; its well-springs are sapped up and its channels are dried, withered, and black as hell! Better for your peace and happiness that the waters had closed over your delicate frame—better that death had clasped you in his icy embrace than that we had ever met, for you are the instrument that must minister to the vengeance for which I have so long panted—you are the victim that must be sacrificed to feed my great revenge!"

"Woman, woman!" shrieked the trembling girl. "what do your fearful words portend?"

"Speak not," continued Madge; "the tones of your voice but add fresh fuel to the fires that consume me: for in them do I hear your mother's tones—sounds as hateful to mine ears as the building gibbet to the condemned man.

"Oh! then, you know my mother?" said Ellen, shrinking still further from the fury before her.

"Knew her!" shrieked Madge—"knew her! She was the serpent in my path whose venomed sting blighted my every hope, crushed my every happiness. She stole from me the love of him upon whose features I now gaze; tore him from these arms, which would have toiled for him, defended him, whilst breath remained within this frame. She it was who made me what I am—the companion of lawless men, a debased and degraded drunkard, a thing lost to all womanly nature, a disgrace to humanity, and a murderess!'

Roused by the words of Madge, which villified her mother, Ellen exclaimed, while her lips trembled with the powerful emotions that tore her breast:

"Oh! shame, shame. Heartless indeed must be the nature that can villify a good and honourable woman! My mother was too kind, too good, too noble-minded ever to wilfully injure anyone. Her honourable nature would have shrunk with horror from any deed that could have inflicted pain upon another."

"She stole the heart of the man I loved,"shrieked Madge; "she wedded with my seducer!"

"Then, by Heaven!" exclaimed Ellen, "she knew it not; for never would she have united herself to the man who had not been true to his love."

"She knew it, girl. I told her all—I told her!"

And a look of exultation lit up the face of Madge with a gleam of triumph as she thought of the agony she had inflicted upon her poor unfortunate rival when she was so soon to become a mother."

"Told her!" said Ellen—"when, when?"

"On the eve of her firstborn, when the pangs of travail were gnawing at her vitals—when the hour was drawing nigh that ushered into this world my murdered babe."

"Wretch! fiend!" exclaimed Ellen, in horror and disgust. "Oh! callous-hearted woman, who, in such an hour, could strike at a woman's happiness. Oh! foul blot upon humanity, how must you stand accursed in the eyes of Heaven! The degraded wretch who forfeits the proud title of man, and lets the arm which should protect fall violently upon defenceless woman, is a thing to be scouted and abhorred. But the woman who can sink to such a depth as to strike at a woman's heart and happiness in the hours of woman's labour, must stand forth the accursed of heaven; and hell disgorge her soul, as a thing too black, too horrible, for fiends to mix with!"

"Ha, ha, ha!" laughed Wild Madge. "The poison works, and I triumph in my revenge."

"Hence, away!" exclaimed the proud girl, roused almost to a pitch of fury by the presence of one so lost to all feeling and self-respect. "Pollute not the air I breathe with your hateful presence. My misery was great before, at the thoughts of the insults I must endure at the hands of the Boy Rover: but his crimes sink into insignificance beside thy black-hearted nature. Away! leave me to my misery; let me not longer gaze upon thy hateful features. Your words have endowed me with a strength that has nerved a daughter's arm to protect a mother's memory. Away, loathsome wretch! away!"

And the poor girl raised her fair white arm to strike the being at her side.

Wild Madge, cowed by the furious looks and gestures of Ellen, retreated a few paces; then, holding the miniature at arm's length towards the fair captive, she exclaimed, in tones rendered hoarse with passion:

"Girl, your words are powerless to sting me. I have sworn never to rest till I have tracked to vengeance and death the being whose lineaments are pourtrayed so truthfully in this small miniature; and all connected or allied to him. And, in the consummation of that revenge, no act, however fearful, no deed, however black, but shall be perpetrated to the gratification of my vengeance. Already have I woven the web around one, which shall consign him to a fearful doom. You are the next whom fate has placed within my power, and terrible shall be your doom. Oh! how I will lacerate the heart of him who blighted mine. To be revenged on him, I will sacrifice you. The Boy Rover awaits to press you to his heart—enfold you to his lustful bosom. You shall fall—not as I fell; for I fell willingly. But still you must fall; and your shrieks for mercy will be music to my soul; and my heart, bounding in the gratification of my vengeance, will swell with joy at my triumph. Ha, ha, ha! my triumph."

"Oh! Heaven," exclaimed Ellen, clasping her forehead in agony, "aid me in this fearful trying hour."

And the eyes of the poor girl were cast appealingly upwards, whilst Madge, with extended arm, held the portrait derisively towards her, and gloated in the misery she had inflicted.

Then a low derisive laugh escaped the lips of the base-hearted woman; but, ere it died away, Ellen, goaded to madness, started from her appealing position, and clasped the throat of Wild Madge with her thin white fingers.

"Fiend!' she shrieked, "I can endure no more. Your taunts have driven me to madness, and a woman's arm shall protect a woman's feelings."

And, as she spoke, with superhuman strength she hurled to the floor the bloated and half-drunken form of her tormentor.

She gazed on her fallen foe for a moment; then, weak as a child, she sank into a chair, and buried her face in her hands.

CHAPTER XXII.

SAD REFLECTIONS—AN UNEXPECTED VISITOR—A FRIEND IN NEED—THE ESCAPE FROM THE IRONS.

WITH limbs cramped and stiffened by the iron which so securely held him a prisoner in the hold of the smuggler ship, Ned, with sleepless eyes and tortured brain passed the weary moments of the fore part of that night away.

He had allowed mercy to enter into his soul, and was now being rewarded for the better feelings which had prompted him to do one friendly act for the brave young lieutenant when under the noose that was to consign him to a fearful death.

In the still darkness of that hold bitter thoughts assailed his breast—conscience was at work, and the young smuggler reviewed the life he had been leading and contrasted his present position and future prospects with what they might have been had he chose an honourable course through which to steer his existence.

In the hours of adversity the human nature is prone to examine into its failings; and when the dark shadow of misfortune enwraps man in its sombre covering, he sees in the darkness those light rays which would have guided his footsteps to prosperity and peace.

Too well he knew that he could expect no mercy at the hands of the Boy Rover, and sure he was that the smuggler captain would invent some terrible doom to warn and deter his crew from any attempt to disobey his orders, or mutiny against his commands.

He expected that ere the sun should again set, he would either swing at the yard-arm or have to walk the plank.

He endeavoured to close his eyes in sleep, but in vain; the drowsy god would not be courted.

Like all men whose lives have been in dishonourable pursuits, the enormity of his sins weighed heavily on his soul, and he feared to die.

If he could expect no mercy at the hands of him whom he had hitherto so faithfully served, and whose dictates he never once before disobeyed, could he expect mercy from Him whose laws he had disobeyed, whose commands he had despised, whose power he had defied!

And as these thoughts preyed upon his mind he shuddered with horror at the approach of death.

The darkness of his prison seemed blacker than ever, and the silence that reigned was painful in its intensity.

And, as he thought, strange sounds rang in his ears ever and anon, and with a start he turned his eyes around.

Strange shapes seemed to people the darkness around him, and his nerves unstrung by the prickings of conscience caused him to tremble with fear at his own imagination.

He tried to whistle to break the silence, but the sound died on his lips.

Like most sailors he was superstitious, and he dreaded the darkness and loneliness of that hold.

How he longed for some human being to keep him company—but for the sound of one human voice, but for the small glimmer of one ray of light.

He felt that he must break the painful silence, he could endure it no longer. He coughed, but to his imagination it sounded so unearthly, that, ere its echoes had died away, a cold clammy perspiration broke out upon his forehead, and the blood seemed to stagnate around his heart in horror.

He closed his eyes, but his brain was peopled with ghastly and fantastic shapes which but added to the sufferings of his affrighted soul.

And thus the time passed on.

Had the Boy Rover have known the fearful sufferings of his follower, he could have devised no punishment greater than that which he was then enduring.

Suddenly Ned fancied that he heard his name pronounced.

His head became bedewed with a cold sweat, and every individual hair seemed to stand on end, as he strained his eyes through the darkness.

"Hist! Ned, Ned!" came the voice again to the ears of the affrighted man.

"Who speaks?" gasped forth Ned.

"Jem," was the reply which came through the darkness.

MURDER OF THE MAN AT THE WHEEL.

Ned recognised in a moment the tones of his friend and companion, Jem Sparks.

A heavy weight seemed to be lifted from his heart, and the horror of his situation appeared less unbearable now that he knew he was no longer alone.

"Where are you?" he asked, peering around in the direction whence the sound of the voice proceeded.

"Hush!" was the reply. "I will be by your side in an instant. Don't say a word above a breath or you may have a companion, and lose all chance of escape."

Ned was silent.

In a moment after a hand was placed upon his shoulder, and Jem stood by the side of the imprisoned man.

"Well, my hearty," inquired Jem, in a bantering tone; "What cheer?"

"Cheerless enough," said Ned, with a shudder. "The darkness of this place is enough to drive a fellow mad!"

"Well, mate, pluck up," said his visitor. "The captain gave orders for us all to have a treble allowance of grog, to wash down the hard day's work; and himself and crew are all as drunk as fiddlers at a village merry-making: he's so pleased at again collaring that girl, that he determined we should all enjoy ourselves.'

"All but me," rejoined Ned.

"Well, you see," continued Jem, not heeding the remark of the ironed man, "we've always been chums as stuck up for each other; and thinks I, I'll wait 'till they're all dead drunk, and then I'll try and take a drop to Ned, 'cos as how he must want his grog down there all to himself. And so here it is. Just lap that little drop down, and it'll put some spirits into you; for it's hard lines to be cooped up, and have your grog stopped at the same time—ain't it, mate?"

"Yes," replied Ned: "and I suppose he means to stop my breath to-morrow, damn him!"

"No doubt of it: so enjoy yourself, mate, while you can. Here," he added, thrusting a flask into the hand of his companion, "take a long pull, and a strong pull, and get as drunk as you can, so as you won't know much about it."

Ned required very little persuasion to drink; and the next moment the liquor was gurgling down his throat. When he withdrew the flask from his lips, he drew a long breath, and said:

"Thanks, Jem; you're a true mate: but I'd a done as much for you, had you been in my place."

"I know you would," returned the other, "and that's why I run the risk of coming here."

"Jem," said the imprisoned man, after a pause, "what do you think the captain means to do with me?"

"Can't say for certain," replied Jem: "scrogging, at the least. It was mutiny, you know; and mutiny's death."

"It's hard lines," remarked Ned, after a pause.

"Well, it is hard lines," said Jem, "very hard."

Then there was a pause, during which Ned took another pull at the brandy flask.

"Goes down like mother's milk, don't it?" said Jem.

"Jem," remarked Ned, "I knew you'd stick up for me. Now, tell me, is there any chance to get free of these cursed irons?"

"Yes," drawled out his visitor, "if you could file the bolts."

"Will you give me a file?" asked the other quickly.

"No," said Ned, "I won't give you one; because, you see, if I did, I might share the same fate. But," he added, stooping down, "I really do think there's one lying at your feet."

The significant tones of the man's voice sent the blood rushing through the veins of Ned.

He felt sure that his companion had brought him means of releasing his imprisoned limbs.

Running his hands over the planks at his feet, he grasped a small file.

"Oh! thanks, mate," he exclaimed, in overjoyed tones. "If I succeed in saving myself, I'll not forget you. We've been palls a long time, and I'll show you as how Ned Waters don't forget a good turn."

"Well, just mind as how you don't blab, if you're collared; or else the good turn you'll do me will stretch my neck as well as your own."

"Never fear," replied his friend. "If I succeed in getting clear of the yard-arm, well and good; but if I must swing, why, demme! I'll swing alone."

"Now, look here, mate," said Jem, "if you've got any of that grog left, just toss it off at once, and hand me back the bottle. I must make myself scarce, if I don't want to be discovered."

Ned swallowed the remainder of the brandy, and returned the flask to Jem. Then, shaking him warmly by the hand, he said:

"Get to your berth as quick as you can, and don't forget that Ned Waters will do as good a turn for you, if it ever lies in his power."

"Hope you won't get the chance, that's all. Go to work quietly as you can; and if any one comes, slum the file, and pretend to be asleep. Good night, and good luck to you!"

And his visitor turned to leave the hold and seek his own berth.

"Jem," said Ned.

"Well."

"Do you think the captain has succeeded with that girl?"

"Didn't I tell you he was drunk in his berth."

"Then she is safe for the present?"

"For to-night she is," remarked his companion; "but I won't say as much for her to-morrow."

"Poor thing!" remarked Ned, "I pity her."

"So do I," said Jem.

"She has suffered enough already."

"Wonder she ain't dead."

"I should like to save here," remarked Ned.

"Look to your own safety," said Jem.

"And then to hers."

"Mind what you're after," said Jem; "look to yourself and let her take her chance, or you'll ruin all."

"Well, perhaps you're right," was the reply.

"Now mind what you're after—good night!"

"Good night," replied Ned.

And the next moment he heard the retreating footsteps of his friendly visitor.

He listened for a few moments and then all was still.

The solitude and darkness that had before so appalled him was now forgotten, and his whole thoughts were centred in releasing himself from the irons which so firmly held him.

He grasped the file and worked it over the rings which encircled his ankles, and the grating sound produced by the operation was music to his soul.

If he succeeded in freeing his limbs and once more regaining his liberty, he resolved to try one more good action, and, at the same time be revenged on the Boy Rover.

He had hitherto been his staunchest friend—now he was his bitterest enemy.

He resolved to stretch forth his arm to save Ellen, when the slightest opportunity presented.

And, thus thinking, he toiled on in the darkness and silence of the hold, now again broken only by the sound of the file, as it worked its passage through the iron. The superstitious dread that had assailed the breast of the smuggler prisoner in his dreary quarters before the arrival of Jem, no longer haunted him; and the sound caused by the friction of the two metals upon each other, which would have driven his guilty mind to imagine it was produced by some supernatural agency had it saluted his ears unknown from whence it came, was now the most soothing music to his soul; for it was a sound heralding liberty and freedom to the bound and imprisoned man.

Ever and anon he paused and strained his ears to catch the slightest sound; but all remained still as the grave, and he would ply the file with redoubled vigour.

In the course of two hours he succeeded in releasing his limbs from the iron bonds, and, with a cry of joy, he sprang to his feet.

But so cramped had his legs become by the confinement, that he tottered a few paces, and sank again to the floor.

Then he commenced rubbing the stiffened joints, to admit of the free passage of the blood through the veins; and in a short time he was enabled to use the benumbed limbs with greater freedom.

Concealing the file in his breast, he groped his way to the opening to the deck; but, as he did so, the sound of several voices saluted his ears, and he hurriedly retreated to his former position.

"What shall I do now?" he thought. "There are several on deck, and to escape being seen by them is impossible; and, if I could, what then can I do—how escape the fate the captain intends for me?"

And the now half-freed smuggler fell into a train of thought upon the best means of ensuring his safety.

"I have it!" he exclaimed, at length. "I must stow myself away somewhere in this infernal hold till an opportunity presents itself of effecting my escape on shore. That I have released myself from the irons is sure to be discovered; but they won't make any search for me: they'll think I've gone over the side, like the young officer. Yes, that's what I'll do. We shall make land in a few hours more; and then will be my time to get clear, and, perhaps, bring down the bloodhounds on the 'Venomed Snake.'"

A few short hours before, the Boy Rover had possesssed in Ned Waters a friend and follower who would have placed his own body before his breast to shield him from harm; but now he would find a foe as inveterate as his friendship had been firm and staunch. Ned only now awaited the moment when he might betray his captain into the hands of justice.

He was not long in stowing himself away behind a heterogenous mass of articles which the hold of that vessel contained; and here awaited the issue of the discovery of his escape.

In the course of a few hours all was life and bustle again on board the smuggler craft, and several men descended to the hold to bring forth the prisoner to his trial on deck.

Bewildered and surprised they gazed on the irons which had bound the mutineer in astonishment.

"Slipped his cable, by Neptune!" said Black Bill, after a few moments pause.

"And showed us a clean pair of heels," chimed in Jem; "wonder how the devil he managed it."

"The captain won't foam and rage a bit," said another, when he discovers the bird has flown; "we'll have to stand clear of him for a time, I reckon."

"Overhaul the ship from bow to stern," exclaimed Black Bill, "he's hid away somewhere, no doubt. He can't have got clear off unless he went over the side."

"And I should say that's just what he has done," remarked Jem, who wished to prevent as much as possible any search for his friend; "Ned is a stout swimmer, and can sail in the water like a duck."

"Well, perhaps you are right; he had good reason for running the risk of being drowned," said Black Bill, not a little pleased at the escape.

"Thought it better, perhaps, than being hung," said Jem; "once in the rope there was no escape, but there was a dozen chances of getting clear off if he took to the water."

"Well, we must go and report to the captain the escape of the prisoner, and it won't be well for him, I guess, if he ever falls into his hands again—come!"

So saying, Black Bill, followed by Jem and the others, returned to the deck.

Ned had overheard every word from his place of concealment, and now strained every nerve to catch the first sound from the deck.

CHAPTER XXIII.

THE SEARCH AFTER NED.

WITH aching head, and bloodshot eyes, the Boy Rover arose from his couch the morning after his capture of the fair Ellen, and the destruction of the brave little revenue cutter.

His temper had been considerably soured by the mutinous conduct of Ned; and that, added to the effects of the previous night's debauch, rendered him surly and peevish in the extreme.

The excitement of the previous day had stirred up his hot blood, and it was altogether in no very pleasant mood that he went on deck.

Nothing was right, and everything was wrong. Not a sailor was properly attending to his duty, not a thing was done right, and oaths and threats alone saluted all who came in contact with him.

He felt that it required something on which to vent his spleen; and he was not long in resolving that Ned should be the object.

Calling to his lieutenant, he ordered him to bring the mutineer on deck, to undergo his trial.

At least, "trial" he said; but not the ghost of a trial did he intend Ned should have, save the trial of whether the hempen string was of sufficient strength to bear the weight of his body from the yard-arm.

It was with impatience he awaited the appearance of the doomed man on deck; and when he perceived Black Bill return from the hold, accompanied by his mates, but bringing with him no prisoner, he yelled out, furiously:

"How is this? Why have you not obeyed my orders, and brought the mutinous dog on deck?"

"Because we couldn't, captain," replied Bill.

"Couldn't! Why?" roared the Boy Rover.

"He has escaped," said Bill.

"Escaped!" yelled the Boy Rover—"escaped!"

"Yes, captain, he has slipped his irons, and escaped."

"You lie!" said the captain, advancing, threateningly, towards his lieutenant.

"It's true, captain," Ned has escaped.

"If he has," exclaimed the Boy Rover, with a burst of ungovernable rage, "look to it!"

"Well, it's no fault of mine that he has done so," replied Black Bill, turning very red in the face.

"No fault of yours," iterated the Boy Rover; "whose fault is it then—whose duty was it to keep safe guard on him?"

"Your orders were to see that he was placed in irons, and then left to himself," returned Black Bill, annoyed at the manner in which the captain was treating him in the presence of the crew.

"Well, and if I did, do you think I meant you to let him escape? But, bah! if he has got shot of his irons he cannot have left the vessel; overhaul every inch of her, and find him, or it won't be well for you."

And he turned upon his heel and strode to the after part of the vessel.

Black Bill gave the order to those around him to search the vessel and see if Ned still remained on board.

This the men immediately essayed to do, and Jem, followed by two others, again returned to the hold, whilst the remainder scattered themselves over the different parts of the vessel.

Black Bill was so annoyed that 'e advanced to the side of the Boy Rover, and exclaimed in a sarcastic tone.

"Perhaps I had better search the cabins, captain."

The Boy Rover turned sharply round, and fixing his eyes upon his subordinate, said:

"What do you mean by that?"

"You ordered every inch of the ship to be searched, and I believe Ned is just as likely to be in the cabin as anywhere else on board."

"Why so?"

"Because I believe he has gone overboard, replied the lieutenant of the smuggler.

"If he has," said the Boy Rover, "then some of you have a hand in it. I remember your unwillingness to seize him last night, or shoot him, as I bid you do, when he threatened me with his knife. I tell you what, Bill, there was a tendency on the part of yourself and the rest to side with Ned, had you dared."

"Captain!"

"You no need deny it was so; for I watched your every look and gesture."

"Captain, do you think that I—"

"No," roared the Boy Rover, "I do not think; I know—know that the turn of a straw would have carried you to his side—know that one word would have made you traitors to me!"

"You're mistaken, captain."

"I hope I am; but I think I'm not. However, it won't be good for any of you to try it on. I am captain here, and captain I remain."

"I hope so," remarked Bill.

The Boy Rover looked piercingly into the face of his lieutenant, to read there the truth or falsehood of his words.

But the eye of the Rover could detect no sign in the immoveable features of the other.

Still, he commenced to doubt the fidelity of the man who stood before him.

He resolved to keep an eye upon his movements; and, if he detected one act to strengthen his belief, he determined that his ends should be frustrated in a speedy and decisive manner.

One by one the men returned to the deck, and reported that they could find no trace of Ned; and each gave utterance to his belief that the smuggler had gained the deck, and, unperceived, leapt over the side of the ship into the sea.

"Then he's a greater fool than I took him for," said the Boy Rover. "He knew not but that I might pardon his act, and suffer him to live; but, if he has indeed dared the waves, he has rushed on to certain destruction."

"Perhaps not, captain," said one, "for Ned can swim like a fish."

"And he shall hang like a dog if ever he falls into my hands," said the Rover. "By heavens! I will teach the man who dares to mutiny against my authority that the Boy Rover is not to be made the tool of any fool who permits his feelings or conscience to disobey my commands. He shall respect the oath of the confederacy, or he dies—dies like a dog—the death of a mutineer. To your duties!"

And, turning from them, he descended to the cabin.

Chagrined and disappointed at the escape of Ned, he flung himself into a seat, and became buried in thought.

He was suddenly awoke from the reverie into which he had fallen by the entrance of Wild Madge.

He started up in surprise as he gazed upon the form of the half-drunk, half-mad woman, who, with dishevelled hair, bloodshot eyes, and foaming mouth, now confronted him.

"How, now?" he exclaimed, peevishly. "What brings you here?"

"To urge you on to the fulfilment of your resolve—to goad you on to the consummation of that girl's ruin. Curse her! she has braved and struck me, and now do I doubly desire the sacrifice."

"She is a courageous girl, said the Boy Rover; "the fiery glance of her black eye almost cows the bold and daring spirit of the Smuggler of the South Seas."

"What?" half-shrieked the virago—"do you fear the girl you have sworn to make your own—do you fear to encompass the ruin of her who is allied to him who has make us what we are?"

"Allied to him—to whom?"

"To the seducer of your mother!"

"What mean you?"

"That girl whom you now hold in your power is the daughter of the man who stole my heart, and then deserted me—the child of her, who, serpent-like, stole the love that should have been mine—who poured the honied poison into his soul, and warped the affections that were mine and mine alone!"

"Can this be possible?" said the young smuggler, in surprise.

"Possible! nay, 'tis true. I tell you I have proof—proof as palpable as holy writ!"

"Where did you get it?"

"From the bosom of that girl."

The Boy Rover became more and more surprised.

"You are drunk again," he exclaimed, after a pause, "and know not what you say."

"I tell you, Richard, that that girl is the offspring of those we both hate, and have sworn to track to vengeance and death. Fate has placed that girl in our hands, and our revenge shall be fearful and deadly. He shall suffer the tortures of hell through his daughter's suffering—he shall feel the misery he has inflicted upon me through his daughter's sufferings. An eye for an eye, a tooth for a tooth—her honour for mine—her sufferings for our wrongs! Oh! Richard, the hour of our triumph is at hand—the moment to strike the blow has arrived. From her fair and spotless neck I tore the portrait of him who has been the curse of my existence; and in the lineaments of her lovely features do I trace the likeness of her who robbed me of my love. Richard, we have sworn to hunt to destruction all connected with that house—remember your oath, and avenge a mother's wrongs!"

The Boy Rover paused for a few moments; even his callous heart was shocked at the horrible vindictiveness of the woman who now stood by his side urging him to perpetrate a deed so fearful that humanity must blush at the bare contemplation of.

Madge eyed his every movement with an impatient glance. She saw that bad as that young smuggler was he hesitated to do a deed which would render him the abhorrence of the greatest miscreant that ever lived, and she trembled with passion lest her vile teachings should go no further.

So strong was the hatred that she had succeeded in planting in the breast of that youth wards one who at least had never done him wrong, that he had never hesitated to do any deed, however black, to satisfy that vengeance; but bad as he was, he could not but think that the fearful wrong demanded at his hands towards a weak and unoffending woman, merely to gratify the fearful longings for revenge of that fell hag at his side, was almost too black to contemplate.

To satiate his own lustful passions, he would not have hesitated to outrage the maiden he held in his power; but when that outrage was counselled by, and perpetrated for the mere gratification of, the vengeance of the woman he called mother, the Boy Rover paused.

There was something so fearfully unnatural in a mother inciting her son to commit so fearful a deed.

"Mother," at length he said, "I have stopped at nothing which you have hitherto counselled—your wrongs have made me what I am—a thief, a smuggler, a branded felon, and a—a—murderer! Crime lies heavy and black on my soul, yet you would make it blacker and more bloody by this crime. I sometimes think that you cannot be my parent, or you could not thus wish to hurl my soul to destruction !"

Madge winced at these words; for well she knew that did the Boy Rover once feel certain that there was no relationship between them, then her hold upon him was lost for ever.

She resolved to prevent this feeling from further stealing upon his breast.

"Not thy mother!" she exclaimed, endeavouring to put on a look of injured feeling—"not thy mother! Oh! boy, boy. Have not your lips imbibed your infant nourishment from this breast; have not these hands guided your footsteps—"

"To what?" said the Boy Rover. "To crimes at which humanity shudders—to deeds of blood and horror!"

"And now does your heart quail? Does the Boy Rover tremble at the deeds he has done to avenge a mother's wrongs?"

Well she knew that if she would rouse him to her purpose, she could find no better means than attributing fear and cowardice to him.

How many a man would have remained an honourable member of society but for the jeer of cowardice! How many a youth would now possess a conscience unstained by sin but from the taunt of fear!"

"I do not tremble for my deeds," said the Boy Rover, after a pause. "Nor do I fear to continue in the ways in which your teachings have led me. I have forfeited all that tends to honour, and am now a wretch, hated and despised, the outcast of society, with every man's hand against me. Therefore, mine must be against every man. I do not fear to encompass the ruin of this girl; but even my degraded nature stands appalled at the vindictiveness of one towards her whose nature as a woman should rise against the deed."

"But whose sufferings call aloud for vengeance!" interrupted Wild Madge, with a burst of passion. "Richard," she added, "can you know that you hold in your power the means by which to strike at the heart of him who embittered the existence of our mother—whose cruelty drove her an outcast from the home of her father, and made her a wanderer in the wide world, the scorn of woman, the jest of man—and yet hesitate to strike?"

She paused for his reply, but the Boy Rover answered not, and she continued.

"Richard, do you recollect the morning of the storm, when, houseless wanderers, we stood on the beach? Do you recollect the blow I received at the hands of him whose arm alone should have been raised to protect the victim of his perfidy? Do you recollect the oath we registered never to rest till we had embittered the very life, and hurled destruction upon the head of him, and all connected with him, who could basely steal a confiding woman's honour, and then add cruelty to the shame and misery his lustful passions and dishonourable nature had inflicted upon her?"

"Well do I remember," said the Boy Rover.

"And now the time has come: fate has thrown in our path the means to satiate the vengeance of a life. Now is the hour to strike at the heart of him who struck at the breast of thy mother; to heap misery upon the head of him who should have been to you a protector and a father."

"By making this girl loathsome to herself?" said the Rover.

"Aye, the more hellish the deed, the greater our revenge. Can the blow sink deeper into her soul than did his perfidy into mine? Are not a mother's wrongs greater than would be that girl's sufferings?"

"But she caused them not," said the Boy Rover.

"Yet she must be the instrument we will use to strike at the peace and happiness of those who did —her father and her mother. Boy," she continued, "this is a fearful life we lead; but we have been driven to it by those connected with this girl. And shall he who has made the gibbet our last resting-place in this life escape the vengeance of his victims—shall he not feel the sting of the worm he has trodden on?"

"The gibbet!" exclaimed the smuggler, and a slight quiver passed around his lips.

"Aye, the gibbet; for such will be our ultimate doom. Are not the bloodhounds of the law even now tracking us over the waves? Is not the wake of the smuggler ship stained with the blood of the officers of justice? And has not he been the cause of the career which you have chosen; and will he not have been the means by which you have merited death at the hangman's hands?"

A shudder passed over the frame of the Boy Rover.

Wild Madge saw in an instant that she was bringing him to her purpose, and she continued:

"Richard, shall we spare him who has not spared us? Shall the doom of the murderer overtake you without one blow at him who has made the gallows your last resting-place on earth?"

With one bound the Boy Rover sprang to his feet.

"By all the furies!—no," he thundered.

Madge saw that the subtle poison of her words had impregnated the blood of the young smuggler, and she could scarcely suppress the smile that played around her mouth.

She had aroused the base nature of the Boy Rover, and too well she knew that she could now easily mould him to her purpose.

"Well spoken, Richard," she exclaimed; "I had almost thought that the son of Wild Madge had deserted his mother's side to lick the feet of her betrayer!"

And a sarcastic sneer played around her lips as she gave utterance to these words.

"By heaven, I will break his heart!" exclaimed the Boy Rover, exasperated by the taunts of the base-minded woman; "I will make him feel the misery he has heaped upon your head—the power of the Boy Rover—"

"And the despised and nameless offspring of his villainy," insinuated Madge.

"Enough!" said the Boy Rover; "say no more—it shall be done. You shall be avenged!"

"And through this girl?" said Madge.

"Yes," was the answer.

"Go, then," she exclaimed, "she waits your coming."

"Not now," he returned.

"When then," she asked, half fearing that he yet would spare the honour of his captive.

"To-night," he replied.

"No time like the present," she urged.

"Not now," he said again. "Last night's debauch has somewhat unstrung my nerves, and I require all their strength to carry out my intentions with that girl."

"She will fall an easy prey," said Madge.

"Think it not," he replied; "she will battle in defiance of her honour while power and sense is left her."

"Then away to her cabin, for she is weak from the dangers she has passed through, "and an easy conquest awaits you."

"Again I say, not now. To-night I will visit her couch—to-night I will revel in her charms—to-night her honour shall be sacrificed at the shrine of vengeance!"

"You swear it?" said Madge, still doubting.

"I do," he replied. "And now return to your cabin; administer to her every want, and make her as comfortable as her circumstances will allow her to be—see to this, I have business on deck."

And the Boy Rover turned to leave the cabin.

"You will not fail," said Madge.

"To-night—no," he replied, as he passed through the doorway and ascended to the deck.

A demoniac smile played around the lips of Wild Madge, as she watched his retreating form ascending the steps from the cabin to the deck.

"The poison works," she muttered—"works well. I shall be avenged—deeply, hellishly avenged. Oh, how I shall gloat in the misery of her sufferings—revel in the cries for mercy which will escape her lips—joy in her shrieks as she falls a victim to his lustful passions: her cries will be like entrancing music to mine ears, and soothe my troubled soul in sounds of melody, for they will be tones of triumph to this revengeful heart. Ha, ha, ha! Wild Madge will make you both the instruments of her vengeance, and a sister's honour shall fall at a——ha, ha, ha! I triumph, I triumph!"

CHAPTER XXIV.

THE APPROACHING SAIL—THE MAN AT THE WHEEL—THE SHADOW ON THE DECK—THE DEATH CRY.

The day wore on, and the "Venomed Snake" glided swiftly over the sea.

With every stitch of canvass set, she bounded over the waters, like a stately swan, ever and anon dipping her proud head to kiss the waves, as with majestic roll they sunk beneath her bows.

Towards evening the sky became overcast, and the Boy Rover ordered sail to be shortened. This was done, and the "Venomed Snake," lightened of some of her sails, made less headway.

The Boy Rover leant over the taffrail, and gazed abstractedly upon the waves as they curled their proud tops over each other; and the smuggler crew, either busied in their duties, or grouped in little knots about the deck, ever and anon cast their eyes upwards at the darkening clouds, or fixed their glance upon the averted face of their captain.

Suddenly rang out, clear and loud, from the mast-head, the cry of "Sail ho!"

The Boy Rover started from the reverie into which he had fallen, raised his head, and, gazing upwards, called:

"Where-away?"

"On the larboard tack," was the reply.

"What do you make her out?" asked the Boy Rover.

"Can't say yet," exclaimed the look-out: "she's too distant."

The Boy Rover took his glass, and, mounting the rigging, surveyed the ocean.

Far out in the distance he perceived the black hull of a ship, bearing up on their track.

He descended from the rigging to the deck, and addressing the steersman, said:

"Ease her off a couple of points."

"Aye, aye, sir," replied the man.

In a few moments the "Venomed Snake" had shifted her course.

Black Bill now took the glass and eyed the stranger.

"Looks like a merchantman," he said, addressing the captain.

"Yes—nothing to be feared from her. Still, we have no wish to encounter her; so keep her on the tack she is now on."

"All right, captain," said Bill, in a half surly tone.

He had not forgotten the manner the Boy Rover had treated him in the morning, when the escape of Ned had been made known to him.

The quick eye of the Boy Rover detected this, and instantly surmised the cause. He felt that he had been somewhat too severe in his remarks, and, as he entertained great respect for his lieutenant, he said:

"Well, Bill, there's no need to be bad blood between us on account of my remarks this morning. They were too severe, perhaps; but they were called forth by the escape of that traitor, Ned."

And, with a frankness which sometimes marked his character, he extended his hand to his lieutenant.

Black Bill took it in his horny palm, and pressed it with a grip that was sufficient to have crushed the bones of any ordinary hand.

The Boy Rover winced under the pressure; but he perceived that it was caused only by the fervour of his lieutenant's feelings.

"Let the boys have a double allowance of grog to-night," said the captain. "The clouds are passing over, and we shall have a fine night: so let them enjoy themselves."

"All right," said Bill, still more pleased at the Boy Rover's returning good humour.

The Rover again scanned the ocean with his glass. Then, looking up at the clouds, he said:

"That vessel is gaining on us now; but a little more canvass, and we shall glide away from her like a hare from a tortoise. Shake out a little more," he added, "and ease her off another point. Keep that course through the night."

"Aye, aye, sir," said Bill, "it shall be done."

"We shall shake off yon ship easily enough; for she rolls through the water like a tub. So let the men have their grog, and enjoy themselves."

The shades of evening were now falling fast, and

the time was drawing nigh which was to consummate the vengeance of Madge, and the ruin of Ellen.

The Boy Rover saw the grog served out to the men; then descended to his cabin, where he threw himself into a seat, and, for a time, became lost in thought.

And thus he remained for some time, when he arose, and, pouring out a tumbler of brandy from a decanter, he drank it off.

Then he listened. The smugglers had commenced their carouse, and loud peals of laughter rang through the ship.

He smiled as he thought that shrieks would soon mingle with them—the shrieks of the pure and defenceless.

He placed his hand upon the handle of the cabin door in which Ellen was a prisoner.

It yielded to his touch, and he entered.

Wild Madge was seated at the table with her head resting on her hand and buried in thought—thoughts that would make the heart shudder.

The poor captive, Ellen, reclined on the couch, with closed eyes, and the gentle heaving of her bosom proclaimed that she slept.

For a time she was lost to the bitter sorrows and misery—for the time she was unconscious to all around.

Worn out by her sufferings, exhausted nature had given way, and her soul now wandered in the dream lands of hope and happiness.

Alas! poor girl—soon to awake to the horrors of thy fearful situation, and the truth of thy fearful position!

The Boy Rover placed his hand on his lips to enjoin silence, as Wild Madge rose to greet him with a gleam of triumph in her eyes.

Even he could not bring his base mind to wake the poor girl from her happy slumbers to all the agonies of her position.

"She sleeps," he whispered.

"Awake her with thy caresses," said Wild Madge.

"Go to my cabin," he exclaimed, "and leave us to ourselves."

A look of horrible triumph passed over the face of the vile woman as she strode to the door.

Then she turned and fixed a fierce glance on the face of the Boy Rover.

"Remember your oath!" she exclaimed. "The victim lies ready for the sacrifice."

"I will," he replied, as he waved her from the apartment.

When Wild Madge had disappeared, the Boy Rover approached the side of the couch on which Ellen lay.

He gazed upon that beautiful upturned face and watched the rise and fall of her gently heaving bosom, and wild thoughts assailed his mind, and the hot passionate blood of his nature ran quicker and warmer through his veins.

He stretched forth his arms to clasp her to his breast, then paused. He hesitated to break the spell which held her in forgetfulness of his presence.

Yet with quickly beating heart and throbbing brow his eyes ravished the form of that fair girl as she lie so still on the couch at his side.

Again he stooped to imprint a kiss upon those rosy lips whose coral beauty bore so charming a contrast to the paleness of her face.

As he did so they slightly parted, and in her sleep Ellen muttered the word "Mother."

The Boy Rover started back.

"Shall I arouse her to misery?" he muttered to himself—"shall these ruthless arms awake her from the dreams of happiness and pleasure that now she revels in to the blackness of despair and misery—shall I wantonly tear her from the fond thoughts that now possess her mind, and plunge her into the dark abyss of despair? No, no!—too soon will she awake to the true situation into which fate has plunged her—too soon will her bright dreams be turned to bitter truths, and misery and despair reign where now happiness and love hold sway."

He paused, and again fixed his eyes on the up-turned face of Ellen.

"She must fall," he continued; "for who can resist beauty such as hers? She must be mine, and the Boy Rover must revel in the charms that now greet his eyes, and once more fire his blood. 'Tis a hellish deed; but who can resist the wild impulses of nature? But not now—not now," he added: "when she awakes it will be time enough to satiate these wild feelings—to curb this throbbing heart, which pants madly to revel in her charms. But not now. Sleep on—sleep on fair girl!—gather strength to return, with all the passionate ardour of my own soul, the burning caresses which I will shower upon thy lips—to return with fervour the pressure of these arms, as they enfold thy beauteous form to this heaving breast, and, in an ecstacy of bliss, unite our souls in one wild dream of love!"

And the Boy Rover tore himself from the side of the couch on which his sleeping captive lie, and, seating himself on the seat which Madge had but just vacated, awaited the awaking of poor Ellen from the slumbers which her worn-out frame so much required to renovate its failing strength.

In the meantime, the sounds of revelry which had pervaded the ship died away, and the drunken carouse of the smugglers was drawing to a close.

One by one the drunken sailors (made so by the fumes of liquor on which the revenue had never seen one fraction duty) ceased their wild orgies, and tumbled into their berths, or lay helplessly intoxicated on the spot where they had been carousing.

Their wild shouts had given place to loud nasal sounds, as they slept off the fumes of the liquor they had been imbibing; and, with this exception, all was silent on board the "Venomed Snake."

In one cabin the form of poor Ellen lie extended in sleep, dreaming of home and happiness; and the Boy Rover, with fascinated gaze, was watching her every breath. In the other, Wild Madge, drunk with joy and brandy, was gloating over her hellish plots for the destruction of poor Ellen. In the forecastle, the drunken sailors snored one against the other, in their intoxicated slumbers.

Black Bill, whose post was on deck, had laid himself under a bulk-head, and gone to sleep; whilst the man at the wheel smoked his pipe, and watched the vapour arising from its bowl, to cheer his hours of duty.

The night was beautiful and calm, with scarcely sufficient wind to fill her sails, which ever and anon flapped against the mast. The waves rolled on with a slow and majestic roll, and the full round moon lit up the boundless waters, and reflected the smuggler vessel in its glassy depths, as in a polished mirror.

There are times when the mind will wander to past years, and long-forgotten events, without any conceivable cause; and so it was with the man at the wheel on board the smuggler ship.

He had been smoking, and watching the wreaths of vapour as they curled upwards in the bright moonlight; and in their fantastic shapes his mind had wandered away from the helm to the little farm-house, and the bright fireside of its old kitchen, where he had sat with his brothers and sisters on many a cold winter's night and listened, with suppressed respiration, to the tales of ghosts and goblins, witches and elves.

So strongly did the awe with which he used to listen to those old tales at the fireside again take possession of his mind, that he laid down his pipe and began to whistle to chase away the fears which these old reminiscences had conjured up.

But in vain; they had taken possession of his mind and held on with a firm hold despite the bright moonlight—bright almost as day—which pervaded the scene.

The more he endeavoured to shake off the depressive feeling which these thoughts conjured up, the firmer hold they took upon his fears; till at length he resolved to leave his post for a moment and arouse one of his messmates to keep him company in his lonely duty.

This he was about to do, when his eye rested upon the shadow of a man on the deck.

He became spell-bound and unable to move. All the superstitious dread of his young days assailed his soul with redoubled violence.

He could but gaze upon that long gaunt shadow and tremble.

As he looked it became taller and taller, till at length it spread nearly the length of the ship.

His nerveless hands let go their grasp on the wheel and he stood gazing in horror upon the fearful object.

He endeavoured to call out but his tongue clove to the roof of his mouth, and his breath became short and quick.

Cold drops of perspiration stood in beads upon his brow, and every hair seemed to stand on end.

His mind reverted to the doom of Captain Waters, and his superstitious nature conjured up that brave man's ghost.

He could not think it was anything human, as he knew that there was not a soul on deck but himself and Black Bill, who lie sleeping soundly beneath the bulk-head, and not a soul could come on deck without his seeing them.

Therefore, it must be some supernatural visitant—some spirit from another world.

And, with horror and dismay, he was powerless to move or speak.

At this moment a wild sea bird in its mad flight crossed the bows of the vessel, and with hideous shriek made the welkin ring.

The steersman felt his strength and power failing him, and felt that in his abject fear he must fall to the deck.

There was a grasp upon his shoulder, but he was powerless to turn. He felt himself lifted from his feet; but he could not resist—so powerful a hold had his fears upon his nerves. He felt himself lifted to the side of the vessel; and the dark-green waters, spangled by the silvery moon, reflected his horrified face in their surface. He felt himself hurled forward over the side; and then, then only, was it that his tongue found utterance, and he gave vent to a shriek.

But too late! His cry was stopped by the waters rushing into his mouth, and changing his call to a half-gurgling splutter; and then down, down, he went into the ocean's bed, never more to rise till the day of judgment!

His mind had found release from his superstitious fears; his body had found a grave in the deep, deep sea.

Aroused from his drunken sleep, Black Bill started to his feet, and looked towards the helms-man.

"What cry was that?" he asked, addressing the man at the wheel.

"The cry of the sea-bird, as it passed over your head," was the reply.

But they were not the tones of him who a short time before had steered the ship over the sea.

Scarcely awake, and half-stupefied by the brandy he had been imbibing, Black Bill detected not the difference.

"Damn the bird!" he exclaimed, savagely, at being aroused in a fright. "Why didn't you knock it overboard?"

"I did," was the answer, "and it will trouble you no more."

"Keep her head right," said Bill, "and I'll just have another snooze."

"All right," grunted out the man at the wheel, as though he had no wish to speak more than he could help.

Black Bill, muttering to himself a curse at being disturbed, laid down again and was soon fast in the arms of Morpheus, as he proclaimed to all within hearing by the long, deep, sonorous tones of a most disagreeable snore.

For some time the man at the wheel gazed around the moonlit sea, and then upwards at the bright blue vault of heaven.

Why did he gaze so intently upon sea and sky?

On the one hand he looked for some star by which to take his bearings—on the other for the white sails of the vessel which had been discovered by the look-out a few hours before.

After a time he bore all his power upon the wheel and brought it round till it would go no further, and then he leant all his weight and exerted all his strength to keep it in that position.

Then, slowly and majestically, the proud ship veered gradually round upon the bosom of the wide ocean.

And, as she turned, the moon-beams fell lightly upon the face of the man at the wheel, and revealed the features of the mutinous smuggler, Ned.

There was a smile upon his mouth, and an expression of determination on his face, as he thus turned the vessel from her course.

He had lain concealed behind the heterogenous mass of goods in the hold during the search which was made for him, and heard every word of the conversation which had taken place between the Boy Rover and his lieutenant on the subject of his escape.

He resolved, therefore, to lie quiet till night, when he doubted not that, flushed with drink, the smugglers would keep but a poor watch on deck, and thus enable him to escape from the hold, and obtain food.

He had resolved then to conceal himself until they touched the shore, and then avail himself of the first opportunity of escaping from the power of the Rover.

But his plans had been altered. He had heard of the approaching vessel, and the orders to alter the course of the smuggler, to prevent a collision; and he felt sure that the Boy Rover must have feared a powerful adversary in the approaching ship.

Could he but get possession of the wheel, and, in the dead of the night, alter her course towards that of the one his captain wished to avoid!

It was a dangerous game to play—but he could but die once.

If he succeeded, he might save his own life and prevent the sacrifice of the fair captive whom the Boy Rover held in his power.

PERILOUS POSITION OF ELLEN.

That would be a glorious revenge on the now hated smuggler.

He resolved to try, and when he found all still and silent as the grave, he emerged from his concealment, and crawling along in the shadow of the bulwarks he now stood behind the doomed steersman.

But here for the first time he feared he should be discovered. The moon cast his shadow along the deck and betrayed his presence there.

In the fear of being disappointed in his resolve, he cursed the moon for shining so brightly. Fool! that bright orb was his greatest friend.

On casting his shadow upon the deck it struck terror to the heart of the only being who was present to oppose him, and had enabled him to overpower without noise or resistance his unfortunate comrade.

It was a desperate and cold-blooded deed, but Ned's were desperate circumstances, and required desperate remedies.

Hence he did not hesitate to steal behind his superstitious victim, and hurl him over the side of the vessel into the sea.

But here another danger had started up to confront him in the shape of the lieutenant of the "Venomed Snake." Black Bill, who awoke from his drunken slumber by the despairing cry of the murdered man, as he disappeared beneath the waves, rose from the shadow of the bulwarks.

But here Ned had sufficient presence of mind to grasp the wheel, and, assuming a feigned voice, replied to the lieutenant's question, who, with his brains still half muddled by his debauch, did not observe the difference between the present steersman and his murdered companion.

It was with a long breath of relief that Ned saw Black Bill once more lie down under the bulwark and hear his loud breathing as he slept off the effects of his indulgence.

Eagerly now he cast his glance across the ocean, in the hopes of seeing the white sails of the previously mentioned vessel glistening in the moonlight, and impatiently did he curse the tardy progress of the vessel through the waters.

Much to his satisfaction Black Bill snored on, never once opening his eyes or making the slightest movement. And Ned, still anxiously fixing his gaze upon the distant horizon, steered the "Venomed Snake," and her disreputable crew in the opposite direction to that which the Boy Rover had commanded her course to be.

Ned had learned from the conversation which he had overheard respecting the vessel, the course she was steering, and he now intended placing the smuggler ship in her path.

Something seemed to whisper to him that she would prove the means of rescuing himself and the captive Ellen from the fates to which the Boy Rover had consigned them.

Strange that such a man as Ned should feel an interest in the maiden. What respect could he entertain for the poor girl, who, had he remained faithful to his allegiance to the Boy Rover, would by the rules of their confederacy, after a time, have been handed over to his tender mercies?

It was not respect or pity for the sufferings of Ellen that had actuated him in the first place to set his captain at defiance, and place himself in the unenviable position in which he found himself. It was a sudden impulse that had prompted him to cut the bonds of the young revenue officer, and when discovered, finding he could expect no mercy at the hands of the Boy Rover, a feeling of hatred took possession of his heart towards the captain under whom he served, and that hatred gave birth to a feeling of revenge.

Thus it was revenge only he sought on the Boy Rover, but with revenge came a wish to save Ellen. He now hated the smuggler and he pitied his captive.

It is the old tale—once friends become enemies, they will love the foes of each other, and hug to their breast the one whom previously they would have scorned.

The Boy Rover made Ned his enemy, and Ned would now do his best to serve all with whom the smuggler was at variance. Ned was the thorn in his path, and ere long he would most certainly feel its sting.

CHAPTER XXV.

THE BOY ROVER AND HIS CAPTIVE.—THE STRUGGLE FOR HONOUR.—THE SUDDEN SURPRISE.

As the time wore on still the Boy Rover continued to watch his sleeping captive.

With rapture his eyes feasted upon that lovely face and gently heaving bosom, as it rose and fell with every breath drawn by the fair and innocent girl.

And the hot passionate blood of his nature coursed through his veins like molten lead, as he gazed upon the half revealed bosom of her who, unconscious of his presence, slept peacefully the calm sleep of the righteous.

The horrors of the day were forgotten in the balmy slumber that now weighed down her eyelids, and her mind was now wandering to scenes of happier and brighter hours than those she had lately passed.

A smile was playing around those coral lips, which, half parted, revealed the pearly whiteness of her teeth, and the veins in her neck looked like thin blue cords upon polished marble.

As the Boy Rover gazed the resolution he had formed not to arouse her to consciousness gradually gave way, and several times did he stretch forth his hand to awaken the sleeping girl.

Fiercer and fiercer became his desires, yet still Ellen lie sleeping unconscious of her danger.

The Boy Rover bent over the couch, and gently drew the coverlid from the bosom of the sleeping girl.

Her dress had become somewhat disarranged, and the white bust of the beauteous maiden was revealed to the sensual gaze of the smuggler.

And with glaring eyes and panting breast the Boy Rover feasted on the half-revealed charms of the fair sleeper.

At the sight of this, the passions of the youthful smuggler became more and more aroused, and his lustful desires now knew no bounds.

His blood was fired, and he trembled with the excess of his unholy passions.

And he resolved that those passions should now be satiated.

He threw his arms around the form of the sleeping maiden, and imprinted a burning kiss upon her lips.

With a shriek Ellen awoke from the bright dream which had usurped her mind—awoke to find herself in the coils of the serpent, and feel its venomed breath upon her lips.

Surprise and horror held her powerless to move or speak.

A faint sickness stole over her frame, and she trembled from head to foot with the power of her emotions.

The grasp of the Boy Rover tightened upon her, and he showered his fulsome kisses upon her face and lips, as he strained her with frantic rapture to his breast.

Who can pourtray the horror of the poor girl at this moment. She gave herself up for lost, and with one wild piercing shriek she closed her eyes to shut out the vision of him who held her to his heart.

So heartrending was the cry, that even the Boy Rover released his hold, and gazed appalled at his intended victim.

And Wild Madge, to whose ears that cry had reached, rubbed her hands, and laughed aloud as she thought of the horrid crime that was being perpetrated.

Finding herself released from the arms of the smuggler, Ellen, with one bound, sprang from the couch into the centre of the cabin.

Recovering from the sudden shock, the Boy Rover sprang towards her. His blood was fired, and his hellish passions now knew no bounds.

Again he clasped her in his arms, and the hot burning kisses rained upon the pale face of the affrighted girl.

She struggled to free herself from his embrace,

but in vain. He only strained her the more madly to his breast.

He strove to bear her again to the couch, to endeavour at length to consummate his hellish purpose.

But Ellen seemed to gain strength every moment, as she saw her doom approaching, and now battled with the strength and fierceness of a tigress.

He forced his rude hands on her now uncovered bosom, and in the excitement of her indignation and despair she fastened her white teeth upon his wrist.

With a cry of pain the Boy Rover released his hold, and the half-maddened girl bounded to the other side of the cabin.

Fully aroused to all the horrors of her situation, the affrighted maiden resolved to sacrifice her life in the struggle, ere she submitted to the unholy desires of her persecutor.

Again the Boy Rover, now maddened with pain, rushed towards her, and Ellen with determined mien awaited the onslaught.

Not a word was spoken.—The silence was fearfully ominous.

On the one side the determination to satiate the lustful passions that consumed him—on the other the resolve to die in the defence of assailed and outraged honour.

The Boy Rover advanced, and the poor girl retreated till she had placed her back against the partition of the apartment.

With a spring he again clasped her in his arms, and once more a wild frantic struggle was commenced.

Resistance but added fury to his dishonourable passions, and he wound his strong arms around the white neck of the panting girl.

In vain she endeavoured to free herself from his loathsome embraces, he held her as he thought in a vice, and his lips were glued to her cheeks.

Wildly, frantically, did he press her to his bosom, whilst the blush of shame and outraged modesty suffused her neck and face.

Never he thought had she looked so beautiful, and willingly he thought he would resign his life to revel in her charms.

Maddened by the sight of the half-nude bosom, he now strove to obtain stronger gratification to the passions which were consuming him.

Shriek after shriek issued from the poor girl's lips, but he heeded them not—his passion was too fierce to be now easily damped.

Still the struggle continued, and the garments of the outraged maiden were torn to shreds in the unequal contest.

Step by step he bore her nearer to the couch, whilst every moment with stronger determination raged the fight between them.

And all the while in the adjoining cabin Wild Madge sat listening and gloating in triumph at the unholy work.

The hands of that base woman which should have been stretched forth to protect her, were but rubbed together in wild glee at her intense sufferings.

Still the fair girl battled with her persecutor, and still the Boy Rover strove to force the beauteous form of that poor maiden upon the couch from which his unholy kiss had previously aroused her.

But when woman battles in defence of her honour, she fights with a determination which nothing but death or unconsciousness can allay.

Ellen strove to fasten her teeth once more in the arm of the ruffian, but he was wary of her intentions, and prevented her accomplishing her object. Failing by any means to release herself from his hold, she now spoke,

"Villain, never shall you triumph in your unholy desires. Never! Death shall claim me for his own ere I fall a victim to your base and fulsome passions."

"To night you are mine," he hissed, and his hot breath fanned her cheek as he spoke. Resistance will avail you nothing—the contest is unequal, and the weakest must succumb at last. Give over this vain resistance, and in one intoxicating draught of pleasure consummate the love I offer you."

"Monster," she shrieked. "Monster, to insult the ears of her you thus outrage.—Release me. Oh God, is there not one heart on board this pandemonium to feel for a woman's wrongs—one hand to strike in her defence."

"Not one," replied the Boy Rover. "By the rules which bind us together, all will share in your caresses, the hearts of each of my followers are bounding in expectation of the hour that commits your fair form to their caresses, so you see how madly absurd is your expectation of succour from any one on board this bark. All have an interest in my success, since once you have returned the love of the captain, he is bound in honour to submit you to his crew.

The crimson blush of wounded modesty that had overspread the face and neck of the outraged maiden, gave place to a deadly whiteness, as the words of the Boy Rover fell upon her insulted ears. Her blood stagnated in her veins, and her heart seemed to cease to beat.

So great was her horror at the doom which was intended for her, that she became powerless as an infant. And the Boy Rover, taking advantage of this moment, raised her in his arms and attempted to lay her upon the couch.

But this action again awoke her stagnated energies, and she fastened her white fingers around his neck, and dug her long nails into his flesh.

The pain inflicted thereby caused the Boy Rover to again release his hold, and once more Ellen, aroused to all the horrors of her situation, sprang to the floor.

The Boy Rover perceived that she would resist to the last gasp, and trembling with the power of the passions which fired his blood, he at last exclaimed—

"Girl, you but waste your strength in the fruitless endeavours to oppose my will. This contest is unequal—you are weak—I am strong, and it is but a work of time that makes you mine."

"Oh! ruffian," she exclaimed, roused to madness by the fearful agony of her feelings, "kill me if you will, but spare me from dishonour. Let the winding sheet encircle my frame, but not the loathsome arms of yourself and crew. Gladly will I welcome death, but spare—oh! spare me, from this hellish villany !"

The tones of her voice would have sunk deep into the heart of any one who possessed one grain of human feeling; but the passions of the Boy Rover were heated to such a pitch that they had consumed every vestige of better feeling, yet he replied—

"Girl, I have told you of the contract which binds myself and crew, but on one condition that contract will I break."

"Oh, speak—speak !" exclaimed Ellen, grasping at the frantic ray of hope, as a drowning man grasps at a straw.

"Be mine," he replied, "submit without resistance to my caresses, and I will save you from the arms of my crew."

"Wretch," exclaimed the indignant girl, "base hearted miscreant, ah, how lost to every spark of honour! Even your base heart can cancel the hellish bond to gratify your own dishonourable ends. Smuggler, as soon would you break faith with the girl you would outrage, could she be brought to submit to thy villanous proposal."

"Do you agree," he hissed, trembling with passion at her sarcasm.

For a moment Ellen did not reply.

Again the question was repeated.

"Give me till to-morrow," she said, after a pause. "Then you shall know my resolve."

The poor girl hoped that the Boy Rover would consent to this, not that for one moment she intended to give herself to his arms by that time, but she hoped that by gaining a delay providence would send her some succour, and release her from the power of the fiend who now held her captive.

It was now the Boy Rover's turn to pause ere he answered, and at length he replied—

"On one condition."

"Name it," said Ellen, a ray of hope again rising to her heart.

"That you swear to unresistingly submit to my wishes."

"I will take no oath," she replied. "Circumstances alone must guide my determination."

"You but delay the blissful moments of ecstatic pleasure that await you," he added.

"No more," said Ellen, fearful of again arousing his passions. "To-morrow night you shall know my determination."

"I must know it now," exclaimed the Boy Rover, as a suspicion crossed his mind that she but sought the delay to effect some means by which she could foil his passions. "Swear that to-morrow night I shall unresistingly press you to this bosom and revel in thy caresses, and I will leave you till that time, but I must have the oath, I will not trust your word."

Like all base natures to whom honour is but a word, the Boy Rover doubted that such a thing as truth could exist unless backed by the oath.

"Leave me now," she continued, "and to-morrow you shall know my determination, more I will not say."

"Then to-night must consummate you ruin and my happiness," he replied, again advancing towards her.

As Ellen had not the remotest intention of surrendering herself to the hateful pollution, she could not find it in her heart to speak the words even to gain the delay which might bring her succour.

"Away!" she exclaimed—"I will lie upon the floor of this cabin a corpse ere I submit to your desires."

But the Boy Rover heeded her not; he again encircled her with his arms, and strove to bear her to the couch.

Once more the battle raged in all its fury—once more lust and despair struggled for the mastery.

But a contest such as this could not possibly last long—the frantic struggles of the young girl but soon expended all her strength, and panting and exhausted she lie helpless in the arms of the Boy Rover.

With a smile of triumph he bore her to the couch, and lay her unresisting form upon it.

Panting, horrified, and despairing, poor Ellen believed now that the hour of her doom had come. She summoned all her strength for the final struggle; and, as the Boy Rover forced her back upon the pillow, she once more fastened her teeth in his arms.

With a cry of pain he raised his hand and struck the poor girl a blow on the mouth.

Goaded to madness by the power which his base passions held over him, he scarcely knew what he did.

The crimson fluid started from the lips of Ellen, and trickled down her neck.

"Cowardly ruffian!" she shrieked. "Strike again, but let the next blow be death."

The Boy Rover, goaded on by the fury of his passions, paid no heed to her words, but strove to consummate his hellish desires.

The garments of the poor despairing girl were torn to ribbons in her frantic endeavours to repel his lustful advances; and her nails were stained by the hot blood of the youth, as she lacerated his face and hands in her frantic struggles to protect her assailed virtue.

Nobly did the poor girl battle for that which is so dear to woman; heroically did she struggle with the wretch who, lost to all feeling or respect, offered her such indignity; but her strength was exhausted, and now, almost powerless as a child, she lay at the mercy of the youth whose dishonourable passions, heated almost to madness by the fearful resistance he had met with, goaded him on to the consummation of his lustful desires.

Throwing the entire weight of his whole body upon the form of the poor girl, he bore her down upon the couch, and his hot breath assailed her cheek, and his burning kisses rained madly upon her lips and forehead.

Shriek after shriek rent the cabin, but still the Boy Rover endeavoured to consummate his ends.

Weaker and more feeble became the struggles of Ellen; and fiercer and more outrageous the indignities that were offered to the poor girl.

The fair girl felt now that all hope of escape from the doom intended for her was gone; and, with one heart-rending cry for help, she gave herself up for lost.

But the eye of Heaven never slumbers, and the guilty are struck down at the very moment of their triumph.

Thus it was that, at the very moment when powerless to aid herself she was about to surrender to the hellish deed, help was at hand to save her.

The cry which she had uttered was answered by a loud crash, and the Boy Rover started up, bewildered and amazed.

Then the voice of Black Bill was heard ringing loudly over the ship:

"To arms—to arms! Treachery—treachery! Wake the captain! Repel boarders! Treachery—treachery!"

Without a word, the Boy Rover sprang to the door of the cabin, and threw it open.

Then a voice, which sent the blood rushing to the heart of the almost senseless girl, fell like the music of heaven on her ears.

Ellen, Ellen! Back, dog!—back, I say! Where is Ellen? I will save her, though I drown the ship in blood!"

And, as the Boy Rover rushed up the stairs to the deck, the poor girl leapt from the couch, and shrieked:

"Here, Charles—here! Save me—save me!"

But here her strength gave way; and, as she tottered towards the door, she fell, just as Wild Madge rushed into the cabin.

———

CHAPTER XXVI.

THE FIGHT—THE LOVERS—THE THREAT.

A TERRIBLE scene of confusion reigned on the deck of the smuggler vessel.

Black Bill had been aroused from his slumbers by the crash which had saved Ellen; as were, also, several of the smugglers.

Scarcely knowing what to attribute the sudden shock to—whether she had struck upon a rock, gone ashore, or met with any other danger with which the vast ocean abounds—they tumbled hurriedly upon deck, there to find the "Venomed Snake" held fast to the side of another ship by the grapnels, and perceive the forms of several men swarming over her sides.

Above the din and confusion, rang the voice of Black Bill, calling the men to arms.

Seizing any weapon they could lay their hand on at so short a notice, the smugglers bravely and desperately endeavoured to drive back the unexpected boarders to their own vessel.

Side by side, their bright cutlasses flashing in the grey dawn, fought, with a furious determination, Charles Lawson and Henry Chambers.

They were the first two who had boarded the smuggler; and as the crew of the "Venomed Snake" endeavoured to oppose their passage they fell before the furious onslaught of the brave young men.

Both, in their anxiety to rescue Ellen from the hands of the Boy Rover, endeavoured to cut their way towards the cabins; and it was as the voice of Charles Lawson rang clear and loud over the scene, when he called upon the girl he so fondly loved, that the youthful captain of the smuggler stood upon the deck, unarmed, save by the knife which he always carried at his belt.

His quick eye took in at one moment the whole state of affairs. He saw that his crew, taken by surprise, were falling back before the furious blows of the two friends, and that all the endeavours of Bill were unavailing to keep them firm.

Once more he was cool, and, as a gleam of hatred shot from his bright eye, he exclaimed:

"Stand firm, men, and let every blow tell."

At the sound of his voice the crew of the smuggler seemed endued with fresh courage, and the confused sailors stood firm, and with greater coolness opposed their antagonists.

But as that voice fell upon the ears of Henry and Charles, they became endued, as it were, with a superhuman strength, and their blows rained thick and heavily as they strove to cut their way to the side of him who had caused them so much misery.

Bill opposed his burly frame to that of the youthful lover of Ellen; but the sword of the devoted youth sunk deep into his shoulder, and, as the smuggler-lieutenant, with a fearful oath, staggered back from the blow, he received a thrust from Henry, which sent him to the deck, and the two youths passed over his body, only to meet fresh opposition at every step.

"Steady, men!—steady!" again rang the voice of the Rover. "Stand firm, and drive them back to their own vessel!"

And the smugglers, forming a more compact mass, drove back the crew of the "Blue Bell" to their own deck, save Charles and Henry, whose swords swept around with such fearful force that they had cleared a space within a few yards of the Rover, and not one of that smuggler crew but feared to venture within reach of their arms.

With an eagle eye, the Boy Rover watched every movement; and, with a coolness which would have done honour to any cause, he stood awaiting the opportunity to again issue his orders.

At the moment when the fierce onslaught of the smugglers had driven back to their own vessel the crew of the "Blue Bell," he exclaimed:

"Stand by and cut away!"

Quick as the lightning's flash the smugglers seized their hatchets and rained fierce and heavy strokes upon the grapnells, and ere their opponents could again force their way to the deck of the "Venomed Snake," the ships slowly parted.

So quickly was this done that even the Boy Rover could not suppress a cry of admiration.

"Ease her off!" he exclaimed.

A man rushed to the wheel and endeavoured to turn her from her adversary.

But the wheel was locked firm.

"Bear a hand here!" called out the man. "She won't answer her helm."

The Boy Rover in a moment stood by the side of the helmsman, and stooping down looked at the wheel.

"Some d—n traitor has done this!" he exclaimed, as he drew his knife and severed a rope which held it. "But he will never have another chance to betray us, but of him anon; we have other things to attend to now," he added, as he perceived the young lovers of Ellen still refused to surrender before the mass of smugglers who now surrounded them.

"Cut them down," he exclaimed, as a shot from the "Blue Bell" struck the man at the wheel and sent his body rolling on the deck at the foot of his captain.

At the same moment Ellen, with a loud cry, rushed up the stairs and darted along the deck.

The Boy Rover heard the cry and saw the form of the maiden as she sped towards those brave youths who strove to fight their way to her, and stretching forth his hand he grasped her by the shoulder and held her as though in a vice.

"Save me!" she shrieked. "Charles—Henry, save me—save us!"

Her heartrending tones fell upon the ears of the young men, and madly, frantically did they strive to force their way to her side.

Blood flowed at every flash of their gleaming swords; but still the smugglers closed before them, and opposed their advance.

Fortunately was it for the two brave youths that, in the hurry and confusion which had prevailed upon the boarding of the ship, not one of that dishonourable crew had armed themselves with a single fire-arm. So sudden had been the surprise, that they had scarcely had time to get even their cutlasses, which were kept in a chest on deck.

Had it been otherwise, a shot from a pistol had doubtless ere this have laid the two lovers of the beauteous Ellen weltering in their blood on the deck.

But, as it was, the brave youths parried the fierce threats and blows of the smugglers, or fleshed their own swords in the bodies of their foes.

They had sworn to save Ellen, or perish; and they would keep their oath.

Nothing but death could turn them from their purpose; they would save her or die.

And the sight of that poor girl, now struggling in

the hands of the Boy Rover, but added fuel to the fire that assailed their brains, and gave fresh strength to their arms.

Sweeping a circle around them with their swords, they strove to near the object of their affections.

And Ellen, her heart panting with hope and fear, still struggled with her persecutor.

Again the "Blue Bell" threw her grapnells on the smuggler's sides and rigging; and once more the two brave youths had to contend with fewer foes, as many of the smugglers rushed to the side to repel the boarders, who once more essayed to make their appearance on the smuggler's deck.

Thus relieved, the friends of Ellen cut down one by one the foes who opposed them, and drew nearer and nearer to the side of her who was so dear to them.

The Rover saw that another minute and they would be at his side. He had no arms to defend himself from their attack but the knife with which he had severed the lashing of the wheel. He could easily have procured arms if he released Ellen; but this he feared to do: so, bearing her backwards, till he stood almost at the extreme end of the ship, he grasped his knife firmly in one hand, whilst he held the poor girl tightly in the other, waiting the turn of events—his eagle eye, all the time, taking in every movement of the vessels, and actions of his crew and enemies.

The smugglers gave way before their foes, although they contested every inch of ground; and Charles and Henry, shoulder to shoulder, fought their way towards the spot where the Boy Rover stood.

"Cheer up, dear Ellen!" exclaimed Charles, as he brought his cutlass down upon the arm of a young smuggler with terrific force—"cheer up! I will yet rescue you from the hands of these hell hounds.

And fervently indeed did the poor girl pray that he might be permitted so to do.

Nearer and nearer to her approached the two brave youths, their cutlasses reeking with blood—the blood of those so unworthy of their steel; and lighter beat the heart of her who watched their every movement with such intense interest.

At any other time the feelings of horror which would have assailed the maiden at the sight of this awful carnage would have driven her to insensibility; but now she gazed on the fearful sight only with feelings of joy at the prospect of her deliverance from the wretches who held her captive.

The fight still raged, and the smugglers continued to fall back from before the fierce onslaught of the brave crew of the "Blue Bell."

The Boy Rover saw that he must now either release Ellen from his grasp, and throw the strength of his own arm into the fray, or stay the further progress of his foes by stratagem.

He resolved to do the latter.

He called to Wild Madge, and in a moment that individual made her appearance at the top of the stairs.

"Lay a train to the magazine," he said, "and stand ready to fire it at the moment I give the order."

"I will," said the fury; and the next moment she had disappeared.

This conversation was carried on in a loud tone, evidently for everyone on board the bark to hear what was said.

Charles and Henry felt the blood curdle in their veins as these words fell upon their ears. Too well they knew the desperate nature of the Boy Rover; and they dreaded lest he should put his designs into execution, and thus sacrifice them all ere they could rescue the much loved girl.

As regarded the smuggler captain, he would have carried out such a purpose ere he would fall into the hands of his adversaries; but her whom he had deputed to fire the train was not likely to obey his order should the worst come to the worst. Wild Madge herself feared to die; and in the bitterness of her revengeful spirit she could not have suffered the Boy Rover to die in such a manner. She would stand by him to the last; but that last must be death—slow, lingering, and fearful, in the intensity of its tortures.

But still the words of the Rover struck a chill of horror to the breasts of all who heard them; and the brave sailors who had so nobly boarded the "Venomed Snake" again wished themselves on board their own vessel.

Those words had unnerved their arms, and they in turn gave way before the smugglers.

Charles saw this and he instantly strove to urge them on.

"Heed not his words," he exclaimed—"such a villain must fear to die, and a ruffian is always a coward at heart. The gallows is the doom that awaits him."

Once more the sailors forced back the smugglers, half ashamed at their fears, and Charles and Henry now stood within arms length of the Boy Rover and the captive maiden.

"Villain!" almost shrieked Charles, as he strove to reach the smuggler-captain with his sword—"villain release your hold of the maiden, and meet your death!"

"Fool!" replied the Boy Rover—"on board this bark none dare command but me. Retire to your vessel, or by hell if you approach one step nearer, I will bury this knife in her heart, and hurl her body into the sea."

And as he spoke the Boy Rover raised the knife above the breast of the affrighted girl.

Ellen shrieked and fell upon her knees at his feet.

"Coward!" exclaimed Henry, as he vainly strove to reach her side.

But the smugglers opposed his passage, and he cut and thrust with the fury of a demon at his assailants.

"Oh, save me—save me!" shrieked Ellen, as she saw the fearful look that gleamed from the eyes of the smuggler captain and the gleam of the knife above her head.

But the smugglers still held the brave youths at bay, who foaming like enraged lions, fought with a ferocity that was truly fearful.

At length they cleared a passage through their foes and stood confronting the Boy Rover, who still holding the knife above the head of Ellen, dared them to move another step.

The fierceness of his tone and manner for a moment awed the young men, and they stood gazing upon the forms of Ellen and the Boy Rover, undecided how to act.

But this indecision was but of a moment's duration; and the next instant, as though prompted by the same impulse, Charles and Henry rushed forwards.

The Boy Rover brought the knife down, with a fearful oath; but ere it reached the breast of the fair girl the arms of Henry were flung around his body.

The young smuggler released his hold of Ellen; and, with a cry of joy, she started to her feet, and the next moment was clasped in the arms of her lover.

In the meantime the Rover was struggling to release himself from the hold of the young lieutenant. They struggled to the side, lost their footing, and fell over into the sea, locked in each other's embrace.

Madge, at that moment, returned to the deck with a lighted match in her hand. She saw the form of the Rover locked in the young lieutenant's arms; and the next moment perceived them both go over the side into the sea.

With a wild unearthly cry she sprang forward, and, for a moment, gazed over the side of the vessel. Then, turning, she exclaimed:

"Curses on you!—you have robbed me of my vengeance. But you shall suffer for it! I care not now to live; for you have robbed me of my revenge; and now you go to hell together."

And she sprang down the cabin stairs with the speed of an antelope.

Charles, half-bewildered, dragged Ellen along the deck, calling out, as he did so:

"To your ship, men—to your ship! or we shall all be food for fishes."

The smugglers, who now knew that their captain had gone overboard, made no resistance to the rapid retreat of the crew of the "Blue Bell; and they soon regained the deck of their vessel.

As Charles was bearing Ellen, more dead than alive, in his arms, a loud cry smote his ears. It was the voice of Wild Madge; and he hurried the fair girl forward to the deck of the "Blue Bell."

CHAPTER XXVII.

SELF-PRESERVATION—THE PARTING OF THE SHIPS. THE ROPE AT THE WINDOW—RESCUE OF HENRY AND THE BOY ROVER—THE COMPACT.

THERE is an undoubted truth in the words that "self-preservation is the first law of nature," and he who affects to despise the action of man when destruction stares him in the face, of endeavouring to save himself, insults that providence which has engrafted in the human frame the feeling of self-preservation.

Men are often actuated by a generous impulse to rush into danger to save a fellow-being, but when perils press him that impulse almost invariably gives way to desire to save himself, and leave the one he would have aided to struggle for his own safety.

If an exception there be to this rule, it is doubtless only that of a mother, who would sacrifice her own life to save that of her offspring.

But in man self-preservation is the first law; he inherits it at his birth, and it leaves him only at death.

It is a question whether this feeling is noble or ignoble; some there are who assert that it is one, some the other: but surely that divine law which has laid it down as criminal to take our own lives has engendered in the breast the desire to preserve them.

But some men there are in this pleading world, who permit the law of self-preservation to take so firm a hold upon their natures, as to bring it to bear upon the ordinary commercial pursuits of life, and thus lower self-preservation to a mean-spirited jealousy; and hence it is we find in the community a class of men, who, when they perceive anything which may be, or they think may be, in opposition to their interests, descend so low in the scale of honour and justice, as to strive by vile subterfuges and slanderous lies to preserve their own commercial pursuits at the sacrifice of another.

Is this self-preservation, or is it only the mean-spirited jealousy of a dishonourable mind—the desire to save ourselves from ruin, or the attempt to rise a step higher by placing the foot on the neck of an opponent in the ordinary pursuits of life?

Surely it is the latter; yet so surely are there those who, at the present day, fall so low as to degrade the nobility of man's soul by any dirty trick that they believe may tend to their own aggrandizement, and the discomfort of those who but struggle honourably in the same fields.

But we have said self-preservation is the first law of nature, and this law it was that now prompted the brave crew of the "Blue Bell" to cast off the grapnells from the sides of the two vessels and endeavour to place a considerable distance between them.

Scarcely had they reached the deck of their own vessel ere they put this operation into practice, and, in a few moments, the vessels parted.

In the panic and confusion they had not perceived one fact. Charles and Ellen were left on board the smuggler ship. The vessels had parted at the moment they were about to leave the deck, and when the scream of Wild Madge was heard.

This was discovered a few moments afterwards; but self-preservation stood in the way of the "Blue Bell" again going to their rescue,

Not one but wished to save them; but not one but feared to be blown to atoms if they again placed their foot on the smuggler's deck. The captain of the "Blue Bell," although he possessed all the generous and noble qualities of a British seaman, did not feel himself justified in sacrificing both vessel and crew for the sake of Ellen and her lover.

At the pleadings of the two young men whom he had succoured on board his vessel, he had consented to board the smuggler, and endeavour to rescue the fair girl from the hands of the Rover, and, if possible, carry him a prisoner to the next port; but now that he heard that a train was laid to the magazine, and a hand ready stretched forth to fire it, he would not lend himself to the sacrifice of so many brave men, and, perhaps, his noble vessel in the bargain.

But he resolved to stand off some little distance from the smuggler, and await the turn of events.

Nobly had the mutineer, Ned, steered the smuggler bark over the dancing waves towards the 'Blue Bell," which he saw gliding over the waters towards him. As the first streaks of early dawn lit up the blue vault of heaven, the vessels had become so near to each other as for every object to be seen by the aid of a glass.

Then it was that Ned, taking his handkerchief from his neck, waved it in the air, to attract the attention of those on board the "Blue Bell."

In a short time he saw his signal returned, and the vessel bearing down upon them.

Ned finding that his purpose had been so far successful, now obtained a rope and fastened the wheel, so that at the first alarm the smugglers would be unable to run from the approaching foes.

He had heard the shrieks of poor Ellen, but he feared to go to her aid lest his designs would be frustrated.

All this time Black Bill slumbered unconscious of the vessel having been turned from her course, and the danger that was approaching.

When the ships were within a short distance of each other Ned discovered the forms and features of Charles and Henry on the deck, and a smile of gratified triumph passed over his face.

Feeling now that the character of the ship would be known, and that the crew of the stranger would be sure to board her, and at the same time not wishing to be discovered as he well knew he would fall a victim to the rage of the smugglers if he were, he descended from the wheel and slowly and quietly descended the stairs to the cabins.

Here he stood in the shade of a projection of panelling and waited with bated breath the issue of his night's work.

Nor had he to wait long ere a fearful crash, as the side of the "Blue Bell" grated against the bows of the "Venomed Snake," told him that his designs had succeeded.

Then he heard the voice of Black Bill as, roused from his drunken slumbers, he gave the alarm to the crew.

He shrunk further back into the friendly shade as he saw the door of the cabin open in which the Boy Rover and Ellen had been engaged in their fearful struggle.

He saw the captain rush upon deck and Wild Madge enter the cabin of Ellen; then noiselessly he stole into the apartment the fury had just deserted.

Fearing lest the Rover should return, or any of the crew have reason to descend, he hid himself behind some furniture, and listened to the strife which was going on above.

From this cabin was the entrance to tne magazine; and it was with horror that, after the lapse of some time, he saw Madge raise the trap in the floor, and stoop down.

With eager eyes he watched her every movement, and a sigh of relief escaped him when he saw her again leave the cabin; but, in a minute more, she returned, with a look of rage and despair upon her features, and in her hand a lighted match.

He saw her approach the trap, and he heard her mutter, "Curse them—they shall die; for they have robbed me of my vengeance!"

By the light of the lamp which hung overhead, and cast its bright rays around the cabin, he saw the working of her countenance, and knew that her resolve was to blow the vessel to pieces.

He stole from his concealment, and, as the fury stooped down with the lighted match to put her design into execution, he rushed forward. With one hand he grasped the lighted match, which he extinguished with his palm; and with the other he clutched the throat of the fury in a deathly grip.

A shriek escaped her lips—that shriek which caused Charles to pause, and was so fatal to his gaining the deck of the "Blue Bell."

The fury struggled in the grasp of the strong sailor; but the fear of death or discovery had nerved his arm with a giant strength, and he held her as though she were a child.

"Silence," hissed Ned, "or I will scatter your brains!"

"Traitor!" she gurgled.

"Silence!" he iterated. "Another word to betray me, and I dash your brains out against the walls!"

Madge ceased to struggle. The look upon that man's face awed even her callous soul.

Ned looked around the apartment, and seizing a cover from a small table, he twisted it round her head, so as to effectually gag her. Then, drawing his handkerchief from his neck, he tied her hands securely together, and, thrusting her backwards, lowered her gently to the floor of the cabin.

The clash of steel had ceased, and nothing but a confused sound of voices, and a trampling of feet, was heard overhead.

Ned looked from the cabin window, and observed that the "Blue Bell" had parted from the smuggler, and was gradually increasing the distance between the two vessels.

Had the smugglers, then, beaten off their foes; and was the Rover once more victorious?"

Ned was in an agony of suspense; if so, his doom was sealed.

Yet, if such were the case, why should Madge wish to fire the magazine?

He was perplexed, and scarcely knew how to act.

He debated in his mind whether it would not be better for him to leap from the window into the sea, and endeavour to swim to the receding vessel.

As he stood thus considering what best to do, he saw the form of Henry battling with the waves.

Scarcely had this object met his sight than he perceived another form in the water, at a short distance from the first; and in a moment he recognised it as that of the Boy Rover.

In a moment he had determined how to act. He looked around the cabin, and his eye lighted upon a new coil of rope.

This he seized, and, flinging it out of the window, held firmly on to one end.

Instinctively, the hands of Henry Chambers were stretched forth to grasp it; but, when he held it in his hands, he seemed to pause, irresolute how to act.

Ned leaned from the window; so that he might be seen by the swimmer, and recognised.

"Come, and fear not," said Ned; it was me who saved you before."

Henry heard the voice, and recognised the features of Ned, and he allowed himself to be drawn up to the window of the cabin.

"Once more, my generous friend," said Henry, as his head was brought to a level with that of Ned's, "you have stretched forth a hand to save me: but I am undecided whether to again place myself in the power of the daring crew of this ship, or trust to reaching the 'Blue Bell.'"

"Come, and fear not; yonder is the captain—we must endeavour to find some means of luring him hither and making him prisoner."

"Your crew have been victorious, I fear, by the "Blue Bell" steering away, and I perceive that my friend and the poor girl are still prisoners on board your bark.'"

"Ah!" exclaimed Ned—"'is it so?"

"I could see their forms gazing at the retreating vessel," said Henry, as he drew himself through the window.

"Then we must secure the captain. How came he overboard?" asked Ned.

"We fell over struggling together," replied Henry.

Ned thought for a moment, then said—

"The captain has not seen you ascend this rope. I will lower it again from the window, and endeavour to attract his attention. Should he take advantage of it, the moment he appears at the window see that you seize him. and I will bind him hand and foot, then we may make terms with him by which we may all escape."

"Be it so," exclaimed Henry, as a ray of hope once more shone upon his heart that he might yet be able to secure the escape of Ellen from the hands of the Rover.

THE HUMAN BRIDGE.

Withdrawing from the window, Henry stood on one side, ready to act the moment the Boy Rover should appear.

Ned, averting his face, so as not to be immediately recognised by his captain, once more lowered the rope.

The Rover was a stout swimmer, and he breasted the waves manfully as he made towards the ship.

Casting his eyes upwards, he saw the rope dangling from the window, and immediately made towards it.

It was not long ere he grasped it in his hands; and Ned, drawing back into the cabin, said, in a low whisper:

"Stand by—seize him the moment he appears."

Henry slightly bowed his head, but said nothing.

Hand over hand, the Rover ascended the rope; and, as he drew his body through the aperture, Henry flung his arms around him, so as to firmly pinion his limbs, and dragged him into the cabin.

In a moment Ned had wound the rope around him, and, thus securely bound, he was forced to the floor of the apartment.

For a moment surprise held him dumb; then, foaming with rage, he exclaimed;

"What does this mean?"

"Simply, captain," replied Ned, with the utmost coolness, "that you are our prisoner."

"Traitor!" yelled the Rover—"is it you, then, I have to thank for this?"

"Yes, captain," replied Ned, "it was me that threw out the rope."

With a demoniac look on his face, the smuggler captain turned to Henry.

"Do you, then, command here; and has the 'Venomed Snake' struck her colours at last?"

"Not that I know of," returned Henry.

"No," said Ned; "for all we know, she is victorious. But, you see, captain, you owe us all a grudge; and all's fair in love and war. So, to save ourselves, we've made you prisoner."

"There is a mystery in all this," said the Rover, after a pause. "Ned, how came you on board this craft? Was it you who brought this vessel down upon us?"

"No, captain, I've never once been off the ship since we set sail; but, whilst you were paying such particular attention to the girl, and the remainder of the crew were dead drunk, I got possession of the helm, altered her course, and bore down on the vessel you wished to avoid. I know not exactly the issue of the affair, for I have been stowed away here since; but I know that not a plank of the 'Venomed Snake' would have remained had I not saved her from that devil there, who was going to blow her to atoms. But look you, captain, I know your devilish nature; you condemned me to death, and you would scrag me now, if you had a chance. That girl and her lover are still on board; and I know you would show them no mercy. Now we must save ourselves. Either give us a free pass ashore, or you must die!"

"What do you ask?" inquired the Boy Rover, feeling he was powerless to oppose them.

"Liberty for myself, for this man, and the girl, and her lover—free and unconditional liberty to leave this ship at the moment we make the land."

The Rover paused ere he answered.

"We are already in sight of land," he replied; "but my own safety demands that—"

"You should submit to our desires," interrupted Ned.

"How?" said the Rover.

"To save your worthless life," replied Ned, coolly.

And, as Ned spoke, he crossed the cabin, took a pistol from a socket in the wall, examined it, and placed it in his belt.

"Look you, captain," continued Ned, "desperate men resort to desperate means. You say we are in sight of land; how far distant is it?"

"About five miles," replied the Rover.

"We can pull that distance from the ship," continued Ned. "Do you agree to lend us a boat, and give us a free pass to the shore?"

"All but the girl," replied the Rover.

"She must go to," said Ned. "Yes or no?"

And Ned presented the pistol at the captain's head.

Again the Boy Rover paused ere he replied. He was taxing his brain for some stratagem by which he might defeat the object of Ned; but the latter guessed his intention and continued—

"No subterfuges, captain. The plain yes or no—yes, saves your life—no, sends a bullet through your skull!"

"Yes, then, since it must be so, you are free, TO THE SHORE!"

But the Boy Rover would have added, not an inch further, had not the barrel of the pistol gleamed before his eyes.

"Enough," said Ned. "Now call for Black Bill, and give the order; and look you, captain, but one glance of treachery and I'll send your soul to hell, with as little compunction as I would

shoot a mad dog—and remember, I never miss my aim!"

So saying, Ned returned the pistol to his belt, and released the bound limbs of the Boy Rover.

CHAPTER XXVIII.

FLIGHT OF THE "VENOMED SNAKE"—DISAPPOINTMENT OF THE LOVERS—BLACK BILL'S AMBITION OVERTHROWN—DEPARTURE FROM THE SHIP.

DURING the time in which the events recorded in the last chapter were proceeding, Charles and Ellen, clinging to each other with all the ardour of the conflicting feelings which had taken possession of their breasts, were left unmolested by the smugglers, who, now that they saw the 'Blue Bell' standing away from them, and had been made acquainted with the fact of the captain's disappearance over the side of the vessel into the sea, had gathered together in small knots canvassing the question what they had best do.

Some were for immediately launching the boats and making a search for the Boy Rover; but Black Bill, mad with the pain he was suffering from the wound inflicted upon his shoulder by the lover of Ellen, and fearing the consequences of his having allowed them to be surprised by the ship which had so unexpectedly run aboard them, opposed this proceeding.

He was now, in the absence of the Boy Rover, commander of the "Venomed Snake," and it would be to him a matter of gratification to keep that command. So, well knowing that if the Boy Rover were by any chance or another to return to the ship, he would surely have to answer for his negligence, he considered the best thing he could do would be to throw every obstacle he possibly could in the way of his rescue.

"Look you, mates," he said, addressing the crew, "yon ship only stands off to see if we fire the magazine; finding that we do not do so she will return and commence the fight again. We are scarcely in a position to oppose her; her crew far outnumbers our own. As for the captain, he has doubtless gone to the bottom with that young fellow he would have slung up to the yard-arm; therefore, I think the best thing we could do would be to put on all sail we can, and give yonder vessel the slip—once clear of her we can mature our plans. So shake out more sail, and show our opponent a clean pair of heels."

There were a few dissentients to this, but the majority were in favour of Bill's plans; so, in the course of a few minutes, the "Venomed Snake" was bearing away from the "Blue Bell" under a heavy press of canvas.

It was evident that the captain of the merchantman perceived their object, for she immediately shook out more sail, and stood after them.

But there was now little chance of her overtaking the smuggler, and this doubtless was soon perceived by those on board the "Blue Bell," for shortly after her topsails were reefed, and she rapidly dropped astern of the smuggler.

With heated breath Charles had watched all that was taking place, and his heart, which a few moments before had bounded with hope, now sunk within him in despair.

Every moment he expected to see the poor girl for whom he had so nobly fought torn from his arms, and, in the agony of the thought, his grasp tightened upon her slender form with a fierceness that was painful to her.

She raised her eyes to his, as though she would read there the thoughts that were passing through his mind, and then, with a sigh, she would drop them to the deck as she perceived the look of anguish that passed over his features.

"Ellen, my own loved Ellen," he murmured, "surely fate is cruelly sporting with our misery. At the very moment when I had thought that I had secured your liberty, to find ourselves deserted by those who had assisted to secure it. The hope that bounded to my heart as I clasped you in my arms has died away, and despair alone holds possession of my breast."

"They will tear me from you; they will consign me to worse than death. Oh, Charles, Charles, would that I were dead!"

And, as the tears gushed to her eyes, her head dropped on the shoulder of him she so fondly loved, and her form trembled with the powerful emotions that shook her soul.

"Oh, Charles," she continued, after a pause, "will your ship desert us thus—will they leave us to misery and death?"

"I know not, dear one," he replied. "Ah!" he added, as he observed the sails strengthen on board the "Blue Bell," "they have recovered from their panic, and will once more bear down to your rescue."

"Heaven be praised!" replied Ellen, clasping her fair white hands together.

Anxiously did they watch the vessel as she strove to make all the headway she could, but a groan escaped his heart as he perceived that every moment placed greater distance between them.

"We are running away from them," he said. "They will never overtake us. This accursed vessel cleaves the waves with a dolphin's speed, and, ere long, will be out of sight of yonder ship."

"Then we are doomed, Charles. Oh, would to Heaven that fate had not brought this misery upon you as well as me; and Henry, too—poor, brave-minded Henry—he, too, has fallen a sacrifice for my sake."

"Heaven forbid!" exclaimed the young man, fervently. "He may have succeeded in gaining yonder ship—he is a stout swimmer."

"Heaven grant it may be so. But how, how did you meet—how knew you that I had again fallen into the hands of this dreaded smuggler?"

"Henry escaped from his power; discovered me upon the raft; and yon vessel saved us both. I learnt from him the fate of his ship and your capture, and together we induced the captain of the "Blue Bell" to steer for your rescue."

"Yes; but you arrived at such a time, and so sudden."

"There was but one man on the deck—and he at the wheel. He steered this accursed bark down upon us, and made signals for us to board. When sufficiently near, Henry recognised him as the man who had severed his bands at the moment when the rope was dangling from the yard-arm which was to launch him to eternity; and, unhesitatingly, we ran alongside, and boarded her, ere the alarm was given."

"But the man—he who saved Henry?"

"Disappeared the moment we were alongside; and I have not seen him since."

"Charles," she murmured, "I owe that man a debt of gratitude which a life cannot repay. He saved me—saved me from—oh! horror."

Charles clasped the poor girl more tightly to his breast. Too well he guessed the meaning of her words; but the thought was, that fate only delayed for a time. Alas! he feared to think; but a half-uttered prayer escaped his lips for the preservation of that girl's honour.

During this hurried conversation, the smugglers had been too much occupied in making their arrangements to give their pursuers the slip to take notice of the lovers.

They knew that they need fear no further resistance from the brave youth; and they also knew that it was impossible for them to escape. So, save a casual glance towards them, they went about their duties as though they were unaware of the presence of that fair girl and her brave and devoted lover.

But Black Bill had not forgotten the blow he had received from Charles, and he determined to repay him for the pain he had caused him, before long. But, for the present, he had other work in hand—to escape from the "Blue Bell," and leave the Boy Rover to perish, and thus make himself captain of the "Venomed Snake."

A short time before, he had cursed himself for slumbering at his post—now he looked upon it as a most fortunate circumstance, since it had been the means of the loss of their captain.

Gradually the "Blue Bell" faded away in the distance, and as it did so, spite of his wound, Black Bill became quite good tempered.

He gave his orders even with a smile and with a cheerful tone. Already he considered himself a captain.

Finding that he had little to fear from the "Blue Bell" now, he turned his attention to his prisoners.

Advancing, therefore, to the side of Charles and his fair companion, he said—

"You will deliver your sword, sir, into my hands, and consider yourself my prisoner. You, miss, will retire to the cabin from which you have but a short time escaped, until such time as I have received the opinions of the crew of this ship as to what course they decide upon adopting with respect to you."

The hand of the brave young sailor tightened on his cutlass, and a glance of ineffable scorn for a moment shot from his eyes as he replied—

"By what right does such a lawless miscreant issue such commands?"

"By the law of might makes right," replied Black Bill. "We sought not your destruction, but you sought ours—you failed, and you must abide by the consequences."

"I deny your right to detain me or this maiden on board this bark, for I perceive that since the fall of your captain you have taken his position; or at least you can frame no excuse for making this lady a prisoner."

"Equally as good an excuse," replied Black Bill—"as had the Boy Rover; and as I am now commander here, I claim all things which our late captain possessed, this girl amongst the rest. By our rules, she would have fallen into my hands in due course of time, but the death of our captain has made her my immediate property."

"Scoundrel!" exclaimed Charles, raising his cutlass; "another such remark and I cleave you to the deck!"

"Bear a hand here," said Bill, turning to the smugglers, and retreating before the threatening weapon of the young sailor, "and stop his prating!"

In a moment Charles was surrounded and disarmed.

"Oh! harm him not," said Ellen, in imploring tones. If ye be men, degrade not yourselves by acts that are unworthy of the beast. He is good and noble: he has but followed the dictates of an honourable mind, and endeavoured to release a weak and defenceless woman from injustice and wrong. Oh! have mercy on us—suffer us to depart—and that one act will counterbalance many a previous crime."

Had it not been for the pain his wound occasioned him, Bill might have been induced to have listened to her pleadings ; but he saw before him the youth who had caused him so much pain, and his was not a nature to feel pity for an enemy, no matter how honourable his cause, if that enemy had inflicted injury on him, morally or physically.

Therefore, Bill paid no heed to the words of Ellen: he resolved to be revenged on her lover.

"Separate them," he exclaimed. Convey the girl to her cabin; and, as for the youth, throw him overboard. It will be the best way to get rid of him, and cause the least trouble."

"Oh! no, no," shrieked Ellen, as she twined her arms around his neck. "Oh! no—do not, for mercy's sake."

"Tear them apart," exclaimed Bill, in a perfect rage, "or it will be the worse for you!"

The smugglers hesitated.

"Damn you!" he exclaimed smarting with pain and rage, "do as I command. "Bear in mind, I'm captain now."

Ellen still clung to the neck of Charles, in an agony of despair.

But the fierceness of Bill's tones aroused the lawless sailors, and they seized the lovers to part them.

As if to belie the words of the dark-featured smuggler, at this very moment a voice, loud and clear, rang over the vessel, and the smugglers to a man started back in surprise and dismay.

The features of Black Bill underwent as many changes as the colours of a camelion, and for a moment he stood gazing first upon one, then upon another of the lawless crew.

Then the voice again rang out—

"Black Bill !"

"The captain, by all that's devilish !" exclaimed Bill: "how, in the name of fury, did he get aboard again ?"

And in a moment Black Bill had sunk fifty fathoms in his own estimation—he was not captain yet!

Still he did not attempt to move till the voice of the Boy Rover once more rang out—

"Pass the word to the lieutenant, wanted in the captain's cabin."

Then he turned away and strode towards the cabin stairs.

"Poor Ellen! the moment that voice saluted her ears a spasm passed through her frame, and had it not been for the supporting arm of her lover, she must have fallen to the deck.

The smugglers released their hold of Charles and the maiden, but still surrounded them to prevent any attempt to escape, though heaven knows how they were to effect that much-desired object.

Black Bill descended to the cabin where he found the Boy Rover standing in the doorway, whom he saluted somewhat coolly, expecting every moment to be ordered into irons for allowing them to be surprised by the "Blue Bell."

But the Boy Rover merely remarked—

"Have a boat lowered, and see that your prisoners, together with this gentleman and Ned Wilton, are allowed to leave this ship unmolested.

Black Bill opened his eyes to their utmost width as Ned stepped forward, and looked first at the captain, then at Henry, and then at Ned. At last, being unable to believe he was not dreaming, he pinched his ear as hard as he possibly could to see if he was really awake.

Finding such to be the case, he gave a long, low whistle, and said :

"What, captain ?"

"Obey my orders," was the cool reply of the Boy Rover. "See they have a free pass from this ship, unmolested."

Black Bill fixed his dark eyes on the captain's face inquiringly, as though he would know the meaning of this order, and gain some explanation of his strange conduct.

But the look he received in return caused him to make a precipitate retreat from the cabin to the deck.

"That's fair and square," said Ned, when Black Bill was out of hearing. "Bill, I know, will obey orders; but now, captain, so that you may not play us false, and counteract the order, and cause us to be again taken as soon as we are over the side, we'll just make you a little bit secure for our own sakes—bind him hand and foot," and, as he spoke, he threw his arms round the Boy Rover and held him firmly, whilst Henry Chambers bound the rope around his arms and legs.

"That'll do," said Ned, when this operation had been performed. "Now, captain, we will bid you good-bye, and thank you for our pass to the shore."

"To the shore," echoed the Boy Rover—"yes; to the shore."

Ned was about to lead the way from the cabin, when he paused suddenly.

"I don't half trust him," he said, addressing Henry. "The moment we are gone he may give the alarm, and have us pursued and taken. Prevention is better than cure, my old grandmother used to say, so suppose we gag him ?"

"A wise thought," replied Henry.

Ned took up one end of the rope which bound the arms of the smuggler captain, and, forcing it into his mouth, brought it round the back of his head, and firmly secured it.

"There, that will do," remarked Ned, eyeing his work with a look of pride. "He learnt me how to do that little job himself."

Then, advancing to the wall of the cabin, he took another pistol from its socket, and a small flask which hung by its side.

"Might be handy," he remarked, as he coolly hid the flask in the breast of his shirt; "and, as he stole them, why can't I rob him? Good-bye, captain," and, seizing Henry by the arm, Ned led him from the cabin up-stairs to the deck.

Arriving there they met the inquiring looks of the smugglers; but Ned and his companion passed on to where Charles and Ellen stood, gazing in mute surprise on all around.

The moment Henry reached the side of his friends, he grasped their extended arms, and whispered:

"Not a word, now; suffice it to say we are free."

"Free," said Ellen—"free ?"

"Yes," replied Black Bill, with a sinister glance; "free TO THE SHORE !"

The friends remarked the emphasis which he laid upon the last words, and the eyes of Henry and Charles met in a meaning glance, whilst the heart of Ellen sunk in her breast. Ned, too, had marked them, but a smile lit up his weather-beaten face as he thought that he had stopped all attempts at treachery by binding and gagging the Boy Rover.

The boat was lowered, and, with beating hearts, Charles, Ellen, and Henry entered it. Ned waited till they were safely in, and then followed. When he had taken his place he called out for them to let go, which was done, and, as she glided away from the vessel's side, he said:

"Black Bill, you ain't captain yet; but, if you order the men ashore to-morrow, you'll find the boat left all right for you. Farewell!"

"We shall meet again," said Bill, with a meaning glance, and a scowl, at Ned's remark of his not being captain.

"Sure to," said Ned; "for I'll come and see you turned off."

"Turned off from what?" growled Bill, as he watched the progress of the boat.

"The gallows," said Ned. "It's sure to come to that."

And, with a loud laugh, he bent to the oar, whilst, assisted by Henry, and guided by Charles, the boat danced over the waters, in the direction of the land, which loomed up black before them.

CHAPTER XXIX.

THE JOURNEY TO THE SHORE—THE PURSUIT.

THERE are few of us who, at some period or another of our existence, have not been placed in imminent danger; few, indeed, who have not felt that overpowering feeling of pleasure with which those so placed have escaped the perils to which they have been consigned: yet that gratification is but of short duration, and the ordinary courses of our life soon render us forgetful of our past fears.

It was, therefore, with a feeling of gratification and pleasure that our hero and heroine saw the distance every moment increasing between the boat in which they were, and the smuggler vessel.

With willing arms Ned and Henry plied the oars; and with equally willing hands Charles guided their course over the waves.

Each thought they had escaped a terrible doom; and, in their thankfulness to Providence, they heeded not what might next befall them. Their thoughts were centred on their escape from the power of the Rover and his ruthless crew; but not one moment's reflection of any danger that might hitherto assail them then crossed their minds.

All thoughts of further peril was lost in their happiness at their escape.

The arm of Charles clasped the waist of the fair girl, and the bright eye of the lovely maiden wandered over the noble countenance of her lover.

They were happy—happier, perhaps, than they would have been had no dark cloud overshadowed their love.

Henry gazed from beneath his brows upon the now smiling lovers, and a sigh escaped his breast.

His was a mind too good, too noble, to feel jealous at their happiness; yet how ardently he wished that he were at that moment Charles Lawson instead of himself.

He loved Ellen with a passion as pure and holy as it was fervent and undying; but even that love warned him to be careful of himself, lest, by one word or act, he should embitter the happiness of her for whose welfare he would have sacrificed his life.

Henry was a brave and noble-minded youth, and would have scorned to have done ought that would have given a moment's pain to the feelings of his rival.

With that true sense of honour, he perceived that Charles well merited the love of the fair girl at his side, and his was not a nature to harm the man on whom the girl so fondly adored had placed her affections. He felt that our hero had wooed and won her with honour and truth, and he would not allow a selfish jealousy to take possesion of his heart, and degrade the noble qualities of his soul, by envying him the possession of that which he himself could never possess.

He loved not wisely but too well; but that love brought out all his generous nature, and made him the firmer friend of both Ellen and his rival.

Ned, too, although gratified beyond measure at his escape, still had his thoughts, and they were not of an over-pleasant nature.

Too well he knew the revengeful heart of the Boy Rover, and he entertained strong doubts as to whether they would be suffered to continue their journey unmolested.

Many an anxious glance he cast towards the "Venomed Snake," expecting every moment to see her bearing down on them; or a boat lowered over her side to pursue them, and, if possible, again make them prisoners.

True he had rendered the Boy Rover powerless to act until such time as he should be discovered by some of the crew and released from the gag and bonds with which he had been secured, but then he knew not how soon the circumstance might happen, and when it did he felt assured that the Boy Rover would not fail to regret that he had suffered them to depart, and take instant measures of again placing them in his power.

However, they were fast leaving the ship, and rapidly nearing the land—a land unknown to them; but they one and all trusted in Providence to guide their footsteps when once they gain·d the shore.

"Thank Heaven!" said Charles, gazing rapturously into the face of his fair companion, "that you are once more free from that accursed vessel. Oh, Ellen, the agonies I have endured, since the moments of returning consciousness, as to the fate which had befallen you, are almost obliterated by the happiness I feel in again gazing upon your lovely face."

A smile rose to the face of the maiden, as she said:

"Charles, words cannot convey what I feel at the providential arrival of the ship in which you came. It saved me from worse than death. Oh, Charles, Charles, your noble mind could not conjure up horrors so fearful as I have endured on board that bark. The indignities and outrages to which I have been submitted, did you know them, would make the blood curdle in your very veins."

An undefinable feeling of horror pervaded the frame of the youth as Ellen spoke, and, fixing a pitying look upon her, he stammered:

"Ellen, Ellen, what do you say—to what do your words portend? Heaven forgive me—but, but, I cannot speak the words. Ellen, Ellen—oh, the thought is madness."

The fair girl threw her arms around the neck of her lover, and, as a deep crimson flush overspread her face, she murmured:

"Charles, I know what you would ask; and no false modesty shall chain my tongue. Charles, I swear by the heaven above us that this heart is as pure as an infant's; that, rather than submit to the vile doings of that ruffian, I would have died a thousand deaths!"

"Forgive me, Ellen—forgive me for the suspicion!" said the young man, clasping her fondly to his heart. "But—but—"

"You feared the worst," she interrupted; "and well might you do so, knowing the hands into which I had fallen, and seeing what you saw in the cave."

"Oh! that I had shot the villain," said Charles; "what misery might it not have saved you!"

"All is for the best," she answered. "We know not what might have been our fate had you done so."

"It would have spared you further outrage," he replied.

"Perhaps not," said Ellen; "and it would doubtless have sacrificed your life. Heaven knows best," she added; "and to Heaven let us trust for future succour."

"You are right, Ellen," he said, after a pause. "Heaven has certainly watched over us, and sent us aid when all hope was lost; otherwise the wild waves would have swallowed us up, and the life of love and peace which I fondly hope to reward us for all our sufferings would have been lost for ever."

And the youth's grasp tightened upon the hand of the maiden.

"Henry has told you how he saved me?" she said, after a time.

"He has told me all," replied the youth; "and never will I forget the service he has rendered you."

"But you have not yet told me how you escaped a watery grave," said Ellen, wishing to draw his mind from the horrors she had endured on board the smuggler.

"He saved me likewise," replied Charles.

"Kind noble Henry!" exclaimed Ellen, extending her hand to the young man, who raised it to his lips, "how can I thank you?"

"I am sufficiently rewarded by a smile from you, Ellen," replied the young man, as a joyous expression passed over his features. "I did but my duty when I put off from the cutter to your rescue; and accident alone threw me in the way of Charles. It was the hand of Heaven," he added, after a pause, "that has decreed that I, by the side of Charles, should struggle for your protection.

"And nobly have you done so," replied Ellen.

"And will till death," he added. "Charles," he continued, grasping the hand of the young man—"I love Ellen with all a brother's love, and shall not a brother's hand be raised in the defence of a sister's honour and happiness?"

Charles returned the pressure of the other's grasp, as he replied—

"From this time forth, in weal or woe, stand we by each other's side in firm and undying friendship."

At this moment an exclamation escaped the lips of Ned, who, looking towards the smuggler, observed that she was taking in sail."

"That means something," remarked Ned, as he pointed to the vessel, "and I don't much like the look of it. Pull with a will, for if they intend to overhaul us, the longer the start we get of them the better."

"What is it you fear?" asked Ellen, with some trepidation.

"Why, you see," replied Ned; "I don't think as how the captain fancies letting us go scot free. He would not consent to your leaving the ship until I shoved a barker under his nose, and brought him to reason. I think he means having us, that's all; but if we once gain the shore he may find it somewhat difficult to lay hands on us again: but in this here blessed element, as you calls it, we ain't got not no chance at all, becos as how he'll send a stiffish crew, and well armed, to take us."

"Then you think he will violate his word?" remarked Henry.

"He'd violate any thing, he would," replied Ned Wilton.

"There is little honour to be found in his composition, I fear," said Charles. "But cheer up, Ellen," he added, as he saw the cheeks of the fair girl blanch with terror—"we have a good start, and another half-hour will place us alongside the land: though I know nothing of the place to which we are steering, yet we shall doubtless find those who will be will be willing to aid us in the event of pursuit."

"Heaven grant it may be so, but my heart misgives me."

"Hope for the best," said Charles; but though he spoke cheerfully his looks belied his thoughts.

"I will plunge myself into the sea rather than again fall into his power," said the poor girl. "I will welcome death rather than a repetition of the agonies I have endured on board his ship."

"There," said Ned, sympathisingly, "don't give way like that. "He ain't got you yet; and he shan't have you, if I can help it."

"We will die before he shall again make you his captive," said Henry.

"Alas!" said Ellen, with a sigh, "better that I had perished when the vessel went to pieces on the rock than that so much misery should be heaped upon us all."

"Here," said Ned, taking the pistols from his belt, "just you take these here barkers. We've got our mawley's, and we knows how to use 'em. You don't; so take care of them. Yer might want 'em; but I hope you won't: 'cos, you see, if the captain collars us, it's a safe case of swing for me."

While this was going on, Ned and Henry bent to the oars with a right good will, and the boat shot over the bosom of the waters like an arrow.

They were but a short distance now from the shore, which appeared to be but one continuous mass of rocks, with scarce a vestige of vegetation to be seen.

"Know you anything of this place?" said Charles, addressing himself to Ned.

"Not a blessed bit," replied that worthy: "never was here in my life before."

"Neither do I," remarked Henry; "and, from all appearance, we shall have to run along the coast ere we find a landing."

While this conversation was taking place, Ned observed that the "Venomed Snake" was slowly nearing the shore likewise.

This fact he pointed out to his companions; and there could now be no doubt that the vessel's course was altered for the purpose of once gaining possession of the occupants of the boat.

Still on they went, hugging the shore, in the hopes of finding some spot at which they could land.

They now perceived that a boat had put off from the smuggler, and, fully manned, was gliding over the sea towards them.

The words of the Boy Rover and Black Bill came forcibly to the minds of the escaped, that they had but a free pass to the shore.

They understood now the emphasis laid on those words; and they knew that they were pursued.

They redoubled their exertions, but could find no place at which they could land. Nothing but high steep rocks met their gaze, and fears that they would again fall into the hands of the Boy Rover and his villainous crew took possession of their hearts.

On they went, and on came the pursuing boat; and it now became evident that if they did not speedily fall in with some spot where they might land, that nothing could prevent them again falling into the hands of the smugglers.

"The treacherous scoundrel," said Charles. "Oh, of what avail was the liberty to leave the accursed ship if only for a short period—raising hopes to hurl them back to despair? Not one spark of honour dwells in the breast of the ruthless captain, not even his word can be trusted."

"He has kept faith with us," said Henry, "for he distinctly said he gave us a free pass to the shore. At the time I heeded not the meaning tones in which he uttered those words, but I see it now."

"The double-dealing villain!" exclaimed Charles, passionately. "But as yet we are free, and, should we once succeed in placing our feet upon the land, may be enabled to remain so; at least, we will not be taken without a struggle. For myself I care not, but for you, Ellen, my mind is in an agony of fear."

"Alas!" said Ellen, "into what misery have I brought you?"

"Oh, speak not thus. I would brave death a thousand times to shield you from harm. Rather say into what misery my love has plunged you. But for me you would not have encountered the horrors of that fearful night when we struck upon the rocks which bound the Cornish coast, and all the subsequent horrors which have assailed you since that fearful night; but for me, Ellen, you would now have been happy with your father, and"—

"Say no more," interrupted the loving girl. "To reward your love I left the home of my parents—left it to share your joys and your sufferings—your weal and your woe. Come what may, I will no more complain so that you are by my side."

And the slender fingers of the poor girl twined with a fervent clasp around the hand of her lover.

Still on came the smuggler's boat, nearer and nearer to the shore, and the pursued strained their eyes along the rock-bound coast for some friendly spot in which to disembark.

"Steer her in shore," said Ned, suddenly, as his eye detected an opening in the rock, forming, as it were, a little bay. "That's the place to land," he added, pointing in the direction. "We can easily climb up them there, for they are not so steep, and who knows but, perhaps, on the other side we find shelter and friends?"

"Let us hope so," said Henry, as he rowed with renewed vigour. "Gold is embedded in the quartz, and the rock-bound shore often hides a beautiful country."

Ned and Henry now pulled for the spot indicated with a right good will, and Charles steered the boat's course directly up to the small bay or cleft in the rocks, whilst Ellen's face once more brightened with returning hope.

Their pursuers too altered the course of their boat. It was evident that they also had observed the place at which the fair girl and her brave companions had determined to land, and it would seem that they intended, if possible, to cut them off ere they reached it.

But renewed hope strengthened the arms of the fugitives, and the gallant little boat danced over the spray with increased speed.

Spite of all their efforts, the boat's crew of the smuggler were unable to overtake or cut them off from the goal which they were now rapidly nearing, and in a few minutes the opening was reached.

Charles guided the little craft between the massive rocks, and in another minute they rode upon the bosom of a small bay.

In this inlet the water was as smooth as a glossy lake—protected from the winds by the huge rocks, which towered some two hundred feet above the sea.

It was with a sigh of relief that the little crew entered this cove; but, as the boat sped over the glassy surface of the bay, a look of anxiety passed over the features of Charles and his friend.

Before and on either side of them the high rocks lifted their towering heads, and shut them, as it were, within the impenetrable walls of a natural prison; whilst behind them was the open sea; and at the entrance to the ocean rode the rough smugglers, ready to pounce upon their prey.

"We are trapped," said Henry, breaking the silence which had been observed by them for some time.

"Alas! I fear it is so," replied Charles. "There appears to be no outlet save by the one which we entered, and there our pursuers await, like angry vultures, to pounce upon us."

Poor Ellen said not a word, but her blanched cheek and trembling hand told her lover the agony of mind which she was enduring at this fresh danger.

"We won't despair yet," said Ned, as he cast his eyes around; "I never seed such a snug shelter for a smuggler craft to run into when pursued by the revenue. Why, the Boy Rover would give something, I wager, to know of the existence of this little bay."

"Perhaps he does," remarked Henry, "and knowing that it could only be here that we should think to effect a landing, allowed us to leave the ship. Like a cat that tortures the mouse ere she kills it—permitted us to escape, well knowing that he could place us again in his hands when he liked."

"Don't think it," said Ned, "or I should have known it too. But if we can't find no outlet save that by which we entered, why, we'll try and climb up the side of the rocks, and see what lies beyond."

"'Tis our only chance of escaping recapture," said Henry.

"It will be our only hope," said Charles, as he threw his arms around the now trembling girl, who sat pale and mute at his side.

"There is evidently vegetation beyond these cliffs," exclaimed Ellen, as she cast her eyes upwards. "Look at that huge tree which overtops the rock yonder."

They looked upwards, and to the left of the bay, at its furthest extremity, and where it narrowed to a few feet, they perceived the branches of a huge tree overhanging the rocks—its bright green foliage rustling in the wind, that bent its branches, with a graceful sway; and the sun, now shining brightly above, reflected it in the surface of the water, at the base of the cliffs.

"Could we but ascend these rocks," said Charles after gazing some time at the object to which Ellen had called his attention, "we should doubtless find behind them some place of shelter from our lawless pursuers.

"We must do it," said Ned, "or we are lost. See, they have entered the cove; and, by all that's holy, we must ascend the cliffs, or they will take us!"

The smuggler boat had entered the small bay, and was making towards them.

CHAPTER XXX.

THE HUMAN BRIDGE—THE ESCAPE ACROSS THE CHASM.

To remain in the boat, and escape them, both Henry and Charles saw in a moment would be impossible; for, even at the widest part of the inlet, they could stand no chance of getting out of the way of the smuggler.

Their only hope was to ascend the cliffs, and trust to Providence. They cast their eyes anxiously around for those which would afford the greatest foothold.

Charles would fain have landed on the side on which the tree grew; for there he thought would be the greatest chance of shelter. But, on that side, the rocks were more precipitous, and the almost unbroken smoothness of their surface held out no hope of escape or ascent in safety.

To the right the cliffs were more on the incline; whilst their rugged and uneven sides presented a much greater prospect of ascent.

"Come, Ellen," said Charles, after he had taken a long survey of all around—"come, lean upon me, and Heaven guide our footsteps!"

Henry and Ned had ran the boat close up to the side of the cliff; and Charles, with Ellen grasping his arm, stepped out on to the rock.

As they did so, a shout arose from the smuggler's boat, and it came bounding over the smooth water of the bay like an arrow.

"They guess our little game," said Ned, "and mean to stop us if they can; but we'll beat them yet, or my name's not Ned Wilton. Just you look after them there barkers, miss, 'cos you might want 'em. You knows how to use 'em—'taint the first time you ever had 'em in your hands."

"Come, Henry," said Charles, "we have not a moment to lose."

"Heed us not," replied the noble-minded young lieutenant. "I care little for myself so that you and Ellen escape. Look to her. We will follow to repel the attack that will doubtless be made. Go!"

Both Charles Lawson and his fair companion hesitated.

"Away at once without further delay," said Henry; "I will follow. But pause not another instant, or you are lost."

And as he spoke he leapt from the boat to the rocks, followed by Ned.

"Now, you varmints," muttered Ned, as he clenched his pistols, "look out for this 'ere mawley; for the first as comes up with me gets it right on his eye."

Holding firmly the arm of the fair girl, Charles led Ellen up the rock.

At every footstep the loose portions of the cliff gave way and rolled down its sides, but still on they went, followed closely by Henry and Ned.

When they had arrived about half way up the cliff, the smugglers drove the boat up to its base, and, leaping from it, commenced climbing the rocks in pursuit of the fugitives.

Charles, encumbered with Ellen, could not make such swift progress as did their pursuers, who rapidly gained upon them, and Henry and Ned, who persisted in keeping in the rear to meet the first assault that might be made, soon found themselves face to face with two of the smugglers.

Not a word was spoken, but, as one of the smugglers reached out his hand to seize Henry, Ned drew back his arm, and struck the smuggler so violent a blow on the face that he staggered to the edge of the cliff, where, struggling for an instant, he lost his foothold, and fell over the side into the water beneath.

"Right fair on his left eye," said Ned, with the utmost coolness, as he waited for his opponent's companion to come up.

But this worthy, somewhat unnerved by the fate of his companion, paused a moment, and drew his cutlass, then, with a cry of rage, he bounded forward, and, as he raised it to strike at Ned, Henry hurled a piece of broken rock with such force, that, striking the man on the shoulder, he fell with a howl of pain.

"Well done," said Ned; "that's one I owe you —you saved me that time."

Charles had paused, and was about to return to the side of Henry and Ned, but the former, observing this called out:

"Keep on. Fear not for us. Save Ellen. We will save ourselves.

"I back we will," said Ned. Then he added, in an undertone: "Don't you see, lieutenant, if we can only keep them at a distance we have little to fear. The captain wants us taken alive; and the men haven't got a single pistol among them. He was too wide awake to let them have them, for fear they'd use 'em. Lor' bless you, that 'ere gal wouldn't be worth not nothing to him dead."

Henry felt the truth of these remarks, but made no reply, and they continued to ascend the rocks, followed at a short distance by the smugglers, who, foaming in rage at the fate their two companions had met with, feared to come to too close quarters.

With palpitating heart and throbbing brain, Ellen clung to her lover; ever and anon turning her head to see if they were still followed by Henry and Ned.

In this way they reached the summit of the cliff, and gazed out upon the scene beyond.

On the opposite side of the chasm formed by the two steep cliffs and the small bay which laid at their base, stretched away a thickly-wooded landscape for some distance, but on the side on which they stood nothing but a huge mass of rock, with the sea washing its sides, met their gaze.

Ellen heaved a heavy sigh, and the grasp on the arm of her lover relaxed.

"Evil destiny continues to pursue us," she murmured. "From here there is no escape—no shelter from these ruthless men. Oh, would that we could leap this fearful chasm, Charles."

"'Tis hard," said Henry, "to meet misfortune everywhere thus. Were we but on the other side of the bay we could defy ten times this force sent against us; but Providence has willed it otherwise, and we must bow to its decrees."

"Indeed we must," she sighed, as, with giddy brain, she gazed down into the clear depths of the water which formed the bay.

Charles drew her back from the edge of the cliff. He feared to trust her upon the edge of that fearful precipice in her present state of mind.

Still closely following them, Henry and Ned continued their way up the rock.

ALONE ON THE DEEP.

The smugglers had recovered somewhat from the fear into which they had been thrown by the fate of their companions, and now came on with renewed courage.

Watching each other's movements, like trained gladiators, for the first opening by which to take advantage of their opponents, both pursuer and pursued continued their way up that steep and rugged cliff.

As they neared the top of the rocks, the smugglers made a sudden rush at Henry and Ned, but were met with a blow from the fist of each which sent them backwards half-stunned.

Ashamed and enraged at being thus beaten back by the young men, the smugglers, now five in number closed together, and made a simultaneous onslaught upon the two determined youths.

Henry observed the movement, and, calling out to Charles to do his best to escape with Ellen, and pay no heed to them, prepared to oppose the further passage of the smugglers, and defend themselves against their attack.

On rushed the five smugglers, with furious determination, upon their opponents.

They were received, as before, with well-directed blows from the clenched fists of Henry and Ned; but the smugglers closed with them, and then commenced a struggle to secure the fugitives.

This struggle lasted for some five minutes; but the unequal nature of the combat could but tell in

11

favour of the smugglers, who, seizing their prey, strove, to the utmost of their strength, to fling them to the earth, and then secure them.

But, one-sided as was this affray, Ned and Henry battled manfully, and the blows they struck told fearfully upon the breasts and faces of their opponents; and, upon more than one occasion, the smugglers found themselves hurled to the hard rocks, with terrific violence.

As the fight continued, the combatants neared the side of the cliff, and, unconscious of their danger, once more endeavoured to secure their prisoners.

As they rushed forward again to the combat, after a moment's pause to take breath, Henry and Ned caught two of the smugglers in their grasp with the intention of once more hurling them to the earth ere they were assailed by the other three; but their strength was gradually becoming exhausted, and the smugglers prevented the kind office intended for them.

The other three now again came to the aid of their companions, and in the struggle which now ensued, Henry and Ned, together with the men in whose grasp they were, struggled to the very edge of the cliff.

In their frantic efforts to keep their foothold, a huge piece of loose rock on the edge of the cliff gave way, and with a loud exclamation of horror Henry and Ned, together with two of the smugglers rolled over the side locked in a deadly embrace.

A cry of horror and dismay escaped from the lips of the lovers who had been a witness to this fearful fall, and as they rolled down the steep and rugged rock, the smugglers stood spell-bound watching their descent to the water at its base.

Charles was the first to recover from the shock caused by this unexpected termination to the struggle, and clasping Ellen in his arms, he exclaimed:

"We must escape to the opposite cliff or we are lost; there are still three of the smugglers remaining, and we cannot entertain a hope of escaping from their hands on this side of the chasm."

"How—how can we hope to escape," asked the trembling girl; "we cannot leap this fearful chasm. Were we to attempt it we should be dashed to pieces.

Charles stooped down and picked up a piece of the rock about the size of his hand, then hurriedly tearing his handkerchief from his neck, he tied the stone in one corner of it, and advancing to the edge of the cliff threw it around a bough of the tree which overhung the chasm from the opposite rock.

The handkerchief held firmly to the branch, and Charles drew the bough as far over the chasm as it would come.

By this means he succeeded in gaining a hold of the branch by stretching his body out over the chasm, and by this means he formed of his own body and the friendly branch a bridge across the abyss.

"Ellen, dear one," he exclaimed, without releasing his hold or turning his head for a moment—"fear not, but cross this chasm on my body: once you have done so I will fling myself across by the aid of this branch—come, and fear not. Cast not your eyes down for a moment, lest your brain grow dizzy, but look upwards and place your trust in heaven and me.

"Oh," she exclaimed—"I fear, dear Charles,

to hurl you as well as myself into the fearful depths beneath."

"Stand firm," he replied, "and you may cross in safety—delay not, or we are lost. Come, love, come."

With trembling limbs Ellen placed her feet upon his body, and moved along this human bridge which the ingenious mind of her lover had formed for her escape.

With slow and nervous steps Ellen moved along over the body of her lover, the bright morning sun shining upon her lovely form, and the silent waters of the little bay lying like a polished mirror afar beneath.

She had moved a few paces along the body of her lover when the smugglers turned, and, recovering from the shock caused by the fall over the rock of their companions and their would-be prisoners, they rushed forward to stay the further progress of Ellen.

They paused a few paces from the strangely formed bridge, and rough and uncouth as they were, they could not but gaze in pleased admiration at the heroic girl and her brave and devoted lover.

But they had a duty to perform—a duty to which they were answerable to the Boy Rover for its commission—and they must perform, or meet the punishment of failure.

Already had their little band suffered reverses, for which the survivors would have to render an account; and too well they knew that should they fail entirely in the object on which their mission was placed, that the disappointment of the Boy Rover would lead him to invent some reason for showering down his vengeance upon their heads.

And the vengeance of that cruel-hearted boy was indeed to be feared alike by his crew or captives.

It would not do for them to return to the ship without having made a captive of the girl at least; and now a splendid opportunity offered itself to them to make her captive.

They once more bounded forward until they stood within a few paces of the human bridge.

But here their career was checked, and they could only stand and gaze at the fair girl as she stood, proud and defiant, upon the body of her lover, her hair streaming in the morning breeze, and a look of firm resolve upon her beauteous features.

And there she stood in that perilous position—in which one false step would have borne her to certain destruction—stood like a tigress at bay, with the bright sun gleaming along the barrels of the pistols which Ned had given her in the boat.

Finding that herself and her lover were likely to fall into the hands of the smugglers, she presented the weapons at the head of her foes and brought them to a standstill, at the very moment when their capture seemed inevitable.

So sudden and unexpected had been the check that the smugglers could but watch her retreating figure as she passed over the body of her lover, keeping her pale face turned towards them, and the barrels of the pistols pointed at their heads.

Surprise and admiration for a time held them spell-bound.

At length one of the smugglers more fearless than his fellows made a motion to move from the spot on which he stood, but the eager eye of the young girl detected the movement, and she said—

"Back, dog! or I will stain the rock with your worthless blood."

The smuggler paused and said—

"We must do our duty. Surrender, and we will no tharm you."

"Surrender!—what, to worse than death?—never! Seek not to molest us, for I would not have your blood upon my soul, but by that heaven above us I swear that if you but advance one step I will lay you lifeless in the waters beneath!"

"Girl," answered the smuggler—"you but enhance the misery of your fate, and call down upon your head the dreaded vengeance of the Boy Rover. Be advised—surrender, and trust to his mercy."

A loud sarcastic laugh broke from the lips of Ellen.

"To his mercy, said you!" exclaimed Ellen, "to his mercy? Fools, cast your eyes down this fearful chasm—what see you?"

The smuggler looked over the side of the cliff, and then raising his face to Ellen, said—

"The rugged sides of these rocks on which your obstinacy will cause you to be dashed to pieces, and the plack pool of water that will form your grave."

"Return to your captain," said Ellen, "and tell him that sooner than place myself for one moment in his power I will dash myself to pieces on these rugged rocks! Too well do I know what mercy to expect from him. Mercy! he knows it not—feels it not. Away, and leave us to our misery—away to your blood-stained vessel, and there pray to Him whose laws you have outraged, to avert the doom of the murderer, and your deaths on the scaffold.

The smuggler shuddered as the last words fell upon his ear, and his base nature would have prompted him to have raised his hand in violence to the utterer of the words.

Turning fiercely to his two companions, he exclaimed;

"Shall we be braved and defied by a girl?—No: I will carry her back to the ship in spite of hell!"

And he bounded forward.

As he did so, there was a quick flash—a loud report—a puff of smoke; and as the echoes of the pistol died away among the rocks, a low groan mingled with the sound—then a loud splash rose up from the waters in the deep abyss, and two smugglers now only remained on the spot where Ellen a few moments before had addressed them.

He who had rushed forward to seize the poor girl had paid dearly for his temerity. The bullet had entered his breast, and the dark waters of the bay had parted to receive his body, and now formed eddying circles around the spot which was now his grave.

But still Ellen stood upon the body of her lover, and still two of the smugglers remained to oppose her passage to the cliff, which she desired to gain.

Charles, unable to move, yet an anxious and painful listener to all that was taking place, still held on to the branch of the tree—still bore the weight of that fair girl upon his body.

His position was indeed a painful and fearful one—with his feet clinging to the projection of the rock—with his hands holding firmly to the bent bough of the friendly tree, and with the weight of that fair young upon his body, as he lay, suspended and unsupported, save by his hands and feet, over that fearful chasm—with the knowledge that close to him were his pursuers, and that one false step would

plunge himself and Ellen into the bay beneath, or hurl their bodies upon the rugged sides of the rocks, a bruised and mutilated mass.

Fearful of receiving the contents of the other pistol, the smugglers stood undecided how to act, and Ellen slowly and carefully stepped along the bridge to the tree.

She seized the friendly branch in her hand, and thus lightend the burden of her lover.

Then she drew herself along the branch, till her feet rested on the cliff, on the opposite side to that on which the smugglers stood. Charles, freed from the weight of the young girl, breathed more freely, and was about to leave the foothold of the rock, and swing his body across the chasm, by the aid of the branch, when the two smugglers rushed forward and seized him by the legs.

So suddenly was this done, that he almost released his hold of the bough. Had he done so, there can be no doubt but that he would have been precipitated head foremost down the rocks, and perhaps have drawn with him the two smugglers.

But, fortunately for himself and Ellen, he kept firm hold of the branch, which swayed and bent in the struggles.

With a cry, the young girl once more presented the pistols at the smugglers. She was loth to shed their blood; but she felt that she must make an effort to release the brave youth from the perilous position in which he was now placed.

"I would not have your blood upon my soul," she exclaimed, addressing the two smugglers; "but I will stretch you dead if you offer further molestation to that brave youth."

There was a determination in her tones that to'd plainly to those lawless men that she would keep her word; and they released their hold of Charles.

The moment that our hero found himself free from their hands, he bounded up, and, clasping the tree firmly, he sprang upwards, and over the chasm.

The sudden strain upon the branch, as it bounded upwards, and then came down again, snapped it at the trunk; and, as the feet of Charles touched the rock on which Ellen now stood, it broke away from the stem, and fell over the side into the abyss, nearly carrying with it the brave youth who had so nobly struggled to save the girl he so fondly loved.

A cry rose in the air: it was that of Ellen, who, as her lover tottered on the brink of the fearful precipice, threw her arms around him, and forced him backwards on to the rock, and he sank exhausted from his gallant exertions at her feet.

CHAPTER XXXI.

HOPES AND FEARS OF BLACK BILL—THE BOY ROVER AND WILD MADGE.

IT was not until the fugitives had placed some distance between their boat and the ship that Black Bill began to consider that it was something strange the Boy Rover should have been so willing to part with his prisoners; but when he did begin to reflect on the affair, he was not long in coming to the conclusion that he had only permitted their departure from the vessel under a pressure of circumstances for which he, Bill, could not account.

He well knew that he was sure to be in disfavour with his chief for allowing themselves to be surprised by the ship which had run alongside them ere they had the least knowledge of its approach; and his wily nature prompted him to devise some means by which he might escape the punishment he felt assured the Boy Rover would inflict upon him for his negligence.

Black Bill, therefore, considered it best to be the first to speak upon the subject; and, as the helmsman could not be found, and all imagined that he had been forced over the side upon the vessels running alongside each other, he resolved to throw the whole blame upon the unfortunate steersman, and, by pleading some excuse or other for his absence from the deck, trust to deceiving his captain, and averting the punishment.

Thus thinking, he descended to the cabin.

Ned had closed the door of the apartment when he had left it, and Bill now knocked with his knuckles upon the pannelling, to announce his presence.

There was no answer, and Bill nervously opened the door of the cabin, and entered the apartment.

But scarcely had he done so, than he started in surprise.

The Boy Rover lay upon the floor, bound hand and foot; and, by his side, Wild Madge, similarly bound, was rolling to and fro, in impotent rage. Bill stooped down and removed the gag; then, for a moment, the lieutenant of the "Venomed Snake" stood gazing down upon them, in a stupified manner.

"What the devil do you stand there like a stuck pig for," exclaimed the Boy Rover, "instead of undoing these cursed cords, and letting me free?"

Bill stooped down and unfastened the cords; and, with a sigh of relief, the Rover started to his feet.

Bill now essayed the same kind office for the prostrate woman, who, the moment she found her hands free, gave the lieutenant such a ringing slap on the cheek, that it sent the blood tingling over his face, and brought a gleam of passion into his dark eyes.

The fury had worked herself into such a passion that she scarcely knew what she did; and there is no doubt but that had anyone else have done her the same service she must have vented her ill-feeling in the same manner.

But she rose to her feet, and then, cramped with her long confinement, dropped suddenly into a chair.

Black Bill looked first from one, then to another, as though he would seek some explanation of how they came to be placed in such a position.

The Boy Rover guessed the meaning of his lieutenant's looks, and said:

"You're a damned pretty fellow to be trusted with the command in my absence!"

"Captain," said Bill, "I—"

"Silence," roared the Boy Rover. "Do you know the fate of a traitor?"

"Yes," said Bill, "but I am no traitor."

"We'll see," replied the Boy Rover. "I believe you are, and let me but have proof of your treachery and you swing at the yard arm. Do you hear that. You swing, aye swing!"

"Captain, hear me a moment," exclaimed Bill, thoroughly alarmed at the tones in which the words were spoken. "You judge me wrongly—you do indeed."

"Look you," said the other, "you shall be judged and fairly, so you need fear nothing if you're not guilty, but let that be for the present. Have they left the ship?—you know who I mean?"

"Yes captain, according to your orders," replied the lieutenant.

"How far are they from land," he asked after a pause.

"Not far—almost half-a-mile," was the reply.

"Do you know anything of that coast."

"Nothing, captain."

"Well, I do."

"You do," said Bill.

"Yes."

"Can they land easily," asked the lieutenant.

"No."

"Then, if you wish, they can be retaken," said Bill.

"I do wish it," said the Boy Rover.

"It shall be done, captain."

"It shall," iterated the smuggler chieftain, "it must, or look to yourself."

"I will have a boat off directly, and take command of her myself," said Bill, only too happy of doing anything that might arrest the anger of his chief.

The Boy Rover paused a moment, thoughtfully.

"No," he said, at length, "you will remain on board. Let Crowther take command of the boat."

"As you will, captain," said the lieutenant biting his lip in disappointment.

"See that the boat be sent off at once, and hark ye, the men are to take them all alive, so see that they take no firearms with them."

"Your orders shall be obeyed," said Bill.

"I will not break my word," said the Boy Rover, with a meaning smile. "I promised them an uninterrupted passage to the shore—they will have reached it ere you can overtake them, but once there their liberty is no longer to be taken in consideration."

"Should they not have reached the shore are the men to take them," asked Bill.

"No, but they will be sure to have reached it ere they can be overtaken. It is impossible that they can escape—there are nothing but rocks steep and precipitous, and they must fall into their hands as easily as I could wish."

Black Bill merely bowed his head, and turned to leave the cabin.

"Stay," said the Boy Rover, "where did that mutineer spring from."

"What mutineer, captain," asked Bill.

"Ned, who do you think I mean?"

"Oh," said Bill, fearing again for himself.

"Why don't you answer," exclaimed the captain as a frown gathered on his brow.

"Because, captain, I don't know," replied Ned.

"Ain't you telling me a lie?" said the Boy Rover, advancing threateningly towards him.

"Upon my soul, captain, I ain't—I don't know no more than the man in the moon where he sprang from."

"Enough," said the captain, "now see to the boat, I will know all about this strange affair when I have him and the others once more on board, then woe be to those who have been playing me false. I'll pay back their treachery in a manner they little expect—go!"

Black Bill darted from the cabin only too glad to get away from the presence of his captain who he felt assured would not pardon him should he discover that his negligence had brought about the boarding of the vessel by the crew of the "Blue Bell."

When he gained the deck the lieutenant gave the order to lower and man the boat for the pursuit of the escaped girl and her friends, which order was instantly obeyed, and in a few moments the boat had left the ship on its errand of villany.

Then Black Bill had the sails taken in and the vessel's course turned a couple of points towards land, in order to take up the boat's crew and their captives on their return.

This being done, he had the wound in his shoulder tightly bandaged—it was very painful but nothing very serious—and with a bravado which is often to be found in the most reckless, he treated it as a mere scratch, and leaned over the bulwarks marking the passage of the boat to the shore.

He followed its course till it had entered the little bay and was hidden from the view of those on board the "Venomed Snake," then he turned away, and seating himself on a bulkhead, soon became lost in thought.

In the meantime all evidences of the affray had been cleared away; the wounded had been placed in their berths, and the dead, of which there were but two, consigned to their last resting place—the vast ocean.

Ropes had been coiled—the decks washed down—arms returned to their chest, and every thing once more bore the semblance of order and strict discipline.

The smugglers who had escaped any hurt in the late fight, lounged about the deck talking of the morning's adventure, their captain's disappearance over the side and sudden reappearance in the cabin, the departure of the young girl with her friends and Ned, for whose presence they were at a loss to account, and the mysterious approach of the "Blue Bell," formed subjects to keep the minds of the smugglers employed; and many and curious were the remarks which they made upon them as they stood upon the deck, looking ever and anon across the ocean, towards the long line of cliffs, for the return of the boat with their captives.

In the cabin, the Boy Rover and Wild Madge were seated, conversing over the events of the night and morning.

The fury, to soothe her ruffled spirits, and drown her disappointment at the non-accomplishment of her hellish wishes, had again had recourse to her favourite medicine—brandy; of which, in the course of a few moments, she had swallowed no less than three glasses: and, as Madge had a perfect horror of a small-sized glass, she had consumed, in a small space of time, sufficient of the liquid to have placed any ordinary lover of the bottle in anything but an upright position.

But the human frame may be brought to bear almost anything; and, in truth, Wild Madge was a proof of how much burning intoxicating poison might be taken into the system after long and continued indulgence had hardened it.

It is strange that the Boy Rover, who had been her almost constant companion, should not have been as much addicted to this degrading habit as herself; yet such was not the case. Indulgence in intoxicating drinks was not one of his failings. Seldom indeed was it that he indulged to excess: and when he did, it was only when some extraordinary good stroke of fortune had overtaken him. But to drink for the mere love of drink, and with Madge to keep him company, he never did.

Having emptied her third glass, Wild Madge, fixing her eyes upon her youthful companion, said:

"I think, Richard, that you are about the greatest fool that ever I came across, to suffer those to escape you who know the secret of your haunt, and the profession which you follow. Twice since we left the shores of Cornwall have we been pursued, and

nearly captured; yet, when you have those in your power who are able to bring down upon you and your crew the bloodhounds of the law, you let them slip through your fingers, instead of giving them a pass from this world at the yard-arm of your vessel."

"Rail on, mother!" answered the smuggler-captain, somewhat peevishly. "What I have done, I have done for the best."

"And a pretty best you've made of it. There's that girl, too—she whose ruin I would have given my life to see consummated; and yet you, who pride yourself upon being the boldest smuggler that ever sailed the main, allow a weak girl to set you at defiance, and laugh you to scorn!"

The Boy Rover bit his lip at the taunt, but was silent.

"And that mutineer, too," continued Madge—"he who guided the vessel into the power of the ship you have just escaped—even he is allowed to escape, to once more bring down foes upon you!"

"Of whom do you speak?" said the Rover.

"Of the mutineer—Ned," answered Madge.

"Yes, yes—I recollect he told me it was he."

"And yet you permitted him to escape!"

"I could not do otherwise—bound and defenceless as I was. But it is not for long. Too well do I know the nature of the coast on which they will try to land. And remember, mother, that only to the coast are they free—once the boat touches the shore, they fall again into my power."

"Perhaps," said Madge.

"Perhaps, said you?"

"Yes—perhaps."

"How—what do you mean?" said the Boy Rover.

"They may outwit you yet," returned Madge.

"Think it not," said the smuggler captain. "Had I not known the utter impossibility of escape, I should not so willingly have granted the request of Ned."

"I am not so sanguine," said Madge. "The youth with whom that girl is so madly in love is brave and fearless, and it is not danger that will deter him from attempting to escape with the girl."

"We shall see," said the Boy Rover—"we shall see."

"And, if they fall again into your power, what will you do?"

"Rid myself for ever from their power," was the reply.

"And the maiden?" insinuated Madge.

"Is reserved for the fate unto which she is destined."

The eyes of Madge lit up with a bright gleam.

'Tis well; I had feared you were afraid to again assail her—I had thought that a mother's wrongs were to remain unavenged!"

"I have not forgotten my oath," remarked the Boy Rover.

"Nor I, Richard—nor I," vehemently replied Madge; "nor never shall, till the grave engulphs me."

"Your's is indeed a revengeful spirit," replied the youth.

"And your's?" said Madge, inquiringly.

"What your teaching has made it," was the reply.

"The avenger of a mother's wrongs," said Madge, passionately—"is it not so?"

"Aye," was the thoughtful reply—"and the hurling of my own soul to perdition."

"Pshaw!—when will you bury for ever these coward thoughts, and—"

"And pursue my bloody and remorceless career

without one pang of conscience,' interrupted the Boy Rover. "I will bury them now and for ever I am steeped so deep in crime that I can never wash away its stain. I am what your teaching has made me, and to the end so will I remain.

And rising from his seat he left the cabin.

CHAPTER XXXII.

RETURN OF THE SMUGGLERS—THE CONDEMNATION—THE IMPALEMENT.

BAFFLED and dispirited, the two remaining smugglers, after a time, descended the rock.

Having arrived at its base they entered the boat, and were about to return to the ship, when they discovered the body of a man lying helpless upon a rugged portion of the cliff, some two or three feet from the water's edge, and some little distance from the spot at which their boat rode.

Believing it to be one of their comrades who had fallen over the cliff, they pulled towards him, but when they laid their hands upon the body to lift into the boat, they discovered the features of Ned Wilton.

Bruised and bleeding, Ned had lain on the spot on which the smugglers had found him for some time. In his descent over the cliff he had clutched at a projection of the rock, in the hopes of saving himself; but though it had broken his fall, it had hurled him upon the rough surface instead of precipitating him into the waters of the bay, and the force with which he fell had shook all sense or consciousness out of him.

The smugglers felt somewhat pleased at this discovery—they could now return to the ship with one prisoner at least.

They placed the insensible man in the bottom of the boat, and taking the oars pulled to the entrance of the bay.

About half a mile from the shore the Venomed Snake rode proudly on the now almost unrippled sea. Her sails furled, awaiting the return of the boat's crew and their looked-for prisoners.

The Boy Rover stood gazing moodily towards the inlet, anxiously awaiting the return of his men.

At length he saw the boat dart out from between the rocks, and a cry of rage and disappointment escaped his lips when he perceived that it contained but three occupants, and one of them evidently injured from the position which it occupied in the boat.

He leant his elbows upon the bulwarks, and his chin dropped into his hands, and in this position he followed the progress of the boat with his eyes, as she made towards the ship.

Not for one moment did his glance stray from the little bark or its occupants.

The boat came swiftly on—there was not a wave to impede its progress, and in the course of a few minutes she dashed under the smuggler's bows.

Ropes were thrown out, and in the space of a few minutes more, the men ascended to the deck of the smuggler, bearing with them the insensible form of the bruised mutineer. It was not until the boat had been made secure to her fastenings that the Boy Rover raised his head and turned inquiringly towards the men who had been so unsuccessful in the expedition on which they had been sent.

"Well?" said the Boy Rover, as a dark frown settled upon his brows, and he fixed his piercing glance upon the men.

The defeated smugglers stood gazing at each other, not knowing what to say, and each anxious that his fellow should break the intelligence to their captain of the utter defeat which had befallen them.

"Well?" added the Boy Rover, in a louder tone; and then his teeth were compressed together, as though he found some difficulty in suppressing the passion which was consuming him.

Still the men did not answer.

"Damn you!" roared the Boy Rover, unable longer to contain himself—"can't you speak? Where are the others?'

"Gone!" said one of the smugglers.

"Gone—where?" said the captain.

"To the bottom," said the man.

"To the bottom, fool?"

"Yes."

"How do you mean?"

"Clean gone!" replied the man.

"What!—all besides yourselves?" asked the captain, in a tone of surprise.

"All."

The captain paused a moment, and then asked:

"How did it happen—did you run foul of the rocks?"

"No, captain."

"How then?"

The man did not answer.

"Look you," said the Boy Rover, as his face became livid with rage; "tell me all—keep nothing from me—or, by hell, it'll be the worst for ye both."

"We are telling you," said the previous speaker, in a sulky tone of voice.

"Go on; tell me all, from the moment you left the ship, till your return."

"Well, you see, captain,' said the man, "we chased the boat into that inlet yonder; and, when we gets in, the tother crew deserted the boat, and ascended the rocks. We does the same, in pursuit of them.'

"Well, go on," said the Rover.

"And, when we gets a little way up, and nearly grabbed the girl and her lover, and that ere young cove as you was a going to hang the other day, Ned and the other gets a struggling, and a great lump of the rock on which we stood gives way, and down we all tumbles into the water—didn't we Bob?"

The man addressed nodded his head in confirmation of the other's words, thinking that his mate had made a first-rate excuse for the failure of the expedition.

The Rover paused, thoughtfully; and the men imagined that he was perfectly satisfied with this account. But they had overdone it. Suddenly the Rover stretched forth his arm, and caught the sailor by the throat.

"You lying thief!" he yelled, shaking the man violently.

"Oh, oh!—don't, captain!" spluttered the fellow, turning almost black in the face.

"You infernal liar!" said his captain, "if you fell into the bay, why ain't your clothes wet, instead of dry—eh?"

The man saw in a moment that he failed to deceive the captain, and he spluttered out:

"Not me, nor Bob, but all the others. We fell on the rocks."

"Where's the girl?" yelled the captain. "Tell me, or I'll throttle you!"

"Escaped, captain—got clean off," said the man.

"Escaped!" iterated the Rover, as, giving the smuggler a final twist, he released the throat of the frightened man—"how could she escape, if you were not a treacherous lot? I know the bay too well. They could but ascend the cliff on the right; and from that there is no escape."

"I tell you, captain," said Bob, "they did escape—escaped over the chasm at the far end of the cove."

"Do you mean to tell me," said the Boy Rover, advancing threateningly towards the speaker, "that that girl could pass over that chasm?"

"She did, captain, upon my soul," said the man, emphatically.

The Boy Rover had clenched his fist to strike the speaker, but the fervent tones of the man caused him to withold his arm.

The tones in which the man had uttered these words carried with them the impress of truth; yet, from his knowledge of the place, he was at a loss to understand how she and her companions could possibly evade capture.

"Are you telling me the truth, or are you giving me another lie?" he said, at length.

"The truth, captain—as true as I stand here," replied the man.

"Then tell me how they escaped."

"Only the gal and her lover escaped, captain."

"I see Ned has not escaped, for there he lies. Where's the other?"

"At the bottom of the bay."

"'Tis well; now for the girl."

"You said, captain, you knew the place."

"I do; so mind what you're at."

"Well, then, you know there's a cliff on both sides?" said Bob.

"I do."

"And you know that at the other end it forms a deep narrow chasm?"

"I do."

"Well, you know there's a large tree on one side?"

"Yes, on the left."

"Well, you see, captain, one of the branches overhangs the chasm."

"It does, I think."

"Well, the lover of that ere gal manages to get hold of it, and, leaning over, made a perfect bridge right across."

"Well, go on."

"And, afore we could lay hold of her, she jumps on to the body of her sweetheart, and walks across."

"And you could not get possession of her," said the captain, looking doubtingly at the narrator, "ere she got the other side?"

"No, captain, we couldn't, for you see she had a couple of barkers, and the moment one of us tried to stop her she fired, and poor Frank received the bullet in his breast, and fell right over the cliff into the bay."

"But how do you account for the loss of the remainder?"

"Ned, the young lieutenant, and two of the crew, went over together; and one, Ned knocked over; and the tother, the lieutenant sent down with a piece of rock. There, captain, that's the truth."

"Why did you not seize the lad then, when the girl had crossed?"

"We couldn't; he swung himself over by the branch."

"Why not have followed him?"

"Because the branch broke with his weight, and we had no means to get over."

"And a pretty mess you have made of the whole expedition!" said the Boy Rover.

Chagrined and disappointed as he was, he could not but admire the courage and devotion of the young lovers, and he turned thoughtfully from the two men, and once more leaned over the bulwarks.

He continued gazing thoughtfully and abstractedly upon the waters for some time, whilst the two men, only too happy to be freed from farther questioning, turned away and joined their companions.

The thoughts of the Boy Rover were not of an over pleasant nature. The present voyage had been a fatal one to him and his crew.

He had started from the Cornish coast with a good and brave complement of seamen, but in the two fights and this last adventure his crew had dwindled down to one half, and several of those were unfit for duty from wounds or illness.

He began to debate in his mind whether it would not be better for him to return again to Cornwall, and endeavour to recruit his crew, but then would it be safe to do so. Could either of those young men have made any one acquainted with his secret rendezvous. If they had he thought it could not have yet been discovered, inasmuch as the crew of the revenue were now one and all disposed of, and that of the Blue Bell were steering far away from the direction of the cave.

But then how could he make up his mind to return, whilst there was a hope of again obtaining possession of Ellen. He felt that she was necessary to his happiness as well as his revenge, and as for her lover it was absolutely necessary that he should be put out of the way. He knew the secret of his haunt, and for the indignities heaped upon the object of his affections, would he not do all that lie in his power to bring him to justice.

The death of the youth was necessary to the existence of himself and his crew.

What then would be best to do, he thought, but he could come to no determination.

He determined to consult Wild Madge, and abide by her decision.

He turned to descend to the cabin, but he recollected that the base-hearted woman, worn out with fatigue and watching of the previous night, had now sunk into a half-drunken slumber, and he resolved to await her awaking.

While these thoughts had been passing through the mind of the Boy Rover, Ned Wilton, the mutineer, had somewhat recovered from the insensibility into which he had been thrown by his fall, and, opening his eyes, he was gazing bewilderedly around.

He was not long in understanding where he was, and, as soon as the truth had dawned upon him, and surrounding objects had made him acquainted with his present position, he endeavoured to rise to his feet.

But he found this no easy task to accomplish, so fearfully bruised and shaken was he that he could scarcely move. He observed Black Bill and gazing at him, he said,

"How came I here?"

"I brought you aboard," replied Bob.

"And the other's," asked Ned, anxiously.

"Got clean off."

"Glad to hear it," said Ned.

"Are you," said Bill.

"You'll have to suffer for 'em," said Bill, with a grin, as the words of Ned on his parting from the vessel came to his recollection.

"Perhaps," said Ned.

"Sir," said Bill, "you won't live to see me hung."

"Don't make so sure of that," replied Ned, raising himself on to his elbow, with some difficulty.

A smile of satisfaction passed over the features of the dark-featured lieutenant as he saw the painful spasm pass over the face of Ned at this exertion.

At this moment the Boy Rover turned his glance towards them; and, observing that Ned had recovered from his insensibility, he strode to his side.

"I kept my word," he said, addressing the mutineer. "I let you have a free pass to the shore."

"Yes," said Ned.

"But no further. Did you think I was such a fool as to let a mutineer escape me—eh?"

"Not if you could help it," replied Ned.

"I'll take good care you don't escape me again," said the captain. Then, turning to Black Bill, he said:

"Call all hands aft."

"Aye, aye, sir," said Bill.

In a few moments all who could leave their berths were gathered on the after-part of the deck.

"Bring him this way," said the Boy Rover, addressing one or two of the smugglers as he strode aft and joined the assembled smugglers.

In a few moments Ned was lifted aft, and supported by two of the smugglers.

Then the Rover said:

"Officers and men of the 'Venomed Snake,' I have commanded your presence to judge this man, who has mutinied against the authority of your captain, broken his arrest, murdered the man at the wheel, steered us into the hands of our enemies, insulted and bound your captain, and killed several of the men sent in pursuit of him this morning. What is the doom of a traitor?"

"Death," said Black Bill.

"Death," echoed the crew.

"Such is the law by which we are bound. You have pronounced his sentence, and it only remains now for me to command the means by which he shall die."

"It does," said Bill.

"It is necessary, for our own safety, that we should make a terrible example of him—Ned Wilton is not the only one on board this bark guilty of a dereliction of duty. You, lieutenant, are blameable for the alteration of the vessel's course, and the consequences attendant upon our being boarded by the Blue Bell."

"Me, Captain?" said Black Bill.

"Yes, you. You were slumbering at your post, and your carelessness has brought about the loss of the girl."

"Captain!"

"Silence! For the inconvenience you have caused me, and the loss of those who went in pursuit of the girl and her friends, I condemn you to become one of the executioners of Ned Wilton. And now," continued the Boy Rover, turning to the two men who had brought Ned back from the rocks a prisoner, "for your failure, I condemn you to assist in the execution."

"Very well, captain," said Bob, glad to escape the consequences of their failure so easily.

"The means," continued the Boy Rover, "by which this mutinous dog shall die, shall be by impalement. Bind him to the mast."

The sailors immediately seized Ned and bore him to the mizen mast, and having procured a long rope commenced binding him to the mast.

This work accomplished, and the bruised and fainting man securely bound in an upright position, the Boy Rover said, whilst a demoniac smile played around his features—

"We are short-handed, and I can ill spare a single man of the crew; but you, Ned Wilton, have sought your own doom, and if you were the last man on board besides myself, you should die. your hour has come, and a traitors death shall be your doom."

The face of the half-fainting man became more ghastly, but he spoke not a word.

"Executioners, do your duty," said the Boy Rover. "Black Bill, you strike the first blow."

And the Boy Rover drew on one side, and, folding his arms, looked steadily and unflinchingly at the doomed man.

Black Bill and the two smugglers who had returned in the boat with Ned, having armed themselves with long Spanish knives, now stood a few yards in front of the doomed man.

"Are you ready," said the Boy Rover.

"Yes," replied Bill.

"One," said the captain of the smuggler, waving his hand.

Black Bill poised his knife lengthwise above his fingers, the handle resting in the palm of his hand, and pointing towards his wrist, whilst the bright sharp-pointed blade gleamed some few inches from his finger's end, then drawing his arm back he threw the knife straight towards the neck of the half insensible mutineer.

The sharp edge slightly grazed the neck of the victim, and struck deep in the mast where it quivered for a moment or two ere it remained stationary.

A shudder passed through the frame of the doomed man, and a cold perspiration broke out upon his forehead.

"That was a well-meant aim," said the Boy Rover, with the utmost coolness, as though the bound man were no more than a wooden effigy on which the executioners were practising. "Now, Bob, let your aim be certain—take him fair in the throat. It will be a good lesson to you all."

The man addressed poised the knife in his hand but stood irresolute.

The captain noticed the hesitation, and a dark frown gathered upon his brow.

"Why do you hesitate?" he said.

The man made no answer.

"You had better not shrink," said the Boy Rover, while a look of fearful meaning gathered around his features, "or you may find yourself in the same position."

The man hesitated no longer. He feared to excite the wrath of the Boy Rover against himself.

He drew back his arm, and the next moment the bright steel, like a flash of lightening, quivered by the side of its fellow in the mast, where it swayed up and down for a moment, and then fell to the deck.

The force with which it had been thrown caused it to oscillate in such a manner as to snap the point.

An exclamation of impatience escaped the lips of the Boy Rover.

The other smuggler now stepped forward and threw the knife. It struck the mutineer in the shoulder, and, as a cry of pain escaped his lips, the blood oozed from the wound and trickled slowly down his arm.

"Well done!" exclaimed the Rover. "The blow was too low, though, to be effectual. But all the better, perhaps, as it will take the longer to despatch him, and make his sufferings the more acute."

A look of agony passed over the countenance of the mutineer as these words fell upon his ears; but he deigned not to sue for mercy.

IMPALEMENT OF THE MUTINEER.

Too well he knew that nothing would so much gratify the hellish nature of the Boy Rover as to hear him plead for his life.

"It is your turn again, Black Bill," said the smuggler captain. "See that you do better this time."

The dark-featured lieutenant once more took the knife in his hand, and again sent it with terrific violence at the throat of his victim.

It flashed for a moment in the bright sunlight, and then was buried again in the mast.

But, in its progress, it had cut the ear of Ned Wilton, and the blood flowed feoely down his neck.

The mutineer gave vent to a howl of pain, and the Rover smiled grimly as he saw the red fluid

start down the face of the ghastly and perspiring man.

Still the mutineer made no appeal for mercy, and Bob again poised his knife.

"Put the poor devil out of his misery," said Jem, who felt some qualms of conscience at the manner in which his mate was being hacked to pieces. "If you must kill him, strike at his heart."

"Silence !" said the Boy Rover, advancing towards the speaker. "Recollect, I command here."

Jem slunk back, and made no answer, but he wished at that moment the knife might change its course and pierce the heart of the captain.

The knife flew from the hands of Bob, and, grazing his throat in its passage, stuck in the mast.

Again a cry of horror and pain rose to the lips of the mutineer, and he put forth his feeble strength to burst the bonds which held him.

"You bound me," said the Rover; "now you are in the same predicament, how do you like it?"

"Monster!" said Ned.

"Ha, ha!" laughed the Rover, derisively."

"Would that I had slain him when I had the opportunity!" muttered Ned to himself. "Oh! would that I had done so."

"See what it is to be a traitor!" said the Rover.

"I see what it is to be a faithful fool, who has sacrificed everything for a villain," said Ned; "but your time will come some day; and then—"

"Stop his mouth," said 'the Boy Rover, turning fiercely to the man whose turn it was to now try his hand at throwing the knife.

The man sent the weapon flying through the air, but this time missed the mark, and, speeding on its way, it passed over the bulwarks into the sea.

A look of passion settled on the face of the captain; and a sigh of relief broke from the poor wretch, as, with a fascinated gaze, he saw the weapon pass him harmlessly by.

"Curse you," said the Boy Rover, "for a set of nerveless fools! Does the gleam of his eye frighten you, and make your hand unsteady? If so, bind his eyes, so that they cannot follow your actions."

"Yes, better bind his eyes," said Jem, who could not but feel some qualms of conscience as the glance of the doomed man rested on his face.

In a moment the eyes of Ned were bound over with a neckerchief; and Black Bill, once more possessing himself of his knife, threw the weapon with unerring aim.

It glanced along the throat of the doomed man, and the red fluid started from his throat, and dyed his breast.

Then his head dropped forward, and he became insensible.

"Now," said the Rover, "have my gig launched; and you, Bill, accompany me to the shore."

In a few moments the Boy Rover and Black Bill had left the "Venomed Snake," and were gliding over the water towards the island.

CHAPTER XXXIII.

THE COUNCIL—THE ABDUCTION—THE ARRIVAL.— THE SHADOW.

MAN proposes and heaven disposes, so says the old proverb; and, like all the old sayings, there is great amount of truth in them.

The Boy Rover had gained possession of Ellen, with the intention of making her subservient to his desires; but resistance had made him think better of the girl he would have outraged, and he now loved her with all the fervour of an honourable lover.

He felt that despite all, it was necessary for his own happiness that he should possess the love of the fair girl, and he resolved to seek her on the island.

Thus it was that he put off from the ship, accompanied by Black Bill and one or two others of the smuggler crew.

A quarter of an hour brought them to the island, and having provided themselves with planks to form a bridge across the chasm, they soon found themselves on the same side of the cliffs as were Charles and Ellen.

Here they rested for a time, and the Boy Rover called a council of his crew.

He mentioned his determination to the members of his crew, and having received their assistance, he now only waited an opportunity to put his diabolical plan into operation.

"She must and shall be mine," he said addressing those whom he had trusted with his secret. "This girl shall grace the cabin of the Boy Rover."

"But, captain." said one of them, addressing the chief, "how will thou gain possession of her, and when will thou put thy plan into operation?"

"No matter how I will secure her. I have said I will possess her, and the determination of the Boy Rover cannot be turned aside."

"But, when?" asked another.

"When the moon has deserted the heavens, and the stars shed no lustre upon the earth, then will we take our way to their retreat, and bear her to the ship. Therefore, hold yourselves in readiness, for the time is not far distant. I shall know no peace until Ellen hath become the partner of my hopes— no matter when the time comes, thou't be ready to aid me."

"We will," answered Black Bill, "we will—to meet death, if so be thy will."

"Thanks, my friends," said the Boy Rover, rising from his seat. "Thy chief will not prove ungrateful. Now leave me, I would be alone."

His followers departed, and when they were no longer to be seen, the Boy Rover threw himself upon the rude couch of dried grass, and fell into a deep train of thought.

Thus the day passed, and night came on.

He turned uneasily upon his couch for some time, and then endeavoured to compose himself for sleep; but in vain did he court the favours of the drowsy god, his mind was too much a prey to the dishonourable thought which played upon his brain.

Feeling that all attempts to sleep were futile, he rose, and gazed upon the scene beyond. The moon shone with a brilliancy high up in the heavens, which rendered every object almost as visible as in day time, save that its light was more mellow and chaste, and the silence which reigned around was broken only by the cry of the night birds, and the distant hum of the waves as they rushed on with their never ceasing and impetuous fury.

He walked forth in the cool night air, which fanned his cheek, and, for a few moments, allayed the burning fever of his brain. But again the image of Ellen rose before his imagination, and nature was forgotten in the whirlwind of passion which again assailed his heart.

"Why should I delay," he muttered to himself, as he gazed upwards at the heavens, "why should I delay my purpose till the moon hath deserted the firmament, and the stars have hid their faces beneath the clouds. I shall never know peace until this girl is clasped within my arms—is pressed firmly to this heart. Would that the mighty waters had never borne her from her distant home, unless it were to become the wife of the smuggler chief. That can never be— not one smile from her can I win—not one look that bids him hope. Nought is to be seen upon her features but coldness; but those looks freeze not my blood, they fire my brain, and dry up the springs of my heart. She shall share my cabin, and if I cannot possess her love, I will triumph o'er her yet."

He took his way along the banks of the inlet until he came to the spot which had been recently cleared of the small trees and underwood, which had evidently grown around in great abundance.

About a hundred yards from the cliffs stood a prettily built one storied house. It was no other than the residence of an old eccentric gentleman, who had lately died. The Boy Rover gazed up at the windows, but all was darkness, the inhabitants had long since retired to rest, and the utmost silence prevailed around.

He approached the door, and listened attentively, not a sound was heard. He peered into the apartment, but nothing attracted his attention. He was about to enter, when looking around he beheld upon the ground the tall shadow of a man.

Instantly he closed the door, and crept rather than walked close along the wall of the habitation, round which he turned abruptly; then, knowing from the position of the shadow, that whoever might be lurking about the house, could not see him from where he was, he darted swiftly across an open space into a clump of trees which grew near, and there taking up his position, he determined to watch, and see who it was that was about at that hour.

But, although from his position he could command a general view of the habitation of his escaped victim, he could distinguish neither the form of a man or beast near the spot; and, after watching for some considerable time, he came to the conclusion that he must have been mistaken, and that no one was about.

Stealing stealthily from his hiding place, like the tiger from its lair, he once more approached the building. He looked again at the window of the room in which he believed the fair Ellen was sleeping, and the blood rushed to his heart, and fired his brain with dishonourable passion.

"To-night," he muttered, through his clenched teeth, and the words came with a hissing sound— "to-night shall the Boy Rover press the fair Ellen to his arms. Another sun shall not rise upon my unsatiated passion. I will not wait for their assistance. There is no one in the house but the girl. Another day must not pass. No, no—there cannot come a better time than this! It shall be done—it shall be done!"

And the Boy Rover approached the door—his tall figure trembling with unholy passion. Again he placed his hand upon the latch, and the door once more opened. He entered the house, and, drawing forth the materials to procure a light, he lit a piece of pine-wood; and then, with steps more stealthy than the panther, crept up the small staircase to the upper rooms.

Arriving upon the landing, he paused to listen. He could hear the measured breathing of the unsuspecting sleeper, as she slept the calm and peaceful sleep of those whose consciences are light and free from sin. He placed his hand upon the fastening of the room which might be considered to be at the back part of the house, and opened the door. Softly, he stepped into the apartment, and his light cast a glare upon every object within.

But his eyes were alone rivetted upon the form of the sleeping Ellen, as she lie upon a couch, on one side of the apartment, little dreaming that her chamber was violated by the presence of a villain.

Slowly he approached the couch, and bent over the weeping girl. His brain turned giddy with the fulsome thoughts that rushed upon it, and a fiendish smile passed across his features. The temptation was too great; he could not resist it; he stooped down to imprint a dishonourable kiss upon her lips, but as he did so, a spark from his pine-stick flew into the neck of the unconscious Ellen, and, with a scream, she started up awake.

Who can pourtray the horror of the poor girl when she saw, standing before her, the form of the Boy Rover? In the glare of the light which he held in his hand, his features looked truly demoniacal. There was a triumph in his looks, a fearful meaning in his scowl, and the heart of the poor girl sunk within her as she contemplated him.

Convulsively drawing the coverlid over her fair, white bosom, she said, in accents of terror—

"Who art thou who dar'st to intrude thyself into my chamber?"

"Doth not the bright eye of my escaped love," he said, in a husky voice, "see that it is the Boy Rover?"

"What want you here?" she asked, more alarmed, as the tones of his voice fell gratingly upon her ears. "Wherefore hast thou come hither, like a thief in the dead of the night?"

A fiendish smile curled his lips, as he replied—

"To tell you that I love you."

"Love!" she said, with a shudder.

"Yes," he replied; "the Boy Rover and chief of the smugglers loves thee."

"Begone!" she said, endeavouring to force a calmness which she was far indeed from feeling. "Leave my chamber. This is not the place nor time to seek an interview with me. You have said you love me; show it then by at once obeying my wishes and immediately leaving the house."

A scornful smile played upon his countenance, as, stooping down until his face was in close contact with her own, he whispered, or rather hissed in her ear—

"Obey, said'st thou? — obey! Knowest thou not that there is but one who dares command—but one whose will is law—and that one is me? Obey! You must be less haughty in your speech."

"How nobly it becomes the man," she replied, as she trembled violently, "who hath power to boast of it before an insulted and defenceless woman. What!" she added, her large blue eyes starting almost from their sockets, and her lip curling with a contemptuous smile, "can the Boy Rover so demean himself by showing himself a coward as well as a villain?"

"I am no coward!"

So saying, he drew himself up to his full height and fixed upon the countenance of the poor girl a scowl of such fearful meaning that her heart sunk within her as she gazed upon his features. But quickly recovering herself, she said—

"I repeat you are both villain and coward. Doth not your acts and words prove it? Is it not the action of a villain to force himself into the chamber of a woman, in the dead of the night, and refuse to quit when bidden so to do? Is it not the act of a coward to threaten the woman he has dared to insult?"

"'Tis well," he replied, biting his lips and grinding his teeth with ungovernable rage. "Thou hast spoken: now heed well the words of the Boy Rover. When from a distant land you arrived with your lover upon upon the shores of Cornwall, I permitted you to live: had it been my will I could have compelled my crew to have put you to death, or forced upon you any torture—for there my will was law. But no; I allowed you to live: I saw you and I loved you—I swore that thou should'st share my roving life— become the partner of my life—the mother of my children; I swore this, and the oath of the Boy Rover is never broken!"

Ellen trembled violently as he uttered these words. Her eyes were rivetted upon the face of the smuggler, but she was unable to speak.

"Thou hast heard," he continued, "the words of the smuggler chief: he now but waits thy answer. Still silent," he added finding that she did not reply. "I say again will you share the cabin with the Boy Rover."

"Smuggler." she answered, it "cannot be, therefore leave me, and go thy way's in peace—

"Cannot be!" he exclaimed, "and wherefore not?"

"It is not for you to question," she replied firmly, then she added in a more gentle tone, go and you will undoubtedly find one who will make you happy, for this I never can."

He gazed upon her for an instant, and then in passionate tones he exclaimed—

"By heaven but you shall become the wife, or the slave of the Boy Rover."

So saying he seized her roughly by the arm, and hissed into her ear—

"Take thy choice,"—either consent to become my wife or my—"

"Help Charles, help!" she shrieked, as she felt his hot breath upon her cheek, and writhed with pain which the ruffian's firm grasp inflicted upon her delicate flesh.

"Silence!" he hissed in her ears; and at the same time he held before her eyes, his long knife, "I have sworn you should be mine, and woe to him who stands between us!"

He turned his head towards the door of the room as he spoke, and there standing upon the threshold, he perceived Charles Lawson attired only in his night-dress, with his arm extended, and holding in his hand a pistol, which was levelled at the head of the Rover.

He slowly advanced towards the ruffian, and placing his left hand upon the Rover's arm, whilst with his right he pointed the pistol fairly at his head, and said—

"Release your hold, for I would not have man's blood upon my conscience."

A scornful smile alone played around the lips of the Boy Rover.

"Oh save me Charles, save me!" almost shrieked the poor girl.

"Once more I bid you release your hold," said the youth, "or I fire."

"Think you I fear thy threats, or that the lamb can defend itself against the wolf, the sparrow against the hawk."

So saying he suddenly struck up the youth's arm with his disengaged hand, and the bullet flew harmlessly over his head.

"Ruffian, release your hold," cried Charles, "for weak and feeble as I am, I will protect her to the last."

He sprang upon the Boy Rover and seized him by the throat, so sudden was the assault that the smuggler released his grasp of Ellen. But the poor youth stood no chance with the powerful smuggler, who, blinded with rage, raised his knife above his head, and then, quick as lightning, buried it deeply in the shoulder of the brave lad, who with a cry fell heavily upon the floor of the apartment.

With a shriek that echoed through the building, and pierced even to the heart of the smuggler, the poor girl fell insensible upon the prostrate body of her lover.

The Boy Rover for a moment stood irresolute, contemplating the two prostrate bodies before him. At first he thought that Ellen was dead, but stooping down he perceived that she still breathed. He was in the act of lifting her up and placing her upon the couch, when the outer door of the house was thrown violently open, and he heard something stumble against some piece of furniture in the apartment below.

Quick as thought he sprang to the door of the apartment and closed it; then placing a piece of furniture against it, secured it against any intrusion for a time. He then approached the window and looked forth. There was no one to be seen. But the shadow which he had observed previous to his entrance now recurred to his mind, and he felt satisfied that it was that of whoever had but just now entered the house. Taking the lighted pine-stick from a cleft in the wall of the apartment, where he had placed it a few minutes previously, he seized the still insensible girl in his arms, and thrusting the torch beneath the couch so as to extinguish its light, he placed his hand upon the sill of the casement and lowered himself and his captive into the open space below.

To dart across this space and beneath the cover of the trees was the work of a moment. He then looked into the face of the still insensible girl and imprinted a passionate kiss upon her lips. As he did so a strange light played upon her features, and, casting his eyes in the direction from whence the glare proceeded, he perceived that the apartment which he but just left was in flames.

Grasping poor Ellen firmly in his arms, he hurried from the place in the direction of the spot where he had left his followers.

CHAPTER XXXIV.

CHARLES RESCUED FROM THE BURNING HOUSE—
THE FRIEND AND THE LOVER—THE VOW.

WHEN the smugglers had departed, and the youthful lovers had somewhat recovered from the fatigue attending their exertions to escape their foes, henry rose from his recumbent position, and assisting Ellen to her feet, they gazed around in the hope of perceiving some desirable place of shelter.

As far as the eye could reach to the right of the spot on which they stood nothing but the open sea met their gaze, but to the left stretched away a thickly wooded country, effectually hidden from the ocean by the high cliffs which bounded it.

Henry took the arm of the fair girl and led her down towards the woods, murmuring at the same time a prayer of hope that they might meet with some friendly hand or hospitable shelter.

At a distance of some hundred yards from the cliff, was a small open space which had evidently been cleared by the axe, and this circumstance caused their hearts to bound with the hope that succour could not be far distant. On they went, and upon turning an angle of the trees they perceived with joy a small wooden built habitation, built in such a manner as to afford shelter and comfort.

They approached it; the door stood open, but all was silent. They entered: the lower room was furnished with a few articles of use, though roughly made, and the dust which had accumulated spoke too plainly to the fact that it had long been deserted.

A rough staircase led to an upper apartment, and our hero and heroine mounted this and found themselves in a room furnished only with a low, rough couch, on which lie a blanket, and coverlet of course cloth; this apartment was formed, too, of logs, the openings between which were filled with a kind of moss to keep out the draughts.

Here they resolved to rest for the present, and as evening came on Charles prevailed upon Ellen to retire to the couch while he kept watch.

Worn out and dispirited, the poor girl complied, and ere the moon had risen she had found relief from her painful thoughts in refreshing slumber.

Charles left the cottage in search of anything which he could find to minister to their wants, and it was not until he saw the shadow of a human form thrown by the bright moonlight that he deemed it necessary to return to Ellen.

He had kept possession of the pistol which was still loaded; and now he drew it from his belt as the cry of Ellen smote his ears.

To enter the house and rush up the stairs was but the work of a few moments, but for an instant he stood paralysed as he saw the poor girl once more in the hands of the Boy Rover.

Then he started forward to her rescue, but in an instant he felt the knife of the smuggler penetrate his shoulder; and as a faintness came over him, he fell, as he saw the Boy Rover grasp Ellen in his arms and bear her to the window.

Then a lurid glare shot across his eyes and he closed them to all around.

There was a loud footstep upon the stairs—the door was thrust violently open, and a figure sprang into the room.

It was Henry Chambers, who had recovered from the shock caused by the fall from the cliff, and was now searching for his friends, when he heard the cry of Ellen and instantly recognised the voice.

He cast his eyes hastily around the room, but no Ellen was there. He was about to search the lower part of the house, when a sight that almost transfixed him with horror attracted his attention.

Lying upon the floor of the apartment, with the blood flowing copiously from a wound in his shoulder, and the flames almost playing around his form, was Charles Lawson. Hastily recovering himself, he seized him in his arms, and rushed from the room, down the stairs, into the open air, and, laying him gently upon the ground, a short distance from the burning house, re-entered the building, to seek for the poor girl.

But vain was his search; no Ellen was to be found: and it was not until the flames had gained such an ascendancy that it would be worse than madness to stay longer, that he, with a heavy heart, gave up the search as hopeless.

He retraced his steps to the spot where the poor youth lay, and bent over his prostrate form. The cool night air had revived him, and he muttered:

"Spare her—spare her!"

"Where is Ellen?" said the young lieutenant, as he raised the head of the youth upon his knee, and looked with a pitiful countenance into his face. "In vain have I searched the house. She is nowhere to be found."

"Water, water!" gasped forth Charles—"water, water!"

"Is she yet in the house?" asked Henry.

The youth's head fell back, and again he was lost to all consciousness.

Henry laid him gently down, and procured some water, which he carried in the crown of his cap, and quickly returned to the spot. Pouring a portion of it over the youth's face, and some into his mouth, he waited patiently in the hope that he would show

some signs of recovery. He bound the wound tightly around with his handkerchief, and succeeded in stopping the flow of blood.

It was a fearful sight to behold the flames encircling the late happy house, as they leapt, and danced, and turned themselves around every inflamable object; and indeed there were many, for the house was built almost entirely of logs. To attempt to arrest their course would have been fruitless, for the weather had been fine and warm for some considerable time past, and they were, therefore, so dry, that instantly the flames came into contact with them they became ignited, and the dense volumes of smoke, as it hung over the burning pile, formed, as it were, a funeral pall to that ill-fated building.

In less than an hour nothing remained to mark the spot where the building had stood but a heap of charred and blackened rubbish.

Henry bore him a short distance to a spot where a young knoll formed a natural couch, and laid the youth gently upon it; and after administering such restoratives as were within his reach, he had the satisfaction of seeing him gradually return to consciousness.

Opening his eyes the poor lad looked around in a state of bewilderment, and seemed to endeavour to recal to his mind the events of the past hour. He attempted to raise himself on the couch, but his wound was so painful, and he was so weak from loss of blood, that he was with difficulty enabled to move.

Gradually a true sense of his position stole across his mind, and his heart sunk within him.

"Ellen! Ellen!" he muttered, in heart-broken accents, "where art thou?"

He closed his eyes as he spoke, and sank back upon the couch.

"Where is she?" asked the young lieutenant, bending over the couch.

The youth opened his eyes and gazed with astonishment upon the form of his friend.

"Ah, villain!" he almost shrieked, "are you still there? Where is Ellen?" He paused, for he recognised the features of his friend; and then added, in a very subdued tone, "Where am I?—where is Ellen?"

"Heaven alone can tell; not I," replied Henry. "But you are safe—saved from the ruins of the burning house."

"What say you?" asked the youth, in tones of surprise. "Has the house, then, been fired, and Ellen fallen a sacrifice to the flames?"

"I think not," said Henry. "I searched; she was not there. You alone I found, with the flames leaping around you, and weltering in thy blood."

"Oh, God!" exclaimed the poor youth, clasping his hands, "has Ellen been wrested from these arms to fall a sacrifice to the foulsome and unholy passions of a villain? Am I doomed to sink down with sorrow to the grave, weeping my last love? Forbid it, heaven, whose ways are just; wrest her from the spoiler, and restore her pure and innocent to these arms."

Henry gazed upon the features of the wounded youth with surprise at the words he was uttering. A sudden light seemed to break in upon him. Had Ellen been carried off from the house, and the fire been the work of an incendiary? It must be so; or where did Charles receive his wound, unless it was in protecting her or the house?

"What mean you?" he asked. "Who has been there?"

"A villain!" replied the youth, in passionate tones; "a villain whose base and coward heart respected neither innocence nor virtue."

"Of whom do you speak?" said Charles, a dismal foreboding crossing his heart.

"The Boy Rover, the hated smuggler, whose accursed villany has caused us so much misery; the black-hearted miscreant, whose base and ignoble nature can respect neither honour nor virtue—whose vile heart is callous to mercy or feeling; the ruffian, whose accursed deed wrecked the vessel on the coast which bore two happy beings to their native land, with hearts filled with hope and gladness! But the vengeance of Heaven will overtake him yet, though his murderous hand has rendered me powerless to save her I so dearly and fondly love!'

And the noble-minded youth sank back upon the earth, exhausted and powerless.

"But, save a few bruises in the fall down the cliff, I am still uninjured," said Henry. "Rest you there. I will seek Ellen. He cannot have yet escaped to his ship. I will track the villain—hang upon his trail as the hungry shark upon a doomed ship. I will save her, Charles—save her from his power, or perish in the attempt!"

"Bless you!" said the wounded youth, as he grasped the hand of Henry, as the brave young lieutenant leant over him. "Oh! would that I could accompany you; but I am powerless—helpless. But, oh! the pain I suffer from this wound is nothing to compare with the agony I endure as to the fate of Ellen."

"Compose yourself," said his friend; "leave her rescue to me. The smuggler can know nothing of my presence here; and he doubtless thinks you have fallen a victim to the flames. He will believe his passage to his vessel safe; but I will be upon his track, and Heaven give me strength to foil the villain yet, and save her you so dearly love!"

"Thanks, Henry! I know not how to show my gratitude—how to –"

"Say no more, but compose yourself. I, like yourself, am a British sailor, and sooner would strike my colours to the enemies of my country than refuse to succour a woman in distress. 'Tis a sailor's boast that his arm is ever ready to defend; and when mine fails, it shall only be when the last drop of blood has been shed in her defence!"

And, once more grasping the hand of the wounded youth, he rushed from the spot, in the direction of the cliffs.

CHAPTER XXXV.

THE BOY ROVER AND ELLEN—THE DESERTED BAY—THE SIGNAL AND REPLY.

WHEN the Boy Rover, bearing the insensible form of Ellen in his arms, took his departure from the vicinity of the burning house, that pile of destruction which his base and ruffian hand had reared—he dashed wildly onwards, his brain fired with success, and his mind a prey to dishonourable and debasing thoughts.

Ever and anon he glanced behind him at that scene of horror and destruction, but not one feeling of compunction took possession of his heart. The demon of evil had got too strong a hold, and would not permit one good thought to enter. No, it was with a smile of fiendish triumph and exultation that he saw the flames rise higher and higher to the heavens, and encircle that house in its all devouring embrace.

Having got some considerable distance from the scene of his hellish works, he stopped and allowed the form of the young girl to slide gently from his arms upon the soft turf, and then wiping the perspiration from his brow, he gazed rapturously upon her features, upon which the silver rays of the moon brightly played.

"Who will say," he half muttered to himself, "that the Boy Rover cannot love. To hold you for one moment in my arms I would brave anything. I would brave the mighty cataracts, descend into the ponderous mouth of the burning mount, struggle with the boa constrictor, or even betray my crew into the hands of mine enemies. There is nothing I would not do to possess thee. But now you are mine, and the Boy Rover is glad, his heart is larger, and his limbs are stronger, and the smuggler is mad with joy."

He placed his arms around her waist and raised her head upon his knee, and gazed with a long and lustful look into her fair face; then, with ecstacy, strained her passionately to his bosom and imprinted his fulsome kisses upon her white lips. She now began to show signs of animation, and lifting her again in his arms, as though she were a mere infant, he said—

"She lives again! but I must hurry forward to the cliff."

He darted onwards as he spoke, and quickly arrived at the edge of the cliff.

He laid the poor girl on the earth, and seating himself near her, waited until she should be restored to consciousness, watching her intently as her bosom rose and fell, with her now somewhat convulsive breathing.

A spasmodic tremor ran through her frame, she heaved a deep sigh, her eyes opened, and she gazed around with a bewildered look. She seemed unable to move, so great was evidently her surprise at the position in which she found herself.

In this manner she lay for some time, the bright moon beams playing upon her face, lending to it a sort of unearthly pallor, and throwing fantastic shadows around. In a few moments she raised herself from her recumbent position, and then for the first time perceived that she was not alone. Straining her eyes in the direction of the figure, she endeavoured to trace the lineaments of his countenance, but the position which the Boy Rover occupied did not enable her to make out his features, as the moon's rays had thrown a deep shade upon the portion he occupied.

The recollection of the night's adventure suddenly flashed across her brain, and the poor girl's heart sunk within her. Springing hastily to her feet she stood before him, and in a voice of the deepest anguish, demanded—

"Who are you? Speak; say who are you, and what place is this."

The Boy Rover rose as she spoke, and turning so as to allow the moon beams to fall upon his features, he said—

"You are answered. The bright moon shows you who he is that stands before you."

"Ah," she shrieked, "villain! where is Charles—the poor youth whom thy coward hand struck to the earth?"

The Boy Rover answered not, but his brow contracted and he bit his lips as the word coward fell upon his ears.

"Speak," she reiterated, "where is Charles?"

"I think only of thee," he replied, endeavouring to evade an answer to her question; for, brutal ruffian as he was, he dreaded to tell her of the fate of her lover, whom he firmly believed had perished in the flames.

"I ask you not of myself," she said, gazing full

in his face with a look of contempt—"I ask you of him whose form you dared to strike to the earth when he would have protected me from a ruffian, a slave, and a coward!"

The Boy Rover writhed at her words, and his chest heaved with the contending passions which her sarcastic expressions called forth. Seizing her roughly by the arm, he hissed in her ears:

"Coward I am none! your lover stood between us, and I struck him to the earth."

"But where is he?" she continued, and her voice trembled as she spoke. "Has he, too, fallen a victim to thy brutal passions—tell me, is he dead?—was the wound which your hand inflicted fatal?"

The Boy Rover did not answer her question, but averted his face from her gaze.

"Smuggler," she said in a more gentle tone, as she laid her hand upon his arm and looked beseechingly in his face—"tell me that he still lives; ah! say that he is not dead, and I——"

"Will love me?" said the Rover, inquiringly fixing upon her a glance from which she shrunk with a feeling of horror and disgust.

"Tell me of him before I answer your question," she said evasively.

The Boy Rover stood for a moment irresolute, then taking the hand of the poor girl in his own he said:

"I did not kill your lover!"

"Thank God, he lives," said Ellen, as she breathed more freely.

The Boy Rover was silent.

"Oh," she said, "let me away from hence; he needs my assistance."

Still the Boy Rover was silent. Ellen attempted to quit the spot, but he moved towards her and arrested her progress.

"Let me begone," she said; "he requires my aid."

"It must not be," replied the Rover: "he needs you not."

The poor girl's heart sunk within her, as she found that the smuggler was determined to keep her a prisoner; and, with tears in her eyes, she exclaimed:

"I must go forth: poor wounded and suffering Charles requires my help. He has no one to care for him but me. You cannot be so callous as to detain me here when he requires my aid!"

"He needs it not," said the other.

"How?" she said, in some surprise, as a fearful presentiment that the Boy Rover had spoken falsely, when he said that he had not killed the youth, stole upon her heart. "Not require my aid, when he lies wounded and suffering, with no one else to attend upon him?"

"No," he replied: "he will never need help, unless it be in the next world."

"My God!" almost shrieked the poor girl—"is he no more—is he dead? Thou said'st but now he had not died by thy hand."

"I spoke truly: he did not die by my hand."

"Then does he live?" she asked, with returning hope.

"No," replied the Boy Rover: "he has fallen a sacrifice to fire, and died in the flames."

With a burst of agony, Ellen sunk upon the ground, and sobbed as though her heart would break.

And thus she remained—her face clasped in her hands, and her form bent forward, weighed down, as it were, with the most poignant anguish. Deep and heavy sobs convulsed her bosom, and the scalding tears trickled through her fingers. She felt that now she was alone in the world, without one friend to aid her—one to love or care for her.

The Boy Rover seated himself again, and gazed intently upon her. The sufferings of the poor girl seemed to have some effect upon his callous heart, and for a moment he felt some degree of compunction for the deed which he had committed; but it was for a moment only, and then his evil passions again took possession of his soul.

After a time he rose from his seat and approached the poor girl with a firm step and a resolute brow, every good thought had vanished from his heart.

Placing himself before Ellen he said, in a tone of the greatest harshness, and with a significant smile curling his lips—

"Need I tell you wherefore I have brought you here?"

"Murderer!—villain!" almost shrieked the poor girl, as the tones of his voice fell gratingly upon her ears and seemed to snap asunder the lethargic chains which had bound her. "Murderer a just God will assuredly avenge the wicked and hellish deeds your hands have perpetrated. Back," she added, rising from the ground, "back! Let me pass, or if you are villain enough, let the same hand which slew him likewise murder me."

The Boy Rover started and gazed at her with surprise and admiration, for this sudden burst of passion for a moment seemed to lend to her features a more than earthly beauty, and her whole mien was stately and grand, as she stood before him with flashing eyes and heaving bosom. But quickly recovering himself, he replied—

"I love you too well to wish to slay you."

"Love!" she exclaimed, in a tone of contempt and disgust, "love! You, the murderer; the blackhearted wretch who, to glut his depraved and bloody appetite, mercilessly tortures those whom cruel destiny have made his prisoners; who degrades the name of man by insulting a defenceless woman, whose weakness prevents her from chastising the contemptible monster as he deserves. A thing like thee talk of love! and to me whose heart thou hast crushed, whose life thou has rendered desolate, whose lover thou hast murdered! Stand aside and let me hence; there is a poison in the very air you breath!"

Trembling with passion, the Boy Rover seized her roughly by the arm, and detained her in his iron grasp.

"By hell!" he hissed between his clenched teeth, "you shall find that I can hate as well as love. Resistance is useless; you are mine."

"Liar!" she exclaimed. "Ellen Hanfield will protect her honour whilst she has life. The great God, who never turns a deaf ear to cries of justice and mercy, will grant a poor girl's prayer, and rescue her from the hands of a villain, who sets alike the laws of him and man at defiance."

The Rover turned, and, fixing a look of fearful meaning upon her, said:

"He must aid you quickly, then; for in a short time you will again be on board."

As he spoke he threw his strong arms around her, and lifting her up, bore her along the cliff till he arrived at the spot on which she and Charles had lay for a short time exhausted after their escape over the chasm.

Then the Boy Rover blew a loud long whistle, and listened intently.

But no response was heard to this, and, muttering an impatient ejaculation, repeated the sound.

Still, there was no reply.

After a few moments pause he called out—

"Bill!"

But no Bill, nor indeed any other voice answered, and, muttering something about carelessness and sleeping at their post, he again raised his voice—

"'Venomed Snake'—ahoy!"

But this had no better effect, and foaming with passion, the Boy Rover cursed and swore in a frightful manner.

He gazed along the cliff, and then over its side into the abyss, but no object met his sight.

"Damn them!" he exclaimed. "I'll make them pay for this. I'll learn them to desert their post and disobey orders. But, come."

And seizing Ellen roughly in his arms, he lifted her from the ground, and placing his feet upon the planks crossed the chasm to the opposite side.

Then again he called upon the boat's crew whom he had left a short time before, but receiving no answer, he descended cautiously the rock with Ellen.

When he had arrived some distance down the cliff he perceived that the boat was gone, and a cry of rage escaped him.

He felt that he was deserted by his followers, and that his chance of regaining the vessel was by endeavouring to attract the attention of those on board from the top of the cliff, from which spot the white sail of the "Venomed Snake" could be plainly seen in the moonlight.

He therefore once more ascended, dragging after him the poor girl.

Arrived at the top, he drew a pistol from his belt and fired it.

In a minute a blue light was seen burning on the deck of the smuggler craft.

Then he took his kerchief from his neck and waved it as a signal to those on board.

Poor Ellen had sunk at his feet in despair, and was bewailing her sad fate and that of her lover, who had so nobly struggled to procure her rescue from him into whose hands she had once more fallen.

He still continued to wave the handkerchief in the air, and in a few moments another light—this time a red one—threw a glare upon the ocean from the smuggler's deck.

With a cry of satisfaction, the Boy Rover placed his neckerchief around his neck and sat down by his captive's side.

That red light had told him that his presence on the cliff had been discovered, and he now only waited the arrival of the boat that was to bear himself and his broken-hearted victim to the ship.

CHAPTER XXXVI.

DOUBTS AND SUSPENSES—THE FIGURE IN THE BAY.

HENRY, with slow and painful steps, took his way towards the cliff.

Fortunately for himself and friends, the shaking which he had received in his fall from the cliff was not so bad as might have been anticipated, when the fearful depth to the bay is taken into consideration. But the fact was, Henry had clung so tenaciously to the smuggler, that the latter had broken his fall; and now, except a few abrasions of the skin, the young lieutenant was comparatively unharmed.

In his passage, to endeavour to save Ellen from the hands of the Boy Rover, his mind was assailed by alternate hopes and fears; and more than once did he pause to think, as he journeyed on his way.

The rays of the moon, as it cast its silvery streaks upon the dancing waves, seemed now to possess no charm for him. He did not, as was his wont, gaze with wonder and admiration upon the reflection of the chaste orb of night. His mind was wandering away to that poor girl, and conjuring up every imaginable evil that could possibly befal her.

He imagined he saw her struggling with the fierce Rover, and endeavouring to break from his grasp, as he imprinted his fulsome kisses upon her lips. He thought he saw her beautiful countenance, which was ever beaming with smiles, distorted with agony; and her fair arms bruised and bleeding, as she vainly battled with the powerful smuggler, to save her honour; and then, fainting and unable to continue the unequal contest, give up in despair. His giddy brain conjured up the look of triumph with which the Boy Rover surveyed his insensible victim; and the blood rushed to his heart, and fired his soul. He bit his lips, and clenched his hands, until the blood almost started from his fingers' ends. The demon of jealousy was taking possession of his brain. He loved Ellen, and to see her willingly become another's would cause him a pang of the most acute anguish; but to feel that she would fall a victim to man she detested, was madness.

"What!" he muttered between his clenched teeth, as he drew himself up to his full height—"shall I know she whom I love is in danger and not go forth to the rescue? Shall the merciless Rover triumph over the woman I would give all I possess, and not try to save her? Have I lost my courage and my strength that he stays here when I should be at her side? No," he added, with a fierce determination—"I will not be idle; I will rescue her from his power, and kill the villain who has outraged the honour of man, and degraded the name of sailor!"

And as he spoke, Henry advanced towards the edge of the cliff.

"I will go and look upon the mighty waters," he muttered, after a pause, for there is a music in their thundering voices, and a grandeur in their ever-foaming surface.

The rays of the moon were throwing their joyous tints upon the leaves of the trees, and upon the waters of the bay, as Henry stood upon their banks. He gazed down upon them with wonder and admiration; and, for a time, he forgot poor Ellen in the whirl of thought which the grandeur of the scene forced upon his senses.

Oh! mighty works of Omnipotence—who can gaze upon those wonders, and not acknowledge the existence of thy being and thy power? Who, as he listens to the roar of the mighty cataract, and sees the spray rise in huge clouds above its surface, will not acknowledge the existence of one superior to man—of one more mighty in his works—more enduring in its formation—more sublime in its grandeur?"

Let the atheist, if such there be, stand upon the brink of the wondrous cliffs, and watch the sun glistening upon the spray, or listen to the thundering voice of the waves as they rush headlong with mad fury against the rocks—let him gaze upon their frantic whirl as they break and recede again to the ocean, and his heart will acknowledge the power of one superior to himself; his mind will tell him how little, how insignificant, he is to that infinite power which formed the "heavens, the earth, the sea, and all that therein is."

THE BOY ROVER BEARING ELLEN FROM THE BURNING HUT.

Down, vain man! thy knee should bend in wonder and adoration at the works of Nature—the arts of man may be great, but the works of God are sublime.

Such were the thoughts of Henry, as he looked forth upon the bay across its waters to the sea beyond. Child of nature as he was, yet he could acknowledge the existence of a power greater than man. The little teaching that he had received from the good old folks at home, his natural generous disposition, and the works of Nature in their wild and uncultivated state, with which he had ever been surrounded, led him to look up with adoration to the Supreme Giver of all things.

He stood upon a huge rock, and watched the gradually changing colour of the vast waters, as the rising moon cast its various tints upon their surface.

Still, there he stood—his noble form clear and distinct, as the rays of the moon played upon him—straining his eyes across the cliff, in the hope of seeing her he sought.

From the scenes around him, his thoughts had reverted again to Ellen, and her prospect of deliverance from the hands of the smuggler. Vainly did he endeavour in his mind to concoct some plan by which he might successfully rescue the poor girl. He seated himself upon the rock, and, leaning his head on his hand, gave himself up to deep thought.

Thus he remained for a few moments, when a

low and plaintive cry was carried by the breeze across the cliffs to his ears.

He strained his eyes in every direction, in the hopes of perceiving any object from which the cry had arisen; but nothing met his sight but the silver rays of the moon upon the dancing stream.

He listened attentively; but nothing but the song of night-birds, and the hum of waters, smote his ears. All was again silent. After a moment, the cry was again repeated. His heart beat violently—a strong feeling seemed to take possession of him. He looked forth upon the waters; for he was convinced that it was from them that the sound came.

Long and earnestly did he gaze upon the stream, which seemed to dance and sport with the moonbeams that played upon its surface. Nor did he gaze in vain; for, at some considerable distance up the bay, he perceived an object which was rapidly floating towards him.

"Yonder," he muttered, "is something which is being carried by the stream in this direction. What can it be? The moon and water have almost blinded me; for I cannot make it out. Ah!" he added, as the object approached nearer, borne swiftly on by the force of the waters, "it is a human being—some one whose boat has turned over, and left him to the mercy of the water. May Heaven send its aid to save him, whoever he may be; for here I am powerless!"

He crossed the plank, and dashed down the rock, for some distance. Then he stood gazing upon the floating object.

On, on, it came—nearer and nearer—quicker and quicker—as though forced along by some invisible hand.

"Ah!" he suddenly exclaimed, as he saw distinctly the floating form—"by heavens! 'tis a woman. Can it be Ellen, whom the Boy Rover has stolen? Can it be her, who now rushes to meet her death? Oh! that my hand could save her. Aid me, Heaven, to arrest for awhile from death the form which now hurries thither! If yon projection would but stay her progress, there might be hope," he said, as he fixed his eyes for a moment upon a portion of a piece of rock upon which the waters dashed. "Ah! no, she is too far in the stream, and she will pass by it; and then all will be be lost—for none can help her then but God! Would that I could bear her safely to this spot! But 'tis vain to think. I must see her die, and my heart must break."

As he concluded, a sudden thought seemed to seize upon his brain; for, with a wild cry of joy, he dashed madly on, until he arrived at a spot where a large projection of rock overhung the stream.

"If the current but bear her to this side," he exclaimed, "the waters, as they break upon this rock, will hurl her far towards this bank ere they again carry her onwards. Oh! may the heavens so let it be; for then my arm may not be streched forth in vain, and my heart broken by her death."

Still onward came the figure, buoyed up on the surface of the water by the air which had inflated her dress. She neared the rock, and a moment would decide now whether there were any hopes of her being saved from so fearful a death.

With the agility of a cat, Henry sprang upon the projecting stone, and crawled along it, until he had almost arrived at its utmost extremity. Nearer and nearer came the poor girl—borne on with fearful rapidity; and quicker and quicker beat the young man's heart.

"She will come on this side!" he almost shrieked with joy, as he saw the poor girl being carried in that direction. "The waters will bear her towards me, and my arm will be stretched forth to save her, and bear her to her lover's arms!"

As he spoke, he flung himself from the rock, clinging to it only by his feet, till his head nearly touched the flowing waters beneath. One false move, and he would be lost to all earthly aid; one moment's hesitation, and all hopes of saving the poor girl were gone.

"She was close upon the rock now, and Henry held his breath, in an agony of suspense. Quickly the waters bore her towards it; and then, as though some unseen hand was there to guide her, carried her, with mad fury, towards him. Swift as the lightning's flash, the arm of the youth was thrust forth, and Ellen was in the powerful grasp of the young lieutenant.

With almost superhuman strength, he drew her towards him; and then, with difficulty—for the fearful weight of the water with which her dress was saturated rendered it no easy task for him, strong as he was—he drew himself and her on to the rock which had done him so much service, and slowly made his way along it, till he reached the cliff. He then lowered his insensible burthen to the earth, and sunk exhausted at her feet.

CHAPTER XXXVII.

THE FEARFUL POSITION OF ELLEN—THE STRUGGLE—THE ESCAPE TO THE BOAT—THE FALLING ROCK.

LET us go back a short quarter of an hour previous to the events described in the last chapter, in order that the reader may be enabled to understand by what means the fair Ellen had thus fallen into the hands of the brave and generous young lieutenant.

Whilst the Boy Rover was casting his gaze over the now moonlit ocean towards his bark, and awaiting impatiently the arrival of a boats's crew to bear him to its deck, Ellen had risen to her feet, and, well knowing the fate which would befal her on board the floating pandemonium which her persecutor commanded, she had resolved to leave no means untried to escape from his power.

With this resolve in her mind, she darted towards the planks which now formed the bridge across the chasm, in the hopes of being enabled to cross them, and make for the woods; but, ere she had taken half a dozen steps, the hand of the Rover grasped her wrist, and she felt herself turned completely round.

She sank down upon the rocks again, and covered her face with her hands; whilst the Boy Rover, in order to prevent a repetition of the attempt, remained standing at the end of the plank—thus effectually barring her passage across the chasm.

Finding all attempts to escape by the bridge were gone, she pondered in her mind the probability of slipping away from her persecutor by descending the rocks, and thus drawing him from the position he occupied, when she might, by some feint or stratagem, succeed in gaining the bridge, and making for the wood, which lay beyond.

She rose, and commenced to descend; and the Boy Rover, the instant he perceived her do so, left the bridge, and followed her down the cliff.

When she had arrived some considerable distance down the rocks, she suddenly turned, with the hope of passing him, and regaining the top. The Rover saw her movement, and stretched forth his hand to avert, when, in her endeavours to avoid him, she lost her footing, staggered, and fell over the side of the cliff into the bay.

Surprise and horror held him for a moment powerless; then, dashing down the cliffs to their base, he looked around for some means of saving her.

It was at this moment that the cry which had smote the ears of the young lieutenant broke from the poor girl's lips; and the smuggler captain drew back from the edge of the bay when he saw the form of Henry spring down the cliff on to the projecting rock which had rendered him so good a service, and awaited the result of the adventure, in painful suspense. He saw the brave youth throw his body over the rock, and he saw his strong arm grasp the fair girl, and bear her to the cliff, and then he crept stealthily up the cliff towards them.

Henry was bending over the half-insensible girl, when the Boy Rover crept stealthily behind him. He drew his knife from his belt, and raised it above his head.

The moonbeams had revealed the features of the young lieutenant; and the Boy Rover felt that it was necessary for his success in again possessing the girl to put out of his way her brave deliverer.

A smile of devilish hatred played around his brow, and he clutched his knife as in a vice; but, ere it descended, a cry from our heroine caused her deliverer to start backwards, and thus averted the blow which the Boy Rover had intended to strike.

At the same moment, Ellen sprang to her feet, and clung to the breast of the youth.

But, ere the young lieutenant could recover from the surprise into which the sudden appearance of the smuggler had thrown him, the Boy Rover had grasped the maiden, and drew her to his side.

"Ah! villain—you here!" said Henry, as he instinctively took a step towards the Rover.

"Aye," replied the smuggler, as he raised his knife, threateningly. "If you value your life, seek not to molest me, or this maiden."

"What would you with her?" said the young lieutenant.

"Bear her back to my bark," was the reply.

"You must slay me first," said Henry.

"I warn you," replied the Rover, "that my knife is sharp, and cuts deeply."

"Too well I know it, villain; for it has rendered prostrate as brave a youth as ever sailed beneath the Union Jack."

"Ah!" said the Rover—"how do you know that?"

"Because I left him but now to seek you."

"And now you have found me, what do you require?"

"Your life, ruffian!" exclaimed the youth, as he rushed suddenly towards the smuggler, and tore Ellen from his grasp.

The Rover advanced threateningly towards him, and endeavoured to bury his knife in the breast of the young lieutenant.

But Henry, now thoroughly aroused from the surprise into which the sudden appearance of the Boy Rover had thrown him, stood upon his guard, and, watching every movement of the smuggler's face, prepared to defend himself from the attack of the knife.

The bold youth waved Ellen back—so that she should receive no harm at the smuggler's hands—and then stood facing his adversary, ready to spring at his throat, or defend his own life, as occasion might require.

But the Rover seemed in no hurry to make the attack. He had felt the strength of the youth before, and he had no wish to come to close quarters with him. He felt that, to ensure success, it was necessary to keep Henry at arm's length, and await the first opportunity to bury his knife in his body. Again, he knew that a boat containing some of his crew would soon arrive, and then all chance of his losing the girl would have passed away. He resolved, therefore, to be cautious, and wait the turn of events.

While they thus stood facing each other, like tigers awaiting for the spring, a loud shout rose upon the air, and a boat glided swiftly into the bay.

A smile of triumph lighted up the face of the Boy Rover, and an exclamation of satisfaction escaped his lips.

His cry was echoed by another from Ellen; but it was a cry of despair.

She felt that she was now indeed lost, and that Henry, like her lover, would fall a victim to the smuggler's vengeance.

Henry, too, saw the danger in which he was placed, and resolved to leave no means untried to subvert it.

Secure, in his own mind, now, the Rover made a step towards Ellen; and, less wary now that he saw his crew ascending the cliff, he paid less heed to Henry's actions.

The young lieutenant retreated backwards, and the Boy Rover grasped the arm of Ellen. Still Henry stood motionless. Ellen struggled; and, the better to prevent her breaking from him, the smuggler captain placed his knife in his mouth, and grasped her with both hands.

This movement was fatal to him; for Henry, with one bound, sprang upon him, and, grasping his throat with one hand, with the other wrested the knife from his teeth.

Henry raised the knife to plunge it to the breast of the Rover; but, with a cry of horror, Ellen flung herself between them. Even she would save the life of him who sought her ruin, and had heaped so much misery upon her and her friends.

Her appealing look unnerved the arm of the young lieutenant, and he lowered the weapon.

The sailors were rapidly ascending the cliff; and, when they had approached sufficiently near, the Boy Rover stepped a few paces backwards, and called out:

"Seize them! If he shows fight, dash him over the cliff."

The crew advanced towards Henry and Ellen.

"Quick!" said Henry—"dash down the rock, into the boat. Away! I will follow you."

Ellen hesitated. She remembered Charles.

"Quick, quick!—'tis our only chance. For the love of heaven, go!"

Ellen cast one look upon his face; then turned, and ran down the cliff, towards the boat.

The Boy Rover rushed forward to stay her passage; but a blow from Henry stopped his career, and he staggered backwards. Two of the new arrivals now rushed towards him; and, when one had arrived within arm's length, he raised the knife above his head, and, quick as the lightning's flash, buried it in the man's throat—and, with a gurgling spasmodic gasp, the smuggler fell.

Awed by the fearful doom of their companion, neither the Boy Rover nor the rest of the newly arrived smugglers attempted to molest the youth, and he bounded down the cliff after Ellen. He came up with her just as she reached the spot where the boat rode on the bay; and, without a word, he lifted her in his arms, and placed her in it: then leapt in himself. To push her out in the stream was the work of a moment; and, as it glided out into the bay, Henry cast his eyes upwards.

The smugglers had recovered from the panic into which the fate of their companion had thrown them, and were now exerting themselves to prevent the escape of the boat.

The Boy Rover, assisted by the new comers, was endeavouring to topple a huge piece of rock over the cliff into the boat; and, as Henry cast his eyes upwards, a cry of horror escaped him, for, at that moment, he saw the huge stone roll over the side.

With a shudder, he closed his eyes; and the next moment the fearful missile struck the boat with such violence that it rebounded over the waters, and shivered like an aspen leaf.

A long, loud, and piercing shriek escaped the lips of Ellen; and, as Henry clasped her in his arms, the boat righted herself on the waters, and slowly drifted towards the opening of the bay.

The little boat drifted on its course, and passed out of the mouth of the bay into the open sea.

The shock caused by the fallen rock had thrown the oars from the craft into the bay, and its occupants were now left to the mercy of the wind and waves.

The bright moonlight streamed down upon them, and cast its mellow rays over the now white-crested billows. A breeze had sprung up, and, as it played upon the forms of Ellen and her noble-minded friend, cooled their heated brains.

Now that they were free of the bay, Henry could not but perceive that the boat had received great injury from the piece of rock which had been hurled upon it, and a cry of horror escaped his lips as he saw that she was rapidly filling.

What was to be done? He had no means of keeping her afloat by bailing out the water; nor could he guide her course to some friendly haven of refuge.

He sat despairingly down, and buried his face in his hands.

Suddenly, he was aroused by a crash, and a loud shriek from Ellen. The boat had struck upon a rock, which appeared but a few feet above the sea.

Driven against this by the fury of the wind, the collision had been of so great a force as to stove her in, and she now rapidly settled down.

With an exclamation of horror, he seized Ellen in his arms, and lifted her on to the rock, following immediately himself.

Scarce were they free of the boat, than, with a loud hissing sound, it whirled round, and disappeared beneath the waters which encircled the spot on which they stood.

They were alone upon the sea, and, in the distance, the white sails of the "Venomed Snake" fluttered in the moonlight.

And the wind freshened, and the waves rose higher and higher, and danced around us, as the flames of a funeral pyre.

Ellen sank down upon the rock, and prayed; and Henry, seeing that they must fall a victim to the coming storm, waved his handkerchief above his head, to attract the notice of those on board the smuggler bark.

"Better," he thought, "that we fall once more into their hands, and trust to Heaven to aid them, than remain here to perish."

But still the waves rose higher and higher; a vivid flash lit up the heavens; and then a peal of thunder shook the massive rock on which they stood, and, as its echoes died away among the cliffs, a huge wave rolled in upon them, and hurled them, like chaff before the wind, into the now foaming billows.

CHAPTER XXXVIII.

AN UNEXPECTED APPEARANCE—THE HISTORY OF AN ISLAND RECLUSE.

THE grey streaks of morning were casting a cold unearthly gleam upon the island, when Charles awoke from a painful stupor into which he had fallen immediately after Henry had left his side; and, raising himself upon his elbow, he gazed bewilderingly around, with aching eyes and throbbing brain.

Standing before him, and gazing intently and pityingly upon his pale and haggard cheeks, was the tall figure of a man, roughly yet comfortably attired, bearing in his hand a rifle.

His long hair and beard, of iron-grey, betokened one of immense strength, and partially hid what had once been a handsome face.

He was leaning upon his rifle, and gazing tenderly upon the wounded youth, when Charles opened his eyes.

As the young man rose with difficulty upon his elbow, he said:

"Exert not yourself, young man; you are wounded, and unable to rise. Let me lift you in my arms, and bear you to my hut. Speak not—you have nothing to fear from me."

And, stooping down, he raised the youth in his arms, as though he were a child.

"Fear not," he said, as he commenced walking from the spot. "You are with one who will befriend you."

Bearing the wounded youth along through a part of the forest for some distance, he came at last to a small hut, built of wood; and, entering which, he laid our hero down upon a soft couch, formed of dried grass, and, still motioning him to silence, procured some water, with which he bathed the wound in his shoulder, and then bound it up again.

This operation rendered Charles more comfortable, and a look of gratitude beamed from his eyes as he thanked the stranger for his kind office. When this had been done, he procured some food, which he placed before his guest; but Charles could not eat—his mind was too much a prey to agonising thoughts.

The stranger, finding that the youth was in a good way of recovering, and that talking a little would do him no injury, and, at the same time, wishing to satisfy his own curiosity as to how he came upon the island, and received the wound from which he was suffering, he questioned Charles as to these circumstances.

The noble youth told him all—concealed nothing from him; and the brow of the stranger darkened when he heard of the indignities to which poor Ellen had been subjected.

When he had concluded, the stranger heaved a sigh, and said:

"Better to live the life of a recluse upon this island than go forth into the wicked world. Alas! I too have had my sufferings."

"I am curious to know your history," said Charles. "Have you been here long?"

"Thirty years."

"By yourself?"

"Yes; but compose yourself; and, while you rest your aching limbs—for I see that you are curious—I will tell you my history.

"I was born in England; but, when quite a

child I accompanied my father to America—my mother being dead. When, at the age of seventeen, my father died, and I was left in the wide world with none to care for me but one frail girl—poor devoted Mary—a friendship had sprung up between us, which had ripened into a pure and holy love.

"I was about twenty, when a rich merchant in New York required an agent in London; and, as by accepting the office I should be enabled to procure sufficient means to support the girl I so fondly loved, we agreed to marry; and the day before I was to sail for England I led her to the altar.

"On the following morning, armed with my credentials, and accompanied by my young bride, I prepared to go on board the 'Sybil,' and bid farewell to America.

"The ship had been towed down the river below Staten Island, and there she lay with her loose sails hanging in the buntlines. At noon, myself and Mary stepped on board the little steamer which was waiting for us, and were soon carried down to the ship, which we boarded without difficulty. In a few moments more the ship's topsail's were sheeted home, the anchor having already been hove up, and the yards hoisted. The noble craft swept gracefully around, and ere long she was on her course towards the broad Atlantic. The lofty sails were set, the courses dropped, and then the men went at work clearing the deck.

"I had gone below to get a glass of brandy and water, to keep off the sea-sickness, and was busy in seeing that our luggage was properly stowed. Mary was left alone upon the poop, where she was engaged in watching the green shore, as it seemed to move past her. The scene was a new one to her, and she enjoyed it much. The dashing foaming water; the distant rocks, over which the waves beat in white surging crests; the receding city; and, above all, the boundless expanse of old ocean which opened before her, all tended to inspire her soul with awe and wonder: and her conceptions at once turned to the Great Ruler, in whose hands all these things were. She was thus standing, and watching the strange scene, when some one at her side spoke.

"'Perhaps this is something new to you, lady,' said the voice.

"Mary turned, and saw the man whom she had at first recognised as commander of the ship. And yet she could hardly realise that she was correct. She had heard him called captain, and she had heard him give such orders as only the captain could give; yet she was puzzled. She had always supposed that a sea-captain must be a rough, stout, dark-featured man, with a coarse face, and huge whiskers; but the man by her side was very young—not over two-and-twenty, if he was so old—tall and straight, and of a noble bearing, and a bright, full, hazel eye, dark, curling brown hair, and features of more than ordinary manly beauty. In fact, he was the very ideal of a noble handsome man, and his peculiar beauty was no more in the conformation of his form and features, than in the beaming light of intelligence and goodness that was manifest in every lineament of his countenance.

"'It is new, sir,' the maiden replied, in answer to the remark she had heard. 'I was never on board a large ship before.'

"'Then you will find much that is new,' replied the captain, in a kind winning tone. 'But I trust we shall be able to make your situation so pleasant that you will not regret having sailed with us.'

"'Thank you, sir,' fervently answered Mary, at the same time raising her eyes to her companion's face.

"'We have a stout ship, lady, and a faithful one,' the young captain pursued, 'and the crew are all excellent seamen and true to their duty. My officers are experienced and energetic, so that my own failings may be easily made up for.' He smiled as he said this, and though he surely meant to have spoken this last sentence in a light tone, yet his voice sank to a low key, and it came out tremulously.

"'Ah!' uttered Mary, looking up with a bright glow, 'I know enough of sea to be aware that inexperienced men are not placed in command of fine ships. And then, too, I think I heard one of the owners tell my husband that Captain Wilson was one of the best commanders he had ever employed.'

"The ship passed into the night, and the land was gone from sight. Both Mary and myself were obliged to give up to the enervating influence of sea-sickness; and, though I doubled and trebled my doses of brandy and water, yet I was the sicker of the two. At the end of four days Mary was well and strong, and she thought she felt better for the short sickness she had experienced.

"It was on the morning of the sixth day out. I had become well again, and now was on deck. The crew had just done their breakfast, and the cook had removed the dishes, when one of the men in the foretop reported a sail.

"'Where away?' shouted the captain.

"'About three points on the weather bow, sir,' was the reply.

"The captain got his glass and hastened forward, and found that the sail could be easily seen from the deck. She was yet hull-down, but the captain could see that she carried square sails.

"'She must be a small craft—a brig, most likely—bound for the Straits,' remarked the captain, as I approached him. 'But we shall soon make her out, for she is coming down fast.'

"The wind was now very near north-east, and the ship was heading as near east as possible, with her bowlines taut. The brig—for a brig it proved to be—bore a very little east of north-east, and was coming down before the wind. In fifteen minutes more the brig's hull could be seen, and it was also seen that she had run up her studdingsails.

"'By my soul!' cried the captain, with his glass to his eye, 'she carries guns; and I can see her bows crowded with men.'

"'How?' cried I. 'What is she?'

"'Are your eyes good, sir?'

"'Yes, as good as ever,' I returned.

"'Then take this glass, and tell me what you see.'

"I took the instrument, and, having raised it to my eye, turned it upon the coming brig. I gazed awhile, and then, as a shudder ran through my frame, I said:

"'I see port-holes in her sides, and guns projecting from them. I see a dense crowd of men upon her forecastle, and they seem very eager. And they are a motley crew, too—not uniform like the crew of a lawful war-vessel.'

"'Aye, sir—so I saw,' responded the captain. 'I think I know the fellow; and to you, sir, who may be cool, I will say—we have fallen into a bad fix. That brig is a Spanish pirate, which has infested this section for over a year. He is a relentless blood-thirsty villain, and we must—'

"At this moment the brig fired one of her bow guns, and, as the report came booming over the water, a shudder ran around among the crew. They now knew the character of the stranger, and they knew, too, that he was a remarkably swift sailer—so much so that he had run away from the swiftest of the British corvettes.

"'Mr. Jameson,' spoke the young captain, calmly and collectedly, 'you must break this matter to your wife, and place her where she will be safe. We shall have some warm work, for I mean to fight to the very last extremity. My ship shall never be given up while I live. You may help me if you will.' Then he turned to his men.

"'Stand by!' he shouted. 'We'll make a run first, and then prepare for defence during the chase. Tacks and sheets. Cast off to leeward—round in on the weather braces. Up with the helm—steadily!'

'In a few moments the ship was heading due south, with the wind fair upon the quarter, and the larboard studding-sails set below and aloft, and she now ploughed through the water swiftly. But the brig had changed her course, also, and was in direct chase; and it was soon evident that the latter vessel was gradually but surely gaining.

"It was a thrilling moment. All knew now the character of the pursuer, and all knew that certain death must follow a capture by him. There is a strange terror in the thought of a pirate at sea, but when that thought becomes reality—when the dread demon is upon the track; and, more than all, when the fearful truth bursts forth that the blood-monster can use the greatest speed—then the night sinks into the night of despair, and the soul turns instinctively to its God.

"So felt those on board the noble ship, as she vainly fled before her fell-pursuer.

"There were some thirty souls on board; and, as the owners were well aware that the Atlantic at that time was infested by pirates, they had the ship well-armed. As soon as it was evident that the pirate was gaining upon them, the captain addressed his crew, and exhorted them to fight like men who were willing to protect their ship and the female on board.

"To this the men gave a cheer, which proved that were were willing to die like men in the defence of the vessel.

"'We must be up and doing,' cried the captain, 'for ere long her shot will rake us easily. Are the small arms all loaded?'

"'Aye, aye, sir,' responded the second mate, who had had charge of that operation.

"Then distribute them at once. Let every man have his full allowance—cutlass, pistols, and carbine. Ah!—Mr. Jameson, will you take arms?'

"Half an hour had now passed from the time when the captain first called his men aft, and the pirate was now not over half-a-mile distant. My wife had been placed in a sort of cock-pit where the powder was stowed, and which was some feet below the water-line. It opened out from the forward part of the steerage, and was the safest part of the ship.

"At length, just as the captain was wondering why she did not fire, the pirate discharged another gun, and the ball ploughed up the water along under the larboard beam, sending the spray over the deck. In a moment more another was fired, and this time with more effect, for the shot struck the starboard stern davit, close into the rail, and shivered it in splinters; and though the flying pieces rained like

hail upon the deck, yet no one was injured. Of course the stern-boat now trailed one end in the water, but as the speed of the ship now amounted to but little it was left hanging there.

"Another gun quickly followed, and, as the ball came tearing through the lower studding sail, an exclamation of sudden interest broke from the captain's lips.

"'See!' he cried. 'She has now shown her colours!'

"All hands looked, and they saw, floating from the brig's mast's head, that dread ensign of sin and death—the BLACK FLAG.

"'Now he means to go at the work in earnest,' said the captain, as he started forward to where the spare arms stood against the fife-rail.

"'Let these be laid under the starboard rail,' he said, 'for, when we heave-to, it shall be on the larboard tack, and of course the pirate will round-to under our lee. Now stand by. Look to your priming. Be ready for my orders.'

"Another and another gun from the brig proved that it would be dangerous any longer to stand on, for she was now so near that she could send her shot with some degree of accuracy. So the captain gave the order for bringing the ship to the wind with the main-topsail to the mast. The studding sails were taken off, the courses clewed up, and then the ship brought to the wind with only the fore and mizzen yards braced up.

"'Now stand by,' cried the young captain. 'Twelve of you lie here under the taffrail, for you will have one good shot from here. The rest of you lie low beneath the starboard rail, and have your pieces ready. Remember you have eight spare carbines. Have them handy, and be sure you know who is to fire them.'

"In a few moments it was arranged who should take the extra arms for a second shot, and also as to how they should pick their men, so that no two should fire at the same person.

"'Look sharp, now. Stand by. Here she comes. Ah! you have a fine shot,' said the captain.

"As the young commander thus spoke, the brig had begun to luff up under the stern, and her men were all huddled together along her larboard rail. There were seventy-five of them at least, and they were dark evil-looking fellows.

"'Now,' cried the captain, 'cock your pieces.'

"'Ship ahoy!' at this moment came from the brig's deck.

"'Up, and fire!' uttered the captain, paying no attention to the hail.

"At the word, the twelve men below the taffrail leaped up, and, with a quick but sure aim, they fired. The pirate was under too much headway to change her course now, and before her crew could make any movement towards overcoming a repetition of this, to them, unexpected movement she was fairly under the ship's quarter. Had she had men in her tops, the pirates might have noticed the disposition of their opponent; but that precaution was overlooked.

"'Up again—fire!' uttered the captain.

"This time there were twenty-six carbines loaded, and eighteen of them were fired with telling effect.

"'Fire the others!' shouted the captain.

"Those who had been selected to fire the remaining pieces were prompt at the work; and by the time they were discharged the twelve men who had first fired had reloaded theirs; and, at a word from their commander, they gave the enemy their contents.

"By this time the ship's crew had become nerved

up to the work before them, and were really eager for the fray. And it came quickly enough. As near as could be judged, about twenty men had been either killed or disabled by the fifty-two shots which had been fired; so that the odds were somewhat reduced, for not a man had yet been harmed on board the ship. The pirates seemed nourishing their revenge until they could gain the deck of their coveted prize, for, as they came alongside and threw their grapplings, they held their cutlasses between their teeth, and their pistols in their hands. As the word came from the pirate commander to board, Wilson started to the rail.

"'Pistols now!' he cried. 'Let every shot tell. Take them as they come. Now!'

"And now the work commenced. For a moment more our men had the advantage; their pistols were discharged, save the extra ones, which were held in reserve by the coolest men of the crew; a score more of the dogs were shot down; and then the conflict came hand to hand. The pirates, to the number of some five-and-thirty, had gained the deck, and with curses loud and deep they went at their fell work. But they had to deal with stout men—with men who feared no open foe, and who now fought for life.

"I grasped my cutlass firmly in my hand, and, with a prayer to God to sustain the right, sprang forward to the conflict. I had once been accounted an excellent swordsman, and I proved now that I had not forgotten my cunning. Within the first half minute two pirates fell beneath my trenchant blade; and on the next moment I struck open the head of one who had just placed the muzzle of a pistol to the captain's head. In an instant more the youthful commander would have been a dead man—he knew it—he saw the movement, but an antagonist in front claimed his whole attention. He saw, too, just as he had given up the last hope of life, my descending blade.

"'God bless you!' he ejaculated; and then he went at the work again.

"The conflict upon the ship's deck had lasted now about ten minutes, and the dead were thickly strewn around. The pirate captain, a huge dark-faced Spaniard, had made his way to the poop, when his eye caught a small silken mantle which lay close by the companion way.

"'Ha!' he cried, 'there are women on board. Ha, ha, ha!—we'll gain a double prize here. By heavens! I'll see what we have below.'

"'Back, villain!' I shouted, springing forward with uplifted cutlass. 'Back, I say!'

"'Ha!—do you think to thwart me? Take that!'

"He aimed a furious blow as he spoke—but he was mistaken in his man; yet he would have quickly overcome me had not Wilson sprang to my rescue. Twice the pirate chieftain's heavy blade was knocked down, and then two more pirates rushed to the scene. They had heard the cry of 'women on board,' and they were eager for the prize. They were both officers. In an instant they engaged the young captain, and thus I was left again with the giant chieftain to deal with.

"Captain Wilson was soon knocked down, and a cutlass was at his heart. He uttered a quick prayer, and then closed his eyes. In the meantime my cutlass had been broken off close to the hilt, and, with a fierce oath, the stout pirate caught me by the throat, and bent me back.

"'Now die!' the fierce chieftain hissed.

"The name of Mary and of God dwelt on my lips in prayer, and then I bowed my head.

"At that moment a wild shriek smote upon my ears, and, opening my eyes, I saw my beloved Mary standing between me and the fierce pirate. A pistol was in her hand; and, as I pronounced her name, the loud report of the weapon drowned my voice, and a pirate, who stood by his captain's side, fell, with a groan, to the deck.

"She had missed her aim: that ball was intended for him whose sword was at my throat.

"The pirates now swarmed on to the deck of our cabin, and our brave captain was pierced by a dozen sabres.

"The pirates had made themselves masters of the ship, and poor Mary had fallen into their hands.

"Heavens!" continued the narrator—"the recollection of that time almost drives me to madness. Suffice it to say I was made prisoner; and Mary, my new-made wife. Oh! God—never shall I forget her shrieks as she called upon me to save her from the fearful doom to which the pirate condemned her. Bound hand and foot, I was powerless to aid her. Oh! boy, you cannot know the agony of that time—God forbid you should ever know it! Let me hurry to the end of my story; for the recolletion drives me mad. Mary fell—fell! And I was powerless to save her! When the wretch had satiated his hellish passion, she escaped from his arms, and flew to the deck. I saw her lovely form, and heard her wild cry of madness, as she leaped over the bulwarks into the sea. I saw the looks of the pirates, as they gazed upon her sinking form; and I tore asunder the bands which held me.

"I was free—free—but I was mad. I rushed to the cabin; I saw him—the fell destroyer of my wife—and I clutched him by the throat. We struggled; but a giant's strength was in my arm. I saw his tongue protrude from his mouth; and his eyes, fast covering with the film of death, starting from their sockets. I felt his grip relax, and, with a loud maniacal laugh, I hurled him a corpse to the floor.

"Poor Mary!—she was avenged.

"I flew up the companion to the deck. The pirates strove to bar my passage; but I struck them down, and fled to the side. With one bound I cleared the bulwarks, and the next moment the cool waters had closed around me.

"I know not what happened after; but the next day I awoke to consciousness and misery, on the rocks which encircle the small bay, a short distance from here, and by which you descended to this spot.

"From that time I have remained here; and here I trust I shall die. The wild solitude of this place is more congenial to my spirits than would be the life and bustle of the city; for here I can nurse my grief for the loss of her whom I so fondly loved."

———

THE STORM—FATE OF "THE VENOMED SNAKE."

THE storm was fast rising, and the rain commenced to descend in torrents, whilst at short intervals lurid flashes of forked lightning, followed instantaneously by loud peals of thunder, lit up the now white-topped waves with a phosphorescent glare.

The sea now appeared like a huge boiling cauldron, and dashed its spray high up in mad fury, forming as it were a dense mist around the smuggler bark.

The sails which had been taken back were now furled and made taut, and not a stitch of canvas was left exposed for the wind to take hold of, and the "Venomed Snake" rode upon the bosom of the angry waters under bare poles.

The anxious eyes of the seamen on board that disreputable bark were casting their gaze in the direction of the island, in expectant hope of the return of the boat sent off to bring the captain aboard.

But all in vain.

Those now on board the smuggler knew little or nothing of the management of the ship, for in the absence of their captain and his lieutenant, Black Bill, not one could navigate her through the storm.

The Boy Rover had never striven to make his men acquainted with the practical rudiments of navigation; he considered it better that they should remain in ignorance of this art: all that he required of them was that they should be well versed in the mechanical labours and obey the orders given by himself and his next in command. He felt it would never do to make them as well informed as himself, for fear that their desperate natures should lead them to rebel against him at any opportunity.

But whilst they remained the mere machines of his will he felt comparatively safe—for should they throw off his authority, there was not one amongst them who could take the command.

Under these circumstances those now on board the "Venomed Snake" were placed at their wits ends how to act, and like most degraded and ruthless natures they were unequal to any task that demanded coolness and judgment.

They stood with blanched faces gazing upon the furious elements, and the distant rocks, but the longer they gazed the more discomfitted they became.

Various were the surmises to which they gave utterance respecting the boats and their crews which had gone to the island—what had become of Black Bill and Jem Wilton, and why the signal had been fired for the second boat.

They guessed that something was wrong, but what that was they were at a loss to imagine.

Through the thick mist, which now almost hid the towering cliffs from their view, they imagined that they saw a boat come from the bay. They strained their eyes towards it, but it was gone; and shortly afterwards they imagined they saw the form of a man standing, as it were, on the waters, waving something above his head. But, ere they could make certain whether they were right or wrong, the figure had disappeared, and nothing but the dense mist caused by the waves dashing in their fury against the rocks met their strained eyes.

Every instant the storm gathered in fury, and the vessel groaned and creaked, pitched and tossed, like some huge monster in agony, upon the bosom of the waters.

"With a majestic sweep, she rose on to the top of the white, foaming, boiling crests; then down into the vortex, with a wall of waters around, and the billows sweeping over her decks, and carrying away every moveable thing in their course, backwards to the boiling ocean.

The men clung to the rigging and the bulwarks, with fear and trembling, and cursed in their hearts the mad infatuation of their captain for the girl, which had led to his absence from the ship at such a time of danger.

Too well they knew that, if the storm did not abate, they must look forward to a fate of horrible suffering.

Should she go to pieces, which, in their ignorance of her management, was more than probable, they could entertain no hopes of escape from a watery grave; for not a single boat was left them; and to live in such a sea, and swim to the shore was impossible.

They were now having a taste of the misery endured by those their base wickedness had often brought about by the false light from their rocky rendezvous: they were now feeling those pangs they had inflicted upon others.

But the wicked are ever the greatest cowards at heart; and those men whose souls had never felt one grain of pity for the sufferings of their victims, now prayed to Him whose laws they had outraged, and whose dictates they had defied, for that mercy which they had denied to their fellow-creatures.

A flash of lightning, so lurid in its intensity that for a moment it blinded with its intense glare the eyes of the seamen, poured its electric fluid down upon the foremast of the smuggler, and, in a moment, her yards shot up a flame, and the mast fell, charred and burnt, with a fearful crash.

A cry of horror escaped the lips of the sailors, and they stood paralysed, gazing upon the flaming mass.

Then a voice rang out:

"Cut away—clear her—or we are lost!"

These words, uttered by one more cool and calm than the rest, broke the stupor into which the others were fallen; and, seizing the hatchets, knives, or cutlasses, whichever were nearest at hand, they set to with a will to clear the ship of the burning mast.

With frantic nervousness, they succeeded in freeing the mast; and it went over the side, and disappeared in the sea, with a hissing sound; and the hull, which had been borne down till her bulwarks lay almost upon the billows, rose upwards with difficulty, shivered from stem to stern; then righted herself again.

But the wind swept over her, and bore her towards the cliffs which bounded the island on which our hero lay wounded; and the wild waves dashed her forward, and seemed to sport in her agony.

At the mercy of the wind and waves, the "Venomed Snake" now rode a helpless log upon the foaming sea.

And her disreputable crew, with throbbing hearts, and cheeks blanched to the pallor of death, clung to the rigging, and prayed for succour.

Oh, thou who in the hour of health and happiness despise the laws and neglect the dictates of the Most High—you, who in the time of prosperity deign not to bend the knee to him who has made the world, rest thou assured that should sickness or adversity overtake you, that your thoughts will fly to him for aid and succour—you, who affect to despise the warnings he has given, will plead to him for mercy—to him whom you have insulted—to him whose power you have trifled with — whose commandments you have refused to obey.

Like the prodigal son, man arises and goes to his father when all else deserts him—seeks life at the footstool of him whom he sets at defiance.

So it was with that bad crew—men whose hands were embrued in the blood of innocence—whose souls were stained by crimes black as midnight—whose deeds had stamped them as outcasts from society, and made them loathsome to humanity, and to heaven!

But still the ship was dashed hither and thither, and still the the tempest burst over it with fearful violence.

ATTEMPT TO FRUSTRATE THE ESCAPE OF HENRY AND ELLEN.

Her timbers groaned and creaked, and her masts shivered like laths shaken in the hands of strong men.

Nearer and nearer to that line of rocks drifted the now helpless hull, and nearer and nearer to destruction floated the demon-hearted crew of that blood-stained bark.

On, on, she went creaking, rolling, groaning, rising, and falling—on, on, propelled by the will of One greater than man—on to destruction—to death.

And the lightning flashed, and the thunder rolled, lighting up the pale faces and striking terror to the hearts of the smuggler crew.

And the waves danced and gambled, and roared in mockery at their sufferings, sweeping over them in derision and giving them a foretaste of their power.

Her guns broke from their fastenings and rolled along her decks with every lurch she made, striking the men in their course and hurling them down in their passage.

The water was gaining in her hold, for she had sprung a leak.

The men strove to man the pumps, but they became choked, and the water rose higher and higher whilst the once trim ship settled lower and lower in the sea.

Flash followed flash—peal followed peal—gust followed gust, and nearer and nearer loomed the dark rocks on the coast.

A long line of breakers foamed and hissed before them, but they were powerless to ease her off from the shore; and they foamed and splashed and roared in mad glee as they swept over the sunken rocks.

Maddened with the fear of death and lost to all control, the smugglers staved in the casks and poured down their parched throats the fiery liquid in the hope that it would drown their sufferings; but it only made them mad, and they ran hither and thither in their drunken and maddened fury—swearing and praying alternately.

One moment sinking upon their knees and appealing for help, the next venting curses loud and deep against the storm and He who raised it.

She had drifted into the white foaming line of breakers, and was lifted high then dashed down again into their midst; there was a loud crash, a fearful cry, a flashing of a thousand lights before the eyes of the seamen, a hissing sound, a sensation of giddiness and suffocation, and the wild waves closed over them.

A moment after they rose to the surface, and were dashed again upon the sharp rocks; a misty foam encircled them like a huge sheet, and the wild waters dashed them hither and thither in sportive glee.

A loud, piercing shriek rose above the roar of the waves, and, clinging with frantic desperation to a portion of the wreck, Wild Madge drifted out from the shore to the open seas.

And high up on the cliff sat the Boy Rover and his two companions, drenched to the skin, watching with painful intensity the fate of his vessel, powerless to stretch forth a hand to save her, and without the means of issuing those orders which had carried her through many a storm.

And lower down the cliff, hidden behind the projection of the rock, Black Bill and Jem Sparks were witnesses to the sad end of the smuggler in which they had sailed for many a voyage, and grateful to think they were not on board.

And in the hut of the stranger, Henry lay listening to the storm and praying for the safety of Ellen and his friend: his mind worried by anxiety for their fate, and his eye gazing thoughtfully upon space as he conjured up imaginary scenes and adventures they might have to pass through. And, with a look of pity, the stranger sat beside the couch of the wounded youth, ministering to his wants and sighing ever and anon as his mind reverted to the fate of his much-loved wife.

CHAPTER XL.

SAD NEWS—MASTER AND SERVANT—THE DEPARTURE FOR ENGLAND.

IN a prettily furnished apartment, some two months from the date of our opening chapter, sat a gentleman of about forty years of age; a newspaper lay open before him, upon which his eyes were fixed with a vacant and painful stare.

He had laid it from his hand as though it had stung him, for in one of its columns he had read the announcement that . . . had been wrecked upon the coast of Cornwall, and all hands lost.

His face was deathly pale, his hands trembled, and his lips quivered, as though he were a prey to some fearful emotion.

After a few moments he raised the paper and again read the article, then heaving a heavy sigh, he placed it again upon the table, and folding his hands, murmured—

"Thy will be done."

Then, bowing his head upon his hands, his whole body became convulsed by the power of his grief.

"Heaven seems to shower down affliction upon me!" he murmured. "My poor girl lost and her lover too, and both so young—cut off when Heaven was showering down happiness upon them. But, alas! life is but a chequered board, and sunshine and showers go side by side."

There was a knock at the door, and, restraining his grief, the gentleman raised his head and said—

"Come in!"

A servant entered the apartment bearing in his hand a letter.

"A letter, sir," said the man.

"A letter," iterated the gentleman holding forth his hand—"for me?"

"Yes, sir," said the man, surprised at the remark as his master was in the habit of receiving many letters daily—"yes, sir, for you: it is addressed to Mr. Joseph Hanfield."

"Yes, yes," replied Mr. Hanfield, hastily, "my mind was wandering."

"You do not look well, sir," said the man, who was an old and faithful domestic.

"No, Jacob, I have had bad news there!" and Mr. Hanfield pointed to the paper which lie before him

"Bad news, sir?"

"Yes."

"Not of—"

"The ship in which Ellen sailed for England!"

"Surely, she arrived safe?"

"No," sighed his master.

"What has happened?" said Jacob with anxiety, for he had nursed Ellen when a child and felt as much affection for her as her parent.

"She is lost!"

"Lost!" said Jacob, letting the letter fall from his hand upon the carpet, and opening his eyes till their lids could extend no further.

"Yes, Jacob," sighed his master.

"Lost!" iterated Jacob.

"Yes, Jacob—lost!"

"How, sir?"

"Supposed to have been wrecked upon the coast of Cornwall."

"And Miss Ellen?" eagerly asked the man.

"Drowned!" said his master, as a tear rose to his eye and twinkled slowly down his cheek.

"And—and—"

"Charles Lawson?"

"Yes, sir."

"Lost, too."

"But, sir, are you sure?" inquired the faithful domestic.

"There can be no doubt of it; portions of the wreck were washed ashore the morning after a storm, but no bodies were discovered."

"But, sir, they may yet live: they may have taken to the boats—they may yet be safe."

"Alas, Jacob, I fear not, if the account of the storm which broke over the coast on that night can be relied on, no boat could have lived in such a sea."

And, overwhelmed by the violence of his emotions, Mr. Hanfield bowed his head and wept.

Aye, reader, wept! The heart of the true man was overcharged with grief at the fate of his child; and he wept tears that relieved the overcharged breast—tears that proclaimed that nature, as the Almighty formed it, sensitive, feeling, and true.

Let those who have never known what it is to

feel the loss of near and dear friends and relatives jeer at the idea of a strong man weeping; let them class him as one lost to all that should proclaim he had thrown away childhood's grief; let them deride the sorrow, and laugh to scorn the weakness: but still let them say he was a man—having man's instincts, man's feelings, and man's nature: for the man that cannot grieve for the loss of those who were once dear to him is no longer worthy the name he would bear, and a thing to be despised by those who would show to the world that manhood embraces those qualites of the heart which raise him above the brute.

Can tears degrade man, when even Jesus wept?

"Give not way thus, sir," said Jacob, commiseratingly. "Hope for the best."

'Twould be hope in vain."

"Perhaps not, sir: nothing is impossible."

".But improbable, Jacob."

"Not so, sir: a boat sometimes lives when even the ship goes down."

"Heaven grant it may be so; but I dare not hope. But the letter, Jacob—I had forgotten that."

"And so had I, sir," said the domestic. stooping and lifting it from the floor. Here it is, sir."

Mr. Hanfield took the letter in his hand, and, turning it round, gazed upon the post-mark.

Jacob turned to go.

"Stay," said his master.

The man withdrew a few paces, and remained watching the countenance of his master as he opened and read the letter.

Mr. Hanfield perused the missive; then laid it upon the table.

"Jacob," he said, at length, "I dare not hope ever again to gaze upon the features of my daughter or Charles Lawson. This letter is from the mother of Charles, bewailing the loss of her son, and making me acquainted with the facts of the wreck."

"But, sir, is she certain of their deaths?"

"Can she entertain a doubt?"

"Perhaps not: but still can she be certain they are no more?"

"No, we can but look upon the chances of life and death; and the chances are many to one."

"True, sir; but still the one may gain the prize."

"Jacob," said Mr. Hanfield, rising from his chair, "I know you would save me the pain of her loss; but I am as sure that you believe in the fate of my child and her lover, as well as I do. Your feeling heart would prompt you to ease my aching heart; but I am not to be misled from facts, which point too surely at their destruction. I have sorrow enough, Heaven knows, of my own; but this poor widow, Mrs. Lawson, has lost even more than me: she has lost her son—the prop of her declining years. I cannot bring him back; but I may sooth her suffering at his loss. I will away to England to-morrow."

"To-morrow, sir!" said Jacob, in surprise.

"Yes, to-morrow. Have everything that is necessary for a hurried journey in readiness. You will accompany me?"

"To the end of the world, sir."

"A vessel leaves to-morrow, I believe."

"Yes, sir."

"Then see that all is in readiness."

"It shall be done."

The man left the apartment; and Mr. Hanfield, drawing his writing-desk to him, commenced writing. This he continued for some time; and, after indicting several letters, rose and retired for the night.

The morning after broke bright and beautiful, and Mr. Hanfield rose from his couch at an early hour, but early as it was he found his faithful domestic already stirring.

Jacob had packed up everything for the journey, and had learned the exact time the vessel intended to weigh anchor and set sail for England.

Having seen that everything was left in good order for his departure, Mr. Hanfield sat down to his breakfast attended by the faithful Jacob.

"We must be abroad before noon said you not, Jacob?"

"Yes, sir, the captain says he must be out of the offing by then."

"And everything is ready?"

"Everything is on board."

"That is well. If we have favouring winds we shall soon get to our destination; but so thought Ellen."

"The weather is fair, sir, and the wind in the right quarter," said Jacob, anxious to turn his master's thoughts from the channel into which they were drifting.

"Aye—but they may change."

Jacob made no remark to this.

"A vessel never started under brighter auspices than did the one in which Ellen sailed," continued Mr. Hanfield, "and yet the storm rose, and—and——"

The poor gentleman heaved a sigh, and his eye became moist as his voice faltered.

"There, there," said Mr. Hanfield, "'tis useless to regret. Now, Jacob, get ready."

And Jacob, glad to escape and wishing to leave his employer to his grief, left the apartment.

An hour later they were on a small brig bound for England; the anchor was weighed, the sails unfurled, and the breeze bellying the canvass, she glided out from the bay into the sparkling ocean, and, bidding farewell to the rock-bound and impregnable shores of Gibralter, sailed with a fair wind and favouring gale for the white cliffs of old England.

CHAPTER XLI.

HORRIBLE SUFFERINGS OF THE SMUGGLER CREW.

THE run rose fiery red, throwing its sickening glare on the turbulent sea that had engulphed the ill-fated vessel that had battled with it so long.

The wind, no longer rough and boisterous, moaned over the crested waves as they rolled onward, as if sighing over the lost and drowned mariner.

Mingled with the voice of the wind, sounds apparently human could be distinguished.

They were sounds of distress.

On a sand-bank lay huddled together some twenty beings. They were all that remained of the crew of the wrecked vessel. A merciful fate had rescued them from immediate death and cast them on to the soft sand of the treacherous shoals that had destroyed their ship.

As the sun rose higher in the heavens, and his genial warmth fell soothingly and healingly on the benumbed and bruised limbs of the wretched men, they one by one shook off the misery that weighed them down and looked about to see how best to improve their fortune.

The sea still came in with what is termed a heavy swell, though the tide was descending, and pieces of the wreck were occasionally washed towards the bank on which the men were grouped. Sometimes a cask or hencoop or chest would surge towards them, and, gathering up their enfeebled strength, they would rush up to their breasts in the foaming surf to bring it to shore.

Shore,—what mockery in the sound! a ridge of sand, not a vestage of anything living on it, vegetable or animal. Though, by the nature of it, they concluded that they could not be far from some mainland; but the spray and height of the waves would not as yet permit any further view than that of the ocean to be visible.

In a few hours they had recovered a great quantity of store from the wreck: several casks of water and rum, one of pork and another of biscuits, spars and rope and planks were all obtained. Then the sea settled down into a calm mood, yet the wind still blew steadily from the south east.

There were twenty in all—poor half-naked wretches who felt, in spite of present safety, that the doom of sin hung over them; however, they attempted to put the best face on the matter they could. They dried their clothes in the sun, and refreshed themselves with the refreshment that had been spared them.

Suddenly they discovered that the tide had turned and was rapidly rising. What if the bark was covered at high water, what would become of them?

Fear and despair filled some of them, but the rest, brave to the last, set themselves in sullen dogged silence to prepare for the worst.

While there's life there's hope! Who will yield up existence to death while a chance remain.

Silently and rapidly the spars and planks, that could be got together, were lashed and formed into a raft. It was finished, and the stores of provision were about to be placed on it, when a fearful cry burst from them, as the rising water showed them too plainly that they were on a quicksand.

In an instant the raft was afloat, and the men scrambled hurriedly and desperately on to it. On came the water, the sand was a moving mass; the men were up to their waste that last clutched hold of the raft.

Help! help!

It was too late; the weight of sand pressing round their bodies was too much.

Down, down, they went, their despairing shrieks smothered by the choking sand.

So perished two of the doomed twenty.

Speechless and horrified, the remainder found themselves afloat on the treacherous element again. But, alas! how much more fearful was the prospect before them now.

Of all the provision, they had only succeeded in rescuing the cask of rum and the barrel of pork.

Hours passed, and they gazed on each other in mute despair.

At last the night came, and with the darkness the gale recovered its fury, dashing the frail raft in scorn over the billows. The sea incessantly dashed over the poor wretches who, laying down clinging to the spars lest they should be washed off, were almost perished with cold and exposure.

Another day broke, but the storm had not abated.

Those on the raft, almost dead from fatigue and hunger (for they dared not moved lest the waves should carry them off), saw with dismay that there remained but fourteen of them.

In the darkness of night four more had disappeared.

The wind abated, the waves moved more sluggishly, the raft more steadily.

Wearily, one by one arose, and sat, in mute despair, looking at each other.

Then their gaze went wistfully round the horizon.

Not a ship, not a spot, was to be seen. Sky and water everywhere.

The gale had driven them far, far away. They had no idea on what part of the globe they were. Yet a growing warmth seemed to suggest to them that they must be drifting towards the tropics.

And now their agonies increased tenfold. Thirst, burning thirst, has laid its fiend-like touch upon their throats.

Some drink the rum, and madness scorches and fires their brain; others eat the pork. Oh! mockery, mockery. Salt food and salt water are abundant.

The sun now shines down with glaring heat; the wind has completely ceased.

They are becalmed.

Another day—the third—and still the breezeless air, and the glaring sun. The rum has gone; for some more thoughtful hand pushed it over into the stagnant sea.

Starvation and thirst had begun their work: gaunt haggard faces, with eyes like coals, glaring from beneath bushy eyebrows, showed how deep the silent agony was within.

And, to add to the horrors of their situation, they were covered with disgusting wounds and sores, caused by the action of the briny waters on their debilitated frames; while the sun, scorching into them, caused them acute anguish.

The stench, too, became frightful—for the sea teemed with life; and the cask of pork was, also, in a state of fearful corruption: but none could remove it—their strength was gone.

And now one by one drooped and died; and their bodies lay festering in the mocking sun.

The fourth day dawned, and seven alone remained, whose eyes alone told that they still lived. Around them lay the hideous corpses of their messmates; and, beyond, the hideous sea.

Who that looked on them could believe them human?—for in their eyes came that mysterious light that is seen only in the tiger thirsting for blood, and ready to spring.

The thought of cannibalism was suggesting itself to them. No word had been spoken: but they understood it too well.

Ravenously stole their looks over each other, as if seeking the best victim.

At last one, in a hoarse whisper, exclaimed:

"Cast lots!"

A slight shudder passed through them at the sound of a human voice.

"Yes," murmured some. Others nodded their assent—too weak even to speak.

The lot fell on the strongest and biggest of the party.

One of them, with a clasp knife clutched in his feeble fingers, attempted to reach him. Crawling painfully towards him, he was about to plunge the steel into the wretch's bosom.

With a yell of fear, the intended victim grasped hold of the uplifted arm. A terrible struggle ensued—terrible, because of their utter prostration of strength.

Strange that, while enduring such suffering and misery, men should cling to that life whose prolongation can but enhance what they already endure!

But with the unfortunate wretches, whose sufferings we have attempted to describe, change was imminent.

The long struggle with nature was over.

Utterly cast down, and worn out with their horrible sufferings, they sank into a kind of stupor.

As in a dream, they lost all consciousness of the surrounding scene; and through their fervid and over-wrought brain passed, in panoramic view, their lives' histories.

Innocent childhood, school days, youth, the first thrill of young love, all were again brought wildly to the memory.

But next came the vision of the first fall of nature, step by step they stride through the long vista of crime.

The dream is ended. Insensible to suffering they lay inanimate across the raft.

Together they rolled. Their hands tearing the rotten flesh from each others' bones. The struggle was brief; the raft swayed with their movements, and helplessly they fell over into the becalmed sea.

Now that five were left, their situation seemed to become more and more awful.

They drew no more lots, but with fear and hate glared at each other; each dreaded that the other would murder him for his blood, and the night passed with eyes wakeful and watchful.

They dared not sleep.

Exhausted and famished, thirsty and fevered, they might have found sweet oblivion a merciful sleep. But, alas!—

They dared not sleep!

Hours passed on, yet still the scene remained unchanged.

Night again threw her mantle o'er the earth, and the red-hot sun, discomfited, retires. The long stagnant waters gradually seem disturbed, at last a faint ripple appears on the surface, another moment the breeze so long withheld speeds past.

The calm is over.

Once more the raft is in motion, but its occupants are unconscious of it.

All through the night the breeze continued gradually freshening till it almost reached a gale, and ere the morning light broke forth the raft had drifted many miles.

IT was morning. A dozen canoes were rapidly propelled in every direction through the smooth waters of a beautiful bay.

Suddenly they espy something on the ocean beyond.

Wind and water together bring the object closer. It nears the breakers—it is lost amid the boiling surf; another moment and it appears again. It is past the bar, it is in smooth water.

Away sped each canoe towards the floating object, and lo! it was a raft freighted with stores for a charnel house.

Astonished, they were about to drag it ashore, but the sickening view and intolerable stench was too much for even savages.

But a slight movement of one of the bodies prompted them to examine and ascertain if any were alive.

They soon discovered some that still breathed, the remainder were passed human help.

Abandoning the raft and its horrible burden to the waves, they bore the four insensible ones to the shore.

On all sides lay extended a most beautiful country. The shore, covered with verdure to the water-edge, sloped gradually for some miles inland till it reached a chain of hills whose tops and sides were black with the dense foliage of the forest, such forests as only Africa can produce.

It was to the shores of Western Africa that the raft had drifted.

The tribe, into whose hands the rescued smugglers had fallen, were not so savage as their neighbours. Their occupations were principally fishing and hunting, the produce of which formed the principal staple of their support; consequently the starved and diseased men were carefully removed.

But days passed ere they could be considered out of danger, and, their being gaunt and careworn, they seemed but the ghost of their former selves; but the lineaments of their faces was the most striking result of their sufferings. There lay the deep furrows that told of mental agony, which would last till the grave closed over all.

All that could please and delight the senses was in abundance at this beautiful spot, and for a time the smugglers enjoyed to the full their luxurious rest from fatigue and danger.

But, as they grew stronger, and the terrible episode they had passed through became more distant, the old love of adventure and change, so predominant in the English character, returned, and they sighed for the blue sea and their ship.

Here they had not room to breathe, they averred. The air was too close—too hot. And on land they could have no clear sailing.

Besides, the friendly natives, though treating them well, would on no account permit them to move unattended. Consequently, in spite of the kindness with which the natives overwhelmed them, they felt as prisoners.

Day after day this became more irksome to them, till at last they resolved to escape.

By dint of signs and a few monosyllables that they had learned by this time, they ascertained they were far from the reach of travellers or traders; but the natives pointing eastward would intimate that several days' journey in that direction white men were in the habit of trading with the warlike tribes that lived there.

All this sank deep into the memories of our smuggler friends, and by signs and whispers when unobserved they had mutually resolved to force their way in that direction, when they could make good their escape.

At last the opportunity presented itself.

There was a great and solemn assembling of the tribe to witness the punishment of two criminals.

The chief, or king, sat on an elevated platform formed of bamboos laid crossways on the top of others fixed in the ground, beside him, on either side, were the chief counsellors and officers of state (for these barbarians had all the traditions of sovereignty and state among their practices of daily life), these all stood in a semi-circle with heads uncovered; beyond, forming a great circle, were the the rest of the tribe, men, women, and children.

Presently, at a signal from the king, the culprits were brought forth.

It was a man and woman. The woman had been accused of unchastity, and the man with being the partner of her guilt.

In this little sovereignty there was no greater crime than inconstancy. The woman's husband had discovered the guilty parties, and their downcast looks and sullen silence too plainly convinced all that they were not innocent.

They knew their doom was death.

A murmur ran through the crowd when, after a brief trial, the king waved his hand.

It was the signal for Justice to do her duties.

The executioners then stepped forward and seized the woman by her arms: they dragged her towards a hole dug in the ground.

As her eyes fell upon it her terror mastered her firmness, and shriek after shriek burst from her lips.

Raising her in their strong arms they lifted her into the hole, the depth of which was sufficient to leave only her head and neck visible.

They then proceeded to throw in the earth, and, trampling it down, fixed the unfortunate woman in her living tomb.

She was buried alive as high as her armpits, and was doomed to perish by starvation.

Smith, Hardy, Tom Lary, and Bond, looked on in speechless horror.

But the worst was to come.

The male culprit was doomed to died a violent death; but, by a species of refinement in cruelty, the woman was to witness it ere her own death released her.

The executioners seized him and placed him before the woman.

They then stripped off what little covering he had on him.

A dead silence prevailed, only interrupted by the moans of the woman, who, closing her eyes, strove to shut out the horrible view from her sight; yet, from some impulse, she would sometimes open them again as if prompted by curiosity.

The executioners then proceeded to fasten two stout and long cords, made of the long grass, to his ankles. Then, throwing him on his back, they called to the people, who, with a shout, rush forward, and a hundred hands grasp hold of the two ropes in opposite directions, and, pulling it with all their might, the wretch's legs are dragged asunder.

The bones crack; the sinews can be seen, like overstrained cords, through his flesh.

The drops of agony lay like beads on his forehead.

More hands clutch at the rope, and with fierce yells of excitement the people tug.

A thrilling shriek bursts from the tortured wretch as his body sinks lifeless to the ground.

But he is not dead. The native's "Medicine" steps forward, and, applying some remedy, and muttering a charm, the poor victim soon reawakens to his misery.

With fresh shouts, the people again pull at the ropes.

This time the culprit does not cry out. His eyes are open beyond their usual extent, and he gazes on all around as if it were but a dream.

Another shout, a run, a confusion of voices, a cry of horror—and, the next moment, some scores of natives are seen tumbling to the ground, over each other, while the ropes are seen flying through the air.

"Good God!" cries Bond—"they have torn his legs out."

"The Lord preserve us!" whispered Hardy. "So they have—the heathenish brutes."

"And that poor cretur, in that ere hole, looking on, too!" said Smith.

"I can't stand this arter to-day," quietly, yet determinedly, said Tom Lang.

It was too true. The legless trunk of the culprit fell, freed from the rope, to the ground. The blood gushed in torrents from the ragged sockets—splashing into the eyes and mouth of the poor buried woman.

In a few moments life was extinct, and the people slowly dispersed, leaving the woman to her fearful death, with the certainty that when darkness came, with it would troop from the neighbouring forests the savage beasts of prey, who would soon end her suffering in this world.

———

CHAPTER XLII.

THE SMUGGLERS DETERMINE TO ESCAPE — THEY RESCUE THE WOMAN BURIED ALIVE — THE FLIGHT.

THAT night, owing to the excitement prevailing in the village, consequent upon the events that had occurred—as related in the last chapter—the four sailors met in secret, to discuss the means and chances of escape.

They met first on the verge of the forest, which lay about half-a-mile from the part of the village where they were located. Though fearful of discovery, still they did not dare to penetrate further into the forest; for the roar of wild beasts was borne on the breeze towards them; and, having no manner of arms with which to defend themselves in case of attack, they stayed without.

The stars shone bright and beautiful—more so than in this Northern clime—and the fire-flies darted about, adding their light to the aid of our plotters, as well as the stars.

A thousand delicious scents perfumed the air; while, beyond, the glistening crest of the waves, dancing, and reflecting the firmament, lent enchantment to the view.

But it had no charms for them. They sighed for freedom; aye, even though it is beneath the sway of a tyrant captain—a fiend, in boyhood's form.

"Mates, we must leave this place," said Bond.

"Aye, aye: but how?" said Hardy.

"Blast me, if I know how!—but go we must." Smith and Lang remained silent.

"Suppose we start now," urged Bond, "and cut across the country, in the direction of the nigger country."

"What! without arms; and these infernal wild beast yelling and howling round us?" said Hardy. "Why, we will all be torn in pieces."

"Better that, than live here all our lives."

"Aye—you didn't say 'better die' while on that cursed raft though!"

An unpleasant feeling crept over all at the mention of that unlucky voyage, and for a moment or so all remained silent; at last Smith spoke.

"I have it," said he, as if a brilliant thought had struck him, "I have it!"

"What is it?" exclaimed the rest.

"Why, suppose we go and rescue that poor woman from that ere grave they've put her in."

"Ah!—well?"

"Well, then, out of gratitude to us, she'll stick to us like a leech, I'm thinking."

"Well?"

"And then, don't you see, she may be useful in aiding us to escape."

"A good idea that, though," said Bond.

"Then let's act upon it," said Lang.

"Agreed," said the other three; "but when shall we begin?"

"Now," said Lang. "No time like the present."

Silently and stealthily they moved towards the village, and arriving at the open space where the execution had taken place they proceeded to reconnoitre.

All appeared still and calm.

The villagers had gone, tired with their revels, to repose.

A faint moan reached their ears, which they had no difficulty in recognising as that of the unfortunate woman's, whose release they were bent on accomplishing.

Guided by the sound they soon reached her side.

It was some time ere they could make it plain to her what they had come about, the poor half-crazed creature believed at first they only came to add to her torture.

But when she could comprehend the purpose of their intention she looked ready to eat them, so great was the revulsion of feeling within her, from deepest despair to hope—hope and life.

It was a work of some difficulty to extricate her, but eventually they succeeded by scooping the earth out with their hands in dragging her forth.

But the long and painful position she had been fixed in, together with the weight of earth, had deprived her limbs of all sensation and power for a time, and she seemed more like one paralysed.

There was no time for ceremony or modesty, so Lang and Smith commenced rubbing her limbs till the blood circulated again in their proper channels.

Bond and Hardy laughed to see their comrades engaged in such tender office.

But they continued their efforts, nevertheless, and, in a few minutes, the rescued woman recovered her usual strength and agility.

They then turned towards the forest and rapidly moved away, the woman acting as guide.

As soon as they again reached the forest the sound that indicated the vicinity of wild beast smote their ears, and again reminded them that they were without arms. They explained this to the woman, who, for a time, appeared buried in thought.

Then starting as if an idea had suddenly occurred to her, she darted off back to the village.

An interval of brief suspense followed. Presently the woman returned bearing in her hands a spear and three heavy clubs, which she had taken from the sides of the sleeping owners in the first hut she came to.

Hope filled the hearts of the seamen as each grasped the weapon offered him, and with less of fear they plunged into the recesses of an African forest.

They had not gone far before they discovered that their progress was not only slow but dangerous, by reason of the dense undergrowth that covered the ground. Day and night were the same in those eternal solitudes; path there was none, and but for the woman who accompanied them, they would ere this have lost all idea of the direction in which they had intended to travel.

After some hours spent in this manner accompanied with numerous alarms, as some panther or jaguar would dash by them trampling and crushing through the bushes, they came to a halt.

Tired and fatigued they desired to rest, but the woman urged them forward by gesticulations expressive of fear of pursuit; besides, she well knew in that terrible climate, away from the sea coast, that death rode rampant over mankind, and life in an African forest would soon end in fever and death.

Bravely they went on in silence and with abated breath.

Morning came; but faint indeed was the light in the forest. The howls of wild beasts gave place to the chatter of monkeys and paroquets, the hiss of serpents to the calls of the gaily coloured feathered birds to their mates.

They now stopped, and, throwing themselves on the ground, waited while the woman gathered some roots and berries for their repast: for food they had none but what the forest produced, and the woman's experience selected.

While the woman was thus occupied, the men, having more leisure now they were beyond pursuit, observed her more narrowly than they had hitherto done, and the result was that they began to think that she was comely enough to be the wife of one of them.

While thus debating within their own minds the appropriation of the dark frail one to their own private uses, the object of it returned with the gathered provision.

It needed no incentive to excite their appetites, fasting and fatigue had sufficiently deprived them of any repugnance they might have had for their coarse and primitive fare. Water they had none, but the woman produced a succulent kind of root which alleviated their thirst.

Having satisfied their demands of hunger, they laid down, and in a few minutes were buried in slumber.

Silent and sorrowful the woman sat a little apart, her thoughts were too painful to allow sleep to visit her eyes. She could not forget that the home of her childhood, friends, kindred, and country were behind her, and that never, never, could she behold it or them again.

Suddenly she started up, her quick ear had detected some sound. After listening a while her face changed from surprise to an expression of fear.

Louder and louder came the sound. Rushing across to her companions she screamed in their ears—

"Elephants! elephants!"

Hastily rising and seizing their clubs they prepared to defend themselves, against what they did not know, for on their first awakening they had not comprehended the woman's meaning. They had not much time for reflection, however, for the sounds were unmistakable.

It was the rush of hundreds of elephants fleeing through the forest.

On they came right in the direction of the spot where the party were resting.

They could not as yet see them, but the crackling of broken trees and the thunder of their hoofs on the ground showed plainly what they might expect if they stood in the way of these infuriated beasts.

For a time they had stood irresolute how to act; but awakened to a sense of their danger, by the warning voice of the women, they plunged in a contrary direction and never stopped till the sounds had become faint and distant.

This little adventure completely disconcerted their plans, and the woman was at a loss to direct them further for she knew not what part of the forest they had reached.

They were lost!

After some hours of fruitless wandering, endeavouring to discover the right direction, they sank down, overwhelmed with fatigue. After resting awhile, one of them suggested that they should ascend the loftiest tree they could see, and have a look-out.

Accordingly they clambered up a lofty tree that

reared its head a hundred and fifty feet high: and, having reached the topmost branch, they gazed around them. A sea of foliage met their eyes on all sides but one; and on that they beheld a vast lake.

No sooner do they espy it, than, rasing a shout of joy, they descend to the ground, and, communicating the fact to their guide, request her to lead them towards these waters.

She shook her head; but, nevertheless, went in the direction indicated, followed by the men.

Night fell around them, and yet they had not reached the lake; so they were, consequently, obliged to wait for the morning, to pursue their route.

So, clambering upon the branches of a tree, they prepare to pass the night in roosting fashion —assisting the woman to ascend likewise.

They soon fell fast asleep, except Smith, who, it appears, had all along a sort of amorous desire for the comely black woman who had followed their fortunes thus far

The language of the eyes is eloquent in love; and Smith found no difficulty in rendering intelligible his passion to its fair, or, rather, dark recipient.

She, poor woman, feeling herself the creature of every chance, suffered, rather than encouraged, Smith's advances.

And, when morning broke, Smith and the woman had disappeared. The three who were left behind were astounded at the perfidy of their friend.

They instantly determined on pursuit, and resolved to have their revenge on Smith.

Steadily pursuing their way in the direction of the lake they had observed on the previous day, they soon have the gratification of seeing through the trees the wished-for haven.

"Oh! how gladly—how eagerly—they rush in the translucent waters! What luxury it was to bathe in an element that is so necessary to life, and yet here is so scarce!"

Refreshed, they returned to the shore; and, ere they could rearrange their dress, to their surprise and consternation they were surrounded, bound hand and foot, and thrown on the ground.

They had fallen into the hands of a tribe who inhabited the village at the back of the lake.

A cursory glance soon showed the captives that they were far different to the tribe they had so recently escaped from. They were taller and stronger built, and more ferocious-looking, and looking sufficiently demoniac; but their paint and arms plainly showed that they were far more warlike than the former.

After they had secured the three men they commenced beating a number of gongs, creating a most deafening noise.

At the sound large numbers of the natives began to assemble from all directions, until an immense concourse surrounded those who had captured the seamen.

Then dividing themselves into two bodies, forming a long and narrow lane between them, and holding clubs in their hands, they untied the bands that confined the limbs of the smugglers.

They were to run the gauntlet between the files of the clubbed warriors, leading from the forest to the water-edge.

Away they sped at the top of their speed. Whack, whack, came the clubs on their unfortunate backs; faster they run, but it is no use the blows descend.

Hardy and Bond sink down bruised and bleeding, but Lang, with a cry of rage and defiance, leaped clean over his messmates and, with a bound, shot clear of the last half-dozen braves and plunged into the lake striking for the opposite shore.

A yell of disappointment burst from the assembled blacks.

Then, rushing towards the lake, they embark in numerous canoes that had laid hid in the bushes at the margin.

At the same moment a canoe shot out in a direction more to the east of the village. There were two persons in it.

They had observed the swimmer struggling to distance his enemies, and, from motives of compassion, strove to reach and rescue him from his foes.

It was Smith and the runaway woman.

They had reached Lang and assisted him into the canoe, and their astonishment was mutual at so early and unexpected a reunion.

They had no time for explanation, for the flotilla of canoes were in hot and swift pursuit.

Away they glide, the woman dexterously applying the paddles.

But the addition of Lang seemed to impede their progress a little, for the foremost of the pursuers were evidently gaining upon them.

Loudly screamed and yelled their swarming foes. On sped the pursued.

At last they could hear the breathing of those in the foremost canoe. They were alongside.

With a shout of triumph they leaped up, and were about to seize the canoe in which Smith and Lang were, when the latter, exclaiming—

"No, I'm damned if we're catched yet!" and leaping into the water he grasped hold of the enemies' canoe, and, with a strong muscular effort, turned it completely over.

Then, swimming back, he regained his seat in the canoe he had left; while the discomfited blacks hung on to their overturned craft till their comrades could reach them to pick them up.

At a little distance beyond, perhaps about half-a-mile, a small tongue of land jutted out into the lake. Smith and Lang thought if they could but run the point they might manage to baffle their enemies. accordingly they redoubled their efforts.

As they neared the point alluded to their hopes grew brighter; but, casting another glance towards their pursuers, they saw with dismay that there was every prospect of their being overtaken ere they could reach the desired goal.

"Curse their black hides!' murmured Lang through his clenched teeth, "they are gaining on us still."

"Never mind, lad, we'll double them yet, I hope," cheerfully replied Smith.

Two canoes, filled with men armed with clubs, now reach them on either side. .

With exultant shouts they bear forward to grasp the overtaken vessel.

But, quick as thought, Smith dashed, with tremendous force, his doubled fist full in the face of the black brave who was foremost.

So powerful was the blow, that the savage staggered backward, and fell headlong into the water, capsizing his comrades, and overturning the canoe.

At the same time, Lang, seizing the club that lay in their canoe, dealt such a terrific blow on the heads of those on the other side, that they all leaped into the water, to escape the onslaught.

Away sped the smugglers again. Smith, seizing the paddles in his powerful hands, soon left a wide gap between them and his pursuers.

CHARLES IN THE HUT OF THE HUNTER.

They reach the tongue of land; they round the point; and, with a shout of joy, they lose sight of their pursuers, as they turn the angle that concealed them from further observation.

"Thank God!" exclaimed Smith — "we can dodge them here, I think."

"Aye, aye," said Lang—"among those little islands: 'twill be odd if we can't find some hiding-place here."

So saying, they darted into a little cove, that seemed to disappear between two grass-covered hillocks. Above their heads the trees met, forming a continuous shade from the burning sun, and rendering it deliciously cool.

"By Jove! a nice crib this," said Lang. "Suppose we go ashore, and rest awhile?"

"No, no; not yet," said Smith.

"Why not?"

"Well, to my thinking, we had better go a little farther ere we have a roost."

"Well, as you like. But what says Nancy, or whatever you call her, to it?"

The black woman pointed silently forward.

They had proceeded some distance in this manner, with little or no change in the character of the scene, when they stopped to listen.

All was silent as death.

They had evidently baffled their foes.

Again Smith dipped the paddles, and, without speaking a word, they went some distance further; and now the stream widened gradually, until it became a capacious river.

On either side they beheld tall palm trees interspersed with the cocoa and banana, growing in wild and dense luxuriance, but no human being met their eyes.

What if the river should lead to some settlement where Europeans might be met with.

Their hearts palpitated with joy as the thought struck them.

To see the shores of old England would indeed be a joy.

Then they remembered Bond and Hardy, and wondered if they were dead.

"Poor Hardy and Bond," sighed Lang, "it was a cruel fate to belabour them with those clubs; ugh! my back and shoulders feel them now."

"Ay, tell us how ye come to be in such a pickle with these savages," said Smith.

Lang accordingly related what the reader is already acquainted with, and then turning to Smith, said—

"But how came you, old fellow, to desert us and take away our fair waiting-woman, without so much as saying good-bye?"

"Oh," laughed Smith, "the fact was I was in love with the beauty; wasn't I, dear?" he added, turning to the woman and chucking her under the chin.

The woman grinned and seemed not at all displeased at this little bit of familiarity.

"Seems to like it," said Lang. laughing.

"Few women that don't, eh," replied his companion.

"Black as well as white," said Smith, "all fond of tickling," and again he chucked the ebony-skinned female under the chin.

"Cut it," said Lang, "she'll be offended."

To this remark Smith gave a grin, which brought the sides of his mouth almost up to his ears.

"You'll have to mind you don't let your head fall in half at that ere fun," said his companion, "blessed if it wasn't nearly off then."

"Ha, ha!" laughed the other, but then seeming to recollect that a still tongue shows a wise head, became instantly silent.

The woman, too, seemed ill at ease, and appeared as though she feared they might be heard by some one who would be more foe than friend.

She raised her hands imploringly, and the smugglers paddled on in silence.

They had gone some little distance further, when Smith paused and listened intently.

"What is it?" said Lang.

"Don't know."

"Did you hear anything?"

"Fancied I did."

"Listen!"

All three listened intently for a few minutes, but not a sound broke the stillness.

"You must have been mistaken," said Lang, after putting the greatest strain he could upon his sense of hearing, "all is still as the grave."

Reassured by silence, Lang again returned to the conversation.

"But how did you get this canoe?"

"Why, when we eloped, we bore up for the lake, and, while we were paddling in the water to refresh ourselves, my sweetheart here discovered that we were near some settlement. She saw smoke through the trees, a little distance off."

"Ah! that must be the same that nabbed hold of us," said Lang.

"No doubt of it. Well, we hurried back to the bank to reconnoitre—not thinking it safe to float about there till we knew the bearings of the craft thereabouts.

"Well, just as we neared the bank, what should we see but this here canoe, hid in among the rushes that grew at the water's edge; and, further off, we could see other canoes all hid in like manner. My companion then peered through the trees, towards the spot where we had seen the smoke; and there she saw enough to convince her that it would be dangerous to place ourselves in their power. So we hastily retreated to the water-side, and, seizing the canoe we had first beheld, we embarked and paddled away.

"We had not gone far ere we heard an uproar of voices, and sounds of beating of gongs; and a turn of the lake brought us in view of the savages, who had collared you, Bond, and Hardy. We watched the whole proceeding, though little thinking that they were old messmates they were bearing so rascally. You know the rest."

Again they lapsed into silence.

CHAPTER XLIII.

THE FLIGHT CONTINUED—A YARN—THE CATARACT.

LANG, Smith, and the woman were still seated in the canoe, silently and swiftly gliding along. They had travelled, they thought, by the far advance of the day, many leagues. Yet they were still in perplexity as regarded their future proceedings; and, like the knight-errants of old, they trusted to their good steeds to extricate them from their difficulty, and set them right.

So the boat, unpropelled by aught save the current, glided onward.

At last the silence was broken by Lang, who said:

"Can't you tell us, old gal, where we are now?"

The woman, who now began to understand the words of her companions, and to speak in broken yet comprehensible English, looked up, and, casting her eyes around, slowly shook her head:

"Me know notink now."

Lang gave a testy sigh.

"Wait till night comes," cheerfully said Smith, "and then we shall see where this river leads to."

"Aye, if the stars can tell us."

"Well, they will tell us."

"But, perhaps, they're different stars in this ere outlandish country."

"Nonsense!" said Smith. "Have you forgotten life on board ship? Don't you know, wherever we sail, we see the old bear to the north, and cross to the south?"

"Aye, so we do: but I'm deuced suspicious about here."

With eager eyes they watched for the coming night.

In these latitudes no twilight heralds her approach; but, suddenly, like the spring of a foe, she falls upon the sun-deserted land, and hides it beneath her mantle of darkness.

Even while watching and expecting the night, Lang and Smith were startled by the sudden darkness, and, for a moment, seemed bewildered as to the navigation of their craft.

Almost as sudden the stars appeared—lighting the scene like enchantment.

"Beautiful!" they both exclaimed, as they beheld the gorgeous canopy above; and then, glancing on the water, saw it reflected around them.

"Now for our bearings," eagerly said Lang.

"Aye, aye, mate."

They gaze slowly around them.

After all, their vision was limited: for, on either

side of the stream the land had gradually increased in height, until, at the moment they were about to take their observation, it rose to the character of hills. Behind and before, the winding of the stream had placed them also between lofty hills ; and far in the distance, forward, they could see the faint blue line of lofty mountains.

What if the river came from those mountains? How could they account for the current flowing towards it? This was a puzzle that time only could solve. So, scratching their heads, they again look round.

But no stars could they see of which they had previous knowledge.

Unfortunately their knowledge of astronomy was limited to the northern hemisphere ; and Smith had only the appearance of the southern cross fixed in his memory: so, not having discovered that, he was fain to express his disappointment and chagrin.

"Damned, if I don't think you're right after all !" he said, addressing Lang.

"Aye, I knew how it would be," said Lang. "This cursed nigger country was only made to worry people."

"What an infarnal row those creeturs on the land are making," said Smith.

"Yes, damn them ! they won't even let a fellow drown his cares in sleep. It is a country !"

The noise of the wild beasts was indeed deafening, and enough to fill the boldest heart with terror to think of being on land.

"Well, if we can't sleep, s'pose you tell us a story ?"

"Well, I don't mind if I do : but what shall it be about—eh ?"

"Oh ! what you like. Tell us about them mermaids : you was going to tell us when we last set round our mess."

"Well, then, I'll begin. You see, when our craft was cruising up the Arctics, we cast anchor, one morning, in deep water, jest abreast of a small island as wasn't down in the chart, and hadn't got no name either. But our captain knew what he was arter, about as right as ninepence ; because a small schooner came alongside, pretty soon, freighted with brandy and wine for the officers, for their own private stores."

"What ship was she?" interrupted Smith. "I likes to know all the facts of the case, you know."

"She was an American frigate : the "Kangaroo" they called her, because she used to jump along at a rare pace in a gale," replied Lang. Then, continuing his yarn, he said:

"Well, the slings were run up to the end of the main-yard, and the waisters were busy hoisting up the barrels, when a cask of brandy slipped from the slings, as it was being canted round, and dropped right splash into the sea, sinking right away. Upon examination, it proved to be the best cask of brandy in the schooner, imported from Bordeaux, for the captain himself.

"He raised a gritty mass, I guess, right off the reel.

"'You etarnal lazy suckers,' says he—'look here! take all the boat's anchors, lash 'em together in twos so as to form grapnells of four points each, and drag all about here for that ere brandy, and mind you find it, or I'll put every mother's son of you on short allowance—aye for the next month !'

"Well, the boats was lowered and a groping we went. I was placed in the jolly with Jones and Tim Whiggins, and a middy to direct. The middy was a pretty considerable smart fellow, and

jest as he was putting off he nodded up to the chaplain, as was leaning over the side, and says —

"'What say you to an hour's float upon this here glassy sea.' The parson was down by the man ropes in a minute, and off we set a-fishing for the brandy tub.

"The current run pretty slick by the side of the little island, and the second luff, who was in the cutter, ordered us to go ahead and watch along the shore, jest to see if the tub warn't rolled up there by the tide. We pretended to look right hard for the tub till we made the lee of the island, and then, if we didn't resolve to take it easy, and run the nose of the jolly into the yaller sand o' the shore, there ain't no snakes. I held on in the starn by the grapnel, and the parson pulled out of his pocket a good-sized sample bottle of the new stuff as he'd jest bought, and wanted the middy to taste ; and, after passing their ideas on the liquor, the chaplain gave us men a pretty stiff horn apiece—now I tell you—and first-rate stuff it was, I swear. It iled the parson's tongue like, all out doors : it took him to talk all about the old original antique names of the islands that laid in spots all about there—classic ground, as he called it ; and a pretty yarn he did spin, too. He talked about the island of Candy, where are the sweetest gals in all creation, or anywhere else : and of a great chief, called Beaulasses, or Molasses, who killed a one-eyed giant of a blacksmith, named Polly Famous, by spitting in his eye ; and about a fireman, named Henearus, who carried out an old man, one Ann Kysis, on his shoulders, when his house was a-fire : for, you see, many of the old Grecian men had women's names, and wisey warsey. But what took my cheese was the parson's telling us about two fellows who got up the biggest chunk of a fight, and kept right at it for ten years—and all about a gal named Ellen, what skeeled from her moorings, and run off to Paris. Then the parson tried to point out the island of Lip-salve, where a conjurer, called Sarey, from her boldness, used to keep a whole class of singing girls, called syringes, 'cos they sucked the sailors ashore, and then chawed them right up, like a piece of sweet Cavendish.

"Then the middy, who'd been keeping dark, and laying low, all this time, showed his broughting's up, and let fly a whole broadside at the parson, about them ere syringes, and other fablous women—such as King Neptune's wife, Ann Thracite, and her she Tritons and Neriads, and river gals, right down to mermaids.

"Well, you see, all this here talk made us dry as thunder ; so the chaplain said he guessed the sun was over the foreyard, and baled us out another horn of liquor all round. Then he took a 'spell-ho!' at the jawing-tackle, and allowed there was a river in Jarminy where all our Dutch emigrants hail from, and that a naked girl used to locate herself in a whirlpool, and come up on moonshiny nights, and sing a whole bookful of songs, as turned the heads of all the young fellers in them parts. Well, reports rung up as she'd a whole cargo of gold stowed away at the bottom of the whirlpool ; and many a wild young Jarman, seduced by the gal's singing, and hopes of gold, leapt into the river, and warn't heard on never arter. These matters hurt the young gal's karracter, and the old folks, who always allowed that she was a kind of goddess, began to think she was not the clean grit ; and the young fellers said her singing was no great shakes, and that her beauty warn't the thing it was cracked up to be.

"Then there was a famous general, who warn't raised in that section of the country, but had swapped a castle on a mountain in Spain for one of them ere water lots near the whirlpool. He began to find himself rather short of cash to buy his groceries, and, concluding that he couldn't do without a leetle whiskey to keep off the ague, he resolved to pay the whirlpool gal a visit, and jest see if he couldn't soft-soap the crectur out of a little rhino.

"Next full moon he toddles to the bluff what hung over the biling and foaming river, and, jest at eight bells, uprose the gal, stark naked, a-sitting on the white froth of the whirling water, and singing:

" 'Won't you come to my bower, what I've shaded for you?'

" 'Well,' says the gineral, not a bit daunted—says he, 'Look here, my gal, I mean to eat a lobster-salad with you to-night, if you promise to behave like a lady, and won't cut up no infarnal shines.'

" Well, the gal gave her word of honour, and the gineral dived into the whirlpool, and down they went, right slick.

"Next morning the gineral was found to turn up with a sighter more gold pieces, bigger round than the top of a baccy-box, and a whole pot-full of the tallest kind of jewels. You see, the soger had carried a small flask of monongahely in his pocket, and the river gal couldn't get over the old rye. Two glasses opened her heart, I guess, and she let the gineral slip his cable in the morning, with just about as much gold as he could stow away. Some of his friends calculated as he'd better drop his anchor there again; and there was some talk in the settlement of forming a joint stock company for the purpose of getting up the gold: but the gineral telled them he guessed he'd got enough for him, and he saw quite enough down there not to want to go no more; and, refusing to say what he had seen, or tell them how they was to go to work, it kinder stopped the joint stock company. The river gal, she fell quite in love with the gineral, right up to the hub, and sat on the biling water, night after night, singing, 'Meet me by moonlight alone.' But the gineral said he'd see her hanged first afore he'd trust her again—'for,' says he, 'no woman was never deceived twice:' which riled the river gal, like mad; and, in revenge, she set the whirlpool biling, like all creation, as if determined to keep the neighbourhood in hot water. From the circumstance of the gineral's getting so much gold out of the river, the Jarmans called it the Rhino; and it's been known by something like that name ever since.

"When the chaplain had expended his yarn, he sarved out another allowance of liquor. I recking that he was the raal grit for a parson, always doing as he'd be done by, and practising a darned sight more than he preached.

"'Tain't christian like," says he, "to drink by ones'self, and raal tar never objects to share his grog with a shipmate."

"Them's the genewine sentiments of spirituel salvashen, and kinder touch the bottom of a sailor's heart.

"The middy then uncoiled another length of cable about the fabblous winner of the sea, and said it was a tarnation pretty idea, that them angels from heaven, as ruled the earth, should keep watch over the treasures of the water. Then he tells a yarn concerning the captain of a marchantman, as was trading in the South Seas, laying at anchor, becalmed, on Sunday morning, about five bells, when a strange hail was heard from under the bows of the craft, and the hands on deck, as answered the hail seed somebody in the water, with just his head and arms sticking out, and holden on to the dolphing striker.

"Well, I guess they pretty soon throwed him a rope and hauled him aboard, and then they seed he was a regular built merman, one half kinder nigger and 'tother half kinder fish, but altogether, more kinder fish than kinder nigger. So, as I was telling you, they got him aboard, and he made an enquiry after the captain, who come out of his cabin, and the merman made him a first-rate dancing squel bow, and says in genewin English,

"Captain, I sarten reckon it ain't entered into your calculation as this here is Sunday, for you've dropped your tarnal big anchor right in front of our meeting-house door, and, I'm hanged if any of our folks can go to prayers.

"Well, the captain was rather taken aback, and the calm, you see, overlaying him in that there hot latitude, had set his back up a bit; and besides, he felt considerable streeked at being roused out of his morning's nap, for nothing; so, altogether, he felt sorter wolfish, and looking at the stranger, darned savage, say,—

" 'Who the ugly are you?'

"This here speech put the merman's dander up, for he says, right sarcy,—

"I guess I'm appointed deacon over all the merman's and mermaid's in these here parts, and I'll just trouble you to treat me with the respect due to a stranger, and a gentleman.

"Well, I guess the captain's ebenuzer was roused for he seized hold of our harpoon that was laying on the fowksell, and hollered to the marman—

"You fishy vagabond, make tracks out of my ship, you sammony-tailed son of a sea cook, or I'll drive the grain slick through your sealy carcass, I will.

"Well, the critter seeing as the captain meant danger, made but one flop with his tail, and skeeted over one side of the ship into the water.

"The captain didn't weigh anchor, nor nothing, only during the night, the cable was cut by the merman, and the ship, drifted on to a coral reef, and rubbed a tarnal big hole in her planking.

" 'That's a good yarn,' said the parson, 'and I believe it's true as gospel.'

"We pulled back quietly to the ship. The barrel of brandy had not been found, and I wish I may be sniggered if the captain did not fly into the biggest kind of quarter-deck passion I ever did see. He stormed great guns, and fired whole broadsides at the boat's crew, swearing they should keep on dredging till the tub was found if it was the day arter eternity. So, you see, the hands was piped to dinner, but I was ordered to keep in the boats and take care they did not stave each other.

"Well, I laid down in the captain's gig, and what with the precious liquor, and the talk about mermaids, and syringes, and water gals, and o c thing and 'tother, a pretty mess began mixing in my brain-pan. So as I was laying comfortably moored in the starn-sheets with my head a lit le over the boat's quarter, I thought it highly unwrong that the brandy tub had not been fetched up, and that the men using the grapnels must have shirked as we did, cos if they sarched as they oughter they must have seed the barrel, for the water was so pertickler clear that you could discarn the crabs crawling over the coral rocks at the bottom of twenty fathom.

"Well, while I was looking into the ocean to see if I could light upon the barrel, a leetle of the largest fish I ever did see come and swum right close to the bottom of the sea, just under the boats. Then it kept rising and rising till I seed its long fins were shaped like mens' arms; and when it come near the surface it turned on its back, and then I seed a human face. I knowed at once that it was a mermaid or a merman, or one of them amfiberous critters called fabblus syringes as the chaplain had been spinning his yarn about.

"So the critter popped his head above the water which was as smooth as glass, and a little smoother too, and says he to me—

"'Look here! stranger! you and your shipmates ain't doing the genteel thing to me no how you can fix it, for they be playing old hub with my garden grounds and oyster beds by scratching and raking 'em all over with them 'ar darned anchors and grapnel fixings, in a manner that's harrowing to my feelings. If the captain wants his thunder-nation liquor tub, let him just send any dacent Christian down with me and I'll give it him.'

"Well I'm not going to say I didn't feel kinder skeared, but the chaplain's yarn had rubbed the rough edge off, and the notion of finding the captain's cask pleased me mightily, cos I knowed it would tickle the old man like all creation, and sartinly get me three or four liberty days for shore going when we returned to Port Mahon. So as I hadn't on nothing perticklar as would spile, only a blue cotton shirt and sail cloth pants, and the weather being not oncommon warm, I just told the merman I was ready and tottled quietly over the boat's side into the blue transparent sea.

"The merman grappled me by the fist and we soon touched bottom now, I tell ye. I found as I could walk easy enough, only the water swayed me about just as if I were a leetle tight, but I didn't seem to suffer nothing from want of breath nyther.

"We soon reached where the brandy cask was lying, right under the ship's keel, which accounts for its not being seen nor nothing by the boats' crews. I felt so everlastingly comical about finding the tub, that I told the half-bred dolphin fellow as pointed it out, that if I knowed how to tap it, I wish I might die if I wouldn't give him a gallon of the stuff, as a salvage fee.

"'What's in it?' says the merman.

"'Why, liquor,' says I.

"'Well,' says the merman, 'so I he'erd them fellows in the boat say, but I guess I've liquor enough to last my time, though I reckon your liquor is something stronger than salt water, seeing it hooped up in that way.'

"'Why, you lubber, its brandy,' says I, 'the real gennewine cony-bach.'

"'And what's that,' says the merman.

"'Why,' says I, 'have you lived to your time of life without tasting spiritous liquors? Well, I swares you ought to be the commodore of all them cold water clubs, and perpetual president of all temp'-rance teetotallers. Go ahead, maty, pilot the way to your shanty, and I'll roll the barrel arter you, I'll soon give you a taste of liquor that will first take the shine out of anything you ever did taste, now I tell you.

"Well, the critter flopped ahead, for you see it's the nature of the merman, seeing as they've no legs, only a fish's tail what's bent under him, to make way by flopping their starns up and down and paddling with their hands—something atween a swim and a swagger—but the way he got through the water is a poser.

"I rolled the tub along the smooth white shining sand, and the crabs and lobsters meeted off right and left, out of my way, regular skeered, and big fishes of all shapes and makes, with bristling fins, swam close along side me, and looked at me quite awful, with their small gooseberry eyes, as much as to say—'What the devil are you at.'

"Bye and bye the merman brought up, in front of rather a largish cave, or grotto of rock and shell-work, kivered with coral and sea-weed. So, you see, the tub was put right on end, in one corner. I axed the merman if he had a gimlet, and he said he believed there was sich a thing in the hold, or cellar. He'd found a carpenter's tool-chest, in a wreck, a few miles to the eastward; and he fetched away six or seven of the little fixings, thinking they might be useful to him. So he opened the back-door, and hailed a young merman to bring him the gimlets.

"Seeing that there was no benches, nor nothing to sit down on—which mermen and mermaids don't want, 'cos they've no sitting parts to their bodies, which is all fish from their waistbands—I just sat on the top of the tub, and took an observation of the creetur before me. His face was regular human—only it looked rather tawny and flabby, like a biled nigger, with fishy eyes, and a mouth like a huge tom cod. His hair hung straight down his shoulders, and was coarse and thick, like un-twisted rattlin. His hands were something like a goose's paw, only the fingers were longer and thicker. Just about midships his body was tucked into a fish's belly, with huge green scales, right down to the tail.

"While I was surveying the merman, fore and aft, the door opened, and a she creetur flopped in, with a young merman at the breast. The little sucker was not bigger than a pickerel, with a tail of a delicate sammon colour, and a head and body just like one of them small tan monkeys with a face as large as a dollar. The merman introduced the she creetur as his wife, and we soon got into a coil of talk, right slick, all about the weather, and the kears and troubles of a young family; and I wish I may be swamped if the mermaid warn't a dreadful nice creetur to chatter. Like all wimmen-folk, she was plaguy kewrous as to where I was raised and rigged; and when I said, 'I guess I hailed from Cape Cod, and all along shore there,' she looked at the merman, and said to me:

"'Well I never, Cape Cod! why stranger I guess there must be some 'finity in our breeds.'

"Well you see, I got kewrous too, and wanted to log the perticklers of the nat'ral history of the race of merman; so I made a few inquiries res-pecting their mode of life. 'I guess,' says I, 'you've a tarnal fine fishmarket about these here parts, and keep your table well supplied with hallibut, and sea bass, and black fish, eh?'

"'Why, stranger,' says the merman, rather wrathy, 'seeing its you I won't be offended, or by heving if that speech ain't enough to make a mer-man feel scaly, why then it ain't no matter. We claim to be half fish in our nature, and I reckon you don't kalkilate that we gobbles up our rela-tions? There's sea varmint enough in all conscience, sitch as oysters, and claws, and mussels, and crabs. We go the whole shoal with them, and then we cultivate kail and other sea truck in our gardens, and sometimes we swim under the wild fowl as they're floating, and jerk down a fine duck or a gull.

"Just then the merman's eldest son-fish fetched in the gimlet, and brought up the mer-man's jawing tacks with a round turn. The young un was about the size of an Injun boy just afore he runs alone—half papoose, half porpus. He got a little skeered when he clapt eyes on me but I give him a stale quid of baccy to amuse himself, and the sugar-plum made the mermaster roll his eyes above a bit, now I tell you.

"Well, I bored a hole in the brandy tub, and picking up an empty clam shell handed a drink to the lady and told her to tole it down. She swallowed it pretty thick, and the way she gulped afterwards, and stared, and twisted her fishy mouth was a sin to Davy Crockett. The merman looked rather wolfish at me as if I'd gin her pison; so I drawed a shell-full and swallowed it myself. This kinder cooled him down, and when the mermaid got her tongue in running order agin, she said she guessed the liquor was the juice of heaven, and she'd be darned if she wouldn't have another drink right off the reel.

"Seeing this the merman swallowed his dose, and no sooner got it down than he squalled right out, and clapped his webby hands together, and wagged his tail like all creation. He swore it was elegant stuff, and he felt it tickle powerful from the top of his head to the end of his starn fin. After taking two or three horns together, the sonny cried out for a drink and I gave him one that sent him wriggling on the sand like an eel in uneasiness. So the merman said as the liquor was real first-rate, he guessed he'd ask in his next door neighbour and his lady, just to taste the godsend.

"Well, in a minnit, in comes a huge merman, of a most awful size, looking just like Black Hawk when he was bilious; he fetched up his lady with him, and his eldest son, a scraggy hobbadehoy merman, and his darters, two young mermaids, or mermisses, jest going out o' their teens, who flapped their yaller-skinned paws over their punking-coloured chops, pretending to be mighty skeered at coming afore a strange man in a state of nature—but they forgot all about that there when the licker was handed to them.

"After taking a few smallers, the fresh merman said he guessed the clam shell was altogether too leetle to get a proper amount of licker, whereby a feller could judge correctly of the real taste of the stuff; so he went to his berth in the next cave, and fetched a large blue and silver shell that held about a pint.

"The news of the brandy tub spread pretty slick, for in half an hour I'd the hull grist of the mermen belonging to that settlement cooped up in the cavern. Sich a noisy swilling set of wet fools I never did see; the drunk come on them almighty strong, for they kept me sarving the licker jest as quick as it could run. I thought if the captain could have seen me astriding his brandy cask, in an underground grocery at the bottom of the sea, sorrounded by such a school of odd fish, how many dozen at the gangway would he have ordered the bosen's mate to have sarved me out?

"The way the drink affected the different creeturs was right curious, now I tell you. One great scaly feller stiffened his tail all up, and stood poppindickler erect on the peaked points of the end fin, like a jury mast, and jawed away real dignified at the rest, wanting them to appoint him a sort of admiral over the hull crew. Another yellor feller, with a green tail, was so dreadful blue, that he doubled himself into a figger 5, and sung scraps and bits of all sorts of sea songs, till he got too drunk to speak at all. Some of the mermen wanted to kiss all the mermaids, and two of the ladies began scratching and fighting like two pusseys, cos one trod on t'other's

tail. Some went flopping and dancing on the sand like mad, raising sich a dust that I could not see to draw the licker—but the party round the tub soon drove them to the rightabout, as interfering with the interest of the settlement. Every minnit some fresh merman dropped on the ground with the biggest kind of load on; I never seed a set of creeturs so almighty tight, yelling, swearing, and fighting, till they growed so darned savagerous that I almost feared for my own safety amongst them drunken moffradite sea aborigoins. So, you see, I up and told 'em that I'd clapt my veto on the licker' and that they should not have any more.

"Well, if ever you did hear a most eternal row, or see a hull raft of drunken fellows cut didoes, then was the time. It was voted that I were a public enemy, and every half drunken merman suddenly became very 'fishus to have me Lynched, and it were settled at last that I were to be rode on a rail, and then tarred and feathered. But, while some of the varmint went arter the rail and tar, the rest of the critters began quarreling who was to serve out the liquor; and as each merman, drunk or sober, wanted so have the care of the precious suff, they soon raised a pretty mess, and kept on tearing at each other like a pack of wolves, Seeing this, I just sneaked quietly away from the cave grocery, till I come in sight of the ship, when I struck upward for the surface, and swum for dear life. I soon seed that the boats' crews were mustering for another bout of the dragging for the brandy cask, so, fearing lest the captain should miss me, I just laid hold of the edge of the gig, and crawled in pretty quickly, and laid myself down in the starn sheets, as if I'd never been out of the boat.

"I hadn't laid there half a second, when I heard a noise just for all the world as if somebody was squeezing a small thunder cloud right over my head. I rose up, and there were the captain and the hull crew looking over the ship's side at me—the officers in a tarnal rage, and the men grinning like so many hyenas,

"'Rouse up, you long-sided lazy swab, and bring the boats in from the boom. Are you going to sleep all day?'

"Ay, ay, sir, said I, jumping up in the boat, when all the water run off me like forty-thousand mill-streams—I'd been so outrageous soaked while down with the mermen. I felt kinder skeered lest the captain should see it, but when I stood up he laughed right out, and so did the hull crew, too.

"'Why, he's not awake yet,' said the captain. 'Bo'sen, give him another bucket.'

"You see they wanted to persuade me I'd fell asleep in the gig, as fast as a meeting-house, and slept there the hull while the crew were at dinner, and that no shouting nor nothing couldn't wake me up—so bo'sen run along the boom, and just give me a couple of buckets of sea-water right over me

"When I told them my yarn about the merman popping up his head, and inviting me down, and all about finding the brandy tub and the rest, they swore that I'd got drunk on the parson's licker, and dreamt it all in the boat. But I guess I know what I did see, jest about as slick as anybody; and the chaplain believed the hull story; and said that, as I'd learned the mermen the value of licker, they'd get hunting up all the tubs and barrels out of the different wrecks in all the various seas; and that intemperance would spile the race, and thin them off till they become one of the things that was—jest like Injins what's wasting away by the power of rum and whiskey given them by the white men.

"I reckon the parsen warn't far out in his calculation. The love of licker has had its effect upon the mermen and mermaids; they must have thinned off surprisingly, for I ain't seen none since, nor I don't know nobody that has, neither."

Having concluded his yarn, they now hurried towards the woman, who had appeared during the recital, totally unconscious of ought around her, and but for the glitter of her dark eyes, as they ever anow encountered the starlight might be thought asleep.

With a sigh of relief she slowly raised her figure, and pointing towards the sky on the right, they looked.

The canopy of stars had passed on in their lasting and restless journey, and the topmost stars forming the Southern Cross, now appeared high enough over the hills, that lined the banks for our travellers to recognise.

There was no mistake, that brilliant and remarkable constellation was palpably before them.

An exclamation of delight burst from the lips of Lang and Smith, simultaneously, as they gazed on the beacon that was to light them homeward.

It was on their right hand, consequently, they were drifting eastward.

Fortune smiled on them. Eastward lay their hope of deliverance.

"Yonder mountains, what are they?" asked Smith, clutching hold of the woman's arm, and pointing to a dark mass beyond, that looked like a giant cloud.

She shook her head, and helplessly and sadly murmured—

"Me don't know."

Smith and Lang muttered an impatient oath, and looking steadily and anxiously forward, seemed to watch the progress of their cause with more interest.

Ere the day broke, however, they noted with some surprise, that as they approached nearer to the mountain, the speed of the current rapidly increased.

Still gazing forward and upward, watching first the stars and then the mountain, they appeared satisfied that this progress was surely and swiftly in the desired direction.

But now a strange sound is heard, like a distant murmur.

They looked inquiringly at the woman.

She, too, has heard it; but her eyes lack the intelligence that can explain it.

Their speed has now become extraordinary, and at the same time they notice that the noise is rapidly increasing.

Day has arrived, as suddenly as he had disappeared, and the stars are suddenly quenched by the bright glare of the sun.

The scene on either side has changed. The river has narrowed, and the banks present a rugged and rock-like surface, still covered with verdure and creepers, and parasitical plants hanging to the water edge. The water, as if furious at being confined in its channel, dashes on at terrific speed. The rocky banks become more and more precipitous, and more and more lofty, till, comparatively speaking, the eddying stream resembles boiling pitch in the darkness below.

The occupants of the canoe are now terribly alarmed. The noise that had first awakened their fears had now increased to a continuous roar—deafening and drowning all other sounds.

They knew now that it was the roar of waters they heard, and, by the awful speed that they were dashed along, felt too certain that they were on some falls.

They struggled desperately to reach the banks—but in vain. They dip the paddles, and, with all their strength, strove to stay the progress of the canoe. In an instant they were dashed like straws from their puny hands.

They tried to catch at the creepers, hanging in festoons beside them: but the river laughed at their efforts, and bore them on.

Horrified and despairing, they held themselves in their seats by clutching the sides of the vessel—for the water bubbled and leaped around them, threatening to dash them to pieces every instant—and gazing on each other, with a look of despairing helplessness.

Fearfully loud was the noise of falling waters.

The canoe no longer sped with the current as before, but whirled from side to side and twisted round like a teetotum, till the unfortunate trio were rendered almost insensible by the giddy motion and the horror of their situation.

They now saw that the river made a sharp curve to the left, leaving the mountain that still loomed in the distance considerably to the right.

Louder roared and swifter flew the waters.

Suddenly it grew lighter.

The banks lessened in height.

Eagerly and anxiously gazed the doomed travellers in the hope of discovering something that might rescue them from the jaws of death.

She looked forward and beheld what seemed the end of the stream, and at the same moment emerge from the gully into a broad expanse of water. It was not yet the end of the stream, though it was no longer so narrow. The banks were farther off, and low, and by the scantiness of lofty trees upon them looked like a marsh or swamp, which probably was under water during the rainy season.

The water was pure, deep, and undisturbed by rocks near the surface, so that it rushed on comparatively smooth. But its speed was terrific.

There was no hope for our travellers.

Miles were passed, and they knew they were rapidly nearing their destruction.

They could see afar off and below them winding from the mountains a large and beautiful river; their eyes followed its course, and they saw with dismay that it seemed to lead towards a point they imagined the river they were on must ultimately reach. They saw also that they were far above it, and consequently thought with horror on the magnitude of the fall that must exist to join that river.

Their thoughts and conclusions were right.

They now observed in the direction from whence the deafening roar proceeded, a dense white mist.

Smith and Lang looked unutterable things.

The woman with her eyes fixed on the bottom of the boat seemed insensible to everything.

Nearer and they approach the pall-like mist.

The surface of the water is like glass, so smooth so polished it looks in its resistless speed.

The canoe now enters the mist.

It is on the crown of the falls.

It quivers a moment, and then it is gone.

Fearful shrieks rent the air, but are instantly hushed in the cyclopean roar.

The waters still dash on, but the canoe has disappeared beyond.

CHAPTER XLIV.

THE BOY ROVER AGAIN—TRAPPED.—AN UNEXPECTED MEETING.

THE storm abated, and the sun burst forth in all its refulgent splendour, and the wearied and saturated smugglers rose from the rock on which they had seated themselves, and watched the destruction of their vessel.

Bitterly did the Boy Rover curse the mad infatuation which had led him to again seek to place Ellen in his power; and he looked upon the loss of his craft, and present helpless condition, as a judgment upon him for all the horror and misery he had caused that poor girl and her brave devoted friends.

Alone with his two companions upon that cliff, with no means of escape, his hopes blighted, and his fortunes crushed, he bowed his head, and cursed himself for his blind unmanly love.

But to remain there and perish would never do. His was a nature that quailed not at the approach of adversity. He must be up and doing.

He ordered his companions to follow him, and ascended to the top of the cliff, intending to cross the planks, and make his way to the woods.

With slow and feeble steps they walked up the rugged rocks; but a cry of horror escaped them as they reached the top.

The planks were gone!

The storm, in its mad fury, had hurled them into the bay beneath, and they were left on that barren rock to starve, whilst, beyond them, upon the opposite side, lay a long stretch of wooded land, and the means of subsistence till succour could arrive.

With black despair pictured in every lineament of their countenances, they stood gazing upon each other.

"Lost!" said one at length.

"Death stares us in the face," said the other; "and we are brought to this through his blind passion for that cursed girl."

The Rover said not a word: he felt that he alone was to blame.

"We may never see a sail from here," said the first speaker.

"Any vessel commanded by anything but a fool," remarked the other, "would keep a long way from these rocks."

The Boy Rover bit his lips, and was silent; but he resolved, if ever it lay in his power, he would be revenged for those words.

His look and word could hold the crew of his vessel in subjection and awe whilst her planks held together; but now he saw plainly that he no longer commanded the men by his side.

His authority, which was supreme on board the "Venomed Snake," was here set at defiance.

Still he felt that his own indiscretions and evil passions had brought about all that they now suffered, and that he deserved the contempt rather than the pity of his companions.

"What is done," he said, after a pause, "cannot be undone. The evil has passed: we must now endeavour to remedy it."

"How?" said one.

"Aye, how?" asked the other.

But the Boy Rover could not answer.

"It is all very well to talk of remedying it," said the first speaker: "but how's it to be done?"

"Let me think," said the captain.

"You should have thought before you led us into this scrape.

"Thinking won't get us out of it," said the other.

"Not a bit of it."

"I have led you out of greater troubles than this," said the Rover.

"That may be," replied one; "but it don't seem to me you will succeed this time."

"Be not too hasty in your conclusions," replied his captain. "Had I given way to despair when danger stared us in the face, the "Venomed Snake" had not met the fate she has, and, instead of finding ourselves on these barren rocks, our bodies had long been food for the sharks."

"Perhaps," said one sulkily.

"Better perish here," said the Boy Rover, "than have swung at the yard-arm."

"But, as we escaped the yard-arm," said the other, "that's no reason we should perish here."

"Nor shall we," replied the captain, "if any means suggest themselves by which we may prevent it."

"If they do."

"Look you, Tom," said the Boy Rover, turning to the man who had last spoken; "and you, too, Sam: you are not more vexed than I am at our present condition; but if you think you can better your condition without me, do so. But if you are willing to trust to me to get us all out of the critical position in which we are placed, then let all ill-feeling and grumbling end at once."

Neither of the smugglers made any remark to this, and the Rover continued:

"How is it to be—trust to yourselves or to me?"

"What do you say, Sam?" asked Tom, turning to his companion.

"Just what you says," rejoined Sam.

"Well, then, since we are all in the same mess, let's stick to the captain," said Tom.

"Agreed," replied the other.

"Then let all animosity and ill-feeling end at once, and strive to aid each in bettering our condition," said the Boy Rover. "But recollect, if you leave it to me, I will be captain ashore, as well as afloat."

"Yes," said Tom, "that's right."

"Then we must endeavour, by some means or other, to cross the chasm," said the Rover, "and find our way to the woods."

"I'm blessed if I can see any chance of that now the planks are gone which you said you had placed across the opening."

"We will return to the base of the cliff. Some portions of the wreck may yet wash on shore here; and, if so, and we can succeed in securing them, we may yet form a bridge across the abyss."

"So we may," said Sam.

"I never thought of that," added Tom—"blowed if I did now."

"And yet you would, in blind passion, have got rid of one who did think of it," said the Rover, with a sarcastic curl of the lip.

"Captain," said Sam, "you said just now let all bickerings cease, and yet—"

"I shall not refer to them again," said the Boy Rover. "Now let us descend the cliff."

Turning, he led the way, and descended the rock, followed by his two companions.

They had descended about half way down the cliff when a cry of surprise arrested their footsteps; and, as they turned, they beheld, creeping from a crevice in the rock, the form of Black Bill.

"It's Bill," said Sam.

"Bill!" iterated the Rover.

"Yes," said the lieutenant, coming forward, "it is me, captain; "and there's Jem."

THE SLAVE CAPTAIN AND THE AFRICAN SHIP.

And, as the lieutenant pointed in the direction, the Rover perceived the form of Jem Sparks issuing from the same spot whence the lieutenant had come from.

In a moment Jem had got free of the opening, and regained an upright position.

"How came you in that place?" asked the Rover, after a pause, in which surprise partook of far the greatest share.

"Sought shelter there from the storm," said Bill: "glad to creep in anywhere."

"Where is your boat," asked the Rover; "and why were you not ready at the post assigned you to bear me back to the ship?"

"Oh! captain, we ain't to blame for deserting the boat, and leaving you here to yourself," said Jem.

"How so? And where is the boat," asked the Rover, "in which I came to this accursed place?"

"Sunk at the bottom of the bay," said Bill.

"How did that happen?"

"Well, you see. captain, while we was a waiting for your return, and spinning a yarn to wile away the time, bang, whizz, comes a shot, close alongside on us—so near, in fact, that the wind it caused in its passage almost turned me round."

"A shot!" said the Rover.

"Yes," said Bill.

"Where did it come from?" asked the Rover, fixing a doubtful glance upon his lieutenant's face.

"Up there," said Bill, pointing to the top of the rock.

"Who fired it?" said Sam.

"There you've done us," said Ned.

"Why have I?"

"Because we don't know," replied Jem.

"Then how do you know the shot came from up there?" asked the Rover.

"Because we saw the fellow that fired it," said Bill.

"Why, you said you did not know who fired it."

"No more we don't. We only know that he was a tall hairy faced chap; but who he was, or what he was, we don't know."

"It was not fired by either of those we sought, then?" said the Rover.

"No."

"Then there must be others on the island beside ourselves."

"Yes, I suppose so. At all events there was one man; and a narrow escape we had from the rifle he seems to know how to handle."

"But did he sink the boat with a gun-shot?" asked the Rover, in sarcastic tones.

"Not exactly, captain," replied his lieutenant: "but when we found we formed such fine targets for him to practice at, we concealed ourself behind the rocks, and, in our hurry to shelter our bodies from the bullets, we threw down a piece of loose rock, and, ere we could stretch forth a hand to prevent it, down went the boat, with a cargo of stone sufficient to sink a vessel ten times her size."

"Strange—I heard neither the report of the gun, nor saw the stranger of whom you speak," said the Rover, musingly. "How many shots did he fire?"

"Oh! three or four; but we only saw him fire one, as we had concealed ourselves. But we heard the report again and again; and, after some time, when all again became silent, and he seemed to have gone away, we were about to creep out of our place of refuge, when bang goes another, and in again we went, like rats into their holes."

"And you were frightened by one man—you and Jem feared to face this stranger?"

"You see, captain, he held the top of the cliff, and could pick us off as easily as I can place my hand on Jem's shoulder. Before we could have made a dozen steps towards him, we should both have had an ounce of lead in our stomachs."

"And that wouldn't have been very pleasant," remarked Jem.

"Well, you see, captain, we lay concealed, listening for your signal, when the rumbling of the thunder broke over us, and we knowed as how a storm was brewing. We sat listening, when we hears a lot of voices; and I says to Jem, 'There's a lot on 'em come from the island to search for us. That fellow with the gun has been and got a lot more, and means to get hold on us.' So we kept quiet, till we could hear they had all gone; and, when we didn't hear them, the storm broke over us, and the rain pelted down in such torrents that we thought we had better stop where we was till it was over: but, as we looked from that hole there, we saw the saucy "Venomed Snake" drift into towards shore, and heard the cry of those on board, as she dashed upon the rocks, and sunk among the breakers. We know'd we couldn't help 'em: so we remained concealed till we caught sight of you, and Sam, and Tom; and then, captain, we came out of our hole to meet you, and say as how we are very sorry for such damn bad ill-luck."

"Ill luck," said the rover, "absolute ruin I mean. But this man you saw upon the rocks, can this island which lies on the ether side of the clift be inhabited." "It must be," said Jim. "we heard a lot of voices."

"It may have been the tones of myself and companions." "What lapse of time was there between the shots you heard?"

"Why, an hour's between the last two, I should say," answered Jem.

"The last shot fired was mine, to attract the notice of those on board," said the Rover. "When I found that you and the boat had disappeared." But come, we must not remain for ever upon this rock— we may find something of which we can form a bridge across the chasm, and reach the opposite side. There are five of us now, and we need have little fear from any one who may be on the island.

Again the boy Rover commenced to descend the cliff, followed by his companions.

The loud roar of the sea had died away, into a sullen murmur, and the waves rolled in upon the rocks slowly, and like exhausted gladiators, whose strength were all but exhausted.

The little bay lie almost unruffled at their feet, and its entrance was chocked up by portions of the wreck.

Broken spars hugged the sides of the cliffs, and bales and barrels floated thither and thither, at the will of the wind or the wave.

A deep sigh broke from the Rover's chest, as he gazed upon the wreck of the fine vessel he had commanded.

He had toiled, struggled, and sinned, to obtain her, and now there she lay, broken into a thousand pieces, and the labour of years scattered to the waves. Scarce one plank held to another, so fearful had been the shock she had met on those jagged rocks.

And the Boy Rover turned his eyes from the scene of desolation, and cursed the ill-fortune which had pursued him since he sailed from the shores of Cornwall, on the morning of Ellen's escape from the cave.

The fate of Wild Madge, too, caused him considerable anxiety. He doubted not that she had met a watery grave; and, base as she was, he could but feel a pang of sorrow for her end, for he thought, "Is she not my mother?"

However, it was not time to give way to grief or despondency. The situation of himself and companions was a desperate one, and some means or another must be resorted to for remedying it; and they walked down the cliff, till they stood at the spot on which each boat's crew had landed.

Portions of the wreck, as we have before stated, floated in the small bay; but not a particle washed up to the spot where they now stood.

The spars and planks hugged the side of the rock —but only at places where the rock was too high for the smugglers to reach them.

Here was another disappointment.

The Rover bit his lips with vexation.

His companions, less cool, gave vent to curses, loud and deep.

The Rover sat himself down, and, leaning his head on his hand, tried to invent some idea by which he could gain possession of the floating pieces of the wreck.

His companions watched, in moody silence, the workings of his countenance.

At length the Rover leapt to his feet.

The smugglers saw that he had hit upon some plan at last.

"I have it!" he exclaimed.

"What is it, captain?" asked Bill.

"What is it?" repeated Jem.

"You see those spars," asked the Rover, and he pointed towards them.

"Yes," said Bill.

"We must have them."

"But we can't reach them," said Jem.

"Yes we can," replied the Boy Rover.

"How," inquired Bill.

"Easily enough," said the Boy Rover.

"Don't see it," said Bill.

"Nor I," said Jem, " Do you Sam."

"Not found here," replied Jem.

"Nor anywhere else," said Bill.

"Yes, we can," said the captain.

"Then be kind enough to explain how."

"Well, you see they hug the rock yonder."

"Yes."

"We must reach them from that spot," said the Rover.

"Your arms are longer than mine then," said Bill, "if you can stretch them out about a dozen feet."

"There is none of us can reach them," said the Boy Rover, "But we can form a chain of our bodies as easily as that young fellow formed a bridge of his."

"How do you mean, captain," asked Bill, with a puzzled expression.

"Are you so dull that you can't see," said the Boy Rover.

"Blowed if I can tumble," said Bill.

"Nor do I wish you too," you must have a steady head and a strong hand. Look here, now, you and Jem stand here, and lower Sam over the side, holding tightly on to his hands, then I will descend Sam's body, and cling to his feet.—my feet will then about touch the water, and I can clasp the spars between them, and you can bring me and the timber to the top of the rock. Do you see now.

"Well, I never thought of that," said Bill.

"Nor I," said Jem.

"Do you see it now," said the Boy Rover.

"Yes," said Jem.

"And a stunning idea it is, captain," said Jem. "But you must mind you don't leave go; or your lost, for certain."

"I'll take care of that," said the captain. "Now, are you ready?"

"Yes," was the reply.

"Then lower Sam over the side."

Bill and Jem grasped the hands of Sam, who gradually slid over the edge of the rock.

"Hold tight, good luck to you," said Sam.

"All right," replied Jem. "Don't be frightened."

"I ain't frightened," said the man; "only I ain't a first-rate swimmer, that's all."

"Well, I am," said the Boy Rover, and if they let go, I'll soon be after you."

This seemed to make the man more satisfied with the part he was about to play, and the Boy Rover, grasping him by the shoulders, lowered himself down his body.

"Dam'd if you won't pull my legs out, captain," said the man, "as the Boy Rover caught the feet of his companion in his grasp."

"No fear of that ;" said the Boy Rover. "I'm not very heavy."

Sam thought otherwise, but made no further remark.

As he had surmised the Boy Rover's feet just touched the surface of the water, and he endeavoured to grasp a spar between them.

But the moment they came in contact with it, it bobbed under.

"Confound it." said Bill, as he gazed anxiously over the side.

"He's hardly low enough," said Jem.

"No, more he ain't," replied Bill. "Catch hold of my legs, and let me slip over a little—that will lengthen the cable."

"So it will," said Jem, catching hold of the legs of the lieutenant, and allowing him gradually to slip over the rock.

This enabled the Rover to grasp the spar with his feet; and, drawing it up, greatly assisted by the buoyancy of the water, he released his hold of one hand, and held it aloft.

In the same manner it was grasped by the others, and, after considerable exertion, safely landed upon the cliff.

"That will do," said the Rover, as he commenced ascending by the way he had got down. "We can draw some more of the wreck towards us by the aid of that spar."

In a few moments they had regained their former position on the rock.

"I tell you what it is, captain," said Sam, as he rubbed his legs: "the next time you try that dodge I'll be last man."

"Why?" asked the Rover.

"Because I'm long enough already. I don't want to be pulled out a yard or two in that manner. You've stretched my legs till you nearly broke 'em."

"You'll have your neck stretched some day," said the captain, with a grin. "That will be worse than your legs, I reckon."

"Cut it," said Sam, removing his hands from his legs, and taking the measure of his throat with his fingers.

"No doubt that is what the rope will do," remarked the Boy Rover.

An involuntary shudder passed through the man's frame at this remark, and he said no more about his legs.

They now descended the rocks to the landing-place, and, by the aid of the rescued spar, drew several pieces of timber towards them, and landed them upon the rock.

By this means they gained sufficient to form a raft; and, as a great quantity of cordage was attached to several of the pieces, they now saw no difficulty in the operation.

The Rover had a strong inclination to form a bridge once more across the chasm, and make his way to the woods; but to this his companions were somewhat averse.

The tale told by Bill and Jem, respecting the shots which had been fired at them, led them to believe that the place was inhabited by those who would prove more foe than friend to the smugglers; and they persuaded the captain to put to sea on the raft, and trust to some passing vessel meeting and rescuing them, when they could invent some tale to disguise their true character.

To this the Rover agreed after awhile; and, the raft being formed, the smugglers launched it, and floated out of the bay, just as the sun was at the meridian.

A stiff breeze was blowing, and they sped over the waves at a tremendous pace.

Worn out with the labours they had undergone, they lay down upon the raft and slept, all but the Boy Rover, whose eyes never for a moment ceased to scan the horizon.

The shades of night were closing around them, and enwrapping the sea a gloomy veil, when the quick eye of the Boy Rover, discovered a speck upon the water.

His heart beat audibly, and his eye followed the object till it loomed larger, and partook of the shape of a hull of a vessel.

Then he awoke his companion, and pointed out to them.

As their glance was rivetted upon it, the white sails gradually became more and more distinct, and they knew that a vessel was heaving down upon them.

They stood up and waved their handkerchiefs, and jackets in the air, and the report of a pistol came across the sea.

An exclamation of joy escaped them, that shot told them they had been seen.

CHAPTER XLV.

THE SMUGGLER'S GRATITUDE—MURDER OF THE CREW.

THE last faint streak of light faded the horizon, and darkness was upon the sea.

The raft upon which the five smugglers had floated over the waves, rode unoccupied upon the bosom of the waters.

They had been saved.

The ship, whose hull had first been detected by the Boy Rover, had borne down upon them, and willing hands had been stretched forth to succour and to save.

The Boy Rover and his villanous companion stood upon the deck.

And pitying glances and kind words met them on every side.

They were among British seamen, and the generous hands and noble hearts of the sailors vied with each other to comfort and aid them.

And the brave man who commanded the small craft, spoke cheering words and extended the hand of hospitality.

They trod the deck on an English vessel, and the proud emblems of freedom floated above their heads.

They told how they had been wrecked in a small trading vessel, which lost her way in the storm; and the sympathy of their saviours was aroused.

The hand of friendship was extended to them, and their every want supplied.

Berths were prepared, and, with kind words and heartfelt wishes for their comfort, they were left to repose.

Night deepened, and all was still on board that bark.

For the weather was now fair, and none but the watch remained on deck.

The Rover left his couch, and so did his companions.

With finger on his lip, and knitted brow, he imposed silence upon his followers.

"There are ten," he whispered, and two passengers. With cool heads, and steady hands, what can we not accomplish?"

"The seizure of the vessel will be easy," whispered Bill.

Jem and the two others nodded, but spoke not.

"We have no arms," said Bill.

"But can soon get them," said the Rover.

"Where?"

"Each arm himself with a marlin-spike. I will go on deck, and enter into conversation with the watch; and then, when he is settled, I will give the signal for you to come up."

"Will you go alone?" said Bill.

"It will be best."

"He may suspect."

"I will disarm all suspicion."

"How?"

"Leave that to me," was the reply.

"But, captain—"

"Silence! When you hear the signal, come—not before."

"As you will," said Bill.

"The ship is ours," said the Rover.

The watch was pacing up and down, humming the air of some old song, as the Boy Rover stood at his side.

"I cannot sleep," he said, addressing the man, as he came to a dead halt upon seeing him.

"Rest yourself," replied the man, "you must need it after what you have suffered."

"I cannot rest," replied the Rover, "the thoughts of my poor lost companions drove sleep from my soul."

"Ah," said the honest, feeling sailor, "it's hard to lose a messmate, but God's will be done."

And as a sigh escaped his breast, at the thought that some day his fate might be the same, he staggered against the bulwarks, and the cry which rose to his lips was silenced by a blow from his marlin spike, which crushed in his skull.

Then with one bound the boy Rover leaped upon the man at the wheel, and ere he could utter a single cry, he fell stunned, and bleeding to the deck.

A long, low whistle escaped the lips of the smuggler's captain, and in another instant the smuggler stood by his side.

"All is well," he exclaimed, hurriedly—"Jem, follow Bill, you and others look to the forecastle,—let none escape."

And followed by Jem, he rushed down the stairs to the cabin.

The captain aroused by the fall of the man, at the wheel, had risen from his cot, and opened the door of his cabin, at the moment that the Boy Rover and his followers stood before it.

As his eyes met the forms of the smugglers, he rushed back, and stretched forth his hand to grasp a pistol, but ere he could present it, a blow upon the forehead sent him staggering and another prostrated him to the floor.

The Boy Rover seized the pistol from the hand of the prostrate man, and rushed from the cabin, followed by Jem.

As they were leaving it, the mate only attired in his shirt, stood before him.

A click, a sharp report, and he lay across the foot of the stairs with a bullet through his neck.

"Come," said the Boy Rover, "our friends may need help."

"The passengers," said Jem.

"Leave them for the present—there is little to fear in that quarter—the crew first." And, as he spoke, he bounded up to the deck followed by his companion.

The sailors now thoroughly roused by the report of the pistol were hurrying up to the deck.

As the head of the first appeared above the hatchway, a blow from Bill sent him down upon his companions.

Surprise and terror for a moment held those below paralysed.

It was for a moment only, and then another head appeared above the opening.

This met the fate of its companion, and the head disappeared.

Six were disposed of, and a smile played round the mouth of the Boy Rover.

The remaining four sailors seemed to be holding a consultation below.

In a few moments a man bounded up the ladder, and sprang upon the deck.

"You dam pirates!" he exclaimed, "you——"

The rest of his speech was stayed by the loud crash of the marling spikes in his brain, and the knife which he had held in his hand fell at the feet of Jem, as his body rolled to the deck.

"Now," said the Boy Rover, "you and Sam look to the passengers. We will do all that is required here."

Bill and Sam strode aft towards the cabins.

"Look out," said Jem. "Here's another coming."

As he spoke, something appeared at the mouth of the forecastle.

It was a hammock, being carried upon the head of a man.

He had adopted this plan to save his skull from the blow which he felt sure he would receive the moment he appeared.

Up it came, till it cleared the opening; then was thrust violently forward, and the man sprang to the deck.

He brandished his knife in his hand, and, avoiding the blow aimed at him by the Rover, plunged it into the arm of Jem.

With a howl of pain, the smuggler sprang back; and the next moment the knife which he had picked up from the deck was buried in the throat of the brave sailor.

With a cry of agony, the man fell to the deck, as another rushed up the ladder.

Poor fellow!—he came to meet his doom. A heavy blow, a sharp cry, and his insensible body rolled down upon the only one now left below.

"We have nothing to fear now, I reckon," said the Boy Rover, turning to his blood-stained companions.

"No; only we must sarve the other one the same, and make all sure," said Jem.

"Yes," remarked the Rover.

"Now, then, come on," said Jem—no skulking!"

But the man, warned by the fate of his companions, remained below.

"Are we to come down and fetch you?" said the Rover.

There was no reply.

"Surrender to us," called out the Rover, "and you have nothing to fear."

The man appeared at the bottom of the ladder.

"You will not murder me?" he said.

"Not if you offer no violence."

"I have your word for it," said the man, still hesitating.

"Come up, and you are safe," said the Boy Rover.

The man ascended the ladder.

"Dam you, why didn't you come before, exclaimed the Boy Rover, as the man's head appeared upon a level with the smuggler's body.

"I——"

"Take that for your obstinacy," said the Rover.

And the hands of the smuggler and Jem descended, and the last of the brave little ship which had rescued them from their perilous position, rolled over with a deep groan.

"That's the last," said the captain, "and the ship is ours."

"The passengers?" said Jem.

"We can dispose of them at any moment."

"We've made a good night's work of it," remarked Jem.

"Better than you would have done by yourself, I reckon," said the Rover, turning to the other man, who had blamed him on the clift for all the mischief he had caused.

"Well, captain, I must say you are the best hand after all," remarked the man.

"Oh, you have come to the decision at last," remarked the Boy Rover, with a sarcastic smile.

"Yes," said the man, "I have captain."

"Well, so far we have succeeded. But the passengers must be cared for."

"What is to be their fate?" asked Jem.

"Why, I think we may as well have a little amusement to-morrow. Then they can walk the plank. So far, we are all right. We will take good care they cannot get out of their berths, so now to rest, till to-morrow."

CHAPTER XLVI.

THE BOY ROVER AND THE PASSENGERS—THE EXECUTION DEFERRED.

NIGHT passed away, and the first grey streaks of early dawn lighted up the eastern horizon.

The passengers, roused by the pistol shot, had known no rest for hours.

Minutes had appeared hours, hours days, yet still they could not understand its meaning.

They had endeavoured to fathom the mystery, but their curiosity was checked—the door of their cabin was fastened.

In vain they strove to open it.

It would not yield.

The united strength of master and servant could not move the barrier which parted them from the stairs.

They knew that something was wrong, but what that something was they knew not.

Had the crew mutinied?

They feared it was so.

A dreadful fear broke over them.

They communed together but could come to no definite conclusion.

The light of day broke through the cabin window and still they were prisoners.

"What can be the meaning of this?" said Mr. Hanfield.

"I cannot think," replied Jacob.

"Something is wrong."

"Doubtless," replied the faithful domestic.

"But why are we made prisoners."

"Heaven only knows."

"I fear the worst," said the master.

"Alas, so do I."

"At the moment, too, when I was seeking my lost child."

"It is hard," said Jacob sympathisingly.

"Hark, I hear the sound of footsteps.

Jacob listened.

There was a step upon the stairs.

The handle of the door moved.

Mr. Hanfield stood ready in case of surprise.

Jacob clutched a chair in his hands with the intention of hurling at anyone who might offer them violence.

The door opened.

On the threshold stood the Boy Rover.

He cast a hurried glance round the apartment, and entered.

The occupants gazed at him in mute surprise.

The Rover started as he looked upon the features of the gentleman.

He had wondered where he had seen that face

before. That he had seen it, he felt certain; yet he was mistaken.

That instinctive feeling for which it is impossible to account had taken possession of his breast.

On the first glance each felt they were enemies, though they had never met before.

"You will consider yourselves my prisoners," said the Rover. "The ship is now mine."

"Where is Captain Hammond?" said Mr. Hanfield.

"Dead," was the reply.

"Dead!" echoed Hanfield.

"Yes, dead," replied the Rover—"as is, also, the whole of his crew."

"Then that pistol-shot I heard—"

"Proclaimed me captain of this bark," interrupted the smuggler.

"Can it be possible that you have repaid the generous hospitality of Captain Hammond by—"

"Taking possession of his ship?"

"That's what I was about to say," remarked Hanfield.

"You are correct in your surmises," said the Rover, coolly. "I wanted a ship, and I have gained one."

"But by what means?"

"The only one left in my power."

"By bloodshed and—"

"Determination," remarked the Rover.

"Villany and murder," said Mr. Hanfield.

"As you will," remarked the Rover. "But come, your presence, and that of your servant is required on deck.

"For what purpose," asked Hanfield, turning a shade paler.

"Come and see," said the Rover.

"Alas! I fear."

"Your colour plainly tells me that," said the smuggler.

"What are your designs," asked Hanfield.

"Merely to make you walk the plank," said the Boy Rover.

"Would you murder me," said Hanfield.

"Willingly," replied the smuggler.

"Boy, boy," exclaimed the old gentleman, have you no fear of justice.

"None," was the cool rejoinder.

"So young and yet so base," remarked the old man.

"Ah, send not your soul to perdition."

"Look you old gentleman," said the Boy Rover "I have taken possession of this ship, and it is necessary for my safety, that none remain who can tell the tale. The captain and crew have gone to their last account, and you and your followers alone remain—you must die—my safety demands it, and my followers will that it should be so.

"Have you no mercy."

"None."

"No fear?"

"None."

"Then your a dam'd scoundrel," chimed in Jacob, unable longer to control his indignation.

"Am I," said the Boy Rover.

"Yes you are," replied Jacob. "And before you shall do my master harm, I'll sacrifice the last drop of blood in my veins."

"Bravely spoken," said the Boy Rover. "You are a noble fellow, and you will join us——"

"Join you—you black-hearted scoundrel," said Jacob, "I would sooner cut my tongue out than take the oath of allegiance to a villian like you."

"It is the only means to save my life."

"Is it."

"Yes it is," said the smuggler.

"Then I'd die a thousand times sooner than have my life spared by such conditions."

"Think ere you decide," said the rover.

"It wants no thinking," replied Jacob. "The honest man's mind is made up in a moment."

"I will give you an hour," said the rover. "And if at the expiration of that time you are still in the same mood you will accompany your master to the bottom of the sea."

And as he spoke the Boy Rover turned to leave the cabin.

"Look here, you pirate," said Jacob, "I know not whether you be commander or not of this ship, now, but I do know you are a black-hearted scoundrel, and if you've got a spark of courage in you you'll give us a chance of fighting for our liberty."

"How!" said the Boy Rover.

"How," replied Jacob, "by meeting us singly and not half-a-dozen on to one."

"Do you think," said the Boy Rover, "that I have run the risk of death in seizing this vessel to become such a fool now?"

"I think you are a most contemptible coward," said Jacob.

"You do?"

"Yes, I do."

"You shall find that it is not blood which makes me so," said the Boy Rover, turning red with passion.

"That is your element," said Mr. Henfield.

"It is," said the Boy Rover, "and I hesitate not to shed it when my own safety demands it."

"Or your own evil passions actuate the deed," said Jacob.

"Which you will, it matters not," said the rover.

"This ship is now in the possession of myself and my friends, and our mutual safety demands your death."

"Will nothing but our blood satisfy you?" said Mr. Hanfield.

"Nothing."

"Not a ransom?"

"Dead men tell no tales," said the Rover.

"If we promise—"

"I would not trust you."

"Then there is no means to escape this fate you have designed for us?"

"Yes—one."

"And that?"

"Take the oath of allegiance, and join us," said the Rover.

"Then you can have my answer now," said Jacob. "I'll see you damned first. So do your worst."

"Peace, Jacob!" said his master.

"It is he who has declared war," replied the domestic—"not us."

"But he may think differently, perhaps, in time," said Mr. Hanfield.

"Do not believe it," said the Rover. "Join us, and live; refuse, and die. There is no middle course."

"And should we refuse?" asked Jacob.

"You walk the plank in an hour."

"Then you walk it, too," said the domestic, rushing forward.

The Rover drew a pistol from his breast, and pointed it at the head of the faithful servant. Jacob drew back, as he saw the polished barrel pointed directly at him.

"Stand back!" said the Rover—"I never miss my man."

"Nor I," said Jacob, suddenly springing forward and striking the weapon from the Boy Rover's grasp, and ere he could recover from the surprise into which he had fallen, dealt him a blow on the mouth that caused him to stagger back several paces.

Mad with rage, the Boy Rover grasped Jacob by the throat, and gave utterance to a loud whistle.

In a moment Bill, Jem, and Sam entered the cabin, and seeing how affairs stood, instantly secured Jacob, and in a few moments his arms were pinioned, and he was rendered powerless.

But the brave domestic quailed not. His eyes was still fixed unflinchingly upon the Boy Rover.

Foaming with rage, the Boy Rover ordered his followers to lead Mr. Hanfield and Jacob, to the deck.

This was done.

Both master and servant cast their eyes across the sea, and up at the blue vault above.

They believed their last hour was come, and murmured an inward prayer for their souls.

But never for one moment did they think of suing for mercy—they were resigned to their fate.

The Boy Rover gave the order, and the planks were placed ready for the sacrifice.

The smuggler's captain moved his hand, and Mr. Hanfield and his servant were led on to the planks.

The sailors now only waited the final order.

With a smile upon his lips, the Boy Rover advanced towards Jacob, and pointing to the water beneath them, said :—

"I never forgive a blow." "I offered you a chance for your life and you refused it.

"And I refuse it now," said Jacob, drawing himself proudly up, even now, when death stares me in the face."

"Stand ready," said the Boy Rover, addressing his men.

"Sail-ho," said Jem, as looking ever the sea at this moment, "he detected the sails of a vessel bearing down upon them."

The Boy Rover glanced in the direction indicated by the finger of his follower, and he paused thoughtfully.

A ray of hope animated the hearts of the doomed men.

The Boy Rover turned to his companions.

"Make all sail." he said hurriedly, "but first take these men below, and see they are safely secured.

When we are out of sight of this stranger, will be time enough for the execution.

CHAPTER XLVII.

THE SLAVE SHIP—WILD MADGE AGAIN.

On the banks of a large and noble river in Western Africa, some few miles from the sea-coast, lay heaped up, in wild and grand confusion, masses of granite and porphry rocks. At the base was seated one of those tawny sons of that oppressed race, the African.

His hands were crossed upon his knees, and his eyes were fixed in dreary vacancy beyond. There was an air of noble grace in the very passiveness of his attitude that seemed to attest that he was at least superior to those who inhabited the villages around.

He was, in fact, the chief of a warlike tribe, whose lives were spent in war, not as the means of attaining glory and renown, but for the ignoble purposes of trade—and such a trade! Yes, they warred against their own kind and colour, that they might supply the demand for slaves that came from the cruel whites!

A tuft of feathers on his head, and a loose robe, formed of the skin of animals obtained in the chase, was his only dress; whilst his lance, or spear, resting idly against his breast, was his only weapon.

About a pace before him stood a man whose dress and complexion showed that he belonged to another and more temperate clime.

Thin, but exceeding tall, and attired in the undress naval uniform of the United States, he appeared as a strange contrast to the African beside him. He was evidently young, and not bad-looking—though the lines around his mouth, and a cruel look in his eyes, would lead one to judge, and, perhaps, not wrongly, that he was vindictive and tyrannical.

He was in the act of gazing across the river that lay before him, and, shading his eyes with one hand, seemed absorbed in the objects before him.

Presently the savage broke the silence:

"Why will not my brother speak?"

"Well, Zambuci, the fact is I am still undecided."

"Is my brother fickle, that he cannot decide?"

"Pshaw!"

"The young men I bring are strong and well, and the white man can afford much."

"But, Zambuci, your price is too high; you must not expect so much."

"Does my brother forget that the blood of my people has flowed, and that many bite the dust?"

"Ah! well; you shall have what you want this time—but not in future."

The savage's eyes glistened with pleasure at the prospect of an accession of wealth, in the shape of powder and trinkets.

But the naval officer, who was no other than a slave captain, still kept his eyes fixed before him.

At last, pointing to some object floating down the stream, he said—

"Look, Zambuci, what seest thou?"

The officer rose, and gazed in the direction the other had pointed out.

"It is some black object—perhaps a sea-horse."

"No, no, your eyes deceive you. I have watched it for some time. I think it is an overturned canoe."

"My brother is right."

"Yes, and is there not something clinging to it, Zambuca, eh,——"

"My brother's eyes are good."

"Well, what see you?"

"Two persons are clinging to the boat."

"Thou art right. By heavens! can we not save them?"

It was the impulse of the moment that prompted the slave captain to feel thus interested in two unknown beings; but the reason was that, in the excitement of their struggles, he forgot the worse part of his nature, and became humane.

Hastily leaving the vicinity where we first introduced them to notice, they walked rapidly in the same direction as the current.

They had not gone far when the captain blew a whistle; and a boat, manned with some half-dozen of stalwart seamen, immediately appeared from some hiding nook, where they had been awaiting their captain's return.

Instantly he embarked, leaving the African behind, who, not caring to trust himself in the power of those who had carried away so many of his countrymen, watched the motions of the boat from the banks.

"Give way, my lads," said the captain to his men, pointing towards the boat that was drifting rapidly down the stream. "Let's see what sort of fish they be."

"Aye, aye," was the response.

"After a few vigorous strokes, they rapidly neared the object of pursuit; and, as they drew nearer, they could distinctly see that there were two men clinging to it.

A few more pulls, and they are alongside Another moment, and Smith and Lang are safe in the American's boat.

Yes, it was them: though insensible, they still lived.

Dashed down the cataract, the dread and horror of their fate lent strength to their arms, and they held on with the tenacity of despair, and though the passage down the falls deprived them of sensibility—yet still, their grasp did not relax, and when once more they floated in still water, the canoe prevented him from sinking, but the poor unfortunate companion of the flight was drowned.

Having recovered the men, the boat was rapidly propelled back to the place from whence they had started, and where the African with folded arms, still stood, watching with evident interest the events that had just taken place.

The captain leaped again on the shore, and turning to the men in the boat, commanding them to lose no time in conveying the still unconscious men on board their ship, and then to return with the long boat besides their own.

The men silently obeyed, and in a few moments the boat was out of sight, being hid from view by a turn of the stream.

"My brethren has done well," said the African breaking the silence. "What will he do with the strangers he has torn from the wives' bosom? Sell them for slaves?"

"A look of malignity crossed the captain's face for a moment, and then as suddenly checking it, he replied in a tone of bland suavity.

"Zambuci, thou art mistaken, white man are brothers, and free—as the air."

Oh," said the African, in a tone of irony, as if he did not believe all white men were free.

"Yes," free; and these men will place under care of a doctor, when—

"Ah, when."

"Well; when they are recovered, they will be—"

"Slaves," echoed the other.

"Liar," he muttered, between his teeth, but checking himself, he added. "Oh, Zambuci, thou art wrong. Thinkest thou that we traffic in each other like ye of this accused land."

As Zambuci was about to reply, a loud report rang through the air, like the firing of a musket.

A thin wreath of smoke curling upwards through the still air, and was seen above the trees that clustered towards the river's brink, about a mile beyond.

Almost as soon as they discovered the smoke, another and another report rapidly followed till the echoes around awoke and perpetuated the ominous sounds.

Surprised and startled, the captain and the chief stood eagerly gazing in the direction indicated by the smoke.

Then, cautiously and silently, they swiftly sped towards the spot, to reconnoitre and ascertain what was going on.

Keeping close to the water's edge. under shelter of the bank, they reached the wood unobserved.

The firing had by this time ceased and the usual silence again reigned supreme.

The African now took the lead, and forced his way through the tangled growth with surprising agility.

After proceeding some little distance, they emerge into a large open space or clearing, evidently the work of fire in some future age, as the ground was entirely destitute of verdure.

On the further side they saw with surprise the retreating forms of several natives. Zambuci saw at a glance that they belonged to a tribe hostile to his, so he at once resumed his more cautious mode of procedure, and plunging again into the wood prepared to make a circuit of the clearing and come upon them beyond.

Some time had elapsed ere they reached the opposite side of the clearing, and there they discovered that the forest extended only a quarter of a mile further.

Having passed through this belt or fringe of wood they found themselves on the verge of an extensive plain, the termination of which was beyond the ken of their inward vision—to their right extended the continuation of the rocky hills, before mentioned, and to their left lay at some little distance the river they had but recently left.

As the eye followed the course of the river it could perceive the grand and boundless ocean into which the river flowed. Nothing interrupted the view, the vast plain bounded by the rocks, appeared almost a part of the sea, towards which it stretched.

Just in the mouth of the river lay a vessel at anchor, her tapering masts gently swaying in the air, as the undulating water moved the hull.

It was the slave ship.

About midway between the ship, and the place were the captain and his African companion were standing, was the boat that had rescued Lang and Smith. They were pulling with all their might towards the shore, and towards the boat two men were seen running at the top of their speed. Behind them, in hot pursuit, were the natives, that the African had seen in the clearing.

Seeing his boat's crew so near, the captain no longer felt the necessity of caution, and at once dashed off towards the same spot where all parties seemed bent on effecting a junction.

He soon came within speaking distance, and saw to his surprise, that the two who were being pursued were Europeans, and that the pursuers, a motley crew, armed with spears and clubs, and in a few instances rifles.

On came the fugitives, breathless, and bleeding, for they were evidently wounded, and nearer came their pursuers.

At last the boat grated on the sand, and the men who had heard the firing as soon as their captain, leaped ashore. They had seen the two poor devils emerge from the wood on to the plain, and pursued by the savage natives, and felt in spite of the service in which they were engaged, the old charm of generous adventures, more the instincts of their nature, to succour the distressed—and consequently they strained every nerve, and swim to reach the land ere the savages could overtake their victims.

THE MASSACRE ON BOARD THE SLAVER.

Dashing forward, the sailors, armed with pikes, which they seized from the boat, as they dropped their oars, neared the objects of their sympathy.

About the same distance off were the natives; and it now became a race of intense excitement—each straining every nerve to distance the other.

Completely exhausted, the two men sank fainting to the ground; and, with a cry of exultation, the sailors leaped astride their bodies, presenting then a bristling row of pikes.

"Save us—save us! We are white men!" exclaimed one of them.

"Aye, aye, my hearties—never fear," cried one of the sailors. "The black devils ain't got you yet."

Exasperated, yet foiled, the savages halted a few paces from the threatening front of the sailors. But, seeing that they still outnumbered them, by three to one, they prepared to attack, and, if possible, obtain possession of those they had so hotly pursued,

With loud cries and yells, they advanced, balancing their spears in a menacing manner.

The captain now reached the scene, and instantly gave orders to the men to raise the exhausted runaways, and bear them to the boats.

Four of the men immediately lifted them up, and hurried towards the boat; while the others slowly followed—retreating backwards, yet still showing the same unflinching front.

They reach the boat, and, by the time they have all embarked, and are about to push off, the natives rush forward, hurling their spears, and other missiles, towards them; but they fall harmlessly around them.

A few minutes, and they stand on the deck of the slaver.

The doctor is summoned on deck, and, after a little attention, he succeeds in restoring all parties to consciousness.

But who can pourtray the astonishment of Lang and Smith when they recognise in the men rescued from the savages their old companions, Bond and Hardy!

Mutual was the surprise; and the joy of once more seeing and recogni ing old faces completely obliterated all traces of ill-will that might have existed.

It appeared that, when they fell into the power of those savages on the lake, they soon recovered the ill-usage they had experienced at their hands, but they were kept close prisoners, and were forced to accompany them on all their expeditions.

On this occasion they had travelled some distance, till they came to a village inhabited by women and children—the men being absent on a hunting expedition. Here, creeping stealthily and silently, in the night, they surprised them, and, with savage cruelty, put them all to death, and afterwards fired the village. Bond and Hardy were so horrified at this remorseless barbarity that they attempted to escape when they beheld the boat on the river, which they knew to be European, by her build; with what success the reader has already been made acquainted.

All was now bustle on board the slave ship. Evening was drawing near, and the deep voice of the captain was heard issuing his commands, in rapid and peremptory tones.

In a little while several of the ship's boats are manned; and the captain, again embarking, leads the small flotilla towards the shore.

As they reach the shore, a strange medley of sounds greet their ears, and a black and moving mass meet their eyes.

Zambuci stands proudly forward to meet the captain, as he steps ashore.

He is surrounded by his followers, who are guarding a dense crowd of poor wretches, who are tied together.

They are slaves.

Zambuci and his warriors have captured, or rather kidnapped, them to supply the cursed wants of slavers.

Like sheep to the slaughter were they driven ot the boats—their piteous wailing cries mingling with the yells and shouts of their captain.

The barter is effected, and the boats return to the ship.

Ere the darkness of night had descended and obscured the land, the good ship, with its bad freight, had made good her way out of the river's mouth.

The rattling of chains, the shout of seamen, and the orders of officers, as the anchors were weighed, mingled with the smothered wail of sorrow issuing from the hatchways, became hushed; and, as the white canvass spread out to the freshening breeze, the spray was dashed aside as the plough cut through the sparkling phosphorescent waves, as if in mockery of the crushed hearts in the hold.

The stars peeped forth with the cold silent light —gazing, as if in pity, on the accursed ship that lent its aid to so cruel a wrong. And, in the dim light, the black outline of the coast could just be discerned in the distance. They were fast leaving the oppressed land behind: the land breeze favoured their progress, and everything conspired to give those on board hopes of a speedy and prosperous voyage.

But they did not neglect the proper caution so necessary to be observed in the nefarious traffic they were engaged in; and, consequently, a sharp look-out was kept, and a course steered that was not usually placed on the chart.

With the exception of the watch and the captain, all were sunk in repose on board the ship.

Even the wretched negroes, for awhile, forgot their miseries. Lulled by the monotonous plash of the waves, as they unceasingly dashed against the oaken walls, they fell asleep.

Poor wretches!—their miseries had scarcely yet began. Another day, with a scorching sun, will awaken them to a taste of the horrors that await them.

Silently, and with head buried in his bosom, the slave captain paced the deck. His steps were hurried, and, by the clutching of his hands, and occasional pauses in his walk, he seemed deeply moved by some inward emotion.

At last he stopped, and calling one of the men to him, said:

"Tell Lieutenant Martiney I would speak with him."

The man touched his hat, and disappeared.

In a few moments the lieutenant stood before him, and, respectfully saluting him, exclaimed:

"I am here, Mr. Wildwell."

The captain, returning his salute, passed his arm through the lieutenant's, and, leading him aside, they walked together.

"Is all well below?" inquired the captain.

"Yes—all's well."

"And the four men we have so strangely discovered, and rescued from impending death, will they join our crew?"

"Well, yes, I think they will, when they are sufficiently recovered."

"Good—it is well for them. Had they proved obstinate, they should have the doom of slavery affixed to them."

The lieutenant shuddered—for at heart he was not so vindictive and cruel as the captain; but he said nothing.

"Martiney," said the captain, sinking his voice, "I know not what to do with that girl. Her very obduracy maddens me. I idolize the ground she walks on, and yet she scorns me. How can I overcome so deadly an aversion?"

"Alas!" said Martiney, "I am a poor hand at subjects of love, and cannot imagine any way by which you can overcome a woman's hate."

"Think you, Martiney, that that woman we found clinging to a piece of wreck off the isle of Madeira, could be moulded to my will?"

"She is in your power; she dare not disobey you."

"True—but I do not wish to use force or harshness. If I could persuade the hag to use all her influence and woman's wit in my service, Donna Iuez might yet be mine."

"Yes, it might be so."

"I will see her."

"Now?"

"No—to-morrow. It is late."

"'Tis four bells in the second watch."

"Ah! then, I'll seek some repose: and do you, Martiney, see all snug. Good night!"

"Good night, sir!"

The captain at length retired, and the lieutenant, musingly, walked towards the man stationed at the wheel.

Lieutenant Martiney was a handsome man, with a profusion of dark hair and whiskers. His complexion showed that his blood had a more Southern origin than his captain: his eye was brilliant and dark, with an expression pleasing and good-natured; he was a few years older, but not near so tall as the captain.

Satisfied with his scrutiny, the lieutenant resumed

his walk, till relieved by the officer of the next watch.

The night wore on—nothing of interest occurred—and the ship careered on its way. Morning came, and bustle succeeded the night's quiet. All hands turned out, and cleaning and swabbing held the sway for a time.

The poor negroes were counted out—none, as yet, were missing—and, with kicks and curses, they were driven back to their wretched prison, heavily ironed, and with scanty food, flung to them like dogs.

The captain sat in his cabin. The door opened, and a woman was ushered into his presence. He motioned her to a seat; but she declined it, and sto d before him.

She was a gaunt and careworn looking woman—age and trouble, apparently, having ploughed deep furrows in her face, which was haggard and pale. Yet, in her eyes there seemed a lurid light that would awaken in the beholder a suspicion that vice and evil passions reigned triumphant in her breast.

Woman, I have sent for you."

"I know it."

Somewhat disconcerted by her bold effrontery and address, the captain paused; but, recovering from his surprise, he continued:

"I have rescued you from a watery grave; and, methinks, that would at least awaken a sentiment of gratitude in your bosom."

Gratitude! I know it not. Rather should I curse you for bringing me back to the hell that is in my heart."

"Indeed!"

"Aye, indeed! What do you want? Have you sent for me to thank you? Do you wish for thanks?"

"Tush, tush!" said the captain, impatiently, and getting angry. Then, looking piercingly and menacingly in eyes that looked back in his as fearless, he continued:

"I want not idle thanks. I want you to serve me—to do me a service."

The woman looked enquiringly, but remained silent.

"Will you aid me as far as in your power? Speak—yes or no?"

"What is the service you require of Wild Madge?"

"Wild Madge!—that's a strange name."

"Aye, and a strange being who bears it," said the woman, bitterly. But what is the service you require?"

"In the inner cabin there is a lady, young and beautiful, I snatched from her happy home, in Mexico. I love her; yet she spurns me."

"Oh! said Madge, and a smile of joy lit her wrinkled face. More woes—more wretchedness! Poor lovers—how delightful! Oh! it fills me with joy to see young maidens' hearts torn as mine was once. Yes, I'll serve you. She shall be yours—she shall fall. Yes," rubbing her hands with demoniac glee together, "she shall become a despised and polluted thing."

"Woman," said the captain, who shrank from so plain-spoken a way of describing his aims, "you mistake me. I seek not to destroy her happiness, but to share her love."

"Love—ha, ha, ha! Love! Go to—the heart of a man knows nought of love, but that of self. Love is a bye-word, ever on their lips, to gain the ends of their selfish desires."

"Enough of that babbling nonsense. Will you attend on her, and endeavour to lead her to think better of me?"

"I will mould her to your will; she shall be yours."

"Enough—I will prepare her for your coming."

Wild Madge retired; and the captain, fastening the door after her, returned to the door at the other end of his cabin, leading to the inner or poop cabin.

He listened a moment—all seemed still—then, turning the handle, he entered.

At the farther end, reclining on a couch, was a beautiful female.

At the first sound of the door opening, she started to her feet.

A look of indignation and alarm crossed her face, as she clasped her hands together, and, in tones of great sweetness, said:

"Signor Wildwell, why intrudest thou on me now?"

She was indeed beautiful—delicately small in feature and form—of that pure classic mould that Eastern poets delight in. Eyes, large and mournful, shot dazzling glances from beneath long silken eyelashes, falling like sunlight on cheeks tinted by a Southern sun. No wonder the captain stood entranced with the vision before him—a peri of loveliness. His eyes gazed with rapture on her form, lighting up with the passion consuming him within. But, with a strong effort, he mastered himself, and, bowing respectfully to her, he exclaimed:

"Lady, I have procured one to await on thee—one of thy own sex."

"Thanks, senor—thanks; that is kind: for it is indeed lonely to be without a companion to confide one's sorrows or fears to;" and she looked gratefully towards him.

"Ah!" thought he, "they say that gratitude is kin to love; I will not yet despair." Then, added aloud—"I am indeed happy to have succeeded in pleasing so fair a lady."

"Ah! senor, if you would but restore me to my friends, I should indeed bless you then. But you will, will you not?"—and she looked tearful and pleading in his eyes. "You will take me back to my dear mother?"

"Lady, it cannot be."

"Cannot!—alas! and why not?"

"Inez, I love you."

"Holy virgin, look down in pity on me, and save me from this man!"

"Inez, why do you fear me? I will not harm thee."

"Why do I fear thee? Ask thine own heart. Is it not there written why I should fly in horror from thee? Oh! senor, senor, do not persecute a helpless girl. I cannot love you—then why seek to make me wretched?"

"Inez, I love you. I have stood at nought that could place her who reigns supreme in my heart beside me. I have torn thee from thy friends, braved the wrath of thy powerful relation, and now—"

"You will relent, and release me."

"Impossible—I have gone too far to retrace my steps. Inez, you must be mine. You will learn to love me yet."

"Never."

"We shall see; for the present, adieu."

In a little while he returned, bringing Madge with him; and, leaving her in the company of Donna Inez, he closed the door, and went on deck.

Bitter were his feelings as he thought on the scornful repulse of Donna Inez. His vanity was deeply wounded, and his heart was a prey to wild and angry passions.

On reaching the deck, he looked savagely around,

as if in the hope of finding some object on which to vent his wrath, and wreak his vengeance.

It was near mid-day, and the sun poured down his beams in scorching heat upon the deck. The slaves now began to experience the terrible reality of their imprisonment. Crowded and packed so close that they could not lay down, it can easily be imagined how terribly great the heat was; added to which, the roof was so low that, sitting down, their heads nearly touched the beams across. In a few hours, dozens died of suffocation; and the stench and heat was so awful, that the poor wretches yelled in agony and fear.

As the captain, in his angry mood, looked round, these heart-rending cries broke on his ear.

"Bring up the lubbers, and lash their black hides: I'll make them dance to their own music."

The hatches were thrown open, the steam issued in fœtid odours, and, in a few moments, the poor creatures stepped with difficulty forward. Lifting their manacled hands, they pleaded ror mercy : but in vain.

The dead carcases were brought up, and, without ceremony, flung overboard to the waves.

The living were, one by one, lashed till the blood and flesh flew in their tyrants' faces. All were whipped—men, women, and even children. Their cries and screams resounded in all directions; and one, a sickly boy, sank fainting to the deck.

The seamen lifted him up, but he was dead.

At this moment, Donna Inez, who had been kept a close prisoner ever since her capture, and, consequently, knew not that the ship was connected with the slave trade, rushed on deck.

The noise had been so dreadful that, in terror and alarm, she had forced her way through the frail cabin door, on to the deck.

Then the sickening sight that met her view revealed at once the dreadful truth that she was in the power of a slave captain.

The captain saw her with surprise and alarm, and, rushing forward, cried:

"Back, lady! This is no place for you. Let me lead you to your cabin."

"Off, fiend — monster! Touch me not. Oh! cruel tyrant—you have killed the boy."

"Damnation!" muttered the captain — "that cursed hag has let her loose. Lady, you must retire;" and again he advanced towards her.

But, quick as lightning, she sprang from his outstretched hands, and, springing on the bulwarks, cried:

"One step nearer, and I leap into the surging sea."

Her nostrils dilated, and her eyes gleamed with indignation, while her cheeks crimsoned with excitement. Her lips were half parted, to give egress to the breath that came from her panting bosom, in quick and rapid succession; and the wind, blowing her light and flowing garment behind, showed the outline of her graceful form, as she stood, with uplifted arms, the impersonation of sublimity and grandeur.

Startled and awed, the captain stood irresolute.

Wild Madge, at this moment, came on deck. She had just missed her charge, and was about to seek the captain, to inform him of it. All eyes were fixed on the beautiful girl, bent on death, rather than infamy. But Madge gave vent to an ejaculation of surprise on beholding the scene we have described.

Her voice startled the seamen standing nearest to her; and they, turning round, beheld with astonishment their old companion, Wild Madge. It was Lang, Smith, Bond, and Hardy.

The recognition was mutual.

"Inez, Inez !" said the captain—"come back. I swear no harm shall befal thee."

"What carest thou for thine oath, bad man? I will not trust thee."

The captain, maddened with the fear of losing her, rushed forward, in the hope of catching hold of her ere she could carry her threat into execution.

But no; with a wild cry, she sprang forward, and leaped into the boiling waves: and, as the water closed over her, a crowd of men sprang in after her, regardless of danger, to rescue so lovely a woman from a watery grave.

For a moment, the captain stood like one paralysed; then, starting forward, he shouted :

"Man the boats—quick!"

Springing on the taffrail, he gazed anxiously, in the hope of catching a glimpse of her white dress: but in vain. Like a madman, he stormed and swore; and, when the boats were ready, he leaped into one, ordering the ship to be put back.

Long and anxiously they searched—but in vain; and sadly and gloomily all returned to the ship, having picked up those who had first sprang into the waters.

On their return to the ship, they discovered, to their surprise, that Lieutenant Martinez was missing.

It was remembered that he was one of the first to rush to the rescue of the unfortunate lady : but no one had seen him since.

It was concluded that he must have struck his head against something as he went in the water, and, being stunned, of course had sunk, and was drowned.

All was gloom and sorrow on board the ship; for the lieutenant was liked by the crew; and the beautiful lady's untimely fate sank deep in the hearts of all.

The captain shut himself up in his cabin, and none dared disturb him.

In the meanwhile, Wild Madge took the opportunity, in the general confusion, to hold an interview with the four seamen who had belonged to the smuggler crew.

CHAPTER XLVIII.

WILD MADGE AND THE SMUGGLERS RESOLVE TO TAKE THE SLAVE SHIP—THEIR DARING ATTEMPTS—THEIR SUCCESS.

THE day wore on and night returned, but the captain of the slaver remained a voluntary prisoner in his cabin. The men marvelled much that he, at all times so stern and immovable, should now be so overcome at recent events as to seclude himself from all active participation in business.

The next day came, and fresh heaps of dead negroes were cast overboard. It was horrible—fearful—like rotten sheep they died in heaps, and still the fever-poisoned air played around the survivors.

The weather was still favourable, and no incident occurred to disturb the monotony of life at sea. The captain had not yet ventured on deck, though he had been seen by the officers of the watch, when they gave in their reports, so they knew he was still in existence, though they at first feared that he might commit suicide.

The night was dark; no star illumined the sky above nor the waters beneath.

Bond, Hardy, Long, and Smith were assembled in the forecastle; they were conversing in whispers when Wild Madge made her appearance, and without a word seated herself on the deck beside them, then, looking around with an air of authority, she said—

"Friends, do you not wish to see Old England's shores again ?"

"Ay, that we do, old gal."

"Well, why should'nt this ship bear us all to the place we wish ?" said Madge.

"Because the skipper never sails in the seas that bear home."

"But what if the skipper did?"

"Well, then the next officer will carry out her commander's intention."

"Ha ! ha ! how dull you are."

"That may be, we've been in an infernal dull place some time now. and I should'nt wonder if some of the dulness got into our brains."

"Ah, I suppose that is it, but—" and her voice sank to a deep whisper, passionate and earnest, "Look you, did you not swear to stand by the Boy Rover in whatever peril may beset him?"

"Aye, aye, that we did."

"Well, he is not dead you know ; at least, he did not perish with the wreck that cast us adrift. He must be still alive, and mourning the loss of his brave crew and his vessel."

"Yes, no doubt he's cut up a bit."

"Shall we not seek him then, and again with joyous freedom dare and defy every power on earth, when in another ship we are are once again afloat?"

"With all my heart," said each of the men, "we'll stick to him as we did afore if we only clap eyes on him again."

"Well," said Madge, "this is a goodly ship; it must be ours."

"Ours ! "

"Yes, ours."

"How?"

"Can we not murder all the crew?" and Madge's eyes looked in the darkness like burning coals, as she hissed those fearful words in the ears of the four seamen.

They remained silent.

"Speak," said Madge ; "are ye afraid to do your captain such service as shall give him another ship and restore a part of his old crew."

"No, not afraid, good mother, but rather doubtful of the success ; you see there is only four of us, while on board this ship there's a goodly crew with a tarnation lot of niggers to settle."

"Harkye ! "

"All right, go on."

"My plan is this—enlist the negroes on our side, kill all the officers and crew, and when once the ship is ours we can steer for the British Channel and seek out the Boy Rover amid his usual haunts, and placing the ship under his command accomplish all that is desired.

For a time the men whispered together, as if discussing the practicability of Madge's scheme, while she, with eager and impatient interest, watched their countenances as if to detect their decision ere they expressed it.

"Well," said she, "what is your answer?"

"Oh, we'll do it."

"I knew you would."

"But we must act with great caution."

"Certainly: but prepare the slaves first. Let us organise them into efficiency ere we carry out the other part of our plan.

They then dispersed.

Climbing over the vessels sides, aided by the darkness, they entered at the ports, and made their way to the hold. Here the stench was enough to knock them down ; but manfully struggling on they bore down upon the dying wretches.

Fortunately for them the weakest had died first, and consequently given the more robust a better chance of life, as they had the advantage of less crowding in their favour.

Desponding, yet full of bitterness, they scarce heeded the smugglers' attempt to come to an understanding. But at last, when they began to comprehend, the love of liberty and life was too strong to resist, and they eagerly and greedily drank in all that was poured into their ears.

The next night the smugglers frequently visited the slaves in the same cautious manner, and each time they conveyed to them arms that they had obtained by stealth and through Madge's aid from the armoury.

With new life thus infused into them by hope, the negroes worked with good and eager will to separate their fetters from each other, and they succeeded.

At last all was ripe for action. The time chosen was night. The wind howled, and the clouds were driven fast and furious across the sky, hiding from view the stars, and exhibiting every indication of of coming bad weather.

Bond and Hardy, each armed with a large knife, crept stealthily towards the companion ladder, and reaching the bottom they felt their way cautiously in the dark toward the guard that were stationed over the slaves.

They were uncertain how many there might be, but yet they thought that once engaged with them the slaves could make good their egress and at once finish the affray.

Guided by the breathing they suddenly dashed forward and plunged their knives into the bodies they knew were before them. A fearful shriek smote their ears, as they felt the hot blood gush over the hafts of the knives and bathe their hands and wrists.

They had killed two, but the shriek had aroused the ship. The next moment the slaves burst through, headed by Smith, carrying in one hand a lantern, and in the other a dagger. He had entered by the port, and marshalled the negroes into something like discipline, and breathless and anxious they were awaiting some signal that all was right. The shriek of the murdered sentries was enough, and dashing forward, Smith called on them to follow him.

By the light of the lantern there was another guard discovered.

With fearful cries and imprecations they rushed upon him.

Mechanically he put out his hands as if to shield himself from the attack, but in vain.

Marling spikes and cutlasses descended with terrific force on his head, and crushed and mangled he fell a corpse at their feet.

On they rushed, like furies let loose ; the negroes looked demoniac in their hate and fury.

In the meantime, Long and Madge had silently approached the man at the wheel, and at the same moment that the shrieks from the hold rent the air, the knife of Long pierced the shoulder of the helmsman, and with a groan he sank dead on the deck.

Now the tramp of the ascending negroes is heard mingled with the din of voices.

The crew, startled and alarmed, rush on deck, but are felled on the instant with the bars and spikes.

The officers now reach the scene, and a fearful

conflict takes place. Armed with revolvers, they deal destruction amid the huddled and crowding negroes, and for a moment the deadliness of firearms check them in their career. But the voice of Madge is heard high above the din, cheering them on, and again they dash forward.

The deck was slippery with gore.

Bravely and desperately the half-armed crew resist the onslaught of the slaves, but numbers eventually overpower them; step by step they yield, till at last they are driven down the hatchway.

Madge, like one of the furies, with hair dishevelled, is seen amid the thickest of the fight, inciting and urging them on, her air and demeanour exhibiting the wildest exultation in the scene of carnage around.

Mad with the excitement and change from imprisonment to liberty, the slaves yield themselves up to every degree of excess. So fearful was their abandonment, that for a time the four smugglers and Madge feared that they had loosened the fiends of hell at their own cost, and that they themselves stood in great peril.

Rushing to the spirit room, they greedily imbibed the contents of the casks that they broached.

At this juncture, the captain of the slaver, who had remained till the present moment in his cabin, became awakened as it were to something unusual occuring on the deck above him. Moodily and hastily he rushed on deck, when, to his extreme astonishment, he beheld the entire change that had taken place in the ship's company.

As his tall form reared itself high above the ordinary height of mortals, a feeling akin to dread crept over the hearts of the black skinned Africans as they beheld him, and for a moment they shrunk back as if unwilling to meet so formidable an antagonist; but the voice of Wild Madge aroused them as she shrieked out—

" There he is, the tyrant who has torn you from home and friends—who has lashed thy backs till the blood flowed from them to the decks—who reaps wealth in exchange for thy carcasses."

" Hell cat! " cried the captain, " cease thy croaking, cursed, jawing tackle, or I'll blow thy mischief making brains to the devil."

" Ha! ha! ha! " she shrieked, " on to him—kill him—slay him—let him die."

The captain levelled his pistol at Wild Madge's head, wild with fury at her taunts—he fired, but the ball whistled high over her head, and she stood unharmed and defiant.

The next instant the mutineers made a rush at him.

Like a lion beset by dogs he hurled them off; again they fly at him, and hanging on every part of his body seek to bear him down, but his size and great strength enabled him to baffle them for a long time; again and again he threw them off, but they thicken and increase around him, till at last, fairly overwhelmed, he is flung on the deck.

Hastily they secure him with ropes, binding his hands and feet in such a manner that he cannot move, and like a log he lays helpless and harmless on the deck, gnashing his teeth in the impotency of his rage.

At first they were for killing him at once, but Madge and the smugglers, from pure cruelty, suggested that they should at present spare him, and in the meantime devise some to cause him proportionate suffering to the agony he had caused them.

They now remembered the remnant of the crew that had retreated below, and wild with the rum they had drank, they rushed down into the midships to hunt out the rest of their enemies.

Brief was the struggle. Worn out with fatigue and outnumbered as they were, they fell an easy prey, and those who survived were quickly conveyed on deck to undergo the death they had at present evaded.

With demoniac yells they seize them, and tying some tackle to their heels they hurled them up to the rigging, till they hung head downwards about a foot from the deck. Then with pikes and capstan bars they dash out the brains of the poor devils till the deck was one mass of blood and flesh.

Horrible and sickening was the scene. Of the crew of that swift-sailing yet ill-fated vessel the captain alone remained alive.

Helpless and bound he lay on the deck gazing into the sky above him. Perhaps at that moment his thoughts reverted to the acts of his past life. Here he lay with certain death before him, and that probably a cruel and painful one. Could he look to Him for mercy and pardon that had so often doomed others?

Worn out and tired, drunk with blood and drink, the mutineers sank into sleep. Scattered in all directions on the deck they lay buried in slumber, and the ship, neglected and uncared for, plunged unguided on her way.

The morning broke. The sea glistened beneath the rising sun, and the roseate east looked surprised to see a brighter hue on the decks of the slave ship. Yes, the morning light revealed the horrors of the night's work. The deck was crimson with blood. The slaves rose one by one, half stupefied and bewildered. Their skins were stiff with the dried gore they had lain and wallowed in.

Madge, with surprising fortitude and daring, instantly assumed the command of the vessel, and gave her orders rapidly and to the point.

Presently all became busily employed, and the disgusting and fearful evidence of the previous night's horrors were silently and expeditiously removed.

By noon the decks were tolerably clean, and the four smugglers, at Madge's suggestion, commenced to instruct the slaves that remained in all the mysteries of splicing and knotting; and ere the evening set in all was once more ship-shape and snug.

Long took the wheel, and after a consultation, they decided to keep before the wind, which was then south-east.

Everything being thus satisfactorily settled, the thoughts of all recurred to the late captain of the ship, now a prisoner in their hands.

What should be done with him?

This was the question all asked.

" He must die! " said Madge.

" Ah, let him perish," growled Smith, " our trade is murder, then why should he be still alive? "

Instinctively they unclasped their knives as if it needed no more discussion, and prepared like butchers for their work.

Calling the blacks around them, they informed them by signs and such few words as they had picked up in Africa, their intention to finish their work by slaying the captain.

Their eyes glistened with joy at the proposal of a bloody revenge, and their white teeth became visible as they grinned with satisfaction.

Rushing below they drag the slaver to the deck.

Too well he knew that he could expect no mercy from those in whose power he now was.

Rearing his lofty form to its full height, he looked around defiantly and scornful.

For like most Americans he detested the niggers, and it was bitter indeed for him to meet his reverse of fortune at their hands.

The sun was sinking slowly in the distant waters. The sky was gorgeously arrayed in crimson and scarlet clouds falling like drapetied curtains over the orb of day and gradually excluding the light, as the eyes of the slave captain wandered round.

He sighed as he thought that that sun was now shining o'er the land of his birth, and that he should behold it never more. Bad as he was, a moment of remorse and tenderness traversed over his heart, when his memory recalled the ill-spent moments of his life. It was but a moment.

His eye fell on the forms of Wild Madge and the smugglers.

As a flash of light, the rage in his heart darted from his eyes. The sight of them called all the mad passions of his nature from the depth of his soul.

"Ah! devils! it is thou that has caused all this," he yelled, and making frantic efforts to reach them he struggled and writhed with the blacks that held him, but his pinioned arms left him powerless.

Wild Madge, looking more like a fiend than a woman, laughed scornfully.

"Accursed hag! could I but clutch thy throat," he cried, "I'd die in peace."

"Ha, ha, ha : 'tis hard to be foiled by a woman, is it not?"

"A woman!—say rather a hell-cat—a she-devil —a—"

"Aye, rail on, but listen—your hours are numbered; have you any message you wish to be delivered ere you quit this scene?" and she looked scornfully and menacingly at him.

He made no answer.

"No message for the beautiful Inez?"

This was too much for his overcharged, pent up wrath. With a terrific yell he bounded from his captors—the cords that bound his arms flew asunder like thongs of straw, and he stood free and unfettered.

For a moment he stood, like a panther at bay, glaring with savage fury on all around.

Like frightened sheep, the blacks scattered in all directions.

Then, springing forward, he rushed towards Wild Madge and the smugglers who stood by her side.

It was a moment of intense suspense.

But Wild Madge was nothing daunted.

Far different was it with the others. Though ordinarily brave in great danger, yet they quailed before the desperation of a madman, whose size and strength was more than that usually allotted to man.

So Wild Madge stood alone before the fierce and deadly avenger.

"Foul witch, I have thee!" he screamed, as with outstretched arms he rushed upon her.

Suddenly she raises her arm, a sharp click is heard, and the next moment, with a cry of rage and pain, the slave captain staggers back shot in the face.

The blood streams down his countenance, and with arms extended he stumbles forward.

The pistol that Madge had fired (fortunately for herself), was, as it turned out, only loaded with powder, consequently the wretched captain was only wounded by the powder.

But terrible indeed was the result to him, for the powder and blood completely obscured his vision, and to all appearance he was totally blind.

Yelling with agony, he rushed forward towards the spot where he remembered to have seen Madge, but she easily evaded him.

Like an infuriated ox, he dashed on in all directions. The crew by this time had recovered their courage, and seemed to enjoy the scene as presenting excellent sport.

For a time shouts of laughter greeted the attempts of the blinded man to clutch at some enemy. And as the sounds of their laughter betrayed their whereabouts to him and he would rush towards the spot, their derisive laughter echoed in the air as the unfortunate wretch stumbled over some obstruction.

At last, tiring of this sport, one gigantic negro hurled with all his force a hatchet at him, it missed his head but sank deep in his shoulder, inflicting a frightful gash.

Others followed, interspersed with knives. He tried to leap overboard, but the deprivation of sight deceived him.

At last, borne down by the shower of missiles, covered with ghastly wounds, and bleeding profusely, he sank to the deck.

Clasping his bleeding hands together, he cried in trembling, agonized tones :

"Inez! Inez! I come—oh God!"

With painful effort he struggled to regain his feet : he stood erect a moment, then, with a deep sigh, sank lifeless on the deck.

It was dark.

The clouds of night compassionately hid from view the scene of inhumanity. Excited with the recent events. the mutineers finish the night in debauch, and the inanimate body of the slave captain lays in his gore, forsaken and neglected.

CHAPTER XLIX.

DISAPPEARANCE OF THE SLAVE CAPTAIN'S BODY —A STORM—A SAIL.

THE next morning all hands were piped up to dispose of the captain's body.

Tired with the previous night's debauch, and oppressed with a feeling betwixt despair and remorse at the bloodshedding they had been guilty of, the men silently and moodily assembled.

Revenge was satiated, and they now looked with loathing towards the spot where the captain had sank to rise no more.

Of all on board, none proved more callous of feeling than Wild Madge. Triumphant and defiant, she resumed her place as commander, and gave directions that the body should be cast overboard with a thirty-two pounder shot at its heels.

The men proceeded to execute her commands, but what was their astonishment to find the pool of blood but no body.

They stared with amazement. He could not have dissolved entirely into blood they thought, though there was plenty of that to give rise to such a supposition.

They searched the ship thoroughly, but not a trace could they discover of the missing body.

At last they concluded that the devil must have claimed him, and in the darkness of night carried him off to the infernal regions.

They were the more confirmed in this idea as beyond the pool of blood, no crimson stains were traced, as would have been the case if the body had been removed in a mortal or ordinary manner.

Once more resuming the even tenor of their way, the ship's company proceeded diligently with the work of the ship.

At noon the wind died completely away, and for nearly the whole of the next day there was a dead calm. Towards the close of the day, the heat which had been almost unbearable all day was more oppressive than ever, and masses of dark clouds collecting in the eastward gave promise of something unpleasant.

Lang, who of all on board knew most about navigating a ship, was now looked up to by his three comrades, and Madge, seeing the threatening aspect above, turned inquiringly toward them, as if for a solution of the difficulty.

"We shall have a breeze directly, my lads," said Lang; "don't you think so, Smith?"

"Aye, lad, I'm of the same opinion; so you'd better give the orders, and we'll touch our peaks to you as captain."

Lang instantly assented, and turning to the crew he shouted:

"Haul down the top-gallant masts and yards—furl every stitch of sail—brace the yards sharp up—and batten the hatches down."

These orders were soon obeyed.

A cloud like the darkness of night now appeared, and bursting from it there flew one of the most furious hurricanes which could be conceived.

The sea which a minute before was like a mill pond, was torn up and flew over them as if it had been smoke; the wind came from all quarters at once, as though each were contending for the mastery; the first decided wind took them on the lee bow, and threw the vessel almost on her beam ends.

Several of the blacks were washed into the sea and drowned, not being prepared for such an event. For a moment the vessel lay in the same position, when she righted a little and gradually fell off to the gale.

The sea was now in a boiling surge, dashing over the ship, which was going at a speed of twelve knots an hour, without a moment's cessation.

The deck was completely flooded, and the wind causing the waves to fall in thick spray around hid the view beyond as if a thick cloud surrounded her.

The crew were thoroughly scared and frightened, especially the blacks, who had never been to sea, and were it not for Lang would have yielded themselves up to despair and death.

Night setting in added to the gloominess of the prospect. At the expiration of two hours thunder, lightning, and floods of rain joined with the other elements in enlivening the scene.

Lang fancied he could detect signs as if they were nearing land, and knowing the danger of hugging the shore in such a storm, he shouted to Smith who had the helm:

"Luff her to, Smith."

"Aye, aye—luff it is."

"Meet her!"

Scarcely had Lang said this, when a great sea came over the weather gangway, completely sweeping the deck.

All night the hurricane lasted, the rain pouring in torrents. Not a stich of canvass was set, and the yards being braced up kept the vessel steady.

As daylight broke some of the clouds cleared away, and the storm gradually subsided.

The sea still ran very high, and no sail being set the ship rolled heavily. So Lang called out to—

"Loosen and set topsails."

As the sun got up the wind slackened, and all on board breathed again more freely.

The danger was past, and the craft was soon got to rights again.

Towards evening a strange sail was reported on the larboard bow.

The smugglers instantly went aloft and made her out to be a small trading vessel running under her topsails before the wind.

For a long time they watched her, at last the darkness hid her from sight.

Strange feelings filled the breasts of the smugglers at sight of this vessel.

What if it should lead to their detection or capture? Or should they endeavour to capture that, and add one more crime to the heap already on their consciences—that of piracy.

Brief was the consultation. Their course was decided—they would hoist the black flag.

They would be Pirates.

CHAPTER L.

THE "SPIRIT OF THE WAVE."—THE HISTORY OF THE CAPTAIN.

GLIDING over the ocean, with her sails set and her bows ever and anon dipping majestically to kiss the white spray as it dashed against them, a fine schooner ploughed her way.

Her low poop scarcely rising from the deck, her masked ports and low-laying build, with her long tapering masts surmounted by a blood-red flag, bespoke her a vessel to be feared and dreaded by the peaceful craft who ploughed the mighty waters in pursuit of commerce.

The bright sun glistening on her ensign revealed in glittering letters "The Spirit of the Waves."

And the peaceful trader, as she swept along on her errand of trade, spread her white sails to the breeze, and prayed that darkness might overspread the sea to enable her to escape from the precincts of that blood-red flag.

The terror of the ocean, she was feared by all.

The scourge of the waves, blood and rapine marked her track, and her planks were stained with the life streams of the good and the brave.

And from her hold and cabin the shrieks of outraged innocence and virtue had ascended, to be stifled by the bloody knife or fatal pistol shot.

She was commanded by a short thick-set man of some forty years of age, whose bloated countenance and blood-shot eyes proclaimed the thing who lost to all self-respect drowned the voice of conscience in drink.

Leaning over the taffrail, his blear eyes gazing upon the waves as they lashed the side of his vessel, and ever and anon squirting from his mouth the juice of tobacco into the sea, or gazing languidly across the ocean, we will introduce him to the reader, and likewise unfold his career up to the present time.

Jean Lavette was born at St. Maloes, in France, and went to sea at the age of fourteen.

After several voyages in Europe, and to the Coast of Africa, he was appointed mate of a French East Indiaman, bound to Madras.

On the outward passage they encountered a heavy gale, off the Cape of Good Hope, which sprung the mainmast, and otherwise injured the ship, which determined the captain to bear up to the Mauritius, where he arrived in safety.

A quarrel having taken place on the passage out, between Lavette and the captain, he abandoned the ship, and refused to continue the voyage.

Several privateers were at this time fitting out at this island, and Lavette was appointed captain of one of these vessels.

After a cruise, during which he robbed the vessels of other nations besides those of England, and thus committed piracy, he stopped at Leychelles, and took in a load of slaves for the Mauritius; but

HENRY DOOMED TO WALK THE PLANK.

being chased by an English frigate, as far north as the equator, he found himself in a very awkward position, not having enough provisions to carry him back to the French colony. He therefore conceived the bold project of proceeding to the Bay of Bengal, in order to get provisions from some English ships.

In his ship of two hundred tons, with only two guns and twenty-six men, he attacked and took the command of a vessel and proceeded to cruise upon the coast of Bengal.

He there fell in with the Pagoda, a vessel belonging to the English East India Company, armed with twenty-six twelve pounders and manned with one hundred and fifty men. Expecting that the enemy would take him for a pilot of the Ganges, he manœuvred accordingly.

The Pagoda manifested no suspicions, whereupon he suddenly darted with his brave fellows upon the decks, overturned all who opposed them, and speedily took the ship.

After a very successful cruise he arrived safe at the Mauritus, and took the command of La Confidence of twenty-six guns and two hundred and fifty men, and sailed for the coast of British India.

Off the Sand Heads Lavalette fell in with the Queen, East Indiaman, with a crew of nearly four hundred men, and carrying forty guns; he conceived the bold project of getting possession of her.

Never was there a more unequal conflict; even the height of the vessel compared to the feeble privateer, augmented the chances against Lavalette; but the difficulty and danger, so far from discouraging this adventurer, acted as an additional motive to exertion.

After electrifying his crew with a few words of hope and ardour, he manœuvred, and ran on board his enemy.

In this position he received a broadside when close to; but he expected this, and made his men lie flat upon the deck.

No. 18

After the first fire they all rose, and from the yards and tops threw bombs and grenades into the forecastle of the Indiaman.

This sudden and unforeseen attack caused great havoc.

In an instant, death and terror made them abandon a part of the vessel near the mizen-mast.

Lavette, who observed everything, seized the decisive moment, beat to arms, and forty of his crew prepared to board, with pistols in their hands and daggers between their teeth.

As soon as they got on deck, they rushed upon the astonished crowd, who retreated to the steerage and endeavoured to defend themselves there.

Lavette thereupon ordered a second division to board, which he headed himself; the captain of the Indiaman was killed, and all were swept away in a moment.

Lavette caused a gun to be loaded with grape, which he pointed to the place where the crowd was assembled, threatening to exterminate them.

The English deeming resistance fruitless, surrendered, and Lavette hastened to put a stop to the slaughter.

This exploit, hitherto unparalled, resounded through India, and the name of Lavette became a terror in these latitudes.

As British vessels now traversed the Indian ocean under formidable convoys, game became scarce, and Lavette determined to visit France; and after doubling the Cape of Good Hope, he coasted up to the Gulf of Guinea, and in the bight of Benin, took two valuable prizes loaded with gold dust, ivory, and palm oil; with this booty he reached St. Maloes in safety.

After a short stay in his native place he fitted out a brigantine mounting twenty guns and one hundred and fifty men, and sailed for Guadaloupe; amongst the West India islands he made several valuable prizes; but during his absence on a cruize this island having been taken by the British, he proceeded to Carthagena, and from thence to Barrataria.

After this period, the conduct of Lavette at Barrataria does not appear to be characterised by the audacity and boldness of his former career; but he amassed immense sums of booty, and as he was obliged to have dealings with the merchants of the United States and the West Indies, who frequently owed him large sums, and the cautious dealings necessary to found and conduct a colony of pirates and smugglers in the very teeth of a civilised nation, obliged Lavette to cloak as much as possible his real character.

At the period of the taking of Guadaloupe by the British, most of the privateers commissioned by the government of that island, and which were then on a cruise, not being able to return to any of the West India Islands, made for Barrataria, there to take in a supply of water and provisions, recruit the health of their crews, and dispose of their prizes, which could not be admitted into any of the ports of the United States.

Most of the commissions granted to privateers by the French government of Guadaloupe, having expired some time after the declaration of the independence of Carthagena, many of the privateers repaired to that port for the purpose of obtaining from the new government commissions for cruising against Spanish vessels.

Having duly obtained their commissions, they in a manner blockaded for a long time all the ports of the royalists, and made numerous captives which they carried into Barrataria.

Under this denomination is comprised part of the coast of Louisiana, to the west of the mouths of the Mississippi, comprehended between Bastien Bay on the east, and the mouths of the river or bayou La Fourche on the west.

Not far from the sea are lakes, called the great and little lakes of Barrataria, communicating with one another by several large bayous with a great number of branches. There is also the island of Barrataria, at the extremity of which is a place called the Temple, which denomination it owes to several mounds of shells thrown up there by the Indians. The name of Barrataria is also given to a larger basin which extends the whole length of the cypress swamps, from the Gulf of Mexico to three miles above New Orleans. These waters disembogue into the gulf by two entrances of the bayou Barrataria, between which lies an island called Grand Terre, six miles in length, from two to three miles in breadth, running parallel with the coast. In the western entrance is the great pass of Barrataria, which has from nine to ten feet of water.

Within this pass, about two leagues from the open sea, lies the only secure harbour on the coast, and accordingly this was the harbour frequented by the pirates, so well known by the name of Barratarians.

At Grand Terre the privateers publicly made sale of the cargoes of their prizes.

From all parts of Lower Louisiana, people resorted to Barrataria, without being at all solicitous to conceal the object of their journey.

The most respectable inhabitants of the state, especially those living in the country, were in the habit of purchasing smuggled goods coming from Barrataria.

The government of the United States sent an expedition under Commodore Patterson, to disperse the settlement of mauraders at Barrataria; the following is an extract of his letter to the secretary of war:—

"I have the honour to inform you that I departed from this city on the 11th of June, accompanied by Colonel Ross, with a detachment of the 44th regiment of infantry. On the 12th, reached the schooner Carolina, of Ploquemine, and formed a junction with the gun vessels at the Balize on the 13th, sailed from the south-west pass on the evening of the 15th, and at half-past eight o'clock, a.m., on the 16th, made the island of Barrataria, and discovered a number of vessels in the harbour, some of which showed Carthagenian colours. At two o'clock perceived the pirates forming their vessels, ten in number, including prizes, into a line of battle near the entrance of the harbour, and making every preparation to offer me battle.

"At ten o'clock, wind light and variable, formed the order of battle with six gun boats and the Sea Horse tender, mounting one six-pounder and fifteen men, and a launch mounting one twelve-pound cannonade; the schooner Carolina, drawing too much water to cross the bar. At half-past ten o'clock, perceived several smokes along the coast as signals, and at the same time a white flag hoisted on board a schooner at the fort, an American flag at the mainmast head, and a Carthagenian flag (under which the pirates cruise), at her topping lift; replied with a white flag at my main. At eleven o'clock, discovered that the pirates had fired two of their best schooners; hauled down my white and made the signal for battle: hoisting with a large flag bearing the words—'Pardon for Deserters,' having heard there was a number on shore from the army and navy. At a quarter past eleven o'clock, two gun boats grounded, and were passed agreeably to my previous orders by the other four which entered the harbour, manned by my barge and boats belonging to the grounded vessels, and proceeded in to my great disappointment.

"I perceived that the pirates abandoned their vessels, and were flying in all directions. I immediately sent the launch and two barges with small boats in pursuit of them.

"At meridian, took possession of all their vessels in the harbour, consisting of six schooners and one felucca, cruisers, and prizes of the pirates, one brig —a prize, and two armed schooners under the Carthagenian flag, both in the line of battle with the armed vessels of the pirates, and apparently with an intention to aid them in any resistance they might make against me, as their crews were at quarters—tompions out of their guns and matches lighted; Colonel Ross at the same time landed, and with his command took possession of their establishment on shore, consisting of about forty houses of different sizes, badly constructed, and thatched with palmetto leaves.

"When I perceived the enemy forming their vessels into a line of battle, I felt confident from their courage and very advantageous position, and their number of men, that they would have fought me; their not doing so I regret, for had they, I should have been enabled more effectually to destroy or make prisoners of them and their leaders; but it is a subject of great satisfaction to me to have effected the object of my enterprise without the loss of a man.

"The enemy had mounted on their vessels twenty pieces of cannon of different calibre; and, as I have since learnt, from eight hundred to one thousand men of all nations and colours.

"Early in the morning of the 20th, the Carolina at anchor, about five miles distant, made the signal of a 'strange sail in sight to eastward;' immediately afterwards she weighed anchor and gave chase, the strange sail standing for Grand Terre with all sail, at half-past eight o'clock the chase hauled her wind off shore to escape; sent acting Lieutenant Spedding, with four boats manned and armed to prevent her passing the harbour; at nine o'clock, a.m., she chase fired upon the Carolina, which was returned; each vessel continued firing during the chase, when their long guns reached.

"At ten o'clock the chase grounded outside of the bar, at which time the Carolina was, from the shoalness of the water, obliged to haul her wind off shore, and give up the chase; opened fire upon the chase across the Islands from the gun vessels.

"At half-past ten she hauled down her colours and was taken possession of. She proved to be the armed schooner, General Boliver; by grounding she broke both her rudder pintles and made water—took from her her armament, consisting of one long brass eighteen pounder, one long brass six pounder, two twelve pounders, small arms, and twenty-one packages of dry goods.

"On the afternoon of the 23rd, got underweigh with the whole squadron, in all seventeen vessels, but during the night one escaped, and the next day arrived at New Orleans with my whole squadron."

At different times the English had sought to attack the pirates at Barrataria, in hopes of taking their prizes, and even their armed vessels. Of these attempts of the British, suffice it to instance that of June 23rd, 1813, when two privateers being at anchor off Cat Island, a British sloop of war anchored at the entrance to the pass, and sent her boats to endeavour to take the privateers, but they were repulsed with considerable loss.

Such were the state of affairs, when on the 2nd September, 1814, there appeared an armed brig on the coast opposite the pass. She fired a gun at a vessel about to enter, and forced her to run aground; she then tacked and shortly after came to an anchor at the entrance of the pass. It was not easy to understand the intentions of this vessel, who having commenced with hostilities on her first appearance, now seemed to announce an amicable disposition.

Mr. Lavette then went off in a boat to examine her, venturing so far that he could not escape from the pinnace sent from the brig, and making towards the shore, bearing British colours and a flag of true.

In this pinnace were two naval officers.

One was Captain Lockyer, commander of the brig. The first question they asked was, where was Mr. Lavette? he not choosing to make himself known to them, replied that the person they inquired for was on shore. They then delivered to him a packet directed to Mr. Lavette, Barrataria, requesting him to take particular care of it, and to deliver it into Mr. Lavette's hands.

He prevailed on them to make for the shore, and as soon as they got near enough to be in his power, he made himself known, recommending them at the same time to conceal the business on which they had come. Upwards of two hundred persons lined the shore, and it was a general cry amongst the crews of the volunteers at Grand Terre, that those British officers should be made prisoners and sent to New Orleans as spies. It was with much difficulty that Lavette dissuaded the multitude from this intent, and led the officers in safety to his dwelling.

He thought very prudently that the papers contained in the packet might be of importance towards the safety of the country, and that if the officers were well watched they could obtain no information that might turn to the detriment of Lousiana.

He now examined the contents of the packet, in which he found a proclamation addressed by Colonel Edward Nicholls, in the service of his Britannic Majesty, and commander of the land forces on the coast of Florida, to the inhabitants of Lousiana. A letter from the same to Mr. Lavette, the commandant of Barrataria; an official letter from the honourable W. H. Percy, captain of the sloop of war. Hermes, directed to Lavette. When he had perused these letters, Captain Lockyer enlarged on the subject of them, and proposed to him to enter into the service of his Britannic Majesty with the rank of post-captain, and to receive the command of a forty-four gun frigate. All those under his command, or over whom he had sufficient influence. He was also offered thirty thousand dollars, payable at Pensacola, and urged him not to let slip this opportunity of acquiring fortune and consideration. On Lavette's requiring a few days to reflect upon these proposals, Captain Lockyer observed to him that no reflection could be necessary, respecting proposals that obviously precluded hesitation, as he was a Frenchman and proscribed by the American government. But to all his splendid promises and daring insinuations Lavette replied, that in a few days he would give a final answer—his object in this procrastination being to gain time to inform the officers of this nefarious project. Having occasion to go to some distance for a short time, the persons who had proposed to send the British prisoners to New Orleans, went and seized them in his absence, and confined both them and the crew of the pinnace in a secure place, leaving a guard at the door. The British officers sent for Lavette; but he, fearing an insurrection of the crews of the privateers, thought it advisable not to see them until he had first persuaded their captains and officers to desist from the measures on which they seemed bent. With this view he represented to the latter that, besides the infamy that would attach to them if they treated as prisoners people who had come with a flag of truce, they would lose the opportunity of discovering the projects of the British against Lousiana.

Early next morning Lavette caused them to be released from their confinement, and saw them safe on board their pinnace, apologising the detention. He now wrote to Captain Lockyer the following letter : —

"The confusion which prevailed in our camp yesterday and this morning, and of which you have a complete knowledge, has prevented me from answering in a precise manner to the object of your mission; nor even at this moment can I give you all the satisfaction that you desire. However, if you could grant me a fortnight, I would be entirely at your disposal at the end of that time. This delay is indispensable to enable me to put my affairs in order. You may communicate with me by sending a boat to the eastern point of the pass where I shall be found. You have inspired me with more confidence than the admiral, your superior officer could have done himself; with you alone I wish to deal, and from you also I will claim, in due time, the reward of the services I may render to you.'

His object in writing that letter was, by appearing to accede to their proposals, to give time to communicate the affair to the officers of the state government, and to receive from them instructions how to act, under circumstances so critical and important to the country. He accordingly wrote on the 4th of September to Mr. Blanque, one of the representatives of the state, sending him all the papers delivered to him by the British officers, with a letter addressed to his excellency, Governor Claiborne, of the state of Lousiana.

"In the firm persuasion that the choice made of you to fill the office of first magistrate of this state was dictated by the esteem of your fellow-citizens, and was conferred on merit, I confidently address you on an affair on which may depend the safety of this country. I offer to restore to this state several citizens, who perhaps in your eyes have lost that sacred title. I offer you them, however, such as you could wish to find them, ready to exert their utmost efforts in defence of the country. This point of Lousiania, which I occupy, is of great importance in the present crisis. I tender my services to defend it; and the only reward I ask is that a stop be put to the proscription against me and my adherents, by an act of oblivion for all that has been done hitherto. I am the stray sheep wishing to return to the fold. If you are thoroughly acquainted with the nature of my offences, I should appear to you much less guilty, and still worthy to discharge the duties of a good citizen. I have never sailed under any flag but that of the republic of Carthagena, and my vessels are perfectly regular in that respect. If I could have brought my lawful prizes into the the ports of this state, I should not have employed the illicit means that have caused me to be proscribed. I decline saying more on the subject until I receive your excellency's answer, which I am persuaded can be dictated only by wisdom. Should your answer not be favourable to my ardent desires, I declare to you that I will instantly leave the country, to avoid the imputation of having co-operated towards an invasion on this point, which cannot fail to take place, and to rest secure in the acquittal of my conscience.

"I have the honor to be, &c.,
"To Gov. Claiborne."   "J. LAVETTE."

On the receipt of this packet from Mr. Lavette Mr. Blanque immediately laid its whole contents before the governor, who convened the committee of defence lately formed, of which he was president; and Mr. Rancher, the bearer of Lavette's packet, was sent back with a verbal answer to desire Lavette to take no steps until it should be determined which was expedient to be done; the message also contained an assurance that, in the meantime, no steps should be taken against him for his past offences against the laws of the United States.

At the expiration of the time agreed on with Captain Lockyer, his ship appeared again on the coast with two others, and continued standing off and on before the pass for several days. But he pretended not to perceive the return of the sloop of war, who, tired of waiting to no purpose, put out to sea and disappeared.

Lavette having received a guarantee from General Jackson for his safe passage from Barrataria to New Orleans and back, he proceeded forthwith to that city, where he had an interview with Governor Claiborne and the General. After the usual formalities and courtesies had taken place between the gentlemen, Lavette addressed the Governor of Lousiana nearly as follows :—

"I offered to defend for you that part of Lousiania I now hold. But not as an outlaw would I be its defender. In that confidence, with which you have inspired me, I offer to restore the state many citizens now under my command. As I have remarked before, the point I occupy is of great importance in the present crisis. I tender not only my own services to defend it, but those of all I command; and the only reward I ask is that a stop be put to the proscription against me and my adherants by an act of oblivion for all that has been done hitherto."

"My dear sir," said the Governor, who together with General Jackson was impressed with admiration of his sentiments, "your praiseworthy wishes shall be laid before the council of the state, and I will confer with my august friend here present, upon this important affair, and send you an answer to-morrow."

As Lavette withdrew, the General said:

"Farewell; when we meet again I trust it will be in the ranks of the American army."

The result of the conference was the issuing the following order :—

"The Governor of Louisania, informed that many individuals implicated in the offences heretofore committed against the United States at Barrataria, express a willingness at the present crisis to enrol themselves and march against the enemy.

"He does hereby invite them to join the standard of the United States, and is authorised to say. should their conduct in the field meet the approbation of the Major-General, that that officer will unite with the Governor in a request to the President of the United States, to extend to each and every individual so marching and acting, a free and full pardon."

These general orders were placed in the hands of Valette who circulated them among his dispersed followers, most of whom readily embraced the conditions of pardon held out. In a few days many brave men and skilful artillerists, whose services contributed greatly to the safety of the invaded state, flocked to the standard of the United States, and by their conduct received the highest approbation of General Jackson.

By the President of the United States of
America.

A PROCLAMATION.

" Among the many evils produced by the wars,
which, with little intermission, have afflicted Europe, and extended their ravages into other quarters
of the globe, for a period exceeding twenty years,
the dispersion of a considerable portion of the inhabitants of different countries, in sorrow and in want,
has not been the least injurious to human happiness,
nor the least severe in the trial of human virtue.

It has been long ascertained that many foreigners
flying from the dangers of their own home, and
that some citizens, forgetful of their duty, had co-
operated in forming an establishment on the island
of Barrataria, near the mouth of the river Mississippi, for the purpose of a clandestine and lawless
trade. The governor of the United States caused
the establishment to be broken up and destroyed;
and having obtained the means of designating the
offenders of every description, it only remained to
answer the demands of justice by inflicting an ex-
emplary punishment.

"But it has since been represented, that the
offenders have manifested a sincere penitence—that
they have abandoned the prosecution of the worst
cause for the support of the best: and particularly
they have exhibited in defence of New Orleans, un-
equivocal traits of courage and fidelity. Offenders,
who have refused to become the associates of the
enemy in the war, upon the most seducing terms
of invitation ; and who have aided to repel his hostile invasion of the United States, can no longer be
considered as the objects of punishment, but as objects of generous forgiveness.

" It has therefore been seen with great satisfaction, that the General Assembly of the state of
Louisania earnestly recommend those offenders to
the benefit of a full pardon. And in compliance
with that recommendation, as well as in consideration of all the other extraordinary circumstances of
the case, I, James Madison, President of the United
States of America, do issue this proclamation, hereby granting, publishing, and declaring, a free and
full pardon of all offences committed in violation of
any act or acts of the Congress of the United States,
touching the revenue, trade, and navigation thereof,
or touching intercourse and commerce of the United
States with foreign nations, at any time before the
eight day of January, in the present year one thousand eight hundred and fifteen, by any person or
persons whatsoever, being inhabitants of New
Orleans and the adjacent country, or being inhabitants of the said isle of Barrataria, and the places
adjacent; provided, that every person claiming the
benefit of this full pardon, in order to entitle himself thereto, shall produce a certificate in writing
from the governor of the state of Louisania, stating
that such person has aided in the defence of New
Orleans and the adjacent country, during the invasion thereof as aforesaid.

" And I do hereby further authorise and direct
all suits, indictments, and prosecutions, for fines,
penalties, and forfeitures, against any person who
shall be entitled to the benefit of this full pardon,
forthwith to be stayed, discontinued, and released.
All civil officers are hereby required, according to
the duties of their respective stations, to carry this
proclamation into immediate and faithful execution."

The morning of the eighth of January was ushered in with the discharge of rockets, the sound of
cannon, and the cheers of the British soldiers advancing to the attack.

The Americans, behind the breastwork, awaited
in calm intrepidity their approach. The enemy
advanced in close column of sixty men in front,
shouldering their muskets and carrying fascines and
ladders. A storm of rockets preceded them, and an
incessant fire opened from the battery, which commanded the advanced column.

The musketry and rifles from the Kentuckians
and Tennesseans, joined the fire of the artillery, and
in a few moments was heard along the line a cease-
less, rolling fire, whose tremendous noise resembled
the continued reverberation of thunder.

One of these guns, a twenty-four pounder, placed
upon the breastwork in the third embrasure from
the river, drew, from the skill and activity with
which it was managed, even in the heat of battle,
the admiration of both Americans and British; and
became one of the points most dreaded by the advancing foe.

Here was stationed Lavette, his lieutenant Do-
minique, and a large band of his men, who, during
the continuance of the battle, fought with undaunted bravery.

Two other batteries were manned by the Barratarians, who served their pieces with the steadiness
of veteran gunners.

In the first attack of the enemy, a column bravely
pushed forward between the levee and the river;
and so precipitate and well-directed was their charge
that the outposts were forced to retreat, closely
pressed by the enemy.

Before the batteries could meet the charge, the
British cleared the ditch and gained the redoubt
throughout the embrasures, leaped over the parapet
and overwhelmed the party stationed there.

Lavette, who was commanding in conjunction
with his officers, no sooner saw the bold and intrepid movement of the enemy, than, calling a number of his best men to his side, he sprang forward to
the point of danger, and clearing the breastwork of
the entrenchments, leaped, cutlass in hand, into
the midst of the enemy, followed by his men, who
while pursuing their piratical course, had fought
many a hard battle upon his own deck, and were
consequently well tried.

Lavette and his crew here made a sudden charge,
which was characterised with the recklessness and
rapidity of practised boarders bounding upon the
deck of an enemy's vessel, and from their superior
force, routed the enemy from the post which they
had by their bravery and undaunted courage so
shortly gained possession of.

All the energies of the British were now concentrated to scale the breastwork, and one brave officer
had already mounted, when Lavette and his followers, seconding a band of volunteer riflemen, formed
an immense phalanx, which, joined with their advantageous position, dissuaded the British from an
assault.

General Jackson, in his correspondence with the
secretary of war, did not fail to notice the conduct
of the " Corsairs of Barrataria," who were, as we
have already seen, employed in the artillery service.
Many of them were killed or wounded in the defence of their country. Their zeal, their courage,
and their skill were remarked by the whole army
who could no longer consider such brave men as
criminals. In a few days peace was proclaimed
between Great Britain and the United States.

The piratical establishment at Barrataria having
been broken up, and Lavette not being content with
leading an honest, peaceable life, procured some fast
sailing vessels, and with a great number of his followers, proceeded to Galvezton Bay, in Texas, where
he received a commission from General Long, and
had five vessels generally cruizing, with 500 men.

Two open boats, bearing commission from General Humber, of Galvezton, having robbed a plantation on the Marmento river, of negroes, money, &c., were captured in the Sabine river, by the boats of the United States schooner, Lynx. One of the men was hung by Lavette, who dreaded the vengeance of the American government. The Lynx also captured one of his schooners and her prize, that had been for a length of time smuggling in the Carmento. One of his cruizers, named the Jupiter, returned safe to Galvezton after a short cruize, with a valuable cargo, chiefly specie; she was the first vessel that sailed under the authority of Texas. The American government well knowing that where Lavette was, piracy and smuggling would be the order of the day, sent a vessel of war to cruize in the Gulf of Mexico, and scour the coast of Texas.

Lavette having been appointed governor of Galvezton, and one of the cruizers having been stationed off the port to watch his motions, it so annoyed him that he wrote the following letter to her commander, Lieutenant Madison:—

"I am convinced that you are a cruizer of the navy, ordered by government. I have therefore deemed it proper to inquire into the cause of your lying before this port without communicating your intentions. I shall by this message inform you that the port of Galvezton belongs to and is in the possession of the republic of Texas, and was made a port of entry on the 9th of October last.

"And whereas the supreme congress of the said republic have thought proper to appoint me governor of this place, in consequence of which, if you have any demands on the said government, or persons belonging to or residing in the same, you will please to send an officer with such demands, whom you may be assured will be treated with the greatest politeness, and receive every satisfaction required. But if you are ordered, or should attempt to enter into this port in an hostile manner, my oath and duty to the government compel me to rebut your intentions at the expense of my life.

"To prove to you my intentions towards the welfare and harmony of your government, I send enclosed the declaration of several prisoners who were taken in custody yesterday, and by a court of inquiry appointed for that purpose, were found guilty of robbing the inhabitants of the United States of a number of slaves and specie. The gentleman bearing this message will give you any reasonable information relating to this place that may be required."

About this time, one Mitchell, who had formerly belonged to Lavette's gang, collected upwards of one hundred and fifty desperadoes, and fortified himself on an island near Barrataria, with several pieces of cannon, and swore that he and all his companions would perish within their trenches before they would surrender to any man.

Four of this gang having gone to New Orleans on a frolic, information was given to the city watch, and the house surrounded, when the whole four, with cocked pistols in both hands, sallied out, and marched through the crowd, which made way for them, and no person dared make an attempt to arrest them.

The United States cutter, Alabama, on her way to the station off the mouth of the Mississippi, captured a piratical schooner belonging to Lavette; she carried two guns and twenty-five men, and was fitted out at New Orleans, and commanded by one of Lavette's lieutenants named Le Fage.

The schooner had a prize in company, and being hailed by the cutter, poured into her a volley of musketry. The cutter then opened upon the privateer, and a smart action ensued, and one of the pirates, an old man, fought desperately with a large hatchet which he weilded with apparent ease, but was eventually cut down, and the conflict terminated in favour of the cutter, which had four men wounded, and two of them dangerously; but the pirate had six men killed. Both vessels were captured and brought into the Bayou St. John.

An expedition was now sent to dislodge Mitchell and his comrades from the island he had taken possession of.

After coming to anchor, a summons was sent for him to surrender, which was answered by a brisk cannonade from his breastwork.

The vessels were warped close in shore, and the boats manned and sent on shore, whilst the vessels opened upon the pirates the boats' crews landed under a galling fire of grape shot, and formed in the most undaunted manner; and although a severe loss was sustained, they entered the breastwork at the point of the bayonet; after a desperate fight the pirates gave way, many were taken prisoners, but Mitchell and the greatest part escaped to the cypress swamps where it was impossible to arrest them.

A large quantity of dry goods and specie, together with other booty, was taken.

Twenty of the pirates were taken and brought to New Orleans, and tried before Judge Hall of the Circuit Court of the United States; sixteen were brought in guilty.

Accounts of these transactions having reached Lavette, he plainly perceived there was a determination to sweep all his cruizer from the sea, and a war of extermination seemed to be waged against him.

In a fit of desperation he procured a large and fast-sailing brigantine, mounting sixteen guns, named her "The Spirit of the Waves," and having selected a crew of one hundred and sixty men, he started without any commission as a regular pirate, determined to rob all nations and neither give nor take quarter.

A British sloop of war which was cruising in the Gulf of Mexico, having heard that Lavette himself was at sea, kept a sharp look out from the mast head, when one morning, as an officer was sweeping the horizon with his glass, he discovered a long, dark-looking vessel, low in the water, but having very tall masts, with sails as white as the driven snow.

As the sloop of war had the weather guage of the pirate, and could outsail her before the wind she set her studding sails and crowded every inch of canvass in chase; as soon as Lavette ascertained the character of his opponent, he ordered the awnings to be furled, and set his big squaresail and shot rapidly through the water; but as the breeze freshened the sloop of war came up rapidly with the pirate, who, finding no chance of escaping, determined to sell his life as dearly as possible.

The guns were cast loose, and the shot handed up, and a fire opened upon the ship which killed a number of men and carried away her fore-topmast, but she reserved her fire until within a cable's distance of the pirate, when she fired a general discharge from her broadside, and a volley of small arms; the broadside was too much elevated to hit the low hull of the brigantine, but was not without effect; the foretopmast fell, the jaws of the main gaff were severed, and a large portion of the rigging came rattling down on the deck; ten of the pirates were killed, but Lavette remained unhurt.

The sloop of war entered her men over the starboard bow, and a terrific contest with pistols and cutlasses ensued; Lavette received two wounds at this time which disabled him. a grape shot broke the bone of his right leg, and he received a cut in the abdomen, but the crew fought like tigers, and the deck was almost ankle deep with blood; the captain of the boarders received such a tremendous blow on the head from the butt-end of a musket as stretched him senseless on the deck near Lavette, who raised his dagger to stab him to the heart.

But the tide of his existence was ebbing like a torrent, his brain was giddy, his aim faltered, and the point descended in the captain's right thigh; dragging away the blade with the last convulsive energy of a death struggle, he lacerated the wound.

Again the reeking steel was upheld, and Lavette placed his left hand near the captain's heart, to make his aim more sure; again the dizziness spread over his sight, down came the dagger into the left thigh, and Lavette became insensible. His men rallied, and drove the sloop's crew to his own vessel, and night coming on they parted company.

Lavette was long confined to his berth, but eventually recovered, and was now scanning the horizon in the hopes of falling in with some sail with merchandize on board.

CHAPTER LI.

THE PIRATE—HENRY AND ELLEN—DOUBTS AND FEARS.

"Deck ahoy!" ran out from the mast head of the pirate.

Captain Latour looked upwards.

"Something floating on the water, on the larboard boy!" exclaimed the man at the look-out.

"What do you make it out?" asked Latour, placing his hand to his mouth so as to form a speaking trumpet, and propel his voice upwards.

"Can't tell—too far distant to be distinct—looks like a man on a spar."

"Hand me the glass," said Latour, turning to a dark weather-beaten man by his side.

This personage obeyed the order, and Captain Latour, adjusting the instrument, leapt into the rigging, and began to scan the space around them.

"Here, Bilton," he said, after taking the glass from his eye.

The man touched his cap in reply, as he strode to his Captain's side.

"Just put this glass to your eye and tell me what you make that object out to be, about two points off yonder."

Bilton looked through the instrument, and after a moment gave vent to a long, low whistle.

"What do you see," exclaimed the captain.

"Man on a spar or a plank, I take it," was the reply.

"Is that all," said the captain, so I judged. "No matter, we can't waste time and put ourselves to unnecessary troubles to pick up every fool that likes to fall overboard."

"Most likely been wrecked, captain," said Bilston.

"Very likely," said Latour, "but that's no fault of ours," and so saying, Captain Latour, leaned over the bulwark and gazed listlessly into the sea.

"Shall I give the order to have the ship put about captain," said Bilton, who occupied the part of lieutenant, on board the pirate.

Latour slowly raised his fat body from the bulwark, and said—

"Were we peaceable traders, I would willingly lay to and send off a boat to his rescue, poor devil, but being pirates we have nothing to gain by any act of mercy. Let the poor devil go to the bottom, or get picked up by some craft of more honourable calling—I don't see the use of saving a man to murder him afterwards."

"How, captain," said Bilston. "I don't understand you." "Don't you, well you may have good proof of my meaning some day, if ever we be defeated, when perhaps, wounded and maimed the officers of justice will use their every endeavour to save our lives and cure our wounds, so that they may pay us afterwards."

Bilston's countenance still wore a blank look.

"Look here, Bilston." What's the use of sending a boat to pick up the poor devil, when should he refuse to join us, we must obey the rule of the ship, and make him walk the plank.

"But he may he willing to join us," said Bilton. "And he may not," said the pirate captain, "and then down he goes into the sea." Let the poor devil be, his chance of life is greater where he is than they would be on board this craft."

"Well, perhaps you are right, sir," said Bilston, raising the glass again to his eye to take a farewell look of the poor object struggling in the waves.

Another long whistle escaped the lieutenant.

"That's a peculiarity of yours," said Latour.

"What, captain?" asked Bilton.

"That whistling."

"It's a habit," said the lieutenant, "I have got somehow."

"Yes; for you whistle at everything."

"There is something here, sir, that would make you whistle, did you see it," said Bilton.

"Aye—what?" asked Latour, suddenly.

"A petticoat, sir."

"What?"

"A petticoat."

"Do you mean a woman?" said Latour, bringing his fat body into an upright position.

"Yes, sir—a woman."

"Just hand me the glass, Mr. Bilton."

The lieutenant obeyed.

"A woman, eh?" said Latour, as he raised the glass to his eye.

The lieutenant watched his commander with a broad grin on his countenance.

"Humph!" he muttered to himself—"the captain would go to the devil for a woman."

"You're right, Bilton—you're right."

"It's a pity we can't waste time to pick her up," remarked Bilton, sarcastically.

"Waste time, Mr. Bilton—waste time!"

"Yes, sir: did you not say it would be a waste of time to lay to, and send a boat off to rescue them?"

Latour winced.

"True, sir—true; but I was not then aware that there was a woman in the case."

And, biting his lip, Captain Latour again raised the glass to his eye.

This conversation had drawn upon them the attention of the crew, who now stood gazing out upon the floating objects with much interest depicted in their countenances.

"Furl topsails," said Latour, taking the glass from his eye, and turning to the second lieutenant, who had advanced to his side—"and just ease her off a couple of points to starboard, Randell."

"Aye, aye, sir," answered the officer; and, turning to the men, issued the order.

In a few moments the pirate was drifting along towards the objects in the water.

"A welcome guest, Bilton, eh?" said Latour.

"What, sir?"

"That woman yonder."

"They do say it is unlucky to have a woman aboard."

"Who do?"

"Sailors generally."

"Ha, ha! for my part, I think differently. It is something to beguile away the time, and break the monotony of the voyage."

"Then you will endeavour to save her?" said Bilton.

"Undoubtedly," replied Latour. "Do you think I am so hard-hearted as to allow a woman to perish in the waves?"

"She might prefer it, sir, to a worse fate," replied the lieutenant, with a meaning glance.

"Humph," exclaimed Latour, dropping his eyes from before the fierce glance of his subordinates.

"Shall I give the order to man the boats," asked Bilston.

"Yes."

"And who shall take command."

"Randall."

"Is he to pick up both," asked the lieutenant.

The captain paused a moment in thought.

"We only want the female," he remarked at length.

"But captain, it is cruel to leave the other to perish," said Bilston.

"More cruel to save and then murder him," remarked Latour.

"He may be willing to join us."

"Perhaps."

"Shall we try."

"You can do so. But I fear he will be more in our way."

"Why so."

"The woman may be his wife, or a sweetheart," remarked the captain.

"We can but see."

"As you will," said Latour, turning away. "But if the fellow has to walk the plank it will be no fault of mine."

"Now the boat," said Bilston, bring the crew who stand awaiting the expected order.

The boat was lowered and manned, and Randall plunged himself in the stern, gave the order, to pull from the ship.

In another moment she was dancing over the crested waters, in the direction of the floating objects.

Latour leaned over the bulwarks, and, watched her progress through the waves, with a meaning smile lighting up his bloated features.

And Bilton followed the course of the little craft, with various emotions conflicting his heart.

He was a strange man, the lieutenant of the pirate bark. Brave as a lion, when the battle cry rang in his ears, his arms were nerved with a giant strength, and his aspect became furious and bloodthirsty.

But in the moments of peace he was gentle as a lamb, tame as the dove, and his heart panted to any act of mercy which fate might throw in his way.

He stood gazing, therefore, after the little boat, as she shot across the waves on her errand of success.

And a sigh broke from his lips as he thought of the fate of the poor woman and her companion.

Not so Latour, though a brave man, his heart felt no compassion, at the fate designed for the poor girl.

He warred with all the world, and blood and rapine followed the bark of his vessel.

With eager eyes he followed the boat, and, in impatience, he awaited the return with its fair burthen.

As he had said, she would cheer the dreariness of the voyage, and break the monotony of a sailor's life.

Love and war was his motto.

How misplaced the words!

Blood and misery had better pourtrayed its meaning.

"Bilton," he said, raising his glance to the face of his lieutenant.

"Captain?" was the reply.

"I am glad your quick eye detected the girl."

Bilton made no remark to this.

He felt sorry that he had said anything about a female, and wished that he had allowed the vessel to take her course over the waters, and left the poor wretches to their fate.

That fate could but have been death; but now what was in store for them?"

Death for the one; dishonour for the other.

Bilton turned away.

He remembered that he had two sisters in England—bright-eyed merry girls—just verging into womanhood; and a shudder broke over his frame as he conjured to memory the bright smile with which they greeted him whenever he paid a visit to his native land.

"What if fate led them to be cast on the mercy of the waves—what if they should fall into the hands of cruel and ruthless men—what would be their sufferings, and his feelings?

Bad as he was, he was still human, and he cursed the words he had uttered, which drew upon the poor wretches the glance of the captain, after he had decided to leave the man to his fate.

But it was too late now to recall what he had done, and he resolved to make amends, if it lay in his power, by doing all he could to avert the doom of the strangers.

The impatience of Latour became more and more manifest every moment, and he sharply gave the order for the vessel to be brought to.

Sails were reefed, and the speed of the pirate stayed; and she now floated listlessly upon the bosom of the deep.

Meanwhile, the boat sped on her errand, and in a short time came alongside the floating objects.

They discovered that those who had attracted the attention of the crew on board the pirate were a youth and a young girl, whose lovely, though pallid features, caused the hearts of the rough sailors to bound again as they gazed upon her.

They were clinging to a spar, and the tenacity with which they had kept their hold had cramped their fingers to such a degree that they could scarcely release their grasp upon the timber.

But the pirates placing their arms around them so as to support their bodies, and prevent them from sinking, loosened their grasp and lifted them into the boat.

The spar, released from the weight it had sustained, bounded upwards, and floated away upon the white-topped billows.

A sigh of relief broke from the breast of Henry Chambers as he saw his fair companion Ellen lifted into the boat; a sigh which would have given place to a cry of anguish had the thought of into whose hands they had fallen crossed his mind,

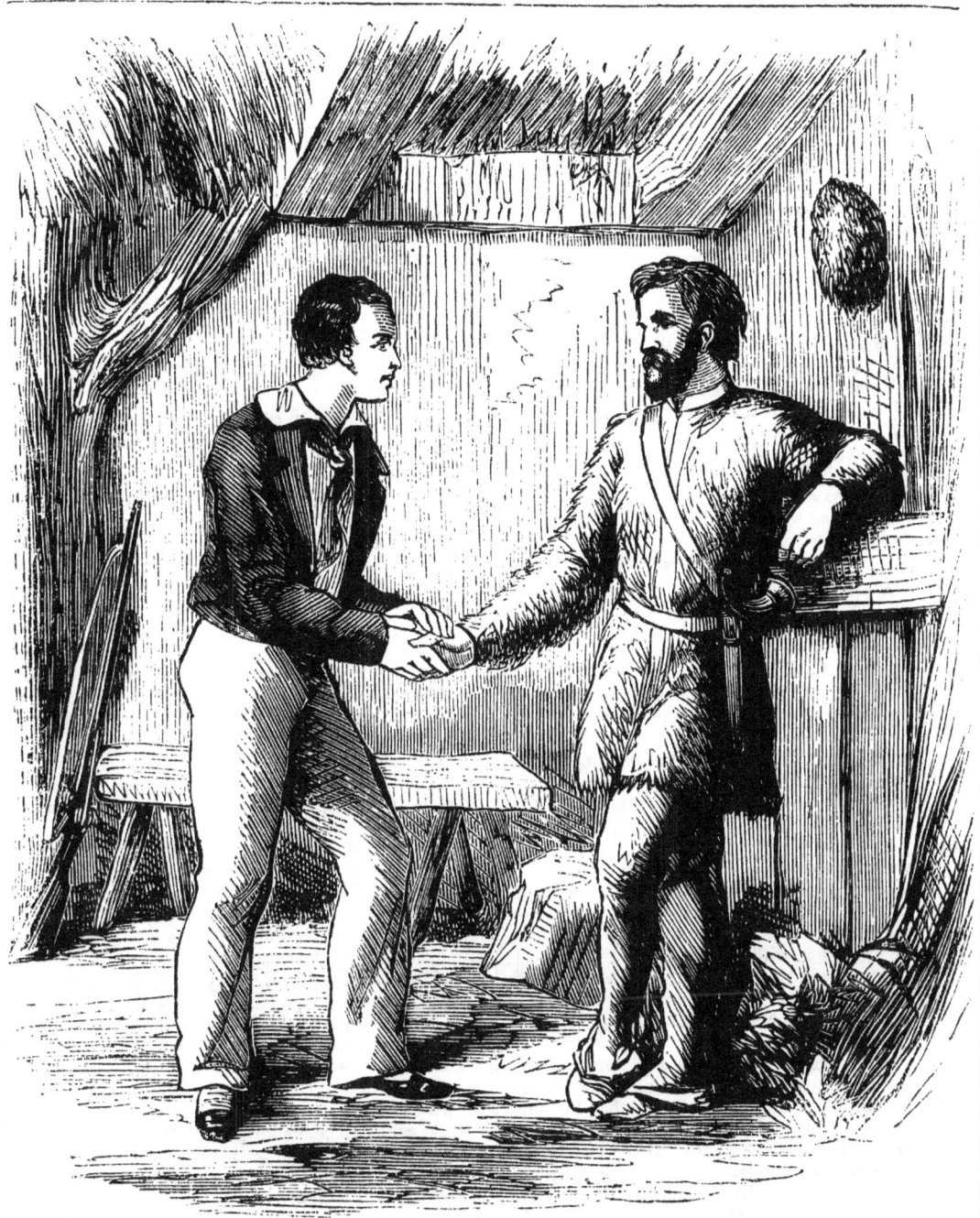

CHARLES CONSOLING THE HUNTER.

But he only saw the poor girl he so fondly, yet hopelessly, loved, saved from the fate which had threatened them, and a silent "Thank God!" spoke his gratitude.

Not a word was spoken by the rough sailors as they lowered her lithe form to the bottom of the little vessel, and gazed with various emotions upon her pale countenance.

Then Randall divested himself of his jacket and threw it over the garments of the fair girl.

Henry was lifted into the boat. The order was given to pull back for the ship, and the little craft shot over the waves towards the pirate bark.

The distance was soon accomplished, and in a short time the poor exhausted girl and the brave and devoted Henry were lifted to the deck of the smuggler.

Latour stood at the gangway to receive her,

and a smile lit up his features as his eye rested upon her lovely countenance.

For beautiful indeed she was, even though the pangs of the suffering she had endured marked their ravages on her pale face.

But he looked blank when his eye rested upon the bold, manly face of the young lieutenant.

He saw that stamped on his countenance which made him feel there was no sympathy between them.

He saw at a glance the superiority of his guest, and he felt that he must be disposed of.

"The plank," he thought, "must be his doom, or my success with this maiden is doubtful."

As he glanced again upon the open brow of the lieutenant, he imagined that he saw a look of hate dart from his eyes.

Nor was he wrong.

That instinct for which we cannot account, had

told the brave youth that he was in the power of a villain, and one whose heart was callous alike to the appeals of honour and justice.

And his heart sank within him as he thought of the poor girl whom he had rescued from the hands of the Boy Rover, and borne so manfully through the waste of waters.

He felt that he had saved her from a fearful doom to meet another equally as dreadful.

Poor Henry, as these thoughts occurred to his mind, a faintness stole over him, and he who had dared so much for the fair and lovely Ellen, now trembled with the excess of his fears.

Ellen, too, as her glance rested upon the features of the pirate captain could not repress a shudder.

There was something in the look of Latour that told her that her sufferings were not yet ended.

"Welcome lady," said Latour, grasping her hand. "I am happy in having been instrumental in rescuing you from a watery grave. Allow me to attend you to the cabin."

Ellen glanced at Henry.

The youth gave her a meaning look in return, and as Latour led her away, Henry followed.

"I regret that we have none of your own sex on board," said the pirate, with a meaning look.

Ellen drew back.

"Nay, fear not pretty one. If my manners are rough my heart is warm. Come, you must need rest and refreshment."

And Latour drew the arm of the shivering girl within his own, and strode towards the cabin.

Henry followed, but when Latour had arrived at the stairs, he turned, and addressing Henry, said:—

"Young man, you had better trust yourself to Bilton there; he will see to your wants."

"I would rather—" commenced Henry.

"Tut, tut—you would not encroach upon the privacy of a lady?" sneered Latour.

Henry turned pale.

"Captain," he said, "It has ever been the proud boast of a British sailor, that he would sacrifice the last drop of blood in his veins in defence of a woman. I would not willingly do you an injustice, but you have said you have no women on board, and my heart misgives me. Give me your word as a man—pledge me your honour as a sailor—that no harm shall come to that poor girl."

A frown gathered on the brow of Latour.

"Young man, you repay my kindness strangely."

"Heaven forbid," said Henry, "that I should do you wrong, but captain, we have passed through dangers which make me fear their repetition. Pledge me your word that the girl is safe on board your bark, and I will believe you, for you are a sailor; one, who like myself, knows that beneath the blue jacket beats a heart ever open to the cries of distress, and that throbs to avenge an insult offered to a defenceless woman."

"Enough," said Latour. "No harm shall come to the girl. Are you satisfied, lady?" he added, turning to his companion.

"I will trust you," she said, "and if you deceive me, may heaven pardon you."

"Come then," said Latour, and they descended the stairs.

Henry watched them with a sigh.

CHAPTER LII.

THE HUNTER AND HIS GUEST—THE HIDDEN DOCUMENTS.

WE left the brave and devoted lover of Ellen lying wounded upon the rude couch of the no less rude hut of the noble-minded hunter, and watched by him with a tender fatherly care.

The good man watched over him with an interest greater than he believed himself capable of taking in any one—smoothed the rude pillow, supported the wounded frame in his arms, bathed the wound, and bound the aching limb with all the tenderness of a woman.

Hour by hour his interest in the youth became greater and greater, and at the expiration of three days healmost felt that he should be sorry to part with him.

The care and attention bestowed upon the wounded part, had the much desired effect, and Charles Lawson walked about again with little pain.

But if the wound of the flesh had healed, there was a wound of the heart, which daily and hourly became more acute in its agony.

It was the loss of Ellen, and the disappearance of his friend.

It doubted not that Ellen was in the hands of still her persecuter, and that Henry had also fallen a victim to the villany of that bold bad youth.

The brave old hunter was unremitting in his endeavours to trace the friends of his guests, but could discover nothing of them on the island or the cliff.

He had observed indications of a rock, but could find no trace of anything human, and he came to the conclusion that the girl had been carried off to the smugglers' vessel, and that Henry in his pursuit, had either been borne away also, or in the darkness of the night have met his death by falling from the cliff into the bay.

It was about midday when the hunter returned to his hut, from an unsuccessful search he had been persecuting at the entreaties of his young friend.

When he entered Charles rose from his seat with a look of anxiety on his pale face, and the question in his look, "Have you found her."

The old man took the hand of the youth in his own and grasped it, with a fervent pressure, as he said.

"I can discover nothing."

"Alas," said Charles, "my worst fears are realised."

"Despair not my boy," said the old hunter. "Heaven may yet interpose to rescue her."

Charles sighed.

"Would to heaven my strength were wholly returned to me. I—"

"Be calm," said the hunter. "Should you excite yourself, you will but render your sufferings of longer duration, and undo the good already done."

"My kind friend," said Charles, taking the hunter's hand in his own, "my love for Ellen, my fears for her safety make me forgetful alike of your kindness and my own health. The miseries I have undergone of late, will, I fear, drive me to despair." I cannot bear them much longer."

"My lad, grief does not always kill, years of misery have marked their deep lines upon my face and heart, but still I live—yes, still I live."

And the old man bent his head to the youth, whose generous heart prompted him to grasp the hand of the man who had suffered so deeply, and so lovingly bore up against his feelings.

"Truly you have suffered much," said Charles, kindly—"

"Indeed, I have," replied the hunter, "but the Lord's will be done."

Charles bowed his head.

"Surely," he thought, "if this man can be calm under the heavy affliction it has pleased God to put upon him, it is wrong in me to complain.

And the brave youth strove to banish the sad thoughts which consumed him. But all in vain.

The image of the loved Ellen would cross his imagination, and the vindictive glance of the Boy Rover ever appeared before his mind's eye.

He threw himself upon the rude seat, and became lost in thought.

The brave hunter watched him for some time in silence.

A look of commiseration was upon his face, and a choking sensation in his throat.

He had learned to love the youth who had been thrown into his path by the villany of others.

And he thought, with a sigh, that the hour drew nigh in which the impulsive young sailor would form some means of leaving the island.

His generous nature had prompted him to succour the boy, but now his inclination would bid him stay where he was.

But he felt that love, that master of us all or would point out the road to escape from the desert island.

"I must suggest something," he thought, to arouse him from this painful fit of thought—some recreation, some labour,to employ the mind, or he will sink under his heavy afflictions."

And again he fastened his glance upon the wounded youth.

Charles was gazing abstractedly upon the floor of the hut, and seemed entirely buried in thought whilst ever and anon a painful sigh broke from his breast, and his pale thin lips quivered with the emotion which beset his heart.

"Charles, at length said the hunter."

"My friend." replied the young man man, looking up.

"You remember the hut in which you took refuge from the smugglers.

"Too well," said Charles. "Was it not there, I received this wound, and was it not from thence the lovely Ellen was born by that accused fiend."

"True?"

"What of it?"

"It has long been uninhabited."

"Well."

"It was formerly occupied by a man, who, like myself had bidden farewell to the world."

"Indeed," said Charles.

"We met once or twice, but there was something in the man, which from the moment I saw him, led me to avoid him."

"Why so?"

"I cannot tell. But the last time I saw him alive, he bid me search beneath the floor of his room when he should be no more."

"And did you so," said Charles.

"No, replied the hunter. "My own sorrows were more than I could well bear, I wanted not those of others, for I fell assured that by so doing I should leave his," Yet now I feel that I should like to comply with his last request.

"What do you expect to find," asked the young sailor.

"I scarcely know, unless it be the history of his life."

"If such had been his wish, you will not now succeed in leaving it, for the fire must have destroyed any document he may have left behind him."

"Not so," replied the hunter. The flooring of that hut is formed only of the earth."

"True," said Charles.

"I have a mind to learn, for such I expect to do, the reason of that man becoming an inhabitant of this island."

"Has he been long dead?" said Charles.

"Some little time now. We held little communication in life, and when he died I buried him beneath the tree where I found you lying and wounded.

"I could not bring myself to enter his hut. I had sorrows enough of my own without seeking out fresh ones. But now the feeling has come over me, to know more of this mysterious release. Will you accompany me to the ruins of his dwelling."

"Willingly," said Charles, rising from his seat.

"Come then," said the old hunter, taking his gun from its usual resting place, in the corner of the apartment.

"I'm ready," said Charles.

The old hunter drew the arm of the youth within his own, saying—

"Lean on me—you are not strong yet—fear not to bear your whole weight, for though I am old and careworn, there is yet sinew and muscle here."

The youth replied with a smile, and they left the hut.

The bracing morning's air played upon their faces, and the wounded youth inhaled it with a feeling of relief.

They were not long ere they reached the spot on which had once stood the log building, from whence Ellen had again fallen into the hands of the Boy Rover.

The debris lie around, charred and blackened by the fire, and a sigh escaped the breasts of both, as they gazed upon it.

The hunter stooped down, and commenced clearing away the charred remains.

Charles watched him intently.

Here must be the spot he meant," said the hunter, when he had cleared a good space of what had formed the floor of the habitation.

"But how will you raise the earth," said Charles.

"You shall see."

And the hunter taking a clasp knife from his pocket, opened it, and commenced cutting a sharp edge to a piece of unburnt wood, some six inches wide.

This accomplished, he used it as a spade, and after some time, at the distance of about a foot, he came upon a small rough made box, which he raised to the surface.

There was no fastening, and raising the lid he revealed to the gaze of Henry, several sheets of dirty paper, on the topmost of which, was written, "The Life and crimes of Murdock the Murderer."

The youth started back as these words met his eye.

The old hunter merely shrugged his shoulders, and said.

"As I expected, I could see the stain of blood on his brow, hence the antipathy,I ever felt for him."

"What will you do with this," said the youth.

"Make myself acquainted with its contents, and then bury it again for ever, from the light of day."

"Why not return it to its resting place, without perusing it?"

"As you will," returned the hunter, "but these manuscripts may furnish our minds with other thoughts for a time, and perhaps prove to us that our sufferings, though great, many have been counterbalance by those endured by him, who has passed for ever from this earth, to let us hope a better world."

And drawing the arm of Charles within his own, he led him back to his habitation.

———

CHAPTER LIII.

THE MANUSCRIPT—A DISCOVERY.

SOMEWHAT tired by the exertions attendant on his walk, Charles threw himself upon a seat, and the hunter doing the same, he said.

"You are still weak, much too weak to bear the least exertion."

"Indeed, I am," replied the youth, "and much I fear the agony I bear at the uncertainty of Ellen's fate, and that of my friend tends but to keep so."

"Do not think of this," said the hunter, "for a time at least strive to banish from your thoughts, that which of a surety must depess your spirits."

"Alas!" said Charles, "it's easier to advise than to perform."

The hunter sighed, too well he knew the truth of these words.

But still he knew that the ultimate recovery of the wounded youth was frustrated by the agony of his mind, and felt that he must use all means in his power to prevent his mind dwelling upon the subject, so holding the M.S.S. in his hand, he said—

"As I have told you, I had a great aversion to holding communion with the writer of these papers during his lifetime.

"There was something so repulsive in his demeanour. God forgive if I misjudged him, but there was that in his manner which when I have met him in my rambles, about the island, which led me to avoid him, I felt that if he suffered those sufferings had been brought on by his own evil passions, and from the words here written, I believe I was right in my conjectures. We both have sufferings enough of our own, yet the manuscript may be the means of pointing out to us that the hand of fate has been ever more merciful to us than it has been to him, and lead us to look upon our own miseries as light compared to his. Rest yourself my friend and let us beguile the hour by their perusal.

"As you will," said Charles, placing himself in a reclining position, and preparing to listen to the tale of Murdock, the murderer.

"I was born in Scotland," commenced reading the hunter "of a good family. My boyhood's life passed, as do most young lives, alternate hopes and fears, clouds and sunshine, and at the age of twenty I fell in love. The courtship lasted some time, and eventually the consent of my friends was given to our union, and here commenced the turning point of my fate.

"My marriage to the girl I had long loved, and who loved me with a love far exceeding my most sanguine hopes, is the point, so far as regards the nice applicability of the past events to present certainties, at which my narrative commences

"Dating from the day of that marriage, there begins a succession of misfortunes, that, insignificant at their birth, were gradually moulded together by extraneous contingencies, culminated to an act foul and terrible, if premeditated or intended, that has made me a branded felon.

"My wife and I never quarrelled.

"We loved and reverenced each other too much for either to trespass or trample upon what the other considered sacred.

"To be sure, in mere levity and exultation of spirit, we perform acts that to persons unacquainted with us and our circumstances, might seemed seasoned with earnestness.

"To such misunderstandings, by a third person, may be attributed the origin of reports that we, my wife and I, lived an unhappy life—a life of turmoil—of blows. Many around us held to such an opinion, but it was from their ignorance of the exact nature of our lives.

"But I, descending rapidly to the grave, do declare that we never, by word or deed, transcended the bounds of our great love for each other; or transgressed those laws that should preserve the person of the wife from blows or contumely.

"If it were possible to exist without jarring discord, to turn the sweetest sympathies into bitter hatred, ours was of that existence.

"Yet it availed me not in the dark day that came upon my household; but rather offered opportunities by which to strengthen an apparent guiltiness.

"'Jessie,' I said to my wife, one evening, 'do you stand on one side of the room, while I take a position on the other. Get me a ball of yarn from the basket, and then whoever is hit the greatest number of times shall make a present to the other. A nice present, of course.'

"'If I lose, my present will be a dressing-gown,' said Jessie; 'but you know you will have to pay for it.'

"'It will be just as acceptable,' I answered. 'But if I lose, you shall have that ring with the emerald and pearls.'

"Then the soft ball of yarn flew quickly from hand to hand—we, all the time, talking and laughing in great glee.

"A knock at the door, and an acquaintance entered, finding our faces flushed with the excitement of the contest, and each uncertain who was the vanquished.

"I declared that she had won the ring and promised to put it upon her finger the next day; which day to her, alive, never came.

"About two o'clock that night I was awakened to consciousness by one of those inexplicable preternatural premonitions of near danger which are often encountered, but generally in a sceptical spirit. My mind was clear to reason—not having its delicate powers blunted by sleep.

"Scarcely were my eyes unclosed before I became cognisant of the presence of a cold clammy nature, by its loathsome contact with my face, and by its pressure upon my bosom, whereby it nearly stilled the beating of my heart.

"Naturally I am no coward, but the knowledge of the presence of this burden, combined with utter darkness—creator of fierce fear—completely unnerved me, and my body shook like a leaf.

"The quiet condition of this body, which appertained not to myself nor my wife—its mysterious situation—and, above all, the moist chilly contact with my face, deprived me for an instant of self-possession.

"The clattering of a blind, or the nibbling of a mouse, seemed like a peal of thunder to my ears; the over-strained eye saw, or seemed to see, ghostly shapes pendent from the chandelier and bed-post.

"I dared not shout aloud, or change my position in bed, for fear that my throat would be clutched by the incubus that sat, like a hideous nightmare, fully developed into a reality, upon my chest.

"I experienced such a sensation as does the strong swimmer or venturesome diver when coming in bodily contact, unforewarned, with a corpse beneath the water—when nature acts like an electric battery, and discharges volumes of fear at the slightest movement; or, like one in the dark who encounters a skeleton.

" I was peculiarly situated; surrounded by an immensity of terror—expansive, inasmuch as it draped thoughts and motions in habiliments that gave them a gigantic appearance; immersed in a sea of dread and doubt, and, finally, completely cowed by fear.

" Now reason made its appeal to the frightened soul.

" The mere consciousness of bodily contact with this invisibility suggested its substantiality; but I hesitated to make the first movement, hostile or otherwise.

" There was a half-formed supposition in my mind that if I stirred there would come upon me an onset by the incubus that I could not withhold. The hesitancy to action I partly overcame by the circumspect rising of my left arm; it was free. I moved my right instantly; and, contemporaneously with that movement, the weight upon my face was removed to my neck.

"A little more stealthy investigation, still fearful of an attack by an insidious enemy, and I found that my right hand and the arm, as far as the elbow was temporarily paralysed, or in that condition usually called 'asleep;' that the hand was cold, and without sensibility, and that it was the object that had rested upon my face.

" Of course I was much elated at the discovery, and ashamed that I had been so easily alarmed at an accident that was susceptible of so easy an explanation.

" In order to give my wife an account of the absurd occurrence, I turned over, my previous position being a reclination upon my back.

" In my relief, consequent upon what I considered a correct explanation of my fright, the weight upon my chest had been forgotten: no, the change of my position recalled it very unpleasantly and inopportunely, even before I had touched my wife.

" Imagine, if you can, the result of this sudden knowledge that my oppressor had not been explained away.

" Think how quickly all the reasons which had been carefully revolved from the mental perplexities in which I had been entangled, were effectually controverted, and how absolutely mystery and frantic horror again swayed the sceptre.

" There was, then, a being of things in the room that did not belong there—never had been there previous to that night—and my deductions were faulty.

"The result was, that I lost all control over my passions — that I was lashed into a fury of despair, by the fear of the presence of a supernatural being.

" Clasping the object upon my breast with my left hand, with my right nerved with terror knowing no restraint, and numbed to all sensation of pain by reason of its paralysis, I struck heavy treacherous blows.

" It had soft hair, and at this I pulled and tugged, in this paroxysm of horror.

" In my great agony of mind I shrieked for aid —notwithstanding my efforts encountered no resistance—and called to Jessie to awaken.

" There was no response.

" The passive submission to blows of the object grasped by my left hand was extraordinary—the silence of my wife unaccountable.

" Then, for the first time during the struggle, did I think of Jessie's remarkably sound slumber, and connect therewith the burden.

" I could not—no by heaven!—I could not separate the identity of my wife from that of the object of my vengeance. Pushing the weight aside, I leaped from the bed and lighted the gas.

" My wife was dead!

" It was her head—that I had so often fondled, playing with its silken tresses—kissing those dear lips—looking into those lustrous eyes— that had so confidently reposed upon my breast.

" Yet not more than five minutes had elapsed since my awakening.

" I can't believe that I am her murderer, even though the law seals me with the crime, and strove to bring me to justice.

" I escaped from their clutches, and flew to the sea coast. The moon shrone bright upon the dancing waters, as I stood upon the beech gazing upon the masts of a vessel which lay off the coast.

" While thus I stood, six drunken fellows rolled down the beech to their boat, which was to convey them on board the ship. I implored them to take me with them—offered to reward them—to give me the means to escape from the justice which was pursuing me. although I told them not of the crime with which I was charged.

" They consented, and I was taken on board.

" When there, the captain of the ship, an old man, interogated me, and suspected from my confused manner that all was not right, blamed the men for taking me on board, and told me that he should consider it his duty to detain me a prisoner.

" I pleaded in vain. He was inexorable in his resolve, and I was placed in confinement.

And thus in an agony of mind I remained for some time, when a youth entered the cabin stealthily.

" You are a murderer," he said, addressing me, " who would escape from justice."

" Yes—yes," I said, scarcely knowing what I replied.

" There is but one means to accomplish this," he said.

" What is it," I asked. " Anything—I will do anything to to escape."

" In your cabin the captain lays asleep. Take this knife, one blow at his heart and you are free."

" Instinctively I grasped the knife, and made towards the cabin."

" Be silent," said the boy, " and let the blow be quick and sure."

Then suddenly recollecting what I was about to do, I exclaimed—

" It is murder ! "

" If you would escape the consequences of the murder, you must commit another, the officers of justice are already on your track, and to morrow will see you in a prison."

" It must not be," I said.

" No one but the captain will prevent your escape, if you would be free, this deed must be done."

" Maddened with the fear of a prison, I crept into the cabin.

"A small lamp swinging from the ceiling, revealed to me the form of the old captain, lying asleep on his cot. I approached him, raised the knife, and then as though all the demons of hell had forced down my arm, I buried the steel in his breast.

"One sharp grasp of agony escaped the lips of the old man, and as the hot blood spurted up over my arms and breast, I threw down the knife and flew from the cabin.

" I have said I could not believe I was the murderer of my wife, but now I stood stained with the life blood of an old grey-headed man, the hand of Cain upon my brow, I knew I was a murderer."

"What have I done—what have I done," I shrieked, as I faced the boy upon the threshold.

"Done! Made me captain of the "Venomed Snake," said the youth, with a demoniac glare in his eye.

"Given me a vessel who shall become the terror of the seas."

"I saw in a moment that I had been made the instrument of others villany, and the thought that perhaps my own death would pay for my crime.

"Then your promise of escape," I began.

"Shall be kept sacred, the boat is already lowered and the open sea lies before and around us, you are at liberty to go."

"Scarcely knowing what I did, I followed him to the deck, and in a few minutes I had entered the boat, and without a word it was cast off.

"Day was dawning, and as I parted company with the vessel, scarcely knowing where I was or what was to become of me, I cast my eyes upwards, and there floating out in to the breeze was the accursed ensign of the "Venomed Snake."

How long I drifted about in the waves I know not, but suddenly I was awoke by the boat striking against the rocks. It had drifted into a small cove or bay, entirely hidden from the open sea.

"I leapt ashore, and drew my boat upon the beech which sloped down in one spot to the water's edge, and as I did so, as though heaven designed to block me out from the world for ever, a high rock fell and filled up the spot on which I landed.

"That boat received no injury, and now lies embedded between the rocks till this day.

"From that moment I have remained on this desolate island, a prey to my own misery, brought me by my own crimes.

"Should this manuscript ever be perused, the reader will know where to find the boat, to me useless, as I have resolved never more to leave this island, and if after its perusal he can feel one pang of pity for a wretch, despised by heaven, raise one prayer for the rest of his soul, and drop one tear of pity for the misery endured for many years by Murdock, the murderer."

The hunter laid down the manuscript, and turned a look of questioning inquiry upon the features of his young companion.

The face of Charles was suffused with a bright glow, and a strange light beamed from his eyes.

"Poor wretch," exclaimed the old man. "No doubt he has suffered for his crimes. In the solitude of this island, conscience never slumbered. In the howling of the blast, how often must that death cry have rung in his ears. For the solitude of that lonely dwelling, how often may not his guilty heart have conjured up to his mind's eye, the features of his murdered victims. Heaven knows, I have suffered enough, but not for all the wealth on the earth would I have had that man's conscience."

"Horrible," said Charles. "That fiend, the Boy Rover, he the prosecutor of poor Ellen, gained possession of the hated vessel, by the blood shed by this man's hand. Heaven's curses light upon him, and his crew."

"The Boy Rover," said the hunter, in some surprise.

"Aye, the fiend whose hand inflicted this wound, the wretch who has torn from these arms the girl I love."

"Can it be possible?"

"It is the same, the captain of that accursed crew of smugglers and cut throats."

"Strange, but the ways of providence are wonderful."

"This boat," said Charles.

"What of it?"

"It may become useful to us."

"How," said the hunter.

"It may enable us to escape from here."

"I have no such wish. I would bury my sufferings for ever in this island."

"Were you to mix again with your fellowmen, this canker worm festering in the heart, might lose much of its force."

"Think it not," replied the hunter.

"Mine is a nature not easily brought to forget. Besides, here I can commune free from interruption with my thoughts. Often in the solitude of this rude chamber do I read and form the features of the sainted being, whose fate has made me what I am. Hold communion with her spirit, which I feel is ever hovering near me."

And as he spoke, a tear dimmed his eye, and his heart heaved with the conflicting emotion his words had called up.

Charles arose, and took the hand of the good man in his own.

"This manuscript has made you sad," he said.

"No, no," replied the hunter. "'Tis not that. I was thinking of her—of her."

"Come, come," said Charles, in his turn becoming a the consoler. "I feel strong now. Let us walk to the rocks and seek for the boat."

The hunter rose. A sigh escaped him. He felt how happy he might be with Charles for his future companion, but at the same time he thought how selfish was the wish to detain him, so putting the youth's hand through his arm, they left the hut and walked towards the rocks.

Having arrived here, they searched about for some time, and close to where the huge tree grew was a fissure, into which they looked, and at the bottom of which, they perceived the boat.

"'Tis there," said Charles, in a tone of pleasure.

"Yes. Strange that I should never before have discovered it. But I suppose the fact of never thinking to search for such a thing, has been the reason of my never before looking into the gap."

But whilst the hunter spoke the face of Charles became clouded.

"And now we have discovered the means of escape we are frustrated."

"How so?"

"We have no means to release it from its hiding place."

"The water in the bay is now low," said the hunter, "but when the tide rises it will float it to our feet."

"Thank God," said the youth, a weight removed from his breast by this remark.

"Then you will leave me," said the hunter. Charles grasped his hand, and a look of pain overspread his face, as he said—

"I would seek and save her."

"Go, then," said the hunter, "and heaven prosper you."

CHAPTER LIV.

THE BOY ROVER AGAIN—THE APPROACHING SHIP—
THE BLACK FLAG.

It was with anxious eyes that the Boy Rover scanned the approaching sail.

Black Bill, too, felt ill at ease, as did also the other smugglers.

There were but six of them, what chance had they then to cope with the coming vessel? None.

Their only chance of escape was in flight.

Every stitch of canvass was shook out, and her masts bent like reeds under the pressure brought to bear upon them.

She careened through the waves like a thing of life, but still nearer and nearer loomed the pursuing ship.

With an oath the Boy Rover turned to his lieutenant.

"I thought there was but one ship on the ocean could skim the waves as does your vessel."

"And what ship was that," asked Bill, moodily.

"The one that's gone to the devil, now," said the young captain.

"What the Venomed Snake?"

"Yes."

"She would be of some service to us now," remarked Bill.

"Aye: Did I now tread her plank, I would not run from that ship," said the Rover savagely.

"But with so few hands we should stand but a sorry chance."

"True. Well we have run into a hornet's nest now, I fear," said the Rover.

"Perhaps not," said Bill, "though she sails well she may not feel inclined to fight."

"We won't strike without a struggle, captain," said Tom.

"Strike, be damned," exclaimed the Rover, "if we strike it must be with the pike and cutlass, but ere I lower the flag and surrender, I'll blow the ship to hell!"

"No surrender," said Bill. "That's only out of the frying-pan into the fire."

And the Boy Rover turned from his followers, and commenced hurriedly pacing the deck.

On they went, her mast almost cracking with the pressure of the sails, and throwing the water high up on her bows, but still the stranger bore down upon them, and by eight bells was so near, that they could make out her colours.

"English," said the Rover, "that's the Union Jack floating at the peak."

"You're right captain," said Bill, "And so much the worse for us."

Nearer and nearer it approached the smuggler's ship, and then there was a puff of smoke, and the report of guns boomed over the waters."

"You be damned," said the Boy Rover.

"Means mischief, captain," said Bill.

"Yes," replied the captain, "that card don't come from the peace society."

There was another flash, another puff of smoke rising from the stranger's deck, and this time a shot ploughed the waves close to her bows.

"Getting hot now, captain," said Bill.

"Rather," was the cool reply of the Boy Rover, as he kept his glance fixed on the pursuing ship.

"What are they at?" he exclaimed, suddenly, as he saw the Union Jack come down with a run.

But the next moment another flag was run up to the mast head, and as the breeze uncoiled its folds, revealed the black flag of piracy.

"Pirates, by Neptune," exclaimed Bill.

The Boy Rover drew a long breath.

"Saved this time," he said. "Dog don't rob dog, "strike," he added, turning to Bill," or we shall have a broadside into us."

"Strike, captain," said Bill, as if he doubted the evidence of his senses.

"Yes, you lubberly fool." It is our only chance to make them acquainted with who and what we are."

"I see now," replied the lieutenant. And the next moment the Rover flag was down.

It was well for them that it was so, for the pirate was about to send a broadside into his bows.

"Ship-ahoy," came through the speaking trumpet of the pirate.

The Boy Rover took up the trumpet, and answered.

"What ship?" he called out.

"The spirit of the Wave," came clear and loud from the pirate.

"Why have you brought us to," said the Boy captain.

"To overhaul you," was the reply. "For what purpose."

"Plunder," answered Latour. "So lay too, while I send a boat, or I'll sink you."

"Come on board yourself," said the Boy Rover. "I have something for your own ear."

"Then speak it where you are. I've no secret from my crew."

"We are on the same track," said the Rover.

"Speak plain."

"Smugglers !"

"What ship is that?" asked Latour, at this.

"The Venomed Snake."

"It's a lie! She's gone to pieces."

This he had learned from Ellen.

"But it is her captain and crew," said the Boy Rover.

"Lay-to," said the pirate, "and I'll come n board."

In a few minutes a boat shot out from under the pirates bows.

It was filled with armed men, with Latour sitting in the stern sheets.

The Boy Rover had taken in canvas, and now calmly awaited the pirates on the deck.

"In a few minutes," she was alongside, and like monkeys, the motley crew came over her bulwarks.

"Who commands this bark," said Latour, leaping to the deck with a bared cutlass in his hand."

"I do," replied the Boy Rover, as he boldly confronted the swarthy pirate.

"You," said the pirate, opening his eyes, to their utmost width.

"Yes, me."

"Well, I'm cursed if you look old enough for a middy."

And Captain Latour strode up to the youth, and eyed him from head to foot, with a disdainful glance.

The Boy Rover bore the scrutiny with a curled lip, and defiant stare.

Apparently satisfied with the scrutiny, Latour at length gave vent to the exclamation.

"Humph."

"Well, sir," said the Boy Rover, "have you taken my portrait."

"I rather guess I have, youngster, but curse me if I can believe you are competent to command a gig, much less a good sized vessel like this, in the name of all that is devlish, how long have you been a captain?"

"Ever since the 'Rockinham' changed her name to the 'Venomed Snake.'"

"Humph," said Latour, still doubtingly.

"You have heard of her, I presume;"

"Well, I rather think I have.

"Then you have doubtless heard of her captain."

"I have heard him called the Boy Rover, and, if indeed you be he, they would have better named you the Baby Rover."

"Thank you for the compliment," said the smuggler captain. "But, nevertheless, I am the Boy Rover, the Smuggler of the South Seas."

"I have heard of your fame," said Latour.

"And I have likewise heard of yours," said the youth. "If I mistake not, you are Captain Jean Lavelette."

"I was," said the pirate. "But the English Government having a great desire to put an end to to my career, and I have heard say there are those who believe they have done so, I deemed it necessary to change my name to Latour, and the deeds of Captain Latour are not imagined to be those of Captain Jean Lavelette."

"A wise plan," said the Boy Rover. "But I presume now Captain Latour, you are satisfied we are no peaceful traders and will therefore allow us to pursue our way."

"A thief don't rob thief as a rule, and I have no wish to do so, but the fact is youngster, I am somewhat surprised that you did not show your teeth in this instance. I have been deceived in your character."

"That is easily explained captain. I have but five men."

"Eh, what," said Latour.

"Five only—all that I am aware were saved from the wreck."

"How did you get this ship?"

"They picked us up, and in the night we seized the vessel," replied the Boy Rover, cooly.

"By way of showing your gratitude, I suppose," said Latour.

"Exactly," replied the smuggler.

"Well, and what chance have you with so small a compliment of escaping from the government sharks," said Latour.

"I hope to soon ship a few brave hands, and start again," said the Boy Rover. "We have our lost fortunes to replenish."

"How are you off for arms and ammunition ?" asked Latour.

"Scarcely a weapon on board."

"Then you will cut a sorry figure if you are overhauled by a cruiser."

"I will sink the ship," said the Rover.

"How was it you did not adopt that measure when you found me in pursuit?"

"I waited to see your character," replied the Rover, "and when you hoisted the black flag I knew was safe."

"Safe indeed, your's is the first vessel I have boarded where a captain imagined the same."

"Doubtless," said the Rover, "but Captain Latour is not in the habit of boarding smugglers, I presume."

"Not exactly."

"Can you spare a few small arms and ammunition," asked the Boy Rover, "in exchange, I can give biscuit and wine."

"Humph," said Latour smiling, "first you should ask me do I intend to let you retain your vessel."

A glance of fire shot from the eyes of the young rover.

Latour saw the look, his mouth relaxed till a broad grim sat upon his features.

"I see there's some fire in you," he remarked.

"And so you would have found ere you had gained a footing on this deck, Captain Latour, did I think you would wished to deprive me of my vessel."

"Well you need have no fear of that," said the pirate.

Then turning to his men, as he sheathed his cutlass he exclaimed—

"Put up your arms for the next ship we meet, and return to your boat."

The men looked inquiringly at their captain.

A frown gathered about his brow, and he waved his hand imperiously.

Bad as they were, the men knew there was danger in disobedience, and sullenly made their way back to the boat.

"Now then, youngster," said Latour—"to business; you want arms ?"

"I do."

"I have not many to spare, but you shall have some for a few bags of buiscuits."

"Agreed."

"Let your men lower them into the boat, and I'll send you the arms when I go aboard."

"Thanks."

"And now, youngster, I have a friend of yours on board my bark."

"A friend of mine," said the smuggler captain, in some surprise.

"Yes,"

"Who," asked the Rover.

"A lady."

"A lady ?"

"Yes."

"Wild Madge ?" asked the Rover, eagerly.

"Wild devils," replied the pirate.

"Who then?"

"A lady, young and beautiful."

"Not Ellen ?" said the Rover.

"Well, I believe that is her name. Ellen—Ellen Hanfield, I think she told me her name was."

"Can it be possible ?"

"Yes."

"Where—where could you get her from ?"

"Off a spar."

"I am delighted to hear it."

"Are you ?"

"Yes, I am."

"Why so."

"Because I would give the world to again posses that girl."

"You would ?"

"I would indeed !"

"You're rather sweet in that quarter, then," smiled the pirate.

"Twice has she escaped me," said the Rover.

"So she told me."

"And to regain her I lost my ship."

"Then you was a fool," said the pirate captain.

"I could not bear to lose her."

"You deserved to do so, if you could not keep her," sneered the pirate.

"How fortunate," said the Boy Rover, "that she fell into your hands."

"So I considered."

"You will send her on board?" asked the youth, eagerly.

"Eh ?"

"You will send her on board, or shall I come and fetch her."

"Neither," said the pirate.

"What you—"

"Mean to keep her till I'm tired of her, that's all," said the pirate.

"You cannot want her," said the Rover.

"You cannot have her," returned the pirate. "She is now my prize, and the value is much enhanced by the knowledge that you did not succeed in your desires."

"Then you would—"

"Play the same part as yourself," said Latour, "though a young fellow that I picked up with her stands somewhat in my way."

"A young lieutenant ?" asked the Rover.

"The same."

"Curse him," said the smuggler.

ELLEN REPULSING THE PIRATE

"No, I mean to drown him," said Latour, with the utmost coolness.

"Make him walk the plank?"

"Exactly."

"Captain Latour. I will give you all this ship contains for that girl."

"When I have done with her you shall have her for half that price."

"When will that be?"

"When she will be no longer worth having."

"Can I offer you no inducement to place her in my hands."

"None."

"Captain Latour," said the Boy Rover, passionately, "I would give this right hand for the 'Venomed Snake' again, and her daring crew."

"Why."

"Because I would wrest her from you".

"Ha, ha," laughed Latour, as he strode towards his boat, into which the biscuit had by this time been placed. "If she gets away from me, and you can lay hold of her, you are welcome to keep her but I shall look sharp after her you may depend."

"You will not grant my request?"

"Just so. Did I feel inclined to grant even hers, I should give her up to the young fellow who bore her so bravely through the waves, for he has the greatest right to her if all had their due. Good-bye, I'll send you the arms, and take your love to the lady. A pleasant voyage. Adieu!"

And entering the boat, he waved his hand to the Boy Rover, who stood watching him with a demaniac glance, in his bright black eye.

"Curse you," he muttered through his clenched teeth. "I would spoil your love, had I but twenty men, but I'll be even with you yet, Captain Latour."

No. 20

And grinding his teeth in impotent rage, he strode to the cabin.

CHAPTER LV.

HENRY DOOMED TO WALK THE PLANK—THE PISTOL SHOT—THE PLUNGE INTO THE SEA.

CAPTAIN LATOUR, the pirate leader, sat in the stern sheets, not a smile upon his face, and his eyes fixed thoughtfully upon the scabbard of his sword, which he was balancing apparently unknowingly between his fingers, whilst the measured strokes of the men propelled the boat along towards the "Spirit of the wave."

The reverie into which the captain had fallen was not broken until the boat was brought up alongside the ship, when leaping up suddenly he cast his eyes aloft and the smile turned to a frown, and his lips became more compressed.

"Humph," he muttered to himself, "while that flag flies that boy had better be disposed of."

He made his way to the deck, and cast his eyes around in search of Bilton, that worthy was by his side in an instant.

"It is the Boy Rover safe enough," he said, addressing his lieutenant.

"And no prize."

"No, Bilton," he answered, "we must make up for the disappointment by the next sail in sight."

"Very well, sir."

"Bilton,"

The lieutenant touched his cap in answer.

"The young smuggler is short of arms and ammunition, I have promised to let him have some—you will see to it."

The lieutenant bowed his head.

"The crew of the boat will remain to take them on board."

"Very well sir," said the lieutenant moving forward to see that the order was performed.

The captain paced the deck thoughtfully while Bilton selecting half-a-dozen cutlasses, and as many pairs of pistols together with a small barrel of powder, saw then lowered into the boat, and gave the order for the men to pull away with their cargo to the smuggler.

Then he returned to the side of Latour.

"The boat has started," he said, "shall I have the black flag hauled down and the union hoisted."

"Not at present, Bilton," replied Latour without raising his glance from the deck, and continuing his walk.

Bilton paced up and down by the side of his captain.

He knew that something unusual either had or was about to occur, from the thoughtful manner of Latour.

Presently the captain raised his head.

"Bilton."

"Sir."

"When the boat returns, order the men aft, and bring the young fellow we picked up yesterday on deck."

Bilton fixed his glance on the face of Latour.

"I fear, captain, your efforts to induce him to join us will be unavailing."

"Why so."

"I have hinted that his service would be advantageous alike to him and us."

"Ah, then does he know our character," said Latour, sharply.

"Not exactly, sir."

"Not exactly—how do you mean.

"He suspects us."

"How know you that."

"He hinted as much to me to-day," replied Bilton.

"How should he suspect," guessed Latour, "and yet how could he be off doing so," he added aloud, "the rig of the vessel—the mixed crew—her armament, and himself a prisoner must tend to raise doubt in his mind."

"Even so," said Bilton.

"And he would not join us."

"He scorned the offer."

"So much the better," said the Captain, "there will be the less need of persuasion from me. Had any doubt remained of our character, he will be satisfied the moment he comes on deck."

"And see the black flag," said Bilton, now perceiving the reason why the captain would not have it hauled down."

"Yes, that will set all doubts at rest," remarked Latour.

Bilton turned away, a pang shot through his heart at the thought of the fate he felt, that brave and youthful sailor would in a few minutes be called upon to meet.

The lieutenant saw that the boat was returning, and almost wished that its pace were slower than it was, so that the time of Henry's existence might be lengthened, although only for a few minutes.

But on came the boat, and in a short time it reached the vessel, and as the men commenced ascending, the lieutenant gave the order for Harry to be brought on deck, and the men to assemble aft.

This the men quickly did, and Henry, his arms bound behind him, was brought upon deck.

Then Captain Latour ceased pacing the deck, and stood with darkened brow before the young lieutenant, and the assembled crew.

"Silence," he said, in a loud, imperious tone. Then turning to Henry he added—

"Lieutenant Chambers, for such I am told is the name you bear. I have to request that you will cast your eyes to the mast head."

The youth turned his glance upwards, and a deathly pallor overspread his features.

"What do you see," asked Latour.

"My worst fears realised," answered Henry.

"I am a prisoner in a nest of pirates."

"Such is the fact," said Latour."

The youth's lip quivered at the thought of Ellen, but he spoke not.

"Lieutenant Chambers," continued Latour, "the man that once steps on board these planks has to choose between two alternatives, either he must join our band and become one of us, or a plank is only placed between him and eternity."

Still Henry spoke not.

"Decide," said Latour, after a moment's pause. "None must live that dare betray us."

"Pirate," said the youth, "it is not the fear of death that pales my cheek, and causes my limbs to tremble. I have braved it too often to fear it now. But—but Ellen—she for whom I have struggled, 'Tis for her sake, her protection, I would live."

The rope was slung from the yard-arm of the 'Venomed Snake,' and I defied its captain's power, the knife has been raised above my head, and the and the foaming billows have threatened me with destruction, and I have braved all—dared all for her—all for honour. Pirate I know that I am powerless in your hands, but death rather than dishonour, is my choice."

"I will give you five minutes to alter your mind, in the meantime the men will fix the plank."

"My determination cannot be shaken."

"Think of her whom you leave behind."

"Pirate will you restore her to these arms pure and holy as she left them."

"By the laws of this ship she is mine," said Latour, "and will you enforce them."

"I will."

"Then villain know that that God who watches over the defenceless and oppressed will yet save her—we have trusted in him, and he has not failed us nor will he do so now. Coward and villain your baseness will yet meet its reward."

"Your answer," said Latour, chaffing at the words.

"You have received it, dog, my determination is irrevocable!"

"To the plank with him," exclaimed Latour.

The plank had been fixed and Henry was placed upon it.

"Ruffian," said the brave young sailor, "May a curse pursue you—may justice overtake you, and the vengeance of an outraged God fall heavily upon your heart!"

"Silence," roared Latour drawing a pistol from his heart and pointing it at the head of the youth.

"Dog, I scorn and defy you!" exclaimed Henry.

"Give him a chance," said Bilton, "when he is over let him have his hands free."

Latour nodded assent and the cord was severed. Henry finding his arms free darted towards Latour, but as he did so the plank was tilted and he fell over the side into the sea with a loud splash.

CHAPTER LVI.

ELLEN AND THE PIRATE CAPTAIN.—THE GOOD RESOLVE.

WITH a smile on his face and a peculiar meaning in his eye Latour entered the cabin appropriated to Ellen.

He found the poor girl seated on a couch with her face buried in her hands.

She was recalling to her mind the fearful scenes through which she had passed during the last few weeks, and wondering whether fate had destined her ever again to see those she so fondly and dearly loved.

Latour stood gazing upon her for some few moments ere she was aware of his presence.

He hesitated a few moments whether or not he should break the reverie into which she had fallen.

And as he gazed a feeling of pity stole into his heart.

But that feeling was quickly chased away by a feeling of a different nature.

He had saved her from the waves.

He now sought her reward.

And that reward was to be her honour.

And he hesitated no longer.

He approached her.

He placed his hand on her shoulder.

Ellen started.

She looked up into the face of Latour.

The expression there alarmed her.

It was such a one as she had seen on the face of Boy Rover when he had sought to trample on her virtue.

A look of anguish overspread her features.

She would have fallen from the couch but the strong arm of Latour was stretched forth to prevent it.

"Sweet Ellen," he muttered.

The girls' cheek became more pale at these words.

"Do you hear me," he said as he observed the poor girl tremble.

"No, no," she remarked, scarcely knowing what to say.

"Then why do you tremble."

"I—I don't know."

"I have come Ellen," said Latour, "to tell you that I love you."

A cry of pain escaped the lips of the poor girl.

"Is my appearance so repulsive," said the pirate, "that it frightens you."

Ellen did not reply.

"Speak," said the pirate.

"No, not that, but—"

"But what."

"Your words alarm me,"

"Do girls tremble at love," asked the pirate, gazing lustfully into her face,"

Ellen averted her head.

"Sweet one," said Latour, taking the white taper fingers of the fair girl in his own. I have come here to tell you that I love you."

Ellen started.

"Oh, speak not this," said the fair girl.

"And why not, sweet Ellen."

And the pirate gazed into her eyes.

A shudder ran through her frame.

A shudder of fear.

"Am I so repulsive then," said Latour.

"'Tis not that, but—but—"

"But what, fair maiden."

"I know not what to say," said the poor girl, trembling.

"Say that my passion is reciprocated," said Latour.

And he strove to draw the poor girl to him.

Ellen drew back.

"Oh, speak not this", she murmured.

"And why not, dearest."

"I am grateful, very grateful, for the act you have done in saving me and Henry from a watery grave, but—but—"

"Well, but what—"

"Spare me, I—I love another," gasped Ellen.

A smile curled the pirate's lips. He thought she meant Henry, should he tell her of his fate.

No, that might ruin all his pleasures.

So he merely fixed a smiling look upon her face' and said—

"Is not the service I have done you worthy of a kiss."

And again he strove to draw her towards him.

"Sir," said Ellen, indignantly.

"A kiss, pretty one. I claim it as my reward for the service I have done you and your lover."

"Oh sir, blacken not that good act by one base deed," said Ellen imploringly.

"Nay—nay, you are coy," said the pirate.

And he strove to imprint a kiss on her fair cheek.

"I am a woman, sir, with a woman's feelings," said Ellen.

"And possess a woman's gratitude," said Latour.

"Yes," replied Ellen, "and never shall I forget your kindness."

"Yet, methinks your gratitude is somewhat cold," said the pirate.

Ellen sighed.

"I do not understand you," she said.

"We shall understand each other better, shortly, I doubt not," replied Latour.

There was something in his tone that caused the fair girl to tremble.

"You are weak," he said. "Let me support you."

And he encircled her waist with his arm.

"Oh, no," said Ellen, "I am strong—very strong.

But her trembling limbs belied her words.

The pirate drew her towards him and imprinted a kiss on her cheek.

The rich blood suffused her face, and in an indignant tone she exclaimed—

"Release me, sir—Blacken not the good act you have done by insulting a defenceless woman."

And she tore herself from his grasp.

A scornful sime curled the lips of Latour.

"Maiden," he said, "I am not here to blush at my actions—know you into whose hands you have fallen."

"I thought with those of a gentleman," said Ellen.

"You are in the hands of Captain Latour the pirate."

"Heaven have mercy upon me," said Ellen.

And the blood which had tinged her cheek rushed back to her heart and left her pale as marble—so pale and cold that Latour himself was frightened.

"Ellen, Ellen," he said, "I will not harm you."

But the head of the poor girl sunk upon her breast.

Latour raised it.

She had fainted.

He bore her to the couch.

He laid her thereon.

Then he imprinted a kiss upon the pale face and left the cabin.

"Bilton," he said, when he reached the deck, "I cannot wrong that girl."

Bilton looked up in surprise.

"Humph," he said.

"You seem surprised," remarked the captain.

"Well, rather," said Bilton.

"You believed me lost to all feeling," said Latour, "Is it not so."

"I have judged by what I have seen," said Bilton.

"Ah, you refer to the youth."

"I do."

"I am sorry that he is dead."

"Are you."

"Yes."

"Were he alive you would condemn him to the same fate."

"I think not."

Bilton mused for a moment.

"Captain," he said, "the youth is safe."

"Ah, what mean you."

"He was saved by the Boy Rover."

"I am glad of it."

"So am I"

"But how know you this."

"I saw the boat pick him up," said Bilton.

"You did—well, I am glad I have not his death to answer for. He is a brave youth and deserves a better fate."

"He does," said Bilton.

"But much I fear," said Latour, "that he will find little mercy at the hands of the Boy Rover."

"Why so," asked the lieutenant.

"They are rivals?"

"Rivals?"

"Aye, rivals in the affections of the girl whom I now hold in my power."

"How know you this," said Bilton.

"I have it from her own lips," said Latour. "It was in pursuit of this girl that he lost his ship."

"Does he know of her existence on board this ship?"

"Yes: I made him acquainted with the fact," said Latour, with a smile, "and he offered to sacrifice his vessel, to again obtain possession of her."

"And you refused to hand her over to him," remarked Bilston.

"I did," said Latour, "for bad as I am, Bilton, had I done so she would have been in worse hands still."

"Then this poor youth will but meet a sorry fate at the hand of the young smuggler."

"I expect so. The revengeful disposition of the young smuggler captain will prompt him to any act of cruelty, in revenge for the less of the girl."

"And yet the youth deserves commendation for wresting her from his hands."

"He does."

"It was cruel," said Bilton, "to separate them. Seldom, indeed, is it that women can be brought to look favourably upon the man who can sacrifice her lover."

"True," said Latour, "but it appears that this youth is not the lover of my captive."

"Ah, not her lover."

"No. The youth she loves lies wounded on an island, surrounded by rocks, several degrees distant."

"Where did you learn this," said Bilton.

"From her own lips," answered the pirate. "She has made me acquainted with all that has happened to her, since she left Gibraltar for England, to become the wife of a young sailor. The vessel was dashed to pieces, on the Cornish coast, and she fell into the hands of the Boy Rover, but was rescued by her lover. Again she was taken by the smuggler, and again she escaped, by the aid of her lover and his friend, who this day walked the plank, but still the Boy Rover pursued them, and wounding her protector, strove to bear her back to his ship, but a storm having arisen his vessel was dashed to pieces, and this youth, who has paid so dearly for his devotion, tore her from his hands, and dared the waves with her frail form. They were rescued by us, and you know the rest."

Bilton paused thoughtfully for a few moments then looking fixedly into the captain's face, said—

"Captain Latour, no man was ever respected more by the crew under him than you, yet I believe, had these men have known what you have now made me acquainted with, they would not have suffered this murder."

Latour started.

"Execution, Mr. Bilton, you mean."

"No sir, foul and unnatural murder, it cannot be called by any milder term."

"But sir, you say the youth is still alive," said Latour severely.

"True, he has escaped the fate you designed for him, but to fall into the hands of him who will condemn him to a worse me."

"I knew not the facts I have told you till after the youth had walked the plank."

"And had you done so," said Bilton, "would it have saved him."

"Yes," said Latour, "for I respect a brave man."

"Then captain let us wrest him from the hands of the Boy Rover."

Latour looked into his lieutenant's face in surprise.

"I cannot break my word with the smuggler," said Latour."

"Your word."

"Yes, I promised not to molest him," returned Latour.

"But did you promise to give this youth into his power?"

"No."

"Then demand him at his hands," said Bilton.

"No," said Latour. "He must take his chance now."

"And the girl," said Bilton, "what do you intend to do with her."

"Make her my own, if I can do so by persuasion, if not, I will not use force," returned the pirate. "If I cannot succeed in bringing her to look favourably on my suit, I will put her on shore."

"Where?"

"At the first spot we touch at," returned the pirate.

"And leave her to do the best she can for herself I suppose," said Bilton.

"She will find little difficulty in reaching her friends," returned the pirate, "if I provide her with the means."

"Well, captain," said Bilton, "oppression has made us pirates, but it can only be our own evil natures that makes us murderers and violators of woman's honour. For the sake of a few moments transient bliss we commit crimes at which humanity stands appalled. I am glad, Captain Latour, that your heart is not all iron."

"Hush," said the pirate captain. "It will not do to let the men observe that our hearts are not adamant; cruel and remorseless themselves, they must be governed as the beasts; brute strength and brute courage only can hold them in subjection."

"True," replied Bilton.

"Enough of this," said Latour, "Now, sir, to your duty."

Bilton saluted his commander, and turned away.

"Haul down that flag," said Latour, after a pause, "and up with the Union Jack."

"Aye, aye," rang out from the seamens' throats.

In a few moments this was done, and the emblem of freedom floated at the mast head.

"Shake out some more canvass," said Latour, "and ease her off a point or two."

This command being obeyed, the Spirit of the Wave rode over the bosom of the waters like a flying dolphin.

Bilton paced the deck with a satisfied smile upon his bronzed features.

He was not all bad.

There lingered still in the inmost recesses of his heart, some of those precepts which a mother's teaching had engrafted on his mind when a child.

Though a pirate he had not forfeited all that proclaimed him a man.

Latour, too, seemed better at ease with himself.

Perhaps it was the thought of the good act he contemplated.

For, strange as it may seem, even the most depraved feel a secret pleasure in a good action—the thought of it throws over the blackened conscience a feeling of light and joy.

The cheerful faces of the captain and his lieutenant seemed to throw an halo of brightness upon all the crew of that piratical vessel as they went about their various duties in a cheerful manner, and the Spirit of the Waves glided through the waste of waters to the laugh and song of the free-hearted pirates.

CHAPTER LVII.

THE CAPTIVES ON BOARD—THE ROVER—AN UNINTENTIONAL BLOW—AND AN UNEXPECTED MEETING.

SUSPENSE is worse than certainty, is an old and a true saying, better to know the worst at once than linger on in doubt and uncertainty.

No matter what our fate, yet if we have a knowledge of it, time will, to a certain extent reconcile us to it, or alleviate in some degree, this pang first caused by it, at least knowledge, but suspense and uncertainty knows no alleviation.

The longer it lasts the blacker it becomes, till eventually it cankers in the heart, and saps up the well springs of life and happiness.

Mr. Hanfield sat in the cabin of the Boy Rover's vessel, with his head buried in his hands, and his mind a prey to agonising thoughts.

Jacob the faithful servant sat by his side, gazing with pitying looks, upon the haggard face of his master.

The good hearted fellow forgot his own sufferings in the contemplation of his master's agony.

Like most domestics, who had lived and grown under the roof of an indulgent master, he entertained a respect for his employer, greater than for any other in the wide world.

He felt that he could willingly suffer, could his master escape, for the knowledge that he was free would cheer his own captivity, or the last moments of his life.

Mr. Hanfield reproached himself, for having, as he considered if, been the means of placing his faithful servant in such a predicament.

Thus they had sat, inwardly praying that the approaching vessel would receive them from the hands of the young fiend, into whose hands they had fallen.

Yet neither of them gave utterance to their thoughts and wishes.

And so they sat, silent, sad, and thoughtful.

Minutes seemed hours, and each had made up his mind that the sails seen from the deck of the Rover, and which, for the time had saved them from the doom to which the base-hearted youth had condemned them, had either been distanced by the Rover, or had changed her course.

If so, their chance of succour was gone.

And their hearts sank as the thought entered their minds.

Boom came over the sea, and simultaneously master and several leapt to their feet.

Their features underwent a sudden change, from despair to hope.

The boom of the pirates gun had instilled fresh life in them.

The sound was music to their despairing hearts.

Each looked into the other's face, and grasped each others hand.

"Heaven be praised," said Hanfield.

"God grant they may overhaul us," said Jacob.

Another boom now saluted the ears of the prisoners.

"They will bring us to," said Hanfield.

"I hope so," replied Jacob.

"But ah," said Hanfield, as his cheek again paled; "how can we make ourselves heard should they board us?"

"I will belabour the door with this stool," said Jacob, raising the article as he spoke.

Mr. Hanfield approached the window and looked out upon the sea.

"An English ship," he said, as he saw the union jack floating at her mast-head.

"Thank God!" said Jacob.

And he placed the stool again upon the ground and went to the window.

He casts his eyes upwards at the long tapering mast, and as he did so, he saw the flag lowered.

"Look master!" he said, "what can that mean. They are lowering the flag?"

"Heaven help us," said Hanfield, "she has struck to this accursed boy."

"Alas! I fear it is so," replied Jacob, and his heart sank within him.

"Ah! what is that?" suddenly exclaimed his master, as the black flag was run up to the masthead of the pirate.

"A pirate!" exclaimed Hanfield.

"A pirate!" iterated Jacob.

"Heaven defend us!" said the old gentleman. "We are sorely tried."

Jacob and his master now gazed fascinated upon the hull of that dark vessel, and as the pirate's boat shot out from under her bows, a sigh broke from their lips.

What mercy could they expect from those men.

Poor Mr. Hanfield! he turned away from the window, and sank into a seat in despair.

Not so Jacob. He could not take his gaze from that black flag.

He saw the boat come up alongside the Rover, and he listened intently.

He expected to hear the clash of arms, the report of pistols, but all was still save the plashing of the waves on the Rover's side.

"This won't do," he said, after a time; "they can but kill us once.

And leaving the window he seized the stool in his grasp, and sent it with all his force against the door of the cabin.

Then he listened in the hope of hearing footsteps descend the stairs.

But not a sound met his ears.

Again he raised the stool, and again he hurled it at the door.

Still there was no response.

"'Tis useless, Jacob," said his master; "they are all of a kidney."

"Damn them!" said Jacob. "I only wish it was that boy's head instead of this door."

And he hurled the stool with such violence against the wood, that it almost split it.

"If they can't hear that," said Jacob, they must be deaf indeed,"

"And if they do hear it," replied his master, "they will pay no heed to it."

Mr. Hanfield arose and again approached the window.

"They are leaving the ship," he said,

Jacob looked forth.

The pirate were entering their boat.

"Hi! Hi!" exclaimed Jacob.

And he waved his hand from the cabin window to attract the attention of the pirates.

But they heard him not or if they did they paid no heed to his signal.

"Curse them all," said Jacob, now fairly losing all command of his temper.

"Hush," said Mr. Hanfield.

"I can't, said Jacob, "to be cooped up here by the scoundrels is more than I can bear."

The pirate boat now pulled out from the rovers side, and the imprisoned men watched her with strained eyeballs as she made her way to the vessel with the black flag.

They then turned from the window and sank into their seats. Hope like a sunbeam had cast a cheerful ray upon them for a moment only to leave the black shadow which succeeded its presence darker then before.

"Lost—lost!" said the old man. "That vessel saved us only to endure a few more hours of agony, I had hoped that heaven had sent a succour, but alas!—aid is not for us."

And the old man's head sank again upon his hands and he was silent.

Jacob fairly foamed with rage and disappointment.

"I suppose," he said, "they mean to do for us."

"Our execution only has been deferred, doubtless," said his master.

"I wish I could only find some weapon, I would not die without a struggle. If I could only bury a knife in that young lads heart I would'nt care what become of me."

Hush!" said his master. "Speak not thus Jacob. Better that we should meet our Maker with clean hands and clean hearts then fly into his presence with murder on our souls."

"Justifiable murder it would be," said Jacob.

"Not so," said Mr. Handfield, "the taking away of life cannot be justifiable."

Jacob thought differently, but he had no wish to cross his master, therefore he remained silent.

"Jacob," said Mr. Hanfield after a pause, "did you ever see this lad before."

"Not that I am aware of," replied the servant.

"Nor I, said Hanfield, "and yet the features are familiar to me."

"Indeed."

"Ay, indeed," said the old gentlemen.

"Yet I do not think fate has ever cast us before into each other's path; still I can trace in those lineaments features familiar to me—a face long since seen, but where I know not."

"Doubtless, sir, you are mistaken," said Jacob.

"I feel convinced I am not."

"There are strong resemblances in some persons," said Jacob. "Yet I can hardly bring my mind to think that this bloodthirsty boy can bear the image of an honest man."

"I cannot think where we have met—yet we must have done so, so strong is the impression left upon my mind."

And the old gentleman fell to musing and thinking, and running over in his mind persons and places, to solve the likeness.

But all of no avail.

And Jacob, worn out with his passions and exertions to make the pirates acquainted with their position, leant his elbow on the table, and leaning his head on his hand, fell into thought also.

And thus they continued for some time, when a hurrying backwards and forwards of footsteps overhead, roused them from their reverie.

"What's that?" said Mr. Hanfield, looking up.

"Don't know," said Jacob. "I only hope they are killing each other."

They listened intently for some moments, and then footsteps were heard descending to the cabin.

A pallor overspread the face of Mr. Hanfield.

"They are doubtless coming to lead us to our doom," he said.

Jacob leapt to his feet.

"We will not die alone then," he exclaimed as he seized the stool in both hands.

"Jacob, I command you," said Mr. Hanfield.

"Master, I have never refused to obey you, but I will not die without a struggle."

And the man strode before his master and awaited the opening of the door.

There was a hand upon the fastening, and Jacob raised the stool above his head.

The door opened, and the faces of the Boy Rover and Black Bill, and two others, appeared at the threshold.

Jacob sprang forward, and brought down the stool with terrific violence.

But it had missed its mark.

The quick eye of the Boy Rover detected the movement, and leaping aside, he thrust forward a youth whose garments were saturated with water, and who received the blow intended for the Rover upon his shoulder, and with a cry of pain, fell forward at the feet of Jacob.

Ere the man could again raise the weapon, the door was pulled too with a loud crash, and Jacob, Mr. Hanfield, and the prostrate man were left alone, while the loud laughter of the smugglers, as they ascended to the deck, came gratingly upon the ears of the prisoners.

Surprise and disappointment for a few moments held Jacob powerless. then a feeling of pity stole over him and he threw down the weapon with which he had floored the now almost insensible youth.

Mr. Hanfield stooped down and endeavoured to raise him, but he was so weak with grief and anxiety that he could not accomplish it.

Jacob stooped to assist him and between them they raised the young sailor and sat him on a chair.

"He's been overboard," said Jacob.

"Poor fellow," said Mr. Hanfield pityingly.

"He's stunned," said Jacob, "but not dead—I didn't mean the blow for him. Let us left him to the window the air will revive him."

Mr. Hanfield and his servant bore the young man to the window, and the fresh sea breeze playing on his pale face revived him and opening his eyes he gazed bewilderedly upon his companions.

Simultaneously all three started and uttered exclamation of "Henry Chamber!" said Hanfield and Jacob in a breath.

"Mr. Hanfield!" exclaimed Henry, for he it was. "My God are you, too, in the power of the Boy Rover?"

CHAPTER LVII.

MARTENEZ AND INEZ—THE ROCKY ISLAND.

When Lieutenant Martinez leaped from the slave ship into the ocean, he struck out boldly towards the spot where he had seen the lovely Inez disappear; in a brief interval of time he reached the spot, and diving beneath the waves, he encountered the form of a lady, as it was rising to the surface.

Seizing her form in one hand, with the other he swam towards the ship, the buoyancy of the waves rendering his task comparatively easy. But what was his dismay, when born by the swell to the crest of a lofty wave, he saw that they were far behind the wake of the ship.

Unfortunately they had drifted to the leeward of the ship, and the crew, who had gazed anxiously and long on the waste of waters, in hopes of discovering the objects they had missed, never thought of looking in the other direction, consequently they were left unheeded and unseen, lost beyond human aid, floating on the pathless ocean.

A feeling of despair came into Martinez's heart, as his eye, in a moment, comprehended their perilous situation, but he was a brave man, and had faced death too often to fear it now.

He raised a shout for help, but his voice fell unheeded on the humid air.

He looked on the inanimate form that his arm was supporting, and in spite of the horrors of their situation, he felt a thrill of joy that he could at least die with so beautious a companion, and thus deprive death of half its terrors.

Silently he battled with the waves, and when exhausted with swimming, he rested by floating, and by slight movements known to the skilled swimmer, kept himself and his burden from sinking.

The ship was out of sight, and still they drifted on.

"We are beyond human aid," thought Martinez, but not Providence. He can still save us, if such should be his will." So bravely and manfully, while strength remained to him he persevered in resisting the approach of death.

But now a new fear crept over him. Inez was still unconscious, and he began to think that she must be dead. So long in the water, though it was not cold, must ultimately rob her delicate form of if, if it had not done so already.

The sun was slowly sinking towards the horizon—a little while and night would descend on them, the air would blow cool and the water chill.

Despair fell on Martinez's heart, as he thought this, added to which fatigue was telling on his robust frame, a brief period, and all would be over.

"Merciful heavens," murmured Martinez, "let us not perish thus."

Weaker and weaker he became, but firmer and stronger was his hold on his companion.

Night came. The cool evening breeze for a moment revived Martinez's drooping energies.

'Twas the dying flicker of the candle ere it expires for ever.

With a sigh of anguish his arm droops nerveless by his side, his eyes closed, and the moaning wind and the murmuring waves together join in a dirge o'er the disappearing bodies.

*   *   *   *

Amongst a cluster of islands, in the midst of the ocean, was one that had never yet been explored. It was well-known to mariners, as presenting a kind of sea mark, and serving to direct them to the pleasant islands beyond it.

It appeared like a vast and lofty rock, precipitous on all sides, and bare and barren. Many had attempted to scale it, but none had succeeded; its circumference was about twelve miles. Standing in the van of the assembled islands, it met the whole force of the Atlantic's swell, and its rocky sides seemed indeed, a protector, designed by Providence, to protect the beautiful and fertile islands beyond.

It was towards this rocky islet that in the moment of their dire extremity Martinez and Inez were drifting, as night fell and hope and sensation died out, the tide that had borne them hither still lent its friendly aid.

The noise of the waves leaping against the lofty rock was like the echo of thunder. They must surely be dashed to pieces against its granite sides.

But no, fortune favoured them here.

The massive rock presented to view many cavernous holes in its surface, worn perhaps by the increasing wear of water upon it.

Into one of these, one of the largest and most spacious, the two inanimate bodies were carried by the waves, and thrown high up on to the soft sand that lay deep on the floor of the cavern.

The waves licked and washed their feet, but their power and control was gone, and the tide presently turned and left them high and dry in an apartment of nature's making.

Were they dead?

All within was dark, but the noise of the water without was tremendous and reverberated with terrible distraction in the cavern.

Some time elapsed, and the moon rode high in the heavens, till through a chink in the roof of the cavern a beam streamed through upon the pale faces of Martnez and Inez.

The action of the noise on his ears and the light upon his face gradually brought Martnez to his senses painfully and with difficulty he opened his eyes, but quickly closed them again, as if to shut out the returning life that providence gave him.

As he laid there with closed eyes, his scattered thoughts began to rearrange themselves into something like order. Memory returned, and with a cry of anguish he started up for the remembrance of the last scene, as he thought of life came with vividness and distinctness before him.

Was this death, and was he now in that world from whence there is no return.

The terrific roar of water filled him with an indescribable dread.

As he again opened his eyes he gazed with surprise on the dazzling scene around him.

The moonbeam that shown through the roof of the cavern is reflected from a thousand stalachtiles and gems that hung pendant from the walls and roof, looking like some fairy grot described in eastern romance.

In a moment he comprehends his situation, he feels that life has not deserted him, and that by some indescribable and mysterious manner he has been rescued from the jaws of death by a merciful and beneficent providence.

Then, remembering his companion, a thrill of agony shot through his heart as the thought came, had she perished.

He looked beside him, and there, to his intense joy, was the object of his solicitude.

The light of the moon fell upon her beautiful face, so placidly calm, as if fixed in the sleep of death. Her dark, damp hair hung dishevelled around her, while her form lay revealed in its classic and beautiful outline, in consequence of her thin wet garments clinging like skin to her form.

But Martinez thought of nought but restoring that lovely being to life.

With trembling haste he raised her head in his arms, and tenderly putting the hair from off her forehead, he wiped her colourless lips with the wet neckerchief from his own neck.

"Could she be dead," he thought ; and a pang shot through his heart at the dire probability.

He placed his hand over the region of her heart. At first he could detect no sign of life, but he waited a moment longer, and to his delight he felt the faintest possible beat.

He now chafed her hands, and used all the means he knew of to restore animation, but the lovely Inez still remained unconscious. Then, as a last resource, Martinez took from pocket a small penknife, and baring her arm, he made an incision in the flesh.

The blood slowly and sluggishly oozed out. With deep anxiety Martinez watched the result of his surgical attempt.

The blood flowed more freely—the faintest tint returned to the fair girl's cheek—a movement of life is perceptible in her form—a deep sigh emanates from her bosom—and then, joy, joy—her eyes open. For a moment the radiant light from them beams full on Martinez ; then a faint smile wreaths her pale lips, and, like a tired infant, she closes her eyes, and in another moment is fast asleep.

Martinez seated himself by her side, and a feeling of calm happiness diffused itself through his being, for he knew by the regularity of the breathing that a few hours of undisturbed slumber would restore her to health.

So Inez slept, and Martinez gazed on the beautiful face, while the light from the moon permitted him ; then darkness came as the moon retired to her rest, and worn out with fatigue and watching, he too fell asleep.

When Martinez again opened his eyes, it was broad daylight. The rays of the sun illumined the cavern far into the interior, and the lovely Inez, still buried in sleep, lay before him.

Refreshed and invigorated by his brief repose, Martinez rose, and casting one rapturous look toward Inez, walked to the entrance of the cave.

On emerging into the open air, he was filled with astonishment at the scene around him. Beyond a stretch of sand, reaching nearly a mile out, lay bound by the surging wave, it being low water. Walking forward, he turned and gazed back, and then the novelty of their position became apparent. The lofty rocks rising in the air some six or seven hundred feet, were totally inaccessible. How then could he reach the mainland, or, if it should prove an island, how could he get to the interior.

Lost in thought and perplexity he gazed for some time on the stony precipices till he remembered with a start that he he had been away from his precious charge longer then he intended.

Hastily retracing his steps he again entered the cavern.

As he advanced towards the interior, he saw Inez was awake and sitting up looking around bewildered and surprised. The moment he approached she look anxiously and scrutinizingly in his face, then apparently satisfied. She murmured—

"Where am I senor—what place is this ?"

"You are safe at present dear lady, but where you are, I'll be hanged if I can tell you."

"Ah, I remember," she exclaimed as a sudden glean of intelligence shot through her eyes, and an expression of fear and agony succeeded. "Oh holy virgin, that man—that ship—the waves— Yes, I remember the sea received me."

And burying her face in her hands, she wept.

"Do not grieve fair lady, you are safe at present."

"And you—why are you here ? Speak, tell me what has happened ?"

"Well lady, you leaped overboard and I followed and bore you up, but the ship sped on and we were left behind."

"Noble man, then I owe my life to your brave efforts."

"Well, I scarce know what to say to that, for I don't know how we came to this place, seeing that I lost all recollection when night came."

"And that bad man, he cannot reach me here, I am safe from him, am I not," she pleadingly uttered.

"Yes lady, he cannot harm you here, neither shall he anywhere else, were I near."

"Oh, thanks, noble senor, Ah I shall soon see my dear friends at home again, shall I not."

"Alas, lady, I know not ; I hope you may, for if it will make thee happy, it will make glad my heart to see it. But—bnt, you see we are cast on this spot, where, as far as I can see no human being ever comes, and worst of all, there does not seem to be anything to eat, except what we might catch from the sea."

"Great Heavens, is it so ?"

MARTINEZ AND INEZ IN THE STALACTITE CAVE.

"It is indeed!"

"Then in thee will I trust, you have nobly and bravely rescued me from death, you have been a brother to me, and my brother henceforth you shall be."

"Oh lady, it cheers my heart to see you so brave and resigned in our present difficulties. I now can endeavour to soften the hardships that may surround us, knowing that you will not despair in my absence.

So saying he turned towards the beach, but had not taken half-a-dozen steps ere Inez called him back.

"Stay, Senor Martinez, let me accompany you, let me see the outside of our prison."

Leaning on his arm they walked forth.

There was no disguising the fact to himself,

Martinez felt that he loved the beauteous being beside him. As the soft pressure of her arm came on his a thrill of extacy leaped through his soul.

Martinez was the soul of honour, yet in spite of that, the thought would intrude poison-like in his mind, that she was wholly in his power.

And the fierce whirlwind of passionate love swept over his soul, and he trembled with mad excitement as his gaze fell on the lovely girl beside him, so confiding, so innocent, and so pure.

His better nature triumped—"I love her, I adore her," he muttered to himself, and shall I injure that I worship—perish the thought."

So they rambled together over the sands, and picking up a few shell fish, they ate some of them raw, for hunger began to tell upon them.

No. 21

Full of wonderment, Inez gazed on the mighty rocks that seemed to shut them out from the world, until the rising tide warned them to retreat to the cave.

Martinez gathered for her sake a quantity of seaweed, and drying it in the sun, made a kind of couch for her.

With grateful looks she smiled bewitchingly upon him, and seated herself upon it.

At last the night came, and tenderly bidding each other good night, they seek repose.

Inez soon falls asleep, in her guileless innocence, and with him near her she feels as safe as when a child, in her mother's arms.

But Martinez seeks slumber in vain, love o'ermaster's him, and the soft breathing of one that is near, drives all repose from him.

A hundred times a feeling he scarce can control urges him to start forward and clasp the lovely Inez to his bosom, and as often the nobility of his nature conquers, and suppresses his feeling.

Early the next morning, he rises, and determining to rid himself of the thoughts that oppress him, he sallies forth, to seek in action forgetfulness of evil thoughts.

For hours he wandered over the sands, and narrowly scrutinised, the base of the rocks for miles, but no trace of pathway to the summit can he find.

Disappointed and tired, he returned to their home, and there he finds Inez awaiting him with tender anxiety.

And now another trouble perplexes him, and that is, what are they to do for food, for himself he did not much care; but the delicate and gentle being before him, how could she exist on raw shell fish.

"My brother, you are tired, and troubled, has ought occurred to vex you?"

"No, lady."

"Nay, call me not lady; am I not thy sister? Call me Inez."

"Well, Inez," and as he uttered the dear name, a thrill passed through his frame.

"Ah, that is right," she said, in tones of pleasure, " now tell me why you look so sad?"

"Because I fear for you, in this wretched place."

"Fear for me, why, while you are near me I am safe."

"Ah, yes," said Martinez, then changing the subject, he said, " but we have not yet explored our cavern—who knows—there may, perhaps, be some mode of egress that way."

This idea seemed to infuse fresh energy into Martinez, for he hastily commenced to make a careful scrutiny.

Walking to the further end, as far as the light would serve him, he looked around; but the sides, floor, and roof, presented the same appearance. Then peering into the darkness beyond, he sought to ascertain if ought different existed there, but in vain, the darkness was too profound.

Bidding Inez patiently to await his return, he walked forward, slowly and cautiously groping his way.

He proceeded thus for some distance, when the passage abruptly turned to the left, and rapidly ascended. After walking some distance further, another turn revealed, to his joy and astonishment, a distant light—evidently shining through some some hole or outlet.

With increased speed he went, the light every moment becoming larger and larger, till he no longer doubted that it would prove to be an opening or outlet to the cavern.

At last he reached the opening, and in another moment he stands in the open air; but who can pourtray his astonishment, as he beheld the most glorious prospect stretched out before him.

He stood on a rocky ledge just outside the cavern—before him lay extended, some hundred feet beneath, the most fertile valley in the world.

For a moment he stood speechless with astonishment and pleasure.

Then, kneeling down, in the flood of feelings that overmastered him, he found relief in prayer.

CHAPTER LIX.

THE THREE CAPTIVES—THE FATHER LEARNS THE POSITION OF HIS DAUGHTER—PREPARATION FOR DEFENCE.

SURPRISE now gave place to the feelings which had usurped the minds of Mr. Hanfield and his faithful follower Jacob prior to the ill-fated young lieutenant being thrust forward into the cabin. Mutual was the recognition, and mutual also were the feelings in each others breast.

Henry knew that the tale he would have to unfold to the old gentleman respecting the terrible adventures his fair daughter had undergone, and the hands in which she now was, and the fate doubtless intended for her by the pirate captain, would wring the heart of the parent, and enhance the sufferings he had no doubt he already endured at the hands by the Red Rover.

Still he did not think he should be acting right in unfolding his knowledge of his daughters sufferings.

He momentarily expected the old man to refer to her, and he was endeavouring to put as good a side upon the misfortunes of his daughter as possible.

He did not imagine for one moment that Mr. Hanfield thought that he knew anything about her, he felt sure that she would be mentioned.

He could see plainly that both the gentleman and his servant were prisoners, but by what means they had fallen into the hands of their captors he could not conjecture.

And he knew also that the Boy Rover trod the deck of another vessel than that which he had endeavoured to capture, though he could not account for this.

He knew nothing of the wreck of the " Venomed Snake," and this circumstance puzzled him not a little.

And then there was Charles, too. left on the desert island, if he had not again fallen into the hands of the smuggler.

Truly he knew enough, far too much to wring the heart of the doting father.

When their surprise at this unexpected meeting had subsided, Mr. Hanfield exclaimed—

" In heaven's name, Lieutenant Chambers how came you here?"

"It is a long story," replied Henry. "In heaven's name how is it that I meet you in such a ship."

"I embarked for England," replied Hanfield.

"For England," iterated Henry.

"Yes, in search of the mother of Charles."

Henry was silent.

"Sad news came to me," said Hanfield, "that the vessel in which he and my dear child sailed for this country was lost."

Henry merely bowed his head.

"Dashed to pieces on the rocks," continued

Hanfield, "and all hands perished." And the old man's voice grew husky at the thought of the sad fate of his lovely child.

Henry hesitated a moment.

Should he undeceive him.

Would it not be better that he should believe her dead, than be made acquainted with her present position.

He scarcely knew how to act or what to say

These thoughts rushed through his mind quick as lightning.

But at length he decided to tell him all·

"Not all lost,' he said.

"Not all," exclaimed the old man.

"No."

"Who escaped." he asked eagerly.

"Two," replied Henry.

"Ah, two."

"Yes."

"And they," he continued eagerly — "speak who were they.

"Charles."

"Charles — yes," he grasped, and—and—my child—my Ellen."

"Yes," replied Henry.

"Oh, deceive me not," said Hanfield.

"I do not deceive you, sir,"

"My child saved?"

"Yes, Mr. Hanfield,"

"Are you sure?"

"Quite."

"You do not say this to spare my feelings?" added Hanfield.

"Sir, I speak only what I know."

"How do you know?"

"I have seen them."

"Where?—when?"

"But a short time since," said Henry.

"Where?"

"Charles, I left on a desert island," said Henry.

"And Ellen?"

"Alas!—"

"Oh, spare my feelings, Mr. Chambers, speak!"

"On board a vessel—" began Henry.

"What vessel?" gasped Hanfield, turning pale.

"Have you seen no vessel," said Henry, "during the day?"

"Yes—one brought us to a short time since."

"A pirate," added Jacob.

"On board that vessel," said Henry, "I—"

"God of heaven! what mean you?" gasped Hanfield, staggering back.

"On that vessel I left your daughter," he said.

"On board that pirate?" almost shrieked Jacob.

"Yes," said Henry.

"Then God forgive you!" said Jacob, as Mr. Hanfield sank into a chair and covered his face with his hands.

"Better death a thousand times!" murmured the broken-hearted father.

"Aye, better death," chimed in Jacob.

"I agree with you both," said Henry.

"Why—why did you leave her to the mercy of those men?"

"Sir, I was powerless to protect her," said Henry soothingly.

"My poor master!" said Jacob, bending over Mr. Hanfield.

"Ah, Jacob," said the old gentleman, "would that savage boy had not spared me to hear this."

Henry watched the poor old man for a few minutes in silence.

He saw that his heart was a prey to the conflicting emotions of grief and despair.

Henry could not interrupt him, as he felt that when the violence of his grief had expended itself he would be enabled to listen with calmness to all that had passed since he parted with his daughter, so full of life, and hope, and joy.

As Henry had expected, the violence of his grief soon abated.

Mr. Hanfield became more calm.

Henry felt that now he could tell him all he knew.

He approached the bereaved parent, and took his hand within his own.

The pressure was returned.

Henry Chambers felt by this that the father of Ellen held him blameless for his daughter's presence amongst the pirates.

And so indeed he did.

Mr. Hanfield, although he knew but little of the young man, yet knew he was a true British sailor.

He was a true British sailor.

As such, he respected him.

He knew that generous hearts beat beneath the blue jacket, and that a sailor's arm is ever ready to defend the weak and defenceless.

"Tell me all," he said, after a pause. "Mr. Chambers, I am calm now; but the thought that my innocent child was amongst the crew of that vessel, from whose mast I saw the black flag wave, completely unmanned me."

"I can easily understand your feelings, sir," replied the brave youth. "You are a father."

"Aye, but I should bear my sorrows like a man," said the old gentleman.

He felt half ashamed that he should show so much grief.

"True sir, but at the same time feel like a man," remarked Henry.

"It may seem womanish in me." said Hanfield.

"On the contrary," interrupted Henry, "It does honour to your nature.

The old gentleman tried to smile, but it was a sickly smile indeed.

"Tell me all you know," he said. "I am calm now."

Henry related to him all that had occurred from the moment that the vessel struck up to the present time, and when he had concluded, the old man grasped his hand fervently within his own, and pressed it to his heart.

"Noble minded boy," he exclaimed, "may God reward you for the agonies you have endured for my poor child's sake. How can I thank you—how show my gratitude?"

"Sir, I am already rewarded by the knowledge that I have done my duty."

"You have—you have nobly, generously, done your duty," said the old man, again and again shaking the young sailor's hand.

Jacob had listened with bated breath, but now he leaped to his feet, and bringing down his hand upon the shoulder of the young sailor, he exclaimed—

"God bless you, sir—you are a true sailor, and a brave man."

"Now, if we could but rescue Ellen," said Henry, "from the hands of the pirates, and Charles, if he still remain on the island, we could be happy."

The old man sighed.

Jacob shook his head.

"We are powerless," said Hanfield, "and in hourly expectation of death."

"Death!" said Henry.

"Yes," replied Jacob. "It was only the approach of the pirate vessel that saved us from death."

"In what manner?" asked Henry.

"Walking the plank!" said Hanfield.

"And did the wretch doom you to this?"

"He did."

"But you have not told me how he came here."

"The captain of this ship picked him up and the others at sea on a raft."

"A raft," said Henry.

"Yes, they had been wrecked."

"Well."

"He had their wants attended to—did all that man could do for a suffering fellow creature, but in the night they rose, murdered the captain and crew, and me and my faithful Jacob alone remain."

"The villains," said Henry.

"Aye, you may well say that Mr. Chambers."

"Dogs that bite the hand that feeds them," remarked Jacob.

"Strange coincidence that you should fall into the hands of the very wretch who strove to violate your child," said Henry.

"Curse him," said Jacob, "but this stool shall do duty yet."

And the good fellow poised the stool in the air as he spoke.

"He knows not that you are her father," said Henry after a pause, "let him remain in ignorance of the fact, the resistance of your child to his vile wishes would but embitter him against you."

"It could not make him entertain more wicked intentions toward us," said Hanfield.

"No," remarked Jacob, "our execution is only postponed."

"How many is there on board," asked Henry suddenly.

"Six besides ourselves," replied Jacob.

Henry mused.

"There is strength in a righteous cause," he remarked, after a pause.

"And if there is," said Mr. Hanfield, "we are but three."

"True," replied Henry, "two to one."

"And one old and weak," said Ellen's father.

"Not so weak after all," replied Jacob.

"Let me think," said Henry, "we may yet find some means to cope with these ruffians."

The old man shook his head.

Jacob looked hard at the stool.

He was conjuring up in his mind how many weapons might be made out of it that could be counted of any service.

The eyes of the young lieutenant followed those of the serving man, and his hand wandered to his shoulder which felt sore now, though his surprise at the meeting had made him forget the blow he had received at the hands of Jacob.

"You strike hard," he said, smiling, "had it been my head instead of my shoulder, I fear the consequences had been serious."

"I am glad," began Jacob.

"I am glad," interrupted Henry, "for it was intended for one who well deserved the blow."

"And who shall have it yet I hope," said Jacob.

"How often do they visit this cabin," asked Henry.

"That was the first visit we received from the time the pirate came in sight."

"Then they do not look in upon you at any stated times."

"No."

"I wish they did, we could be prepared for them," said Henry.

"We can hear them descend," said Jacob.

"Yes, true—now if only half the number were to come we might succeed in overpowering them, ere they could bring the rest upon us."

"But they are armed," said Mr. Hanfield, "while we are powerless."

"Not so," said Jacob, "this stool."

"It is of little use against cutlass or firearm," quietly returned his master.

"Still we may take them unawares," said Jacob.

"I fear they will be too wary now that they have seen you are determined to resist them."

"The Boy Rover is not to be caught napping," said Henry.

"So young, so bold, and yet so wicked," remarked Mr. Hanfield, "yet surely he cannot be so bloody-minded as to murder us who have never wronged him."

"He murdered the crew," said Jacob.

"And will show us no mercy," said Henry, "me at least he will not."

"Then we must do our best to murder them," said Jacob.

The old man shook his head.

"Thou shalt do no murder," he said.

"Surely it would not be murder," remarked Henry, "if we slew these men in self-defence."

Mr. Hanfield was silent, but Jacob raised the stool again from the floor, and said—

"Murder or no murder, if I can only get a fair blow at the head of either of them they won't live long after."

"Let us break up that stool," said Henry, examining it carefully, "the legs will prove very effective weapons."

"So they will," said Jacob, turning it upside down and placing his foot upon the seat, commenced tugging away at one of the legs.

But he was unable to sever it.

"Here—I'll bear a hand," said Henry; and, placing one foot on the seat, as did Jacob, commenced pulling at another leg.

It was a well-made article, and it required all the strength they could put forth; but, after some time, it began to crack, and, with a little working backwards and forwards, they succeeded in dismembering it of two of its legs. There was no difficulty now in working the other two out of their sockets; and, when this was accomplished, Henry said:

"Now, Mr. Hanfield, there is one each for us, and one to spare."

Mechanically, the old gentleman took the weapon which the young sailor handed to him.

"Now let them come as quick as they like," said Jacob, flourishing his stick, "and we'll show them that three honest men are a match for double their number of robbers and cut-throats."

As if in answer, they heard footsteps descending.

"Stand firm," said Henry, "and let each bring down his man."

Jacob grasped his weapon tightly, and set his teeth firm.

He was resolved this time that he would hit the right mark.

Mr. Hanfield, spite of his dislike to commit murder, as he considered it, grasped his weapon firmly, and took up a position beside the door of the cabin.

Henry stepped in front; but Jacob drew him away.

"That's my place," he said.

"The position is the most dangerous," said Henry; "let me take it."

"No," returned Jacob—"here I stand; for I mean to make no mistake this time."

Henry saw he was determined; so stepped to the opposite side of Mr. Hanfield.

Jacob motioned them to be silent.

The footsteps still descended, and they knew from the sound that there were at least three.

They halted at the cabin door.

The captives almost held their breath.

A look passed between them, and determination sat on every face.

There was a movement outside.

The fastenings were being removed, and each stood ready for the spring.

CHAPTER LX.

CHARLES VISITS THE CHASM—ARRIVAL OF THE HUNTER—THE LANDING OF THE BOAT.

THE sun rose bright and glorious, streaking the clouds with golden azure, and tinting the tops of the trees with its gorgeous rays, and played upon the waters of the little bay, as they rippled against the cold, grey, frowning rocks, which rose like giants on either side.

Charles awoke from an uneasy slumber—a slumber in which the vision of the boat he had seen embedded between the rocks had taken a most prominent part.

He cast his eyes on to the face of his companion, and saw that he still slept; and he arose noiselessly from the couch, and approached the rude window.

He looked forth upon the luxuriant vegetation, which abounded on either side, and a sigh broke from his lips.

So calm, so peaceful, seemed all around!

Were Ellen by his side, he could live and die in that lovely spot—away from the troubles of the world; but without her he could not rest. His soul yearned for the presence of that fair and lovely being whose image had filled his eyes and heart from the moment she had been torn from him by the ruthless Boy Rover.

"Where was she now?" he thought. "Perhaps on board the Rover's vessel, crying for mercy and succour.

And as the thought passed through his mind, he imagined that he could see her battling with the smuggler captain to protect the honour he strove to outrage.

His brain turned giddy, and his breath came quick and short.

He would save her—rescue her from the villain's power. His whole life should be devoted to this object. Sea and land should not stand between him and her. He would track the villain till he had found her—and then—then he prayed that Heaven would give him strength to avenge the insults she had been subjected to.

Yes, he would go. He was not yet strong, but still his wound had healed, and he felt no pain now.

He would leave the worthy hunter, and once more dare the dangerous wave in search of the girl he so fondly, madly loved,

He believed that it was the will of Heaven that he should learn the position of the hidden boat.

It was revealed to him that he might have the means to pursue the reckless smuggler, and save his soul's idol.

And he would do it yet.

The Rover should not escape his vengeance.

Ellen should not fall a victim to his unholy passions.

He would save her, or die in the attempt.

Heaven would preserve her innocence in the meantime.

And when they again met, the terrible smuggler should tremble.

Such were his thoughts and resolves as he stood gazing out in the direction of the rocks where he had seen the boat with which the murderer had gained the island some years before.

He turned from the rude hole which served as a window, and once more approached the couch on which the hunter lay,

He still slept.

A calm serenity was on his countenance.

A peaceful smile played around his mouth.

The measured breathing showed that his slumbers were not harrassed by anxious dreams.

And yet he had suffered much.

Much more than had the youth who now bent over his sleeping form.

Charles silently stole away from the couch.

He could not find the heart to arouse him from the calm sleep in which his senses were bathed.

He would not arouse him to the true reality of his position.

Perhaps he was dreaming of early days, when all was hope, light, and joy.

Dreaming of the bright heaven he had pictured to himself in the love of his fair young bride, and the happiness that he fondly thought would attend them through life's stormy path.

Charles dared not awaken him as those thoughts passed through his mind.

It would be cruel.

It would transplant his mind from heaven to hell —from brightest joy to stygian despair.

Charles stole cautiously to the door of the hut and opened it.

The cool morning air fanned his fevered temples, and cooled his heated brain.

And the bright sun threw his shadow along the moss-grown earth.

He stepped out into the air and closed the door.

Then he started in the direction of the rocks.

His step was more lithe than it had been for some time, and he felt better and stronger.

He hurried on.

But the recollection that he was still weak from the loss of blood, stayed his impetuous course.

Charles therefore slacked his speed.

The beauties of the surrounding vegetation were forgotten or unheeded in his anxiety to once more gaze upon the hidden boat.

That boat which he hoped would lead him to Ellen.

He soon reached the rocks, and rested for a moment ere he attempted to ascend.

In a short time he went on again.

He gained the summit of the cliff which shut the little vessel from sight, and gazed down into the chasm.

There rode the boat on the water which found its way between the huge blocks of stone.

The boat was much higher up than it had been the night before.

The tide was rising.

A thrill of joy shot through the heart of the young lover.

He gazed long and anxiously upon the little boat as it rose higher and higher up the chasm.

But suddenly his faced paled.

What if the tide should again recede ere the boat rose sufficiently high for him to grasp it.

And again, if he succeeded in holding it, had he sufficient strength to lodge it upon the rock.

His mad joy was damped.

He was weak and the boat was heavy.

Charles paused to consider how he could best surmount the difficulty which now, for the first time, presented itself to him.

He must seek the assistance of the good old hunter.

But then he must arouse him from the peaceful slumber in which he had left him.

This he had no wish to do.

Yet if he did not the boat might again sink to the bottom of the chasm, and his departure from the island thereby be destroyed.

And an hour's delay might be fatal to Ellen.

In his own mind he felt certain of again meeting with her.

Love is so hopeful that it leaps barriers insurmountable.

He resolved, therefore, to return to the hut and arouse the hunter.

He turned to descend the cliff.

A report met his ear and caused him to pause.

He looked around him and saw a puff of white smoke rise from the trees in the direction of the hut.

Charles now saw that the hunter had arisen.

It was his rifle he had heard.

He was in search of game for the morning meal.

Our hero felt pleased at this, and in another minute he saw the old man come from the shade of the trees towards the rock.

Charles called to him.

The hunter looked up and saw the youth waving his hand to him.

The old man returned the salutation and made towards him.

"You are up betimes," said the hunter, when he had gained the foot of the rocks.

"Yes," replied Charles, "I could not sleep."

"Ah," said the old man with a smile, "the boat has broken your rest."

"It has," said Charles. "all night have I seen it in my dreams.'

By this time the old man stood by his side.

He looked down into the chasm, and perceiving the boat was rapidly rising, he said—

"In a few minutes the water will bear it within grasp."

"Yes," replied Charles, "and I was about to return to the hut to seek your assistance to land it on the rock, when the crack of your rifle announced that you were stirring."

"I was seeking something for the morning meal," said the hunter.

Chrales still intently watched the boat.

As it rose, so did the spirits of the young lover.

"And when we have succeeded in landing her," said the old man, "what do you propose to do?"

"Launch her in the bay, and then seek for Ellen."

The old hunter shook his head.

"She has neither oars, rudder, nor sail," he said.

A look of blank despair sat on the youth's face.

He had not observed this circumstance before.

In his anxiety to gain possession of the boat he saw not that she was entirely without the means of guidance, and his heart which a minute before had bounded with joy now sank within him.

The hunter watched him narrowly.

"How impulsive," he muttered to himself, "but it is the failing of youth."

Charles down upon the rock, and gazed thoughtfully upon the still rising boat.

He felt almost ready to burst into tears at the disappointment.

But Charles was not the lad to remain long without striving to remedy any disaster.

He saw now that if they succeeded in bringing the boat to land it would be useless without the means of guidance.

He began to think how he could best render it in some way serviceable.

He had heard of men who being cast adrift upon the ocean, had gained the shore by means of planks, spars, and a thousand other contrivances which they have used instead of oars.

Had not he himself drifted upon the heaving waters without sail or oar, and had not heaven sent him succour.

Still the chances of falling in with some vessel or inhabited coast were greater when he had the means of steering his bark.

But without these he resolved not to forgo his cherished hopes.

He rose from the rock with a brighter face.

The old man had watched the workings of his countenance with intense interest, and a smile broke over his weather-beaten face as he saw the flush of determination return to the youth's features.

He wished not to part with the poor lad whom fate had thrown in his way; but he felt a pride in him when he saw that no obstacle would be allowed to deter him from his cherished scheme.

Brave and noble himself, he could but admire and praise those qualities in others.

The boat had now risen so high that by stooping over the rock they could touch it.

Once or twice, in his endeavours to get a good hold, Charles nearly lost his balance, and bid fair to be precipitated into the chasm.

The hunter's arm, however, was stretched forth to grasp him.

"Be patient," he said; "a few minutes more, and you can grasp it with safety."

"I dread the receding of the tide," said Charles

"It will not turn yet," said the hunter, as he cast his eyes upwards.

Reassured by the hunter's words, Charles, watched and waited.

Moments appeared minutes, minutes hours, to the impatient youth.

But the longest day must have an end; and in the course of another quarter of an hour the boat could be grasped in safety.

"Now," said the hunter, "hold firm, and I will draw her up, stern first."

They both got a firm hold of the stern end of the little vessel, and raised her in the water.

The buoyancy of the salt fluid greatly assisted them, and they drew one end over the edge of the rock.

Then they paused for breath—still holding on to the stern of the little craft.

In another minute they set to work again, and, bearing on the stern all their weight, at the same time drawing it shorewards, they had the satisfaction to hear her keel grating on the hard rock. Having got thus far, they had little difficulty, and, by dint of strength and persuasion, the boat was released from her hidden cave, where she had lain so long.

When fairly landed, the hunter and his young friend gazed at each other, as they rested from their exertions.

The old man saw on the face of the youth a beam of satisfaction and joy.

But the weather-beaten face of the good old man bore the impress of grief and sorrow.

———

CHAPTER LXI.

LATOUR VISITS ELLEN.—A PIRATE'S LOVE.—A WOMAN'S REFUSAL.— MERCY TRIUMPHANT.

THE " Spirit of the Wave " danced over the crested billows, dipping her proud head into the foaming waters, and kissing the silvery spray as it leapt up to her figure head, whilst her white sails glistened in the sunlight and bellied with the passing breeze, and the union jack, which had taken the place of the dreaded black flag, floated proudly out from her mast head, and danced in the air as if it fluttered a proud defiance to the world.

The crew were gathered here and there in little knots, spinning yarns, or singing and smoking.

Bilton paced the deck thoughtfully, with his hands clasped behind him.

He was conjuring up to his mind the various scenes of his life, and comparing his boyhood's days, so full of happiness and peace, to his manhood's actions of bloodshed and crime.

Latour, as was his wont, was leaning over the taffrail, gazing at the billows as they dashed against the vessel and broke into a thousand globules of silver, and picturing in the wild waves the furious passions which assailed his own breast.

Thus the time passed, the breeze continuing steady, and the crew having little or nothing to do.

Latour, evidently tired of the position he had occupied so long, drew his stout form up to its full height, and casting an eagle glance around the deck, made his way to the cabin.

He knocked gently at the door thereof to announce his presence.

There was no answer.

He turned the fastening and entered.

As he did so, the fair, delicate form of Ellen rose from the couch on which she had been reclining, and retreated to the further end of the apartment.

She feared that the pirate captain had again come to make his dishonourable overtures to her.

And her face became paler, and her lips trembled.

Latour closed the door and advanced towards her.

He saw that she feared him, and he endeavoured to reassure her with a smile.

" Lady," he said, endeavouring to take her hand.

But the poor girl drew back in fear.

" Lady," he continued, " why do you fear me?"

" Because you are cruel and unmerciful," replied the poor girl.

" Nay, there you wrong me," said Latour.

" Heaven grant I do," said Ellen coldly.

" Indeed you do," said Latour. " Had I been so, I should have complied with the wishes of one whom I have this day met, and placed you again in his power."

A look of surprise overspread the face of his captive, as she said—

" Of whom do you speak? "

" The Boy Rover! "

A cry escaped the lips of Ellen.

" The Boy Rover! " she iterated.

And her face became pale as marble.

" Aye, lady—the Boy Rover. But a short time since I boarded his vessel, and he demanded you at my hands."

" And you would not give me up? " said Ellen.

" No, lady, I would not."

" And why?" said Ellen, in a sarcastic tone.

" Because I would not see you in the power of one you so much despise," replied Latour.

Ellen was silent.

She felt that she hated equally the pirate and the smuggler.

Their ends with regard to her were the same, at least, so she believed, although Latour had been the more tender of the two.

" Where is Henry?" she said, at length. " Let me see him, if but for a moment."

Latour's eyes sank under her gaze.

" Lady, I cannot," he replied.

" Why not," she asked.

" Because he is not on board my vessel," replied the pirate.

" Not on board," said Ellen.

" No, Lady."

" Where is he then," said Ellen, her heart beating violently,

Latour hesitated ere he replied.

" Lady," he said at length, "though I am captain of this vessel, I must obey the rules of our confederacy even with the lowest man in the ship."

" Go on," said Ellen, " tell of him—of Henry."

" The youth refused to join us," said Latour, " and his obstinacy brought about his ruin."

" Oh heaven," grasped Ellen.

" He was condemned to walk the plank," continued Latour, " and like a brave youth he met his fate unflinchingly."

Ellen sank down upon the couch, and buried her face in her hands.

Latour approached her and strove to assuage her grief, but the girl repulsed him and starting to her feet again she exclaimed—

" Murderer !—murderer !"

" Hear me," said Latour, again striving to get her hand in his.

" Away," she exclaimed, " touch me not with those blood-stained fingers—away."

" Be calm," said Latour, " and hear me."

" Calm—calm," almost shrieked Ellen, " Oh, villain—villain."

Latour stood gazing at her in admiration so superbly beautiful did she look.

But a pang of regret shot through his breast at the deed he had committed.

He would win that girl's love—but dare he hope to succeed in gaining even a smile from her after the death of Henry.

His heart was softened towards her.

He had intended to make her his own in spite of all resistance, but his better nature had stepped in, and he resolved to woo and if possible to win her.

With this intention he had entered the cabin.

But now he saw how fruitless would be his endeavours.

But at all events he resolved to inform her that Henry was not dead.

This he thought will at least be some small satisfaction.

" Ellen," he said, " be calm and hear me."

The poor girl's sobs were the only answer he received.

" Ellen," he said, " the youth lives."

Ellen started.

" Oh," she exclaimed, " speak the truth man, first you say he is dead then that he lives."

" Ellen" returned the pirate, " I have not lied, I told you that according to our rules he was doomed to walk the plank."

"You did," said Ellen.

"But I said not that he was dead," said Latour, "the youth lives for ought that I know to the contrary."

Ellen looked questioningly upon the pirate.

"He was pecipitated into the waves, but was rescued from death.'

"How—by whom?"

"By a boat of the vessel we lately passed."

"The Boy Rover's," exclaimed Ellen.

"The same."

"Then he is lost."

"Why so?" said Latour.

"The Rover seeks his life," exclaimed Ellen.

"Why should he?"

"Because he has befriended me," replied Ellen, "because he has dared to stand forth in the defence of an outraged and defenceless woman."

"Fear not," said Latour.

"Say rather fear the worst," said Ellen.

"The Boy Rover may spare him," said Latour.

"Think it not," exclaimed Ellen, "He thirsts for his blood, and will slay him.'"

Latour was silent.

The wild life he led had thrown him among men of different passions, and he could read their natures in their looks.

He had read the Boy Rover's.

"Blood-thirsty, brave, and cruel," were written, as in a book, upon every lineament of his countenance.

"Ellen," continued Latour, "had I felt disposed to save the youth, I had not the power. If I, the captain of this bark, should attempt to break through the rules laid down and agreed to by us all, where would my authority be? I could not save him; but the Boy Rover has. It is useless to regret what is past; we can but hope for the future. Something may turn up to save him from the vengeance you so much dread."

"Alas! I fear not," sobbed Ellen.

"I am more hopeful than you. The Boy Rover sails now in a very different vessel from that in which he held you captive: without arms, and without men, he is comparatively harmless. Therefore, the probability is that the youth you so deeply respect will yet be saved."

This somewhat reassured Ellen, and she became more calm.

Latour seated himself upon the couch, and watched her for some time without speaking.

At length, when she had become calm and cool he rose, and taking her hand he said—

"Ellen, king's ere now have sued for favours at the hands of their subjects—I, captain of this bark, whose will is law, ask at your hands that love which I have the power to force—nay, hear me to the end," he added, as Ellen strove to tear herself from his hold. "I supplicate you to look mercifully upon me? there is that in your nature which I feel would lead me to become worthy of that love. Share with me the wanderings of my life, my joys, my sorrow, and I swear by the heaven above us that my whole life shall be devoted to you, you shall rule where you are now a prisoner, your every wish shall be granted, your every command obeyed. The world calls me pirate, but it has made me so. Cruel laws have driven the man whose honour was once stainless, whose aspirations were noble, and whose career left behind a lie without a blemish to the road I have now taken. Men call me cruel, but then injustice has made me so, I but repay them in their own coin. I am not all bad, and the evil that is within me may be turned to good by you, Ellen when I saw your

beautious form buffeted by the waves, I resolved to save you that I might make you mine—mine in spite of all, but I have learnt to love you, love you with a passion pure and holy as ever man felt for woman; that love I throw at your feet, deign to accept it, and the dreaded pirate Latour becomes your slave."

He ceased speaking, but still he'd the hand of the affrighted maiden in his own.

Ellen trembled, and would have sunk to the floor, but the pirate threw his strong arm around her waist and held her up.

"Speak," he said, "tell me that you return my passion,"

Her lips opened, but she spoke not.

The pirate drew her towards his breast, then a low cry broke from the pale lips of the maiden.

She strove to tear herself away from his hold, but Latour still held her gently but firmly.

"Spare me—spare me," she murmured.

"By heaven, I swear I will not harm you," said the pirate.

"Then go—leave me," murmured the poor girl.

"Give me the assurance that you love me," said Latour, and your wish shall be a command.

"I cannot," she said. "Oh, spare me."

"Cannot, why?" asked the pirate.

"I love another," said Ellen.

"He who has fallen into the hands of the Boy Rover," said Latour.

"No."

"Who then?"

"A youth, brave as a lion, gentle as a lamb," she murmured. "Oh, man, man, I cannot love you—my vow is plighted, and never, never will I forget it."

"Is this your resolve?"

"It is. I know that I am weak and powerless—you strong and determined; but though you may break my heart you cannot win my love, and a just heaven will in good time punish your wickedness."

Latour led her to the couch and released his hold of her waist.

"Ellen," he said, "I will not wrong you. Your beauty has triumphed, and bad as I am, I cannot harm you. At the first opportunity I will send you on shore. Farewell! we must not meet again lest my good resolves be overthrown, Farewell!"

CHAPTER LXII.

A PERILOUS POSITION—THE ESCAPE.

FOR some time Martinez gazed in silent admiration of the scene before him. Then, recollecting that he had left Inez alone and anxious behind him, he hastened to return, without making any further investigation.

"No, no," he thought. "It will be sweet and pleasant pastime to revel in this paradise together. "Oh! if she were my Eve, this would indeed be Eden."

Pale and breathless, Inez stood where Martinez had left her. As the last faint echo of his retreating footsteps sounded in her ear, a feeling of utter loneliness fell like a shadow on her heart; and so oppressive did her thoughts become at the idea that Martinez might by some accident be prevented from rejoining her, that she clasped her hands in an agony of terror.

But time wore on, and, though it seemed an age to her, Martinez soon returned.

With a cry of joy, she rushed towards him; and then, as if remembering her position, she stopped short, and blushed.

THE CAPTIVES ON THE SPRING.

Martinez briefly related to her the discovery that he had made; and, together, they at once start for the paradise beyond, and forsake the barren rocks and sand without regret.

Silently they threaded the rocky passages that led to the interior of the island—Martinez leading Inez by the hand, the soft pressure of which thrilled him to the soul.

As they proceeded through the gloomy darkness, Inez, in thought, recurred to her present position; and it startled her not a little as she reviewed it.

Snatched from almost certain death through the instrumentality of a young and handsome man, she could not feel other than grateful; but when thrown, as she was now, in his society, with none other near, a feeling, she confessed to herself,

akin to love, if not love itself, was gradually taking the place of gratitude. Alas! what could she do if the same feeling should influence him, and passion carried him beyond prudence—how could she, with love burning in her heart, resist him?

But her thoughts were cut short by the light bursting on her vision, revealing the lovely valley before them. With an exclamation of joy and surprise, she murmured:

"How beautiful! Oh! Martinez, what a paradise."

"It is indeed beautiful; but it wants one thing to render it perfect."

"And what is that?" she said, turning her lovely eyes full upon him, with surprise that he should think aught wanting to complete the scene.

But Martinez turned away his face, and only sighed.

By the intuitive perception that belongs to love, she knew what he meant, and remained silent.

"But how are we to reach the valley?" said Inez, after a long pause, during which they had been scrutinising the place on which they stood.

Martinez looked puzzled.

"By heavens!" he exclaimed—"this would be a more cruel death than starving in our cave, if we can only feast our eyes on this."

"These rocks can never be so cruel as to refuse us the means of descent," murmured Inez.

"Stay thou here, Inez, lest we lose our cavern's mouth, while I will endeavour to find some way of reaching below."

"Ah! leave me not long," she said, sadly. "I'm very lonely without thee."

"Nay, I'll not be gone long. Would," he murmured, in a lower tone, "that I might never have to leave thee."

Martinez soon found that the place on which they stood was a sort of ledge of rock, some few feet wide at the entrance to the cavern, but narrowing at either end, till at the distance of twenty yards it ceased altogether. Like a caged lion he paced this narrow belt of rock, minutely examining every inch in the hope of discovering some indurations on the side of the steep precipice. He stooped down on his knees, and peered over the side. It did not appear to be more than a hundred feet in depth, yet the rock seemed smooth as a glass, and was completely bare of verdure, forming a strange contrast to the luxuriant foilage below.

Not a tree or a shrub projected anywhere, that might have served for hold or otherwise.

Martinez stood erect, and looked at Inez in despair.

Her sweet eyes had watched his every motion, and returned his look with one exhibiting the concern she felt, more for his sake than her own.

"If I only had a rope!" he sighed.

They could hear the song of birds rising sweetly and faintly on the air towards them—they could see the waving foilage, and in fancy beheld the luscious fruit. They could even descry the silver thread of a small brook among the trees. Surely it was indeed a lovely place, and yet beyond their reach.

Presently Martinez happened to cast his eyes upward, and he saw that the rocks were not so steep from where they stood.

What, if by ascending these they could reach beyond the limit of the ledge on which they stood, and perhaps find a less precipitous part of the rocks farther off.

Without a moment's hesitation, Martinez communicated to his companion his hopes and determination.

She looked with blanched cheek at the rock, and gazed almost appealingly on him not to try it.

But Martinez was a seaman, and for a lady's b hoof what would he not dare, more especially if love accompanied him in his peril.

With a pressure of hands they parted, but a yearning, soul-meeting glance told how deep in the heart of each existed the passion of love.

With a bound, Martinez sprang up a few feet of the rock before him, and then began his toilsome ascent.

Spell bound, Inez gazed at Martinez as he toiled upwards. It was solid, hard rock, so nothing was displaced—nothing fell to endanger the safety of Inez.

Slowly and painfully was his progress now; his fingers were lacerated and bleeding, still he persevered.

At last he reached a similar ledge of rock to the one he had left, about forty feet above it. Here his further progress was stopped.

Sitting down, he rested himself awhile to recover breath and strength.

He waved his hand cheerily to Inez below, so as to reassure her. Then, apparently reinvigorated, he rose and pursued his researches.

As he suspected, this ledge led farther than the other round the rock, and he was enabled to proceed nearly half a mile: here the ledge rapidly inclined downward.

Martinez's heart beat high with hope—if it should continue thus to the bottom, how easy then would be the path for Inez.

Still he walked on, and the path was still the same, though doubling and winding it yet inclined downward. More than half way down the rock had been accomplished, already the songs of birds and the rushing of water told how near he was to the accomplishment of his hopes, when—

"Ah! confusion," he exclaimed, and with a groan of despair sat down on the ground and tore his hair with vexation.

Before him further progress was cut off by a yawning gulf or chasm, and beyond on the other side he could see that the path to the valley was easy and complete.

Oh, how to bridge this chasm, it was their only hope.

Again his brave undaunted heart came to his aid, and springing up he cast despair to the winds.

Had he not succeeded so far, and should he yield to despair and death when only a few feet separated them from the goal they sought.

He looked around him.

Huge masses of rocks lay heaped in wild confusion. As he suspected, the chasm was a rift in the rocks, the action of water for ages had worn it through the hard granite, and around lay heaps of rock displaced by the same means.

One enormous mass lay on the very verge of the gulf.

Martinez measured it by his eye, and a glance satisfied him that it would bridge over the chasm if it could be moved in that direction.

He went close up to it, and pushed it, to his great joy it moved.

It was balanced in such a manner that he could cause it to sway to and fro. Oh, if he could move the mass down the incline all would be accomplished.

But it defied his strength.

Then Martinez decided that he would return to Inez and bring her back with him, and he thought perhaps that her little aid might serve to turn the scale and move the hugh stone from its place.

Hastily returning, he retraced his steps, and after a while reached the spot above where he had left Inez.

She was there rigid as a statue. But the moment she beheld him a cry of pleasure brust from her lips and she waved her hands.

Martinez returned the salutation, and was preparing to descend, when to his horror he found that though he ascended it with some difficulty—yet to descend was an absolute impossiblity.

There was nothing to prevent him being dashed to the bottom if he attempted it. What was he to do? And how could Inez reach him?

The day too was rapidly declining, and the

night would come and find them separated from each other. Inez, lonely and terrified, might find shelter just within the cavern, but Martinez dared not let sleep seize him lest he should roll off the rocky ledge and be dashed to pieces below.

Their situation was indeed terrible. Despair black and gloomy fell on their hearts, for worst of all were they not separated. Even the solace of dying together was refused them.

Martinez groaned in anguish to behold the mute agony of Inez. In vain he racked his brain to derive some scheme or plan to master their present difficulty.

At last he thought it is but forty feet, and though scant of clothing, he surely might get enough strips out of it to make the required length.

So tearing off all under garments, he proceeded to cut them with his knife into strips, and then securely tied them together.

Ever and anon he would throw his impromptu rope over to ascertain if it was long enough.

At last it hung low enough for Inez to reach. Hope again began to draw on their hearts, and in obedience to Martinez's request she pulled it with all her might to test its strength.

All seemed right and ready.

Telling her to hold tight, Martinez planting himself firmly began to draw the light and fragile form of Inez up.

Bravely she grasped the line, fear and hoped lending strength to her fingers, and soon she hung suspending in the air, a feeling of difference came over her, but closing her eyes and murmuring a prayer she placed her trust in Providence.

Another moment she was safe beside Martinez.

Again a feeling they scarce could control urged them to rush into each other's arms, but they did not.

The sun was now sinking towards the west, so they knew they had no time to lose. Leading her by the hand, Martinez hurried down the path he discovered, and in a little while they reached the chasm that barred their further progress.

Martinez explained to Inez what he had hope they might together accomplish, so smiling and cheerfully she asserted.

They reached the enormous stone, and with united efforts strove to move it from its place.

Inez's efforts proved as Martinez expected, it turned the balance in their favour.

Slowly the mass turned over, till getting fairly on the incline it plunged forward.

A noise like thunder echoed among the rocks, and when recovered from the shock of the concussion they beheld it firmly fixed between the chasm forming a rough but massive bridge.

Overcome at the new prospect of deliverence and fatigue she had gone through, Inez fainted.

Catching the tender burden in his arm Martinez clambered over the new formed bridge, and with a cry of exultation ran down the remainder of the incline.

In another moment he stood beneath the branches of the trees.

They were saved.

CHAPTER LXIII.

THE PIRATE SHIP AGAIN.—THE CHASE.—A YARN. —THE BURNING VESSEL.

The sun had sank to rest in its golden bed, and the dark shades of night had fallen over the sea. The bright blue canopy of heaven was reflecting glitter-ing stars upon the boundless waters, and the young moon, like a thread of silver, looked like a golden crescent in its satin case, surrounded by sparkling jewels.

Ellen, assured by the pirate's promise, had unrobed and retired to rest. Latour had sought his cot and slumbered free from the passions of his nature. The crew, save three of the watch, lay slumbering in their hammocks, and Bilton, who was for the time officer of the watch, paced the deck gazing upon the bright blue vault of heaven and thinking of the home of his childhood.

The "Spirit of the Wave" rode over the billows gently, and the sails ever and anon flapped against the mast, for scarcely a breath fanned the cheek of the men on deck.

All was silent save the lazy plashing of the waves on the vessel's bows, and the measured tread of the lieutenant in his thoughtful walk.

Suddenly Bilton raised his eyes from the deck on which they had been fixed for some time, and gazed far astern of the ship,

An exclamation escaped him which brought one of the crew to his side.

"Get me the glass," he said, addressing the sailor.

The man stepped back to obey the order.

"Stay," said Bilton. "Look yonder. What do you make out that light to be?"

The man shaded his eyes with his hand, and looked in the direction indicated by the lieutenant's fore finger.

"If it's a star it's a bright one," said the man dropping his hand.

"Do you think it is a star?" said Bilton.

"Can't say I do," replied the sailor, "'taint low enough for that."

"Go down to my cabin and fetch the glass."

The man pulled his forelock and departed on his errand.

"I'm much mistaken," muttered the lieutenant, still looking at the bright object, "if it is not a light from some vessel," and he strained his eyes towards it.

The man returned with the night glass, and handed it to the officer.

Bilton raised it to his eye and gazed long and earnestly at the light.

Then he lowered the glass, and handing it to the man, said—

"Take a glance. Harvey."

The man obeyed.

After the lapse of a few moments he brought the glass down from his eye and gave vent to a long low whistle.

"Well," said Bilton, "do you make her out?"

"Yes," replied Harvey.

"And what is it?"

"A vessel."

"What's her course?" asked Bilton.

"Bearing down full upon us."

"You think so?"

"I do."

"And so do I."

The lieutenant again took the glass and looked anxiously through it.

"Whew!" he whistled. "We have not been watchful to let her get so near ere we discovered her, Harvey."

"Sir?"

"She looms up large through the glass, and has got the weather gauge of us."

"Yes," replied the man, "we're almost calm—hardly a breath."

"Confound it, and she has got the wind."

"Can you make her out sufficiently, sir," said Harvey, "to tell her character?"

"She is a large sloop of war, I take it," replied Bilton.

"Can she suspect our character?" said Harvey.

"I fear she does," replied the lieutenant. "She steers as if she knew it."

"Been on the look out for us, perhaps," suggested the sailor.

"Doubtless," replied Bilton.

And after another long look he lowered the glass and commenced again pacing the deck.

Harvey watched him in silence.

Presently he stopped in front of the sailor.

"Harvey."

"Sir."

"That craft means mischief."

"You think so, sir?"

"I do."

Harvey looked as if he though so too.

"Pipe all hands."

The man bowed his head.

"We must have the ship cleared for action," said Bilton.

"She will be some time ere she can come up with us, sir," remarked Harvey.

"No, no—she has got the wind, whilst we have scarcely a capful. Look again."

The man did look, and found that the vessel was not very far distant of their own, and was coming down upon them at a good speed.

"What do you think," said Bilton.

"That she's too near to be pleasant," replied the sailor, "if we are not prepared for her."

"Right. Call up the men, I will awaken the captain."

And as Harvey walked forward Bilton descended to the cabin of Latour.

The pirate captain still slumbered.

Bilton leant over him and placed his hand on his shoulder.

Slight as was the touch, the pirate captain started up, and grasped a pistol which lay on a chest beside his cot.

"Captain," said Bilton.

"Ah, Bilton, is that you?" said Latour lowering the pistol.

"Yes."

"What is it?"

"We are pursued."

"Eh!—what?" said Latour, leaping from his cot.

"Pursued."

"Yes."

"By what?"

"A ship of war," replied the lieutenant.

"The devil!" said the pirate.

"I hope not, sir," said Bilton, smiling.

"Hope not what?" said Latour, scarcely awake.

"That we are pursued by the devil," replied the lieutenant.

"No, I suppose not. We are devils enough ourselves, Bilton, eh?"

Bilton shrugged his shoulders as much as to say yes.

Latour commenced hurriedly robing himself.

"On what tack is she?" he asked after a time.

"Right astern."

"How's the weather."

"Bright," replied Bilton.

"And the wind?"

"Calm."

"The devil!" said Latour.

"Scarcely a breath," remarked the lieutenant.

"No matter, we are both alike."

"I think not, sir—"

"Why?"

"Our pursuers have got the wind, whilst we have scarcely a breath."

"Ah!" said Latour, pushing his arm hastily through the sleeve of his coat. "Have the hands piped up."

"I have done so, sir," said Bilton.

"Right. See that all is clear for action."

"The order has been given."

"Have the long gun manned," said the captain. Bilton bowed.

"See the men are all at their quarters."

Bilton bowed again, and left the cabin.

Latour buckled on his cutlass, and stuck his pistols in his belt.

Then he walked across the cabin, and opening a small box which stood on a table, he took therefrom a small thin dagger.

"You have done me some service before," he muttered, "I may want you again,"

And thrusting it in his belt he left the cabin and ascended to the deck.

So well were all on board that ship trained, that in a few minutes all were at their posts, every gun loaded and manned, and all made ready for action.

Bilton handed the glass to his commander.

The pirate gazed through it for a moment, and a flush overspread his face.

It was the flush of excitement at the coming contest.

All the passions of his nature were aroused now, and he stood with flashing eye looking upon the light which every moment became more bright and distinct.

"Bilton," he said, in an imperious tone.

"Sir."

"Down with that rag, and up with the black flag. Let them see our calling. It may serve as a decoy, but damn me if I fight under it. Show them that we neither give nor receive quarter."

Bilton saluted the pirate, and in another moment the black flag was run up to the mast head.

"That's it," said Latour, when he saw the dread ensign floating above his head. "The sight of that rag nerves my hand and steels my heart, and there's not a man on board but knows if he is taken fighting under it, that he'll get a short shrift and a long rope, so he'll fight like the devil,"

"We have few cowards on board," said Bilton.

"Few!" said Latour, "not one!"

"True, sir,—a bolder crew never sailed the salt deep," said Bilton, looking round with a feeling of pride.

"Nor a worse set of scoundrels," remarked Latour.

"And that's true, captain," said Bilton.

"Bold and bad—one and all."

"Humph!" exclaimed Latour, as he turned away to give some order.

The pursuer gained rapidly on them still.

"Curse this calm," said Latour.

"Yes," said Bilton, "if we want to run it will play the devil with us."

"Run be damned!" said Latour savagely, "it will baulk our manœuvres, that's all I care for."

"We trust but little to that as a rule," said the lieutenant.

"True—a broadside or two and then board, is our plan; but we have an enemy now to cope with, or I am much mistaken, that can fire and board as well as us.

"We must board them if possible," said Bilton.

"Yes," replied Latour, "you will lead the boarders."

Bilton bowed.

"There she comes," exclaimed the pirate, as a sharp flash lit up the sea.

"Now she'll show her teeth," said Bilton.

As he spoke a shot whistled over the stern of the pirate.

"And that flash has shown us her position," replied Latour.

The light which had first attracted the notice of the lieutenant was now doused, but the flash had laid her open to the pirate's fire.

"Harvey," said Latour, "did you mark her well,"

"I did, captain," replied the gunner.

"Take your aim."

"All ready."

"Fire."

Harvey applied the match—a bright flash—a loud report—and a shot flew from the long stern gun and struck the pursuing vessel, carrying away a portion of her figure head.

Latour kept his eye fixed upon the ship through the glass.

"Well done," he said.

The breeze now freshened and filled the sails of the pirate, and she moved more swiftly through the waves.

The pursuer hauled off a bit after the shot of the pirate struck her.

"She don't admire your card Harvey," said Latour, "and it strikes me she'll haul off till daylight."

Better if she does, perhaps," remarked Bilton, "boarding in the dark is awkward work."

"Give her another shot," said Latour, "before she hauls out of range."

"Aye, aye, sir," replied the gunner.

"Raise your piece a bit."

This was done.

"Ready" asked Latour.

"Aye, aye, sir," was the reply.

"Apply the match then," said the pirate, again raising the glass.

Harvey applied the match to the touchhole, and another shot opened on its errand.

But it fell short of its object, the stranger having hauled too far out of range.

"Turn in," said Latour, "and rest while you can, at daybreak you will have hard work and hard knocks,"

This order the men cheerfully obeyed.

The pursuing vessel still continued to haul off, but Captain Latour felt certain that she would again endeavour to come up with them in the morning as soon as light.

When all had been secure, Latour invited Bilton and the second officer to his cabin, resolved himself not to again seek his couch lest the stranger's ship should suddenly bear down upon them.

This Bilton accepted after ordering a sharp look out to be kept on their pursuer.

Ellis, the second officer, was a man of about forty years of age, and had previously been the captain of a small trader, but having after a long and honourable service, lent himself to smuggling his ship had been seized and himself imprisoned, and ashamed to again face his fellow men in the station of life he had hitherto trod, and feeling that his character was gone, he joined the celebrated pirate, and was made a second lieutenant.

This at first gave umbrage to the crew, but when they were made aware of the fact that he was a skilled navigator, they were content that he should fill that position on board the Spirit of the wave."

In a short time the two were seated round the table in Latour's cabin, with the wine bottle and brandy-flask before them.

"Let's see," remarked Latour, "it is three hours to daybreak, and time hangs heavy when you have nothing positive to do, and yet look forward for hard work, how shall we kill the hours till then.

"Give us a song, captain," said Ellis.

"No, no," said Latour, "that is an amusement I never indulge in, I should like to hear a yarn of your own spinning Ellis, one with a little truth in it, about your smuggling games, eh!"

Ellis shook his head.

"Captain, had I not descended to that line, I should never have been a pirate, and as I even now believe it better to be an honest trader than a pirate, I will not refer to them, but I will tell you an incident in my life before I forgot that a good name is worth keeping. It occurred soon after I took the command of the 'Cousin Alice,' as fine a little brig as ever danced over the billows with a bale in her hold."

"Go on then," said Latour, gulping down a deep draught of brandy.

"Here goes then," said Ellis: "You must know that the good brig Cousin Alice was new when I took charge of her. Her owners lived in Mobile, and in that port we shipped our crew and took in our cargo.

"On the day before we had planned to sail, eight of my men had permission to go on shore, and while there they got into a drunken row and killed one of the citizens. Instead of returning to the brig they fled from the city inland, and we were obliged to hunt up a new lot of hands.

"This detained us nearly a week; but we finally got under weigh, and with a fair wind stood out in the bay. We were bound for Smyrna, and for three weeks not an event occurred to mar the peace of myself nor the success of the voyage.

"One evening, when within four days' sail of Gibralter, as I sat in the cabin alone, my first mate, Mr. Gould, came down and sank into a seat close by me. He was pale as death, and trembled in every joint.

"'What's the matter?' I asked him.

"'The brig!' he gasped, catching hold of my arm. 'The crew have mutineed!'

"I started to my feet, but Gould pulled me back.

"'Don't go on deck!' he cried. 'They'll kill you if you do.'

"But I was not to be deterred. It was my vessel and I meant to go and see what was to pay. Breaking from my mate's grasp I rushed up the ladder, and just as I reached the deck I met one of the men, named Luton—Walter Luton, his name was, and I had looked upon him as one of the best seamen on board. I had never seen a movement in him that was out of the way, and had I thought of mutiny, he would have been the last one I should have suspected.

"'Luton,' I said, 'what's the trouble up here?'

"'Nothing that I know of,' he answered me.

"I had just turned to the wheel when I felt some one grasp my arms from behind. I struggled to break loose, but to no purpose. It was Luton who held me first, though he quickly had a man to help him.

"'It's no use,' he said, while some one passed a cord round my wrists. 'You are nabbed and you can't get away. I want you to understand that I am skipper of this craft now!'

"I asked the fellow what he meant to do, and he told me I'd find out in good time. Then I called out for my men to come to my aid; but I soon found that all who were friendly to me were in the same position as I occupied myself.

"In a few moments I saw my mate led up from the cabin, with his arms pinioned, and shortly afterwards, Mr. Orne, who was a passenger, was led up in the same situation. There were two more passengers in the cabin—Mrs. Elizabeth Banks, and her daughter, a little girl about twelve years of age. I had began to feel more than usual apprehensions for them, when I saw them both led up.

"Once more I turned to Luton and asked him what he meant.

"'I should think you might guess by this time,' he said. 'But,' he added, 'you need not be afraid, for we don't mean to kill ye.'

"It was too dark for me to distinguish faces at any great distance, so I was totally unable to see how matters stood with the crew. I knew that three of the strongest men had been engaged in securing me, and I had not been able to see any one at hand who seemed to be willing to help me, so I concluded that the whole crew had joined the mutineers, or else such as had not already been secured. As soon as the woman and her child were brought up I was led forward and stowed away against the bowsprit, and the others who had been secured were placed about me, and then one of the men, a stout, hard-looking mulatto, named Sam Goldbush, mounted guard over us with a cocked pistol in each hand.

"'There,' said Luton, as he had thus arranged matters, 'now rest easy.'

"I was too deeply moved by wrath and indignation to make any reply, and in a moment more the villain walked aft. My first impulse after he was gone was to look around me and see who were to share my fate.

"There were Gould and Truil, my two mates; Charles Emmerson, a young man who came out for his health, and who had engaged to act as supercargo; Manuel, my black cook; Mrs. Banks and her child, and Mr. Orne—eight souls in all. This left thirteen men to be accounted for.

"I could not think they had all become villains. There was one in particular whom I felt sure would rather die than join in such a wicked scheme. That was Peter Ames, a youth some five-and-twenty years of age, who had been with me ten years. And if he had not joined them, then perhaps others had not.

"In the course of half an hour after we had been put under guard I saw the men go at work breaking out some spare spars from amidships. Some of them went down in the hold and brought up a lot of boards, and shortly afterwards they began to spike them to the spare spars. They had a main-top gallant-mast, a main top-sail yard, and a spare jib-boom, and across these they were spiking the boards. My heart sank within me! They were making a raft! The spars were placed across the sail at the gangway before they commenced work, in order that they might have no difficulty in launching the frail thing.

"I heard them querying as to whether the raft would be sufficient to hold up all who must go on it, and I heard Luton remark that it made little difference to him whether it held them or not. I could not see all of the work, but could hear the heavy clank of the hammers, and the occasional words of command from Luton.

"I tell you plainly, it is of no use for me to attempt to describe the feelings I had at that time. I had known that some of the men were reckless and bad, but I had never seen one act of insubordination, nor received one word of insolence, nor

had I, or any of my officers, detected anything which could have been by any means tortured into a suspicion of mutiny.

"The whole thing had been carried on most secretly, and they had everything repared for the final stroke. Mrs. Banks was calm and quiet. I asked her if she had any fear of being set adrift on that raft, and she said that she had been praying that they would send her off on it. Her first fears were so terrible that the thought of the raft was like the bestowal of new life.

"It was near midnight when I heard the raft plunged into the water. There was but little wind, the brig not going over three knots, and the sea was quite smooth. I saw some of the men bringing something out of the hold, and I supposed it to be bread. Half an hour after the launching of the raft Luton came forward with some of his companions and helped us to our feet.

"'Now, captain,' he said, 'I'm going to give you a bit of a lift. I suppose ye've seen enough to show ye what we're up to. We'd have spared ye a boat if we could, but as we can't we've done the next best thing: we've fixed ye out a nice raft, and ye'll find it all tight and snug. I may be a hard sort of a boy, but a harder one than I might have put you to death.'

"'And what but death are you preparing me for now?' I asked bitterly.

"'Oh,' he quickly returned, with an oath, 'if you don't like it I can change the plan. Anything to suit. Just say the word and I'll put a bullet through your head quicker! What say ye?'

"I knew that we were on the track of vessels bound to and from the Mediterranean, and that we might be picked up, so I told him I'd take the raft.

"'Then keep quiet,' he cried, 'and come along.'

"I saw that several of the men were armed with pistols, and I dared not make any opposition, for I knew that those who would thus steal the vessel, with worse crimes in view, would not hesitate to kill any of us who should give them trouble. And I had seen, too, that Luton was a determined fellow and I very quickly made up my mind that I must take what he chose to give and put up with it.

"The raft was hauled up under the lee gangway, and the main topsail laid aback. I was sent over first, and the mates next. Mr. Orne followed; then came Mrs. Banks, and then Mr. Emmerson, and lastly Manuel, with the child in his arms. They had made several attempts to win the black cook over to them, but without effect; and when I afterwards asked him how he dared to hold out against them, he informed me of their purpose. He said they told him they were bound for the coast of Africa, after a cargo of slaves, and that he told him he would sooner die than help to drag his own countrymen away from their homes in that manner.

"As soon as we were all on the raft the painter was cast loose, the topsail given to the wind again, and ere long the brig was out of reach.

"Do you think you can imagine our position. The raft was not over twenty-five feet long at the longest part, the space covered by boards being not over ten feet long by about eight wide. At every undulation the water swept over the surface, and we were very quickly convinced that our first attention must be turned to fixing some means of securing ourselves to our frail bark.

"It was nearly half an hour before the brig was entirely out of sight, and during that time our conversation was wholly upon the subject of the fearful crime by which we had been forced into our present situation. We learned, upon mutual consultation, that none of us had suspected anything out of the way until the moment of action came. Of course our position was a terrible one, but as we had all feared death this seemed a great relief, and hence we did not then fully realise all the horrors surrounding us. It was like a temporary respite to the condemned criminal. There was room for hope.

"As soon as the vessel was out of sight I began to look around for some means of making our position more secure. The only line or rope of any kind we had was the painter. This was about five fathoms long, but it was sufficient for our purpose, being firm and strong, and of good size. For provisions they had given us a small basket of biscuit, and a very small breaker of water. That night we took counsel with each other, and fervently prayed, and agreed to live or die together.

"The first thing I did after daylight had dawned was to fix the rope so that it might afford us the means of safety from being swept from the raft. One end was firmly knotted to the heel of the topgallant mast; then carried to the other end and there secured, and then brought back and fastened to the end of the boom. Thus we could all get inside of the life-line, and hold on upon it when occasion required. We had no seats but the boards of the raft, so that keeping dry was out of the question.

"The brig was out of sight, and no sail was to be seen. We ate a frugal breakfast, and then sat down to watch the horizon. The day passed and the night came, but we saw no sail. On the following day we discovered a sail about noon away to the southward. We used all means in our power to attract attention, but to no effect. The sail remained in sight about an hour and then disappeared. The rest of the day passed without seeing anything to move our hopes.

"Another, and another day passed without our seeing another sail. On the evening of the fourth day the last biscuit was eaten and only about a pint of water remained! On the following morning we drank the rest of the water, and from that moment our thoughts were turned towards heaven! All day we watched with straining eye, and night came without hope. A day without food and drink! The single day of privation would not be much if we thought the night would bring us relief; but when the commencing pangs are but the forerunners of what must increase and deepen, perhaps unto death, then they are rendered painful even in the beginning.

"There was no dew in the night, and when the daylight came again we were faint and weak. We had had no rain for many days, and our first thoughts in the morning were of clouds and fresh showers. There were clouds in the heavens! At eleven o'clock it commenced to rain. We quickly pulled off our garments, such as we could use, and having taken the breaker from Mrs. Banks, who had used it as a seat, we prepared to replenish it. It required nearly half an hour to rinse the salt from the garments, and after this we quenched our thirst, and then squeezed the water into the breaker. We got the breaker nearly half full before it ceased raining. At two o'clock the sun came out, and the clouds were soon gone.

"We now had water, but the cravings of hunger were upon us. The beverage cooled the tongue, but it could not bring strength to the starving. Night came again—and morning followed. Three days without food! I had become so weak that I could scarcely stand, and I looked only to death for relief. Mrs. Banks had not yet uttered a word of complaint, but I saw that she could not stand it much longer.

She had kept bread from her own store for the child but that had been gone some time, and when her little one began to cry for food she became nervous and unhappy. The afternoon crept on, and we felt that we could not pass another day. We gazed upon each other vacantly, and I wondered if I looked as haggard as the others did.

"'God have mercy!' groaned Mrs. Banks as she clasped her child to her bosom.

"It was painful to hear the poor child cry. The little one knew not why she must be hungry. She begged for something to eat, and it made my heart bleed to hear the poor thing promise to be good—very, very good—if her mamma would give her something to eat.

"Towards the middle of the afternoon, Enoch Trull, my second mate, who was a stout, rough man, and who had been uneasy for some time, turned to me and said—

"'Captain, have we got to die?'

"I told him our only hope was in God.

"'But what's the use,' he returned. 'Why need we all die, when by one's dying the rest may live? I must either have food or I must die.'

"Finally he came out with the idea of drawing lots to see who should be put to death for the saving of all the rest. I saw Mrs. Banks clasp her child and try to hide it, for Trull had been eyeing it sharply.

"'No, sir,' I said, 'when we first came on board this raft we pledged ourselves to live or die together. So let it be. My life is valuable to me, but it is not worth saving at the expense of another.'

"Trull found himself alone and he abandoned the idea.

"Night came at length, and as I lay down and wound my arm about the life-line, I expected to see no more daylight. I offered to assist Mrs. Banks to a place of rest, but she would not move from her seat on the now empty breaker. She feared for her child. I could see very plainly that the looks and words of the second mate had frightened her. But I was too weak to urge her, so I left her to herself. Emmerson was too weak to speak, and once Trull hinted at the idea of putting him to death, but I dissuaded him, I laid down and tried to sleep, but I could not. The night was very dark, with thick, heavy clouds in the heavens, but the wind had died away almost to a calm. I could not feel any wind, though ever and anon a light wave would dash over the raft. There was a slight current here settling to the southward, though not enough to be perceptible to us.

"It must have been near midnight when I was aroused from a state of stupor into which I had sunk, by feeling some one crawling past me. I looked up, and could just see Trull creeping towards young Emmerson with a knife in his hand. I had strength enough to reach forward and grasp his arm.

"'Don't do it,' said I.

"'I must!' he said, 'let me go. I am mad! I must have blood if I cannot have water. Let me go, I say!'

"But I held on. I urged him to go back and leave the poor supercargo alone. But Trull gave one more struggle, and had just succeeded in breaking from me, when I was startled by the raft's striking against some solid body. The concussion threw Trull from his feet, and caused me to start upon mine. I gazed up and saw a dark mass looming up by my side. At first I supposed it must be a rock; but my mistake was soon discovered by hearing the cry from Trull's lips—

"'A ship! A ship!'

"The others were upon their feet in an instant, even the supercargo raising himself to a sitting position. Mr. Gould, who seemed to be the strongest of the party, soon found a rope which hung from the side of the vessel, and ere long we found that we were just at one of the gangways. We called out with all our strength for help, but no one came.

" 'I'll go up,' said Gould, 'and see what's to pay.'

" Trull suggested that the crew might be frightened at our voices, which seemed very probable. However, Gould succeeded in working his way up into the main chains, and having let down some ropes, Trull quickly followed him. They went on deck, and when they returned they assured us they had not been able to find any living thing on board.

" ' But never mind,' said Trull; 'they've probably hid somewhere. Let's all get aboard, and then we'll hunt them up.'

" They soon prepared a sort of ladder by which Mr. Orne and Manuel made their way up. Next they sent down a sling and hauled up the child, and then Mrs. Banks was hauled up, though the task was a severe one, the men being so weak that they could scarcely stand. As soon as the mother was up I helped Emmerson to his feet, and having got him to the deck, I followed him.

" When I reached the deck of the vessel I could see that it was a brig, but it was too dark to make anything out in detail. There was no light in the binnacle, nor could we see a soul save our own party. Yet the sails were set, and the yards nearly square. I had worked my way around to the wheel, and was searching for the cabin bulkhead, when I stumbled over what seemed to be a human body. I stooped down and found my impressions correct. I pushed and punched the prostrate man, and cried in his ear. He gave a quick cry and started to a sitting posture.

" 'Who is it?' he cried.

" 'Eh?' exclaimed Trull, who was close by, 'Wasn't that Peter Ames's voice?'

" 'Hallo!' returned the roused man. 'Who's that?'

" 'D'ye know Enock Trull?' responded the mate.

" 'And Captain Ellis?' added I, giving him a shake.

" 'It's my captain! Where am I?'

" 'By the holy poker! but it's the old brig!' cried Gould, feeling the binnacle.

" We had, most assuredly, found our way back to the 'Cousin Alice' once more, though for awhile it seemed more like a dream than a reality. Ere long Manuel brought a light from the caboose, and we began to see things about us.

" 'Where are the rest of the crew?' I asked, as Ames got upon his feet.

" 'They're gone,' he returned, at the same time gazing half wildly at us. 'But where did you come from?' rubbing his eyes and gazing as though he might be mistaken after all.

" But that was not the time for question. Food and drink were uppermost in our thoughts. Wine and water were prepared, and all got up again without trouble. We had sense enough to be careful, and hence we saved our lives.

" It was well into the day before we began to understand each other—I mean young Ames and myself, His story was simple. On the third day after leaving us the villians overhauled a Spanish brig, and Luton had the boat lowered, and into it he called all hands, save Ames and the mulatto, Goldbush. There was but very little wind—not enough to fill the sails, and hence they had taken the boat. They were armed to the teeth, and meant to make one or two hauls before they reached the slave coast. Peter saw them board the Spaniard, and he saw a short conflict. He watched their movements, and saw them fill their own boat with goods, and then the Spaniard's boat was lowered, and that was also filled. After this, some half-dozen of the vessel's crew got into the boats with their captors, and Goldbush made the remark that they were going to have more hands. When the two boats had got some few fathoms from the captured vessel, a wreath of smoke and flame was seen to curl up from her hold. At the same moment a breeze sprang up from the southward and eastward, and the brig's sails filled. The mulatto stood at the rail leaning over. The thought of escape from the accursed crew came upon young Ames like a flash. Quick as thought he caught up an iron belaying-pin and knocked Goldbush overboard. The blow was given in just the right spot, and it took but a slight lift at the heels to tumble him over. The wind had taken the brig on the quarter, so that the main-topsail's being taken aback made no difference as far as starting was concerned. But Peter secured the helm, and then went and cast off the weather main braces, and ere long he managed to get the yards into their proper places, and then he resumed the helm. He saw one of the boats pick up the mulatto, and he saw Luton, too, standing up in the stern-sheets of his boat making the most frantic signs for the brig to turn back. But the bold youth took no notice of it. He kept his place at the helm until night, and then only left it for the purpose of obtaining food and drink. He had seen the Spanish craft burn nearly to the water's edge, so he knew that the villians could not find refuge there.

" All that night he kept the helm, and it was not until the close of the next day that he even dozed. On the evening previous to his meeting with us, he had become so utterly exhausted that he could stand up no longer. He had run far enough north, he thought, to strike the track of vessels bound up the Mediterranean, and he meant to take an easterly course; but as the sun went down the wind went with it, and as it seemed to be perfectly calm, he lashed the helm, and then lay down by it. And it was in this position we found him.

" Peter told me that Luton had threatened him with instant death if he did not join them, and that when he signified his assent he did so with the resolution to embrace the first opportunity to leave them or expose them. And I also learned that to him and three others we owed our lives. They agreed to join the mutineers only upon the condition that no lives should be taken, though Peter was the only one who was not willing to go into the business for the sake of the profits.

" We ran the brig to Gibraltar without much trouble, and there we managed to obtain eight good men. We went on to Smyrna, and when we touched at the Rock on our return, we learned from the captain of a Tangier fellucca that a boat with the name 'Cousin Alice' on the stern, had been picked up near Mansoriah. Of course we were sure that Luton had met the fate he so richly deserved; but what became of the other boat we never knew. I never saw any of the mutineers again, and I think it safe to assert that they all found the cold graves to which they had consigned us."

Captain Latour who at first listened intently to the story of his second officer, gradually allowed his head to drop on his breast, and drowsiness to steal over his senses.

THE REWARD OF FIDELITY.

Whether it was the narrative or the brandy‘ it is impossible to say, but by the time Ellis had finished speaking, the pirate captain was in a profound slumber.

Bilton and Ellis, however, still kept their eyes and their ears open, and their mouths too pretty well, for they ever and anon took copious draughts from the flasks before them.

Suddenly they both started to their feet. The boom of a gun saluted their ears.

"Hallo," said Bilton, "at it again, are they. Wake the captain, while I go on deck.

And the lieutenant rushed from the cabin, while Ellis placed his hands on Latour's shoulders to arouse him.

"Captain! Captain Latour," said Ellis, roughly shaking him.

With an effort the sleeper started up.

"The vessel is firing again, captain," said Ellis, "Hark! there goes another gun."

And as he spoke, the low booming of a cannon came over the water.

Latour darted up to the deck followed by Ellis.

"It is off here," said the captain, taking his glass and pointing over the starboard quarter.

"There goes another," said Gurney, the old boatswain.

This remark was called forth by seeing a dim light upon the dark horizon. But no report followed, yet the light did not disappear.

It grew brighter and broader, and the glare shot higher into the heavens.

Latour brought the glass suddenly from his eye, exclaiming—

"She's on fire! Tacks and sheets! Stand by the braces! Port your helm carefully—Let go the starboard braces—Round in on the larboard. Port, port! Round in handsomely. Haul aft the sheets here, some of you."

The noble ship obeyed her helm quickly, and ere long she was upon the starboard tack, and standing towards the strange light, which now bore very near south-west.

There could no longer be any doubt that the fire was from a burning ship, for the flames now shot high up, and the lurid glare spread wider and wider.

"Gurney," said the captain, turning to his grey-headed old boatswain, "how far off is that fire?"

"I should say nothing short of two miles," replied the old salt, after having measured the distance carefully in his mind.

"Just what I should have said," added Ellis.

"Then we must put on more sail. All hands. Lively, boys. Clew up the top-gallant s'ls, and then lay aloft and shake the reefs from the tops'ls. Quick, now, for there may be lives to be saved."

The reefs were cast out, the yards hoisted, the top-gallant sails sheeted home again, and then the ship began to plough the water handsomely. The wind was only a couple of points forward of the beam, so she carried her sheets flowing freely.

Ellen, who had been aroused for the second time by the report of the guns, could remain no longer in her cabin, but hastily throwing her garments around her, she made her way to the deck, and stood beside Latour, gazing out into the waste beyond.

"Heaven have mercy!" ejaculated Ellen, who was the first to speak. "Is it not a ship on fire?"

"It must be—Ha! See—look now," cried Latour. "See the flames shoot up into the rigging—'tis a heavy ship."

A cry of horror went up from the deck as the captain thus spoke, for the whole mass of the burning ship's top-hamper could now be seen as the flames now shot up amongst it. Like serpent's tongues the angry fire lapped the illumined spars, and along upon the stout tarred ropes the red demon leaped and danced. The sails were in flames, and away up to the very trucks the angry forks of living fire now made their way. The noble hull was one mass of surging flame, from which three pyramids of red fire arose, thence shooting out madly into the lurid sky as though they would bound away from the horrid monster that gave them birth.

It was a grand, an awful scene, and the hearts of those who in safety beheld it seemed hushed to a deathly stillness beneath its fearful power. Anon the picture became more distinct, and moving men could be seen rushing to and fro upon the burning deck.

"See!" cried the boatswain. "They are throwing over spars and boxes.—Ha! and now they leap into the sea!"

"God help them!" ejaculated Ellen, turning away her head for a moment to shut out the scene.

The pirate vessel was now within a mile of the unfortunate ship, and everything upon the latter's deck could be plainly seen. The crew seemed to be all gone, for no moving thing of life was any longer to be seen. The fire was now at its height, and the huge sheets of flame swayed to and fro like a fiery forest. The roar of the raging element could be plainly heard, as could the loud hissing of the the huge brands that ever and anon fell into the water. In another moment a new cry went up from the deck. The foremast of the burning ship was seen to sway to and fro for an instant, and then over it went crashing and hissing into the sea.

The deck must have been burnt away, for hardly had the foremast gone ere the mainmast followed, taking with it the mizen-top-mast, the stays not having been burnt off.

"Stand by to bring-to here," shouted Latour. "We must not venture nearer. Main-topsail braces! Stand by to clew up the courses, some of you! Lay the maintopsail to the mast!"

"Will you go no nearer?" asked Ellen, in surprise.

"Not with our ship, lady," the captain returned. "We must do the rest with our boats. Perhaps you don't understand this."

"I think I do not, sir."

"I will explain: The heat of that burning ship has so rarified the atmosphere all around it, that for a short space a sort of vacuum is produced, and from all quarters the tendency of the air is towards the fire. Vessels have been thus drawn towards a burning craft even at the distance of a quarter of a mile; and you will readily see, that when once within the circle of that influence, a vessel's sails become useless to her."

Ellen understood it now, and she saw how easily an inexperienced man might have allowed his own ship to run on to sure destruction.

As soon as the ship was hove-to the boat was was lowered, and six of the strongest men called to go in her with Ellis and the boatswain.

"You will pull as fast as possible," said Latour to his mate, "and be sure that you keep a bright look-out for any poor fellows who may be in the water."

"Aye, aye, sir," responded the mate; and then he leaped into the boat and pushed off.

The stout men bent over the oars with a will, and ere long they were in the vicinity of the burning mass. They could not go very near, for the heat was intense. The ill-fated ship now lay with her head to the wind, and shortly after the boat began to pull around her, her mizen-mast went by the board, and came crashing and hissing into the water. The bulwarks were mostly gone, and along by the waist the sides were all burnt out—so much so, at any rate, that the boatmen could look through into the fiery gulf between decks. The flames were still shooting up in the sky, but not so high as before; though the surface of the sea for some distance around was light as day. Eagerly did Ellis gaze about him for some sign of life. He knew well that nothing could be alive within the flaming hull, and of course he supposed that some of the crew must have leaped into the water with something for support. He had pulled nearly around when a loud shout arrested his attention. Instinctively the men backed their oars, and in a moment more the mate saw two human forms clinging to a box, not over a rod distant. The boat was quickly pulled for them, but ere it could reach them they had sank to rise no more.

For nearly an hour Ellis cruised about the scene of the terrible disaster, and he might have remained longer, but a cry from the old boatswain called his attention to the burning hull, and he saw it swaying to and fro like a dying beast. He called to his men to pull away, and while yet they bent at the oars, the illumined mass gave one mighty throe, and then, reeling back, her stern went down. The water hissed and boiled—the seething mass sent forth huge balls of flame—the hot steam belched up in gigantic clouds—and, in one short moment more, the troubled waters gathered over the charred and blackened wreck! She had been heavily armed, and hence she sank more quickly than she might otherwise have done.

For awhile the boatmen could see nothing. They were left in a gloom, to them like the blackness of a tomb. But gradually their eyes overcame the effects of the sudden transition, and they easily made out the light which hung at the peak of their own ship. Of course they could search no more in such darkness, and with sad and heavy hearts they pulled for their vessel. The boat was dropped around to the stern and there simply made fast by the painter, for the captain had resolved to lay-to until morning, and then see if any lives could be saved by daylight.

When the boat's crew were once more on board, Latour turned to Ellen, who had all the time stood by his side gazing upon the spot where the burning vessel had gone down into the vortex, and said—

"A beautiful sight that, Ellen, was it not?"

"And a sad one," replied the maiden.

"Indeed it was," said Latour. "But the air is damp and cold, and you had better again retire to your cabin."

And the pirate offered his arm to support her.

Ellen hesitated.

Should she accept the proffered aid?

She gazed up into the face of the pirate through the darkness, as if she would read there his thoughts.

"Ellen, I will keep my promise," said the pirate, as he observed the hesitation of the young girl.

There was a frankness in his tones, and Ellen took the arm of the pirate and walked towards the cabin stairs.

She cast one long lingering look in the direction where the burning ship had sank, and then descended to her cabin.

Latour left her at the door, and with a grateful sigh she again threw herself upon the couch.

CHAPTER LXIV.

CHARLES AND THE HUNTER.—THE APPROACHING SHIP.—DEPARTURE OF CHARLES FROM THE ISLAND.

THE bright orb of day rode high up in the heavens, pouring down its warm genial rays upon the little island on which our hero and his noble-minded friend, the hunter, reposed after their exertions in landing the boat upon the rocks.

What varied emotions passed through the minds of both as they reclined on the rude cliff beside the long-hidden vessel which had borne the murderer to those shores.

Emotions widely different—emotions of grief and joy.

Charles thought only of the dear one far away, and the hopes of again beholding her! now engendered by the little vessel at his side.

Like the drowning man who grasps at a straw in the hope that it will bear him safe to shore, our hero looked upon the little bark as the means of again seeing his beloved Ellen.

But the old hunter was filled with grief at the prospect of parting with his young companion.

He had been as happy as the recollections of his griefs and sufferings would permit him to be on that lonely island, ere the youth by his side had been thrown across his path.

But he felt that if again left alone he should become miserable.

The warm flood of love so long extinguished had gushed back again to his for the wounded boy. A love that he had not felt for years.

And now he was about to lose him.

He wished they had never met, for the genial nature of Charles had cast a warm ray on his lonely dwelling, only to be obliterated by his absence.

The light of his rude hut was to be extinguished, and his home rendered more desolate.

Like the bright star which for a moment illumines the black cloud, then disappears and leaves it darker than before.

Yet he could not blame the youth for his intentions.

Love was his attractive star, and it would lead him on till that love was consummated, or till death laid its icy hand upon, and bid him go no farther.

And death he would bravely dare to seek the object of his affection.

He could not live without Ellen.

But he would die for her sake.

Hence he would dare the dangers of that wild vortex of waters which encircle the earth in that small boat.

Without rudder or compass, sail or oars, he would trust himself to the rolling element beneath whose crested tops the wealth of ages lie buried.

In his heart love was stronger than fear, and he would obey its dictates, come weal or woe.

Such were the thoughts that passed through his mind as he lay upon the rock.

The old hunter was the first to break the reverie into which both had fallen.

"Let us now return to the hut," said the old man, "and refresh ourselves after our toil."

Charles rose.

"I do not care to eat," he replied. "I feel so happy now."

"At the prospect of escape from this island," said the hunter.

"No. At the prospect of meeting with Ellen."

The old man sighed.

He thought of the time when on the wings of love he bounded to meet his outraged wife.

But he dashed the tear away that rose to his eyes, and taking the arm of the youth led him towards the hut.

The meal was eaten in silence, the thoughts of each absorbed their minds.

When it was concluded, Charles said—

"Kind friend—for kind indeed have you been to me—a stranger thrown across your path, I must leave you soon, but let me hope not for ever. I pray that heaven may place the means in my power to rescue Ellen from the hands of the wretch who holds her, and then I will come back to bear you from this lonely island to my home, in gratitude for all your kindness to me."

The old man shook his head.

"If heaven spare you," he replied, "my prayers shall be for your happiness, but heed not me, here let me live and die."

But Charles determined if ever it laid in his power, to return to the island and bear the old man to his home.

"I will now go back to the rock," he said, "and endeavour to launch the boat in the bay ere the tide has receded."

"You are too weak yet," replied the hunter.

"Not so. The hope of again seeing Ellen has nerved my arm, and I am strong."

The old man believed that it would be useless to persuade him from his purpose, so silently followed him to the rocks.

"We must get it across the chasm," said the hunter, "but how."

"This was a difficulty the impulsive youth had not thought of.

But he set his mind to work to conjure up the means.

"Oh, for a couple of planks," he muttered, "that would reach from rock to rock."

"Yonder lie some uprooted saplings," said the hunter, pointing to the base of the cliff.

The heart of Charles bounded with joy.

With the speed of an antelope he bounded down the cliff, and in a few moments returned, dragging up a small trunk of a tree, whose branches had long since perished.

By the aid of the hunter it was thrown across the chasm, a work rendered somewhat easy from the opposite cliff being lower than that on which they stood.

"I feared it would not reach," said Charles.

And again he bounded down the cliff.

In a short time another was placed in its position, and a bridge formed over the chasm.

Then the boat was drawn towards it, and balanced crosswise after some considerable exertion upon the bridge.

"I shall have no difficulty in getting it to the other side as it is on the decline," said Charles, "if you will prevent the trees from slipping."

Then he worked the boat a little way down the bridge, and holding the side of the boat so as to prevent it shifting from the centre, threw himself astride the rude passage, and working his body down forced the boat before him, taking care that the little vessel did not shift too far on either side so as to over balance itself.

By this means it was safely landed on the opposite rock, and with a cry of joy, Charles threw himself fainting and exhausted by its side.

The greatest difficulty was passed.

The hunter crossed the bridge and stood by his side.

"Charles," he said, "this resolve of yours is madness, thus to cast yourself to the mercy of the waves; see, from this cliff nothing but the vast ocean is to be seen, and outside this bay rocks abound on which this frail craft must be dashed to atoms. I seek not to detain you here, but fly not thus into the face of your Maker."

"I must seek her or die," said the youth.

"Wait and watch," continued the hunter, "vessels sometimes approach these rocks in fair weather, then you might put to sea with some chance of success."

Charles paused for a few moments in thought.

"The weather," he said after a pause, "is now beautiful and fair, did I think a ship would pass within sight to-day, I would be advised."

"If not to-day," said the hunter, "one may to-morrow."

"To-morrow never comes," said Charles bitterly, "and the day after to-day may be too late."

"Heaven works all for the best," remarked the old man.

"I cannot delay," he said, "minutes seem hours, and days years to me."

"I must seek her—save her."

"Wait then but for one day," said the hunter, "and then if no sail is to be seen, I will speak no more."

Charles looked up in the face of his friend and grasped his hand in his arm.

"Kind, generous man," he said, "I know and feel your anxiety for my safety alone prompts you thus to urge my stay. But I place my faith in God—that God who never deserts the just and the true—he will protect and aid me—but I will not leave the island to-day if no sail appears in sight, but to-morrow I go, come what may."

"Then heaven grant a vessel may near this rock bounded coast," said the hunter."

"Heaven send it may," replied Charles, "but my kind friend assist me to get the boat down to the waters edge, so that it may be launched the moment a sail appears, if heaven should send one this way."

To this the hunter consented, and in the course of an hour the boat was got down to the spot where Charles and Ellen had landed when pursued by the smugglers.

"Now," said Charles, "she can be launched in a moment."

"She can," said the hunter, turning away with a sigh.

Charles followed him up the rocks and over the rude bridge.

Casting his eyes seaward he scanned the horizon.

The day was beautiful and clear.

The youth gazed far out to where sky and water seemed to mingle.

There was a speck not larger than his hand.

He shaded his eyes and gazed intently.

"Can it be," he muttered, "heaven send it may."

"What," said the hunter.

"A ship."

"Where?"

"There yonder."

And Charles pointed in the direction.

"I can see nothing but sea and sky," said the old man.

"There—just where the sea and sky meet," said Charles, again pointing in the direction.

The hunter shaded his eyes with his hands, and looked intently in the direction the youth indicated.

But he could see nothing.

"Your anxiety pictures it to your imagination," said the hunter; "or else my eyes are dull."

"It looms up larger and larger," said Charles, still keeping his eyes fixed upon it.

"I cannot see it," said the hunter—"yet my sight is generally good. I fear you are mistaken."

"No, no," said Charles; "I have seen a ship when farther distant than that with the naked eye."

"And, if it be a vessel, how far distant is she?"

"Some miles," said Charles; "but an hour or two will bring her well in sight; and the wind sets fair on this island."

"Then you think she will come this way?"

"I do."

"Heaven grant she may."

"Amen!" said Charles.

"Supposing her to come near this island, how long will she be?" asked the hunter.

"That will depend greatly upon her sailing qualities, which I cannot form any idea of at this distance."

"If of moderate speed, how then?"

"At near sundown."

"Then let us return to the hut," said the hunter.

Charles turned, and together they descended the cliff.

With beating heart he walked beside his companion.

"Heaven grant she may not alter her course, or the wind change!" said Charles.

"I trust she may not, for your sake," said the hunter, "since you are resolved to go, at all hazards."

And a look of sadness passed across his face.

He felt even more wretched now that the boat was ready, and a vessel in sight, than he had done before.

His companion sighed as he marked it.

In silence they gained the hut.

In silence the mid-day meal was eaten.

They were wretched.

But not another word of dissuasion did the hunter utter.

The time wore on.

Five hours had passed since Charles first saw the speck on the horizon. Then he arose, and said:

"If she has not changed her course, she must now be near the island."

They walked forth again, and soon stood upon the rocks.

The speck had become a fine ship—the white sails of which, bellied by the breeze, sparkled in the fast setting sun.

Charles turned his glance from the ship to the hunter's face.

Their eyes met.

And in that glance more was said than words could pourtray.

Charles extended his hand, and the hunter grasped it fervently.

Without speaking they descended the rock to where the boat lay.

Charles pushed it down into the bay, assisted by the hunter.

Then he leapt into it; and, again looking up into the face of the recluse, he said, while a tear dimmed his eye:

"Come!"

"It must not be," was the reply: "here I remain; but take with you an old man's blessing."

Charles bowed his head, to hide the tears which rolled down his cheeks; and the hunter, extending his arms, exclaimed:

"May He who commands the winds and the waves have you in his keeping! Farewell for ever!"

"Farewell—but not for ever! We shall meet again."

And, as he spoke, the boat floated from the side of the rock: and Charles, with his eyes fixed in gratitude upon the face of the hunter, was borne rapidly out of the bay.

CHAPTER LXV

THE PIRATE AND THE OFFICERS—ADVENTURES AND RECOLLECTIONS.

CAPTAIN LATOUR sat in his cabin sipping his brandy from a tumbler, and puffing huge volumes of smoke from a large Dutch pipe. In this manner he had continued to amuse himself for the last hour, but all in vain, for his was a nature that required excitement. When he could find nothing to keep his mind employed he became miserable.

Solitude in the present instance became irksome to him, and as there was not a sail in sight, and he had promised in no way to molest Ellen, he knew not how to kill the time.

After shifting uneasily upon his seat, once or twice, he seized a small hand bell and rung it violently.

This summons were immediately answered by a young man of foreign aspect.

"Petro," said Latour, "tell the officers I should be glad of their company here."

Petro bowed and departed on his errand.

In a short time Bilton, Harvey, and a young man named Redwood entered.

"Where's Sharp," said Latour, "and Harris."

"On deck," replied Bilton.

"Is it necessary they should remain there."

"No."

Again Latour rang the bell, and again Petro made his appearance.

"Send Sharp and Harris here," said Latour.

In a few moments the men made their appearance.

"Gentlemen," said Latour, "I intended to make for the first port. This voyage has been a dull one, we have fallen in with nothing worth powder and shot. The vessel requires some repairs, and the men would like a run on shore, so unless we are overhauled, we'll not put ourselves out of the way to seek for prizes at present, but as I hate to sit moping here by myself, I beg you will join me. We shall make land in twenty four hours, and in the meantime, as we cannot devote it all to sleep, I propose we make each other's better acquaintance over a glass or two of grog—so pull round and help yourselves—no ceremony."

The order was cheerfully obeyed, and in the course of a short time the fumes of the tobacco smoke, coupled with that of the brandy, which by the way had not paid duty, loosened the tongues of the party, and from natural compliments and common place conversation, they drifted on to the various adventures which they had met with in their nautical career.

Latour related some of his hairbreadth escapes, as did also Bilton, but Redwood who had been the least talkative of the company, intimated that the adventures which had made him a pirate was the strangest of them all.

"Let's hear it then," said Latour, "you never told us how you came on that raft, I got you off although you joined us willingly enough."

Redwood took a deep draught and said—

"Well, you see captain, after a somewhat unusual long stay at home, caused by the death of my mother, I got shipped as mate aboard a brigantine, named the 'Volante,' commanded by Captain George Grayson, who was a singular compound of the practical man and the dreamer. In matters of business and professional routine, no one could be more sharp, shrewd, and clearheaded; but outside the line of his duty, he was visionary as a poet. He was thoroughly imbued with the romance of the ocean. With its legendary history he was intimately acquainted, and what was more singular, all the nautical fables that had gathered about his favourite element in the lapse of ages, found in him an unquestionable believer. He had as firm a faith in the existence of the great Norway kraken, as the good bishop who has chronicled its marvels. He fully believed that Vanderdecken, in command of the Flying Dutchman, was still endeavouring to double the Cape of Good Hope, and he expected, in the course of some of his long voyages, to hear with his own ears the song of the syrens, and to see with his own eyes the ocean mermaids combing their long hair, and smiling at the charms reflected in their mirrors. As he dwelt on some of these marvels to his mate, his dreamy blue eye would light up with a strange fire, and his voice tremble with emotion. He was altogether a strange person.

"One night, at the completion of my watch, I went below, leaving the deck to the second mate. I was preparing to turn in, when the door of the state room opened, and Grayson came forth into the cabin, partially dressed. He moved with a stealthy, gliding step, his countenance exhibited a deadly pallor, and his eyes, wide open, gazed straight before him with an expression of terror I had never before noticed, for he was a remarkably brave and self-possessed man. It at once occurred to me that the captain was walking in his sleep. With a view of rousing him, I called him by name.

"'Hush!' said the captain, pointing with his fore-finger. 'Do you see it?'

"'I see nothing, sir,' I answered, after gazing in the direction indicated.

"'Nothing!' cried the captain in amazement. 'Impossible! She stands there—as clear to my eyes as you yourself.'

"'Who, stands there, captain?'

"'My mother,' he answered in a hollow voice.

"'I thought your mother was dead?'

"'Ay—dead and buried long ago,' replied Grayson, in the same hollow tone. 'But she comes to see me, for all that, when danger threatens me. And she never appeared to me except as the herald of peril and disaster. There she stands, in her long white robes, as they dressed her for the grave—ineffable sweetness but ineffable sadness, in her face. Look! look there! she beckons me with her wan finger."

"'This is a delusion, captain. You are feverish—delirious.'

"Captain Grayson looked at me, sadly and earnestly, but shook his head.

"'You will never believe it,' he said, 'but I—I am *sure* of the reality of the vision—as sure as I am of the truth of this book,' and he laid his hand on the bible which lay upon the cabin table. Then, turning his face in the direction in which he had been previously gazing, he added, 'The figure is growing dimmer—is fading away like an expiring flame: the mission is accomplished, the warning is given!'

"The positive earnestness of the man—the loneliness of the scene—the chill midnight hour, all contributed to affect me with a strange and unwonted superstitious terror. I felt my strength failing me, and I grasped the captain's arm convulsively, as my eyes instinctively followed the direction of Grayson's look. And, strange as it may appear, I seemed to feel an electric current flowing from my companion's person, and thrilling through all the nerves of my frame—the sensation being like that experienced when circulation is returning to a limb in which it has been temporarily suspended. But more appalling yet was my conviction, that I saw, on the opposite wall, the figure of a shrouded woman, whose faded features bore a striking resemblance to those of the captain. This figure was very dim, it is true, and seemed formed of a wan light, like that of phosphorus, flickering and wavering, like the pallid billows of a faint northern aurora. And then these waves of flame grew fainter and fainter—the outlines of the Awful Shape more and more indistinct, till they finally faded out utterly.

"'It is gone!' gasped I.

"'You saw it, then?' said the captain. 'Thank God! I am not insane, as I have sometimes suspected. You see there are more mysteries in life, young man, than philosophy can fathom. But I must go on deck, for we shall have a change of weather soon—I know it.'

"Left alone, I soon partially recovered my ordinary healthy tone of mind. Discarding, as utterly puerile, the belief that I had actually been confronted with a visitant from beyond the grave, I fell back, for explanation, on what is the usual resort of strong-minded persons, in these cases, the theory of the strength of the imagination. The captain, whose reason had been weakened by perpetually dwelling on supernatural marvels, had imagined that he had seen a spectre, which he described minutely. I, brought into *rapport* with him, by the contagious force of sympathy, had also imagined that I saw the same thing. It was a temporary mania, so powerful as to have the effect of reality; that was all. Such, at least, was the manner in which I succeeded in calming my shaken nerves, when I threw myself into my berth, and courted the coy damsel, Sleep. She came at last, and sealed the heavy lids, but my slumber was uneasy, and peopled with a thousand vague shapes of terror. I was aroused at last by hearing my name called, and I sprung into the cabin to listen for a moment to a hundred wild noises, and then to rush on deck and bear my part in trying to foil one of the wildest tempests that ever howled its wrath off Hatteras.

"Captain Grayson stood on deck, as calm in the midst of the elemental warfare, as ever he had been in the golden sunshine and mild breezes of a summer's day in the tropics. His orders, given in a sharp, incisive tone which becomes the hour of peril, were obeyed by men whose hearts were as true as steel. The white canvass, so lately clothing the spars of the brigantine with a robe of radiance, were reduced to the smallest compass: she was nearly under bare poles. Still the storm raved through her rigging, and the fierce waves glittering with phosphoric radiance, threatened every moment to engulph her. They lifted her prow to the skies—they sank down with her into inky gulphs from which it seemed she could never raise her quivering timbers—they followed her, rearing and roaring like wild beasts with ravenous jaws seeking to devour her. Two men, lashed to the wheel, sought to keep her steady to her course. Hark! that ominous cracking! The foremast bends—breaks—and the weight of the top-hamper coming down by the run, careens the Volant to the water's edge. Ready—axes, tomahawks, knives! work with a will and clear the wreck! The mainmast must be sacrificed, and soon, in that black midnight, with the wind howling like a legion of unloosed demons, with the waves plunging like masterless coursers, in the midst of a horrid chaos, that seems like the eve of doom, the late beautiful Volant, the pride of the manly hearts that trod her deck, is weltering an almost helpless hulk upon the world of waters.

"'What think you now of the warning?' whispered Grayson, hoarsely, as he stood beside me. I was silent.

"Long before morning the fury of the storm had abated, and when the red sun rolled upward from the eastern horizon, its slant rays fell on billows yet heaving angrily, but shorn of more than half their terrors.

"The seamen were employed in rigging a headsail on the stump of the foremast, while from a temporary staff, the colours of the brigantine were displayed, union down, when a sail was signalled bearing down on us.

"The stranger was a large schooner, clipper built and sharp, but having unusually high bulwarks, and she showed, on nearing, American colours. She seemed to have passed unscathed through the tempests of the preceding night, and when within hailing distance, the sound of a fiddle was heard on her deck. Two or three bonnets and veils flitting to and fro showed that she was a passenger ship. In a few minutes her topsail was thrown aback, she lost her headway, and a boat, lowered and manned with some difficulty, for the sea was still running pretty high, pulled for the wreck of the brigantine. The light craft was soon alongside, and then, while a seaman in the bow held her fast with a boathook, a person who appeared to be an officer, followed by four or five men, clambered up the brigantine's sides and bounded lightly on her deck.

"The first who sprang on the deck of the brigantine, was one 'prime in manhood where youth ended.' Slender, yet firmly knit, erect and graceful, he might have been pronounced eminently handsome, but it was beauty which had been scaled by the repellant end of the magnet. His jaunty sea-cap rested on curls black as the raven's wing, but the coils of which reminded one of the tortuous involutions of a nest of vipers. His eye, too, had a hard snaky fire in its lustre, and the beautiful full lip that sardonic smile, at once sensual, contemptuous, and defiant, which the fallen archangel, the prince of darkness, might have worn. There was nothing particularly striking in the costume of the stranger. His loose blue jacket and pantaloons were of superfine cloth, however, and the ends of his scarlet neckerchief, as they floated away on the sea-breeze, disclosed linen of matchless fineness and spotless purity, while a line of rare diamond studs glittered on his bosom. A crimson shawl of Indian workmanship knotted round his waist, sustained a brace of ivory-handled pistols.

"His nearest companion was a handsome boy similarly attired. The rest of the group were only noticeable from their ruffianly look, and the sinister circumstance that they were armed to the teeth with pistols and cutlasses. But the peculiarities I have noticed, to the eye of a seaman like myself, who received the party, at once announced that the visitor who came on board in this style, could be no other than one of those pirates who, in spite of the vigilance of the cruisers of all nations, still prowled about the Spanish main, and sometimes far from the Antilles, and spread their canvass even on the broad Atlantic. Nor did this conjecture long remain without confirmation.

"'Have I the honour of addressing the commander of this fine vessel?' asked the pirate, if such indeed he was, accosting me in a tone of mock civility.

"'No, sir; I am the first officer—Captain Grayson is below.'

"'Please give him the compliments of Captain Brandon of the Rattlesnake, and tell him that I shall do myself the honour of waiting on him in a moment. Stay, young man. What is the name of your vessel?'

"'The brigantine Volant, of New York, for Cardenas.'

"'Cargo?'

"'Hogshead and box shooks.'

"'Enough. Now do my errand.'

"Feeling the folly of disobeying, and anxious to apprise the captain of this new disaster as soon as possible, I went below. The weary and jaded crew of the Volant, gathered on deck, were huddled together, gazing on the people who had taken possession of their craft, with looks of wondering anxiety.

"Captain Brandon surveyed them with a keen eye.

"'A fine set of fellows,' he muttered, to the boy who stood beside him. 'They would be no unwelcome addition to our crew, Eugene. We are short handed, you know. Antonio is down with the fever—Baptiste lost his leg when we were chased by the Vincennes, Black Ralph went to Davy Jones last night. My lads,' he added, addressing the Volant's crew—'what say you to a cruise under a flag that owns no master on the main? What say you to a doubloon a week instead of eight dollars a month—grog without limit—plenty of liberty—lots of pretty girls, and the luxuries of the tropics at your command? Let those who are willing to swing in a rover's hammock, step forward.'

"Not a man stirred from his place, though one or two of the younger seamen seemed wavering, and whispered to each other.

"'I give you one more chance, my lads,' said the pirate; 'who speaks?'

"No one volunteered a reply.

"'Fools!' muttered the pirate; 'and worse than fools—madmen!'

"He strode aft, and pausing, gazed upon the American flag that streamed from the jury-mast to which it was nailed, while his brow grew black as night.

"'Cursed ensign of tyranny!' he cried. 'You revive the memory of all my wrongs. Yet I remember the time when a foolish boy, I hailed the stars and stripes as the emblem of all that was glorious and honourable in war and peace. Sailing under its folds, I, too, dreamed of winning honours for myself, and of one day walking the quarter-deck, the honoured champion of the constellated flag. But I lived to see it float above my head as the bloody scourge was laid upon my naked back. Down! down! vile rag!' And he seized the banner with his clenched hand.

"There was one, however, who could not tamely see that ensign humbled. An old grey headed seaman, named Hardy, from Old Essex, rushed forward, and snatched the flag from the pirate's profaning hand.

"'Man and boy,' said he, ' I have honoured the old gridiron flag, and I swear I won't see it dishonoured.'

"'Fool!' retorted Brandon; 'leave you hold?'

"'Never, while I live.'

"'Then die, dog, in your folly?' cried the pirate; and pulling a pistol from his belt, he levelled it full at the head of the bold seaman. I give you one more chance,' he said, waving in his purpose. 'Surrender the flag and live.'

"'Never, said old Hardy.

"A flash—a report—and the gallant old seaman fell dead on the deck, his hand still grasping the ensign that he died to save from dishonour, and his life's blood adding a deeper die to its crimson rays. There was a murmur and movement among his shipmates, but the pirate crew unsheathed their cutlasses, and their chief stood backed by a wall of steel. Resistance would have been suicide. They were doomed to see the ensign they worshipped torn from its staff, trampled under foot, and spit upon.

"'And now,' said Brandon, turning to his followers, ' drive these dogs below, and bar en down the hatches, while I attend to the captain.'

"With these words, he left the deck and entered the cabin. Captain Grayson and myself were seated on the transom. The former was stern and collected, and made no reply to the mocking salutation of the pirate.

"'Captain Grayson, I presume?' said Brandon, doffing his cap.

" There was no reply.

" You are aware, I presume, that you are my prisoner ?'

" ' I am aware that you are a pirate! answered Captain Grayson.

" ' Indeed, your supposition does great credit to your penetration.'

" As he spoke, Brandon had opened a locker, from which he took a bottle of spirit, some glasses, and a decanter of water, and sat down mixed a tumbler of grog, with great coolness.

" ' Gentlemen, I hope you will join me,' he said pushing the bottle towards Grayson and myself. ' I hate to drink alone. No, well, then, we'll proceed at once to business. Your cargo, captain, such as it is, is quite useless to me ; but you must have money—species—on board ; and hard cash is exactly the commodity that suits my occasions. I shall trouble you to make an immediate transfer of your cash.'

" If I had money on board, ruffian, replied Grayson, ' I would never surrender it, and you could never find it.'

" ' I infer from the last clause of your remark, old gentleman,' said the pirate, 'that you have money concealed somewhere. Leave me alone to find it. I'm as keen on the scent of gold as a Spanish bloodhound on the track of blood.'

" With these words he arose, and commenced a thorough search of the cabin, having first called to his assistance two of his men. They rummaged every locker, lifted a trap beneath the cabin table, and explored the recess it covered, demolished the panelling, searched the persons of the captain and myself, our trunks, every hole and cranny that could hide a dollar.

" ' You can't have thrown it overboard,' cried Brandon, with a black look.

" ' You shall never be a dollar richer for this day's work, you black-hearted villain,' cried Grayson.

" ' Miserable idiot,' cried the pirate, stung to madness. ' You shall never live to boast that you have baffled me.'

" Quick as thought he drew and fired a pistol, and with one deep groan the captain fell forward on the cabin table dead, But almost simultaneously with the flash and the report, a hatchet which had been used in breaking up the panelling, was caught up by myself and sent whizzing through the air at the captain's head. It struck him in the forehead, and inflicted an ugly gash, felled him to the floor. But he was up on his feet in an instant, looking more like a fiend than ever, but shouting to one of his crew, who was preparing to avenge his wound.

" ' Alive, don't harm him, alive I say. Bind him with the lashing of that chest and bring him on deck. By all the fiends that fell from heaven, I would'nt have a hair of his head hurt. You shall see sport anon, I promise ye.'

" Mastered after a desperate struggle, my arms were tightly secured, and I was dragged on deck.

" ' Toss me this dog into the bottom of the boat,' said Brandon, as he followed, and then whispering certain directions to one of his followers, he went over the brigantine's side and dropped into the stern sheets of the gig. The ruffian who had been left behind soon rejoined him.

" ' Is it done ?' asked Brandon.

" ' Ay—ay, captain,'

" ' All right,' replied Brandon. ' Now pull with a will for the Rattlesnake.'

" The gig was shoved off, the oars fell into the rowlocks, and impelled by the long, deep, steady strokes of the rowers, the light craft bounded over the billows.

" ' Lift up this fellow's head,' said Brandon, pushing me with his foot as he spoke ; ' let him look his last at the brigantine.'

" In spite of the anger, loathing, and grief that possessed me, I was impelled by curiosity to ascertain the meaning of the pirate's speech. When my head was raised above the level of the gunwale, I looked eagerly in the direction of the Volant. There she lay rolling on the glittering waves, a helpless hulk. But as I looked, I beheld light puffs of black smoke rising from her decks, followed almost instantly by tongues of yellow and crimson flame. Swift as snakes they coiled up the remnants of the masks and rigging, and then I heard, with indescribable agony, the stifled cries of men in anguish. The fell cruelty of the pirates burst upon my mind with awful emphasis. They had bound the crew and fired the brigantine.

" Averting my eyes from the spectacle, I turned them on the pirate. ' I little thought,' I said, ' ever to implore your mercy ; but I do so now, humbly, abjectly, if you will. I do not beg for my life, but for the lives of yon poor men. There is time yet to save them.'

" ' They chose their fate,' answered the pirate, coldly, ' I offered them service under my flag.'

" ' And they rejected it !'

" ' Like fools.'

" ' Like heroes. You have sent them to heaven on a car of fire.'

" ' Very likely. Look, look! see! the decks are in a sheet of flame now. And hark! don't you hear wild screams above the roar of the fire? That is music—eh, Eugene ?'

" But the boy whom he addressed had shut his eyes, and was pressing his hands to his ears, an action which seemed to enhance the enjoyment of the pirate, who laughed long and heartily.

" ' Who was it offered a prize for a new sensation ?' said he. ' I'm glad I find I'm not utterly blasé. I relish this.'

" There was a strange fascination in the spectacle, which rivetted even my gaze. But it was of brief duration. The doomed vessel was soon wrapped in a shroud of fire, and then, as the air below became intensely heated, the decks blew up with a loud explosion, and the remnants of the once fair fabric, the pride of the builder, the merchant, and the seaman, sunk, hissing into the waste of waters—a cloud of heavy smoke, gradually wafted away by the wind, alone indicating the scene of her destruction.

" When the gig's crew stood on the deck of the rover, the ruffians who sailed under the black flag gathered around their captain, eyeing curiously the bloody bandage which swathed his forehead.

" ' It is nothing, my lads,' he said ; ' a scratch from a hatchet thrown by a lubberly hand. Be careful there with your prisoner, men. Use him as though you loved him. Close the cabin door, and set him up against it. So—well done.''

" Lifted over the vessel's side, I was placed against the closed door of the deck cabin, facing the wondering crew of the ' Rattlesnake.'

" The captain took his revolvers from his belt, examined them carefully, supplied the place of the two charges he had fired off on board the brigatine, and then, measuring off fifteen paces from

WORK OF THE WRECKERS.

ne spot on which I was placed, wheeled and faced me.

"'You know, my lads,' he said, addressing his crew, 'that I never boast of what I cannot do. You have heard me say I was a good pistol-shot; now I mean to prove it. I have twelve shots here. Now, you shall say where you will have me put them; the first that speaks shall be attended to, and so on in turn. For every shot I miss, I promise a glass of grog to every man of you; but I give you my word that you stand a poor chance of getting drunk at my expense."

"'Captain,' said the one-eyed boatswain of the pirate, 'put me a ball through his starboard flipper—the one that flung the hatchet at ye—to begin with.'

"Good,' said the captain, with a grim smile.

And he deliberately raised his pistol.

"Motionless as a statue, and as pale—for I was but a man—I awaited the terrible ordeal to which I was subjected. The pirate captain levelled his arm, and drew the trigger. The cap snapped.

"'Hurrah!' cried the boatswain, with an oath. 'It's the captain's treat.'

"'How so?" asked Brandon, with lowering brow.

"'A snap's as good as a shot," said the boatswain.

"'Is that so, gentlemen?' asked Brandon, appealing to the crew.

"A unanimous and thundering 'ay' decided the case against the popular commander.

"'The steward shall pay the fine when the shooting is over. Who speaks for the next shot?'

"'I do,' said the carpenter. 'Douse his starboard glim 'or him.'

"'The right eye, eh?' Here goes, then!'

"Again was the pistol levelled at me. But, at this breathless moment, the boy Eugene walked into the line of fire.

"'Out of the way, Eugene!' cried the captain, angrily.

"But the boy folded his arms, and faced the captain without moving.

"'How is this?' asked Brandon. 'What does this mean?'

"'It means,' answered the boy, 'that I have something of the utmost importance to say to you. Leave this sport for awhile—let the men have their grog—and grant me a few words.'

"The red colour rose to the captain's swarthy cheeks, and the red fire glittered in his serpent-eyes for a moment; but, letting down the hammer of his pistol, he thrust it back into his belt, and motioned the boy aside.

"'Now, then, what means this folly?' asked the captain, sternly.

"'I have a boon to ask of you, Paul,' was the reply.

"'What is it?'

"'The life of that brave young man.'

"'Of the man who sought my life?'

"'Had you fallen, I would have avenged you, and then died of a broken heart. But, though the weapon was aimed at your life, you must admit that the deed was a brave one.'

"'Was ever caprice like this?' muttered the captain. 'But it is like a woman.'

"'And you may well wonder,' said the other, 'that any womanly feeling can have survived in this floating pandemonium. Oh! how different a life from what I pictured in the romantic dreams of my youth, when I left all, father and mother, and followed you.'

"'You repent it, do you?'

"'The woman who loves truly never repents. It is only when I see you sink to the level of the fiends who follow that my blood curdles in my veins. I have stood beside you in action—but then your foes struck at you red-handed; but to see you murder a pinioned prisoner in cold blood is more than I can endure. It is unworthy of your manhood. Hardened and degraded as I am, I cannot bear it.'

"'But, suppose I deny your suit, my pretty minion?'

"The girl unsheathed a dagger, which she wore in her belt, and directed it to her heart.

"'I will sheath my dagger here, and end my shame and misery together.'

"'Hold!' cried the pirate captain. 'Put up that toy. I command you.'

"'Command!' said the girl, haughtily.

"'Implore you, then,' said Brandon, in a softer tone.

"The poignard was hastily returned to its sheath.

"'What if I make you a present of this fellow's life—what would you do with him? The crew will demand some punishment.'

"'Set him adrift in a boat. His offence was committed against you—not them: they cannot murmur at a commutation of his sentence.'

"'Let me hear the dogs murmur at anything I decree!' said the captain. 'Well, then, I spare the fellow's life.'

"'A thousand—thousand thanks—not for his life, but for the proof that you have given me that you still love me.'

"'Love you, Eugenie! Never doubt that!' said the corsair. 'In this dark heart there is at least one virtue—loyalty to my lady-love. Come, you shall see with what a good grace I yield to you. Unbind this man,' unbind this man.'

"Wondering, but not daring to murmur, two of the crew, leaving their liquor, which had just been served out to them, obeyed the captain's command, and I stood unshackled on the deck of the rover.

"In the same brief, peremptory tone, Brandon next proceeded to order a boat to be lowered, and oars, biscuit and water to be placed in her.

"'Here, then, young man,' he said, as he led me to the vessel's side, 'we part company. There is your only chance for life.'

"I looked at the threatening sky and rolling deep, but said nothing.

"'I wish you luck,' said the pirate, 'for I bear you no malice. Give me your hand.'

"But I drew back

"'I cannot clasp that hand,' I said.

"'Be it so,' said the pirate, haughtily. 'You have your way of thinking—I mine. Circumstances make men. Had you been in mine, you might have been this day what I am. Adieu! we may never meet again.'

"'If we do,' I said, 'I give you fair warning. We meet as enemies.'

"'Defiant to the last,' said the pirate, with a smile.'

"I dropped into the boat and took the oars. The captain and Eugenie watched the frail craft from the quarter-deck, till it was a blurred spectre on the face of the great deep. After drifting about for many hours, I was picked up by you, Captain Latour, and the kindness I experienced at your hands, led me to respect you as much as I condemned Brandon. After a great deal of hesitation, I resolved to join you, as I had neither friends nor means of starting again in the position I held on board the Volant; having lost all, and as I saw that although a pirate you could still be a man, the little qualms of conscience I experienced at first soon died out, and I believe, captain, I am as good a pirate as any on board, but I must protest against cold-blooded murder of helpless prisoners."

Latour winced at this last remark.

The pirate's mind reverted to Henry.

But the shade of displeasure soon passed away as he thought, "at least, my act has not killed him."

"You see," remarked Bilton, "that it is seldom that pirates can be merciful. Their own safety demands often the blood of those whom chance has thrown in their way. Every man's hand is against the pirate, and his own, must to a certain extent, be against them."

"Still," said Latour, who like most men who have sunk low in the scale of honour and rectitude, "piracy is not so bad as slave catching. Bad laws make men pirates. Injustice drove me to run up the black flag, and wage war with all the world."

"I'd rather be a pirate than a slaver," said Linton. "We get hard knocks, and stand a chance of being turned off at the yard arm, but a slaver only kidnaps or buys a lot of poor ignorant devils who can't help themselves, and if he should get overhauled, he escapes with the loss of his slaves or his ship. It's only cowards who take to that trade."

"They meet with rough work sometimes," said Harris. "I was once on board one, and the captain was killed by one of the slaves he had purchased."

"Tell us all about it," said Latour.

"Just pass the brandy first, captain," said Harris, "and when I've moistened my throat I will do so."

The brandy was passed across the table, and

Harris, after filling and nearly emptying his tumbler, said—

"It was a bright moonlight night, I recollect, when the little vessel I sailed in lay off the coast of Whictaion, Lower Guinea, with her sails flopping lazily against the mast.

"Among the slaves the captain had purchased that day were two young stalwart men, brothers, one some four or five years older than the other. On their way to the vessel, the elder brother managed to release his arms from the cords which bound them, and also succeeded in releasing his brother, when, watching an opportunity, they made for the woods. They were immediately missed, and the captain and several of his crew started in pursuit of them. The younger brother escaped, but the eldest fell into their hands.

"So desperately did he struggle with his captors, that one of them was seriously injured before they could succeed in binding his arms and legs. The captain was so exasperated at the injury the sailor had received, that he gave orders to his men to form a gallows and hang the black upon the spot. This order was obeyed, and in a short time the poor wretch was suspended by the neck as a warning to the African never to try to escape from the vengeance of the white man.

"A few hours later, the crew had turned into their berths, only one man being left, as watch, on deck, and he, overcome by the excessive heat of the day, was slumbering at his post. Not a sound was to be heard but the plashing of the waters against the vessel's side, the flapping of the sails against the mast, or the creak of the cable, as she rose and fell gently upon the bosom of the waters.

"A dark object was floating towards the ship, but so silently that had it been seen by the watch he would scarcely have suspected it to have been anything worthy of notice. On it came until it had gained the side of the vessel, and there became stationary for a few moments, then silently floated towards the cable, two black arms grasped the chain, and then the body of a black man rose out of the water, crawled along the cable, and climbed on to the deck.

"Slowly he crept towards the cabin—his foot was upon the first step, when a voice demanded—

"'Who's there!'

"The black turned quickly, and encountered the sailor who had been slumbering at his post. He uttered no sound, but sprang upon the seaman and grasped him by the throat. In vain the man struggled to release himself, the black's grip only became tighter. Shortly the sailor's muscles relaxed, and the black lowered him gently and insensible to the deck.

"The African then crept stealthily down the cabin stairs, and placed his hand upon the fastening of a door; it yielded to his touch, and he stood within the cabin. By the light of a lamp, which hung suspended from the roof, every object was to be seen distinctly. He approached a couch on which a form reposed, and the contortions of his features were fearful; but in an instant he started back in surprise. It was not the form of the captain, whose life he sought, that lie on the couch before him, but that of a young girl of some ten or twelve years of age. The captain's cabin was upon the opposite side of the stairs, and the one he had entered was devoted to his daughter, who had accompanied him on his present voyage.

"The African stood for a moment irresolute, then, as a sudden thought seemed to strike him, he sprang to the couch, tore off the coverlet, grasped the form of the young girl in his arms, and rushed from the cabin, up the stairs to the deck.

The child, thus rudely awakened from her sleep, uttered a piercing shriek which awoke her father, who instantly leaped from his couch, and rushed to his daughter's cabin. As he did so, he caught sight of the retreating black, with the form of the child in his arms. He seized a pistol, rushed up the ladder, and, in an instant, stood on the deck.

The African, at this moment, was at the vessel's side, and perceiving the captain, who was attired only in his shirt and drawers, he uttered a cry of defiance, and plunged over the side, with his burden, into the sea.

The captain raised the pistol and fired, but the next moment he saw the black making towards the shore with the child.

By this time several of the crew were on deck, aroused by the report of the pistol, and the cries of the young girl.

"'Man the boats!' almost shrieked the captain. 'Fifty guineas to the man who saves my child!'

"The men wanted no second bidding. In a few minutes more the boats were launched and manned, and sweeping over the waters in pursuit of the African and his captive.

"But although they plied their oars quickly they were unable to overtake the black, who gained the shore, but some distance down the stream from the spot where he had intended landing. The place where he went ashore was a rock, whose rugged side was washed by the waves. To clamber up this rock was a work of some difficulty, and by the time he had gained its summit, which was some seventy feet above the water, his pursuers were at its base. The captain too had put off from his vessel and stood with his hands clasped in the bows of the boat which came rapidly to shore.

"'Climb the rock,' he shouted to his men' 'and wrest her from him.'

"The men commenced to ascend its rugged sides, and the captain, leaping from the boat, cheered them on. But ere they got two thirds of the way up the African exclaimed as he held the young girl at arm's length—

"'White man, you have killed my brother, this is my revenge.'

"As he spoke he hurled the child over the rocks into the rushing waters beneath.

"The captain uttered a cry of horror and sprang madly upwards until he stood face to face with the black,

"'Hell-hound!' he shrieked, as he seized the African by the throat.

"Fierce and deadly was the struggle which now ensued. The captain was a powerful man, but the black, what he lost in strength, made up for in suppleness of limbs. The crew stood as it were paralysed for the time, watching the fearful contortions of the combatants, as they writhed and twisted in each other's grasp. Nearer and nearer the edge of the rock they strangled, until they stood upon its very edge, and then both dropped over its side.

"With a wild cry, the seamen rushed down the sides of the rock to its base, and there discovered the mangled bodies of the slave captain and the young African, locked in each other's embrace.

"Both were dead.

"The child was never seen after the African had hurled her from the top of the rock. It was supposed that her head came in contact with some of its rugged portions, and that she sunk never to rise again.

With heavy hearts, the crew returned to their vessel, and the next day we sailed from the shores of Africa with our living freight.

"I could not but think the fate the captain met with," continued Harris, "was well merited, and I resolved to forsake the vessel the moment she entered the port with here unnatural freight."

"And did you," asked Bilton.

"Yes, and after knocking about for some time, I was thrown into the company of Captain Latour and agreed to serve under him, and here I am, and here I trust I shall be for many a long day."

"Then you don't repent joining us," said Latour.

"Not a bit of it, captain, I was a little bit nervous at first, but I soon got over that."

"Nervous," said Latour with a laugh, "well that's a feeling that I never experienced."

"Well, some cannot help the feeling," said Bilton, "I have felt it very often, but have soon overcome it, but there are some who never conquer it till reason has left them."

"Not much chance of getting over it then I reckon," said Latour.

"You recollect Crazy Joe, don't you," said Bilton.

"I should rather think I did," replied Latour, "we lost a good man when he fell, struck down by a bullet at my side."

"Who was he captain," said Harris—"what made him crazy."

"Why you see, his friends sent him to sea when he was about fourteen, and, unfortunately for him, he was placed under a captain, whose strictness and cruelty was hardly ever equalled, and at the slightest hesitation of man or boy to obey an order, he brought the cat into requisition.

"Now Joe always hesitated to go aloft, but, by the captain's orders, was forcibly put in the main rigging, and then a boatswain's mate was commanded to lash him like a dog until he learned to run aloft. The poor fellow's legs and arm trembled, he grasped the shrouds—he cried—he prayed the inhuman captain for God's sake to have mercy on him; but all in vain. The boatswain's mate was ordered to lay on harder and harder, regardless of the boy's piercing screams, which made even veteran seamen turn from the brutal scene with disgust. His clothes were rent from his back, the blood followed the lash, and still the tyrant roared out, 'Lay on, boatswain's mate!' With one wild scream he spang from under the lash, and bounded up the rigging with amazing rapidity. He doubled the futtock rigging like a cat, passed up the topmast and topgallant rigging with undiminished speed, shinned the unrattled royal rigging, and perched himself like a bird alongside of the pennant which streamed from the masthead.

"Here he paused, looking fearlessly upon the deck below. All hands came up to see him—his cries and cruel treatment had already enlisted their sympathy, and, if possible, had increased their hatred of the captain.

"The monster was smiling complacently at the success of his experiment; he was one of those tyrants who boasted that the cat, properly applied, could make men do anything. Still he was apprehensive that the boy might destroy himself, and the circumstance be used against him at the Admiralty, where he knew representations of his cruelty had already been made. The men gazed in silence, looking first at the boy and then at the captain, who was seated near the taffrail. They dared not be seen speaking to one another—it

was a flogging offence; even at night spies passed under their hammocks to ascertain if they whispered. The officers walked the lee side of the quarter-deck, occasionally casting their eyes aloft, but were as silent as the men.

Still the boy clung to the masthead, playing with the pennant, apparently unconscious of the interest he excited below. Tired with gazing aloft, the captain sung out, through the speaking-trumpet—

"'Down from aloft; Down?'

"The boy sprang upon the truck at a bound, and raising himself erect, waved his cap around his head; then, stretching his arms out, gave a wild, laughing scream, and thew himself forward.

"The captain started to his feet, expecting to see the boy dashed to pieces on the deck; but when clear of the shade of the sails, he saw him sliding along the main royal stay towards the foretop-gallant masthead, and heard him laugh and chatter like a monkey, as if enjoying the sport. He reached the masthead in safety, and then descended along the top-gallant back-stay hand-over-hand.

"The captain looked at him, and was about to speak, but could not find words. The boy frothed at the mouth and nose; his eyes seemed starting out of his head; he rolled upon the deck in convulsions, staining it with the blood which still trickled from his back. He was a maniac. The surgeon's skill in the course of a few weeks restored his bodily health, but not his reason.

"From that time forward he was fearless. In the darkest night, the fiercest gale, he would scamper along the deck like a dog, and bound aloft with a speed no one on board could equal. He would run over the yards without holding, pass from mast to mast on the stays, ascend and descend by the leeches of the sails, and run upon the studding-sail booms. He was nimble as a cat, and had forgotten fear. Some of the light duties aloft he learned to discharge in company with the men—he did as they did, but could not be trusted to do anything himself. One order he always obeyed without hesitation. At the command, 'Away aloft,' he was off, and never paused until he reached the mast head.

"As he was harmless, and rarely spoke, the captain kept him on board, and, in the course of a year, sent him aloft for amusement. His strength increased with his years, but his bulk and height remained nearly the same at eighteen as when he became a maniac.

"His ribs, breast, and back seemed one case of bone, and his sinews and muscles made his legs and arms appear like pillared columns. He was fair, with light blue eyes, and delicate skin; his face oval and full, but void of expression—neither love, fear, revenge, or pleasure could be traced in its stolid outline. His eyes stared at everything without appearing to see, and, when he spoke, there was rarely any meaning in his words. He followed the men in their various duties like a dog following his master.

"Whenever he was struck or started by a boatswain's mate, he ran up the main rigging, screaming at the top of his lungs, and never paused till he had performed the first evolution which had made him a maniac.

"The ship arrived at Plymouth to be docked and refitted. The captain, availing himself of the leisure, was going to be married, and the news was communicated by his servant to the cook, who soon circulated it on the berth-deck among the men, who cursed his and all his kin.

"His servant came on board of the hulk where

the men were lodged, the evening when the captain was to be married. Crazy Joe (the name the boy was known by) met him at the gangway, and asked intelligently if the captain would be married that evening, and where ? The servant gave him the information he desired and went about his business.

"That night, whilst undressing, the captain was seized by the throat, and dragged to the bridal-bed.

"Look, fair lady, on me," said Crazy Joe, "but do not scream, or I will kill you. Look on me. I hold within my grasp a devil, who delights in cruelty—a merciless fiend, who has scourged the backs of hundreds of brave men—a ruffian, who has robbed me of my reason; I hold him within the grasp of death, at the very moment his black soul thought itself within the reach of bliss. Monster! look upon your lady—think a moment of the heaven of earthly joy almost within your reach—then think of me, poor Crazy Joe ! and of the future to which I send you ! Die, wretch—die ! "

"When the alarm was given, the strangled body of the captain was found lying alongside of the bridal-bed; but the maniac who killed him was never recognised afterwards. He belonged to Cornwall, and found shelter from pursuit in the mines until the excitement passed away.

"The lady stated at the time, and many years afterwards, that the attack of the maniac was so sudden and silent, that she knew nothing of it until the curtains were pushed aside, and she felt the pressure of the captain's body bent over the edge of the bed. Joe held his victim around the neck with the right hand, and turned him from side to side as easily as if he had been a child, while the forefinger and thumb of the left hand grasped her own throat, ready to extinguish her life if she attempted to raise an alarm.

"His face was pale and death-like, his eyes started but were motionless, and every word he uttered seemed to issue from the very depths of his soul. The captain's looks were terrible beyond description —death left the impress of ferocity upon his darkened features. How the maniac entered or left the room she never knew ; his departure was as noiseless as his entrance. So paralyzed was she with fear, that an hour elapsed before she could muster courage to call for help; but she thanked God, when the captain's cruel character became generally known ashore, that she had been rescued from his alliance.

"Some time after this I fell in with him, and he joined us, and proved as good a man as ever walked the deck, but he fell, poor fellow, while interposing his own body to save mine, and I don't think I ever felt so much grief before in my life as when we consigned his body to the waves, for though reason had left him, his bravery was undoubted, and he would have sacrificed the last drop of blood in his veins to save any one who could give him a kind word."

CHAPTER LXVI.

THE FIGHT IN THE CABIN.—THE CAPTIVES TRI-
UMPHANT.—THE SMUGGLERS MADE PRIZE.

A FEW moments passed, moments of anxiety and suspense to the trio in the cabin of the vessel, which the Boy Rover had made his own by deeds of violence and bloodshed.

Not a muscle of their faces relaxed.

Not an eye was withdrawn from the panels of the door.

And each, with his upraised weapon stood with body bent forward and determination fixed on their features, ready for the first appearance of the smugglers.

They had not long to wait.

The door was unfastened and thrust quickly open.

Simultaneously Henry, Jacob, and Mr. Hanfield sprang forward, and brought down their weapons with all their force upon the party outside.

So sudden was the onslaught, that the three smugglers staggered from the effects of the blows they had received.

Black Bill was sent reeling backwards till his further progress was stayed by the panelling of the opposite cabin.

Jem and Sam were more fortunate, though both had been struck, the start they had given on seeing the prisoners armed to attack them, saved their skulls, and the well-intended blows fell wide of their mark, and in a moment they recovered, sprang forward, and Jem, clasping Jacob in his arms, rolled with him on to the floor.

Sam soon disarmed Mr. Hanfield, and turned his weapon upon Henry, and a combat with the legs of the dismembered stool was quickly the result.

Black Bill soon recovered, and pulling himself together, as he termed it, he rushed forward to assist his companions.

Striking Mr. Hanfield a heavy blow on the forehead, he sent the old gentleman reeling across the cabin, but received in return a blow between the eyes from the fist of Henry, which caused them to emit a volley of sparks like the bursting of a sky-rocket.

Meantime Jacob and Jem rolled over and over each other, striking and kicking in their endeavours each to beat the other.

In their struggles, Jacob managed to seize hold of the only remaining leg of the dismembered stool, and grasping it firmly, raised it above his head, and delivered such a crushing blow upon the forehead of the smuggler with the seat, that Jem released his hold of the serving man, and fell back senseless.

To leap to his feet was the work of a moment, and again poising his weapon in the air, Jacob sent Sam rolling on to the floor bleeding profusely.

The quick eye of Black Bill saw the state of affairs in an instant, and feeling that he had no chance with the three captives, he rushed for the door.

But ere he reached it, a blow from Henry caused him to stagger, and before he could recover himself, Jacob struck him on the back of the head, and down he went.

Then the three captives looked at each other.

A sigh of relief escaped the breasts of each.

One half of the smuggler crew were defeated.

They had but three to cope with now.

"So far, so good," said Jacob. "What is the best move now ? "

"To endeavour to surprise and overthrow the remainder," said Henry. "We are now man to man, but delay is dangerous, these rascals may soon recover."

"Perhaps I had better give them a finishing touch," said Jacob, raising the broken stool.

"Hold ! " said Mr. Hanfield. "It would be murder."

Jacob lowered his weapon.

"Let us rush upon deck," said Henry, "before they are prepared for us. I do not think they have heard the affray, and we may take them unawares."

"So we may," said Jacob.

"Leave the captain to me," continued Henry. "We have an account to settle."

"Be it as you wish," said Jacob.

"Come then," said Henry.

He moved towards the door.

Jacob and his master followed.

They listened a moment.

But there was no sounds to intimate that those on deck knew what had taken place below.

Henry commenced to ascend, followed closely by Jacob.

Mr. Hanfield brought up the rear.

The Boy Rover was leaning over the taffrail, gazing moodily into the sea.

He saw not the arrival on deck of Henry.

The brave young lieutenant pointed out the man at the wheel to Jacob, and rushed forward to the Boy Rover.

Suddenly the smuggler captain turned towards him.

A loud cry from the man at the wheel had broken the reverie into which he had fallen.

It was a cry of pain.

The wretch had given utterance to it upon receiving a stunning blow upon the head from Jacob's weapon.

The Boy Rover started back upon seeing Henry, and strove to open the long Spanish knife he wore at his belt.

But ere he could accomplish this, Henry sprang upon him.

The Rover raised his arm to ward off the blow aimed at his head, and the knife was dashed from his grasp.

Jacob sprang forward and possessed himself of it, and instantly buried it in the breast of the remaining smuggler, who, also aroused by the cry of the steersman, had leapt to his feet.

With a howl of pain, the Boy Rover flew at the throat of the young officer, who, dropping the *** of the stool, grasped the smuggler, and strove to hurl him to the deck.

But this was no easy task.

The Boy Rover was a powerful youth, and Jacob sprang to his side and raised the knife.

"Hold," exclaimed Henry, "I command you hold."

"He shall not escape," said Jacob,

"Leave him to me," said Henry, as placing his leg behind the smuggler, he threw his whole weight upon him, and hurled him backwards. Over and over they rolled along the deck, but Henry succeeded in getting his fingers round the neck of the smuggler, and finally pinning him to the deck.

"A rope—a rope," exclaimed Henry, "Quick—quick."

Jacob seized a piece of rope and threw it round the legs of the Rover.

This he tied securely.

In another moment his arms were bound, and Henry releasing his hold, rose to his feet, and wiped the perspiration from his brow, with the sleeve of his shirt.

Not one word did the Boy Rover speak.

But the glare of his eye was fearful. He foamed at the mouth, and ground his teeth in furious rage.

But he was powerless, and the three men stood gazing in triumph upon him.

"The ship is ours," said Henry, after a pause.

"He is secure now, let us bind the others before they recover.

"And throw them overboard," said Jacob.

"No," replied Henry, "hand them over to the first vessel we meet with, to be conveyed to prison."

"That is right," said Mr. Hanfield, "the laws they have outraged will then be vindicated."

"Better save all unnecessary trouble," said Jacob.

"Vengeance is not for us, said Mr. Hanfield.

Jacob shrugged his shoulders.

He thought they might as well send them overboard, and thus get rid of them at once.

But he was overruled.

In a short time, the smugglers were all rendered powerless, by being bound with cords.

Then they were carried one after the other below.

The Boy Rover was the last taken down, and when they laid him beside his companions in crime, he spoke for the first time.

"You triumph now," he hissed between his clenched teeth, but beware yet of the vengeance of the Boy Rover."

Henry only replied with a look of contempt.

"So young, and yet so brave," remarked Mr. Hanfield.

"You may well say that, Mr. Hanfield," remarked Henry.

The bound Rover started at the mention of his name.

"Hanfield," he exclaimed.

"Yes, Hanfield is my name," replied the old gentleman.

"Of Gibraltar."

"Yes."

"Then the resemblance is no lie," murmured the Rover.

"What mean you," asked the old man, in some surprise.

"Mean," said the Boy Rover, "Ha, ha, ha, you have me now in your power, but I will wring your heart, old man, and turn your smiles to tears. You have a daughter, young and beautiful."

"I have," replied Hanfield, "and pure and innocent as the new born babe."

"It's a lie," exclaimed the Rover, "she has—

"What?"

"Fallen."

"Fallen."

"Aye, now, do I triumph," exclaimed the Boy Rover, as he saw the pallor which overspread the face of the old man.

"What mean you?"

"That she is innocent no longer," said the Rover.

"Villain, have you dared"—

"I have."

"Heaven's curses rest on your soul," exclaimed the father, passionately, then he exclaimed sorrowfully, "My poor, poor child."

A look of pleasure passed over the face of the Rover, as he saw the anguish his words had caused the old man.

"Liar!" exclaimed Henry, "she is yet as pure as ere she fell into your accursed power, you have dared to assail her honour, but you have not triumphed."

"But another has," said the Boy Rover, in freezing tones.

"Who."

"Latour, the pirate," said the Rover.

"She would never yield," exclaimed Henry. "My soul upon it, she never would."

A scornful smile played around the mouth of the Rover.

"Accursed dog!" exclaimed Hanfield. "But you, at least, shall pay dearly for your villany. Justice shall deal with you. The laws you have outraged shall yet be avenged."

"Justice holds me not in her power," said the Rover.

"But she soon shall."

"I will find means to baulk both that and you," said the Boy Rover, in cool calm tones.

"We will prevent you," said Harry.

"Come sir, leave him with his own worthless companions and his own bad conscience."

And taking the arm of the old man, Henry led Mr. Hanfield from the hold followed by the faithful Jacob.

The sea was calm and the air still, and the ship glided slowly over the waves.

Henry cast his eyes aloft and around him, then turned them upon his companions faces.

"Night will soon come on, but there is every prospect of this calm continuing, I am glad to see, and doubtless we shall fall in with some ship ere long."

"I trust we may," said Mr. Hanfield, "for should we be overtaken by foul weather, it would go hard with both us and the vessel."

"Indeed it would," said Henry.

"Especially as there is only yourself to work her," remarked Jacob.

"I wish we could assist him," said Mr. Hanfield.

"We will place our trust in providence, sir," said Harry, "and hope for the best."

Night came on.

Still the ship glided over the waters, the only object on the dancing waves.

The smugglers, who had now one and all recovered the effects of the blows they had received, lie bound chafing in the hold, swearing and cursing at their ill-fortune, and blaming themselves for not having prevented their present position by putting their captives to death when the vessel of the pirate hove in sight, and vowed if ever they escaped, to be less merciful for the future.

CHAPTER LXVII.

THE NIGHT WATCH.—THE STORY OF THE WRECKER BOY.

THE bright stars were reflected in the now almost motionless waste of waters, and the hum of the blue sea had subsided to a monotonous hum, when Jacob stretched himself on a cot in the cabin and courted the favours of the drowsy god.

Henry, on whom the whole working of the vessel had devolved, stood at the wheel guiding the motions of the ship, and taking his bearings from the star-spangled heavens.

By his side stood Mr. Hanfield, lost in thought, and with his eye gazing on vacancy and his mind lost to all around him.

He was thinking of his child—his beautiful Ellen, and muttering an inward prayer for her safety and honour.

The trio had arranged that one should rest and two should watch alternately, till succour should arrive, and to Jacob was consigned the morning watch, whilst Henry and Mr. Hanfield kept a look out through the darkness.

The young lieutenant ever and anon fixed his eyes upon the thoughtful face of his companion.

He guessed the subject of his thoughts, and endeavoured to arouse him from their melancholy influence.

"I fear we shall never meet again," said Mr. Hanfield, in answer to a few words of consolation spoken by his companion.

"Hope for the best, sir," said Henry. "The ways of providence are wonderful, friends long parted are often thrown together again after years of parting. But I trust that your daughter may again be clasped in your arms ere long."

"Alas, I fear not. The villanous hands into which she has fallen, make me feel I have gazed the last upon her on earth."

And seating himself, the poor old man buried his face in his hands, and trembled with the excess of the emotions his daughter's uncertain fate conjured up in his breast.

Tired and exhausted as the young lieutenant was, he felt that he must arouse the father of Ellen from the state into which he had fallen, and he tasked his mind to do so.

"Cheer up, sir, cheer up," he said. "Give not way to despair. You will yet meet again."

"In heaven we shall," said Mr. Hanfield. "On earth, I feel, never. Had she not have fallen into the hands of those cursed pirates, smugglers, wreckers, or whatever they be, I might still hope."

"Hope on then," said Henry, "I have met with one after a parting of thirteen years, was cast by the hand of providence, into the hands of his father. Like your daughter, he was thrown upon the rocks of the cornish coast."

"But fell into the hands of friends, then not enemies," remarked Hanfield, with a sigh.

"It is seldom that in the hour of adversity, but we meet a friend somewhere—there is a silver lining to the dark clouds—why should there not be in your case, or that of your daughter's."

"Alas, I know not, but I fear the worst, but this meeting, who and what was it?"

Henry saw that the old gentleman's curiosity was aroused, and wishing to draw him from the apathy into which he feared he would sink, he said—

"I will tell you how this youth, after a lapse of so many years, met with one, of whose existence, he knew not, and as the years of parting were passed on the very coast where your daughter and her affianced husband were wrecked, through the machination of the accursed smugglers and wreckers, whom we have this day overcome, it may interest you and lead you to hope for the best."

Henry cast another long glance across the ocean and then turning to his companion, remarked—

"Of the time between the wreck of the vessel, which placed him in the hands of the wreckers, till the day on which he so strangely met with his parent, I know nothing, and I only give you the events of the day and night on which providence so strangely restored him to the arms of one who had long believed him dead."

And easing the vessel half a point, Henry commenced his story of the Wrecker Boy.

"By the seaside, on a high cliff, which formed part of a long reach of rocky coast, stood Maurice—a lad of some fourteen or fifteen years, he was a stout, handsome youth, with more thought and manliness in his bearing than is common to that age.

"His dark eyes scanned the waste of rolling waters with a calm, steady, melancholy gaze, as, leaning upon an oar, a net which he had been repairing at his feet, he awaited the approach of a boat which was rounding a headland some three miles distant.

"He was attired in a fisherman's garb, and as the ribbon from his tarpaulin hat, and the red scarf about the half-exposed throat, fluttered in the breeze, he stood a picture of humble and unconscious grace, such as an artist's eye would have delighted to dwell upon.

"Behind him, at the distance of about a quarter of a mile, stood a number of rude fishermen's huts some hundred rods apart, and before the doors of some of them the fishers or rather wreckers—for such they were—were busily engaged repairing their fishing-tackle, or otherwise providing for the equipment of their boats.

"'Ronald is coming,' said one of them, 'for see, Maurice is making the sign to us. Rely upon it, he sees a storm in the wind's eye as well as we do. Heaven send us a good wreck this time! The last was all work and worry, and little profit.'

"'The devil send you a wreck, you mean!' at this moment interposed a rude, weather-beaten, hard-visaged woman, who was standing in the doorway of one of the cottages, and had been watching Maurice with interest long before he made the sign. 'You don't flatter yourself that heaven has anything to do with your murdering and robbing the poor, helpless castaways, whom the less cruel sea surrenders to your clutches, do you?'

"'How now, old woman?' returned the wrecker who had spoken; 'what has stirred you up this morning? You must have got out of the wrong side of the bed—eh? How should we live except by knocking the brains out of those who were half-dead already, as they were washed ashore? Our lives are as good as theirs, and we're not going to starve. If they don't want to be killed, they mustn't come ashore, and cheat the sea of its due. Let 'em drown! What we get, we'll have.'

"'You'll have a rope round your neck one of these days, and I shall live to see it,' retorted the woman. 'I only hope poor Maurice may never learn to do as you have done.'

"'Oh! let Maurice alone,' said one of the wreckers; 'he'll be the very prince of wreckers yet, if you don't make a weak fool of him with your nonsense. He's nigh as strong as a man already, and there's not a better hand among us with a boat. He pulled me from the undertow, the last stormy night we had, when I thought nothing could save me. And nobody else would have risked it but him. Perhaps it may be in my power to do *him* a service some day. If so, I'll do it at any sacrifice, as sure as my name's Bob Hammer.'

"'And as sure's my name's Joe Darby,' said the one who had first spoken, 'if Roland don't do better by me than he has done the last three or four times, in sharing, I'll take what proportion I earn, come what may. I won't be fooled any longer with his captaincy and his equal divisions —not I!'

"And he took a huge chew of tobacco to fortify and give emphasis to his resolution.

"'Ha, ha!' laughed the woman.

"'Don't laugh at me!' fiercely exclaimed Darby.

"'Ha, ha!' repeated she; 'you will if you can, Joe Darby—not without. Both my husband Ronald and you are brutes, sure enough; but, as he is the bigger brute, he'll have his own way, I reckon.'

"And, without another word, she went into the hut, Darby still muttering to himself.

"'Here comes the captain, with Maurice,' said Hammer, as the twain were seen leaving the cliff's edge. 'It's blowing a stiff breeze already, and those clouds tell us there'll be work to-night.'

At the appearance of Ronald Marksley, seven or eight men from the various huts of the group were seen hastening towards his house, where, on their arrival, a conference was had regarding his disposal of the common stock of plunder, the tidings from the neighbouring town, preparations for the storm, torches, etc., etc.; and, after half-an-hour's talk, the breeze, meanwhile, having increased to a strong gale, and the rain pouring in torrents.

"'Why do you act so mysteriously, mother?' asked Maurice of Dame Marksley later in the day, as she beckoned him, with significant looks, from the apartment where her husband lay asleep, stretched upon the floor. 'What is it you would say to me?'

"'Maurice, my boy, long have I wished to disclose to you an important secret, but fear of him, and the thought that it might do no good, prevented me. But he treats me like a slave, and so I wish that you may not follow in the bloody track of these dreadful men, that I will reveal it to you—and may God turn your knowledge to good account. Maurice, you are not our son.'

"'Is it possible?' exclaimed he, starting and turning white. 'What, are you not my mother?'

"'Hush! Ronald may feign sleep and overhear,' replied she, with her finger on her lips. 'You are the sole surviver of a ship which was wrecked on yonder shore when you were about four years old. You, too, would have been murdered, as was he in whose arms you were washed ashore by a mighty wave, had I not stayed Ronald's ruthless arm, after he had given the finishing touch to the unhappy man who had folded you to his breast to save you or perish with you. Yielding to my prayers, he consented to let you live, and adopt you as our son. Whether the murdered man was your father, I know not; but certain it is you are not our child, and I thank God that you are not. I tell you this, my lad, that you may turn with loathing from the bloody ways of these relentless monsters, who fatten upon misery, and who take a mortal's life with as little compunction as they would hook a fish. Keep this secret, Maurice, and while you stay with us, do all you can to save, instead of taking life. Be a saviour, instead of a destroyer, and by every safe means thwart the assassins in their dark hours of cowardly pillage. So God will prosper you, and his vengeance, which will surely light upon them, will be averted from your head.'

"'I will save all I can hereafter,' replied the wrecker boy, gravely. 'I never liked their ways and have never harmed a castaway. But oh, this news makes me feel so strangely. I don't know whether to feel glad about it or not. You don't think,' he added, earnestly, pressing her arm, 'that it is my father that he murdered—do you?'

"'Perhaps not, my boy—perhaps not. I remember his face; I don't think he looked like you.'

"'Oh, I hope it wasn't. But then, even if he were not my father, perhaps my father was on board, and then—then,—and he burst into tears and sobs—' he must have died at any rate.'

"'Here, Maurice! Run over to Bob Hammer's and ask him if my knife is ready. He was to put a new handle on, and sharpen it. Be spry.'

These words proceeded from Marksley in the room, he having just awoke.

"The forlorn wrecker-boy brushed away his tears hastily, and went upon the errand—his heart heavier than it had ever been before.

DEATH OF LATOUR, THE PIRATE.

"He now felt alone in the world—and amid such associations!'

"As night came on, the sky became changed with furious clouds, and there was a mighty moan which swept across the black ocean, seeming like the noise of some monster of the waters yawning for his human prey.

"The vaulting billows appeared to leap in fiendish gladness to the clouds, which were preparing food for them, and their white crests smiled in anticipation; while their steady rolling, irresistible gush as they swayed along together, sounded like whispers of the fury which was to come.

"Awful was the voluminous gloom of the waste of dark and billowy hills; awful the Cimmerian canopy which made earth and ocean cower beneath its frown and portentous sigh.

"'Oh!' he thought, 'who are on the deep today?'

"'Will they reach their port or their doom tonight, or struggle triumphant through an open sea?'

"'How many thousand prayers are offered for them!'

"'Will they be answered by Him who poured the flood, or shall they be as fruitless as the seabird's cry?'

"The league of wreckers—some eight or ten, sworn solemnly to stand by each other in secrecy to the death—were prepared to answer such a question in their own way.

"For many miles, the coast, of which they were the hunting demons, presented no point upon which, should a vessel be driven there, there was the most remote chance of escape from ship-wreck.

"Many were the stout ships which had dashed to pieces on the dread shore, the terror of the mariner, and the delight of the ravenous fish and ocean-fowl, and of the wreckers, more savage than they.

"'Oh! this is a glorious bluster, men,' exclaimed the remorseless Marksley, as they assembled on the cliff just as day went down, with sad face, behind the veil of heaven, as if hiding in grief for the wretchedness which was impending. 'And see!—four—five—seven ships in the offing. We shall be the most luckless dogs alive if some of them are not ours.'

"Repairing to a boat-house on the beach, the party, of whom Maurice and Mrs. Marksley were members, with provisions for a rude lunch, and with bludgeons, knives, etc., awaited the expected sounds of distress — signal-guns booming, or lights glaring, over that mighty graveyard.

"Nor had they long to wait.

"A gun was heard—the sound muffled by the roaring waves—and the men sprang to their feet, and went forth upon the rocky shore to watch.

"Other guns, nearer and nearer, were fired in rapid succession, and a light was seen not more than a mile from the frowning shore.

"'Poor wretches—God have mercy on them!' ejaculated Mrs. Marksley, who had remained in the boat-house with Maurice.

"Tears started into the wrecker boy's eyes, for he thought of all she had told him that day, and had brooded, ever since, over the probable fate of his father.

"The old woman continued:

"'Wind and wave are driving them directly on these accursed rocks. There's not the slightest hope for them. Merciful hands might save a few, but they would as well fall into the tiger's clutches as among these. Better that they should drown at once.'

"The wreckers had kindled a bonfire—sad misnomer—on the shore, as if in sign that friendly aid might be expected; and the helpless vessel, a ship of large size—all management of her having finally been abandoned as useless—drove headlong upon the rocks, horrible cries of despair mingling with the noises of the storm, as she went to pieces in the dark.

"'Maurice, you may have a chance to-night to do God and man service,' said Dame Marksley, hurriedly, as they prepared to go forth. 'If you do, lose it not. Thwart the demons if you can. Remember your own wrongs, and should you see a struggle going on, give aid to the unfortunates, not to our men—not even to Ronald, should he be in peril of his life. I will be at your side to direct you.'

"'I will do as you say,' said Maurice firmly, "as surely as I hope to see my father in heaven, where, you have taught me I can never reach, should I shed blood of any human creature. On, my poor father!'

"They stepped forth from the boat-house into the wild scene of darkness, danger, and death.

"The crash of broken timbers mingled with the roar of the elements and the cries for help.

"The surging waves answered with relentless dashing, and engulphed many a hapless wretch for ever.

"'They are about it. Look, Maurice—they are dashing the brains out of those men yonder. And see! Ronald is struggling beyond, with one of those who are washed on shore. If we have not strength

let us use craft. If he prevails, let us try what art will do to save the man. Come.'

"The two hastened to the place where, stumbling and struggling among the rocks, sometimes knee deep in the breakers, Ronald and the stranger tugged for life.

"The latter proved a match for his antagonist, despite the exhaustion resulting from the shipwreck.

"'Here, Maurice, Helen, help!' cried the wrecker chief as his strength began to fail him.

"Maurice ran to the stranger, and fastening about his neck, exclaimed in his ear—

"'Fall, friend! fall, and I will save you. Fall!'

"Whether the man believed, or whether his feet slipped at that moment on the sea-weed which mantled the rocks beneath his feet, the desire of Maurice was gratified—he did fall: and Maurice, as if by accident, stumbled between the legs of Marksley with such force, as to pitch him headlong upon the sharp rocks, where a wave rolled over him, bruised and bleeding by the fall.

"'Blundering fool! Is this the way you aid me?' were the first words which escaped the lips of the enraged and baffled wrecker, as, pretending to be anxious for his safety, Maurice hauled him roughly away from his adversary up the beach. 'Where is he?' he added, looking round in the darkness for his opponent in vain.

"'I saw a heavy wave roll back with him into the sea,' said Dame Marksley. 'It's all over with him by this time.'

"'Are you there, Helen?' exclaimed Marksley, feeling for her. 'I would you had been here in time to have hit him with a bludgeon. But we shall find his body, I suppose. Where's Maurice?'

"Maurice had suddenly disappeared; through all the excitement of the scene, he had not lost sight of the stranger, and had now gone to his relief.

"The man was scrambling, exhausted, up the rocky acclivity slowly on hands and knees, when, just as Maurice put forth his hand to assist him, a broad and awful mountain wave thundered over them both.

"Quick as thought, the hardy wrecker boy sprang forward and fell, clutching with an iron gripe the rocks on which he lay prostrate.

"The retiring wave left him there; but not so fortunate was the stranger.

"He had been borne back into the trough of the sea.

"Maurice sprang up, and at this juncture Bob Hammer came along with a coil of rope which he had found, upon his shoulder.

"'Is that you, Bob?'

"'Ay, ay, my hearty—how goes it?'

"'Bob, I saved your life once,' said Maurice, hurriedly. 'Now return the favour. You see that man. I'll hold the rope. Fasten it round you and plunge. Quick, or it will be too late.'

"'I'll do it, my lad, if it costs me my life.' And in less time than it takes to relate it, the grateful wrecker bounded forward into the yawning, death-fraught element, white with the hissing foam.

"'Hold hard, boy, and I'll save him,' gurgled Bob Hammer; and rising on the top of the billow he disappeared behind it.

"The huge hill of water rolled forward and fell, bathing the legs of Maurice, to whose aid was lent the strength of some mighty stones, behind which he had taken foothold.

"And now, by the dim light of the distant torches on the shore, Maurice saw two dark objects floating in the trough of the sea.

"He heard a faint, bubbling cry—that of a

'strong swimmer in his agony'—and knew that it was a signal for him to haul; and with all his might he did so, but the burden, and the force and weight of the waters would have proved too much for him had he not fortunately been aided at this crisis by the timely arrival of Dame Marksley.

"'Pull; pull! or they'll drown—pull!' cried Maurice, panting with fatigue and excitement, and the wrecker's wife bent to the task, and her sinewy arms were exerted to good purpose. A rising wave assisted their last efforts, and brought the rescued twain high up the rocks, several feet beyond them.

"'Whew!' sputtered the woman, as, drenched by the billow, and with her mouth full of salt water she scrambled up from the awkward position into which she had been thrown, 'that was the biggest wave of to-night.'

"'Bob,' cried Maurice, running to him, 'how do you feel?'

"'Well enough, only a little out of breath.'

"'Will you do me another favour?'

"'Yes, a hundred!'

"'Then help me to carry this man to a place of safety; any nook high up in the rocks will do, and keep this a secret; this man must not die.'

"'Not if he bean't dead already, you mean.'

"The man lay motionless where the wave had left him.

"'We'll see how that is; but let us be quick, or we may be seen by the captain.' And they lifted the insensible man along to a more secure place, while Mrs. Marksley repaired to where the other wreckers were busy securing their plunder, as the waves gave it to them; ever and anon giving a fatal rap on the head of some half-drowned creature, that the morning might bring no disputants for their prize.

"When Maurice disappeared, Marksley, taking it for granted that his late adversary was drowned, had hurried toward that part of the beach where the most of his men were engaged, and on the way he ran against Joe Darby, whom he found busy rifling the pockets of a corpse which had been flung ashore.

"'Ha! are you there, Darby? A prize, eh?'

"'Ay, and a rich one, too; and mine, mark you, mine, all mine. No shares in this, you may be sure of that.' And Darby held up a gold watch and chain, and a large and apparently well-stuffed leather pocket-book, dripping with brine. 'Who knows but there's a fortune there?'

"'If there is, or whatever there is, it will be shared equally among us.' insisted Marksley.

"'Will it, though?' sneered Darby, about to stow it away.

"'Ay, will it!' quickly returned Marksley, enraged at this dishonest braving of a compact which he had sworn to observe; 'and this—and he adroitly snatched it as he spoke—'this to make sure of it.'

"In the next instant they were engaged in a deadly embrace.

"Mutual hatred so absorbed them, that while they grappled they would have been engulfed by the breakers had they not suddenly been parted by three or four of their comrades, who came up crying.

"'Boat, boat. Wreckers ahoy.'

"A boat, bottom upwards, to whose keel clung half a dozen men, was on the point of being hurled ashore, and the wreckers were desirous of mustering all their strength at that point, that not one should escape to tell the tale of that awful night.

"'Fighting among ourselves. For shame, Let's look to the boat first,' exclaimed the remorseless villains. 'Let us attend to their welfare, and then, when they're sent home, fight after, if we please. Hurry.'

"The combatants desisted, and all sped to the spot whereon the boat was now cast, like a toy, by the mighty sea.

"It had evidently come from some vessel which had foundered, since otherwise no boat would have ventured to try that wrathful waste of billows, and miraculous indeed was their preservation thus far.

"The wreckers, with murderous intent, had grouped together to make short work of those whom the hand of God had protected; and just as the boat dashed with a thundering shock upon the dark beach, Dame Marksley arrived, and seeing how matters stood, hastily collected such sticks as she could find, which might be used as weapons, designing them for the shipwrecked strangers, should they be so fortunate as to be able to wield them.

"'Now, men,' shouted Marksley, 'death to all,' And they brandished their clubs, as the helpless men were jolted, sprawling among the surf-boiling rocks.

"'Death to you, first,' at this instant shouted Joe Darby.

"And he plunged a dirk deep in the side of his unsuspecting leader, who turned upon him, the blade still sticking between his ribs.

"Thus two of the wreckers were prevented from at once pouncing upon their intended prey, and the odds in number were now made about equal.

"The renewed strife between Marksley and Darby so disconcerted the others of the gang as greatly to paralyse their efforts, and ere a blow was struck, four of the strangers were on their feet and were armed and warned by the resolute Dame Marksley: and at this juncture, Maurice providentially appeared with Bob Hammer, and together they dragged the remaining two from the surf, just as they were being swept back into the roaring, tumultuous waters.

"Blindly obedient to the wrecker boy, in fulfilment of his gratitude, Bob Hammer sided with the strangers, Maurice and he each lending them a knife; and when the onset came, the wreckers met with a stout and most unexpected opposition.

"Their leader, still contending with his implacable foe, Joe Darby, rolled with him beneath their slippery feet, scarce minded by them in their new-born apprehensions for their own lives.

"'Take that, traitor!' said one of them, dealing a deadly blow at Bob Hammer, as he was found arrayed against them.

"'Thank you, I'd rather not,' expertly dodging the unfriendly manifestation?' and the force of the blow, spent upon the air, precipitated the giver headlong among rocks and seaweed.

"'Take this with my compliments, Pete Wyvil,—and it's the last you will ever want, I hope,' said Bob, bringing down a crashing blow which fractured the fellow's scull.

"The conflict was now general, and as fierce as may be imagined among men striving for life.

"Though much exhausted by the struggles with the waves, the men who had just escaped shipwreck—the value of the life, and the hope of it having now grown stronger and dearer than ever—became inspired with a new energy, which made them equal to the fearful occasion. And they were doubly encouraged at finding friends in the midst of their dastardly enemies.

"The wrecker boy moved in the thickest of the conflict—which was waged by the solitary glare of a torch, stuck in the rocks a few rods higher up the shore—like a sprite, dashing in where he could render assistance to the strangers, and ever and anon dealing a serviceable stroke upon the arm or head of some wrecker at the very moment when he imagined victory secure.

"Deep and ferocious were the curses heaped upon him, upon the old woman, and on Bob Hammer, by the baffled, panting, bruised, and bleeding wreckers, as they found themselves forced finally to yield, step by step, and to fly before their desperate opponents, leaving three of their number dead and horribly mutilated upon the resounding beach.

"'Victory!' shouted Bob Hammer, as the last of his late comrades fled up the cliff, or along the shore. 'Victory! Maurice, my lad, I never felt the joy of doing a good action as I do now.'

"You did nobly, Bob, and I hope this will be our last occasion to do anything like it throughout our lives. But see, friends," added the wrecker boy, as the strangers gathered round their preservers, tendering them their thanks in half-exhausted accents—'who are those coming this way with lights?'

"'More enemies!' exclaimed some, grasping their weapons with what remaining strength they had.

"'No, no—you are mistaken,' said the wrecker boy; 'they are people from the town. You will find no more fiends to deal with.'

"He was right.

"In a few moments a crowd of men arrived, and, learning the story of the affray—having been attracted to the beach by the signal guns that had been fired long before—they attended the exhausted participants in that terrible struggle up the cliffs to the habitations of the wreckers, all of which were now deserted, save by their wives and children.

"Among these was not forgotten he with whom Marksley had first striven that night.

"He was found still stretched motionless on the spot where he had been left; but Maurice, as he bent anxiously over him, perceived with joy symptoms of returning consciousness.

"When morning broke, the golden sun shed not more light upon the brightening sea than did the news which enraptured the soul of the wrecker boy.

"In the stranger he had first been the means of rescuing, he found—his father; learning from his lips the strange tidings that he, with a few others, had alone escaped the wreck which thirteen years before had sent, as he had thought, all other of his fellow-voyagers to eternity, including his brother and his infant son. That brother had died by the hand of Marksley.

"Explanations on both sides were now followed by a vigorous pursuit of the old offenders, who had been for years 'unwhipt of justice,' the terror of the coast, no evidence before having been positive against them.

"Some escaped, and the remainder, though murder could not be proved upon them, were condemned to expiate their crimes in prison.

"Against Bob Hammer no proceeding was made—the story of his services on that thrilling night making him the object of general sympathy and applause.

"But where was Marksley and his brother murderer and plunderer, Joe Darby?

"On the ensuing morn, when, beneath the smile of the refreshing sun the subsiding ocean danced in silver, and search was made for the victims of the storm and of the fight, a dark mass was seen floating not far from the shore, rolling slowly towards it.

"The anxious searchers waited till it came within reach, and then pulled it from the reluctant serf.

"It was found to be the dead bodies of Marksley and Darby, fast locked in each other's arms.

"The waters had evidently been their winding-sheet, as they had fallen in the death-grapple.

"They, and the other wreckers who had been slain, were buried on the shore they had so long contaminated.

CHAPTER LXVIII.

CHARLES IS TAKEN ON BOARD A FRIGATE—ELLEN IS PUT ON SHORE BY THE PIRATE—THE FIGHT—DEATH OF LATOUR—BLOWING UP OF THE VESSEL.

THE shades of night were fast gathering over the sea and o'ershrouding in darkness the white sails of the vessel which our hero and the noble-minded hunter watched from the cliff which bounded the ocean, and shut out from the view of a passing vessel the luxuriant country behind them.

The frail little bark, as it danced over the billows with the hopeful lover of the fair Ellen, had been seen by those on board, and signals had been exchanged between them.

The ship had altered her course and bore down upon the boat, but her commander, well knowing the danger of hugging a rock-bound shore, used the utmost caution.

As the twilight deepened, and the ship became more dim, the heart of Charles beat anxiously; a fear took possession of his heart that the vessel might lose sight of him in the darkness, and that he might lose the present opportunity of again walking the deck of a well-armed ship.

For as she came nearer and nearer the young midshipman had no doubt as to her character.

She was a British frigate!

But as the shade deepened the vessel showed a blue light.

Charles strove his utmost, by paddling with his hands to guide the boat towards the ship.

The sea was comparatively smooth, and the little vessel, obedient to the touch, glided over the waters.

A boat was now lowered from the vessel, and was propelled over the undulating waves by the willing hands of British seamen.

Oh! how the heart of the young sailor bounded with joy as the boats touched each other.

There was music in the sound as they grated their sides together, for our hero felt that he was safe.

He stepped into the ship's boat and was hastily pulled to the vessel.

As he stepped on to her deck a feeling of pride and joy took possession of his breast, and as he cast his eyes aloft at the flag which for ages has braved the battle and the breeze, a tear dimmed his eyes, and his frame seemed to be nerved with fresh strength.

Proudly he looked back to the cliff he had so short a time before left, and as he did so he perceived a bright flash, and the crack of a musket sounded over the waves and died away in echoing cadence.

Charles sighed.

He felt that it was his friend the hunter wishing him farewell, and making him acquainted with the fact that he knew he was safe.

Being ushered into the captain's cabin, our hero gave the commander of the frigate an explanation of how and by what means he came upon the sea as he was found by those on board; and upon being introduced to the other officers he found among them one young man with whom he had previously sailed as middy.

The recognition was mutual—the greeting warm; and Charles and his now found friend retired together to the latter's cabin, where an hour was spent in conversation respecting the adventures of Charles, when he retired to rest; and the next morning accepted a post in the vessel, which was on a cruise in search of the pirate Latour.

The doings of this man had awakened the government to the necessity of driving him from the seas, and the 'Swallow' frigate was sent in search of him.

From passing vessels the route of the pirate had been learned, and Captain Perry was now keeping a sharp look out, as he knew the famous pirate could not be far away.

Thus two days passed, when early on the third morning after Charles had been taken on board, a vessel was sighted by the look-out.

As the day wore on, and she loomed up larger and larger, till her build could be made out by the aid of the glass, Captain Perry gave orders to clear for action, as he doubted not that the vessel was the Spirit of the Wave, and commanded by that daring freebooter, Captain Latour.

The ship was soon cleared, and every stitch of canvas set to give chase, lest the vessel should endeavour to fly.

But there was no need for this last, as Latour would have scorned to fly from before a seventy-four.

The pirate was a brave man, and at his back fought as brave a crew as ever sailed the salt waters.

But as the time wore on, the Spirit of the Wave, for such indeed was the vessel, changed her course, and made for a small island at a few leagues distance.

"She will show us a clean pair of heels I fear now," said the captain, turning to our hero, who stood watching the movements of the pirate by the commander's side.

"It would seem that such is her intention," replied Charles.

Had Charles have known the pirate's intention, how would his heart have beaten.

But he knew it not, and was cool and collected as ever.

When Latour discovered the vessel to be a frigate he resolved to fight her, and had every thing made ready for that purpose, but wishing that Ellen should be found on board, he resolved to run to an island a few leagues hence, and there place her on shore, when he would turn and meet his rapidly advancing foe.

The Spirit of the Wave was a good sailor, for such purpose had she been built, and Latour doubted not that he could soon destroy his adversary, but he scorned to fly for other reasons than that which we have stated.

The frigate was no mean sailor, and with her masts bending like reeds before the wind, she careened through the waves in pursuit of the buccaneer.

But the "Spirit of the Wave" gradually placed greater distance between them, and by nightfall was scarcely visible.

Biting his lips with vexation, the commander of the frigate retired from the deck, giving strict orders to continue the chase through the night.

And over the moonlit sea her sails bellied by the breeze, and her masts bending under the strain of canvas, and her hull creaking from the pressure, the Swallow dashed over the waves in pursuit.

Meantime Latour gained the island, and when he had ventured as near as prudence dictated, he entered the cabin in which Ellen sat.

"Lady," he said, advancing towards her and taking her thin white hand within his own, "I am here to keep the promise made to you, that of placing you on shore.

A look of pleasure beamed from the eyes of the maiden.

"Now," she said.

"Even now," replied Latour, "I would fain have placed you on shore in some more inhabited spot, and where you might have easily found means of again rejoining your friends, but I may not be enabled to do so. We are pursued by a heavily armed vessel, and though I would scorn to run from a fleet, I have turned tail for your sake. We are near a small island, I will place you safely on it, and leave you to the care of the hospitable inhabitants. Here," he added, drawing a well filled purse from his breast, "is money for your wants.

But Ellen put it from her.

"Tush," said the pirate, "on that island among strangers, what will you do without money; the rough inhabitants may be hospitable, but money will gain your desires. Take it, it will be needful and useful, it will support you and procure you a passage in the first trading vessel that touches here."

Ellen still hesitated, but the pirate thrust the purse into her hand and said—

"Come."

In a few moments they were upon deck.

The first gray streak of early dawn floated in the eastern horizon, and the air was cold and damp.

The island on which she was to be landed, rose sloping and grey up from the waves, and could just be discerned from the deck.

A shudder crept over the form of the poor girl, as she gazed over the bulwarks into the boat which had been launched to convey her to the shore.

Latour led her to the ladder, and then pressing her hand in his own, he said—

"Lady, you are now free—yonder you will meet with those who will give you every information how you may again meet your friends. If bad thoughts with regard to you have for a time usurped my mind, and bad passions have prompted me to do you wrong, they are for ever gone. I have been a bold bad man, but my heart is not all iron, your beauty softened it and I would not harm you. I know not how soon my time may come, perhaps ere to-morrow's dawn, Latour the pirate may lie at the bottom of this boundless ocean, for I have no mean enemy to cope with, and I now go forth to meet him, but whether I live or die will matter little to you. Go, and be happy, and should the name of Latour the pirate be heard by you, give him credit for having done one good act, and remember that he has one bright spot in his black and callous heart. Farewell!

The pirate handed her into the boat, and ere she

could give utterance to her thoughts he had turned away, and the boat shot out from the ship's side rapidly for the shore.

Like a thing of life it darted over the bright moonlit sea, and struck on the shingly beach.

"There you are," said one, as he held forth his hand to assist her from the boat, "keep on up the beach, and you'll find plenty of fisherman's huts.

And accepting the man's assistance, Ellen left the boat and stepped on to the sands.

Then the boat was pushed out again into the waves, and Ellen was left on the beach alone.

The murmuring of the slowly rolling waves was all that broke the silence around, as they washed up over her feet as she stood watching the retreating boat.

Behind her the beach went up to a few huts, evidently occupied by those who gained a livelihood by fishing around the island.

When the boat had regained the ship, and the vessel which had been put back for them, tacked and stood upon her course, Ellen turned and ascended the beach.

The increasing light began to reveal objects more distinctly to the gaze of the fair girl, and she bent her steps in the direction of a small wooden edifice erected on the top of the beach.

Meanwhile, the vessel commanded by Latour had turned to meet her pursuer.

The sun was rising in all its brilliancy when the vessels again came in sight of each other, and Latour bade all those of the crew, whom it was not necessary to remain for the working of the ship to seek what rest they could as he saw hard work before them.

Nearer and nearer the two vessels became to each other, and higher and higher they loomed as the day crept on.

Every preparation was made for a desperate combat on board of each, for both were heavily armed and well manned.

About midday the two vessels were within range of each other, and Latour opened fire with the long pivot gun amidships.

The ball struck the frigate, but the distance being somewhat great, it did little injury.

The frigate now bore upon the pirate's bows, and discharged a broadside, which, but for the beautiful manner in which the pirate was made to answer her helm, would have proved anything but pleasant.

After striving for the best position, and each endeavouring to bring its guns to bear upon the other's bows, the fight became general, and the broadsides were poured from each vessel in quick succession.

Latour cared little for fighting at long distance, hand to hand was the game that he preferred, and therefore he kept nearing his adversary as fast as he could.

After several rounds had been fired, the battered hulls were brought alongside each other.

Latour well knew that his men could be trusted and prove as brave as any in boarding, and the grapnells having been thrown, the vessels firmly locked together, the order was given to board the frigate, Latour himself leading on the boarding party.

The crew of the frigate stood ready to repel the boarders, and a desperate conflict now raged.

Oaths and shrieks now mingled with the report of pistols and the clashing of steel, as the pirates strove to gain the frigate's deck, and the British sailors hurled them back upon their own.

"On—on, follow boy—follow!" rang clear and loud from the throat of the pirate captain as he urged his men on.

And leaping upon the bulwarks of the frigate he dealt death and destruction around him.

His heavy cutlass fell upon the heads and arms and bodies of the sailors, as they strove to drive him and his men back to the deck of his own vessel.

He had cleared a passage for himself, and was about to leap down on to the frigate's deck, when Charles drew a pistol and fired.

The bullet struck Latour in the forehead, the cutlass dropped from his hand, and he fell backwards into the space between the two vessels, which being rapidly closed by their bulwarks grating together, his body was crushed in a most frightful manner ere it fell with a loud splash into the waves.

With a loud cheer the crew of the frigate pressed forward, and drove the pirates back to their own decks.

The death of their captain had had more effect upon the crew of the pirate, than had the pikes and cutlasses of the man-of-war's men.

They were disheartened, and a panic seemed to have seized upon them.

But Bilton upon whom the command now devolved, leapt upon the bulwarks of the frigate, and waving his sword around his head cheered on the men.

"Death or victory!" he exclaimed, "remember we can neither give nor receive quarter. On then men, drive them beneath their hatches. On—on!"

The pirates rallied, but the fate of Latour had so depressing an effect upon them that they fought not with half their usual spirit.

Again were they driven back by the seamen of the frigate, whose duty it was to repel the boarders, and headed by Charles they swarmed on to the deck of the Spirit of the Wave.

Bilton and the other officers fought like demons and endeavoured all in their power to excite the men to imitate them.

Again the pirates drove the crew of the frigate over their bulwarks to the deck of their own vessel, the sides of which now poured with blood.

Many had fallen on either side, and the decks were slippery with gore.

But the voice of Charles urged the men on, and though they could not succeed in again gaining a footing on the deck of the pirate, they repelled all attempts of the pirates to board the frigate.

The pirates were fast becoming demoralised, and could not be brought to follow the orders of Bilton and the other officers, and without receiving any order for so doing, they cast off the grapnels, and the ships parted.

Foaming with rage, Bilton struck one of the men who done so, to the deck.

"Cowards," he exclaimed, "Can you only fight with women and unarmed men. Glad am I that Latour has not lived to see you run from a foe strong as yourselves. Will you surrender and swing at the yard arm?"

"We've no chance," said one of the men, "we are outnumbered and must be beaten."

"Then die like men, back to back—foot to foot—shoulder to shoulder."

"Run her aboard the frigate," he added, addressing the steersman.

"She won't answer her helm," said the man surlily.

And as he spoke a terrific broadside was poured into the hull of the pirate.

With such effect had been the aim, that the splinters flew about in all directions.

Two of the pirates were killed, and several received severe contusions from the pieces of timber knocked from the hull by the frigate's shot.

Then the frigate bore down upon them, firing again as she came, and raking the pirate fore and aft.

Bilton saw that the game was nearly played out; he felt convinced from the manner of the crew, that they had lost all their heart and that nothing could now save them from falling into the hands of the frigate, if she once more threw the grapnells on her.

He resolved never to surrender the vessel, for too well he knew a pirate's doom would be meted out to all who were taken prisoners.

The black flag floated defiantly at the mast head, and several of the crew called out for it to be lowered.

"Look you lads," exclaimed Bilton, "I have sailed and fought under that flag and under it I will die. Never shall the Spirit of the Wave strike to a British man-of-war. It has fluttered defiance to the world, and proudly and defiantly shall it sink with the shattered hull which has so long been the terror of the seas. A train is laid to the magazine, if we cannot conquer we can die, and ere an enemies' foot shall again press the deck of this vessel, I will blow her to hell, and her coward crew who fear to defend her!"

And darting swiftly down the hold Bilton was lost to sight.

The pirates knew that what he had threatened he would do, and several of them stepped forward to prevent him, but as they looked down they saw the bold man with the lighted match in his hand and became paralized.

A few of the sailors cut the lashings of the long boat, and succeeded in launching her.

A scramble took place to get into her, and their weapons were turned upon each other.

The desperation of fear now lent a strength to their arms which had it been used against their enemies would have told fearfully on them, and oaths, curses, and blows resounded on both sides.

Some few leaped into the boat, and then pushed off from the side of the ship, amid the yell of those left on board.

But their cries were soon drowned, with a rumbling noise and a fearful shaking of her timbers, the vessel trembled for a moment and then with a loud report her decks were lifted into the air.

A volley of flame and smoke shot upwards, and her hull parted.

The slightly rolling waves were lashed into a fury and beat over the wreck of the vessel.

And when the smoke had cleared away, the charred and blackened planks floated on the waves.

Bilton had fired the train, and the once dreaded Spirit of the Wave was no more.

CHAPTER LXIX.

THE PIRATES IN THE LONG BOAT AND WHAT BEFELL THEM.

THE long boat containing the few pirates which had escaped from the vessel ere her brave officer Bilton had fired the train which communicated with the magazine, had been pulled some distance from the ship ere she was blown into a thousand pieces and launched so many of her daring crew into eternity.

But distant as they were the shock nearly lifted the frail bark out of the water.

It had thrown two of the men forward on their faces, and the shaking which the boat received threatened all with destruction.

But she soon righted, and when after the shock they sufficiently recovered to look around them only one vessel met their gaze.

The pirate ship was no more, save and except the planks which were being tossed upon the bosom of the water.

Fearing pursuit from the frigate, they bent to their oars in the hope of avoiding falling into the hands of the frigate's crew.

Though they gazed anxiously expecting every moment to see boats coming in pursuit of them, not one appeared, and gradually they placed distance between themselves and the frigate.

The sun was now sinking, and ere long darkness would be upon the waters.

Black clouds were drifting up from the north, and hanging threateningly in the horizon.

A storm was brewing, and the eyes of the men were fixed anxiously upon the sky.

No longer could the frigate be seen, the fast coming darkness had shut her from their view.

In a short time the gale rose, and amid wind and rain the boat was dashed over the now furious waves.

All night long the boat buffed bravely with the billows, plunging her way through the darkness like a living thing, and seemed to defy the tempest.

Grey dawn found her flying before the gale, with no prospect of more quiet weather, for the wind was in the north-east, and rain and hail beat down upon her as though the windows of heaven were indeed opened.

All that day the storm lasted, yet the boat lived, and night changing the dim grey light to pitchy darkness brought no change, but sunrise brought some relief, and the men became more hopeful than they had been of falling in with some vessel or finding some shore on which they might land.

But the day passed on and night once more cast her sombre mantle over the seas.

There was a lull of the storm at sunrise, and a few hours afterward the sea became comparatively quiet. In an hour or two the storm was almost over, and before the day passed the sky began to clear, and the hearts of those in the little boat to grow light—all save Bill Gibbons.

As the day passed on they comforted each other by assurances that it could not last long now, and that the very length of time which had elapsed since the blowing up of the pirate should give them hope on an ocean where vessels sailed every day of the long year.

But faces grew wan as time passed on, and voices weak, and the hope faint; and when at last the long-diminished rations which they had secured dwindled to crumbs and sips, and Bill Gibbons made known the terrible fact that the bag contained but one biscuit, and that the cask was empty, despair seized upon them, and the blood-shot eyes, half-blinded by the sea spray and the searching wind, grew dull and leaden. Anxiety warded hunger off awhile, but her fangs were fixed upon their vitals at last, and turned them first into desponding imbeciles and then into wolves.

Food! food! food! This was all the cry, all the thought. A crust, a bone, a piece of raw, tainted flesh—anything to eat. Bill Gibbons could have torn a living thing to pieces, and sucked its blood with joy. A young officer clutched the boat's side with his one hand and had s range thoughts of horrible feasts which sickened, even while they tempted him. And then Bill Gibbons saw dancing before his eyes rare viands, exchanged strange glances with the young officer, and felt at a knife stuck in his belt. The knife with which he had served the rations, as though he had some horrible food in contemplation.

But man predominated over wolf as yet, and they waited.

For what ?—all knew, but none gave utterance to the words. The restless hand played upon the knife-handle. If no one died soon it would be made use of as it had never been before.

One died about an hour after this, and the eyes of the other four were fixed with a strange glance upon the corpse, but the officer thrust it over the side of the boat into the sea with a shudder.

But the pangs of hunger were gnawing at their vitals and gradually driving them mad.

During the day another sickened and died, and he like the previous one was thrust over the side of the boat.

But the eyes of Bill Gibbons followed the body till it disappeared, and his hand played nervously with his knife.

Three now remained, and the fearful gleam of their eyes, as they rested upon each others countenance told too plainly their thoughts.

Thus time wore on, when suddenly Bill Gibbons started hurriedly to his feet, his dagger flashed for a moment above his head, and then descended to the haft in the heart of one of his companions.

"We must have food or die," he exclaimed, turning to the officer, "it is prepared, come."

And in another moment their lips were glued to the wound as the red blood spurted forth, and they drank of it greedily.

Starvation had maddened them, and they feasted horribly.

In an hour from the completion of the hideous banquet, Bill Gibbons and the young pirate officer were raving maniacs. They shouted, yelled, cursed, howled. All the horrors of insanity came upon them, and in their mad fury they grasped each other by the throat and rolled over the side of the boat into the sea, and sank never to rise till the day of judgment.

CHAPTER LXX.

THE SEARCH FOR THE BODIES OF THE PIRATES. — THE CHARRED FORM ON A SPAR.—CHARLES LEARNS THE FATE OF ELLEN.

AFTER the first shock caused by the daring act of Bilton, which had sent the once defiant Spirit of the Wave into a thousand fragments, and strewed the waves around for some distance with the charred and blackened remains of the vessel, and the numerous articles which she contained, the commander of the frigate, with that impulse which ever prompts the British sailor to succour and to save even those who have turned the deadly steel against their hearts, ordered the boats to be launched and manned, and every effort made to save any of the pirate crew who might have escaped the fearful explosion.

The sailors obeyed the command as soon as issued with an alacrity that spoke well for the noble feelings that found a home in their breasts.

A few minutes before they strove to kill those whom now they as willingly went forth to save.

Charles was the first to leap into a boat of which he took the command, and ordering the men to pull to the spot where the Spirit of the Wave had gone to pieces, he scanned the space around in the hopes of seeing some of the crew of the pirate, to whom he might extend a helping hand.

The huge timbers of the once noble vessel, were tossing about on the crests of the billows, and ever and anon hurled against the sides of the frigate's boat, so thickly was the space around strewed with the blackened debris of the ill-fated ship that it was with the greatest difficulty Charles succeeded in guiding his boat safely among them.

But no human being met his sight for some time.

It was after he had determined to give up the search as hopeless, and had commanded the men to pull for the frigate, that an object flung as it were across a spar caught his gaze as it rose and fell upon the waves a short distance from the boat on the larboard side.

Pointing it out to the men he bade them pull for it, and the long strokes of the men-of-war's men soon took the boat alongside of it.

It proved to be the form of a man, but so disfigured as to render it impossible to distinguish the features.

The hair was all burnt from the head and face, which was charred and blackened, and the shirt and vest had been partially burnt, revealing the chest blackened as the face.

Charles could distinguish that he was an officer by the portion of dress which remained uninjured.

He placed his hand upon his heart to discover if any pulsation remained, and found that his heart still beat.

Our hero had him placed in the boat, and then gave order to pull for the frigate.

The men bent to the oars with a will, and the craft darted over the waves with rapid strides.

They were not long in reaching the frigate, when the blackened form of the pirate was handed as tenderly up to the deck as if he had been a sick child in the hands of a tender nurse.

Detested as was the name of pirate by the British sailors, they felt no small commiseration for the charred and blackened wretch whom Charles had found drifting on a spar amid the debris of the pirate vessel, and tenderly he was borne below, and the surgeon summoned for the duties he was performing to those of his own vessel, to attend to the stranger and the pirate.

But after an examination of the blackened form of the pirate, the doctor shook his head ominously.

"What do you think of him sir," asked Charles, who stood by the side of the surgeon, gazing pitifully upon the burned man.

"There is no hope of his recovery, Mr. Lawson, not the least."

At these words the man opened his eyes, and fixed them intently upon the doctor and the youth.

"That name," he said, "Lawson."

"That is my name," replied the youth in surprise. "What is yours, for I grieve to say that it is impossible to recognize your features."

"Mine is Bilton," gasped the man.

"Bilton, I have never heard it before that I am aware of," said the youth thoughtfully.

"You have heard of Latour," again grasped the sufferer.

"I have."

"It was your hand that slew him," said the pirate, you fired the fatal shot that sent his soul to the other world."

"Was that Latour," asked Charles.

"It was—but your name is Lawson—Charles Lawson—is it so ?"

"It is," replied our hero.

"Then" gasped the man with difficulty, "stoop down, there," he added, as the youth bent over him, "You love Ellen Hanfield."

"Ah !" exclaimed the youth, "what of her—speak—speak."

"She lives."

"Yes—yes."

THE SLAVER IN SIGHT.

"And is safe," gasped Bilton. "She fell into the hands of Satan; but he harmed her not."

"Where — where is she?" exclaimed Charles, eagerly. "I feared she was in the hands of the Boy Rover."

"No; Latour placed her on shore, when your ship came in sight."

"Where—where?"

"On the island. Oh! I cannot see you. Stoop lower. I—I—"

"Where — what island? Speak, in mercy's name!" gasped Charles, bending his head down, till his ear laid almost on the lips of the dying man.

But Bilton answered not.

"Speak, I conjure you," pleaded the youth.

"Ah! cowards," exclaimed Bilton, raising himself on to his elbow, and glaring wildly around—won't you fight? Then I blow the ship to hell, Ha, ha! 'tis done, and a pirate's doom shall never be ours. Ha, ha!"

His head fell back—he was dead!

The spirit of the brave man had fled to the footstool of his maker, there to render an account of his fearful life, and receive the punishment of those crimes which, by his daring acts, he had failed to receive at the hands of human justice.

Charles bent over him with a look of pity in his handsome countenance: pirate though Bilton was, still he was a man, and our hero could but feel how sad was the fate of one who had evidently borne in his nature the stamp of all that ennobles the human mind—but his talents and bravery had been prostituted to a wicked life, and he died as he had lived, defiant to the last.

CHAPTER LXXI.

HENRY ON THE LOOK OUT — A SAIL — THE BOY ROVER AND HIS COMPANIONS PLACED ON BOARD A MERCHANT SHIP AS PRISONERS.

THE night wore away; and Mr. Hanfield, worn out, sank down upon a bulk-head, and slept, leaving Henry to his work at the wheel, and the thoughts which usurped his breast.

Day broke; the white fleecy clouds gradually chased the sombre pall of night from the scene, and the first rays of the glorious sun shot athwart the heavens.

Higher and broader it rose—tinting the white-crested billows with hues of golden brightness, and giving a fairy-like lustre to their crested tops, as they rolled and sported against the hull of the ship, to leap backwards again into the waste of waters—myriads of globules, of various hues.

Higher and higher, brighter and brighter, till a sea of red spread over the horizon. Then, in the midst, rose the large round red orb, which, as time advanced, changed his colour to golden yellow—becoming smaller and smaller in its disc—and the red streaks faded away before its refulgent brightness.

Now the white sails gleamed in the bright sunlight, and the eyes of the young lieutenant became heavy, and he longed for rest.

Jacob had risen from his couch, attired himself, and made his way on to the deck.

The gorgeous scene rivetted his attention for a time, and he was lost in wonder and admiration.

He turned to where his master lie sleeping, and placed his hand upon his shoulder.

The old gentleman awoke at the touch, and, starting to his feet, shuddered with cold.

The night air had struck into his frame.

"Retire now to your couch, sir," said Henry, "whilst myself and Jacob work the vessel."

"You must need rest," said Hanfield, addressing the young officer. Cannot me and Jacob remain on deck, while you seek a few hours' repose? I have been a sorry companion; but, worn out with fatigue and anxiety, my eyelids closed ere I myself knew it."

"No," replied Henry. "I am young and strong, and better stand the fatigue than yourself. Besides, I am used to the sea, which you are not; and, while I sleep, we may lose the opportunity of meeting with a passing vessel, as, should one appear in sight, you will scarce know how to steer this bark towards her."

"But you need rest," said Jacob.

"I could not rest," replied the young sailor; "at least for the present. You, sir, seek your cot for a few hours; then I will turn in.

Mr. Hanfield saw that it would be useless to persuade Henry further; so, shaking the youth by the hand, the old gentleman turned, and descended to the cabin.

"Jacob," said the young sailor, after Mr. Hanfield had gone below, "take the wheel, and keep her thus, while I run aloft, and take a survey."

Jacob took the wheel, and Henry darted up the rigging with the agility of a cat.

Mounting to the cross-trees, he viewed the horizon.

An exclamation escaped his lips. It was an exclamation of joy.

There was a speck on the horizon: a speck like a small black cloud, rising from the sea.

But the experienced eye of the young sailor knew what this was.

It was a vessel. It was hope.

He congratulated himself that he had not yielded to the solicitation of Mr. Hanfield to seek rest; for he felt, had he done so, this chance of succour would have been lost.

And doubtless he was right.

Neither Jacob nor his master would have discovered a ship in that small black speck.

Even had it met their gaze they would have taken no notice of it.

The day wore on, and the vessel which Henry had sighted from the mast-head loomed up larger and larger, till her build could be distinctly made out by the young officer, and he discovered her to be a merchant vessel.

Hoisting signals, she bore down upon them, and towards evening sent a boat alongside.

Henry explained to those in the boat that he wished to speak with the captain of their vessel, but could not leave the ship, as there were only two others to work it, and two out of the three knew nothing of the handling of a ship.

The merchantman which had laid back her topsail to await the return of the boat, was communicated with by signals from the men who had charge of the boat, who furled more sail as the boat sped back to the vessel.

Mr. Hanfield, who had been now some time on deck, Jacob, and Henry watched the boat reach the side of the vessel, and anxiously awaited her return with the captain.

In the course of a few minutes they perceived the figure of that officer enter the boat, and the little craft was urged once more towards them.

She was soon alongside, and a gentlemanly-looking man made his way on to the deck beside Henry, who saluted him respectfully.

"You have requested my presence on board your vessel," said the captain of the merchantman; "may I ask the cause?"

"I had done myself the honour, sir, of waiting upon you, had I been enabled to do so, but in truth myself and this gentleman and his servant are all that are here to work the ship."

"Where are the remainder of your crew—have they deserted?"

"No, sir, the crew of this vessel have been foully murdered."

"Murdered!"

"Even so."

"By whom?"

"By the Boy Rover and some of his followers."

"Ah, the Boy Rover, the Smuggler of the South Seas. I have heard of him often, but never met with him."

"You can soon do so, sir."

"How?"

"He is a prisoner in the hold of this vessel," said Henry.

"Here—in this ship?"

"Yes, sir, here."

"But is this his vessel?"

"No."

"Then how came he here a prisoner?" asked the captain.

"You must know, sir," said Henry, "that this gentleman and his servant took passage in this vessel from Gibraltar to England. A raft was made out, upon which were six persons, and the captain brought them off and did all that he could to assuage the sufferings of the men, whom he believed to have been wrecked in the storm which swept over the ocean on the day previous. In the night they rose and murdered the captain and the crew, leaving only these gentlemen, whom they intended should walk the plank, but a sail coming in sight, their execution was deferred. On board that vessel which had prevented the murder of my friends here, I myself was a prisoner, and doomed to walk the plank, because I refused to join the crew who were pirates. The ceremony was performed on myself, but I was rescued from the waves by the Boy Rover, who had taken possession of this ship, and placed in confinement with the doomed men. It was no act of mercy which prompted the smuggler to save me from a watery grave, but one which would gratify his revenge, for we had met before, and he owed me much ill-will for having protected a lady whom he had carried away, and who, strange to say, is none other than this gentleman's daughter. Knowing well that a fearful doom was intended for us, we resolved to protect and defend ourselves to the last, and when three of the crew entered the cabin where we were confined, we overpowered and made them prisoners. The Boy Rover, ignorant of what had occurred below, we surprised on deck, and now have them all safely secured in the hold."

The captain listened intently to the explanation, and when Henry had finished, he asked—

"What do you require of me?"

"That you take these men on board your vessel and hand them over to the authorities of the first port you enter."

"Your request shall be granted," said the captain.

"And I would beg the assistance of a few of your crew to navigate this ship into port.'

The captain thought a moment, and then replied—

"Willingly would I send you a few men on board for that purpose, but I am short-handed myself, no less than four of the crew being on the sick list."

"I should be sorry to abandon this ship," said Henry.

"We must avoid the necessity of that," replied the captain, "but the utmost I could spare would be one man."

"If he be a practical seaman," said Henry, "I doubt not with the aid of my friends here, and by our keeping in company, I can succeed in taking this vessel into port."

"Then let it be so," replied the captain, "you shall have the man, and I will take your prisoners on board."

"I thank you."

"And every true sailor should thank you for the benefit you have conferred upon mercantile profession, by having made prisoner this terror of the seas. I will take them on board and put them in irons."

Then leaning over the bulwarks he orders one half of the crew in the boat to come on deck to assist in removing the Boy Rover and his companions to the boat.

The Boy Rover and his companions were brought up from the hold.

With a look of hatred and defiance he stood before Henry and the captain.

"You will be removed to yon vessel," said Henry, addressing the young smuggler, for the better keeping of yourself and bloodthirsty companions, and will be placed in the hands of justice when she arrives in port."

A scornful smile curled the lip of the smuggler, and drawing himself proudly up, he suffered himself to be led to the side.

Then he turned and addressing Henry, exclaimed—

"We have met before and we shall meet again—beware of the vengeance of the Boy Rover."

Henry turned scornfully away.

Then turning to Hanfield the smuggler said—

"And so shall we meet again, for there is something here tells me my hand must be at thy throat. You triumph now—but beware, my turn will come.'

He then relapsed into silence and was launched over the side into the boat together with his two companions.

"Guard them well and pull for the ship," said the captain, addressing his crew, "then return for the other three.

"Aye, aye, sir," responded the sailors as they pushed off.

In the course of half-an-hour the boat returned, when the others were placed in it, and the captain of the merchantman also entered to be conveyed to his own vessel.

A noble looking seaman was left on board, and the two vessels set sail in company for England.

CHAPTER LXXII.

ELLEN AT THE FISHERMAN'S HUT.—THE ROBBERY.

COLD and damp struck the morning air into the thinly clad frame of the Beautiful Ellen, as with the purse which Latour had forced upon her pressed between her fingers, she made her way up the beach towards the hut.

Cheerless and desolate in the grey light of the early dawn looked the few rude habitations towards which she wended her way.

She sighed on the thought of her wretched fate, and wondered when her troubles and sufferings would end.

She was free now from the power of the Boy Rover and the pirate Latour—free, but in a place where she was a stranger, and where everything bore indications of unworthiness and wretchedness.

Arriving at a small hut, which stood overlooking the sea, she paused and listened for any sound that might indicate that its inhabitants were stirring.

But no sound came to her ears, and she hesitated to make her presence known.

But the cold dews struck so acutely into her tender frame, and she trembled so violently, that she feared lest by remaining longer without shelter she might bring upon herself an illness which would prevent her seeking her friends at an early moment.

She, therefore, approached the door, and, lifting a stone from the ground, knocked with it upon its rude panels.

This she did several times; and, after the lapse of a few minutes, she saw through the chinks of the habitation the gleam of a light.

Anxiously she awaited, and listened; and, in a short time, a man, rough and uncouth in appearance, habited in a flannel shirt and canvass trousers, with a striped flannel cap on his head, made his appearance on the threshold.

He started back in surprise as the frail delicate form of the young girl met his gaze.

"May I crave shelter in your habitation?" said Ellen, timidly.

"Where did you come from?" said the man, in a rough voice.

" From the sea," replied Ellen.

" From the sea! Ye ain't a witch, are you?" said the man, recoiling backwards a few paces.

" Oh! no; I am only a poor girl, who has suffered much, and would rest here, till some passing vessel could bear me to my home."

" Aye; but how came you here? That's what I want to know," said the man.

" I was sent on shore, a short time since, from a vessel which has stood out to sea."

The man looked suspiciously at her.

" Sent ashore, and the vessel gone away without you! What were you sent ashore for?"

" That I might return to my friends," said Ellen.

" But few ships touch here," said the man. " What vessel have you come ashore from?"

" The Spirit of the Wave," replied Ellen.

" What!" exclaimed the man—" 'The Spirit of the Wave?' Why, that is the vessel commanded by the pirate Latour."

" The same," said Ellen.

The man looked rudely at her, as he remarked:

" I see; Latour took you on a cruise, and, when he got tired of you, put you ashore here. That's it, ain't it?"

The pale face of Ellen became suffused with blushes; but she spoke not.

" Well, come in," said the man, after a pause; " and you've no need to blush. You ain't the first girl as Latour has had, I'll wager. The next port he makes he'll find another; and, when he's done with her, he'll serve her the same way. He came down handsome, though, didn't he, when he turned you adrift? If he didn't, it ain't like what I've heard of him—that's all."

" I do not understand you," said Ellen.

" Well, gave you money to go on with, then?" said the man.

" Oh! yes, yes," replied Ellen, hastily, wishing to let the man know that she had the means of paying for any accommodation. He gave me this purse; and I can pay for anything I require."

The eyes of the man feasted greedily upon the purse, as Ellen held it extended before him.

Gold is the talisman which opens the portals of the soul, it would appear: for the man, hitherto so rough in his bearing, immediately altered his manner, and pressed Ellen to enter the hut, lest the cold air should effect her delicate frame.

Ellen entered the place, which was strewn around with fishing-nets, pieces of rope, and all the implements of those engaged in the fishing-trade. Smoke-begrimed and miserable indeed this place appeared; and the heart of poor Ellen sank as the door closed behind her.

" Take up your quarters there," said the man, pointing out a chest which stood in one part of the room; " and I'll soon get a fire to warm you; and wake up the old woman."

With a sigh Ellen complied, and seating herself on the chest, watched the man as he piled some wood in the rude grate and set light to it.

A cheerful blaze illuminated the dirty apartment, and shed a warmth throughout the place.

" There," said the man, " now I'll go and call up the old woman to look to you and make you as comfortable as she can."

And lifting a piece of dirty sailcloth which hung across one end of the apartment he passed into a room used as a sleeping place, and Ellen heard him calling upon some one to arise.

Ellen cast her eyes around the rude place, everything seemed dirty, and the smell of tobacco and fish pervaded the whole.

In the course of about ten minutes the dirty sailcloth was again raised, and the figure of a woman about fifty years of age, of anything but a prepossessing appearance stepped into the apartment where Ellen sat.

She came up to our heroine and gazed long and rudely into her face, and after having satisfied her curiosity, she gave vent to a kind of hoarse cough and remarked—

" You want to stay here till some ship passes, do you?"

" I seek such favour at your hands," replied Ellen.

" But we are very poor, and fishing has been bad lately."

" I will willingly repay you for any expenses incurred on my part," said Ellen. " I should be sorry to be a burden on you."

" We are too poor to be generous or hospitable," said the woman, " if you have the money to pay for all you require, you can make yourself comfortable here."

In a short time a meal was prepared, but in so rough a manner, and with such coarse viands, that had Ellen been at all inclined to eat, she would have turned from the rough fare placed before her.

" I cannot eat," she said " I would seek repose,"

" This way then," said the woman, leading her towards the canvas partition.

This being raised, Ellen saw a dirty bed on the floor of a dark apartment.

" There," said the woman, " that is the best we can offer you, but it is better than none, I have no difficul t in sleeping, nor has the old man, for we work hard, and if is not as soft as what you have been used to, no doubt you can make it do."

Ellen hesitated.

" You need have no fear of being disturbed," said the woman, " the old man has gone to the boat, and will not be back till nightfall.

With this assurance Ellen threw herself upon the rough couch, and the woman departed.

Worn out with anxiety and fatigue, Ellen sunk into a deep slumber.

When her senses had become firmly bathed in sleep, the woman who had been watching her through the canvas, opened the door of the rude habitation and beckoned to two men who sat some short distance from the hut on the keel of an overturned boat.

Rising hastily at the signal they approached the house.

" Hist," said the woman, laying her fingers on her lips to enjoin silence.

" She sleeps."

" All right," said her husband, " where's the purse?"

" In her bosom," replied the woman.

" That's awkward," said the other, " we shall be sure to wake her."

" Well, she'll know of her loss Dick," said the husband of the woman, " sometime, so she may as well know it first as last."

But if she cry out, she may betray us," he said.

" Not much fear of that, the boys are all out at sea now."

" But the women aint," remarked the other.

" We must prevent her hollowing," said the man.

" But how?" asked Dick.

" With this here little bit of steel," replied the other, drawing a knife from his side.

" I tell you I won't agree to that," replied the other, " I don't mind the robbing part, but I won't shed blood."

"Then she'd betray us."

"No need of that," remarked Dick, "when we've got the money we can just put the tarpaulin over her, gag her mouth, and carry her to the vaults of the old fort."

"Well, as you like," replied the other," but she's best out of the way."

"So she will be," said Dick, "and I'll agree to nothing else."

The man who had first opened the door of the hut to Ellen's summons, seemed somewhat dissatisfied, but he entered the hovel without further remark.

Stealthily they both crept into the apartment where Ellen lay, and bending over her, Dick thrust his hand into her bosom and drew forth the purse.

The act caused Ellen to start up with a loud cry, but the hands of the man were upon her mouth, and in another moment the old piece of sailcloth was torn down and thrown around her, and she felt herself lifted from the couch and borne away.

She struggled for a moment, and then lost all consciousness.

CHAPTER LXXIII.

A CHAPTER OF YARNS.

THE sun rose bright and beautiful, and the sea though not absolutely, yet lay almost like, a mirror in which the reflection of the ship could be seen as accurately as in a glass.

The seaman which the merchant captain had left on board, enabled Henry to obtain a night's rest, and he awoke refreshed and strengthened.

But when he cast his eyes around after coming upon deck, he was much chagrined to find that during the night the ships had parted company, and the merchantman was no where to be seen.

Scarcely a breeze fanned the cheek, and the sails flapped against the masts.

Mr. Hanfield and Jacob were upon deck, looking wistfully across the ocean and leaning over the taffrail.

There is perhaps nothing more monotonous and wearying than a sea voyage, especially in a calm, and they none of them knew how to chase away the oppressive feelings which were caused thereby.

But Bob Bittern, the sailor who had come on board to help work the vessel into port, had been a sailor all his life, and was ever ready for a yarn, and having made himself quite at home, proposed that till a capful of wind bellied the sails they should spin a yarn or two to kill the time.

This was agreed to by the others, and Bob, seating himself on a bulk head, took a fresh quid, and said—

"You must know that about twelve years ago I was aboard a man-o'-war off Algiers, and as we had very little to do, we often got leave to go ashore. I was very fond of hunting, as was also several of the young officers and men aboard.

"I occasionally made excursions into the surrounding country, in quest of the smaller game which abounded in that vicinity; and though far from being one of the best marksmen of the crew, I seldom returned to the ship with less than a dozen brace of partridges, and numbers of hares, wild geese, plovers, quails, and so on. This success in a short time made me quite infatuated with the sport, and I began to think of quitting the service, my time being up, and turning hunter altogether. Perhaps I should have done so but

for a serious adventure which befel me afterwards, and which completely weaned me from the desire of making my home in the forest.

"One bright morning in September I set off with a companion, at a very early hour, and shaped my course for a swampy field, distant some three or four leagues, and which, owing to the rough country intervening, we did not reach until the sun was from one to two hours above the eastern horizon.

This swampy field stretched along the base of a steep, rocky, and wood-covered ridge, dividing the latter from a clear, beautiful lake; and the rich alluvian was so soft and miry in some places as to require considerable caution on the part of the explorer to avoid a fatal engulphment. The thicket was filled with legions of snipe and other small game; and as these had been our chief attraction to the spot, we gave but little thought to the risks of the undertaking, but boldly plunged into the darker recesses of the swamp and began our work of destruction.

"I soon tired of it, however, for it was literally slaughter, and not sport. No skill was required, All we had to do was to load with shot, point ours guns at the nearest cloud of birds, pull the trigger, and pick up the spoil by dozens.

"'This will never do for me, Victor,' said I to my companion. 'I am not partial to any unusual trouble in bringing down game—but then I do like a chance to aim once in a while, if only for the sake of keeping my hand in. The idea of shooting birds as they are in the act of alighting on the muzzles of our guns! Bah!'

"'My dear fellow,' replied my companion, 'it may be very fine sport for you to go stumbling about through the woods, and getting a shot now and then from a distance too great for a poor marksman like me; but the fact is, I like to shoot often, and kill something every time I fire; and where can I find a place better suited to my tastes and abilities than this?'

"'If you were to get a large coop, cram it full of domestic fowls, and fire a cannon, loaded with small grape, into it, you might possibly kill more at one shot than you do now; but I am not sure the sport would be any more exciting, or that you would have a chance to display any greater amount of skill.'

"'Ah, well, you may laugh at me, if you will,' he answered, with a peculiar shrug; 'and, meantime, I will shoot snipe.'

"'Victor, there are more lying dead around us now than we can carry back to the ship; and so pray let us quit, and try and find something more worthy of us.'

"'And all because you are obliged to shoot at two yards instead of thirty. Nonsense! I care not for such work. Let me do my work here, and do you go and fire from yonder hill. Then we shall both be satisfied—I because I shall kill my game at close quarters, and you, because you will do the same from a skilful distance. What do you say?"

"'That I will go up the hill, contemplate the surrounding scene, and give you a couple of hours more to carry on your butchery. But be ready by that time to depart, or I shall leave you alone in your glory.'

"'All right, my friend; I shall do wonders in two hours.'

"'Kill a thousand poor innocent snipe at least,' said I, as I turned away, with a smile of contempt, and began to pick my way out of the thicket.

"On quitting the swamp, and gaining the hard ground at the base of the ridge, I did not immediately ascend the latter, but sauntered along the level for a couple of hundred yards, my mind occupied with thoughts and reflections that led me far away from the scene around me. In this manner I approached a large beautiful spring of clear cold water, that bubbled up through the roots of an immense tree, whose dense foliage threw over it a most delightful shade, and I mechanically stooped to gaze upon it before my mental vision took any cognizance of what the material saw.

"At length my attention was arrested by what appeared to be the recent footprints of some wild beast, made in the soft moist earth of the margin; and a close and deliberate examination led me to believe the animal to be a panther, which had stopped and drank at the spring within a few hours, but whether before or since daylight I could not determine.

At all events, here was something with which to amuse myself during the two hours allotted to my companion, and I forthwith began to trace the course of the retreating beast, with a view to following its trail for a short distance, and happily finding its lair somewhere in the vicinity.

"My companion was still busy at his destructive work in the swamp—scarcely a minute passed that I did not hear the report of his piece—and resolved not to disturb him, or venture beyond the sound of his gun.

"I began to follow the tracts of my nobler game.

"For fifty yards the trail ran along the edge of the swamp, and then turned up the hill, where it was lost on the harder ground; and as I had no dogs with me to take up the scent, I should never have thought of looking further for the animal if there had been anything better with which to amuse and occupy my mind.

"As it was, however, I went up the hill, giving all the denser undergrowth a cautious inspection before entering it, and carefully examining the rocky ledges for some crevice, hole, or cave, in which the beast might have its home.

"An hour thus passed, found me upon the top of the ridge, leaning my back against a large old tree, whose lower lateral branches were showing signs of decay.

"I had already given up my search for the beast, and had stopped here to rest and take a quiet survey of the scene below, with its narrow belt of swamp, its glistening lake, broad, level, open plain beyond, and once more had my mind begun to wander away to still brighter scenes in a distant land, when I suddenly became interested in a peculiar whining sound, that seemed to be made close to me.

"I looked down at my feet, and beheld hard, solid earth; I walked around the tree, and could not discover the smallest hole for any animal to burrow in; I carefully inspected all the branches overhead, but did not detect even so much as a bird among them.

"Where had the sound come from?—and by what had they been made?

"I listened, but all was again still.

"Had it been mere fancy on my part?

"For some ten minutes I stood perplexed, lost in wonder and conjecture; but not hearing anything more during this time, I was on the point of moving away to seek my companion, when I was almost startled by the same sounds being repeated as near to me as before.

"What were these sounds?—and whence came they?

"Again I went around the tree, and carefully examined everything, above and below, but could not perceive a single spot where an animal half the size of my fist could be screened from my view.

"As the first and main crotch of the tree was not more than ten or twelve feet from the ground, I resolved to ascend to that, and see if I could possibly gain any clue to the mystery; and laying my gun flat down on the earth, so that by no accidental discharge its contents could be lodged in my body, I was soon at the point designated.

"Here, much to my surprise, I found a large cavity, or hollow, in the very centre of the tree; and at the bottom of this hollow, or about four feet below me, were a couple of sleek, fat animals, with shiny eyes, and more resembling two medium-sized, yellowish cats, than anything el   to which I can liken them.

"On seeing me, the little fellows exhibited signs of fear and dislike, by drawing back as far as they could, bristling, and spitting like kittens; and I wondering what they were, was watching them with a feeling of interest and curiosity, when suddenly there came to my ears a wild cry or scream, that seemed to thrill through every nerve and fibre of my body, almost causing me to lose my hold, and fall to the ground.

"A second wild cry followed closely on the first; but it needed not this repetition to tell me what it was, and warn me of my danger.

"The panther, whose trail I had followed, and the mother of the little animals in the hollow before me, was returning to her offspring. and already I could see her yellowish form gliding along through a cluster of bushes, scarcely a hundred yards distant.

"In the name of Heaven, what was I then to do?

"My gun, loaded only with shot, was on the ground below, and should I leap down for it, the ferocious beast might be upon me before I could gain a place of safety; and the charge, not being powerful enough to kill, would still leave me at her mercy; while, if I remained where I was, with nothing but a knife for defence, I should undoubtedly be torn to pieces in a very few moments.

"Under ordinary circumstances, or away from her young, I should have had little fear of the beast; but here, where I was, I felt certain she would attack at once, and ferociously fight to the death.

"But what was I to do? To remain where I was would be certain death, and to leap to the ground seemed to promise nothing better.

"I thought rapidly—a thousand ideas flashed through my mind in a moment—and my plan was fixed by a sort of lightning impulse.

"I would ascend the tree to its highest branches —to a height which the heavy panther could not reach—and there be guided by circumstances.

"No sooner resolved upon, than I began to put in execution my design; but ere I was half way to the top, I heard a terrific screech below me, and looking down, perceived, to my horror, the fearful beast fast making her way up the body of the tree towards me.

"It is needless to say that I used every exertion of which the human frame is capable when prompted by the fear of an appalling death, and I crashed upward through the leaves and branches with a rapidity that has always been a matter of wonder to myself.

"When I had gained one of the topmost limbs, that bent under my weight and swayed to and fro, the terrible panther, lashing her tail with rage and fury, was scarcely more than ten feet below me; but I thanked God most fervently that, though only that distance divided us, it was beyond her power to lessen it.

"She had already reached the highest point that the slender limbs and her great weight would permit, and I was therefore safe so long as I could keep my place.

"But it was not a pleasant thing to know that I had as little power to harm her as she had to injure me, and that she could remain on the watch below as long as I could possibly cling to limbs above, and that on account of her young, she would probably not leave again while I should retain my position, unless drawn off by an attack from another foe.

"My only hope was now in the aid of my companion; and though, considering his poor marksmanship, I regarded his appearance as a fearful alternative, yet, as there was no other means of escape, I forthwith began to shout his name with all my vocal strength; while the panther, as if comprehending my design, uttered a few menacing growls, and one terrific screech, and then thrashed about the tree in a manner that shook the upper limbs frightfully, and once so disturbed my footing, that I came near falling to the spot she occupied.

"At length I heard the faint reply of Victor, to which I responded with my loudest cries for help.

"In a minute or two I heard the sound of his voice nearer, and I continued to scream for help, in order to hasten his movements and guide him to my rescue.

"At the end of perhaps another two minutes, but which really seemed like ages to me, I caught a view from my elevated position of his slender figure darting among the bushes.

"I could now easily reach him with my voice, and in a few hurried words I informed him of my perilous situation and the danger of an unguarded approach.

"In another moment he had mounted a large rock, from which he could both see and be seen; and in a tone tremulous with fear and emotion, he inquired what he could do to aid me.

"'Put two balls in each barrel, put on good caps, and then advance steadily and firmly, and keep your presence of mind!' I shouted back to him.

"'Should the beast descend to attack you, do not fly from her, but pour in your fire at close quarters, and pray God to make your shot fatal!'

"Scarcely had I spoken, when another slight shake of the upper limbs drew my attention to the panther, which I now perceived was in the act of lightly and stealthily descending the tree.

"That she had seen my companion I did not doubt, nor that she was now retiring from me for the purpose of attacking him; and these facts I instantly communicated to him, with the injunction to stand firm, keep calm, and be prepared for the worst.

"I could see that he was excited even to trembling; but he replied, in a tolerably steady voice, that he would do the best he could.

"'And if possible,' I rejoined, 'I will get down and come to your aid.'

"With an interest the most intense—such an interest as we feel when life and death are in the balance—I watched the descent of my foe.

"She paused over her young for a few minutes, uttered a peculiar whine, and then leaped to the ground and darted off to the nearest thicket.

"Now, I thought, was my time; and telling my companion what had happened, and to be on his guard, and what I proposed to do, I hastily descended the tree, seized my gun, and dropped a couple of balls into each barrel.

"This I had accomplished, and was in the act of examining the caps, when, with a wild roar of fury, the beast, which I supposed to be some distance away, sprung out of the nearest covert and rushed upon me.

"There was no time for an aim, and no necessity for it. Quick as lightning I cocked both barrels, brought the piece to a level with my breast, and pulled both triggers.

"The furious animal was even then leaping upon me, and received the entire contents of the gun—balls, shot, and wadding, in her face and breast, and came down upon me, mortally wounded, hurling me to the earth, and seriously lacerating me in her dying agonies.

"With the most desperate exertions I struggled beyond her reach, and, then, with torn garments and covered with blood, leaned against a tree for support.

"My alarmed companion now came running up, and put an end to the dying beast by pouring the contents of both his barrels into her already wounded head.

"After killing the two young panthers, my friend assisted me back to the ship, where, for two or three weeks, I remained unfit for duty, secretly vowing I would thenceforth leave the hunting of wild beasts to whoever might feel disposed to engage in the dangerous occupation. Since that eventful day I have seen some years of service in strife with men, but have ever steadily refrained from engaging in any profession aside from my line of duty."

As the old tar told his tale, his face became bedewed with perspiration. The recollection of the fearful moments passed in that tree, he could never forget, and he said, that often when sleeping in his hammock he would wake up with a start, and see the glaring eyes of the panther, in imagination fixed upon him.

"You had a narrow escape," said Jacob, after a pause.

"Indeed I did," replied the seamen, "and never shall I forget it till my dying day."

"Well, I never was placed in anything of a dangerous position," said Jacob, "till I came on board this bark, but you have met with a few adventures, I believe, sir, in your time."

"Yes," replied Mr. Hanfield, to whom these words were addressed, "like most men, I have been placed in a few awkward positions. Like our friend here, I was fond of hunting when quite a young man, and good scope was given to that propensity during the few months I was in India transacting business for my father."

"One day I accompanied a gentleman in a tiger hunt. The spot selected was the edge of a tank, where a tiger used to drink. There was a large tamarind tree on its banks, and here I took up post to watch, and soon after sunset we took up our position on a branch about twelve feet from the ground, after having fastened an unfortunate bullock under the tree for a bait.

"Well, we remained quietly on our perch for a couple of hours, without stirring. It might be eight o'clock, the moon had risen, and so clear was the light that we could see the jackals at the distance of half-a-mile, sneaking along towards the village, when a party of Brinpassies, passing by, stopped to water their bullocks at the tank. They loitered for some time; and becoming impatient, I got off the tree with a singlet rifle in my hand, and walked towards them, telling them that I was watching a tiger.

"I was sauntering back to my post, never dreaming of danger, when my friend gave a low whistle, and at the same moment a low growl rose from some bushes between me and the tree. To make my situation quite decided, I saw my friend's arm pointing nearly straight under him, on my side of his post. It was very evident I could not regain the tree, although I was within twenty yards of it. There was nothing for me but to drop behind a bush, and leave the rest to Providence.

"If I had moved then, the tiger would had me to a certainty; besides, I trusted to his killing the bullock, and returning to the jungle as soon as he had finished his supper. It was terrible to hear the moans of the wretched bullock when the tiger approached. He would run to the end of his rope, making a desperate effort to break it, and then lie down, shaking in every limb, and bellowing in a most piteous manner.

"The tiger saw him plain enough; but suspecting something wrong, he walked growling around the tree, as if he did not observe him. At last he made a fatal spring, with a horrid shriek rather than a roar. I could hear the tortured bullock struggling under him, uttering faint cries, which became more and more feeble every instant, and the heavy breathing, half growl, half snort, of the monster, as he hung to the neck, sucking his life-blood.

"I know not what possessed me at this moment, but I could not resist the temptation of a shot. I crept up softly within ten yards of him, and kneeling behind a clump of dates, took a deliberate aim at his head, while he lay with his nose buried in the bullock's throat. He started with an angry roar from the carcase when the ball hit him. He stood listening for a moment, then dropped in front of me, uttering a sullen growl. There was only a date bush between us; I had no weapon but my discharged rifle. I felt for my pistols, they had been left on the tree. Then I felt that my hour was come, and all the sins of my life flashed with terrible distinctness across my mind. I muttered a short prayer, and tried to prepare for death, which seemed inevitable. But what was my friend about all this time? Oh, as I afterwards learned, he, poor fellow, was trying to fire my double rifle; but all my locks had bolts, which he did not understand, and he could not cock it.

"The tiger made no attempt to come at me; a ray of hope cheered me; he might be dying. I peeped through the branches, but my heart sank within me when his bright green eyes met mine, and his hot breath absolutely blew in my face. I slipped back upon my knees in despair, and a growl warned me that slight movement was noticed. But why did he not attack me at once? A tiger is a suspicious, cowardly brute, and will seldom charge unless he sees distinctly.

"Now I was quite concealed by the date leaves, and while I remained perfectly quiet I still had a chance. Suspense was becoming intolerable. My knees were becoming bruised by the hard gravel, but I dared not move a joint. The tormenting mosquitoes swarmed round my face, but I feared to raise my hand to brush them off. Whenever the wind ruffled the leaves that sheltered me, a harsh growl grated through the stillness of the night.

"Hours that seemed years rolled on; I could hear the village gong strike each hour of that dreadful night, which I thought never would end.

At last the welcome dawn! and oh, how gladly did I hail the first streak of light that shot up from the horizon, for then the tiger rose and sulkily stalked away to some distance. I felt that danger was passed, and rose with a feeling of relief which I cannot describe. Such a night of suffering was enough to turn my brain, and I only wondered that I survived it. I now set off for the elephant. It was all over in five minutes. The tiger rushed to meet me as soon as I entered the cover, and one ball in the chest dropped him down dead."

"You did'nt go tiger hunting again after that," said Jacob.

"No indeed," said the old gentleman with a shudder, "but come Mr. Chambers, as we cannot do anything better till the winds springs up, have you no adventure to recount."

"In course he has," said Bob, "why the youngest boy in a ship can spin a yarn."

Henry, like most sailors, was fond of yarn spinning, and as he wished to make the voyage as comfortable as possible for Mr. Hanfield, and feeling sure that a breeze would soon spring up, he commenced.

"I'll just tell you of a little adventure which befell me while on the coast of Peru, sailing under the brave old captain Waters, whom the hell hound we have just captured had tied to the mast while he sunk the vessel. Well, that's nothing to do with my story now."

"As I said we were on the coast of Peru, and I had occasion to proceed into the interior to receive a sum of money which was due to me. I engaged a horse, and after two hours hard riding through a country abounding with natural beauties, I arrived at the house of my friend, Don Zauletti, threw my bridle to a groom, and entered.

"'Ha! Don Spunyarn,' exclaimed he; 'you look warm—riding does not suit you north-men, so near the equator.'

"'No, perhaps it don't; but, for heaven's sake, my good fellow, if you've anything drinkable in the place let's have it.'

"Quick as the word a bottle of champagne sparkled on the table.

"'And now, I suppose, you are come for your money?'

"'Why, yes: the truth is I came on purpose.'

"'Well, drink your wine, and we'll talk about it. You smoke, of course?' said he, handing me a box of cigars.

"'Yes,' said I, helping myself, and lighting one of exquisite flavour.

"'How shall I remit your cash?'

"'Oh! I'll take it with me.'

"'You had better not.'

"'Why?'

"'The roads are not safe; 'tis not many day since two foolhardy Englishmen, who boasted that they always carried about them twenty or thirty ounces of gold, were robbed and shot.'

"'You be hanged! don't think to scare me, my friend,—hand over the cash.'

"'I'll do so with pleasure, but, if you take my advice, you'll not trust yourself on the road with so much money. I'll give you an order on Don Carlos La Joanja, and you can receive the money tomorrow.'

"'No, no—give me the cash; I'm a match for a dozen such vagabond robbers as you have in this country.'

"Without further hesitation he paid me, saying—

HEAVE-TO !

"'I do not want to hurry you, but with all that gold about you, I hope you'll get back by daylight.'

"'Stow your gaff, my good fellow: you'll not frighten me? I shall dine with you, finish another bottle or two of your wine, and get home in the cool of the day; and, trust me, if I should come athwart any of these scoundrels, I'll give them pepper, or my name's not Harry. But come, pass the cigars.'

"Towards evening I again mounted my horse to return; the sun was slowly setting in the west, casting a mellow tint over the surrounding scenery. The blue mountains rose in awful grandeur, towering one above the other, clothed with trees, which probably had stood there for ages; my senses were oppressed with the magnificence of the scene.

"It was a delicious and balmy evening, and as I rode, a soft cold breeze floated gently from seaward, forming a pleasant contrast to the stifling heat of the morning.

"Darkness, which in tropical climates followed immediately after the setting of the sun, surprised me many miles from my destination; presently I came to a part of the road which was narrow and had trees on each side. Now, thought I, if what Zauletti said be true, this is just the spot the wretches would select. The thought had scarcely entered my head, when crack went a rifle and I was rolling in the dust—my horse shot under me and I stunned.

"'Give me your gold,' were the first words which saluted my ears when I recovered my consciousness and found I was disarmed and bound;

"'May I be hung up by a lanyarn, like a parson's shirt on a washing day, if I give it you—if you want it you must take it.'

"They did not want a second invitation, but soon stripped me, not only of my gold, but of hat, jacket, and waistcoat. A tall, ugly fellow, with an enormous crop of black hair on his face, took a fancy to my boots and laid hold of my leg to pull them off. Not fancying the loss of my understandings I gave the fellow a straight-forward kick in the centre of his stomach.

"'Caramba!' exclaimed he, cocking his gun.

"The captain, who had been listening all this time to something, was aroused by the click of the lock, and turned round.

"'Joachim, on your life disobey my orders—put up your piece : now drag the beast (pointing to my horse) out of the road, and see all clear ; here comes another.'

"I was now moved, under charge of the gentleman who wanted my boots, and placed under a low wall. By this time the clank of horses' hoofs was plainly to be heard ; my friend now produced a long knife, which he kindly promised to insert in my windpipe if I made the least noise.

"'A single horseman, captain,' said one of the robbers ; 'shall we serve him as we did the other ?'

"'No, no; he don't ride so fast.'

"On came the horseman, singing an Irish song in an accent which plainly told the land of his birth ; when he came abreast of us, three of the men rushed out, one seized the horse and the other two capsized him from the saddle.

"'Och! by the soul of Saint Patrick, it's a mighty ungenteel way you have of asking a man to stop,' and then surveying the group, he exclaimed—'By the Lord above, you ugly specimens of humanity, what may you be going to do with me? Let go me arms, you devils, bad manners to you; don't you know how to treat a gentilman when he comes among you?' continued he, struggling to free himself. 'Fair play's a jewel any how, and I'd fight you two to one after a potathy breakfast, bad luck to your ugly mugs.'

"Eight to one was long odds; he was soon bound, and placed alongside me, when he said—

"'It's wrong to rejoice at another's misfortune, but, by my sowl, I'm glad to see you here; a companion in misfortune is like butter in your gruel, darling: it softens it down.'

"And then, turning to our guard, he said—

"'Is it hungry you are, that you open your mouth in that way to swallow what I'm saying ?'

"'Silence! unless you want the knife to keep silence,' said our friend of the black muzzle.

"Again the sound of horses was heard. As they came near how I longed to be able to give them warning, but durst not, as Joachim's long knife gleamed in the moonlight, threatening death at the least noise. Onward came the horsemen as hard as they could gallop.

"'We must shoot the beasts,' said the captain, in a whisper; 'they ride so fast—steady aim—fire.'

"No sooner were the words out of his mouth, than down came the foremost rider; the second horse, not being hit in a vital part, plunged terrifically ; his rider drew a pistol from his belt and fired, bringing down our friend of the black muzzle, who fell at my feet, covering me with black blood, which spouted from a wound in his forehead.

"The captain, who had reserved his fire, now sent a bullet right in the horse's head; it was a

sneezer, and down he came, throwing his rider some distance.

"Don Manolia!" said the captain, recognising the fallen man.

"'Serve him right,' said one of the band; 'he won't give information against us again.'

"The wounded man rose on one hand, and with the other suddenly drew from his bosom another pistol. Quick as thought, one of the robbers, who was standing by, swung the butt end of his gun round, and before he could discharge it the pistol was flying in the air.

"'Not so fast, Don Manolia,' said the captain. 'I am surprised at your want of gratitude; the first time we robbed you, we treated you like a gentleman, only took your money and sent you home unhurt, and in return you sent the patrol after us ; the second time we stripped you of everything; that did not satisfy you, for you again set the blood-hounds on our track. This time I'll not give you the chance of doing so: bind him to a tree. An ounce of gold to the man who first puts a bullet into his head, 'twill teach others not to interfere with Juan Alaga, or his Black Band.'

"While their attention was thus directed, my companion crept close to me, and told me he had a knife in his pocket. After some trouble I succeeded in getting it out. Our cords were soon cut. This was a moment of intense interest to us, and in breathless silence we crept on under cover of the wall; my heart beat audibly, and seemed ready to burst from my bosom with excitement. I was in momentary expectation of hearing a bullet whiz over my head, or perhaps come in closer contact, yet could not suppress the exultation I felt at a chance of escaping with our lives. We had now reached the end of the wall and found further progress checked by a large piece of water.

"'Now, honey, can you swim?' said my companion.

"'Yes.'

"'Then strike out silently; when you reach the opposite side squat down under the bank with your head just above the water.'

"When in the middle of the water we heard the report of a rifle, and then another, an then—oh! horror—the death-scream of poor Manolia.

"'Quick, honey, quick, or they'll be down on us before the ripple's off the water.'

"We had scarcely reached the opposite side when two of the band mounted, scoured the bank, one on each side. I was in great trepidation ; every moment expecting they would discover us—and when one of them dismounted within a few yards of us, I felt almost choked, the fear of discovery was so great. To my infinite satisfaction, they gave up the search and departed.

"Rising from our bath, considerably refreshed, we now started for Lima, which we reached in safety; and entering my lodgings, astonished the people by appearing in my shirt, trousers, and boots.

"'What's the matter? Is he mad ?' was asked.

"'Och, botheration to you,' said my Irish friend; 'we're not mad, but took with a fit of the shivers, give us some brandy, ye spalpeens.'

"They all crowded round us, eager to learn our adventures.

"'Don't you hear we've been tumbling in a bog, and have got a crow in our throat. For the love of the Blessed Vargin, give us some brandy, or it'll be eating our livers.'

"Having fortified our inward man with a good topper of hot brandy, and satisfied the curiosity of our friends, we turned in for a snooze. After passing a troubled night, during which I was continually waking up with the death-scream of poor Manolia ringing in my ears, I was aroused at day-break by the landlord coming into the room.

" 'Come, sir, rouse out: these fellows have made a nice finish to their night's work, by rifling the house of old St. Moy, reported to be the richest man in this part of the country. They knifed his servants, all but one girl, who escaped and brought the news to Lima. They tortured the old man, in every way, to make him give up gis money. He gave them what he had; but they insisted that he had more; and then they ham-strung him, to make him confess. He offered to give them any sum they should name if they would wait till the morning; but they thought it was only a trap, and fancied he had gold secreted. The captain swore if he did not give them more gold he'd shoot him. The old man clung to life with all the intenseness of despair, and with tears in his eyes implored them to spare him.

" 'But the old man had spoken truth; he had no more gold, and they shot him like a dog. Disappointed in their object, they have decamped to the mountains. A strong detachment of soldiers are going in search of them. Your last night's friend, Don Sullivan, goes. You'll join them, of course?'

"I assented; dressed myself in haste, and descended to the common room.

" 'Ha! Harry, my boy. Is there any of devil left in you, after the ducking you got last nigh? By my soul, them was the devil's pet chickens; and wouldn't I like to see them strung up like stockings on a clothes-line! My service to their black muzzles,' said he, tossing off a glass of raw whiskey; 'may they never grow ragged or squint, is the sincere wish of their friend, Pat Sullivan. My blessing on the rope that hangs them, if they ever reach such an exalted situation. But come, eat,' said he; 'eat, honey, get your breakfast: sure the soldiers 'ill be here before you're ready.'

" 'Ugh! having a man or two shot before your eyes over night is not a great incentive to the appetite; but as there's small chance of a ship working to windward without plenty of ballast, I'll tackle that fowl.'

"I was interrupted by the entrance of our quarter-master, who informed me that we had a slant of wind; that the ship was hove short, and everything ready for a start. In half an hour I was alongside, and with a spanking breeze we bore away. In a few hours the blue mountains of Peru were hull down in the distance. On our return to Lima, I learned that the Black Band was broken up; and all, save the captain, were captured, and had suffered the penalty of their crimes."

CHAPTER LXXIV.

THE SLAVER IN SIGHT—WILD MADGE SENDS HER CARD ON BOARD.

As Henry concluded, the breeze sprang up, and the wind bellying the sails of the ship, she sped over the waters with redoubled speed.

Each had returned to their duties, for even Jacob and his master had some work assigned to them.

And cheerfully, indeed, did they perform it.

The day wore on, the breeze freshenin gas it did so.

Bob Bittern had gone aloft, and presently he was heard hailing the deck—

"Sail on our starboard bow!" he called out.

"What do you make her out?" asked Henry, placing his hands to his mouth the better to throw his voice up to the seaman.

"Can't say yet, sir."

"Do you think it is the vessel we have parted company with?" asked Henry.

"Can't be certain," called out Bob, "but don't think its her rig."

"Keep your eye on her."

"Aye, aye, sir."

"Jacob," said Henry, turning to that personage. "Be so good as to go below and bring me the glass."

Jacob turned and descended the cabin, and soon returned, bearing the glass in his hand.

"Here you are, sir." he said.

Henry took the glass, and placing it to his eye scanned the horizon where sky and wave seemed to meet.

Long and anxiously he looked.

"What do you make her out to be?" asked Mr. Hanfield, who stood beside the young man, anxiously awaiting his opinion.

"She is too far yet, sir, to speak with any certainty," replied Henry.

"Do you think it is the vessel in whose company we wished to remain?" asked Mr. Hanfield.

"I do not think so, from what I can see of her at present," replied Henry, "but the distance is great, and the atmosphere may interfere in our obtaining a fair opinion of her build. Still I think this vessel is too long and tapering in her build."

"The merchantman was not a very bulky built vessel," said Mr. Hanfield.

"True," replied Henry; "but if I were asked my opinion of that vessel, I should say she was built for speed, not for strength."

"Indeed!"

"Yes."

"Then what do you think she is?" asked Mr. Hanfield, anxiously.

The mind of the old gentleman was filled with pirates.

But should it be the vessel on which he believed his daughter was a captive—"The Spirit of the Wave."

He might then meet her; might once more gaze upon her lovely features and clasp her in his arms.

But then came the horrid thought, would they meet as they had parted, in purity and innocence.

Alas! he hoped so, but feared almost to hope.

"She looms up larger now," said Henry. "She is a swift sailer, let her be what she will."

"Do you think, Mr. Chambers," said the old man, "do you think—"

"What, sir?" interrupted the young man.

"That that vessel is the ship from which you was hurled into the sea?"

"The Spirit of the Wave?" asked Henry.

"Yes."

"Oh, no," replied the young man. "Her build is vastly different. Take the glass, sir, and follow her course," he added, wishing to prevent the old gentleman's mind from dwelling on his daughter, "while I take the wheel."

The gentleman took the glass, and carried it to his eye.

Henry returned to his post at the wheel—still

keeping his gaze fixed upon the course of the coming ship.

"It is as well to be prepared for emergencies," remarked Henry to Bob Bittern, who had descended to the deck; "so just run down into the cabin, and bring me the sword which hangs on the wall."

"Aye, aye, sir," said Bob.

In another minute he had returned with the weapon, which the young lieutenant buckled to his side.

"I don't like the look of her," remarked Bittern. "There's something very rakish about her."

"What do you think she is?" asked Henry.

"Well, I think I could guess," said Bob, pulling out his bacca-box, and picking off about three inches of pigtail.

"What?" asked Henry.

"I should like to bet a can of grog I hit her calling in a minute—there!" and Bob forced the pigtail into his mouth, as if he were ramming a charge into a cannon. "I've had a shindy with them ere craft afore now, I can tell you."

"But you have not told me what you think she is," said Henry.

"Oh! didn't I, sir?"

"No."

"Well, I'll bet a day's allowance of grog, to a chew of bacca, that she's fishing for blackberries."

"For what?"

"Blackberries."

"What, a slaver?" exclaimed Henry.

"To be sure she is," replied Bob Bittern, pointing towards the vessel, which now seemed like a toy boat. "Look at her hull—look at her rig. She's built to run—not to fight or trade; unless it's trade when they steals a lot of poor blacks 'cos they ain't got milky chops as we has."

And Bob Bittern laid his hand upon his tanned and weather-beaten face, to give greater force to his words.

A smile rose to the face of Henry; for Bob Bittern's exposure to the heat of the tropical climates had rendered him almost black.

"That's what she is, sir," continued Bob—"depend upon it; and I shouldn't wonder if she ain't got a first-rate cargo aboard.,

"You think so?"

"I do; and I tell you what I wish, sir," he continued—"and that is, that this here vessel was well manned and well armed, and that she'd just come athwart us. I should like to show some of there slave hunters what strength there is in a freeman's fist. But, Lord love you, sir, they've felt that afore!"

"Then you've had some experience in that line?"

"To be sure I have; and many's the poor black devil has gone quite red in the face with gratitude to us for rescuing them from the hold where they was all but suffocated. You should just see the whites of their eyes, sir, when they comes on deck, after their chains is knocked off. It would do you good—it would: Their eyes goes right up in their head, and don't come down for nearly three weeks arterwards; so werry thankful is they for their deliverance.

"Three weeks!" said Henry, with a smile.

"Well, sir, I knows it's quite three minutes. A man could chew out a foot of pigtail while they was examining their brains to see whether or no they wasn't a dreaming it all or no."

"Well, we shall soon see what this customer is, unless she changes her course, and bears away from us."

"Shouldn't wonder if she don't do that," said Bob, advancing to the side of Mr. Hanfield, who still looked through the glass at the approaching ship.

Henry left the wheel and stood by his side.

"She is bearing down upon us," he said, after shading his eyes with his hands and taking a long look at the vessel.

"Evidently so," said Mr. Hanfield, lowering the glass.

"That's to take off suspicion," said Bob. "Oh, they are an artful lot, they are. Lor bless you, the captain of a slaver is generally one of the smoothest spoken, kind-hearted individuals in all creation; can put on the modest, and no mistake. But it's only when you're bringing 'em too, that's all."

"What," said Mr. Hanfield, "is that ship a slaver?"

"In course it is—can't you see it by her build."

"I cannot tell one from another," replied the old gentleman.

"You can't?"

"No."

"Well, I never! Why a cabin boy would know her."

"But I am not a cabin boy," said the old gentleman, smiling.

"Well, I reckon you ain't quite," said Bob, "or you'd know that ere vessel aint engaged in any legetimate trade—there's a word for you. Blessed if it didn't nearly make me swallow my quid."

And the good humoured face of the honest tar was covered for the moment with the most comical grimaces.

"Ah, that is something else which I cannot understand in your line."

"What's that, sir?" asked Bob.

"Chewing tobacco."

"Can't you chew?"

"No."

"Then you is a innocent, you is, and no mistake," replied Bob, almost looking upon the old gentleman with disgust. "You knows nothing of the real joys of life. But I suppose you bacca?"

"Smoke, you mean?" said Hanfield.

"Exactly."

"I occasionally take s cigar."

"I am very happy to hear it. I can't abear a man as don't smoke, acos it aint natural. But give me a pipe, one as black as a tarpaulin. That's the way to taste the wirtue of the weed, as some people calls it."

"It would make me ill," said Mr. Hanfield.

"Would it."

"Yes."

"Well it wouldn't me, I can tell you," said Bob, "if you once get used to it. And then, why you wouldn't give a chewed out quid for a cigar."

"Ease her off a point, Bob," said Henry, at this moment, and the stalwart sailor, touching his forelock, darted away to obey the order.

"A strange fellow that," said Mr. Hanfield, turning to Henry.

"Yes, but a thorough seamen," replied the young lieutenant.

"So it would appear, from his love of tobacco alone," said the old gentleman, with a smile.

"It is not by that I judge him," said the young man, "but from the manner in which he goes about his duties."

"We were somewhat fortunate in gaining his assistance," said Hanfield.

"Indeed we were."

"What do you think of yon vessel, Mr. Chambers," asked Hanfield, after a pause.

"I believe her to be that which Bob has stated," replied the young man.

"A slaver."

"Yes."

"Have we anything to fear from her?" asked Hanfield, eagerly.

"Nothing, I should say," replied Henry. "Her object is to avoid meeting with any vessel, rather than molesting us."

"Then we can hope for no assistance from her either?"

"None."

"Yet she seems bearing down upon us," said the old man, looking over the side at the vessel which came rapidly towards them.

"So she does."

"Then how do you reconcile that fact with what you have said?"

"Indeed, I scarcely gave the circumstance a thought," replied Henry. "If she really be a slaver, and such indeed I believe her to be, it is strange that she should not avoid us."

"So I think."

"She herself may need assistance, and seek it from us," remarked Henry.

"What assistance could she possibly need?"

"She may be short of rations."

"True. But her captain must likewise know the abhorrence in which he would be held by all honourable men."

"But he would doubtless, if such were the case, disguise his real character."

"Could he do so?"

"He would pretend he was other than he was."

"Just so. And such you think the intentions of this one?"

"I do."

"You do not think he can have any guilty designs on this vessel?" asked Mr. Hanfield.

"Oh, no. A slaver is not a pirate," answered Henry, with a smile.

"That is true."

"Therefore we need have no such fear," said the young man.

Reassured by this, Mr. Hanfield left the deck and descended to the cabin, where burying his face in his hands, he became lost in the thoughts which the sight of the approaching vessel had revived in his mind.

Thoughts that racked his heart.

Thoughts of his fair and beautiful child—his loved one—his Ellen.

Meantime Henry, Bob, and Jacob remained on deck, attending to the working of the ship, and watching the vessel which Bob had sighted that morning, as she careened over the waves, under a heavy press of canvass.

Henry entertained no fear of her; but he had likewise given up all hopes of obtaining any assistance from the approaching vessel.

Having parted company with the merchantman, he knew how desperate would be their position did rough weather set in; as, should such be the case, there was but himself and Bob to work the ship.

Though Bob was every inch a sailor, still they could cherish but little hope that they would be enabled to carry the vessel into port if overtaken by rough weather.

But it is not in a sailor's nature to despair; so Henry placed his faith in Providence, and hoped for the best. Meantime, the vessel sailed nearer and nearer to them, and every rope in her could be distinctly seen and traced in the bright sunlight.

Henry had again taken the wheel, and he steered his own vessel full upon the stranger.

The slaver (for such indeed she had been, but now bore a very different character) still kept on her course—her long tapering mast bending under the pressure of her broad sails, and appearing like dark lines upon a light-blue ground.

Proud and stately was her motion as she cut through the sparkling waves—ever and anon dipping her bows to kiss, as it were, the billows that rose before her, and sprinkled her figure-head with showers of silvery spray.

Nearer and nearer the vessels approached each other; and Henry, with a true sailor's love for a taut little craft, gazed upon her with admiration.

"She's a fine craft that," he said, addressing Bob Bittern, who stood by his side.

"Aye, that she be, sir," replied the sailor—"as pretty a bark as ever sailed the salt seas; but it's a damn shame that she should be used for trapping poor niggers. I arn't had much learning—for, boy and man, I have sailed the briny deep; but this much I know, that the smoother the face, the more callous the heart; and the prettiest girl is the most deceitful one. And so it is with the craft that I have fell across: the firmer her build, the blacker her dealings."

"You may perhaps be right as regards the latter," said Henry with a smile, "but I cannot think you are serious as regards the ladies Bob."

"Can't you sir, well then I am, I would'nt give a chew a bacca for a fine lady. I've had a little experience of 'em, I has."

"You, Bob."

"Yes sir, me."

"Why how can that be, when you have spent your life on the ocean," asked Henry.

"I been in port sometimes you know," replied Bob.

"Yes, I suppose so."

"And I've learned to read 'em a bit, I can tell you sir," said Bob, in a sort of confidential tone.

"And your experience has been with the ladies on shore."

"That's it sir,"

"But surely, not all the fair ladies on shore are deceivers," said Henry smiling.

"I tell you they are sir, and I've found it out. They hoist false colours, takes you in tow, and runs you on the breakers, and there they leave you a helpless hulk, without a rudder to steer with, or a sail to hoist."

"I'm afraid you have got into bad company Bob in your runs on shore."

"Not always I aint, I've learned to steer clear of the land sharks. If I go ashore now and see a nicely painted tight-laced little craft steering down upon me, I set all sail on another tack, for I know I sha'nt have a shot in the locker left once she throws her grapnels aboard of me. But when I make out a bark, bearing no more sail than will carry her along under a fair wind, then I heaves to, and lets her take me in tow, and she's safe to pilot me back to the ship without the loss of every likeness of his blessed majesty."

"It would be a good thing for many sailors if they acted like you on shore Bob," remarked Henry.

"In course it would sir. But there, a fine painted figure head takes their fancy, and they're safe to be run down. I hate your neatly trimmed craft I do."

And Bob evidently smarting under the recollection of some of his foolish freaks ashore, turned away and went about his duties.

The vessels continued nearing each other, and it was evident that before sundown they would be close enough to hail.

Thus the time wore on and the two ships came within half-a-mile of each other.

Henry could plainly see the union jack floating from the mast of the stranger, and a ray of joy took possession of his heart.

A look of pride beamed from his eye as the time honoured flag met his gaze, and he felt certain that any assistance he might require would be readily granted by the commander of the vessel.

The idea of her being a slaver entirely died away from his mind now, though her build somewhat puzzled him.

But that flag—it floated not over a slave.

He hoisted signals and they were answered, but not as he had expected.

A wreath of smoke rose from her deck and a shot ploughed the water at her bows.

In a moment Henry saw what was the character of the vessel and his cheek turned a shade paler.

Mr. Hanfield came on deck and cast an anxious look upon the young lieutenant.

Bob Bittern turned his gaze also upon the face of Henry.

"She aint a slaver," he exclaimed, "but a pirate."

"A pirate!" exclaimed Hanfield.

"'Tis too true," said Henry, "and there goes the black flag."

And as he spoke the union jack was lowered and the black flag run up to the mast head, as another shot bounded over her bows.

CHAPTER LXXV.

MARTINEZ AND INEZ ON THE ISLAND.—LOVE.— THE SHADOW IN THE MOONLIGHT.

THE moon had risen in all its splendour, and threw its silvery rays upon the luxuriant valley, tinting the foliage of the trees and the moss covered earth with a fairy-like glow of subdued light, when Inez awoke from the fainting sleep into which she had fallen, to find herself clasped in the manly arms of Lieutenant Martinez, her head pressed upon his bosom, and his breath fanning her pale cheek.

In a moment the truth of her position flashed upon her, but she strove not to raise her head from the spot on which it was pillowed, nor to release herself from the warm, fervent pressure of the young seaman.

A strange feeling was in her heart; a feeling she had never before experienced; a feeling she could not define, and she closed her eyes again and heaved a deep sigh.

The pressure upon the slender waist tightened, and she felt the heart of the young seaman throbbing against her brow.

"Will she never wake?" murmured Martinez. "Oh, can this sleep be the forerunner of death?"

Inez rose her head from his breast and fixed her large dark eyes upon the handsome face of the young man.

"Heaven be praised!" he exclaimed. "Lady I had feared that your sufferings had killed you."

A sweet smile played around her beauteous mouth as she murmured—

"No, thanks to you I am saved."

"But for what?"

"What heaven shall destine," she murmured.

Martinez sighed.

"And what is that?" he said. "Away from friends and home, in this beautiful but uninhabited spot."

"Away from friends," she exclaimed; "ah, no, for are you not near me?"

And she placed her small white hand in his.

Martinez pressed it fervently, and a thrill of joy ran through his frame.

"You do not fear me, then?" he murmured.

"Fear you?" said Inez, looking up in his handsome face, half surprised.

"Yes, lady—fear."

"Why should I fear you? You who have rescued me from a watery grave."

"Lady," said Martinez, looking searchingly in her dark eyes as the bright moonbeams played upon her lovely features. "We are alone, with none but the eye of heaven to gaze upon us— none but the hand of heaven to guide us—alone in a strange place, distant from our homes and from man."

"What then?" she asked innocently.

"Aye, what then?" he answered.

"We are safe from the wiles of the wicked— safe from the designs of cruel and designing man," she said.

Martinez fixed his glance upon her, but the same placid sweetness sat upon her marble brow.

He turned away his gaze and sighed.

"You are unhappy," she said, placing her hand in his and looking into his face.

"Why do you think so?" he asked.

"That sigh."

"No," he replied, "I am not unhappy. I know of no greater happiness than being by your side—no greater joy than gazing upon your lovely features—but—but—"

"What, senor?"

"I fear."

"Fear?"

"Yes, lady—fear for you—for myself," he exclaimed.

She looked questionably upon him.

His gaze fell before the innocent look, but his heart beat with a wild throe of emotions.

"Why should you fear for me?" she said, after a pause.

"Alas! I know not—I—"

"Your exertions, senor," said Inez, "have been too much. You are unwell."

Martinez again sighed.

"Ah," she murmured, "for my sake you have struggled too much. For my sake—"

"For your sake lady, I would dare anything," said Martinez pressing the taper fingers of Inez in his own, "for you I would sacrifice all, life, everything."

Inez looked her thanks.

Gradually he drew her towards his breast.

"Lady," he said, dare I speak. Here alone in this place; but no, no it must not be."

And again he turned his gaze away from the face that nearly pressed his own.

"There is nothing senor that you can say I would not listen to," exclaimed Inez.

"My words might give you pain," exclaimed the young seaman.

"You have been too kind, too good to me to lead me to think so," she replied.

And the look of gratitude she fixed upon him, caused him a pang of such exquisite agony that he drew her head upon his breast and said—

"Inez, together have the rude waves carried us to this place, from which I fear there is no prospect of escape. We are doomed to live and die here alone. It is a paradise free from the evil passions of wicked men—free from the doings of a cold and callous world. In such a spot as this must Eden have been. Inez could you live and die here."

"I could," she murmured.

"But could you be happy."

"I think I could."

"Alone," he murmured.

"No, but you are by my side," she replied.

"Yet held aloof by honour," he exclaimed

Inez raised her head and fixed her eyes upon his.

"Can we not be to each other as brother and sister," she murmured, "loving, peaceful, and happy."

"Inez," he murmured, "man is not free from sin for he is mortal. Adam sinned with all the beauties and blessings of Eden around him.

The eyes of Inez fell from before the gaze of Martinez.

But she tore not herself away from his arms which pressed her with a fever almost painful.

"Inez," he murmured after a pause. "Love is sinful, but to sin is human."

She made no reply.

"Inez dare I speak—to offend I fear is to love you—but remain silent is to die."

Her small white hand trembled within his own, still she tore not herself away.

"Lady may I hope for your forgiveness," he said.

"For what," she murmured, "for what can Signor Martinez ask my forgiveness."

"For to love you," he exclaimed.

Inez strove to disengage herself from his hold.

"Lady," he said in pleading tones, gently resisting her endeavours to free herself from his embrace. "Hear me, I must speak, though your reply drive me for ever form your lovely presence. I love you, love you with a fervent and holy passion, engendered by the dangers we have passed through. Honour bids me smother that love, but nature prompts me to lay it your feet. In this place, away from the hearts of man, cut off from the world by the impenetrable barriers which nature in her wonduous works has formed, we are destined to live and die on this beautiful island. Life is sweet but without your love death will soon set his seal upon my existence, you can bid me live, you can seal my doom Inez, lady, Inez, speak."

But Inez was silent.

"Bid me live or die."

A deep sob escaped her bosom.

Martinez bent his head till his lips touched her cheek.

It was cold as death.

Martinez started in horror.

"Inez, Inez," he exclaimed, "speak to me in mercy speak to me."

Still was she silent.

"Oh God, I have killed her," he exclaimed in agony.

He raised her head from his breast, and allowed the moonbeam to fall full upon her face.

A shudder ran through his frame.

So pale so cold was that beautiful face.

"Inez, Inez," he exclaimed.

Still no answer.

He drew her head again to his breast, and pressed it there.

A sigh escaped her lips.

She had fainted.

"Inez—Inez—dear Inez!" again he moaned.

Inez opened her eyes, and looked pitifully upon him.

"Speak, dear one," he exclaimed—"speak! Oh! say that you forgive me."

"Forgive you?" she whispered.

"Yes, dear one—forgive me the pang I have caused you. Drive me from your presence, if you will; but, oh! forgive me."

She placed her hand in his.

"What have I to forgive?" she murmured.

"My rash words—my——"

Her pressure tightened on his hand, and the blood which had become stagnated again darted like electric fire through his veins.

"Oh! Inez, speak—tell me, can you love me?"

She buried her face in his bosom, and her slender form trembled with emotion.

He drew her closer to his breast, and whispered:

"Shall I live or die?"

"Live," she sighed.

"For you?" he exclaimed, passionately.

"For me," she murmured.

"Then you love me?" he exclaimed, frantically. "Oh! speak the word, sweet one. My heart is bursting with suspense."

"I love you," she murmured.

But so low, so soft was the tone, that it came to the ears of the enraptured Martinez like the soft sighing of the breeze amid the foliage of the trees.

Enraptured, he strained her to his breast, and showered kisses upon her coral lips.

What music to his soul were those words! They intoxicated his senses; and a heaven of delight seemed showered upon him.

And Inez nestled on his bosom, to hide the blushes that rose to her cheeks.

"Thanks, dear one—thanks!" he exclaimed, fervently. "You have given me new life; you have bid me live."

"You have saved me, and I am thine."

"My wife?" he whispered.

She pressed his hand.

"Beneath this bright moon," he exclaimed, "I swear to love thee ever—to shield thee from harm, come it in what shape it may. Though no church rite can bind our souls, yet love shall cement our holy alliance. On this island the ceremonies of marriage cannot be performed; but they are but the conventionalties with which we can dispense. True love needs no rite to bind us. Our own vows are sufficient—vows plighted beneath heaven's canopy, and registered in our own hearts. Shall it not be so?"

Closer to his breast clung the beautiful Inez; but she answered only with a sigh.

A sigh, so soft, so sweet, so full of love and tenderness.

Martinez cared not now for the world, his whole thoughts were centered on the fair being reclining on his breast.

What were the dangers he had passed through to save her, when the reward of his labours was the love of the beautiful Inez.

And the moon rose higher in the blue vault of heaven, and bathed the lovers in its silvery rays—smiled, as it were, upon their happiness, and threw around them an halo of joy.

"Come," whispered Martinez, drawing the fair girl with him as he rose from the ground. Yon grassy knoll on which the bright moonbeams play shall form our nuptial couch. There love shall hold his revels and the night bird sing our epithalamium. Come, dear Inez, come."

Inez burst into tears, but they were tears of joy and with one deep sob she flung herself upon his bosom.

He clasped her to his heart, and as he did so a shadow fell upon the ground at his feet.

Inez saw it, and with a scream she raised her head.

So also did Martinez.

It was the shadow of a man.

They turned hastily, and there, in the bright moonlight, standing contemplating them, was the tall form of a man!

CHAPTER LXXVI.

THE VAULTS OF THE FORT.—THE DISCOVERY.—DESPAIR.

It was with a painful feeling of cold and numbness that Ellen awoke from the fainting fit into which she had been thrown by discovering the two men bending over her in the hut of the fisherman.

For some few moments she could not recall to her senses what had happened, but after a few moments of painful thought she realised all the horrors of her situation.

She was alone and in darkness,

Not a ray of light penetrated the place in which she found herself.

She stretched forth her hands in horror, and they came in contact with the slimy walls of some place.

But what place was it.

She could form no conjecture.

With a cry of horror she rose to her feet.

But so cramped and benumbed with the cold were her limbs, that they refused their office, and she sank down again in the spot from which she had arisen.

A painful feeling took possession of her.

She believed she was incarcerated in some cold damp dungeon, and left to die.

In vain she strove to rise.

She placed her hands upon the wet slimy walls of her prison house, and a feeling of horror ran through her frame.

She felt in her bosom. Her purse was gone; and she now understood why she had been placed where she was.

But what place was it?

She could not think.

Whichever way she stretched her hand it came in contact with cold slimy stones.

In an agony of fear she listened for any sound that might come to her ears.

But all was silent.

Silent as the grave.

She buried her head in her hands, and wept.

Her tears seemed to relieve her overburdened heart; for, after a time, she again struggled to rise.

The blood had commenced to circulate through the benumbed limbs, and she could move along by placing her hands against the damp walls for support.

She tottered forward.

But no outlet could she find.

She turned, and struck her arm against a projection; and, feeling around it, discovered it to be a stone pillar.

She was evidently in some vault or dungeon; but in what part of the island she knew not.

Round and round she walked—keeping one hand upon the wall, and the other stretched out before her. Still no outlet could she find; and, after continuing her search for some time, she sank down upon the cold damp stone floor, and burst again into tears.

Poor girl!—her fate was indeed a sad one.

Nought but sorrow and affliction had been her portion since she had left the house of her father to become the wife of the brave youth she fondly loved.

And, as she sat there, she reviewed her sufferings, and wondered how she had been enabled to bear up against so much misery and insult.

But now she thought an end had come to all.

She believed she had been placed in the position in which she now found herself, to die.

To die a lingering death of starvation!

The doom was a fearful one, but it would end soon all her sorrows and her sufferings.

And she bent her head upon her breast and prayed.

Prayed for her father—for her lover, and herself. Then she lay down and awaited death!

But it came not to the worn and weakened frame of Ellen.

Hours past away—hours of darkness and silence in which nothing but the loud beating of her own heart was audible.

A heart lacerated with care and sorrow.

She had closed her eyes, and given way to a dreary sort of apathy, when suddenly she was startled by the flash of a light across the closed eyelids.

She started up and looked eagerly around her.

The figures of two men appeared at one end of the vaults in which she was confined, one bearing on his shoulder a tub, whilst the other carried a lantern in his hand.

She strained her eyes to trace the lineaments of their features, and saw that he who carried the lantern, was none other than the man who had answered her summons at the door of the hut after being placed on shore by Latour—the other she fancied to be the man whom she had seen but for a moment, and whose hand was placed upon her mouth to stifle the cry which arose to her lips when awoke from the slumber into which she had fallen in the inner room of the fisherman's hut.

She rushed forward as well as she could to beg of them to release her from that horrible place, when she suddenly paused as the words of one of the men smote her ear.

"The Boy Rover won't be much pleased at not getting a better cargo than this," said the man. "But there, we'll square it all up with him by handing over that girl."

Ellen trembled as these words fell upon her ears. Could she hope for mercy from those men whom she now felt sure, instead of being honest fishermen were contrabandists, and who were in league with none other than the wretch who had striven to violate her, and who had caused her so much bitter misery and suffering.

She felt that all appeal to their feelings would be in vain, but she determined to watch by which means they entered and left the vaults.

With this intention she crept stealthily forward keeping close to the wall till she had placed herself opposite to the two men.

THE DISCOVERY OF ELLEN.

These worthies, after having fixed the tub or barrel on the top of several others which were piled up at the farthest end of the vault from that where our heroine had been lying, took the lantern from where they had placed it, and commenced ascending a ladder which led to a trapdoor in the roof of the vault.

Suddenly the man who carried the lantern paused when he had gone about half way up the ladder.

"What's the matter?" said his companion, who was waiting to ascend.

"Why, I just recollect that girl we put down here aint got anything to eat or drink, and if we mean giving her to the Boy Rover it won't do to let her starve."

"No," replied the other; "better fatten her."

"Well, I'll get the old woman to prepare the provender for her, and bring it down when its ready."

And the man passed on up the ladder, lifted the trap, and disappeared all but his arm to which the lantern was suspended, and which he held down the opening to light up his friend.

When the second man had stepped from the last round of the ladder on to the floor of the apartment above, the trap was closed, and Ellen heard with horror the small door bolted in its frame.

With a heavy heart she sank again upon the ground and gave way to tears.

The fate she had fondly hoped she had escaped from a few hours before, was still held over her, and the words these men had uttered struck a greater chill to her heart than did the damp vaults to her blood.

Was she then destined to fall again into the hands of that inhuman youth—was she then reserved for fresh insults at his hands?

Rather death, she thought, a thousand times, than a repetition of that which she had already undergone.

In fear and trembling she awaited the appearance of the man with the food he had spoke of to his companion, resolved to appeal to his feelings to save her.

"All men are not lost to feeling," she muttered to herself. "There must be some bright spot in their black and callous hearts."

In a short time she heard the bolts of the trap withdrawn, and the rays of the lantern penetrated the darkness of the vault.

The man descended the trap, bearing the lantern in his hand, and a loaf of brown bread and a piece of cheese beneath his arm, which he presented to Ellen, who stood at the foot of the ladder.

"Here," he said, "there's food for you."

"Oh," exclaimed the poor girl, bursting into tears. "Why am I confined in this dark place?"

"Better be confined here than have your throat cut, aint you?" growled the man. "But there, women never are grateful shew 'em what kindness you will."

"For mercy sake let me out from this place!" pleaded Ellen.

"Here, catch hold of the bread if you want it," growled the man, savagely.

"Oh, for the sake of your own soul, let me get out of this place," pleaded Ellen.

"It aint safe to do that," said the man.

"Why not?"

"Because you'd soon get us into trouble," growled the man.

"I swear I will not harm you," said Ellen.

"I'll take good care you don't, neither," replied the man; "so lay hold, if you don't want to starve. You'll get out in good time."

"When will that be?" sighed Ellen.

"When the Boy Rover anchors in the bay."

And ascending the ladder he closed and secured the trap, leaving Ellen in darkness and despair.

CHAPTER LXXVII.

THE PIRATE'S FIRST TRIAL—THE HURRICANE— THE WRECK—THE CAPTIVE.

IT was not long after Wild Madge and her white companions, Lang, Smith, Hardy, and Bond had resolved to become pirates, that they found means to manufacture a black flag which they ran up to the mast head, and calling all the liberated slaves around them, explained to the blacks the life they proposed to lead, and exhorted one and all to join them and take the oath.

Wild Madge was to have the supreme command, Lang was to hold the next office, Smith the next, and Bond and Hardy were to follow, each holding equal rank.

The inducements held out to the blacks, were revenge on their oppressors, rapine, and robbery upon those who had sought to make them slaves.

Incentives which drew one and all to join.

The slaver had been well armed so as to be enabled to cope with the vessels ever on the look out for them, or to put down any revolt on the part of their black cargo.

To Hardy and Bond was assigned the care of the arm chest, and these worthies commenced distributing them among their men, and exhorting them to use them without mercy upon all who should offer resistance.

Meantime they drew nearer and nearer the sail which they had made out.

Wild Madge leant over the bulwarks, her eyes never for a moment taken from the white canvas of the unsuspecting vessel which kept on her way across the bosom of the deep waters.

When they were within a mile of each other, Wild Madge beckoned Lang to her side.

The captain, for such he now was called by all on board, obeyed the summons.

"What craft is that?" she asked.

"A trader, I should say," replied Lang.

"You think so?"

"I do."

"And one that will make little resistance," said the woman.

"Resistance would be useless," said Lang, "against us, if the blacks stand firm."

"They will do so." said Madge.

"I hope they will."

"I am sure they will."

"Why so?"

"Are they not actuated by revenge?"

"True, yet they may be struck with fear," said Lang.

Wild Madge shook her head.

"They are sensual beasts," she said.

"What of that?"

"There may be females on board yon ship."

"And if there be?"

"To possess them the black skins will fight like demons"

And that fearful meaning look spread over the face of the fury.

"But we take first pick," said Lang.

"Who?"

"The officers."

"True."

"I don't half like the idea of white women being ravished by these blacks."

"Why?"

"I can't say—it don't seem natural."

"Ha, ha," laughed Madge. "I shall enjoy the scene. How musical will sound their shrieks. Oh, it will afford me pleasure indeed, if on board that ship there be a woman for each of the crew."

"Humph!" said Lang, half disgusted, "there's not likely to be so many, but suppose there should only be one short."

"Well."

"It would cause unpleasantness," said Lang, leering round at the virago, "unless you gave yourself to the last man and so make up the deficiency.

Wild Madge turned fiercely upon the speaker.

Her blessed eyes started almost from her head with passion.

"Me," she shrieked.

"If you counsel rapine, you alone would be to blame for any violence offered to you."

"Who would dare offer violence to me," shrieked Madge.

"I cannot say, I merely speak of probabilities returned Lang.

"Speak of them no more then," said Madge, "or I will put you in irons."

Lang turned away but spoke not.

Wild Madge again lent over the bulwarks and fell into a strain of thought.

Thoughts called forth by the words of the seaman.

"Was she not foolish in exciting the blacks by hopes of feeding them lustful natives?

Yet her hatred to her sex could not be obliterated.

The shrieks of a violated woman were music to her soul, the groans of an outraged maiden fell upon her ears like balm upon a wound.

Still there might be truth in the words of Lang. But then again she thought age and the disgusting appearance which a life of passion and drunkenness had given to her, would prevent any overture offered her from even the ignorant negroes.

So she dismissed all anxiety from her mind on that score, and became as inveterate as ever against virtue and innocence.

The love of suffering and misery in others seemed to be so strongly engrafted in the heart of Madge, as to be unable to exist without seeing or hearing it.

Closer and closer came the vessel, and the crew were beat to quarters.

Lang again approached Wild Madge.

"We are sufficiently near now," he said, "to hold parley with them."

"Do so then," replied Madge.

"Bond," called Lang.

Bond advanced, placing his hand to his cap.

"Captain."

"Send a shot across her bows."

"Aye, aye, sir," replied Bond.

And the next minute a long brass gun which stood amidship belched forth a sheet of flame and smoke, and a shot ploughed the waters a few yards from the bowsprit of the stranger.

Lang watched as it crochetted over the waves and finally sank into the bosom of the ocean.

"She'll know what that means," said Lang, turning his gaze from the course of the missile to the masts of the vessel.

The sails of the stranger were hauled back.

"Sensible captain that," said Lang.

The captain of the pursued ship had given the order to lay to.

Gradually the pirate vessel neared her victims; and, when sufficiently close, Lang raised the trumpet to his mouth, and called out:

"Ship, ahoy!"

"Ahoy!" came back over the waves.

"What ship?" called Lang.

"The 'Mary Ann.'"

"Where from?"

"Liverpool."

"Where to?"

"America," was the response.

"What's your cargo?"

"Hardware—passengers."

A smile played round the mouth of Madge as these words fell upon her ears.

Then the voice of the commander of the stranger again floated towards them.

"What ship?"

"The 'Scorpion,'" replied Lang—for such had they named her.

"Where from?"

"Africa."

"Where to?"

"Any sea in which prizes may be taken, answered Lang. "Up with the colours," he added, "and run her aboard."

The flag of piracy, which had been lowered after the men had taken the oath, was now run up, and fluttered in the breeze.

The moment that its folds spread themselves out over the pirate ship, the "Mary Ann" made all sail to fly from her assailants.

At this Lang gave orders for all sail to be set and chase to be made after the vessel, which thus flew from them.

The crew set about obeying the order, and in a short time every stitch of canvas she would carry was shook out, but swift sailer as she was she fell away from her intended victim.

As if by magic, the breeze had dropped and the pirate was becalmed, while the Mary Ann kept on her course.

Her sails dropped and flapped against the masts, and her black flag hung like a wet rag, loose and drooping.

The crew stood around the decks watching the countenance of Lang as he stood with folded arms gazing intently upon the horizon, then turning his looks to the trader as the dying breeze carried her further from him—

"Curse them!" he muttered, and as if to echo the words, a long, low, but air-filling moan came over the sea. It was that sound which ever precedes a terrible tempest, a sound which will cause the bravest seaman's cheek to turn pale whenever he hears it, for it is like the knell of death unto the dying.

"Down with every thread of canvass," cried Lang, "show not an inch, or it will be stripped from the spars by the blast which is coming from yonder cloud."

As he spoke, he pointed to a mountain-like cloud which was sweeping from the north-west, which he could see bounding, writhing, and falling before the coming hurricane. The crew hurried to obey their leader, and soon the snow-white sails, which contrasted so strongly with the spars and hull of the vessel, were lowered to the deck.

"Four men at the helm! Brace yourself well, and let every man secure himself ere the squall strikes us!" shouted Lang, grasping at the same time one of the after shrouds.

Thus prepared for the gale, the pirates again glanced toward the trader, which still kept her canvass spread, seeming to choose the alternative of being wrecked or dismasted by the gale to being overtaken by the pirate.

And now the gale, passing over the sea, came sweeping along the water down towards the ship.

A sound like the rustling charge of a mighty army of horsemen, could be heard in the distance, and then could be seen the rising wall of foam as it seemed to be lifted up before the terrible blast. On, on, it came—the cloud, the wind, and the snow-white foam.

"Hold hard—stand firm at the helm, and bear off dead before the wind!" cried the thunder-like tones of the pirate captain, and its echoes were mingled with the sound of the storm as it swept down upon him.

One moment the vessel seemed to sink into the waves, to press forward and downward under the fearful weight, whilst each spar bent and creaked and seemed almost with human voices to speak.

Then she rose upon the crest of that huge roller of foam, and away like a frightened thing of life, away over the madly boiling waters, she sped swift as the clouds above her.

Now she was wrapped in clouds and foam, and the pirates could not see the trader any more, for they were veiled by the storm.

Yet their course lay towards where she was last seen, and though under bare poles, the pirate was swiftly cleaving her path towards the spot.

Oh, heavens! is there—can there be a more magnificent sight in nature than a hurricane—a real hurricane! The waters seem to rise and mingle with the clouds, your vessel seems first to be with one and then the other; to be a thing with wings, rising and falling like a feather, or pitching and leaping about as if mad or drunk with the very excitement you feel. You have no time for terror, no thought of danger; all is wrapped up in the grandeur of the scene.

But let us step on board the trader.

They looked as if every man was determined to die where he stood, rather than yield: yet their look told of despair, a despair which in itself is almost invincible. And ever and anon their glances wandered to the quarter-deck of their own craft, where was a sight which, while it made their case more unhappy, and added to their desperation, was one that would but add to their bravery if they were men.

There, beside an old, white-haired, but noble-looking and richly-dressed gentleman, stood a young girl, scarcely sixteen years of age, clinging to his tall, slender form, as a daughter only can cling to her father.

To say that she was beautiful, would not be half enough to convey to the reader a picture of her.

She was tall for her age—her thin dress, as she leaned against her father, showed the outlines of such a figure as was given to Venus when she arose from the sea; full, perfect, voluptuous, without losing one line of virgin grace and modesty. Her eyes were full of tearful expression, and so large, so soft, so dewy, where those jetty orbs, as she looked up toward her father's anxious brow, that a very fiend could not gaze into them unmoved. Her face was pale—pale as her father's cheek.

He strained his daughter's form to his breast, he gazed with a sad eye and quivering lip towards the pirate, then looked down upon the beautiful frail flower at his feet, and groaned in the agony of his heart as he seemed to think what might be her fate.

"Child," he murmured, "must I lose thee, my last and only joy."

"Oh, my father, let us yet hope," sighed the girl; "God is merciful, HE cannot thus let us perish."

"If it were but death, my Bianca, if it were but death for me, I would not care; but for thee, it is death, or worse."

"We may yet escape them. See those rising clouds— at other times they would be terror to me; now I hail the black-winged heralds of the tempest with delight."

The father turned to a young man dressed as an officer, who had stood with his glass in his hand, steadily regarding the pirate during the scene, and addressing him—

"What think you, captain—is there a chance of escape?"

"We may hope, senor, yet have we but hope."

"Can we not hope to beat them off?"

"No, senor; yet we can die in the trial. In this combat no quarter will be asked or given. We will save your daughter, or perish, for she alone would be preserved of all on board, if he overtakes us."

"If you die, my father, I will die with you!" cried the fair girl; "I will not live to fall into their ruthless hands; no, not if my own hand doth the deed."

"My brave, blessed child," murmured the father.

And the old man strained his daughter to his breast.

The young captain again raised the glass to his eye, and looked anxiously at the Scorpion.

Then lowering it he turned to the old man.

"He prepares for the storm," said the young captain. "It is coming, and 'tis a fearful blast, yet in it lays our only hope of safety. If our spars will only stand its strength for a few hours until darkness comes on, I may hope to elude him—if they fail, we will either founder at sea, or fall into his hands. I shall not stir tack or sheet, my ship must sink or bear it."

"Bravely spoken," cried the old man, turning to the captain, "so be it—we may better perish thus than by the merciless hands of those fiends in human form; touch not a sail; if the canvass must be taken in, let the storm do it for us."

"Come away from the guns, and secure yourselves for the storm!" cried the captain, to his crew; then he took his place beside the two men at the helm, and gazed back at the coming storm.

"It will be upon us in another moment," he cried; "now it shuts in the pirate, she is hidden in its mist and clouds of spray; hold fast for the love of life, for it is upon us."

With a cry the girl clung to her father.

"Seize the netlings of the taffrail," cried the captain—"hold on or you are lost."

Bianca and her father grasped the netting at the taffrail, as directed by the captain, and now each one on board of the galleon turned their eyes towards the coming tempest. They saw the rushing clouds, heard the roar of the winds as they rolled up the waters into a foamy heap, and then with trembling anxiety awaited the result, when it should reach their tall-masted vessel.

On—on it came—now the foam was close behind them, then their loose, flapping sails filled with its first breath—another second, and the storm was upon them with all its terrific force.

Down—down, as if she was driving to the depths of the ocean pressed the noble bark, her bows sinking deeper and deeper each second. Her sails filled almost to bursting, the spars bent forward over the bows, not an inch forward did the hull seem to move but rather pressed bodily downward.

Then, when it seemed as every sail must burst and each spar snap asunder, she lifted upon the white rollers of foam, and off like a great white-winged bird she dashed—now swooping down into the eddying foam, then rearing up towards the very clouds.

Breathless, pale, trembling, clung her crew to the rigging, while the noble captain and her staunch helmsmen strove to keep the ship before the gale, for they knew that certain death to all would ensue if she but varied a single point: for that gale if brought upon her beam could not fail to capsize her, or drive her to the bottom.

With her long hair streaming out upon the gale, and her white robes fluttering in the wind, half sheltered behind her father's side, stood Bianca, gazing with a mixed terror and wonder upon the great wreaths of foam which were flung out like the arms of following spirits behind the vessel, seeming to try to wrap her dark hull in their cold embracings.

The gale howled on—the clouds, and foam, and the strained ship, all rushed on together in a wild, indescribable confusion.

"If she will but bear this blast four hours, we will be saved!" shouted the captain, as he braced his shoulder to the helm: "for we now are wrapped in mist and darkness, and it were impossible for the dreaded pirate to keep upon our track in a time like this."

The gale seemed to increase, even so high that the waves could not raise, and the sea became almost a level sheet of foam. Still the sails clung to the yards, though each spar bent as reeds in the forest when the gale bows them to the earth.

Then, while the captain and crew were watching these with breathless fear lest they should give way, a shriek from Bianca, so loud and piercing that it could be heard even above the gale, called their attention to another and yet more fearful sight. There, close in their wake, and with his red hull—his dark fearful flag flying, and but one snugly reefed sail set—was the pirate, bounding lightly over the water, and gaining fast upon them. They could see his tall form as it towered above his terrible crew; and that flag with its horrible motto was poised like a black-winged vulture above them. This they saw, and paler than before became every cheek; but yet they did not yield them to despair. Every man grasped his weapon, and as they looked each other in the eye, each could read but one thought, that, "together we live, together we die."

On came the pirate closer than before, and now they could more plainly see its dreaded form.

As those on board the galleon saw with agony that, inch by inch, slowly, but surely, their terrible enemy was gaining upon them, they prepared for the struggle of death which must ensue when he attempted to board them. But while this was doing, one cloud darker than the rest was seen sweeping along over the distant sea, casting its shadow upon the foam. The quick eye of Lang saw it, and he shouted to his crew :

"In with your sail—down with every thread, and hold fast for your lives!"

Then, when the captain of the trader saw this, he shouted to his men:

"Hold fast the sails, touch not a rope; let this destroy us rather than yon fiend. It is even now gathering gloom for nightfall, and we will yet hope."

His last words were drowned in the fearful yell of the blast, as it now broke still stronger upon them.

One moment the ship bounded forward; then her strained spars, with a terrible crash, bent forward, and, snapping in a mass close to the deck, fell in a confused wreck, while the driving foam covered them, the decks, everything, with its boiling eddying waves.

Death and their sepulture were close together then.

Of all the trader's crew, the helmsman, captain, and his two passengers, were all that stood now upon her decks. They were abaft the falling spars, and thus they were saved.

And there she lay trembling in the foam; beyond her the dark spars; and here and there a struggling dying man could be seen, battling for life amid the waves.

And, far out in the distance, the "Scorpion" rode upon the billows, under bare poles.

Still howled the gale above their heads, yet drove the eddying clouds along the war-spirits of the storm; but their water-logged, sparless hull pitched and heaved with a dead weight as the waves tumbled and tossed about them. No longer did they dash on and leave the huge rollers behind.

And now it was pitchy dark above and around them save when some long, ragged flash of lightning would break from the dark clouds and throw its lurid glare over their shivered, shattered hull. And when it did, what a picture for a painter did it illumine.

The farthest aft upon the wet deck, with her dishevelled hair made glossier by the spray, and streaming out over her father's bared breast, knelt Bianca, one hand clasped to her brow to shade her eyes from the glare, the other arm encircling her father's neck, and half-hidden in his long white hair which hung heavy and wet close to his neck.

Her pale lips were moving in silent prayer, that prayer which, though spoken in a breath, is the surest of all to reach "our Father's" ear.

And upon one knee, with one arm clasping his daughter's waist, the other clinging with the strength of desperation to the netting, was Bianca's father. His brow wore the same anxious look, but his eye, bent only on her, showed that of her alone he thought, for her alone he feared.

The two helmsmen clung yet to their useless helm, their weather-stained faces calm and composed; calm with the dead apathy of despair, calm with the knowlege that they must die, and with the determination to meet their fa'e as became men.

And the young captain, he was now upon the wreck of his first command, stood near them, calm too, as they, but looking sadly upon the poor girl, who knelt so helplessly at her father's side.

Little cared the young and manly brave for himself, yet it was painful to think that she, so young, pure, and beautiful, must soon become the prey of the ravenous shark, or still more ravenous pirate.

The night wore on, and with it the gale seemed to abate; and though the spray still swept wildly over their decks, the sea was getting smoother.

Then the captain again spoke of hope to that miserable father, and said—

"If the pirate has been blown far to leeward, he may not find us again, and we may yet keep our strained hull above the water until some friendly sail, sent by God's holy mercy, may cross our path!"

And yet there was not one spar left upon the trader's deck whereby to hoist a signal of distress, or to raise a scanty sail to move her onward over the waters.

Still, Hope, that last blessed boon of heaven, which clings to the soul when all things else have fled, cheered up the seaman's heart, and determined him to struggle to the last.

The two mariners who had clung so desparingly to their helm, raised their heads as they heard their brave captain's words, and their eyes too grew brighter, as if they felt that their time had not yet come. But that grey-haired father looked sadder still upon the frail and beautiful child of his heart.

The waves sank down, and the foam began to give way to the glorious blue of the ocean. The storm was over, the elements, tired of their own fury, had sunk down to rest, and a quiet calm came upon the water and in the sky. And soon the east began to grow bright, and then the upper edge of the sun came up from the blue line of the horrizon. As this illumined the water, with eager and straining eyes the poor survivors of the wreck gazed around them to see if their dreadful foe was yet in sight.

A cry of agony escaped them.

The Scorpion was bearing down upon the wreck with every sail set.

The father clasped his daughter to his heart, and prayed—not for himself but for her.

In a short time the Scorpion was alongside, and

a boat having been launched, Lang and Hardy with several of the blacks boarded the logged hull.

Like demons they sprang forwards to the spot where Bianca surrounded by her father, the captain and the helmsman stood.

The men threw themselves before her, but the weapons of the blacks fell upon their heads, and they were struck bleeding to the deck.

Lang seized the girl by the arm, and drew her fainting form to the boat.

"My prize," he muttered.

A wild shriek broke from her lips and her head dropped.

Lang laid her down in the bottom of the boat and returned to direct the removal of the stores.

All that was deemed worth taking was soon carried on board the Scorpion, together with Bianca who for the present was placed under the care of Wild Madge.

CHAPTER LXXVIII.

THE SMUGGLER PLACED IN GAOL.—THE WARDERS SURPRISED.—MURDER OF THE TURNKEY.—THE ESCAPE.

CONFINED in the hold of the merchantman, together with his five companions, the Boy Rover chafed like a caged lion.

Bitterly did he curse the ill fortune which had befallen himself and his followers, and bitter indeed were the invectives he heaped upon the head of the noble young lieutenant.

"Curse him!" he muttered, between his set teeth. "He has been a thorn in my side. It would seem fate has destined that he should ever stand between me and my desires. Fool—fool that I was to take him on board. Better have let the waves close over him when Latour made him walk the plank."

"Of course you had," said Black Bill, sulkily. "But you are so cursed strongheaded. Can't see what you wanted to get him aboard for at all. You knew the fellow hated you, and had got the pluck to show it too. You should have let him gone to the bottom, and then we might have been free."

"I am aware of it now," said the Rover. "but the hatred I bore him was so strong that I could not see him die so easily. I wanted to torture him—kill him by inches. Was it not to him I owed the loss of our vessel; was it not to him I owed the loss of the girl?"

"Curse the girl!" growled Bill; "we've had no luck since you first caught sight of her baby face."

"Not a day but some bad luck has beset us," remarked Jem.

"Well, I suppose it would have done so if we had never seen her," said the Boy Rover.

"No it wouldn't," remarked Bill, who was of rather a superstitious turn of mind.

"Well," chimed in Sam, "it aint no use quarrelling about that now. The captain has got us into an infernal scrape, and he had best try to get us out of it."

"It's all very well," said Black Bill, "to talk like that, but it strikes me there isn't much chance of his doing that."

"I reckon not," said Jem.

"At present there seems little prospect of doing so," said the Rover, "but I feel sure that we shall yet give the bloodhounds of the law the slip."

"Do you?" said Bill.

"I do," replied the Rover.

"Then I don't," surlily exclaimed the smuggler mate.

"You are too desponding," said the Boy Rover.

"No I aint," said Bill; "only it's no use fancying we're going to do things we can't, for how can we escape with these cursed irons upon us."

"Why, we can't, of course," said Jem.

"Perhaps not, but we shall not always have them on us I hope," said the Boy Rover.

"No, but they won't take them off till they have made us equally secure," said Jem.

"I shall not give up all hope of escape yet, anyhow," replied the Rover.

"Then I shall," growled Bill.

"Do as you please," said the Rover.

And he lapsed into silence.

The ship sped on her way to her destination, the captain taking every precaution to guard against escape, either by treachery or accident.

Not for one moment were the smuggler's limbs released from bondage, and even the Boy Rover himself began to despair.

In a few days the vessel ran into Portsmouth harbour, and the smugglers were brought upon deck to meet the officers of justice who were to take charge of them and convey them to prison.

Strongly ironed, they were placed in a boat and taken ashore.

Although their capture had been kept as secret as possible, it nevertheless became known to many, and ere the boat reached the landing a considerable concourse of people had assembled, eager to catch a glimpse of the youthful captain and his disreputable companions.

They were landed under a strong guard, and as they stepped on shore, groans and hisses resounded on all sides.

But the Boy Rover walked in the midst of those who guarded him with head erect and unflinching eye.

Not so his companions.

Black Bill hung his head as did also his companions, and the groans struck terror to their guilty souls.

They were hurriedly marched to the prison, and placed in the keeping of the governor of the gaol, and as the door closed with a loud bang behind them, and they heard the key rattle in its ponderous locks, hope deserted all but the Boy Rover.

Not a muscle of his face changed, not a look betrayed the least fear or anxiety.

They were placed in three separate cells, the smuggler captain and Sam sharing one, Jem and Bill the second, and Tom and Ned the third.

Here for the first time was freedom granted to their limbs.

But of what avail was that.

They looked around them.

Four walls encircled them, high and smooth.

Sam sat down upon the rude stone bench and covered his face with his hands in despair.

But the Boy Rover stood gazing around him calculating the thickness of the stone, the position of the cell, and the prospects of escape.

And poor indeed they were.

Not foothold for a spider did there seem in that cell.

Still the Boy Rover did not despair.

He sat down beside his companion and placed his hand upon Sam's shoulder.

Sam started.

"Come, cheer up," said the young captain, "don't give way like a woman."

A sickly smile which faded almost ere it was born rose to the face of the smuggler.

"What makes you so downhearted," asked the Boy Rover.

"There's little here to make a fellow cheerful," replied his companion.

"There's nothing to cause you to despair," said the Rover.

"Ain't there?"

"No."

"Not these walls," asked Sam.

"No," replied the Rover, "I know it is difficult to reconcile myself to fresh habitations, but the feeling soon wears itself out."

Sam shook his head.

"You don't mean to say," exclaimed the Rover, "that the sight of these grey stones can cur the spirit of one who has dared danger and death as you have done upon the ocean."

Sam looked rather ashamed of himself as the words of his youthful captain fell upon his ears.

"I don't know how it is captain," he said, "but I seem to have all the pluck taken out of me here. You know I never hurled down my colours to any enemy, let him be ever so strong. I never turned tail upon a pistol or cutlass, but damn me, I can't help feeling down here."

"We have faced many dangers," said the Rover.

"So we have captain."

"And been in some very hair-breadth escapes."

"That's true."

"But we have got out of them," said the captain,

"Yes."

"Then why daspair now."

"I don't know, but I can't help it," replied Sam.

"Cheer up man," said the Rover, "cheer up, there is still hope."

"Where," eagerly asked Sam.

"Here."

"How."

"The governor of this prison has forgotten something."

"What is that."

"He has placed two of us in one cell," said Dick.

"What of that."

"A great deal to our advantage."

"How so."

"It will enable us the better to effect our escape."

"I cannot see it."

"But I can."

Sam only shook his head.

"I tell you it will, it is not likely that more than one turnkey will visit us."

"Well."

"We can overpower him."

"But he would soon get assistance did we attempt to escape."

"He would be unable."

"Why?"

"Anyone of us could bind his limbs, while the other stopped his breath."

"But we have nothing here to bind him with, even allowing that we could overpower him," said Sam, his face becoming a little brighter.

"Yes, we have."

"What?"

"Our neckerchiefs."

"But even if we should succeed, what then?"

"We could release our companions."

"Well?"

"There would then be six of us," said the Rover.

"Still we could not escape."

"We could overpower the warders, seize their keys, open the prison doors, and make for the coast."

"You think so?"

"I know so," replied the young smuggler, in a tone of conviction.

"Will the risk pay for the trial?"

"Certainly it will. If we remain here we shall swing. They can but make us do the same if we murder every official in the prison."

"When would you make the attempt?" asked Sam.

"To-night—when the turnkey visits us, to see that we are safe."

"You are so sanguine."

"I am but resolved never to throw a chance away," replied the captain.

"And you think we shall succeed?" said Sam.

"I know we shall," replied the Boy Rover, "if you but stand firm, and flinch not."

"No fear of my flinching, if there is a chance of liberty," said Sam.

"There is not only a chance, but a certainty," replied the Rover.

"Then I am with you."

"Bravely spoken."

"To-night, then, we shall try?"

"To-night; for every day's incarceration in this place will add months of age to my frame."

"And yet you do not seem to care much for it," said Sam.

"I will not give way to despair," said the smuggler captain, "till the rope encircles my neck. While there's life there's hope; and, when hope leaves me, farewell to existence."

The cheerful tones of his companion soon roused Sam from the desponding state into which he had fallen; and ere the coming night shut out the little ray of light which straggled through a small window, near the roof, his spirits had become as light and buoyant as those of the Boy Rover.

Seating themselves upon the stone bench they awaited in silence the visit of the turnkey.

The prison clock had just struck the hour of nine, when they heard a key turned in the lock of the cell door.

Silently the Boy Rover rose to his feet.

He placed his finger on his lip to enjoin his companion to silence.

Placing his hand to his neckerchief, he drew it from his throat and stood behind the door of the cell.

A look passed between them, but not a word was spoken.

Sam also rose and removed his neckerchief from his throat.

The door opened and the turnkey stepped just within the cell.

At that moment the Boy Rover rushed upon him.

The turnkey raised his hand to defend himself from the sudden spring of his assailants, but it was grasped by Sam, who coiled the handkerchief around his arm.

At the same time the Boy Rover threw his neckerchief over the head of the man, and drew it tightly over his mouth.

The man struggled but was unable to free himself from their hold, and in an instant his arms were lashed to his side by Sam, while the Boy Rover fastened his own so securely that the surprised turnkey could not utter a sound.

Tearing his keys from his grasp, the Boy Rover looked from his cell door into the long stone passage,

Not a sound met his ears, nor the form of a living soul met his sight.

An oil lamp suspended from the roof threw a dim light along the passage.

The Rover turned to his companion with a triumphant look upon his features.

"Sam," he whispered, "the coast is clear."

"Hurrah!" exclaimed Sam.

"Hush, you must not halloa till out of the woods."

Sam became silent in a moment.

"Force him on to the bed," he whispered, pointing to the turnkey.

This was done.

"Come," said the Rover.

Sam followed the captain from the cell into the passage.

Then the Boy Rover closed the door of the cell and locked it.

"He can give no alarm now," he whispered to his companion.

"We done that job clean," whispered Sam, with a grin.

"Yes, now to release the others," said the Rover, moving along the passage.

"Did you notice which cell they were placed in," asked his companion.

"Yes, I took the bearing."

"All right."

"This is one, I think," said the Rover, as he stopped before the door of a cell.

Placing his ear to the door, he motioned Sam to be silent and listened.

A sound came to his ears.

The Rover smiled.

It was the voice of Black Bill.

"All right," he whispered. "Keep a look out Sam."

"Aye, aye, captain."

The smuggler applied a key to the door but could not turn it.

"Curse it," he said, " I may have to try them all before I get the right one."

He selected another from the bunch with the same success.

Impatiently he selected another.

As he did so he detected that it was numbered.

He cast his eye up the door and saw that a number was also painted thereon.

"Ah," he muttered, "the key bears the number of the cell—good."

And searching over the keys he found one bearing the same number as that of the cell.

He placed it in the lock and it yielded.

The door opened.

Bill sprang forward, then came to a dead stop.

The Boy Rover placed his finger on his lip to enjoin silence.

"Well I'm blowed," exclaimed Bill, unable to prevent giving expression alike to his surprise and joy."

"Hush!" hissed the Rover.

"Captain."

"Silence, if you would not have every turnkey in the prison upon us."

Jem, too, had started up from the seat on which he had been sitting, and stood rubbing his eyes as if he wished to make sure that he was really awake.

"Come," whispered the Boy Rover, "follow me in silence."

"Where to?" said Bill.

"Liberty!" answered the captain.

"Liberty!" exclaimed Jem, in a whisper, " you don't mean it?"

"I do—come."

And he left the cell followed by Bill and Jem.

Turning, he closed the door.

"Now for the others," he said, moving stealthily along the passage.

Confused and bewildered at finding themselves free from the cell in which they had endured several hours of misery, the men followed silently the Boy Rover till he stopped at the door of a cell near the end of the passage.

Here too he placed his ear against the door and listened, but not a sound could he distinguish.

"I cannot hear them," he whispered, "yet I feel sure this is the cell in which Sam was placed."

"Let's see, captain," whispered Bill, looking up at the door, "it's number three they give him for a lodging—yes, that's right."

The Boy Rover selected the key, and placed it in the lock.

It yielded easily to the pressure of his fingers, and he pushed the door silently open.

The light from the passage penetrated the cell and revealed the forms of the two men fast asleep on the bed.

"Well," exclaimed Bill, looking in, "that beats me. Just shows you what it is to have an innocent mind and a pure conscience. Blowed if they aint both snoozing!"

"Sound asleep," whispered the Rover. "Keep a sharp look out for any sail that may heave in sight."

"Aye, aye, captain," said Bill, looking up and down the passage.

The Boy Rover laid his hand upon the shoulder of Tom, and shaking him gently, he said in a loud whisper—

"Turn out."

"It aint my watch," growled the man, half asleep.

"Breakers ahead!" whispered the Rover into his ear.

"'Bout ship," exclaimed the man, leaping from the bed, and stumbling across the floor of the cell.

The Boy Rover caught him by the arm to save him from falling, exclaiming—

"Hush Tim—hush."

"Ah," said the man, looking half frightened. "Captain?"

"Silence," hastily exclaimed the Boy Rover. "I have come to release you from this cursed place, but your noise has almost betrayed us."

The man was thoroughly awake now.

"I thought I was in my hammock and had further to jump," said Tim. "But captain—"

"Not a word now, but follow me. Ned is awake I see—bring him along."

In surprise they followed the rover from the cell into the passage, where they found their companions.

Having also closed this door, the Rover, fixing his eye upon the faces of his companions, said—

"Thus far we are free, but there is much yet to do. Be silent and be calm. We must seize the turnkey at the door and obtain his keys ere we can get outside these cursed walls, but we must be silent or we shall bring heaven knows how many upon us—then farewell to any chance of escape. Follow me, and seize and stop the mouth of any one we may meet."

The men nodded in answer to this, and the Boy Rover led the way along the passage.

Arriving at the end of this, another passage turned off leading to the porter's room and principal door of the prison.

"Keep close together," said the Boy Rover, "but, above all, be silent."

WILD MADGE AND MR. HANFIELD.

Then he moved stealthily along followed by his companions.

They had got within a dozen yards of the porter's room, the door of which stood open, and the reflection of a large fire burning in the grate, cast a warm glow upon the opposite wall, when a loud thumping noise was heard.

Simultaneously each one of the part paused and listened anxiously.

The noise continued.

"What is it I wonder," whispered Bill.

"Curse it," whispered the Boy Rover, "it is the turnkey.

"Where is he?" asked Bill, turning rather pale.

"In our cell, his mouth and arms are bound, but his legs are free and is kicking at the door."

"Curse it," exclaimed Sam, "he will betray us to the others."

"Shall we go back and cut his throat," said Bill.

"How can you do that," asked the Rover. "Where's your knife."

"Oh," said the man, suddenly recollecting that none of them had a weapon of any description.

"Forward," said the Boy Rover, "we must endeavour to get clear before he is discovered."

The kicking noise still continued, each moment sounding louder than before.

"Hallo," came a voice to the ears of the smuggler, "what' that."

"One of them smugglers, I expect," said another voice, in the porter's room.

"'Taint much good there kicking here," said the first speaker.

"Lockett will soon stop their row," said the other.

The smugglers, who had paused to listen to this colloquy, now moved forward again; but their progress was stopped by the loud cry of "Help!"

No. 29

"Fury!" exclaimed the Boy Rover, "he has got his jaws free. Quick, quick—or our escape will be frustrated."

It was evident, too, that those in the porter's room also heard their cry, as sudden exclamations and quick movements emanated therefrom.

"They are coming," said the Boy Rover, hastily. "Stand firm, and pounce upon them."

Scarce had the words left his mouth than two men, each bearing a naked cutlass in his hand, dashed from the room into the passage.

Scarce had they taken three steps when their eyes encountered the forms of the smugglers.

With a cry of surprise they halted; but, ere they could recover themselves, the Boy Rover dashed forward, and struck one of them a heavy blow upon the forehead, with the bunch of keys.

The man staggered; but his companion raised his weapon.

Ere it could descend, Sam had caught the arm of the man in a vice-like grip.

"Disarm them," said the Boy Rover, in a loud whisper.

In an instant the smugglers threw themselves upon the warders, and forced them to the ground.

But, ere they could prevent them, the men shouted:

"Escape—escape!"

"Blast you!" roared Bill, seizing one of the cutlasses, and raising it above his head—"another word, and I'll strike you dead."

"Escape—escape!" shouted the man.

Bill raised the cutlass above his head; then brought it down with fearful force upon the forehead of the warder.

It inflicted a fearful gash; and, as the warm blood spurted from the wound upon the faces of the smugglers, with a deep groan, the man fell forward upon the floor.

The other warder, frightened by the fate of his comrade, made no further resistance, but suffered his mouth to be bound by the handkerchief of Jem, in silence.

The Boy Rover possessed himself of the other weapon, and, holding its point to the man's breast, he exclaimed, hurriedly:

"The keys—quick—the keys!"

The man pointed to the room he had just quitted.

The Boy Rover strode to the room and looked around.

His quick eye immediately detected the objects he sought hanging by a hook beside the fireplace.

Eagerly he seized them.

Making his way from the room, he beckoned to his companions.

The men left the warders and advanced towards him.

"Have you got them?" asked Bill.

"Yes."

"Then we are all right."

"Don't make too sure."

"Why?"

"We are not free yet."

"But soon shall be."

"I hope so."

The noise of the men in the cell still came to their ears.

"I fear that fellow will bring others upon us," he said advancing toward the iron bound door.

"Curse him!" said Bill.

"For what?" asked the Rover.

"For making that row."

"He but does his duty."

"Damn his duty," exclaimed Bill. "I'd duty him if I had him here."

The Boy Rover placed one of the keys in the lock, but all his force could not turn it.

He then tried another.

Still the result was the same.

He tried the third and last, but it would not move in the wards.

"Furies!" he exclaimed. "I can turn neither."

"Let me try," said Bill, advancing and laying his hand upon the key.

But all his efforts proved unavailing.

Still the kicking and shouting of the men in the cell continued.

"Curse that fellow," exclaimed Bill, "he will do for us yet, I'm afraid."

"He will certainly bring others upon us, if there are others to bring."

The other smugglers gathered round Bill anxiously as he strove to open the door.

"See if there are not other keys in the room," said the Boy Rover turning to his followers.

Tom and Sam entered the porter's lodge and searched around it.

But no other keys could they find, and chop-fallen they returned to the door, where Bill, perspiring with his efforts, had given up the task in despair.

And still the kicking and shouting continued in the cell and echoed along the passages.

"Trapped, by all that's devilish!" said Bill.

At this moment there was the sound of approaching footsteps.

"Some one comes," said the Boy Rover, hurriedly.

"Look out," whispered Bill, grasping the cutlass.

The footsteps sounded nearer.

The Boy Rover made another effort to turn the key in the lock.

Nearer and nearer came the approaching footsteps towards them.

In an agony of suspense the smugglers waited and watched.

The tall figure of a man appeared at the end of the passage.

It paused for a moment, then raised its arm and shouted—

"Ring the alarm bell! Lockett, Potter, the prisoners are loose! Ring the alarm bell! warders—warders!"

"Curse you," roared Bill, unable longer to keep cool and calm, "I'll cut you down like a bit of salt junk."

But ere the words had left his lips, there was a sharp flash—a puff of smoke, and a loud report echoed through the passage.

The warder who had been bound and stood leaning against the wall watching the movements of the smugglers, turned quickly round and fell to the ground.

The bullet had entered his breast.

At the same moment the Boy Rover had turned the key the reverse way in the lock, and the door opened.

With a cry of joy the smugglers sprang through it, and gained the open air as the loud tones of the prison bell smote upon their ears.

———

CHAPTER LXXIX.

THE PIRATES AT WORK.—THE RECOGNITION.—HENRY
DOOMED TO DEATH.

With cheeks blanched with feelings of dread and horror, Mr. Hanfield gazed upon the dread ensign as its black folds curled in the wind and hung like a funeral pall over the beautiful tracery and cordage of the Scorpion.

Henry too, stood for a few moments irresolute how to act, he had not forgotten the indignation which had been offered to him on board the Spirit of the Wave, nor the doom to which Latour had consigned him.

Bob Bittern looked anxious but decided, and his horny hand tightened round the marlin spike he held in his grasp.

Jacob turned his eyes from one to the other of his companions, in the hope of reading their opinions respecting the pirate bark, then cast his eyes with a shudder upon the dreadful black flag.

After a pause Henry said—

"To run from that ship would be madness, to think of resistance would be worse."

"What will you do?" asked Mr. Hanfield anxiously.

"Strike your flag," asked Jacob.

Henry cast his eyes aloft, then turned to Jacob.

"No," he exclaimed, "at least," he added, "mine shall not be the hand to hurl down the saucy rag. They may sink us, but we will go down with the colours flying."

"Hurray!" shouted Bob, flourishing the spike around his head. "Man and boy I've sailed under that flag, and blow me it shall be my winding sheet afore I strike to a pirate."

"But resistance is useless," said the old gentleman.

"But that would be cowardice," replied Bob.

"I cannot reconcile cowardice and discretion," said Hanfield.

"That's because you're a landsman," replied Bob. "Why I'd never break a biscuit again if I struck my flag."

"But situated as we are—only four—surely it is not cowardice to surrender. Resistance will but add to the cruelty of the natures of miscreants, such as those."

"Perhaps you are right, sir," said Henry, "but I have a sailor's feeling respecting such a set."

"I honour you for it," said Hanfield, "but I will say no more."

"In a few minutes they will clap their grapnells aboard of us," said Henry. "We are powerless to prevent them, therefore must submit with a good grace."

"But you won't stand quiet and be murdered, will you?" exclaimed Bob.

"I consider the best plan would be, not to offer resistance as that would but inflame their bloody passions. We can only hope to beat them off."

"But I must leave my mark upon the skull of one or two of them," said the sailor.

"Not unless you are first assailed," said Henry.

"The first blow is half the battle," said Bob, in a dissatisfied tone.

"Sure; but in this instance a blow from us may prove our death warrant," remarked Henry.

"Of course, if you command, I must obey," said Bob; "but still I should like to try the strength of some of their skulls with this little bit of iron."

And Bob whirled the marling-spike about as though it had been a switch.

Another gun was fired from the pirate, to bring the vessel to.

"It's getting warm now," remarked Bob. "The next shot will make our timbers shake, I reckon."

"Yes," said Henry; "but still I will take no notice, and keep on our course, till they run alongside us."

The "Scorpion" bore down upon her, like a hawk upon its prey.

Shot after shot was now fired from the pirate—each one striking her hull, and sending splinters flying in all directions.

Still Henry kept on his course—not a sail was furled.

This seemed to exasperate the pirate, for, through the speaking-trumpet, came to their ears the words:

"Heave-to, or I'll sink you."

"You be hanged!" roared Bob.

"Heaven have mercy on us!" exclaimed Hanfield, as another shot struck the bowsprit, and carried it away.

The ship rolled and shook like a giant in pain for a moment; then became steady.

But the pirate was upon them; and, in another minute, the two vessels were locked together by the pirate's grapnells, and some thirty blacks, headed by Lang and Hardy, leaped upon the deck of Henry's ship.

Bob sprang forward, but the voice of Henry recalled him.

The brave but thoughtless sailor retreated slowly and grumblingly to the side of his commander.

Lang approached to where the young lieutenant stood, surrounded by Bob, Jacob, and Mr. Hanfield.

"You are commander here, I suppose?" he said, addressing Hanfield.

"No, sir," replied that gentleman. "My friend here holds that position.

Lang turned to Henry.

Their eyes met.

Simultaneously, both Henry and the pirate captain started back.

The recognition was mutual.

Lang was the first to speak.

"The devil!" he exclaimed.

"You introduce yourself by your right name," exclaimed Bob.

Lang turned fiercely round upon the honest sailor with a dark scowl upon his face, but the unflinching eye of Bob somewhat cowed the pirate for he turned again to Henry.

"We have met before," he said.

"We have," replied Henry, "on board the Venomed Snake, if I mistake not."

"You are right. Do you command this bark?"

"I do."

"Then I beg to inform you, that it is the intention of myself and crew, to take possession of anything we may think proper which is on board."

"I am powerless to resist you," said Henry.

"And wise not to attempt it," said Lang.

"Is he," muttered Bob. "I only wish he'd say the word, and I'd brain him—the cursed shark—I would."

Lang turned to his followers, who stood close behind him, with every species of weapons in their hands ready to murder or rob as the circumstances might require, and gave the order for them to search the vessel, and bring on deck everything worth removing to their own bark.

Henry still stood silently against the masts.

"You aint over polite to an old acquaintance," said Lang, after several of the men had departed on their mission.

Henry turned away indignantly.

"Is that your way of treating one you haven't seen for some time," continued Lang.

"I had no wish to see you now," replied Henry.

"Suppose not," said Lang, "and I had no thought of meeting with you. But I reckon your'd rather see me than the Boy Rover."

"I have seen him," replied Henry.

"On have the island."

"Since then."

"Where ?" asked Lang.

"On board this vessel."

"The devil you have," exclaimed Lang. "He got off the island then ?"

"He did."

"And where is he now ?" exclaimed Lang eagerly.

"Where he will never more be able to break the laws—insult and outrage defenceless women—and murder in cold blood honourable men."

"What's he dead ?"

"No."

"Where then ?"

"In prison I expect by this time, or at least on his road there," answered the young lieutenant.

Lang looked hard at Henry.

"Aint you telling a lie ?" he said, after a pause.

An indignant flush overspread the face of the young officer.

"What!" he exclaimed.

"There, don't get your dander up," said Lang, "or you may find the point of a dozen cutlasses picking out the softest part of your belly."

"Do you take me," said the young man indignantly, "for one so base as yourself."

"Don't come any of your palaver," said Lang, "for it won't serve you much. If you are so very sensitive, you ought to have been a tailors's trotter not a seaman. But there, I suppose you are sore a little at the honour we have paid you, in coming to see you."

"Honour," iterated Henry, "such a thing has been dead in the hearts of yourself and companions for years. But, thank heaven, some of the vile crew are about to meet the reward of their evil deeds."

"Ah ! the Boy Rover you mean."

"Yes, and some of his companions."

"Then the sharks have clapped their hands on him have they," asked Bill.

"They have, and ere long I trust will have the rest."

"Much obliged to you," said Lang. "but I don't mean to give them a chance if I can help it."

"You may escape for a time," said Henry, "but punishment will sooner or latter overtake you."

"You talk like a parson," said Lang, getting rather out of temper.

"I speak like a man," replied Henry.

"I should advise you to be very careful how you speak to Wild Madge."

"Wild Madge ?" iterated the young man.

"Yes, and happy she will be to see you, I know," said Lang.

"Where is she ?"

"On board ; and as I know it will put her in a good temper to meet with you again, I'll just introduce you to her."

"That fiend ?" exclaimed Henry.

"Yes, if you like ; she's commander of the vessel."

"Curse her," said the young man bitterly.

"I should advise you not," said Lang. "that is if you have any respect for your life. Here," he added, turning to the blacks who stood behind him, "just see this gentleman safe on board."

The blacks advanced.

"Stand back," said Henry. "I am powerless to prevent your sacking the ship, but I will defend myself against any indignity you may offer me."

And Harry drew the sword from the sheath which he had fastened to his side.

"I'm with you, captain," said Bob, springing before him and raising the marlinspike above his head. "Come on, you black varmint. Cuss you, I've broken open the hatches many a time to set you free when you've been going to slavery, and this is the return you make, you cussed pirates : but I'll show you what I think of your gratitude."

"Down with that fellow," said Lang, pointing to the old sailor.

The blacks rushed upon him, but swinging the marlinspike round he struck one of them so heavy a blow on the head that the fellow rolled, covered with blood, upon the deck.

Henry sprang forward to Bob's assistance, but in a moment they were both disarmed and held firmly by the negroes.

"Cuss you," growled Bob.

A powerful black raised a cutlass above his head in a threatening manner.

"Hold," said Lang.

The man dropped his weapon.

"He can offer no further resistance," said the pirate, "take them on board. If they attempt to escape from you then brain them."

The blacks led them to the side, and Henry and Bob feeling that all resistance was now useless, suffered themselves to be carried on board the pirate.

Turning to Hanfield and Jacob, Lang said—

"You're both land lubbers, I see now, so I don't think but what you can stay here and go to the bottom."

The face of Hanfield paled, so did also Jacob's, for they doubted not, by that remark, that it was the purpose of the pirates to scuttle the ship.

But neither spoke.

The blacks, headed by Hardy, had been ransacking the vessel from stem to stern, and now mustered on deck.

In a short time every article worth removing was placed on board the pirate, and Lang then gave the order for holes to be made in the bottom of the ill-fated vessel.

This was done, but in such a manner that the vessel would take a long time to sink, and so as to render the doom of the two men more horrible and lingering.

Then Lang, followed by the men who had remained to perpetrate the hellish work, left the vessel with the doomed men looking imploringly upon them, and gained their own ship.

At this moment Wild Madge, who had been standing on the quarter-deck of the pirate, caught sight, for the first time of the features of Mr. Hanfield as he turned with an imploring look to the demon faces of the pirate crew as they gazed with hellish looks upon the doomed ship.

She started, and her face became pale.

Then her eye gleamed, and the colour again rose to the face of the fury. The large blue veins on her forehead swelled almost to bursting, and darting to the side, laughed so hideous a laugh that even that crew of black demons shrank back affrighted.

Hanfield turned his pleading gaze upon her, and a shudder ran through his frame.

"Ho, ho!" shouted Madge, "at last—at last." And she threw her arms above her head, in wild glee.

"What's the matter?" asked Lang, making his way to her side, and looking upon the woman as if he thought she had taken leave of her senses.

"Ha, ha!" she screamed, rather than laughed—"look, look."

"Where?" said Lang.

"There—there. Do you not see him?" and she pointed to Hanfield, who, pale as death, stood leaning against the mast of the doomed ship.

"Well, what of him?" asked Lang.

"What of him? Ha, ha!—the hour of triumph has come, and Wild Madge will be avenged."

Lang, who believed she had been practising her old habits, and imbibing too much brandy, turned away, with a shrug of his shoulders.

"Cast off the grapnells," he exclaimed to the men who stood around.

Then Wild Madge turned her gaze from Hanfield to the sailors, as they hastened to obey the order of their officer.

"Hold—I command you!" she shrieked.

The men fell back from the sides and nettings.

"Why," asked Lang, in surprise, "do you stop them?"

"Because I will not be baulked of my revenge—revenge for which I have waited and prayed—for which I have sinned and lived."

Lang looked more and more surprised; but, knowing the temper of the furious woman, he remained silent.

"Look," she exclaimed—"look upon his pale face; see his trembling limbs. Ah! my revenge shall be fearful: his sufferings shall be great—greater than I have endured—endured through his accursed wiles, his smooth tongue, his treacherous heart. Oh! joy—joy; 'tis the first moment of gladness this seared heart has known. Man—man, you shall now feel the power of her you have wronged and scorned."

With bewildered stare, the men gazed upon her; and even Henry, as he stood guarded by the ferocious blacks, paled and trembled as he gazed upon the workings of her bloated and besotted face.

"Here, Madge," said Lang—"here is an old acquaintance I have brought off the ship."

Madge turned at these words, and her eyes fell upon Henry.

She recognised him in a moment.

"Ha, ha!" she laughed, "fate is kind to me. So—so you two are in my power; you who have been the cause of my boy losing his vessel; you who have left him to perish ere my revenge was fulfilled!"

"What's to be done with him?" asked Lang.

Madge paused a moment ere she answered; then, with a fearful look, she exclaimed—

"His fate shall be the same as that which his superior officer suffered when first his accursed face was seen on board the "Venomed Snake." Let yon ship be scuttled."

"It is already done," said Lang.

"'Tis well—'tis well. Away with him to his own deck, there bind him to the mast as was his master. Oh, the music of his shrieks shall cheer my soul, and my boy shall be avenged! Away with him to the mast—to death!"

"Hell hound," exclaimed Henry, "I defy you."

"Ha! ha!" laughed Madge. "Look your last on heaven for your grave yawns to receive you."

"Wretch!"

"Away with him; but bring me yonder man."

she exclaimed. "Bring him before me, but beware you injure not a single hair of his head. No torture but that inflicted by me must he bear, but oh! that shall be torture, more hellish than fiend ever conjured up. Quick! quick! that I may gaze into his hated face and hear the loud beating of his heart. Oh! Wild Madge, thou shalt be avenged."

And she strode along the deck, flourishing her arms above her head in the wild paroxysm of passion which now held sway over her soul.

A soul black as midnight—guilty as hell.

Lang waved his hand, and the blacks forced Henry along the decks towards the doomed ship.

"You black-minded old wretch," exclaimed Bob Bittern, struggling to free himself from the grasp of his captors. "I wish I could just get your cursed windpipe between my fingers, I do. Let go, you ugly black brutes; let go, I say, or shiver me, I'll kick your shins to a pulp."

And suiting the action to the word he kicked out with such force that he sent a tall black howling upon the deck.

"Bind his legs," exclaimed Lang.

"Cuss you," roared Bob, "you had better stand clear, I tell you, and haul off your cowardly swabs. Let go my arms and I'll take the whole ship load of you, one after the other."

But his struggles were soon stopped: a rope was passed round his legs and arms, and he was laid helpless on the deck.

"You cowardly hounds," he yelled, as after an ineffectual struggle to free himself he sank exhausted. "Let me only get my hands free, and I'll show you what a British sailor is made of—you piratical sharks."

But now that he was secured no one took any further notice of him; all turned their attention to Henry, who was being bound to the mast of the sinking vessel.

Proudly and defiantly the youth looked upon his executioners, but not one word did he speak till securely bound and the men moved from his side.

Then he fixed an agonizing glance upon Hanfield, and said—

"Farewell my friend, these friends have doomed me to the same death as that inflicted by the son of that brave woman, the Boy Rover, upon the brave and gallant Captain Waters. No cry for mercy will I utter, no hope will I entertain of pity from their callous hearts, but like him whose name I ever revered, whose memory I have ever respected I will die with the brave flag under which I have sailed and fought with, that proud emblem of freedom floating above my head, and trust to the country of which it is the ensign to avenge my death, and hurl destruction upon those merciless fiends—farewell—a long farewell."

"Bless you Henry," said Hanfield, "would that I could save you."

"'Tis needless to regret, may your fate be less bitter."

"Now then bring them along," said Lang.

Hanfield and Jacob were seized by the negroes and forced away.

Henry heaved a deep sigh as he saw them borne over the side of the pirate vessel, and a prayer rose to his lips.

A prayer for the safety of that man whose daughter he so fondly yet hopelessly loved.

Then he looked upon the blue clear vault of heaven—out, far out upon the white crested sea.

Never to him had the sky looked so bright the waves so beautiful.

He believed he was taking his last look upon the world, and he prayed now for himself.

The grapnells were now cast loose, and the two vessels parted.

Henry was left alone to die.

To die a slow lingering death upon the waste of waters.

Hanfield was borne to the deck of the pirate ship.

She who had commanded that he should be brought before her, stood with folded arms and firm set teeth, in the centre of the vessel.

The veins upon her forehead swelled larger and larger till they stood out like cords, and the fearful glew of her eye told of the workings of her evil mind.

There was a look of triumph now upon her face a fearful meaning in her fiery eye.

She moved not, spoke not, as they bore the old man towards her.

When Hanfield had been placed before her, she moved her hands to his captors, and they drew back, leaving her and the trembling man face to face.

With a start Hanfield gazed upon the eyes of the woman as she fixed her penetrating orbs upon his pale face.

For some moments they gazed at each other in silence then the lips of Madge moved, and she uttered the name—

"Joseph!"

For a moment Hanfield stood as though he were paralysed, then gasped forth — "Madge, oh, God!" staggered and fell upon the deck.

CHAPTER LXXX.

THE DOOMED YOUTH IN THE SINKING SHIP.—THE RESCUE.

SLOWLY the vessels parted and every minute increased the distance between the doomed youth and his executioners.

The holes which the blacks had bored in the bottom of the ship were few in number, just sufficient to allow the water to enter, consequently, hours must elapse ere she finally settled down in her ocean grave.

They had shown more mercy had they have made more openings.

But mercy was not a feeling which entered the hearts of that demon crew.

Strong indeed is the passion of revenge in the heart of man.

The negroes who had been stolen, or decoyed from their homes, could not realise the truth that the poor youth whom they had left to die would have sacrificed his life for them, would have fought and bled to have saved them from the fearful doom to which heedless unfeeling men would consign them.

They only knew that the white men was their enemy.

Knew that he would sell them to a life of bondage.

And their ignorant notions could not grasp the truth that all whites were not alike.

They felt them to be their enemies, and cheerfully and willingly would they inflict punishment upon those who so often inflicted torture upon them.

The pirates had released them from a fearful fate; and to them only they now clung, with feelings of gratitude.

They thought not of the horrible life which they had entered upon; they only thought of that which they had escaped.

Gratitude and their natural passions prompted the rest.

And so, without one pang, they consigned to a fearful doom a brave and honourable youth.

Left to misery and death one who would have defended them at the sacrifice of his blood.

And this at the bidding of men who were worse than those from whom they had been released.

The day wore on, the sun sank down to rest in his golden bed, and darkness was fast stealing over the wide expanse of waters.

Inch by inch the ship to whose mast the brave and devoted youth was firmly bound sank lower into the bosom of the waves.

Drifting hither and thither, at the mercy of the winds or waves—rising and falling, a helpless log, upon the dark blue sea.

Oh! the moments of agony that youth endured.

Moments which, in their passage, pointed to but one end.

And that end was death.

No hope of succour did that brave youth entertain.

Alone upon the sea.

Alone to die.

No more would he gaze upon the face of the lovely Ellen.

Never again would he drink in the sweet music of her tones.

No, never.

She was lost to him for ever.

And Charles, too—his much esteemed friend Never more would they meet on earth.

And the poor old man, Mr. Hanfield — what would be his fate?

He feared to think.

Yet his heart would turn sick at the thought.

Too well he knew the natures of those men.

But he had heard the words of Wild Madge.

What could they import?

Alas! he could not divine.

Yet a feeling of fear for Hanfield crept upon his heart.

A feeling for which he could not account.

Still he could not banish it from his mind.

It would force itself upon his thoughts, although he strove to bury it, by preparing himself for the death which threatened him.

The shades of night closed over the ocean, and one by one the stars peeped forth from the dark blue canopy.

How brightly they twinkled.

How deeply hued was the blue sheet of clouds that covered that vast deep.

Henry sighed, and thought of home.

The home of his childhood—the days of happiness.

Days ere sorrow had stolen over his heart, ere care and anxiety had forced themselves upon his soul.

In that fearful hour he reviewed his boyhood's days.

In that time of suspense he fancied he could hear the sweet voice of his loved mother ring in his ears.

How bright the picture his imagination formed of the old house at home.

How vividly did every room in the old house appear to his mind's eye—every nook and corner summon forth some old association.

Oh, happy did those bye-gone times appear now.

How bright the sunshine, how beautiful the flowers, how kind the deeds of all connected with the home of his childhood.

But the old house vanished from before his mind's eye; the voices of loved ones faded, and the murmur of the sea alone smote his ear.

On, on through the darkness; down, down, inch by inch into the deep blue sea.

The wind sighs through the cordage, the stars sparkle in the heavens, the white-crested billows roll sportingly along past the hull as she sinks lower and lower, and seem to mock at the doomed youth.

He closes his eyes and prays.

But still thoughts of earthly things will creep into his mind, and he opens his eyes to see in imagination the beauteous face of Helen before him.

He endeavours to stretch forth his hands towards her, but shouts and mocking laughter ring in his ears, and the face fades away.

He strives to dart forward to the spot on which she stood but he is powerless to move.

The cords that bind him lacerate his flesh, and in vain he strives to burst the bands asunder.

With a sigh he wakes to the truth of his position.

Lower and lower sinks the doomed ship.

How long before she will fill and settle down.

Not long, for the waters are rising in her hold and she labours heavily.

He will pray—not for aid, but for salvation.

Again his eyes close, and his lips move in prayer.

A faintness steals over him and his brain whirls.

The splashing of the waves against the sides of the ship sound louder and louder, and the wind was fiercer and fiercer, and he fancied that the vessel is driving over the sea at a fearful rate.

A terrific gale is springing up, and straight before the ship is a long line of breakers.

Still the ship keeps on her course, and he is powerless to guide her from the rocks.

Again the face of Ellen appears before him, but this time her features are convulsed with pain and fear.

She points to the long line of white foam, then clasps her hands beseechingly.

She is praying of him to save the vessel from carrying them to destruction.

But he is powerless to do her bidding.

Again he beholds the beseeching glance, and he strives to burst his bonds.

They yield—he rushes forward, but ere he can reach her side, he is grasped in the arms of the Boy Rover.

And a loud mocking laugh falls upon his ear.

He struggles to free himself, but in vain.

The smuggler captain holds him firmly, and the fingers that grasp his arms burn like red-hot iron.

He sinks upon his knees at the feet of the Rover, but a loud demoniac laugh breaks from the lips of the smuggler as spurning him with his foot he clasps the form of Ellen in his arms.

He hears the wild shriek of the maiden as the burning fingers clasp her tender flesh and he starts to his feet.

He rushes forward to tear her from the grasp of the ruffian, but ere he can reach her side he is again paralysed.

He sees her borne along the deck, and hears her cries for mercy, still he is unable to move.

In agony he strives to pray.

And his prayer is answered.

A form springs to her side, and hurls the smuggler to the deck.

It is the form of Charles.

He clasps the lovely Ellen to his heart, and as he bends his head to imprint a kiss upon her cheek, a loud report rings in his ears, and Charles falls bleeding to the deck.

He hears the loud shriek of the maiden as she throws herself upon the prostrate body of her lover, and the loud laughter of the Rover at his hellish work.

He sees the smuggler draw another pistol from his belt and place its muzzle to the head of the bleeding youth—sees the bright flash—hears the loud report—as the bullet penetrates the brain of Ellen's lover.

With a cry of horror he bounds forward.

But alas! his arms are bound and he cannot move.

The voice of Charles rings in his ears, calls upon him by name.

With a loud cry he strives to reach the prostrate man, but cannot move.

Still the voice rings in his ear—still the loud laughter of the smuggler falls upon his senses.

Gradually their features fade, and the tones of their voice die away.

With a start he awakes from the dream into which he had fallen, awakes to the reality of his position in the sinking ship.

The dawn is breaking, and cold grey clouds have taken the place of the blue star-bespangled canopy.

Suddenly he turns his gaze from the sky to the sea as the boom of a gun echoes across the billows.

A vessel is bearing down upon him, and a voice salutes his ears, but the words are indistinct.

He lifts his eyes to heaven, and a feeling of joy takes possession of his heart.

A prayer rises to his lips, a prayer of thankfulness for the aid sent to him.

How his heart throbs as a boat is lowered from the vessel, and comes bounding over the waves towards him, it gains the side of the sinking ship and a youth clambers over the bulwarks, their eyes meet, a loud cry simultaniously breaks from their lips, and Henry is clasped in the arms of Charles Lawson.

———

CHAPTER LXXXI.

THE FRIENDS ON BOARD THE FRIGATE.—THE PURSUIT OF THE PIRATE.

THE sun rose higher and higher in the heavens, and lit up the vast waters till the waves seemed to dance and sport in the golden rays like fiery demons in robes of burnished metal.

Lower and lower sank the doomed hull into the bosom of the waters; past all hope of being saved so effectually had the pirates done their work, and so high had the waters risen within her hold.

And the "Swallow," the frigate which had taken Charles on board, and been instrumental in the destruction of the pirate Latour, stood away from the fast foundering ship, lest as she went down into the vortex she drew them within the eddying circles which would roll around her grave.

And on the deck of the "Swallow" two young men stood side by side watching the sinking ship.

One was pale and weak, and he leaned upon the shoulder of the other for support.

There was a look of gladness upon the features of both, a look of brotherly affection beaming from their eyes, as ever and anon they turned their gaze from the sinking ship to each other's face.

The sympathizing looks were genuine ones, for each could feel for the others sufferings—both had suffered deeply.

At length, with a hiss and a roar, a sweep and a whirl, the doomed ship plunged beneath the waves, and the wild waters as they closed over her boiled up fiercely and curled their foam-crested tops high above the spot where the ill-fated ship had disappeared.

For a moment the friends on the deck of the "Swallow" gazed upon the spot where the vessel had rushed for ever from their view; then they turned their eyes upon each other's face and a deep sigh escaped their hearts.

"Gone at last," exclaimed Charles. "Thank God! The inhuman fiends doomed you to a lingering death, Henry, for had they been more merciful, she had gone long since, and we should have met no more."

A warm pressure of the hand was the grateful reply.

"Come, Henry," said Charles, "come to my berth: you must need repose after the sufferings and horrors you have endured."

A long, deep drawn sigh escaped the lips of Henry as a shadow ran through his frame at the contemplation of the fearful doom intended for him by the pirates, and the horrors of that night, as bound to the mast, the vessel every moment sank lower and lower into her grave.

The grave from whose portals he had been arrested by the hand of his friend Charles Lawson.

The dawn of day had revealed to the officer of the watch the doomed ship; and to Charles had been entrusted the command of the boat which was sent to his aid.

With what feelings of surprise and joy did he awake to the knowledge that his bonds had been severed, and that his cramped and stiffened body was being supported in the arms of his friend!

That friend whom he believed he should never see more.

How tenderly had Charles borne him to the boat; and thence to the ship, where, after a brief introduction, and some stimulants being administered, he could not be persuaded to leave the deck, and seek rest, till he had seen the last of the doomed vessel.

All attempts to save her would be fruitless; so those on board the "Swallow" made no attempt, but stood anxiously watching the sinking ship, and uttering exclamations of satisfaction at having been enabled to rescue the prisoner from his dreadful position.

But now that the ship had gone down, leaving nothing but the eddying waters to mark her grave, Henry suffered himself to be led away to the berth of his friend, where, worn out with the sufferings he had endured, he was soon lost to all consciousness, in balmy and refreshing sleep.

This time his dreams were bright, for his heart had been lightened.

Charles returned on deck to his duties, leaving Henry to his peaceful slumber.

Pacing thoughtfully up and down, his eyes fixed upon the deck, he had become lost in thought, when the captain of the Swallow approached him.

"Mr. Lawson, has your friend said what course this pirate steered?" said the commander.

Charles started.

"No sir; only too anxious that he should seek some rest, I made no inquiry as to the possible whereabouts of the pirate."

"It will not do to let him escape with impunity," said the captain. "We have swept one demon crew from the seas and must endeavour to sweep the others. Such crimes as these men are guilty of makes humanity shudder, and we must not rest till we have hurled them to destruction."

"I will seek my friend, and learn this pirate's course," said Charles.

"Stop sir, rouse him not now, when he awakes, tell him I would speak with him," said the captain.

Charles bowed, and the captain turned away.

A brave man was the commander of the Swallow, and one too, who, when once he had resolved upon anything, never rested till he had carried it out.

He had resolved to track the slaver-pirate; and Wild Madge and her hellish crew, would soon have a determined foe upon their track.

The shades of night had again closed over the sea, when Henry awoke from the refreshing sleep into which he had fallen, and rising from his cot, seated himself upon a chest, and awaited the appearance of his friend.

It was not long ere Charles Lawson made his appearance, and as he entered, Henry rose and grasping him by the hand, he exclaimed—

"Oh Charles—my friend—how can I thank you—how—"

Charles held up his hand deprecatingly.

"Not a word of thanks, Henry," he said, "I have but done my duty, rescued the friend that saved me from death.

A look of admiration beamed from the eye of the young lieutenant, and silently, yet fervently, he pressed the hand of his friend.

"Sit down," said Henry, "we have much to tell each other since we parted on the island."

"Much," said Charles, "but the captain wants to see you. Go to him first, and then we can listen to each other without fear of interruption."

Charles led the way, and in another moment stood in the presence of the commander of the frigate.

With a dignified, yet courteous demeanour, the captain greeted the youth that his vessel had been instrumental in saving him from death, and having questioned him as to the bearings of the pirate, her build, strength, and armament, questions which Henry answered as best he could, and as truthfully as possible, the young men once more returned to the berth of Charles, and having seated themselves, each prepared to listen to the recital of the others adventures—Charles eager to learn anything respecting Ellen—Henry hoping, yet fearful, to learn that she was safe.

With what interest — with what intensity of feeling did not Charles listen to the recital of the adventures of Ellen and the brave Henry on the rocks.

With admiration he listened to the account of how the poor girl, to escape the Rover, had sunk into the bay—how his hopeless yet noble-minded rival, plunged himself head-downwards, clinging only to the rock by his feet, had succeeded in bringing her safely to the huge blocks of stone uninjured.

How anxiously he listened to the account of their escape from the cliff into the boat, and a shudder ran through his frame as Henry told him how the villanous smugglers strove to dash them to pieces by toppling over upon them the high piece of loose rock as the boat floated out from their base towards the entrance of the bay.

Intently he gazed upon the face of the youth as he recounted how the storm rose and dashed the boat upon the sunken rocks, and how, clasping

HENRY OPPOSING THE FISHERMAN.

Ellen in his arms, he laid upon the huge block of granite, over which the billows, lashed to fury by the storm, broke in thundering roar, and blinded their vision in showers of spray.

He could not repress the cry that broke from his lips when Henry recounted how the gale drove the "Venomed Snake" on to the long line of breakers which roared and hissed, and howled around them; how, with a thundering crash, she broke to pieces on the hidden blocks of stone hurling the bodies of the smugglers hither and thither, bleeding and lacerated; how the shrieks of the wretched rovers mingled with the howlings of the blast, and how the huge wave as it rushed upon him and the almost insensible girl, lifted them high off the rock on which they stood and bore them far out into the boiling sea.

How fervently did he press the hand of the youth as he listened to how he struggled to sup-

port Ellen on the bosom of the furious waves; how he exerted all his strength to swim with her towards the white sails of a vessel which his eyes, half-blinded with the spray, could detect through the mist, and how, when strength and senses alike were leaving him, and he could hold out no longer, they were lifted into a boat and taken on board.

Henry spoke of the feeling of gratitude which rose to his heart at their deliverance from a watery grave—gratitude that was so soon to turn to indignation and horror when he discovered that he had been saved by a pirate.

Then he spoke of the agony of mind he endured whilst a prisoner in the hold of the "Spirit of the Wave," not for his own fate, but for the fate which threatened Ellen, whom the pirate captain had marked out for his own.

Charles listened with horror to the recital of

the sufferings of his friend when doomed to walk the plank, and surprise almost held him dumb when Henry spoke of his rescue by the Boy Rover and the circumstance of meeting with the father of Ellen a prisoner on board the ship which the murderous hands of the Boy Rover had made his own.

Then he spoke of the fight in the cabin and the defeat of the smugglers, who had been conveyed to England and a prison; spoke of their being boarded by a portion of the crew of the smugglers who had turned pirates; of the doom to which they had consigned him, and of the commands of Wild Madge that Hanfield should be brought before her; likewise the ominous words she had spoken, and the fearful doom he believed was intended for the poor old gentleman.

Here he paused, for the rest was known to his anxious listener.

Charles, in compliance with the questioning look of his friend, then explained how, wounded and bleeding, he was discovered lying on the spot where Henry had left him, beneath the tree, on the island, by the good old hunter—and loud indeed was the youth in the praises of the good old recluse; how he had watched and tended him, till health and strength had been restored.

He recounted to his friend how he had found the manuscript of Murdock, the murderer, and had learned therefrom the fact of the concealed boat in a cleft in the rocks; how they had succeeded in extricating it from the place where it had lain buried for so many years; and how it had borne him from the island to the vessel in which they now were.

Then he spoke of the chase of Latour, and the engagement with the pirates; the death of the captain, and the famine of the crew; the blowing-up of the vessel, and the finding of the blackened body of Bilton; and the last words of the brave though misguided man.

Words that both caused his heart to beat with joy, and stilled its throbbings with despair.

Words that assured him that the lovely Ellen's honour had not been assailed by the pirate, but left him in doubt and suspense as to her situation.

Charles paused—for he had concluded his tale of what had befallen him since they last met on the island—and Henry became absorbed in thought.

Suddenly he raised his eyes to his friend's face, and said:

"Where did you find Latour?"

Charles explained.

"Then he must have landed her on the island of Barbat. Its inhabitants have the semblance of gaining a subsistence by fishing; but, in reality, are engaged mostly in smuggling."

"Ah!" exclaimed Charles, "if such be the case, then Latour, doubtless, only landed her there with the intention, if he had been victorious, of again returning, and bearing her away."

"I am inclined to think so," said Henry. "When sailing under Captain Waters, in the revenue cutter, we made a descent upon the island; and discovered that the vaults of an old ruined fort had been used for the storage of contraband goods, although, at that time, it was empty, and we could find nothing to legally criminate anyone on the island; but we had great suspicions as to the real character of the place and its inhabitant, and doubted not that it was there the Boy Rover obtained many a cargo."

"Indeed!" said Charles. "Then Ellen is in great danger."

"Doubtless."

"And I am powerless to aid her," exclaimed the young man, bitterly.

"Unless," suggested Henry, "the commander of this frigate might be induced to sail to her rescue."

Charles shook his head.

"Captain Parry," he said, "is a true sailor, and a man that would not flinch from his duty; but the pursuit of a female is no part of that duty."

"Then you think he would not aid you?"

"I fear he would not."

Henry again became thoughtful.

"Charles," he said, after a pause, "we may perhaps induce him to make for the island."

"How?"

"He would fall in with the crew of Wild Madge."

"Doubtless."

"He could take no better course than that to the island."

"Why so?"

"The pirate is more likely to make for that than any other spot."

"Do you think so?"

"I do."

"If we could but bring Captain Parry to think the same," said Charles, a ray of hope brightening up in his face, "we might search for Ellen, and perhaps save her."

"We will endeavour to do so," replied Henry. "I will seek the captain, explain to him the character of the island, and the probability of his there meeting with the pirates."

"If you would do so," said Charles, "we might discover her."

"We might."

"Unless," added our hero, a look of pain again crossing his handsome features, "she already has been borne from there, heaven knows where."

"I do not think so, as it was evidently understood by those on the shore that Latour would return for her; if so, they could not have received the intelligence of the pirate's destruction yet, and Ellen is doubtless a prisoner awaiting his return."

"Poor girl, her sufferings have indeed been great," muttered Charles.

"Heaven grant they may soon be at an end!" exclaimed the young lieutenant. "Let us hope for the best. I will now seek Captain Parry, tell him of my suspicions, and induce him, if possible, to turn his vessel's bows in the direction of the island."

With this intention the youth rose from his seat, and accompanied by Charles sought the captain's cabin.

Captain Perry listened intently to what they had to say, and when they had concluded he ran his finger over the chart till it rested upon the place Henry had indicated, then, summoning his first lieutenant, ordered the vessel's course to be turned towards the island.

With smiling faces and beating hearts the friends retired to their berths as the vessel made her way for the island where they hoped to fall in with Ellen.

CHAPTER LXXXII.

THE SEARCH.—THE DISCOVERY.

It was towards evening that the frigate made the coast of the island where Captain Parry hoped to fall in with the pirate.

In vain had the look out scanned the horizon for the sails of Wild Madge's vessel.

But Captain Parry resolved to cruise about the island, in hopes of falling in with the vessel, for some time, ere he gave up the chase as hopeless.

Henry and Charles asked permission of the worthy officer for leave to go on shore, which was granted, and the two youths were soon rowed to the island.

Henry, who had before been on shore in this part, acted as guide, and by taking a circuitous route they came upon the ruined fort unobserved by any of the inhabitants.

It was now quite dark, and our friends took counsel of each other which was the best way to proceed.

Neither of them had any doubt that Ellen was on the island, but how to trace her they were at a loss to imagine.

"I believe that if she is here at all," said Henry, "she is confined within the ruined fort. for I do not believe that Latour would have put her on shore unless he had intended again calling for her after the engagement, should he have proved victorious."

"May she not be in the hut of one of the fishermen?" asked Charles.

"I think not."

"Why so."

"These men who inhabit the coast are but fishermen in name, in reality they are smugglers," said Henry; "and there can be no doubt but they had a perfect understanding with Latour to keep the girl prisoner till his return."

"But why confine her in the fort?" asked our hero.

"Other vessels touch upon this course besides pirates and smugglers," replied the young lieutenant, "and it would not do to run the risk of her being seen by any honest trader, as it might reveal the true character of the inhabitants, and cause much unpleasantness."

"True."

"So Charles, I feel convinced that if she be now upon the island, she is confined somewhere within the fort," exclaimed Henry in tones of conviction.

"Can we obtain an entrance into it, think you?" asked the lover of Ellen, anxiously.

"We may be enabled to do so." replied his friend, "but as our vessel must have been seen on the coast, there is doubtless a watch kept lest suspicion fall upon their real pursuits and the fort be surprised."

"True," said Charles, with a sigh.

"But still, we will not despair," replied his friend.

"Despair," replied Charles; "no; we are armed, and, if necessary, will fight."

"Aye," said Henry, "it shall not be said that we came here to rescue a female and ran away at the sight of resistance."

"Have you ever been in the fort?" enquired Charles.

"Yes."

"Then you know the best means to obtain an entrance?"

"I do."

"Lead on then, and woe to them who attempt to bar our passage," said Charles.

And as he spoke he looked to the priming of his pistols, then drew his cutlass from its sheath, and grasping the hilt firmly in his hand, was prepared for any surprise that might present itself.

"We must be cautious and wary," said his companion; "for although everything at present seems silent, and not a soul is in sight, we know not where danger lurks."

"True."

"This way then."

And keeping within the shadow of the ruin, Henry led his friend round to a small doorway at the eastern side of the building.

Then he stopped and listened.

All was now still save the plashing of the waves as the tide rolled up upon the beech.

Not a light appeared in any of the huts which lay scattered under the shadow of the fort.

All seemed buried in slumber.

"Hist!" said Henry.

"It was but the waves," replied his friend, "as they roll in upon the beach."

"I have been through this doorway before," he remarked, "when I commanded the party who searched the vaults, and the darkness, if I remember right, was most intense. Mind how you step, for hereabouts is a trap with a ladder descending to the vaults."

"But how can we hope to find anything in a strange place and in the dark?" asked his friend.

"How foolish; in my anxiety to get on shore I forgot that we might require the means of obtaining a light."

"But I did not," said Henry.

"Oh, can you procure one?—how fortunate," exclaimed Charles.

"Yes, I have some tarred rope in my pocket which will serve us as a link," replied his friend. "But let us work our way round towards the trap before we light it, lest it be seen from the outside of the building by any person who may be on the watch."

"It will be best," said Charles.

"Here, lay your hand upon my arm, and follow me closely. I will feel the way with my feet, lest there be any other opening in the floor than that with which I am already acquainted."

Charles did as his friend desired.

Henry moved forward, and cautiously followed closely by his friend.

Slipping his feet along the floor of a sort of passage, Henry felt for any opening in the ground, till at length he reached the spot where he believed the trap was situated.

Here he stooped down, and ran his hand over the boards.

His fingers came in contact with an iron ring.

"All right," he said, in a loud whisper. "I have found the entrance to the vault."

"Good," replied his friend.

"Now for a light," said Henry. "They cannot see the reflection now from without. Stand still—don't move any—lest we lose each other."

In a minute a light was procured, and the tarred rope ignited.

As the link burned up brighter, Charles saw that they were in a large stone passage, and that at their feet was a trap door, evidently leading into the vaults of the fort.

"Here it was we believed the smugglers concealed their contraband goods." said Henry; "but whether they were prepared for our visit, and so removed the articles, we could not determine. However, we found nothing here, and had to leave the place, after a fruitless search. Still I could never reconcile it to my mind that they were honest folks. The little they could get by fishing on the coast would never support them."

"We may find more here now," replied his friend.

"I hope so."

"Aye," said Charles, "it would be joy indeed to find Ellen."

"Heaven grant we may!" said Henry. "Though I could wish to find her elsewhere than in these vaults."

"Poor girl—poor girl!" sighed Charles.

Throwing the light of the torch around, and upon the ground at their feet, Henry stooped down to raise the trap.

An exclamation escaped him.

"What is the matter?" asked his friend, anxiously.

"Look, here is a lanthorn," replied Henry, lifting from the floor a large horn-covered lanthorn which the man who had brought Ellen the food had left outside the trap door for further use.

"How fortunate," exclaimed Charles. "But does it contain a candle?"

Henry opened it.

"Yes," he said.

"Then light it, and we shall be enabled to get on better with the two."

Charles took the lanthorn and held it while Henry applied the burning rope to the candle, then closing its horn door, he held it up above his head and threw its rays around him.

"Capital," he exclaimed.

"We shall be enabled to proceed the better," replied Henry, "but be on the alert lest we are surprised and molested."

Raising the trap, Charles stooped down and lowered the lanthorn down the ladder as far as his arm would reach.

The place was dark as pitch, but in a few moments the youth could distinguish the floor of the vault.

Then he placed his foot upon the first step of the ladder.

He paused.

A strange thought had struck him.

What if the trap should be closed and fastened upon them.

He turned to Henry and mentioned what he had thought.

Henry stood for a moment considering how he could possibly prevent such a circumstance from occurring.

He looked around the passage.

His eye fell on a broken stave.

Raising it from the floor he forced it between the trap door and the box into which it fitted, then placing his foot upon the end of the stove, forced it down till it would go no further.

"That will prevent the trap being closed in a hurry," he said, "and I do not think it can be got out very easily."

With a nod of satisfaction Charles commenced descending the ladder, followed closely by his friend.

If any doubt could have existed in the mind of Henry and his friend as to the purpose to which these vaults were applied, it was instantly dissipated upon their arrival at the bottom of the ladder.

Around in every direction casks of spirits and wines were piled one above another, together with bales and packages.

In fact, the vaults were nearly filled with contraband articles, despite the vast area which they occupied, and which in former days had been devoted to the storage of munitions of war, and articles for the furnishing of vessels at sea.

"This place," said Charles, as a damp chilliness struck upon his frame, "is well adapted for the storage of goods, but surely none could be so inhuman as to confine a poor defenceless girl in such a place?"

"Heaven only knows," said Harry; "yet I could not help thinking that if Ellen were on the island she would be placed here for security."

"If she be I will bear her afar from it or perish in the attempt," exclaimed the young man.

"And I will aid you," replied his friend, "while one drop of blood circulates within these veins—whilst one particle of strength is contained within this arm—whilst one breath remains within this body."

"Noble, generous friend, how can I express my gratitude for your devotion to me—to her?"

"Speak it not," exclaimed Henry, "so great is the love I bear to Ellen that I would willingly die to see her happy."

And as the words left his lips a sigh escaped his breast as he thought of that love he could never hope returned.

Henry, too, could not but feel for his friend.

He knew how fervently, yet hopelessly, he loved the girl who had centered her affections upon himself.

But feelings of jealousy never entered his soul.

He knew the noble self-sacrificing nature of his friend.

He could feel for him—pity him—but did not fear him.

Knowing, as he did, that he possessed the undivided affections of Ellen, he felt sure that Henry would never wrong him, either by thought or deed; but thought his true and holy passion, though unrequited, would prompt him to shield, rather than to destroy, his happiness.

Knowing and feeling the pain any mention of of their love must inflict upon his friend, he strode on, holding the lantern above his head with his left hand, whilst he bore his bared cutlass in his right, without making any further remark.

Section after section of the vault was examined.

But no indication did they meet with of the presence of Ellen.

It was a fortunate circumstance for them that they had discovered the lantern; for the rope was nearly consumed, and it gave at best but an indistinct light.

Eventually it burnt so low that Henry could no longer hold it without burning his hands; so he was compelled to hurl it from him.

The light of the lantern was now all they had by which to take their course through the vaults.

Through the glare, into every corner of this subterranean place, the friends walked on, side by side, pausing every moment to listen for any sound that might give indication that their presence was suspected or discovered.

They had arrived at the farthest end of the vaults, and nothing save bales and casks had met their sight; and, with a sigh of disappointment, they turned to leave the place.

"She is not here," said Charles. "Fearful as this place is, I had almost hoped to find her."

"I had felt sure we should," replied the friend.

"Our labour and anxiety has been of no avail," said Charles.

"Yes, it has," replied his friend.

"What?"

"We have discovered the hiding place of these smugglers, packed with contraband goods, and can bring down upon them the crew of the frigate."

"Fine—but no Ellen!"

And Charles turned away disappointed.

A low groan at this moment saluted their ears.

"Hark!" exclaimed Charles.

"What cry was that?" exclaimed Henry.

Both listened.

All was again silent.

"'Twas nothing," said Charles.

"Yet I thought I heard a groan," said the young lieutenant.

"So did I," replied Charles.

"But we must have been mistaken," replied his friend.

"Yes."

And again they moved along the vault towards the ladder.

They had got but a few paces when the sound which had before arrested their footsteps saluted their ears again.

Simultaneously both paused.

"Surely that was a human voice," exclaimed Charles.

"What could it be?" said Henry, "if not the tones of some human being?"

"Hark!" exclaimed Charles.

They stood still and again strained every nerve to listen.

Again the sound came to their ears, but so low that it seemed more like the dying cadence of the wind than aught else.

"There it is again!" exclaimed Charles.

"Yes," said Henry.

"Is it human, or but the wind forcing its passage through this place?" asked his friend, half doubtingly.

"It was the tones of some one in distress," said Henry.

"Heavens!" exclaimed Charles, "can it be the voice of Ellen?"

"Alas, I know not."

"By heavens! if she be within these accursed walls I will cut my way to her side," exclaimed the youth. "though all the spirits of the damned stood forth to bar my passage. Ellen! Ellen!" he called loudly, "if you be in this cursed place, speak—oh! speak! It is I—Charles."

The tones of his voice reverberated in loud echoes through the damp vaults, breaking against the pillars which supported the roof and died away in the arched roof of the damp, cold place.

This was succeeded by a silence so profound as to be truly painful.

Still the friends listened for any reply that might come to their ears.

Any sound that might denote the whereabouts of the being from whom that groan had emanated.

A few moments passed in breathless anxiety—moments, that in the intensity of their feelings, seemed hours.

But the sound again came to their ears, and simultaneously each turned in the direction from which it proceeded.

"Here! here!" exclaimed Charles. "This way Henry—this way!"

And holding the lanthorn above his head he darted round a stone pillar which supported the roof, followed by his friend and companion Henry.

On, on, they went in the direction from whence the sound proceeded, casting anxious looks around at every step.

Section after section, arch after arch was passed through, but nothing in the shape of a human being met their gaze.

The rays of the lanthorn glistened upon the green, damp wall and slimy flooring, but no indication of human life was revealed to their sight.

Once more they paused.

They looked inquiringly into each other's eyes to unravel the meaning of the sound.

But the blank look on the features of both, showed that each were equally puzzled and confounded.

"What can be this mystery?" exclaimed Charles, after a pause.

Henry shook his head.

"Think you that any one has discovered our presence here?"

"No," replied his friend.

"What then can it be?"

"Alas, I cannot determine."

Again that low moan echoed through the arched chamber of the vault.

But this time more distinct.

Indeed, it seemed close at their sides.

The friends started and turned pale.

Soon they recovered themselves, and Charles raising the lanthorn above his head and grasping firmly the hilt of the cutlass, darted forward.

Henry followed.

"Speak! speak! Who is here?" exclaimed Charles in an excited tone.

"That voice—oh, heaven! I thank thee! Saved, saved!" fell upon the ears of the two brave youths.

With a cry of joy they both bounded forward.

"Ellen! Ellen!" shrieked Charles; "My God, I thank thee! 'Tis her—'tis her!"

He turned swiftly round one of the pillars, and the rays of the lanthorn falling upon the damp ground revealed to his view the figure of a female seated upon the earth, her hair hanging dishevelled down her shoulders and back, and her face pale as death.

The youth dropped the lanthorn from his grasp and sprang forward at the same moment the figure arose.

Henry fortunately picked up the lanthorn from the ground, and as its light streamed around the vault it revealed Charles and Ellen clasped in each other's arms.

CHAPTER LXXXIII.

WILD MADGE AND MR. HANFIELD.—MAN'S HONOR AND WOMAN'S VENGEANCE.

IT was with a bewildered look upon his face that Mr. Hanfield sat up in bed and gazed around him.

For a few moments he was unable correctly to realise his position.

But slowly and clearly the truth dawned upon his mind.

He was in bed in the cabin of the Scorpion, to which he had been conveyed by the pirates by the orders of Wild Madge.

His late sufferings, combined with the shock his system had received at recognising in the bleared and bloated features of the triumphant woman the same once beautiful girl in whose caresses he had revelled, and in whose smiles he had basked.

But oh, what a change since then.

A change so great, so fearful, that it caused reason for a time to totter on its throne.

Had he caused the fearful change. Had his acts brought about this disgusting metamorphosis.

His heart smote him for his guilty deed.

He raised himself up in the bed, and as he did so the figure of Wild Madge, enveloped in a long cloak, stood before him.

A shudder ran through the frame of the man as he gazed upon her.

"Ha, ha," she laughed, "the change is great since last we met, Joseph, is it not?"

"Indeed it is," he answered with a shudder.

"Aye, Joseph, look upon the thing you once

professed to love—gaze upon the wreck of her your base heart professed to worship."

"I have wronged you Madge, and I ask your forgiveness," said Hanfield.

"Forgiveness," she exclaimed; "for what? for making me what I am—a thing loathsome even to myself? Forgiveness! Joseph, I have but lived for revenge."

A look of pity stole over the face of Hanfield as he gazed upon the repulsive features lit up with a look of triumph.

"Listen Joseph. I swore a bitter oath on the day that you led to the altar that baby face you made your wife—swore that I would encompass your ruin, and sow the seeds of bitterness in the hearts of both. You spurned the woman whose love you had sought, whose honour you stole—spurned from you when purity and innocence were sacrificed to you. From that moment I have never known rest."

"Spare me, Madge, spare and pity me," gasped Hanfield.

"Pity—ha, ha! What pity had you for me? None. Shall I yield thee that which you refused to yield to me? No, man, the victim of your perfidy has lived and longed for vengeance on the head of her seducer. Day and night my thoughts alone have been centered on revenge."

"Heaven forgive you!" sighed Hanfield.

"I have forfeited all hope of heaven," said Madge. "My crimes are too black even to merit forgiveness—crimes of which you have been the author!"

"Me!" exclaimed Hanfield.

"Aye, you," said Madge. "Was I not pure and innocent ere your shadow fell upon my path, and your honied words upon my soul? You professed to love me, and I believed you. Believing, I yielded to your persuasions—fell, never again to rise."

Hanfield sighed.

"Your passion consummated, you flung me from you as a thing unworthy for you to spare your affections—left me to shame, misery, and despair."

"Forgive me, Madge—forgive me!" exclaimed Hanfield.

"From that moment love turned to hatred, and vengeance only usurped my heart—vengeance that should be as deep and bitter as your own villany. Oh! how I have sighed for this hour."

"Madge," said Hanfield, "that I have wronged you, I both feel and know; and bitter indeed has been the remorse for my acts. But I was young and thoughtless—unable to feel the full extent of the wrong I did you. Forgive me, Madge; and believe me that in forgiveness your soul will find rest. It is human to err, and it is noble to forgive."

"Can I forget?" she exclaimed.

"Alas! no; but you can forgive," said Hanfield.

"Never!" she almost shrieked. "Hear me, and then ask your own heart if mine can feel pity. Deserted by you, with the brand of shame upon my brow, and the stamp of infamy upon my soul, I wept in sorrow the weary months away, till I became a mother—till I gave birth to an offspring on whom I should have looked with pride and joy. But its first cry smote upon mine ears like a death knell; for it was the evidence of shame hitherto hidden from all save myself. In the rude fisher's cot, on the sea shore, at the same time as, in the proud mansion in which you dwelt, the one for whom you deserted me, and I your

victim, gave birth to offsprings, having but one father. What were my feelings, do you think, when I knew that my child was a nameless babe, and the offspring of shame; and that the child of her for whose love you spurned mine would, in the eyes of the world, be the superior of mine? Though both possessed the same father, one only could bear his name! I, whose love you had sought and won, was left to the jeers of the cold world—the scorn of the virtuous. My grief would have killed me, but for the determination to be revenged on her who had torn you from me, and on you."

Hanfield shuddered—so fearful was the glance she fixed upon him."

"This feeling grew with time, and the misery you had inflicted upon me I would inflict upon others. I could not bear to know that others were better than me—more virtuous, more pure. The knowledge of my shame drove me to seek relief in brandy, for only when my senses were steeped in forgetfulness by the burning liquid could I rest. See what it has made me. Look upon these bleared eyes, this bloated face—'tis drink, drink has done this—drink taken to drown the memory of what I was, the feelings of what I had become, of what your villany had made me. Oh! man, man, what crimes might you not have spared me—what hours of bitter anguish might you not have shielded me from."

Hanfield sighed deep, and covered his face with his hands.

"Oh, that I could recall the past," he faintly murmured.

"Aye," exclaimed Madge, "could I recall the past, I could forgive."

"And you will, Madge?" exclaimed Hanfield, looking up.

"Never! the shrill voice of my drowning infant floats over the waves telling me that vengeance is mine."

"The infant?"

"Aye, Joseph Hanfield; my child—your child. The little innocent whom these hands destroyed," exclaimed Madge, holding forth her arms.

"Destroyed?" gasped Hanfield.

"Aye—murdered."

"Murdered?"

"Even so, Joseph Hanfield. Your child I murdered that it should not know it was the offspring of guilt. Hark!" she added, her eyes lighting up with an unnatural fire, "do you not hear its cry as it floats upon the waves? See! it raises its arms towards me, but I spurn it from me, and the billows carry it down—down. Ha, ha!"

"Madge, Madge, you are crazed. Poor thing, heaven have mercy on her," exclaimed Hanfield.

"No, no," said Madge, recovering herself, "it is gone long since, nothing lives but revenge now—nothing but revenge."

"Madge."

"Peace, speak not. I will read your doom. You have a daughter, beautiful as her mother; I, a son, with a nature black as hell. She, your child, must feel the pangs which I have felt; she must fall—surrender her honour to the keeping of him whose hands are stained with the blood of his fellow man. Ah, it will be a noble vengeance—the child of my seducer ravished by a murderer. Ha, ha, ha!"

Hanfield shrunk back upon the pillow in horror as Wild Madge gave vent to these words.

"Madge," he gasped, "you know not what you say."

"Would that I did not, for then my heart would be at peace. This is the revenge I have sworn to have. For the present she has escaped, but it will not be for long. She must fall, and when honour is to her but a recollection and a name, Wild Madge will be avenged on the man whose acts have made her the loathsome, despised, and bloody-minded thing she has become."

"Oh, heaven!" gasped Hanfield, "can this woman have fallen thus? Is every noble quality of the soul obliterated?"

"Aye, Joseph Hanfield," exclaimed Wild Madge, "my heart, like my face, has changed. On these cheeks the bloom of youth and beauty sat, but that beauty has gone, and repulsive ugliness reigns supreme; in this heart feelings of love, joy, and peace have held their sway, but that too has changed; its well springs are dry and withered, burnt up by the black passions which now hold dominion over it—charred with crime and misery."

"Alas, alas!" sighed Hanfield.

"Oh, it will be a great revenge," yelled Madge, "to hear her shrieks for mercy as the arms of the spoiler encircle her form, and the breath of pollution fans her cheek."

"Woman, if you are not all lost, forbear," cried Hanfield.

"Ha, ha," laughed Madge. "Joseph Hanfield, the victim of your perfidy will gloat in triumph over the wreck of your child—the offspring of your baby-faced wife.'

"Peace," exclaimed Hanfield.

"'Tis dead for ever here," answered the besotted woman, laying her hand upon her heart. "I can feel no joy now but in the sufferings of my own sex. Woman has been my curse, and I will be hers, no matter who or what she be. I hate the name, for it reminds me of her who robbed me of your love."

"Wretched being, speak not of her whose noble soul shed a halo of joy upon the path of all who knew her. She merits no ill-will for she never did you wrong."

"Not wronged me," yelled the fury, her bleared eyes almost starting from her head.

"Never."

"Liar!"

"Never, by word or deed," iterated Hanfield.

"Did she not scheme and plot to draw you from these arms?" asked Wild Madge.

"Never."

"Did she not win you for herself, and cause you to leave me in shame and wretchedness?" said Madge.

"She knew not of our connexion," answered Hanfield.

"Still did she wrong me."

"How so?"

"By marrying you."

"She believed me true."

"Aye, but soon she knew you false," chuckled Madge. "Oh! that was a glorious triumph when I poured into her ears the secret of our love."

"Wretch!" exclaimed Hanfield, in tones of indignation and disgust.

It was the first bitter drop, and it poisoned her soul."

"Fiend!"

"Ha, ha!" methinks I see her now, as on the beach I told her that my unborn child claimed for its father her husband. Ha! what joy did that look of anguish shed upon my heart—with what pleasure did I mark the quivering lip, the tearful eye, and the heaving bosom. Oh! it was triumph to know that she was as wretched as I—I, your despised victim."

"Devil! Ah, lost—lost to all feeling and self-respect."

"Curse her," exclaimed Madge—"curse her! She embittered my existence; I embittered hers. Would that I could have planted a thousand daggers in her heart."

"Woman, forbear."

"I will taunt you, Joseph Hanfield, till madness creeps upon your brain, as it has upon mine. I will taunt you till every moment of your existence is a misery to you. Bitter hours of agony shall be your potion. Here, on board this vessel, I hold supreme command till the Boy Rover once more treads the deck of a vessel gained for him by me. This is a pirate bark, and within its timbers are, and will be, perpetrated deeds at which your soul shall shudder. The shrieks of outraged women shall ring in your ears, as the black crew feed their unholy lustful desires. You shall hear their cries as the ravisher gloats upon his victim, and learn the horrors of the fate intended for your child: for I feel assured that she cannot escape the doom I have meted out to her. Hark!" she added—"do you hear that cry? It is the cry of a maiden for aid, to save her honour. Ha, ha! she calls in vain. The pirate has her in his fangs, and the hell-hounds wait the remains of their master's feast. Ha, ha! there's music in the sound; it falls like balm upon my soul. Listen, Joseph Hanfield—'tis the doom intended for your young child!"

And, throwing her arms about wildly, Madge darted from the cabin, as Hanfield pressed his hands to his ears, to shut out the cries.

CHAPTER LXXXIV.

THE HORRIBLE FATE OF BIANCA ON BOARD THE SCORPION.

THE pirate ship of which Lang acted as captain and Wild Made as superior, danced over the sparkling waves towards the island of Borrabas.

She had left behind her a trail of blood, but a deed worse than murder was being perpetrated in the cabin of Lang.

The young girl, Bianca, whom the ruffians had taken on board the Scorpion after slaying her father and the young captain, had been placed under the care of Madge, till she recovered from the stupor into which she had fallen.

Better that death had sealed her eyelids a thousand times than that she should have awoke to the fearful reality of her position.

As soon as she recovered, Wild Madge made her acquainted with the fearful doom to which she was consigned, gloating in the anguish of the poor girl with demoniac pleasure.

In vain were her prayers and tears.

She could not move that stony heart.

She threw herself at the knees of her tormentor and prayed for protection from the ruffian crew.

But her prayers were answered with jeers—her tears with laughter.

She appealed to Madge as one of her own sex; alas, poor girl, she but enhanced her position.

She clung to the furious woman's dress, but Madge hurled her away from her with boisterous laughter.

At length, in utter despair, she flung herself upon the ground and tore her hair in agony.

But the sight of that pale, beautiful girl softened not the heart of the hell-hag; it served but to amuse the base soul of that callous woman.

Tired at length with her torturing words and wicked acts, Madge left the cabin and went upon deck.

Lang was leaning over the taffrail and gazing thoughtfully into the sea.

The fury approached him, and laid her hand on his shoulder.

The man started.

"Lang."

"Madge."

"She has recovered."

"Who?"

"The girl."

"Well?"

"She awaits you in my cabin," said Madge with a meaning glance.

The eye of Lang brightened.

"Go," she said, "and let no softness of heart interfere with your objects."

"I expect there'll be a row with the others," said Lang.

"Why?"

"Because they've not got one as well as me," replied the captain.

"There was no other woman on board," said Madge. "I wish there had been one for each."

"They have as good as said I must hand her over after I have done with her," remarked Lang.

"Who says so?"

"Smith."

"He is next in command."

"Yes."

"He would take the next prize," said Madge.

"True, but then you see we may overhaul a dozen ships and no females on board."

"Yes, we might."

"And if I hand her over to Smith, then there's Bond and Harvey, and the blacks," said Lang.

"Well, you must settle that amongst yourselves," remarked Madge; "but mind there must be no mutiny."

"Humph."

"You understand me—no mutiny," continued Madge.

"Well, of course I am satisfied," said Lang.

"Then endeavour to satisfy the others," said Madge.

"But how?"

"Let her fall into the hands of the others according to their rank," returned Madge.

"But this would be horrible," remarked the man.

"What would?"

"To consign her to such a fate."

"Nonsense," replied Madge; "the girl is ruined if she submits to you, therefore she may as well go the round of the ship as not, and better too, if there is any likelihood of mutiny by her not doing so."

"But—"

"But what?"

"'Tis fearful—horrible!"

"Tush, man, your heart is too soft," said Madge. "Go."

And Madge turned away and descended to the cabin of Hanfield, which adjoined the one in which the doomed girl sat wringing her hands in despair.

"Well, if you aint an infernal unfeeling and unnatural wretch my name's not Lang," said that worthy, looking after the retreating form of Wild Madge. "You aint a woman—that's certain.

You are a cursed hell-cat, and nothing else. Ugh! I'm disgusted, bad as I am."

But if Lang was disgusted with Wild Madge, he was not with himself, for he strode down into the cabin, and fastening the door, approached his weeping and heart-broken victim.

Not one qualm of conscience did he feel as he gazed upon her pale face; not one compunction as he looked upon those tear-bedewed eyes.

With a look that would have melted the heart of a less callous man than the pirate captain, the poor girl slunk back from the lustful gaze of the sailor.

"You ain't frightened, are you?" exclaimed Lang, advancing towards the retreating girl.

"Oh! spare me," she gasped, in tones so pleading that even Lang hesitated for a moment to lay a hand upon her.

But the sight of that beautiful countenance and heaving bosom fired the blood of the man; and, stepping to her side, he threw his arms around her neck.

With a shriek, she strove to tear herself away—a shriek that was heard by Wild Madge in the next cabin.

"Hold your row!" yelled Lang. "I ain't agoing to hurt you? What do you want to squeak like that for?"

"Mercy."

"Well, you ain't got nothing to fear," exclaimed Lang, drawing her towards a seat on which he sat: then pulled the pale trembling girl upon his knees.

"For the love of heaven, spare me!" she gasped.

"Just you keep still," said Lang. "If you go twisting and twirling about in this manner you'll dislocate your neck; for you'll never get your head out of my arm, I know."

With a groan, the trembling girl tried no longer to free herself from the pirate's embrace.

"There," said Lang, "that's better. It's all nonsense to be obstropolus: because you only hurt yourself—not me. We shall soon understand each other, we shall. Now, my dear, just give me a kiss, to begin with."

But the girl started, and nearly succeeded in tearing herself from the grasp of the pirate.

Lang's grasp, however, tightened around her.

"Oh! if you be a man, insult me not thus," she cried, her tears bursting forth afresh.

"If you be a woman, just show yourself a sensible one, replied Lang. "Now, look here: I suppose you know why I have come to see you."

"To give me my liberty, eh—is it so?" exclaimed the girl.

"Well, not exactly."

"Oh, you have the power," gasped the maiden.

"But I aint got the will," replied Lang.

"Be merciful," pleaded the girl.

"I've come here to be happy," said Lang, leering round at her as she endeavoured to turn her face from his gaze.

The young girl sighed deeply.

Her bosom rose and fell with the violent emotions which assailed her breast.

"Come, kiss me," said Lang. "Don't be so shy: it aint any use being shy here. Lor bless you, the more free you are the better for yourself. It's always best to give away what is sure to be taken."

And the ruffian drew her head down till her lips touched his own, and he imprinted upon them a shower of fulsome kisses.

In vain the poor girl struggled.

MARTINEZ RESCUING LUCY FROM THE TORRENT.

The blood of the pirate was fired by the embraces in which he revelled; and, despite her shrieks and struggles, he pressed her madly to his breast.

The cries of the poor girl became fainter and weaker every moment; and, ere long, worn out and rendered prostrate with her fearful efforts to escape, she lay upon his arm, panting and almost unconscious.

He bore her to the cot on which Wild Madge slept; and, spite her cries and tears, consummated the hellish villany which the base heart of Wild Madge had brought about.

There was no friendly hand stretched forth to save her; and in about an hour Lang left the cabin, and returned on deck, flushed with his unholy victory.

With a mind bordering upon distraction, and a heart broken and crushed, Bianca lay panting and sobbing upon the cot, till, casting her eyes around, she discovered Smith had intruded upon her presence.

With a deep groan of agony, she sprang up in the cot; but the pirate was by her side in an instant, and his unmanly arms thrust her back.

Again was she assailed—again was she subjected to treatment at which the heart must shudder, and the soul shrink in abhorrence.

She prayed for death to end her sufferings.

But, alas! those sufferings had only begun.

The inhuman wretches who formed the crew of that floating pandemonium treated her to indignities so vile, so base, that nature stands appalled at the bare contemplation of them.

Not one feeling of mercy entered the breasts of those rough men; not one hand was stretched forth to save her from further insult.

Throughout that day and night was the poor weak girl subject to brutal tortures.

Her cries penetrated the walls of the cabin, and smote upon the ears of the guilty wretches, but found no response save further insult.

Wild Madge listened with joy.

There was music, she said, in the sounds of woe.

As each shriek smote her ears, a smile gathered on her bloated face; as each cry penetrated the walls of that cabin in which the unholy work was going on, the fury rubbed her hands together in mad glee.

Oh! how must she have fallen—how low, how deep.

And the woman had once been pure and innocent—gifted with all those qualities which ennoble the soul. To what depths had she descended, to be able to sit and listen to the cries of one of her own sex, and know the fearful nature of the hellish deeds which were being perpetrated, and not raise hand or voice to check them!

Fallen she must have been—fallen deeper than the darkest depths of hell.

But the cries ceased, and the groans were heard no more.

Nature had given way at last; and that fond and beautiful girl, but a few short days before so full of life and joy, had succumbed to the horrible indignities which had been heaped upon her.

Death had been more merciful than her persecutors, and saved her from further insult and degradation.

The angel of death had borne her pure and guileless spirit away from that fair body which the lustful demons of that ship had contaminated by their unholy presence and wicked unmanly actions—borne it away from that floating hell, to realms of joy and peace.

Loud and deep were the curses of that portion of the crew whom death had disappointed of their unholy desires; and loud and derisive were the taunts of those who had assisted to murder that fair being who now lay cold in death upon the little cot in the cabin of Wild Madge.

Heaven had thrown around it that shield which man denied her—mercy.

CHAPTER LXXXV.

THE MUTINEER AND THE LOVERS ON THE ISLAND—THE NUPTIAL COUCH.

With mingled feelings of surprise and rage, Lieutenant Martinez gazed upon the form of the stranger, as it stood before him, in the full moon's rays.

At any other moment his heart would have bounded with joy at the knowledge that the island was inhabited by another human being besides himself and his fair companion; but now such a fact was the most unpleasant that he could learn.

He felt as if he could have sprang at the throat of the man, and forced the life from his body.

The knowledge that there was another human being in that island would destroy the consummation of that love Inez had given him—destroy, too, at the very moment when its consummation was at hand.

Inez turned pale.

She feared lest the stranger had overheard their words, or observed their actions.

If he had done so, what would she appear in his eyes?

And a shudder ran through her frame.

That she loved Martinez, she doubted not; but that, in the eyes of God, she was wrong, situated even as they were alone in that island, in surrendering herself to him without first undergoing the marriage ceremony, she felt assured; and the warm love which had fired her blood, and heated her passions, now cooled rapidly, and she strove to tear herself away from the ardent embrace of her lover.

"We are not alone," she said. "Surely Heaven has been instrumental in saving us from this sin."

"Curse him!" muttered Martinez. "To appear at such a moment is sufficient to drive one to madness. At the moment, Inez, when I had hoped to——"

"Hush!—perhaps it is better as it is," exclaimed the young girl, in a low tone. "He is, doubtless, some poor fellow who, like us, has been borne hither by the cruel waves."

"To-morrow I could have welcomed his presence with joy; but now—"

Inez hung her head, and a tremor shook her frame.

"See—he comes towards us," she interrupted.

The figure approached.

The light moonbeams playing more fully upon his form, as he advanced nearer, revealed to their gaze that he was habited in the garb of a sailor, but without hat or jacket.

Martinez angrily and impatiently awaited his approach.

Inez, tremblingly and blushingly, did the same.

In a few moments the man was by their side.

"Heaven be praised that there is another human being in this spot save myself!" he exclaimed, in tones of thankfulness.

"Hell be cursed for it, thought Martinez," for it has robbed me of that for which I have sighed.

But Inez only hung her head.

The knowledge of what she was about to submit to brought the blush of shame to her cheek, and she feared the stranger might read her thoughts in her face.

"Whoever you be," continued the man, I rejoice to see you. To one like me who has spent weary days of loneliness in this place, the sight of another human being is happiness. Stranger, let me grasp your hand.

For a moment, Martinez hesitated, could he forgive the man for making his appearance at such a moment. Yet, how could he have known that his presence was distasteful.

The anger of Martinez evaporated.

The generous nature of the young lieutenant rose uppermost, and he extended his hand. Fervent was the pressure inflicted on it by the stranger.

"Thank God, he murmured," I am no longer alone.

And he extended his hand to Inez.

The young girl placed her taper fingers in the horney palm of the stranger, but they trembled in his grasp, and as he fixed his gaze upon the face of the beautiful maiden, the hot blood mounted to his forehead, and bathed her features in a rich red glow.

"Who are you," asked Martinez," after a rather long pause?"

"A poor sailor."

"How came you here?"

Alas, I know not."

"Know not," said Martinez, in some surprise, looking hard at the same time in the face of the stranger.

"Indeed, I know not," replied the man.

"That is strange," said Inez.

"Not so lady." Having offended the captain of the vessel in which I sailed, I was condemned by him to be impaled. Fastened to the mast, three seamen were ordered to impale me with their knives, and I fell bleeding and insensible. Heaven, and the inhuman wretches who were my executors only know what followed. When I recovered consciousness, I was lying upon the shore of this island. Weak and almost powerless, I dragged myself high up to prevent the waves carrying me out into the ocean. Oh, lady, your heart would indeed shake did you know the sufferings I had undergone, till heaven in its mercy gave me strength to search for food and shelter. I found it, and day by day my strength returned, but never till this moment have I gazed upon a human being.

He paused.

A sight of pity escaped the breast of the fair girl.

Even Martinez felt a pang for the man's sufferings.

"By what means came you hither," asked Ned Wilton, the mutineer, who had been condemned to the fearful fate we have already described, some time previous by the Boy Rover, and who, when the ship struck had floated away on some of its timbers, and been landed on the island on which Martinez and Inez had been thrown.

"A calamity at sea," replied Martinez, not feeling desposed to explain all the circumstances of the case. "My wife fell overboard, and I plunged in after her. The waves bore us hither."

"Was no attempt made by those on board to save you," asked the man.

"Oh yes, but in the darkness I presume, they could not distinguish our forms, and at daylight all trace of the vessel had disappeared."

"And the lady is your wife," asked Ned.

"Yes," replied Martinez, at the same time pressing the hand of Inez, to name her not to make any remark that might give the lie to his words.

Martinez thought that by asserting Inez to be his wife, the stranger would have no suspicions of the real facts of their conduct, should he have observed it, nor feel any surprise at anything which might occur, and besides, it would induce him not to force himself upon them more than possible.

"It's hard," said Ned, "for man to meet with such a fate, but for a woman, it is fearful. But heaven has been merciful to her in keeping you by her side."

"Indeed it has," said Martinez.

"I shall be able to rest now," said Ned, "that I know there is another human being besides myself in this accursed place, though it may seem uncharitable and wicked to feel glad that others are as miserable as myself, but to be alone is fearful. Moments seem hours, hours days, days years. No one to speak to, no one to look for. Oh, God, loneliness is worse than death."

Inez felt for the man, his sufferings she thought must have been hard to bear.

"How have you procured food," asked Martinez.

"Oh, there is an abundance of vegetation," replied Ned. "On this island man need not want for that. I could be happy here, did not loneliness make me miserable, but for that, I could rest in peace. I have prayed for the sight of a human being, and my prayer has been answered.

"Yonder have I formed a rude shelter from the winds and rain by the boughs of trees. Come and share it. The night air though warm is filled with dews, and the tender form of your fair partner should not be exposed to them."

"I thank you," said Martinez, "but I cannot accept your generous offer."

Ned looked up in surprise.

"No!" he exclaimed.

"I cannot—my wife—"

"I had forgotten," interrupted Ned. "True there is but one apartment. No matter, she must not be exposed to the dews lest she suffer. Come, I will show you where it is, for to-night you can rest there, as I will lie beneath the shadow of a huge tree which grows some hundred yards from the hut."

"We cannot deprive you of your shelter," said Martinez.

"You must not expose that fair being," replied Ned.

"For her sake, then," said Martinez, "I will accept."

The hand of Inez trembled on the arm of the lieutenant.

"Come, sweet one," he whispered, "come."

But Inez hesitated.

The knowledge that another save themselves was on the island had shaken her resolve to sacrifice herself to her love.

Martinez fixed his eye upon her and the pressure upon his arm tightened.

But still her hand trembled.

Her bosom rose and fell as the emotions of love and fear shook her breast.

Martinez saw the struggle which was going on within her, and he drew her form close to his breast.

He could almost feel her heart beat.

But she suffered herself to be led along by Martinez, preceded by Ned Wilton.

"I had almost feared," whispered Martinez in the ear of his companion, "that the consummation of our love had been delayed by this meeting."

"It must, it must," exclaimed Inez in a whisper, whilst the tell-tale blood mounted to the roots of her hair.

"Why so, dear one?"

"We are not alone," she murmured.

"But I have proclaimed you my wife," said Martinez.

"Still I tremble," she murmured.

"Fear not," replied Martinez, "all will be well."

A sigh broke from her lips.

She felt that the meeting with Ned Wilton had been designed by heaven to save her from committing sin, but the love she had avowed for the brave young seamen—the love which she felt for the saviour of her life, her passion, which his words and caresses had exicted, all combined to persuade her to throw herself into his arms, and consummate their happiness in one soul-entrancing embrace.

After a walk of about a quarter of a mile, they came upon a rude hut formed of the branches of trees and long grass woven together, and sheltered from the rain by a green hill which rose some little height above the rude habitation.

"This is the place which I manufactured to sleep in," said Ned, "feeling assured that I should ever have to end my days on this island. Use it to-night, and to-morrow I will assist you to build one for yourselves."

"You are kind," said Inez, "very kind. But where will you yourself seek rest?"

"The boughs of yonder tree will shield me to-night," answered Ned.

"I thank you," said Martinez, a gleam of pleasure sparkling in his eyes as he cast his gaze around the small place, half hut, half bower, and which he could clearly distinguish in the moon's light, "for the sake of my partner I will consent to deprive you of your own shelter till I can form one for ourselves."

"And welcome you are to it," said Wilton.

"We are grateful, for Inez needs rest. The sufferings we have endured is more than her tender frame can well bear."

"The couch is rude," said Ned pointing to one corner of the place which was bathed in darkness, "it is but leaves and long grass, yet it is soft and comfortable. You are worn, no doubt, so I will leave you till the morning, when we can each tell our sufferings and our hopes of escape from this accursed place. Rest lady in safety. Good night."

"Good night," sighed Inez.

"Good night," hurriedly exclaimed her companion.

Ned Wilton turned away, and strode in the direction of the tree, beneath which he had it to be his intention of sleeping.

Martinez and Inez stood gazing after his retreating figure, with varied emotions in the breasts of each.

A strange feeling seemed to seize upon the heart of the fair girl, a feeling as though she had hurled a friend from her side in the hour of danger.

Martinez on the contrary watched the retreating form of Ned with a feeling of joy at his heart, a relief to his breast, it seemed every step he took which placed a greater distance between them.

Then he turned his gaze to the features of his fair companion—she was pale, and tears stood upon the long dark lashes—tears she knew not which of joy or sorrow.

But Martinez believed they were the former, and stooping down he kissed them away. He drew her within the place, and pointing to the bed of dried grass, he said :—

"Inez, dear one, heaven smiles upon our love, for see, has it not led us to our nuptial couch."

A deep sigh only broke in answer to his word.

"Inez, do you regret your vow," said the young lieutenant, as he observed her deep drawn sigh ?

"Regret—no—but——"

"But what dear one ?"

"I would that we were wed," she replied.

"Can love be less true because no ceremony binds it. Believe me dear one, he that could forget the vows made without the marriage ceremony, would do so with it. True love needs no binding vows, registered on earth, recorded in heaven, and providence will punish the guilty one who breaks his oath, whether worldly ceremonies have been resorted to or not. True love—love like ours, can never die."

"And you will love me ever," sighed Inez, allowing her head to fall upon the breast of her companion ?

"Ever till death," he exclaimed.

"Then I am thine Martinez—thine."

The young man strained her to his breast, showered kisses upon her cheeks and lips, and lifting her beautiful and slender form in his arms, he bore her along to the couch of dried grass.

Inez sank down upon it with a feeling of conviction that the love of her companion would ever remain green, and throw around her a shield of protection and happiness in that deserted place, from which there seemed no escape.

The night wore on, one by one the bright stars faded in heaven's blue vault, the chaste light of Luna's orb faded, and the cold grey clouds of early dawn broke over the sky.

On the rough yet soft couch of dried grass, in the corner of that rude shelter reared by the hands of Ned Wilton the mutineer, the fair and beautiful Inez lay in the arms of the man who had saved her from the waste of waters, her head pillowed upon his breast. She had sank to sleep confident in the love of him to whom she had yielded her maiden's purity and innocence.

CHAPTER LXXXVI.

THE LOVERS ON THE ISLAND.—THE FAIRY TALE.—LOVE AND MUSIC.

THE sun was high in the heavens ere Inez awoke from the entrancing slumber which had sealed her eyelids, awoke to the knowledge of what had passed in that simple place, awoke to the fact that she had had one in the wide world to look to for love and peace.

Martinez had risen and gone forth to meet the man whom he had seen so unexpectedly on the previous night, and Inez appreciating this mark of respect to her feelings, left the couch and approaching the opening, used as a doorway, looked forth upon the island.

The bright sun was tinting the tops of the trees in golden splendour, the birds carrolled forth their musical notes in melodious tones, and the air was fragrant with the balmy breath of myriads of flowers.

The beautiful woman gazed and listened in rapture.

"Oh," she thought, "is not this a paradise, blessed by the love of Martinez, I can resign all hopes of again mixing with the world. Here, with him, could I live and die, but the continuance of his love is all that is necessary to make this place a heaven of delight."

Her dark eyes was fixed raptuously upon the light clouds as they floated in the broad expanse of heaven, when a hand was laid upon her shoulder and she started round with a cry of surprise.

Her eyes met the smiling face of Martinez, and the blush mounted to her forehead, as the young man placing his arm around her slender waist imprinted a kiss upon her lips.

"My own, my loved one," he murmured.

Inez replied not, but laid her blushing face on his breast.

"Is not this a beautiful spot," he said.

"Indeed it is," she murmured, looking up in his face, half smiling, half fearfully.

"With you by my side Inez, with your love, here could I live and die."

"So could I" replied the maiden.

"Here we are free from all the conventionalities of the cold deceitful world, here we can ramble hand-in-hand amid flowers, whispering love's tenets in each others ears, dwell with rapture in each others tones, gaze with love into each others eyes. "Oh, Inez, here away from the heartless world, happy in each other's love may we wander contented and in peace."

Inez nestled closer to his breast, she was happy, happy in her love.

"Have you seen the stranger," she asked, after a pause.

"Yes, dear one. He will be here anon. He has kindly offered to assist me in building a place like this to shelter us from the nights dews, and has now departed for another part of the island to procure for us the long grass with which to bind the branches together that is to form our house. I would have accompanied him, but I feared you would miss me and become uneasy at my absence.'

"I should have been so, Martinez," she murmured.

"So I feared, otherwise the beauty of the place would have tempted me to wonder with him.

"It is a delightful spot," said Inez.

"A fairy land," exclaimed Martinez, "but one thing only is required to make it a paradise."

"And that, Martinez," she asked.

Content," he replied.

"Oh, I am contented," she exclaimed. "As I looked forth and saw this place bathed in the beautiful sunlight, I thought of the fairy tales I oft had read when a child, and how like this spot is to what I then formed of them."

"You are fond of fairies then," said Martinez, with a smile.

"Oh, yes, I love a fairy tale, for though they are often absurd, yet they lead the mind to acknowledge the truth that a contented soul renders us more happy then will the possession of all the wealth for which men sin and lie.

"True, dear one, and contentment is all that we require to render us happy here. Come, let us walk forth till the stranger shall return, and stroll amid the flowers of this fairy land, and as we go I will tell you a story."

Inez looked into his face with a sweet smile, and taking his arm they strolled over the flower-bespangled sward, crushing the scented petals beneath their feet at every step, and surrounding themselves with an atmosphere of fragrance almost overpowering in its intensity.

"In such an atmosphere must fairies dwell," said Inez.

"And thou art the queen of all, sweet one," exclaimed the young man gazing rapturously upon the fair being at his side.

"But you promised to relate a fairy tale," said Inez.

"And I will do so, Inez," replied Martinez. "It will do to pass away the time till the man's return."

Inez smiled her thanks and Martinez commenced.

"It was a bright autumnal day when two boys wandered forth to gather nuts. One was keen-eyed and self-important in his gait, the other had mild, deep eyes, and his motions were like flowers bending to a gentle breeze.

"Alfred, the keen-eyed, mounted on a tree, and shaking it, exclaimed—

"'I should like to own a dozen such trees,' said he, 'and have all the nuts to myself.'

"'Oh, see how beautifully the setting sun shines slanting through the boughs on the trunk and branches! It glows like gold!' exclaimed Ernest.

"'If the sun were like old Midas, that we read about at school, there would be some fun in it,' replied Alfred; 'for if it turned all it touched into real gold, I could peel off the bark and buy a horse with it.'

"Ernest gazed silently at the golden sea of clouds in the west, and then at the warm gleams it cast on the old walnut-tree.

"He stood thus but a moment: for his companion aimed a nut at his head, and shouted—

"'Make haste to fill the basket, you lazy fellow.'

"The nuts were soon gathered, and the two boys stretched themselves on the grass, talking over school affairs. A flock of birds flew over their heads towards the south.

"'They are flying away from winter,' said Ernest. 'How I should like to go with them where the palms and cocoas grow. See how beautifully they skim along the air.'

"'I wish I had a gun,' rejoined Alfred; 'I would have some of them for supper.'

"It was a mild autumn twilight.

"The cows had gone from the pastures, and all was still, save the monotonous boss of the crickets.

"The fitful whistling of the boys gradually subsided into dreamy silence.

"As they lay thus, winking drowsily, Ernest saw a queer little dwarf peep from under an arching root of the walnut-tree. His little dots of blue eyes looked cold and opaque, as if they were made of torquoise. His hands were like the claws of a bird. But he was surely a gentleman of property and standing, for his brown velvet vest was embroidered with gold, and a diamond fastened his hat-band.

"While Ernest wondered who he could be, his attention was attracted by a bright little vision hovering in the air before him.

"At first he thought it was a large insect, or a small bird; but as it floated ever nearer and nearer, he perceived a lovely little face with tender luminous eyes.

"Her robe seemed like soap-bubbles glancing in the sun, and under her bonnet, made of an inverted white petunia blossom, the little ringlets shone like finest threads of gold.

"The stamen of a white lily served her for a wand, and she held it towards him, saying, in tones of soft beseechment—

"'Let me touch your eyes.'

"'You had better touch my wand. You will find it much more to the purpose,' croaked the dwarf under the walnut-root. 'Look here! wouldn't you like to have this?' and he shook a purse full of coins as he spoke.

"'I don't like your cold eyes and your skinny fingers,' replied Ernest. 'Pray, who are you?'

"'My name is Utouch,' answered the gnome; 'and I bring great luck wherever I go.'

"'And what is yours, dear little spirit of the air?' asked Ernest.

"She looked lovingly into his eyes, and answered, 'my name is Touchu. Shall I be your friend for life?'

"He smiled, and eagerly replied, 'Oh, yes! oh, yes! Your face is so full of love.'

"She descended gracefully, and touched his eyes with her lily-stamen.

"The air became redolent with delicate perfume, like fragrant violets kissed by the soft south wind.

"A rainbow arched the heavens, and reflected its beautiful image on a mirror of mist. The old tree reached forth friendly arms, and cradled the sunbeams on its bosom.

"Flowers seemed to nod and smile as if they knew him very well, and the little birds sang into his inmost soul. Presently he felt that he was rising slowly and undulating on the air, like a winged seed when it is breathed upon; and away he sailed on fleecy clouds under the arch of the rainbow.

"A mocking laugh roused him from his trance, and he heard Utouch, the gnome, exclaim, jeeringly—

"'There he goes in one of his air-castles, on a voyage to the moon!'

"Then he felt himself falling through the air, and all at once he was on the ground.

"Birds, flowers, rainbows, all were gone. Twilight had deepened into a dreary evening; winds sighed through the trees, and the crickets kept up their mournful creaking tones.

"Ernest was afraid to be alone. He felt round for his companion, and shook him by the arm exclaiming—

"'Alfred—Alfred—wake up! I have had a wonderful fine dream here on the grass.'

"'So have I,' replied Alfred, rubbing his eyes. "Why need you wake me, just as the old fellow was dropping a purse full of money, into my hand.'

"'What old fellow,' enquired Ernest.

"'He called himself Utouch," answered Alfred, 'and he promised to be my constant companion. I hope he will keep his word; for I like an old chap that drops a purse of gold into your hand when you ask for it.'

"'Why, I dreamed of that same old fellow,' said Ernest, 'but I didn't like his looks.'

"'Perhaps he didn't show you the full purse?" said Alfred.

"'Yes, he did,' replied Ernest; but I felt such love for the little fairy with tender eyes and heart-melting voice, that I chose her for my little-friend And, oh! she made the earth so beautiful!

"His companion laughed, and said, 'I dreamed of her too. So you preferred that floating soap-bubble, did you? I should have guessed as much. But come, help me to carry the nuts home, for I am hurry for my supper.'

"Years passed, and the boys were men.

"Ernest sat in a small chamber that looked towards the setting sun.

"His little child had hung a prismatic chandelier drop on the window, and he wrote amid the rainbows that it cast over his paper.

"In a simple vase on his desk stood a stalk of blossoms from the brilliant wild flower called the cardinal.

"Unseen by him, the fairy Touchu circled round his head and waved her lily-stamen, from which the fine gold-coloured dust fell on his hair in a fragrant shower. In the greensward below, two beautiful yellow birds sat among the catnip blossoms, picking the seed while they rocked gracefully on the wind-stirred plant.

"Ernest smiled as he said to himself—'Gone are the dandelion blossoms, which strewed my grass-carpet with golden stars, and now come these winged flowers to refresh the eye. When they are gone to warmer climes, then will the yellow butterflies come in pairs; and whenever they are gone, here in my oboe sleep the soft yellow tones ever ready to wake and cheer me with their child-like gladness.'

"He took up the instrument as he spoke, and played a slight flourish.

"A little bird that nestled among the leaves of a cherry-tree near by, caught the tones of the oboe and mocked it with a joyous trill, a little sunny shower of sound.

"Then sprang the poet to his feet, and his countenance lighted up like a transfigured one; but a light cloud soon floated over that radiant expression.

"'Ah, if thou wert only not afraid of me!' he said, 'if thou would come, dear little warbler, and perch on my oboe, and sing a duet with me, how happy I should be! Why are man and nature thus sundered?'

"Another little bird in the althea bush answered him in low sweet notes, ending ever with the plaintive cadence of a minor third. The deep, tender eyes of the man-child filled with tears.

"'We are not sundered,' though the. 'Surely my heart is in harmony with nature; for she responds to my inmost thought, as one instrument vibrates the tones of another to which it is perfectly attuned. Blessed, blessed is nature in her soothing power!'

"As he spoke, Touchu came floating on a zephyr, and poured over him the fragrance of mignonette she had gathered from the garden below.

"At the same hour Alfred walked in his conservatory, among groves of fragrant geraniums and richly flowering cactus.

"He smoked a cigar, and glanced listlessly from his embroidered slippers to the marble pavement, without taking notice of the costly flowers.

"The gardener, who was watering a group of japonicas, remarked—

"'This is a fine specimen that has opened to-day. Will you have the goodness to look sir?'

"He paused in his walk a moment, and looked at a pure white blossom, with the faintest roseate blush in its centre.

"'It ought to be handsome,' said he, "the price was high enough. But after all the money I have expended, horticulturists declare that Mr. Buncan's japonicas excel mine. It's provoking to be outdone.'

"The old gnome stood behind one of the planks and shrugged his shoulders, and grinned.

"With perceiving his presence, Alfred muttered to himself, "Utouch promised my flowers should be unequalled in rarity and beauty.'

"'That was last year,' croaked a small voice which he at once recognised.

"'Last year,' retorted Alfred, mocking his tone. 'Am I then to be always toiling after what I never can keep? That's precious comfort, you provoking imp!'

"A retreating laugh was heard under the pavement, as the rich man threw his cigar away, exclaiming impatiently—

"What do I care about the japonicas!—they are not worth fretting about.'

"Weeks passed, and brought the returning seventh day of rest.

"The little child who made rainbows flicker over the father's poem, lay very ill, and the anxious parents feared that this beautiful vision of innocence might soon pass away from the earth.

"The shadows of a Maderia vine now and then waved across the window, and the chamber was filled with the delicate perfume of its blossoms.

"No sound broke the Sabbath stillness, except the little bird in the althea bush, whose tones were sad as the voice of memory.

"The child heard it, and sighed unconsciously, as he put his feverish hand within his mother's and said—

"'Please sing me a hymn, dear mother.'

"With a soft clear voice, subdued by her depth of feeling, she sang Schubert's Ave Maria.

"Manifold and wonderful are the intertwining influences in the world of spirits.

"What was it that touched the little bird's heart and uttered itself in such plaintive cadences? They made the child sigh for a hymn; and bird and child together woke Schubert's prayerful echoes in the mother's bosom.

"And now from the soul of the composer, in that far off German land, the spirit of devotion comes to the father, wafted on the wings of that beautiful music, Ernest bowed his head reverently and sank kneeling by the bedside.

"While he listened thus, Touchu glided softly into his bosom, and laid her wand upon his heart. When the sweet, beseeching melody had ceased, Ernest pressed the hand of the singer to his lips and remained awhile in silence.

"Then the strong necessity of supplication came over him, and he poured forth an earnest prayer.

"With fervid eloquence he implored for themselves an humble and resigned spirit, and for their little one, that living or dying, good angels might ever carry him in their protecting arms.

"As they rose up, his wife leaned her head upon his shoulder, and with tearful eyes whispered—

"God help us this and every day,
To live more nearly as we pray."

"That same morning Alfred rode to church in a carriage, and a servant waited with the horses till he had performed his periodical routine of worship. Many coloured hues from the richly stained windows of the church glanced on wall and pillar, and imparted to silk and broadcloth the metallic lustre of a peacock's plumage. Gorgeous in crimson mantle, with a topaz glory round his head, shone the meek son of Joseph the carpenter, and his humble fishermen of Galilee were refulgent in robes of purple and gold. The fine haze of dust on which the sunbeams fell, gleamed with a quivering prismatic reflection of their splendour. From the choir descended the heavenly tones of Schubert's Ave Maria. They flowed into Alfred's ear, but no Touchu was there to lay her wand upon his heart.

"To a visitor who sat in his cushioned pew he whispered that they paid the highest price for their music and had the best that money could command.

"The sermon urged the necessity of providing some religious instruction for the poor, for otherwise there could be no security to property against robbery and fire.

"Alfred resolved within himself to get up a subscription immediately for that purpose, and to give twice as much as Mr. Duncan, whatever that sum might be. Utouch, who had secretly suggested the thing to him, turned summersaults on the gilded prayer-book, and twisted diabolical grimaces.

But Alfred did not see him; nor did he hear a laugh under the carriage when, as they rolled home, he said to his wife—

"'My dear, why didn't you wear your embroidered crape shawl? I told you we were to have strangers in the pew. In so handsome a church, people expect to see the congregation elegantly dressed, you know.'

But though Utouch was a mocking spirit, Alfred could not complain that he had been untrue to his bargain. He had promised to bestow anything he craved from his kingdom of the outward.

"He had asked for honour in the church, influence on 'change, a rich handsome wife, and superb horses. He had them all.

"Whose fault was it that he was continually looking round anxiously to observe whether others had more of the goods he coveted?

"He had wished for a luxurious table, and it stood covered with the rarest dainties of the world.

"But with a constrained smile he said to his guests—

"Is it not provoking, to be surrounded by luxuries I cannot eat? That pie-crust would torment my sleep with a legion of nightmares. It is true I do not crave it much, for I sit at a loaded table 'half famished for an appetite,' as the witty Madame de Sevigne used to say.'

"Again and again he asked himself why all the fruit that seemed so ripe and tempting on the outside was always dry and dusty within.

"And if he was puzzled to understand why he seemed to have all things and yet really had nothing, still more was he puzzled to understand how Ernest seemed to have so little, and yet in reality possessed all things.

"Ernest was a painter; and it chanced that they met in Italy.

"Alfred seemed glad to see the friend of his childhood; but he soon turned from cheerful things to tell how vexed he was about a statue he had purchased.

"'I gave a great price for it,' said he, "thinking it was a real antique; but good judges now assure me that it is a modern work. It is so annoying to waste one's money.'

"'But if it be really beautiful, and pleases you, the money is not wasted,' replied Earnest; 'though it is certainly not agreeable to be cheated. Look at this ivory head to my cane. It is a bust of Hebe, which I bought for a trifle yesterday. But small as is the market value, its beauty is a perpetual delight to me. It troubles me that I cannot find the artist, and pay him more than I gave. Perhaps he is poor, and has not yet made a name for himself; but whoever he may be, a spark of the divine fire is certainly in him. Observe the beautiful swell of the breast, and the graceful turn of the head.'

"'Yes, it is a pretty thing," replied Alfred, half contemptuously; "but I am too much vexed with that knave who sold me the statue to go into rapture just now. What makes it more provoking is, that Mr. Duncan did purchase a real antique last year for less money than I threw away on this modern thing.'

"Having in vain tried to impart his own sunny humour, Ernest bade him adieu, and returned to his humble lodgings, out of the city.

"As he lingered in the orange groves, listening to nightingales, he thought to himself:

"'I wish that charming little fairy, who came to me in my boyish dream, would touch Alfred with her wand; for the purse the old gnome gave him seems to bring him little joy.'

"He happened to look up at the moment, and there, close by his hand, was Touchu, balancing herself tip-toe on an orange bud.

"She had the same luminous loving eyes, the same prismatic robes, and the same sunny gleam on her hair.

"She smiled as she said:

"'Then you do not repent your early choice, though I could not give you a purse full of money?'

"'Oh, no, indeed,' replied he. 'Thou hast been the brightest blessing of my life.'

"She kissed his eyes, and, waving her wand over him, said, affectionately:

"'Take, then, the best gift I have to offer. When thou art an old man, thou shalt still remain to the last a simple happy child.'"

Inez smiled her thanks for the story.

"Oh, Inez," said Martinez, "may the good fairy learn us to be content; for then we shall be happy. If we can but rest satisfied with the position into which it has pleased Providence to place us, we need have no care; but, in each other's arms, we can make this island an Eden of peace, happiness, and joy.

And he stooped to kiss the ruby lip of Inez.

"Inez," he said, after a pause, "often have I listened with rapture to the tones of your sweet voice, when pacing the deck of the accursed Slaver. Often have I paused and drank in the melodious sounds as they rose from your cabin. Here upon this flowery knoll, sit and sing me one of those melodies which have so charmed me when sailing over the ocean wave."

With a smile, Inez seated herself at the feet of Martinez, and fixing her large dark eyes so full of love and tenderness upon his face, she sang with deep pathos, the following lines :—

Be on your guard ! for kindred ties,
    By falsehood may be broken ;
The heart may wear a deep disguise,
    Though friendship be its token.
The man who smiles with blandest grace,
    Perchance may seal your sorrow,
For by his words, 'tis clear to trace—
    The dullness of to-morrow.

Be on your guard ! and look afar,
    Believe not all thou hearest ;
And look at mortals as they are,
    And trust the one who's nearest.
The hope that brightens Time and Fate,
    May charm thee as it's flowing ;
But like the sun at heavens gate,
    'Tis sinking while it's glowing.

Be on your guard ! by day and night,
    When beauty's smile is glist'ning ;
For though your deeds be out of sight,
    The angels may be list'ning.
Calm pleasure has her garlands wove,
    By fancy's snowy fingers,
And truth can turn a charm to love
    And music, while it lingers.

Be on your guard ! for life may end
    As youth's gay dreams are shining ;
The charm on which you lean may bend,
    Though joy be round it twining.
The lips that whisper soft and sweet
    From whence bright words come streaming,
Bedew a wreath whose flowers meet,
    And kiss love's soul while dreaming."

Martinez sat enraptured, and as the last tones died away in the perfumed breeze, he pressed the beautiful girl to his heart and murmured his thanks in her ear.

"Martinez," she said, "sing to me."

"Alas ! Inez, there is no music in my voice," he replied.

She raised her eyes archly to his, and murmured—

"How then could you have won my love. It was the music of your voice that penetrated the portals of my heart and entered my soul."

"That was the music of love Inez." he replied.

"Then sing me a love song," she said, "for love and joy is in our hearts."

"I fear to try after what you have done, but I can refuse you nothing.

With a smile, Martinez sang in a full toned musical voice, the following:—

Come sail with me, o'er the bright blue sea
    And list to the billows roar ;
Come sail with me, o'en the ocean free,
    Far out from the rock-bound shore.

Come keep the silent watch with me,
    As we journey o'er the deep ;
I'll whisper words of love to thee,
    Where the hollow winds ne'er sleep.

I'll show thee beds of coral rare,
    Beneath the rolling waves,
And point thee out sweet places where
    Are conceal'd the mermaid's caves.

As o'er the crested waves we steer.
    And watch the glist'ning spray,
I'll speak with thee of friends so dear,
    Of love one's far away.

We'll gaze down into the waters deep,
    And fancy there we see,
Lov'd features now in death's long sleep,
    Ever lost to you and me.

Then come, love, share the watch with me,
    The stars shine bright above ;
And as we sail o'er the deep blue sea,
    I'll whisper words of love.

As Martinez concluded, a glance from the eye of the beautiful girl repayed him for his song.

"Oh, Martinez, how happy may we be here," she murmured.

"Happy as the day is long he replied," no dark cloud will hither come to mar our happiness. Peace and joy alone must reign.

"Heaven grant it may be so," she answered.

"It shall be dearest—it must be," exclaimed the young man.

At this moment they saw Ned approaching, carrying on his back a quantity of long grass.

Martinez and Inez rose, and walked forth to meet him.

Kind was the greeting of Inez, and deep and heartfelt the thanks she tendered to the mutineer for the kindness he had shown them.

Ned wanted not thanks—he was only too happy to know that there were human beings besides himself on the island.

In a short time, Ned Wilton had plucked sufficient fruit and berries for a morning's meal, of which he invited Martinez and Inez to partake, and seating themselves upon the grass at the foot of a tree, they partook of the viands, after which Ned and Martinez proceeded to form a kind of arbour, in which to shelter Inez and her lover

---

CHAPTER LXXXVII.

A SAILOR'S FAILING.—LANG TRIES TO CURE BOND OF SUPERSTITION.

PERHAPS there are no class of men in the world more given to superstition than sailors, and Bond and Hardy formed no exception.

They were superstitious. Perhaps it was the voice of conscience ever whispering to them of their crimes, gnawning at their hearts, and burthening their lives.

Be this as it may, they were fearful cowards in the dark, and murderous fiends in daylight.

Lang had ordered his vessel's head to be turned towards the Island of Barrabas, where he intended to unship the cargo of merchandise which they had stolen from the vessels in their voyage, and take in a cargo of brandy ; resolved to combine the pursuits of smuggler with that of pirate.

The shrieks of the murdered girl had died away, and the vessel sailed on her course.

Bond and Hardy whose watch it was, kept close together. The evil deed which they had that night perpetrated, brought forth the workings of conscience, and in deep yet silent tone that small voice upbraided them for their villany.

WRECK OF THE CYCLOPS.

The wind as it tore through the cordage, caused them to start in fear, and the flapping of the sails ever and anon as the breeze lulled for a moment smote upon their hearts like sounds of another world.

Both felt uncomfortable, yet neither liked to confess his fears to the other, and whistling or singing they endeavoured to keep up their spirits.

A night bird had flown over the vessel so low that its wings almost touched the faces of the guilty men, and caused a cold shudder to run through their frames.

Bond had paused for a moment, and lent over the topsail, his mind still a prey to the superstitious fears which possessed him, when a hand was laid suddenly upon his shoulder, and he turned with a loud sharp cry of fear.

"What the devils the matter with you," said Lang, who a moment before had come upon deck unseen by Bond, and placed his head upon his arm.

"How you frightened me," exclaimed the other.

"Did I—what are you got to be frightened of," asked Lang, with a grin?

"I—I don't know—but——"

"Did you think the devil had come for you at last?"

"No, but I almost thought it was the spirit of that girl."

"Pshaw—do you believe in such things," asked Lang?

"Do I believe in them," asked Bond. "To be sure I do. You know ghosts haunt the world after they are dead."

"Did you ever see one," asked Lang.

"Can't say I have, but I know they do."

"How do you know they do," asked the pirate captain.

"Because I've heard them."

"Where?"

"Here."

"Nonsense," said Lang.

"I tell you it ain't nonsense. They make all manner of noises if they don't show themselves."

"Come, come," said Lang, "if you have heard any noises depend upon it that they can be accounted for, and come from natural causes."

"Did ever anybody find out what caused noises in haunted places," asked Bond?

"Yes, many."

"I should like to know a single case?"

"Should you."

"Yes, I should, for I don't believe they ever discovered a ghost noise to be anything but a ghost."

"Well, I have come on deck, because I cannot sleep," said Lang, "so I'll just relate to you how a strange-minded woman upset all the tales connected with a haunted house, and proved that a search was only necessary to account for any sound which the superstitious believe to be caused by super-human agency.

"I should like to hear it," said Bond, "but I'm very much mistaken if there ain't such things as ghosts, and sprites, and spirits, although I ain't really seen one. Just sit down on this bulkhead," said Long, "and I'll tell you a story of a supposed haunted house, which I have myself seen. It was an old stone building covered with moss and ivy, and looked more like a prison than a human habitation, and was known by the name of the haunted house.

"It was supposed to have been, at some previous time, the abode of a gang of murderers and robbers, whose ghosts still lingered within these gloomy walls, and nightly held the most frightful revels.

"The ghosts of the murdered victims were thought to be there still; and, on dark and dismal nights, the terrible crimes that had been perpetrated there were acted over again, and rendered ten times more horrid by the ghostly actors.

"Several different families had successively tried to live there, but it was impossible.

"No consideration could induce anyone to stay more than one night. It was said that all night long were heard the most unearthly groans, the most heart-rending wails, and the most agonizing shrieks that ever fell upon the ears of mortal man; for, be it known, the ghosts of those days, though they themselves were but ethereal substances—the spirits or shadows of being passed from earth, yet they were believed to have the power of moving ponderable objects, and making the most frightful noises.

"All who had ever been at the old stone house in the night-time agreed as to having heard these horrid sounds; and some positively declared that they had seen the white ghost of a murdered man rushing through one of the rooms with an expression of unutterable anguish and agony on his features, and the crimson gore streaming from his side, and uttering the while a piercing shriek.

"How people were deluded and made to believe such absurd and foolish things, it is impossible for us at this late day to tell; but it probably originated in some trivial circumstance at first, which they were unable to explain, and their frightened and superstitious imaginations supplied the rest. It seems incredible that imagination can create a horrible monster of hideous sounds, but it surely does under certain circumstances.

"At the commencement of my story the old stone house had not been tenanted for many years; and such an object of dread was it, that the more timid would not pass in its vicinity in the night, and bold indeed must he be who would dare to enter it.

"In this neighbourhood there lived John Smith and his wife Susan. They were both past the meridian of life. They lived alone and always had, for they had never been blessed with children to cheer their lonely fireside.

"Mr. Smith was about the medium height, thickset and rather corpulent. His face was broad——broader than it was long—his cheeks protruded something like the little young squirrel, when going to his hole laden with nuts for winter use. His dull grey eye was almost expressionless, and was shaded by very heavy jet-black eyelashes. You must not for a moment suppose that John Smith was not an intelligent man—for intelligent he certainly was. He did not believe in witches, ghosts, &c.—oh, no! he had too much sense for that.

"Whenever he talked, which was most of the time, it was in a loud elevated key, as if he was speaking to some one at a great distance. If he chanced to cough, which he frequently did, being somewhat asthmatic, he was heard a mile off.

"The fact was, as he himself used to say, he intended to do or say nothing that he was not willing everybody should hear and know.

"He boasted of his courage, and evidently believed and tried hard to make others, and especially his wife, believe that he was incapable of fear.

"Mrs. Smith was small of stature, delicately formed, and had once been very beautiful. She possessed superior intelligence and great penetration of mind; and the main object for which she lived seemed to be to make her husband know and acknowledge her superior intellect.

"This, however, he had not done. She was very quiet and unobtrusive in her manner, not a great talker, but uniformly speaking in a mild and pleasant tone, and the only indication she ever gave of ruffled passions was the flashing of her jet-black eye. She, like her husband, did not believe that disembodied spirits returned to earth to torment the living.

"One evening, when John Smith returned home from his daily labour, he entered the house, as was his wont, by making a great deal of noise—slamming the door and stamping his feet—and commenced talking to his wife in his usual manner, that is, as if she had been at least a quarter of a mile away.

"'Wife,' said he, 'I've a great notion of buying that big house down on the five corners, and moving down there. What d'ye think of it?'

"'Why, John, that's the haunted house, isn't it?'

"'Haunted—fiddle! Now I hope you are not so silly as to be afraid to live there because of such foolish stories. I am not afraid; and the fact is—in fact you know that I am afraid of nothing. The fact is, that house can be bought real cheap—in fact for one-tenth of its real value, just because everybody is afraid of it, and the owner can't sell it; and the fact is, I am going to buy it. I don't believe it is anything more than the wind, or noise of rats among some old rubbish, that has frightened the people so.'

"'Now, John, you know that I do not believe those ghost stories. I am willing that you should buy the house, but one thing I wish to say. Wherever we move to next, it must be for a permanent residence. We have always been moving from place to place, till the saying that the 'rolling stone gathers no moss' has nearly proved true with us. Whether we move to that house or some other, it must be the last time.'

"'I know we have moved a great many times; but, Susan, the fact is, you know that I have always done what was best, and, in fact, you ought to know that I always will do for the best.'

"'I don't know any such thing. Well, never mind, you think I don't know much; perhaps you'll find out your mistake before you die. But, Mr. Smith, if you move to the old stone house, we, at least I, shall never pack up and move to another house.'

This ended the conversation, for John Smith knew by that emphatic 'Mr. Smith,' and the flash of his wife's eye, that the matter was irrevocably settled.

"After considering the subject for a few days, John Smith finally bought the old house, and they were shortly installed within its prison-like walls.

"On the first day he went through all the great house, exploring every room. It cannot be denied that his heart beat faster as he opened some of the closet doors which had not been opened before for perhaps a century. But he went with a bold step, while he kept saying to himself:

"'I am not afraid, I never fear anything.

As he expected, he found no bones of murdered men, nor blood-stained walls, nor any other evidence of the horrible crimes that were supposed to have been committed there.

"For the first week of their residence nothing unusual occurred. To be sure, sometimes at night the wind howled dismally around the sharp angles and jagged corners of the ancient house, and the rats frequently capered and squealed above their heads; but this was nothing more than they had expected, and they began to feel themselves quite at ease in their home.

"One night John Smith did not return home till late, and his wife had retired. He shortly retired also, and was soon in a sound sleep.

"In the course of an hour or two his wife aroused him, and said that some one was knocking at the door. He shouted, with stentorian voice:

"'Who's there?' But there came no answer. He sprang out of bed, and opened the door, but there was no one to be seen. 'Wife,' said he, considerably vexed at being awakened from his comfortable sleep, 'there is no one here; it is all your own imagining.'

"'I am certain I heard a rapping; but never mind, you think I don't know much.'

"Smith went to bed again, but in a short time rap, rap, rap was heard—not loud, but very distinct. He went to the door again, but nothing could be seen.

"He thought of the house being haunted, but did not mention it. He said:

"'The fact is, I believe somebody is trying to fool me by rapping on the door, and then running away; but, in fact, I'll put on my clothes, and the next time he raps, you see, I'm out after him.'

"Soon the raps were heard again, and out he rushed, and went completely around the house, looking into each of the dark corners; but no one was to be seen. Now he was indeed puzzled.

"'This is very singular,' said he. 'Wife, what do you suppose makes that rapping?'

"'Oh, I think it is the wind or rats.'

"'There is not the least breath of wind, and rats could not make such a noise as that.' After a moment's thought he added—'If it is anybody around the house, in the morning I can find out something about it; for a little snow fell in the evening, and there are no tracts in it but mine, and the fact is, you see, I can track 'em out.'

"Thus trying to calm his troubled mind he lay down, but not to sleep.

"Thoughts of frightful ghosts were continually in his mind, but he kept them to himself, for fear his wife should think him a coward.

"The raps were heard but once or twice more, and morning came at last.

"John Smith went out to see what discoveries he could make; and his wife, who rather suspected that the raps were in the room, commenced searching for the cause, and soon found it.

"But she resolved to keep it a secret for awhile, thinking that she would have a good opportunity to convince her husband that she did know something. Soon he came in, with a troubled countenance, saying:

"'There has been no one around the house—what did make that rapping?'

"'Now, Mr. Smith, I hope you are not afraid?' said his wife, with a mischievous twinkle of the eye, which, however, he failed to perceive.

"This was enough for him. He said no more, but soon went away to his work, and did not return till night.

"Mrs. Smith thought he would speak of what happened the night before, but he did not mention it, neither did she.

"The first half of this night nothing happened. But about midnight, when everything was silent as the grave, they were startled by a low long-drawn groan, which seemed to proceed from an adjoining room, where Mrs. Smith kept her loom, spinning-wheel, &c.

"'What's that?' said Mr. Smith; and, for the first time in his life, he spoke in a low tone.

"'Don't know; you'd better go and see, John. It's in the other room.'

"He got up, lighted a candle, and went into the other room, but could discover nothing that could make a noise.

"He extinguished the light, and for an hour all was silent.

"Then came another groan, more startling than the other.

"Again he examined the room carefully, but with no success.

"He was becoming greatly alarmed, and said:

"'Susan, what does infest this house?'

"'It is the wind, or—'

"'Stop, Susan; don't talk so foolish.'

"He said no more, but inwardly resolved to live in the house till *she* was satisfied; 'for,' thought he, 'I can stand it as long as she can.'

"The groans continued to be heard at intervals all night—always coming from the same place—but each time they seemed more startling and awful.

"The next day Mr. Smith went away, as usual, and his wife exercised all her wits to solve this new mystery, but in vain.

"At night the same groaning was heard; and it seemed more terrible each time.

"John Smith turned and tossed himself in bed in mortal agony, but he said not a word.

"The next day, while he was gone, Mrs. Smith pursued her investigations, and, to her great joy, discovered the secret.

"'Now,' thought she, 'I will certainly make my husband acknowledge that I know something.'

"When John Smith returned home his wife noticed that his face was haggard, and his eye wild, and she feared for his reason.

"She longed to explain the mysteries to him, but thought the right time had not come.

"As they sat speechless that night by the fire, the wind howled and shrieked dreadfully around the rough corners of the old house, and once or twice when the wind died away that same awful groan was heard.

"Mr. Smith was writhing in agony as if he were sitting on live coals, till at length his pent-up anguish broke forth in thunder tones.

"'Susan, we can't live here; the fact is; this house is filled with infernal demons: ha! hear them! that sound is more terrible than the wailing of the damned. Hear that hiss! The hissing of the fiery serpents, as they coil their wreathing forms around the dwellers in the bottomless pit, while lapping their forked tongues in the faces of the wretched victims, is nothing to it.'"

"When he ceased speaking, his wife said, with most provoking coolness—

"'Mr. Smith, you seem excited; I hope you are not afraid.'

"'No,' he thundered, 'I am not afraid; but I cannot, will not stay here and have my life tormented out of me. But,' he added, 'why does it not trouble you?'"

" 'Because I believe as you used to tell me, that there are natural causes for all these things,' and as we are to spend our lives in this town, I wish to make the best of it.'

" 'Oh, Susan, I wish you would not be so set in your way: but it can't be helped, and, the fact is, I shall leave.'

" He started up as if about to go, but his wife stopped him, saying—

" ' Wait a little while, John, and listen to reason. Wouldn't you like to have the cause of all these strange noises explained ?'

" 'I would ; but it's impossible ; no mortal could do it.'

" 'I can,' said she quickly ; 'and, although you think I don't know much, if you will sit down and calm yourself so as to be able to understand, I think I can do it to your satisfaction.'

" 'Well you can try—go on.'

" 'The causes are all very simple when understood. What we have heard to-night is the whistling of the wind, which has been magnified by yous excited imagination into the most dreadful wails and hisses, and if you will fasten a board over that deep notch under the cornice here on the east side, in that short corner, it will stop it. As to the rapping we heard the other night, that was caused by a turkey. You know you brought up a live one, with his legs tied together, and it being late you put him under that bench close by the door, and being, I suppose, in an uncomfortable position, he made the rapping on the floor. And now for the terrific groaning. My reel stands in the other room with half a skein of yarn on it. The end of the yarn lies on the floor close by a mouse-hole. A mouse comes out and endeavours to carry the yarn into his nest, which turns the reel slowly, and, being ungreased, makes the groaning, which frightens the mouse, and he runs off to return in an hour or so. I saw it done to-day myself.'

" Mr. Smith said not a word, but took up the light and went into the other room and found the reel just as his wife had said.

" He turned it slowly and it made the groaning, but now it sent no thrill of terror to his heart.

" He then went out and placed a board where his wife had told him, and the peculiar whistling of the wind ceased. He then came in and said—

" 'Wife, you are right ; I am convinced. I never should have found it out. You know more than I do.'

" At last he was convinced of his wife's superior intelligence, and she was satisfied.

" In time they passed from earth, and the old stone house was again untenanted, and so it has ever since remained.

" The inhabitants in the neighbourhood still believed it was haunted ; and said the reason why John Smith and his wife could live there they were in league with the devil."

" And so they were, I believe," said Bond, only half convinced.

" Nonsense man. There are natural causes for every sound, no matter how difficult they may be to discover. You confess you have never seen a ghost ; then why believe there are such things, whilst there are others who have imagined themselves to have come in contact with supernatural beings, but having mustered up the courage to fathom the mystery, have discovered the real source to arise from natural causes."

" There may be for some, but not for all," said Lang. " When I was a boy at school, I have often passed an old house on the road to Brentford—that house was haunted. It was overgrown with ivy and sinking to decay. It had at one time been a fine building, with ornamented front and tastefully carved door posts and window frames, but they were rotting with damp and crumbling with age ; not a whole pane of glass remained, for what time had spared, man had destroyed."

" No one cared to occupy the house, although it might have been rented for absolutely nothing ; the sparrows seemed to be the only living things that cared to approach it, even the children, who are so fond of romping in the fore-courts of empty houses and making their hollow rooms echo with the sound of the knocker, always avoided this one, and not a boy in the neighbourhood, who had played truant from school, would have dared hide himself behind the tall, straggling bushes which grew in its front garden, had he suddenly perceived his master coming along the road—he would rather brave his teacher's anger, than trust himself within the precincts of the haunted house.

" But I have heard my mother say that the old house had once rang with shouts of laughter and the sound of merry voices, and over its mouldering front, where now the rank ivy clung so tenaciously, the trailing rose, and the sweet-scented jassamine shed around their sweet perfume.

" It had formerly been occupied by a young man named Jessop, the son of a substantial country gentleman, but a man who considered it necessary that everyone should be a useful member of society, no matter whether he be rich or poor, In his young days he had studied for the bar -- not for a living, but because a life of idleness was distasteful to him—and he resolved that his son should likewise make himself the master of some profession, as he remarked, ' We never know what may happen, and it is a good thing to be able to labour for your bread."

" With this determination young Jessop was sent to London to study medicine, and having a fine house, a good supply of money, and being withal a jovial fellow, he soon had a large circle of friends around him, and the homes of his fellow students were open to him, at many of which he was a favourite visitor.

" Among his fellow students was a young man named Charles Verner, and between him and Henry a strong friendship had ripened, and after their duties at the hospital one day Charles invited Henry to accompany him to the house of a friend at which he had an engagement.

" Jessop agreed, and the two friends went to the house of a lady, whose husband, a medical man, had died a few years previous, leaving her with an only daughter and a small annuity to comfort her declining years.

" Charles Verner was a constant visitor at her house, for he loved the fair Mary with a true and holy passion, although he had not yet mustered up courage to declare his attachment to her.

" No sooner did Henry Jessop see the young girl, in the fresh bloom of eighteen summers, than his breast was fired by her beauty, and he resolved to brave everything to win her for himself.

" From that night Henry Jessop became a constant attendant at the home of Mary, and his insinuating manner, his free disposition, and apparent kindness to the old lady soon won the love of the daughter, and in an evil hour, firmly believing in his love and honour, poor Mary fell.

" The passionte feelings of Henry, which had almost consumed his reasumed reason, now gradually died out, and the poor girl was neglected. Now, and not till now. did he perceive that Mary was beneath him in worldly station, and to wed her would incite his father's anger.

"From coldness and neglect came absolute cruelty, and to the young girl's prayers and remonstrances he replied with jeers, and when she reminded him of his vows and begged of him, as a man, to fulfil his promise, he would turn from her with scorn.

"At last he refused to see her at all, and the poor girl, tired with waiting and watching for him, would return to her home with tearful eyes and aching heart.

"Months flew by, and Mary, finding it impossible longer to conceal her shame, determined to see him, and once more appeal to his feelings—to his honour—to repair the injury he had done her, and should he then refuse she could but end her misery in death.

"She wended her way to the hospital and inquired for him, but he refused to see her, and after waiting for some time she bribed one of the servants to show her where he was to be found. She knocked at the door of the apartment, and a voice bade her enter. She did so, and found herself in the presence of her faithless lover and several gentlemen.

"'I would speak with you, Henry,' she said, addressing Jessop.

"'I decline to hold any communion with you,' was the reply. 'This is no place to seek an interview with me—therefore, begone.'

"'Henry,' she sobbed, 'I have sought you everywhere—my heart is breaking. If you have one spark of manly feeling, save me from worse than death.'

"'What does this lady require?' asked an old gentleman, rising from his chair and approaching Mary.

"'Nothing,' said the young man, greatly confused, "that is—I once condescended to notice her, and now she follows me with annoying persistency.'

"'But she must have some motive for so doing—what can it be?'

"'I don't know—that is, I expect it is to extort money from me. I think my best plan would be to give her into custody.'

"Poor Mary pressed her hand upon her heart to stay its beating. She felt as though she would be suffocated, and tearing apart the strings of her bonnet, she let it fall upon the floor. Now, indeed, was she satisfied of the heartless nature of the man before her, and the deep love she had borne him turned to hate.

"'Oh, villain—villain!" she almost shrieked; 'thou disgrace to the name of man—thou foul blot upon creation. Oh, gentlemen, forgive me, but my heart is breaking. This wretch won my love—I listened to his promises—I believed him, and I fell; brought misery upon a happy home—broken spirits where all was gladness. Oh,' she added, raising her arms above her head, 'may the curse of a just heaven fall heavily upon him! may he live to bear the misery which he has caused me, and die alone, unpitied and unwept!'

"A stream of blood gushed from her mouth as she uttered these last words, and then she fell forward on her face to the floor.

"Two of the gentlemen present raised her from the ground, bore her to a couch, and endeavoured to reanimate her; but all in vain, the soul of poor Mary had fled to happier realms.

"Henry Jessop left that room with a weight upon his soul, and a feeling in his heart that those who had witnessed the scene looked upon him with contempt; so, pulling his hat over his brows he hurried homewards.

"Arriving there, he seated himself in a chair, buried his face in his hands, and sank into a deep reverie. Suddenly he was startled by hearing the room door open, and looking up, he saw Charles Verner standing before him.

"'What do you want?' gasped Jessop, an icy chill stealing over him. 'What do want here?'

"'Revenge!' was the reply.

"'I have done you no wrong?'

"'Done me no wrong?' said Verner. 'Have you not, when under the solemn bond of friendship, stolen away the heart of the woman I loved? Have you not made her fair name a bye-word?—brought her to disgrace and misery—then, villain as you are, refused her that reparation it was in your power to give. Was not this enough, but you must murder her?'

"'Murder her!'

"'Aye, coward, they were my words. I have heard it all, and I am here to revenge the death of poor Mary.'

"'Leave me. I have enough to bear.'

"'Never, till one of us has joined the spirit so lately flown.

"As he spoke, Verner grasped Jessop firmly by the throat.

"'Let go your hold,' exclaimed Henry.

"'Never with life,' was the reply.

"'Then your blood be upon your own head!' cried Jessop.

"Long and fearful was that struggle, chairs and tables were overturned, and the carpet tore from its fastenings to the floor, knocking down the ornaments from the chimney-piece, smashing anything that came in their way, dashing each other against the walls of the apartment, with foaming mouths, disordered dress, and lacerated hands they struggled out of the room on to the landing, where dashing against the balustrade it gave way, and the two men, still grasping each other by the throat, lost their footing and fell over the well-staircase into the hall below, crashing their skulls on the floor.

"Here they were discovered, still grasping each other's throat, quite dead, and from that time no one would reside in the house, for in the stillness of the night there is to be heard the noise of the awful struggle in the room above, and the fall of the two bodies into the hall below."

"Nonsense," said Lang. "It is but the imagination which pictures these sights and sounds. But the day is breaking, and if I mistake not, yon speck is a vessel. I will get the glass and see what I can make her out."

Lang procured the glass and gazed at the speck upon the ocean.

"Whew!" he muttered. "A frigate, by her build. Ease her off a couple of points, and make all sail. We can run into the hidden cove long before she can come up with us."

CHAPTER LXXXVIII.

THE ESCAPE FROM THE VAULTS – THE FIGHT OUTSIDE THE FORT—A SURPRISE—CHARLES AND ELLEN ONCE MORE IN THE HANDS OF THEIR ENEMIES.

WITH what wild paroxysm of joy did the brave and devoted Charles Lawson strain the beauteous and suffering Ellen to his breast, with what fervour did he rain down kisses upon her pale cheeks, and with what feelings of boundless gratitude did he murmur the words—

"Thank God she is saved."

Who can pourtray the emotions which filled the breast of the lovely Ellen, at the unexpected meeting. Her bosom rose and fell in one wild throe of convulsive joy, as she suffered her head to droop upon the shoulder of her lover.

Henry, too, was not an unimpassioned witness to their meeting. His heart bounded with the generous feeling of his nature—he was happy at their discovery—overjoyed at their felicity—but a shade of sadness sat upon his brow.

He loved Ellen and he respected his friend, he would have sacrificed all but honour to their happiness. Yet he felt sad when the arms of the youth encircled her form, and Ellen sobbed upon the shoulder of his friend.

But Ellen was not unmindful of his presence, nor unthankful for the sacrifices he had made.

With a sweet smile she extended her hand, and as the youth grasped it fervently in his own, a thrill of pleasure ran through his heart.

"My own—my loved one," exclaimed Charles, "heaven be praised that I have found you."

"Oh, Charles, how your noble heart would bleed did you know the agony I have endured within this place."

"Cheer thee, my own sweet Ellen," exclaimed the youth, I have come to bear you from this accursed place."

"Heaven be praised," exclaimed Ellen.

"Myself and Henry have sought you here—it was he who led me hither," said Charles.

"Kind generous friend," exclaimed Ellen, "how can I ever repay your kindness to me."

And Ellen raised the hand of the young lieutenant to her lips and imprinted a kiss upon it.

"I am more then repaid by a smile from you, Ellen," said the youth.

But as he spoke, a sigh escaped his breast.

"Oh, Charles," she murmured, again laying her face on his shoulder. "I had feared we should never meet again."

"Providence," exclaimed the youth, "is merciful though fate has been cruel. For what purpose can you have been consigned to this fearful place."

"To await the coming of that bloody-minded fiend, the Boy Rover," she replied with a shudder.

"The Boy Rover," exclaimed Henry and Charles in a breath.

"Even so."

"I thought you had been placed here by Latour," remarked Henry.

"Mr. Latour set me on shore, and gave me the means to procure a passage to my friends, but a fisherman in whose hut I sought shelter, robbed and placed me here."

"It must have been done to await the the return of Latour," said Charles.

"I think not," replied Ellen, "Latour had long promised to send me safe on land. His vessel was pursued by a ship of war, and he placed me on shore in this island."

"It was our frigate." said Charles.

"Yours?" exclaimed Ellen.

"I was on board the frigate, dear one, which gave chase to the pirate. He accepted our engagement, and himself and wicked crew are all destroyed."

"Alas! his end has been a fearful one," said Ellen.

"It was one he merited Ellen, and sooner or later justice is sure to overtake the guilty."

"True—true," she replied.

"But the Boy Rover," began Charles.

"I overheard the man who brought me here," interrupted Ellen, "say that it was their intention to keep me prisoner here till the Boy Rover should call at the island."

"Indeed."

"Yes, these goods that are in this vault but await her. Oh heaven be praised that you have come, for to fall again into his hands, to receive once more from him the insults and indignities to which I have been submitted would cause reason to totter from her throne, and drive me to madness."

"Fear not, Ellen," exclaimed Henry—"the Boy Rover is powerless to harm you more."

"Ah!" exclaimed Ellen.

"His sting is plucked," said Charles. "Henry has captured and handed him over to justice."

"Brave youth!" she exclaimed — "a nation's gratitude has become your due."

"So fear not for him, dear Ellen," exclaimed her lover. "He is safe, Latour is dead, and the bright light of peace and happiness is breaking through the black cloud of misery and despair which has so long overshadowed your destiny."

"Heaven grant it may be so!" exclaimed the young girl, fervently, raising her eyes, and clasping her hands.

"Come, sweet one," exclaimed Charles; "let us leave this accursed place. I shudder as I gaze upon it, and wonder how you could have existed here."

"Alas!" I know not myself," sighed Ellen "unless hope, which never deserts the innocent and true, has buoyed me up amid my sufferings."

"Sufferings, Ellen, for ever at an end!" exclaimed Charles.

But, ere the words were fairly uttered, a sound, as of angry voices, smote upon their ears.

"We are discovered!" exclaimed Henry.

And, bending forward, all three eagerly listened. The blood rushed back to the heart of the maiden, and she trembled so violently that she would have fallen had not her lover supported her.

Again the sound of voices came upon their ears. This time in loud and angry tones.

"Quick!" said Henry—"we must gain the open air, or we may be blocked in."

"We must be sure they do not close the trap upon us," exclaimed Charles. "Come, Ellen—come, and fear not."

And he drew the trembling form of the young girl towards the opening.

"Look to her, Charles—do not leave her side," exclaimed Henry, darting hurriedly forward, with his bared cutlass grasped tightly in his hand.

"Whither would you go?" asked Ellen, in half frightened tones.

"To keep the path clear for your flight to the boat."

"Hold!" said Charles—"rush not into danger for my sake: together we will escape, or perish."

"Look to Ellen," exclaimed the youth.

And darting forward he hurriedly ascended the ladder into the passage above.

The passage was clear, but the tones of men in loud and threatening conversation came to his ears from the direction of the door by which they had gained access to the vaults.

Henry paused and awaited the appearance of Ellen and his friend.

In a few moments they ascended the ladder and stood in the passage.

Henry silently withdrew the wedge and closed the trap.

Then turning to Charles and his trembling companion, he whispered—

"There are several, I judge by their voices, around the door through which we must pass."

"Oh, heaven!" exclaimed Ellen, "we are lost."

"Do not despair," whispered Henry. "They must cut the life from this frame before they shall harm you."

"Oh, into what dangers does not your devotion to me lead you."

"It is a labour of love," said the youth.

Ellen sighed.

"We must pass through that door, Charles," he said, "pass through it with Ellen. Keep close to me, and be silent. When we are a few paces from it I will dash through them; you follow instantly with Ellen. Once outside the fort the crew of the boat may be summoned to our aid should they attempt to bar our passage."

A meaning pressure of the hand was the reply of Charles.

A smile of thankfulness from Ellen.

They moved stealthily forward, grasping their weapons firmly, till within a few paces of the small doorway.

"Be on your guard," whispered Henry, placing himself in front of Charles and his fair companion.

Charles replied by a nod.

"Follow me, I will clear a passage for your escape."

And raising his cutlass above his head he sprung forward through the doorway.

A loud shout rose on the air, and Charles, grasping Ellen by one hand whilst with the other he wielded his sword, hurried forward after his friend.

The suddenness with which Henry dashed among the little group of smugglers and fishermen took them so much by surprise that they had not recovered themselves sufficiently to act, when Charles leading the fair girl passed through the door into the open air.

But the sight of Ellen seemed to arouse them, and giving vent to their surprise and chagrin in a volley of oaths, they rushed forward to prevent her further passage.

The fisherman in whose hut she had sought shelter sprang towards her, but as he stretched forth his hand to grasp her wrist the cutlass of Charles descended upon his arm and inflicted a cut to the bone.

With a howl of pain he sprang back, and the wounded member dropped powerless by his side.

"Down with them," he yelled as the others sprang forward.

But Henry was by the side of his friend in an instant, and their weapons gleamed in the air.

The men drew back.

The look of firm resolve to escape with the girl or die which sat upon the features of the two brave youths, cowed the brutish nature of their opponents and they hesitated.

"Fly to the boat," exclaimed Henry, addressing his friend; "I will bar their pursuit."

"What? leave you to fight alone?" exclaimed Charles, with a look of injured feeling. "No, no: we escape or die together."

"Go, go," said Henry, "ere it is too late."

"Impossible. I will not leave you," said Charles kindly but firmly.

"Then we will retreat fighting to the shore," exclaimed Henry, as the fishermen having recovered from the panic into which the blow delivered by Charles upon the arm of the man had thrown them, now made threateningly towards them.

Ellen trembled in every limb, and her agitation was so great that it placed her lover in the greatest danger, so fettered as it were his actions, and rendered him almost powerless to defend himself and his fair charge.

"Take my pistol, Ellen," he exclaimed—"it is loaded—and hesitate not to use it."

Ellen drew the weapon from the belt of her lover, and cocked it.

Her hand trembled as she did so, but she resolved to defend herself and Charles, should necessity demand it.

The fishermen, who were seven in number, were armed with various weapons, and now rushed towards the two brave youths, with the determination of cutting off their retreat to the boat.

One, armed with a huge bludgeon, struck a heavy blow at Charles, which the youth parried with his cutlass; but so violent was its force, that it struck the weapon from his grasp to the earth, and left him at the mercy of his adversary.

With a cry, Henry sprang forward to protect his friend; but Ellen had pulled the trigger of the pistol, and the ruffian fell to the earth, with the ball in his chest.

"Bravely done!" exclaimed Henry, as, flourishing his weapon around before his friend, he kept the others at bay whilst Charles regained his weapon.

"Infuriated at the fate of their comrade, the smuggler-fishermen again threw themselves upon the sailors.

But the sharp cutlasses of the friends kept them at bay, and the brave youths slowly retreated step by step, keeping their faces to their foes.

"Perdition!" exclaimed one of the fishermen, "shall we suffer them to escape us? Down with them—tear the girl from them."

And he flung himself upon Ellen.

The poor girl shrieked aloud as the horny fingers of the man rudely grasped her wrist.

But the shriek of Ellen was drowned in the roar of pain which he gave utterance to as the sword of Henry descended upon his head, and inflicted a gash upon his forehead from which the blood flowed in a copious stream and blinded him.

With a howl of rage the remainder of the fishermen flung themselves upon the two friends, and bore them down by the impetuosity of the attack, and for a moment Ellen was left standing alone in despair.

But the youths soon recovered themselves, and were up again striking heavy blows to the right and left.

Charles saw his friend in danger and held his own weapon to parry the blow, and Henry leaping back struck forth at random, and Charles receiving the full force of his friend's cut as well as that of his adversary upon his sword, it was shivered to the hilt, and he stood unarmed at the mercy of his assailants.

With a cry of fear Henry sprang before him to shield him from the threatening weapons of his foes.

"Fly, Charles," he exclaimed, inflicting a wound upon the foremost of the fishermen. "Fly with Ellen to the boat."

"I am unarmed, but I cannot leave you at such a moment," answered Charles resolutely.

"If you have no care for yourself, have mercy for her," answered his friend. "If she again fall into their hands her fate will be certain."

"Still honour tells me I must fall by your side," said Charles.

"In mercy to her—in mercy to me—to yourself—I implore you to go," exclaimed the brave youth still keeping his opponents at bay with the point of his weapon. "Carry her to the boat, and leave her in the care of one of the crew; you can return with the others."

"And in the meantime you may fall," exclaimed Charles, dealing a tall young fisherman a fearful blow between the eyes with his fist as he endeavoured to clutch at the pale trembling girl.

"Fear not for me, but go. Look to her safety or it will be too late. If you respect me—if you love Ellen—if you would save her from worse than death, I implore you, go!"

"It would be cowardly," exclaimed Charles.

"It would be manly to save a woman's honour at the sacrifice of your own," answered his friend.

Charles hesitated.

He knew, unarmed as he was, he could do but little to assist his friend, and he knew also that if Henry fell Ellen would be again in the power of those ruthless men, yet he could not bring himself to leave the brave youth to die alone.

"Oh, for a weapon," he gasped.

"Go, in heaven's name!" said Henry, "the knowledge of the danger to which Ellen is exposed unnerves my hand. If you would save her and save me, I implore you, fly."

With a look so full of thankfulness to his friend he grasped the hand of Ellen and urged her onwards towards the beach.

His heart beat violently as the shouts of the combatants, and the noise of the unequal combat came upon his ears.

The view of the beach was shut out from the gaze by the walls of the fort, around which they must turn to arrive at the spot where the boat awaited their return.

Charles wished to heaven that it were not so, as were it not for this their danger had been seen and known by those who had charge of the boat, and the smuggler fishermen would have had strong arms and willing hearts to contend against.

Hurrying so as to be able quickly to return to the side of his friend, Charles turned the angle of the fort.

The beach lay before him, and the boat rode upon the waters, kept steady by the constant dipping of the oars.

Scarcely had Charles and his companion come in view of this than he felt himself grasped from behind.

He struggled to free himself, but a bandage was placed quickly over his eyes and mouth, and his hands were fastened behind him.

He strove to call upon Ellen, but the ligature was drawn so tightly that his words died away in a sort of groan.

In another moment he was borne to the earth as a cry from the girl, who but a few short minutes before he had rescued from her prison, fell upon his ears.

Then all was silent.

Cold drops of perspiration broke out upon his brow and his heart beat convulsively.

In vain he strove to free his arms from the bonds, in vain he tried to call upon Ellen, and in an agony of despair he almost fainted.

Then a voice fell upon his ear—a voice that he felt assured he had heard before, but could not divine when or where—a voice which chilled his blood as it gave utterance to the words—

"Bear her to the ship. Wild Madge will be overjoyed to see her again; and just move this fellow out of the way of being seen by that boat's crew, till I can make up my mind what to do with him."

Then all was silent for a minute, when Charles felt himself lifted from the ground and carried along some little distance.

Then he was laid down again and all around was silent.

For a few moments he listened intently in the hope that he might hear the voice of the beloved Ellen, then with a burst of heart-rending anguish he murmured—

"Lost to me again! Oh, God! my heart will break!"

A strange dizziness came over him—a sound as of rushing waters filled his ears, and he lost all consciousness.

Meantime Henry defended himself from the attacks of the smuggler fishermen with the utmost bravery, and dealt blows thick and fast on every side.

Not for a moment did he turn to look after his friends, but when he judged they must have gained the beach, he turned hurriedly and fled after them.

"I don't like flying from the cowardly hounds," he thought, "but I will soon return with two or three brave fellows and show them what stuff the true British seamen is formed of."

He had gained the angle of the fort, and just come in sight of the beach, when a powerfully-built fisherman, grasping in his hand a cutlass, dashed right before him and opposed his further progress.

In a moment Henry was upon his guard.

"You don't go so easily," said the man. "Now youngster you've got one to deal with as knows how to handle a bit of steel."

And the man struck a heavy blow at the youth's head.

Henry parried it, and at the same time he leapt backwards.

Enraged at the ease with which the youth prevented his intentions, the man dashed angrily forward, but Henry leapt on one side, and the fisherman losing his balance staggered like a drunken man.

Henry raised his weapon and hesitated.

But he saw those with whom he had previously been engaged wending towards him, so he hesitated no longer, and ere his new opponent could recover his balance, he brought his cutlass down with such terrific force upon his head that he rolled stunned and bleeding upon the beach.

With a cry of triumph Henry bounded forward towards his boat.

CHAPTER LXXXIX.

FLIGHT OF THE SMUGGLERS—ATTEMPTED CAPTURE ESCAPE TO THE COAST.

THE loud tones of the prison bell echoed far and wide over the now slumbering town of Portsmouth.

"Curse that bell!" exclaimed the Boy Rover, as, followed by his companions, he darted on towards the beach.

"It will bring the whole town after us," exclaimed Bill.

Scarce had the words left his mouth than a man turned abruptly in the street, and grasped the Boy Rover in his arms.

"Surrender!" he exclaimed.

"You be d—d!" said Bill, striking the man a blow on the head with the cutlass which he had brought with him from the prison.

AN ADVENTURE IN THE FAR WEST.

The man staggered, and released his hold.

"Take that for your interference!" exclaimed the smuggler mate, dealing him another blow on the same spot.

The man dropped to the earth, and the smugglers again dashed on their way.

"Thus perish all who oppose us!" said Bill, with a theatrical air.

"We cannot stand upon trifles now," said the Boy Rover. "It will be their own faults if any-one else molest us."

"And it'll be my fault, captain, if I don't drop 'em down with this here weapon, if they only tries it."

"Hush!" exclaimed the Boy Rover—"don't speak so loud, or you will bring pursuit down upon us."

"To be sure you will,' said Jem; "you never speaks but you hollers."

"Keep your eyes open," said Sam. "I saw a chap steal back into a doorway down there; and I expect he means pouncing on us."

"Be wary, then," remarked the Rover.

"Shall I slit his wizen, captain?" asked Bill.

"If he attempts to molest us," replied the cap-tain.

At this moment there came upon their ears a loud voice, exclaiming:

"Here they are—here they are!"

"Hallo!" exclaimed Jem.

"Silence!" said the Rover; "we are pursued, and discovered."

"Curse it!" said Sam.

"Be silent," said the Rover; "we are not yet recaptured.

"Nor do I want to be," said Bill. "I've had enough of that place; and sooner than go there again, I'd open my jugular vein—I would."

"Look out, or you may get it opened for you," said the Rover.

"Stand firm," said Bill, as the quick tramp of several feet echoed through the silent streets.

In another moment the figures of four men were seen hurriedly approaching.

"Stand back in the shadow of the wall," said the Rover.

"Aye, aye," replied the smugglers.

And they drew back, and stood in a row, close to the wall of a large building.

Never slackening their pace for a moment, the men in pursuit, headed by the turnkey, who had been released from the cell in which the Boy

No. 33

Rover had imprisoned him, by a duplicate key possessed by the governor, drew near the spot where the smugglers stood.

"Do not move till I give the order," said the Boy Rover, as they each endeavoured to strike down his man.

Dashing up to the smugglers, the pursuers paused before them.

"On them!" said the Rover.

And, ere the men could raise a hand to defend themselves the smuggler struck out at them, and three out of the four rolled upon the ground from the force of the blows.

The turnkey alone remained firm. Dashing forward, he grasped Jim by the collar of his jacket.

Jem raised his hand, and struck him a heavy blow between the eyes.

But the man did not relax his grasp.

He pressed his knuckles into the neck of the smuggler till that worthy fairly yelled out at the pain inflicted.

"Let go," shouted Jem.

"Not so fast," replied the man.

But ere the words died away he fell half-blind by a blow from the fist of the Boy Rover.

Two of the others had regained their feet, and once more rushed upon the smugglers.

But the odds were now two to one, and they were instantly knocked down by the iron hands of the escaped prisoners.

"On again!" exclaimed the Rover, and he darted on, followed by his companions.

The men again rose to their feet, but the punishment they had received deterred them from following.

But they raised their voices, and the dark street echoed with their loud cries of—"stop them!—stop thief!"

"Curse them!" exclaimed the Boy Rover, "They will bring the whole town upon our heels, and in spite of all resistance we shall be re-taken."

But for some time they continued their flight without further interruption.

Yet the loud tones of the prison bell came upon their ears, and put everyone upon the alert.

They had placed a considerable distance be-tween themselves and the prison, and were begin-ning to congratulate themselves upon having suc-ceeded in escaping, when another party of men suddenly made their appearance from a bye street and confronted the smugglers.

"Stop!" exclaimed one, "or I will shoot you down like dogs."

"Blaze away, old fellow," exclaimed the Boy Rover, with the utmost coolness, "we can stand fire."

"'Tis useless to resist," said the man who had threatened to fire upon them. "Surrender, and you shall be well treated."

"I never strike my colours," replied the Boy Rover in the same cool tone.

Black Bill, who during this conversation kept the cutlass as much hidden behind him as possible, sidled up to the side of the speaker.

"Surrender, or I fire!" he exclaimed.

"Didn't you hear the captain tell you to fire?" said Bill.

The man enraged at the cool taunting tones raised his arm, and the muzzle of a pistol flashed before the eyes of the smuggler.

Quick as the lightning's flash, Bill swung his weapon round and struck the pistol from the man's grasp.

"Secure it," he exclaimed.

The Boy Rover stooped down hurriedly and secured the weapon.

"Fire!" said the man who had been struck by Bill.

There was a sharp flash and a loud report, but the bullet flew harmlessly over the heads of the smugglers.

"Down with them," shouted the man who had given the order to fire.

"Down with you," said Bill, dealing him a blow with the cutlass. "That'll stop your croak-ing, I reckon."

The Boy Rover raised the pistol to the level of the heart of the man who fired, and as its echoes died away he saw the man fall heavily to the earth.

The three which remained now turned and took to flight, and once more the smugglers were free to move forward.

But the Boy Rover well knew that the report of the fire-arms would reveal their whereabouts, and he doubted not would bring down upon them numbers with whom they would be unable to cope.

So turning to his followers, he exclaimed—

"Quick! Follow me—this way."

And darting on for some short distance fur-ther, he turned abruptly down a narrow street.

"Do you know your way, captain?" asked Bill, who ran by his side.

"No," replied the Rover, "but we must get away from where the pistol was fired as it will be sure to bring more than we can hope to cope with to the spot."

"That's true."

"Let us get on some distance this road. I don't suppose it will take us far from the coast."

"I hope it won't," said Bill, "for curse me if I can feel at all safe out of the scent of salt water."

"Nor I," replied the Rover. "I have taken my bearings, and I think I shall steer the right course, though it will carry us a few points out of our track."

"Well then, we must tack to get right again," said Bill, pausing to get breath.

"Yes," replied the Rover. "But are all here? We must not leave any behind."

"All right, captain."

"That's well. The coast appears clear, so sup-pose we furl sail and haul to for a few minutes," said the Boy Rover, now fairly out of breath with his run.

This proposition found no opposition as one and all were only too glad to pause and rest for a few minutes.

The Boy Rover cast his eyes eagerly round in all directions.

There was no one to be seen—not a human form appeared in sight.

"I think we have done them all first rate," re-marked Sam.

"Yes, for the present," replied the Boy Rover, "but the alarm bell still rings, and the news of our escape has spread through the place doubt-less by this time, and every one is on the watch for us."

"If they don't come no nearer than they are now," said Jem, "we aint got much to be frigh-tened of."

"But I am afraid we shall yet have to fight our way to the coast," said the Rover.

"I don't care how soon it comes in sight," said Black Bill.

"Nor I neither," said Sam.

"How far are we off it, do you think, captain?" said Bill.

"Off what?"

"The coast."

"Not far."

"What point of the compass does it lay in?" said Jem; "for I have lost my bearings altogether in this confounded run."

"Yonder," said the Boy Rover. "We must steer to the left."

"All right," captain," said Bill: "lead the way."

"Keep a good look-out for breakers," said the Rover, as he once more started off at a quick pace.

"Aye, aye," replied the smugglers, following in the wake of their captain—not a little pleased at the smoothness of their journey.

The bell still continued to toll, and its tone was ever and anon borne by the wind to the ears of the escaped men.

"The fellow that cast that instrument," said Sam, "ought to be hung just now to its tongue."

"Why?" asked Jem.

"Because he'd make it hold it," replied Sam.

"Hold what?"

"Its tongue, to be sure," said Sam, laughing at what he considered a bit of wit. But Jem was too dull to take it so. He only replied with a sort of grunt, and strode after Bill and the captain.

Still bearing off to the left, in a short time the fugitives felt assured that they were making a direct course to the coast.

The air was more fresh, and the wind more keen.

"Captain," said Bill, "I can sniff it."

"Sniff what?" asked the Boy Rover, suddenly.

"The salt water."

"Aye," replied the Rover.

"There's something refreshing and cheering in that, for it savours of freedom."

In a few moments more they caught a glimpse of the sea stretching away before them.

"Now," said the Boy Rover, with a bright gleam in his dark fiery eye—"now I can defy them. For the first time since that cursed lieutenant put the irons on my limbs do I breathe freely. They thought they had me secure; but the career of the Boy Rover is not yet ended. They shall hear of me again, and shall tremble at the name of the smuggler of the South Seas.

CHAPTER XC.

ONCE MORE ON THE ISLAND.—TALES AND ADVENTURES.

DAYS wore on, and Martinez and Inez, basking in the sunshine of each others love, were happy.

To them the desolate island was a paradise.

Ned Wilton too was happy.

He had met with friends in this place to which cruel fate had consigned him.

He was anxious and willing to do all that he could for the comfort of his fellow castaways, and never was so happy as when doing some little office for the beautiful Inez.

But time brings with it its changes.

It is almost impossible to exist for ever on love alone.

It is not that love cools in ardour, for true love will remain bright and green when the sear and yellow age shall bow the body and wrinkle the polished brow.

Still Martinez longed for something beyond love, a something by which they might kill the long hours of the day—longed for some kind of employment.

Hours pass wearily away when the mind cannot find employment; so it was agreed that Ned and Martinez should endeavour to construct such rude weapons as the means at their command would enable them to do, and start on an hunting expedition.

Ned was no less anxious to seek adventures than his new found companion, and together they set to work with right good will.

But by the time they had succeeded in forming a couple of rude clubs and bows and arrows, the weather, which had hitherto been fine, changed, and for two or three days they were unable to start out in pursuit of game or dare the chase.

This was a sad disappointment, but there was no help for it, and the friends assembled in the hut or arbour of Martinez, which was made larger than that of Ned's, and endeavoured to pass away the time by the recital of their various adventures and listening to the dulcet melodies of the beautiful Inez.

The rain came down in torrents, and the earth was so much saturated that all hope of putting their projects into execution must be abandoned for some time.

But as Ned had a good stock of fruit and berries laid by in case of any unforeseen circumstance arising, they were well provided with food, so they resolved to await the return of fair weather with resignation, and strove to amuse each other as best they could.

Having procured a fire, which was done by striking a spark from two flints upon some powdered bark, the three castaways seated themselves around it, and after the genial warmth had penetrated their frames and conversation had flowed till each felt no restraint in the others company, Martinez, turning and addressing himself to Ned Wilton, remarked—

"Like me, you are but a young man; still, a sailor's life is ever full of danger, and I should like to hear some of your adventures, and so would Inez, poor girl, for she feels dull. The different epochs of a man's life are often instructive as well as amusing, and serve to kindle friendship, as by the knowledge of each others sufferings men learn to love, to pity, and to respect.

"Well, I can't say as I have met with many adventures in my time as can be at all instructive or amusing," said Ned, "unless it was an hunting excursion I was once on. However, it will serve to pass away the time, so here goes. It was when I was quite a boy, and before I joined the 'Venomed Snake.'"

"It was a bit of adventure I once had above Calcutta a-bit. It wasn't very pleasant sport at the time, though it's well enough to think of now."

"One morning a heavy lighter came alongside, manned by half-a-dozen natives.

"Our captain had engaged her to go after fresh water.

"About ten miles above Hoogly—and I don't know but what it may be more—there was a fine stream of water, and there we were going, intending to be gone over one night.

"Our first mate, a stout good-hearted fellow, named Bill Gillott, was to take charge; and Sam

Willis, Jack Springer, and myself were to accompany him.

"We got our guns and pistols aboard the lighter—for, ye see, there were likely to be robbers about wherever Europeans ventured off in small parties—and having put our bedding and provisions in, we made sail up the river.

"We had a fair wind, and by noon we reached the mouth of the stream, up which we were to get our water.

"It was quite a little river, coming in from the north'rd and west'rd, and, as we turned into it, we could feel that it was cooler and sweeter than the water of the Hoogly.

"About four miles up we came to the camp where the native water-carriers were in the habit of stopping; and here we came-to, and made fast.

"Some forty or fifty feet from the bank, on the edge of a thick deep jungle, there was a spring which sent out water enough to supply quite a stream. It was at this spring we meant to get our water, and, as soon as all was ready, we set our natives at work, carrying the buckets to and from the lighter, we filling them at the spring.

"As we five could fill much faster than the porters could carry, and as it was not in the contract that we should lug water under the hot sun, Gillott and I left the other three filling, while we went to explore the jungle.

"But we did not go a great way. The reeds were so thick and stout that we could with difficulty make our way amongst them; and, in fact, we could not, save where a sort of path had already been beaten.

"While we were in there, the mate made some remark about the tiger.

"The very sound of the monster's name was enough to make me tremble.

"When we returned, we asked the natives if tigers were ever seen about that neighbourhood. They said they had never seen one, though there had been tracks found upon the edge of the spring, which were supposed to have been made by the tiger.

"The oldest of the Indians, and the one who hired all the others, said he had been engaged in work that called him to this spring more or less for fifteen years; but he had never seen anything that looked like the animal in question.

"Most of the people of this country have a mistaken idea of the tiger. The few specimens which have been carried round to show are not much like the real Royal Tiger of Bengal.

"There are certainly three different sorts of tigers, and they vary in size as well as in colour. The smaller kind have the same general characteristics, and are coloured after the same pattern as the larger ones, but the colours are not so bright.

"The Royal Tiger has a yellow ground to his skin; and then the stripes are a beautiful black, running over the back and down the sides, about in the same course with the ribs. But it is with regard to the size of the animal that there is the greatest mistake.

"When I tell a man I have seen a tiger ten feet long from his nose to the end of his back, and then five feet of tail added to that, making fifteen feet in all, he don't want to believe me. But it is so.

"The royal tiger has been seen to carry off a full-sized buffalo.

"An old Hindoo merchant—an honourable man, and one who could have no earthly reason for deceiving me—assured me that his men had killed a tiger in one of the deep jungles of the Burracoor whose body alone was thirteen feet in length! I might have hesitated about believing this had I not seen one myself nearly twice as large as I supposed they ever grew.

"You can imagine something of the strength of such an animal.

"It is very fortunate that they are scarce, for their destructiveness is beyond all precedent.

"They kill for the mere sake of killing. Let one of them make his way among a herd of cattle and he will kill without eating a morsel while there is a living animal to be seen.

"While they can get blood they will not taste flesh. They do not eat to appease their hunger only; they eat to gorge themselves; they will gulp down blood while they can stand.

"It is said by those who best understand their habits that they love human flesh more than anything else, and will leave the blood of any animal for a man. Such taste as that, though it may flatter humanity, I must say I fail to admire or appreciate.

"When night came we hauled our lighter into the middle of the stream and then turned in.

"When we awoke in the morning one of the natives said he had heard a low, howling noise during the night, not far off.

"At one time he thought it was a tiger, and was upon the point of arousing us; but as he listened more attentively it sounded nearer like the yelping of a dog, and he concluded to let us sleep.

"As soon as we had eaten our breakfast we hauled our lighter to the shore, and commenced work.

"The sun had got high enough to throw down an uncomfortable heat, when I plainly heard a crashing in a distant part of the jungle, and in a few moments more one of the natives started the cry—

"'The tiger! The tiger!'

"In all the various sounds of earth I doubt if there is another which can strike such terror to the souls of the natives of that country as does that cry. No sooner did it break upon the air, than the rest of the Indians took it up, and at the same time rushed for the lighter.

"They had just gained it, and we, who stood beneath the awning which had been spread over the spring, were about to follow, when a low, deep cry, like the snarl of a cat a thousand times multiplied in volume and depth, broke upon our ears, and on the next instant a dark object came with a sort of blurring sensation, distinctly before our eyes.

"We started back, and as soon as I could look fairly, I saw a huge tiger crouching upon the hard sand, about half way between where we were and the boat!

"He was gazing upon the natives.

"They knew his habits well enough not to run any further then.

"They had gained the bows of the lighter only when the tiger leaped from the jungle, and the cuddy, or little cabin, was in the after part.

"They knew if they turned to seek that place the monster would leap upon them, so they stood in a body and faced him, while he lay in a crouching posture, with his tail lashing the sand, and his claws gathering for a spring.

"We had taken our guns up with us to the spring, for the report of the native who had heard the noise in the night served to put us on our guard.

"The pieces were common heavy muskets, and we had loaded them with two bullets each. We seized them as quickly as possible, but there was a difficulty in the way of our firing.

"The tiger was directly between us and the natives. The place where we stood was some feet higher than the shore, and the place where the monster was crouched was in a direct line with the bows of the boat!

"A ball passing through his body from one of our guns would, if it kept on in a straight line, strike the natives at the breast.

"It was very evident that no time was to be lost, and yet our best course was not so easily decided. However, we were just upon the point of moving around so as to bring the tiger out from that fatal range, when I noticed that the natives were not only conversing eagerly, but were also changing their positions. I saw they were up to some plot, but what it was I could not tell. They saw how we were situated with regard to firing, and hence they seemed to have studied for themselves. Presently one of them spoke to us—

"'The tiger means for leap at us! He looks find if we got swords and guns. He find no—he leap. When you see him on boat you fire. Fire at him—

"The Indian probably meant to tell us where to aim, but that moment a movement in another quarter arrested his attention. They had each gained a position to suit, and then watched the tiger with the most intense eagerness. I saw the monster's fore legs move—I saw the claws open upon the sand — and then came that peculiar gathering of the body which shows that the muscular power is all concentrated. On the next instant the huge body left the earth, and as it did so the six natives disappeared, as if by magic. They had dropped down into the spaces between the casks, doubling themselves up just like hedgehogs.

"The tiger struck the tops of the casks, and seemed for the moment to be utterly confounded, and during that moment we raised our muskets. The beast stood slightly quartering, with his head from me, so that my best point of sight was just behind his shoulder. We fired together, or very nearly so.

"While yet the ring of our reports was upon the air we heard a deafening howl, and before the smoke had cleared away, so that we could see the lighter, the tiger was upon the sand, very near the spot where he had crouched before. He saw us, and with another yell leaped towards us. I clubbed my musket, and struck him upon the head as he passed me, but the blow seemed to make no impression upon him. He kept on some yards beyond us, and then turned. He did not stop to gather for a spring, but rushed directly towards us. We moved quickly aside, and he passed us again.

"We now knew, of course, that he was bewildered, and to such an extent that he could not reason.

"As he turned a second time, the mate caught the axe, which we had brought with us for ordinary use, and stood by to use it.

"He grasped it with a steady nerve, for there was little danger now, and as the tiger came on again, hesitating and half-turning when he reached us, Bill brought him a blow upon the top of the head that split his skull.

"The mighty beast staggered sideways a few steps, and then fell dead.

"The natives now came up from the lighter, and their shouts of joy and exultation were beyond anything of the kind I ever heard before.

"They claimed a good share of credit in the monster's death, and we were willing to grant it, for had they not acted as coolly and resolutely as they did, the tiger would not have been killed as he was, and beyond that it was impossible to judge what might have happened.

"At all events, I don't believe that we, had we been exactly in their situation, would have done so well as they did.

"We should not have resorted to stratagem so easily and naturally, but should have been more likely either to have made for the cabin, or to have faced him and made the best of it—in either of which cases we should probably have come out second best.

"The tiger measured seven feet and a half in length of body, and nearly eleven feet from nose to tail, inclusive.

"Two of our bullets had passed within half-an-inch of his heart, one had entered his head, while one was lodged in his shoulder.

"We voted the skin to our mate, and he was thankful and proud.

"It was lucky that we had the skin to show when we returned to the ship, else the crew might not have believed that we had slain such an animal so easily."

"That put me in mind," said Martinez, after a pause, "of a fearful adventure myself and a friend had with a large snake."

"You!" said Inez.

"Yes, dear one, me," replied the young lieutenant.

"Oh, do tell me all about it," said Inez.

"It will make you shudder."

"Never mind."

"You will say I had a lucky escape," said Martinez.

And he placed his arm around her slender form.

"That of course I am only too happy to know, without having heard the adventure," said Inez. "Still you must not refuse to let me hear the dangers which you have undergone.

"Well then, Inez, it was when I was a younger man than I am now by some years. It was when I was in the last of my teens, and I had a strong desire to sail round the world.

"My father was a merchant, and had an interest in several ships; and from the time that I left my academy until I was nineteen—a space of about a year—I gave him no peace. At length he concluded to let me go. It was on the very day that I was nineteen years old. I was as tall as I am now, and though not so muscular and firmly knit in frame, yet I was very near as stout in body. My father obtained me a berth as supercargo, and I considered myself the happiest man on the face of the earth.

"The old ship, 'Trident,' was ready for sea, bound for a trading voyage around the earth, and I was ready to go in her. We sailed with a fair wind, and I promised myself a fair voyage. We stopped first at the Cape Verde; next St. Thomas; then we doubled the Cape of Good Hope, and stopped at Zanzibar. Then we sailed to Muskat; and so on, trading as we went, and making money rapidly. At length we reached Canton; and from there we ran down, through the China Sea, to the

Sea of Calebes, and stopped at Manado, a town on the Island of Calebes, which island, however, is more generally known by the name of Macassar.

"Here we sold cutlery, cloth, and manufactured articles of various kinds, taking in exchange coffee, spices, and a choice lot of medicinal drugs, all of which we got at cheap rates.

"I had seen some most beautiful birds flying about on shore, and as I knew how to preserve and mount them, I wanted very much to get some of them. One of the natives informed me that, some four miles to the southward and westward of us, where a small stream emptied into the sea, I could find plenty of birds of all kinds.

"On the following morning I asked the captain if I could have the small wherry during the day, and he told me yes. The wherry was a small, snug little affair, which we had on purpose for a sort of errand-boat when only one or two persons wished to go in her. But the day promised to be a very hot one, and I came very nigh finding no one who would go with me. I had asked all whose society I had fancied, and they all said no. Finally, our second mate, whose name was Spinnet—Jack Spinnet, and who had once told me no—came and asked me if I had found a companion. I told him I had not, and then he said he would go with me. I was pleased with this, for he was the first one I had asked, and the very man I most liked for such companionship.

"We got our guns and knives; and, having taken a few articles we fancied we might need, we got into the boat. The short light mast was stepped, the small sail set, and away we went down the coast, under a creeping breeze, at the rate of three miles an hour.

"We found the river without trouble, and, as soon as we had got well up into it, I proposed unstepping the set mast—the sail might frighten the birds. They might be used to seeing boats, but not white sails. So the mast was taken down, and we plied the oars.

"The day was a hot one, in right good earnest; but we were in for it, and did not complain. We shot several beautiful birds; but the one I most wanted we had not yet seen. It was congenerous with the bird of paradise. I had only seen two. They were quite large, with a body nearly as heavy as the body of our common pigeon, and with the most luxuriant profusion of gaudy plumage I ever saw. The body was of a bright scarlet, the wings nearly all black, and the tail consisted of a perfect rainbow, both in colour and shape.

"We made our way up the river very slowly—sometimes rowing and sometimes sculling, and sometimes pushing ourselves along by means of a pole which we had for that purpose.

"It was now near noon, and the sun poured down his heat with a prodigality which we could have spared without the least inconvenience. To row with any force was out of the question. We kept in the shade as much as possible, and lazily crawled along. The banks were covered with heavy timber, all interwoven below with vines and tangled wildwood of all descriptions.

"Here and there dark, dismal-looking bayous, made up from the river, almost entirely covered with reeds and old trees. The stream itself was not deep, as we could use our setting-pole anywhere, though in some places we could sink it beyond reach in soft mud; and, save where these small bayous made out, it was not over twenty yards wide.

"At length I saw the bird I wanted. There were two of them upon the opposite side of the river from where we were, and a little farther up. I caught my gun, and examined the priming; and having laid it across my knees, so as to have it ready in case the birds should fly over us, I took my oar and started the boat out. The birds were standing upon a branch, which made out from an old tree of the cypress species, and nearly, if not quite, over the water.

"My only fear was that we might frighten them away. Jack proposed that we should pull across and down at the same time, and then work up towards the birds under cover. This was a good plan, and we at once acted upon it.

"When he had gained the opposite shore, we were covered from our game by the overhanging foliage, so we worked up without fear of alarming it. I took my position in the bow of the boat, with my double barreled gun in my hand, and already cocked; while Jack sat in the stern-sheets, pushing noiselessly up with the pole.

"At length I turned, and whispered to my companion to push carefully, for I knew we were coming very near. In half a minute more I saw the birds through an opening in the foliage, and I quickly called upon Jack to stop, and he did so. The birds were still upon the same branch, and my chance was a good one, though a rather longer range than I would have chosen could I have had everything my own way. I fired—and I saw one of the gorgeous fellows drop. I threw down my gun, and caught an oar, and we were soon near the spot.

"The shore was low, and we could see the wounded bird struggling, some fifteen or twenty feet from the water. We drove our boat ashore as quickly as possible, and as she touched I leaped out. I had hardly touched the soft, grassy earth, when a sharp terrified cry from my companion arrested my further progress. I turned, and I saw him standing in the boat—his face pale as death—a look of utter horror prevading every feature; and his frame quivering like an aspen. He seemed to be strangling—he seemed to be trying in vain to either breathe or speak. One hand was extended, and the other hung by his side shaking with sudden palsy.

"'Jack,' I cried, 'in mercy's name, what is the matter?'

"'Come, come to the boat!' he gasped, in a frantic burst.

"'But what is it?' I insisted, becoming frightened by his deathly look.

"Pretty soon the power came to him.

"'Jump for the boat!' he cried. 'Don't stop to look to the right nor left! Jump! jump for your life, jump!'

In an instant the thought of some venomous reptile flashed upon my mind, and without further hesitancy I started. When I reached the boat I looked back upon the ground where I had stood, but saw nothing. I was just upon the point of asking Jack what he had seen when, accidently, I raised my eye to the huge tree above me. A cry of horror burst from my lips, and but for the need of action I should certainly have sunk down with absolute terror.

"Upon the tree—coiled around and around—with his great broad, flat head lapped over the very limb upon which the birds had sat, and over the spot where I had stood, his cold diamond eyes glittering like gems in the sunlight, was a monster anaconda! the largest I had ever seen larger, much larger than I believed they ever grew. The tree was over three feet in diameter, certainly seven feet in circumference, and the monster was coiled about that five times, and had certainly eight feet to spare from the tree to his head. That head was right above us now, and the forked tongue was darting out angrily.

"As soon as I was in 1 sprang to the stern-sheets and caught the pole. I pushed the boat off—the stern struck a sunken limb—it swept the shore—and we were in the mud!

"'Push! push! For your life push! See! see! He means to strike us!' cried Jack, pointing up to the monster's head as he spoke.

"I pushed—pushed with all my might—but to no effect. The boat would not budge an inch! The bows would swing around, but the stern was fast.

"'Can't you push her off?' asked Jack,

"'No,' I returned. 'Something's got her foul!'

"Just as I spoke the serpent threw his head back, and carried it to the opposite side of the tree.

"What he meant to do we did not then try to consider. We only thought of getting our boat out of his reach. Jack caught an oar, and we both pushed together; but the thing would not budge! What could it be? we were not held thus by the mud—that was impossible,—and yet we only had soft mud to brace against when we pushed.

"I was growing crazy! There was a monster, whose power might crush us as though we had been worms, within an easy reaching distance, and yet we could not move! To move the boat was impossible. What held her I could not tell. To leap overboard would only be sure death; for the water was not over eighteen inches deep, and below that was a bed of mud. Our pole, which was twelve feet long, could be run down nearly the whole length; and that was one reason why we could not get purchase enough to move the boat.

"Oh! Heavens! what a sight it was! The huge body of the monster gleamed with a thousand varying colours as it worked in the almost vertical rays of the sun, and the broad head was coming around from the opposite side of the tree! I had pushed the pole into the mud, straining and torturing every muscle, until I knew that I could do nothing thus. Meanwhile Jack Spinnet, who had caught up an oar, had been doing the same. The shore was too far off to be reached by a leap, and there was no tree within reach save the one the anaconda occupied.

"Suddenly I saw Jack fall over backwards—a dark mass flashed before me—there was a sickening sinking sensation, as though the gushing, spurting head of a decapitated mother or wife had been held up by the hair before me—and then my eyes involuntarily closed.

"A horrid shriek from my companion aroused me. I opened my eyes and looked. There lay my friend, upon his back, across two thwarts and the monster serpent's head lay flat upon his breast!

"Oh! My soul! my soul! what a sensation was that! Pain was not in it. It was the very essence—ten thousand times refined—of the soul's most agonizing horror. The serpent had placed his head there, and the expression of his face was the deepest we can ascribe to the most exultant Tartarian demon! Oh; there was expression there—such expression as I pray to God I may never see again! As his head lay thus, those glittering eyes of his could look into his victim's face. His body was loosening from the tree—he had made up his mind for a dainty meal!

"And here let me dispute a false idea which has become universal wherever the serpent is known. It is printed in school-books; set down in works upon natural history: and sustained by travellers. It is this; that the anaconda, the boa, and others of that tribe, prepare their food before swallowing it by licking it all over, and thus covering it with a sort of gelatinous substance which causes it to slip down more easily. Now, this is not so. The serpent does this no more than does every animal that lives! Let a man work for an hour at trying to swallow a mass beyond his capacity, and I think you will find it pretty thoroughly gelatinised. The truth is this: the serpent swallows his food as all other animals do that swallow it whole. All animals within his capacity he swallows instantly, without even maiming them. But when a huge serpent has been a long time without food, and he chances to strike upon something with a larger circumference than his own body, he must work ingeniously to destroy it. First, he knows he must kill it, and this he does as he fights his own kind—by crushing. When it is crushed he commences to swallow. His muscles are all relaxed, and their tension is great. He works and works—the glands of the mouth are overtasked and irritated, and they discharge their secretions for their own ease, as the eye weeps when it is in pain. Thus, of course, that part of the food which has been in the mouth will become covered with saliva. Sometimes a huge anaconda will lie two weeks with a deer, or some other large animal, not much over half swallowed!

"The serpent has the same kind of salivary glands that other animals have—no more, no less; and if an animal is sometimes found half swallowed by him, and all covered with saliva, it is simply because he has been a week about it! The presence of the saliva is the result of overtasking the mouth, and not a natural preparation of food.

"For a single instant after I opened my eyes, and saw the position of my companion, I was utterly powerless, but a stifled groan from the poor man quickly startled me into action.

"'Martinez, save me!'

"Never did three words operate upon me as did those. They not only touched my heart, but in an instant all fear was gone, as if by a miracle, and every nerve was strung to action. One of the barrels of my gun was yet loaded with a heavy charge of buck shot. I caught it up and cocked it. I determined to run a risk. I moved a step forward and then knelt down. The side of the snake's head was exposed to me. I placed the muzzle within twelve inches of it, aimed for the broadest part, just at the back of and below the eye, and fired!

"I saw that same black mass sweep upward, and in a moment more came a thrashing and crashing that was frightful to hear. The folds of the monster's body had tightened about the tree, and his head, with some twelve or fourteen feet of neck and trunk, was thrashing to and fro upon the ground and amid the branches overhead. For a few moments I feared he would smash our boat, but he had neither sense nor sight, and, as the position of his folds naturally carried his head from us, there was no more danger.

"Jack Spinnet arose from his recumbent position, but he could do no work. He was weak and faint—the terrible, the awful fear of those few moments having left him utterly nerveless.

"I assured myself that he was not bodily injured, and then I took the pole and tried once more to push the boat off. I had sense enough to look now and see what was the matter; and the result was that I found an unearthed root, probably from the large tree close by, under the water, which had worked its way up between the stern-post and the rudder. I quickly pushed it out, and then pushed off.

"I asked Jack if we should stop and see the serpent die.

"'Oh! in Heaven's name, no,' he answered. 'Get back as soon as you can. I am not well, Walter—I am not well.'

"Of course I hesitated no longer. I sculled down the river, there set my sail, and, with the evening breeze, I ran up to Manado.

"On the following day some of us went out and found the serpent dead. I had blown his brains half out from his flat saucer-like skull. There was some muscular activity remaining, but not enough to amount to anything. We towed the monster's carcase to Manado, and there had the skin taken off and stuffed. The Dutch consul there offered a large sum of money for it, and we sold it to him.

"Jack Spinnet received a shock on that occasion from which he will never recover, though he is by no means an invalid. His nervous system is shattered, and there is an oppression upon the chest; and if he ever chance to sleep upon his back, he is sure to be seized with a most horrible incubus—the serpent is upon him, as he was in that terrible hour, and his whole frame quivers with fright. He awakes with a cold sweat all over his body, and sleeps no more for the night."

"Indeed the adventure was a terrible one," said Inez. "Oh! had that cruel snake have encompassed your ruin, I—I—"

"Would not now be sitting beside me, dear, listening to the words of him who so fondly loves you."

"Indeed, no," said Inez. "Fate would have robbed me of all worth living for—your love."

And she flung her arms around his neck, and imprinted a kiss upon his glowing cheek.

"Ah! dear one," he said, "I have seen some adventures in my chequered life."

"Then the snake adventure is not the only one?" said Inez, looking up in his face.

"No, darling: in America I have nearly lost my life through the buffalo."

"The buffalo?"

"Yes."

"When?"

"Oh, some time since."

"Oh, let me hear it."

"Well, then, it was whilst I was with a party hunting through the western part of Missouri.

"We had horses and tents; and our baggage was carried by a heavy wagon, drawn by mules.

"We left Jefferson city, and struck the Osage at Warsaw; and from that we took our course to the westward.

"One pleasant afternoon we came across buffalo tracks, and from their appearance we knew there must be a large drove of them.

"As soon as we came to a good place we hauled up and drove down our stakes.

"It was very near sundown when we got fairly encamped; so we got supper, and then concluded to wait till the morning, for further work out of doors.

"In the morning we got an early breakfast, and then started out.

"We took the open way, across a sort of rocky plain, beyond which was a splendid grove of maples; and just as we entered this grove we heard the tramp of buffaloes.

"We put on at full gallop, and in a few minutes came in sight of a fine drove upon the edge of a stream.

"Part of the herd turned down the stream, and part started up.

"There were eight of us hunters; and, as the herd separated, five of the party turned their horses' heads up the stream, where the largest number of buffaloes had gone.

"The other three, of whom I was one, turned the other way.

"There were fifty animals, at least, in the lot we gave chase to, and they started off in fine style. We had followed them half a mile, and shot two cows, when we saw that the stream went to the right and made a bend round a wooded hill.

"I told my companions I'd cut across and head the buffaloes off; they liked the idea, so I turned short to the right, feeling sure that I should hit the river in that direction.

"We had seen a stream a mile or so back, and I knew this must be the same one, and if it was then this bend kept on till it made over half a circle.

"I had ridden about half a mile, when I came to a deep gully, where the water had at some time dug its way into the earth.

"My dog, who was ahead, leaped over easily; and I knew my horse could do it too.

"So I put him up to it, and he made the reach.

"He cleared the gully with four feet to spare; but he stumbled and fell, and when I got him up I found he had badly sprained his right fore foot.

"He had struck a small rolling stone, and turned the ankle.

"I tried to lead him, but he could not walk, at least, not without great difficulty.

"I had but little time for considering.

"I could hear the buffaloes away to my left, and I knew they would be around before long.

"I drew down the rein and tied it to a small tree, and then seizing my rifle I kept on afoot.

"I ran most of the way, only slackening into a kind of dog trot once in awhile to rest, for having been so long used to the saddle it rather took hold of me to run.

"By-and-bye I came out into an open prairie that is, if you call such a place a prairie. It was covered with short crisp grass in some places, and in others it was bare sand.

"On the further side of this opening, I saw the stream, and to the left, half a mile off, I saw a dozen buffaloes coming down.

"I wondered where the rest were; but I saw there would be a chance for a good shot if I could get near enough, so I left the wondering for another time, and put off for the stream, hoping to reach a place where I saw a small clump of bushes were growing.

"I reached the bushes just in time, and called my dog in.

"The buffaloes were not far off, and were evidently going to pass between me and the stream, which was only a few rods distant.

"I supposed the animals must have seen me, and I feared they would turn off, but they did not.

"There was just twelve of them, and mostly cows and yearlings, but there were two huge bulls in advance looking as ugly as you please.

"I had never seen a buffalo before to be shot at, and I had an idea that they were afraid of man.

FOUNDERING OF THE "PRETTY LASS."

"But just at that time I was too excited to think.

"I had heard my companions talk so much about killing buffaloes, that I had become so eager to put a bullet through one of their hearts, that I should have fired if I had known all about them.

"However, I didn't think of danger.

"My only thought was that I'd shoot one of them, and the rest would run like mad.

"Presently they came.

"They were not more than three rods off, and I thought the shot a sure one.

"I cocked my rifle and brought it to my shoulder. I was sure I pressed the trigger, and at that instant my dog gave a quick sharp howl. I fired, but the howl startled me, and the shot was not true.

"I hit the buffalo—the largest of the two bulls—and he stopped and shook his huge head and shoulders.

"In a moment more he turned and saw me.

"The rest of the herd had gone.

"He gave one ugly defiant roar, and then turned his body for a change.

"I saw blood trickling down the long hair upon his right shoulder, and from the place where the crimson drops started out I judged that the ball had only struck some two inches out of the way.

"But it might have been a foot for that matter, for when my dog howled I was so startled that I lost my aim entirely.

"I thought he was going to spring out, and my first impulse was to stop him; so I just lost all, for my finger was already too hard pressed on the trigger to be stopped.

"Something must have bitten the dog; but I had no time to look.

"As soon as I saw the bull turned towards me I knew he would attack me.

"I knew enough of the animal for that.

"He went between me and the stream, so I had a run across the opening before me. I had no time to lose—not an instant—and I started.

"The distance to the wood was all of fifty rods.

"My only idea was to reach it.

"What I should do when I got there I did not stop to consider—I only wished to get there.

"I was as tall then as I am now, and with not an ounce of superfluous flesh upon my bones.

"I ran as I never ran before nor since. I heard the tramp of the infuriated monster behind me, and I knew he was gaining.

"Out from the edge of the wood—just a few yards out—stood a clump of maples which seemed to grow from one immense root.

"There were two large ones and two small ones.

"Could I reach them?

"I was not over half way across yet. I told ye before that I wasn't used to running. It took my breath from me.

"Every nerve in my body was strained, and every muscle was beginning to relax.

"I heard the tramp of the bull not two rods behind me!

"My rifle was heavy, and it bore me down.

"It was of no use to me as it was, and it might be the cause of my death if I hung on to it.

"It prevented me from a free swing of my arms.

"I knew the brute was gaining, and I felt the eight and twenty pounds of steel and wood wearing me out. I let it drop; and then I ran more easily.

"The maples were now ten rods distant, and the bull not a rod behind me.

"My dog was at his heels, but he paid little attention to him; though I am sure it made a slight difference.

"Had it not been for the annoyance of the dog I think the bull would have caught me before I had run twenty rods. I am sure of it.

"Four rods remained to the trees.

"Could I reach them alive?

"I heard the puffing of the buffalo, almost like the snort of a locomotive; and I fancied I could feel his breath as it struck my back!

"One rod more!

"Had it been two rods I should have sunk down.

"The trees had become indistinct—the earth seemed rising up before me—my head was almost bursting, and my heart was in my throat, aching as thought it were broken!

"One more effort—a wild plunge—a low painful groan—and I turned the trees and fell against the largest one.

"The bull kept on a few yards, and then stopped and turned.

"His eyes were glaring wildly; his mouth was foaming; and the foam, mingled with blood, streamed down his swart breast.

"He was tired as well as I; for he had been on the run a long while; and he stopped now to take breath.

"Had he kept up the chase — had he attacked me then—I should have been at his mercy, for I could not have moved around that tree to have saved a dozen lives! I was completely, utterly exhausted.

"I would have given all I owned in the world could I only have thrown myself full length upon the ground; but of course I dared not do that.

"Pretty soon my dog started out; but the first movement the bull made was to take him on his short sharp horns and toss him over his back.

"Shrieking with pain, the poor dog crawled back to the trees and crouched down at my feet, where he lay and regarded the buffalo with anything but pleasant looks.

"But this movement of the dog's served to start the monster up, for as soon as he had disposed of his tormentor he turned towards me and ploughed his head into the ground.

"This operation he repeated several times—thrusting his horns into the earth and tossing up the dirt—and then he plunged towards me.

"I had gained a very little of my strength—at any rate, enough to enable me to move around the trees—and I did so.

"One thing was fortunate for me.

"As I told you before, these four trees seemed to grow all out from one root, just as you often see maples, and hence I had more surface of barricade between me and my enemy.

"I could move around them, or in between them, as I pleased.

"Their stumps, or butts, were together at the surface of the earth, but they spread apart sufficiently to admit my stepping through between them anywhere.

"But at first I passed wholly around them.

"In a very few moments the fear of death was upon me again? The bull seemed to feel sure of me when he first plunged towards me; but when he found that I avoided him by slipping around the trees he stopped, and fairly spoke his rage and disappointment. He stopped—he shook his head—he gave a roar that made my heart quake—and then gazed savagely at the trees around which I had passed, as though he would wreak his vengeance upon them.

"I never saw so much pure hatred and ugliness expressed in any other face as I saw in his then.

"While the bull stood there calculating how he should work, the thought occurred to me of climbing one of the trees.

"If I could gain a perch up there I should be sure, for of course my companions would be after me before a great while.

"I cast my eyes quickly up—I gazed around—and the hope was gone. There was not a limb anywhere within my reach!

"For a little while after this hope failed me I felt weak; but I overcame it by an effort, and was just in time to avoid the infuriate beast as he came dashing around the trees.

"He seemed determined now.

"With his head down, his eyes glaring like coals of fire, and his long tail high in the air, he bounded after me.

"Round and round we went, I keeping close in to the trees, and he performing a circle some thirty feet in diameter, every once in a while taking a cut and then flying off on a tangent, and coming back straight for the trees.

"I began to look for my companions.

"I could stand it no longer.

"You cannot form any idea of how I felt.

"I cannot tell it; but I tell ye I can remember it.

"I looked in all directions, and yelled with all my power; but I saw no one—I heard no one.

"I felt sure that in a few minutes at the furthest I should be tossing, a mangled, helpless mass, upon the monster's horns.

"The buffalo was opposite to me, and I had stopped from absolute exhaustion.

"He saw me stop, and he dashed towards me.

"He was coming directly between the trees and I dodged around.

"As he saw me make motion he changed his course.

"Around I went again, sustaining myself by the trees—actually holding myself up by them!

"Faint—weary—dying, almost—I staggered on.

"I looked off once more to see if my companions were coming. I tried to cry out, but I was too weak.

"I gazed down upon my dog.

"Poor Lion! He knew that his master was failing! He looked up and whined, and there were tears in his eyes. He surely wept then—wept because he knew we had met an enemy which had cowed him.

"'Good-bye!' I said. 'Good-bye Lion!'

"The faithful creature understood me, for he reached up his paws, and then turned away as though he would have me run for home.

"The bull had stopped again, and was glaring at me as before—glaring at me as though he would rush through the very trees that separated us."

"At that moment a thought came to me that sent the blood rushing with power through my system.

"In an instant a supernal hope darted to my soul, and under its influence every nerve and muscle of my frame were operated upon as though by the shock from a galvanic battery.

"I felt sure the bull had become so utterly carried away by anger and chagrin that he was blind with madness.

"He had no thought but to overtake me—but to wreak his vengeance out upon me.

"I felt assured that if I had remained still when he dashed at me before, he would have tried to pass between the trees.

"Even he might have known better in his sober moments; but he knew it not now.

"He had surely thought of trying it once—why might he not try it again?

"As I said before, the thought gave me fresh strength.

"You know how a dying man will momentarily put forth a wonderous power beneath the influence of sudden hope.

"It was so with me.

"I drew my knife—it was a stout, keen bowie—and moved to the space between two trees—it was between the two smaller ones.

"There I confronted him, and shook my left fist in his face.

"My soul! how he did make the dirt fly.

"He ploughed his horns deep into the earth, and then shook his head aloft.

"There I stood, and still shook my fist.

"Presently I saw him gather for a plunge, and as he did so I moved back a single step—not to the right hand or left, but only back as though I would move off.

"He took the hint, and in a moment more he made a dive.

"Would he turn?

"No.

"On he came—I still facing him with that defiant shaking of the fist. His head passed between the trees—his broad shoulders struck them; they quivered beneath the shock, and the smallest one bent from its very roots under the mighty strain.

"My heavens! what a gasp of agony burst from my lips at that moment!

"The huge monster was coming through.

"Instinctively I turned; but I knew I could not run. I could not stand much longer.

"I looked again upon the buffalo.

"His swart shoulders had entered between the trees—they had passed through—but he got no further.

"The bended maple, like the jaw of a trap, had sprung back into the hollow behind the shoulder, and there he was held, with his fore-feet quite twelve inches from the earth.

"Oh! what a moment was that for me.

"I saw the position of my enemy in an instant.

"I had not thought it possible for him to thrust his shoulders through that place.

"I had hoped that he might have run his head through, and jam his shoulders in far enough to hold him while I could strike.

"But when I saw how the stout tree sank into his flesh, I knew he could not help himself; and especially so since his fore-feet were useless to him.

"I walked up and looked at him. I slapped his black nose again and again. I kicked him with all my new found strength.

"Then I moved around to his right side, and felt for the socket above the breast-bone. I found it, and, with one plunge, I sent the broad blade of my knife home to his heart.

"The blood spurted forth as though from an engine—the pressure of the trees having held the life-tide bursting in the huge arteries of the throat.

"The beast glared at me once more—his eyes sent forth one more volume of fire—there was one more rumbling effort at that old roar—and then his head dropped—the fire of the eye went out—there was one mighty throe of the huge frame—and the monster was dead.

"At that moment I heard my name pronounced. I looked around, and there were my two companions coming up.

"They had found my horse, and had then started after me.

"And they found me; but I tell you plainly they found but a weak specimen of a man.

"They had to lift me upon a horse, and then one of them got up behind to hold me there.

"But I was quite well in the morning; and when we made a meal from the meat of that buffalo bull, you may be sure I had some thoughts running in my mind that did not accompany every meal."

"And so I should think, too," said Ned.

"Yes, much as I enjoyed the meal, I could not relish the recollection of the dangers I had passed through."

In this manner several days were passed by the castaways, the weather still continuing too stormy to allow them to go forth in quest of game or adventure.

But bad weather, like all things else, must have an end; and the elements had expended their furies, and the bright and glorious orb of day again shone forth in all its warm and refulgent splendour.

Still the little island bore a very different appearance to what it had done before.

The various small streams which intersected it had become so swollen by the heavy rains, that they had overflowed their banks, and had more the appearance of rivers and brooks.

This was a sad drawback to Martinez and his companion; but nothing daunted, they bid farewell to the beautiful Inez, and started forth, full of hope, in quest of food for their rough-made weapons, and sport for themselves.

Inez stood watching their manly forms, as they strode over the flower-bedewed earth, on their journey in search of game.

She almost feared to be left alone; yet the assurance that they would return by nightfall, and, if possible, bring with them the skin of some animal to make a garment for her in the cold damp days, reconciled her to her first parting; and she waved a kind adieu, as, entering a wood, they became lost to her sight.

CHAPTER XCI.

THE CASTAWAYS—INEZ AMONG THE FLOWERS—BREAKING OF THE WATERS—A PERILOUS POSITION—THE ESCAPE.

THE day wore on, and Inez busied herself about the hut, and strove to kill the long hours with singing or humming snatches of songs.

But she soon wearied even at this, and though the day had but half gone, she ever and anon looked forth as though she were anxious for the return of Martinez and his companion.

The sun was high in the heavens, and its golden beams tinted the beautiful landscape with gorgeous hues.

Inez was tempted by the fineness of the day to stroll away from the hut, and putting a hat made from the long grass which grew so luxuriantly around them, and bedecked with wild flowers she left the arbour and walked slowly in the direction from whence she expected her lover to return.

Musingly, almost pensively she strolled over the verdant ground, crushing into the earth at every footstep the luxuriant and beautiful variegated flowers which reared their heads in such rich abundance, and encircling herself in the luscious fragrance of their dying breath.

On she went, scarcely for a moment raising her large dark eyes from the ground, save and except to take a long look far out in the distance where she believed her lover to be pursuing the chase.

On she went for some time, till she approached the boundaries of a stream shut in by hugh stones, which upon one side formed a beautiful chasm, down whose sides the most magnificent flowers grew in luxuriant clusters.

Charmed by the sight which they presented, Inez sit herself down upon the bank upon the miniature chasm to gaze upon the beauties of the floral world beneath and around her, and likewise to rest her weary limbs.

Her natural penchant for music became excited by the beauty of the spot, and as she heedlessly plucked the flowers by her side, she sang in a low sweet tone the lines of one of those beautiful and charming ditties which she had oft sang at the feet of her father in her native land: --

"Where the mussel and scollop shine,
    Brighter than flowers;
Where the seaweed and coral twine
    Into sweet bowers—

"Oh! come with me, child of earth—
    Come with me home—
To the place of our spirit-birth
    Under the foam.

"Come to the pearly strand
    'Neath the sea green—
Trust me so fair a land
    Ne'er hast thou seen!

"Where life is a passion
    Too lovely to tell—
And the sea-nymphs shall fashion
    Around thee a spell.

"We follow the joyous beam
    Gilding yon mountain;
We glide o'er the glassy stream,
    Roam by the fountain.

"With the wild bee in summer.
    We float o'er the wave;
With the sea-bird in winter,
    We fly to the cave.

"Say, wilt thou be one of us,
    Maiden, oh, say!
Ere the sea-king advancing,
    Shall lure us away?

"Oh! come with us, child of earth,
    Come to our home—
To the place of our spirit-birth
    Under the foam.

"Where the mussels and scollops shine,
    Brighter than flowers;
Where the seaweed and coral twine
    Into sweet bowers."

"Ah, me!" she sighed, when she had finished her song, "I love to sing, yet it makes me sad, for the tones of my own voice carry me back to happier days—happier did I say? Ah, no, not happier, for am I not happy now? Happy in the love of him who risked his life to save me from the death I tempted? Oh, I am happy—so happy for he loves me truly, dearly. Yet why do I feel so sad? Alas! I cannot tell. I must chase away this fear—this foreboding, and bring smiles again to my cheek—smiles to welcome him home."

And still plucking the flowers by her side she began to sing again :—

"Come to the sunset shore, darling,
    When the winds sigh soft and low,
When the fleecy clouds, with motions light,
    O'er the moon's face come and go.

"I'll meet thee there to night, love,
    Just by the bright lake's side,
And the ripples will dance in the moonbeams
      pale.
    As smiles on the face of a bride.

"There's a moss-grown seat 'neath a bending tree,
    Arched o'er with many a flower;
'Tis a lovely spot in that wild retreat—
    Fit place for a fairy's bower.

"I've a tale for thee to-night, darling,
    To tell to thee alone;
For I could not say it when others were by!
    Say, lov'd one, wilt thou come?

"When the star lights up its tiny lamp,
    And mirrors itself in the sea;
When the birdling sings the last good night,
    Then, darling, I'll look for thee."

For some time she continued the work of destruction among the flowers, despoiling them of their beauty, but impregnating the air with their perfume, till casting her eyes upwards she perceived by the position of the sun that she had sat longer than she intended, so she rose to depart.

"I must away soon," she murmured, "lest the shades of night overtake me, and Martinez return to our humble but happy home and find no smile to greet him."

So rising from her seat she sang again the following lines, brought to her memory by the words she had uttered—

"Away to thy home in the glade,
    For the track of the red man is there,
And thy wife listens faint and dismayed,
    As their war-cry rings out on the air;

"While thy children have ceased from their play,
    And are shrieking in helpless affright;
Oh, why did their father delay,
    While the savage had come with the night?

"And well might the rose-tinted cheek,
    In that perilous hour grow pale;
And well might those helpless ones shriek,
    As the war-whoop is filling the vale.

"Then turn from the buffalo chase,
    And fly to thy home in the glen,
Or the scalps of thy loved ones will grace,
    The wigwams of demon-like men.

"Ho! swift bear me onward, good steed,
　There is death in the steps of delay;
Fail me not in the hour of my need,
　We must come with the dawn of the day.

"The wild savage foe little deemed
　The horse and his rider were there;
Of the rifle's sure aim never dreamed,
　Till its bullet had sped through the air.

"And then over the prarie they flee,
　Like the wind or the wolf-hunted deer;
And thy loved ones are saved unto thee,
　Though the angel of death had been near.

"Then turn to the One in the skie,
　Who the hand of the spoiler hath stayed;
And let prayers of thanksgiving arise
　From the hearth of thy home in the glade."

"Ah me!" she sighed, "I must delay no longer, but away at once or night will overtake me ere I can reach home."

As she spoke she cast her eyes down into the small chasm and perceived, growing right at the bottom, a beautiful large white flower.

"I will pluck that," she murmured, "and twine it in my dark tresses. How lovely it is."

And as she spoke she descended the embankment to the foot of the rock which shut out the further progress of the stream.

She bent forward and grasped the coveted treasure, and as she drew it from the stem a strange noise broke upon her ears.

She started and turned pale.

"A storm is brewing," she muttered. "That sound surely was thunder. I must haste. If I am overtaken by the storm, I shall not be able to find my way back.

And hurriedly she turned to ascend the bank.

But the noise again sounded upon her ears, and she grasped at the long reeds which grew around.

She cast her eyes upwards, and a cry of terror broke from her lips.

A cry of anguish; for she thought her last hour had come.

She strove to fly; but she was powerless to move.

She was chained, as it were, to the spot. But her eyes were rivetted upon the rock, which shut out the further progress of the stream.

Oh! horror.

The late storm had swollen the stream till it burst its boundaries, and was forcing itself over the rock, into the flowery chasm.

Slowly at first.

Then fiercer and fiercer—till a huge sheet of water formed a large and beautiful cataract.

Hissing, tearing, roaring, it thundered into the chasm, as though in mad glee at its escape from its usual course.

It rose higher and higher at her feet each moment, and she struggled hard to fly before it.

But terror held her powerless.

She saw death staring her in the face.

She saw the means to fly from the foe which assailed her.

But she could not move.

She thought of Martinez, and her senses seemed to be deserting her.

The rushing of the waters made her giddy, and she would have fallen forward into them, but she still had presence of mind to cling to the long reeds.

But otherwise she was powerless.

On, on, they came—swifter, swifter.

Up, up, they rose—higher, higher.

In another minute they would encircle her lovely form in their all-devouring embrace.

She cast her eyes upwards, and a prayer rose to her lips.

It was answered only by the wild birds, as they flapped their wings, as though in joy, above her head.

The waters reached her feet, and rose higher up her ankles. Still she felt powerless to save herself.

She uttered one long loud cry.

Echo alone answered her.

In despair, she gasped forth:

"Martinez, Martinez, save me! Oh! save me."

Then her brain whirled, her sight faded, her grasp on the reeds relaxed, and she tottered.

But at that moment an arm encircled her waist, and a voice rang in her ears:

"Inez, I will save you, or die."

She turned—the spell which held her was broken—and, with a loud cry, she flung her arms around the neck of her lover.

Grasping her slender form tightly with one arm, he clung to the projections of the rocks with the other, and drew her up—up till he had gained their summit, where he paused to rest and thank Heaven that her voice had assailed his ears, and enabled him to stretch forth an arm to save her from death.

CHAPTER XCII.

THE SEARCH FOR THE MISSING ONES.—THE WRECK OF THE CYCLOPS.—AN INHUMAN DEED.

To gain the beach and alarm those who had charge of the boat, was a work of short duration.

Henry, panting and breathless, made the crew of the little bark acquainted with the true state of affairs.

But where was Charles and Ellen.

He looked around him expecting to see them both.

But no.

Their forms were nowhere to be seen.

"Where are they?" he asked, turning anxiously to the sailors.

"Who?" asked one of the men.

"Charles—Ellen!"

The men looked surprised.

He imagined the officer had been drinking whilst on shore.

"Have you not seen them?" he added.

"Who, sir?"

"My friends who accompanied me," he replied.

"We have seen no one, sir. Have you lost him?"

"He came this way with a young girl we have rescued from the hands of these accursed villains. Where—where can he be?"

"Perhaps we had better search for him, sir," said the man who had before spoken.

'Yes—yes, one remain in the boat, the rest all follow me."

The men obeyed, and Henry led the way back to the spot where the affray had taken place.

On their way they passed the inanimate body of the fisherman who had endeavoured to bar the passage of Henry to the beach.

But contrary to expectation no one else was to be seen.

"Strange," said Henry. "What can all this mean? I see the contemptible curs they can only war with women, and have flown at our approach. But Ellen—Charles; where are they?"

Frantically he tore around the old fort, followed by his companions, but no trace could he discover of Ellen and her lover.

What was to be done?

He knew not.

The more he endeavoured to think, the more undecided how to act did he become.

In vain they searched everywhere.

Down on to the beach, along the rocks, but no trace could they discover of the missing ones.

Henry knew not what to think—what course to pursue; and after wandering about for an hour, during which time no one attempted to interrupt them, he finally gave up in despair all hopes of discovering what had become of them.

In a low and desponding state of mind he returned to the boat, followed by the men.

He resolved to return to the ship and seek the advice of the commander.

So he gave the order to pull for the ship, and the men, bending to their oars, the little boat glided swiftly from the shore.

They were not long in reaching the ship, and as Henry and his companions clambered over the side they observed the officers in anxious consultation, and the captain with a glass at his eye scanning a distant portion of the shore of the island.

As Henry approached him, he lowered his glass and looking hard and full at the young man, he exclaimed—

"Your boat has just returned in time, as there is a vessel foundering away there on the rocks."

"Where, sir?" asked Henry.

"To eastward there," said the captain, pointing in the direction. "Man the boats there and pull off to her rescue."

"Captain—" commenced Henry.

But the captain only waved him off without taking the glass from his eye.

"Quick there, bear a hand all of you," he exclaimed, "she is sinking fast."

Henry panted to tell the captain that Charles was missing, for it was evident in his anxiety to render aid to the suffering vessel that he had not noticed the absence of the young officer, but the commanding tones of the captain checked him, and he dropped into the boat which was already manned and anxious to be off on their errand of mercy.

Away they went with a will.

A long pull, a strong pull, and the boat clave through the waters like a wounded whale flying in vain from the harpoons of the hunters.

After about an hour they came up with the sinking ship.

She was a large merchantman, who had been disabled in her rudder, and drifted out of her course, till she had struck upon a sunken rock outside the island.

She was named the "Cyclops," and belonged to the port of London.

At the time that Henry and his companions came up with her, she had become a total wreck.

They had succeeded in carrying lines to the rocks which bounded that part of the coast, and many had endeavoured to escape by their means.

Her stern was under water, having gone down stern foremost.

Her bowsprit and forecastle alone remained above the water; and over this the waves washed, threatening destruction to the poor wretches who clung to her timbers.

Her masts were gone, and several who had been carried over with them were battling for life in the surging waves.

Henry forgot for the time his anxiety for the safety of Charles and Ellen, in his hopes to save the unfortunate beings who were making such frantic endeavours to retain life.

Cheering his men on, he exerted himself to the utmost to succour and to save.

Nor were those efforts fruitless.

They picked up eight souls—wrested from death—eight exhausted wretches.

To attempt to take on board more would have been fatal to their own safety; so they called upon those who still remained on board to trust to the lines, and draw themselves ashore, lest other boats should not arrive in time to take them off.

This advice was followed.

Along the ropes went the sailors, swinging in the air.

There were five ropes, made fast from the vessel to the rocks.

The men who had trusted themselves upon them had gone more than half the distance to the rocks, when, as if by one accord, they were precipitated into the boiling sea, and the ropes dropped into the waves.

They had been cut on shore; and the inhuman wretches who had perpetrated this hellish deed hurled to destruction five as brave fellows as ever sailed the salt deep.

A cry of horror broke from the lips of the boat's crew.

Unconscious of what they were doing, they pulled in-shore to their rescue.

But Henry, more cool, bid them hold.

He was as near to the shore as he dared approach, lest he met the same fate as the foundering ship.

But this was not all which caused him to give the order.

The victims had fallen upon the rocks which were scarcely covered by the foam of the sea.

They would never rise more.

Stunned and mutilated the waves would bear them away to furnish a meal for the sharks or wash their shattered remains upon some shingley beach.

With heavy groans, like a giant in agony, the Cyclops parted her timbers, and with a soughing sound down she went into the waters which leapt and danced, and sported around her, throwing high above the spot where she had disappeared, her winding sheet of foam, and hissed and bubbled her death song as the waves filled up the vacuum caused by her descent.

"Pull—pull for your lives," exclaimed Henry, grasping the tiller and turning the boat fairly round. "Pull men—pull—or she will carry us with her."

But the men needed no second bidding.

They saw the danger to which they were exposed, and they bent to their oars for dear life.

When the fury of the waves caused by the sinking ship had somewhat abated, Henry looked around.

There were several men battling in the waves and making towards them.

Another boat too, sent from the frigate, was close at hand, and leaving this to save those now in the water, he gave the order to return to the frigate with the eight unfortunate sufferers he had been instrumental in saving from a watery grave.

CHAPTER XCIII.

THE CAPTURED YOUTH AND HIS KEEPERS.— ADVENTURES AND DANGERS.

IN a cleft in the rocks Charles lay insensible, guarded by two of the smuggler crew.

Henry and his companions had passed and repassed the spot within a dozen yards, yet so secure from observation was it that they had not the least idea of the existence of such a place.

This was the spot to which he had been conveyed by the orders of Lang, and the men only now awaited the presence of the captain to know whether the youth was to be carried on board the Scorpion or put to death in that place.

He had lain there for some time closely watched and his guardians, annoyed at the prolonged absence of their captain, began to complain.

"What a devil of a time he is gone," said Bond, "does he mean keeping us here much longer, I wonder."

"Whether he does or he does not we can't help it," replied Hardy. "Here, just take a pull at this flask and make your life happy."

Bond wanted no second invitation to this, so taking the flask of brandy from his friend's hand he applied it to his lips, and a long gurgling sound emanated from his throat. Then, drawing a long breath, he said as he handed back the bottle to his companion—

"I wouldn't care about being left here if we could only have a game at cards, or something to kill the time, but I do hate having to stand looking at nothing and wondering what's to come next."

"Ah—like to keep your mind employed," remarked his companion.

"To be sure I do."

"Then why don't you spin us a yarn—anything is better than nothing."

"Well, suppose I do," replied Bond, who had a sailor's love for a yarn, no matter how much slack could be wound up off it. "Just let's sit down then and here goes. You know as how I was once aboard a northern whaler."

"No I don't," said Hardy.

"Well you knows it now then. Well I was, that's afore I turned smuggler or pirate some time—Well you see one day as several of us stood on deck looking at a very beautiful iceberg which was slowly drifting away to leeward, I fancied I saw something move upon it, and remarked the same to my shipmates.

"'What do you make it out—I can't see anything but a mass of ice,' says one.

"'It's a white bear!' observed the mate, who had overheard my first remark, and now stood quietly looking at the object through a telescope.

"For the last two or three days we had not had any special excitement, and several of us were eager for some daring adventure.

"We asked leave to go in quest of the bear, and our captain, one of the kindest-hearted men in the world, assented, but with several words of caution, which I fear were too much disregarded.

"Our vessel was run down to what was considered a safe distance, and hove-to, and ten of us, armed with guns, pistols, axes, spears, harpoons,

boat-hooks, &c., pulled away merrily for the scene of action.

"As we neared the mighty floating fabric of the polar regions—built without hands by one of the immutable laws of the Great Architect of Nature—stretching its glittering towers, and dome, and pinnacles, and spires, far up into the clear sunlight, which was flashed back, as from mirrors and prisms, with a brightness and gorgeousness that made it seem a fairy palace of silver and gold and precious gems—I confess I for a time forgot the object of our expedition, and yielded my senses to a sort of rapt contemplation of the beauty, grandeur and glory of the icy structure before me.

"'There she blows!' was the jocular remark of the boatswain, recalling me to myself.

"We had been approaching at an angle which had hid the bear from our view; but at the moment of the exclamation, we had just turned a sharp point from which Bruin again became visible.

"He was sitting in a sort of niche, about fifteen feet above the water, and looking very contented and unconcerned, till he got a sight of us in such close proximity, when he seemed to suddenly change his placidity into a condition of temper more befitting the ferocious brute he really was, growling hoarsely, showing his teeth, and thus giving us fair warning that we might expect trouble should we venture to assail him on his own domain.

"He was, indeed, a most formidable-looking antagonist — measuring at least twelve feet in length, with a corresponding height, breadth, and bulk—and I remember wondering what chance a man would have for his life if once fairly within the stroke of one of his tremendous paws.

"I know that the lion of Asia and Africa is acknowledged to be the king of beasts and lord of the wilderness ; but I am inclined to believe he does not compare in either strength or ferocity with this dangerous monster of the polar seas.

"As our boat was brought round in front of the brute, at the distance of some two hundred yards, I ventured to suggest the laying on our oars, and holding a sort of council-of-war, before proceeding to an attack which clearly promised to be a most dangerous one, indeed; but my suggestion was unheeded—the boatswain confidently asserted there would be little or no danger in advancing close and pouring a volley, as the beast would be too badly wounded from so many balls to do us any harm—even if not killed outright.

"So we rowed up to within perhaps seventy-five yards—the bear grinning and growling at us all the while—and then the boat was brought round, broadside to, and every man took up his gun and got ready to fire at the word. Sailors, as a general thing, are not good marksmen, and I readily calculated that not more than half our balls would hit the beast, even at that short distance, and thought it more than doubtful if either one of the balls, or all combined, would give him a mortal wound.

"But I was not the commander, and had only to obey orders ; and so, taking the best aim I could, I fired with the rest, and had the instant mortification and alarm of seeing the savage animal leap from his perch into the water and make directly toward us, swimming with a swiftness and vigour that showed he was more angered than hurt.

"All was now confusion and dismay, even the boldest and coolest getting fearfully excited.

"We knew how to manage whales, but we had

not served an apprenticeship at attacking polar bears, and every man now thought of the worst story he had ever heard of the almost fabulous power and ferocity of the beast.

"If he should reach us, what might he not do?

"'Give way, lads! give way! for the love of God, give way!' shouted the boatswain.

"It needed no incentive but his own personal danger to make every man do his best; but a single minute's labour convinced us that we could not escape in this manner—for though we were sending the little boat over the light waves at its greatest speed, we could see that the bear was gaining on us at every stroke.

"It was now arranged that a part should keep at the oars, and all the rest be ready with our axes, knives, pistols, and so forth, to assail the monster as soon as he should come within our reach.

"Our guns, already discharged, were useless, nobody seeming to think it worth while to reload them.

"It was my lot to be stationed at the stern, armed with an axe. As I watched the approach of the beast, showing his teeth and growling savagely, I thought it not improbable that I should be the first to feel his vengeance, and my friends at home be left to mourn the untimely death of the wanderer.

"But with all this I felt no disposition to shrink from the danger, and stood prepared to do my duty, and die, if I must, like a man and not a coward.

"Pale, I was unquestionably, but I knew I was calm externally, and I grasped my weapon with a firmness and determination that I flatter myself did me no little credit·

"On came the beast, blowing, snorting, and growling, his eyes in his anger looking like balls of fire; and as he came up within a few feet, I swung my axe for a blow at his skull.

"But at this moment some of the men behind me, commenced firing their pistols at his head, which seemed to disconcert him a little and check his progress.

"The men at the oars, encouraged by this, now pulled with a will, and began to increase the distance between ourselves and the animal, which now seemed undecided whether to continue the pursuit or beat a retreat.

"There is no doubt, if we had kept steadily on, that we might have escaped—as the bear, without being further molested, would probably have returned to the iceberg; but the very moment he showed hesitation, we all became fixed in a resolution to conquer at all hazards; besides two other boats were now putting off from the ship, and we were not disposed to see another party triumph in our place.

"We had a harpooner with us who was anxious to try his skill, and we now gave him a chance. With the precision of a master of his art, he hurled the weapon through the air, and buried it just back of the fore-shoulder of the beast.

"With a perfect howl of pain and rage, the bear half leaped from the water, and then plunged forward for his revenge, fairly lashing the waters into foam.

"We saw there was no chance of escaping by flight now, and therefore did not attempt it, but every man seized upon some weapon and prepared himself to fight it out to the death.

"As the furious beast came up near enough for my blow, I struck him with all my might, aiming for his skull, just as he was in the act of seizing the gunnel with his teeth; but at that moment the boat rocked, my foot slipped, my mark was missed, and I was pitched head foremost into the water, almost into his very clutches.

"Fortunately for me he was so very intent upon attacking the men collectively as not to perceive there was one already in his power; and retaining my presence of mind, and being a good swimmer, I immediately dove, passed under the boat, and scrambled in again near the bow.

"The fight meantime had become quite desperate on both sides.

"The men, being huddled together in a small space, were having as much as they could possibly do, with all their weapons, to keep the ferocious beast from crushing and upsetting the boat, or lacerating them with his teeth and claws; and the bear on his part, being determined upon his revenge at all hazards, was making constant efforts to throw himself into the boat right in the teeth of blows from axes and boat-hooks, and thrusts from knives and spears.

"By one bold, rapid movement, he did succeed in getting one foot over the gunnel, when, before he could make good use of this advantage, one of the men by a well directed blow with his axe, chopped it clean off. Even this seemed rather to madden than daunt the brute, and he continued his assaults with more fury than ever.

"At length, when covered with blood and wounds, his efforts began to slacken, as if growing too weak to maintain the unequal contest, and we were beginning to congratulate ourselves that at last the victory was ours—just at this moment, by what impulse or power I never could conceive, the dying monster, with a hoarse, awful roar, that rings in my ears yet, suddenly leaped half out of the water, and came down with his four-quarters upon the stern of the boat, crushing it as if it were a mere cockle-shell, knocking down two of the men, seizing one poor fellow in his teeth, and pitching the rest of us into the sea, and some of us into his very clutches.

"Merciful God! what shouts and screams, and what a scene of wild confusion, as each man sought to save himself, regardless of every other! and oh! what a wild, despairing, appalling shriek came from the poor fellow whose very bones were now being crunched in the jaws of the monster!

"No human power could save him, and no one changed his course to offer human aid. No one knew whose turn it might be next. and every man struck off for the approaching boats to save himself.

"But the bear did not follow us. As if satisfied with his revenge, he remained almost stationary, growling over and crunching his victim, till the two boats picked up the rest of us on the way, drew up near him and poured in a volley, which almost riddled him and ended the bloody contest.

"Then we collected the mangled remains of our poor comrade, for decent burial, and towed the slaughtered monster to the vessel, every man secretly vowing he would never be caught in another foolhardy attack upon the animal lord of the polar regions."

"'Well I reckon you had enough of that fellow," said Hardy.

"Yes, almost as much as I have of waiting in in this confounded place for the captains return.

"'Then take another pull," said Hardy, "and I'll spin another yarn, to try and make you comfortable.

Bond took another pull, and prepared himself to listen.

ELLEN PROTECTING HER FATHER.

"It was when I was on board my father's craft, trading to Egypt," commenced Hardy, "that one bright morning I entered the boat, intending to go up the river Nile a few miles and try my luck at fishing.

"We had a wind fair for both ways, if it only remained steady; so I took no help with me, save my two companions, Abdac and Mada.

"Had there been a prospect of having to row against the wind or against the current, I should have taken two oarsmen.

"But the wind was likely to hold steady, so I started off with only my own crew. We took our fire-arms and fishing materials, and started.

"We reached the place where I had been told I should find fish, and there we dropped our sails, and let go a huge stone which was made fast to the painter.

"At the end of half an hour we had caught four small fish, somewhat resembling the common horn-pout of our fresh-water ponds, and which Abdac called 'skarl.'

But these were not the fish we wanted; so we up anchor, and, having hoisted one of our sails, we ran a mile further up, when we came to a wide place in the river, one bank being high land, while from the other swept away a wide marshy tract, covered with tall reeds.

"This seemed a fine place for fish, the kind we were after being mostly found under the shade of high banks.

"Our boat was going through the water at a pretty good jog, and I had just told Mada to let go the halyards, when we struck something with such force that I was knocked over on my side.

"Mada fell sprawling into the bottom of the boat, and Abdac had me by the knee to hold himself up. We were thrown around into the wind, and as the boat began to fall back I started forward to see what we had fallen foul of, supposing it to be either a stump or a bit of sunken land.

"I had just reached the forward thwart, and had one hand on the foremast, when I saw a sudden commotion about four feet from the bows, and on the next instant came a loud bellowing noise followed by a cloud of spray, which came dashing over me.

"For a moment I was so startled that I could not even think. The loud bellow and the blinding plash of water in my face, were enough to startle any man; but my thoughts quickly returned, and I knew just what had happened.

"We had run foul of an hippopotamus!

"His huge ugly head was above water, and he was making for the boat.

"I had never seen one of these animals at large before; but I had seen a pair of tame hippopotami at Zanzibar and knew most of their peculiarities.

"They are often found as large as an elephant, and full as heavy: but their legs are very short, and upon land they are so clumsy and unwieldy that a smart child could run away from them.

"They grow to be twelve feet in length and about the same in circumference, and seem to be very solid and compact. Their skin is thick and tough, almost as much so as that of the rhinoceros and without hair, save here and there a few bristle like affairs, which are generally white in colour. The feet are divided into four broad toes, which are not connected by any membrane, as we might expect from its amphibious nature. The head is immense, and the mouth, which looks terrible enough when the huge teeth are all exposed, can be opened to the distance of a foot and a half. The peculiarity of this mouth is, that the lower jaw is stationary, while the upper one has the motive power.

"The hippopotamus is not an angry beast unless he is starving or molested; but when attacked he becomes at once vengeful and formidable.

"In the water he can handle his massive body with surprising quickness, turning and darting about with an agility which seems utterly anomalous when considered in connection with his size and form.

"His tail, which is short, is flat and pointed, and no doubt serves both as a scull and rudder.

"As soon as I had discovered the character of the snag against which we had run I sprung aft for my rifle.

"I had just grasped it and turned to go forward again, when a quick cry from Abdac broke upon the air, and, as he started back, I saw the monster spring up and seize the bows of the boat between his huge jaws.

"Our frail craft was taken under water as though a mountain had fallen upon it. I saw it going, and, lifting my rifle as high as I could above my head, I leaped towards the shore.

"We had run close under the high bank, where I had meant to anchor, but the boat had been driven some four or five rods from the shore by the wind; but I was a good swimmer, and easily reached dry land without getting my rifle wet enough to damage anything.

"The bank was not perpendicular, but afforded a landing almost anywhere, so we had no trouble on that score.

"As soon as I reached the shore I turned to see how matters stood with my companions.

"Abdac was very near the shore swimming with all his might, while Mada was not quite so well off.

"The latter had been sitting down as the boat went under, and he was taken under with it.

"The boat came to the surface up in its beam ends, the masts and sails preventing it from turning over, and Mada came up under its stern, puffing and blowing like a porpoise.

"When I first saw him he was upon one side of the boat holding on to the gunwale, while the hippopotamus was upon the other. I could see that the poor fellow was frightened.

"And well he might be, for what protection had he from the deadly monster? The boat could be smashed like a bubble, and as quickly.

"The beast was some five or six feet from the boat, and was gazing upon the frightened Arab. I saw that there was not a moment to lose, and a lucky thought flashed through my mind.

"If Mada was attacked that would be the last of him, in spite of all we could do.

"'He's waiting for Mada to move,' said Abdac, who had joined me. 'If he moves the brute 'll snap him up.'

"I called out for the poor fellow to remain perfectly quiet. I believed that if I could attract the animal's attention, and then wound him, he would make for me. Abdac hinted that I had better step a little way into the water.

"I improved upon the advice, and having waded in up to my knees, I commenced to cry out at the top of my voice, my companion joining me.

"As I had supposed, the hippopotamus turned his head towards me, and on the instant I took aim and fired. I then bade Abdac to take my place and divert the animal while I re-loaded my piece. My powder was in a metal flask, and of course it had been kept dry.

"The huge monster uttered a terrific roar, and made a plunge for the shore. His roar, or cry, is just about like what the grunt of a hog would be if it could be lengthened out. He came swiftly enough until his feet touched the land, and then his passage became slow and lumbering.

"The blood was running from a wound in his head, just below the back of the left eye, and he was maddened into fury.

"As Abdac ran back upon dry land and clambered up the bank, the brute bellowed savagely, and hastened after him. The bank was not very steep, so he made his way up without slipping back.

"Just as his head appeared above the edge of the bank I had finished loading my rifle; but was not a good time to fire.

"He was in such motion—pitching and tossing his wounded head—that I was not sure of my aim. The eye was the only point I dared trust. His heart lay beneath such a mass of tough skin and flesh that I feared I should not be able to touch it.

"There were quite a number of trees at hand, and I at once sprang in front of Abdac, and succeeded in getting the brute to give me chase, which he did with a will.

"In about five minutes the hippopotamus began to show signs of fatigue, and I thought I might then try an experiment. So I ran around in a circle some half dozen times, and then dodged behind a tree and cocked my rifle.

"As I had hoped, the beast came to within a few yards, and there stopped, as though he would consider whether he should run against the tree, or follow me around it.

"But I gave him little time for reflection. I had worked too carefully for this position to lose its result now.

"The moment he was fairly still, and his gaze fixed upon me, I took a deliberate aim at his right eye, and fired. He gave a terrific howl and plunged towards me, hitting the tree with a force that almost cracked it.

"As he felt this shock he staggered back, and then came at me again, and again he hit the tree. He was past seeing plainly, even if he could see at all; for the left eye must have suffered a severe nervous attack in the damage which had been done to the other one.

"A third time the monster plunged towards me, and a third time he hit the tree, which had fairly become loosened at the roots by the repeated shocks. But his power of locomotion was about expended.

"As he staggered back from his third attack he reeled and fell, and after a few struggles his life was gone.

"At this moment Mada made his appearance, creeping carefully up over the bank, as though he would be sure not to fall into the jaws of his enemy.

"As soon as he had satisfied himself that the amphibious monster was past all power of doing harm he went back with us to the river's edge.

"We found that the boat had floated down some distance, but she was easily overtaken, when Mada swam out, and brought a line on shore.

"We hauled the light craft to the land, and found the two muskets safe beneath the thwarts; and having turned the water out, we set her afloat again. The bows were crushed almost down to the foot of the cutwater; but by all three of us sitting aft we raised the forward part so high that no water came in, and thus we sailed safely back to the town.

"In the afternoon the natives went up and cut the huge carcass in pieces, and brought it home, some parts of it being esteemed by them very highly for food."

When Hardy had concluded his yarn, he took a long pull at the flask, and offered it to his companion.

Bond, not at all loth, followed his friend's example, and, rising from his seat, went to the entrance of the nook and looked out.

"Well, do you see anything of the captain?" asked Hardy.

"Devil a bit," replied his companion; "and I am cramped to death, waiting, cooped up in this place."

"I expect he is amusing himself with that gall," said Hardy.

"Well, then, it's pretty well time he had done," remarked the other. "I'm blessed if I don't think we had better get back to the ship."

"We must obey orders," said Hardy.

"Orders be blowed!—and that chap's a coming, too: I saw him move."

"He can't move far," said Hardy, "seeing as how he's spliced up so precious tight."

"Perhaps Lang has forgot all about us," said Bond, after a pause.

"More likely the coast ain't clear," said his companion. "So I should advise you not to put your piratical jib so far out again; for your figure-head is safe to be known."

"Why?"

"Because it is so precious ugly," replied his companion, with a grin.

"Stow it," said Bond.

"Here, come and sit down, and make your miserable life happy," said Hardy. "Depend upon it the captain will be here the moment he can safely come. So sit down, and pitch us another yarn; and, if he don't turn up then, why, we'll be off, and chance it."

"I reckon you don't half believe my yarns when I tells them yon," said Bond, sitting down, with a very bad grace.

"Yes, I do," said Hardy—"every blessed word."

"Do you now?"

"Yes."

"Then I'll tell you an adventure I had in the swamp in America, some two years ago."

"Do so."

"Well, you see, I started on a voyage of discovery, with my gun and a dog; and, entering a swamp, found it very decent travelling, until I got in beyond the point of a great lake.

"Here the way became more difficult, there being great tracts of soft mud, overgrown with grass, besides many bogs and pools.

"I found the timber to consist mostly of willow, honey-locust, cotton-wood, pawpaw, and buckeye, with any quantity of wild vines and creepers.

"I knew there was an immense bayou not far in, and this I wanted to find, so I looked sharp, and pushed on.

"At the end of an hour I found the object of my search.

"I reached the shore of the bayou by a sort of natural causeway formed by the trunks of trees which must have been gathering sward there for ages.

"I stood and gazed off upon the dark dismal-looking water, and made up my mind that I'd have a boat as soon as possible, and thus explore this vast solitude of forest sea.

"Birds were plenty there. They flew about in all directions, and so near me did they come, that I caught several with my hand, and, after examining the plumage, I let them go again.

"But pretty soon I saw something else besides birds.

"A motion of the water close by where I stood arrested my attention, and, upon turning my eyes that way, I saw a huge alligator come up, and place his fore feet upon the bank.

"He saw me, and stopped, but he did not retreat at once.

"He turned his ugly head towards me, and reached further up on the bank, as though he would see what manner of thing I was.

"My dog barked and howled, but showed no disposition to attack the monstrous reptile there.

"But had the fellow been on dry land old Tiger would have given him battle.

"The dog—we called him Tige, or Tiger, was a cross between the English bull and the large mastiff, not full-blooded howsumever, as his father was between the bull-dog and the regular Newfoundland.

"So you can imagine something of his size and strength.

"He was really a magnificent dog.

"I watched the alligator for a few moments, and then I aimed at his eye and fired.

"He slid back into the water, and, tell ye, for awhile there was considerable of a kick-up in the neighbourhood. In less than a minute there was a dozen alligators flying about there, and I supposed they were going to make a meal of their unfortunate companion.

"By and bye the monsters saw me, and three of them started directly up the bank at my feet.

"One thing was certain. They weren't afraid of me; and I wondered if they wouldn't make a meal of my flesh.

"One of the fellows that had started up the bank—a very large one, certainly thirteen feet long—was coming towards me without any hesitation.

"I had reloaded my rifle, and with a quick aim I destroyed his left eye. He fell back, and the other two quickly followed him.

"I had frightened the alligators for a moment, but I knew enough of their habits to know that they would very soon come back, so I thought I had better be moving out of that.

"I withdrew a short distance and reloaded my rifle, and then started on.

"My intention was to go back by the same way I had come, but I missed it, and came out at another place. Yet I knew my course - or supposed I did—and kept on. Ere long I came in sight of water again. It was a point of the great bayou.

"I stopped a moment to consider, and then struck across into a narrow opening toward the extreme point of water.

"I had come to within a few yards of the shore when I was stopped by a narrow strip of shallow muddy water.

"It was not over five feet wide, and upon the opposite side the grass grew tall and rank.

"I could leap it easily, and I gave a spring to do so.

"I touched the grass—I touched the sward—I touched a very soft spot. I was in the mud to my knees! I attempte raise one foot—the other settled! I attemped to raise that one, and the first one settled! I was now in to the thighs!

"I laid my gun across the sward and attempted ta raise myself that way.

"But it was of no use. The more I struggled the deeper I sank!

"Down—down—down I sank, until finally I had settled in up to my arm-pits!

"Oh, my heaven! You can have no idea how I felt at that moment.

"That I should ever get out of that mud appeared impossible. I dared to move my feet no more, for I could feel that there was yet soft mud beneath them.

"Of course my arms helped to hold me up, but they would not do so if I should draw my body down by attempting to draw one of my feet up.

"I thought of my dog.

"Could I but pull myself up by him?

"He came at my call, and immediately tried to draw me out by seizing my frock in his teeth; but his own feet sank in, and he then relinquished the task.

"I at length succeeded in getting him in front of me, but as I commenced to bear my weight upon him, and he found himself sinking, he sprang away, and once more made a fruitless attempt to set me free.

"Now can you imagine my situation? Just think of it; my arm-pits rested upon the sward, and I could feel that I was slowly, but surely, settling further and further.

"There was an oppression about my heart, and my lungs could not move freely.

"My breath came hard, and I had every reason to believe that ere long it would be gone for ever!

"I had torn up all the grass within reach in my vain struggles.

"Thus was I situated, when a new object of terror presented itself.

"I saw a shadow upon my right hand, and upon turning that way I beheld the head and shoulders of an immense alligator.

"He saw me in an instant, and came quickly up the bank. I knew at once he meant to attack me.

"My rifle was well bedaubed with mud, but the priming was dry.

"The monster came straight on, and the sluggish movement of the hot heavy air, was enough to bring to my nostrils the strong, rank, musty odour of the foul reptile.

"As soon as I could fairly collect my energies I levelled my piece and fired. I think the ball entered his mouth, which was partly open.

"At any rate he turned as quickly as he could, and lumbered back to the water. I heard his heavy plash, and saw my dog spring back and bark.

"I now saw plainly what had brought the alligator up.

"It was the dog.

"He had been frisking about, crying out with pain and fear on my behalf, and the horrid creature had seen and scented him.

"If this was so, then might not Tiger's barking draw up more?

"I tried to call him back.

"He would come and gaze in my face for a moment, and then rush back again.

"Presently I saw him start back, and utter a quick yell. My heart sank within me, for I knew another alligator was coming!

"And so it proved. Tiger slowly retreated, yelping as he did so; and pretty soon the great ugly head appeared above the edge of the bank.

"This one was larger than the other. He was all eighteen feet long!

"He stopped a few moments after he gained the bank, and turned his long horrid snout towards me.

"Then he looked at the dog, which stood at a safe distance, barking furiously, and then turned his gaze once more upon me, and began to slowly advance.

"I clubbed my rifle, and as he came near, I brought it down on the top of his head, breaking the stock short off.

"He drew back, and at the same time opened his mouth, and then shut it with a crash.

"I noticed one thing; and that was that the alligator did not yet sink into the mud.

"His fore feet were some two yards from me, so I saw that at that distance the sward was tough enough to bear my weight.

"But I had not much time for study or reflection.

"The monster was approaching me again. I had raised the barrel of my rifle to give him another blow, when old Tiger sprang upon him.

"Under other circumstances the dog would not have ventured thus, but to save me he forgot himself.

"The alligator gave one snap of his teeth, and the dog sprang towards his tail.

"In another instant that tail was raised, and quick as thought it came down on Tiger's devoted back.

"He gave one sharp, piteous howl; and as he struggled in the mud with his spine broken, the monster turned, and seizing him in his huge jaws, made off into the bayou.

"I heard the last stifled groan of my dog, and for a few moments I forgot my own danger. Poor old Tiger!

"He had been my almost constant companion for years, and to see him die thus, in his efforts to save me, was painful indeed.

"And after he had gone I reflected upon the use I might have made of him had I only thought of it in season.

"I could easily have sent him home, and of

course when once there he would have drawn some of the household out.

"But it was too late to think of that now. He was gone, and I was left alone. But I was not to be left alone a great while.

"During the presence of the last alligator, I had been slowly sinking deeper into the mud! My shoulders were now just above the surface—the mud was almost up to my collar bone.

"Oh! my soul—my soul! how I yelled and groaned! I shouted with all my might—I groaned in agony the most torturing—and then I cried like a child. I clapped my hands, and called out to God for help!

"What a death! What a death for a stout, strong, healthy man! To be strangled in that mud, to gradually sink—sink to the chin—to the lips—to the nose; the neck stretched, and the eye glaring—the nostrils finally submerged, and the death-struggle commenced while yet the eyes could drink in the scene! I might tear away the mud with my hands for the while, but it would only be to prolong my agony.

"Under the fearful impulse of such thoughts I involuntarily made one more struggle. The only result was to draw me deeper into the mud.

"Just as I stopped my worse than vain efforts, and my voice had failed me from exhaustion of the lungs, I saw another alligator coming up over the bank.

"It was not the one which had taken the dog.

"It was, if anything, a larger one. He came fully up ere he stopped to take an observation.

"He hesitated but a moment, however. He seemed to see that my head and shoulders offered something that would suit his palate, and he moved towards me.

"I had seen, from the tracks of the dog, and the movements of the second alligator, that at a distance of four feet from me, towards the shore, there was a firm footing.

"I had evidently sunk into a sort of mud-pot which made out from the narrow strip of water over which I had leaped.

"As I saw the monster start towards me I thought of my rifle barrel. I looked for it, but 'twas lost in the mud.

"On the next instant I thought of my knife.

"It was at my left side, and I knew it could not be very deep down, as the sheath hung loosely upon my belt. I plunged my left hand down, and reached it.

"It was a large hunting-knife, with a buckhorn handle, and very strong and sharp.

"I had heard of the way the African savages sometimes killed crocodiles, by covering the arm with thick leather, and then forcing a knife down the capacious throat of the victim.

"So I seized my knife in my right hand, and prepared for the meeting.

"My arm was free, as I had made quite a hollow in the mud below the shoulder

"It was not even a case of life or death with me then.

"It was simply a choice of deaths; whether I would sink to my own grave in the bosom of the swamp, or be made the food of an alligator.

"So I had no fear of my enemy beyond the mere horror of being eaten up.

"As he came nearer he found that the ground was soft, but he worked his way along, for though his legs should sink down, his huge belly would offer a resistance sufficient to prevent his legs from sinking further.

"At length his snout was close upon me, and his mouth was open.

"He struggled forward still further, his fore feet were now in the mud, but they were still serviceable.

"He dropped his lower jaw—his mouth was fairly yawning—his terrible teeth gleamed like so many spikes—and he was ready to bite.

"With a quick movement I thrust the knife deep into his open mouth, striking the centre of the lower jaw beyond the tongue. He closed it, and started back.

"Or he closed it all he could.

"The knife was nearly perpendicular, and as the handle came in contact with the roof of the mouth, of course the jaws were stopped. The front teeth were six inches apart.

"I instinctively clung to the knife, and as the monster started back he at the same time gave me a start from my miry prison!

"He raised me all of four inches!

"In an instant more he threw his mouth open, and as he did so I thrust my arm forward with all my might.

"The blade was driven into the bone at the bottom of the mouth, and this last movement turned the handle down to the opening of the throat, where it became buried and braced in the tough flesh.

"In his agony he struggled back. He found he had bitten something that hurt him. He shook and reared his head, but he could not break my hold.

"No, no—my life lay then in the gripe of that right hand!

"Did the fingers relax but one grain I should be lost!

"Up—up—up I came from the sticky mud, the wounded suffering monster leaping and working his way back as fast as the nature of his foothold would allow.

"Why—I couldn't realise it! I knew I was coming out—out—out; but it seemed more like a dream than like reality.

"But at length the alligator got his feet upon good foundation, and with one mighty effort he broke from me, and turned towards the water with the knife still braced in his throat.

"And where was I?

"I was stretched at full length upon my belly along the crushed and bedaubed grass.

"The powerful creature had just drawn me clear of the mud, and laid me out so that I could not sink again.

"Carefully I crept upon the hard sward, and, when I regained my feet, I started.

"I simply looked over into the water, but saw nothing of my enemies or their canine victim.

"Carefully I picked my way over the narrow stream, and then struck for home. I was weak and faint, and my garments were heavy with mud. But I struggled on.

"I reached my vessel just as the last tints of day were disappearing in the west, and night closing in upon the scene.

"I was safe—I was uninjured; but I had lost my dog, and, in return, I had gained a bit of knowledge, which has probably been of much service to me since:—Never make a leap in a strange swamp until you know where you are going to alight."

"Well, I do believe every word of that, I do," said Hardy.

"Upon my soul, it's true," said Bond.

"In course it is," said Hardy. "But don't you

think you had better wash some of the grit out of your mouth?"

And he handed the flask to his companion.

"Well, I almost fancies I can taste the mud now, I do."

"No doubt of it," said Hardy; "and I dare say you always will. But what a pity the crocodile didn't swallow you!"

"Why?"

"It would save you being hung some fine morning."

"Stow it," said Bond. "You know I don't like such chaff."

Hardy was about to reply, when a low whistle saluted their ears; and the next moment Lang entered the nook in the rock.

CHAPTER XCIV.

ELLEN CONVEYED ON BOARD THE SCORPION—JOY OF WILD MADGE—ARRIVAL OF CHARLES A PRISONER.

THE "Scorpion" rode at anchor in a small bay or cove, sheltered from a sea view and hidden by the high rocks which surrounded it.

It was a bay well adapted for smuggling.

It had often been used by the Boy Rover when chased by the revenue cutters, or for the purpose of embarking contraband goods.

Wild Madge had had the 'Scorpion' run into this bay for a double purpose.

To seek shelter and escape from the frigate which they had sighted, and dispose of their ill-gotten spoils, whilst they could take on board a cargo of taxable articles, and run into some of the numerous creeks which abound on the coast of Cornwall, where she knew willing hands and willing customers would be found to cheat the revenue and purchase the contraband cargo.

But little had she expected to take on board one who now in an insensible state was being pulled rapidly to the ship.

The attention of Wild Madge had been called to the return of the boat with a female lying at the bottom.

Eagerly she gazed over the bulwarks, shading her bleared eyes with her hand.

"Some girl Lang has taken a fancy to," she murmured. "Ah! it does my heart good to feel that others must suffer as I have done; yet he disobeys orders. Still it gratifies my revenge, and I must overlook this dereliction of duty."

And the hag chuckled with glee at the prospect of another victim to the unholy passions of her demon crew.

"There will be music in her shrieks," she murmured; "music that can cheer the heart of this unhappy wretch; 'tis the only solace to my soul, the only joy of my heart, for though formed by nature for a woman, I glory in woman's fall and woman's suffering, for man's villainy has made me a devil, and I revel in hellish deeds."

Swiftly the boat cleaved the waters of the bay, and in a few minutes was alongside the vessel.

Wild Madge rubbed her hands in glee as Lang lifting the insensible form of the girl in his arms, mounted to the deck.

Staggering under his burden he approached the fury.

"Madge," he said.

"Well?"

"I have brought some one on board."

"So I perceive."

"Do you know who it is?" he asked.

"Yes—a woman," she replied; "another victim."

"True, but do you not recognise her?" asked Lang.

And he raised the head of the insensible girl, and revealed to the bleared eyes of the wicked woman the pale features of Ellen.

Madge started back.

A gleam of pleasure shot from her eyes.

She threw her arms wildly in the air.

"Ha! ha! ha!" she laughed.

"You know her now?" inquired Lang.

"Know her!" echoed the fury.

"Yes."

"I do—I do!" she shrieked rather than spoke.

"Are you not pleased that I have brought her on board?" asked the captain.

"I am overjoyed," she replied.

"I thought you would be," said Lang.

"I am, I am."

And the wretch rubbed her hands together in wild glee.

"Ah! fate seems propitious," she exclaimed, for it places her father in my power, and now yields the daughter up to my vengeance as it did her lover. Oh! that was a glorious revenge! I will hiss his fate in her ears, and break her heart with a recital of his agonies.

"Whose?"

"Her lover's."

"He lives."

"Ah!"

"'Tis even so."

"Why say you this?" asked Wild Madge in a tone of surprise.

"I have seen him," replied the pirate captain.

"When?"

"To-day."

"Where?"

"On the island."

"You mistake."

"I do not."

"Are you sure it was he?" asked Madge.

"Quite."

Madge shook her head.

"It cannot have been him."

"I tell you, Madge, it was. The girl and him were together, flying towards the frigate's boat when I captured them."

"Where is he then?" asked the fury.

"On shore."

"Then he has escaped you?"

"No, no; he lies bound hand and foot in a cleft in the rocks watched by Bond and Hardy."

"Ah! then he is in our power," said Madge.

"He is."

"A power terrible and fatal to him," remarked Madge.

"You owe him no good will," said Lang.

"Curse him—no. Oh, I will make their hearts ache—heap sufferings upon them which nought but death can allay. My boy—my poor boy shall be terribly avenged."

"And so will you," said Lang.

"Aye, aye—so will I. I will tear their hearts and make them groan in anguish. The vengeance I have lived for shall be satiated—aye, and terribly satiated!"

"Shall the lad be brought on board?" asked Lang.

"Why did you ask?" exclaimed Madge, fiercely.

"I did not know—"

"Yes," she replied—"so that each may know the other's fate."

"Then I will carry this girl to the cabin, and return for the youth," said Lang, lifting the insensible form of Ellen in his arms.

"Do so," replied Madge.

"You will look to her?"

"Aye," hissed the fury; "she shall not escape me so easily as she did my boy."

Lang carried Ellen down to the cabin of Wild Madge, and laid her upon the cot.

"Go," she said, "and bring her lover on board."

Lang turned to go.

But he hesitated on the threshold.

"Madge," he said.

"Well?"

"Do you think it is wise to bring him on board?"

"My revenge would be but half gratified now were he to escape," she replied.

"But—"

"But what?" interrupted the shameless woman.

"Would it not be better to drown him in the bay?" said Lang.

Madge thought for a moment.

"He would sink like a stone," said Lang, "now he is securely bound."

"No," said Madge, "for the present he must live to see the agonies endured by the girl he loves."

"As you will," said Lang.

"Besides it will torture her heart to hear that he is in my power."

Lang said no more but departed to bring Charles on board.

When he had gone Wild Madge bent over the beautiful girl.

A look of demoniac pleasure overspread her bloated features.

A gleam of fearful meaning lit up her bleared eyes.

"Ha, ha," she laughed. "Oh, how I will wring her heart, and that too of her father—the betrayer, the seducer! He shall feel the fearful vengeance of the woman he loved, then scorned. He shall hear the shrieks of his child as I pour the venomed words into her ears, and embitter her existence. Oh, my vengeance shall be slow, sure, and terrible. We will sail for England, and rescue my boy from the prison to which he is consigned, so that he may fulfil the destiny I have marked out for him, and minister to my revenge. Ha, ha, I triumph now, Joseph Hanfield, and the bitter seeds you have sown in my heart you shall reap in your own. I loved you once, but you then scorned me, and that love is turned to hate—fierce, undying hate. You cannot escape the vengeance of her you scorned—vengeance, bitter, fearful, and devilish!"

And the woman sat down beside the girl, and watched and waited for the first signs of returning consciousness to that fair creature who lay so pale and cold before her.

Poor Ellen! her sufferings were not yet at an end.

Hers was a hard fate.

The dark clouds had not yet floated away and revealed their silver lining.

And there she lay, pale and insensible, upon that bed on which the poor Bianca died, watched by the fiend who could listen unmoved to the cries for mercy of an outraged and defenceless woman—who had forfeited the right to that title, and steeped her soul in crime till every spark of humanity had flown her heart for ever.

Meantime Lang had returned to the shore to fetch the ill-fated Charles Lawson on board the pirate bark.

Bond and Hardy were not a little pleased when he made his appearance in the cleft of the rocks, for their patience had fairly become exhausted.

"We thought you never meant to come back," said Bond, surlily.

"Did you now?" said Lang.

"Yes, we did," replied Bond.

"Then you see you are mistaken," said Lang.

"Well, so I am, but we were just a coming on board to see if the gal was holding you so tight you couldn't get away."

"No fear of that," said Lang, "she hasn't opened her peepers yet."

"A jolly good job for her if she never does," remarked Hardy.

"Well, let's get aboard," said Lang.

"How about this chap?" said Hardy, pointing to the bound youth, who lay listening intently to every word but powerless to move.

A shudder pervaded the frame of Charles at the mention of the name of Wild Madge.

Too well he knew the fearful nature of that base and degraded woman.

He feared the worst now he learnt Ellen was in her power, and a prayer rose to his lips for the safety of the girl he so fondly and purely loved.

The bandage over his mouth prevented him giving utterance to a sound, so in silence he was lifted from the ground and borne down the beach to the spot where the pirate's boat was in waiting for them.

In this he was lain, and Lang, Bond, and Hardy entered after him.

The boat was pulled to the ship, and he was hauled up the side on to the Scorpion's deck.

Then was the bandage removed from his mouth and he gave utterance to a deep groan as he felt that he had failed to save Ellen, and was a prisoner in that pirate bark.

CHAPTER XCV.

THE SMUGGLERS AT WORK AGAIN—THE WRECK OF THE 'SAUCY LASS.'

DARK clouds were gathering in the sky.

The wind blew in cold and fitful gusts, and the air was laden with moisture.

On land the pedestrian sought shelter, and at sea the vessels ran for the nearest harbour.

The fishing-boats made for the coast, and the 'old salts' turned their quids and gazed mysteriously and knowingly at the horizon.

The wind blew in shore, and the waves were crested with a white foam.

A noble ship was ploughing the billows and making all speed to reach port before the threatened storm broke forth in all the fury which the heavens indicated might be expected ere the night.

Away past the Eddystone lighthouse and Lizard's Point, towards Mount's Bay, the "Saucy Lass" took her course.

But the wind filled her sails and drifted her along; and as night closed over sea and land she was bearing direct upon the rocks, where we first saw the Boy Rover and his base hearted companions.

She was heavily laden and rose so low in the waters that the waves ever and anon washed her decks, and her captain with a look of anxiety paced the deck.

The coming storm had cast a shade over his heart.

He saw danger to his vessel in sight of home after escaping it during a long and tedious voyage.

Presently the storm burst in all its fury, and a squall rising the "Saucy Lass" was driven by the force of the gale on to her side.

"But, with a creak and a groan, she righted herself; and the captain gave the order to brace up every stitch of canvas, and run her along under bare poles.

This order the crew rushed hurriedly to obey; and in a short time she lay upon the foaming waters without a thread for the gale to hold on.

But the storm became fiercer, and the darkness denser and blacker, and the crested waves rolled higher and higher, and broke over the ship, carrying away, as they receded, everything upon her deck.

The sailors clung to the rigging, and the men were lashed to the wheel.

Suddenly the fearful cry of "breakers ahead!" rang out over the ship.

"'Bout ship!" exclaimed the captain; and the men at the wheel hastened to obey the order.

For some time the captain had directed the course of his vessel by a lurid light which shone bright and clear over the seething waters.

A light which had been placed to mislead the mariner, and cause him to hurry his vessel to destruction.

We have seen this light before, in the opening chapters of our tale.

It was in the opening of the rock in which was situated the cave of the Boy Rover.

Once more was the smuggler and his companions at their hellish work—once more had they kindled the betraying fire.

After having eluded the pursuit of the officers of justice, who endeavoured to recapture the daring band, the Boy Rover and his companions had found means to return to the scene of their former villainy.

Again they had taken up their abode in the secret cave, whose whereabouts had not been discovered, and of whose existence none knew save those we have before met there, and now turned their hellish minds to the fell work in which they so much delighted; resolved to amass a sufficiency to obtain a fresh vessel, and once more ply their old avocation.

On the night of the storm the opening had been uncovered and the fire lighted.

There was prospects of plunder in that fearful gale.

"The coast will be strewn with wrecks in the morning," said the Boy Rover to his companions, as he heaped more fuel on the fire, "if the gale but lasts."

"I reckon it will," said Black Bill, "for the wind sets dead in shore, and no vessel can ride with safety in such a storm."

"All the better for us," remarked Sam.

"Rather," said Jem.

"It's an ill wind that blows nobody good," said the Boy Rover, with a smile. "If it robs the owners of their cargo it places it in our hands."

"And we know what to do with it, I reckon," said Sam.

"Well, pretty near," said Jem; "we have had a little dealing in that line in our time."

"Yes," said the Rover, "but the business of the wrecker is fast dying out. The cutters keep such a sharp look out round the coast that a fellow don't get a chance of picking up a honest living as he used to do."

"A what?" asked Bill.

"Honest living," replied the Rover, sticking his tongue in his cheek.

"Ah, yes—that's the right name for it, I dare say," exclaimed Bill, with a laugh.

"In course it is; we never call anything out of its name—do we?" said Sam.

"Hilloh!" exclaimed the Rover suddenly, "there it goes."

"What?" said Bill.

"A signal of distress."

"Then there's a vessel on the coast," said Sam.

"If there is, nothing can keep her off the rocks," said Bill.

"So much the better," said the Rover.

"It's all up with her once she gets alongside the breakers," said Bill.

"Not much chance for her then," said the Boy Rover, coolly lighting a cigar at the treacherous fire.

Again the report of a gun boomed over the waters and saluted the ears of the men watching in that wild cavern.

"Come on, old fellow, we are waiting for you," said the Rover, puffing a huge cloud of smoke from his mouth.

"Why don't you go and help them?" said Sam.

"We'll go and help ourselves as soon as she strikes," said the Boy Rover.

"And the sooner the better; for it's dull work sitting here doing nothing," said Black Bill.

"Very," said Jem.

Boom again came the gun to the ears of the assembled smugglers.

"That's a little nearer," said the Boy Rover. "She is fast drifting to her doom."

"We shall hear them howl soon, I reckon," said Black Bill, knocking the ashes from his pipe, and commencing to refill it.

"I don't suppose they'll meet their fate very quietly," said the Boy Rover. "If they do, it's more than the others have."

"I can't see what they have got to squeal for," said Bill.

"Nor I neither," said Sam.

"It's when their heads come bump agin the rocks, I take it," said Jem.

"Oh, they must holler then," said Sam, "acos it hurts them."

The gun continued to be fired at intervals; and at length it sounded so near that the Boy Rover leapt to his feet.

He approached the opening, and looked out over the white surf at the base of the rocks, against which the waves now struck in fury, and threw sheets of sparkling foam high up the cold grey stone.

But for a moment he could see nothing. Shading his eyes with his hands he endeavoured to penetrate the darkness.

At length they rested upon a huge black mass surging and swaying like a wounded giant, just outside the line of breakers which stretched far away on either side.

"There she is, reeling about like a sailor on leave with a full cargo of grog aboard him," said the Boy Rover, pointing out of the opening.

Black Bill took his pipe out of his mouth, and shading his eyes from the glare of the large fire, looked in the direction indicated.

THE WRECKERS AT WORK.

"Humph," he exclaimed, " she's a large ship."

"Yes," replied the Rover, " such a one as I wish was my own now."

"What a pity we can't get one," said Bill.

"It is ; but we will have one ere long," said the Rover, "unless fortune frowns on us."

Boom went ehe signal gun again.

The watchers could see the flash as it lit up the darkness for a moment.

"They're holding on pretty tight to the rigging I could see," said Bill.

"Yes, but they will soon have to leave go, for they are close on the breakers," said the Boy Rover, as coolly and calmly as though he were conversing about the most common-place affairs.

"We had better turn out now, captain, hadn't we ?" inquired Black Bill.

"There will be plenty of time when she strikes, and that won't be long first," replied the Rover.

"Whew ! the wind blows cold," said Bill, drawing back into the cavern.

"You had better wrap yourselves up," said the Rover; "you won't find it too warm on the rocks."

The men drew on their pea-jackets and sou'-westers.

"I suppose, captain," said Black Bill, with a comical expression of countenance, "if any of the crew comes ashore they are to be tenderly treated and well cared for ?"

The Boy Rover turned his gaze from the opening to the face of his follower.

"In the usual way," he said, " thrust them back again into the sea."

"And so put an end to all their miseries," remarked Sam.

"Nothing like being charitable," remarked Jem. "Can't abear to let them suffer, so put them out of their misery as soon as possible."

"That's it," said the Rover.

"Besides, dead men tell no tales," replied Black Bill.

At this moment a loud crash echoed far out over the waters, and ere it had died away, loud cries of anguish filled the air and penetrated the cavern where the smugglers stood jesting so heartlessly.

"She has struck," said the Rover, throwing the end of his cigar into the fire; "now to the rocks and the beach—there is work to do now."

"Hurrah!" said Bill, "and fortunes to be made captain."

And with the cries of the wrecked mariners ringing in their ears, the pirates laughed heartily at the prospect of plunder.

"Close up the opening," said the Rover, "and then to your duty."

The opening through which the bright rays of the treacherous fire had lured the brave bark to destruction, was covered, and the smugglers turned to leave the cavern on their unholy expedition.

As they departed, a smile lighted up the features of the Boy Rover.

"More plunder," he murmured, "more plunder. We shall get another ship, and again become the terror of the seas'"

And loosening his knife in its sheath he left the cavern to join his companions in their wicked work.

The Saucy Lass had broken her back upon the sunken rocks, and was fast going to pieces.

In vain had the signal gun been fired for assistance.

Its echoes had only come back as though to mock them,

In wild and frantic agony the sailors clung to the cordage.

But the huge waves swept over her and tore them from the ropes and tossed them into the boiling sea.

In vain did they call for aid.

The furious winds drowned their cries, and the beating rain nearly obscured their vision.

One by one they were swept away, or dropped cramped and benumbed into the sea.

The cries of the seamen became less frequent and more feeble as one by one the sea received its victims, or the wild waves dashed them upon the rocks lacerated, bleeding, and inanimate.

Some strove hard to reach the shore, but when they held out their hands to those upon the rocks to assist them, they were thrust back into the boiling surf.

The disabled ship groaned and creaked as her timbers parted.

Once or twice the waves lifted her bodily up, only to dash her down again with redoubled fury upon the sunken and treacherous rocks, over which the white foam spread the winding-sheet of the brave mariner.

The waters burst in through the rents in her bottom and sides, and floated her cargo up out of the hatchways, to be carried away by the next wave which should mercilessly sweep her decks.

The last sailor, unable longer to retain his hold, had relaxed his grasp of the friendly rope, and fallen into the waves.

Not a single cry for help was heard now; and nothing but the raging storm, and the groaning and creaking of the parting timbers, as the hull rose and fell amid the breakers, saluted the ears of the merciless wretches who had brought about the destruction of as fine a vessel as ever sailed the blue waves, or bore a crew of British seamen over the deep, or the union jack into a foreign port. Her masts had gone over the side; but the fury of the gale had prevented their being cut away, and

the waves dashed them against the hull, in fury.

Gradually the bolts started, and the noble ship went to pieces.

Her timbers were hurled furiously upon the rocks, and split into splinters with the force of the concussion.

And the Boy Rover and his heartless companions smiled at their work of destruction, and searched eagerly along the beach and among the rocks for all that came ashore.

A dead body was washed up to the feet of the Boy Rover.

He drew it up out of reach of the waves, and, having rifled the pockets of the corpse, thrust it back into the sea.

To himself and his companions the murdered seamen was worthless.

No feeling of pity or remorse took possession of their breasts for the guilt they had committed; no sympathy for the corpse of him whom their villany had laid at their feet.

Bale upon bale, and chest upon chest, was washed on shore.

These were eagerly grasped by the wreckers, and conveyed by them to their secret hiding place.

All night long did they continue their work.

When morning broke, and discovered the beach strown with portions of the wreck, they ceased from their dishonourable labours.

Fatigued with their exertions, they returned to their secret cave.

Like beasts of prey they hid themselves away in their lair, and feasted upon their spoils.

Around the rude table they sat, and jested over their wicked work; drank off the wines and spirits which had been washed on shore from the wreck; feasted their eyes upon the bales and chests which had rewarded their night's toil: but not one feeling of regret for the homes they had rendered desolate—the widows and orphans their hellish work had made—entered their hearts.

CHAPTER XCVI.

THE CAPTIVE AND THE FURY.

NIGHT had fallen upon the ocean and the stars glittered in the blue canopy ere Ellen awoke.

With a sigh the fair girl opened her eyes and looked bewilderedly around her.

Where was she?

The place was strange to her, and as she looked around the cabin a feeling of horror took possession of her.

For a moment she closed her eyes, and when she opened them again they rested upon the form of Wild Madge.

With a scream she started to her feet.

That form—those features—too well she knew them; and her heart sunk and her frame trembled, whilst the bleared eye gleamed malignantly upon her.

"God of Heaven!" she gasped. "Am I once more in the power of this fearful being?"

"Ah, ah!" laughed Madge—"the beautiful and scornful daughter of Joseph Hanfield recollects then the features of her enemy."

"Too well — too well," cried Ellen. "Oh, woman, where am I—why am I here?"

"To minister to my vengeance," exclaimed Madge—"to feed the burning fires that consume me."

Ellen covered her face with her hands and sobbed.

"Girl," said Madge, "this is the second joy I have known for years. I have sworn that you should fall that I might be avenged upon her who gave you being."

"Mercy!" gasped Ellen.

"As I have said before, it is dead within me; mercy can never more enter this breast. I have lived but for vengeance, and that vengeance must be satiated. Fate plays into my hands, and I shall yet enjoy that for which I have so long prayed."

"Woman, woman!" exclaimed Ellen in tones of agony.

"Ha, ha! no longer woman, but devil!" said Madge. "Woman's nature left my soul when your father scorned my love—when I placed the offspring of our guilty love upon the sands on which the waves rolled; then I became a fury. From that moment I have never known peace—never known rest—and never shall till the fearful vengeance I have planned shall have been consummated."

"Forbear—forbear!"

"Girl, you plead in vain. I have sworn to encompass your ruin in retaliation for the sacrifice of all my hopes. I have sworn that you shall become a thing loathsome to yourself, as I have become. I have sworn that the child of him who wronged me should atone for the guilty work of her father—that father who now lies in my power."

"My father!" gasped Ellen.

"Aye, girl, your father—my seducer. Fate has placed him in my hands, as it has done you. I will rack your hearts as mine has been racked. He shall hear your shrieks for mercy, and I will laugh to scorn his pleadings. The Boy Rover lies in an English prison, but we will tear him from it to place him by your side. Once have you escaped him, but you shall not escape again. You will fall, and your father's ears shall be pierced by your shrieks for mercy."

"Fiend!—fiend!" exclaimed Ellen. "Oh, thou disgrace to woman! Heaven has been merciful to me, and sent me aid; and so it will again. Providence will prevent this hellish work. A just God will still succour the innocent, and confound the guilty."

"We shall see," said Madge—"we shall see. But, if my boy fall a victim to the laws of the country ere we can rescue him, you shall not escape. There are those on board this bark who will pay no heed to a woman's pleadings or a woman's tears. I will wring your heart till death would be a mercy. Know that your father and your lover are here, and that I will devise such tortures for them as shall make you consent to my desires, to save them."

"Wretch—devil!"

"Rail on—I heed you not," said Madge.

"My poor father!" gasped Ellen.

"Ha, ha!"

"Woman, do you speak truly when you say he is here—here in this floating hell?"

"Rise, and I will show him to you," said Madge.

Ellen rose from the couch; and Wild Madge, crossing the cabin, lifted a kind of curtain which hung against the partition between the cabins, and, pointing to a small round hole in the wood-work said:

"Behold him!"

Ellen placed her tearful eye to the hole in the partition.

"Father—father!" she gasped.

She saw her father seated in the adjoining cabin, with his elbow resting upon a small table, and supporting his head with his hand.

Pale, thin, and attenuated, his hair silvery white, and his whole appearance betokening much physical suffering.

"Does Wild Madge lie?" she asked, in a thoughtful tone.

"Oh, why—why is he here?" said Ellen.

"To minister to my vengeance—to hear the shrieks of his child—her child—as she surrenders her honour to a murderer."

"Oh, God!"

"To feel the fury of the woman he wronged and scorned."

"Scorned!" exclaimed Ellen. "Could he do otherwise than scorn and loathe you, base, degraded, heartless fiend?"

"Ha, ha!" laughed Madge. "He trod upon the worm; it turns upon him with a scorpion's sting. Would it were your mother I had within my power; but that cannot be; and the daughter must quench the fires of revenge that consume me."

"Hell-fire will burn your soul for ever for the crimes you perpetrate," exclaimed Ellen. "The wrath of a just heaven will overtake you, as it has your guilty son, and a fearful doom will be your portion."

"Not to save my soul from all the torments of hell would I forego my revenge," exclaimed Madge, "for that alone have I lived—for that alone would I die."

"Woman, have you no thought or fear of hereafter?" asked Ellen.

"None."

"Oh, shame—shame!"

"Shame—who brought me to it? exclaimed Madge. "Your father: on his head, then, rests my guilt. He spurned me; left me and my child to shame and misery. I had been more than woman had I borne it."

"If he wronged you, why should you wrong me?" she asked.

"Because I have sworn to have vengeance for that wrong, vengeance upon him and all connected with him. My oath is registered in heaven, and by hell I will not break it."

"Heaven's vengeance will avert the blow," exclaimed Ellen.

"Vain hope," said Madge. "You shall not escape this time; you shall be too well guarded for that. I will watch you as the tiger does the hunter, and be ever ready to spring upon and prevent any attempt to avert your doom. You have no foolish boy now to play with, but a woman rendered furious by her wrongs."

Ellen sunk down upon a chair and buried her face in her hands.

"Fiend!" she exclaimed; "the vengeance of heaven will yet overtake you, and save a father and his child from the fearful doom you would hurl upon them."

CHAPTER XCVII.

THE SMUGGLERS IN THE CAVE—TALES AND ADVENTURES.

THE wreck of the 'Saucy Lass' brought several cutters to the coast on which the unhappy ship met her doom, and for several days the Boy Rover and his followers were unable to leave their hiding place.

To the restless mind of the Boy Rover this was torture, and his ill-temper rose hour by hour. But Black Bill, to assuage his ill-humour, proposed that they should pass away the time by spinning a few yarns.

This was eventually agreed to, so they sat round the rude table and, broaching a keg of brandy, Black Bill commenced—

"When I was in America hunting was not only a pastime, but one of the means of procuring a comfortable living, and I will tell you a story which was there told to me by an old trapper whom I chanced to meet."—

' When I first located myself in the western part of the State of New York (said the veteran pioneer, who narrated the thrilling adventure I now record), ' wild game, especially deer, was quite plenty in that region, and hunting was not only a pastime, but one of the means of procuring a comfortable living.

' The most of our meat we obtained from such animals as we could kill; and the skins were not only valuable for our own use, but as the articles of traffic for whatever we were compelled to get from a foreign source—such as tea, coffee, sugar, salt, powder, lead, and so forth.

' Deer, as I have said, was the most plenty of the more valuable wild game; but the large timbered tracks, which might be dignified by the name of forests, also contained bears, wolves, and now and hen a ferocious cougar, sometimes called the American lion, but more generally the panther.

' The last mentioned beast, which is about four feet in length, and something over two in height, is both savage and powerful, and is more dreaded by the hunters than any other.

' Concealed among the branches of a thick-leaved tree, he often awaits his prey, and woe to the man or brute upon which he makes his unerring spring.

' I had been more than a year in my new home before I got a sight of this ferocious animal, and the acquaintance I then formed with the stranger led me to hope that I might never be brought in contact with another of his species.

' At that time we had three methods of hunting the deer—namely, by stalking, by dogs, and by fire-light.

' The first was the most common mode, and consisted simply in approaching the animal under cover from the leeward, and shooting him while he was yet unconscious of an enemy being in that vicinity; the second was to rouse him by dogs, and fire at him, until killed, from different stand-points along some path of his own, which he would be certain to follow in his endeavour to escape; and the third was to carry a lighted torch into the woods on a dark night, and keep a sharp look-out for the eyes of the animal, who, arrested by the strange and novel sight, would thus allow the hunters to approach so near that a good marksman would seldom fail in his shot.

' In saying that these three methods were then practised by us, I do not wish it understood that I mean them to have been peculiar to our section; for the same means, I believe, are common wherever the deer is hunted, and especially in Virginia, and other Southern states, even at this day.

' For the first year my favourite plan was hunting by fire-light; and, with my eldest son, then a boy of fourteen, to carry the blazing brands just in front of me, I, for the first season, made the business quite profitable, generally killing from one to six animals in a night; but, after the thrilling adventure happened which I am about to relate, I gave up this mode of hunting entirely, and adopted the less dangerous one of stalking by daylight.

' One very dark cloudy night, my son and I, equipped as usual, struck off into the woods surrounding my clearing, and shaped our steps for one of the favourite haunts of the deer, about two miles distant from our dwelling.

' I carried my rifle, and he the resinous knots, which we usually did not light till near the field of sport.

' The night was so dark that we had to literally grope our way through the tangled wood, often stumbling over trees and rocks, and plunging into holes, and thus getting more than one serious fall.

"It took us an hour to get over these two miles, and I really felt not a little fatigued when we reached our destination, which we might never have found had not the way been so familiar to us that we could always tell by the peculiarity of the ground exactly where we were.

' Well, we reached the place at last, lighted one of our torches, and proceeded to the hunt. There ever was to me something strangely solemn and impressive in picking my way through the dark wood and deep thickets just behind the lurid glare of the smoking and blazing torch, looking for two small fiery eyes in the black wall of night surrounding the lighted scene, in which trees, rocks, bushes, and in fact every object, seemed to take a wild, gloomy, and fantastic shape; and this night, from some cause, I felt more strongly impressed and depressed than usual—an undefinable dread allied to fear, creeping coldly through my frame, and causing me to start at every sound and be constantly on the alert for a hidden danger.

' I resolved to say nothing of this to my son, reasoning to myself that it only arose from some peculiar state of the nerves, and would soon pass away. I observed, however, that he occasionally started at the sharp breaking of a stick, and now and then glanced cautiously around him, with a perceptible shudder, and I asked him what was the matter.

"Nothing, father," he replied, hurriedly — "nothing."

' Soon after this, our eyes simultaneously fell upon two small shining balls; and as we both advanced cautiously toward them, I brought my rifle forward to an aim; and when near enough to get a dim outline view of the timid animal, who was watching the firelight in surprise and wonder, I pulled the trigger.

' But the piece did not fire, and an examination of the lock showed me that the flint was crushed; and on searching for another to supply its place, I ascertained, much to my chagrin, that I had left them all at home.

' This was not an agreeable discovery—for one of us must either go back for the flints, or both of us return and let the deer go free for the night.

"It is too early to think of giving up the hunt, father," said my son. "I think I can go and get back in an hour or an hour and a half at most."

"Do as you think best, William," I replied, "If you choose to go, I will remain, for it seems a pity that we should even lose one night at this important season. We have need to kill all the deer we can provide for our winter's store."

"I will be back shortly, father," rejoined the

stout-hearted youth, as he handed me the torch, and dashed off into the surrounding darkness.

'While I remained alone, holding the blazing brand, and wondering what could have caused my recent dread, which had now nearly passed away, some five or six deer approached within a few paces of me, and there (for a while) stood, snuffing the air and gazing at the firelight, just as if they knew it was impossible for me to harm them; and then suddenly, with a wild bound, they disappeared together, and went crashing through the bushes, as if pursued by some terrible enemy.

'This did not cause me as much surprise as regret for their loss; and, seating myself upon a fallen tree, I had begun to ruminate upon the mishaps of the night, when, chancing to turn my head on one side, I saw two fiery eyes fixed upon me at no great distance, and again felt that undefinable dread shiver through my frame.

'This induced me to wave my torch from side to side, and call out after the manner of a frightened child.

'The eyes quickly disappeared, with a rustling of the leaves and bushes, and the next minute appeared on the opposite side of me, and a strange, ferocious growl saluted my ear.

'I bounded to my feet in an instant, feeling as if my hair were standing on end. I had suddenly comprehended all.

'It was no gentle, timid deer I had to deal with now, but probably that terror of the forest, the voracious cougar, who was only kept from attacking me by his instinctive fear of the light I held in my hand.

'What was to be done? My rifle was useless, and my only other weapon was a knife, which would afford me but poor defence should the terrible beast ever get to close quarters.

'And then my son, who was abroad in the dark—what a horrible fate would be his should the beast leave me and fall upon him.

'Would it not be best for me to start towards the dwelling, and while keeping the animal at a distance by waving my torch, thus attract his attention, till I could warn my son of his dangerous position.

'This certainly seemed the best I could do under the circumstances, and immediately I set forward.

'My first steps were arrested by a savage growl, a disappearing of the eyes, and a rattling of the bushes, and I felt my heart stand still as I grasped my knife and prepared to defend myself against a sudden spring.

'But the beast only changed his position to my right; and, as I glanced hurriedly around upon the encircling wall of darkness, I again perceived the two fiery eyes at about the same distance as before.

'Again I waved my torch and set forward, and again the furious animal, with growls that made my blood curdle, darted around me to a new standpoint.

'I continued on, keeping a keen watch for my enemy, and, as it seemed to me, carrying my life in my hand.

'In this way, by slow degrees, often stopping for the dread encounter when I fancied the beast might be about to make his fearful spring, I succeeded in getting over some half a mile of ground in the course of half an hour.

'By this time I had become somewhat accustomed to his ways, and began to move forward, with more haste and less fear, cheered with the hope that I might ultimately reach my home in safety; when, in crossing a sort of boggy glen, I stumbled and pitched forward, and the torch, slipping from my hand, was extinguished in a small pool of water.

'"Heaven have mercy on my soul!" I prayed, as I comprehended how near I was to the gates of death.

'In that awful moment I had no hope that I should live to see my dear family again, and the agony I suffered from the thought is beyond the power of language to pourtray.

'Happily my presence of mind did not desert me; and instantly dropping my useless rifle, I instinctively stretched my hands upwards and grasped the limb of a tree that spread above me.

'With a desperate effort— such an effort as a man in an appalling situation may make for his life—I bounded upward, and balanced my body upon the limb; and at that instant a rushing sound, accompanied by something, and the sudden appearance below me of two fiery eye-balls, too truly told me how narrowly I had escaped the clutches of my foe.

'The cougar now became more furious at my escape, and, with something like whining growls, encircled the tree rapidly a few times; and then, horrors! began to climb it.

'I was not safe where I was; and hurriedly gathering myself upon my feet, at the risk of falling to the ground below, and actually dropping my knife, my only weapon of defence, in my terrified haste, I seized the next limb above me, and drew myself upon it, just in time to clear myself from the claws of my ferocious pursuer.

'In this way I went on, limb after limb, till I at last reached a giddy height from the ground, and a point where the slender, bending branches warned me that I could venture no further; and all the way up the panther kept me company along the body of the tree. whining and grumbling forth his eager hope of his human prey.

'At last we were upon the same level, and within a few feet of each other; and most terrible to me was the gleam of his fiery eyes, as, in his efforts to get hold of me, he stretched his body along the limb as far as his own safety would permit, and thus brought them in such close proximity, that it seemed to me I was actually in his power and only remaining unmolested during his pleasure.

'And from that moment I date a scene of the most thrilling and painful excitement it was ever the lot of poor mortal to experience.

'I was upon a small, bending limb, which swayed to and fro with the slightest movement of my person, and which was barely strong enough to sustain my weight; I was obliged to support myself in my uneasy position by keeping a firm hold of the smaller branches with which I was surrounded and enveloped.

'Within a few feet of me—in fact so near that I more than once felt his breath — the panther was crouched, watching me with his eyes of fire, occasionally growling forth his displeasure, and stretching himself along the limb till I seemed to be in his very jaws, and then drawing himself back to rest and make a new trial.

'And all the time the cold night-wind sighed mournfully through the great, dark forest, as if singing a dirge to my hopes.

'When, as was often the case, my limbs began to grow numb from remaining too long in one position, I was obliged to make a change; and this I always did at the risk of slipping from my perch to the ground below, where certain death from my fall, or the wild beast, or both together, would have ended the scene.

'When I thought sufficient time had elapsed for the return of my son, I began to shout his name, and continued it at short intervals, the panther keeping up a growling accompaniment, till a faint answer reached him from a distance; and then my heart beat strangely with the joy that I was not altogether alone, and could communicate once more with a human being, and the fear that by coming too near the panther might leave me to fall upon him.

'There was nothing that he could do to assist me without drawing the danger upon himself; and as soon as he was near enough for me to make my voice distinctly heard, I informed him of my perilous situation, and ordered him, as he valued his own life and mine, to go home at once and remain there, but not to tell any of the rest of the family what had occurred.

'He begged and pleaded to be allowed to come to my assistance; but I was inexorable; and at last he bade me farewell in a wavering voice that told the anguish of his noble heart in leaving his father to a night of such awful peril.

'That night was an eternity of suffering to me, for every minute seemed an age.

'Would the morning ever come to release me from my terrible foe? And then again, would he depart with the light, or still remain on guard?

'At least, assistance would then arrive, sooner or later, and I should be able to see as clearly as himself, and, therefore, I hoped and prayed for the dawn.

'Oh, with what joy I beheld the first grey light in the east, and with what anxiety I watched it grow brighter, and the red fiery gleam fade from the eyes of my savage guard, as his brownish-red body became more and more visible!

'With the return of light he began to grow restless and uneasy, more than once looking cautiously around him, till at last he commenced to retreat and descend, growling his displeasure all the way to the ground, and then quickly disappearing from my view.

'With a fervent prayer of thanksgiving for my own wonderful preservation, I now, believing the danger past, began to descend myself; but so cramped and benumbed were my limbs from the cold and my long protracted and painful position, that I at length lost my hold, and fell some fifteen or twenty feet, but, fortunately, without any serious injury.

'Almost the next minute I was swooning upon the neck of my son, who, in company with a couple of the neighbours whom he had aroused, had thus early come to my assistance.

'It was a long time before I fully recovered from the effects of that night of horror, and I never think of it even without a cold shivering sensation, as it might be the approach of death itself. As I have already said, it was my last night of hunting deer by fire-light.'

"You see, captain, the old chap hadn't a very pleasant time of it that night," said Bill.

"No, indeed," said the Boy Rover. "Come, Sam, it's your turn now."

"Well,' said Sam, " here goes:

'Some years ago I was travelling through Egypt on a tour of pleasure and curiosity. I had two companions—an intimate friend and his sister.

'The later was then eighteen, and possessed all the charms and romance of that delightful age.

'I could dwell upon her attractions, her beauty of person and refinement of mind—her graceful step and merry wit—her enthusiasm, courage, fortitude, patience, and many other virtues and accomplishments—were it not for the simple fact that she is at this present moment my wife.

'At Cairo we chartered a Nile-boat and crew, to convey ourselves and baggage to the ruins of Thebes and intermediate points of interest; and on a clear, beautiful day we embarked and set sail, with a fair up-river breeze.

'Our little vessel was worked by twelve ordinary boatmen, commanded by a *rais*, or captain who was himself under the charge of a janizary, and with all of whom, not being able to speak their language, we could only communicate through our dragoman, or interpreter, who was likewise to serve us in the capacity of servant and guide.

'Although we had done our best in selecting our boat and crew, yet a more dirty, ferocious, piratical looking set of fellows I never saw collected into the same compass; and had our intended voyage laid across the Mediterranean, instead of up the Nile, I certainly should have refused to embark.

'For several days, however, as we progressed slowly up the river—by sails when the wind was favourable, and by oars and towing when adverse—nothing occurred to excite any serious apprehension.

'At length, on reaching a dreary part of the river—a region rather abounding in crocodiles than human beings—it set in to rain, with low clouds and a thick fog, which almost changed the day into night, and the night into Egyptian darkness indeed.

'Long before sundown we were compelled to tie up to the bank; and, whether by accident or design, the boat was run up into the mouth of a wooded creek, at a point the farthest from human habitation.

'"How is this?" I said to the dragoman; "why do we not stop at some village?"

'"There is none near," he replied, lowering his eyes upon my fixed penetrating gaze; "and the rais says he fears to keep upon the river in this fog, and the mud of the shore is so deep and soft, it is impossible for his men to tow the boat; besides, your honour will bear in mind it is now nearly dark."

'"All of which excuses are doubtless very good," rejoined I, turning away as if satisfied with the explanation.

'My friend and I occupied a small cabin near the stern, and my friend's sister another just forward of and adjoining ours—the rest of the men, including the dragoman and janizary, having the remainder of the boat at their disposal.

'As I turned from the interpreter I went down into the after-cabin, where I found my friend getting ready for a game of cribbage, his sister being in her own apartment.

"George," said I, in a low tone, I do not wish to alarm you unnecessarily, but the truth is, I do not like the appearance of things just at the present time."

"Why, how now, Frank?" he said quickly, turning slightly pale. "What new discovery?"

"Only this—that the villains, as I believe the whole of them to be, have run us ashore in just the worst place in the world for us to get assistance, in case they should take a fancy to cut our throats."

"Oh, my God! and Helen here with us!" he

exclaimed in horror. "For myself, merely, Frank, I should not care so much; but the thought that, if they should overpower us, she might be reserved for a fate ten thousand times more horrible than death, quite unnerves me."

"If we are to die by the hands of these wretches, she must die first by ours, George."

"I understand you."

"But you cannot know the agony this terrible thought costs me," said I.

"I can guess it from my own, Frank, for I know we both love her. But perhaps we are mistaken as to the designs of these fellows, who may be more honest than they look."

"God grant it!"

"You know we have suspected them from the first, and have watched them closely for several days, without discovering anything to confirm our suspicions."

"True, George; but then you should remember they have never had an opportunity like the present."

'Just now I questioned Azem concerning our stopping in this out-of-the-way place, and I did not like his hang-dog look as he assured me in reply, that it was necessary to quit the river at once, as the banks were too muddy for the men to tow."

'I affected to be satisfied, for if harm is meditated, it will be best for us not to let them think we suspect them till we are ready to strike in turn; but as I know they might have landed us at some small village instead of here, I cannot shake off the fear of some wicked design."

"Well, it is best to be prepared," replied my friend, producing a brace of fine revolvers, and a large, heavy bowie-knife. "There are ten shots," he said, "and yours added, make twenty, to say nothing of these two good knives in the hands of two desperate men. I tell you, Frank, it will cost the scoundrels something to murder us."

'At this moment Helen came into our cabin from her own, and we informed her what we suspected and feared, and what, in the last extremity, we had resolved on concerning herself.

She listened quietly and calmly, scarcely changing colour; and when we had done, she drew herself up, and with the look and manner of a true heroine, replied—

"If we are assailed, which heaven forbid! give yourselves no uneasiness about me. At Cairo, unknown to either of you, I purchased a beautiful stiletto, which I have since carried concealed about my person, prepared for whatever might happen. Rest assured, if you both perish, I shall not fall alive into the hands of these wretches, and may God forgive me if I sin in the only sure defence which will then be left me!"

"There speaks my noble sister!" exclaimed George.

"And did your mind then, have a fore-shadowing this trouble, Helen?" inquired I.

"I hardly know. I did not like the appearance of the men we were to sail with, and thought it best to be prepared for the worst."

"But you said nothing of this Helen?"

"No, for the time had not come for me to speak. Before I left home on this long and perilous journey, I considered all the dangers, and resolved that no idle fears or superstitions of mine should ever intrude upon your social pleasures: but since you have been the first to mention your apprehensions, I feel free to express mine."

'We now held a consultation as to the best course for us to pursue under the circumstances—

whether to call down the interpreter and endeavour to frighten him into a confession, or wait for events to determine our offensive actions.

'We decided to adopt the latter alternative, believing it safest to give no one an idea of our suspicions.

'It was not, perhaps, till a couple of hours after sunset that anything unusual had occurred, and then we suddenly became aware that the boat was in motion, but propelled so quietly and silently, that, had we not been on the alert for danger, we should not have detected it.

'We placed our dim light where its feeble rays would fall directly upon any person entering our little cabin, and drawing back into the deeper shadow, with our revolvers ready for instant work, awaited further developments in a suspense that was really painful.

'An hour—a long, dreary hour—passed, with the boat all the time in motion, and then it gently rubbed against the bank, and stopped.

'We held our breath and listened.

'All was still, except the pattering of the rain, and a very low murmur of voices.

'Then we could hear feet stealthily approaching, and we silently grasped our weapons more firmly, and riveted our eyes upon the point of entrance.

'Presently we could see two or three dark, hideous faces peering down, and endeavouring to ascertain if we were asleep.

'We had so disposed ourselves that they could not see us, and we held our breath and watched.

'Presently they began to descend very stealthily, and we could see they were all armed with pistols and ataghans.

'There could be no mistake—they intended to murder us while we slept. A fourth face appeared.

'It was Azem's, our dragoman. He whispered something and made ominous signs. This was sufficient, I thought. It was time for us to act.

'"Let me have the first chance, George," I whispered, so low that, with my mouth to his ear, he barely heard me. "Be ready, but do not discharge a shot till mine are expended. Helen, when I rise, do you lie down at once, and screen yourself as much as possible. Ready now!"

'I quietly reached forward my hand, and aimed my first shot at the head of our treacherous interpreter.

'I fired, and Azem pitched headlong, with a yell and a groan.

'His yell was more than echoed by his surprised and terrified companions, who instantly turned to fly.

'Three more shots were among them in as many seconds; and then my bowie knife was flashing in the hand of a temporary maniac. In less than ten seconds it was red from point to hilt, and the three ruffians were bloody corses at my feet.

'New faces appeared above, and my friend's revolver began to play.

'Then came wild yells, and a flight of terror.

'I rushed on deck—more mad than ever; but every foe had fled—some upon the bank, some into the water.

'Nothing was to be seen, and therefore we could not pursue. I was perfectly wild with rage, and athirst for bloody vengeance.

'I dared them to come back, and called them cowards, forgetting they could not understand a word I uttered.

'It was ten minutes before I became reasonable, and then I found George one side of me, and Ellen the other, both piteously begging for me to be calm.

'The affray was over, and we were masters of the boat. The three villains who had entered the cabin were dead, the dragoman was badly wounded, and all the others, including the janizary, were missing.

'I need not dwell upon the scene—a terrible one to me when I came to comprehend it; and yet, though my hands were red with the blood of my fellows, I could not regret the course I had taken to preserve our lives.

'They were murderous wretches, and I felt they had deserved their fate.

'We spent a gloomy night, waiting for daylight, and guarding against the return of our foes, who did not reappear.

'We dressed the wound of Azem, our interpreter, which, though dangerous, was not necessarily mortal; and we drew from him a confession, by which we learned that it was the design of the crew to murder my friend and myself, divide all our money and effects, and reserve the girl for the fate I had feared.

'The storm cleared away towards morning, and we found our boat about two miles up the creek, in a dreary place.

'We pushed it into the current, and slowly floated down into the Nile.

'On reaching that river, we continued to float down till we came to a large town, where we went ashore and reported to the governor what had occurred.

'Our statement was subsequently confirmed by Azem; and the governor not only exonerated us from all blame, but offered to supply us with a trustworthy crew, if we wished to continue our voyage.

'We thanked him, but declined his offer, and returned to Alexandria, whence we sailed to another country.

'We subsequently learned, through our consul, that all the pirates were arrested, tried, condemned, and executed, and I never had reason to think that one of the wretches died unjustly.'

"Ah, you wasn't sorry—wasn't you?" said Bill.

"No," replied Sam, "I wasn't—they deserved it."

"Why?"

"Because they were pirates," said Sam.

"Well, certainly that's something," said the Boy Rover; "but I can't help thinking there's not much difference between them and us."

"Well, not now, perhaps," said Sam; "but at that time I was what people calls a decent member of society."

"Oh, ah!" said Bill—"I see—but certainly your opinion's changed with your position."

"Stow it!" said Sam—"and push the brandy this way."

"It's a good thing we have got plenty of it," said the Rover, as Bill complied with Sam's request; "for the devil only knows how long it will be before another storm visits the coast, or the cruisers make themselves scarce in this locality."

"They can have no suspicion of our secret cave," said Bill.

"I think not at present," said the Boy Rover. "But we can't hope to keep it a secret for ever; so I shall only be too glad to procure another vessel as soon as possible."

"Ah, they'll never find the place out," said Jem.

"Why not?" asked Bill.

"Because it's too securely hidden in the rocks," replied Jem.

"Why, you talk like a madman," said Bill. "If the captain could find it out, why shouldn't they?"

"Well, that's true," said Jem, "so they might. But talking about madmen, did I ever tell you of an adventure I had with a wild man a few weeks before I made your precious acquaintance."

"No—what was it," said Bill.

"Let's hear it," said the Boy Rover, lighting another cigar.

"It's true, captain," said Jem.

Oh, of course," said the Boy Rover—"no one would believe you guilty of telling a lie."

"Well, you see captain, when I was aboard of the 'Pelican,' a small trading vessel, that on one occasion a small party of us went ashore on an island in the South Pacific, for the triple purpose of searching for water, hunting for game, and general exploration.

'Our party gradually became separated, and in the course of two or three hours I found myself entirely alone, in eager pursuit of an animal something between a goat and a deer in appearance, which had just vanished from my view over the summit of a rocky acclivity.

'The scenery around me was wild and romantic—rocks, trees, hollows, caves and chasms on the right and left—a steep high ledge before me—a dense jungle behind, through which I had just made my way.

'The strange animal I had seen had disappeared from the summit of the ledge in front, and I was hastening to follow it by taking a course to the right, where the hill seemed to present fewer obstacles to my ascent.

'But I had by no means an easy task, and was often turned aside by here and there a chasm, gully, or precipitous rock, so that at least half an hour was consumed in making an ascent which in a direct line was only a few hundred feet.

"I reached the summit of the ledge at last, however, and found there was still another before me, equally wild and inaccessible.

'On debating with myself whether to go on or turn back I perceived the animal I was in quest of quietly walk out from a clump of bushes on the top of the second elevation, and with a stare of confidence as quietly walked away.

"So," muttered I, apostrophising the animal, "you think you are safe now, do you? Well, we shall see!"

'With this I set forward again, clambering up rocks, leaping narrow fissures, and now and then pulling myself up some steep earth-ascent by means of bushes growing here and there.

'I had much trouble in keeping my rifle safe from damage, and once I nearly lost my life.

'I had come to a fissure or chasm about five feet wide, running far away to the right and left, and opening down a dark pit into the very bowels of the earth.

'It would be perfectly safe to leap across it I thought, and more especially as there were some bushes growing close to the opening on the other side, which I could catch hold of, if necessary, the moment of my feet striking against the edge.

'Perhaps this apparent security against losing my balance made me less cautious than I otherwise should have been.

THE ENGAGEMENT.

'At all events, I slightly stumbled as I leaped, instinctively threw my gun forward to save myself, struck on the very edge of the chasm, which gave way under me, caught the bushes with both hands, and found myself dangling over the awful abyss, upheld from certain destruction only by a frail support.

'The minute which I occupied in drawing myself up and getting safe footing under me, was an age of horror, and then I sunk down, weak, trembling, and exhausted, and fervently thanked God for my preservation.

'It was at least a quarter of an hour before I thought myself able to stand, and when I did get up, my knees trembled so that I was obliged to take hold of the bushes for support.

'I picked up my rifle, and found to my great joy it had not been injured by the fall; and after waiting a few minutes longer to compose my nerves, I again set forward, though with much less confidence in my weak, human abilities.

'On finally reaching the height at which I aimed, I found it to be the most elevated point of the island.

'The scene was beautiful.

'It was near the middle of a warm, pleasant day, and all nature around me was in sweet repose.

'On two sides of me, at the distance of a couple of miles—the breadth of the land here being about four, and my position near the centre—I could see the mighty waters of the Pacific, slightly rolling under a gentle breeze near the shore, and blending in the distance with a soft sky.

'Our vessel lay at the southern point, distant some four or five miles, and hidden by an intervening hill; but I could perceive its exact locality; and by some peculiarity of the atmosphere, it appeared as if with a little exertion, I might cast a stone to its very deck, though I knew this to be an optical illusion, and that, by the rough, perilous route I had come, it would take me some hours to go back to it.

'Southward were rocks, chasms, precipices,

woods, and jungles, with little rills trinkling and flashing here and there like threads of silver; but northward the hill sloped down into a soft, quiet, beautiful valley, where occasional bright-hued flowers and blossoms made a pleasing contrast with the dark trunks and branches of gigantic trees, the long, brown, spiral stems of interlacing vines, and the differently-shaded green of the surrounding, overshadowing, enclosing and fluttering leaves.

' A few birds were flitting from point to point and twittering forth their music of joy, and these were all the signs of life I could see.

' My strange animal had completely disappeared, and it was quite probable I had beheld the last of him, though I doubted not there was game in the valley, which I now resolved to explore, if only to find a less fatiguing and perilous route back to the vessel.

' Accordingly, after a rest of a few minutes, I went slowly down the slope of the hill, keeping my eyes warily about me, but seeing nothing remarkable till about two-thirds of the descent had been made, when, directly at the lower base of a huge, overhanging rock, I espied a large spring of clear water.

' Now the spring itself was not remarkable, since one might have looked for it in just such a place; but it had evidently been deepened and rounded out by human hands, and was so nicely and artistically walled-in by shells of different colours as to produce a most pleasing and beautiful effect.

' Besides this, the drain had been rounded and shelled in like manner for a distance of twenty feet down the hill, where the tiny stream had an aboubt fall of a few feet into a natural channel, and was thence allowed to pursue its way undisturbed.

' Now, who, in this wild place had taken the trouble to collect these shells, and perform a work, which, setting aside the skill required, must have cost the labour of days? Was the island inhabited? I had seen no other signs of such being the case.

' Had it been the fanciful work of some idle sailors?

' It was very strange and curious, to say the least, and for some time I stood gazing at it with wonder, and then, feeling very thirsty, I leaned myself against the rock, and laid myself down to drink.

' I had nearly quenched my thirst, but was still drinking, looking down in the pool, when suddenly there was reflected in the water an apparition that made my hair stand and my blood run cold with horror.

' With a startled cry I sprang to my feet, and found myself confronted with something in human shape, but whether man or beast I could not at first determine.

' The object was about five feet six inches in height, shaped like a man, entirely naked, but covered all over—face, limbs, and body—with a natural growth of hair, varying in length from an inch to a couple of feet, the longest being about the head, face, and breast.

' I could see it had human features, concealed under a shaggy, grizzly beard, and the hair of the head swept down in long tangled masses, and partially shaded, small black, wild, piercing eyes, which were now fixed upon me with an expression of blended wonder and ferocity.

' In its hands, which, with its hairy arms, resembled the paws of a bear, it held a formidable club, that it was swinging to and fro, as if undetermined whether or not to crush in my skull with a single blow.

' Terrified almost out of my senses, I still had a glimmering idea that I should make instant exertions to rid myself of the monster, and with the thought I threw out my hands and grasped my rifle, but before I could bring it to a level, it was struck with so much violence as to bend the barrel, and it fell, lock downwards into the pool, a totally useless weapon.

' Quick as thought I next drew my knife, but in an instant this was sent flying with a whiz through the air, and the wrench from it almost dislocated my wrist.

' I was now unarmed in the presence of the monster, who, with a wild, horrid laugh, suddenly threw down its club, as if disdaining so unequal a combat, and flew at my throat.

' I grappled with him in self-defence, but though larger and heavier than he, I was only a mere child in his hands, and in a moment I was hurled to the earth with such violence as to deprive me of consciousness.

' When my senses returned, I found myself bruised, bleeding, and naked, lying on the ground near the spring, with the monster dressed up in my clothes, strutting proudly to and fro, and jabbering and laughing to himself.

' The sight was a ludicrous one—for he had got on my trowsers wrong side out, and my jacket hind part in front, and was putting on the airs of a military coxcomb—but I was in no mood for laughing then.

' A sudden remembrance of all that had occurred induced me to feign death, in the hope that he would go away and thus leave me a chance to escape.

' With my eyes closed, I watched him from under the lids for several minutes, and came to the conclusion that he was a human being, who had been so long upon the island as to have become wild – perhaps some young sailor put ashore here for punishment, or washed ashore here from some wreck—or perhaps an Indian blown hither in a canoe from some distant island, to which, from the loss of his little craft, he could never more return.

' At length he came and threw himself down beside me, and began to roll, pinch, and rub me, uttering at the same time a low, moaning sound, as if regretting that I did not return to life. Presently he seemed to grow angry, and then suddenly buried his teeth in my arm.

' At this, in spite of myself, I gave a yell of pain, and the monster instantly sprang to his feet, and danced, capered, screamed, and laughed for joy. Then quickly returning, he gathered me up with ease, swung me over his shoulder, and started for a thicket, but whether to preserve or destroy me I could not tell.

' At all events, I now struggled to free myself, and wildly shouted for help, though without expecting any response. To my unspeakable joy, however, my call was answered by some of my comrades.

' The monster, also, heard their voices, and stopped to listen.

' " Help! help! help!" I cried. " Quick! quick! in the name of God."

' There was a rustling and tramping sound, and

then three of my comrades hove in sight at a distance of not more than fifty yards.

'The monster saw them, and dropping me, and, uttering a howl of fury, bounded towards them.

'The next moment three rifles cracked together, and, with a piercing yell, he pitched headlong upon the earth, where, for a short time, he floundered like a dying fish, and then suddenly regained his feet, and rushed furiously upon his enemies.

'Wounded, covered with blood, and dying though he was, he met the foremost, wrenched his gun from his hands, and might have brained him, had not the knives of the others at that moment reached his heart.

'Thus he died, and thus was I saved.'

"Of course it is all true, captain?" said Bill, looking across the table at the Boy Rover.

"Jem assures us that it is," replied the captain.

"And so it is, too," said Jem, a flush of rage mounting to his cheek. "I didn't say your yarn was a lie, did I?"

"Nor did I say your's was," said Bill.

"Didn't you? Well, you meant it," retorted Jem, angrily.

"Silence!" said the Boy Rover, rising: "we must not quarrel among ourselves. We only war with those whose hands are against us. It's now dark, and we can steal out upon the rocks and see how the coast lies."

And, throwing his jacket over his shoulders, he made toward the entrance of the cave, followed by his companions.

The Boy Rover feared lest words might come to blows, otherwise he had no wish to leave the cave; but well he knew that when thieves fall out, honest men sometimes get their dues.

CHAPTER XCVIII.

HENRY CHAMBERS AND CAPTAIN PERRY — THE DETERMINATION TO SEEK FOR THE MISSING ONES.

CAPTAIN PERRY, who never once left the quarter-deck, had watched the foundering of the "Cyclops" through his glass, till she disappeared beneath the waters.

Then he turned his gaze to the boat, which, propelled by the willing arms of the seamen, and guided by Henry Chambers, was making its way rapidly towards the frigate, with the shipwrecked mariners they had been instrumental in saving from their threatened doom.

The boat having come alongside, and the fainting sailors assisted on to the deck, Henry followed, and stood before the captain.

Saluting his commander, he gave an account of what had happened upon the rocks, where the "Cyclops" had broken up, and spoke in high terms of the behaviour of the men under his command.

After having listened to the report of the young man, Captain Perry said:

"Mr. Chambers, in my anxiety to forward relief to the sinking ship, I had not noticed the absence of your friend."

"It was of that, sir, I was so anxious to speak when I reported myself as come aboard," said Henry.

"Why did not Mr. Lawson return with you?" asked the captain.

"Alas! sir, I know not," replied the young man.

"Know not?"

"No, sir."

"How do you account for this?" asked the captain, in a tone of surprise.

"I am at a loss to account for his absence," replied the youth.

"Strange!"

"Yes, sir, but if you will grant me a few moments interview in your cabin, I will explain what befel us on the island."

"Certainly," said Captain Perry, turning towards his cabin.

Then the youth followed him, and having been requested to be seated, he complied with the captain's desires, and said—

"You must know, sir, that we had a double object in going ashore."

"A double object!" said Captain Perry.

"Yes, sir. Firstly, we were in hopes of discovering anything which might lead to the conviction that the pirate of which we were in pursuit was likely to touch the island; and, secondly, the desire to rescue a poor girl, whom we had reason to believe was a prisoner within the ruined fort, whose walls could be seen from the deck of this ship."

"What girl?" asked Captain Perry, in some surprise.

"A young and beautiful girl, the affianced wife of Charles Lawson. He was bearing her from Gibraltar to England, when the vessel in which they sailed was decoyed on shore in a storm by wreckers, headed and commanded by none other than the Boy Rover, the smuggler of the south seas."

"Ah!" exclaimed Captain Perry.

"Even so, sir."

"But her lover, in his endeavours to save himself from a watery grave, found himself, by accident, in the very cave to which the Boy Rover had carried his affianced bride, and succeeded in escaping on a raft, which parted on the wave, and they were separated. The girl was picked up by myself whilst sailing under Captain Waters, but in an engagement with the Rover, the revenue cutter was overpowered, and Captain Waters consigned to the doom which the pirates had consigned me when I was rescued by my friend. The girl once more fell into the rover's hands, and from whom she received indignation, at which the soul shudders."

"Go on, sir," said Captain Perry.

"I, too, was taken prisoner by the Boy Rover, but succeeded in escaping from his vessel, when I fell in with Charles Lawson, and together we tracked the Boy Rover till we succeeded in wresting her from his grasp; but fate still was against us, and myself and the lovely Ellen fell into the hands of Latour the pirate. I was condemned by him to walk the plank, but was picked up by none other than the Boy Rover, whose vessel having been wrecked, he had succeeded in murdering the crew of another and getting possession of her, but with the aid of the father of the girl, of whom I am speaking, and who was a passenger on board, we succeeded in overpowering the villians, and sent them to England, by a passing vessel, prisoners. But, sir, misfortune still pursued me. As we were endeavouring to make for an English port, we were overtaken by the pirates, who were none other than the crew of the 'Venomed Snake,' and I was bound to the mast and the vessel scuttled, from which fate I escaped by the fortunate vicinity of this frigate. What Charles Lawson had been told by the dying pirates after the destruction of Latour's vessel, convinced him that his affianced bride was a prisoner on the island; and, having some knowledge of the character of the place and its inhabitants, we resolved to search for her. In the vaults of that fort we discovered the poor girl, and bore her towards the beach, but in endeavouring to convey her to the barque, I have lost sight of both her and Mr. Lawson. In vain we searched, no trace of them could we find, and now, sir, I appeal to you in the name of humanity to assist me in recovering my friend and the poor girl who so fondly loves him, and has suffered so much in the hands of base and designing villains."

Captain Perry paused thoughtfully for some moments.

Then he rose and paced the cabin.

Suddenly he paused before the youth.

"Mr. Chambers," he said, "you say you have some knowledge of this place?"

"I have, sir, having visited it before when on board the revenue cutter."

"With what object?"

"That of searching for smuggled goods," replied Henry.

"And did you succeed in finding any?" asked Captain Perry.

"No, sir, we did not. But I am satisfied now of the existence of great quantities in the vaults of the fort; and from what the poor girl stated, they but awaited the Boy Rover to convey them to England."

"Are you sure of this?" said Captain Perry.

"Quite, sir."

"Then the inhabitants of this coast are ———"

"Not what they seem, sir. To all appearance they are fishermen, but, in reality, they are smugglers."

"And you are certain of the existence of evidence to that effect?" asked Captain Perry, anxiously.

"I am, sir."

"Then I will have the boats manned and armed. I had hoped to fall in with the pirate, but if we can destroy his emporium, we shall not yet have sailed out of our course in vain."

"In the vault of that fort, sir, are bales and barrels, which can have been placed there for no other purpose than to be secretly conveyed away at the first opportunity. Besides, the inhabitants would be unable to exist on their professed avocations. It is by aiding and assisting pirates and smugglers that they can do so."

"We will soon find out their true characters Mr. Chambers, and if your friend and his lover are still on the island, we will leave no means untried to bring them off."

"Thank you, sir," said Henry, a gleam of joy lighting up his features.

"I will have the boats manned at daybreak; and you, sir, shall guide us to this fort."

"They will, doubtless, expect a visit from us, sir, and endeavour to destroy all evidence of their guilty avocations," said Henry.

"No doubt they will do so," said the captain; "but it is too late to start on such an expedition now. At daybreak we will pull for the shore."

"Would it not be advisable, sir, for a boat to be sent to the beach to watch, as, during the night, they may consign to the waves the barrels and bales with which the vaults are stocked?

Captain Perry thought a moment.

"Perhaps it would," he said; "so I will have a crew told off for the purpose."

And he left the cabin, and ascended to the deck, followed by Henry.

"In a short time one of the boats was manned and armed, and started to keep watch along the beach.

This done, Captain Waters mentioned the business he had in hand for the morrow, and recommended Henry to seek rest, so that he might be ready to start with the expedition at daybreak.

CHAPTER XCIX.

THE PRISONERS IN THE HOLD OF THE "SCORPION" — THE DRUNKEN PIRATE — ONE STEP TOWARDS FREEDOM.

THE gallant old tar, Bob Bittern, whom we last saw bound hand and foot on the deck of the "Scorpion," was confined, together with Jacob, the servant of Mr. Hanfield, in the hold of the pirate vessel.

Bitter indeed were the invectives Bob breathed against the pirates; and deep and deadly the vengeance he vowed, if ever he found an opportunity to get out of the cursed place, in which lay, beside, his no less indignant companion.

Several times had Lang offered them liberty, on condition of joining them,

The pirates sadly wanted able seamen to assist in working the vessel, and gladly would they have welcomed Bob into their confederacy. But Bob treated all the overtures with scorn and derision.

So also did Jacob; and together were they kept in the dark, with the vain hope that their sufferings would induce them to throw aside all qualms of conscience, and become pirates.

Jacob's anxiety was principally for his master, to whom he felt certainly some horrible doom was intended; whilst Bob only panted to avenge the fearful death he believed Henry had suffered at the pirates' hands.

"The tarnation sharks!" he said. "I only hope as I shall get a chance to bear up alongside that hell-hag as gave the order to have him bound to the mast—I only hope I shall get a chance to throw my grapnells aboard her—I'll pour such a broadside into her hull as'll shake her timbers a bit. I wouldn't run foul of a woman; but she ain't no woman. Look at her figure-head, and you'll see that, in a minute, she might have been built for one; but, demme, if she ain't spoilt in the building —a piratical old sea-tiger—curse her!"

"She is an inhuman brute," said Jacob, "and bears some fearful ill-will to my master, for which I cannot account. I fear the worst for him, poor gentleman."

"So do I," remarked Bob. "In the hands of that infernal wretch and her hellish crew he will meet but little mercy, unless we could manage to escape and batten down the hatches when the devils are all below."

"We have little chance of that," said Jacob.

"Aye," said Bob, "at present we are too closely watched. But let us keep our weather eye open, and should an opportunity occur, be ready to take advantage of it."

But no opportunity occurred till the Scorpion had anchored in the little bay of the island on which Ellen was confined.

It was whilst Lang, Bond, and Hardy were on shore that Smith, in a state of absolute drunkenness, descended the hold to see after the prisoners.

Staggering up to where Bob and Jacob were, exclaimed, in tones intended to be extremely affable—

"Well, shipmates, what cheer?"

"Damn bad," replied Bob, in a sulky tone.

"Well, don't come foul of a fellow like that," said Smith, staggering about, scarcely able to stand. "You ought to be very comfortable and happy."

"Ought we," said Bob.

"To be sure you ought. I'm comfortable, and why shouldn't you be. Plenty of grog, and everything else you like to have. No splicing the main brace aboard the Scorpion, but take part what you like, and drink all you can. I'm very comfortable, I am—very."

And as Smith gave expression to the last word, he staggered forward, and fell upon Bob Bittern,

"What the devil did you do that for?" exclaimed the drunken sailor. What do want to run foul of me for. Can't you steer clear of a craft sailing under bare poles, but you must set out of your course and bear down on her like that."

And Smith floundered, and staggered, and rolled about like a Chinese junk in a high wind, but still hugged the head of Bob, who hardly knew whether to be angry with the man or pleased at what might turn out as something to their advantage."

"Steer off a point or two," said Bob, "you've lost your bearings."

"I'm blowed if your bowsprit aint got entangled in my rigging," said Smith, who could not recover his equilibrium, but fairly lay upon the bosom of the old sailor.

"Then why don't you cut the lashings?" said Bob.

"To be sure," said Smith, fumbling for his knife, "right you are, messmate. I never thought of that."

"Look sharp," said Bob, "or damme we shall sink together."

"So we shall, messmate," said Smith, clutching at his knife, and making several attempts to open it with his teeth before he succeeded, and swaying to and fro on the chest of Bob.

"We must clear the wreck, to be sure," stammered Smith, turning the blade of his knife towards the face of Bob.

"Hold on, messmate," exclaimed Bob, "you're going the wrong way to work—cut through this first."

And the seaman held up his arms, which were bound together at the wrist.

"Aye, that's it," said the other, becoming more and more overpowered with the fumes of the liquor every moment.

And after several ineffectual attempts to cut the lashing, much to the fear of Jacob, who expected to see the drunken brute cut the wrists and the cord, and the bonds which held Bob powerless fell from his wrists to the floor.

The moment they did so, one hand grasped the pirate by the throat, and the other tore the knife from his grasp.

Then Bob flung the drunken man from him, and Smith fell heavily to the ground.

Quick as lightning, Bob stooped and severed the cord around his ankles.

This done, he turned to Jacob.

"Quick!" he exclaimed — "hold up your hands."

Jacob obeyed, and the cords around his wrists were instantly severed.

Then those at his ankles underwent the same operation.

"Free—free!" he exclaimed.

"Yes, from those bonds; but not from this accursed ship."

Then he turned hurriedly towards the prostrate man.

Smith made two or three attempts to rise to his feet; but he was so drunk now that he could only raise himself on to his hands.

"Struck upon a rock," he murmured, "and shall go to the bottom; for I can't hold off. I say, messmate, just take us in tow."

"Aye, aye," said Bob—"right willingly. Bear a hand here, Jacob."

And taking the cords in his hand, with which himself and companion in misfortune had been bound, he directed Jacob to put a tow-line round the pirate's ankles, whilst he bound his arms.

This operation took very little time; and before it was completed Smith was in a profound slumber, and his snoring might have been heard half over the ship.

Bob turned his eyes to Jacob, with a look of thoughtfulness.

"He will, no doubt, soon be missed, and search made for him," said Bob.

"Then we shall be none the better off," said Jacob.

"Perhaps worse," remarked Bob, "if they find him here in this condition."

"What had we better do?" asked Jacob.

"Shiver my timbers, if I know," said Bob.

Jacob paused, thoughtfully.

"It would scarcely be safe to attempt to go on deck till night sets in," said Bob, "as we should be instantly discovered. But, if he is not sought for till then, we may stand some chance of either escaping from the vessel, or secreting ourselves in some out of the way corner, till a favourable opportunity present itself."

"But I fear ere that this fellow will be discovered, and then all will be known," said Jacob.

'Sure to be," remarked Bob. "Let us carry him up here, behind these barrels; and then, should anyone come down, if we keep in the dark, their suspicion may not be excited."

"That will be about the best thing we can do," said Jacob, stooping down and taking hold of the legs of the slumbering pirate.

Bob Bittern seized his arms, and they lifted him up, and carried him to the spot indicated, where they laid him behind several barrels which had been taken from one of the vessels the pirates had destroyed.

"I should like to bury his knife in his gullet," said Bob; "but it would not be wise to do so now. A time may come for that yet; and, if it does, I won't spare him. Now I don't care how soon the shades of night set in."

CHAPTER C.

MR. HANFIELD SURPRISED BY UNEXPECTED VISITORS—THE ATTEMPTED ESCAPE — THE FATE OF JACOB AND BOB BITTERN — THE VILLAINS FOILED—A WOMAN'S DEFIANCE.

HEARTSICK, weary, and miserable, old Mr. Hanfield sat in a chair beside the table in the cabin in which he was confined.

His mind a prey to torturing thought, he

sought not his cot, but remained hour after hour buried in a deep and painful reverie.

Suddenly he started.

His cheek blanched.

His form trembled.

Eagerly he bent forward his head and listened.

But all was still.

He rose and paced the cabin for a few minutes; then reseated himself, and murmured:

"My nerves, shaken by all that I have passed through since I sailed for England, conjure up sounds long, long since heard. I could have sworn that I heard the voice of my child—my poor suffering Ellen. It was but fancy; I shall ever hear it more. She is lost to me for ever!"

And he buried his face in his hands, and sighed heavily.

But again he started.

Again he fancied the voice of his loved child floated in the air.

And again he listened, in anxious suspense.

"Surely it was her voice; surely I heard the word 'Father' pronounced, as she was wont to speak it! There—there it is again!" he continued, rising from his chair.

But all was again still in that floating pandemonium.

"It must be but the workings of an overcharged heart," he muttered. "She is lost to me for ever."

He was about to seat himself again when he heard the bolt on the outside of his cabin door draw back.

"That hell-hag!" he thought, "coming again to torture me. Do I not suffer enough, but she must add to my misery with her hated presence Heaven forgive her! she has wrung my heart to madness already."

And, retreating to the farthest end of the cabin, he stood awaiting the appearance of Wild Madge.

But slowly and silently the door opened, and Jacob stood upon the threshold.

Hanfield sprang forward.

Jacob placed his finger on his lip to enjoin him to silence.

Scarcely able to repress the cry of surprise he was about to utter, Harfield immediately drew back.

Jacob entered, followed by Bob Bittern.

As silently as they had opened it they closed the door behind them.

"Hush!" said Jacob. "Do not speak above your breath."

"How have you escaped?" said Harfield, in a tone of pleasureable surprise.

And he extended one hand to his faithful follower, and the other to Bob.

"No matter now," said Bob. "The enemy is on the watch, we must stand to quarters, and be ready for action."

"We have come to save you," said Jacob, returning the pressure of Hanfield.

"Thank God!" exclaimed the old man, fervently.

"At least we are going to try," said Bob, in a whisper. "There's a boat moored astern. If we can succeed in getting into it, we may cut her adrift, and get ashore."

"But are there none of the pirates on deck?" asked Hanfield.

"They are all drunk below, I think," said Bob, "don't you hear them bawling and howling like a lot of savages as they are?"

"I have heard nothing but savage sounds in this accursed ship," said Harfield.

"We only caught sight of one fellow on deck," said Jacob, "and he had his back turned towards us—he was leaning over the side."

"Come along, old gentleman," said Bob, "but keep your weather eye open, and if one of the damn pirates run foul of you, hit out straight, and send him to the devil! Once in the boat; I'll give them leave to catch us if they can. Come on, follow me."

A gleam of joy shot from the old man's eyes.

His heart leapt at the prospect of escape, and buoyed with hope, he prepared to follow the honest tar and his faithful servant.

Stealthily Bob mounted the steps to the deck, and anxiously gazed around the vessel.

The man on the watch still leant over the bulwarks, gazing into the sea, with his back towards them."

"Silence!" whispered Bob—"all right."

And, followed by his companions, he stepped as stealthily as a cat towards the place where the boat rose and fell on the undulating waters of the bay.

"Now, old gentleman, you drop in first," said Bob, in a whisper, "and your man next."

Mr. Hanfield placed his hands on the bulwarks, then started back, as the man leaning over the side turned suddenly round, and revealing the features of Bond, roared out at the top of his voice:

"The prisoners are escaping, by God!"

"Damn you," yelled Bob Bittern, furiously, as Bond rushed towards them, "I'll cleave you to the brisket if you move another step."

And the old sailor raised the knife he had taken from Smith in the hold above his head in a threatening manner.

The fierce demeanour and the determined tone of Bob caused Bond to start back a few paces.

"Into the boat," exclaimed Bob—"in with you, old gentleman—"you at least can escape, if you look alive—in with you, and I will cut her adrift if I cannot follow."

"No, no," said Hanfield, "you could have escaped without me, but in your anxiety to save me, you have ruined yourself. No, if we cannot escape together, we at least will remain together."

"You're a brick," said Bob, "but you're a fool as well."

"You get into the boat and save yourself," said Harfield.

"If I do I'm damned!" exclaimed the sailor.

The cry of Bond had reached the ears of Lang and Hardy, and, seizing the pistols and cutlasses, they rushed upon deck.

"What's this?" exclaimed Lang, in a loud tone.

"The prisoners are attempting to escape," answered Bond.

And at the same time he pointed towards Mr. Hanfield, his servant, and Bob.

"The devil!" ejaculated Hardy.

All three of the pirates advanced towards them.

"Back to your berths," exclaimed Lang, "or I will cut you down."

"Cut away, my hearty," exclaimed Bob. "Why, you cowardly swabs, if you will only lay down your toasting forks, I'll lick the three of you in less than a good seaman takes to run aloft."

"Back to the hold!" roared Lang.

"I'll see you damned first," retorted Bob.

"Then, curse you! take that," roared Lang, and swinging his cutlass over his head, he brought it down towards the form of the bold sailor.

But Jacob, anxious to save his friend, darted before Bob, and the weapon, descending upon his head, he fell bleeding and insensible to the deck.

"Blast you!" roared Bob, rushing upon Lang, and seizing his arm, he endeavoured to tear the weapon from his grasp.

Hardy now seized him, and raised his cutlass to strike.

Bob flung him off, and as he staggered, Bob buried the knife in his throat.

With a loud shriek he fell at the feet of his companions.

But he died not unavenged.

Lang and Bond raised their weapons, and the brave sailor fell beside his fellow-prisoner.

Both weapons had struck him and inflicted deep wounds on his heart.

But he uttered no cry of pain as he fell.

He turned his eyes upon the pale and awe-struck Hanfield, and gasped:

"Fly—fly—the boat—the shore—ah, pirates dogs—sharks—I—I—"

His head sunk back. Bob Bittern was dead.

Like the tiger who has once tasted blood, and knows no rest till it is satiated with the life-fluid, Lang sprang towards Hanfield, who, overcome with horror, sank upon his knees beside his faithful servant, and, raising the weapon above his head, was about to deal a death-blow upon the head of the old man. when the weapon remained suspended in the air, and he drew back in surprise.

"Coward and villain!" shrieked Ellen, as standing defiantly before him, she presented a pistol at his head. "Stand back, lower but your weapon one inch, and I stretch you dead at my feet."

"Stand aside!" exclaimed Long, "or——"

"A daughter's hand shall protect a father's life," exclaimed the defiant girl, "and rob the gallows of its due."

CHAPTER CI.

THE SMUGGLERS ON A NEW COURSE—THE QUARREL —BLACK BILL DOES NOT HAVE IT ALL HIS OWN WAY.

THE night was fine ; there was no moon, but the bright stars twinkled in the dark canopy of heaven's vault, as the Boy Rover, followed by his companions, went forth from the cave to the beach.

"It's a beautiful night," said Black Bill— "but tarnation cold."

"Yes, and a dead calm, too," replied the Boy Rover. "There's not much chance of work to-night."

"No," replied Bill : "for my part, captain, I think we might as well have remained where we was ; for, see, yon light shines from the port-hole of the revenue-cutter that has been sailing up and down the beach to look out for wreckers."

"True," remarked his companion; "and I only wish that we were strong enough to board and seize her."

"Ah, captain," said Bill, "then we might be off again on the old game."

"Yes," replied the Rover; "but there don't seem much chance of it, anyhow, at present. We shall have to remain in the cave till better times set in."

"I shouldn't much mind that," replied Bill, "if we had only got some pretty girls to keep us company, and cheer the monotony of our existence."

"Confound the girls!" exclaimed the Rover— "they seem to bring nothing but misfortune with them."

"Oh! not at all," chimed in Sam. "I should like to run the risk, captain."

"Should you?" said the Boy Rover, with a smile.

"Yes."

"And so should I," said Bill. "What do you say, captain? Don't you think we could hunt up one or two to share with us the hours we remain on shore?"

"As to that, I dare say we could do it," said the Rover ; "but I begin to doubt whether a woman is not the worst thing we can get in our camp."

"Oh, no," replied Bill. "They ain't all like the girl you got off the rocks."

"Perhaps not."

"Why, there are plenty as would be too happy to fall into our arms," said Sam. "What do you say, captain, to make a descent on the borders of St. Ive's. and see if we can't do a little business ?"

The Boy Rover shook his head.

The opposition he had met with from Ellen had somewhat shaken his belief in the weakness of woman.

"Not that his soul had become one jot less black ; but he had learned the truth that woman will not always fall without a struggle.

A struggle that oft ends in death.

Woman's honour was a thing not lightly to be assailed.

Her resolve to resist the wiles of a villain is firm to the last.

Still, he well knew that his companions were fast getting dissatisfied with their present position.

He felt assured that it would soon become irksome.

And then dissatisfaction might lead to revolt.

This he wished to prevent.

For then he would be left alone.

And that he feared most of all.

Alone, he would find some difficulty in starting again in his former career.

But, backed by his companions, should a favourable opportunity present itself, he might procure another vessel, and once more become the terror of the coast.

So he felt that he must give way somewhat to their desires.

"As you will," he said; "but remember that there are but few of us, and caution must mark our doings."

"Bravo !" exclaimed Bill—"I knew the idea of getting a girl into the cave would be just the thing to suit you."

The Rover made no reply.

It was just the thing that did not suit him.

Had he a vessel on board of which he could have carried her, he would not have hesitated.

"Then shall we start at once, captain?" asked Bill.

"If you like," said the Rover.

"You will go with us?" exclaimed Sam.

"No."

"No?"

"That was my answer," replied the Rover.

"But why?"

"Oh, you must come, captain. It's a dangerous piece of work, and where more kicks than favours may await us. You won't leave us to fight out any row by ourselves?"

This remark altered the Rover's decision.

It would never do for him to shirk danger.

"If he did so, he would but bring down upon himself contempt, where he now found respect.

Should he allow them to believe he feared to encounter any danger, his power was gone.

So he turned to Bill, and said:

"I had forgotten you might get into trouble, or I had not refused to accompany you."

"I thought you didn't mean it," said Bill.

"In course he didn't," exclaimed Sam.

"Not likely," remarked Jem, "because we have stood beside him in danger."

"And one good turn deserves another," remarked Bill, "and nobody knows that better than the captain."

"Away then at once," said the Boy Rover, "or we shall have daybreak before we can again return to the cavern."

And so saying, he started off in the direction of the spot indicated by his followers.

A walk of two hours brought them in front of a small cottage, which stood alone and distant from any other habitation about half a mile.

Here Bill paused, and, turning to the Boy Rover, said:

"Captain, there's a pretty girl lives in this cot."

"How do you know?" returned the Boy Rover.

"Because I have seen her many a time. She keeps house for her father, an old sailor, who has assisted to work a revenue cutter, which has more than once chased us along the coast, and from which we have only escaped by gaining the bay, where we were hidden from their sight."

"Ah!" said the Boy Rover, his evil nature prompting him to revenge himself upon the man who sought his destruction, although he did but his duty, and obeyed the orders of his superiors.

"Yes," said Bill, "and the last time I was this way I learnt that the old boy had retired from the service, and now lives with his daughter on his pension."

"And do they reside here alone?" said the Boy Rover.

"They did," replied Bill, "and I dare say they do now."

"And so you fancy this girl," said the Rover.

"Fancy her!" exclaimed Bill. "I love her."

"Ah! ah!" laughed the Rover and his comrades.

Bill turned fiercely towards Sam.

"What are you laughing at?" he exclaimed.

"You love her!" replied Sam. "Ah! ah!"

"Yes, I do, is there anything strange in that."

"Rather."

"What!"

"Because you can't love anything but yourself," replied Sam.

"Can't I."

"No."

"You're a liar!"

"A what!" shouted Sam.

And he sprang forward with his hands clenched.

"Order!" exclaimed the Boy Rover, starting between them.

"A liar! am I," said Sam, foaming with rage.

"Yes, you are," retorted Bill.

"I'll knock the words down your throat," yelled Sam.

"Silence!" exclaimed the Boy Rover. "Sam, do you forget the rules and the oath!"

Sam dropped his upraised arm, and stepped back a pace.

"Curse the oath!" he said.

"Remember Bill is your officer, and mutiny is death," said the Rover.

"And I shall be called a liar!" exclaimed Sam.

"No," said the Boy Rover. "Bill, keep a curb on your tongue, for though Sam cannot resent an insult I can. If you are his superior, remember I am yours."

Black Bill gritted his teeth, and cast a malignant scowl upon his opponent, but said not a word.

"There must be no quarrelling," said the Boy Rover. "Remember, it is in the power of each to hang the other."

"Well, what did he jeer at me for?" said Black Bill, sulkily.

"Because, Bill, you made use of a word wrongly. You asserted that you love the girl you say resides in that cottage."

"Well, so I do."

"Nonsense."

"Why nonsense?"

"Because, if you loved her, you would not have her," replied the Rover. "You may desire to share her favours, but that is not love."

"Ah, well, I calls it love," growled Bill, "and it's all the same to me."

"But it may not be to Sam," said the Rover.

"I don't care what it is to him. Let him keep his laugh to himself, that's all.

"And just keep your tongue to yourself, that's all," said Sam.

"Silence! Let there be no more of it," exclaimed the Rover, "or you may both have cause to regret your hasty tempers."

The angry men relapsed into silence, and in a few minutes the affair was forgotten.

"How do you propose to get possession of this girl who has so charmed your heart, Bill?" asked the Boy Rover.

"Well, I hardly know," returned Bill, looking up the little casement before which they now stood.

"She is doubtless in bed, or asleep," said the Rover.

"No doubt of that."

"It would never do to carry her to the cave in her night-dress," said the Rover.

"Why not? There are plenty of women's clothes in the chest washed ashore from the wreck."

"To be sure there is," said the Rover.

"So that won't much matter, you see, captain."

"But the night is cold, and the air damp," said the Rover.

"I'll throw my pea-jacket over her," returned Bill. "I shall be warm enough carrying her."

"If you succeed in getting her," said the Boy Rover.

"What's to prevent me?" asked the mate.

"Nothing that we see at present," said the Rover; "but we can't make sure till we have her in our power."

"*We?*" said Bill, in a tone of surprise.

"Yes," replied the Rover—"*we!*"

"But I intended this girl for myself," said Bill.

"Did you?"

"Yes."

"But you know our rules," said the Rover.

"What rules?"

"Share all plunder."

"But not this girl."

"Why not?"

"Because I don't think it fair. You didn't share the girl you found on the rocks," growled Bill."

"True—but I did not succeed in my desire," said the Rover. "Had I done so, I should have acted fairly by you."

"Humph!" growled Bill. "I think it would be better if I kept the girl for myself, and helped you each to get another for yourselves."

"Oh, one's enough for all," said the Rover.

"We do not want too many in the cavern. So either our old rule must be carried out, or the g r. shall not be molested."

"That's fair, captain—quite fair," said Sam, who felt a secret pleasure at the chagrin of the smuggler mate.

"It would be fairer to act as I propose," said Bill.

"No, it wouldn't," said Sam. "We have got rules; so let us abide by them. If we take the girl, she is the property of us all, *after* the captain has done with her."

"Curse it!" roared Bill, fairly goaded to fury by the remarks of Sam—"I won't have nothing at all to do with it, then. The girl may go, for what I care!"

This caused a burst of laughter from the smugglers, in which the Rover joined.

"Silence!" said the Boy Rover, at length. "We must get to work now we have come so far from the cave. I had rather this expedition had not been taken; but, as it has, it must not be a fruitless one, if we can help it. I, Bill, and Jem will enter the house, and seize the girl, while the rest keep watch."

So saying, the Boy Rover strode towards the door of the cottage.

CHAPTER CII.

MURDER OF THE OLD SAILOR—ANOTHER VICTIM TO BRUTAL PASSIONS.

THE house which was occupied by the old sailor, Henry Cordage, an intrepid seaman, who had retired on his pension, and his daughter Mary, a buxom lass of nineteen summers, was a little cottage fronting the high road to St. Ives, and in a deserted part of the country.

But the good old seaman had little fears of residing in so lonely a spot.

Too poor to tempt the avarice of thieves, he believed no other danger would assail them; so the old salt retired to rest without even calling into requisition the aid of locks and bars to secure his dwelling.

Whilst the smugglers were wrangling outside his habitation, himself and his fair daughter were peacefully slumbering within.

Old men sleep lightly, and Harry Cordage was awakened from his slumbers by hearing a noise which sounded like a footstep on the stairs leading to his own and his daughter's sleeping apartments.

For a moment he listened to hear if it were his daughter Mary.

But the footstep was heavier than his daughter's and the old man starting up in bed called out loudly—

"Who's there?"

Then he listened again.

There was no answer.

The footsteps ceased.

"Who's there?" again asked the old man.

Still there was no answer.

Bounding from the bed the old man made his way to his chamber-door.

A strange fear seized him.

He felt anxious for his child,

Throwing open his chamber-door he called out "Mary—Mary!"

"Yes, father," said a voice in the opposite room.

"Get a light, girl," he exclaimed.

"What's the matter, father," said the voice of Mary.

"I want a light," replied the old man, peering into the darkness of the staircase.

But he was unable to see anything but the darkness around.

Click, click, went the flint upon the steel, as Mary strove to obtain a light in compliance with her father's request.

Still the old man listened, and peered into the gloom.

He was certain that he had not been mistaken. He felt assured that some one had entered his dwelling.

But he likewise began to think that whoever it was had decamped at the sound of his voice.

He resolved to go down as soon as his daughter procured the light, and secure the door of the house.

Suddenly a bright gleam shot through the chinks of the door of his daughter's chamber.

"Shall I bring you the light, father?" said the voice.

"Yes—yes; quick!" answered the old man, stepping on to the landing, and placing his hand upon the latch of his daughter's bed-room door.

He was about to lift it when he uttered a sharp cry of pain and staggered backwards, striking heavily as he did so, against the door of his own room.

At the same moment his daughter opening her door to give her father the light, uttered a loud scream, and let it fall to the floor.

She had caught sight of her father wounded and bleeding in the doorway of his own room, and the faces of the Boy Rover and Black Bill upon the stairs.

As the gleam of the candle penetrated through the chinks of the girl's chamber it revealed to the smugglers the position of the old seaman, and then the Boy Rover sprang forward and buried a long Spanish knife between his shoulders.

The glance the Boy Rover had of the poor girl, as she dropped the light to the floor, was but momentary; but, slight as it was, it served to reveal to his gaze a fine-built pretty-faced girl, attired only in her night-dress, the spotless whiteness of which lent an unmistakeable charm to her appearance.

He bounded forward, and clasped her in his arms, as the last flicker of the fallen candle died out and left the place in darkness.

Another scream she uttered, and struggled to free herself from his grasp.

"Be quiet," hissed the Rover in her ears, "or I will drive my knife into your heart."

The girl trembled violently, and seemed for a moment to have lost all consciousness.

But she roused herself, as Black Bill bounded to her side.

"Let me go—let me go!" she shrieked. "Oh, help—thieves!"

"Silence!" said the Rover, still holding her firmly.

"Oh, my poor father—you have murdered him!"

"And I'll murder you, if you ain't quiet," said the Rover.

"Oh, oh!"

"Listen to me," said the Rover. "We intend taking you away from here."

"Oh, spare me!"

"Be silent, and listen."

"I will—I will."

"We intend taking you away from here for a time. You can go as you are, or you can dress yourself—which you like; only you must be sharp about it—that's all."

"Take me away?" gasped the frightened girl.

"Yes."

"What for?"

"To make you happy," said Black Bill.

"Happy!"

"Yes, happy. Don't you like being happy, eh?"

"My poor old father!" sobbed the girl, endeavouring to make her way to the spot where the old man had fallen, and was now breathing his last.

"Curse your father!" said the Boy Rover. "Just pay attention to me."

"He is dying!"

"So much the better; you won't have him to trouble you," said the Rover.

"Wretch!—let me go to him," exclaimed the girl.

"Will you dress yourself?" asked the Rover.

"Let me go to my father!" she pleaded, in tones of agony.

"You can't do him any good," said the Rover; "he is dead as a herring."

"Dead!" gasped the girl.

"Yes; and you won't be long first, if you don't be careful. Here, bear a hand, Bill: if she won't dress herself, take her as she is—that's all."

"Oh! for God's sake, no—no," exclaimed the girl, now shuddering at the knowledge that she was held in the arms of a man only attired in her night clothes.

Her horror and anxiety respecting her father had prevented her paying much heed to her own condition: but, now that Bill also seized her, to assist in carrying her from the house, she became but too plainly aware of her position.

"Well, then, be sharp," exclaimed the Rover; "we can't waste time."

"Oh, leave the room—do leave!" exclaimed the girl.

"Oh, you've no need to be alarmed. We shan't look at you—because we can't. It's too dark. So look alive, or you must go as you are."

"Where—where would you take me?" gasped the trembling girl, feeling for her clothes.

"Oh, you'll see in time," said Bill.

"Oh, do let me go to my father!" she gasped, again striving to pass them.

"Now be wise," said the Rover. "Get your things on at once, or you go without them; and that you won't find at all pleasant, for it's freezing cold, and there are four more of us you will have to accompany."

"Oh, where—where?"

"You will see in time, I tell you. Now, will you dress, or go as you are?"

With a heavy sigh the poor girl drew on her clothing.

"Now, are you ready?" said the Boy Rover, at length, when he could perceive in the dim light which entered through the small casement that the girl had placed on her frock.

"Are you men," she gasped—"and can torture a poor girl in this way?"

"You will find in good time we are men," said the Boy Rover.

"Oh, prove it, and leave me here alone with my father," exclaimed the girl in pleading accents.

"I might comply with your wishes," said the Rover, "but have not time."

"Oh, yes—yes!"

"Oh, no—no!" replied the Rover; "indeed I have not. Ere long it will be daybreak, and I have no wish to be seen in this locality."

"You fear the consequences of your wicked work," said the girl. "But if you escape now, you will not escape for ever. The blood of that poor old man calls for vengeance, and it will sooner or later have it."

"Curse your preaching," exclaimed the Boy Rover, seizing her by the wrist. "Catch hold of her arm, Bill, and drag her down the stairs."

"Oh, for the love of heaven let me look upon my father!" exclaimed the girl, as they rudely forced her from the chamber on to the stairs.

"It's too dark, you can't see him," said the Boy Rover.

"Let me press my lips to his," she pleaded.

"You will have other lips to press soon," he replied, brutally forcing her down the stairs.

She started with a loud cry as the remark of the Rover met her ears; then, as the meaning of his words dawned upon her she became powerless as a child, and they led her unresistingly from the house.

CHAPTER CIII.

THE RETURN OF INEZ AND HER COMPANIONS TO THE HUT—THE FLOOD IN THE WILDERNESS—A WOMAN'S PETITION FOR THE ENEMY OF HER PEOPLE.

PANTING and breathless, yet with a feeling of thankfulness in her heart for her preservation, Inez lay upon the breast of Martinez.

Thus a few moments passed—the hearts of both being too full to give utterance to their thoughts.

Martinez was the first to recover; and, straining the beautiful form of the dark-eyed girl to his heart, he exclaimed:

"Inez, Inez, thank God your voice reached my ears, or you had been lost to me for ever; and cold, blank, and desolate would have been my existence."

"Ah, Martinez," she replied, "but for your aid I had met the fearful doom which threatened me. My limbs were paralysed with fear, and I was powerless to move. Heaven be thanked that you were so near!"

"Heaven be praised that it was so!" he exclaimed, fervently — "for, if it saved you from death, it likewise saved me from despair. Come, love, lean upon me and our kind friend, and we will bear you to our rude but happy home."

Ned, who at this moment had arrived at the spot, extended his arm for the aid of Inez.

The mutineer saw all that had happened in a moment; and a shudder pervaded his frame as he perceived the danger Inez had so providentially escaped.

Still throbbing with emotion, the fair girl clung to the arms of her lover and friend; and silently they took their way to the hut, or arbour, which sheltered them in that island on which the rude waves had cast them, and separated them from the world.

Arrived there, Inez seated herself upon a heap of dried grass, and Martinez took his seat beside her.

He saw that her nerves had been greatly shaken. and he endeavoured all in his power to chase away the gloom which her narrow escape had thrown around her heart.

Meantime Ned busied himself in preparing the game which they had been fortunate enough to hunt up for supper.

In the course of a couple of hours the mutineer had prepared the meal; and Martinez, with a cheering word and a kind smile, led the beautiful girl to the rude table on which it was spread.

Ned and Martinez, who had fasted for some hours, did ample justice to the viands; but Inez, unable to forget the fearful danger from which she had been rescued, was sad and silent.

Martinez strove all in his power to bring the smile back to her face, and chase away the sad effects of the adventure.

"Inez," he said, "strive to forget it, and be happy that we are now all assembled here together. Come, come, cheer up; we all in the course of our lives meet with danger."

"Yes, true," she replied; "but not so fearful a doom as that with which I was threatened. Oh! those rushing waters; I can see them now—hear them—as they dashed over the rocks into the chasm."

" No doubt—and will see and hear them in imagination as long as you think upon the circumstance."

" Oh! water is a fearful thing," she shuddered.

" Yes, indeed, when it becomes man's master," said Martinez. But, come, Inez, brighten up, my girl. Your adventure was indeed a fearful one; but not near so fearful as was one which happened to a person whom I once met in America, when we dropped down the coast, after landing a cargo of blacks—Heaven forgive me for ever joining in such hellish work!—an adventure which must have appalled the stoutest heart, and unnerved the strongest hand."

" What was that?" asked Inez.

" Call a smile to your face, dear one, and I will relate it to you in the words of him who told it to me, and to whom the adventure happened. We were seated in the public room of an hotel, when the conversation turning upon adventures and hairbreadth escapes, he said :

' Early in my life I gained a livelihood as a travelling pedlar, and during that time it was my lot to endure many hardships and encounter many danger .

' Travelling from place to place as I did, through the more thinly-peopled sections of the country, exposed to heat and cold, sunshine and storm ; sometimes riding the whole day without food, and often passing the night in the most unhealthy and wretched quarters ; continually meeting with incidents and accidents of the most disagreeable nature—all this is very trying to one poor human system, and there are few men so constituted as to be able to endure it for any great length of time.

' During the few years which I spent in this manner, in what I may call the wilderness of the West, many events occurred, which, could I now recall, and had I time to relate, I believe would deeply interest you ; but I will only give you the most remarkable one of all, and the most closely interwoven with my life and destiny.

' One dull, gloomy, drizzling day, during the spring of the last year I served in the capacity I mentioned, I found myself, near the setting-in of night, passing through a long dreary wood, where for miles I had not seen any habitation.

' In fact, since noon of that day, I had passed but one dwelling, a poor, miserable log-hut, where for myself I had obtained rather a lunch than a meal, but had not been able to procure anything for my weary horse.

' How far I had yet to go to reach a habitation where I could find shelter for the night I could not say, and in consequence I began to feel quite uneasy.

' My horse was fatigued and hungry, and myself cold, wet, and uncomfortable.

' Spurring on my jaded beast, however, in the hope that I should yet find some comfortable lodging on the way, I rode some two miles further, and descended into a steep, narrow valley, through which flowed a swift mountain stream, and across which led the narrow road I was pursuing.

' It was now getting quite dark; and as I reached the stream and heard the gloomy murmur of its swollen waters, he knew not if it were safe to attempt the ford, I felt quite disheartened, and was half tempted to turn back and encamp as best I could.

' But looking around me, as my poor horse pricked up his ears and uttered a pleading whine

I espied a light a few rods below, and riding down to it I was greatly relieved and rejoiced to find it proceeded from a neat and comfortable dwelling, which stood back some fifteen yards from the stream, and probably as many feet above the level of its waters.

' On knocking at the door, it was opened by a very genteel-looking woman, some forty-five years of age, who, from her dress and appearance I judged to be in deep mourning.

' To my statement of who and what I was, and my application for permission to pass the night beneath her roof, she replied in a kind and gentle tone, that she would be very happy to entertain me, if I would accept her humble fare.

' Procuring a lantern and some corn for my horse, I led him, by direction, to the other side of the hill, where I turned him out to graze in a partially cleared field.

' On returning to the house I was agreeably surprised to find a pleasant fire, a smoking supper well under way, and, gracing the apartment with her mother, a young lady some eighteen years of age, whom, at a single glance, I considered one of the most beautiful and fascinating beings I had ever seen.

' She was of the medium height, with light hair, blue eyes, and a pale lovely face, upon which every noble virtue seemed to have set its seal.

' She was modest, retiring, and intelligent, and her voice was one of great sweetness and melody.

' From the very first I became deeply interested in her—to me she was a delicate flower blooming in a dreary wilderness—and consequently I became more than usually interested in the family history as related by her mother.

' The elder lady was a widow by the name of Arlington, who, some three years previous to the time I speak of, had, with her husband and two children, removed from the eastward, and settled in the lonely place where I now found them.

' Some half a mile above their dwelling, and some two miles below what was then a small but very flourishing village, Mr. Arlington had erected a saw-mill and grist-mill.

' He had just got them completed and in good working order, when, one dark stormy night, going out to raise the floodgate, he had fallen into the water, been swept down into the torrent, and drowned—the body being discovered the next day, some two or three miles below.

' Of the two children mentioned, the eldest, a son, some twenty years of age, had taken the place of his father since his death, and was now away at the mills ; and the other, the daughter, Julia Arlington, was the one I have already described.

" It was on a night similar to this, Mr. Perry," pursued the widow, addressing me in a sad tone of deep feeling, " that we met with that great misfortune which time can never repair; for what can compensate for the loss of a beloved husband and kind father ?

" Never do I hear the hoarse murmurs of yonder stream, amid the dark and dismal watches of the night, that my mind is not borne back to that night of all nights of suffering, suspense, and that awful realisation which followed when the remains of him we so devotedly loved were brought here and placed before us, as if only for one final farewell of his clay-cold form !

" Oh! the anxious hours I pass thinking of my son, who, for aught I know, may come to the same untimely end; and on nights like this, when he is compelled to be away from home, I spend a great portion of my time in prayerful anxiety, and even the presence of a stranger is most heartily welcome, as a slight relief to the painful gloom, though we are seldom called upon to entertain one.''

'Mrs. Arlington shed tears as she spoke, and the fair Julia wept almost convulsively.

'I offered what consolation I could; told them to put their trust in Providence; that all seeming evils were for our good; and, after some further conversation of a similar nature, and a narration in part of my own history, I retired for the night.

'The house was a small frame, some story and a half in height, containing two or three rooms on the ground floor, and two above, one of which was assigned me for a lodging, the widow and her daughter remaining below.

'Being greatly wearied with my day's ride, I quickly turned in, and, thinking of the fair Julia, her bereavement, loneliness, and consequent desolation, I soon fell asleep, to see her again in my dreams.

'I might have slept for a couple of hours; I cannot say; but on awaking, as I did, with something like a start, I heard the rain pouring down in torrents, and even fancied the hoarse murmurs of the mountain stream, as it dashed swiftly past over its rocky bed, were sounding in my ear.

"Thank God for this comfortable shelter!" was my mental prayer; and again I fell asleep.

'From this second sleep, which was more sound than the first, I was aroused by several wild appalling shrieks.

'Starting up in bed, I was horrified, almost paralysed, at hearing the terrible roar and rush of heavy waters around me, and of feeling the whole building tremble and shake, as if it were about to be wrenched from its foundation, torn asunder, and scattered in fragments.

'For a few moments I knew not where I was, and could not comprehend what had happened; but the continuous shrieks for help, and a fancied recognition of the voice of Julia Arlington, brought back my recollection to the point of retiring to rest, and then the whole truth seemed suddenly to flash upon me.

'And, merciful God, what a truth—what a horrible reality! The mountain stream had burst its former boundaries; had ascended its banks in a wild, roaring, raging flood; had partially submerged the dwelling of my kind hostess, and was now surging past with that terrific power which no strength or art of man can check, and which, in its awful force and sublimity, seems to mock his weakness, and tell him how frail, how helpless, how insignificant he is before one single element, when guided by the almighty hand of Omnipotence.

'As shriek on shriek still rose above the creaking and groaning of the swaying timbers of the dwelling, above the moanings of the blast, the plashing of the rain, and the gurgling, rushing, surging murmurs of the angry flood, I sprung from my bed, threw on a part of my clothing, hurried to the stairs, and commmenced descending them rapidly.

'When a little more than half way down, I found to my dismay and horror that my feet were buried in water, and I knew that the parties below must be struggling in the liquid element to keep themselves from drowning.

'Labouring as I knew they must be under the most intense and terrible excitement, they might naturally want the presence of mind which would enable them to escape immediate destruction by gaining the second story; and, shouting to them that help was at hand, I plunged boldly downward

into some four feet depth of water, and went knocking about in the deep darkness among the different articles of furniture, but struggling forward to the point whence came the continued shrieks of fear and distress.

'The flood was still rising rapidly; it appeared to me that I could feel it gaining upon us every moment; the groaning and trembling house seemed about to be borne away, or come crumbling down around us; and I felt, if there were indeed any salvation for us, our lives depended upon the action of the momentous seconds which were so rapidly bearing us to the verge of eternity.

'Happily I soon reached the widow and her daughter, whom I found clasped in each other's arms, nearly beside themselves with terror, but instinctively keeping their heads above the water in which their bodies floated; and, speaking to them some soothing words of hope, which I little felt myself, I dragged them forward, found the stairs, and assisted them to the story above.

'By this time poor Julia Arlington had fainted; but the mother, with a slight revival of hope, seemed to regain her presence of mind; and, as we both bent over her daughter, chafing her limbs, and dashing water in her face, till she began to show signs of returning consciousness, she said to me, with the deep feeling of a fond and grateful parent:

"May the Lord Almighty bless you for this! You must have been providentially sent to our rescue; for, without your aid, I am certain we should have been drowned below."

"Alas!" said I, somewhat gloomily, as the rising waters seemed to roar around us even more fearfully than ever—"we are not yet saved! we are not yet saved! and the good God alone knows what fate is in reserve for us!'

"God help us!" exclaimed the restored Julia, a few minutes later, as she stood trembling and clinging to her mother and myself, and endeavouring to peer around her into the awful darkness: "I fear we shall yet be swept away by this terrible flood."

"I have my fears, too," I replied; "but we will rely on God's mercy, and hope to the last."

'Almost as I spoke, there came a louder creaking and groaning; then a crashing as of some breaking timbers; then a rocking to and fro, like a boat upon the waves; and then a seeming whirling and plunging downward and forward.

"God help us now, indeed!" I exclaimed; "for we are already afloat—already in the grasp of the angry flood—and should be prepared for the worst, as becometh those who put their hope and trust in a Higher Power and a better world.''

'I need not dwell upon that never-to-be-forgotten night.

'I could not, if I would, describe our feeling of alternate hope and despair; our unspeakable anxieties, as we went whirling down with the rushing tide; rocking, rolling, plunging through the seething, bubbling waters; now striking some rock or tree with almost force enough to crush our frail tenement; now checked in our progress till some feeling of hope would revive; now torn from our moorings and sent onward again, a frail bubble upon the bosom of a maddened flood, till despair would awe us to silence in view of the impending death!"

'All that dark and awful night was passed in a manner which, if you cannot imagine, I have no language to describe.

'Reaching at daylight a long, broad level, we

floated out of the main current, and made a lodgment upon rising ground, as Noah's ark might have rested upon the summit of Mount Ararat.

'Here we remained through the day, in painful anxiety—watching the timbers, drift-wood, and wrecks of buildings which went floating past us—and humbly thanking God for our own wonderful preservation.

'Before noon the storm had begun to abate, and we saw the sun of that day set gloriously in the west, with the water subsiding around us.

'We passed another night beneath the same roof; but on the second day we were enabled to walk forth, and make our way to a settlement in the vicinity, where we were hospitably received, and where the anxious mother and sister were joined by the son and brother, whose escape had been almost as miraculous as our own.

'In conclusion I have only to add, that the acquaintance of two, begun amid such fearful and trying scenes, soon deepened into a friendship, which ripened into a pure and holy love; and Julia Arlington is now the wife of him who laboured for her salvation through that terrific night of tempest and flood."

"There, Inez," continued Martinez, "you perceive that you should be grateful for not meeting with sufferings more acute. Had you been borne away with the waters, Heaven only knows what might have been your fate."

Inez sighed.

She pressed the hand of her lover.

"But for you I might have been dead," she said. "Oh, truly the devotion of man—the promptings of his generous heart, and his heroic deeds—oft saves woman from a fearful doom!"

"And so does the devotion and tenderness of woman oft save man."

"Aye, you may well say that," remarked Ned. "Many a poor fellow has owed his life and liberty to a woman. Many a brave man can look back with joy and thankfulness to the time when a woman's voice was raised in his favour—when a woman's heart pleaded for mercy with his foes. In every land are records of woman's tenderness, and woman's struggles to save a poor wretch from death or torture — not only in the civilised parts of the world, but even among the wild tribes of Indians, away far from the influence of teachers and religion."

"True," said Martinez.

"True—yes," said Ned. "As a proof of woman's will to save a fellow creature, I'll tell you of a poor Spaniard who was saved from a fearful doom by a young Indian girl:

'Romance never pictured a more attractive hero than the brave Hernando de Soto, the successful invader of Florida, the worthy path-finder after Columbus.

'Leaving his wife, after a brief year of marriage, he had proceeded with a fleet of his own providing, and nearly a thousand men, to take possession of the Island of Cuba.

'De Soto and his followers soon possessed themselves of a village upon Tampa Bay, then called Espiritu Santo, where were the head-quarters of the cacique, Hiriga or Ucita.

'This old chief had become so utterly embittered by the outrageous conduct of Pamphili de Narvaez, ten years before, that no conciliation on the part of De Soto could restore his confidence and goodwill.

'One of De Soto's scouting parties had one day attacked a troop of Indians and put them to flight.

'One of the horsemen, in a charge of one of the number with a lance, was startled to hear a voice speaking the Spanish language saying—

"Good sir, I am a Christian man. Save my life and those of these poor men."

'The lance was dropped into its rest, and the horseman eagerly inquired the man's name.

"It is Juan Ortez," he answered, "and I have abode with these people ten years. I was with Narvaez in his expedition, and came near being sacrificed with my companions; but, thanks be to heaven, I was spared."

'The wanderer and exile—for such was Juan Ortez—was welcomed to the camp of De Soto, and recounted his adventures in words that brought tears to the eyes of his listeners.

'Not the celebrated Captain Smith ever passed through more thrilling or romantic scenes.

'The name of Narvaez was terrible among the Indians, from the enormity of the cruelties he had practised.

'Ucita, especially, had imbibed a deep unconquerable hatred against him and his followers; and when a little band, sent out by the leader, fell into the hands of the savages, and were brought to the chief to be disposed of as he pleased, it was not wonderful that the long cherished feelings of hate and revenge should find vent in cruel deaths.

'Of the number which had fallen into their hands, all save one were despatched instantly. Juan Ortez was this man; and it seemed that he was kept for more refined barbarities, which could not be so quickly decided upon.

'He watched the terrible preparations that seemed to herald his death with a heart that almost ceased to beat.

'Even his firm Spanish bravery quailed before them; and their mocking tones and gestures struck even greater terror into his soul than any physical demonstration of cruelty could have done.

'At last, when they had ceased to be amused with torturing or terrifying him, the chief gave orders that he should be bound to a stake, and fire kindled beneath him.

'The soul of Ortez was shaken within him. His courage and prowess in war had been indisputable; but this cold-blooded and deliberate butchery was more than he could face.

'A woman's cry startled him as the cruel sentence passed the chief's lips; and, turning, the captive beheld an Indian girl fall fainting into the arms of one of the warriors.

'He had no time to witness more, for he was dragged to the place of execution.

'The preparations were soon completed, and the fire was lighted.

'The heat of the blaze soon reached his limbs; and he closed his eyes, praying for immediate death rather than prolonged agonies.

'Just as he seemed to be parting from earthly things, the pleading tones of a woman's voice again aroused him, and he opened his eyes once more.

'A moment before, he had seen the old chief Utica, with hate and revenge pictured upon his countenance, apparently enjoying the commencement of his victim's agonies.

'Now the fierce look was partially melted, and another expression was coming over the face.

'On the ground, before the chief, knelt the Indian girl who had before attracted his attention, whose dress and adornments seemed to distinguish her as his child.

'Her face, though dark, was very beautiful and the grace of her kneeling figure, as she wound her arms passionately about the old chief, as he sat upon the ground, had rarely before been surpassed even by that of the haughty dames of Spain.

'Evidently she was pleading for the prisoner, for she cast rapid and pitying glances at him, and then turned with a wilder earnestness to the chief.

'A little shame mingled with Unita's softer mood, as he glanced up to see what his braves were thinking of this scene; and during this mute council, the slow flames were heating the poor captive's limbs!

'One look at him seemed to give the maiden strength and courage.

'She snatched the hatchet from the hesitating hand of the chief; and, with a single bound, she cleared the intermediate space between him and the captive, and cut the thongs that bound him to the stake.

'Half stupefied by the heat and smoke, Juan Ortez scarcely comprehended what she had done, until the brave girl took his passive hand and led him from the spot.

'The warriors seemed to approve her proceedings, or at least to take them quietly, for they drew off from the scene with an exquisite grunt.

'As they filed away, the maiden eagerly caught the arm of the oldest-looking, and, by her rapid gestures, and earnest pointing to the now half fainting captive, seemed to ask his assistance.

'She drew him hastily towards him as he lay upon the ground.

'From a pouch which hung from his belt, the Indian produced something which he rubbed gently upon the bare and scorched limbs.

'As soon as the sufferer seemed relieved, she beckoned to four of the Indians, and appeared to be directing them to make a litter of some of the branches which had been intended for his funeral pyre.

'Upon this litter three stout savages, at a nod from her, lifted the poor bruised frame, and carried it away to the hut of an old squaw, who spread upon her floor a number of buffalo-skins, on which they laid him—the girl leading and directing all their movements.

'It was many weeks before the captive's wounds were all healed.

'During that time the maiden came every day to watch his progress to health; and an animated, but to him unintelligible, conversation took place between the old squaw and his young protectress, which seemed to result in unmistakable satisfaction on the part of the latter.

'Gradually Ortez learned enough of the language of the tribe to understand them; and, after a fashion, he could express his gratitude to the maiden, Monica, for her interposition in his favour.

'After awhile she supplied him with the Indian costume, and bade him paint himself in imitation of the tribe.

'His burns were now healed, and he found himself appointed to a station of trust, which, however, involved a certain amount of danger.

'This was to watch by the dead at the place where the Indian custom is to bury them.

'Some of the tribes west of the Mississippi place their dead upon a sort of scaffold, after binding them in buffalo skins.

'These scaffolds are placed in the open air, and, from their height from the ground, are perfectly safe from wolves or other animals.

'But the Florida Indians build a sort of rude temple, or mausoleum, which does not, however, bar the approaches, and sometimes the devastations of the monsters of the forest.

'Their only resource, therefore, is to give the sacred edifice in charge of some one of approved valour; and to this charge Ortez was deputed.

'One terrible night he distinctly heard a sound that seemed different to those which had often appalled him before.

'There was no mistaking the mighty roar of the forest monarch.

'He knew all the danger that beset him now; but his duty was to maintain his post.

'On this night it so happened that the only dead form within the temple was that of a child—a beautiful little girl, the daughter of one of the chiefs.

'From time to time during the night, Ortez had withdrawn the curtain of soft-dressed skin which hung before the body, and watched it with feelings of interest and grief.

'The child had often played around him before he was appointed to this dangerous post, and a sort of friendly intimacy had been established between them.

'Besides, she was the frequent companion of her whom, of all women, he loved and honoured—Monica.

'Now she lay here in her childish beauty, perhaps to be a prey to a monster which even his strong arm might not be able to repel or vanquish.

'Nearer—nearer came those terrible sounds, rendered still more awful by the perfect stillness of the night.

'A bound through the forest, a sharp quick rush, a hasty convulsive snuffing of the air, and Ortez was sure that the lion had already scented his prey.

'Through the darkness, he could not detect his approach.

'Only his ear, and that exquisite sense of which not all men are possessed when danger is near, confirmed him.

'He drew aside the curtain that hid the beautiful little form which, at his previous look, had lain so straight and still upon its leafy couch.

'O! horror—the lion had already forced its way where the branches were less impervious, and had seized the child with his teeth, attempting to drag it to the ground.

'A moment, and he might have left the dead for a living prey.

'There were but two ways—one, to flee instantly to some small tree; or, to try the effect of his arrow.

'Bravely, he chose the latter.

"It entered between the eyes of the animal, and the form of the child fell from the now quivering mouth.

'A moment of blind rage—a swift spring, which Ortez, who had caught up the child was fortunate enough to avoid—and the animal stumbled forward and fell.

'Laying the child upon its couch, gently and reverently, as one of keen sensibility ever touches the dead, he drew his bow again, and the mighty monster breathed his last.

'The morning light showed the savages how

trustworthy and brave was their guest—not now their captive, for he was in freedom to go or stay. How could he but choose the latter, when Monica's presence was as the sunlight to his soul !

' But when nine years had glided by after this, and Monica had been given by her father to a warrior of her own tribe, the desolate Spaniard began to yearn after that far land which he still called home.

' There was as yet no opportunity for him to embark ; and, while waiting for one, he was suddenly called into action.

' Another expedition had been fitted out against the people who had adopted him.

' He was one of them still—wearing their costume—yielding to their habits. There was no alternative, and, uncertain as to what nation the invaders belonged, he joined a small body of warriors, and met in the enemy his own countrymen.

' Attaching himself to the expedition under De Soto, he performed numerous deeds of courage and bravery, enduring hardship and fatigues which his Indian life had made more endurable for him than for others.

" It is not always woman who is the sufferer and man the saviour," said Martinez.

" No," replied Ned: " and it only proves that there is implanted in the breast of all a heart which, properly trained, ever pants to extend aid and mercy to the suffering or oppressed."

Inez had now somewhat recovered from the confusion into which her adventure had thrown her.

The bloom again returned to her pale cheeks.

Her eye brightened.

The sombre look gave place to a smile.

And once more she felt happy.

Happy in the love of him to whom she had surrendered all that woman holds dear.

The remainder of the evening was passed in pleasant conversation.

Fresh arrangements were made for the morrow, the day's success far exceeded the expectations of either Martinez or the mutineer.

Not yet were either of the lovers tired of the life they were leading on that deserted island.

Love smoothed their path, and strewn around them a halo of brightness and peace.

The good night was spoken, and Ned retired to his own hut.

With a feeling of gratitude and love Inez and Martinez retired to their rude couch, and the beautiful girl sank to sleep upon the breast of him who was now all and all to her.

CHAPTER CIV.

THE CASTAWAYS ON THE ISLAND—HOPES AND
FEARS—THE UNLOOKED-FOR ADVENTURE—THE
RECOGNITION.

DAYS passed, and the castaways on the island spent the time in the chase, or wandering about the place in search of fresh novelties.

In the latter Inez always accompanied them ; and with a most childish glee did she fall into rhapsodies on the beauties of the scenery, which was, indeed, charming in many parts of the island.

Starting one morning a few hours earlier than usual, they extended their walk further than they had hitherto done, and came to a spot where the sea washed high up a sort of cutting, or bay, between the rocks which bounded the island.

The hearts of the two men bounded with joy as they gazed out upon the white-crested waves, as they rolled and sported in the bright sunlight.

An indefinable feeling took possession of their breasts.

But the features of Inez became sad.

" Look, look!" exclaimed Martinez. " Inez, there lies the road to the world—the bright joyous world which for some time has been dead to us. Oh, is not this a sight to make the heart leap with joy! See how the waves roll in at our feet ; then hurry back, with a murmur, as though they bade us come with them!"

Inez heaved a deep sigh.

" Why do you sigh, dear one?" asked Martinez.

" The sight of the sea saddens me," replied Inez.

" Saddens you?"

" Yes."

" Why so?"

" I know not."

" It is because you think of that fearful time we passed on its bosom till we were thrown upon this island," said the lieutenant.

" No, it is not that," she replied.

" What then?"

" Alas !——"

" Speak Inez—tell me what it is that makes you sad," said Martinez, taking her fair hand tenderly in his own.

" Is not this island beautiful?" she asked.

" Aye," replied Martinez—" beautiful as a fairy land."

" Have you not said, that here with me you could pass your life in happiness and peace," she asked.

" Surely, yes."

" Yet the sight of these waves would lure you from this place," said Inez.

" But not from you, Inez—not from you," he replied, hastily.

" Are you not content here?" she asked.

" Yes—yes. But——"

" But you sigh to again join in the giddy throng—sigh to once more return to your native land.

" And do not you, Inez, dear one?" he said.

" No."

" No?" he iterated.

" Indeed, no. Here, with you alone, is far preferable to the inhabited city," she replied.

" Why so, Inez?"

" Because I love you, Martinez ; because here we are happy, basking in each other's love. There—what there?"

And she extended her arm, and pointed over the billows.

" What there?" said Martinez. " Love still."

" For who?"

" For you—you only, Inez," he replied.

" Still would I remain here, Martinez ; here, where all is lovely and peaceful ; here, where the foul breath of scandal penetrates not ; where I am a wife, though no ceremony bound me to you, save my love ; where our home is but the rude branches of trees intertwined ; where our couch is but the dried grass, plucked from the hill-side ; where all is peace, and joy, and love."

" I have no intention of leaving the island," said Martinez.

"No," she replied; "but the thought—the hope—was there," she said, placing her thin white fingers upon his breast.

Martinez replied not.

"Was it not so?" she asked.

"Inez," he said, "I will not deceive you—it was."

"I knew it—I felt it," she said.

"But why should you regret it?" he asked. "Would it not be a joy to return to our native land—to gaze once more upon the features of those we love—to mingle again in the world?"

"To you, Martinez, it might," she said, sadly.

"And to you also, dearest Inez," he said.

"No—to me it would be pain and misery," she replied. "I care not—need not the company of others than yourself. In your love I would live and die,"

"Still could you do so" he replied; "still would you be to me the same as now."

Inez shook her head.

"Martinez,' she said, and her voice quivered as she spoke, "in our native land I should be looked upon with scorn—treated with contempt."

"Why so?"

"Ask your own heart," she said.

"It would reply, 'Your fears are groundless,'" he said.

"It would reply—did it reply truly,' said Inez—"that she who sacrificed all for love of yourself was a wanton whom the lips of chaste and virtuous women should censure and avoid. It would tell you that among the innocent and pure Inez has no place."

"What need you care for the opinion of others?" he asked.

"What need I care?" she iterated.

"Aye, what need you care, or fear my love will not last? Spite of all, you are my wife in the eyes of Heaven. Sheltered by my affections, you could hurl back scorn for scorn," he exclaimed. "You were cast away upon a desert island with me only. Friendship ripened into love. What then?"

"I fell."

"Not so. There were none to perform the formalities which society are pleased to dictate; and which, upon many of those who undergo them, are no more binding than a rotten cord. We consummated that love without the idle ceremony—we registered a vow in heaven, beneath its spangled canopy, to be true to each other till death. That vow never shall be broken, come what may; for I hold it sacred as that uttered before the altar. True love heeds not—fears not—the ungenerous censures of a heartless world; but turns the brighter for them. No, no Inez—if you think that by again joining with the world I should love you less, you wrong me, Inez—wrong me deeply!"

"I would not wrong you for all the wealth of worlds!" she exclaimed, passionately, throwing her arms around his neck—"but here we are happy. No word of censure meets our ears; no glance of coldness meets our gaze. But love—true love—reigns supreme, and turns this uninhabited island into a paradise. Let us, then, remain here—free from the contamination of heartless men and women—surrounded by the beauties of nature, happy in our affections, and at rest from the world."

And she drew the head of the lieutenant down to her lips, and imprinted an ardent kiss upon his cheek.

"As you will, dear one," he said. "I can deny you nothing; so fondly do I love you."

And Martinez strained her passionately to his breast.

Meantime, Ned, not wishing to intrude upon them, when he perceived that Martinez and Inez were in conversation, had strolled some distance away from the spot where they stood.

Suddenly the lovers were aroused by a loud cry from Ned; and, looking in the direction whence it proceeded, observed the mutineer running hastily towards them, and waving his hand for them to meet him.

"Something has alarmed him," said Martinez. "Stay here, Inez; I will go and see what it is."

"Oh, no. no," she exclaimed, hastily; "do not leave me!"

"What do you fear?"

"I know not; but there is a weight at my heart—a foreboding of coming evil."

"Well, we will wait till he comes up to us," said Martinez.

They had not to wait long.

Ned, panting and breathless, stood before them.

"What is the matter?" asked Martinez, eagerly.

"Oh—oh!" panted Ned.

"Speak—speak!" gasped Inez.

"Wait a bit," gasped Ned, "till I get my breath."

Martinez and Inez waited impatiently.

"Well," continued Ned, "seeing as how you was a talking to each other, and knowing as two's company, and three is none, I just strolled a little way on, when all of a sudden I see—"

"What?" exclaimed Martinez.

"What?" gasped Inez.

"A man!" exclaimed Ned.

"A man?" echoed both Martinez and Inez, in the same breath.

"Yes," said Ned—"a right-down real living man."

"Where?" asked Inez.

"There," said Ned, pointing with his finger in the direction from whence he had come.

"What sort of a man?" asked Martinez, in a tone of surprise.

"A short man."

"Yes, yes," said the lieutenant; "but was he an Indian?"

"An Indian?" said Ned.

"Yes."

"No,"

"An European?"

"Yes."

"How came he here?" asked Martinez.

"I didn't stop to ask him," said Ned; "I was so frightened.

"Frightened?" said Martinez.

"Well, not exactly that," replied Ned. "I was so surprised, that directly I see him I turned round and came to tell you."

"Did he see you?" asked the lieutenant.

"I think not," said Ned; "for he had his back towards me."

"What was he doing?"

"Nothing."

"Was he armed?"

"No."

"How was he dressed?" asked Martinez.

"In shirt and drawers."

"Nothing else?"

"No."

"Then, doubtless, he is some poor sailor, cast away, as we have been."

"That's just what I thought," said Ned.

"Shall we seek him, or return without making him acquainted with the fact that there are other human beings on the island beside himself?" asked Martinez.

"It's fearful to feel yourself alone," said Ned.

"It is so," said Martinez.

"Indeed it is. I believe if I had not seen you I should have died with the oppression caused by the loneliness of this place. Let us seek him. Perhaps the sight of us may be as cheering to him as was the sight of you to me."

"Come then, Inez," said her lover—"come, and let us welcome to these shores a fellow-sufferer."

Inez clung to her lover's arms; and they all three moved forward in the direction whence Ned had seen the stranger.

But Inez felt a sad foreboding of evil as she did so.

She knew not why; yet in vain was it that she strove to shake off the feeling.

An instantaneous feeling of dread had taken possession of her breast. Not even the presence of Ned and Martinez could remove it.

On the contrary, it deepened as they went on, and her limbs trembled.

Fain would she have urged them to return.

Yet she feared to do so, lest Ned might believe her cold and callous to the sufferings of others.

On they went, for some distance, when they suddenly came in sight of the figure of a man habited in the manner Ned had described.

He was standing with his back towards them, shading his hands with his eyes, and looking far out into the distance.

"Poor fellow," said Martinez—"he has, doubtless, like us had his sufferings—and more; for evidently he has no clothing to cover him but that in which he stands."

"Been shipwrecked, I expect," said Ned.

"Looks like it," said Martinez.

Ned placed his hands to his mouth, so as to form a kind of speaking-trumpet, and called out:

"Shipmate, ahoy!"

With a bound, the man sprung round, and looked towards them.

Then he clasped his hands together, and stood for a few moments gazing in wonder and surprise upon the running trio.

Then, giving utterance to a wild shout of glee, he sprang forward to meet them.

In a few moments he stood before them.

" God be praised!" he exclaimed—" we are not alone."

As the man gave utterance to these words, Martinez and Inez started.

The fair girl turned deathly pale, and trembled violently.

" Not alone, shipmate!" exclaimed Ned—"not alone!"

" Thank God !" ejaculated the man.

Then he raised his eyes to the face of Martinez, and started back.

" Martinez!" he gasped.

" Ridley!" exclaimed Martinez—"you here!"

" Yes, lieutenant ; and never did I feel more joy in my life than I do at meeting you now."

" How came you here?" asked Martinez, in a tone of bewildered surprise.

" Oh, it is a long story," said the man ; "I will tell you anon. But there is another here beside me. He is very ill. Come—come and see him."

And the man turned and walked rapidly away, ere Martinez could enquire who it was of whom he spoke.

The three castaways followed him till they came to a spot over which the luxuriant foliage of a large tree cast a pleasant shade.

There, lying upon the ground, was the tall figure of a man. Martinez and his companions stepped forward at a sign from the sailor, and gazed upon the prostrate form. Then, starting back, Inez and Martinez simultaneously gasped forth:

" Captain Wildwell !"

CHAPTER CV.

THE ESCAPE FROM THE SLAVER—THE WOUNDED CAPTAIN AND HIS SAVIOUR—LAND IN SIGHT.

WE left Captain Wildwell lying covered with wounds and bathed in blood on the deck of the slaver where he had been prostrated by the inhuman wretches after the mutiny, and where he was left to die, whilst the mutineers drowned the recollection of their bloody work in the fumes of the various spirits which they had broached.

When satiated with drink, and they lay scattered in all directions sleeping off its influence, a man suddenly crept up one of the hatchways, and darting behind a bulkhead stooped down and listened.

Assuring himself that all was still, he stole along the deck, and untying the lashings which suspended a boat at her stern, cautiously lowered it till it rode upon the waves.

Then he returned, and descended the hatchway; and soon again appeared on deck, with a bundle.

He was making his way towards the cabin, to assure himself once more that all was silent, when his foot struck against the prostrate body of the captain.

Stooping down, he examined the features minutely.

Then he placed his hand upon its breast. He suppressed the cry which rose to his lips, and simply murmured:

" He still lives!"

Rising to his feet, he hurried again to the stern, and threw the bundle into the boat. Then he returned to where Wildwell lay, and, raising him in his arms, carried him to the side.

Here he fastened a rope around his waist, and, lifting him up, with some difficulty, held fast to the rope, and lowered the bleeding man tenderly in the boat. Then he seized one of the ropes which still held the boat fast, and slid down it into the boat, beside the captain.

Drawing the knife, he severed the fastenings, and the boat floated away from the ship which had been the scene of such fearful work.

This man was Jack Ridley—a good sailor, and one who had sailed on board the slaver from the time she first started on her unholy work.

For him Captain Wildwell entertained a greater respect than for any other common seaman on board ; and, in return, found a staunch follower in Jack.

He had been forced down the hatchway when the mutiny first broke out, and had been unable to render any assistance to his comrades.

It was not long ere he discovered that the ship was in the hands of the mutineers ; and he knew that if he attempted to make his way on to deck he would assuredly meet the fate of his fellows.

So he secreted himself away in the hold, intending to await the first opportunity that might present itself to escape from the vessel.

In a fearful agony of mind he passed the hours away.

He could hear the rude song and the ribald jest bandied about, as the mutineers sat drinking.

Gradually the uproarious noise grew less and less ; and he knew that they had fallen into a drunken slumber.

Then, he thought, would be his time to endeavour to escape.

With this resolve to try, he groped about the hold to find the steps which led to the deck.

As he did so, his hand came in contact with a bundle.

He pressed his fingers into it, and discovered it to contain biscuits.

They have been given to the slaves by the mutineers, to induce them to look favourably upon the project ; but had not been eaten.

Jack secured these, as, should he be enabled to put his project into execution, they would be of service to him.

Finding the steps, he groped his way up ; and what followed has been already related.

Further and further the boat drifted away from the ship ; and when Jack Ridley had thought he had got sufficiently far out of hearing, he stooped down to get the oars, which were always kept in her, ready for any necessity ; but, to his horror, they were gone.

This was a sad blow; for now there was nothing to guide her but the rudder.

Still Jack knew it was useless to despair—so resigned himself to his fate.

He cast his eyes upon the body of the insensible captain, and, taking off his jacket, he rolled it up, and laid it under the head of the wounded man.

The air was cold ; and the waves, as they dashed upon the little bark, threw the spray over him, and soaked him to the skin : but the rough sailor could not deny his jacket for a pillow to the wounded man.

Ridley cast his eyes up to the heavens, in the hopes of seeing a star by which to direct his course.

But, as though they disdained to shine upon the scene of such hellish slaughter, not one brilliant speck could he detect.

So he sat himself down, and allowed the boat to drift whithersoever it would; and, as the first grey streak of dawn appeared in the eastern horizon, Captain Wildwell showed signs of life, and gasped forth:

"Water—water!"

But water was there none, and Jack Ridley, as he gazed compassionately upon the wounded form before him, cursed himself for not having tried to obtain water before he left the ship.

"It might save him," he thought. "Oh, for a drop of water!"

There was water all around, but not a drop to drink.

He bent over Wildwell.

"Captain," he said.

"Who speaks," gasped the wounded man.

"It's me, captain—do you not see it is me—Jack Ridley?" said the man.

"I cannot see," gasped Wildwell—"all is dark, Jack, have you escaped the hell-hounds?"

"Thank God—yes!"

"Jack, you would do much for me?" exclaimed Wildwell.

"I would, captain."

"Then bury your knife in my heart, and save me from these demons."

"Captain," said Jack, "I will save you if I can, but I will not murder you."

"You will not murder me, Jack—you will but put me out of my misery—free me from fresh tortures these fiends will yet subject me to."

"Fear not, captain," said Jack; they cannot now harm you. You are far from the ship; the glimmer of her sails cannot be seen."

"How—far from my ship?" gasped the poor man with difficulty.

"Yes, captain; I waited till all were drunk and asleep, then I lowered you into a boat and pushed off."

"Ah!" gasped Wildwell, "Jack, I thank you, but better I had been left to die."

"Live, captain, if only to be avenged on the wretches who can repay your kindness by such torture."

"Alas! I am blind—what is life without sight."

"Blind," exclaimed Jack—"Oh, God!"

"Aye," gasped Wildwell!—"I cannot see you, though I hear your voice. Oh, kill me, Jack—be merciful—kill me!"

"I cannot—I cannot," gasped the seaman.

"Then give me a drop of water, I am parched. My tongue cleaves to the roof of my mouth—water, Jack—water!"

"Captain—captain, there is not a drop!" exclaimed Jack.

"Then death will soon come," gasped the captain. "Heed not me, save yourself. I—I—oh!"

And the head of the wounded man rolled uneasily for a moment and then he again sank into insensibility.

"Heaven be merciful to him!" sighed the good-hearted sailor—"and let him die thus, unless some friendly shore or passing vessel appears in sight."

The sun rose over the vast expanse of waters, and poured down its refulgent beams upon the pale face of the wounded man, as he lay so still in the bottom of the boat.

Higher and higher in the heavens it rose, and nearer and nearer became its rays, till at length even Jack Ridley could not bear them.

He took off his guernsey shirt and spread it over the face of Wildwell to protect him from the heat of the sun.

And now it played furiously upon himself—scorched and blistered his arms and body.

His lips became dry and parched; his tongue clove to the roof of his mouth, and the waters danced before his eyes like liquid fire.

Thirst was telling upon him and fast driving him to madness.

Several times did he stretch forth his hand to dip it into the sea, but the recollection that to drink of the salt water was death restrained him, and with a sigh he drew back his hand.

The sun sank in golden glory into its western bed, and night once more cast her sable mantle over the sea.

Jack Ridley was fast sinking into unconsciousness when a drop of rain fell upon his face.

With a cry of joy he looked upwards, and as he did so a bright flash of lightning illumed the dark heavy clouds above him.

Then the thunder rolled along, and ere its echoes had died away the portals of heaven were opened and a deluge of rain poured down from the clouds.

"Saved—saved!" gasped Jack, as he hastily snatched the guernsey from off the form of the insensible man, so that the cool refreshing drops might fall upon his fevered brow and parched lips.

All that night the storm raged and the wind drove the little boat over the billows with terrific speed.

Towards morning there was a lull in the storm, the flashes of lightning were less frequent and less intense in their brilliancy, and the wind dropped and the boat glided smoothly along.

Morning broke—the cold grey clouds floated up and spread themselves over the dark sky.

With anxious gaze the wearied Ridley looked around, and with a cry of joy he perceived that their boat hugged the coast of, to him, an unknown island.

CHAPTER CVI.

DEPARTURE OF THE PIRATES FROM THE BAY—THE SLOOP OF WAR—THE ENGAGEMENT.

FOR a few moments Lang stood cowering before the haughty glance and defiant mien of Ellen, as, proudly erect, she held the pistol pointed at the head of the pirate captain.

His cutlass fell by his side, and he stepped back a pace.

"Father!" exclaimed Ellen, never for a moment taking her eyes from the face of the pirate.

"My child — my Ellen!" gasped Hanfield, rising to his feet.

But, as he was about to fling his arms around her, Wild Madge, foaming with rage, her eyes bloodshot, and her limbs trembling with passion, sprang between them.

"Ha, ha! you thought to escape me," she exclaimed; ' but you shall find that there is no flying from my power."

"Back, wretch!" exclaimed Ellen—" or I may be goaded to rid the world of a fiend more inhuman than painter ever drew. Back, I say, or, by heaven, I will kill thy worthless body!"

" Fool!" shrieked Madge, "think you I fear your weapon, like those cowardly hinds? Imagine not that because you caught me slumbering, and took from my breast the key of the door, and that pistol, that you can escape. No, no; there is no escape for you or him! Fire—if you can. Fools, idiots! tear the weapon from her grasp."

But Lang and his companions hesitated.

"Cowards!" shrieked Madge—"do you fear an unloaded weapon?"

At these words Bond rushed upon Ellen, and grasped her arm.

The fair girl pulled the trigger.

The pistol was not loaded.

A loud and scornful laugh burst from the lips of Wild Madge.

With a cry of despair, Ellen hurled the pistol with all her force at the fury.

It struck Wild Madge on the cheek ; and, as it fell heavily to the deck at her feet, a thin stream of crimson gore trickled down her bloated face.

With a howl of pain, she sprang forward; she seized Ellen by the hair, and shook her violently.

Old Mr. Hanfield forced himself between them.

"Curse you both!" roared Madge; " but you shall suffer for this. By hell! I will torture you till your lives are rendered unbearable. Away with them to the cabin!"

Lang seized Ellen, and Bond grasped the old gentleman, and forced them down to the cabins they had previously occupied, in which they fastened them, and returned to the deck.

At this moment a boat which had been sent to keep watch at the mouth of the cave in which the slaver rode at anchor, concealed by the high rocks, returned to the ship, and gave intelligence that a frigate was on the coast, and that one of her boats, manned and armed, was evidently watching the shore.

"The loss of the girl and her lover, doubtless, has caused this," said Lang; "and should the boat discover our hiding-place, it will not be long before the frigate is bearing down upon us."

"Weigh anchor then" said Wild Madge, " and cut to sea before daylight."

"There is a cargo on shore."

"No matter: not for fifty cargoes would I have that girl and her father escape me. Besides, I am anxious to return to England, and see if something cannot be done to rescue the Boy Rover and his friends."

"As you will," said Lang.

Then pipe up all hands—and to work at once," said Madge.

And she turned and descended to the cabin.

As Madge disappeared down the stairs which led to the cabin, Lang and Hardy piped up the hands.

In a few moments the blacks were on deck.

Surprised at being thus called from their berths, they looked inquiringly at Lang.

"Furl the awnings, and run the anchor up to the bows," said Lang, in a tone of command.

The crew were immediately on the alert. The awnings were furled ; and all the men stretching aft the spring cable hauled the anchor up to her bows.

"Well done, my lads," said Lang.

In a quarter of an hour the slaver was gliding from the bay.

As she passed out from the cover of the higher rocks, her sails began to expand, and she darted through the smooth water with the impetuosity of a dolphin.

The slaver's course was steered in the opposite direction to that in which the frigate lay riding at anchor.

The breeze was favourable, and every stitch of canvass was shook out ; and, when morning broke, the dark outline of the rocks which sheltered the bay looked dim and ghostly.

The sun rose, and the shore faded from the sight.

Nothing but the waste of waters around the slaver could be seen.

Then Lang turned in, after giving a few directions to Bond as to the course he was to keep the vessel.

It was not till the shades of evening began to lower, that Bond, surprised at not seeing anything of Smith, made search for that worthy; and, after some time, discovered him bound, as Bob Bittern and Jacob had left him, in the hold of the vessel.

He had fully recovered from his debauch ; and, in answer to how he had been made a prisoner, stated that the captives had pounced upon him unawares, and bound him before he knew their limbs were free.

Bond released him, and together they retired to the deck.

Night came on, and the vessel still rode safely over the sea, with its freight of misery, and crew of demons.

But when morning broke Lang discovered that the vessel had drifted some distance from her course, and close upon them the white sails of a sloop of war was distinctly visible.

"Confusion!" exclaimed Lang, as his eyes encountered the vessel for the first time ; " we shall have to fight."

"True," said Bond. "We can run, perhaps; but I doubt if it will serve us much. Besides, she cannot carry so many men as us, and if we succeed in capturing her the guns will swell our armament."

"Pipe all men to quarters," said Lang.

This was done.

In the meantime the sloop came steadily on, and her commander believing from the build that the vessel ahead of him was a slaver, made every preparation for battle.

The long gun in the centre was cleared from the encumbrances which surrounded it. Other guns had been cast loose, shot handed up, and every thing prepared for action, with all that energy and discipline which characterises a man of war.

The eyes of Captain Newcome, for such was the name of the commander of the sloop 'Firefly,' were fixed upon the pirate as his vessel bore down upon her.

When she was within a cable's length of her he called out—

"Heave-to, or I'll sink you!"

But the only answer he received from the pirates was a broadside of carronades and heavy volley of musketry.

The broadside, though too much elevated to hit the low hull of the sloop, was still not without effect.

Her fore topmast fell.

The gear of the main gaff was severed, and a large portion of the standing as well as the running rigging came rattling down upon the decks.

The volley of musketry was more fatal, six of the seamen were wounded.

Two fatally.

"Well done," exclaimed Captain Newcome, who was a man who admired bravery and the clever handling of their weapons, even by his foes—"they know how to handle their guns though I should never have given them credit for such work."

"Which they shall pay dearly for," said the lieutenant, who stood by the captain's side.

Captain Newcome gave the order to pour a broadside into the pirate's hull.

The next moment a volley of flame, smoke, and shot was belched from the port holes of the government ship.

"Bravo!" exclaimed the commander. "Starboard; ease off the boom sheet—let her go right round—so—steady, lads!—well done!"

The sloop wore round and ran astern of the pirate.

When Lang observed this he imagined that the sloop, finding she had met with more resistance than she had bargained for, had sheered off, and he gave a loud cheer.

"The last you will give," exclaimed Captain Newcome, as it saluted his ears.

In a few minutes the sloop had run some distance astern of the pirate.

"Now, then," said Captain Newcome, with a smile, "let her come to and about. Man the long gun, and see that every shot is pitched into her, while the rest of you set up a new foremast, and knot and splice the rigging."

The sloop's head was again turned round towards the pirate.

Her position was now right astern of the pirate, and nearly a mile distant.

The long gun amidship was now regularly served—every shot telling upon the pirate, and raking her fore and aft.

"This won't do," said Lang.

"We must try close quarters," remarked Bond.

"We must," said Lang: "her guns are superior to ours."

And he advanced to the wheel, and steered the vessel himself down upon the sloop.

Then he resigned the wheel to the steersman, and, seizing a cutlass, he exclaimed:

"Throw the grapnells aboard of her."

This was done.

The two vessels were locked together.

"Remember," shouted Lang, "that every man fights with a halter round his neck. Follow me!"

Armed with pikes, cutlasses, and pistols, the pirates endeavoured to force their way on to the deck of the sloop.

But several times were they driven back by the brave British tars, who fought with a courage never superseded.

But the blacks were four to one; and their impetuous onslaught told fearfully on the British sailors, and they fell back before them, contesting every inch, and making the passage of the pirates slippery with their blood.

Captain Newcome received a blow on his head from a cutlass; and a young sailor, springing over him, as he fell, dealt a death blow at his assailant; but, ere he could again raise his weapon, the cutlass of Lang had sunk deep in his skull, and he fell heavily upon the body of his commander.

With the fall of their captain, the courage of the seamen sank low; and the blacks, headed by Lang and Hardy, poured on to the deck, and drove the sailors down the hatchways, and over the side of the sloop, into the sea.

Then a loud shout rose from the throats of the demons, as Lang rushed to the mast, and tore down the colours.

The ship was now in the hands of the pirates; and, although the loss they had sustained in their crew was great, their gain in arms and ammunition was still greater; and a smile of gratification lit up the features of Lang, as he shouted:

"Victory! victory!"

CHAPTER CVII.

THE PIRATES PLUNDER AND SINK THE SLOOP—
THE DEBAUCH—FATE OF THE MERCHANTMAN.

At the first report of the guns Wild Madge had come on deck; and, despite the danger to which she was exposed, she remained there during the whole time of the engagement.

The pistol which had been wrested from Ellen she had loaded; as also another one, which she had taken from a chest in her cabin; and she concealed them both in her breast.

She resolved that should her vessel be conquered, that Ellen and her father should never escape.

There was a bullet in each of the weapons she carried.

And, in the event of the pirates falling into the hands of the British, they were destined to find a home in the breasts of her victims.

Wild and extravagant was her joy when she saw the colours of the ill-fated "Fire-fly" lowered, and heard the shouts of the blacks proclaiming their victory.

Then she returned to her cabin, and pouring out a tumbler of brandy, drank it off, as though it had been water.

Her bloodshot eyes lit up with an unnatural lustre, and a demoniac smile played around her mouth.

"More blood," she exclaimed—"more misery! Oh, how it glads my heart! Ha, ha!—my boy shall yet have another well-armed ship, to carry desolation in its wake, till my revenge is satiated."

Again she drank of the fiery liquid, and once more returned to the deck.

In a few moments Lang stood beside her.

"You have done well," she said.

"We are victorious," he replied, wiping the perspiration from his face with the back of his hand.

"Are all dead?"

"No," he replied—"the greater number are; the rest are under the hatches."

"That is well."

"What is to be their fate?" asked Lang.

"Will any of them join us?" asked Madge.

"I don't think it is likely," replied Lang.

"Why not?"

"Because they are the real sailors—the pride and boast of England," said Lang.

"Were they foreigners they would save their lives," said Madge.

"They are English," said Lang, "and prefer death to dishonour."

"Fools!"

"So I think."

"Let them have their own way," said Madge "If they prefer death, 'tis their own fault. Give them the chance to live; for wo need more white men on board. But, if they refuse, let them go down with the bark."

"Then she is to be scuttled?" said Lang.

"Of what use is she to us? She would but encumber our movements. Take all out of her that is worth the having, and then let her be scuttled. Dead men tell no tales; sunken ships bear no evidence."

"True," replied Lang.

"See to it quickly, or a passing vessel may learn our character."

"Down with the black flag," said Lang, "till we wish to announce our character again."

In an instant the black flag, which had been run up to the mast-head as the "Fire-fly" poured in her first volley, was lowered.

"Throw these bodies overboard," said Madge, pointing to the blacks who had fallen from the fire of the sloop.

This order, too, was quickly obeyed; and, one by one, the dead Africans were thrown into the sea.

One or two were only wounded, but Madge motioned with her hand to hurl them overboard.

"We cannot be hampered with dying men," she said.

And so they consigned them to the deep.

"Now we will get the guns and ammunition of the sloop on board of our own ship," said Lang.

With a cheer the men rushed to perform their duties.

It was again night ere the pirates rested from their labours; and the pirate ship rode lower in the trough of the sea from the increased weight of her now superb armament.

Then an appeal was made to the sloop to become pirates.

But one and all refused.

Then Lang gave the order to scuttle her. Holes were bored in the bottom of the vessel; and, as the moon rose over the dancing waters, the sloop sunk into her ocean-bed, with the brave fellows in her hold, who scorned to live at the sacrifice of honour.

Then the sails of the "Scorpion" were once more unfurled, and she danced proudly over the waves.

Success but engendered a longing for fresh conquests; and Lang, placing the glass to his eye, scanned the horizon.

But they were alone upon the deep, and the pirates descended to end the day in debauchery and drunkenness.

Elated by their victory, and fired with drink, it was not long ere a scene of riot took the place of the quiet and orderly conduct which had prevailed so lately on board the "Scorpion;" and, one by one, the Africans fell, and sunk into slumber, completely overcome by the fumes of the liquor which had been broached for them to drink success to their future undertakings.

The ship was now allowed to go pretty nearly her own course; and, had an avenging hand be nigh, she would then have fallen an easy prey to any vessel with a few brave men on board.

But her career of crime and blood had not yet ended.

It was just at daybreak on the second morning after the ill-fated 'Firefly' found a grave in the bosom of the boundless deep, that the look-out hailed the deck with the words—

"A sail on the larboard bow!"

In an instant Lang, who was on deck, seized a glass, and leaping into the rigging gazed out in the direction indicated.

The vessel sighted by the man at the mast-head was bearing down upon them in an opposite course to the pirate, and keeping on her way, all unthinking of the character of the ship which in a few hours they would pass.

"What do you make her out?" asked Smith, advancing to the side of Lang.

Lang took the glass from his eye, saying—

"I can't tell yet, she is too distant."

Then he handed the glass to Smith, and leaped down on to the deck.

Smith made his way into the rigging and looked the glass.

But like Lang he could not discover with any certainty the character of the advancing vessel.

So he descended to the deck.

"Well," said Lang, "what do you make her out to be?"

"Can't judge anything of her till she looms up larger," said Smith.

"It won't be long first," said Lang.

"No, for she is evidently sailing the opposite course to us."

"I imagine so."

"We shall doubtless be within hail about midday," said Smith.

"About that time, I reckon."

"Do you mean to fight?" asked Smith.

"I do," said Lang—"but it will depend upon Madge.

"Yes," said Smith. "But don't it strike you as something strange."

"What?"

"Why, a female commander!"

"Well, it does a little."

"A little?"

"Yes."

"It does me a great deal," said Smith. "I don't half like her interference in things she don't know anything about."

"Well, it's hardly worth while altering it for the present, anyhow," said Lang.

"We are going home to England," remarked Smith, after a pause.

"Yes, and it won't be long before the white cliffs of Old Albion will be seen from the masthead, if nothing happens to us," said Lang.

"Of course you will anchor in the old bay where the 'Venomed Snake' always took up her quarters?"

"I don't know of a better or more secret place," said Lang.

"Nor I. But what shall we do then," asked Smith.

"Unload our cargo, I suppose," answered Lang.

"Yes," drawled Smith, "but what next?"

"Go ashore."

"For what purpose?"

"What purpose?" iterated Lang.

"Yes."

"Why, what do sailors generally go ashore for—have a lark—get drunk, and do as we like," replied Lang.

"Humph!" exclaimed Smith, "is that all."

Lang stepped in his walk, and fixed his glance upon his companion's face.

"What are you driving at," he said, after a pause.

"Ain't we going to try and release the Boy Rover," said Smith.

"Yes, if we can," replied Lang.

"And bear him from limbo to the ship?"

" Yes."

" And make him captain of this ship, and take up your old position of ordinary seaman yourself," said Smith.

Lang started.

" Now a sailor generally wishes to become an officer," said Smith—" but I never knew an officer before now as wished to become a common seaman."

" Whew !" whistled Lang. " I see your drift now : you mean to say that, if we lend a hand to rescue the Boy Rover we reduce ourselves."

" Just so."

" Then I'm blowed if I do," exclaimed Lang, " I've been captain of this ship ever since she fell into our hands, and I'll command her while I can tread her planks !"

" You ought to."

" And I will !"

" Wild Madge intends this vessel for her son," said Smith.

" Does she ?"

" Yes."

" Then perhaps she will find herself greatly mistaken."

" She would if I were captain," said Smith.

" And she shall while I am," said Lang.

" I should not pay much heed to her commands," said Smith.

" I can scarcely do otherwise."

" Why not ?"

" Because though I am captain I am not the chief in command here."

" Then you should be."

Lang turned and paced the deck thoughtfully for some moments.

Smith watched him closely.

He knew full well that if the vessel were handed over to the command of the Boy Rover, his position in her would be no better than any of the blacks.

He was now an officer.

He held a command.

He would still do so.

But he felt assured that he would be deprived of it the moment the Boy Rover stepped on to the decks.

Hence he had only been too happy to set the power of Wild Madge at defiance.

He must induce Lang to do so ere they arrived at England.

He believed he had said enough to lead Lang to do so.

Lang had never thought of losing his position if the Boy Rover should be rescued.

But the words of Smith had set his mind at work.

Presently he stopped before his companion, and said :

" Take no notice about what we have been speaking of for the present. I will think of it. Now we have something else to do."

And, taking up the glass, he again looked in the direction of the vessel.

She was keeping on her course, and now loomed up larger and clearer, and Lang had little difficulty in making out her build.

" Can you make her out now ?' asked Smith.

" I think so."

" What is she ?"

" A brig."

" Her build ?"

" English."

" What do you take her to be ?"

" A merchantman."

" Good," said Smith.

" Run up the union jack," said Lang ; " it may avert any suspicion as to our real character."

This order was obeyed.

" Ease her off a couple of points," said Lang.

This was done.

" Now clear for action," he said ; " for, if the wind keeps fair, we shall soon be within hail."

The men set to work with a will, encouraged by their late victory, and the hope of further reward.

The two vessels still kept on their course—each rapidly nearing the other.

Wild Madge came on deck, and enquired the cause of the preparations.

" A vessel in sight," replied Lang.

The eyes of the fury sparkled ; but she said no more.

The eyes of all were now rivetted upon the stranger, as she came up, hand over hand, at a good speed.

As Lang had predicted, it was mid-day before they were in hailing distance of each other.

Then he gave the order for all hands to go to their duty ; and the utmost silence reigned throughout the ship.

Then seizing his speaking-trumpet, Lang leaped into the nettings, and bawled out :

" Ship ahoy !"

" Hallo !" came back in reply from the stranger's deck.

" What ship ?"

" The ' Mermaid.'"

" Where from ?"

" London."

" Where to ?"

" Cape of Good Hope."

" What cargo ?"

" Merchandise and passengers.

At this the eyes of the blacks lit up with a demon glare.

There were women on board, they doubted not.

This was an inducement to fight, if nothing else had been.

" What ship ?" came from the deck of the " Mermaid."

" The ' Scorpion,' " replied Lang.

" Where from ?"

" The seas," was the reply.

There was an instant commotion on the decks of the merchantman, and fresh sail was instantly rigged.

" She has a suspicion of our character now," said Lang. " Down with the Union, and up with the black flag, let her be satisfied as to who and what we are."

Down came the Union Jack with a run, and up went the dreaded emblem of piracy.

Sail was now shook out on the ' Mermaid ' and her course was changed.

" She's going to run for it," said Lang.

" Seems like it," said Smith, shading his eyes with his hands to get a better view of the ' Mermaid's return.

" Shot the long gun, and give it to her point blank," exclaimed Lang, at the same time descending from the nettings and hurrying to the side of the man at the wheel.

The " Mermaid" now used her best endeavours to show the pirates her stern ; but Lang seized the wheel, and brought the " Scorpion's" broadside to bear full upon her.

The gun was loaded, and the match applied, but the shot fell short of its intended work.

" Crowd on more sail !" exclaimed Lang.

"Crowd on more sail," exclaimed Lang.

This was done, and the 'Scorpion' darted through the sea at a pace which left no hope for the 'Mermaid' to escape by flight from her pursuer.

Then Lang left the wheel and gave the order to load the long gun again with canister shot.

He took the match himself this time, but waited till he was nearly abreast of the 'Mermaid'

Then he directed the aim and fired.

The cry of pain which arose from the deck of the merchantman told but too truly how unerring had been his mark.

"Lower your boat ;" shouted Lang—" and send your captain aboard, or I'll sink you !"

But the 'Mermaid' only crowded more sail.

During this chase the people on board the 'Mermaid' were in the greatest alarm, but however their apprehensions might have been excited that courage which is so characteristic of a British sailor never for a moment forsook the brave captain.

He boldly carried on sail, and although two or three of his men had fallen, and the ravages of the shot where everywhere around him, he resolved not to strike his colours to the pirate.

But unfortunately for him he had not a single gun on board, and no small arms that could render his courage availing.

The tears of the women, for there were several on board, and the advice of the male passengers overcame his resolves at last, and he permitted himself to be guided by the general opinion.

One of the passengers volunteered himself to go on board the pirate ship, and after a little hesitation a boat was lowered over the side of the 'Mermaid' for that purpose.

Both vessels now lay to within fifty yards of each other, and a hope arose in the breasts of those on board the merchantman that the passengers who had volunteered to go to the pirate might be enabled to avert at least the worst of the dreaded calamity.

Lang awaited the arrival of the person in the boat with some impatience, and as he came over the side he asked—

"Are you the captain of the ship?"

"No, sir," replied the man.

"Why did he not obey my command, and come on board as I requested?"

"The passengers objected to that course."

"What passengers have you on board?" asked Lang.

"Eight women and twelve men."

"Eight women?" said Lang—"that's good."

The face of the stranger paled as he shuddered at this remark.

"Enough," said Lang, "return to your ship and tell your captain to come on board, or I will sink you!"

The man hesitated for a moment then turned to plead for the safety of the females.

But Lang drew a pistol from his belt and presenting it at his head exclaimed—

"Begone, and do my bidding, or I will stretch you dead on the deck!"

"Without a word the man hurried over the side into the boat.

"Hark, you!" said Lang, calling after him—"tell the captain, if he attempts to run I will send such a broadside into his hull as shall shiver her from stem to stern."

The boat returned to the 'Mermaid' and the long gun was once more loaded ready for any emergency.

The passenger was met by the captain at the gangway, and a cry of horror rose from the throats of the females, as they eagerly crowded around him to hear what success his messenger had met with.

The captain resolved to go on board the pirate, and without hesitation he stepped into the boat, taking with him five of the crew—the mate and four able seamen—and pulled for the pirate.

Lang stood by the mainmast with Smith by his side, as the captain and his mate and two of the sailors came on board.

The pirates had armed themselves with cutlasses, and Lang desired the captain to approach while Smith ordered the mate and two sailors to go to the forecastle.

For a moment they hesitated, but at a sign from Lang they were surrounded by several of the blacks, armed to the teeth, and they suffered themselves to be forced away from their captain's side.

Then Lang turned to the captain of the merchant man.

"Why did you not come on board, when I first ordered you to do so?" asked Lang.

"Because I complied with the wishes of my passengers and remained on board my own vessel," replied the captain haughtily.

"It had been better for you had you complied with my orders," said Lang.

"I am not in the habit of obeying the orders of a pirate," replied the captain.

"Keep a civil tongue in your head," said Lang, somewhat chafed by the haughty reply, "or I'll——"

"What?" interrupted the captain.

"Strike you to the deck," exclaimed Lang.

"I expected to meet a coward as well as a villain!" said the captain of the 'Mermaid' in a cool sarcastic tone.

"Damn you!" yelled the pirate, Lang, raising his cutlass.

But the brave sailor flinched not.

"Strike, pirate!" he said—"for I scorn to strike to you."

"Have, then, your wish," exclaimed Lang, goaded to fury by the cool, sarcastic tones of the officer.

And he struck the brave unharmed man a fearful blow on the head with his weapon.

Not a cry—not a groan escaped the lips of the merchant captain.

For a moment he stood erect with the blood pouring down his face, then he staggered and fell heavily at the feet of his murderer.

The two men who remained in the boat had pulled out some little distance from the pirate's side and had seen the murder of their brave captain.

As he fell they bent to their oars and endeavoured to pull to their ship.

But Lang and Smith darted to the side and fired their pistols.

Their aims had been unerring, and the two men fell forward to the bottom of the boat.

"Man the boats," said Lang.

In a few minutes two of the boats were manned by the black demons, each man armed with a cutlass and pistols.

Lang took the command of one, and Smith the other.

When they were ready to push off for the merchantman, Lang, addressing Bond, said:

"Stand ready with the match by the long gun, and if you perceive the least resistance offered to our boarding, rake her decks fore and aft."

Then he gave the order to pull for the ill-fated ship.

As the boats approached the ship the terror of the females became excessive.

They clung to their husbands in despair; and the men, blanched with terror, endeavoured to allay their fears by assuring them that if no opposition was offered the pirates they would only plunder the vessel and depart without doing further violence.

But a few minutes undeceived them.

The pirates rapidly mounted the sides of the merchantman,

As they leapt on to the deck the blacks cut furiously right and left at all within reach.

The females screaming hurried to hide themselves below as well as they were able, and the men fled before them leaving them entire masters of the deck.

Bleeding and terrified the men lay huddled together in the hold, while Lang and his companions proceeded in their work of pillage.

Every thing was hauled on to the deck—every portable article of value heaped for the plunder.

Money, plate, charts, nautical instrument, and everything of consequence, were seized by the pirates and piled on the deck for removal to their own ship.

When nothing more of value could be found, Lang ordered the hatches to be battened down; and when this was done, and the escape of the men from the hold utterly prevented, he descended to the cabin, accompanied by Smith and several of the blacks.

Here he found the females trembling with horror and calling aloud for mercy.

But their agonized cries—their pleading looks, and half-fainting forms—excited no compassion in the breasts of these ruthless men.

On the contrary, it seemed only to fire their blood, and urge them on to deeds at which the soul revolts.

They were ruthlessly seized by the pirates, and dragged from their knees, on which they had sank to plead for mercy, and indignities and insults, of the most revolting description, heaped upon them.

Their cries for mercy were heard by those inoffen-

cerated in the hold, who were unable to render them assistance.

But the cries grew fainter and fainter, and agonising sobs only rose from the cabin, where fiends, bearing man's shape, disgraced God's image, and hurled their souls to perdition.

In the space of a quarter of an hour the pirates returned to the deck, and lowered their plunder into the boats.

Then they returned and fastened the half-fainting women in the cabin, and bored holes in the vessel below the surface of the water.

Then the inhuman wretches ascended to the deck, and lowered themselves over the side into their boats.

Lang gave the order to pull away from her side.

As they did so, the cries of the helpless creatures smote their ears, as they called upon the pirates to save them from the waters, which rose higher and higher every moment in the hold of the doomed ship.

But they bent to their oars with loud and mocking laughter, and gained the side of the "Scorpion."

The plunder was thrown on board the pirate, and the wretches made their way on to the deck.

But in a few moments there was a considerable commotion among the blacks; and Lang, who was about to descend to the cabin, was hurriedly called back by Smith.

"What is the matter?" he enquired.

"The blacks are furious," was the reply.

"At what?"

"Their comrades have made them acquainted with what has occured on yonder bark; and they demand that the females be released, and brought on board.

Lang shook his head.

"That won't do," he replied. "The ship is fast sinking; besides, we have women enough on board now."

"There are only two, and they are blacks," said Smith.

"Quite good enough for them," said Lang.

"They swear they will have the white women out of yonder vessel," said Smith.

"And I swear they shan't," exclaimed Lang.

At this moment several of the blacks who had remained on board hurried to the side.

Lang drew his pistol from his hilt, and strode towards them.

"What means this?" he exclaimed.

None answered.

"Speak—what means this?" he yelled, furiously.

A tall African turned and said:

"We are going for the women."

"By whose orders?" asked Lang.

"Our own," replied the man, laying his hand upon the lashing which secured one of the boats.

"Take your hand from that rope," exclaimed the pirate, firmly.

But the man only gritted his teeth, and cast a look of malice upon the pirate captain.

"Take your hand from that rope," exclaimed Lang again, "or, by God, I'll send a bullet crashing through your brain!"

"We will have the women," said the man.

And he commenced unfastening the lashing.

Lang strode forward a couple of paces, and levelled the weapon full at the head of the African.

But the black stirred not.

Lang pulled the trigger.

The report was mingled with a roar of pain;

and, as the smoke curled up over the deck, the defiant black fell forward with a bullet in his brain.

For a moment his companions stood as it were paralysed.

Then they bounded towards the captain.

But Lang had drawn his cutlass.

He struck the first down that came within his reach.

The suddenness and the determination with which Lang met their attack caused the others to fall back; and they stood glaring upon him, undecided how to act.

"Lend me your pistol,' said Lang to Smith, holding out his hand for the weapon, but never for a moment averting his gaze from the row of blacks who stood before him.

Smith placed the weapon on full cock in his hand.

"Look you, men,' he said, in a loud determined voice—"I am captain here. Go to your duty instantly !"

But the men still stood gazing upon him.

Not one stirred.

"To your duties !' exclaimed Lang. "What —do you mutiny?' Fools! is there one among you can navigate the vessel should you succeed in becoming its master? To your duty, I say! Yon vessel is fast sinking, and you would find nothing but corpses in her hold did you board her. Away to your posts at once, and let there be an end of this revolt! It will serve no good purpose. I speak not again; but, as I have slain your leader, so I will you, if you return not to your duty on the instant."

The fierce tone of determination in which these words were uttered, and the knowledge that none on board but the whites could navigate the vessel, caused the men to go to their posts without another word; and, in a few moments, all was again order on board the " Scorpion."

The pirate ship was steered away from the sinking vessel, and she was left to the doom which the murderous hands of the villains had consigned her to.

Lower and lower she sank, till the waves washed over her decks.

Down, down she went, till not a vestige of her could be seen—hiding the fearful evidences of the deeds of those ruthless men in the deep, deep sea!

CHAPTER CVIII.

A MAN OVERBOARD—BOND DARES THE DANGEROUS WAVE—A GALLANT RESCUE.

ORDER being restored, the ' Scorpion' kept on her voyage; but in the course of a few hours she fell in with a gale which lasted several days, and consequently she was kept under close-reefed top sails and storm staysails.

The lengthened period of the gale raised a monstrous swell, but it was long and regular.

On the fourth day the wind abated, but the swell continued and in the evening there was a little wind.

It was just then that a circumstance occurred which nearly put an end to the career of Bond.

During the day-watch, between seven and eight, some hands being employed in the foretop, the other watch at supper, and Lang and Smith seated smoking in the cabin, Bond being at the helm, he heard a cry apparently rising from the sea.

Surprised he ran to the side of the ship.

Looking over he saw a youthful black struggling in the water and fast going astern.

He had fallen out of the fore chains and it was his voice that Bond had heard.

One hasty look the pirate gave at the struggling wretch, and then he shouted loudly—

"A man overboard!—a man overboard!"

The cry reached the ears of Lang and his companion in the cabin.

With a bound the captain sprang to his feet, and rushed upon deck followed by Smith.

Scarce had his foot touched the deck than Lang called out—

"Helm a-lee!"

A man sprang to the wheel.

The ship went about and then fell round, driving first before the swell, till at length she was brought to.

But as soon as this was done, and the men, who now scrambled on deck were awaiting the next order, Lang looked out at the struggling swimmer and shook his head,

"He must perish," he said—"for the swell is so high, that to send out a boat would be perfect madness.

"Why so?" asked Smith.

"She could not live in such a sea—and we can better lose one man than a whole boat-load," replied Lang.

"He is not more than a hundred yards from the ship," remarked Bond, coming to the side of Lang—"and there is a possibility of swimming to him with the aid of the deep water line, which is quite strong enough to haul two or three men on board."

"And who would be likely to undertake such a foolhardy task?" asked Lang. "Not you, I think, Bond?"

Piqued at the tones of the captain, Bond exclaimed—

"I'll go myself."

"You?"

"Yes, me!"

"Are you mad?"

"No—I am not," replied Bond; "only it shall not be said I hadn't got pluck enough to save a messmate."

And as he spoke he flung off his cap and jacket and made the line fast to his body.

"You'll never reach him," said Lang,

"I'll try, at any rate," answered Bond—"so here goes."

And mounting the bulwarks he leaped from the ship's side into the sea.

A shout of admiration broke from the lips of the assembled blacks.

And eagerly they rushed to the side to gaze at him as he struck out to reach the unfortunate black.

The sea line was new and stiff in the coil, so that Bond, not drawing it close round his body, it slipped and he swam through it.

But fortunately he caught it by his feet and made it secure by putting one hand and arm through the noose.

He then struck out direct for the black, and found that he could swim with ease, owing to the buoyant nature of the water.

Bond had not swam more than half way before the line got foul in the coil on board and checked

the swimmer so suddenly that it pulled him backwards and under water.

He, however, recovered himself quickly, and struck out again.

During this time, to clear the line on board they had cut some of the entangled parts, and in the confusion and hurry, severed the wrong portion.

Through this, Bond had half the coil of line hanging to him; and was likewise adrift from the ship.

Lang noticed this in an instant, and immediately hailed him to return.

But, from the noise of the waves, he could not hear what those on board said.

He believed they were encouraging him to proceed.

He swam on with increased vigour.

He shouted in return, to show that he had confidence in himself.

He easily mounted the waves, as they breasted him; for he was a superb swimmer.

Still he made but slow headway against such a swell; and it was only at intervals that he could get a glimpse of the struggling African when on top of the white-crested waves.

But on he went, resolved to prove to Lang and the others that he had a little courage in him.

But soon Bond began to feel the weight of the severed line upon him.

Then it was he began to fear he would be unable to hold out.

His strength too was becoming exhausted, and his strokes less powerful.

He began to repent his rashness.

He thought he had only sacrificed himself without any chance of saving the African.

He persevered, nevertheless; and having, as he guessed, come to the spot where the black was, he looked, and, not immediately seeing him, he was afraid he was gone down.

But, when he had mounted the next wave he saw the poor fellow in the hollow, almost spent with his long exertions to save himself from a watery grave.

Bond swam to him, and, hailing him, found he was still sensible, but utterly exhausted.

Bond stretched forth his hand.

With a cry of joy, the black seized it.

"Hold on to my hand," exclaimed Bond; "but if you cling to my body we shall both perish."

The black promised to obey.

Bond then signalled to those on board to haul him to the vessel.

For then he had not the least idea that the line had been cut.

But, as he cast his eyes towards the ship, a cry of horror escaped his lips.

He perceived that the vessel was at least a quarter of a mile distant.

His heart sank within him.

Full well he knew that the line was but one hundred fathoms in length.

In a moment he realised all the horrors of his position.

He saw at once that he had been cut adrift.

All the horrors of his situation rushed upon his mind.

He felt that he was lost.

But, although death appeared inevitable, he resolved to struggle for life.

But the weight of the rope was now weighing him down more and more.

While swimming forward, it trailed behind; and

although it impeded his way, he did not feel half its weight.

Now, however, as it was slackening, it sank deep, and drew his body down with it.

The waves, too, which while he breasted them, and saw them approach, he rode easily over; but, being now behind them, they broke over the heads of the two swimmers, burying them under, and rolling them over, with the force which they struck upon their exhausted frames.

Bond endeavoured to disengage himself from the line; but the noose was so jambed—and having the black in one hand—he could not possibly effect it.

He was about to give up in utter despair, when he saw that the pirates were getting out the boat.

Lang, who would not have the boat put out to save the life of the black, now that he saw a prospect of losing his old messmate, altered his mind, and gave the order to lower the boat to their rescue.

It was, indeed, an anxious time for Bond; but, in a few minutes, he had the satisfaction of seeing the boat clear the ship, and pulling round her bows.

The danger, however, was so great, that, when Lang had her launched, he could only prevail upon three men to go with her on her errand of mercy.

Her course through the mountainous sea was indeed slow; but the sight of her endowed Bond with renewed courage and strength.

The exertions he made were almost incredible.

He was often under water with the black, and rose again to fresh exertions.

Thus they struggled for life.

At length a crested wave broke over them, and down they went, several feet under the water.

The force of the sea drove the affrighted black against him.

The African seized Bond now by the loins, with his head downwards.

The bold sailor struggled to disengage himself.

It was impossible.

He gave himself up for lost.

He kicked and plunged with all his force to shake the black from his hold.

But the African only clung the tighter.

What was to be done?"

A thought struck him.

Being head downwards, he dived deeper, although he was nearly suffocated from holding his breath so long under the water.

But that had the desired effect.

The African, perceiving that Bond was sinking, instead of rising with him, let go his hold, that he might gain the surface.

Bond turned and followed him and drew his breath once more.

Another moment and both had perished.

Bond now no longer thought of saving the black.

He struck out for the boat which was now fortunately near him.

Perceiving this, the African called pleadingly upon him to save him.

For a moment Bond hesitated.

He feared that the black would again endanger his life.

But bad as he was he was not wholly lost.

He felt somewhat recovered from his exhaustion. and he perceived the boat was close at hand.

He resolved to turn and help the black.

He gave him his hand charging him not to grapple with him or he would leave him to his fate.

Again he renewed the arduous struggle of keeping himself as well as the black above the water.

His strength was now all but gone, and every few moments they sunk and rose again.

Oh! how slowly the boat appeared to move towards them.

Fainter and fainter became their struggles, yet they held up.

Gradually his senses deserted him, and his mind wandered away to long-forgotten scenes. The home of his childhood was before him—he stretched forth his hand to grasp at his mother's dress, and he fell heavily to the ground.

A cry of pain escaped his lips, and he opened his eyes to see those who manned the boat lift the African over its side and lay the black beside him in the bottom.

Then he closed his eyes again and was lost to all consciousness.

There was great danger and difficulty in getting again to the ship.

More than once the boat was half filled with water from the following seas.

When after much exertion the boat gained the ship there was great difficulty in getting the sufferers out, as, had they approached too near, the boat would have been dashed to pieces.

Lang seeing this gave orders for lowering the tackle from the yard-arms.

This was speedily done.

The three men who had so gallantly volunteered to man the boat clambered up them leaving the sufferers in the boat to take their chance of being got on board, or the boat being stove in pieces against the vessels side.

This, however, was not the case or Bond and the African must have inevitably perished.

They got them on board at length, but not without considerable damage to the boat.

Few cared for that so long as their comrades were saved.

When Bond was hauled on board the line was still round his form, and the poor fellow had been supporting the weight of seventy yards of rope.

They carried him to his hammock and poured some brandy down his throat, and in spite of the adventures he had passed through, the next day saw him pacing the deck as well as ever.

CHAPTER CIX.

THE EXPEDITION—THE ASSAULT ON THE FORT—DEFEAT OF THE ISLANDERS—RETURN TO THE FRIGATE.

AT the hour named for the expedition to start from the frigate, Henry Chambers came upon deck, armed with a pair of pistols and a cutlass.

The crews of the boats which were to start on the expedition were all mustered on deck.

Captain Parry stood on the quarter-deck, scanning the shore with his glass, when Henry, placing his hand to his cap, announced himself as ready to start.

"Good morning, Mr. Chambers," said the captain; "and I trust it may prove a good morning to us."

"I hope so, sir," replied the youth.

"It strikes me there will be hard work for you,"

said the captain. "There is an unusual amount of bustle on shore."

"Indeed, sir!"

"Yes."

"They cannot suspect a visit from us, I should say," replied Henry.

"Those whose acts will not bear the strictest investigation are often suspicious; and they may fear that the presence of this ship bodes them no good."

"And are making preparations to defend themselves, sir," remarked Henry.

"Such I believe to be the cause of the bustle on shore," said Captain Parry, taking the glass from his eye, and turning to our young friend.

"If there be resistance to be met with," said Henry, "the men who tread the deck of the "Swallow" well know how to meet it.'

"Aye, sir," said the captain, as a proud smile curled his lip — "a braver crew never broke a biscuit."

"They will do their duty, sir."

"Or die," said Captain Parry.

Then, turning, he gave the order for the men to embark.

In a few minutes the pinnace and cutter were manned.

Captain Parry watched them eagerly as they passed over the side into the boats.

Then, as Henry prepared to follow, the captain extended his hand to him.

The youth grasped it fervently.

"You have a double object in view, Mr. Chambers," he said—"that of doing your duty to your country, and rescuing your friends, whom you believe to be concealed on shore. I wish you every success; and I am well assured that your anxiety to accomplish the one will not lead you to forget the other."

"Sir," said Henry, with kindling eyes, "I trust that I shall never forget that my first duty is to my country. My friends are indeed dear to me, but the honour of the flag under which I serve is far more dear."

"I am sure of that."

"And, sir, no act of mine shall ever induce me to forget it. I love the old rag, and, whilst I have strength to wield a cutlass. I will fight to keep her flying and untarnished."

"Bravely spoken!" exclaimed the captain— "but they are words that would come from the lips of every true sailor."

"They are, sir; and I trust that we shall return to the ship with the proof of them proudly floating in the breeze."

And, once more shaking the hand of the captain, Henry dropped into the stern sheets, and, waving an adieu, gave the order to pull for the shore.

With a loud cheer, the gallant fellows bent to their oars, and the boats bounded away from the vessel's side, under the long and even strokes of the men-of-war.

Each boat was armed with a pivot-gun—to be worked to cover the landing of the men should they meet with resistance on the beach from the fishermen smugglers.

A grim old tar stood ready—match in hand—to send a shower of grape and canister among those who were inclined to dispute the passage of his messmates towards the ruined fort.

But all along the beach seemed to be deserted.

Not a soul was to be seen.

The inhabitants of the island, however, were on the watch.

Feeling assured that the escape of Henry to his vessel would bring down upon them a visit from the frigate, and knowing that what he had seen in the vaults of the fort must have revealed the true motive of their calling, they had armed themselves to repel any force that might be sent from the ship.

Counting upon the aid of the crew of the slaver they believed that they could defend themselves in the fort.

But this hope died away with the approach of morning.

The slaver was discovered to have weighed anchor and put to sea.

This was a sad blow to their hopes, but knowing that they would certainly be arrested and punished for aiding and abetting pirates and smugglers, they resolved to defend themselves to the last.

Every person, therefore, capable of bearing arms took up their position in the fort and resolved to fight to the death.

With the first streak of dawn the approach of the boats was observed, and barricading the entrances the fishermen smugglers awaited the summons to surrender.

In the course of half an hour after the boats were sighted from the fort, Henry gave the order for his men to land.

This order was followed by the captain of the other boat.

When the men had stepped on to the shore, Henry and his fellow officer consulted for a few moments as to the means of attack.

It was decided that each boat's company should march towards the fort, Henry's crew taking one side and Bentley's the other; and on with even and determined strides the sailors marched.

Still, not a soul was to be seen, but Henry knew too well that he would have to expect anything but an undisputed passage.

He kept his eyes anxiously fixed upon the fort, but moved steadily onward.

They had got within a hundred yards of the building when he perceived the heads of several men just above the walls.

"Quick march!" he exclaimed—"or a shower of bullets will be amongst us."

The sailors started forward in a quick run.

And well it was they did so, for the next moment twenty muskets belched forth their murderous messengers.

But the bullets flew over the heads of the sailors, and with a loud cheer they dashed on right under the walls.

Henry led them to the small door through which himself and his friends went on the day before, and ordered the men to cut it down with their hatchets.

Several of the sailors, who were supplied with this weapon, struck heavy blows upon the door, and endeavoured to break it open.

"Stand close to the walls," exclaimed Henry, "and don't leave them a mark for their aim."

The men in the fort poured volley after volley down from the ramparts; but the sailors stood close to the wall, and the bullets fell harmless some feet from them.

The repeated blows of the axes soon told upon the door; and, in the course of a few minutes, it was almost beaten to splinters.

Then, with a cheer, Henry drew one of the pistols from his belt, and, waving his cutlass above his head, dashed into the narrow passage, followed by the men.

It was quite dark, and anxiously he felt with his foot for the trap in the flooring.

It was open.

He stretched forth his hand, and hurled it down into its rest, and dashed on.

Just as he had gained the end of the passage, which led into a large square apartment, the report of several muskets reverberated like thunder through the passage, and the balls struck the wall above his head.

The flash of the pieces, and the dim light of the early morning, revealed the forms of several of their foes at the farther end of the apartment.

With a cheer to his men, he dashed towards them.

The impetuosity of the attack seemed to strike them with terror; for they fled towards a broad staircase, that led to the ramparts.

Henry discharged his pistol—as did also several of the sailors—and again dashed forwards.

Two of the defenders of the fort were wounded, and fell upon the steps; and the seamen bounded over them, grasping their weapons tightly in their hold.

Henry gained the top step, and stood upon the ramparts.

Hurriedly, he cast his glance along on either side.

The ramparts were filled with the rough uncouth men who inhabited the beach, armed with every available weapon.

The moment that Henry appeared at the head of the stairs, they raised a loud cry, and dashed towards him. But the youth was on his guard.

"Close in," he exclaimed to his followers, "and let every blow tell."

A lusty cheer, from the throats of the brave seamen, answered him as he sprang forward and aimed a blow at the head of his foremost opponent.

But the man received the blow upon his own steel; and, as the weapons clashed together, the sailors poured in a volley from their pistols, and the fight became general, all along the ramparts.

The clashing of steel, the report of pistols, the shouts of the combatants, and the groans of the wounded and dying, made up a fearful din, which could be plainly heard by those left in the charge of the boats on the beach.

The sunbeams now tinted the grey clouds, as the refulgent orb of day rose from its bed beyond the waters, and shed a brighter light upon the combatants.

The smuggler fishermen fought with a courage worthy a better cause; and inch by inch did they dispute the passage of their assailants along the ramparts.

The report of the pistols was stilled, for there was no time or opportunity to reload them; but the clashing of the cutlasses, and the loud shouts of the sailors, echoed over the beach.

Many a hard blow was given and received—many a cry of pain rose above the ramparts, and was echoed back from the surrounding rocks; but still the defenders gradually fell back before the furious onslaught of the brave seamen.

Thus the fight continued for about half an hour, when Henry, parrying a blow at his head from a tall powerfully-built fellow, his weapon was struck from his grasp, and he stood at the mercy of his assailant.

With a shout of triumph, the fellow again raised his cutlass; but the young lieutenant drew the discharged pistol from his belt, and hurled it with such violence into the man's face, that he fairly staggered, and the intended blow fell short of its aim.

As the blood poured from the wound inflicted in his forehead, and nearly blinded him, Henry sprang upon him, and grasping his wrist, gave it a fearful twist, at the same time forcing the arm of the man behind him.

With a howl of pain, he relaxed his hold on his cutlass; and the youth, tearing it from his grasp, dealt him a blow on the head with his own weapon, and he fell, stunned and bleeding, at the feet of his gallant foe.

Leaping over the body, Henry still pressed forward, followed by his men.

The defenders gave way; and the seamen, perceiving this, pressed on with increased vigour.

It now became but a work of time—the tide of victory had sat in their favour.

One by one the defenders of the fort were cut down, or sought to fly.

But to escape was impossible.

The second boat's crew, under Bentley, when they had arrived at the top of the broad staircase had turned to the left, whilst Henry's men had turned to the right, and the consequence was that the defenders on the fort were placed between two divisions of their foes, and had to fight, as it were back to back.

As Henry and his men pressed them they fell back upon Bentley's, and were cut down easily, as being so crowed together they could not fight with that freedom possessed by the sailors.

Seeing their companions falling so rapidly, and feeling that it was useless to further extend the battle, the remainder of the defenders called for quarter and laid down their arms.

A loud hurrah broke from the seamen!

The fort was taken!

Henry gave the order to have the prisoners secured, and then the Union Jack was waved over the walls of the fort.

As the wind extended the folds of the proud old rag, a gun was fired on board the 'Swallow,' and those in charge of the boats stood up, and waving their hats cheered lustily.

Securing their prisoners, Henry ordered them to be conveyed to to boats and carried on board.

This was done, Henry accompanying them to obtain further orders of his commander, leaving a few men, under Bentley, in charge of the fortress.

CHAPTER CX.

YARN ON THE SLAVER — CAPTAIN BRADY'S MIRACULOUS ESCAPE.

RATHER stiff with his exertions in the water, Bond was pacing the deck on the following morning, when Lang and Smith strolled towards him.

"Well, I reckon you had a very narrow escape from your foolhardy adventure of yesterday," remarked Lang.

Bond merely shrugged his shoulders.

"I like to see a man of courage," said Lang—"but I dont like to see foolhardiness of the danger you encountered."

"It has served a good purpose, anyhow," said Bond.

"Well, it saved a fellow's life, to be sure."

"It saved all our lives, I think," said Bond.

"How so?" asked Lang.

"It has propitiated the blacks. They hadn't

forgot the death of their comrade by your hand, and only awaited a favourable opportunity to mutiny. But my risking my life for one of their people has made us popular again with them."

"Ah?" exclaimed Lang—"Is it so?"

"Yes," said Bond. "So if I run into danger to save the blacks I have the satisfaction of knowing that I also saved ourselves."

"It's the most narrow escape I ever saw," said Smith.

"It aint so narrow a one as Captain Brady had with the Indians," said Bond.

"Captain Brady—who was he?" asked Lang.

"Haven't you heard of him?" said Bond.

"No."

"Nor I," said Smith.

"Well I'll tell you who he was and what he did," said Bond—"if you like to listen for five minutes."

"Do so," said Lang, seating himself on a bulkhead. I like to hear of adventures, they sometimes suggest a means of escape when danger threatens,"

Smith and Bond seated themselves by the side of their captain, and the latter commenced.

"I've had a narrow escape, it's true, but then I had at least friends to help me ; now this man I have mentioned was alone with none but enemies around him, and yet in spite of the danger in which he was placed his courage never for a moment forsook him, and it is almost wonderful how he escaped an apparently inevitable doom :

'During the early settlements in the western part of Pennsylvania and the north-western portion of Virginia, the hardy adventurers into those then wilderness solitudes at times suffered severely from the incursions of the Indians.

'In 1780, a very large body of warriors, from the vicinity of the Cuyahoga Falls, came suddenly down upon the unprotected frontier.

'Before any check could be put to their ravages they succeeded in murdering and plundering a great number of the whites, and effected their retreat in safety.

'At this time there was a well-known Indian hunter in that vicinity—one Capt. Samuel Brady, whose many daring exploits and hair-breadth escapes had rendered him as famous throughout that region as his contemporary, the celebrated Daniel Boone, was in Kentucky.

'He had under his leadership a goodly number of as brave and daring spirits as himself, and he at once called them together, selected a certain number for the expedition, and set out on the trail of the savages, hoping to overtake them and inflict a severe chastisement before they should reach their villages.

'In this respect, however, the captain and his friends were disappointed, for the Indians had gained a start which enabled them to reach their towns in advance of their pursuers ; but, as they belonged to different tribes, it was discovered that they had separated on the bank of the Cuyahoga—one part crossing it and going to the northward, and the other turning to the westward, as it was supposed, to the Falls, where it was known there was a village.

'It was the design and expectation of the gallant captain to take the Indians by surprise ; but the latter, expecting to be pursued by the whites, were prepared to receive them, and it was only by a mere accident that the borderers were saved falling into an ambuscade which would have proved fatal to all.

'Seeing that the Indians were fully prepared for them—that there was no chance of taking them by surprise—that their numbers were at least four times as many as our own—our friends judiciously determined upon a retreat ; but they had not got far when the Indians, uttering their wildest warwhoops, set after them in a body.

'Knowing that if his men continued together there would be no hope for any of them, Captain Brady, in order to save as many lives as possible, called out to them to disperse in every direction, and each man to look out for himself.

'By this means he expected to divide the Indians into small parties in their pursuit of single individuals ; and this might have been the result had they not, unfortunately for his own safety, discovered in them their most vindictive and troublesome foe, and at once resolved upon his capture.

'Captain Brady was well known to the Indians. In former times he had hunted with them over those very grounds ; but he had subsequently become their most implacable enemy.

'He had done them so much injury as to create in them a fiendish desire to take him alive and put him to the torture—they well knowing that the accomplishment of this purpose would not only rid them of the man they both hated and feared, but would deprive the whites of their bravest and most daring leader, and would thus strike a more effective blow against the latter than would the destruction of a dozen or twenty men of lesser note.

'For this reason, therefore, the moment it was ascertained he was one of the party, his capture was determined on by all ; and, turning from the pursuit of the others, the whole yelling crew set after him.

'Near the spot where Brady was standing, a rude plank bridge stretched over the Cuyahoga River ; and across this he determined to attempt his escape.

'Some of the Indians, divining his purpose, placed themselves on the bridge to intercept him. The brave captain, nevertheless, did not hesitate. Dashing across the plank, he hurled several of his assailants into the stream, and, eluding the others, he reached the opposite bank, and fled at his utmost speed.

'Captain Brady had something of the start, and was one of the fleetest runners on the border. That he could distance and escape from a few he was sanguine enough to believe ; but when he saw the whole body of savages in chase of himself, his very heart seemed to die within him.

'What chance had he of escape, indeed—single-handed and alone—afar from the refuge of even a wilderness fort—and with fifty infuriated Indians in hot pursuit, urged on by a spirit of revenge, and resolved, above every other earthly consideration, upon taking him, alive or dead?

'Near the point were the race first started, the Cuyahoga makes a bend to the south, so as to nearly enclose an area of several square miles in the form of a peninsula.

'The direction taken by Brady soon brought him within this enclosure ; and the Indians, by extending their lines to the banks of the stream, at the point where they most nearly approach each other, considered him as in a net, and announced their satisfaction by yells of triumph.

'There was now, in fact, no chance for him to escape through their lines or across the Cuyahoga River ; and considering that the foremost pursuers were not fifty yards behind him, either of these chances were regarded as impossible.

'Still the hardy and gallant captain did not despair. He had many a time hunted over this very ground, and knew every inch of it, and all the windings, turnings, and peculiarities of the rivers, as well as the Indians themselves. He knew, too, there was one point where the river, compressed within a few feet, rushed roaring and foaming through a rocky gorge; and it at once occurred to him to shape his course for this point, and make a bold desperate leap for the other shore.

'He might fall short, and be dashed to pieces upon the rocks beneath, it was true; but this would only be a quick and sudden death. The awful tortures of the stake awaited him if taken alive; and to take him alive was unquestionably the design of his pursuers.

'Bounding forward with renewed energy, and with a bare hope of life before him, he fled with a speed that few could equal, slightly gaining upon the fleetest of his foes, but not sufficiently, during the whole race, to take him beyond the easy range of a rifle-ball.

'Nearer and nearer he came to the rushing and foaming stream; and as he heard the roar of the waters, and saw that but a few seconds could intervene between the present and the awful leap which might save or destroy him, his heart beat wildly, and his whole frame seemed to tremble with the intense concentration of his mind upon the fearful venture.

'Nearer and nearer he came; louder grew the roar of the waters; the awful chasm gradually yawning before him, and the white spray of the fearful torrent rising to his view; the Indians yelling behind, and his only hope here: and then contracting his muscles, as his feet lightly pressed the precipitous rock, and throwing into them all the power of his concentrated will, he leaped into the air, like a bounding ball, and landed safely upon the other rocky verge of the abyss, striking a little below the height from which he sprung, but passing a clear distance of twenty-two feet between the mural shores.

'Instantly grasping some bushes which fringed the verge of the awful chasm, to prevent himself from falling back into the seething stream, the gallant captain stood for a few moments, panting from his exertions, and striving to recover his breath for still another flight.

'In those few moments the Indians appeared upon the opposite bluff, expecting to find that he had been dashed to pieces on the rocks below; but on discovering him safely on the opposite side, their astonishment was so great as involuntarily and simultaneously to draw from them some two or three short approving whoops, forgetting, in their first surprise, that he was clearly beyond their reach, and not seeming to recollect it till he had begun to vigorously climb the ridge above him in his further efforts at escape.

'Then, drawing up their rifles, with a quick aim, they poured in upon him something like a regular volley, most of the balls whistling close around him, and one of them lodging in his hip, and inflicting a severe and painful wound.

'Notwithstanding this, the gallant fellow continued his ascent, and, on reaching the top of the ridge, gave a yell of defiance, and disappeared on the other side.

'Captain Brady was now aware that the Indians would have to make a considerable circuit in order to reach him; and, had he not been so severely wounded, he would have considered his escape as almost certain; but knowing he would still be followed, and finding his wound very painful, and the cords of his leg fast stiffening, he cast about him for some place to secrete himself from their search.

'After running a short distance, he discovered a pond, and near the shore a large oak which had fallen into it.

'There might be nothing better than this; and, hurrying forward with all all his might, he boldly plunged in, and swam under water to the tree, and came up beneath the trunk and among the branches, in such a manner as to be barely able to breathe without exposing any portion of his person to his enemies.

'Here, in a state of mind which may be imagined, but cannot be described, the gallant borderer remained for a long time, watching his enemies as they collected, one by one, along the shore at the point where his bloody trail had disappeared in the water.

'Still resolved upon finding him, either living or dead, the savages were by no means disposed to give up the search; and, after running along the shore for a considerable distance, on either side of his trail, to ascertain, if possible, where he had emerged from the water, several of the party plunged in, swam out to the oak, and actually seated themselves upon it, while they conversed in their own language, which he understood, concerning his wonderful escape.

'At last, with such feelings of joy as no one not similarly circumstanced might comprehend, he heard them state their belief that he was drowned, and his body lost to them by being sunk in deep water; and soon after this, to his still greater joy, they quietly returned to the shore, and, one by one, all gradually disappeared.

'Remaining in his uncomfortable position till he considered it safe to leave, the captain swam back to land, and set off on his journey home, which he eventually reached, more dead than alive, and where he found the companions of his perilous expedition.'

"Well, I reckon he stood about as near a chance of going to Davy Jones's locker as you did yesterday," remarked Lang, when Bond had concluded his recital of the adventures of the famed Captain Brady.

"And a little more," remarked Bond.

"Well, I still think as I did before," remarked Lang—"that you were a confounded fool to run the risk you did to save the black varmint."

"Well, if he was a black, he was still a man, wasn't he?" exclaimed Bond.

"And a brother," answered Lang, sarcastically; "though I don't care much myself about such relationship."

"Any how, he was a comrade," said Bond.

"So he is," drawled Lang; "and if he had been a white man I might possibly have felt some sympathy for him, but being a blackey, why, I don't care a fig whether he sank or swam, that's all."

"That ain't standing by the rules," said Bond, "which makes all on board equals."

"Do they?" said Lang. "Then I don't acknowledge the justice of *that* rule: I can't make a thick-lipped black the equal of a white man, let him be ever so stained in crime."

And, rising from his seat, he strode away towards the cabin.

CHAPTER CXI.

THE SECOND EXPEDITION TO THE BEACH—THE FRUITLESS SEARCH—THE TIMELY DISCOVERY—FATE OF THE RUINED FORT.

THE anxiety of Henry Chambers to gain some knowledge respecting the fate of his friend Charles Lawson and the beauteous and unfortunate Ellen, induced him to question his prisoners as they were conveyed to the frigate.

But from them he could gain no satisfactory information.

At first he attributed it to the fact that they felt an animosity towards him, and a pleasure in his suspense.

But their manner soon led him to believe that they spoke truly when they denied all knowledge of the whereabouts of the young lovers.

Scarcely knowing what to think he lapsed into silence, and spoke not another word till the boat was brought up alongside the frigate.

Captain Parry, who had been anxiously awaiting the boat, greeted him kindly as he came over the side.

"I knew that the old flag would fly from the walls, yonder," he said.

"Yes, sir," replied Henry, "and I am happy to say our loss is but trifling."

At this moment those who had remained on board gave a loud cheer for their comrades who had gone the expedition.

Captain Parry turned quickly and a shade of displeasure passed over his face.

But in a moment it died away, and a smile lit up his bronzed countenance.

Raising his hat, he waved it above his head as the sailors leapt on to the deck, and another loud cheer at once broke from the throats of the crew.

When silence was obtained the captain ordered the prisoners to be brought on deck.

This was soon done, and those who had endeavoured to defend the fort stood ranged before him.

"I am at a loss," said Captain Parry—"how to deal with you. Honourable foes, whom the chances of war place in our hands, are treated as such, but you are not honourable foes — you are but a set of ruffians who have thought proper to set the laws at defiance and war against your own kindred. I shall therefore feel it my duty to convey you to England in irons, where you will be given up to the civil authorities. Take them below!"

The men stood gazing in moody silence upon the captain of the frigate as he spoke, and they were led away to the hold.

When the last had disappeared down the hatchway Henry said—

"I await your further orders, sir."

Captain Parry thought for a moment ere he replied.

"Bentley's force is now in the fort."

"It is."

"Was it in the same state as when you last left it?" asked Parry

"For all I know to the contrary. Thinking it best to bring our prisoners on board ere anything further was done, I have not yet visited the vaults."

"Nor seen anything of your friends?" asked the captain.

"No, sir; nor can I learn any tidings of them.

"Strange!"

"Very strange, sir."

"They are doubtless prisoners somewhere on the island."

"Such I believe to be the case," said Henry.

"They must be discovered if possible," said Captain Parry; "for Mr. Lawson is too valuable an officer to lose. Can you form no conjecture whatever as to their whereabouts?"

"None—unless they are confined in the fort."

"You will return to the fort, sir, and have the goods, if not already moved from the vaults, sent on board."

Henry bowed.

"At the same time you can institute a search for Mr. Lawson, whom I hope to see return with you."

"I sincerely hope he may, sir," said Henry, fervently.

And he left the captain's side and gave the order for the boats to be again manned.

In the course of a few minutes Henry was once more on his way to the shore.

How he thought, as the boat danced over the waves—"if Charles and Ellen be in the fort, I will release them, but if they are not there then I know not where to seek them."

The boat was pulled up on to the beach, and Henry and the sailors, save two who were left to look after the boat, disembarked and made their way to the fort.

The young man informed his fellow officer of the commands of Captain Parry to have the property in the vaults taken on board, and then advanced to the trap which we have before seen, and raised it.

Several of the sailors had provided themselves with lanterns at the request of Henry, and these they now lighted and descended the steps into the vaults, headed by Henry, after he had placed sentries at different points to give notice of any attempt to surprise them.

The vaults presented the same appearance which they had done on the previous visit of Henry.

The barrels and bales were still there, not a thing had been removed.

Taking a light from the hand of one of the seamen, the youth drew his cutlass, and commenced a search for the missing ones.

Not a single spot of those extensive vaults escaped his observation.

But no trace of our heroine or her lover could he find.

It was evident that they were not confined in that part of the place.

But he could not but think that they were concealed somewhere in the building; so mounting the steps into the passage he made his way along it into the large square apartment, or kind of hall, from which several smaller apartments opened. Into each of these he went.

But all were empty.

He strode up the broad staircase to the ramparts and walked around them.

Still no trace could he discover of his lost friends.

Leaning his back against the wall from which the Union Jack now floated so proudly, he gazed down upon the beach beneath him.

He could see the rude huts of the fishermen smugglers; but not a living soul met his sight, save the sailors who kept guard at the different entrances to the fort.

With a sigh, he turned to descend the broad staircase, and found his companions in the vaults.

The brave seamen were busily engaged in rolling up the casks of spirits into the open air, through a large opening at one end of the fort, which had been discovered by Bentley, concealed by rubbish.

"I can find no trace of Mr. Lawson," he said, addressing Bentley.

"It is a strange affair," replied the young man. "Where can he be?"

"I can form no conjecture. It is not likely that he can be concealed in any of the huts on the beach; for I do not think there is one strong enough to hold him."

"Not if he had the free use of his limbs," said Bentley; "but he may be bound, or wounded; and in either case he would be unable to escape."

"True," remarked Henry—"it may be as you say. I will demand an entrance into every one of them. I will away at once, and leave you to see that the men carry out the orders of the commander."

And the youth strode towards the steps.

"Stay," said Bentley.

Henry turned.

"You will not go alone?" said Bentley.

"Why not?"

"There may be danger."

"I fear it not."

"I am aware of that," said Bentley: "but it would perhaps be advisable to take a couple of stout fellows with you."

"I will do so," said Henry, after a pause.

Then, bidding two of the men follow him, he left the fort, and made his way to the hut where Ellen had sought shelter on the morning that she had been sent on shore by the pirate Latour.

The rude door was closed, but Henry struck a heavy blow upon its panels with the hilt of his cutlass.

In a moment it was opened by the woman who had procured breakfast for Ellen.

She started back when she saw Henry and the sailors; and, thinking they had come to search for her husband, she exclaimed, hurriedly:

"He is not here—he is not here!"

"Who is not here?" asked the young man, jumping to the conclusion in an instant that his friend was concealed in the hut, and darting past the woman as he spoke into the dirty dingy apartment.

"My husband."

"I seek not your husband," said Henry—"but a young officer. Search the place," he added, turning to his followers.

And, without waiting to hear the woman's reply, Henry darted into the space which was parted off by a dirty piece of sailcloth, and served as a sleeping apartment.

But no trace, of course, could be found of Charles.

Disappointed and annoyed, the youth made his way from the hut, followed by the two sailors.

Henry summoned admittance at the next habitation—and indeed all of them; and, in spite of the closest scrutiny, nothing was to be found to speak of the whereabouts of his lost friends.

It was evident that he must return to the ship without finding them; and sadly he made his way back to the fort, with his two companions.

The men had worked hard during his absence.

The vaults had been nearly emptied of their treasures, which stood ready for transit along the beach to the boats.

Henry was about to acquaint the young officer, Bentley, with the failure of his expedition, when, casting his eyes down upon a spot of the ground of the vault from which two of the sailors had that moment rolled a heavy cask of spirits, he perceived a spark travelling slowly along under some bales which stood piled one upon another.

Starting forward, he bent down his head to obtain a better view.

With a cry of horror, he stretched forth his hand to grasp at it; but he clutched at tinder.

Still he could perceive the spark under the cotton bale.

In a moment the fearful truth had flashed upon him.

It was a slow match, leading to a mine beneath the bales.

He called loudly to the men, and told them of what he had seen, and ordered them to instantly remove the bales, in order to extinguish the match. But the bales were piled high up, and were of enormous bulk and great weight.

Henry rushed to the other side of the bales, and then became certain that the mine, if one there was indeed, must be beneath them.

In a few minutes then it would explode.

Calling upon the men to leave the vault, the sailors rushed up the steps, and into the open air.

When the last had gone, Henry followed.

"To the beach!" he exclaimed. "If the place is mined, a few minutes will decide its fate."

The men hurried down the beach towards the boat, and then stood and gazed at the frowning walls of the fort.

Suddenly a rumbling noise smote their ears, and the ground trembled beneath their feet.

Then a loud report followed; the walls of the fort cracked in every direction; and the next moment, amid a cloud of dust and smoke, the whole building fell a heap of rubbish to the earth.

CHAPTER CXII.

THE SAILOR'S DAUGHTER AND HER PERSECUTORS IN THE CAVE—BLACK BILL DISSEMBLES.

THE first streak of dawn threw its cold light aslant the grey rocks as the Boy Rover and his dishonourable companions bore into the secret cave the poor defenceless Mary Cordage, the wretched girl whom they had torn in the dead of the night from her humble home.

Feeling how vain was all resistance, she had suffered herself to be led or rather carried to the hut of the smugglers

Too well she had divined the meaning of the words uttered by the Boy Rover, as he led her from her chamber.

There could be no second thought as to their fatal meaning.

They told her but too plainly that she was to become the victim of their base and sensual passions.

But the horror of her situation—the fate of her father, whom she so fondly loved, and the presence of these bold base men—awed her into silence.

This silence was construed by the smugglers into resignation to her fate.

And no little pleasure did they exhibit at what they believed to be an easy conquest.

Save Black Bill, whose dark features became even more black.

He had intended the girl for his own and great indeed was his chagrin when he discovered that the Boy Rover stood upon his rights, according to their rules, and asserted his determination to abide by them.

This was a blow that rankled in the heart of Black Bill.

He ground his teeth in rage.

He clenched his hard hands till the nails almost lacerated their palms.

But he was silent.

He could see, too, that his annoyance caused no little gratification to Sam and the others.

This was wormwood to his soul.

He began to think of revenge.

But he resolved to bide his time.

Bold and bad, still he was crafty.

His was not a nature to forgive an injury.

But he would dissemble.

He would appear to be satisfied and wait an opportunity to reveal the true state of his feelings,

Even though he had to wait for years.

He entered the cave with the rest, and now joined in the conversation as lively as the others.

Even the Boy Rover himself believed that his anger had abated and that he was quite willing that the arrangements should be carried out to the letter.

If Bill appeared to coincide with them it was appearance only, for he changed like a caged tiger.

However, the poor girl was conveyed into the cave.

The lamp was lighted and a shudder of horror pervaded her frame as she cast a glance around the rude place.

"This is your new home," said the Rover.

A sigh deep and prolonged was her only reply.

Then, overcome by her feelings she sunk down

upon the very spot where Ellen had herself lain, and burst into tears.

They were indeed tears of agony.

But no look of pity did they call forth from the inhuman monsters into whose hands she had fallen.

On the contrary, they seemed to gloat in her misery.

"This is your new home," continued the Rover, "and you can now make yourself as comfortable as you like.

"Comfortable!" gasped Mary.

"That's the word—what's to prevent you," said the Boy Rover.

"Is not the fate of my father, and my own misery sufficient," she replied.

"It's no use to regret his death," remarked the smuggler captain, brutally.

"What could profit you to commit so hellish a deed?"

"Revenge."

"Revenge?" she said.

"Yes."

"He never harmed you."

"Didn't he."

"Nor none else."

"He did."

"How?"

"He sought my destruction."

"Your destruction?"

"Yes."

"Impossible."

"It is true."

Mary shook her head incredulously.

"He has sought the destruction of myself and band," said the Rover—"many a time has the accursed vessel in which he sailed chased my own along the coast."

"Then you are——"

"The Boy Rover——"

"The Smuggler of the South Seas!" gasped Mary.

"The same."

"Then heaven help me!" exclaimed the poor girl, who had heard from her parent the character of him whom now held her in his power.

"I don't suppose heaven will interfere much in your cause," said the Rover, brutally.

"Oh! why am I brought here?" she asked.

"To minister to my pleasure," he replied.

"Your pleasure?"

"Yes."

"I do not understand you," exclaimed the poor trembling girl.

"Don't you."

"No."

"Then you are more dull than I took you to be," said the Boy Rover.

And he fixed upon her a glance full of deep meaning.

"Ah, ah!" sighed the girl.

"Sigh away, it will relieve you, perhaps," said the Boy Rover.

"Villain!"

"Curb your tongue," said the Rover, "abuse will serve you little."

"Let me return to my father," she said.

"That cannot be."

"Why not?"

"Because I require your presence here."

"For what purpose?"

"You shall soon know."

"I must go home."

"Go you shall if you like," said the Rover.

"Oh, then I will go at once!" she exclaimed.

"No, you won't," said the Boy Rover, placing his hand upon her arm; "I have not yet done with you."

"What do you require of me?" gasped Mary, as her face paled till she was as white as a spectre.

"That which a woman can surrender but only to one."

"And that?"

"Your honour!"

"My honour!" she gasped.

"Yes," he replied—"if it is still in your own possession."

"Oh! heavens, why am I destined to be thus insulted?" sobbed Mary.

"You must blame Heaven for your fate," said the Rover.

"Blame Heaven?"

"Aye."

The girl looked surprised.

"Had Heaven denied you less beauty you had scarcely excited a passing thought in the minds of myself and my friends," said the smuggler captain.

"Would then that I was ugly as sin," she muttered; "for then had my father been spared, and myself left free from insult."

"But you are pretty," said the Rover; "and myself and companions cannot do otherwise than admire you."

"I want none of your admiration," said Mary. "I only want to leave this place."

"I am sorry that I cannot comply with your desires at present," exclaimed the Rover. "In due time you will doubtless be allowed to quit this place."

"I would go now."

"Doubtless; but that cannot be," said the Boy Rover, firmly.

"Have you the heart to keep me from the side of him who now lies cold in death?" she asked.

"I have," he replied.

"Monster!"

"As you will. It can afford you no pleasure to be by the side of a corpse; but it may to be beside the living."

The girl shuddered.

"He is my father."

"I am your lover."

"My persecutor."

"No—your admirer."

The girl turned away from him with a look of disgust.

"Wretch!" she muttered.

"Softer language will serve you better," he said.

"I can find none sufficiently strong to express my feelings towards one so degraded and lost to all feeling," she exclaimed.

"It is a pity," he said, sarcastically: "but no matter what the language you use towards me—it can have but little effect upon me. You have been brought here to minister to the gratification of myself and friends; and when we get tired of you we will allow you to go—but not before. So you had better reconcile yourself to your fate, and make the best of it."

"Reconcile myself to my fate!" she iterated, with a sad tone of voice. "Oh! Heaven, I'm sorely tried."

"Not to the extent that you will be," said the Rover.

The girl raised her eyes reproachfully to the face of her persecutor; then turned away with a sigh, and sank sorrowfully down upon the chest on which Ellen had reclined, as her eyes encountered the look of fearful meaning which the youthful villain fixed upon her face.

Her bosom rose and fell with the violence of the emotions which shook her breast, and she buried her head in her hands, and sobs loud and deep emanated from her bosom.

Poor girl! she was sorely tried. The anguish of her own situation was somewhat despised in the grief she experienced at the fate of her father.

But she saw that it was useless to plead to that inexorable villain to suffer her to return to his side; and she gave way to despair.

Meantime the smugglers had been listening to every word that had passed, and seemed greatly to enjoy the scene.

Mary lacked the bold defiant spirit of Ellen, and the ruthless men fancied that she would prove an easy conquest.

This thought placed them in the best possible humour—save Black Bill, who only clenched his teeth the tighter, and glared the more furiously upon Sam and the captain.

As to Sam, that worthy seemed to enjoy greatly the interest taken by the Boy Rover in the poor girl.

He felt that Black Bill was being slightly brought down a bit in having his prize taken from him; and, like most degraded natures, Sam felt pleasure in the others chagrin, as it ministered to his own revenge.

He chuckled with himself at the disappointment of the mate in not being able to monopolise to himself the pretty Mary.

But Bill's mind was not idle.

He was endeavouring to think of some means by which he could forestal his captain in the caresses of their prisoner.

He resolved to appear satisfied, although he was far from being so.

When the Boy Rover, leaving the side of the weeping girl, seated himself at the rude table on which provisions had been placed by Jem, Bill remarked:

"Well, I suppose you mean to give her a little time to compose herself before you resorts to extremities?"

"Why?" asked the Rover.

"Because time may soften her down a bit—that's all," said Bill. "One volunteer is worth two pressed men. You know so, I suppose. One consenting woman is worth a dozen forced ones."

"Humph!" exclaimed the Rover—"I daresay she will be left to herself for some hours. I am more inclined for rest now than anything else, after the journey we have had."

"So I should say," remarked Bill. "But if I had thought you had meant to collar her first, I'm hanged if I had put you afly to where she was to be found."

"You wouldn't?"

"No."

"Ha, ha!" laughed the smuggler captain—"you don't half seem to like it, Bill. But fair's fair. You know she falls to my share first."

"And mine next," growled Black Bill, sulkily. "Well, since such are the rules, I suppose I must abide by them. Still I don't like it—blowed if I do."

"I never refuse to act fairly by any of you," said the Boy Rover; "so I cannot see why you should be angered at my claiming my rights."

Bill shrugged his shoulders, but made no reply.

"Drink, man," said the captain, filling a can with brandy, and handing it to Bill, "and don't let there be any ill-feeling on the subject. I only stand upon my rights; and I will see that your's are never encroached upon. I can't say fairer than that."

"In course you can't," said Sam, with a wink at Jem.

Bill turned, half furiously, towards the speaker; but, suddenly recollecting that he had resolved to appear satisfied, he took the can, and drank deeply, to hide the passionate flush on his cheek.

"It won't do, Bill, for us to fall out," remarked the Boy Rover, as the mate placed the can on the table. "We are bound together by no ordinary ties; and ill-feeling but tends to weaken our already enfeebled band. So now let there be no more bad feeling amongst us; and act fairly towards each other."

"Well, I suppose what you say is best," said Bill, appearing to be satisfied.

"To be sure it is," said the Rover. "So now let the subject drop; and, when the meal is finished, let us all seek rest—for we know not what may occur to need our strength.

CHAPTER CXIII.

BLACK BILL TRIES A LITTLE BUSINESS ON HIS OWN ACCOUNT—AN UNEXPECTED INTERRUPTION AT THE MOMENT OF SUCCESS.

ALL was hushed in the cabin, save the low sobs which ever and anon broke from the room of the poor victim of the smugglers.

The Boy Rover had retired to rest, as the sun rose out of the waters, and threw its fiery tints upon the ocean's bed.

His followers, worn out with the night's adventure, had done the same; and now all, save Black Bill, were slumbering heavily.

The smuggler mate, on the contrary, was awake.

His passionate nature was aroused, and he lay thinking how he could outwit the Boy Rover, and rob him of the prize he had wrested from him.

Impatiently did Bill listen to the measured breathing of the sleepers.

Several times he was about to rise from his rude slumbers; but a movement of one or other of the smugglers caused him to assume the recumbent position again, and feign slumber.

At length all seemed quiet.

Bill raised his head, and listened intently.

The even breathing of his companions showed that they slept soundly.

The crime of that night had not driven slumber from their eyelids.

Their callous hearts felt no compunction at the work of their guilty hands.

So hardened can the soul become with crime, that it hears not the voice of conscience.

After a time Black Bill rose stealthily from his couch.

He cast an anxious glance around him.

Then he moved forward to that part of the cabin where the poor girl sat weeping in agony.

Sam moved restlessly.

Black Bill paused.

The mate gritted his teeth, as he gazed towards the uneasy sleeper.

Again all was quiet.

The smuggler moved forward.

"Curse him!" he muttered to himself—"I should like to bury my knife in his heart. But for him, the captain had never demanded the girl; but I'll be even with them all yet—I'll be even with them!"

And he shook his clenched hand menacingly towards the sleeping man.

"I am half a mind," he continued, "to murder them all, as they lie asleep. But no, that will not do. Still I will be revenged on them at some time or another. For the present I will turn my thoughts to vengeance on the captain. The girl's mine by rights; and I'll have her too."

And, again casting his glance anxiously around the cave, he strode forward.

The girl, lost to all but her own misery, was seated still on the chest, with her face covered by her hands, through the fingers of which the tears of grief at the loss of her father, and her own fearful position, found their way.

Black Bill silently approached her.

The girl heard him not.

His shoeless feet made no noise upon the ground floor of the cabin.

The smuggler stood before her, and looked upon the bowed head, with a fiendish gleam in his dark eye.

Once or twice he stretched forth his hand to arouse her.

But each time he drew back his arm.

It was not pity for her sufferings that prompted him to do this.

Such a feeling did not enter his breast.

But something, for which he could not account, caused him to pause ere he made his presence known to the weeping girl.

Perhaps he feared she might start and scream, and thus awaken those who slumbered all unconscious of what he was doing.

This he felt he must prevent, if possible.

For too well he knew his treachery would be severely punished by the Boy Rover.

So he paused, and considered how best to act.

Still the girl remained unconscious of his presence.

Every moment's delay was fraught with danger; and yet he hesitated to announce his presence.

He could not be seen by the smugglers—as the various bales and other articles in the cave hid him from sight.

But, if the girl should give utterance to any sound, they might awake; and his absence from his couch would be instantly discovered.

He scarcely knew how to act.

He wished that she would raise her head from her hands.

This she did at length.

With a deep sigh, she looked.

She started.

A cry rose to her lips.

But, ere it escaped them, the hand of Black Bill was laid gently on her mouth.

"Hush!" he hissed in her ears—"utter not a sound, or you are lost."

The girl fixed her eyes, with a frightened expression, upon his face.

"I will befriend you," he whispered.

"You!" she gasped, in surprise.

"Yes, me."

The girl involuntarily clasped her hands.

A beam of joy shone in her tearful eyes.

The thought struck her that Black Bill, pitying her position, had waited till his companions were asleep, to assist her to escape from that fearful place.

His dark and repulsive features, at which she had trembled before, now seemed to be veiled with a look of pity, and she rose silently from her seat and stood beside him.

"You would save me?" she exclaimed in a whisper.

"I would."

"Oh, do so, and heaven will bless you."

"Listen, but speak not above a whisper," said Will. "I have said I would save you from those men : you know for what you have been brought here."

"Too well can I guess," she shuddered.

"Then hear me."

"I will."

"Would you escape them?"

"Heaven knows I would," she exclaimed.

"I can lead you from this place," said Bill.

"And you will," she exclaimed.

"I will," he replied.

"Oh, thanks—thanks."

"But on one condition," he said, grasping her wrist, and drawing her trembling form towards his own.

"Speak—speak !"

"That you——"

"What ?"

The arm of Black Bill encircled her waist, and his hot breath fumed her cheek.

"Consent to become mine ere I lead you to liberty," he hissed in her ear.

The gleam of pleasure that had risen to her face departed on the instant.

Her eyes dropped to the ground.

She strove to force herself away.

A shudder ran through her frame, and a sob broke from her lips.

"I—I—cannot." she gasped.

"Would you destroy yourself—do you refuse to leave this place ?"

"No—no; give me my liberty, and I will bless you," she exclaimed.

"On that condition you are free," said Bill.

"You can save me?"

"I can."

"And you will, without demanding of me a recompense so fearful," she muttered. "Oh! be merciful—pity and save me!"

And she clasped her hands and looked pleadingly up into his face.

"Hark, you !" said Bill—"in a short time the others will awake from their slumbers, then shall I be powerless to aid you; then you will find that there is no escape from this place.

"They have sworn to bask in the sunshine of your caresses, and they will keep sacred their oaths. Be wise; surrender yourself to me—to me alone—and fly ere they awake. But hesitate or refuse, and you become the victim of all and remain a prisoner here."

"Oh, God !" gasped the girl.

"Why then refuse to save yourself from such a face ?"

"Enable me to escape from here," she said—"enable me to return to my poor dead father's side, and you will be rewarded by the knowledge of the good act. Oh! be a man, and pity me—spare me—help me !"

"On the conditions I have named," he said.

"Urge it not," she gasped—"you know not what you ask."

"Nor you the risk I run in befriending you. Your escape discovered, I shall perhaps be found out, and then death will be my reward. If I run the risk of death for your sake, is that I ask of you more fearful."

"'This death to me," she replied, with a deep drawn sigh.

"And will it not be worse than death to you if they awake and find you here."

The girl hung her head.

She was silent.

The pressure of Bill's arm tightened around her slender waist.

She felt herself dragged towards him till her bosom was pressed against his heart.

She feared to tear herself away, lest she should awake the others, and all hope of escape be frustrated. Yet she shuddered at the contact with the smuggler mate.

What could she do?

How could she act?

These were questions she asked herself, over and over again.

But she was unable to reply to them.

"Did she refuse to listen to the overtures of Black Bill, might she not consign herself to a worse fate?

Should she accept the fearful alternative, would not her life be blighted—her existence become a misery?

In truth, she was sadly perplexed how to act.

She felt it was in vain to appeal to the manhood of the villain who held her now to his breast.

Either way she considered she was lost; and she burst again into tears.

The gentle resistance which she made served only to fire the blood of the ruffian.

Black Bill felt that he had only to urge his suit to succeed in his desires, and be revenged on the Boy Rover.

He drew her closer to his breast.

He could feel her heart beat against his own.

His lips touched her cheek, and he imprinted a kiss thereon.

As though an adder had stung her, the old sailor's daughter drew back her head.

"Oh, release me!" she said.

"Be wise," he hissed.

"Be merciful!" she replied.

"I would," he muttered.

"Oh, do so!"

"Accept the terms, and escape from here," he said.

"Are there no other means?"

"None."

"I—I—cannot."

"Then you are lost."

"Oh, say not so!"

"It is true."

"You can save me," she gasped: "do so—oh, do so!"

"I will: but the risk I run must not be unrewarded."

"It—it cannot be rewarded as you wish," she muttered.

"Then you must take your chances; and I tell you, your fate is certain," said Bill, relaxing his hold of the poor maiden.

"Save me!" she gasped.

"Surrender."

"I cannot—dare not."

"Then you rush upon a fate more fearful a thousand times," said Bill, coldly.

"No—no!"

"Yes—yes."

And Bill turned, as if about to seek his couch again.

The girl sprang forward. and grasped him by the arm.

"Have mercy!" she said.

"I have offered it, and you have refused it," he replied. "I must again seek my couch. Already have I run a fearful risk to save you."

"Oh, do not desert me—do not refuse to aid me to escape!" she pleaded, still clinging to his wrist, and looking up tearfully into his face.

"Do you consent?" he asked.

"Think of what you ask!" she exclaimed.

"I have thought."

"And you will forego your desires?" she said, hastily.

"No."

"Yes—yes!"

"No," he replied, firmly. "I risk my life; and it is not too much to ask a few short minutes' bliss in return."

"To me it would be eternal misery," she sighed.

"What then will be the doom intended by those who now slumber, and from whom you may fly?"

"Oh, Heaven!" she gasped.

"Look calmly at the offer I make you," said Bill, in a whisper.

"I cannot," she replied.

"Evils encompass you on either side," said Bill.

"Alas, alas!" she groaned, as her bosom shook with emotion.

"If you abandon the lesser, you fall upon the greater," said Bill. "I offer you freedom: they will consign you to a life of imprisonment. If you accept the terms I offer, you are at liberty to leave this place. They will consign you to the same fate, and keep you immured here in this cavern. Be wise—submit to my desires—and I unbar your passage to liberty. Refuse, and you become the mistress of each of us, and end your days in this prison-house!"

"Is there no other means of escape but this," gasped the poor girl.

"None," replied Bill, again clasping her waist.

"Heaven guide me how to act!" she said.

"Quick!—your answer. Yes, or no, for the last time!" and he feigned to leave her side.

"I—I know not what to say," she gasped.

"Then you are lost."

"No—no. I—oh, God!"

"You submit," exclaimed Bill.

"I—I must!—Heaven, forgive me!"

A look of triumph broke over his dark features as he exclaimed—

"You are saved!—you are saved!"

"Liar!" exclaimed a voice behind him, and turning hurriedly he perceived the Boy Rover presenting a pistol at his head.

CHAPTER CXIV.

THE STRUGGLE IN THE CAVE—RAGE OF THE BOY ROVER AND DEFIANCE OF BLACK BILL.

WITH an exclamation of surprise Black Bill released his hold of the wretched girl.

For a moment he stood glaring like a tiger at bay upon the tall youthful form before him.

Mary started back with a cry, and stood trembling like a frightened fawn.

For a few moments the Boy Rover stood eyeing his follower, with a scornful curl upon his lip, and an indignant gleam in his bright eye.

Without lowering the pistol, he advanced steadily to within a few paces of Black Bill.

Then his lips parted, and he exclaimed, in a loud tone:

"Traitor!"

The sound of his voice awoke Sam and Jem, who instantly sprang from their beds, and hurried to the side of their captain.

"Traitor!" again exclaimed the Boy Rover, through his clenched teeth—"is it thus you dare presume to set me at defiance? Speak, or I will blow your brains out!"

One look Black Bill cast around him; then, drawing himself proudly up, he yelled, rather than spoke:

"It is!"

"Mutiny, by G—d!" exclaimed the Boy Rover —the blue veins on his forehead starting out like cords upon his pale brow. "By all the furies of hell! I am captain here, and will have my will

obeyed. Dare you defy me, reptile?—me, the Boy Rover, the Smuggler of the South Sea?"

And he gritted his teeth, in impotent rage, as he stepped still nearer his lieutenant.

But Black Bill quailed not.

He kept his ground.

His eye was fixed upon that of his captain.

Not for a moment did it drop beneath the piercing gaze.

"Traitor, you know your doom!" he exclaimed, in a loud tone. "'Tis death."

"You lie!" yelled Bill.

"Lie, dog?" roared the Boy Rover. "This—to prove my words!"

"And, as he spoke, the Boy Rover pulled the trigger.

But the quick eye of Bill detected the movement of the finger, and, with a bound, he sprang upon the Rover, and struck up his arm.

"It was well for him that he had done so."

It saved his life.

The bullet struck the rock above his head; then fell, with a heavy sound, at his feet.

So sudden and unexpected had been the movement of Black Bill, that, for a moment, the smuggler captain stood surprised and powerless.

Never before had he experienced such resistance to his will.

Foaming with rage, he glanced upon the burly form of his dark-featured officer.

Then he turned to his followers.

"Seize him!" he exclaimed. "By h—l! he shall soon know who is master here."

For a moment Sam and Jem hesitated.

"Curse you!—do you too defy me?" he yelled.

And he stamped his feet as he gave utterance to the words.

Sam and Jem sprang forward to secure the detected man.

This was too much for Black Bill.

He had not forgotten the taunts and threats of Sam before the cottage of the old sailor.

With a yell, he seized that worthy by the throat, as he sprang at him; and, throwing all his force into his arms, he dashed him to the ground; and then struck out, with all his might, at Jem.

"Curse you!" he roared—"keep back, or you'll find you have no child to play with."

"Down with the traitor!" exclaimed the Rover, rushing back to the spot where he had been lying, to secure another weapon.

But this was no easy matter.

Black Bill was a powerful man.

And so Jem found, to his cost, as he essayed to place his hand upon the furious Bill.

He received a blow on the forehead, which sent him sprawling beside the already prostrate Sam.

Then, guessing the reason of the hurried movement of the Boy Rover, and knowing the determined character of his captain, Bill sprang after him, and tore a pistol from his hand, at the moment the Rover had secured it.

"Look you, captain," he exclaimed—"your own deceit has brought about this: so I warn you not to try hard lines with me. That girl I marked for myself; but you thought proper to take her from me. I know what I have sworn to; but I am not to be made the slave of your will, at every turn of fancy. You have called me a traitor; but you have made me one, by professing to assist me to procure the girl, and then claiming her for yourself."

"Put aside that weapon!" exclaimed the Boy Rover.

"I hold it in my own defence," said Bill.

"Lay it down, I tell you!"

"No, no."

"Put it down, I command you!" said the Rover.

"Do you think I am a fool?" exclaimed Bill. "You sought my life; why should I hesitate to take yours?"

"You dare not," exclaimed the Boy Rover, firmly.

"I dare," said Bill.

"Fire then," said the Rover; "for, by all that's devilish, I had rather lay there a corpse than be other than commander here!"

"I have not disputed your authority," said Bill.

"You have set it at defiance," said the Rover.

"And will do so, spite of all," said Bill.

"Seize him!" cried the Rover, foaming with rage, as Jem and Sam, having risen from the ground, came once more towards him.

"I warn you—keep off," yelled Bill, "or there'll be murder!"

"Do your duty," exclaimed the Boy Rover—"seize the traitor!"

"The first that places his hand upon me," said Bill, gives the signal for your death!"

And he presented the pistol full at the head of the Boy Rover.

But the smuggler captain kept his eye fixed unflinchingly upon the long shining barrel.

At this moment Mary, who had been tremblingly watching all that passed, tottered to the spot.

"Oh, men—men!" she gasped—"can a poor defenceless girl be the cause of perhaps murder? For the love of heaven, let me hence from this place, and save yourselves from crimes which sooner or later will bring down upon you a fearful punishment!"

And she stepped between the furious Bill and the no less furious Boy Rover.

Black Bill placed his back against a tall pile of bales, which had been washed on shore from the wreck, so as to keep his foes in front of him, and watched eagerly for any advance on their part towards him.

The Boy Rover rudely seized the arm of the poor girl, and pushed her savagely from between himself and his lieutenant.

"What," he exclaimed, "shall one traitor defy us all!—or, are you all leagued against me?"

"No," said Sam.

"No," exclaimed Jem.

"Shall I be defied?" he exclaimed. "Shall my authority be set at nought—and by a mutineer? No, by h—l, it shall not! I have been captain since the crew was formed; and so I will remain till it is entirely broken up."

And he sprang towards Bill, to disarm him.

But, as he did so, Mary darted between them.

"Hold!" she exclaimed.

"Stand aside!" roared the Rover.

"I will not," she replied.

"Will not?" iterated the Boy Rover, raising his arm, menacingly.

"No, will not," she replied, firmly. "Strike, if you will."

"Tempt me not," yelled the Boy Rover, "or I may do so!"

"I believe you will. The wretch who can murder an old and feeble man, and tear from her home his child in the dead of night, can scarcely be expected to be other than a coward."

The Boy Rover bit his lips, and a flush of shame rose to his face.

"I would not offer you violence," he said; "but I warn you not to tempt me. Stand aside, and let me look the traitor in the face."

"Let there be no murder," she exclaimed. "Already are your hands stained with blood."

"Stand aside, or, by all that's furious, the blood of the child may mingle with that of the father!"

And he hurled the poor girl from him with such force that she must have fallen to the earth had not Sam caught her in his arms.

With a shriek, she tore herself from his hold.

The Boy Rover sprang forward towards the still defiant Bill.

"Keep off," yelled Bill, "if you value your life!"

"Lay down your weapon!" he exclaimed.

"And trust to your mercy!" sneered Bill.

"He has but one shot," exclaimed the Boy Rover. "Arm yourselves, and avenge me if I fall."

And, as he spoke, he sprang upon the mutineer, and strove to wrest the weapon from his grasp.

But this he failed to accomplish.

Black Bill grasped his throat with his left hand, and held him at bay.

Meantime, Jem and Sam had each secured their

weapons, and now advanced threateningly towards the lieutenant.

Black Bill saw in a moment that the chances were against him; and, exerting all his strength, he hurled the Boy Rover from him, and sprang across the cavern.

"Look you, mates," he exclaimed, pointing the muzzle of his pistol into a small keg against the side of the wall of the cave: "advance one step nearer, and I discharge my pistol into this barrel of powder, and blow us all to hell together!'

CHAPTER CXV.

A SAIL IN SIGHT—TERRIFIC COMBAT BETWEEN THE PIRATES AND THE BRITISH MEN-OF-WAR.

For three days the 'Scorpion' kept on her course without meeting with any incident worth recording; but on the fourth day, Bond hurried into the cabin where Lang was seated, exclaiming—

"There's a small vessel bearing down upon us, captain."

"What is the cut of her jib—is she a merchantman?" asked Lang, taking a cigar from his lips and puffing forth a mouthful of smoke.

"She's a Britisher, I think," answered Bond, "but from what I can make out of her she isn't any merchant, but a small vessel of war."

"Whew!" whistled Lang.

"I am half afraid that's what she is," replied Bond.

"Afraid be d—d!" roared Lang, starting to his feet; if she is a three-decker I am not afraid of her."

"I don't see any pull in fighting a craft of that kidney," said Bond; "it's generally hard knocks and little prize money."

Lang cast a contemptuous glance upon the other, and strode to the deck.

Now taking his glass he raised it to his eye.

He was enabled to make out that the vessel in the distance was British, and there was not the slightest doubts but that she was a ship of war, but of no very formidable dimensions.

She appeared to be bearing down upon the 'Scorpion' with all sail.

The pirate was going over the surface of the waters leasurely, but seeing the other ship astern Lang gave orders to his men to pull the canvas.

The topsails followed the top gallant sails, and even the royals were sheeted home, for there was not much wind astir; the spanker jib and stay sails were all set and away flew the 'Scorpion.'

"You are going to run, then," said Bond.

"Run, be hanged!" exclaimed Lang; "I only want to see her metal."

Believing that the pirate was about to endeavour to escape, the stranger put on more sail, and fired a gun to bring her to.

Lang smiled.

"Now I know what she is," he said, turning to Bond.

"What?"

"A ship of war."

"I to'd you so."

"But I had my doubts."

"Now you are satisfied."

"I am."

"And will get away if possible?"

"No!"

"No?"

"I shall fight her."

"As you will," said Bond, turning away.

Lang now ordered the hands up to reduce the canvas, and the speed of the 'Scorpion' was instantly slackened by being stripped of all her light sails.

The stranger gradually neared, still signalling to the pirate.

Finding that the 'Scorpion' paid no further heed to her summonses, the stranger sent a boat which pulled alongside the pirate believing her to be a merchantman.

But those in the boat were soon undeceived, for they were instantly made prisoners.

The look out on board the 'Damon,' which those captured stated to be the name of their vessel, must have been somewhat lax, for they had not observed the fate of the boat but fired a gun to recall it.

But ere its echoes had died away, Lang gave the order to raise the black flag.

Then it was evident that the true character of the pirate was known by the commotion on the deck of the 'Damon,' for as the black flag ran up to the gaff, and the drums on board the war-ship beat to quarters, and she was cleared for action. Lang had the topsails of his vessel backed and lay to, while the 'Damon' crowding all sail she could carry, come rapidly up.

When the two vessels were within pistol shot the guns of the pirate were unmasked, and the men stood at their quarters awaiting the next order.

But Lang was silent.

The 'Damon' now ran right up to them, and her captain perceiving the pirate lying so quietly, leapt into the lashings and called out to know if she had surrendered.

"Surrendered, be d—d!" roared Lang. "Now, pirates, show them a taste of your metal!"

Ere his words had died away, the pirates discharged a tremendous broadside, which made the 'Damon' quiver from stern to stern.

It was returned by the 'Damon' with equal force; and was kept up with fierceness on both sides—for both vessels discharged their broadsides with fearful rapidity; and Lang found the precision of the enemy's fire, and the admirable discipline they exhibited, would soon sink his ship if he did not manœuvre, and, by stratagem, counterbalance the disadvantage under which he laboured from the fact of the enemy's metal being greater than his own.

With the number of blacks on board, he could spare several, without weakening the guns of any of the people; and he resolved to try what could be done by raking.

He gave the necessary command, and succeeded in laying the pirate broadside across the bows of the 'Damon,' and pouring in a terrific fire, which completely swept the decks with a shower of iron hail.

The 'Damon,' however, speedily cleared herself from the dangerous position.

She laid herself broadside to broadside, and kept up a steady but destructive fire.

Lang now sent a party of blacks into the tops, with hand-grenades and rifles.

The hand-grenades were hurled down with terrible precision; whilst those with the guns killed a great number on the British vessel.

Still the crew of the 'Damon' fought fiercely,

as British sailors will ever do under any circumstances.

Their shots told with a power and certainty which, in spite of the devil-may-care courage of Lang, made him uneasy for the result.

But he cheered his men, and flew from one part of the vessel to the other, with a rapidity that was marvellous.

Still the tremendous charges from the 'Damon' caused the pirates to waver; and it was only by the greatest exertions that Lang could keep them to their task.

At length the gaf of the 'Damon' was shot away.

Seeing this, the blacks shouted out, in ecstasy:

"She's struck—she's struck!"

But the practised eye of Lang could detect no slackening in the firing; and the next moment himself and crew saw the English colours nailed to the mast.

And, as the wind spread them defiantly out over her decks, she poured in such a broadside that the slaver rocked and groaned beneath it in agony.

Lang saw that his men again wavered.

He knew that to fear now was to fall; and to fall was death.

Not a very honourable one either; for they were pirates.

Should they be conquered, a long rope and a short shrift would be their doom.

Knowing and feeling this, he animated his men by his own example.

Scorning all fear, he rushed into the very thickest of the fray.

Now directing the men abaft—now cheering on his crew—with a voice of thunder, he bade them stand to their quarters, and die rather than surrender; for surrender was death at the yard-arm.

The foremast of the pirate was shot away, and several important stays were cut; the mainmast was riddled, and several of the guns were silenced; whilst a mass of dead and dying Africans lay around.

The 'Damon' had suffered almost as much.

The foretop and maintop mast were down, with the loose rigging and tackle lying upon the deck, and creating the greatest confusion. The mizen topmast was also gone by the band; and every mast bore terrible evidence of the 'Scorpion's' guns.

Twice she caught fire; but each time it had been extinguished by the noble fellows, who were compelled to leave their guns to accomplish it.

Still the effect of the Britisher's fire was terrific; and Lang found his vessel so crippled, that he resolved to make an attempt to board the enemy.

Turning to Bond and Smith, Lang said:

"We can't hold out at this game; and, if we strike, we shall swing to a certainty."

"No doubt of that," said Bond.

"Now I have an objection to dance a hornpipe in the air," said Lang. "So I go in for death—from pike or cutlass—or victory."

"What do you mean?"

"We must board her."

"'Tis our only hope."

"Call up the men," said Lang. "I will lead them myself."

This was done.

Lang selected the best among them, and bade them be firm and bold, and the vessel would yet be their own.

So saying, he leapt into the mizen chains of the 'Damon'—for the guns were now muzzle to muzzle—and climbed up the sides, followed by Bond and the African whom he had selected for the duty.

A tremendous hand to hand contest now ensued. The English fought with that bravery and resolution which ever characterises them; whilst Lang and his followers, having everything at stake, fought with a desperation amounting to a perfect frenzy.

The struggle was terrific.

The British seamen were cut down, wherever they stood, rather than give way an inch; and the Africans, warmed up into action by the knowledge of their superior numbers, fought with a courage worthy of a better cause.

Lang and Bond plunged into the wildest and fiercest points of contention, and opposed the most steadfast and skilful; and fortune smiled upon them wherever they stood and struck; and their cutlasses were deluged with the blood of the brave sailors from point to hilt.

The battle raged with a fury that made it certain that it could not last long. The firing, the crashing, the groans and cries of the wounded, mingled with the oaths and shouts of the combatants—the hot suffocating clouds of smoke in which they were enveloped, lit up every now and then by the flashes of fire from the guns, as they were discharged with murderous animosity by the foe—all told how desperate was the conflict.

Lang and Bond still maintained their ground, though at the expense of the lives of many of their followers.

Still they fought on, cutting down their opponents with a strength equal to their skill, which in itself was great.

Muskets and pikes were levelled at their breasts, cutlasses gleamed around their persons, pistols flashed in their faces—still they were unhurt, though in a complete storm of bullets. Their clothes were rent in several places, their hats were perforated with balls; but, by some special providence, they had not as yet received one slight wound.

On they moved, though every step they took was severely contested, and hardly gained. Several times they concluded they had gained a victory; but as often the determined resolution of the English compelled them to acknowledge that the important object was neither obtained, or so certain of being so as they could desire.

Even in the moment when success appeared less doubtful, the men were gradually repulsed, and nearly driven from the vessel; but they rallied them by strenuous exertions, and, by hard fighting, gained the ground they had lost.

Fiercer and hotter the fight raged, the men seemed actuated by the spirit of devils, and, with unrelenting fury, did their utmost to slay each other.

At length, one of the blacks, who still remained in the tops, succeeded in shooting the lieutenant of the 'Damon.'

Captain Featherton, the commander of the British vessel upon seeing his lieutenant fall by a shot through his heart faltered.

This was fatal to himself and his crew, for the sailors lost heart, and ere they could recover the momentary panic at which this circumstance threw them, the pirates pressed them back, and in a few minutes the victory was their own.

The few sailors who remained out of the brave crew were quickly disarmed and made prisoners, but the captain scorning to surrender his sword to a pirate so goaded Lang, that he shot him through the head, and the brave man fell at his feet a corpse.

After the sailors, whom Lang hoped to be able to induce to join him, had been removed on board the 'Scorpion,' some of the guns were taken out of the 'Damon' and put on board the pirate, and every article of value met the same fate.

When the pirates had taken all they could conveniently find room for they scuttled the British ship, and the noble little vessel sank proudly into the bosom of the deep waters, with the proud flag of England still floating from the mast, where it had been nailed by the true-hearted British sailor who hurls defiance to the world.

CHAPTER CXVI.

THE PIRATE LAYS UP FOR REPAIRS—THE OLD TAR'S TALE OF HOW HE SERVED HIS OFFICER.

THE damage caused to the pirate by this engagement was so considerable that Wild Madge and Lang did not consider it advisable to continue their voyage to England; so they resolved to run into a small bay of an island which had often served the purpose of the Boy Rover in his smuggling voyages, but which was uninhabited, and seldom or ever visited unless by the crew of a passing vessel to procure wood or water.

This island lay some ten leagues distant from the spot where the engagement had taken place, and the vessel's bows were therefore turned thither in order that she might be repaired ere she sought the coast of Cornwall.

The weather continuing fine nothing occurred to prevent the consummation of their object, and the 'Scorpion' soon rode in the smooth waters of the little bay, and every man on board strove his utmost to repair the damages which she had received.

Lang thought this a favourable time for endeavouring to prevail upon the prisoners to take the oath and become pirates.

The question was asked and refused by all, save one Jack Snipe, a noble-looking tar, who gave way to the inducements held out to him by Lang, under the assurance that several of his fellow-prisoners had taken the oath, and whilst the men were under the influence of drink, with which he had been well plied.

But great was his grief when he found how he had dishonoured the colours under which he had served, when the fumes of the liquor had worked off.

Then he discovered that his messmates had been made to walk the plank, and that he was the only one out of the brave crew who had so disgraced the name of British seamen.

But he had taken the oath and he must make the best of a bad bargain.

Still he could not help brooding over what he had done, till at length he became miserable and dejected.

Lang saw this and endeavoured to win back the usual spirits of the old tar; and finding that brandy was not at all obnoxious to him the pirate gradually brought him round to care less about his fall.

He invited Snipe to his cabin—treated him with great kindness—was ever ready to do anything he could to reconcile him to his new life, till at length the old sailor became more satisfied with his position.

"Come," said Lang one day to him as they were seated in the cabin—"it's no use being down about what can't be helped. Life has its changed, and it is best to make them work as smoothly as we can. Let us indulge ourselves in a can of grog, and kill time with a yarn—a sailor has ever got a good coil of that commodity at his finger's end.',

Snipe shook his head.

"I ain't," he said—"only yarns as will remind me of what I was."

"Tut—tut, man!" said Lang; "you are desponding again. Come, pitch one out, and a devil for care."

"Well, if you must have it," said Snipe—"here goes."

The speaker replenished his lower jaw with a choice roll of weed, which he deposited to his satisfaction; and then making a short pause, as if to recall events, commenced his narrative:

'You see, I ain't much of a fist at palarvering, as you are. My edecation has been only ship-shape and Bristol fashion. However, I can do a seaman's duty. I make steam-way when I clap on the jawing tackle. So you must make allowance; and, when I am jammed hard up for lingo, you must get me out of irons as best you can.

'The whole matter is well coiled away; and, when once I cast off, I can pay out fast enough.

'It was on board the 'Agrippa' that I first became acquainted with Mr. Girdler. He was middy aboard that ere vessel; and the way I first got into his notice was, while we were up the Mediterranain, we had a third lieutenant, who was a sour ill-tempered son of a swab—a know-nothing demme eyes, you see, sort of a chap, who was always for shirting the men with a rope's-end when they did their work better than he knew how to give orders.

'He was fond of jeering Mr. Girdler, and telling him he crawled aboard through the cabin window; and would set him on duty he could not do himself, and jeer and sneer at him if he did not know how to do it.

'I never in my life saw a middy do the duty he made Mr. Girdler do; and he always did this when he had the watch, and our cap'n wasn't by, or, for the matter of that, the other lieutenants.

'Well, Mr. Girdler happened to be liked on the berth-deck — uncommon he was — and the third lieutenant hated. There was not a hand but would show Mr. Girdler how to do what he was ordered, if he could get near, when he was at fault; or who would have stopped to turn their quid if they could have shoved the lieutenant over the side.

'Howsomever, one day — I remember it as though it were but yesterday—he happened to be a jawing Mr. Girdler at his work. Well, you must know the blackguard didn't stop there, but got to taunting him about his family.

'My eye! he nabbed it then. He'd no sooner slipped the words out of his ugly mouth—I was aft at the time on the mizen rigging, and heard it all —Mr. Girdler ups with his fist, and down goes the lieutenant, bang upon the deck. If he had been struck with a six-pounder, he couldn't have dropped quicker.

'Well, up he jumps again, and down he goes again. Then he springs up again, and shows fight. But it warn't of no manner of use. Mr. Girdler let fly at him right and left, and fairly hammered him all over the quarter-deck, until he laid down, and roared out murder and mutiny, with all his might.

'Then, up comes the first and second lieutenant, the master, the master's mate, doctor, purser, cap'n—and all hands as could get near looked to see what the upshot would be.

'Well, as soon as the cap'n heard that a mid had licked a lieutenant, he ordered the mid into irons for striking his superior officer; and it was said he would be run up the yard-arm for it.

'He was tried by a court-martial when we got back to England—and I don't know what else besides. But, you see, Mr. Girdler happened to be a cap'n's nephew; and, when the whole on it came to be overhauled, the cap'n was in a jolly rage with the third lieutenant.'

Here the old tar paused to take a pull at the can of grog before him, and substitute a quid for the one he had been indulging in, and which he now threw into the crown of his hat. Then he continued:

'In course I was brought before the cap'n to say what I knew of the matter; and didn't I stretch out when I had the offing clear. I made no more ado, but up and told the cap'n how many tricks he had played on Mr. Girdler—making him do topmast and master's duty: and I said as how the ship's company would bear me out in all that I had said; and then I told them all I had heard of the quarrel.

"I didn't forget to make known all the nasty spiteful sneers the lieutenant had flung out as I could overhaul; and, when my yarn was spun out, the lieutenant said as how I was in Mr. Girdler's pay—a lying varmint.

'Well, the cap'n said he should judge himself about that, and summoned some of the crew aft; but they all stood on the same tack as myself. And then the cap'n told the lieutenant, if he forgot his situation—no, his position, that's it—as a officer, he must expect his subordinates—they're hard words for the jaw—he must expect they would not respect him, and so he should settle the business with ordering Mr. Girdler into the tops for striking his superior officer.

'The third lieutenant looked evil enough at me as he made for the deck; and, as he went along, he whispered to me:

"My man, I will remember you for this."

"Thank you, sir," says I, with a laugh, and followed him.

'Mr. Girdler's irons were cast off, and, with a clean pair of heels, he went into the tops.

'Soon afterwards it came to blow very hard, and we were not long in getting everything snug alow and aloft. I was in the maintop, and, when I had spare time, I said what I could to cheer Mr. Girdler, for he looked very much as if everything in the shape of happiness for him had gone by the board.

'In the middle of one of my speeches, he drew a paper parcel from his pocket, and said:

"Snipe, you are my friend—that I know. Will you do me one favour—will you give this to my father?"

"In what latitude am I to find him?" I asked.

'Well, before I had finished, he jumped by me, was on the foot-rope of the mainyard in a minute, sided out until he was at the yardarm, and then he leaped into the water. Mind you, there was a heavy sea running at the time; and so, you see, he made up his mind to slip his wind.

'I sprang after him the minute I saw what he was up to; and, being more nimble on the foot-rope than him, I was at the yardarm almost in time to hook on to him: but I missed the grab I made, overboard he went, and then me arter him.

'I knew I could swim like a duck in a pond, and he couldn't, and, if I could lay hold on him, I could keep him above water till we were picked up; and if not, why we in course must both of us go to Davy Jones together.

'I didn't care much about that, seeing as I should die in good company, and there wasn't any-one to pipe their eyes because my life-lines were unrove.

'As soon as my head was above water, I found myself lifted up by the same sea as Mr. Girdler, and, with a hard struggle, managed to reach him. I seized him by the collar, and held on like grim death.

'The crew had seen us jump from the yard-arm; the ship was laid to, the jolly-boat was lowered, aye, and very nearly capsized was it, too. But, to cut the story short, we were picked up.

'Mr. Girdler had no more life in him than there is in a half-starved marine; and I'd swallowed enough salt water to float a four-oared cutter. How-somever, we soon got on our pins again. I got five guineas from the cap'n; and Mr. Girdler had the articles of war read to him in a long palaver which was paid out to him in the cap'n's cabin.

'The third lieutenant did not have a very easy berth of it after that. He minded what I had said of him, and roused me out whenever he had a chance, until one day he called out to me:

"Here, you sir, start the maintop-men aft to haul in the weather braces. You sir, I don't see the maintop-men coming aft, and I shall order the bo'swain's mate to start you with a rope's end if you crawl to your duty in that way."

'Now, you must know, we were hauling in the main brace at the very time he was bellowing out this. The captain happened to be at his elbow, and, tapping him on the shoulder, he says to him:

"Don't you know his name, Mr. Partridge? If you do not, it is time you did. It's my practice to know the name of every man on board my ship; and, if you don't know a man's name, ask it, Mr. Partridge, and don't sing out, 'You sir, here;' and 'you sir, there.' People have names, and will answer to them when so addressed; but you must not look for any particular man to do what you command when nobody but yourself can tell what you mean."

The lieutenant showed in his face as many colours as a dying dolphin; but he didn't say nothing. Why? Because he daresn't. But he didn't forget though to carry a heavy freight of spite for all this —not so much for me, as for Mr. Girdler, for the licking he'd got. He happened to be some relation to the lady whose flag Mr. Girdler carried out at the fore; and, when he got ashore, after being paid off, he made use of it to pitch such a lying yarn to her as to make her shove her boat off when hailed by her true lover.

'As soon as he was safe on blue waters she was brought home, and when our ship was paid off at Portsmouth, Girdler asked me to keep in his wake until I went to sea agin, which I agreed to, for some how or other I had taken a fancy to him.

'Well, I went to his father's house in London with him, and sure enough it's a grand place, and grand folks live there. Why the young lady's father and mother wouldn't let Mr. Girdler splice with her is more than I can overhaul now, it gets to the windward of me, for if they are richer than him they must live in king's houses.

'Let that be how it may Mr. Girdler made sail to range up alongside the lady, but she luffed, bore away, and kept clear—she wouldn't see him, and he was desperately cut up about it.

'His dispatches were sent back, and he was told that the lady intended to part company with him for ever.

'Well, you never saw a craft that had parted with her rudder yaw about as he did.

'I looked out sharp, for I expected he'd a cut his life-lines adrift, but he didn't. He tried hard for another ship to make for any sea or port, to the devil, or anywhere, so that he didn't stay in England.

'Well, one morning I was making a stretch from his house at Wapping for a splice in the main-brace with some messmates, and not being over clear as to the bearing, I ran right out of my course and was brought up in a large open land full with trees, lying to the sou'ard and west'ard, I take it.

'While I was trying to find out the latitude I feels a tap on the shoulder, and I looks round and if ever I saw a hangel it was then.

'The Agrippa going with all her sails set was never half so beautiful—my eye she was such a clipper—such top lights—such a clean run along the bends—such—I never! She spoke in a voice sweeter than any mermaid's as she said—

"I beg your parding, but I perceive you belong to the 'Agrippa'"

'We had the name of the ship worked in gold under a crown on the sleeves of our jacket.

"You are right, miss," says I—"cap'n of the main top, at your sarvice."

'Well, she overhauled my log as to our voyage and sich like, and at last, turning the colour of the inside of an Indy shell, she says—

"Did you happen to know Mr. Girdler?"

"Know him?" says I—"I should rather think I did; and a better hearted youth never trod the deck of a vessel in the sarvice."

"Ah! I am glad of that, but does he not drink and swear?" she said.

"Not near so much as a man ought to do," says I; "he's to 'tickler, he is, for when even he had to rouse a l us, or hail a sleepy topsman, he never would use a word that you mightn't find in the Lord's book, and it isn't every officer as can say that."

"Nor drink?" says she.

"Lor, love you," says I, "as for his drinking, it's many a time as I've his share of grog and my own too!"

"I'm glad of that," says she—"but wasn't he fractious and insubordinate? Wasn't he ordered in irons for mutinous conduct?"

"Begging your parding, miss," says I—"did you ever happen to know of a gentleman called Mr. Partridge?"

'With that she turned the colour of a scraped carrot.

"Yes," says she.

"Then, saving your presence, you have heard of one of the greatest rogues a honest tar ever came athwart on."

'So I up, and told her what I told you; and, when I had run to the end of my line, she raved some pretty words to me, gave me a grimace, and said that she had heard a good many stories from Mr. Partridge, but now she would log them; for she was sure my yarn was not for the marines to believe, but what anyone might hoist in; and asked me if I was likely to see Mr. Girdler soon

'I told her I should before I turned in that night.

"Then," says she, "say to him, if he will be at the same spot, at the same hour, that he visited a month afore he went to sea, he will meet with Agnes."

'Them's the words—for I made her say 'em agin and agin, until I logged 'em, as sure as print in a book.

'Well, she cast loose her foretop sail, and was weighing anchor, when I asked her to give me the points and heavings of Wapping. But—would you believe it?—she didn't know anything about it, although I told her that it lay due east; nor know'd nobody that lived there; but she showed me a long, narrow, dirty-looking street, called the Strand, and told me if I stood on tacking until I was brought up to the Bank of England, where they keeps all the ochre, I should find plenty of landsmen who would shape out my course for me; and so we parted company.

'Soon after I had gathered headway, it struck me that this angel might be the very craft Mr. Girdler had laid down his Jack, ensign, and pennant to!

'Whew! I was brought up all standing as soon as the thought laid itself aboard of me; and, when I came to overhaul matters, I was certai it must be so.

'Well, I 'bout ship at once, and stood on the other tack, and made for Mr. Girdler's house. I crowded sail, and, arter running now and then a little out of my course, I made it.

'When I asked for him, the steward's and cook's mate said he'd gone out of town two bells before I reached there, down to a place called Cambridge.

"I soon found that there was a craft on four wheels that made a voyage every day; so I bore away to it, and found it just ready to run into port.

'It was full upon deck—had its reg'lar complement—but there was room for one cabin passenger.

'I knew my duty better than to stow myself there; and, as there were some upon deck amidships, I scrambled up aloft; but, before I had made my anchorage good, a fellow claps on my leg to haul me down; but I gave him a lurch with my starboad fin, and down he tumbles into the mud.

'Well, there was a reg'lar shine; but, arter I had swore I'd keel haul anyone who laid a grappling iron on me, they hauled their wind, and hoisted a flag of truce, by proposing me to pay the cabin fare for a young woman on deck, who was to go into the cabin, and I was to have her berth.

'This put us all in good trim, and then four horses which were made fast to the hull, went off with a smack of a cat, and we went cracking on at six knots an hour until we got to Cambridge, and hang me if I ever saw such a set of lubberly fellows as I saw there; for arter axing half a hundred on 'em where Mr. Girdler was, none on 'em could tell me: I knew he was there, because his father's people told me so, and they ought to have known, I should think.

"But did they tell you where he hoisted his colours?" said Lang.

"Not they, neither did I ask," returned Snipe, with an indignant expression at what he deemed the most unmitigated stupidity of the town's people. "I was told he had gone to Cambridge, and then I was at Cambridge, and nobody know'd nothing about him.

"'Spose I had been on the Agrippa, and you

had come aboard and axed for Jack Snipe—'Oh, says the bo'sun's mate,—'that's the cap'n of the maintop,' "and he'd have passed the word for'ard for me—yet we'd five hundred aboard."

'Well, I run foul of half a dozen parson looking young luffs, with a kind of square shaped truck rigged on their tops, laid athwart ships, and they'd bent a black spanker something of the same cut as the chaplain's.

'I hailed them, and thought to show a ship-shape breeding, so I called 'em parsons, and they began bawling out a lingo I couldn't understand; but I soon found they were skylarking, and up to mischief, for they began to run foul of each other and try to run athwart of me.

'Well, I was not going to spoil sport, so I sided out with a bend, and clearing the decks for action I let fly at the nearest fellow's figure head, and I think I nearly carried away his dolphin striker.

'I capsized one of his mates, and laid on to another broadside to broadside; but mates all came on to action, and I should have been raked out fore and aft and sunk, if two or three youngsters hadn't bore up to my help; they then began to sing out a sort of war cry—

"Town! town!" and the parsons "Gown!"—'by the way that's what they call the black spanker they had rigged on.

'Well, in the midst of a crew of these black-rigged fellows who bore down upon us in answer to the signal, was Mr. Girdler, ready to pitch into the young fellows who had stood by me, so I hailed him, and he luffed up short, both crews drew off by his orders while he spoke, and when I told him all, both sides wore ship and bore away; then I explained to Mr. Girdler what I had given chase to him for, and he was like a madman.

'He made me repeat a hundred times the message which she had given me for him—he made me describe her build, the bend of her sails, her trim, everything, every word she said, and then wanted to make sail for London at once.

'But I begged to turn in first, or at least to make a stretch along the eating haliards, for I had ccme better than fifty knots without having anything but a little grog; for though they had piped to dinner on the road, afore I could get my grinders into a bit of meat, in comes the skipper as held the tiller lines, and sings out "Coach is ready," so we were obliged to drop knife and fork and get on board, and were under weigh in the turning of a glass up'ard, but not until the thieves who kept the grog shop had made a haul of our money for what we never had.

'When I represented this to Mr. Girdler, he made me bring myself to anchor before enough grub to provision a ship's crew; and then went to finish the night with his friends, who he said belonged to a first-rate univeremy. But all I know is, if she is manned by such a crew as I saw, she must have an howdacious rum set aboard.

'He roused me out by day-break. He had been drinking wine the whole blessed night. Howsomever, we jumped into a poshay. Then went along at a spanking rate.

'We made the voyage in about six hours; and, as Mr. Girdler looked white about the gills—for I must tell you that he was three sheets in the wind when we started—I persuaded him to turn in for about eight bells. He followed my advice; and then, with a clean shirt and a shave, he looked as lively a young fellow as you'd wish to see.

'As night drew on, he prepared to make for the spot where he was to meet Mrs. Agness. He pressed me into the service; and I was glad enough to go,

for I wanted to catch a sight once more of the pretty creeky craft.

'So we set sail; he piloted the way; and, tacking, we were brought under the lee of a hugh wall. Mr. Girdler managed to find the door; and, giving it a push, it went open.

'We entered the garden, and crept round the bushes, until we made the house, and got in front of some windows, with a little gallery in front of them; and then we dropped anchor among some bushes, and so close that nobody could make us out unless they ran foul of us.

'Well, there we lay till the moon came up; and, arter we'd been out two bells watching the window, we saw the pretty face peep out of the window; and up jumps Mr. Girdler and I together, and nearly frightens her out of her life. She jist screamed like the cry of a Mother Carey's chicken, and then she whispered "Eustace," and he sung out, gently:

"Agness, my precious angel!" or something like that; and then said:

"Here, Snipe, give me a lift up to the head-rail; and, if any footstept draws this way, pipe a call. Lay down among the bushes, and don't stir a pin."

'I nodded to him, and, giving him a hoist on to my shoulder, he scrambled up like a nimble topman up the to'-gau'nt shrouds until he got over the gallery; and then he took a pull at her lips, and talked sentimental.

'I daresay each of 'em had a great deal down in their logs which they read to each other; for he staid long enough with her.

'At last, out he comes; and, as he came over the gallery, and stood with his feet at the outer edge, saying a few things afore he parted company, I hears a footstep coming along very slow and cautious, stepping short, and then standing on again. I piped; and Mr. Girdler, giving the young lady a parting salute, dropped to the ground. We rattled along for the door, as we heard a voice sing out, "Thieves, thieves!" and bellow away as if he'd a top chain in his throat. If I'd run athwart him, I'd a spoilt his music.

'As we crowded sail, still keeping under the lee of the bushes, Mr. Girdler says:

"You make for the door, and bring up somewhere until I join you."

'With that he drops beneath the bushes, and I stood on.

'I got out of the door, and made sail down the road, until I thought I made a long stretch enough of it; and so I lay to. But there I stopped, I don't know how long, until I got tired; so I up stick, and bore away for the garden agin.

'When I reached it, all was quiet.

'Mr. Girdler wasn't in sight.

'I tried the door, but somebody had made it fast. I peeped through the keyhole, but I could see nothing. I put my shoulder to the door, and answer the signal but no, nothing stirred.

'I turned my quid, and wondered where away he'd stowed himself.

'At last I began to think he might have been overhauled for a thief, and put in irons.

'If he had, it was my duty, you know, to be alongside of him; and I gave a fresh lurch at the door to break it open.

'While I was shoving away as hard as I could, I finds my collar suddenly laid hold of, and a fellow with a drawn cutlass standing over me.

"Hollo, my fine fellow," says he, "what's up?"

'I shook off his grappling irons, and bid him be hanged.

"You're a blue jacket," says he, "and are waiting for Mr. Girdler."

"Am I?" says I; and found out at the same moment that I was talking to Mr. Partridge. I knew his voice, and then altered mine, that he shouldn't know me.

"Yes," says he, "you are; and you shall tell."

"Shall I?" says I. "Perhaps I shall, and perhaps I shan't; and I don't think I shall."

"But I am sure you will," says he.

"Are you?" says I.

"Yes," says he, "I am. I've served out your master, and will do the same for you; so mind that, my man."

"Thank'ee, sir," says I. "I'm much, much obliged." But I doubled my fist as I spoke these words.

"Are you?" says he, mocking my voice most beautifully. "Your master's laid by the heels; and so shall you be if you don't tell all you know."

"Arter you," says I, as I got clear offing for my arm; and, throwing it out, I sent it bang between his toplights, and down he went.

'I threw myself upon him, and twisted his

cutlass out of his hand, and threw it away. Then I told him to stand up, and fight like a man; but he wouldn't, and was roaring out blue murder. So I roused him up to his feet, and paid him over the head and eyes, until I clapped a stopper on his jaw, and he dropped down like a log.

'I flattened his gib-sheet in handsomely. He sung out like a marine seized up to a grating, and his noise brought up a lot of people; but I sheered before anyone laid me aboard, and hung about a short way off—half a knot, perhaps—hoping to see Mr. Girdler. But the sun came up, and he did not heave in sight; so I thought it best to heave ahead for his house.

'I made it about eight in the morning, and found everybody in a commotion. Mr. Girdler had been brought home in the middle of the night dangerously wounded.

'The servant said the doctor was with him, and he warn't expected to live, and they wouldn't let me see him, and said as how he was gone clear out o' his mind, and raving all sorts of nonsense.

'Well, it struck me that this was the work of

No. 43

Partridge. I remembered what he had said to me, and I thought I'd go and have a look for the cutlass, as perhaps that might help to make my suspicion certain. So, without saying anything to anybody, I went back to the place; and, hunting about, I picked up the cutlass, in the hedge, opposite to the garden wall.

'I looked at it, and it was stained with blood all over the blade.

'Now, as I had not used it on Mr. Partridge, I concluded that it was stained with the blood of Mr. Girdler; and a sickening sensation came across me as I thought of this.

'Well, as I was looking at this here weapon, I thought as how I heard the voice of Mr. Girdler. With that I jumps over the garden wall, and steered towards where the voice came from. I looked round, but no Mr. Girdler could I see.

'Presently a land lubber comes up to me, and says:

"Is your name Snipe?"

"I am called Jack Snipe, for want of a better," says I.

"That'll do," says he. "Come along."

"But where are you bound for?" says I.

"Mr. Girdler wants to see you," says he.

"Ah, then, it's all fair and above board," says I; and so I followed.

'Well, this ere chap took me to a small house; and in one of the rooms of this lay Mr. Girdler. He appeared very bad; but the doctor who was attending to him said as how I was not to pay out his jawing tackle: so, after a few words had passed between us, he told me to come next day; and so I left him for the night.

'Well, after this, Mr. Girdler got worse and worse. He was in a bad fever—so the doctor said—and knew nothing or nobody; but talked of a thousand things, which nobody could fathom. He laughed, and then he sang, and then his lee scuppers would overflow — and all within the striking of a bell.

'I knew somebody must keep watch over him; so I asked them to let me have the night watch.

'Well, they granted it to me; and I used to sit by his side till morning, and then turn in.

'I used to hear him order, as though he were on deck; and he would fancy himself yardarm and yardarm with Mr. Partridge, and would then speak so soft and low about Miss Agnes.

'I felt I had work to keep the weel clear. One night I was sitting by his side, and he had been rattling away as usual, and was just dropped into a sleep. It was midnight, and had been raining all the evening: but the wind, which had been southerly, with a little west in it, got round more to the westward, and was getting to blow a gale. I was thinking of my own life; I was earthed down, and sad thoughts came upon me: for, you see, I was overhauling the black days of my log. As I was a doing this, I cast up my eyes; and what do you think I saw?'

"Can't say," said Lang, taking a deep draught from the can of grog.

"Why, a young 'oman in white."

"Well, what did she say?"

"Ah, but she was all in white though, and with a figure-head as white as her rigging."

'She looked steadfastly on me, but I was taken flat aback. I stared at her, with my toplights like portholes, and a mouth like a main-hatchway.

'She didn't speak a word, but advanced towards me.

'I never heard a footfall. She came like a schooner with a light breeze; and, after staring at me, as if she would speak, she turned her head away, and stood by the bed: she clasped her hands, and knelt down by the side.

'After she had been there a little while, she rose again, and leant over the bed, and kissed Mr. Girdler's forehead, that, with his dark hair, appeared as white as spray. Then she raised her toplights to heaven, while the salt water ran out of them like pearls. Then she embraced him again; and then she turned to me, pointed to Mr. Girdler, pressed her two white fins together, and left the room, keeping her bows towards us.

'Just as she reached the door, Mr. Girdler sprang up in the bed, and stared at her. She smiled—and, ah! that was a smile—and then vanished like a beautiful vision.'

"Vanished?" said Lang.

"Yes," said Snipe, with a grave shake of his head—"vanished!"

'Mr. Girdler gave a loud cry, and fainted.

'I sang out for help: but I never told anyone the ghost of Miss Agnes came to his bedside.

'Well, after a time, the doctor said as how Mr. Girdler would recover; and so he did; but he never knew how he got wounded.

As soon as he was well enough to get out, he made for the place where Miss Agnes lived. I went with him, but we found the house was let to some other folks, who know'd nothing about Miss Agnes and her parents, only that they believed they were gone abroad, but where they couldn't say.

'Well, every place he tried; but he couldn't overhaul the whereaway; but we did find Mr. Partridge gone, as a third lieutenant, in a seventy-four, upon a five years' station, in the East Indies, after he got well.

'An old messmate of mine told me this, and said he'd seen him afore he sailed, and his figure-head was so altered that his friends hardly knew him.

'Well, after knocking about a little longer, Mr. Girdler was made first lieutenant, and arter then Captain of the 'Agapemone;' and as she had her full complement of petty officers, I could only be made foremast-man, and I declare that Mr. Girdler, or Captain Girdler was a staunch friend to me for life.

"Then how was it you left him?" asked Lang.

"Why, you see I sailed with him as fought his ship bravely, and is now dead and gone—Captain Feather-tone—cause you see the Agapemone was pretty well blown to pieces by the bursting of her magazine.

'That's how it was I came on board the 'Damon,' as pretty a craft, and manned by as brave a crew as ever fought under the colours of Old England.'

"Colours which they never disgraced," said Lang—"for rather than see them lowered they nailed them to the mast. With such a crew what would I not do?"

The pirate looked thoughtfully upon the floor of the cabin as he gave utterance to those words.

CHAPTER CXVI.

THE CASTAWAYS—LOVE AND JEALOUSY—A WOMAN'S APPEAL, AND A MAN'S RESOLVE.

STRANGE, intense, and conflicting were the emotions which raged within the hearts of Martinez and Inez as they gazed upon the prostrate and disfigured form of the captain as he lie upon the earth beneath the spreading branches of a huge tree.

For some moments after the utterance of his name neither Inez nor Martinez spoke.

Each were busied with their own thoughts.

To Inez this meeting was anything but a pleasant one.

She could not forget that Wildwell had torn her from her home to make her his.

She ran through in her recollection all that had transpired on board the slaver, and she trembled now that her eyes encountered the man who so madly loved her.

Nor were the thoughts of Martinez the less uneasy.

He saw before him a rival.

He knew that Captain Wildwell was a man not to be easily put from any design he had planned.

He knew that he loved Inez to madness.

And he dreaded his presence there, lest his return to health bring with it a return of that passion for the beautiful woman who had surrendered all her virgin purity to the keeping of his lieutenant.

Martinez was not the man to wish a fellow-creature ill, but the demon of jealousy began to rise in his breast, and fain would he have gazed on the corpse rather than the still breathing form of the man before him.

He felt sore at ease.

The first shadow had crossed the sunshine of his existence on that Island.

Ned Wilton, on the contrary, was almost mad with joy.

It was happiness indeed to him to know that there was still others on the island besides himself and the lovers.

In a few minutes he and Jack Ridley were hale fellows well met.

They had run over their logs, and each given the other a bit of their adventures.

And something more still.

Something which Ned looked upon with greater pleasure than aught else, and which cemented the friendship of the two sailors in an instant.

Jack Ridley took a string of pigtail from his pocket and, twisting off several inches, placed it in the hands of Ned.

Ned's eyes sparkled with pleasure.

He looked at it for an instant; then opened his mouth to its utmost stretch.

In the next instant half the pigtail he had received was being twisted and twirled about by his teeth; and the glow of pleasure on his face was spoiled only by the swollen appearance of his cheeks.

Had anything been required to make Jack Ridley and Ned Wilton friends, it had certainly been found.

The baccy had done it; they were the firmest of friends.

At the mention of his name, Captain Wildwell opened his eyes, and gazed vacantly up at the luxuriant foliage above his head.

Then, with a sigh, he closed them again.

"Poor fellow!" said Ned, speaking with difficulty, from his mouth being so full of tobacco, as he gazed down upon the captain of the slaver—"I reckon it will be some time afore he can walk the quarter-deck again."

Jack Ridley stooped down, and smoothed the pea-jacket which served as a pillow for the wounded man.

"It will," he remarked, in answer to Ned—"for he has been sadly treated. I only wish I had the wretches here, and I could get at 'em one at a time. I'd show the piratical sharks a specimen of what a true sailor can do—if I wouldn't, split me!"

A smile broke over the face of the wounded man as these words fell upon his ears.

"There, you will lay more comfortable now, cap'n," said Ridley, easing his head on the jacket. "You'll soon get well, I reckon, being watched by two pretty eyes like those what's a looking at you now. It's the lady, cap'n, as jumped overboard from the vessel."

"What—what!" gasped Wildwell, opening his eyes again, and looking up in the face of his follower.

"The beautiful lady, cap'n, as was lost at sea, you know."

And Jack moved away from the spot where he stood, to allow the eyes of the prostrate man to encounter the form of Mary.

Weak and suffering as he was, the slaver captain fairly started into a sitting position as his almost dimmed sight encountered the slender form of the dark-eyed Mary.

For a moment he gazed in speechless amazement upon her.

Then, in a tone so fervent, he gasped forth:

"Inez—beloved Inez!"

And, as the words left his lips, he fell back on his rude couch, exhausted and powerless.

The heart of Martinez beat violently.

It seemed as though it would burst from his bosom—so fierce were its throbbings.

His teeth clenched tightly together.

His hold upon Inez tightened, till it became almost painful; and his eyeballs were strained to catch the workings of her countenance.

His hot blood was fired.

He loved the girl at his side with a passion so fierce that it amounted almost to frenzy.

But, if he could love, he could likewise hate; and jealousy was goading him on to believe the look of pity on the features of Inez to be one of love for the prostrate man.

Bitter, indeed, were the thoughts that took possession of his heart.

He turned his gaze upon Wildwell.

He took one step towards him.

Then he paused.

A blush of shame overspread his face.

The man before him was powerless and ill.

Could he allow the demon to tempt?

Could he forget his manhood?

Could he assail the wretch so weak and exhausted at his feet?

Those words had stung him to madness; but his better nature rose in time to save him from offering insult or violence to one whom he had hitherto respected and loved.

"Come away, Inez," he said—"come away!"

Inez hesitated.

Martinez drew her a few paces from the spot.

"Inez," he said, fixing a penetrating glance upon her now pale features, "the sight of this man is more than I can bear."

"Why so?" she asked.

"Why so!" he iterated.

"Aye."

"Can you ask?"

Inez raised her eyes to his.

The fiery glance he threw now frightened her. Never had she seen him look so fierce. The fair girl trembled. Yet she knew not why.

"What is the cause of this emotion?" she said, softly.

"Can you not guess?" he asked.

"That man?"

"Yes."

"But why should he cause you so much uneasiness?" she said.

"Why!"

"Aye, why?"

"Because——"

And he paused.

"Because what?"

"I fear."

"Fear!"

"Yes."

"What can you fear?" said Inez, placing her hand on his.

"Alas! I know not, Inez; but—but my heart is ill at ease," he replied.

"And so is mine."

"From what cause, Inez, does it spring?" he said, looking fixedly at her.

A purple blush suffused her pale cheeks. Her eyes dropped to the ground. Martinez observed all this, with compressed lips.

"Speak!" he said.

"I would we had not met again," she murmured.

"Would to heaven we had not!" he said, hastily. "Would that the sea had swallowed him up, or death closed his eyes, ere he landed here."

"Martinez!" said Inez, reprovingly.

Again a flush of shame rose to the face of the lieutenant.

"Inez," he said, "I know not what I say—mean not what I say: but I am wretched. Your love is all in all to me. To lose it, is to make existence miserable—turn the sunshine of joy into the black and Stygian darkness of hell. That man loves you, and I fear him!"

"Fear him!"

"Aye."

"Why should you fear him?" asked Inez.

"Because I love him to distraction."

"And do not I love you?" she said, as the tears rose to her eyes. "Do I not love you with all a fond woman's love? Oh, Martinez!"

And a violent sob choked her further utterance. Martinez caught her to his breast.

"Have I not proved how deep is my love for you?—Have I not sacrificed the dearest treasure that woman possesses to my love?"

"You have—you have!"

"And yet you doubt me," sighed Inez, in a tone of bitterness.

"I—I, doubt you not," he said—"I only fear the——"

"What?"

"That man!"

"What can you fear from him?"

"His influence!"

"With whom?"

"With you!"

"Me?"

"Yes!"

"Martinez—what influence can he possibly possess over me?"

"I know not."

"No?"

"And yet——"

"Martinez," she interrupted—"Is it possible that jealously could have laid so firm an hold of your heart?—It is possible that you can believe my love to cool towards you, because the man from whom I strove to escape, even at the sacrifice of my life, lies there but a ruin of his former self. Oh! Martinez, 'tis not *my* love that will change, but—but——"

"Mine?" he interrupted—"Never!"

"And yet you doubt me?"

"I cannot—cannot help this feeling that has taken possession of my soul. I dread something, I know not what. I feel, I cannot describe how. Inez, would to heaven we were away from here—from him!"

"Oh! would that we were, could it but make you happy: for heaven knows, your happiness and your love is all I care for in this world."

"And thine is the same to me. A look—a smile bestowed upon another is agony to my soul. So fervently do I love you that I envy almost the passing wind that kisses your cheeks, and could quarrel with a breeze for assailing your beautiful form. A love like mine is fierce and passionate, and I cannot help the fears that rise within my heart."

"For your love, and your's alone do I live," exclaimed Inez; "and when our affections towards each other alter, then let me die, for existence will then be worthless."

"We will leave this place," said Marinez, after a pause.

"How can we do so," she asked.

"Did I not point out the way," said Marinez, "when we discovered that others besides ourselves were on the island."

"The sea?"

"Yes."

"And whither would you go?"

"Anywhere."

"Anywhere?"

"Aye, from here—from him!" said Marinez.

Inez sighed.

"Martinez," she said.

"Inez?"

"You would go and leave *him?*"

"I would!"

"To die?"

Martinez answered not.

"To die without a thought of what you do—leave him to perish here, and refuse to attend to a fellow-creature a helping hand? Martinez, think not I care the less for you because I feel as a Christian. He lies there weak and powerless—away from the home of childhood—away from those who could assist him to health and strength. Shall we refuse that which we might have cause to ask for ourselves? Shall we turn from him in anger, whilst death hovers around his brow? Shall I forget that I am a woman, and that a woman's mission on earth is mercy? Can you forget that you are a man and a sailor, and refuse to succour the suffering and oppressed?"

Martinez cast his eyes to the ground.

"No, Martinez—no! That noble nature which won my heart has not deserted your breast; that noble spirit for which I sacrificed myself has not flown your soul! He I love is still a man in nature as well as in name; and one who, though shut out by circumstances from the world, can still cast his eyes heavenwards, lay his hand upon his heart, and say 'I am a Christian,' and that 'faith, hope, and charity are not obliterated from my heart.'"

For a few moments Martinez stood gazing upon the ground at his feet.

The glow of shame deepened on his cheek.

His bosom rose and fell like the waves on the shingly beach.

Then he raised his head.

He stretched forth his arm and caught Inez to breast.

He parted the dark locks upon her brow.

He imprinted a kiss upon her quivering lips.

"Inez," he exclaimed, as he gazed proudly into the liquid depths of her dark lustrous eyes—"Inez—my love, my life, my soul, my guardian angel—how do you teach me to know what I should become! I was jealous: but that is past. I forgot that I was a man; but your words recall me to myself, and show me what I might become, and what I should be. Inez, I will succour this poor fellow-creature; I will watch and nurse him, and strive to restore him to his former self: for such deeds are more worthy a man or a sailor than hatred or jealousy. Inez, your love shall light me on in the path of mercy, and save me from staining my name with dishonour."

—————

CHAPTER CXVII.

THE WOUNDED SLAVER CAPTAIN TAKEN TO THE HUT, AND NURSED BY MARTINEZ AND INEZ. THE TALE.

THE bright smile and the look of affection on her face repaid the young lieutenant for the good resolve which he had made.

Martinez now felt thoroughly ashamed of himself for allowing the feelings which had taken possession of him to find for a moment a home in his breast.

But there is seldom love without jealousy; so Martinez may well be excused if the canker-worm for a time gnawed its way to his heart at the sight of one whom he knew to be a rival.

However, the words of Inez had dispersed the dark cloud, and the sun again shone in his heart.

He turned and strode towards the spot where Wildwell lay.

Inez followed him.

Reaching the side of the prostrate man, Martinez stooped down and bent over him.

A look of pity stole over his face as he gazed upon the disfigured features of the once handsome slave captain.

"Captain," he said, softly.

The eyes of the invalid opened.

"Captain, do you know me?" asked Martinez.

"I should know that voice," murmured Wildwell; "but it is the tones of one some time dead."

"It is Martinez."

"Martinez!" gasped Wildwell.

"Aye, captain."

"Impossible!"

"In truth it is he."

"He is dead."

"He lives."

Wildwell shook his head.

"Look upon me, captain," he said. "Am I not Martinez?"

And the lieutenant bent further over the wounded man.

"'Tis the voice of him you name," said Captain Wildwell.

"And the features?" said Martinez.

"Alas!"

"What?"

"I cannot see them," said the captain, in a tone of agony.

"Cannot see?"

"No."

"I will raise your head."

And Martinez placed his arm beneath his head.

"'Tis useless," said Wildwell.

"You can then be sure that it is Martinez who speaks.

"Alas! I cannot."

"How so?"

"I am blind!" exclaimed Wildwell.

"Blind?" said Martinez.

And a shudder of horror ran through his whole frame.

"Yes, blind," sighed Wildwell.

"Merciful heaven's!—can it be," gasped the lieutenant.

"But too true. Oh! Martinez, what have I not suffered since last we met," exclaimed Wildwell. "Give me your hand. There, it trembles in my own. You pity me—me, the slaver captain, who has been so fearfully punished for his wicked deeds. Oh! 'tis sad to be thus, with the light of heaven denied to me. Better death—death!"

"Give not way to despair, captain; you were not wont to do so."

"No," exclaimed Wildwell—"but then I could see, but now this fearful blackness is upon me—now that eternal night has settled on my soul, I fain would die!"

Martinez cast his eyes towards the spot where Inez stood.

She was gazing with a look of anguish upon the prostrate man.

And tears filled her eyes as she heard the fearful affliction of him who had persecuted her so fearfully.

But she was silent.

Martinez beckoned her towards him.

Inez obeyed him.

She stood by his side.

Beside him whose presence she had once feared, and from whose power she had leaped into the foaming billows to escape.

"Blind," he whispered to her.

Inez sighed.

"The hand of fate has fallen heavily upon him," said Martinez—"and in truth he needs our aid."

"Shall he ask for it in vain?" said Inez, gazing at the face of Martinez.

"No, by Heaven!" exclaimed Martinez.

"That voice again," said Wildwell. "the tones on which I loved to dwell. Can it be? Speak, Martinez, speak. That voice, 'tis music to my soul. 'Tis—'tis—"

"Inez," interrupted Martinez.

"Heaven be praised!" exclaimed Wildwell; "for then I am not guilty of her death—that sin at least is spared me."

"It is—it is," said Inez, bending down and placing her hand in that of the invalid.

"Now I can die happy," said Wildwell. "Inez can you forgive me?"

"I can," she said.

"And will?"

"And will!" she replied.

"Heaven bless you!" said Wildwell. "The sufferings I have endured were nothing compared to those I experienced at what I believed to be your fate. Oh, Inez, to hear you speak again is music to my soul! Would that I could once more gaze upon your lovely features! But there—there I see thee in imagination as plainly as ever! I can see the sweet smile wreath your lips; and the long dark lashes shading the fiery glance of your eye. Heaven be thanked that you are saved from the doom you courted through my work!"

"Compose yourself," said Martinez. "Do not talk; it but serves to weaken your already weakened frame."

"True—true," gasped Wildwell—"I am faint enough already."

And the pressure of his hand on that of Inez relaxed, and he suffered his head to fall back upon the pea-jacket—from which he had slightly raised it at the sound of Inez's voice—and lie motionless.

For some minutes the lovers remained gazing upon the altered countenance of the sufferer.

Gradually the slaver captain's breath became more regular, and they perceived that he slept.

Then they simultaneously rose from his side.

Their eyes met.

A look of pity passed between them.

With a sigh, they both turned to join Jack Ridley and Ned Wilton, who were talking over their adventures, and chewing the pigtail to a pulp.

As the lovers approached them, the two sailors rose from the ground, where they had been sitting.

"Well, lieutenant," said Ridley, "what do you think of the commander?"

"Low—very sad," was the reply.

"Yes, he's had something to put up with from the piratical fiends," said Jack.

"Fearful," said Inez. "His sight is injured."

"And that's what I most fear," said Ridley.

"It is horrible to lose the sight," said Martinez, with a shudder.

"If it warn't for that," said Jack Ridley, "I should think he would stand a chance of getting all right agin, now that he has lived so long after the injuries he has received. But the loss of sight makes him fretful; and he has got enough to bear up against without the thought of that."

"How did that come about?" said Ned.

"What?"

"His blindness."

"Well, you see, when the pirates let loose the blacks to mutiny, they were commanded by one Wild Madge."

"Wild Madge!" exclaimed Ned.

"That's what they called her," said Ridley.

"And wild indeed she was, in appearance and manners," said Inez.

"Wild Madge!" exclaimed Ned again, as though he could not believe he had heard aright.

"Yes, and an infernal fury she is—the confounded hag!" said Ridley. "But you don't seem to believe it. Ask the lieutenant."

And Ridley pointed to Martinez as he spoke.

"Wild Madge—the mother of the Boy Rover," muttered Ned. "Well, I never!—how the devil did she get aboard?"

"The captain picked her up at sea."

"Then he didn't know as much of her as I do," said Ned, "or he would have thrust her over the sides into the waves."

"You know her, then?" said Ridley.

"Know her," exclaimed Ned, "to my cost; and so does everyone with whom she runs foul. A beastly drunken wretch—lost to all womanly nature—with a mind as evil as the devil's. Know her? Yes, curse her, I do know her!—saving your presence, ma'am. I do know her; and her hateful cub of a son into the bargain!"

"Is she the mother, then, of the celebrated Boy Rover?"

"She is."

"I should like to know a little more about her and her companion," said Ridley.

"Not now," interrupted Martinez. "First convey the captain to our hut, and when he is comfortably and safely disposed, then we can learn what we wish to know—how he came to such a state, and who were those who brought him to it."

"So we can," said Ned. "Bear a hand, messmate, and we will put the poor fellow under shelter, where he can be better watched and cared for than he can be where he lies."

And Ned and Ridley, darting to the side of Wildwell, raised him tenderly in their arms and slowly bore him to the hut of Martinez, preceded by the lovers.

In a short time Captain Wildwell was laid on the bed of dried grass which had served for the couch of Martinez and Inez.

Once or twice he opened his eyelids, and his features were lit up with a smile.

But he uttered not a word.

However, it was evident that he felt all was being done for him that could be done; and when, at length, Inez had smoothed the grass, so as to form a by no means uncomfortable couch, he sank into a quiet slumber.

Covering him with the pea-jacket of Jack Ridley, the four castaways sat down, and partook of a humble, yet plentiful, meal; and, when this was ended, and Jack Ridley and Ned Wilton had replenished their mouths with the pigtail, Jack told them all what had happened on board, from the moment of Martinez leaping after Inez into the sea; and how he had succeeded in hiding from the mutineers, and found the captain bleeding and wounded on the deck, and contrived to escape with him to the island on which they now were, and where he little expected to meet with those whom he believed had perished in the deep waters of the ocean.

Ned also recounted what he knew of Wild Madge; and, in fact, disguised nothing of his whole career; and, when he had recorded the whole of his adventures, he concluded, by saying:

"You see I haven't got much to boast of in my life. I've been a bad youth, and a bad man; but it's never too late to mend. I have thought so more since the 'Venomed Snake' went down, and I was thrown ashore here, suffering from the wounds I received at the command of the Boy Rover, and at the hands of my messmates, when bound to the mast, and impaled with their knives. But there—it was a just punishment for a guilty life; and I mean, if ever I have the chance to leave this island and return to my native land, to be a good man for the future, and, by a life of honesty and truth, strive to win a good name, and atone for the sins I have committed when serving under one whose callous heart could so cruelly torture one who had served him too well."

"And Heaven give you strength to keep to your good resolve," said Inez. "There is no heart so callous but there is one green spot within it: there is an oasis in every desert, which glistens like a star in a dark sky, to show us how to steer to comfort and peace."

"If men would but only think so," said Martinez. "But, alas! some are lost beyond all retrieving.

"Then I don't believe there is any green spot in the hearts of those inhuman fiends who brought about the mutiny on the slaver," said Ridley. "They are nothing but a cursed lot of pirates; and pirates, you know, never have hearts at all."

"They have; for they are men," said Inez.

"They ain't—acos they are devils," said Ridley. "Nobody ever heard of pirates having such a feeling in his heart as mercy or pity."

"You are wrong, Jack," said Inez: "I have."

"You!"

"Yes, me."

"Then its more than I have," said Ridley.

"But not more than you shall," said Inez; "for I will tell you a story of one, told to me many years since, by an old friend of our family, whose hand had been sought in marriage by one who hoisted the black flag over the blue sea."

"Will you?" said Ridley, turning his quid round in his mouth—"I should just like to hear it. But, you see, I ain't much of a scholar; so, if you'll tell us all about him without putting a lot of long words in, I shall be glad; 'cos, you see, it spoils half a story when you don't know what the long words means."

Martinez laughed, and Inez could not repress a smile, at the request of the sailor.

"I will tell you it in the same words, as near as I can recollect them, as she told it to me when, a young child, I sat at her feet, one night, in the home of my youthful days."

Ned and Ridley composed themselves on their seats to listen; and Martinez, having taken up his position beside the sleeping man—so as to be enabled to render him any assistance necessary, if he awoke—Inez commenced:

'When I was about eighteen years of age,' said the old lady, looking down upon me, as I sat peering up into her wrinkled yet still handsome face, 'a young man, by the name of Walter Crawford, made me an offer of his hand.

'He was rather good-looking, had a fine manly figure, was considered quite respectable, and, on the whole, I liked him, though I cannot say I ever had any violent passion for him.

'But he had for me—at least so he said—and he frankly declared that if he failed to link his fortune with mine he would be ruined, body and soul. I considered this very extravagant language, and told him so; but he repeated it more than once, and confirmed it with an oath, which I did not like.

'However, my father, for some reason, had taken an utter dislike to young Crawford, and said I should never marry him with his consent; and, as I would not wed against his wishes, the affair ended in a dismissal of my passionate suitor, who parted from me in anger, and immediately left for parts unknown.

'Six years after that I married one who at that time was master and part owner of a vessel trading between Liverpool, the West Indies, and different parts of Mexico and the Caribbean Sea.

'As he continued his vocation for several years after our marriage, I used occasionally to make the voyage with him.

'Our last voyage was made in the year 1725, and of something that happened then I am now going to tell you.

'At the time I now speak of, the navigation of the Gulfs of Mexico and Bahama, and contiguous waters, was a dangerous business for merchantmen and traders, owing to the hordes of pirates which infested that region.

'My husband had several narrow escapes, and I was all the time uneasy for fear something would happen to him.

'When I was with him I was afraid, and when he left me at home I was miserable all the time of his absence.

'Well, one night, when about six hours' sail from Havana, on our last homeward voyage, my husband came down to me in the cabin, and reported all going well.

"A few hours more, my timid wife," he said, with a cheerful smile, "and we shall be beyond even the apprehension of danger, and then I trust I shall see you yourself again, for really your dejected, anxious looks are enough to give one the blues."

"I wish for your sake, William, I could be more cheerful," I replied; "but when I think of the danger we run, and what we have at stake, I cannot help feeling somewhat nervous and frightened."

"Well, I cannot blame you, Anna, all things considered: but as this is my last voyage, let us hope your fears may be soon overcome! I will read a chapter from the Bible, and turn in, for I am very much fatigued. We have a favourable breeze, and nothing at present to give us any alarm."

'I felt strangely uneasy, even while he was speaking; but I kept my fears to myself; and taking up the Bible he began to read a chapter, as was his custom before retiring for the night—for, unlike many sea-captains, my husband was a religious man. The chapter for this occasion was the Fourth of Job; and he had just finished the words "Remember, I pray thee, who ever perished, being innocent? or where were the righteous cut off?" when he was suddenly interrupted by the sharp, startling cry:

"Sail-ho?"

"Where away?" he shouted, as he dropped the book and rushed to the deck, leaving me trembling with fear, but somewhat comforted by the sacred words he had just read.

"Close on our weather beam!" I heard a voice reply.

'There was a quick movement of feet on deck; and while I sat holding my breath with fear, there rang out upon the still air the sharp reports of a volley of musketry, followed by the gruff, savage hail:

"Ship ahoy!"

"Hillo!" was the answer.

"Heave-to, and let us send a boat abroad, or we'll riddle you with a broadside, and be —— to you!"

'Then came several quick orders, a hurried tramping of feet on deck, the rattling of cordage, the flapping of sails, and then a death-like silence.

'Presently I heard a step upon the stairs. I looked up and saw my husband slowly descending. His knees quivered, and his face was deadly pale. He spoke, but in quavering tones:

"Anna, my dear wife," he said, as he reeled forward and threw his arms around me, "your worst fears are confirmed—we are in the hands of pirates. For myself, I could die like a man; but you! you! oh, my God, you!" and, sinking heavily upon a seat, he groaned like one in pain.

'It was my turn to be supporter and comforter

now. The poor, weak, timid woman was to change places with the strong courageous man.

"William," I said, solemnly and firmly, and feeling a calm holy thrill of security and protection pass through my late fainting and shrinking frame— "William, in our hour of trouble, remember the sacred promises of the Lord : 'Who ever perished, being innocent? or where were the righteous cut off?'"

"Then none are innocent, and none are righteous," he replied, gloomily ; " for all perish—the lamb as well as the wolf. It is our turn now. We can scarcely expect these wretches to spare ; for they have run up the black flag, and their motto is, 'Dead men tell no tales.' There—hark! Even now they are boarding us! Oh, my dear wife, it is the thought of you that unnerves and makes a coward of me! I could die bravely if you were dead ; but, oh, to leave you behind to a doom a thousand times worse than death!—this is the fear that pierces my very soul! Oh, merciful God, let this cup pass from me!"

'There was now a fearful noise on deck—rough voices, shuffling feet, shouts, and blasphemous oaths.

'I arose and stood before my husband—firm as a rock—unnaturally calm in that moment of terrible peril.

'Three or four men, frightful-looking fellows, armed with pistols and cutlasses, appeared descending the stairs.

"Ho! ho! what have we here?" said the foremost, in a gruff voice, and with a coarse laugh. "A woman, as I live! This will be sport for the captain, who always takes the women for a part of his share."

"Send your captain here," said I, with a calm firmness that surprised myself.

"All in good time, my beauty! You'll see him soon enough. Come, sirrah! you're wanted on deck," he continued, addressing my husband. "All your lubberly crew are going to walk the plank, and they want you to lead off. Up with you—be lively—for we've got no time to spare!" he added, putting a pistol to my husband's head.

"Will no amount of ransom save our lives?" asked my husband.

"No, we don't do business that way. So up with you, or I'll scatter your brains where you stand, and they might soil the lady's dress!"

"Farewell, my dear, dear wife!" said my husband, in a choking voice, as he threw his arms around my neck, and pressed his trembling lips to mine. "Let your dagger save you from dishonour," he whispered, as he tore himself away.

'Oh! my dear child, it was a terrible moment; but still I was calm—unnaturally calm—and the reassuring words of the Lord were still ringing in my ears.

"Men," said I, "you have had mothers and sisters—perhaps sweethearts and wives—and still, in your inner hearts, must beat some feelings of human sympathy. Oh, by all you hold sacred, I adjure you not to stain your hands with the blood of those who never injured you ; but let a daughter, a sister, a wife, a mother, appeal to you for mercy! Take all our money and goods, if you will ; but let us escape with life!"

"Ho! ho! ho!" laughed the spokesman, who was the second in command—"you talk like a woman ; and all women are fools."

"At least, then," rejoined I, "before you sacrifice any lives, let me see your captain; for I have something to tell him of importance, which may

make it to his interest to spare some of your prisoners."

"Aye, aye—that's fair enough," said the man, as he turned and marched my poor husband before him to the deck, leaving me alone, but still upheld by a Superior Power.

"I knew not what I should say to the pirate captain—it seemed as if I only needed to gain time for something to interpose and save us.

'In a minute or so a quick step descended the stairs, and a voice said, impatiently :

"What is it, woman—what is it? I am the captain of the pirate, at your service."

'I was standing with my features in shadow, but the light fell clearly upon his. Years had passed—with him long, bitter years of passion and strife—since I had looked upon that face ; but through the heavy beard, the bronze of exposure, the scars of battle, the knitted brow, the merciless eye, the deep furrows of grief, anger, hate and remorse, I recognized the comely youth, who had once sued for my hand.

"Walter Crawford," said I, "it is Anna Mervale who stands before you."

'He started and staggered as if struck a heavy blow, and then, catching hold of me and turning me to the light, he looked eagerly and wildly into my face.

"Gracious God!" he cried, sinking down upon a seat, and burying his face in his hands.

"Walter Crawford," said I, " I will not say I ever loved you, but for long, long years, as a maid, a wife, and a mother—I have prayed for your happiness. My husband commands this vessel. He and I, and nearly all we possess, are now in your power. Will you save or destroy us ? Shall our prayers go up to Heaven for your salvation, or shall our spirits appear at the Judgment Seat against you ?'

'He groaned and sobbed like a child.

"Oh, Anna," he replied, "I told you your rejection would destroy me, body and soul!"

"No, Walter Crawford! If you are destroyed, body and soul, it will be by your own evil deeds. No disappointment can be an excuse for crime. What a life is this! Quit it, repent, reform, and be saved!"

"It is too late!" he groaned, starting up, and pacing hurriedly and unsteadily to and fro. "And we meet thus! Oh, my God! my God!"

"Will you save or destroy us ?" said I, calmly.

'For nearly a minute he did not reply, during which period he must have undergone an age of torture. Then he turned and grasped my hand—presenting the most haggard, wretched, woe-begone countenance I ever beheld.

"Farewell," he gasped—" farewell for ever!"

'He turned, reeled, and rushed on deck.

'Then I heard hurried orders and hurried movements.

'Spellbound, I was standing like one in a trance, when my husband rushed down, clasped me in his arms, and exclaimed :

"My dear, dearest Anna, what magic is this? The pirates are gone, and we are saved!"

'I could not reply. Nature, which had done so much, could not sustain me against the rush of this new and happy emotion. I pointed to the open bible, and fainted upon his breast.

'We were saved indeed.

'Long years have passed since then, my child. My husband sleeps in his grave ; but I still live, and pray that God will forgive that man who dates his ruin from his love of me."

"Well, I reckon he warn't so bad, after all," said Ridley—"though I believe he is the only pirate as ever had a heart, for all that."

"It has served to pass away the time," said Inez—"if for nothing else; and there is always something to be learnt even from a tale."

"That's true," said Ned—"and I should like to hear another whilst the captain sleeps; for there is nothing more wearisome than sitting silent with only a poor suffering wretch to fix your thoughts on."

"Well, ain't you got a yarn you can spin us till he wakes up?" said Ridley.

Ned shook his head.

"I only knows a love yarn; but then, you see, I knows it's true, acos it happened in the neighbourhood where I was born, and from where I used to watch the waves a rolling in on the beach, and sigh for a voyage round the world. But, if it's a love story, it's about a shark as well; and it happened in a cosy little nook, nestling amid white cliffs:

'One day two pretty girls strolled close to where

I was standing, wishing I was a sailor, and gathering the pretty shells on the beach.

"Isn't it sweet here?" exclaimed Stephanie Calderton, untying the ribbons of her broad 'flat,' so that the wind might play unhindered with her loose brown ringlets.

'There was no answer. Rosa Miller was walking slowly on, with her blue dreamy eyes fixed vaguely on the far distance, while a faint rose-colour came and went across her cheek.

"Why don't you answer, Rosa?" persisted Stephanie, merrily. "I know, though—it's because you are vexed at John Darrell's flirtation with Katy Arnott."

Rosa shook her head.

"John Darrell need render no account of his proceedings to me," she said, curving her lip. "He is at liberty to play chevalier to any lady he likes: I refused him this morning."

"Refused him! Refused John Darrell!"

'Stephanie opened her round black eyes in surprise.

"Refused John Darrell, the handsomest fellow

at the sea-side, and the noblest, and a man who loves you better than his own heart's blood! Oh, Rosa, how could you?"

"He does not love me," returned Rosa, quietly. "It is a mere passing fancy—an evanescent partiality. The man that wins *me* must be no such cool calm wooer. *I* want a love stronger than life itself."

"And so," exclaimed the indignant Stephanie, "John Darrell is to be discarded because he don't think proper to shoot himself, or go insane, or perform any other little piece of theatricals! Rosa Miller, I think you are an unmitigated goose."

'The sunset was glowing redly across the sands, when a merry little party came out upon the beach, where bathing machines were standing.

'A grey-haired old fisherman was busily engaged with a messmate in caulking the seams of their boat. He looked up, and greeted the newcomers with a nod.

"Why, here's old Jackson again!" exclaimed Marmaduke Calderton, gaily. "What's the matter with your boat, old True-penny? If it's out of order, we'll have to be content with a bath, instead of a sail."

'The old man shook his head, and replied:

"The less you have to do with salt water the better when sharks is around; and, true as you're alive, I saw one o' them ugly demons off the rocks not three hours ago."

"Nonsense!" laughed Calderton. "You were dreaming, Jackson. Who ever heard of a shark in these waters?"

"No, sir, I warn't dreamin'; and I calculate I've lived by the sea long enough to know the white belly of a shark when I see it. Hows'ever, you can believe it or not, just as you please."

'The gay party laughed at the fears of the old man, and proceeded towards the bathing machines.

'There never was anything half so bewitching as Rosa Miller looked in her dark-blue bathing suit, edged with vivid scarlet. The sunset seemed to leave its carmine shadow on her cheek; the blue sparkle of the waves seemed to concentrate in her eyes; while her long golden tresses gave a careless grace to the whole.

'John Darrell, as he walked listlessly along the shore, saw how lovely she was, and his heart sank within him.

"The shark! the shark!"

'How wildly that awful shriek rose into the air, reaching Darrell's ears, and causing him to turn abruptly towards the little group of bathers!

'Was it indeed the deadly hunter of the sea whose white glimmer flashed through the waves? or was it but a line of evanescent foam?

'He knew not; yet instinctively he sprang towards the shore, as the terrified bathers fled shrieking landward. Katy Arnott, Stephanie Calderton, and her brother, and Charles Maygood, and—

'Where was Rosa Miller?

'Poor Rosa!—poor little Rosa! She had incautiously ventured too near the deep water; and, when the blind shock of terror fell on them, all had unconsciously turned in a wrong direction.

'Before the bewildered faculties of the dripping group could fairly take in the circumstances of their escape, and Rosa's peril, John Darrell had sprang into the sea, and was striking out with swift strong impulses towards the girl.

"Are you mad, Mr. Darrell?" the old fisherman had cried, seizing his arm. "You can't save the poor lassie, and you're only perilling your own life."

'But John Darrell's set teeth and blazing eye had spoken too truly his determination. A thousand remonstrances—nay, ten thousand—would have fallen on a deaf ear.

'As it happened, neither Calderton nor Maygood could swim; and they watched the lessening distance between Darrell and Rosa with breathless interest, which made every second seem like an age.

"There!" he's got his arm around her," ejaculated Jackson. "Them's good strong strokes for a feller that swims with only one arm; but I misdoubt me he's come too late. D'ye see that white shine by the Point Rock? That's the shark."

'He paused, while his sun-browned face turned a dull, dead, saffron hue.

"They'll never reach *this* shore alive," he muttered. "See how the ugly creetur gains on 'em. If he could only leave the gal, and save himself—but I guess he ain't made o' that sort o' stuff. There! he's steering for the left. I have it—he's goin' to try landing on the rocks under the headland."

'A deep awful silence fell on the witnesses as the desperate swimmer shot beyond the intervening cliffs, and, at a little distance, the white flash surely and steadily followed.

* * * *

"There, give her a dose o' brandy, hot and strong, and she'll be all right; it's nothing on airth but a swoon," ejaculated old Timothy Jackson. "I ain't so sartin', though, about that ugly cut on Mr. Darrell's forehead. He must ha' got it struggling up them wild rocks. I never s'posed we should ha' seen either on 'em alive agin."

'Slowly Rosa opened her blue wondering eyes, and gazed with a shudder round the room, as sense and remembrance came back to her.

"Am I safe?" she murmured; "and did *he* save me from that cruel death?"

"That he did, young lady, and at the risk of his own life, too, if it's Mr. Darrell you mean," said the old fisherman, solemnly.

"I must see him," said Rosa, firmly.

"But you can't; for he ain't fit to leave his room."

"Then I must go to him."

"Well, I don't know as there's any harm in that; my old woman don't seem to make no objections," said Timothy, opening the door for her.

'And Rosa went up the narrow creaking stairs to old Huldah Jackson's 'best room,' where the calico curtains were drawn, and the blinds all shut, so that she could but just discern the prostrate figure on the lounge beyond.

"John," she faltered, under her breath.

"Rosa, my darling!"

'Kneeling on the carpetless floor beside the wounded man, Rosa Miller sobbed out her incoherent thanks, never once trying to withdraw the little hand he kept so tightly prisoned between his own.

"I never knew how brave and noble you were, John," she murmured. "I never dreamed you cared so much for silly little me."

"Then, Rosa, will you reconsider this morning's decision?" he asked, in deep tremulous accents. "Again I plead my cause; you have answered 'No' once."

"But I answer 'Yes' now," she sobbed, hiding her face upon his arm.

'To this day Rosa Darrell never regrets the

hour of deadly terror that revealed to her the noble depths of her husband's true heart.'

"Hush!" said Martinez, at this moment—"he wakes."

Inez flew to the side of her husband.

Captain Wildwell raised himself on his elbows.

"Inez," he gasped—"Heaven be praised I can see you, though but through a haze!"

"Then your sight is not lost," said Inez.

"No, not entirely," he answered. "Oh, what joy I feel at that knowledge! Now I shall soon get well; for there is hope at last."

CHAPTER CXVIII.

THE IMPRISONED YOUTH AND THE PIRATE.

WHILST the events recorded in the previous chapter were taking place, Ellen and her father remained prisoners in their respective cabins; and Charles lay heavily ironed in the hold.

It would be no easy task to describe the feelings of either.

Various and conflicting were they indeed.

Each bemoaning their own fate, and the fate of each, could find little rest for their agonised minds.

Chafing like a wounded tiger, Charles Lawson daily became more worn and dispirited.

He could bear his own sufferings; for he cared not for himself.

But for Ellen he feared.

His mind conjured up the worst for her.

In imagination he saw her beauteous face covered with the blush of shame—her soul lacerated by the inhuman and diabolical work of the fiends into whose hands she had fallen.

Did he sleep, he awoke startled and frightened; for every sound that fell upon his ears appeared to him like the shrieks of Ellen, as she pleaded for mercy from her inhuman captors.

Then he would train every nerve to listen; and lacerate his hands and legs, with the vain endeavour to tear his chains asunder, and fly to her rescue.

Then, fatigued and exhausted, his head would sink upon his breast, and he would give way to despair.

In vain he examined the features of those who visited him, either to bring his food, or see that he remained properly secured. In vain he sought in the countenances of these rude men for the slightest trace of pity or commisseration.

He could find none.

Stern, cold, and pitiless were his jailors; and hope fled the breast of the brave youth.

With what feelings did he listen to the roar of the cannon, and the clash of steel, as the merciless pirates pursued their unholy calling!

How fervently did he pray that the black flag might be lowered, and that Ellen might be rescued!

But, alas! hitherto his prayers had been in vain. The dread ensign of piracy still unfolded its fatal emblem—still cast its fearful shadow over the seas.

Thus the time wore on, till the "Scorpion" was run into the bay for repairs.

It was about two days before the time she was reckoned to be prepared to start on her homeward journey, that Charles sat with his face buried in his hands, in the hold of the pirate vessel.

So absorbed was he in thought, that he observed not the descent of a tall African down the hatchway.

Nor was it, indeed, till the black placed his hand upon the youth's shoulder, that Charles raised his head, with a start.

"White man sleeps," he said, in a low tone of voice.

"Sleeps!" replied Charles.

"You close your eyes, and sleep."

"Not so," said Charles. "I cannot sleep in this floating pandemonium."

"Not sleep!"

"No."

"Why not?"

"Can you ask?"

The black nodded.

"Were you a prisoner, as I am—kept from your friends, and heavily ironed," said Charles—"you, too, could not sleep."

"I am away from friends," said the black. "The African friends are a long way off—and cruel white men tore me from them—yet I can sleep."

"It is because you are now free," said Charles.

The black shook his head.

"Are you then a slave?"

"No."

"Then you are free."

"Yes—to fight for white men," replied the black, bitterly; "but not to share with him in all his spoils."

"I thought pirates always shared equally."

"The plunder we do—but the white women—"

"Ah!" exclaimed Charles, his mind reverting in a moment to Ellen.

"The captain take big ship and many women, but he keep them all, and sink the ship," said the black.

"What then?"

"The Africans swear to have the women, and he shoot one dead," continued the black.

"Well."

"The Africans fall back and obey," said the black—"but they wait—"

"For what?"

The black stole up close to Charles, and stooping down till his thick lips almost touched the cheek of Charles, he hissed:

"Another captain."

"Another captain?" iterated Charles, in a puzzled tone,

"Yes."

"What other?"

"One who know how to steer de ship over the sea."

"And such a one you seek," said Charles.

The black nodded.

"And should you find him, what then?' asked Charles, anxiously.

"Captain Long die."

"Then you would mutiny?"

"We would."

"All of you?"

"Not all."

"How many?"

"Half, quite."

Charles looked steadfastly into the African's face.

He wished to read if possible the thoughts of the man who had so cautiously made his appearance in the hold.

He doubted whether the man spoke truly, or if

it were but the work of Madge or Lang to learn if he would be induced to take the command should the blacks revolt.

But he was soon satisfied by the manner of the men that the words he had uttered came from himself and were not dictated by others.

Charles saw in a moment that there was discontent amongst the blacks.

He was not long in divining its cause.

This set him thinking for some moments.

At length fixing his eyes upon the African who had stood silently by his side, he said—

"Why have you sought me?"

"Because you are a prisoner."

"Well?"

"And a sailor."

"True."

"You can steer ship?"

"I can."

"You know when storm comes, and wind, and the ship rocks—you know how to make her skim along through all this?"

"I do."

"And you are a prisoner?"

"I am."

"And would like to have *them* taken off."

And the black pointed to the irons.

Henry sighed.

"I would—I would."

"You can."

"How?"

"I will tell you."

"Go on."

"The captain shot one of our race, and we hate him."

"Well?"

"You hate him?"

"I can bear him no love."

"You would kill him?"

"In fair fight, yes."

"With your knife."

"Not in the dark, or whilst he slept," said Charles, thinking that the black was coming to the offer of liberty if he undertook to murder their captain.

The black looked as if he would not hesitate did a chance present itself.

This Charles perceived, and he shuddered.

But he made no remark.

He was thinking how best to reply to the fellow whom he now perceived had sought him with some object.

After a pause the African whispered:

"Would you be captain of this ship?"

"No," said Charles.

"No?"

"Certainly not."

"Do you like imprisonment?"

"No."

"Is not liberty dear to you?"

"Aye, indeed it is."

"Then be free."

"I would."

"You can."

"But how?"

"Listen," said the African. "Myself and several of my race are dissatisfied with the present captain. We would mutiny, but not one of us can navigate the vessel."

"Well?"

"If you will be captain and carry us home, we will set you free."

"And those besides on board?" asked Charles.

"The man paused.

"Speak!"

"We will be avenged on them," said the black.

"What, on that poor girl?"

"Her in the cabin?"

"Yes."

"She is our prize."

"You would not harm her?" said the young sailor.

"She is white, and the whites are our foes."

"Not all."

"Yes."

"No."

"But they are—they seek to make us slaves."

"Some do, but not all."

"They who rescued us pretended the same, but we are slaves now as much as we were before."

"But I tell you were I to consent, I would steer the vessel to your own land and set you free.

"You would?"

"I would."

"Then be our captain."

"On one condition."

"What is that?"

"That you swear not to harm, by word or deed, those I shall command you to respect."

"Is the captain one of these?" asked the black, showing his teeth.

"No."

"And that woman?"

"Which?"

"Her who pretended to be our friend—her who fight like a demon."

"Of whom do you speak—Wild Madge?"

"Yes."

"It is unmanly to offer violence to a woman—no matter how depraved or fallen she has become. I tell you what: those who have induced you and your fellow-countrymen to join them in their unholy calling, have broken the laws of humanity; and justice demands them. I will take the command of this ship if they are placed in my hands to carry them to justice and the punishment of their crimes. Will that do?"

The black paused, thoughtfully, for some time. At length he said:

"I will ask the others. I will return and tell you what they say."

"Very good," said Charles. "But remember—we only make prisoners; we shed no blood."

"I will say so."

"On no other condition will I consent," said Charles. "I pant for freedom; but I accept it not if it must be stained with crime."

"To-morrow I will come again," said the man.

"I shall await you with anxiety," replied Charles.

The man grinned, and commenced cautiously to ascend the steps to the deck.

CHAPTER CXIX.

THE MUTINEERS IN COUNCIL—CHARLES RELEASED FROM HIS BONDS.

NIGHT had cast her sable mantle over the sea.

The bustle and activity which had remained throughout the day had ceased; and those who laboured hard to get the vessel ready for her homeward voyage now rested from their toil.

The wind was light; and, sheltered by the rocks, the "Scorpion" rode upon the waters like a sleeping babe nestling upon the breast of its mother.

The cordage flapped idly and softly against the mast; and the low waves plashed mournfully and languidly against the timbers.

Wild Madge had resigned herself to her favourite occupation—sipping brandy from a huge tumbler in the cabin, and thinking of the revenge she gloat in on their arrival in England.

Ellen sat at the farther end of the cabin—pale and still—with her long lashes moist with tears, and her thin lips quivering with emotion, as she gazed upon the degraded woman before her.

Not a word passed between them.

Ellen had long since found how futile was her pleading.

She could only wait and hope.

Hope for the time to come when fate should rescue her from the power of that fearful woman.

She had placed that faith in Providence, and become resigned, to a certain extent, to her sufferings.

She felt sure that Heaven, to which she prayed for succour, would, in its own good time, rescue her from the threatened doom.

In the next cabin Mr. Hanfield lie upon his cot —a broken and shattered form.

His hair was now white as silver—his form bent with care—his eye lustreless.

His anxiety for his child had made sad ravages on his frame; he was but a shadow of his former self.

Truly, he had suffered enough.

His sins had found him out; and the seeds sown in youth he had reaped in sorrow in age.

Lang, Smith, and Jack Snipe were regaling themselves over their grog and cigars in another cabin.

The latter, though a brave sailor, and one who honoured the flag beneath which he had served so long and faithfully, had been talked over by his companions; and Jack daily became more reconciled to his new life.

There were times when his heart smote him for remaining among those against whom he had fought; but he always excused himself, by saying: "Well, it's my luck; and, perhaps, it's for the best."

And so, instead of leaping overboard, to escape becoming a pirate, as he once or twice thought of doing, he washed down his qualms of conscience in a stiff glass of grog, which was always to be had in the captain's cabin.

Smith had command of the watch; and this was loosely kept.

Having no fear of being surprised, and foreseeing no danger, the men were allowed to do pretty well as they liked.

Smith sat on a bulk-head—a cigar in his mouth, and a glass of grog at his side—in a half dreamy state, paying no heed whatever to the men, who, one by one, slunk away from their posts, till the deck was occupied alone by the officer.

Watching the smoke curling upwards from his cigar, his mind wandered far away from the deck of the "Scorpion," and the deep, deep sea.

The days of his boyhood were before him, and, for a time, he lived again in innocence and peace.

There is a charm in recalling to the mind days long past—hours never to return—and dwell with rapture upon occurrences in former life, which then possessed no delight, but to which time lends a lustre.

Lost in reverie, he observed not the men leave the deck; nor did he perceive them, after the lapse of about a quarter of an hour, return silently to their posts.

Indeed, it was not till the cigar had burned down so low as to become dangerous to hold in the lips, that Smith cast his eyes around the deck.

Perceiving each at his post, he took another cigar from his pocket, and lit it from the burning end of the one he had been smoking.

Then, flinging away the end of the consumed one, he rose and took a turn round the deck.

As he did so, the head of the tall black who had been in conversation with Charles Lawson disappeared quickly down the forecastle—from the steps of which he had been watching the thoughtful man and joined his companions below.

Smith paused before the entrance to the forecastle, and, taking the cigar from his lips, he called out down the stairs:

"Now, then, lights out there!"

"Aye, aye," replied a dozen voices from below; and the next instant the forecastle was in darkness.

Having satisfied himself of this, Smith rolled away towards the quarter-deck.

But he was mistaken. The blacks—and there were at least thirty assembled in the forecastle— had only placed a pail, turned upside down, over the light.

It was a rule, strictly enforced on board the "Scorpion," that no light should remain burning at a late hour.

And a very necessary rule it was—as the pirates invariably got intoxicated, and, whilst under the influence of spirits which had never paid duty, might have been the cause of enveloping the ship in flames.

No sooner was the pail placed over the light than the tall black crept cautiously and noiselessly up the steps, and watched the form of Smith, as he strode along the deck.

Then down he went again.

"All right," he said.

The pail was removed, and the black features of the pirates were once more lighted up by the glimmer of the candle.

There was a look of determination upon their faces, as they sat there; and it was evident that something more than ordinary formed the topic of their conversation.

And so it did.

They had all met there to hear the effect of their countryman's interview with the prisoner in the hold.

From the moment that Lang fired the shot which laid the mutineer a corpse on the deck, these men had resolved to be revenged on the death of their countryman.

It was only the fact that there was not one among the Africans who could navigate the vessel that induced them to return to their duty.

But, though they did so, and though they fought like fiends with the crew of the "Damon," they had neither forgotten nor forgiven the death of their comrade and leader in their insubordinate conduct.

They only waited some favourable opportunity to mark their sense of the injustice done them.

This opportunity they believed was now at hand. The man who had visited Charles in the hold had given his report; and it only remained for the others to decide whether they would accept him as captain on the conditions he had named.

To this there were a few dissentients.

The fair face of the lovely Ellen had been seen by them; and their brutish natures desired her for a victim.

But it was evident that Charles never would consent to this; so, after much cavilling, carried on in whispers, it was agreed that the youth should take the place of Lang, and act as he liked towards all the whites on board.

Now there remained but one thing to be done before they rose and declared that the command of of Lang was at an end.

That was the release of Charles from his irons and the hold.

But how was this to be accomplished?

Lang only could release him: he kept the key of the lock fastened to the bolts to which the youth was secured.

After some conversation on this subject, one of the men produced a strong file, which had been used that day in the repairs.

This was given to the black before mentioned; and he was despatched to the hold to endeavour to sunder the iron bands which held Charles a captive.

Cautiously ascending to the deck, the man made his way to the hold unseen by Smith, but observed by those on the watch, to whose inquiring looks and motions he only nodded in reply.

Charles had sunk into an uneasy slumber, from which the man awoke him by stumbling over his legs in the dark.

"Who's there?" he exclaimed, in a loud tone.

"Hist!" exclaimed the black. "I have come to release you."

"Ah!" exclaimed Charles.

"Hush!" replied the man. "If you speak so loud you will have to stay where you are; for you will bring down the whites upon me."

"I will be cautious," said Charles—a gleam of joy rising to his heart at the prospect of deliverance.

"Then hold this ring tight," said the man, seizing the band of iron which encircled the ankle of the youth, "and I will soon cut through it."

Charles grasped the ring with both hands, and a strange feeling of hope ran through his heart as he heard the file grate across his bands.

He thought of Ellen, and his heart bounded in his breast.

Every move of the file seemed to him to give utterance to the word freedom.

The black worked the tool swiftly over the ring; and, for some minutes, nothing but the sound of the steel upon the iron could be heard.

There was music in the sound now, though at any other time it had grated harshly upon the ears of the youth.

But not so now.

Every movement of the file carried him nearer to the loved object of his affections.

And he almost laughed for joy as the black, having cut clean through the ring, wrenched the band open, and released one leg of the captive.

But prudence warned him to silence, and he stifled the cry that rose to his lips.

But his heart beat wildly—throbbed in unison with the movements of the file—till the second ring was severed, and his limbs were free.

He could remain silent no longer. Springing to his feet, he exclaimed:

"Ellen, I come to save you, or to die!"

CHAPTER CXX.

THE SLEEPING OFFICER SECURED—THE MUTINEERS' FIRST ORDER.

THE watch is changed, and Smith turns into his berth, giving place to Bond.

That worthy answers to his call with a thick husky voice, and staggers up to the deck with an oath at being disturbed.

He is more than half intoxicated; and, after swearing at the blacks who form his watch, he reels against the bulwarks, staggers half across the deck, and finally seats himself upon the very bulk-head which was occupied by Smith a short time before.

Here his head drops on to his breast, and his loud breathing proclaims that he sleeps.

Nothing could be better for the object the blacks have in view.

After making sure that Bond was in a sound slumber, those who formed the second watch stole away to the forecastle, where they reported to their comrades that no watch was kept on deck, and began to indulge themselves with potations of grog, of which there was no stint on board the "Scorpion."

Suddenly two persons ascended the hatchway from the hold to the deck.

It was Charles Lawson and the black sailor who had filed asunder his fetters.

As Charles placed his foot upon the deck, he drew a deep sigh of relief, and gazed around him.

Not a soul met his sight but the man at his side.

"Has no watch been set?" he whispered to his companion.

"Yes."

"I do not see them."

"No," said the man.

"How is that?"

"They are below."

"Who is the officer of the watch?" asked Charles.

"Bond."

"And he?"

"Is there."

And the man pointed to the bulkhead on which the sleeping man sat.

A smile broke over the face of the youth.

"Is it thus a watch is kept on board this vessel?"

"Not always," said the man.

"She would fall an easy prey to a foe," said Charles.

"And she will to us."

"I trust so."

The man motioned him to the forecastle.

Charles paused.

"No," he said.

"No?"

"Not yet."

The man looked questioningly in his face.

For a moment he entertained a doubt of the youth's intentions.

Did he mean to play the mutineers false.

It must be so, or why did he hesitate?"

The eyes of the black glistened.

He placed his hand to his belt, and his fingers clutched the handle of his knife.

Charles saw all this.

He guessed the cause in an instant.

He felt it necessary to disabuse the mind of the black.

Laying his hand upon his shoulder, he said—

"Whilst I am in the forecastle he may probably awake."

"What then?"

"He may discover my presence there," said Charles.

"And if he do?"

"He would instantly give the alarm," said Charles.

"Well?"

"And our intentions would be frustrated."

"How?"

"By Lang and his followers."

"There is no fear of that," replied the black.

"Why not?"

"Because they are few and we are many."

"Well?"

"And can defy them."

"Are you armed?"

The black drew his knife.

"And your companions?"

"The same."

"Only with knives."

"That is all."

"You have no firearms?"

"No."

"That is well."

"Well?"

"Yes."

"But we very soon will have them," said the blacks.

"For what purpose?"

"To defend ourselves."

"Against whom?"

"The captain."

"If, as you say, you are strong in number and he is weak, you will need no weapons to become masters of the ship; and mark me, before I take a step further in this business, there must be no unnecessary bloodshed, or I will return to the hold and await the arrival of some vessel to rescue myself and fellow-prisoners from the hands of the inhuman fiends."

"You have but to command, and we will obey."

"That is well. Now let us first bind the sleeping man."

The black sprung a few paces from the side of his companion, and grasping the end of a coil of rope placed it in the hands of Charles.

"Good," he said. "We can become masters of the ship without slaughter."

And as he spoke he threw the rope over the head of the drunken pirate, and allowing it to slip down over his shoulders, tied his arms firmly to his side.

Bond opened his eyes, and looked wildly and confusedly around for a few moments.

Then, suddenly, he seemed to awake to the reality of his position.

Starting to his feet, he was about to call out, when Charles sprang upon him, and, placing his hand over his mouth, he said, in a whisper, to the black:

"Pass the coil around his legs; then give me the end."

In a moment this was done.

Charles took the rope in one hand, and, drawing the other from the mouth of the suprised pirate, forced the rope therein, and, passing it round the back of his head, secured it ere he could utter a sound.

"There," said Charles, turning to the black, "he can give no alarm now. He is securely gagged. You see it is not necessary to bury your knife in his heart to stop his tongue. Blood should never be spilt if it can be avoided."

So saying, he placed his arms around the bound man, and lowered the body of the unfortunate Bond to the deck, where the pirate lie powerless to speak or move, but inwardly cursing his unlucky stars for sending him to sleep when danger lurked so near.

The speed with which this operation was performed so took the black by surprise, that for a few moments he could but stand and gaze with admiration upon the late captive.

Then, casting a contemptuous look upon the prostrate man, he laid his hand upon the arm of our hero, and led him towards the forecastle.

But Charles declined to descend.

"Go below," he said, "and announce to your companions that I am on deck."

The man hesitated.

"Go," said Charles—"why do you hesitate?"

"You are not going to play us false?" said the black.

"Play you false!"

"Yes."

"How can I play you false?" said Charles.

"By giving the alarm yourself," replied the man.

"Look you," said our hero "my greatest desire is to escape from those who brought me hither; and to surrender to justice the inhuman fiends who have heaped misery upon my head, and on her's I so fondly love."

"The woman?"

"Yes, the same."

In an instant the black seemed to understand him: so, nodding his head, he descended to the forecastle.

As the black descended the ladder, Charles laid his hand upon his breast, and muttered:

"Lie still, my heart! Oh, how violently it throbs! What a blessed boon is freedom! How much more so must it be when it may also secure the freedom of Ellen! Heaven grant that I may be enabled to bear her spotless and innocent to England; that I may rescue her from those who seek her ruin; and consign to their doom those who have so long and cruelly sought our destruction! Oh, Ellen, Ellen! these limbs are again free; and my heart pants to gaze once more upon your face, and tear you from the power of these worse than fiends!"

One by one the blacks ascended to the deck, and arranged themselves around Charles.

When the last had come up from the forecastle, and Charles had surveyed the dusky group with feelings of pity and abhorrence, he said:

"You have called upon me to become the commander of this vessel till such time as you are safely landed on the shores of your native land?"

"We have."

"And you promise to implicitly obey my every command?"

"We do."

"Then on those terms I agree," said Charles. "In a few moments your resolve must be known to those who have command of this vessel, and they will take every precaution and adopt every means to prevent us taking possession of the ship if we delay. Therefore, I order five men to proceed to the cabin in which the officers now are, and to make them prisoners without shedding a drop of blood, save in self-defence."

Five tall blacks instantly stepped forth.

Then turning to the African who had been with him in the hold, he said—

"You will follow me to the cabin of that fiend, Wild Badger; the others will keep watch and be ready to render assistance in any case that may require their aid. But remember, the vessel is not yet in our hands, and that silence must be observed."

The men nodded.

"To your posts and your duty!"

The five men instantly proceeded to the cabin of Lang.

One more glance Charles cast around the black crew who stood beside him, then motioning to the African he strode proudly along the deck to the stairs leading to the cabins.

Oh! how his heart beat now with alternate hopes and fears. Hope that he should clasp Ellen to his arms, pure and spotless as when the rude waves flung her senseless body on the rocks at the feet of the Boy Rover—Fear, lest the hand of the spoiler had robbed her of all woman holds dear, and embittered her existence, and ruined his hopes for ever in this world.

———

CHAPTER CXXI.

THE FIGHT IN THE CABIN—LANG AND SNIPE MADE PRISONERS.

LANG was in the act of raising the glass filled with hot rum and water to his mouth, when the door of the cabin in which he sat was thrust open and the five blacks who had been told off from those who came up from the forecastle stood upon the threshhold.

With an exclamation of surprise Lang sat with the glass half raised to his lips, and his eyes open to their utmost, looking first at Jack Snipe, and then at the Africans.

It was some moments ere he could sufficiently recover himself to speak.

But when he did he dropped the glass hurriedly upon the table, and sprang to his feet.

"What is the meaning of this," he exclaimed, in a loud tone.

"Captain," said the foremost of the Africans—the ship is in our hands."

Lang staggered back, and Jack Snipe sprang to his feet.

"Liar!" roared Lang, recovering himself in a moment:

And thrusting his hand hurriedly into his belt he drew forth a pistol.

A demoniac gleam shot from the eyes of the Africans.

It was the same weapon with which he killed their leader when they wished to launch the boat to fetch the women from the sinking ship.

"Dogs!" he roared—"do you mutiny? You have had a taste of how I punish a mutineer. Back to your posts, or by hell I'll stretch the first man dead at my feet that dares to hesitate.

And as he spoke he placed the weapon at full cock.

A derisive burst of laughter broke from the lips of the blacks.

"What—ho, there!" shouted Lang—"Bond! Smith!—mutiny, by God!"

Another defiant burst of laughter broke from the blacks.

"You may call for Bond as long as you like," said one—"for he can't come."

Lang's features became pale as marble.

"Dogs!—you have slain him," he roared.

"No—but we have secured him," said a tall black; "and he can't help you."

"Smith—Smith!" roared Lang. "Jack Snipe, down with them!"

And he sprang forward, firing his weapon as he did so into the midst of the Africans.

For a moment they gave way before his impetuous onslaught; but the ball lodged in the partition of the cabin.

Furiously he struck at the blacks with the butt-end of his weapon—shouting the while for Smith and Jack to aid him.

Jack Snipe could not stand calmly by and watch the unequal contest; so, darting to the side of Lang, he struck out right and left upon the faces of the blacks with his clenched fists.

Hitherto the Africans had not drawn their knives; but now that blows rained upon them fast and fierce, their blood became fired with passion, and they brandished their knives menacingly.

But this did not deter Lang.

Madly he struck at the blacks, inflicting fearful blows upon their heads and shoulders with his discharged weapon.

"Put up your knives, you cowardly snobs," said Jack, "and stand up like men—or, demme, I'll close your toplights for you in the twinkling of a bedpost! Take that, you black viper!" he added, dealing one of the blacks a blow between the eyes, which sent him reeling to the table, and smashed the glasses of grog to the floor.

"Come on! Who's the next?" he roared, warming up with excitement.

"You are!" shouted a tall black, springing upon him, with his knife raised above his head.

But Jack leaped aside, and struck the fellow so violent a blow on the ear, that he fell stunned and insensible to the ground.

"Hurrah!" shouted Jack. "Demme! we'll never strike our colours to a set of black warments as is fit only to be food for sharks."

And, rushing to the side of Lang, he joined that worthy, by raining blows thick and fast on the three remaining blacks, who, seeing the fate of their comrades, slowly retreated to the stair.

"Hurrah! Victory—victory!" shouted Jack, still pressing on, despite the blows aimed at him with the knives.

But here the blacks called upon those on deck; and, in another moment, the stairs were choked up with their sable forms.

With a howl of rage, Lang retreated again to the cabin, followed by Jack Snipe.

"I reckon," said Jack, "we're just in a pretty mess. I don't like to knock under—especially to a Ingine; but I don't see much chance of keeping afloat now, even if we nail the colours to the mast."

"Curse it!" roared Lang—"I did not expect this."

And he drew the short sword he wore from his belt, resolved to sell his life dearly.

There was a cessation of hostilities now, and each party eyed the other fixedly.

"Look you," said Lang, as the cabin again became filled the Africans—"what good can you do to yourselves by seeking my death?"

"We will no longer obey your commands," said one.

"Why not?"

"Because you do not act fair towards us."

"How so? You all share equally," said Lang.

"We do not."

"Tell me your grievance; and, if it is a just one, it shall be seen into and altered."

"You would not let us go to the ship for the women."

"The vessel was sinking, and it would have been useless."

"You should have brought them on board."

"It would have interfered with the discipline."

"You slew our countryman."

"He mutinied."

"Because you were unjust."

"Not so.'

"It was."

"Had he obeyed my commands, he had now been living; he refused, and he died."

"We are here to avenge him."

"You seek my life?"

"No."

"What then?"

"To make you prisoner."

"How will you work the vessel?"

"No matter."

"Yes it is; for you'll be taken by a king's ship," said Lang.

"We shall not."

"You will; for you know not how to work the ship either in a chase or an engagement."

"We can obey orders."

"And do you think, if we are made prisoners, that we will give them?" asked Lang.

"No."

"Whose orders, then, can you obey?'

"Those of the white captive."

"Who?"

"The youth whom you put in irons in the hold," said the black.

"Ah!"

"He is captain now."

"Charles Lawson?"

"The same."

"Captain of the ship?"

"Yes."

"Of a pirate?"

"He is."

"Fools!" exclaimed Lang—"he does but inveigle you to your destruction. Make him captain of this ship, and he will steer you to the yard-arm of a man-of-war."

"He will steer us to our home—land us on the shores of Africa, from whence we were torn to become slaves."

"From which fate I rescued you," said Lang.

"To endure a worse," said one of the blacks.

"To make you free."

"Yes, to obey your commands, and receive a

bullet in our skull if we refuse," said one of the Africans.

"Fools!—return to your duty. If you have released the prisoner in the hold, confine him there again. He but lures you to destruction. Trust him not, or you are doomed."

"We will trust him," said one of the blacks, advancing towards Lang—"and you shall take his place in the hold."

And the man stretched forth his hand to grasp the pirate captain.

But Lang sprang back; and, as the man followed him, he thrust the weapon into his breast.

The black fell back, with a howl of pain.

This was the signal for a fresh onslaught.

Howling like demons let loose, the Africans sprang forward.

In vain Lang endeavoured to keep them at bay with his short sword.

In vain Jack Snipe rained blows thick and fast upon their sable faces.

The Africans pressed on, and Jack was borne to the floor, and secured.

Lang's sword was torn from his grasp; his throat was clutched tightly by the fingers of a powerful black; his arms were pinioned behind him; and, despite his kicks, blows, and plunges, he was borne to the floor, beside Snipe.

Then a loud shout of triumph arose from the lips of the sable pirates—a shout that penetrated to every part of the ship, and caused a thrill of fear to run even through the veins of Wild Madge herself.

CHAPTER CXXII.

BOND RELEASED FROM HIS IMPRISONMENT—PREPARATION FOR DEFENDING THE SHIP FROM THE MUTINEERS.

SMITH, who had sank to sleep almost immediately after he had turned into his berth, which he did as soon as his watch was relieved, was suddenly awoke from his slumber by the report of the pistol fired by Lang among the black mutineers.

Starting up in his cot, he listened intently.

A confused sound came to his ears—a sound for which he could not account.

Straining every nerve to catch its import, he was not long in discovering that something unusual was going on in the aft part of the vessel.

Leaping out of his cot, he hurriedly attired himself, and threw open the door of his cabin.

At this moment the tones of Jack Snipe came to his ears, as that worthy shouted the truly English "hurrah!"

His first thought was that Snipe, having indulged deeply, was drunk; and that the fumes of liquor, having made their way to his head, had opened his mouth.

But, as he looked forth, he perceived the steps leading to the deck crowded with the dark forms of the Africans.

In a moment he conjectured the real cause of their presence there.

He hesitated for a moment how to proceed.

The voice of Lang came to his ears, as the captain shouted his name.

What was best to be done?

It was evident that the blacks had mutinied,

and that the whites were so greatly outnumbered that resistance would be madness.

Retiring into his berth, he flung up the lid of his chest and took therefrom a pair of pistols and a long Spanish knife.

Assuring himself that they were loaded, he sprang to the door, and again looked forth.

The Africans were peering down the staircase, and into the cabin of Lang.

He still stood undecided how to proceed.

He could hear the voice of Lang, and listened to the conversation which took place between him and the Africans.

Once or twice he was prompted to spring forward to his rescue.

But prudence told him that it would be of no avail.

He thought, perhaps, that if he could get to the deck unseen by those below, he might find those there who were averse to the mutiny, and induce them to stand firm to the whites, and thus render more assistance than he could do by showing fight below.

Watching his opportunity, he sprang up the stairs to the deck.

All was quiet there.

Not a soul was to be seen.

Anxiously he looked around him.

He felt assured that all the blacks were not below in the cabin.

Therefore, all were not engaged in the mutiny. In this he was right.

The mutiny had been formed only by those we have seen in conclave a short time before.

For many reasons the mutineers had not enlisted all their countrymen in their cause. They felt assured of gaining them to their side when once the ship was in their hands; but they feared the least indiscretion might betray them ere the prisoner in the hold was released.

So they decided to trust only those on whom they could depend.

Whilst hesitating how to proceed, or what to do, Smith struck his foot against an object on the deck.

Looking down, to see what it was, a cry of surprise and pleasure broke from his lips.

It was Bond.

The man whom Charles Lawson and the black had bound with the rope.

In an instant Smith bent over him and severed the lashing which held the pirate dumb and powerless.

With a sigh of relief, Bond bounded to his feet. He was sober now.

The fumes of the grog he had imbibed had been effectually dissipated by what had passed.

"How came you bound and lying there?" asked Smith.

"There is mutiny."

"I know that."

"That youth has been released from his irons, and the ship is in his hands."

"We must outwit him."

"How?"

"We must devise some means," said Smith.

"Can you think of any?"

"Where is the youth? I have not seen him."

"I think he is in the cabin of Wild Madge."

"Is she a prisoner."

"I know not; but I heard him order one of the blacks to follow him thither."

"Only one?"

"Yes."

"Then we'll get him into our power, and stay

this mutiny," said Smith. " Come—there is not a moment to be lost. The Africans are in Lang's cabin. Without a captain, they must go back to their duty. If we can secure this youth, the mutiny is at an end."

" True."

" Then to the cabin of Wild Madge," said Smith.

" Stay," said Bond—" the odds are against us; but I, for one, will not fall unavenged. Should we be compelled to retreat again to the deck, we may yet die in company with several of those who seek our destruction."

" Well?"

" This barrel of powder will serve us well," said Bond, laying his hand upon a cask which stood upon the deck beside them, and which had been placed there owing to the repairs. " Let us knock the head in; and, if the worst comes to the worst, we will draw the mutineers hither, and fire our pistols at the cask, and blow us all to h—l together."

" We should destroy ourselves."

" True; but we should also destroy them."

" That would be a deep revenge," said Smith.

Bond moved a few steps, and, taking a marling-spike from a bulk-head, he returned to the side of his companion.

" The blacks want the ship," he said—" and the youth, who has brought more trouble on us than anyone, to be captain. Let them have it; but, if they are victorious, they shall pay dearly for the prize."

And raising the iron bar above his head, he brought it down with all his force upon the head of the cask.

Another and another blow, and the head of the cask gave way.

" There," said Bond, throwing the shattered wood upon the deck, and leaving the powder exposed—" a pistol fired into that will blow a few of them to h—l before their time."

" True," said Smith; " but, if we load the pivot-gun, and stand by with a match, we have the ship in our own hands. We can sweep our own decks as easily as those of a foe."

" But, while we go below for the shot, the blacks may come upon deck, and defeat our first resolve."

" So they may," said Smith. " But no—you go below for the shot: I will stand here, with my pistol pointed into the barrel. If they return to the deck, I fire; if not, the gun can be loaded."

" We will show them how to mutiny," said Bond, darting from the side of his companion, and down the hatchway, with the speed of an antelope.

Smith stood beside the opened cask.

The muzzle of his pistol was pointed fairly into it.

He could not but feel that, if necessity called upon him to pull the trigger, it would be the signal for his own destruction, as well as that of the mutineers.

But he likewise felt that it would but hurry his death for a short time; and that by firing the powder he might escape tortures which the cruel natures of the blacks might induce them to inflict upon himself and his fellow-countryman.

Impatiently he awaited the reappearance of Bond from the expedition on which he was gone.

And nervously, too, he listened to every sound that rose from the cabin where the mutineers were.

In a short time Bond returned to the deck, loaded with grape and canister shot.

A feeling of relief seemed now to take possession of the minds of both, as they commenced hurriedly to load the long pivot-gun amidship.

Performing their work as silently as possible, yet putting in a more than ordinary charge, Lang and Bond smiled with satisfaction at the idea which had suggested itself to their minds.

The weapon loaded. Smith said:

" Where's the match?"

" Here," said Bond, taking a straw match from his breast, which he soon succeeded in lighting. " Now let them come!"

" Had we rushed to the rescue of Lang or Wild Madge we should certainly have fallen," said Smith; " but, doing as we have, the ship is in our hands; and, despite the numbers opposed to us, we may yet succeed in quelling the mutiny, and teach a lesson to the Africans that it is dangerous to oppose the white man.

CHAPTER CXXIII.

THE SLAVER GAINS HIS SIGHT—JEALOUSY FINDS A HOME IN THE BREAST OF MARTINEZ.

WITH a long deep-drawn sigh, Captain Wildwell opened his eyes.

A cry of joy broke from his lips.

He started up in the bed.

But so weak and faint was he, that he instantly fell back again, ere Martinez could throw his arm around his shattered form.

But, ill as he was, a smile broke over his features as he sank back upon his pillow.

A cry called forth, from his heart, by the fact that his sight had returned.

That blessed sense, of which he feared he had been bereft, came back to him in that long sleep from which he had just awoke; and, with a feeling of gratitude to Heaven, he bounded up on his couch, only to find that if Providence had vouchsafed to him the blessing of sight, it had not yet granted him a perfect restoration to health and strength.

In that look, his gaze had fallen upon Inez.

Never had she appeared to him so lovely as now.

In an instant all the former feelings he had entertained for her returned.

And he lay, panting and almost breathless with his exertions, gazing upon the now pale face of the beautiful woman he had borne away from her friends and her home.

" Inez—beloved Inez!" he exclaimed—" oh, what joy to gaze once more upon thy lovely features; to look into those dark lustrous eyes—those orbs which have before fired my soul with love and adoration! Ah, that I had strength to rush to your side—to clasp you in these arms—to feel your heart throb against my own! But no—no!—such happiness is not for me. You looked coldly upon me, and repelled my advances; and I dare not hope—no, I dare not hope—that that love I have covetted will ever be mine."

" Never!" exclaimed Martinez, in a tone so deep that it seemed like a voice from the grave.

Wildwell turned his gaze upon the face of his lieutenant as he bent over him.

His features were pale as marble.

But there was a strange gleam in his dark eye.

It seemed to flash fire as it looked down upon the disfigured features of the invalid.

Wildwell saw it, and shuddered.

He closed his eyes for a moment, only to open them again upon that look.

In a moment he guessed the cause alike of the exclamation and the glance.

In an instant he perceived, by the pale face and averted glance of Inez, that his thoughts had steered in a right direction.

His bosom rose and fell with the powerful emotions which now shook his frame.

His agitation became so powerful as to deprive his weak frame of all its remaining strength; and he closed his eyes with a groan, and became insensible once more.

For a few moments Martinez still bent over him.

His dark flashing eye still fixed with a terrible meaning upon his haggard features.

His bosom heaving, like the waves in a storm, from the violence of his feelings.

Feelings called forth by the words of the wretched man.

And these feelings were—jealousy!

The demon was thoroughly aroused—the hot blood of the lieutenant had boiled up till it almost threatened to drown his senses.

The veins on his forehead stood out like thick cords.

His fingers twitched nervously, and his nails pierced deep into his palms.

There was agony in his soul now—agony too fearful to bear.

Wildwell still loved Inez, and he still lived.

Martinez felt assured of that by the slow measured breathing of the prostrate man.

As the lieutenant looked upon him, a hope rose in his mind that the slaver captain would die.

The life of Wildwell was now a hell to his soul.

His death alone could render him happy.

And his glance wandered from the pale inanimate face before him to the dark-featured Inez.

He clenched his teeth tightly.

Why was her glance fixed upon the floor of the rude hut?

Why had the smile fled her cheek?

Why was she sad?

Did she then, after all, love the slaver captain?

Had his words called back the fleeting passion to her heart?"

He doubted.

Who?

Inez.

Doubted the woman who had preferred death in the foaming billows to life with the man who lay so helpless in a corner of that rude cabin—doubted her who had sacrificed herself to her love for him.

Yes, Martinez doubted her true feelings; for the demon of jealousy had him now, body and soul, in his coils.

Impregnated his soul with its poisoned venom, till all the nobleness of his nature had been driven from his soul.

And thus he stood—his glance wandering first from the face of Wildwell to that of Inez; and then back again to the pale features of the prostrate captain.

Inez rose from her seat, and approached him.

She laid her hand upon his arm.

Martinez started, as though an adder had stung him, and hurriedly withdrew his arm.

Inez looked up in his face, in surprise and alarm.

Their eyes met.

Inez started now in turn.

Never before had she seen such a look on his features.

Never before had she seen him appear so strange.

An instinctive feeling of dread crept over her.

A sigh broke from her lips, her eyes dropped from before those of Martinez, and she trembled.

"Well?" he said, after a pause, in a whisper.

"Martinez," she said, "why do you look so strange?"

"Can you not guess?" he said, bending down till his lips met her ear, and uttering the words in a low hissing whisper.

"No," she replied.

"You cannot?"

"No—are you ill?"

"Aye, in mind."

"In mind?"

"Yes."

"What—what—"

"Look there," said the lieutenant, interrupting her, and pointing to the prostrate captain.

"Poor fellow!" she said, following his motion with her eyes.

Martinez winced.

"Heaven be praised that his sight is restored!" said Inez.

"Aye."

"Are you not glad to see it?" asked Inez.

Martinez grasped her wrist, and fixed a penetrating look upon her face.

"Inez, are you?" he said.

"Heaven knows that I am," she replied.

"Ah!" hissed the lieutenant, his features turning pale as marble, and flinging her arm from him.

For a moment Inez gazed upon him in speechless amazement.

Then her bosom heaved, and the hot scalding tears gushed to her eyes.

"Martinez," she gasped—"oh, Martinez!"

Then, with a sob, she retreated back to her seat, and buried her face in her hands.

For a moment Martinez stood looking upon her.

Then he bounded forward, and stood by her side.

"Inez," he exclaimed, "forgive me!"

The young girl raised her eyes to his face.

The look she fixed upon him went to his heart. Never before had he felt so base and degraded.

He held his hands supplicatingly towards her.

Inez rose.

A flush suffused her face.

Inez sprang forward, and encircled his neck with her arms.

At this moment Ned and Ridley, who had observed that something unusual was passing between the lovers, rose from their seats, and left the hut.

When they were gone, Inez, looking through her tears, exclaimed, in a voice choked with emotion:

"Martinez—dear Martinez!—what is the meaning of this?"

But Martinez replied not.

"Speak, in Heaven's name. Oh! has your love so soon cooled—has your affection for me so soon died out? Am I then hateful?"

"No," he exclaimed.

"It must be."

"No, no!"

"What is the meaning of this strange conduct?"

"Ask me not."

"Hear me, Martinez. I must know the reason of this change in your manner towards me. But a few days since, and I believed you would have laid down your life for me; but a short time ago, and you swore that nothing in heaven or earth could lead you to look coldly upon me. I believed you, and I surrendered myself to you. Oh! Martinez, was your love then a lie; and do I now find, when honour and purity are lost to me, that I have but fallen a victim to a designer and a villain?"

"Inez—"

"Is it so?" she gasped. "Speak, let me know the worst, though it break my heart to hear the truth."

"A villain, Inez—me a villain?" he exclaimed, a flash rising to his very temples.

"Aye, or why this change?" she said. "Have you not sworn that you loved me?"

"And I do."

"No, Martinez—no!"

"I swear it."

"And you prove your love by—by—"

"It is the fierce, undying love I bear you, that makes me forget——"

"That I am a woman—the woman whose love for you was above all else—whose belief in your honour and nobility of soul led her to sacrifice herself to you. But, oh! what a change: how fearfully have I been undeceived."

"Deceived?" he exclaimed. "No—by heaven I love you to madness: so fervent is the passion I bear you, that it drives me frantic to see you even look upon another. Inez, this man is a shadow on the sunshine of my heart: he loved you—still loves you, and I fear—"

"What?"

"That love."

"Martinez, the love of Inez was given to the man who alone could win it," she said; "that man was yourself. My love can never change, come what may. Drive me from you with scorn and cruelty, and still the love you won will be yours and yours alone. To love once is to love for ever, it will live whilst life remains, and go down with me into the cold and silent grave!"

CHAPTER CXXIV.

JEALOUSY—THE RESOLVE—BETTER THOUGHTS—
THE GOOD TRIUMPHS AT LAST.

THE eyes of Martinez fell before the glance of his companion, and he remained silent for some moments.

At length he looked up.

"Inez," he said, in a subdued tone.

The young girl sighed but spoke not.

"Inez," he said, dropping his eyes again to the ground, "I fear—"

"What?" she interrupted.

"What?" he iterated, "that my happiness is gone for ever."

"For ever?" she echoed, scarce knowing what she said, and laying her small white hand upon his arm.

"Aye, for ever."

"Wherefore?"

"Alas!" he replied, "I know not, yet I feel that all my hopes of joy are for ever flown. Oh, Inez, you would pity me, did you but know what I suffer."

"Why should you suffer?" she asked, in a soft tone—"are you not happy?"

"Happy," he iterated bittterly; "happy, and he there?"

And he pointed to the prostrate form of Captain Wildwell as he spoke.

Inez followed the motion with her eyes, then she fixed her glance on the rude floor, and a deep sigh emanated from her breast.

"How can I be happy," exclaimed Martinez—"with the knowledge that another loves the woman I adore? How can I know with peace that your love is coveted by another? Inez, we must leave this place—we must fly his presence as we would a pestilence."

"Do you fear him?" asked Inez.

"I fear, I know not what. I fear him—you—myself. Inez, if you still love me, let us hence from this spot made accursed by his presence. I cannot rest and feel that he is near you—you, whose love he sought—still reeks. There is madness in the thought. It makes my brain dizzy, and drives me almost to distraction."

"Martinez," she said, throwing her arms around the neck of her companion, "is it possible that the demon of jealousy has taken possession of your soul—that soul I believed so generous, so noble?"

"I know not what to say," he replied, "nor what to think. Inez, I love you to madness; and it is a barbed arrow in my heart to see you smile upon another."

A look of pain crossed the face of Inez.

"Oh! Martinez," she said, with a sigh, "how have you changed, in so short a time!"

"Changed!" he exclaimed—"not to you. The love I felt for you when cast upon this island is still as strong, and will remain so till death. Changed it is not—never can be. I worship the very ground you tread upon—could kiss your footprints in the earth, and die to feel that I alone possessed your heart. But the serpent has stolen into our Eden, and poisons my soul with its breath—my happiness with his presence. He sought your love once—he will seek it again."

"But never can possess it," said Inez, hastily.

"The hope is enough to drive me mad. I know not whether it be jealousy that gnaws at my heartstrings; I only know and feel that there is danger in his presence—danger to you—to me. I will fly this place—I will leave this island; go anywhere, so that he be not near us. No binding ceremony makes you mine: you are still at liberty to bestow your love on whom you please. Were you my wife, I—I—"

"Martinez," she interrupted, "would to Heaven that I were! Oh! if you can think that because no legal rite has made me yours, my love can wander to another, how basely, cruelly do you wrong me. No, Martinez, in the sight of men I am *not* your wife; but in the sight of Heaven I am. There our vows have been registered; and, when I prove false to that love I gave to you, may Heaven desert me, and shower down upon my head its direst vengeance!"

A look of joy stole over the face of the lieutenant. He raised his right hand above his head:

"Inez," he said, "by that Heaven I swore to love and cherish you. Day by day, and hour by hour, my love has grown stronger and fiercer—till one glance from your beauteous eyes bestowed upon another strikes a dagger to my soul. I wrong you—I feel I wrong you basely to doubt your love for me; but I cannot shake off from heart the oppressive feeling that he loves you: and that makes me fear for my own happiness. Inez, my Spanish blood is soon heated; and, when it is, I know not what I may do. I fear for myself—for him—for you: fear that I may be goaded to commit a deed at which mankind would shudder."

"What mean you?" asked Inez, in alarm.

"I know not myself," he replied; "but there is a something working in my heart that goads me on to slay the man who dares to look upon you as other than my wife."

"Martinez, would you—"

"Murder him," hissed Martinez, "did he win a smile from your eyes—a kiss from your lips!"

"Oh, Heaven!" she gasped.

"As fiercely as I love, so fiercely can I hate," said Martinez: "I feel it here."

And he laid his hand upon his breast as he gave utterance to the words.

Inez cast a glance upon him so full of pain and fear, that he hurriedly said:

"Not you, Inez—not you is it that I can hate. My love is too deep-rooted for that. But him—him who dares to raise his eyes with admiration to your face—dares to utter one endearing word to you."

"Hate him," said Inez—"a poor weak, dying man. Ah, Martinez, you know not what you say. Is this your generous nature? No; you are not yourself, you are—"

"Mad, Inez—mad," he interrupted.

"Heaven forbid!"

"Yes, Inez, I feel that I am mad, or soon shall be if I fly not from here. But for his presence I had been happy and content, but now—heaven forgive me if I do wrong him—I hate him—fear him, for he loves you. Inez, we will leave this island, we will go whither the winds and waves shall take us; but go we must, or I shall die!"

"And leave him to perish?"

"Curse him!"

"Martinez!"

The tone of her voice called a blush of shame to his cheek.

"Curse him who never harmed you?"

"He does harm me," said Inez.

"How?"

"By loving you."

Inez turned away with a sigh.

Oh, Martinez!—is this generous?" she said.

"I know not, care not," he replied. "I could pray for him were he miles away from you. But we must fly from him: if you love me, Inez, as you swear you do, you cannot hesitate to go."

"Where?"

"Anywhere, so that he is left behind," replied the lieutenant.

"To die?"

"Aye, if he will."

"Without aid—without succour," said Inez. Oh! man man, can you do this—can you leave even an enemy to die uncared for and alone. Where is that generous heart, that nobility of soul which Martinez once possessed?"

"Dead," replied Martinez.

"No!" she said. "It may slumber for awhile, but it will yet awake. Never can the man who won the love of Inez fall so low as to degrade his being by so base an action—never can the name of sailor be coupled with that of wretch, who, in time of adversity, refuses to extend the hand of help to a suffering fellow creature. On the battle field and on the dark blue waves man seeks the life of his enemy, but never does he refuse to aid that enemy when he lies helpless at his feet. If that man be your foe, he is weak and powerless, his sufferings call for aid, and shall they call in vain? No, Martinez, they will not; for though jealousy has turned your brain, you are still a man and a sailor."

A flush of shame suffused the face of Martinez.

His eye quailed before the glance of Inez.

He felt that the part he acted was far from creditable to him.

He saw that the love of the woman before him would be turned to scorn did he persist in his resolve.

He loved her to madness.

To lose her would be destruction to his peace and happiness for ever.

But if he allowed the demon that had possession of his heart to triumph over his better nature, would she not despise him?

And then, though she had fallen, though she was his wife in all but name, would she not perhaps sunder the fetters that bound her to him, and leave him to misery and despair."

All these thought rushed like lightning through his mind.

And a struggle commenced between the good and bad natures striving for mastery in his breast.

Inez watched the workings of his face with intense interest.

She saw the struggling going on, and she inwardly prayed that the good would triumph.

And her prayer was heard.

The noble soul was not wholly subdued by the demon who had forced its way into his heart.

After some time he took the hand of Inez in his own.

She felt it tremble as she did so.

"Inez," he said—my better angel—you have triumphed. I will not disgrace the name of man by suffering the wild passions of my nature to triumph, I will remain by his side till health and strength return to his shattered frame. Then—then will I depart from this place; leave his presence, and seek a home where we can be happy."

"Can we not be happy here?" said Inez, fixing her large lustrous eyes upon him.

"Were we away, we might. But, Inez, I would repair one evil—I would make you my wife in name, as well as nature. I will bestow on you my name; I will chase the shame from your brow which men can see there. We will strive to gain some civilised shore; and there I will lead you to the altar—make you my true and lawful wife."

No ceremony can ever bind me more firmly to you—no rite performed can ever make my love the stronger. But still it will render me happy; for it will bestow upon me the name of the man I love beyond all else on earth. But, Martinez, we will first perform our duties, as Christians, and extend to you suffering wretch all the care and succour which lays in our power. Believe me, Martinez, were we to refuse to extend to him the hand of help, we should never feel happy again; for the deed would ever remain a black spot upon our happiness and peace."

———

CHAPTER CXXV.

THE SLAVER SETS SAIL—THE STORM—THE FATE OF THE FRIGATE.

ALL search having proved unavailing, Captain Perry gave orders for the "Scorpion" to weigh anchor; and once more her sails were spread to the breeze, and she danced over the waters like a thing of life.

Henry Chambers was sad and moody. In vain he endeavoured to learn from the prisoners the fate of Ellen and her lover.

One and all denied all knowledge of them; and, thinking that spite alone caused them to withhold all information of their whereabouts, he gave up in despair, and waited, trusting to Providence to, sooner or later, solve the mystery.

For some days the course of the vessel was calm enough. There had been what sailors term a swift breeze, or what landsmen would call storms; but they were of an ordinary nature, such as are met with in the most easy passages across the ocean.

Captain Perry, according to his reckoning, expected to be in the course of a few days in sight of land, when a dead calm fell upon the sea.

Scarcely a ripple disturbed the waste of waters.

The surface of the waters presented the appearance of a polished mirror.

It was towards evening that Henry leaned over the taffrail, and was gazing listlessly into the smooth sea.

Pompey, the black cook, who had been chewing pigtail, and expectorating over the side of the vessel for some moments, suddenly shaded his eyes with his hand, and looked toward the horizon.

Then, wagging his woolly head ominously, he slowly approached Henry, and, laying hold of his short crisp curls, bobbed his black head, saying, as he pointed up to the heavens:

"Massa Chambers, we shall have it smartish, fore long."

Henry look with anxious eye towards the spot indicated by the black.

"You are right, Pompey," he replied—" we shall have our work to do, or I am very much mistaken."

At this moment Captain Perry came on deck, and Henry, pointing to the horizon, the captain instantly called out :

"Reef all sails !"

"Aye, aye, sir," sang out the sailors.

And the next moment the crew were at work, obeying his orders.

An inky mass of clouds were now fast drifting up before the coming blast.

Soon the sky was obscured, and darkness was on the sea.

Then the wind rose with a terrible rush, as of a thousand furies let loose.

The sea, a short time before so smooth, was now lashed to fury.

The vessel was driven before the force of the tempest like leaves before the wind.

Her bare poles strained and creaked, and then yard snapped asunder with a sharp crack.

Presently mountainous billows swept the deck, and the crew lashed themselves to the bulk-head and rigging.

But in spite of this the waves in their mad fury tore some of them from their holds and they were carried overboard.

The voices of Captain Perry and his officers were heard giving orders, which, whatever they might have been it was now impossible to obey.

A perfect darkness enshrouded their path, save at intervals when the lightning illumined the angry roar with a momentary gleam; then when the fury of some large wave had spent itself upon the labouring vessel, a cry for aid was heard, which amidst the dreary darkness of the night was even more awful than the raging of the storm.

A crash, sounding to the affrighted ears of those who still gasped for breath like the dismemberment of a world, ensued; and the main-mast, with all its top-tackle and rigging, was gone.

Still, for a moment or two, it held on to the ship by its main shrouds; and the mass of tackle dragged heavily after the vessel.

A few of the men endeavoured to clear it with their hatchets, and eventually succeeded in their task.

The frigate rose upon the sea now, as if the hand of a giant were lifting up some mimic vessel in sport—the whole fabric shuddering from stem to stern, as though prescient of the fate awaiting it.

Presently the timbers cracked—her sides opened —as she rose on the summit of the waves; and then down, like the rush of an overwhelming avalanche, she went into the deep abyss made by the trough of the sea.

Another mast was rent into splinters.

The cheeks of the hardy sailors paled; and a low muttered prayer, as it fell from their lips might be heard amid the lull of the tempest.

Water-logged, a sheer hulk, at the mercy of the winds and waves, the once trim "Swallow" floated on, struggling on her fatal course, like some huge living thing who, wounded to death and blind with passion, yet of rare instinct, sought some place of rest in which to lay down and die.

How many are there in their happy homes, reclining in soft luxury, and fanned only by the breezes of fortune, who give not thanks to Him who stills the tempest for the peaceful security vouchsafed them ! How many are there who, all unmindful of the blessings bestowed upon them by a wise and omnipotent Creator, give no thought to those who, from a wreck, look up to the angry sky, in hope to see some opening gush of light— some gleam afar off—that might whisper to their hearts of safety !

On board that ill-fated frigate, the "Swallow," despair and confusion prevailed.

Some of the crew yelled in mad intoxication— having stoved in the heads of the spirit casks, and drank of the burning liquids. Others laughed wildly, or prayed frantically.

In vain the cool tones of Captain Perry rang through the ship; in vain the voice of Henry endeavoured to call the crew to their duty. All discipline was at an end.

Captain Perry, finding that his orders were not obeyed, rushed about the deck, exhorting the men to be calm, when the second mast fell, and he was carried overboard.

To save him was impossible—so high ran the waves—so fiercely blew the gale.

Not a man stretched forth a hand to rescue him from a watery grave.

But there was one on board who strove to save him.

That one was his dog—a fine Newfoundland— who, the moment his master was carried over the side into the sea, jumped over the bulwarks into the waves, and swam towards him.

But the force of the waves prevented the noble animal from reaching its master ere the brave captain sank to rise no more.

As his body disappeared beneath the foaming billows, the dog set up a long dismal howl; then dived beneath the billows, and was lost to the view of those who strained their eyes to catch a sight of the faithful brute, as the quick lurid flashes of lightning lit up the angry sea.

Still the ship drifted on.

In the course of half an hour from the time of Captain Perry being carried overboard and lost, the tempest slightly lulled.

Hope began to dawn upon those few who had not wholly lost their reason.

Henry Chambers, who was lashed to the rigging, began to think the fury of the tempest had past.

Near to him was Pompey, the black cook.

"Massa Chambers," said Pompey, as the pitch-like darkness was penetrated for an instant by a lurid flash—"are you safe."

"Thank heaven, for the present, I am spared!" said Henry.

"The worst has passed now, I think," answered Pompey.

He had scarcely spoken these words when the wind, which seemed only to have left them for a time to gather yet more stormy spirits to add to its fury, rose with still greater force.

The squall seemed to clutch the ship in its invisible arms, and—helpless hull as she was—dashed her through the waters headway to destruction.

The elements seemed all confounded together, as the gale ploughed up the deep waters to the murky sky.

Several broad flashes of lightning showed the wretched mariners that the vessel was being hurried on to a reef of rocks.

They closed their eyes in agony; a few more minutes of anxious suspense, and above the roaring of the wind, and the dash of the waters, a harsh discordant sound was heard.

The ship had struck! she was lifted up again by the force of the wind and waves, who had her now, like a helpless log, to dash about whither they pleased.

They seemed to delight in making cruel sport of her.

She was lifted up from the breakers and let go again in mere wantonness, and fell again upon a coral reef with a crashing sound.

Wonderful is it that she still held together.

She must have been a rare piece of man's handywork to have held so bravely on.

Her crew knew that she could not hold together much longer, as each succeeding wave struck her sides against the rocks.

How, in that black expanse, they prayed for light, for the darkness was horrible.

It would be some comfort, they thought, to die, if die they must, by the light of day.

The tempest seemed to have spent its fury; a few streaks of heavenly light were visible in the horizon—the dawn was coming.

When the first few faint glimmers of the new day made their appearance, and tinged the edge of the waters with a line of beauty, the waves seemed to shrink before the glance of morning, and the wind subdued its voice.

The sea changed its colour—an emerald green shone upon its surface. The white foam, as it broke into thousands of particles upon it, looked like floating pearls.

The wind was no longer raging—it had subsided, as though its stormy period of passion was over.

The waves still washed about the wreck, decking it with sea-weeds of all hues and shapes, from the bright green to the sombre black, as they receded and left these memorials of the deep behind them.

An amphibious bird—one of the deep divers that, with collapsed wing, can seek its prey beneath the waves—took a devious circle as he flew round the shattered vessel, and, with a hoarse scream at intervals, seemed questioning the strange object in that lonely region.

But what of those who, amid the storm and blackness of the preceding night, occupied the frail craft?

Some of them for awhile had lost their reason; whilst a few anxiously surveyed their position by the morning's light.

No speck of land or coast was visible—nothing but a dreary waste of waters.

"It was impossible the vessel could hold much longer together. Indeed, it was surprising she had weathered the night.

A few of the crew, assisted by the carpenter, set to work to hastily construct a raft.

Spars were obtained and firmly lashed together, and when completed it was found incapable of holding more than two-thirds of the crew.

The majority of those on board the vessel jump on the raft and nearly swamp it.

The first lieutenant, however, who was mindful of his duty and discipline, took the command of the frail structure, and would only allow a certain number on board.

Taking what provisions and water they could obtain, the raft drifted out from the vessel with its living freight.

While this was taking place, Henry Chambers, the black cook Pompey, and a few others, were engaged in constructing a smaller one for themselves.

Obtaining several empty barrels, they lashed spars across them, interlaced them with shorter pieces, and formed a tolerably strong and buoyant structure.

On this, Henry, Pompey, and seven others of the crew took up their quarters.

The ship was breaking to pieces, and three or four of the crew, who were madly intoxicated insisted upon remaining with her.

It was in vain that Henry endeavoured to persuade them to accompany him.

Abuse and brutish answers were all he gained in reply to his humane endeavours.

With a sigh, Henry sat down, and the raft floated away from the doomed ship.

Her occupants watched her eagerly as she diminished in the distance.

And, as they strained their eyes towards her, they saw her break to pieces; and shortly not a vestige of her remained visible.

The brave ship had paid the debt of nature; had gone whither all things, animate or inanimate, must go at last—to ruin.

Not a vestige of her was left above the foam-crested waves, which leapt, and danced, and roared, as though in mockery at her fate.

The white spray washed over her grave; the winds roared her funeral song, and the mist hung like a funeral pall, as her timbers opened and her bolts were forced from her sides.

It was a sad fate for so gallant a craft, which, a few short hours before, had sailed so majestically over the broad expanse of waters—her sails bellying to the gentle breeze, ever and anon dipping her proud bows, like a stately swan, to kiss the diamond-crested billows as they leaped upon her; then receded, like a bashful maiden, from the salutation they had wooed, only to return again, and leap, and sport, and sing around her, as she disdainfully glided by them.

Now she would glide no more over their surface; for the tempest had thrown its coils around her—held her for a time writhing in its fearful folds—then hurled her mangled remains to the bottom of the ocean.

CHAPTER CXXVI.

THE SUFFERERS ON THE RAFT—LAND IN SIGHT —HENRY AND THE BLACK ARE WASHED ON SHORE.

OVER the still foaming and angry billows glided the frail structure on which Henry Chambers and his few companions sought to escape the doom so

No. 46

many of the crew of the "Swallow" had met during that fearful night and early morning.

Shortly after the vessel had disappeared, the brave dog, who had so vainly sought to save his master's life, swam alongside of the raft; and Henry, with whom the animal was a great favourite, instantly stretched forth his hand and dragged the exhausted beast on board.

It lay down at his feet for some minutes—panting and exhausted; then leapt to its feet, and, with a low whine, fixed its glance upon the face of the youth.

Henry caressed it, as was his wont; but his heart was too sad to allow him to speak to the animal.

The brute, as though it could read all that was passing in the youth's breast, curled itself at his feet.

Henry scanned the horizon; then dropped his glance to the sea.

They had nought but a few spars between themselves and eternity.

Hour after hour passed.

With anxious eyes they endeavoured to discern some sail on the horizon; but none appeared.

Night came on apace—bright and beautiful now.

The sky was spangled with myriads of stars; and the young crescent moon tinged the water with silvery streaks.

But when the morning sun again shone upon the shipwrecked mariners, two of their company were gone.

They had either been washed off the raft by the waves, or fallen over its sides whilst they slept.

Another day!

Several birds of prey, with distended and blood-shot eyes, wheeled round them, as though anticipating a meal from their dead bodies.

In the after part of the day they saw a sail in the distance—very far off.

Every eye was strained to catch a glimpse of her course.

A flag was hoisted, as high as their pole would admit; and they shouted with all their might, fondly hoping that the sound of their voices would be carried by the breeze to the vessel.

They thought the ship was steering towards them, and shouts of joy burst from every lip.

But the shouts changed to groans in a few short minutes.

Their hopes were cruelly disappointed; for they beheld the vessel recede from their sight, and nothing but the tops of her masts were visible.

Then they, too, disappeared.

She was sailing from them.

The next day passed, and their provisions began to get short, and were obliged to be husbanded with greater care; but there were less mouths to consume them—for they lost three more of their companions. One had been dragged off by a shark; another had died from cold and exhaustion; and the third from a fever which he had when leaving the ship, and when, from cold and exposure, his disease had become augmented, in delirium he drank madly of the salt water.

Still Henry Chambers and Pompey, the black cook, bore up bravely; but another day passed, and still no sight of either a sail or land.

The sufferings of the poor occupants of the raft were now of a horrible nature—their provisions were almost exhausted, and famine stared them in the face.

One more of the party died.

Worn with anxious watching, their bodies saturated with the salt water, and their limbs benumbed with cold, the wretched occupants of that frail fabric had to endure a still greater horror; their food was now entirely exhausted.

Henry, Pompey, one sailor, and the dog were now the sole survivors on the raft.

Hunger was gnawing at the vitals of all; and the sailor, Charles Kepple by name, looked anxiously towards his companion, and then the dog.

His meaning was at once understood—as well as if he had spoken.

Henry shook his head, and turned his gaze upon the horizon.

Bitter tears rose to his eyes.

The black observed the looks of both, and was at no loss to interpret their meaning.

He stooped down, and, placing his arm around the dog, embraced him fondly.

The dog, too, who was as pensive as possible, seemed conscious of the fate in contemplation for him.

Hunger makes savages of man.

A few more hours passed, and Kepple leaned forward and whispered a proposition in Henry's ear that they should slay the dog.

Henry shook his head, and averted his face.

"I starve," growled Charley.

"Here—I have a trifle of my own rations left," said Henry: "take them."

And he threw towards Kepple a few crumbs of biscuit, which he had husbanded.

Kepple devoured them greedily.

Meagre as was the meal, Kepple seemed grateful for it; and, though his glance ever and anon wandered to the dog, he made no further proposition that the animal should die to furnish them with food.

He had resolved to wait till the morrow.

Another day passed, which, in despite of hunger, misery, and despair, saw the poor mariners wrapped ever and anon in a fitful but heavy sleep.

The next day the horrible pangs of hunger seized more powerfully upon the wretched occupants of the craft.

Still no hope of succour—no sail in sight. A bright and scorching sun lit up the surface of the ocean; but, in the far-off distance, Henry could observe no trace of land.

The occupants of the raft were now more like horrid spectres than living beings.

Kepple sat in moody silence, as though he was now determined to suffer to the last without complaint or murmur.

The day wore on; and Pompey, touching Henry on the shoulder, pointed to Kepple.

The man lay upon the raft, as though bereft of life.

Henry crawled towards him—spoke to him—but received no answer. Then he turned away, with a sorrowful countenance.

At the further end of the raft crouched the half-starved dog. The black stood by the side, holding him by the neck with one hand, whilst with the other he pointed at him.

Henry saw that Kepple was dying, and knew that it was from want; but he shook his head to the black's mute appeal.

The dog looked wistfully up in his face, as if he understood his meaning.

"Not yet," he said—"not yet. We will wait another hour: then—then—"

The black nodded; and Henry sat down, and buried his face in his hands.

An hour had passed, and Henry rose and approached the prostrate form of Kepple.

He stretched forth his hand and touched him.

A shudder ran through his frame—the sailor was dead.

With a sigh, he beckoned to Pompey; and, together, they pushed the corpse over the side of the raft into the sea.

Then Pompey returned to the side of the dog, and stood over the poor animal, waiting for a sign from Henry to act as his executioner.

Henry cast one glance around the horizon—a sob broke from his breast, and he moved his hand to the black.

The negro clasped the dog's neck firmly with his left hand, and with his right drew a long knife from his belt.

Henry turned his head away; he could not bear to see the faithful creature sacrificed, though he was starving.

As he did so, a loud cry of joy broke from his lips, and he leapt to his feet.

"Hold, Pompey—hold! Heaven be praised—land—land!"

And he pointed to the distant horizon.

The black dropped the knife, and bounded to his side.

He looked in the direction to which Henry

pointed, and beheld, in the far-off distance, a faint indication of a small island.

The raft was drifting speedily towards it; and, as it approached nearer, they beheld an island distinctly visible above the surface of the waters.

The raft drifted on: night came—a black and gloomy night—enshrouding the ocean in a dense fog: but, when the morning sun appeared, the island was close at hand.

Oh! how the hearts of Henry and his black companion bounded with joy.

Who can describe their emotions as each moment they saw the frail structure on which they stood float nearer and nearer to the haven of refuge!

They laughed and cried by turns—they grasped each other's hands—they patted and fondled the poor brute who had been so nearly sacrificed to provide them with food, and who, as though he partook of their joy, licked their hands, and caressed their legs.

Presently the raft struck against the jutting point of a rock with such force that it was nearly dashed to pieces.

But, when the wave passed on, the raft was found to be fairly fixed on the rock.

Wave after wave came on now in quick succession; and, as each succeeding one arrived, the frail fabric was carried away piecemeal.

This was continued for some time; and then a heavy sea dashing over it, crushed it down upon the rocks, and dashed it to pieces.

Henry and Pompey clung to the spars, and they struck out, as well as they were able, for the shore.

But so weak and exhausted were they, that the waves, as they broke upon the rocks and beach, and hurried back to their ocean bed, carried the two poor starved men back with them, only to hurl them again upon the rocks, and threaten them with destruction.

At length one wave, more furious than its fellows rolled in, bearing the two shipwrecked sufferers on its bosom high up the beach.

As it receded, they stretched forth their hands and grasped at the shore; and the wave retreated back to the vast expanse of waters, leaving them lying on the sands, bruised and bleeding.

CHAPTER CXXVII.

ON THE SAND-BANK—THE STRUGGLE—DEATH OF THE BLACK.

BLEEDING and exhausted, Henry Chambers and the black cook lie upon the barren shore on which the waves had cast them.

Almost deprived of their senses by the violence with which the waves had hurled them upon the sand-bank—for such indeed it only was—they lay, panting and breathless, inwardly murmuring a supplication to Heaven, to prevent the furious element, as it rolled in, from again carrying them back into the waste of waters, which boiled, and seethed, and foamed around them, more and more

And that prayer was answered.

Gradually the waves receded.

At each roll their fury became spent.

And, as the poor shipwrecked seamen observed this, their strength returned.

They scrambled up, and dragged their wearied bodies higher and higher up the bank, till, at length, they were out of danger of the waves.

Here they sank down, and gazed in horror around them.

Neither spoke.

Their hearts were too full for utterance.

They could but gaze alternately into each other's face; then turn their glance towards the sea.

For in that direction alone dared they hope for succour.

What if it came not soon?

They must perish.

Perish upon that bank of sand, on which not one root grew.

Truly, their position was a terrible one.

Still it was better than that from which they had just escaped.

Thus they sat for some time in silence.

Then Pompey raised his head, and fixed his eye, now bloodshot and dim, upon the face of the youth.

"Massa Chambers," he said—"Pompey starve"

There was something so fearful in the tones of the black, that Henry sprang to his feet.

"And I starve, too," he exclaimed.

"No food here," said the black—"no ship on the sea—no hope for life, for the dog is gone!"

Henry looked around him.

He had not observed this fact before.

The dog was not to be seen.

"True," he said—"and our last hope is gone!"

The black's teeth were clenched firmly together, and a strange light shone in his eyes.

He stepped close up to the youth, and laid his hand upon the handle of his knife.

"Massa Chambers," he hissed—"two men live —two men starve: one man die—one man live."

"Ah!" exclaimed Henry, bounding back a few paces—"what do you mean?"

The black drew his knife from his belt.

"One must die to save the other," he exclaimed.

"Stand off!" said Henry. "Would you kill me, that you may live?"

"Massa Chambers got a knife," said the black. "Him can defend himself. Perhaps him kill Pompey.

Horror and disgust for a moment took possession of the mind of the young officer; then, with a sigh, he said:

Pompey, while there is life, there is hope. Heaven may yet be merciful, and send us succour. Ah! do not let this horrible feeling take possession of you. We have shared the same dangers together; together let us live and die."

"I starve," said Pompey, gloomily.

And, as he spoke, he stepped forward with his upraised knife.

"Think, Pompey," said Henry Chambers— "think what will you gain by my death? A few hours' life, perhaps: that is all."

"Pompey must live," exclaimed the black, in ferocious tones—"Pompey must live!"

And he flung himself upon Henry.

The young man was not unprepared for this assault.

The look, the tones of the African told him but too surely that there was danger; and he stood ready to meet it.

As the black threw himself upon him, he grasped his wrist, as his hand was about to descend; and, lent fresh strength by the horror of his situation, he gave it so severe a twist that the black dropped his knife with a howl of pain.

At the same time, worn with hunger, he fell upon

his knees; and Henry stood triumphantly over him, with his knife held above his head.

But the youth lowered not his steel one inch.

Hungered as he was, he could not slay the wretch who sought his life to appease his appetite.

A feast of human flesh was indeed too repulsive to the soul of the young officer; and, with a shudder, he released his hold of the black.

"Pompey," he said, "you would slay me, and eat me; but I will be more merciful to you, though I starve. In Heaven's name, let us seek to comfort each other in our fearful affliction!"

The black struggled to his feet, but answered not.

The generous nature of the youth prompted him to believe others actuated by the same impulses and feelings as himself; and, no sooner had he given the black his life, than he turned away, fully believing that Pompey, out of gratitude, would never more attempt his destruction.

With a sombre look, the black picked up his knife, placed it in his belt, and sat down again upon the sand; and, with an aching heart, Henry followed his example, sitting down some distance from his companion.

He strained his eyes to catch the slightest sign of a sail upon the horizon; and, after an hour's anxious gaze, he permitted his head to drop upon his breast, and sank into a deep reverie.

He thought that now his last cruise had come; that he was destined never more to see his native land—to look upon the features of those he loved.

And, as he sat gazing sadly on the waves, as they rolled in upon the bank, he burst into tears.

Suddenly he started, and looked up.

A cry of horror broke from his lips, and he bounded to his feet.

Pompey had crept behind him, and the black's knife was again raised above his head.

As he sprang up, the black closed with him.

Henry had no time now to open his own weapon; and, grasping the black in his arms, he strove to prevent the African from using his knife.

Long and fearful was the struggle.

The black goaded to madness by hunger; and Henry by the resolve to sell his life dearly.

Over and over, on the soft wet sand they rolled, twined in each other's arms—the black struggling to release his wrist, and bury his knife in the heart of his companion—and Henry fighting for life, from his desperate foe.

Truly it was a fearful time.

Kicking, plunging, striking, the fight continued, till at length Henry succeeded in tearing the knife from the black's grasp.

But the instant he possessed himself of it, Pompey grasped the youth by the throat, and pressed his fingers so tightly into the flesh that the young officer could scarcely breath.

Still Henry did not strike.

He could not bear to kill the man who pertinaciously sought his blood.

Once or twice he raised the weapon.

But it fell harmless by his side.

He hoped that Pompey would desist.

But he hoped in vain.

The black, rendered more furious by the loss of his knife, now attempted to strangle him.

Tighter and tighter the African's fingers were pressed into the flesh.

Weaker and weaker the youth felt himself becoming.

His eyes were starting from his head—his tongue from his mouth.

He felt that in a few moments the black would dance in triumph over his breathless body, and he once more raised the knife.

But the black's hold became the fiercer.

With an inward prayer for forgiveness, Henry mustered all his strength.

The glittering steel descended, and with a strange hissing sound penetrated the throat of the African.

One loud shriek broke from the black's lips—one convulsive shudder ran through his frame.

Then his grasp relaxed, and he fell backwards drawing the knife from the wound as he did so; and the purple stream gushed from his throat as he fell dead at the feet of him whose life he had sought.

CHAPTER CXXVIII.

THE BOAT—THE HURRICANE—THE WRECK—THE RAFT—THE STRUGGLE IN THE SEA—HOPE.

FOR a few moments Henry stood like one in a dream, looking down upon the prostrate body before him.

The bloody knife he threw with horror from him far out into the sea.

A shudder ran through his frame as he thought of the fearful deed he had committed.

A deed which had been none of his own seeking.

On the contrary, gladly would he have spared the wretch at his feet.

But the black would not have it so.

He had brought about his own destruction.

But still Henry could not but gaze with horror upon his work.

And for some time he was irresolute what to do.

The sight of the body caused him feelings of such horror that he deemed it best to hide it from his view.

He could not, with the pangs of hunger gnawing at his vitals, do what Pompey had done had he been the victim—appease those pangs by devouring human flesh.

A sinking sensation stole over him as he dwelt upon this, and fearful lest he should be tempted to feast of the dead African, he resolved to consign the body to the waves.

Stooping down he seized the legs of the black, and drew the body to the edge of the bank.

Then he knelt down, and summoning up all his strength he pitched it as far as he could out from the bank.

The waves rolled in, they seized the dead man in their embrace and carried him out from the fascinated gaze of the youth, who with a fervent "Thank God!" staggered back up the bank, as it was lost to his view for ever.

Now he was alone.

Alone on that bank of sand, with the white-crested waves around him.

Alone, without shelter and food!

He felt now more wretched than ever.

Whilst the African remained there was at least something near him on which to rest his gaze; but now there was a blank in his heart—he was alone.

And he sank down upon the wet sand praying for death.

And thus an hour passed.

He felt that it was in vain, but still he once more allowed his gaze to wander over the sea in search of succour.

Far—far out he looked.

But not a speck upon the horizon.

With a deep sigh he withdrew his gaze, and his glare dropped to the waves as they lashed the bank.

A cry of joy broke from his lips.

His dim eye kindled.

His heart heaved.

A black mass lie rocking upon the foam at the foot of the bank.

He rushed towards it.

He almost leaped with joy.

A small boat, carried by the waves, hugged the bank at his feet.

He stretched forth his hand, but the receding waves bore it from him.

But the next wave dashed it back, and he grasped its side and drew it up upon the soft sand out of their reach.

He felt strong again now—for there was some hope.

Hope for him—hope for Pompey too, would he but have waited; for in the little vessel which it would seem heaven had guided thither, was a small chest of food and a beaker of water.

In the bottom of the boat were also two oars and a sail.

With a cry of gratitude Henry sank down on his knees and gave thanks to heaven.

After a time he arose, as deeming his position somewhat bettered by the circumstance. He began to turn his thoughts as to the best means to take.

He hauled the little boat still further on to the beach.

Fixing one of the oars firmly into the sand he attached a painter firmly to it.

He then proceeded to survey the bank.

He found that but a small portion was uncovered at high water ; for trifling as was the rise of the tide the bank was so low that the water almost flowed over it.

The most elevated part was not more than fifteen feet above high water mark, and that was a small knoll about fifty feet in circumference.

He returned to the boat, and having lifted out the water and provisions, dragged them up one by one until they were all collected on the spot he had chosen, he then took out the oars and little sail.

His last object was to haul the little boat up to the same spot, but this demanded the whole of his exertions.

After considerable labour, he contrived to accomplish this, by first lifting round her bow, and then her stern.

He then repaired to one of the beakers, and took a long deep draught.

As the day advanced, the heat became intolerable.

But refreshed as he now felt himself, it only stimulated him to fresh exertions.

He turned over the boat, and contrived to rest her stern upon two hillocks, so as to raise it above the level of the sand beneath it, a few feet.

He then spread out the sail from the keel above, so as to keep off the sun.

Dragging the beakers of water, and the provisions under the boat, he left the chest outside, and having thus formed for himself a sort of covering, which would protect him from the heat by day, and the damp by night, he crept into shelter himself.

He calculated that he was on one of a patch of sandbanks, off the coast of Soango, and about seven hundred miles from the Isle of St. Thomas.

Still he might be fortunate enough to fall in with some trader, and slight as the hope was, it still bouyed him up.

We do not know, but we think it is hardly possible to conceive a situation much more deplorable, than the one we have just described, to have been that of Henry Chambers.

Alone, without a chance of assistance—with only a sufficiency of food for a few days, and cut off from the rest of his fellow creatures, with only so much terra firma as would prevent him from being swallowed up by the vast unfathomable ocean, into which the horizon fell on every side around him, and his chance of escape, how small!

Hundreds of miles away from any from whom he might expect assistance, and the only means of reaching them a small boat—a mere cockle shell, which the first rough gale would inevitably destroy.

Still he resolved not to give way to despondency yet.

He was young, courageous, and bouyant with hope, and there is a feeling of pride, of trust, in our own resources and exertions, which increases and stimulates us in proportion to our danger and difficulties; it is the daring of the soul, proving its celestial origin and eternal duration.

So intense was the heat, that he almost fainted for sufficient air to support life, as he lay under the shade of the boat during the whole of that day.

Not a breath of wind disturbed the glassy wave—all nature appeared hushed into an horrible calm.

It was not until the shades of night were covering the solitudes, that he ventured forth from his retreat; but he found little relief.

There was an unnatural closeness in the air—a suffocation unusual even in those climes.

The youth cast his eyes up to the vault of heaven, and was astonished to find that there were no stars visible, a grey mist covered the whole firmament.

He directed his view around the horizon, and that too was not to be defined, there was a dark bank all around it.

He walked to the edge of the sand bank, there was not even a ripple, the wide ocean appeared to be in a trance, in a state of lethargy or stupor.

He parted the hair from his fevered brow, and once more surveying the horrible, lifeless stagnant waste, his soul was sickened, and he cast himself upon the sand.

There he lay for many hours, in a state bordering upon wild despair.

At last he recovered himself, and rising to his knees, he prayed for strength, and submission to the will of heaven.

When he was once more upon his feet, and had again scanned the ocean, he perceived that there was a change rapidly approaching.

The dark bank on the horizon had now risen higher up, the opaqueness was everywhere more dense, and low murmurs were heard, as if there was wind stirring aloft, although the sea was still glassy as a lake.

Signs of some movement about to take place were evident, and the solitary occupant of the sand bank watched and watched.

And now the sounds increased, and here and

there a wild thread of air, and as rapidly disappearing, would ruffle for a second a portion of the stagnant sea.

Then came whizzing sounds and moans, and then the rumbling noise of distant thunder.

Louder and louder yet.

A broad black line is seen sweeping along the expanse of water—fearful in its rapidity it comes, it comes, and the hurricane burst at once and with all its force, and all its terrific sounds upon the isolated and dejected youth.

The first blast was so powerful and so unexpected, that it threw him down, and prudence dictated to him to remain in that position, for the loose sand was swept off, and whirled in such force as to blind and prevent him seeing a foot from him, he would have crawled to the boat for security, but he knew not which direction to proceed.

But this did not last, for now the water was borne up upon the strong wings of the hurricane, and the sand was rendered firm by its saturation with the element.

He felt he was drenched, and he raised his head, all he could discover was, that the firmament was mantled with a darkness horrible from its intensity, and that the sea was in one extended foam, boiling everywhere, and as white as milk, but still smooth as if the power of the wind had compelled it to be so, but the water had encroached, and one half of the sand bank was covered with it, while over the other, the foam whirled each portion, chasing the other with wild rapidity.

And now the windows of heaven were opened, and the rain mingled with the spray, caught up by the hurricane, was dashed and hurled upon the forlorn sailor; who still lay where he had been first thrown down.

But of a sudden a wash of water told him that he could remain there no longer.

The sea was rising fast, and before he could gain a few paces on his hands and knees, another wave, as it chased him in its wrath, repeated the warning of his extreme danger, and he was obliged to recover his feet, and hasten to the high part of the sand bank, where he had drawn up his boat and his provisions.

Blinded as he was by the rain and spray, he could distinguish nothing.

Of a sudden he fell violently.

He had stumbled over one of the beakers of water, and struck his head against the chest.

Where then was the boat?

It was gone.

It must have been swept away by the fury of the wind.

Then all chance was over.

And if not washed away by the angry waters, he had to prolong his existence but for a short time, and then to die.

The effect of the blow, combined with the shock the loss of the boat caused him, threw him for some time into a state of insensibility.

When he recovered the scene was again changed.

The broad expanse was in a state of wild and fearful commotion.

The waters roared as loud as did the hurricane.

The whole sand bank, with the exception of that part on which he stood, was now covered with tumultuous foam, and his place of refuge invaded ever and anon, when some vast mass overloading the other waves, expended its fury at his feet.

Henry believed all hope of life was now gone.

He prepared to die.

But gradually the darkness of the heavens disappeared.

There was no longer a bank upon the horizon.

And the youth began to hope.

For what?

That he might be saved from the impending danger, to be reserved perhaps for a death still more horrible; to be saved from the fury of the waves, which would swallow him up, and in a few seconds remove him from all pain and suffering, to perish from want of sustenance under a burning sun; to be withered, to be parched to death, calling in his agony for water.

As Henry thought of this, he covered his face with his hands, and moaned aloud in his agony of mind.

Then he prayed that the waters might rise higher and higher, and relieve him from his sufferings.

But the waters did not rise higher. The howling of the wind gradually decreased, and the foaming seas had obeyed the Divine injunction—they had gone so far, but no further!

The day dawned, and the sky cleared, and the first red tints announcing the return of light and heat had appeared on the broken horizon, when the eyes of the despairing mariner were directed to a black mass on the tumultuous waters!

It was a vessel with but one mast standing, rolling heavily and running before the gale right on to the sand bank where he stood; her hull one moment borne aloft, and the next disappearing from his view, in the hollow of the agitated waters.

"She will be dashed to pieces," thought the youth; "they cannot see the bank."

And he would have made a signal to her if he had been able to warn her of her danger, forgetting at the time his own desolate situation.

As Henry watched, the sun rose bright and joyous over the scene of anxiety and pain.

On came the vessel flying before the gale, while the seas chased her as if they would fain overwhelm her.

It was fearful to see her, and agonising to know that she was rushing to destruction.

At last he could distinguish those on board.

He waved his hand, but they perceived him not: he shouted, but his voice was borne away by the gale.

She was within two cables' length of the bank when those on board perceived their danger.

It was too late. They rounded her to. Another wave hurled her towards the sand.

She struck.

Her only remaining mast fell over her side, and the roaring waves hastened to complete the work of destruction and death.

Who shall paint the horror of the unhappy and now despairing beings who were on board of her?

Who shall describe the cry that was sent forth by them for succour and assistance in this their last hour of imminent peril?

The youth's fascinated gaze now fastened upon the doomed vessel, over which the sea broke with fearful violence.

There appeared to be about eight or nine men on deck, who sheltered themselves under the weather bulwarks.

Each wave, as it broke against her side, and then dashed in foam over her, threw her with a convulsive jerk still further on the sand-bank.

At last she was so high up that their fury was partly spent before they dashed against her frame.

Had the vessel been strong and well-built—had she been a collier, coasting the English shores—there was a fair chance that she might have withstood the fury of the storm until it had subsided, and that, by remaining on board, the crew might have survived; but she was of a very different mould, and, as the youth justly surmised, an American brig built for swift sailing, very sharp, and, moreover, very lightly put together.

Henry's eyes, as may be easily supposed, were never removed from the only object which could now interest him—the unexpected appearance and imminent danger of his fellow-creatures at this desolated spot.

He perceived that two of the men went to the hatches, and slid over them to the leeward. They then descended, and, although the seas broke over the vessel, and a large quantity of water must have poured into her, the hatches were not put on again by those who remained on deck.

But in a few minutes this mystery was solved.

One after another at first, and then by dozens, poured forth out of the hold the kidnapped Africans who composed her cargo.

In a short time the decks were covered with them.

The poor creatures had been released by the humanity of two of the sailors, that they might have the same chance as themselves of saving their lives.

Still no attempt was made to quit the vessel.

Huddled together, like a flock of sheep, with the wild waves breaking over them, there they all remained, both Europeans and Africans; and, as the heavy blows of the seas upon the sides of the vessel careened and shook her, they were seen to cling in every direction, with no distinction between the captain and their oppressors.

But this scene was soon changed.

The frame of the vessel could no longer stand the violence of the waves; and, as the English captain watched, of a sudden it was seen to divide amidships, and each portion to turn over.

Then came the struggle for life or death.

Hundreds were floating on the raging element and wrestling for existence, and the white foam of the ocean was dotted by the black heads of the negroes who attempted to gain the bank.

It was a horrible and terrible scene to witness so many at one moment tossed and dashed about at the mercy of the waves — so many human beings threatened with eternity.

At one moment they were close to the beach, forced on it by some tremendous wave; at the next the receding water and underflow swept them all back; and, of the many who had been swimming, one half had disappeared, to rise no more.

Henry watched with agony as he perceived that the number decreased, and that none had yet gained the shore.

At last he snatched up the haulyards of his boat's sail, which were near him, and hastened down to the spot to afford such succour as might be possible.

Nor were his efforts entirely in vain.

As the seas washed the apparent inanimate bodies on shore, and would then have swept them away to return them in mockery, he caught hold of them, and dragged them safe on the bank.

Thus did he continue his exertions until fifteen of the bodies of the negroes were spread upon the beach.

Although exhausted and senseless, they were not dead; and, long before he had dragged up the last of the number, many of those previously saved had, without any other assistance than the heat of the sun, recovered from their insensibility.

Henry would have continued his task of humanity, but the parted vessel had now been riven into fragments by the force of the waves, and the whole beach was strewn with her timbers, and the stores were dashed on shore by the waters, and then swept back again by the return.

For a short time the severe blows he received from these fragments of the vessel disabled him from further exertion, and he sank exhausted on the bank.

Indeed, all further attempts were useless. All on board the vessel had been launched into the sea at the same moment, and those who were not now on shore were past all succour.

Henry walked up to those who had been saved. He found twelve of them were recovered; the rest were in a state of insensibility.

He then went up to the knoll where his chest and provisions had been placed, and, throwing himself down, surveyed the scene.

The wind had lulled, the sun shone brightly, and the sea was much less violent.

The waves had subsided, and, no longer hurried on by the force of the hurricane, broke majestically and solemnly, but not with the wildness and force which but a few hours before they had displayed.

The whole of the beach was strewed with the fragments of the vessel, with spars and water casks; and every moment was to be observed the corpse of a negro turning round and round in the froth of the waves, and then disappearing.

For full an hour did he watch and reflect, and then he walked again to where the men who had been rescued had been sitting, not more than thirty yards from him.

They were sickly, emaciated forms, but belonging to a tribe who inhabited the west, and having been accustomed from their infancy to be all day in the water, had supported themselves better than the other slaves, who had been procured from the interior, or the European crew of the vessel, all of whom had perished.

The Africans appeared to recover fast by the heat of the sun, and were now exchanging a few words with each other.

The whole of them had revived, but those who were most in need of aid, were neglected by the others.

Henry made signs to them, but they understood it not.

He returned to the knoll, and pouring out water in a tin pan from the beaker, brought it down to them.

He offered it to one, who seized it eagerly, water was seldom a luxury obtained in the hold of a slave vessel.

The man drank deeply, and would have drained the cup; but the youth prevented him, and held it to the lips of another, and he was obliged to refill it three times before they had all been supplied.

He then brought them a handful of biscuit, and left them, for he reflected that, without some precaution, the whole sustenance would soon be seized and devoured.

He buried half a foot deep, and covered over with sand, the beakers of water and the provisions, and by the time he had finished his task, unperceived by the negroes, who still squatted together, the sun had again sunk below the horizon.

Henry had already matured his plans, which were, to form a raft out of the fragments of the vessel, and with the assistance of the negroes, endeavour to gain the main land.

He laid down for the second night, on this eventful spot of desolation, and commending himself to the Almighty's protection, was soon in a deep slumber.

It was not until the powerful rays of the sun blazed on his eyes, that he awoke, so tired had he been with the anxiety and fatigue of the preceeding day, and the sleepless and harrowing night, which had introduced it.

He rose and seated himself upon the chest.

How different was the scene from that of yesterday!

Again the ocean slept—the sky was serene—and not a cloud to be distinguished — throughout the whole firmament, the horizontal line was clear, even, and well defined—a soft breeze rippled over the dark blue sea, which now had retired to its former boundary, and had left the sand-bank as extended as when he had been cast on shore.

But here the beauty of the landscape terminated; the foreground was horrible to look upon—the whole beach was covered with the timbers of the wreck, with water casks, and other articles, in some parts heaped and thrown up, one upon another, and among them lay jammed and mangled, the bodies of the many who had perished.

In other parts there were corpses thrown up high and dry, or still rolling and turning to the rippling wave—it was a scene of desolation and of death.

The negroes who had been saved, were all huddled up together, apparently in a deep sleep, and Henry quitted his elevated position, and walked down to the low beach, to survey the means which the disaster of others, afforded him for his own escape.

To his great joy he found not only plenty of casks, but many of them full of fresh water, provisions also in sufficiency, and, indeed, everything which could be required to form a raft, as well as the means of support for a considerable time, for himself and the negroes who had survived.

He then walked up and called to them, but they answered not, nor even moved. He pushed them, but in vain, and his heart beat quickly, for he was afraid they were dead from previous exhaustion.

He applied his foot to one of them, and it was not until he had used force which in any other case would have been dispensed with, that the negro awoke from his state of lethargy, and looked vacantly about him.

Henry had some little knowledge of the language of the Kroumen, and he addressed the negro in that tongue.

To his great joy, he was answered in the same language, which if not the same, had so great an affinity to it, that communication became easy.

With the assistance of the negro, who used still less ceremony with his comrades, the remainder of them were awakened, and a palaver ensued.

Henry soon made them understand that they were to make a raft, and go back to their own country, explaining to them that if they remained there the water and provisions would soon be exhausted, and they would then all perish.

The poor creatures hardly knew whether to consider him a supernatural being or not.

They talked among themselves—they remarked at his having brought them fresh water the day before—they knew that he did not belong to the vessel in which they had been wrecked—and they were puzzled.

Whatever might be their speculations, they had one good effect, which was, that they looked upon him as a superior and friend, and most willingly obeyed him.

He led them up to the knoll, and, desiring them to scrape away the sand, supplied them again with fresh water and biscuit.

Perhaps the very supply, and the way it was given to them, excited their astonishment as much as anything.

The casks were collected and rolled up—the empty ones arranged for the raft; the spars were hauled up, and cleared of the rigging, which was carefully separated from the lashings; the one or two sails which had been found, rolled up, or were spread out to dry; and the provisions, and articles of clothing which might be useful, laid on one side.

The negroes worked willingly, and showed much intelligence.

Before the evening closed, everything which might be available was secured; and the waves now only tossed about the lifeless forms, and the small fragments of timber which could not be serviceable.

It would occupy too much time were we to detail all the proceedings of Henry and the negroes for the space of four days, during which they laboured hard.

Necessity is truly the mother of invention, and many were the ingenious resources of the party before they could succeed in forming a raft large enough to carry them and their provisions, with a mast and sail well secured.

At length it was accomplished, and, on the fifth day, Henry and his men embarked; and, having pushed clear of the bank with poles, they were at last able to hoist their sail to a fine breeze, and steer for the coast before the wind at the rate of about three knots an hour. But it was not until they had gained half a mile from the beach that they were no longer annoyed by the dreadful smell arising from the putrefaction of so many dead bodies—for to have buried them all would have been a work of too great a time.

The last two days of their remaining on the sand-bank, the effluvium had become so powerful, as to be a source of the greatest horror and disgust, even to the negroes.

But before night, when the raft was about eight leagues from the sand-bank, it fell calm, and continued so for the next day, when a breeze sprang up from the south-east, they trimmed their sail, with their head to the northward.

This wind, and the course steered, sent them from off the land, but there was no help for it, and Henry felt grateful that they had such an ample supply of provisions and water, as to enable them to yield to a few days contrary wind, without danger of want.

But the breeze continued steady and fresh, and they were now crossing the Bight of Benin. The weather was fine, and the sea smooth, the flying fish rose in shoals, and dropped down into the raft, which still forced its way through the water to the north-ward.

Days passed over, but still Henry and his negro crew were floating on the wide ocean, without any object meeting their anxious gaze.

Day after day it was the same dreary sky and water, and by the reckoning of Henry, they could not be far from the land, still none as yet had greeted their eyes.

While his eyes were strained to catch a glimpse of land, what was his joy to discern two sails to the northward

The youth's heart bounded with joy and gratitude to heaven. He had no telescope to examine them, but he steered directly for them, and about dark he made them out to be a ship and a schooner in full sail.

He and his negro companions shouted out at the top of their voices, and Henry thought the two vessels slackened sail, for he certainly began to lessen the distance between his own raft and the two ships. Those on board the former were now still more vociferous in their demands for assistance, and their attempts to attract notice.

In their anxiety to do so, the poor wretches rushed all on one side of the raft; and, before the imprudence could be discovered, the weight of the men caused it to career over, and all were precipitated into the sea.

This was indeed a sad circumstance.

At the very moment when succour was in sight, those who had suffered so much were doomed to disappointment.

As Henry, who with the rest had been overturned, rose to the surface, he cast his eyes despairingly around him.

The raft had floated on, and was now, carried by a stiff breeze, some distance from where himself and his companions in misfortune were struggling in the waves.

He struck out, with the hope of reaching the raft, and soon succeeded in obtaining a hold of its side; but it darted from his hands, and he sank swiftly down into the bosom of the waters.

When he again rose to the surface, the raft was a long way off; and, with a cry of despair, he cast his eyes around, in search of his companions.

He saw several of them struggling in the waves, and heard their cries for aid, as they were borne to his ears by the wind.

But those cries became less, as, one by one, the poor wretches sank never more to rise.

He struck out again, resolved, if possible, to reach the raft; and eagerly strained his eyes to catch a glimpse of the vessel which had caused so sad a circumstance.

But he saw them not.

No. 47

The wind had borne them far out of sight or hearing.

De pair now took possession of his soul, as, farther and farther, the raft drifted from him.

Still he swam on, although he felt his hour had come.

Suddenly he saw a black object before him.

What could it be?

A boat.

He struck out for it.

Larger and larger, it loomed up, till, with a shout of joy, he reached its side.

It was the boat which he had found at the sand-bank, and which had been washed away by the storm.

He clasped it eagerly with both hands; he drew his body up over the side, and sank down, exhausted, with a prayer of thankfulness upon his lips, to the bottom.

But, the next moment, a dozen hands laid hold of it, and he was flung out into the sea.

CHAPTER CXXIX.

ONCE MORE ALONE ON THE DEEP—THE SWIMMER
AND HIS PURSUER—SAVED.

No sooner had Henry Chambers swam for the boat than his companions struck out for the same object; and such was the impetuosity, occasioned by their anxiety to scramble in all on one side, that the boat was instantly turned over.

Some had got across her keel—whilst several of the others were holding on to her like grim death—when Henry once more rose to the surface.

In an instant he saw how matters stood; and, his usual calmness returning to his aid, he began to point out to those who surrounded the boat the improbability of their being saved if they continued in their present position; for those who were on the keel would shortly roll off, and exertion and fatigue would soon force the others to relinquish their holds, or urge them to endeavour forcibly to dislodge the possessors from their quiet seats.

He pointed out the necessity of righting the boat—of allowing only two men to get in her to bale her out, whilst the others, supported by the gunwales, which they kept upright, might remain in the water until the boat was in such a condition as to receive two more, and thus, by degrees, to ship the whole crew in security.

At the order from the lieutenant for the men on the keel to relinquish their position, they instantly obeyed.

The boat was turned over, and once more the experiment tried; but quite in vain; for, no sooner had the two men began to bale out the water with a couple of hats, and the safety of the crew to appear within the bounds of probability, than one man declared he saw the fin of a shark.

No language can convey the panic which seized upon the struggling mariners.

A shark is at at all times an object of horror to a sailor; and those who have seen the destructive jaws of these fish, and their immense and almost incredible power, their love of blood, and their bold daring to obtain it, alone can conceive any idea of the sensations produced by the cry of—"A shark! a shark!"

Every man now struggled to obtain a moment's safety. Well they knew that one drop of blood would have been scented by the everlasting pilot fish—the jackalls of the shark—and then destruction would be inevitable if one of these monsters should discover the rich repast, or be led to its food by the little rapid hunters of its prey.

The boat again turned keel upwards. One man only gained security to be pushed from it by others. And thus their strength began to fail from long continued exertion.

As, however, the enemy so much dreaded did not make its appearance, Henry once more urged them to endeavour to save themselves by the only means left—that of the boat. But, as he knew that he would only increase their alarm by endeavouring to persuade them that sharks did not abound in these parts, he used the wisest plan, of desiring those who held on by the gunwales to keep splashing the water with their legs, in order to frighten the monsters at which they were so alarmed.

Once more had hope began to dawn—the boat was clear to her thwarts, and four men were in her. A little forbearance, and a little obedience, and they were safe.

At this moment, when those in the water urged their messmates in the boat to continue baling with unremitting exertion, a noise was heard close to them, and about fifteen sharks came right in amongst them.

The panic was ten times greater than before—the boat was again upset by the simultaneous endeavours to escape the danger, and the twenty-three sailors were again devoted to destruction.

At first the sharks did not seem inclined to seize upon their prey, but swam in amongst the men, playing with the water—sometimes leaping about, and rubbing against their victims.

This was of short duration. A loud shriek from one of the men announced his sudden pain: a shark had seized him by the leg.

No sooner had the blood been tasted than the long dreaded attack took place.

Another and another shriek proclaimed the loss of limbs.

Some were torn from the boat—to which they vainly endeavoured to cling. Some, it is supposed, sunk from fear alone. All were in dreadful peril.

Others, who had not been so seriously injured by the monsters of the deep, endeavoured to get up the keel of the boat, which was again upset. But, worn out with excessive fatigue, and smarting under the keen pain, they gave up the chance of safety, and were either eaten up by the sharks, or, courting death, which appeared inevitable, they threw themselves from their only support, and were drowned.

And, in the short space of a few minutes, all that remained of the ill-fated crew of the raft were Henry and one black.

The sharks seemed satisfied for the moment; and they with gallant hearts resolved to profit by the precious time, in order to save themselves.

They righted the boat; and one getting over the bows, and the other over the stern, they found themselves, although nearly exhausted, yet alive, and in comparative security.

They began the work of baling, and soon lightened the boat sufficiently not to be easily upset, when both sat down to rest.

The return of the sharks was the signal for their resuming their labours.

The voracious monsters endeavoured to upset the boat—swimming by its side, in seeming anxiety for the prey. But, after waiting for some time, they separated.

The two rescued seamen now found themselves free from their insatiable enemies, and, by the blessing of God, saved for the present, at all events, although it was impossible to tell what might occur.

Tired as they were, they continued their labour until the boat was nearly dry, when they both lay down to rest—the one forward, and the other aft. So completely had fear operated on their minds, that they did not dare even to move, dreading that an uncertain step might again capsize the boat.

They soon, in spite of the horrors they had witnessed, sunk into a sound sleep, and day had dawned before they awoke to horrible reflections and apparently worse dangers.

The sun rose clear and unclouded, and the cool calm of the night was followed by the sultry calm of the morning; and heat and hunger, thirst and fatigue, seemed to settle on the unfortunate men, rescued by Providence and their own exertions from the jaws of a horrible death.

They awoke and looked at each other. The very gaze of despair was appalling.

Far as the eye could reach, no object could be discovered. The bright haze of the morning added to the strong refraction of light; one smooth interminable plain, one endless ocean, one cloudless sky, one burning sun, were all they had to gaze upon.

The boat lay like the ark, in a world alone.

They had no oar, no mast, no sail by which to steer.

It was now about half-past six in the morning; the sun was beginning to prove his burning power, the sea was as smooth as a looking-glass, and save now and then the slight catspaw of air, which ruffled the surface of the water for a few yards, all was calm and hushed.

In vain they strained their eyes—in vain they turned from side to side to escape the burning rays of the sun. They could not sleep—for now anxiety and fear kept both vigilant and on their guard. They dared not court sleep—for that might have been their last of mortal repose.

Another night passed.

A night of horror, agony, and despair.

But the morning came at last.

And, with the first beams of the morning sun, Henry sprang to his feet, with the cry on his lips of—

"A sail—a sail!"

The black bounded to his feet, also, as Henry pointed out, far away in the distance, the sails of a vessel.

Every means of making a signal was resorted to.

One stood upon the thwarts, and flung his jacket in the air; whilst the other, although the stranger was miles distant, endeavoured to hail her.

Sometimes they hailed together, in order to produce a louder sound; and occasionally they both stood up to make a signal.

Their eyes were never off the vessel; they thought no longer of the burning sun, of hunger or thirst, for deliverance was at hand—at least, so they flattered themselves—and no time of the greatest joy could have beat the excitement and gratification of that moment.

Whilst they stood watching in silence the approach of the vessel, which slowly made her way throug the water—and at the very instant that they were assuring each other that they were seen, and that the vessel was purposely steered on the course she was keeping to reach them—the whole fabric of their hope was destroyed in a second.

The ship was kept away about three points, and began to make sail.

Then was an awful moment. Their countenances saddened as they looked at each other; for in vain they hailed—in vain they threw their jackets in the air. It was evident they had never been seen, and that the brig was steering her proper course.

They endeavoured, by heeling the boat on one side, to propel her by their hands; but they were soon worn out with fatigue, and obliged to relinquish the attempt; for, independently of the impossibility of success in such an undertaking, they lost the better opportunity of being seen by the vessel.

It was after a long-drawn deep sigh from the man in the stern-sheets, and after wiping away a stream of tears as he looked at the vessel, then two miles and a half distant, that he broke into a loud lamentation on the utter hopelessness of their situation if they were not seen.

The black, now that he discovered the ship was sailing from them, lost all control of himself: and, leaping and shouting, in the hopes of attracting the notice of those on board the distant vessel, he lost his balance, and fell into the sea.

Henry stretched forth his hand to save him; but in vain. The poor fellow never rose to the surface; but the water around the boat was tinged with blood.

The sharks had followed the little vessel, and received their reward.

Henry closed his eyes, with a shudder of horror; but the next moment he leaped up.

"There is but one hope—one!" he exclaimed. "It is to swim to yonder ship. But the sharks! Well, it will but give them their meal a few hours sooner. Heaven help me! To remain here is to die; to hazard the attempt can be no more. Guard me, Heaven!—but it is my only hope."

And, glancing towards the white sails, he sprang up, and far over the side of the boat into the sea.

Not a fin was in sight when he took the daring leap; and Henry fondly hoped that, satisfied with the black, they had taken their departure: but, feeling assured that if any of the monsters had seen him they would not be long in following him, he kept kicking the water, and splashing, as he swam.

When he had swam some distance, Henry saw by his side one of these dreaded monsters. Still he swam on bravely, and splashed and splashed, and kicked the water, as much as possible.

He had made up his mind for the worst; and he had little hope of success.

In the meantime, the breeze had gradually freshened, and the brig passed with greater velocity through the water—every stitch of canvass was spread.

To the poor swimmer, the sails seemed bursting with the breeze; and, as he used his utmost endeavours to propel himself, so as to cut off the vessel, the spray appeared to dash from the bow, and the vessel fly through the sea.

He was now close enough to hope his voice might be heard. He hailed, and listened anxiously for a reply to his summons.

And it came.

Over the sea, borne by the wind to his ears, came the sound of a human voice.

" Oh, joy—joy !

Again it salutes his ear.

He raised his head.

He strained his eyes towards the ship.

He saw the sails put back, and her course altered.

A boat was lowered from her side; and into it half a dozen men descended.

It made towards him—propelled by long and steady strokes.

But, horror—horror !—the shark has also seen the boat, and makes for his prey, ere he can be torn from its fangs.

Henry saw his danger, and dived.

It was providential for him that he did so; for, by the act, the monster missed his prey.

Again he rose to the surface.

So did the shark.

It now became a fearful race for life or death.

He struck out frantically for the boat. He reached its side; he grasped the hands extended to him, and was drawn into the boat as the monster grasped at his heel, and tore away his shoe.

——

CHAPTER CXXX.

INSUBORDINATION IN THE CAVERN—THE PRISONER RELEASED—THE AGREEMENT—THE VENGEANCE OF BLACK BILL.

WE left the Boy Rover and his dissolute companions—Black Bill, Sam, Jem, Tom, and Ned—together with the poor old sailor's daughter, Mary, in the cavern, where a scene of violence was taking place, and the authority of the Smuggler of the South Seas was being defied by the next in command.

The noise occasioned by the struggle, and the loud and blasphemous language of the smugglers, aroused Tom and Ned, who, having partaken too much of the spirit which never paid duty, had slumbered heavily through the first part of the broil.

Starting from their rude couches, they both became sufficiently alive to all that was passing in the cavern, at the very moment that Black Bill had uttered his threat to blow them all to hell together.

This threat had a wonderful effect.

As Bill levelled his weapon at the keg, the others drew back in terror.

They could see by the workings of the smuggler lieutenant's countenance that he really meant what he said.

They drew back in horror.

As though paralysed, they stood gazing upon him from a greater distance.

They feared to molest him further, lest he should put his threat into execution.

Bold as they were, they stood appalled before his haughty glance.

For haughty and defiant indeed was the look which Black Bill fixed upon them.

He knew the cruel and unforgiving nature of the Boy Rover.

He felt that he could expect no mercy at his hands.

He saw that it would be useless to ask for pardon; and there was, therefore, nothing left him but to sell his life dearly.

So, if he must fall, he resolved not to fall alone.

The barrel of powder was before him, at his feet.

His enraged captain, panting for revenge, stood eager for the spring.

The weapon was in his hand—the long bright muzzle pointed to the fatal dust.

And thus he stood at bay before his awe-struck and guilty assailants.

As for Mary, she knew not whether to hope or fear.

Were Bill made prisoner by the Rover, and the threatened doom averted, would her danger be increased or lessened?

This was a question she asked herself, as those bold bad men stood glaring like wounded tigers upon each other.

But it was a question she could not satisfactorily answer.

Either way, she believed, was destruction to her.

Perhaps, after all, it would be better that she died of the explosion than of grief and shame.

For, if Bill's resolves were defeated, there was no hope for her that the Boy Rover, or his inhuman followers, would allow one grain of pity to enter their souls towards her.

She dared not hope they would be merciful to her.

She had no right to hope.

The indignities they had offered her — the murder of her father—told but too fearfully that mercy or pity were dead to them for ever.

She cast an appealing look upwards towards the rude stone roof of the cavern, and her white lips parted, as she breathed forth :

" Lord, have mercy upon me !"

Poor girl !—heaven was her only hope of succour now ; and to that she appealed.

Chafing like an angry tiger held at bay by the hunters, the Boy Rover could only glare upon the lieutenant, who thus threatened his own destruction, and that of his comrades.

" Ha, ha !" laughed Black Bill, hoarsely. " You see, captain, I am no chicken to be played with."

The Boy Rover, goaded to fury by the remark, took one step forward towards him.

" Back !" roared Bill, a demoniac scowl suffusing his face, and levelling the barrel of his weapon fair into the centre of the keg.

One hasty step backwards the Boy Rover took.

And a sigh of relief broke from the lips of his followers as he did so.

" You are wise," said Bill. " Now, captain, you know me to be a man of my word."

The Boy Rover remained silent.

" You know that what I say I mean," said Bill, after a moment's pause.

Still the Rover answered not. He only watched intently every movement, however slight, of Black Bill.

" You are not the only one of the crew," continued Bill, " who, when he says he'll do a thing, will do it."

" We shall see," remarked the Boy Rover.

" We shall," replied Bill. " In all connected with our profession I am willing to obey you; but in these little private bits of business I own no commander."

" Remember the oath."

"I do."

"And you refuse to keep it?" said the Rover.

"I do not refuse to keep it—or, rather, that part of it which is just. I only refuse to permit it to bind me when the interest of none but myself are concerned. In this business I hold that you have no right to interfere. I knew the girl, and sought her for myself—not for you."

"And I claim her according to our rules," said the Boy Rover.

"You would never have thought of doing so, but for that varmint of a Sam."

"Perhaps not."

"And never have wanted to have had anything to do with her, but for him."

"That may be; but having decided on putting into force the rule which gives me power to claim her, you, as one of my crew, had no right to dispute it."

"I had."

"No, you had not."

"I had every right, said Bill.

"Those rules you agreed to with the rest."

"Still I do not hold that particular rule binding," said Bill—"nor would it have been enforced but for him."

And Bill pointed to Sam.

"Still having resolved to put forward my claim I shall not swerve from it," said the Rover.

"And being resolved to send you to hell with myself if you persist in holding me liable to punishment for what I have done, I shall not swerve from it," said Bill, pointing to the barrel of the pistol in a meaning manner.

"You wont?"

"No!"

"We shall see."

"So we shall."

"Will you surrender that weapon and trust to my mercy, said the Boy Rover.

"As well might the lamb trust to the mercy of the wolf," said Black Bill. "Captain, I will not trust you."

"Don't be a fool," exclaimed Tom; "listen to reason."

"You shut up," said Bill.

"Well, I only advice you for the best," replied Tom.

"Then I don't want your advise," said Bill. "That gal's mine by fair rights, and it's the captain's fault that I now stand here on my own defence.

"Lay down the pistol," said Jem, "and it will be all right—I dare say."

"Silence!" said the Boy Rover—"I alone make terms here."

Jem bit his lips, and retreated a few paces.

"Will you surrender, and trust to my clemency?" said the Boy Rover, once more.

"No," said Bill—"unless you swear not to seek to harm me."

"I will swear nothing."

"Then I refuse."

"You do?"

"I do."

The Boy Rover turned to his followers.

"You have each a pistol," he said. "Fire!"

"To h—l with you then!" said Bill, placing his finger on the trigger.

"Oh! for mercy, hold—hold!" shrieked the poor girl, once more springing forward.

Bill hesitated.

"Oh! men—men," she added, "have you no fear of a hereafter? Think what you would do—think, think! You would not rush with your sins heavy on your soul into the presence of your Maker! Oh! forbear—forbear."

"I tell you," said Bill, "I'll blow the place to the devil, and all in it, before I will submit to this arbitrary work. He would have some fresh sport, to wile away his time: perhaps have me impaled, as he did Ned Wilton, on board the "Venomed Snake." But he won't, though. I have stood by him, and fought for him, many a time; and this is the return he makes—tears the girl from me, and then threatens me with death! But Black Bill won't die without a struggle. If I must go to Davy Jones's locker, why, demme, he shall keep me company there, too—that's all!"

Mary approached the Boy Rover, and placed her hand upon his arm.

Her eyes were filled with tears, and her lips trembled, as she said:

"I know not how you can have wished to harm me—me, who never did you wrong. I know not what can have induced you to slay my poor old father, and tear me from his side. It must have been some evil influence which worked upon your soul. Some demon took possession of your heart, and urged you on to this guilty work. Oh! think, if you consent to listen to his promptings, what must be your portion. Can the gratification of ruining a poor defenceless girl induce you to plunge your soul to perdition? No, no—it cannot! Your heart is not all iron. There must be one soft spot that my sufferings and my tears may penetrate. Oh! be merciful to me—to him—to yourself. End this fearful strife, by permitting me to depart from here! A bad deed is sure to bring a train of bad works with it; a good one is sure to be followed by better. I alone have been the cause of this—though it has been none of my seeking. Be merciful! Let me hence to him whose blood stains the once happy cot—to him who lies cold and dead—my father!"

The Boy Rover listened, without interrupting her, to the end.

A calm smile played around his mouth.

Not a feeling of pity seemed to take possession of his soul.

His heart was still callous to the sufferings of Mary.

Her pleadings had no power to turn his cruel nature.

Still he thought that by appearing to listen and consent to her desires, he could best draw back from his word, without appearing to do so.

His courage had not been subdued by the bold daring of Black Bill; but he was wise enough to see that the smuggler lieutenant had the power to destroy not only him, but all in that place, together with the cave.

But for this power, which Black Bill possessed, the Rover had never swerved from his threat to carry out the punishment of mutiny.

He saw, too, the eyes of his companions fixed anxiously upon him.

After a pause he said, turning to the poor girl:

"You plead well, and I almost feel tempted to comply with your request to set me free."

"Oh! bless you—bless you!" she exclaimed, clasping her hands together.

"But on one condition will I consent to do so," said the Boy Rover.

"Speak it—oh! speak it," she said, hastily.

"That he whose love for you led him to mutiny against me, instantly surrender himself prisoner," said the Rover.

The eyes of the poor girl dropped to the earth.

Her bosom rose and fell with emotion.

Her limbs trembled violently.

She shook her head despairingly.

She believed there was but little chance of her freedom on such conditions.

She dared not hope that Bill would consent to die to save her.

Yet, after a few moments' pause, she looked up in the face of the mutineer.

The glance she fixed upon him, so full of despair, would have been sufficient to strike deep into the most callous heart.

Bill heard the words of the Boy Rover—saw the look of the half-fainting maiden—and he spoke :

"Captain," he said, "smuggler and murderer though I am, I am still a man. Open the door of this cavern—give that girl her liberty—and swear not to molest her yourself, or allow any of the others to do so—and, though I would defy you to my last breath, for her sake I will surrender: I swear it !"

With a loud cry, Mary tottered towards him—her hands clasped—her eyes filled with tears.

"You will—you will ?" she gasped, eagerly.

"I will," he replied.

"Bless you !"

"For your sake I will," continued Black Bill—"though, by so doing, I sign my death-warrant."

"Heaven will reward you," she gasped, as the scalding tears chased each other down her cheeks.

"And he will torture me," muttered Black Bill. "But no matter. I have lived a bold and reckless life, and will die a bold defiant man. Perhaps it is better it should be so. There can be no good feeling between us after this. And, though I shall perhaps perish, I shall at least have the satisfaction of knowing that I have done one good deed in my life; and that he will not die so honourable a death as I shall. The tree is well-grown, and the hemp spun, which will end his days. It would, after all, be but a poor revenge were I to deprive the gallows of its due, and rob the hangman of his fee. And there will yet be one in the world to say that Black Bill, the smuggler, could sacrifice his own life to save a woman's honour."

"And one whose prayers shall be raised to Heaven for your forgiveness," exclaimed Mary.

"Lead her forth," said the Boy Rover, waving his hand to Sam. "But first bind her eyes; so that she cannot bring the sharks down upon us. See her to the slopes beyond the rocks; and then leave her to go her way."

The eyes of the poor girl were bound, and Sam led her from the cabin.

The moment she had disappeared, the Boy Rover turned to Black Bill, who still kept the muzzle of the pistol pointed at the keg of powder.

"Surrender," he said—"the girl is free."

"When Sam returns," was the reply, in a cold calm tone. "Captain, I know you too well to trust you."

"Ah, traitor !"

"You would instantly start in pursuit of the girl, and bring her back, were I to surrender this weapon. No, no! Let Sam return, and the girl place some distance between herself and this cave, then will I keep my word—you may depend on it."

"You would play me false," said the Rover.

"I have sworn to do an act of justice—and I will do it," said Bill. "The conditions were, the girl should be free."

"She is free."

"But will she remain so ?" said Bill.

"Yes."

"You promised to aid me to get her into my power; then tore her from me," said Bill. "If you would be false to me once, you would be so again."

"Then you refuse to surrender ?" exclaimed the Rover.

"Till Sam returns."

The Rover was silent; but he resolved that Bill should suffer for his obstinacy.

In about half an hour Sam entered the cavern.

"Now," said the Boy Rover.

"Is the girl safe," asked Bill, "and beyond pursuit ?"

"She is," replied Sam.

"You can have no further excuse," said the Boy Rover.

"None," replied Bill. "The girl is free, and far away from here. You demand my life; you shall have it. But, Rover, Black Bill dies not alone. He has lived a bold and fearless life, and he will die a bold and fearless death. Thus do I keep my oath—ha, ha!"

And he pulled the trigger of the weapon, and fired it into the keg of powder.

A fearful explosion followed; and, through the walls of the cavern, rent by the force of the shock, poured a dense volume of smoke over the waves.

CHAPTER CXXXI.

THE REVENUE CUTTER — THE SEARCH IN THE CAVERN—DISCOVERY OF THE BODIES.

LOUD was the report, and fearful the shock, in that secret cave of the smugglers.

The heterogenous mass of bales, barrels, and trunks, which were piled around, toppled and fell in one confused mass.

The opening to the sea, before which the deceitful fire had been so often kindled to allure the unsuspecting mariner to his doom, was laid bare.

In some parts, even the thick stone walls of the cave were rent in several places; and huge volumes of black smoke poured out into the open air.

Black Bill had indeed been avenged.

He had triumphed in his death.

Feeling that there was no hope for him, he had determined to sacrifice those who sought his life.

And fearful were the means he employed to bring about his vengeance.

The sun was high in the heavens when the dark cloud of smoke issued from the cavern, and curled up over the glistening waves towards the bright blue expanse above.

The little revenue cutter, the "Royal Blue," which had been sailing round the coast since the last work of the wreckers, in the hope of picking up something from the wreck, was lying idly at anchor, some three miles from the cave.

But the cloud of smoke, as it curled up over the rocks, could be seen plainly from her decks, on which two of the officers, and several of her men, were; and, though the roar of the explosion had been somewhat deadened by the fact that the wind was blowing in the opposite direction, still sufficient had been heard to cause a more than ordinary interest to those on board.

"There's one of the rocks dying of spontaneous combustion, I should say," remarked a young middy to the second lieutenant, as, happening to cast his eyes in the direction of the cave, his gaze encountered the huge column of black smoke, as it curled up towards the clouds.

The officer thus addressed shaded his eyes with his hand, and looked intently towards the spot.

"Humph!—something wrong there, I should say, Mr. Canning," he remarked, addressing the young officer, without once turning his gaze from the spot.

"What do you take it to be, sir?" asked the youth.

"Can't say," was the reply—"but I should think that it was an explosion."

"It certainly would seem to be the best guess," replied the youth; "for I was struck, a few minutes since, with a strange sound in the air."

"So was I," replied the lieutenant—"but did not think it anything worthy of notice at the time. Oblige me with the glass, Mr. Canning."

The young officer instantly complied with the request of his superior; and the lieutenant, placing it to his eye, fixed his gaze eagerly upon the spot, over which the smoke hung for some moments.

"Are you any nearer the real cause, Mr. White?" asked the middy.

"No, sir," replied the lieutenant—"only a little nearer its locality."

"And that, sir?"

"Just where the brig went to pieces a few nights since," was the reply.

"And do you still think it an explosion, sir?" enquired the youth.

"I do; for I can make out no other cause," replied the lieutenant.

And he presented the glass to the young officer.

The middy took the telescope and having placed it to his eye took a long look at the spot.

"Well, sir?"

"It is as you say, lieutenant," answered the youth.

"And do you still think it an explosion?" said the lieutenant.

"I do, sir."

The officer looked puzzled.

"And yet," replied the middy—"I was not aware that any powder was stored about the coast thereaway."

"Nor I."

"There are no mills?" said the youth.

"None."

"Strange."

"Very."

"The smoke still rises," continued the youth, again placing the glass to his eye—"and seems to ooze from out of the very rocks."

"So it appeared to me," replied the lieutenant.

"The distance is not so great as to deceive us," said the youth.

"No."

"It certainly comes out of the rock and not from behind it."

"Well, it is a strange affair," remarked the lieutenant, pacing up and down the deck.

"Will you order a boat off, sir," to ascertain its cause," said the youth.

"I can scarcely see the use of doing so," was the reply.

"There may be lives in danger," said Canning.

"Sure'y you do not think that people live in the solid rocks." laughed the lieutenant.

"Well, no," replied the youth.

"Then of what avail would it be our despatching a boat to the scene."

"I cannot say."

"Nor can I see," said the lieutenant.

"Yet the peculiarity of the circumstance, sir, might warrant the mission," said the middy.

"And appease the curiosity of Mr. Canning, eh, sir!" grinned the lieutenant, looking fixedly in the youth's face.

The middy slightly blushed.

"Well, to confess the truth, I should certainly like to ascertain the cause of this strange phenomenon," replied the youth.

"You would?"

"I should."

"Then I will not disappoint you," replied the lieutenant.

"Thank you, sir."

"Have a boat lowered and manned," said White.

The youth laid down the glass, and sprang away to see the order executed.

In a few moments a boat was lowered and eight seamen seated in her.

The youth rebounded to the side of the lieutenant, who, in the absence of her captain who had gone on shore, had the command.

"Is all ready?" asked White.

"All!"

"You will take the command of the boat yourself, Mr. Canning.

The youth saluted his superior, and hurried over the side into the boat.

Seating himself in the stern sheets, he gave the order to pull directly for the rock where the brig had gone on shore.

The men bent to the oars; and the youth, taking the lines in his hand, nodded an adieu to White; and the boat flew over the almost becalmed sea, towards the rock in which was the secret cavern of the Boy Rover.

The wind being in their favour, and the sea almost as smooth as a looking-glass, the cutter's boat sped rapidly on, till she was just outside the long line of breakers on which more than one vessel had met an untimely fate.

But now the waves rolled lazily in—scarcely deigning to curl their heads over the low sunken rocks.

The water, too, was clear as crystal; and the young officer could distinctly see the sharp points and rugged surfaces of the line below the waters.

By this means he was enabled to steer up to the beach.

Just as he was about to step on shore, he happened to cast his eyes up to the rock from whence the smoke had issued, and perceived the large opening through which the glare of the wreckers' fire had so often shone out over the angry waves.

But the opening was too high up for him to hope to reach it.

So he leapt on shore, accompanied by two of the sailors, and commenced ascending the rocks.

But nothing unusual met their gaze; and they descended the other side, down which we saw, in the first part of our tale, the Boy Rover bear the beautiful and insensible maiden, Ellen Hanfield, on the fearful night when the waves threw her at his feet.

Disappointed at not discovering the cause of the volume of smoke, Canning determined to make a circuit of the rock; and, in so doing, he came upon the opening through which the Boy Rover had borne the insensible Ellen into the cave; and, still later, the poor unfortunate sailor's daughter, Mary.

Into this he penetrated, followed by his two companions.

The cave was now well lighted, from the sun pouring in at the opening on the side to the sea.

It soon became evident that the explosion had occurred there; for their senses were soon made cognisant of this fact, from the strong smell of powder which pervaded the place.

With a request to the two seamen to keep close to him, the youth hurried along the narrow passage, till he arrived at the cavern.

Here he paused, in surprise.

A loud cry broke from his lips, as he saw that the huge rock was hollow, and that it was filled with an immense amount of goods, of every description.

In an instant the truth flashed upon his mind.

Those bales, barrels, trunks, and heaps of cordage and sailcloth, told but too certainly he was not mistaken in his conjectures.

It was a wrecker's cave.

A place where ruffians, of the deepest dye, concealed the rewards of their unholy labours.

For a few moments the youth paused at the opening.

But, in that short space of time, his eye had encompassed all that it contained.

"There has been an explosion here," he said, addressing his companions; "the wreckers have taken less precaution than was necessary, and, by their carelessness in placing powder with their other goods, have brought about the discovery of their hiding place."

"That's it, sir," said a true type of a British seaman, giving his trousers a hitch and turning the quid in his mouth to allow him freedom of speech—"that's it : the varmints are unkenneled now though, and if we can't get 'em into our clutches, I reckon we shall the booty, anyhow, the land sharks."

"They are no doubt those we have been so long on the look out for," replied the young officer; "but now, having discovered this place, we will return to the vessel for orders how to proceed.

He was about to turn up the passage again, but he suddenly paused.

"Stay," he said. "First we had better be certain that there is no fire about the place, or when we return we may find our prize a heap of tinder."

So saying, he advanced into the cavern, and looked eagerly for the least signs of fire.

But not a spark could he distinguish.

Still continuing his search, he made his way to the spot where Black Bill had stood holding his weapon presented at the bag of powder.

A cry of horror broke from his lips, and he leapt back several paces.

"What's the matter, sir ?" asked one of the sailors.

The youth only replied by a motion towards the ground.

The sailor advanced and stooped down to examine the spot.

But with a cry of horror he too shrunk back.

At their feet lay the blackened and charred remains of a man.

Not a feature was distinguishable—one arm was blown completely from the trunk, and the face, black and scorched rendered it impossible to detect anything to his appearance.

It was the remains of Black Bill, the smuggler lieutenant.

A sickening sensation seized upon the three seamen as they gazed upon it, and they closed their eyes to shut out the horrible sight.

But the young officer felt that he must not allow his feelings to interfere with his duty, and thinking that perhaps there had been others in the cave at the time of the explosion, he gave orders for a rigorous search to be made.

They were not long before they came upon the remains of Sam and Jem, who, like Bill, were so scorched and mutilated, as to leave nothing by which to trace the lineaments of their features.

There being no signs of life in either of these blackened and mutilated bodies, the young officer and his companion turned away from them with a feeling of pity not unmingled with disgust.

A few paces further they went, and the body of Ned encountered their gaze.

His face was not so blackened as that of his companions; but life was extinct.

The seamen, having assured themselves of this fact, passed on in their search.

In a short time they came upon the body of Tom, who, being the farthest from the barrel when it exploded, did not present anything near so shocking an appearance as that of his guilty companions.

Life was still fluttering in his breast; and the sailors instantly lifted the poor wretch towards the opening.

But, as one of them threw off his jacket to form a pillow for his head, he gave vent to a feeble sigh, and expired.

With a shake of the head, the sailor put on his jacket again, saying :

"A wrecker don't deserve any sympathy; but I couldn't help offering him a pillow. But there—he don't want it now. I only hope as how the Almighty will extend as much mercy to him."

"You are a noble fellow, Jack," remarked the young officer, who could not but admire the feelings of the rough but honest tar.

"Well, sir, you see, I'm a Christian," replied the man—"that is, I hope so."

"It was a Christian act that, anyhow," replied the youth. "But let us hope that we have seen the last of these sad sights."

"I hope so, too, sir," said the man, looking round the place.

"We will return to the boat now," said the youth, "and pull for the ship. Mr. White will, doubtless, come hither himself."

"If I was him, I should stop where I was," said the sailor, taking another quid. "He won't see anything to make him feel comfortable here—eugh !"

And the man turned the tobacco from his mouth, with disgust.

"The sight has quite spoilt the flavour of the 'bacca—that it has."

The young officer shuddered, and led the way to the passage.

"Hallo !" he exclaimed, suddenly coming to a stand-still—"what was that?"

The seamen paused, also.

Then each listened intently.

A low moan came distinctly to their ears.

"There's some one in the place," said the young officer.

"And alive, too," said the sailor. "None of the charred bodies made that noise—did they sir, do you think?"

And the bronzed face of the brave fellow, which would have scorned to pale before the belching cannon, became colourless.

"Psha!" said Canning—"how can the dead speak? No—there is still some one in the place who has not yet paid the debt of nature. We must not leave him to die, for, though they are wreckers, we are men."

"And Christians, sir," chimed in the old tar. "Why, demme, the sound comes from under these here bales!"

And the sailor kicked a heap of bales with his foot.

"Clear away my hearties!" said Canning.

In another moment the three seamen were exerting themsleves to the utmost to topple over the bales.

In this they succeeded: and, when they came to the last, they perceived a young man lying on the floor of the cavern, crushed and bleeding.

They raised him up, and gazed upon his face.

They were the features of the Boy Rover—the Smuggler of the South Seas.

CHAPTER CXXXII.

ONCE MORE ON THE ISLAND—THE SLAVER'S STORY.

IT was towards the close of a warm day, some two months after the last scene recorded in the hut on the island, between Martinez and his lovely partner, Inez, that Captain Wildwell, borne in the arms of Jack Ridley and Ned Wilton, issued from the rude habitation.

Martinez, whom the beautiful girl had brought to a true sense of reasoning, had smothered the feelings of jealousy which had taken possession of his heart, and had assisted, all in his power, the endeavours of Inez to bring back the glow of health to the cheek of the slaver captain.

Watched and tended in turn by Inez, Martinez, and the two sailors, Captain Wildwell's health and sight were gradually becoming restored to him.

In her company, the wounded man became gradually better; the kind offices she performed for him seemed to strike deep into his soul.

There was a music in her voice which drowned

for a time the pain he endured. The soft touch of her hand upon his cheek, as she smoothed his rude pillow—the melody of her voice, as she sang some pleasing ditty to cheer the long, tedious, and painful hours—all seemed to bring back the fleeting breath to the form of the man who had torn her from her home and her friends.

And in this kind work Martinez assisted. The better feelings of his nature had triumphed; and, indeed, he now vied with the others in any little office which could please, or assuage the sufferings of his former captain. To wile away the long days and suffering nights, he would tell his adventures, or conjure up some romance to smooth the weary hours in their passage.

Nor was Captain Wildwell ungrateful for all the kindness he received at his hands.

He could but thank him—but then in so heartfelt a manner, that Martinez often looked back to the moments of his wrath with a sigh of shame and redoubled his exertions to assist and assuage the pangs of the half-blinded captain.

It was the first time that he had been lifted from his rude couch to the open air.

His dull eye kindled, and his cheek flushed, as he felt the cool breeze upon his brow.

He turned his gaze to those who had borne him from the hut, and, in tones of heartfelt gratitude, thanked them.

He seemed to grow strong in an instant; and, after sitting some time, gazing around the place, he said, addressing Inez, who sat on the grass-covered earth at his feet:

"Sing me one of your old ditties, Inez. There is a charm in your tones; they carry my spirit back to younger and happier days."

"Not to-night," she said, in a low voice—"I feel too melancholy."

"Are you sad?" he said, anxiously. "Alas! alas! I have much to answer for."

And his glance dropped to the ground as he spoke.

Fearful lest he should relapse, Inez and Martinez instantly commenced to cheer him.

In a few moments the depression had worn off; and Martinez, anxious that he should forget his sufferings, remarked:

"Captain, Inez is not in a humour to sing this evening; and I have exhausted all the little stock of yarns. Now, you have seen a great deal of the world; and, if you feel strong enough, you will, perhaps, tell us a story. It will tend to chase away the dullness which has fallen upon Inez, and render you, perhaps, forgetful for a time of your own sufferings."

Only too happy to make some return for all the kindness and care he had received at the hands of those around him, Captain Wildwell promised compliance with this request.

Seating themselves comfortably beside him, Inez and Martinez exchanged a look of gratification, and awaited for him to commence.

Ned and Jack Ridley also seated themselves—but in such a position as to be enabled to support the sufferer, should necessity require it.

"I wish I could do more justice,' he said,' to the tale which I am about to relate; but I have not the language at command which some men have: but this much I can say, that what I relate is strictly true, and is to be found on the records of the criminal statistics of America.

The time at which my story opens was at that period when America was but a thinly populated country; but it will still prove interesting for all

that; and, what's more, it is one of those tales which conveys a moral to the thinking mind.'

Having been placed more comfortably in his rude seat, and a support formed for his head and shoulders, by a bundle of dried grass, he proceeded:

The scene in which my story commences was a wild clearing in the heart of a Webster forest.

A tall and athletic man was at work in one corner; and dark lusty strokes of his axe, as he swung it into the heart of a giant chestnut, reverberated cheerily through the woods.

The morning was bright, and the air rich with the commingled perfumes of mosses, flowers, and foliage, gathered up from the wilderness.

The early sunshine dawned among the boughs over the woodman's head, and every blow of his axe brought a storm of dew down to the daisies and strawberry vines which he was treading to death beneath his heavy shoes.

Though the morning was deliciously cool and breezy, the workman stopped now and then to inhale a deep breath, and wipe the perspiration from his forehed; and, at each time, he cast a glance of goodnatured anxiety over the logs rolled together in heaps, and the forest of newly-made stumps that stood glistening in the sunshine, yet ful of sap, and with tufts of green still clinging to their broken bark.

But, though his eye took in every object which lay between him and the log cabin that stood on the opposite side of the clearing, it invariably lingered last and longest on the thong of newly-cut leather, which, from the distance, he could just see dangling through a gimlet-hole in the door from the wooden latch which secured it within.

Honest David Hunt! There was hunger, and some little desire for rest, in those frequent glances towards the slender cloud of smoke that went curling up from the stick chimney of his dwelling.

At last he planted his axe against the massive trunk which it had half cut away, and was rolling down his shirt sleeves, when the latch-string began to vibrate before his eyes, and, after a moment, the cabin-door opened, and a young man came out with a rifle in his hand, and dressed in a green hunting-shirt.

"Hallo!" exclaimed David, with a sort of half whistle, as he buttoned his waistband, "airly and late that chap is always hanging around my premises. I calc'late it ain't very difficult to guess why that gal was so long gettin' breakfast."

David had scarcely buttoned his second waistband when a young girl appeared in the cabin door with a napkin in her hand, which she flung up as a signal for breakfast.

"Oh, yes, she can call me now," said David, taking up his old straw-hat from the grass; "but before I eat or drink, I must know what brings that Ike Shaw to these diggins so often. When foxes begin to prowl around a hen-coop in the day time it looks dangerous. I say, Ike Shaw—Ike Shaw, hallo!—this way a minute!"

And, as David Hunt uttered this shout, he swung his hat in the air—an unnecessary signal for his voice might have been heard far in the woods.

The young hunter turned, and came across the clearing; and, though he swung his rifle about with a dashing air, David could see that his face was crimson as he drew near. But a fine handsome face it was. David could not deny that though he did exert himself to look ferocious, an got up a frown as he approached, that seemed much out of place on that broad frank forehead.

"Well, Ike, what brings you in these parts so soon again?" inquired David Hunt, putting on his old straw-hat, and folding his arms over his broad chest, after a fashion he much admired in 'Othello,' during the only visit he ever made to the theatre, while on his journey 'out west' from the New England States. "Don't think of settling in these diggings, nor anything, do you?"

"Well," said Isaac Shaw, blushing still more deeply, "I don't know how it will be. A chap can't always make his home in the woods; you'll agree to that, I suppose?"

David nodded his head, and replied:

"Just so, Ike."

"Well," continued Ike, gathering courage from his companion's assent, "I have a sort of notion to settle down before long, and clear up a farm for myself. Game is getting scarce, and I begin to feel rather lonesome in camping out nights so much."

"And how are you going to pay for the land?" inquired David, folding his arms more tightly over his chest. "Wild land is cheap out here—true enough; but yet government won't be satisfied with anything less than cash on the nail."

"I know that," replied the young man, with a brightening eye; "but I haven't been so idle as some folks might think. I've got three hundred dollars out at interest with Judge Church down on the Bend."

"Well, but you haven't been taking a notion to my property here, have you?" inquired David, with a shrewd smile. "You don't wan't me to sell out for nothin'?"

"No," stammered the young hunter, crushing a tuft of wild pinks beneath the butt of the rifle, to hide his embarrassment; "but I've been thinking—"

"Well, there isn't nothing very uncommon in that, is there?" said David, laughing, as the young man hesitated and blushed like a girl.

"No, Mr. Hunt, no; I may as well out with it," cried Shaw, setting down his rifle hard, and speaking with desperate rapidity. "I mean to speak to you about it in a day or two; but, as we are on the subject, suppose we finish it at once. There is Hannah—your daughter; we have been acquainted three years come fall; and if you ain't willing to let her keep house for me, it don't make much odds whether I have a farm or take to the woods again. One thing is certain, I shan't be very contented anywhere."

"There now, you've spoken up like a man," replied David, frankly extending his hand. "I cannot spare the gal, for, since her poor mother died, she's all I have to depend on; but don't look so down in the mouth about it. I'll tell you what we can do: take up three hundred dollars, and buy the lot that lies next agin mine. There is my cabin already built, and a housekeeper in it. Hannah won't make a worse daughter for me because she's your wife."

And David Hunt pointed to his dwelling, with a smile on his face; yet a single tear brightened in his eye, for the love which he bore his daughter was the most holy feeling of his life.

"I never was so happy," exclaimed Shaw, grasping the rough hand of the father-in-law, and giving it a vigorous shake. "And Hannah, dear girl, she thought you must miss her help, and would not consent to go away. I left her with tears in her eyes."

"Hannah is a good gal," replied David, drawing the back of his rough hand across his eyes. "I only hope she'll make you as good a wife as her mother was to me: and she will. But now I think of it, Ike, there is that young fellow, Bill Wheeler, from the Bend. He's been hanging around here a good deal lately, and seems determined to get my gal away from her old father. He's a ferocious chap to deal with, that Bill Wheeler; I shouldn't wonder if he gives us some trouble yet."

"Let him attempt it," replied Shaw. "I know that Hannah loves me—she told me as much this morning. What can Bill Wheeler say against that, I should like to know?"

"Nothing, of course, nothing," replied Hunt— "though Bill is a savage fellow when anything goes agin the grain with him. But see—Hannah is at the door; the breakfast will get cold. Come in, and we will talk it all over."

Shaw took up his rifle, and the two went towards the house together.

Scarcely had David Hunt and his companion closed the cabin door after them when a horseman came from a cart-path leading through the woods; and, dismounting near the chestnut, he looked cautiously around, saw the great gap cut in the trunk of the tree, and, driving his horse back into the woods again, tied it to a sapling down in an abrupt hollow, which concealed them from the clearing.

When the man appeared once more in the open space he took up David's axe, examined it closely, while he dislodged the tiny chips that clung to its edge, and tried its sharpness with the ball of his thumb.

"The chips are green and warm yet, the helve is warm with the old man's handling. I may as well make myself scarce at once, for the old man will be hanging around home till night. I am certain of that from the way he has begun his day's work."

As William Wheeler muttered these discontented words to himself he sat down the axe and moved away, as if to seek the woods again.

As he turned his head and cast a surly look towards the cabin, he gave a start, his heavy eyebrows worked and knit themselves over his flashing eye, and with a half-suppressed oath he looked around as if to ascertain some means of reaching the cabin which might not expose his person to the inmates.

"There were two. I saw them through the window. Who is he? Let me make him out— let me but fasten an eye on him, and I warrant he's done for."

Once more he sent an oath through his grinding teeth, and plunged into the hollow where his horse was tied.

The fine animal turned his head and greeted his coming with a low neigh; but his brutal master lifted his heavy boot and gave the poor creature a kick that made him wheel and run back with a violence that almost tore the sapling up by the roots.

"By Jove! you had better stop that," exclaimed the man, infuriated by the noise, and giving the bridle a savage jerk. "Stand still, stand still, or I'll bleed you with a new-fashioned lancet," he exclaimed through his shut teeth.

And drawing a bowie-knife from beneath his hunting-shirt, he plunged his arm back to drive it into the heart of the rearing animal.

But, as if comprehending his danger, the beast

leaped b ck with a violent impetuosity that broke the sa. ling sheer in twain, and plunged down the hollow just time enough to escape the fearful blow aimed at his chest.

So fierce had been his attempt upon the horse that Wheeler lost his balance and fell forward to the ground, ploughing the rich earth up with his knife before he could recover himself.

The furious man started up, gazed after the horse on instant, then shaking the soil from his knife, he thrust it back into his bosom with a low savage laugh.

"You have saved me ten pounds by that plunge, old fellow," he said, still gasping with passion. "I was a double fool to let you break loose though, Mike, Mike!—easy, boy, easy! Come back, so-ho—so-ho!"

It was surprising that a voice so fearfully savage the moment before could have been modelled on the instant to the low, silky and wheedling tones which this man adopted in persuading the horse back to his keeping again.

It sounded through the woods like the mellow tone of a bird calling for his mate.

But the horse plunged on till the call terminated in a low, sweet whistle.

He had leaped across a rivulet, which ran gurgling along the depths of the hollow, and his front hoofs were buried deep in the opposite ascent when that whistle came singing through the bushes.

He stopped suddenly. with his ears still laid back and his hoofs on high. A shiver ran through his limbs.

His ears began to tremble as they arose to their natural position—his fore feet sunk slowly down, and wheeling gently around, he re-crossed the brook and crept up the hill like a hound called back from the chase.

"So, old fellow, you've come back, have you?" muttered Wheeler, tying the broken bridle and tightening the knot across his knees with both hands. "It's well for you that I have no other horse to carry me to the Bend. Now, see if you can stand quiet, will you?"

This speech terminated with another oath, while Wheeler knotted the bridle on the splintered trunk of the sapling, and turned away.

He crept stealthily around the edge of the clearing, taking care to conceal his progress by the underbush that grew thickly in that portion of the wood.

At length he reached the little patch of vegetables which lay between the forest and the little back windows of the cabin.

Here he paused a moment—peered anxiously through the thick foliage to the right and left—then. parting the branches with his hands, he stole softly forth, and, darting across the garden, crouched down beneath one of the windows, where he lay for two or three minutes, holding his breath, and afraid to stir a limb, lest he should agitate the creeping plants that clung around the window, and thus give notice of his presence.

At length he rose cautiously: first on one knee; then to a stooping, and, at last, to an upright position, which brought his face to a level with the window.

He lifted his hands and parted the network convolvulus and flowering beans that draped the sash, with a cat-like caution that scarcely shook a drop of dew from the host of purple bells that clustered around him.

Having thus made an opening which commanded the interior of the cabin, he remained motionless, except that now and then his fingers clutched themselves together; and, once, he unconsciously crushed a cluster of the scarlet bean flowers which fell against his palm with a violence that shook the whole vine.

What a tranquil and happy scene it was that the bad man gazed upon!

In the centre of the cabin stood a small table, covered with a coarse cloth of snow-white linen. A plate of savoury ham—the ruddy colour of each slice relieved by the pearly and golden circle of an egg, which formed a tempting mound upon it—stood in the centre: warm corn cake, a plate of potatoes, with their dark coats torn just enough to reveal a tempting and mealy richness at heart, a saucer of wild honey, and another of golden butter, composed the wholesome repast of which David Hunt and his guest were partaking.

The farmer had filled his plate a second time. Hard labour and the morning air had given him a keen appetite: and his thirst seemed in proportion; for Hannah was holding forth, but without lifting her eyes to his face, his third cup of rye coffee, on which the heavy cream was mounting like a foam, when Wheeler looked in upon the peaceful group.

Shaw ate but little; and Hannah—the noble warm-hearted Hannah Hunt—did nothing but blush every time she lifted her eyes from the bright tin coffee-pot, and deluge every cup she filled with a double quantity of cream—that little brown hand of hers was so very unsteady.

It seemed so strange for her to sit there, with her father directly opposite, and Isaac Shaw lifting those bright saucy eyes to her face every other minute, and then dropping them, as if he knew perfectly well that he ought to be ashamed of himself there before her father.

It was as much as Hannah could manage to sit still and wait on the table.

It seemed a marvel that her dear old father could eat so heartily.

Everything seemed looking at her with a peculiar meaning. The old house-dog there on the hearth—the cat, as she moved demurely across the room — the purple morning-glories, trembling around the windows—all seemed perfectly aware that everything was settled between her and Isaac Shaw, but rather astonished that the old man should take it all so quietly, when they had every one of them heard him protest a thousand times that it would be the death of him if she were ever to think of being married.

Hannah tried to act as if nothing had happened. She was frightened to death at the idea of meeting her father's eyes: and as for Ike Shaw, it was really too bad!

What for on earth did he keep looking at her from under those long eye lashes?

She was perfectly certain in her own heart that she had never once looked at him since they had sat down to breakfast; nothing in the world would tempt her to do anything so forward.

Dear, pretty Hannah Hunt! How did she know that the young man at her left, in the green hunting-shirt, was looking at her, if she never turned her eyes that way?

At length when David Hunt had transferred the last morsel of ham to his lips, and drained his cup of coffee for the third time, he drew back his chair and looked at Shaw.

"Well, now, Ike, I am ready to talk over the business as soon as you have a mind to——"

David Hunt was here interrupted in his speech, for Hannah recollected that moment that she had no spring water in the house, and the haste which she made to get her sun-bonnet, and lift the pail to her arm, quite disconcerted the whole party, but it was only for a moment.

David settled back in his chair again, after giving a glance at her burning face as she lifted the wooden door-latch, and commenced muttering to himself.

"Well, well, it's only human nature; I was once young myself," he addressed Shaw again.

And there was that vile man listening to every word that passed between the honest farmer and his son-in-law.

He was crouching amid the vines as Hannah passed him, with the water-pail on her arm and the love-light brightening her blue eyes and sending its red to her cheeks.

Her garments almost touched him as she turned a corner of the cabin, but he held his breath and shrunk close to the logs, listening to the conversation within, even while his kindling eyes follow the young and happy creature as she passed with a light step into the woods.

When she had entirely disappeared he turned his eyes inward again, bent his ear like a hound, and pressed his face close to the matted foliage, that no word passing between the two men at the table might escape him.

After some ten minutes he drew stealthily back, dared into a patch of early corn that came up to almost one end of the cabin, and winding noiselessly through it, cautious as a serpent not to shake a single silken tuft that streamed from the half-ripened ears, he entered the woods again.

"To-morrow! to-morrow! quick work; but I am ready—the job pleases me—it pleases me—so, so, fool—stand still. What, afraid of the knife yet? It has better fare on hand—so, so!"

These words were uttered after Wheeler entered the hollow where his horse was tied.

He had been fingering the haft of his knife while muttering to himself, and partly drew it from his bosom as he came up.

The still restive animal started at the gleam of the blade, which gave rise to the half-savage, half-soothing words which his master uttered as he unknotted the bridle.

After looking cautiously over his shoulder, Wheeler mounted to his saddle, and crossing the cart-path, rode leisurely toward the spring where Hannah Hunt had gone just before.

A happy girl was Hannah Hunt as she passed through those thick woods down to the little spring which supplied the household with water.

Everything around her bore a thrice pleasant look.

When she turned down the little footpath, and came in sight of the fountain, it was gushing up quick and bright, with a sweet impetuosity, like the sensations of her own pure heart.

It seemed rejoicing with her—smiling with her.

How sweetly it flashed up from its mossy basin, dimpling and laughing as the arrowy sunshine darted through the heavy masses of foliage overhead, and broke into a golden shower on the rivulet that danced down through the rich turf, carpeting the earth all around.

It fell athwart the roots of that gnarled oak that twisted in and out among the rocks just above, like a knot of huge serpents charmed to sleep by the soft lulling of the waters—and on the little hollow, choked up with brake leaves, where the pretty stream lost itself, and plunged into the earth again.

Hannah came down the path, smiling.

She sat down beneath the shadow of the rock, with the water almost kissing her feet.

A bird was overhead, and it began to sing till the leaves around its hiding-place shivered again. But Hannah did not listen to the bird. Why should she?

There was music enough in her own heart.

She had trodden upon a tuft of wild blossoms, and the air was perfumed with their dying breath; but she only knew that everything was very lovely and tranquil around her.

The very foliage, and the glimpses of sky shining through, seemed rejoicing overhead, like old friends, longing to come nearer and bless her.

Her heart was brimming with joy; tears, the highest and most blissful drops that ever fell from the blossoms of a young heart, sparkled in those soft eyes: and there she sat, so quiet and motionless, bending a little forward, like a wood lily on its stalk; and none but the Almighty, who loves the joy of an innocent heart, knew how pure and entire that joy was.

All at once a shadow fell upon the spirit of that young girl.

One of those strange intuitive feelings, which seem like spirit-tones in the heart, came over her.

There was no unusual noise in the forest, and yet she bent her ear to listen. Still no sound, save the soft hum of summer insects, and such beautiful things as love the solitude, arose to startle her.

But the feeling of dread was in her heart. She put back the mass of golden curls that had fallen over her shoulder, and listened still more intently.

It *was* a sound—the tramp of a horse—mellowed and broken by the forest turf.

Certain that it was the approach of an enemy, Hannah snatched her sun-bonnet from the ground, and, hastily filling her pail from the spring, turned breathlessly into the path.

It was too late for escape.

Scarcely had she advanced half a dozen paces when William Wheeler appeared in a curve of the path.

She turned into the wood, though the undergrowth was so thickly tangled there that it seemed almost impossible to force a passage through.

Wheeler sprang from his horse, and left it standing across the path, as he came quickly toward the breathless and startled girl.

"What, Hannah, are you determined to fight shy yet?" exclaimed the vile man, pressing close to the struggling girl, and attempting to take the pail from her hand. "Come, come—give it up—it's too heavy. You bend under it like a sugar-cane in the wind. Let me carry it, I say."

He took the pail forcibly from her hand as he spoke, and dashed half of the water to the earth.

"Never mind," said he, with a disagreeable laugh—"we can go down to the spring and fill it again. I want to talk with you."

"What do you wish to say?" faltered the terrified girl. "I thought you would not come again. I must go home—my father is waiting."

"Thought I should not come again? A pretty fellow I should be to take you at the first word. No, no, Miss Hannah, I do not so easily give up an idea when it once gets into my head. Such girls as you are scarce here in the bush."

While he spoke, Wheeler swung the half empty pail on one arm, and, forcing Hannah's hand through the other, dragged her toward the path.

"I do not wish to go down there—I will not, unless you drag me from the spot by force," said Hannah, wringing her hand suddenly from the hold he had fixed upon it, and darting up the hill with the speed of a deer.

Wheeler sprang after her. A hound in full cry could not have leaped more fiercely forward. He grasped her hand—turned her round with a jerk; and, when her pale face was close before his, he laughed — not, as might have been expected, a coarse ruffianly laugh, but low and sweet, with a tone that thrilled through the heart it reached.

"Come, girl, come : I do not want to frighten you. Go down to the spring—I have a great many things to talk over. How can you tremble so close by the man who loves you better than anything else on earth !"

And, with a reed-like bend of his fine form, William Wheeler threw his arm around Hannah's waist, and again attempted rather to persuade than force her toward the spring.

"I will not move a step. I cannot. Oh, Mr. Wheeler, pray let me go—you frighten me almost to death !" cried the poor girl, trembling in every limb, while her ashy lips quivered with terror.

"How foolish you are, Hannah Hunt, to fear from one man—an old lover and true friend—that which pleases you in a fellow like one I could mention. Now, I'll wager my horse there against a Canada pony that you did not shrink, and tremble, and quiver all over with disgust when Ike Shaw came to your house this morning," said Wheeler, girding her waist more firmly with his arm, and speaking in a mellow and persuasive voice—a voice which sounded so like that of Isaac Shaw that Hannah raised her large eyes to his face in wonder and new dread ; but they sunk to the earth again, shocked by the conflicting passions which had met their gaze in that handsome but evil face.

"Come, have you done with all this childish nonsense ?" continued Wheeler. "I only want a fair hearing. You were too hasty the other day when I came like an honest man and asked you to marry me ; and I, like a fool, went off with my cause half argued. Stop, stop, there is no getting off, I must be heard."

Still Hannah writhed in the clasp of his strong arm, and looked wildly over his shoulder in hope of aid from the house.

"Say what you wish here, then," she said, almost wild with terror. "I will listen—take your arm away, and let me sit down on the log a little further from your horse. I will hear all you have to say if you do this."

"What, you would get a little nearer the house and scream if I only lifted my eyes to that pretty white face of yours ? No, no, Hannah, I am not to be cheated in that way."

And flinging his disengaged arm around her person, Wheeler lifted her from the ground and moved rapidly away.

The poor girl struggled, her head fell back on his shoulder, and her terror found voice in a single sharp cry.

"Hush," said Wheeler, turning his face till she could feel his warm breath as it poured from his clenched teeth. "Hush, I say, or I shall be forced to quiet you with my handkerchief."

He moved towards his horse as he spoke, set her on the ground, still grasping her arm with one iron hand, as he sprang to his saddle, and attempted to drag her up after him.

Another cry, sharp with terrible agony, broke from the lips of that poor girl.

It was followed by a rushing sound in the path above, the crash of branches, the leap of a strong man, and the shout of a fierce voice—

"Villain !—villain !"

And with this fierce cry David Hunt plunged like a lion down to the spot where his child was lying pale and senseless.

He sprang over her body with his arms outstretched and his eyes on fire—for one instant his iron hand clutched the folds of Wheeler's hunting shirt, but it was wrested from him by the violent leap taken at that instant by the goaded horse, as he darted up the path.

"Oh, if I had my rifle !" exclaimed David Hunt, in a hoarse whisper, as he lifted his child from the earth and laid her down again—for the stout man shook with rage, and at that moment was as weak as an infant—"Oh, if I had but my rifle !"

For a few moments the sufferer paused for breath.

Then he continued :

"About ten miles from the residence of David Hunt one of the largest tributary streams of the Mississippi made a sudden sweep inward, like a bent bow, embracing a rich tract of alluvial or bottom land in its curve, and forcing its outer banks back into the shelter of a range of hills, more broken and picturesque than is usually found in scenery composed almost equally of wood and prairie land.

Just within the curve of this bow, or directly on the 'Bend,' as the inhabitants called the plain which swept out from the embrace of the river, stood the country-seat.

The entire district was but sparsely inhabited; and, as yet, the country-town consisted only of a few log-cabins, half buried in luxurious cornfields ; two or three young orchards, filled with trees that had only decked themselves in the blossoms of a single spring ; and one great frame-dwelling, with verandahs running across the front—the two chimnies of new bricks standing on the expanse of glistening shingles like members of a volunteer militia company in flowing regimentals, whose pride it was to keep guard over the humble log-cabins and stick-chimneys which lay below.

A blacksmith's shop—so open in front that you could see the glowing iron even in winter as it poured a torrent of sparks up from the huge hammer which ground it to the anvil—stood opposite to the tavern : and this, with the noise of carpenters still at work in the interior of the building, lent a sort of bustle and business aspect to the Bend, which those who visited it found rather cheerful and exciting after the dim solitude of their forest-home.

A flour-mill, too, clattered cheerfully night and day in a hollow close by the river ; and there was scarcely a day in the week when a group of men might not have been observed loitering around Judge Church's tavern.

It was Saturday, about five days after the visit of William Wheeler to David Hunt's farm, and the strangers gathered around the Blacksmith's shop and tavern towards sunset were more than usually numerous.

Three or four farmers had come from a remote part of the county with waggon loads of grain, which could scarcely be converted into flour the next day.

Others had brought their horses to be shod, and, meeting with cheerful company at the tavern, were in no haste to return home.

The evening was warm and sultry, and the dusk was come on, but the blacksmith was heard at work; the sound of his anvil rang out over the village, and the glare of his forge reddened around him as the beautiful sunset fell through a bank of hazy clouds on the landscape without.

A horse, of light bay colour, finely-limbed, and with the look of a high-blooded racer, was tied with a stout bridle to an iron ring at the door-post; but, though the hot sparks flashed close to his eyes, they only kindled up a little, as if some of the fire had shot beneath the lids; and, though the nostrils dilated, he neither pulled at the halter nor seemed restive in the least, for once when he had run back a little, a voice from the opposite tavern checked the fretful impulse, and left him standing with his eyes to the flame but with slack halter and shrinking limbs, for to the poor animal there was something in that voice more terrible than the shower of hot sparks that rained over him.

The voice came from a young man seated in the lower verandah of the tavern.

His chair was tilted back, and his right foot rested on his left knee, and, though the fringe of his hunting-frock swept over a portion of the boot, its small size and unusually neat workman-ship could not be entirely concealed.

The man wore a fine otter-skin cap, which, being drawn over his face, left the upper part in shadow; but waves of light hair curled up among the rich fur about his temples, and his somewhat prominent chin, upon which the light lay strong, was so delicately moulded that in repose his fea-tures seemed almost effeminate.

This man sat with half-closed eyes, smoking.

Now and then, as he bent slightly forward to knock the ashes from his cigar against the sole of his boot, he glanced his eye through the bar-room window, which was open a little to the right, and seemed to listen.

At such times the shadow which fell over his eyes was thrown on the temple, and the whole character of his face changed.

It was a restless wicked eye, which lighted up every feature with evil fire.

It must have been a natural expression, for there was nothing calculated to excite or annoy him in the bar-room.

Two or three persons only were gathered about the bar, joking each other, while the judge him-self was busy crushing lumps of sugar in one of the small tumblers of greenish glass, which gave a dingy hue to the brandy he had just poured out for one of his customers.

William Wheeler, for it was he, had just drawn back to his old position when two men on horse-back came round the corner, and, as if rejoiced by the sight of company, urged their horses to a trot, and, drawing up in a cheerful dashing style, dis-mounted before the tavern.

Wheeler started and dashed down his foot with a violence that drew the chair forward till the front feet rang against the floor.

The light struck full upon his face. It had, all at once, become white as a corpse; and his eyes glittered like those of a housed serpent.

The two travellers had been busy tying their horses to the post of the verandah, and, before they were at leisure to notice anything, Wheeler had fallen back to his old position.

"Does not that look like Bill Wheeler?" said the youngest of the two, as they came up the wooden steps together.

David Hunt cast a quick glance towards the seemingly half-sleeping man, knotted his huge fingers tightly together, and moved a step for-ward; but Shaw caught his arm.

"Remember your promise to Hannah," he said, in a low voice; but his own limbs trembled with rage as he restrained the vengeance of the old man. "Remember, we have both promised," he added, drawing Hunt towards the door. "But for that, I have the best right."

"I have never broken my word to the poor girl yet," muttered Hunt, moving reluctantly on. "I never will. But it's tough work to keep my hands off him."

And, with these words, David Hunt and Isaac Shaw entered the public-house; but the cheer-fulness with which they had dismounted at the door was entirely dispersed; not even the hearty welcome which they received from the persons at the bar had power to restore them to a moderate composure.

"Why, who on earth is this? David Hunt?" exclaimed the judge, laying down the sugar-stick and holding out his right hand, with which he shook his neighbour's vigourously, while he passed the tumbler of brandy to a customer with the other.

"It seems an age since we've seen you at the Bend—and you, too, Shaw; we began to think you had taken to the bush for good. I was just calculating that your money would be so much clear gain in my hands, and had half dunned my-self for the interest, when I heard that you were coming down to scrape it up, interest and all, for the land-office. What's in the wind now, Ike? No gal in the way, is there? I'll tell you what," continued the judge, folding his arms over the railing of the bar, and shaking his head, "this whole affair looks rather suspicious."

Isaac blushed like a girl; but he was about to stammer out some reply, his face flushed still more deeply. It was not embarrassment then, but indignation, for in turning his eyes he had seen the white face of William Wheeler peering in at the window; the face disappeared instan-taneously, but Shaw felt as if those glittering eyes were still fixed upon his burning forehead. It was rage rather than terror that arose in his heart at the sight of those eyes; but to a less brave man there would have been something starting in their shape and fiendish glare. The evidence of emotion, visible in Shaw's face, was mistaken for embarrassment by the good-natured judge.

"Well, well, if you want the money, that is enough put up with me to-night, and I'll try to make it out in the morning."

"Not here. I will not sleep under the same roof with that man!" said David Hunt, drawing Shaw aside, and speaking with great earnestness.

"I would rather go myself," said Shaw, also in a low voice; "but it looks like a storm. If a hurricane should come up we could never get through the wood alive."

"No matter, alive or dead, I will not stay at the bend to-night!" replied Hunt, with sup-pressed energy; but his words reached the per-sons around the bar, and they looked at each other a little surprised at his obstinacy and the stern wilful tone in which his determination was expressed. It seemed to them as if harsh feel-ings existed between the men.

"Very well, I'm ready to start the moment our horses have had a feed," replied Shaw, moving towards the bar. "I suppose an hour or two won't make much odds to the judge?"

"None at all," replied the judge, pointing to an old-fashioned chest of drawers in the corner, "the money is already in the old desk there. Go in and take a bite of supper while the horses are feeding. Come along, all of you."

The whole group put itself in motion and followed the judge into a back kitchen, where supper was served in no very delicate style, but in rough and hospitable confusion.

William Wheeler had been standing with his back to the railing of the verandah, his arms folded tightly over his chest, and watching with cat-like eagerness every thing that passed in the bar-room.

The moment Judge Church went out, followed by the company, he glided softly down the steps and across to the blacksmith's shop.

The smith was busy at his bellows, and the roar of the air escaping into the bed of glowing coals forced Wheeler to draw close to the forge before he could make himself heard.

When he felt the red light of the fire upon his face he turned it away instinctively, or the honest smith might have been startled by its pallor and fiendish expression.

An ostler, coming round from the barn with a measure of oats in his hand, saw him standing there, enveloped, as it might seem, in a crimson mantle by the flames, and wondered what traveller had entered town without his knowledge; for, though Wheeler was a boarder in the tavern, and well known to the man, his face was so changed with the working of evil passions, that it seemed like that of a strange man.

"Have you fastened the shoe?" said Wheeler, hoarsely, touching the blackened arm of the smith with his finger—for he had spoken twice, yet could not hear the sound of his own voice. "Have you fastened the shoe?"

"No," said the blacksmith, leaning upon the pole of his bellows, and wiping the perspiration from his forehead with the coarse sleeve that was rolled above his elbow.

Wheeler uttered an imprecation.

"I haven't fastened that shoe," continued the smith, quite unmoved by the fierce words that had reached his ear, and resuming his hold on his bellows with one hand, while he raked the hot coals over a half-formed circle of iron glowing in the forge. "But I have put on a new one, that fits like a lady's slipper. That horse of yours has got a neat hoof—rather too delicate for common workmen. I had to make undersized nails, for fear of breaking it."

"Is he shod—have you done with him?" exclaimed Wheeler, sharply.

"Half an hour ago;" and, taking up a huge pair of pinchers with which he dragged forth the iron from its bed of fire, and seizing his hammer, the good man gave it one swing with his arm, and it came crashing down upon the anvil with a force that sent a storm of fire-sparks over the young man as he passed and untied his horse from the iron ring at the door.

Wheeler led his horse across the street, and flung the bridle toward the man who was removing the bit from the tired animal from which Hunt had just dismounted, while Shaw's horse was quietly munching the oats which were before him.

"Here, take care of the creature, will you?" he said, testily. "You need not stay to rub him down, he is half starved."

The ostler caught the bridle with a dexterous movement of one arm, and quietly drawing the head stall back to the neck of Hunt's horse, pushed the measure of oats towards him with his feet, and then moved away.

"Hallo, blockhead! where are you going?" cried Wheeler, with an oath; "I don't want him taken to the barn; turn him into the white clover lot, and see you put up the bars."

The man wheeled round sulkily, and grumbled below his breath.

After crossing the road he took down a set of bars, slipped off the bridle, and gave the spirited animal a slight blow with it, which sent him bounding into a field which was hedged in from the highway by a heavy rail fence, and swept back from the tavern some ten or twelve acres of short but fragrant sward, where it was lost in a forest of heavy timber.

The tavern itself stood in one corner of this field, and a cross road bounded the opposite end which ran up from the forest and intersected the turnpike some thirty rods below the house.

Wheeler stepped within the hall, but stood watching the man till he put up the bars and flung the bridle down in a corner of the verandah; then he turned away and went into the supper-room.

He took his seat at the lower end of the table so noiselessly that his entrance was unobserved, till Judge Church happened to look that way and uttered an exclamation at his paleness.

The rest of the company fastened their eyes upon his face, the moment his exclamation escaped the host.

A spot of living fire flashed into either cheek, and he clutched his knife and fork hard as if angered by the general observation.

"I have the tooth-ache; have been racked to death with it a l day," he said, in a clear and low voice, strongly at variance with the expression of his face.

"I will not sit at the same table with him," muttered David Hunt, grasping Shaw by the arm. "Come let us go."

They both arose, but, as if overcome with pain, Wheeler left his seat and went out.

Obeying the impulse given by his younger companion, Hunt sat down again, and no one observed that they had intended to leave the table.

When they went into the bar-room after supper, Wheeler was walking up and down the room.

He seemed to be agitated, or in great pain, but there was only one small candle in the bar, and he kept in the shadow.

Meanwhile the judge was busy counting out the money which Shaw had come to take up.

It was much of it in small silver coin, with two or three pieces of gold, and several bank notes of small account.

After it had been counted over two or three times, the judge emptied it into an old shot bag—where it had been previously stored—tied it up with a piece of twine, and handed it to Shaw, taking his promissory note from the young man as he delivered the money.

"Come, now, we have nothing to keep us here," exclaimed Hunt, drawing a deep breath, for the presence of Wheeler seemed to oppress him. "Where are the horses?"

"They ought to be in the stable," said the judge, turning a key in the sloping lid which closed a desk in his chest of drawers. "There is a storm coming up, or I am no judge of signs."

Hunt had heard only the first part of the speech. He was eager to leave the room; and, hurrying out to the horses, forced the bits into their mouths, though scarcely half the oats had been consumed.

"Come, Shaw, come, we shall have to ride fast, or the storm may come on us in the woods," he called out from the verandah.

Shaw went out, followed by all the persons in the room except Wheeler.

He stood motionless, near the window, listening to every word that passed, till the two men mounted and rode away.

Then he stepped hastily to the bar, seized a decanter, and pouring out a tumbler half full of clear brandy, drank it off.

"Is your tooth no easier?" said the good-natured judge, returning to the room just as the young man was in the act of taking his hand from the tumbler.

"No, it keeps getting worse; I will go to bed and sleep it off: that is, if I can," he replied, turning his face from the light, and pouring out a spoonful of brandy which he held in his mouth as he went up stairs.

"That's a strange sort of fellow," said one of the guests, who had been a boatman on the Mis-

sissippi. "I have seen that smooth face of his somewhere before. How long has he been in these parts?"

"About six months," replied the judge, to whom the question was addressed—" off and on; he's been hanging about all that time, if not more."

"What does he follow for a living?" persisted the guest.

"He's got some business with the land-office, I believe," said the judge; "trades in fur, and wanders off with the hunters sometimes when they take to the woods."

"Just so; said the guest; "but where on earth have I seen him; that voice of his sounds nat'ral as can be. I've heard it before, and shall remember it by-and-bye."

"Oh, as to his voice," said the judge, laughingly—"he can speak sharp enough one minute, and soft as a girl the next."

Wheeler was not again mentioned that night, but as if some association had been aroused unconsciously in the mind of the boatman, he began to talk about his wild life on the great river, and late in the evening was describing the fearful scenes which attended the hanging of the Vicksberg gamblers.

It was a fearful subject, and told at a fearful hour, for the hurricane had burst upon them strong, and loud, and terrible.

It came blowing up from the forest, and swept by in its wrath till the great half-empty house rocked like a cradle. The chimneys toppled over and crashed upon the roof overhead.

The verandahs were torn away like a handful of rushes, and yet that little group of men sat, awe-stricken and fascinated, listening to the rough eloquence of the boatman as he described the storm of human passions that he had witnessed amid the terrible but still less awful storm of the elements that raged around them.

William Wheeler went to his room and sat down the light, reaching it far away with his hands that it might not shine upon his face.

He felt as if his thoughts were branded in crimson writing on his forehead, and that some eye might read his purpose there.

His conscience whispered falsely.

That forehead was white as marble, but shrunk and knitted together with dark passions.

Foolish man! why did he thrust away that candle so fiercely? the Almighty required no human light—no letters of blood upon the brow—to read that which was passing in his heart.

He took his bowie-knife from his bosom and felt the point; tried it against the seat of a chair till it seemed as if the well-tempered steel must have broken off in the wood.

Then he drew a portmanteau from under the bed, and took out a hunting-frock, darker than the one he usually wore, and without the yellow fringe.

Having put this on, and supplied its place in the portmanteau with the one he had flung off, he drew the otter-skin cap over his forehead, and blowing out the light crept from the room.

He had nearly reached the stairs, when a thought seemed to strike him; for he stole back, and after searching in the dark, found the leather string suspended from the wooden latch in the door of his room.

He tied a knot in the end, which he tightened with his teeth, and drew it back so far into the gimlet-hole which perforated the door that any one anxious to enter would have supposed the thong drawn through by some person within.

He listened a moment at the door, and then glided with quick and noiseless steps down the stairs.

There was no light in the hall, but the ceilings were yet unplastered, and a net work of faint rays fell through a thousand crevices of the new lath, which was the only partition between him and the bar-room; the door was partly open, and directly before it sat a group of travellers, eagerly listening to the exploits of the boatman.

This man checked his speech an instant and looked up as Wheeler darted by; but the movement was quick as the flight of an arrow, and, satisfied that it was but a passing shadow made by the flaring candle, the man went on in the description as the storm rose.

Once out of the house, Wheeler crept, in a stooping posture, around the verandah, thrust his arm through the railing, and softly drawing forth the bridle that had been cast there, followed the windings of the fence till he came to the cross-road.

He turned the corner with a bound, and drawing one sharp breath, ran swiftly towards the woods.

He turned again, followed the line of brush-fence that separated the forest from the clover-fields, and keeping himself in the wood, looked around for his horse.

The noble animal was grazing near the centre of the field.

A low, sweet whistle made him pause just as the tuft of fragrant and dewy clover was folded to his lip; again that whistle came from the wood still faint but a little sharper than before.

Without staying to crop the handful of blossoms which were even then filling his mouth with fragrance, the animal gave a start, flung up his head, and sprang away.

With a single bound he cleared the fence and stood by the side of his master.

Wheeler took a heavy silk handkerchief from his pocket, tied two corners together with a piece of cord, and slipped it over the horse's head, where he arranged it with cord knotted across the chest, and the square of crimson silk spread out upon the animal's back like a saddle-cloth.

"No saddle, no blanket to-night, old boy," he muttered hoarsely, while the horse bent his head for the bit.

He put on the bridle, drawing the throat-latch so fiercely that the horse shook his head and ran back.

Wheeler clenched his hand, opened it again as suddenly, and patted the restive creature on the arching neck.

"So—so," he muttered, loosening the strap which cut cruelly against the poor animal's throat. "No noise—no prancing here. So—so, be quiet, boy: take care of the brush, and you shall be coaxed like a girl for once: so—so."

With these words, uttered scarcely above his breath, though the mustering storm would have drowned his loudest tones, Wheeler sprang upon his horse, and, guiding him cautiously through a corner of the wood, came out into the cross-road, about half a mile from the town.

"Now for it!" burst from his lips in a whisper which seemed like a shout suppressed with difficulty—"now for it!"

There had been a moon that evening; but the coming storm overwhelmed and shrouded it from sight.

Still, a pearly glow now and then shot along the small and gloomy clouds that came surging up from the north, and spread themselves over the sky, like a leaf-coloured pavement, torn and agitated by unseen hands.

But soon even the pearly gloom disappeared. It had lingered among the clouds—the last smile on the face of heaven. Now it was swept away, and left nothing but blackness and gloom behind.

The air seemed pressing down to the earth—thick, stagnant, and sultry.

A dismal sound came up from the forest, as if the elements were chained among those giant trees, moaning at their captivity, and wrathful with each other.

Still, amid darkness and gloom, that horseman sped on.

The road was narrow and full of ruts. Stumps in some places, stood half crumbling away in the very waggon track; but, with a loosened rein, and knees pressed hard to his fleeting animal, the doomed man plunged onward to his fate.

The thunder, which had been all the time muttering on high, now pealed and crashed above him. The lightnings came down in sheets of lurid fire, shedding a bluish tinge over the corpse-like hue of his face.

Still his horse plunged on, amid sheets of flame or black darkness—never checking his speed for an instant.

All at once that desperate rider drew the curb with a sharp pull which brought the horse's foaming mouth down upon his chest.

He staggered, fell back upon his haunches, and recovered himself with a smart of pain.

But, all the time, the rider was bending forward, till his face almost touched the arched neck of the beast—his knees were pressing convulsively to the drooping sides of the stumbling animal—and he strove again to catch the sounds of hoofs which had for an instant reached him through the storm.

"On, on!"

The words came hissing through his shut teeth; but scarcely had the gallant horse made a bound forward when the curb was fiercely drawn again.

"It is somewhere close by. Oh, if the lightning would but strike again!"

It did strike, with a crash that made the brave horse leap in the air, though he had never shrunk from the lightning.

Not three yards before them a dry tree was shivered in ten thousand pieces; and every splinter shot forth a stream of fire.

For one moment the horseman recoiled; the next he recognised the spot.

"Thank God, there it is!" he exclaimed aloud; and, with his blasphemous thanksgiving on his parted lips, he struck the horse, and dashed into a cart-path, revealed by the stricken tree.

On, without swerving from the path an instant, he passed directly under the burning tree, and was engulfed in the dark woods beyond.

David Hunt and his companion had ridden hard in hopes of making their way through the woods before the storm came on; but there was full six miles of forest, cut only by the narrow and broken road, through which night-travellers passed with some danger even in the best of weather.

They had scarcely cleared a third of their way when the rain began to fall in great heavy drops, and the storm mustered around them with terrible force.

The heavy farm-horses which they rode stumbled in the deep ruts, and became almost unmanageable, as the thunder came crushing, peal after peal, overhead, and the woods around seemed a-fire with lightning.

Still the riders urged them forward; for the peril seemed equal if they returned or pursued their way home.

"Great heavens! did you see that?" exclaimed Shaw, reining in his horse with a firm hand, and pointing in the direction whence they had come.

"I thought it had struck somewhere," replied Hunt, checking his horse for a moment, and looking back. "Ha! it is the old tree at the crossroads. How the flames shoot up—it was as dry as tinder! Thank heaven, while it burns we shall have light enough to keep our horses from breaking their knees in the confounded mud-holes!"

"Hear that!" exclaimed Shaw, and his face changed in the red light.

"Heavens and earth!—it is right upon us. What shall we do?" cried Hunt, wheeling his horse suddenly; and the light from the burning tree revealed his face, also, white with terror, as he rode back a few paces, and drew up again, agitated and irresolute.

"We may as well go forward—there is nothing to choose. It will be upon us long before we can clear the wood, either way," shouted Shaw, looking back.

"Lord, preserve us! It will be an awful gust; and Hannah is alone!"

For a few moments Wildwell paused; then, having refreshed himself with a draught of water from the hand of Inez, he continued:

'Hunt spoke loud, and joined Shaw; but the noise of the elements would have overwhelmed a band of trumpets, and no one heard him.

Terrified into almost supernatural exertion, the two horses plunged on, leaping, and sometimes staggering, through the fearful storm, like drunken creatures.

The riders spoke to each other again and again—shouted even—but the rushing wind swept away their voices; and, but for the quick flashes of lightning, which every instant revealed their pallid faces each to the other, they could not have kept together.

Still the terrific storm was not upon them in its full might.

The thunder boomed and crashed overhead—the giant trees were laced together through and through with fiery lightning—the wind was strong and high; but far down in the forest came a still more terrible sound.

The whirlwind was coming up from the dark north—heaving onward with a fierce rushing roar, and crushing down the mighty forest in its path.

On and on it came, like a mighty ocean heaving loose from its foundations.

And now it was upon them!

The two horses stood still, quaking with terror. Their riders cast themselves forward upon the shivering beasts—clung to their dripping necks; and they, too, were motionless.

On it came—gathering new strength and terror.

The hoarse winds, the thunder, and the noise of giant trees, uprooted like the reeds, and dashed to the earth, mingled together, and threatened the very heavens.

The air was black with clouds of mingled foliage. Great limbs of trees, masses of loose leaves, vines twisted asunder, and saplings torn up by the roots, went rushing by.

The wind now scattered them abroad—now drove them together in masses.

The lightning shot its fiery tongues through them, and the rain mingled with it all—not with the soft lulling sweetness of water-drops, that fall gently from the clouds, but blent with all the turbulent elements that made the night horrible.

Still the horses crouched their limbs together, and buried their hoofs deep in the earth; and the riders clung to them, awe-stricken and breathless.

All at once the ground began to heave under them.

The earth was torn up all around. A great oak, whose roots were tangled under the soil across the road, fell crashing close behind them.

The maddened horses leaped forward; the outer branches of the falling tree almost brushed the riders from their seat; and the huge trunk fell across the road, just where they had been an instant before.

The horse which David Hunt rode cleared the tree first, and was plunging on in the darkness, when a sharp cry cut his ear, even through the storm.

Hunt grasped the bridle with both his strong hands, and, putting forth all his strength, wheeled his horse round, for Shaw was still behind.

A flash of lightning revealed his horse without a rider.

Shaw was upon the ground.

A black mass, that might be a heavy limb of the fallen tree, or a human being stooping over him, was betrayed for an instant, and all was black again.

"Shaw, are you hurt? Answer me—answer —if you are not killed!" shouted the former.

He listened.

No sound; nothing but the fierce storm.

"Speak! do speak! I dare not ride on, the horse might tread you to death in the dark. Are you calling out? the storm is so loud I might not hear you if you did; try, try: the least shout will tell me where you are!"

Another flash of lightning revealed Shaw's horse, and, with a shout of joy. Hunt saw the figure of a man rise from the earth and spring upon his back.

The next instant all was darkness again; but Hunt felt the horse of his companion pressing close to his side as the two animals urged their way, breast to breast, through the unabating storm.

"Were you hurt?" shouted Hunt, anxiously, feeling in the dark for his companion's hand, which hung motionless and dripping wet by his side.

"No, no; a limb swept me from the saddle, that was all."

"Thank God, it was no worse!" exclaimed Hunt, in a voice which bespoke the hearty gratitude which he felt, and wringing the damp hand which he had seized, the good man uttered another fervent "thank God!"

That instant a glare of lightning passed over them. Hunt saw the face of his companion, and his warm fingers tightened on the hand they had enlocked.

"How white—how strange you look!" he said, powerfully agitated. "Shaw, own it, you are hurt; I hardly know you with that face!"

The hand which David held was wrung harshly from his grasp, and the reply which reached him, like all that had gone before, was broken and half drowned by the storm.

"No, no, it is only the lightning. My horse is lamed though. You must break the way for us."

As these words were uttered the speaker fell back and rode behind Hunt till a light gleamed from a little window in the distance, like a star braving the stormy night to guide the wanderer's home.

"There, there, Hannah is up and waiting for us," cried the glad father, and urging their horses on, the travellers dismounted at the cabin-door.

"The horses have had a rough time of it," said Hunt, shaking the water from his garments; "they must be fed first."

"I will take care of them; go in, go in," exclaimed his companion, holding forth the bag of mone—"put this away; I will come back in a minute."

David took the money with one hand and pulled the latch-string with the other; his companion turned abruptly when the light fell on him through the door, and led the horses away without answering Hunt, who shouted after him to hurry back, for Hannah was waiting with supper on the table.

Sure enough supper was on the table; a cake of rich corn-bread, warm from the fire, a young chicken nicely broiled, and a saucer of golden butter just from the churn stood temptingly ready on the snow-white tablecloth.

There was pretty Hannah, her cheeks all rosy with the heat, pouring a stream of sparkling hot water from the clumsy kettle into a little britannia tea-pot, battered with long use, but bright as silver, which had been standing on the hearth at least two hours, with the lid temptingly thrown back and ready to receive the boiling water at any moment.

"So you *have* come; I thought it was you," exclaimed Hannah, closing the lid of the teapot, and going up to her father, her sweet face sparkling with gratified joy, she flung her arms around the old man's neck and kissed his wet cheek.

"Have you been frightened, darling?" said the old man, tenderly taking her hand in his.

"Oh, yes, very much, till I heard you coming. I was so afraid that you would get hurt in the woods. I have been crying here alone half the evening; and yet it seemed as if it would all turn out well. And so it has: here you are. But Isaac—he did not let you come back alone?"

"Oh no—he is turning out the horses. But a tree fell close by us, and he got a fall. Nothing to speak of, though," added the kind man, observing that the cheek of his daughter turned pale.

"You are sure no one is hurt?" said Hannah, in a low voice, winding her fingers around the huge hand which was clasping them.

"Yes, yes: but what is the matter—what ails your hand? You are not afraid of a little water, are you?"

Hannah turned to the light, and looked earnestly at the fingers her father had been clasping. They were crimson with blood.

"Father, father, you are hurt, and will not tell me!" she exclaimed, turning towards him, and holding up her hand. "Oh, father, how could you deny it? See, your sleeve is spotted; your hand is wet with it. Tell me—tell me, where are you hurt?"

"Hurt!" exclaimed Hunt, going close to the light, where he examined the sleeve of his linen coat, and his crimson hand, in a state of painful bewilderment—"hurt! no, I am not hurt! But where did this come from?"

His ruddy cheek became a shade paler as he shook the drops from his fingers—for there was water as well as blood upon his hand; and an expression of doubt and anxiety stole over his face.

"It must be Shaw," he muttered, at length, stealing a glance through the door, as if anxious for the appearance of his friend. "His arm may be cut. Ah, I remember—that made him fling off my hand so savagely. Well, it may not be much after all."

Hannah stood watching her father as he muttered these words in a voice so subdued that it scarcely reached her ear.

"Father," said she, at length, laying her hand on his arm, "tell me all! Where is Isaac?"

"Out there with the horses, I tell you," replied Hunt, shaking off the strange feeling produced by the blood upon his hand, and speaking out with his usual frankness. "There—put away the money in my chest: I had forgotten it."

Setting the bag of money on a corner of the table, Hunt began to examine his garment over again, muttering to himself, with seeming wonder at the state they were in.

Hannah took up the bag with a shudder—for the

canvass had a red stain upon it. She placed it in the chest pointed out by her father, and gave him the key with a forced smile, which looked ghastly on lips as pallid as hers had become.

"Come, now, bustle about, and get some dry clothes ready against Shaw comes in. He will be dripping wet, I can tell you," said Hunt, with renewed cheerfulness. "But first bring me a basin of water to wash my hands. Where on earth can this have come from?" he muttered, while laving his hands in the basin; and once more his face took an anxious expression.

Hannah had already prepared dry garments, both for her father and his guest.

Hunt went into his own little bedroom, and came out dry and comfortable.

Still Shaw did not appear.

Hannah seated herself at the table, broke the corn-bread, and poured out a cup of tea.

Hunt took the cup, set it down untasted, and, leaning his elbows on the table, waited for his companion to come in.

At last he started up, and went to the door.

A horse was standing near, with his saddle on, and his bridle dragging along the wet grass.

The old man started out into the rain, caught the horse, and led him towards the stable, where he expected to find Shaw.

All was still in the log-stable. The door was open: but no living thing stirred within.

Hunt shouted aloud, again and again.

He went into the house for a lantern, and searched everywhere for his friend.

Hannah followed him in silence, the tears rolling down her pale face, and oppressed with anxiety such as had never filled her heart before.

It was all in vain — no voice answered the anxious shout of David Hunt.

Once he heard something like the quick tramp of a horse down in the woods. The sound lasted but an instant.

At length, both father and daughter went into the house, filled with trouble and consternation.

The whirlwind went by, the rain ceased, and the wind died moaning amid the torn foliage.

The moon came out in the firmament once more, smiling, like the eye of an unconscious child, over the wild scene below.

It looked calmly upon the earth — torn and ragged, and harrowed up as it had been with the storm—on the shattered trees—the herbage broken and soiled, and heaped together in ridges on the places it had beautified when the sun went down.

Like a Christian soul, eager to fling a mantle of charity over the ruin which sin has made, that peaceful moon wore a veil of misty silver amid the devastation which, but for it, would have been dreary indeed.

But there was one object lying in the cart-road, deep in the forest, which the pure moonbeams but rendered more horrible.

It was a human form, flung, like a slaughtered animal, across the trunk of the oak which Hunt had seen uprooted but an hour before.

The lax limbs were entangled in a bough, which was broken, bent, and crushed by their weight. The face was turned upward—white, cold, and ghastly—among a mass of leaves matted together by the dark stream which trickled heavily down from the body upon them.

There were none of those pleasant sounds of dropping water which would have followed a common storm in the forest; for the winds had swept the rain away as it fell, and a hush, like that of death, was all around.

But, that small current of blood, welling slowly down over the drenched hunting-frock, which hung around the body, through the crushed leaves of the earth, drop by drop, fell upon the sweet air with sluggish and horrid monotony.

Still, the moonbeams smiled upon the scene, as they had smiled upon the blossoming turf the night before.

The smothered hoof-fall of a horse, smiting his way through the mud, gave another sluggish sound to the still night.

It grew slower, and more laborious, as the jaded horse drew near, and stopped altogether some paces from the uprooted oak.

A man, whose thin face looked sharp and haggard in the moonbeams, dismounted, and struck a fierce unsteady blow, with a stick he had gathered up from the wayside, which sent the poor animal tearing down the road.

The branches of that fallen oak crashed under him as he rushed through it.

The body slid downward a little, and the horse plunged, with clanking stirrups and loose bridle, deep into the forest.

When this sound had entirely died away, the horseman crept towards the oak, softly, as if he was afraid of rousing the body to life.

He looked neither to the right nor left, but with his face towards the body—though his glittering eyes were fixed on the dark trees beyond—not on the gloomy object itself.

The man stooped down as he drew near the tree —crouched lower and lower, till his knees sank in the mud and herbage, as if in search of something.

His hand touched the blade of a knife—half buried in the earth. He grasped it by the point— sprung to his feet with a sharp breath—and, holding it before him, clenched it eagerly with both hands, laughing a horrible choking laugh as the blade shook in the moonlight.

"You will bear no evidence against me now, old friend," he said, in a voice that fell upon the air so strange and hoarse, that he started, and looked over his shoulder, as if another man had spoken his thoughts.

All was still, but the murderer had been frightened by his own voice, and slunk away, with his face still turned toward the body, though he had never once looked upon it.

Another horse was tied in a hollow—scarcely twenty paces from the road—through all the hurricane; and, with the lightning firing his eyes, he had stood without wincing. But, now that he saw his master coming heavily toward him, he began to paw the mud with his hoof, and gave a faint neigh.

The man parted his lips, and tried to check this manifestation of joy; but the words died in his husky throat, and, mounting with difficulty, he rode away, faint, and wavering to and fro on his seat."

Once more Wildwell paused in his narrative, and allowed his head to sink back against the bundle of dried grass.

"You are getting weak," said Inez, "do not exert yourself further, but retire to your resting place.

"No, no," said Wildwell, with a faint smile, "a few moment's pause, and I will continue my narrative; besides, the cool breeze is refreshing and pleasing to my senses, and I would fain stay here for a time."

"Let me smooth your pillow," said Inez, rising

to her feet and smoothing the dried grass against which his head leaned.

"Thank you," replied the slaver captain—"that will do nicely. I am strong again now, and will continue my story if it does not tire or disturb you."

Receiving the assurance that they were but too happy to listen to him, he once more began.

CHAPTER CXXXIII.

WILDWELL'S NARRATIVE CONTINUED.

'THREE weeks after the events I have related a horseman rode slowly through the clearing before David Hunt's cabin, and dismounting beneath the huge chestnut, which was yet standing with its trunk cut through to the heart, and all the foliage on the upper branches hanging withered and crisp in the morning sunshine.

As the man passed from under the tree his foot struck something upon the ground.

It was David Hunt's axe, rusted and wet with dew, which had been lying upon the same spot till the grass and strawberry vines had crept over and tangled themselves around it so completely that, but for his accidental stumble, it might not have been discovered.

The man lifted the axe, examined it closely, and muttered—

"There is nothing here but rust—downright honest rust."

And resting the implement against the tree, he moved across the clearing.

David Hunt's cabin stood desolate and uninhabited, like a forsaken bird's nest in the midst of its little vegetable garden.

No wreath of smoke went curling up from the stick chimney in the quiet morning air, and, though it was near the breakfast hour, no snowy napkin streaming from the window proclaimed the waiting meal.

The door was unlatched, and our horseman had but to touch it with his foot to gain admission into the dwelling.

How lonesome and neglected it was!

A few ashes lay upon the hearth, caked together with the water that had rained down the open-mouthed chimney.

A bed stood in one corner, neatly made, and covered with a pretty patchwork quilt, but the pillows were spotted with mildew, and the damp mould had eaten its way in many a broad spot over the glowing colours of the quilt.

The back window, close by, was open, and a mass of morning glory-vines, entangled with scarlet-runners in full flower, had forced their way through and crept along the wall.

They had twisted themselves around one of the bed-posts, and were creeping over the head-board, where they hung in a light and graceful wreath, rendering the decay and stillness around yet more melancholy by contrast.

The man who gazed upon this scene was but a backwood's constable—rough and uncultivated; but even he was affected by this picture of home comforts so completely abandoned.

He had come to search the house, but moved about with a soft tread, and unlocked the cupboards and that large chest with a bunch of keys which he took from his pocket stealthily, as if his heart would not permit him to handle roughly the household gods of another man.

He started up from his knees by the chest, and dropped the garment he was examining, like a guilty one, when a noise at the window disturbed him.

It was only the house cat—gaunt and thin with hunger—who had just come in from the woods, and stood staring at him from the window-sill, with a flying squirrel in her jaws.

The poor animal had attained a fierce and savage look, from solitude, and the wild search she had been compelled to make for food; but she dropt her prey, and crept towards the man, purring mournfully, and rubbing herself against his thick boots.

"Poor puss, poor puss," murmured the man, stooping down to smooth her rough coat with his hand.

But, as if she had not seen that he was a stranger before, the cat snapped angrily at his hand, and darted away to the squirrel, which she seized in her mouth, and carried under the bed, where she remained growling fiercely, and peeping at the stranger from under the valance, with her round savage eyes, as she devoured her victim.

After he had examined everything below, the man went up a ladder which led to the garret, where he continued his search among the barrels and bunches of dried herbs which it contained, but evidently to no effect, for he came down the ladder muttering:

"There's nothing here—nothing on arth that can tell agin him—and I'm glad of it as if I'd caught a bear in a coon trap. Burn me, if I can believe the old chap's guilty, arter all."

With these words the constable went out, closing the door carefully after him, and, mounting his horse, made the best of his way to the Bend.

Judge Church was walking up and down the verandah in front of his tavern, when the constable rode up.

"Well, neighbour, well," exclaimed the kind-hearted man — "what news? How have you made out?"

"Just as I expected. There's nothing in the cabin but the fixens that belong there; and they are nigh upon spiled. For my part, I never could see the use of goin' there agin."

"Never mind, Johnson—never mind; that flinty lawyer would insist on it; and you know it won't do for me to interfere. They mistrust me—I can see that; but they needn't — they needn't! I always liked Hunt. It goes agin my feelin's to believe him guilty; but, if they prove it—if he has killed that young fellow, and then robbed him—I shall do my duty, Johnson: I must do my duty."

"And I must do mine, too," replied the constable; and he added, bending down nearer to the judge, "but it will be a tough job to tie the halter round that old man's neck. Between you and I, judge, when you have done your part of the business, and my turn comes, there may be a log missing from the jail there."

A bright gleam shot to the judge's eye, but he shook his head reprovingly.

"No, no, Johnson—that will never do. Law is law. But hush—hush! Don't think of anything of the kind yet. We must do our duty, the laws must be maintained, Mr. Johnson."

The judge spoke these last words in a raised voice, and accompanied with a warning look, which the constable understood, for just then

Wheeler came sauntering round a corner of the house and slowly approached them.

The appearance of this man had been so much changed since his presentation to the reader, that his features had become sharp and thin; a restless expression would constantly break over them notwithstanding the listless air which he at times assumed.

His figure had shrunk away till the hunting-frock which he always wore hung loosely about him.

All this gave a neglected look to his person, combined, as it was, with the disorder visible in the remainder of his dress.

"Halloa, Wheeler!" cried the constable, glancing at the young man's dress, which was even more roughly put on than it was the day before, and resting his eyes at last on the clumsy boots, which gave a still more slovenly air to his person—"you are so much like one of us that I did not know you at first. Glad to see you taking to the brush like a man at last. There was no living sociable with a chap who wore a silk handkerchief week days, and had his calf-skin boots blacked every morning. I tell you what, it makes us plain, homespun fellows, mistrustful."

Wheeler had approached them with the heavy restless air of a man who had known but little sleep for many nights.

When Johnson uttered the last word he lifted his eyes, which seemed almost black from the dark shadows around them, and cast a keen glance at the constable, and then at the judge.

"Mistrustful?" he said, with a forced smile; "mistrustful of me?"

"Not now, that you dress like a man, and have given up pinching your feet out of all shape," replied the constable. "But what have you done with the rights-and-lefts? Give them to old Brown; let him hang them up at his door for a sign. Come, bring the things out, and I'll leave them as I go along."

"You would only get one of them at best," said Wheeler, with an unnatural laugh. "The ostler got tired of blacking them, I suppose, though I paid him well enough for the trouble."

"So he rubbed them with tallow, and spoilt the polish," cried the constable, laughing.

"No—worse than that. He lost one boot altogether; so I was obliged to patronize Brown," he replied, with affected carelessness.

"A cunning fellow, that ostler of yours," said Johnson, nodding to the judge and taking up his bridle.

"I say, Wheeler," he added, turning again to the young man—"you wanted an order to see David Hunt, one day last week; I am going to the jail now, you can walk along, and I will let you in."

Wheeler hesitated a moment.

"Is his daughter there now?" he inquired

"Oh, yes, poor gal, she never leaves the poor old man."

"Well, wait a moment, and I will go with you," replied Wheeler, turning to mount the steps of the tavern.

"Is he acquainted with Hunt?" inquired the judge, addressing Johnson the moment Wheeler was out of hearing.

"Not that I know of," was the reply; "but he is hand and glove with the prosecuting attorney, and it would not answer to refuse him."

"Just so," said the judge, rather anxiously; "but give the prisoner a hint before he goes in; the fellow is silky as an eel or green corn, but I

don't like him. He may be put up to this by the attorney, and so take advantage of anything he can get out of poor Hunt—put the old man on his guard—you understand?"

"Yes, yes, I will see to it," replied Johnson hastily. "Come to think, now, I may as well ride on, and leave orders for the jailer to let him in. If we go together there will be no chance to caution the old man."

"Ride on then," replied the judge, "I will tell him how it is." And with a friendly shake of the hand, the judge and the constable separated.

After a little time Wheeler descended from the room, where he had been arranging his dress, and walked hurriedly down the road toward the county jail, which stood on the outskirts of the town.

The jail was built of logs, and erected after the usual fashion of such buildings; but the windows were heavily grated, and the huge logs were bolted together with iron bars, which formed a massive wall, scarcely less vulnerable than granite itself.

The doors, too, were knobbed with great spike-nails, and bolted with massive bars, just as they came from the forge.

Altogether, though rudely built, the jail was not only strong, but well-guarded, and it must have been a desperate man indeed who could hope for escape when once immured within its rugged walls.

But the stout farmer, who was the only important prisoner in the building, had little thought of escape.

If the massive logs could have crumbled to dust at his feet, David Hunt would not have fled one step from the captivity in which his friends and neighbours had placed him.

Still, imprisonment was a weary trial to an old man who had been all his life an active tiller of the soil—a healthy, enterprising, and cheerful farmer.

He felt restive, and sometimes almost sullen—cooped up, as he expressed it, like a barn-door fowl with its wings clipped.

Sometimes he gave way to fits of childlike melancholy; for, innocent or guilty of Isaac Shaw's death, the old man could not but feel the event deeply—the more so as his gentle and suffering daughter was always near to remind him, by her sad and mournful attempts at cheerfulness, how terribly she felt the event which had rendered her young heart desolate.

Sometimes David Hunt would give way to fits of sturdy indignation against those who had placed him in confinement; and again he would admit, with simple-hearted candour, that appearances were strong against him, and he could not blame those who, on evidence so conclusive, had dragged him from his quiet home, and shut him up, to undergo a disgraceful trial for the murder of a man whom he had loved as a son.

"I would not have cared," said David to his daughter, on the morning after constable Johnson had been at the jail to warn him of Wheeler's visit—"I would not have cared a bean-stalk about being shut up here, if I didn't have to see every scoundrel that chooses to come in and ask me impudent questions. It's bad enough to think that poor Ike is gone. Don't turn pale—don't cry so, Hannah! You did not think it was me, if I did bring home the money with red hands! You don't—I know my own daughter will never believe it."

"No, no, my dear good father!—never will I think it again," exclaimed Hannah, winding her arms around the stout old man, and kissing his brown cheek, while she trembled and wept with agitation. "But he is dead—dead and gone—and oh, father, how I did love him!"

"I know it, gal—I know it well enough," said the prisoner, bending the pale head of his child back between both his great hands, and kissing her forehead, while his stout form trembled, and tears ran down his cheeks. "I know you loved him; and he was as good a fellow as ever lived. But if he's in heaven, Hannah—and why not?—he was good enough to go there, though he wasn't a member of any church—if Ike Shaw can only look down from heaven now, he knows that I didn't do it. I!—why, Hannah, I loved him almost as well as you did!"

David Hunt sunk down to a bench that ran across his prison-room, and, covering his face with both hands, sobbed aloud, though he was ashamed of his tears, and struggled hard against them.

Hannah crept to his side, and, bending her fair head upon his breast, tried to comfort him.

"I didn't do it, Hannah—the God of heaven knows I didn't. I'm growing thin. I look down-hearted sometimes—I know that—but it isn't a guilty conscience. They may hang me to-morrow, if they like; but I'll cry out 'not guilty' with my last breath. They shan't point you out, Hannah, arter I'm gone, and say, 'There goes the gal whose father owned that he had killed a man just as they swung him off.' They shan't, I say—they never shall do that, Hannah!"

And, pressing the poor weeping girl to his broad bosom, with both his arms, David Hunt swayed to and fro on his seat, protesting that he was innocent, and trying to sooth her grief.

But, when she moved on his bosom, and tried to murmur words of confidence and hope through her tears, he broke forth:

"Never mind, gal, never mind; they may do it if they like — my own old neighbours, too. Let them hang me—let them hang me!"

He paused, thoughtfully, for a few moments, and then added:

"I will take you with me. We will go together; for it would kill you to see them strangling your father like a dog—wouldn't it, Hannah? That will be best; and we can be buried in one spot, down in the woods, by your mother."

The emotion of the poor girl became more intense, and her tears flowed faster.

"Don't take on so," he said—"don't take on, Hannah! We shall find them both in another world—poor Ike, and your mother, too. But you must go with me, Hannah; for the first thing that she will ask for will be the little gal she left behind for me to take care of; and I shan't dare to tell her that I've left you all alone in a world where an honest fellow can be hung for nothing—by his own neighbours, too!"

"Yes, father, we will go together: neither of us have anything to live for now," said Hannah Hunt, rising from her father's arms, far enough to wind her own around his neck, and laying her pale wet cheek feebly upon his shoulder. "I am glad, father, that you want me to go with you. The world would indeed be lonesome after—after that!"

David Hunt laid his check down to the pale face upon his shoulder, and began rocking her in his arms again, without any other reply; for this rush of passionate feeling had exhausted even his strength.

By degrees, father and child became more calm; but David was still holding the strengthless girl in his arms, when the prison door opened, and William Wheeler entered the room.

David Hunt sprung to his feet, set Hannah down, and, dashing the tears from his face with an impetuous motion of the hand, walked quickly to the further end of the dungeon, where he turned, like a stag at bay, and waited, in stern silence, for his visitor to speak.

Almost for the first time in his life William Wheeler was at a loss for words.

He turned pale; but, shaking off the fascination which the prisoner's eye seemed to fix upon him, he moved gently to the bench were Hannah was sitting, and placed himself near her.

Hunt took a step forward; but, before he could do more, his daughter had left her seat, and stood by his side, pale, and still trembling, but with the tear quenched in her eyes.

"Well, sir, what do you want here? This roof belongs to the State. If I were a free man, it could not cover us both half a minute longer."

"I have come as a friend; pray hear me with patience," said Wheeler, rising and moving toward the prisoner.

Hunt flung one powerful arm around his child, and motioned Wheeler back with the other.

"Stay where you are, Bill Wheeler; I care nothing about the place you stand in, but my gal here, trembles as if a rattlesnake were crawling this way; keep where you stand, I can hear you well enough."

"Why do you treat me in this way?" Wheeler said, soothingly. "You may believe me or not, but I only came to see if I could help you. The trial comes on to-morrow."

"To-morrow!" exclaimed Hannah, faintly, and drawing closer to the old man.

"The evidence against him is enough to convict any man," continued Wheeler, still drawing towards the unfortunate pair. "The people are excited against you, Hunt. There is but one way to save your life—for, the trial once over, they will hang you at once."

"But how—how can he be saved?" she cried, in a voice of eager hope, which overwhelmed every other thought in her heart.

"By escape, Hannah, by escape," he replied, drawing still closer to the excited girl. "It will be easy to break the jail if he has a friend on the outside—I will be that friend—by to-morrow morning we can be safe in spite of all the constables in the country. I have money enough for us all—leave every thing to me."

A flash of joy shot over the broad face of David Hunt as this prospect of liberty was presented before him. But it passed away; and, grasping his child's hand very hard, as if to prevent her speaking, he gazed on Wheeler's face earnestly a moment, and then said—

"And what do you expect to gain by it if I should break out of jail?"

"Nothing—nothing but your own good-will, Hunt, and the kind feelings of your handsome daughter here," replied Wheeler, stammering.

"And this is all you would be at?" continued Hunt, still with coolness.

"Why, Hannah knows how well I love her, but she does not know that I can take her down the river and make a lady of her—that I sometimes take money enough in one night to buy out your farm twice over."

"Oh, how—how?" inquired Hunt, as if much interested. "How can you clear so much money in a night?—how can you make a lady of my gal here?"

"Why, I will marry her the minute we get to one of the river towns; and money—money makes a lady when nothing else can, all over the country."

"Yes—just so," muttered Hunt, grasping his daughter's hand still more firmly, as he felt her start and tremble. "But would you be kind to Hannah?"

"She shall sleep on gold, if she wishes it," replied the young man, with flashing eyes; and, emboldened by the quiet way in which Hunt seemed to be dropping into his plans, he attempted to withdraw Hannah from the protecting arm of her father.

But Hunt put a hand against his breast, and pushed him back.

"Not yet—she is not yours just yet. Look here—do you think I murdered the poor young man in cold blood?"

No. 50

"What else can one think? He has disappeared. His money was found in your chest. What else can be thought?

"You believe this, and yet will help the old murderer to break out of jail, and then marry his daughter?"

"I would do a great deal more than that for her sake," replied Wheeler, casting a look of revolting tenderness on the helpless girl.

"Well, then, let me tell you, Bill Wheeler—if I was the cold-blooded murderer that you think I am, I should consider my gal here disgraced by marrying a man who would help me to escape: but I am no murderer, nor robber either. I wouldn't run away if these jail doors were hung wide open, and a troop of horses outside. If they want to try me for my life, let the neighbours do it. If they want to hang me, let them do that, too. We are ready, Hannah, we are ready;" and, wringing his daughter's hand with a sort of mournful exultation, the old man looked firmly in the face of his anxious visitor. "She would sooner be with her old father on the gallows than your wife. Wouldn't you, Hannah," continued the firm old man, folding the poor girl in his arms.

Wheeler began to expostulate again, but the prisoner cut him short.

"It's of no use, I tell you; I am determined to stand trial. I'm not guilty, and I won't sneak away as if I was."

"But they will hang you. Even Judge Church is turning against you now," persisted the young man, becoming more and more anxious.

"Well, let him," cried Hunt, with a broken voice, and dashing a tear from his rough cheek—"I shouldn't have believed it of him, though!"

Wheeler was about to urge his purpose still farther, but that moment the jail door was swung open, and our old friend the blacksmith came in. He cast a sharp glance at Wheeler as he entered, and shook Hunt warmly by the hand.

"Well. I have just seen the judge, and he says your trial will sartinly come on to-morrow," exclaimed the good man, with a degree of cheerfulness which seemed remarkable under the circumstances. "They are all ready. The attorney has got evidence enough to hang fifty men: the whole would be complete as a nailed horseshoe if they could only find the body. It's a pity they can't find the body, though—isn't it?"

Hunt shook his head, and muttered:

"It is strange."

"Got any lawyer feed yet?" inquired the smith.

"No," replied Hunt—"I have no money. Besides, what could a lawyer do for me?"

"True enough—true enough!" rejoined the smith, folding his dusty arms, and laughing. "I will be your lawyer. What do you say, Hannah—shall I be his lawyer?"

"You have always been a good friend," said the young girl, smiling faintly through her tears. "You have brought us our meals, and tried to cheer him up every day. No one has ever given us any hope but you."

"Yes, yes—depend on it the truth will come out at last. Such thing always do—one time or another."

The blacksmith turned half round as he uttered these words, and cast a keen glance from under his heavy eyebrows at Wheeler, who still lingered in the room.

The young man turned a little pale; but he tried to smile, and murmured, in the low silky voice which he could so well assume:

"Certainly, the truth always makes itself known at last."

"Well," continued the smith, wiping his hand on the leather apron which he always wore, and patting Hannah kindly on the head before he took leave of Hunt, "keep up your spirits, both of you—that is half the battle. I have left some provisions with the jailor: don't let the thoughts of to-morrow spoil your appetite. Come, Wheeler, are you going my way?"

Wheeler hesitated, and looked anxiously toward the prisoner; but, meeting no encouragement to remain, he followed the smith out, with evident reluctance.

On the following day the Bend was a scene of great bustle and excitement.

News of the murder had spread all over the country; and every man or woman who could make business at the country-seat went there to witness the trial of David Hunt.

Long before noon, the main street was alive with people. Waggons stood by the way-side; and a line of saddle-horses extended far down the fence which separated the house lot, in a corner of which the tavern stood, from the highway.

There was no court-house at the country-seat, and Judge Church had made arrangements for the trial to take place in the bar-room of his tavern, which was the most capacious apartment at the Bend.

Benches were placed in the body of the room; and, in order to give an air of magisterial dignity to the whole proceedings, a huge arm-chair was raised on a platform within the little enclosure which usually served for a bar.

A host of decanters and glasses were removed from the little shelf which ran along the front; and two or three portentous-looking law books, in new sheep-skin covers, occupied their place.

As yet, the judge had not taken his seat; and a dense crowd was gathered before the tavern, which filled the street almost across to the blacksmith's shop, where our friend, the smith, was hard at work, preparing shoes for one of the half-dozen horses that had been brought to his door.

Never had the good man worked with so much vigour as on the morning when all else seemed to have taken a holiday.

His face glowed in the fire-light, great drops of perspiration rained from his brow, and he swung the heavy sledge-hammer over his head with an impetuosity that made the anvil ring with deafening noise over the crowd of persons jostling each other—talking warmly about the trial, with their faces turned in eager curiosity towards the county jail.

The murder of Isaac Shaw had caused great excitement in the country—not only because the young man himself was a general favourite, but from the fact that David Hunt, the person about to be arraigned for trial, had ever been held amongst the most peaceable and honest farmers in the country.

Notwithstanding the strong evidence against him, there might have been many found in that crowd who openly expressed a firm conviction of his innocence; while others seemed willing to pursue him with that reckless and wild persecution which is apt to follow a man accused of a capital crime all over the world, and which has but little restraint in many frontier states, where the will of the people, even now, often usurps the place of law and justice.

At length there was a slight confusion manifested near the jail, and, while the crowd swayed round that way, David Hunt appeared, walking firmly up the street between two constables.

His port became more erect as he drew near the crowd; and, though somewhat pale, his countenance was both firm and mild in its expression.

Once or twice a look of sorrowful reproach came to his eyes, as they happened to fall upon the form of some old friend shrinking back in the crowd, as if afraid that an accused man might address him; and again those deep-set eyes flashed gratefully when a hand was thrust towards him, and a friendly voice called out:

"Keep up your courage, neighbour: the darkest hour is just before day."

As he approached the tavern, the crowd in the hall and verandah made a rush for the bar-room; while the remainder fell back, and formed a line for the prisoner to pass.

He was followed close by two females—the blacksmith's wife and poor Hannah.

A rough, hard-featured, but good-hearted woman was the blacksmith's wife.

She was proud of her courage in thus standing by the unfortunate—as she expressed it—and walked through the throng, supporting the feeble steps of that young girl, with the mien of a newly-enlisted grenadier.

Her navarino bonnet, which had been fashionable some ten years before, was set back on her head; and its immense sugar-scoop front, flaring up from her honest face, gave a still more decided military dash to her appearance.

She waved a plump hand, encased in its yarn glove, to her husband, who stood at the shop-door, nodding his round head in approbation of her proceedings, as she mounted the tavern steps, and followed the prisoner, almost carrying her companion into the temporary court-room, and sat down near the bar.

The judge had taken his seat in the bar when they brought the prisoner in.

On his right hand, but outside the railing, stood the prosecuting attorney, turning over one of the new law books with intense interest.

On the left side was constable Johnson, with a large sugar crusher in his hand, which he now and then struck down upon the railing with great emphasis, as he called the court to order.

CHAPTER CXXXIV.

THE SLAVER'S NARRATIVE INCREASES IN EXCITEMENT.

DAVID HUNT was brought in, and placed upon a bench opposite to the judge, who scrupulously averted his eyes from the prisoner's face while the jury was enpannelled, and the whole preliminaries entered upon.

Never had a court been conducted with so much of imposing form at the Bend before.

Everyone looked grave—some even solemn—as the prisoner was arraigned.

Hunt stood up, his lips turned white, and his hands, which he clasped over his breast, shook a little; but his eyes were bent full on the judge, and he answered, "Not guilty—not guilty—so help me, God!"—in a voice that swelled clear and full through the listening crowd.

As the prisoner sat down, Hannah cast a look over the crowd, rose to her feet, and, supporting her faltering steps by pressing her hand to the wall, went round to the bench he occupied, and crept timidly to his side.

He did not turn his head, or seem to be conscious of the action; but the lines about his mouth began to quiver, and he shut his heavy eyelids hard together once or twice, as if determined to force back the moisture from his eyes before it had time to form into tears.

This stern effort to subdue the feelings tugging at his heart, joined to the feeble and desolate air with which the poor girl had performed her simple act of devotion, had its effect upon the impulsive and ardent beings who surrounded them.

That gentle creature, so young, so pure and helpless, as she crept through the outskirts of the crowd, like a pretty fawn following the hunted stag even among the hounds, and crouched down by the only being left her on earth, touched their sympathies more than a thousand orations would have done.

Though rude backwoodsmen, feeling—good and generous feeling—was vigorous in their tough hearts.

A whisper ran through the crowd, many an unequal breath was drawn, and more than one heavy lip trembled, without speaking.

The foreman of the jury—a bluff, hale, old fellow—drew his coat sleeve across his eyes two or three times.

The judge turned uneasily in his chair, and seemed to be diligently counting the glasses crowded on a shelf behind him.

The blacksmith's wife lifted a flaring cotton handkerchief to her face, shook her huge navarino bonnet mournfully, and sobbed aloud.

"This will never do," whispered the prosecuting attorney, leaning towards William Wheeler, who stood close behind him. "Who put the girl up to this stage effect?"

Wheeler replied only by a sarcastic and yet ghastly smile.

The pompous young lawyer then turned to the judge.

"May it please your honour, I desire that the young woman there may be removed from the court until she is called up as a witness," he said, pointing toward poor Hannah.

The blacksmith's wife flung back her navarino, grasped the handkerchief in her hand, and gave the lawyer a look that would have demolished a man of common nerve.

The judge turned hastily on his seat.

"I'll see you——"

He checked himself just in time—took up one of the law books, as if to seek for some authority—and then replied, with solemn dignity:

"The court has decided that it is no business of yours where the girl sits."

David Hunt, who had grasped his daughter's hand, and half risen, sunk back to his seat again as these words fell on his ear, and a murmur of approbation passed through the crowd.

The attorney turned very red, muttered something to Wheeler in an undertone, and, after a good deal of ostentatious preparation, arose to open his case.

The chain of evidence which he proposed to lay before the court was indeed such as left but little doubt of the prisoner's guilt.

He was ready to prove that Hunt and the deceased had come to the Bend together on the night of the murder—the one with no ostensible business, and the other to receive a large sum of money.

Eager words and gestures had passed between them at the tavern. Hunt had insisted on riding home through the storm, though the deceased more than once exhibited great reluctance to go.

After the two disappeared in the woods together Shaw had never been seen again; but, two days after, his horse was found wandering along the highway, with his saddle torn and soiled with blood, one of its stirrups gone, and the bridle hanging in tatters about his head.

Wheeler, and two other men from the Bend, had gone to the forest in search of the body; but nothing was to be found except the marks of some violent struggle near the cross-roads.

Footprints, both of man and horse, sunk deep in the mud, were trampled all over the road, just where a huge oak had been flung across it by the storm.

Two or three small branches of the oak, which seemed to have been crushed by some heavy weight falling upon them, were broken, and some of the leaves matted together with blood; while a purple stream had flowed over the trunk, and stained the earth half a yard round.

Most of the blood must have flowed after the rain had ceased, or it would otherwise have been washed away.

But, further than this, no trace of the body could be found, which would have been the case had the death been accidental.

The same company had proceeded to Hunt's dwelling, who would give no account of Isaac Shaw's disappearance, but persisted that they had ridden home together the night before, safe and well.

A bag of money was found locked in Hunt's chest; a linen-coat, with blood-stains on the sleeve, was discovered beneath the bed; and Hunt's daughter had acknowledged that the stain was fresh and wet upon it when her father returned home on the night of the storm.

When the attorney had prepared the court for this evidence, he sat down, and the examination of witnesses commenced.

Several persons who had been at the Bend that night were called up; and among them the Mississippi boatman.

William Wheeler was among the last.

He gave his evidence in a clear straightforward manner, as if every word had been studied by heart; but his face was ashy pale, and he never once fixed his eyes on any man, but kept them bent upon the floor, or turning restlessly from one thing to another all the time he was speaking.

When he sat down, Hannah Hunt was called for. She rose very feebly, but did not move from her father's side.

When the attorney began to question her, she made an effort to speak—and thought she did, poor thing!—but the whisper that escaped her lips was so faint that no one heard it.

"Tell the truth, gal—tell the truth," murmured the prisoner from beneath the hand which shaded the agony working in his face. "Tell the whole truth."

The girl cast one look of anguish on the old man, and, summoning all her energies, found voice to speak.

She admitted that her father had reached home late at night, that he came alone, with blood on his hand, and gave her some money tied up in a shot-bag, which she had carefully locked up in his chest.

But she said, also, that her father had insisted that Shaw rode home with him to the door, had watched and waited for him all night, and that he was about setting forth for the Bend in search of him, when persons came to arrest him.

She sat down trembling and faint, amid the murmurs of an excited audience.

The judge asked Hunt if he had any witnesses to produce, and if he had no counsel.

"No," said the old man, lifting a face on which the agony of a strong spirit was written. "No, 'Squire Church, you won't believe me, and I have no other witnesses. I don't want any counsel."

The good judge sunk back in his chair with a disappointed look, and the attorney arose, wiped his mouth, swallowed a drop or two of water, and commenced a bitter and cruel attack upon the prisoner; but neither the judge nor jury were accustomed to the restraints imposed on their comfort by this protracted flood of eloquence.

They sat restlessly in their seats; and the judge turned with an air of desperation towards the shelves behind him, and, taking down a box half-full of cigars, selected one for himself and passed the box over to the jury.

The judge lighted his cigar and smoked with grave composure, only stopping now and then, as some lofty flight of eloquence broke from the lips of the lawyer, to knock the ashes away from his Havana against the railing of the bar.

"Pass it to him, pass it to him—have you no manners?" whispered the judge to constable Johnson, who was leaning forward over the bar in order to place the box upon its shelf again.

The constable started back and went eagerly up to the prisoner, but Hunt refused the kind offer, at which the judge shook his head two or three times, for he took the refusal as an evidence of downheartedness which nothing could overcome.

As the lawyer drew towards a close the judge became much agitated; the cigar went out between his lips, and his face looked pale amid the smoky atmosphere that hung around him.

When the man sat down there was silence for more than a minute—profound, death-like silence, and then the judge arose.

"David Hunt—neighbour, neighbour!—have you nothing to say for yourself?" he exclaimed, with a burst of feeling that even made the jury start.

David Hunt rose to his feet; a clear strong light was in his eyes; and, though somewhat pale, he stood firm and collected among his old friends.

"Yes, I have something to say. You will not believe me, but I speak for myself. All that they have sworn against me is true, and yet all that I have said is the truth also. I did come to the Bend with poor Isaac Shaw, for I loved the fellow, and in one week he would have been my gal's husband. We came to get the money which Judge Church owed him. I found that man in the tavern."

Here the old man lifted his hand and pointed to Wheeler, and continued—

"He had insulted my daughter—he had tried to carry her off by force. My blood boiled when I saw him. I had promised the poor gal here not to touch him, and yet I found it hard work to keep my fingers from his throat. This was the reason I wanted to get home—this was what I was saying to Shaw.

"We started home. The storm was awful—trees fell around us like grass before the scythe. It was terrible dark, but we kept together till a great oak was torn up and crushed almost over us. Then I thought Shaw was knocked from his horse.

"I saw him on the ground, and—so help me God, I speak the truth!—for one moment it seemed to me as if some man was bending over him. I rode towards him but the lightning ceased, and, while I was calling to him he rode up to my side. I had his hand in mine once.

"The lightning struck again, and I saw his face—it was white as a corpse, and did not look natural, but the voice sounded like his, though it was smothered by the noisy wind. I left him at the door to put out the horses, and went into the cabin with the bag of money, for he put it in my hand as I gave up the bridle. The gal was right, my hand was wet with blood when I went in. I was not hurt—the blood was not mine. It might have been his. The God of Heaven knows I did not shed it!"

The prisoner then sat down, but rose again in an instant.

"Neighbours," he said, stretching forth his hand to the jury, while his eyes flashed and his stout form dilated with intense feeling; "neighbours, I have told you the truth, the whole truth, and nothing but the truth, so help me God!"

He sat down amid the breathless crowd; no one spoke, no one moved, but a sound rung over them from the blacksmith's anvil, clear and full, like the quick toll of a bell.

All at once that ceased, and the silence was profound.

It was broken at length by the blacksmith's wife, who started up, and, forcing her way to the door, went out.

When she came back her husband was in her company.

He made way for himself and wife up to the bar, and addressed the judge, who had just arisen to commence his charge to the jury.

"I say, 'Squire, supposing you give me a chance first," said the smith, rolling down his sleeves; "I reckon as likely as not I shall have a most considerable finger in the pie before it's cooked."

"Do you wish to give evidence? Do you know anything about it?" inquired the judge.

"Well, I should think it likely that I did, so just give me the oath. But first bend down your head here."

The judge bent his head, while the smith whispered something in his ear.

He then gave some directions to the constable in a low voice, and that dignitary moved round to the other side and took his station by the door.

The oath was administered, and then the blacksmith unrolled a dirty handkerchief which he carried under his arm, and took out a muddy boot, a horseshoe, and a scrap of red silk.

He had scarcely laid down these things before the judge, when some confusion arose at the door of the court.

William Wheeler had attempted to pass out and the constable was forcing him back again.

In the struggle Wheeler's face was turned to the crowd; it was ghastly and white, and when he raised his voice to expostulate, it was choked, and so husky that few heard him.

"Order, order—keep still!" resounded through the crowd, and Wheeler, as if restored to some presence of mind, drew back again to his old station.

"Well," said the blacksmith—"I want to tell you how I came by these things, and get back again to my work.

"Well, neighbours, you remember the night of the storm; some of you were in town, I shod your horses, and worked late to get through. Well, among the rest, Bill Wheeler, there, came in a terrible hurry and wanted a shoe put on that handsome black critter he rides. It's got a delicate hoof, so I was obliged to make nails purpose for it—small nails, such as I never made for any other horse on earth.

"Wheeler took the horse away just before the storm came on. He never took that trouble before; but yet I thought nothing about it till a good while after.

"I saw Hunt, there, and young Shaw ride away from the tavern; and, just after that, a man came prowling round the stoop and along the fence.

"Still, I didn't think much about it, but, after I'd done work, went home, feeling rather uneasy

about a coal-pit that I had set burning on some land of mine, down below the cross-roads.

"I got up in the morning before day-light, and rode down to the coal-pit, expecting to find it blown into ten thousand pieces by the hurricane.

"The road was choked up by trees and bush; but I got along tolerably well till I came to the cross-roads, where I meant to cut through the woods.

"I found a tree choking it up, and was walking my horse around it, when what should I see but the body of a man lying among the branches.

"It was Ike Shaw—as dead as a door-nail: at any rate, I thought so then."

"Was he alive? Was he murdered? What did you do with him?" exclaimed several voices from the crowd.

"Keep cool, neighbours—keep cool!" cried the smith.

"There—you have nigh about set that poor gal into fits," he continued, pointing to Hannah, who was bending towards him, with clasped hands, and a look of wild anxiety in her face. "I should not wonder now if she faints when I tell you that the poor fellow was cold and stiff, with a knife-hole in his side; but yet there was a breath of life in him."

His predictions were right. With a single gasp, Hannah fell across her father's lap, quite senseless. But every one present was so occupied with the witness that she remained unnoticed.

"I have powerful strong arms," continued the blacksmith, extending his great hands; "so I took the poor fellow up, and carried him down to the coal cabin.

"There was a bunk full of straw in one end, and a spring of water close by.

"After I had worked over him awhile, he came to a little, and asked where I had found him.

"Of course I was rather curious to know how he came to be bleeding in the brush.

He seemed loth to tell; but at last owned that when he was riding with David Hunt through the storm, some one fell upon him in the dark, flung him from his horse, plunged a knife in his side, and left him senseless on the ground.

"He suffered terribly, poor fellow; and the thought that Hunt had attempted his life seemed to hurt him worse than his wound.

"He begged me not to mention the matter, as he was determined not to prosecute the old man; and he feared that the affair could not be hushed up if people knew he was wounded.

"It came hard for me to believe that Hunt was a murderer and a robber. I was in hopes that something would turn up to clear him; so I made up my mind to keep quiet.

"I doctored Shaw up as well as I could, and went home, promising to come back after dark with a waggon, and take the poor fellow home with me.

"When I came to the cross-roads again on my way home, I searched about among the brush to see if I could find anything.

"There was a little hollow close by the road; and, up one side, I saw that the sods were torn, as if a horse had lost his foothold, and slipped down.

"A sassafras bush, close by, was broken, and one of its roots torn up; and, right there, tangled with the root, I picked up a horse-shoe.

"I knew it in a minute; for the small nails had been torn from the hoof, but stuck in the shoe yet: and I declare, for the first minute, my heart flew into my mouth.

"Well, I searched round, in hopes of finding something more; but this scrap of silk, with a bit of twine tied to it, was all that I could find. It did not seem of much consequence: but I brought it home with the horseshoe.

"As I came into town, Wheeler's horse stood in a crook of the fence down in the judge's house-lot. So I just climbed the bars, and examined his hoofs. The one that I had shod the night before was bare as my hand.

"By this time I was pretty well satisfied who was the murderer; but yet any other man might not have been certain as I was.

"I went over to the tavern, and asked about Wheeler of the folks in the kitchen.

"They told me that he was sick in bed, and had been all night half-dying with the toothache.

Just then the ostler came down with Wheeler's dandy-boots in his hands. He had brushed one, when I happened to see something that made me anxious to get the dirty boot. The ostler went out a minute, and I snatched up the boot and made for home.

"Well, 'squire, I took the horse and waggon, and went after Shaw that night.

"My old woman, here, is a first-rate nurse; and he began to get better after awhile: but this minute he's as weak as a baby—trying to set up a little for the first time this very day.

"I never told him a word about Wheeler, nor anything concerning the trial of Hunt; for he was so weak that it might have killed him. Besides that, I wanted to see what kind of a lawyer I should make.

"Now, 'squire," continued the good blacksmith, "I've taken oath that this shoe is the one which I put on Wheeler's horse at eight o'clock on the night of the storm; and that I found it just after daylight, on the very spot where Isaac Shaw was stabbed.

"Now, observe this boot. The clay upon it is red; such as can be found at no spot hereabouts, except just at the cross-roads. I took the boot with my own hands, and measured it by half a dozen of the tracks left on the spot. They fitted it like a glove.

"Now, 'squire, here is the piece of silk. It seems to me that if you will just examine the pattern closely, it looks very much like the silk handkerchief that Mr. Wheeler, there, has got round his neck. He had on the same concern the night I shod his horse."

Every eye in the room was turned upon Wheeler, who cast a sharp glance behind him, and made another desperate effort to force his way through the door.

By this time the crowd was in a state of wild commotion; those outside pressed up against the windows, eager to learn what was passing in the court-room, where the excitement was increasing every moment.

"Off with the handkerchief—off with it!" issued from various parts of the room.

But Wheeler flung the officers back, and struggled desperately against their attempts to untie the square of crimson silk twisted carelessly around his neck. But it was secured at last, and handed to the judge.

The jury crowded around the bar, eagerly watching the judge as he unfolded the handkerchief.

A corner was torn away, and the fragment produced by the blacksmith perfectly fitted it.

Besides this, a pattern of black ran over the crimson groundwork, which rendered the handkerchief somewhat peculiar; and this pattern was also in the fragment.

The jury had scarcely satisfied itself on the fact, when a portmanteau was brought into court, which an officer, who had been sent to search Wheeler's room, had found under the bed.

It was hastily unstrapped, and a hunting-frock drawn forth, torn and mouldy; but, notwithstanding this, traces of blood were found upon the shirt.

When this object was held up before the jury, the excitement was intense.

Three or four men leaped through the window into the bar-room—packing the crowd more closely together. The hall was filled with stern eager faces, pressing forward to the door; and men stood so thickly together, that lights had to be passed from hand to hand overhead, as those who carried them found it impossible to force a passage into the court-room.

"Make room—make room, I tell you!" cried a female voice from the crowd—"she will be stifled." And, with her arm flung around the drooping form of Hannah Hunt, the blacksmith's wife forced a passage for the girl where half a dozen men would have failed. Wherever her immense navarino rose upon the crowd, men fell back, and made way for her where no room seemed to exist.

As she passed through the door, Wheeler darted forward; and, in a moment, would have been safe in the dense mass of human beings that filled the darkened hall: but Johnson saw the movement just in time, and flung him back against the bar.

"He is trying to escape—he will get clear!" cried a voice from the window.

The cry was followed by a moment of comparative silence; men bent their faces together, and whispered in groups; while the crowd outside uttered words that made the judge turn pale.

The accused man heard them also, and, springing over the bar, drew his knife, and called upon the judge to protect him, in a voice of sharp agony, that rang over the throng like the cry of a hunted animal.

His cap was off, his throat was bare, and the breath as it panted through seemed choking him. His face and hands were deadly white; but a spot of scarlet burned, like a live coal, in either cheek, and specks of foam flew from his mouth.

The sight of a knife, drawn in their midst, exasperated the crowd; and, when the desperate man leaped over the bar, with the weapon gleaming in his hand, many thought that he was about to attack the judge.

Those in front were pushed against the bar, till the railing cracked beneath the sudden pressure. Half a dozen hands were outstretched to pull the man away; but he drew back of the judge, and made an insane effort to intimidate them with his knife.

"Ha! I know him now—that face, like ashes, and his eyes burning," cried the Mississippi boatman, springing up to a bench. "He was among them at Vicksburg—a blackleg—a gambler—the worst of all that infernal gang I told you about the other night. I saw him with a knife in his hand there, looking just as he does now. The rope was almost around his neck, but he stabbed the man who held him, and got away. They hung his mates—but he escaped: he will escape now."

The object which had possessed the crowd to the

moment had only been a vague determination to secure the accused man and lodge him in some place of confinement. The people were greatly excited; their sense of justice had been outraged; an honest and innocent neighbour had been hunted within a step of the gallows, before their eyes, by the wicked man who stood armed and menacing them in the very bar of justice.

All the elements which led to violence were aroused in their hearts; still the wretched man might have been safe but for this speech of the rough boatman; and his words concentrated the wild passions already fermented in a stern resolve.

There was no shout, the tumult grew less than it had been, men turned fierce eyes to each other, and a hoarse whisper ran through the crowd.

"He escaped the mob then—he will escape the law now."

These were the words that went hissing through the room, out from the windows and along the street.

Still there was no tumult—but the crowd closed slowly up, till the bar gave way.

A sea of eyes—dark, fierce, terrible eyes—met the wretched man everywhere; they glared on him from beneath the light, they glared on him from the dark windows, and far down a vista in the hall.

He dropped his knife, his limbs gave way, and like a branch lopped suddenly from an oak, he sank down behind the judge, who spread forth his arms and tried to protect him.

It is vain—all in vain !

The good judge pushed some of the foremost back; he besought them to respect the laws—he shouted to those in the street, entreating them to come up and save their neighbours from a great crime.

But still they closed in around him—stern and silent, and fierce with a thirst for blood which no heart present had ever felt till then.

They tore the miserable wretch out from behind his protector.

They passed him, on a bridge of uplifted hands, to the window, and out into the street.

The blacksmith had returned to his work, and the blaze of his forge reddened over the fierce crowd as it fell in towards his shop and formed a wall of human beings around it.

"The handkerchief !—the handkerchief !" passed from mouth to mouth.

Instantly a mass of crimson silk was disentangled from some fragments of the bar, and tossed over the crowd.

The red light shone through it as it rose and fell, and a hoarse cry followed its progress.

Oh! the next scene was horrible—I cannot describe it !

When David Hunt recovered from the stupor which had fallen upon him, with the conviction that his innocence could no longer be doubted, he was sitting in the midst of the court-room, perfectly alone.

A noise—a strange murmuring noise—came surging in through the windows.

He arose, and staggered a few paces forward, wondering what had become of his child.

A crowd of human beings blocked up the street —dark as death close to him, but lighted up on the opposite side by a fierce ruddy glare.

It fell on a platform of stern faces, uplifted, with a sort of savage awe, toward a human form swinging from a post directly before a huge opening cut through the blacksmith-shop, instead of a window.

Hunt cast one look toward the form, framed, as it were, in the rude opening, on a back-ground of fire.

He recognised his enemy, shrunk back with a groan, and, covering his face with both hands, shuddered from head to foot.

But let us turn to a scene less terrible.

The first words of Hannah Hunt, on reviving, were to ask for her father.

He was beside her—safe and free—but still visibly affected by the dreadful event of the day.

The thought of both turned to Shaw; and the inquiry for him came from the lips of each simultaneously.

Though still weak, he and Hannah bore the interview better than could be expected. No pen, however, can adequately describe the emotions of the poor girl—they were a strange mixture of joy and gratitude, of horror and dread.

The lovers were soon left to themselves; for a dozen neighbours were waiting to press the hard hand of David Hunt, and, among them, Judge Church was the foremost.

There is another clearing now in the forest, immediately adjoining that of David Hunt; but the old cabin, with some additions, answers for the home of the young couple, as well as for that of the father.

An air of comfort, and even of comparative elegance, marks the spot; and, perhaps, there is not, west of the broad Alleghanies, so happy a household."

Inez and Martinez having thanked the slaver captain for the recital of the narrative Wildwell, who in truth was far more exhausted than he felt willing to admit, yielded to their solicitations to retire into the hut and seek his couch.

Ned and Jack Ridley lent him their aid, and when they had laid him down upon the rude bed of dried grass, he fixed his gaze with a thankful glance upon the faces of all, and soon sank into slumber.

Inez and Martinez watched him for some few moments, and the same thoughts ran through the minds of each. Both felt happy now that they had remained to succour the wounded man.

CHAPTER CXXXV.

THE BOY ROVER TAKEN ON BOARD THE REVENUE CUTTER—THE OFFICER AND THE SURGEON.

THERE is ever to be found in the heart of the British sailor, the one noble quality—pity !

With all the wild passions of a tiger let loose, he will fight for his flag or hurl destruction upon the guilty wretches who prey upon the commercial ship which sails the ocean, or those demons who traffic in human flesh; but his duty done, he becomes as tender as a woman, and is equally as eager to assist a foe, as aid a comrade.

Hence it was that though the men of the revenue cutter felt assured that the place in which they found themselves was a wrecker's cave, and that the black and charred remains of the bodies they had discovered were those who preyed upon the vessels their diabolical artifices brought to destruction upon the rocks, they were eager and willing to extend a helping hand now that misfortune had overtaken them.

They saw that the Boy Rover was suffering, and pity took possession of their hearts.

They thought not then of what he was—of the misery he might have inflicted upon others.

They saw only that he was powerless and suffering, and they were willing to do all in their power to assuage his agony.

Tenderly they bore him fuom the cave to the open air.

Softly they pressed the painful limbs.

Slowly they carried him along the rocks to the beach.

And gently as a mother tending a sick babe, these rough seamen laid him in the boat, and pulled for the cutter.

Arriving there, he was as gently lifted on board, and conveyed to a cot.

The surgeon was summoned, and his injuries speedily attended to.

The young officer stood silently by his side while the surgeon examined the nature of his wounds, and prepared such appliances as were necessary; and when, at length, the doctor turned away from the cot with a dubious shake of the head, he asked:

"What hope, sir?"

"Little," was the reply.

"I am sorry for that."

"And I, too, sir."

"His sufferings must be great," said the sailor.

"Yes—but heaven, in its infinite mercy, has closed his soul to them for the present," replied the surgeon.

"But he will awake to them?"

"Ere long, I hope."

"Hope?" said the sailor.

"Yes, sir," was the reply. "Not, heaven knows, that I wish the poor wretch to experience them; but, if he awake not soon to consciousness, all will be over."

"Ah, I see, doctor. I thought—"

"That I wished him to suffer—as, doubtless, he deserves to do: for, from what I hear of the description of the place from which you have brought him, he is a wrecker."

"Such I believe him to be," said the young sailor.

"Then Heaven has punished him for leading such a guilty life," said the doctor. "Still, it is not for us to judge him—but to do all in our power to assuage the agonies he must suffer. The rest we must leave to justice and to God."

"True," said the young man—"but, surely, he is punished enough by the fate he has met with."

"That is not for us to decide, sir."

"True."

"The captain, when he comes on board, will act according to his judgment. In the meantime, we can but act as Christians."

"Such would be the desire of every man in the ship," said the young sailor.

"Yes, seamen are ever merciful to a fallen foe."

And, as if to prove his words, the doctor tenderly raised the head of the cruel unconscious youth, and smoothed the pillow of the little bed.

"Nothing more can be done for him now," said the doctor, after he had adjusted the pillow, and placed the head of the Boy Rover in the most easy position.

"You think he will recover?" asked the young sailor.

"I hope he will."

"Yes; but which way does your mind trust, doctor?"

"Science can do much," was the reply; "but life and death are in the hands of God."

"Then you are doubtful of the issue?"

"I am. Still, I think, with care he will yet recover," said the surgeon.

"Thank God for that," said the young officer.

"It will be a triumph for science if he does recover," said the doctor. "But, perhaps, it were better for him that he died."

"Why so?"

"Justice, sooner or later, demands her dues," said the doctor significantly.

"I see," replied the young man; "you think if he die now he will escape further punishment.

"I do."

"And yet he may be innocent of sin," said the young man.

The doctor shook his head.

"I doubt it," he said.

"Do you?"

"I do."

"Why so?"

"He was in the cave?"

"True."

"The cave appeared to be the hiding place of wreckers?"

"It did."

"An innocent man would not be there."

"Why not?"

"Dishonest people do not make confidants, or expose their secrets to honourable men," said the doctor.

"Perhaps not."

"Depend upon it, he is one of a band," said the surgeon—"and perhaps of that band we have been so long in search, and which have baffled all our endeavours to capture."

"The Boy Rover's?"

"The same."

"You think so?"

"I do."

"Why so?"

"Because the bodies of all you discovered in the cave appeared to be young, I am told," replied the surgeon.

"As well as we could judge from the disfigured features."

"And the band of the Boy Rover are most of them young men."

"So I have been given to understand," said the young officer.

"Then why not he be one of that gang?"

"I scarcely think so."

"Why not?"

"Because the Boy Rover's band were much more numerous than the number of bodies which were found."

"They may not all have been present in the cave."

"True."

"How many were there captured and sent to jail?"

"Six, I believe."

"That was the number."

"And they escaped."

"True. And six bodies, in all, you found?" said the surgeon.

"Yes."

"Then that alone would lead me to believe this poor wretch to be one of them."

"I begin to think so, too," said the young sailor.

"And, again, if I recollect right, his vessel always mysteriously disappeared about that part of the coast in which the cave is situated."

"It did."

"Then that is another reason why I think him to be one of the dreaded band," said the surgeon.

"Your surmises are doubtless correct," said the youth.

"I feel assured they are," was the reply.

"I had much rather have captured him in health," said the youth, after a pause.

"It would have been an honour to do so," was the reply. "The name he bore—the terror he spread around the coast—had rendered him so famous, that doubtless promotion would have repaid the act."

"No doubt."

"But," said the surgeon, with a smile—"although I believe this sufferer to be one of the band of the Smuggler of the South Seas, I am not so sanguine of his being the Boy Rover himself."

The young man's countenance changed in an instant.

"Well, no."

"But you had almost leaped to the conclusion that he was," said the doctor, looking fixedly at his companion.

"I had, indeed," said the seaman, with a smile.

"I thought so."

"But do you think it is?"

"I cannot say."

"Do you think?"

"I never saw him," replied the surgeon.

"But have heard of him?"

"Yes."

"The description of him?"

"Yes."

"And was he like him?"

And the youth pointed to the cot on which the Rover lay.

"No."

"He was not ?"

"Indeed, no."

"Then it is not him."

"That I cannot say.

"You say his description would not tally with this man ?"

"It would not."

"Then that is conclusive."

"No, it is not."

"How so ?"

"The description I have had of the Boy Rover was that he was handsome."

"Well ?"

"Is he handsome ?"

And the doctor turned his eyes to the cot. The youth's glance followed his companion, but his eyes dropped with a shudder.

"Indeed, no."

"Still it may be him. The explosion had its consequences, has obliterated all trace for a time of his features. It may be none other than the Boy Rover, and it may not, but time will show if he recover."

"I hope it is he."

"Why so ?"

"Because——"

"Of promotion. sir." interrupted the surgeon.

The young man blushed.

But he answered not.

"Such were your thoughts ?"

"I must confess that was the channel into which they wandered," replied the youth.

The doctor smiled.

"Well, well," he said, after a pause—"youth is ever ambitious.

The young sailor coloured to the temples.

"Lieutenant is higher than midshipman, and captain higher still," remarked the doctor. "But there, sir, I hope to live to see the day when you will be the latter."

"I thank you,"

"And trust that you will earn the post by honour and bravery," said the doctor.

The youth smiled.

"Doubtless, the capture of the Boy Rover in health and strength would have given you the first advancement. But whether this man be he or no, you must bear in mind, sir, that it required no extraordinary amount of courage to capture a dying man ; though the anxiety you showed to alleviate his sufferings does your heart as much credit as would his defeat in open flight have done your courage."

The young man blushed, but the doctor taking him by the arm, said—

"Never mind. I do not blame you for hoping to raise yourself by any means so long as they be honourable ones. A kind man is ever a brave man, and the soul that can prompt a generous action can perform a brave deed. Whether yon poor disfigured wretch be the veritable Boy Rover, or only one of his followers, you have done your duty like a true British sailor; and as such must commend yourself to your superiors, who are ever anxious to reward merit in whatever shape it may present itself."

The young sailor bowed.

"Come," continued the surgeon—"we can do nothing further for him at present : rest and time is all that is required now."

And he led the young man from the cabin, leaving the Boy Rover lying unconscious that he was in a cot on board a revenue cutter.

CHAPTER CXXXVI.

THE HUT AND ITS INMATES—INEZ'S STORY.

DAYS flew by, and Captain Wildwell gradually recovered his sight, health and strength.

Never was he so happy as he felt now in the company of Inez, Martinez, and the two sailors; and the hours were passed away in the recital of adventures and pleasing tales, which tended to break the monotony of the life circumstances compelled them to bear, and assuage the bitter feelings which otherwise might have crept into their hearts.

In the cool of the evening, seated before the rude habitation, the castaways gathered around the wounded man and recited in turn the little incidents which they had encountered during their eventful lives, and which we trust may not be uninteresting to our readers till we once more return to the various characters of our tale, and take up the thread of their adventures on the deep blue seas.

INEZ'S STORY.

CLICK, click! Tap, tap! A summons, positive yet timorous, as of one who would be heard by only one listener.

It clicked through Ernestine Kennard's light slumbers, and she awoke with a sudden start.

A quick thrill at her heart told her what wanderer stood outside her window.

She drew a dressing-gown from the foot of her bed, and folded it round her. Then she opened the casement, and stepped out upon the verandah.

It was a woman—a girl rather, scarcely seventeen, albeit she held a baby in her arms—who had given the summons. and who now crouched, as one utterly exhausted, on the low settee which the climbing roses, twining round the pillars of the verandah, overhung.

Her face was ghastly in the moonlight—a passionate, beautiful, brunette's face, with strong lights and shadows, and great, brilliant, black eyes, with a strange fire in their depths.

Ernestine, herself, had much the same features. Nose, mouth, and forehead, and the pretty chin with a dimple in it, were the same; but all Ernestine's tints were cooler and softer. Her hair and eyes were brown, and in her look was tender patience, rather than undisciplined self-will.

For one moment she gazed silently—yet with tears almost choking her at the beautiful ruin she saw. Then she cried, in a voice of infinite tenderness :

"Laurette—sister Laurette !"

The wanderer drew her breath with a long shuddering sigh. She looked at Ernestine curiously, and then pulled back her shawl from the little creature sleeping on her breast.

" Do you see what is in my arms ?"

" Yes."

" Do you know that I was never Robert Hawthrne's wife ?"

" I feared so."

" And yet you say, 'Laurette—sister Laurette !' God bless you, Ernestine! Heaven take pity on you !—the world will give you a cold shoulder 'oon enough if you allow one such as I am to claim kinship with you. And yet the world need not be too relentless. All I shall ask of it soon will be a few feet of earth to lie down and be forgotten in. Ernestine, I am dying."

Ernestine Kennard looked at her sister a moment more, and read the fatal truth in the hollow cheek and eye too fiercely bright.

Shame had killed that gay young creature, who, only one year ago, had been the pet and darling of the household—loved with a caressing tenderness that Ernestine, good and perfect as she was, had never inspired.

The old fond love which had linked those two orphan girls together, during all the years when they had been the nearest things on earth to each other, thrilled in the elder sister's heart now.

She took the hapless ones into her arms together — young mother and infant child; and then she half-led, half-carried them through the casement, and made them lie down on her own bed.

The little one woke now, and opened its eyes. It had a wan pinched face; but those great black eyes—eyes like it mother's—lit the wee features with a strange beauty.

It was a patient little thing; for it did not cry even now—only looked around with that imploring passionate gaze.

Once more Ernestine pressed, with her cool tender lips, a kiss on the burning wasted cheek of poor Laurette ; and then, whispering that she would be back in a moment, she went resolutely to her father's room.

It was no pleasant duty this of rousing that determined resolute man—that iron old soldier—and telling him that she had openly disobeyed him.

She went in, opening the door firmly, and starting him from his sleep, as was always easy enough with one who had kept so many perilous bivouacs.

Raising himself on his elbow, he looked to the intruder for an explanation.

She gave it, readily enough. She had been forbidden, under direst penalties, ever to breathe her sister's name in that house ; but her whole soul was roused, and she heeded no prohibitions now. She spoke with a certain steely ring of determination in her voice.

" Father, Laurette is here—dying. She has brought home her month-old baby. They must stay there. In the name of humanity, you shall not refuse that shelter to your own child which you would grant, under like circumstances, to the commonest vagrant !"

" How dared you," the old soldier cried, in tones of strange fierceness— ' how dared you bring them in ? Have I not told you my daughter Laurette is dead ? I recognise no such person any more."

" Then, sir, your roof must shelter a Laurette who is nobody's daughter. I shall not turn my dying sister away. If you would have such work done, you must do it yourself; and then bethink

yourself what you will say to my mother when she stands before you in heaven, and asks you what became of her youngest child."

The strong old soldier quailed at those words. They conjured up before him a vision—another face, like what Laurette's was once—so beguiling, so passionate, so darkly bright—his own Laurette —the only woman he had ever loved, and who laid the second Laurette in his arms, and died.

His face whitened with a strange pallor.

If her mother had but lived, he thought, Laurette would never have fallen. What was he —rough soldier as he was, and away from home so much during all her earlier years—to guide that passionate, charming, undisciplined girl ?

He called Ernestine back as she reached the door. He spoke with a strange humility:

" You are right, child. Laurette was your mother's daughter—her legacy. She has claims on me which I dare not set aside. Care for her— nurse her well—comfort her if you can. Dying, did you say ? I will come to her—poor little Laurette !"

How the old love swelled in the man's strong heart as he dressed hurriedly in the midnight !

Laurette had always been his darling—ever since her mother's death, the nearest thing the world held to him.

She was more brilliant than Ernestine, and he had loved her better. A wayward, self-willed, headstrong creature ; but he had never thought of crossing her—had been, rather, the most servile of her worshippers.

Accustomed to no discipline—no control—it was not strange that when Robert Hawthorne came, and she was forbidden to see, or hear, or love him, she rebelled.

Opposition only strengthened his hold on her.

He was a bold, bad, unscrupulous man ; and he followed up his advantage.

The worst fact of all—that he was the lawful husband of a living wife—Major Kennard had not even suspected.

It was reserved to Laurette to make the discovery, after she had supposed herself for eight months legally married to him.

She saw him gay, handsome, loving. His presence imparted a new flavour to her tame insipid life —a career which had never had half stimulus and excitement enough to satisfy her.

The very difficulty of meeting him lent to their stolen interviews a piquant charm ; and, hurried on by her own emotional, intense, unreasoning nature, she had eloped with him before she fairly knew it.

While she believed herself his wife she had been able to forget the rest of the world, and be happy. But her nature was too proud and high to bear quietly the sense of wrong, or the stings of self-contempt.

After learning the truth, she had waited only until the first hour she was able to travel before leaving him for ever, and coming home with the death arrow rankling in her breast.

She looked up with her great, beseeching eyes, when at length her father entered the room.

A sudden blush stained her face—then she closed her hands tightly round her child, and spoke to him.

" Father, this is kind. I disobeyed you, and I have forfeited my claim on your love, or your pity. But I did not voluntarily disgrace myself. Until two months ago I thought I was that man's wife, and the knowledge that I was not brought me home to die."

The old soldier listened to her with a mist before his eyes, and a quiver at his heartstrings.

Looking at her, it was his youth's own Laurette whom he saw—the tones he heard were those that thrilled, long ago, the pulses of his youthful manhood.

He bent over her, deeply moved, and kissed her wasted face—the face where years so few and sorrows so bitter had left traces.

He said, gently—

"I forgive you, Laurette, for the sake of one who stands to-day in Heaven, and whose mother-love, if she were on earth, could never fail you. Live for me, if you can: if you die, your babe shall never want home or care."

"Will you—can you—take her, Ernestine, and be her mother in my stead?" and the pleading eyes sought the tender, loving face bending over the bed.

"While God spares me," was the answer, strong, solemn, and binding, as any oath could have made it; and Ernestine lifted the baby from its mother's side, and laid it with a sweet tenderness against her own breast.

In the soldier's heart the fountains of the deep waters were broken up.

He was glad to be able to make an excuse to himself for taking his favourite child back to his home.

For the time he forgot outraged pride, humbled self-complacency, and only remembered watching over that dying girl, for whose sweet sake she bore the name by which he called her.

As the night drew toward the dawning, a light flashed into Laurette's face, like the gleam which a taper sends forth before it expires.

She looked up with an imploring gaze.

"Father," she cried, "I have a request to make—only one—you will grant it, your child's last prayer?"

"Speak, darling!" The old soldier's voice was husky and tremulous, and the eyes with which he searched his daughter's beseeching face were dim.

"I know you, father; you have a soldier's notions of honour: you punish wrongs with the sword, but you must not punish my wrong so. Promise me you will never seek Robert Hawthorne's life. Let God avenge me. Promise! I shall not die easy unless you do!"

Major Kennard besitated.

Already the thought of the vengeance he was to take had been sweet to his heart.

There was no other sacrifice he would not have made more willingly to that dying girl.

She watched him eagerly.

Soon she reached up her hand and touched his appealingly.

"Father, you torture me. Do promise. Baby's grandfather must never take her father's life. I have but a few moments between me and eternity —must I spend them all in pleading with you?"

Then he kissed her.

"Child you have conquered. Never will I hurt one hair of Robert Hawthorne's head, but the curse of a bereaved father shall be upon him. Worse than that of Cain shall be the brand upon his forehead. No fear but his punishment will find him out."

"But not by your hands, father; thank God, not by your hands. I am glad I am dying, father, taking my blighted life out of the world. That is God's mercy to me. His answer to my prayer, His

token that I am forgiven. When my child gets old enough to know my story, tell her, and teach her to pity her mother's memory, and forgive her. Remember, Ernestine, she is——"

The sentence was never finished.

A sudden convulsion shook her, and when it passed, and the face upon the pillow grew still, no breath passed the lips, no pulse throbbed in the wrists. Laurette—the beautiful, betrayed, suffering Laurette—was dead.

Laurette had been dead a month, and Ernestine Kennard sat with her lover.

It was her first interview since her sister's death.

Norman Kensett resided in York, where he was just establishing himself in business; and his visits to his betrothed were, of necessity, not very frequent.

It had been six weeks since their last meeting, and there had been much to talk over between them.

Ernestine had been telling him the whole sad story of her sister's death, and the responsibility she herself had assumed, for the future, in undertaking to be a mother to the child, Laurette Kennard, as they had resolved to call her.

Norman Kensett had been listening with the air of one not well pleased. He was come of a proud stock, and it was not pleasant—nay, it was scarcely endurable to him that disgrace should enter the family of the woman he loved and expected to marry.

At length he said, interrupting her:

"Ernestine, you were to be my wife this autumn. Can you reconcile all your duties? How can you occupy the position I intend you to fill— go into society, receive calls, make and do justice to the acquaintances my bride ought—and yet burden yourself with the care of a young child? I think you promised too much when you undertook to regard the poor little object as your own. It is hard enough that there should be such a child, any way, without your sacrificing to it the best years of your life and mine. I do not like to cross you, Ernestine; but I think I ought to insist on your finding a suitable nurse for the child, and leaving it here with your father. There would be gossip which I could never bear if we should take it to York with us."

For a moment Ernestine Kennard looked at her lover with eyes full of sad longing tenderness; then she spoke patiently, sorrowfully, humbly:

"You have anticipated me, Norman. I do not mean that I had thought, or could think, of the plan you propose of leaving little Laurette to the care of a stranger. That would be impossible; for I promised my dead sister that I would never part with her—and I must keep my pledge. But I had begun already to realise that I could not do my duty to the child, and still be to you all that you had a right to claim in your wife. Nor do I think I ought to leave my poor father to bear this—the heaviest grief of his life—utterly alone; to abandon him to solitude, with no one who loved him to care for his comfort. I could not blame you, either, for shrinking from the gossip and the disgrace which that poor baby would bring upon you. I have thought it all over in the last month many times, and I know it is my duty to give you back your freedom. I had looked forward, perhaps, to a future too bright, and God sees fit to take away my heart's desire. There is no escape from my duty. God gave me my father and my sister. I must do my duty to them before I dare to make new ties for myself. If I had been already your wife, perhaps I should have had no right to make the promise I did to that poor dying girl. But I was not your wife—the vow is made, and I must keep it, even though it be to my hurt. I see plainly that we must go apart. I cannot be unjust enough to force you to assume a share in my sacrifices and duties, or unreasonable enough to allow you to continue bound to me, when I know not how many years must pass before I could possibly be to you what you wish."

Norman Kensett looked at her—a man's unreasoning anger kindling in his eyes, and flushing his face.

His reproaches burst forth in words, at length:

"So this is your love—your boasted love? This is the union that was to have been eternal—the heart that was to know no law but my love—the life that would spend itself only too gladly for my happiness! This is that miracle of constancy, of self-sacrifce, of devotion—a loving woman: this one, ready to throw away the whole future of the man she has promised to marry, for the sake of a sister who—"

" S op!" (Earnestine's voice was clear, and cold, and strong now.) "Stop! I will not hear you speak one word against that dead girl. She did not sin knowingly. She thought she was that man's wife. It is time enough that we should part when you can speak to me like this. Were I all alone in the world, with no other tie to bind me —no other duty to hold me back—I should be loth, after the experience of this hour, to trust myself to your tender mercies. Once for all, I release you from the pledge which binds you to me. I will go my own way, live out my own life, and you shall live out yours."

Ten days afterward Norman Kensett received a package directed in Ernestine's hand. He tore it open eagerly; but there was not a word in it from her—only his own letters.

Until then she had not been able to force herself to part with them. Womanlike, she had read them over and over, every one, until each word that told he had ever loved her was engraved upon her heart.

In three days more she received back all her own in return, and, with them, this note:

"ERNESTINE,—I cannot write to you coldly, however much I may blame you for the shadow which will darken all my future. I *have* loved you wildly; I love you yet—tenderly, longingly. Why should I not tell you so once more? When this reaches you, I shall be far enough away. To-morrow I sail in the 'Atlantic' for France. The mercantile house of which my uncle Golding is at the head has need of a resident partner in Paris. I am to be that partner. I welcomed the opportunity eagerly, for, since destiny flows between us two, it is well that the billows of the ocean should roll between us likewise. Good-bye, Ernestine. God bless you; and may you never see cause to regret the manner in which you have decided our future.

"NORMAN KENSETT."

Ernestine Kennard read those words calmly.

It is not in our hours of mortal anguish that we make most bitter moaning.

In one season all the roses of her life had blossomed and fallen. Leafless and bare would be the tree henceforth, for ever. Would any birds sing in its boughs?

It was no pleasant task to tell her father of the change that had overtaken her life.

Stern, and strong, and proudly noble himself, Major Kennard was not patient with weakness or selfishness in others.

She loved Norman Kensett so well still, that she was resolute to shield him from her father's displeasure.

She made the separation seem wholly her own work; and then had to bear a little reproach at the sacrifice she was making of herself and her lover.

Perhaps, though, the old soldier was secretly not ill-pleased that he should still retain his one daughter with him; and that poor Laurette's child was thereby ensured care as tender as any mother could have bestowed.

The little creature looked quite another being now from the pinched, wan, little morsel the dying girl had brought to her home. Under Ernestine's fond care the cheeks had filled out, the lips learned to smile, and at three months you could have nowhere found a more loveable baby.

After a short pause Inez continued:

Ernestine Kennard did not die: she was not the kind of woman to die of heartbreak. She had too much reverence for God and her own soul.

She was never the same after her parting from Kensett. The buoyancy of youth, the June of her life had passed by, but she was not less lovely.

She seemed to have forgotten herself only to remember others the more sweetly and tenderly. She was never melancholy or absent-minded.

No one knew how her nights were passed, what presence haunted her dreams, or what tears fell on the brown curls of the little child—her sister's child—which slept on her bosom.

She was to her father the most cheerful, affectionate and attentive of daughters; to little Laurette the tenderest and most patient of nurses; to the poor an unfailing friend.

With society she was but little brought into contact.

Since her sister's death she had been out very seldom.

Major Kennard did not choose to run the risk of being received coldly; and since the epoch of what he considered his disgrace, he had voluntarily withdrawn from associating with all his neighbours, save that class who were dependant on him for aid and comfort.

Time had swept away ten years into that sea where all the past lies buried.

Little Laurette was ten years old, and in all this time not one note of intelligence had ever reached Ernestine concerning Norman Kensett; yet those ten years of care had scarcely dimmed her beauty.

Many would have pronounced her even more attractive at twenty-eight than she had been at eighteen.

Her brown eyes were as clear, as bright, but more tender—her brown hair was as glossy and as luxuriant—her complexion as pure and as delicate—yet there was a subtle change by which you knew she was older.

It was in the deepening of the expression; the clearness with which the soul looked through the face, and hinted of sad and tender experience, of many prayers and some tears.

Such was the woman who stood firm yet tender by the side of the old soldier when he fought his battle.

It was on a winter day. The snow lay white and high outside the house. The wind swept with a cry passionate and bewailing, through the trees which shook in all their icy armour—the sky was light blue, cold and pitiless.

In-doors, where the fire was warm, and the crimson curtains hung their luxurious folds about s bed piled with eider-down, lay the stout old soldier.

He had struggled long with that deadly enemy who sounds no trumb t, or utters no war-cry.

He had surrendered a' last, and was waiting now for Death—grim conqueror—to bear away his captive.

In this last hour no thought of battles or vengeance stained his soul.

All was loving, peaceful, happy !

A boy—he seemed to wander again over hill-top and dingle. and ever beside him was his elder brother, the bold sailor, in whose sunny curls, many and many years ago, the sea-weeds twined and tangled.

Oi c · more his mother seemed to kiss and bless him—how many years was it since her last kiss froze on her dead lips.

She has been waiting for him since, in the Upper Country.

Then his feet wandered through the paths of his young manhood.

He talked to the Laurette he had loved and wooed then, as if she were again beside him.

Then he seemed dimly to remember that she had died ; and he asked longingly for the child she had left him.

In mercy, all that experience of shame and sorrow connected with his youngest daughter seemed to have been obliterated from his mind.

Turning his head, with a slow painful motion, he saw the little Laurette, his grandchild, standing beside his pillow, and at once his thought seemed to accept her as his daughter.

He put out his trembling hand, and touched her hair. He murmured :

" Dear child—blessed child—I am going to your mother. She waits for me. She knows that I have been faithful to her memory. Ernestine, where are you? You are oldest—steadiest. You must watch over your sister. Kiss me, both of you, my daughters, my darlings !"

They bent over him, both of them ; but his brow was so cold, little Laurette shrank back in terror.

Ernestine pressed her lips to his, long and fondly.

When she lifted her head she was fatherless ; the old soldier's soul had gone forth on the winter wind, toward the land beyond the stars and the sun.

Then, for the first time, her fortitude gave way.

She was sinking back insensible, and would have fallen to the floor, but the arms of one who was just entering caught her and saved her.

He laid her tenderly on a lounge—this new comer.

Then, glancing at the frozen pallor of the face upon the bed, he understood all.

He held a bottle of some pungent aromatic salts to her nostrils : he bathed her face ; and presently he was rewarded by seeing her eyes unclose.

" Where is the doctor?" he asked, as soon as she was able to listen. " I wish I, too, might have been with you. Were you in the room with him alone—you and that child ?"

" Quite alone. It was so fearfully sudden. Dr. Graves was here an hour ago, and he said nothing o such immediate danger ; and I saw no signs, save that his mind wandered. He seemed to live all his youth over again. He took Laurette for

her dead mother ; and his very last words were to ask us both to kiss him. It is a great comfort, Mr. Duncan, that you were able to see so much of him as you have since he was ill. He talked to you more freely of his religious feelings than he ever has to any one else."

" And I truly think he has gone to a happier home. Oh, Miss Kennard, if I could only comfort you. There seems so little one can say in such an hour of sorrow ; and I know you are left very desolate. He loved you so."

By this time Ernestine's tears were falling fast, and she clung, with almost the simplicity of a child, to Walter Duncan's hand.

He was the village rector; a young man who had been settled in his new parish of Grantburgh but a single year.

A studious, scholarly, thoughtful-looking man he was—one whom all who knew him recognised as the very soul of everything pure, noble, and of good report.

He had admired Ernestine from the very first time he had met her ; but it was not until he had seen her in her father's sick room that he had approached her nearly and intimately enough to learn to love her.

In these last few weeks she had grown, quite unconsciously to herself, to be the one hope and guiding star of the minister's future.

He stood beside her now, longing, with a wild irrepressible tenderness, to take her head to his heart ; to whisper comfort to her as no mere friend might ; and to make her feel that earth was not desolate for her—that it still held one to whom she was the first and dearest in the world.

But it was no time to tell her this now, with that white frozen face lying on the pillow.

He almost reproached himself for the longing that surged through his heart.

She had never dreamed that she was more to him than one among many friends : and she kept him with her, clinging instinctively to the only comforter she had.

Soon Laurette drew near, and, with the child-like freedom of her petted ten years, made him sit down, and climbed into his arms, resting her tear-stained face against his shoulder.

" Be sorry for me, too," she said, childishly. " Grandpapa is gone, and I have only Ernestine. Because I am little and young, no one guesses how sorry I am."

It was a relief to Walter Duncan's overflowing heart to hold the little creature close to him, and lavish on her the tender sympathy he dared not offer to Miss Kennard.

Slowly the long days passed on, until the day when the dead man was carried out of his home, away from his children, and laid by his own Laurette's side, where the sunshine sifted down through the churchyard willows.

During those weary days, friends and neighbours who had long held aloof, repelled by the reserve of Major Kennard and his family, came with the eager spontaneous kindness of a country village to insist upon assisting Miss Kennard in her hour of bitter sorrow,

She welcomed all kindness, all sympathy—poor desolate girl !—with a thankfulness which it was very touching to see.

It was all over at length ; and she settled down, with a sad piteous resignation, into the slow routine of her daily life, as it was to be.

She had not even the relief of domestic cares. Mr . Jones had been the housekeeper and matron of the establishment ever since the death of Mrs. Kennard; she was still to continue so.

Hitherto a great part of Ernestine's life had been devoted to her father. She had read to him, talked to him, walked with him—been his companion, adviser, and friend.

Now those long unoccupied hours hung like a weary weight upon her hands.

She could not, at such a time, go into society; she could not always be teaching Laurette; she was too melancholy to read.

It was no wonder that she welcomed the frequent visits of Walter Duncan with a satisfaction which deceived him into the belief that his presence made her as happy as it made him, even to sit in the same room with her, and watch the slow, pensive smiles creep over her face, or the play of her features as she talked.

For four months he rejoiced in this hope silently, and then he asked her the question which had been so long hovering on his lips.

It was a spring twilight; the sun had just set; and the air was fragrant with the breath of opening blossoms.

Miss Kennard stood alone at the window, watching the castles in the air, whose turrets yet flamed with the ruby and topaz and amethyst of the sunset.

Her long black dress swept downwards in folds to the floor, and its dusky hue made her face, neck and hands look almost spectrally fair in the contrast.

Her gaze was fixed, her attitude one of intense thought, and she did not hear Mr. Duncan's step till he stood beside her, and called her as he had never called her before—

"Ernestine!"

She turned, with a surprised air, and met his eyes.

His look, so full of absorbed tenderness, told his story before his words did. But his words came, earnest, manly, freighted full with the gift of his heart.

He told her how well he had loved her, and how long—how patiently he had waited for an hour when he might venture to speak to her—how he longed to consecrate the whole of his life to make her happy.

She did not interrupt him.

As if spellbound, she listened to it all: but no blush stained her cheek, no thrill of responsive love stirred the drapery that lay so still above her woman's heart.

"I am so sorry," she said, at length, "so very, very sorry. Believe me, I never thought of the chance of this."

And then she told him all.

It was his due—he had given her so much love —to know why her heart held no response to his pleading.

She told him the whole story of her early love; the manner and cause of her parting with Norman Kensett—and the tenderness which, long after parting, clung desperately to his memory.

Love was over for her, she said—as dead as the dead day, which could never in all the years come back.

Esteem she gave him—he was her best friend; but there was no hope of resurrection for the youth of her heart.

Walter Duncan listened, as a criminal listens when the judge puts on the black cap; but was ever criminal who listened without some hope of reprieve?

There was a faint hope in his heart through it all.

Time works wonders—time makes grass grow even on graves, healing into greenness and beauty the wounds which rend the earth's sad bosom.

When she stopped speaking, he said—

"Permit me one question, Ernestine, only one. Do you still love Mr. Kensett, or is the old dream dead?"

"The dream is dead, utterly dead; but hope nothing from that, for the power to love is dead with it.'

"To love, perhaps, as you loved once, but not to give me a love which would be worth more to me than the uttermost passion of any other woman's heart. I will not let you refuse me now. Wait awhile, till you have accustomed yourself to think of me in the light of a lover, and then tell me whether you do not think life would be much happier shared with one who loved you beyond everything save Heaven—cherished and honoured as the mistress of a happy home—than it would be to live on, lonely as you are.. Never fear that such love as I believe you can give yet would not satisfy me. You must be my wife, or I must go alone through my life; so I have time enough to wait. We will leave it so."

In three months time Walter Duncan and Ernestine Kennard were—betrothed lovers, I was about to write, but that would hardly be a true statement, since Miss Kennard still protested that she could not give him a love worth acceptance; so I will use a more matter-of-fact mode of expression, and say that in three months they were engaged to be married.

When Laurette was informed of the betrothal, she received the intelligence like the queer, perverse creature that she was — in some things younger than her years; in others far older.

Returning, with childish frankness, Mr. Duncan's proffered kiss, she cried, with a wise little shake of her head:

"You'd a deal better have taken me. Ernestine doesn't begin to love you as well as I do. I'm sure I'm as pretty as she. Why didn't you ask me instead?"

"You weren't old enough, dear," was the playful answer; and the sprite walked musingly away, muttering to herself:

"Not old enough! Why, doesn't he see that I'll grow older every day? That fault is mending; and I know somebody that said aunt Ernestine was too old."

It was a still and bright afternoon, toward the last of August; and Mr. Duncan, and Miss Kennard, and little Laurette were out on a large pond popularly known as Stillwater Lake, in an expedition for water lilies.

They were in a frail-looking but strong little plaything of a boat, in which Mr. Duncan was accustomed to row, and of which he understood the management perfectly.

They had been enjoying themselves and the expedition.

Seldom during the month since her engagement to Walter Duncan had Ernestine been so light-hearted.

The sunshine of the golden summer day exhilarated her like wine. The perfume of the great creamy blossoms thrilled her senses with subtle delight.

Laurette was merry, too.

She was a strange, capricious, loving, teasing, fantastic creature—of unaccountable moods, and uncontrolled impulses—her mother's child.

To-day she was in the humour to be amusing; and no one could resist the contagion of her mirth.

With jests and merry sallies, and now and then a snatch of song, they glided along, stopping once in a while to gather a bunch of lilies, which seemed larger or sweeter than its neighbours.

At length, with an impetuous motion, Laurette sprang from one side of the boat to the other, and bent over to reach a blossom which had caught her eye.

As she leaned, she lost her balance; and, before a hand could be outstretched to save her, the elf-child was in the water.

For an instant Walter and Ernestine looked at each other—pale with terror.

The water was six feet deep, at least.

As they watched, they saw her sink.

Miss Kennard looked at her companion with a gaze of passionate terror and entreaty.

He was leaning far over the boat, as if striving to be ready to catch her when she rose.

He met Ernestine's gaze with one as full of anguish.

"If I could only save her," he cried, piteously; "but I cannot swim! If I should jump after her, it would only be to abandon you to your fate. I should but die with her."

Even as he spoke, she had risen and sunk again, just out of his reach.

They were not more than twenty yards from shore, and they saw now a stout swimmer making bold swift strokes toward her.

Sooner than I can tell it he had caught her—he was struggling back with her to the shore.

Silently, swiftly, Walter Duncan rowed after him.

As Miss Kennard stepped on the dry land the stranger laid Laurette at her feet.

It was no time for words. Only two passed between them."

"Ernestine!"

"Norman!"

"It was Walter Duncan's task to bear the senseless child to the nearest house; and it was almost an hour before she was fully restored.

Then, going out to look for the preserver of her niece, Miss Kennard found no one save Walter Duncan, waiting with a carriage to convey them home.

That evening, sitting beside Laurette's bed, Miss Kennard received a card.

"The gentleman is in no hurry. He says he will wait in the parlour till you are at liberty to see him," said the servant who handed it to her.

A slow smile stole over Miss Kennard's face—the message was so characteristic of one whom she used to know and love.

She rose, and looked in the glass.

She was engaged to another. The old dream was dead—or she thought so. But she wanted to look well in Norman Kennett's eyes.

She smoothed the heavy folds of her brown hair, adjusted her collar, and then remembered the ten years which had passed since she left her girlhood behind her.

Then, going down, she blushed, until it seemed as if the lost girlhood had come back again.

"How am I to thank you?" she said, warmly, giving both hands to her old friend. "And how came you there, just at the right time."

His answer was very earnest:

"That child—or, was it our own proud tempers?—separated us once, Ernestine. Shall she not restore us to each other again? Thank me, by giving me back yourself. I have never known happiness since we parted. I have been faithful to your memory. No other woman has had power to charm me for a moment. I have hungered and thirsted for your love. I should have come back to you long ago, but I was too proud. I thought you gave me up too hastily; and I doubted your love. I did not come until I could live without you no longer. I did not know, until I came here this afternoon, that your dear father was dead. I came prepared, if you should feel that duty called you to live here with him, to live here also, and make your duties mine. I came ready to sacrifice all things for your sake, if only I should find you the same Ernestine Kennard whom I had left. I learned from Mrs. Jones of your father's death. She told me you had gone out on the lake; and I was pacing along the shore in the hope of seeing you when I was so happy as to save the child. Shall I have the reward I claim, Ernestine? Shall the child I saved be our child henceforth?"

Miss Kennard blushed, and drew away the hand he had taken.

"It cannot be," she faltered, "I am not the same Ernestine."

"Not the same?"

"No; it was your Ernestine whom you left. Now I am engaged to Mr. Duncan."

"What, the hero of your sail? But I beseech you never to go boating with him again. You might have to be on the water with him if you married him. Seriously, I don't see how you can think of risking such a step. He can't swim."

Miss Kennard caught the merry, roguish, old-fashioned twinkle out of the corners of those two laughing blue eyes, and answered it—she could not help it—with a laugh.

At that very moment Walter Duncan came in. She went up to him, and gave him her hand. She spoke frankly.

"Walter, this is Norman Kensett, about whom I told you. He has come back over the sea to ask me to marry him. I told him the old dream was dead: I thought so; but I was wrong. His voice has awakened it again. I have told him I am no longer my own. This hand is yours. Do with it what you will."

He took Ernestine into his arms.

He kissed her once, with such a kiss as one gives to the beloved dead whom the grave is about to shut from our eyes for ever. Then he led her forward, and placed her hands in those of Norman Kensett's.

"The hand must go where the heart does," said he, in tones which he strove to make firm, though the words almost choked him. After a pause he continued—

"My own happiness was never worth half as much to me as yours is, Ernestine. May God bless both of you; and may the man you do love be all to you that I, whom you could not love, would have tried to be."

When he had said these words he went away, alone, out into the night.

I am not sure that Miss Kennard had not sacrificed the best love, after all: but she was satisfied.

"He is a noble fellow—a true man," Kensett said, warmly, after he had gone. "I don't see how you have helped loving him, darling."

"Because I had known you first," whispered Ernestine, looking as shy and rosy as in girlhood.

The next morning Laurette heard it all.

"It serves him right," she muttered, "for loving Ernestine, when I told him I loved him better."

The next time she saw Walter Duncan she told him the same; and he bent over and kissed her with a warmth of tenderness he had never felt for her before.

To a man whose love had been scorned, it is something to know that even a child loves him best of anything in the world.

———

Five years had passed since the wedding-day of Ernestine Kennard—five happy years—when the surrender of Fort Sumter flashed over the wires,

and a great nation shook with one tumultuous throb of indignation, and, standing up in its might, armed itself for the contest.

Among the first to seek an appointment as chaplain was Walter Duncan.

He has been heard of since—rushing fearlessly into the thick of danger, and carrying comfort to the wounded and dying, on many a battle-field.

At home, one watches for him; dreams of him; prays for him; reads his name when it occurs in dispatches, with kindling eyes.

Laurette is sixteen now, and to her he is still the first and noblest of men.

He has never spoken to her a single word of love; but I believe that he will some day.

Surely a patient heart will not go unrewarded!

When he comes home, and finds her blossomed

from childhood into woman's ripe splendour—above all, when he reads her faithful heart in her eyes—I think he will learn again the sweet duet of love; and, this time, she who will sing the air will be the child who loved him all the time."

Thus ended the narrative of the beautiful Inez; and, after receiving the thanks of her hearers, she asked Ned for a story, which the mutineer gladly complied with, and which ran as follows.

NED'S STORY.

"Some years ago a gentleman of considerable fortune married a young lady whose name was Eliza Downing, and hired a fine house in the then fashionable part of Bristol.

Shortly after Mr. Lawrence's marriage, a young lady, of the name of Mary Benson, whose parents had lately died, leaving her considerable property, came, at Mrs. Lawrence's request, she being a distant relation of the family, to reside with her and her husband.

Mr. Lawrence, who was a handsome and highly-educated gentleman, appeared to be devoted to his young wife; and Mrs. Lawrence and Miss Benson, both being amiable and accomplished ladies, lived together very happily, and were much respected and esteemed by a large circle of friends and acquaintances.

Within a year, however, of Mr. Lawrence's marriage, his wife took sick, and, after a long lingering illness, she died, leaving the widower inconsolable with grief.

Indeed, so overwhelming were his regrets, that his friends began to fear for his sanity; and, after trying change of scene in his own country, and every other means that could be thought of to dissipate his affliction, he at length, by the advice of his physician and friends, undertook a long tour to Europe, where he would be out of the way of everything that could remind him of his loss.

Miss Benson, on the death of her cousin, had gone to Clifton, to reside with an aunt; and the house was left untenanted.

Soon after this the owner died; and, some dispute occurring in relation to his will, his property—this house among the last—was thrown into chancery.

Twenty years elapsed, and the property at length came into the possession of a gentleman named Carr, who endeavoured to let the house formerly tenanted by the Lawrences to a respectable family.

But twenty years had made a vast difference in the city of Bristol. Fashion had begun to travel westward, and no family could be found willing to occupy so handsome a mansion, and to reside in the no longer fashionable neighbourhood in which the house was situated.

At length Mr. Carr, in despair of securing an eligible private tenant, let the house to a widow lady, of the name of Hutchins, who intended to establish a first-class boarding-house.

The mansion was commodious in every respect, and was soon filled with boarders.

One day Mrs. Hutchins received a letter from a lady of her acquaintance, whom she had her own reasons for wishing to oblige, informing her that the lady, whose name was Nesbitt, was coming to reside for some time in Bristol, and intended to take up her abode at her (Mrs. Hutchins') house, with her servant-maid.

The widow was very glad to receive the letter, and immediately set about preparing rooms for her expected visitor.

Her house was, however, so full, that she was at a loss where to find a bed-room for the servant of Mrs. Nesbitt.

At length she bethought her of a room in the rear of the first-floor, which had been packed full of old furniture when the Lawrences left the place, twenty years before, and which, through all the long years the house had been untenanted, had remained there.

She found, when this lumber, almost rotten with age, was removed, that the apartment was really one of the handsomest in the house; but, before she had got it quite ready for occupation, Mrs. Nesbitt and her servant arrived.

The old furniture had been all removed, with the exception of a mahogany escritoire, still in excellent preservation, which, being fastened to the wainscot, was allowed to remain.

The charwoman had been busy all day; and in the evening, after Mrs. Nesbitt's arrival, her maid offered to assist in completing the arrangement of the apartment she was to occupy, which was immediately adjoining her mistress's bedroom.

"Shure it wants but little doin' to it, marm," said the charwoman, as she and the servant-maid ascended the stairs together. "I've made the bed, and there is but to set the chairs, and tidy up a bit, and shure it's the handsomest room in the whole house."

Mrs. Nesbitt had entered her bedroom, and sat down to write a letter.

Presently she was startled and alarmed by a frightful shriek; and the next moment the charwoman and her own maid came rushing into the room—the former uttering a variety of ejaculations, while the latter sank down lifeless on the sofa.

When, after some difficulty, quiet was restored, and the servant-maid had recovered her consciousness, Mrs. Nesbitt, Mrs. Hutchins, and other ladies who had been drawn to the apartment by the cry, asked for an explanation.

Both the servant and the charwoman said that, on entering the room, they had lighted a candle, and, looking towards the bed, had discovered that a young lady, clad in white garments, and with long flowing yellow ringlets, was lying asleep outside the coverlid.

Thinking that some lady boarder had mistaken the room for her own, both had stepped to the bed, and both at the same time had lightly laid their hands upon the arm of the supposed sleeper, in order to awaken her, and inform her of her mistake.

To their surprise, the arm was cold as marble.

The charwoman had remarked that the lady would get her death of cold sleeping there, and, finding that she did not wake up, they touched her cheeks.

Their astonishment was now changed to horror. The lady's cheeks were firm and cold as her hands and arms; and another glance had satisfied them that they were gazing upon a corpse.

They both shrieked, and fled from the apartment.

The ladies listened to this explanation with astonishment.

Had the servant-maid alone seen the lady, they would have thought that her nerves had been excited by the fatigue of travelling for so many days, and that the supposed corpse had been a freak of her own imagination; but that the stout Irish charwoman, whose nerves might be supposed equal to anything, should have seen something, convinced them that they must have seen some one in the apartment.

And yet Mrs. Hutchins said there was not a young lady, nor a lady with long yellow ringlets, boarding in the house!

After some deliberation, they agreed to proceed to the room in a body.

They did so; but, lo! the apartment was empty.

Yet, on examining the bed, they could plainly discern the hollow made by the weight of a human body.

The servant and charwoman were questioned and cross-questioned together and apart; but they still adhered to the same story.

The report was soon spread abroad that the house was haunted.

Crowds came to see the room where the apparition was discovered.

A weekly newspaper published an engraving of the apartment, with the figure of a corpse dressed in white, lying on the bed; and furnished a full and particular account of the charwoman: a story embellished and exaggerated by the editor, to suit the taste of his readers.

For several weeks the mansion was the attraction of the city. Nothing more, however, was seen of the ghost; and the whole affair would probably soon have been forgotten, but for the circumstances which sprang out of it.

Amongst the gentlemen who boarded at Mrs. Hutchins' was one Mr. Eldrige, a retired lawyer, who, now that he had given up practice at the bar, amused his abundant leisure by examining curiously into other people's affairs, and prying into the secrets of everything he could get hold of.

This gentleman, twenty-two years previous, had been an intimate friend of the deceased Mrs. Lawrence, prior to her marriage; and he had once visited the house where he now boarded, when it was tenanted by Mr. and Mrs. Lawrence and Miss Benson; and he either recollected, or learned by some means or other, that the room where the apparition had been seen was that in which Mrs. Lawrence had died.

This became known, and gave new life to the mystery; and at length an old gentleman, named Downing, an uncle of the deceased Mrs. Lawrence, was attracted by curiosity to come from a long distance to visit the haunted house.

He had not been very friendly with his deceased niece—not from want of affection, but from his cold cynical nature—but he had, nevertheless, deeply and sincerely mourned her untimely death.

He had once visited the house while his niece resided in it, and he also identified the haunted room as her bedroom.

Mr. Eldridge and he soon fell into conversation.

"Very singular affair," said Mr. Downing. "If I believed in such things as ghosts appearing at all, I should say that the ghost was Eliza's—my deceased niece's."

"Are we any of us sure that the spirits of the departed do not appear sometimes?" replied Mr. Eldridge.

"I don't believe they do," returned Mr. Downing; "at all events, without there is some extraordinary cause."

"Ah—yes—exactly so," answered Mr. Eldridge. "Here's where the puzzle lies. You know Eliza Downing—Mrs. Lawrence I mean—your niece, had bright yellow, long, silky ringlets; and she

was the only person who has ever died in this house. Now, it is not likely that the ghost of a person who did not die here should visit it after death. Again, there is not, nor has not been, any lady answering the description given by Mrs. Nesbitt's maid and the charwoman, living in the house, nor visiting here: yet they described just such a woman as Mrs. Lawrence, neither of them having seen her while living.'

"Very strange!" repeated Mr. Downing.

"Yes, because one would think Eliza would rest comfortably in her grave. She died very young, it is true; but she has nothing to make her unhappy, and was almost worshipped by poor Lawrence."

"Humph!" exclaimed Mr. Downing.

"Do you think not?" replied Mr. Eldridge. "Recollect how he grieved when she died. I thought he would never get over her loss. He went to France, and I don't believe he's ever been in Bristol since."

"Those who make the most violent demonstrations are not always those who feel the deepest," replied the cynical Mr. Downing.

"You have reason to think Lawrence was not devotedly fond of his wife?"

"Perhaps not any particular reason; but I heard she died very suddenly. I was in Clifton at the time; and, if it was her ghost that really did appear, what should cause her to appear if she did live and die happily?"

"True — very true," said the lawyer: and, coming round, as was his custom, to other persons' opinions, he added—"and, as you say, people can't judge from appearances."

"I said nothing of the kind," replied Mr. Downing. "I said that the greatest demonstrations are not the surest signs of the deepest feeling; and that my niece died very suddenly. Where is Lawrence now—is he living?"

"I can't say. He returned from France, after travelling for two years, and went to reside in the country: where I don't know; nor whether he is still living. But I can find out."

"I wonder whether the physician who attended my niece during her last illness is still living?"

"That I don't know either," replied the retired lawyer; "but I can find out, and I will, and about Lawrence, too."

And he rubbed his hands in ecstasy at the idea of having a task just suited to his inclinations thus, as it were, imposed upon him.

"If you can find out, I should like to see the physician," said Mr. Downing—"merely to ask a few questions relative to my niece's last illness: though I believe this ghost story is all a humbug."

"You stay here to-night?"

"I do."

"Then I will let you know what I can find out to-morrow," replied the lawyer.

And the two old gentleman separated.

Mr. Eldridge soon discovered that Dr. Harmon, who had been Mr. Lawrence's family physician, was not only still living, but was in Bristol, and in a very extensive and lucrative practice.

He then called at the doctor's residence; but he was from home.

"Can I see Mrs. Harmon?" he asked.

He was shown into a parlour, and very soon the lady made her appearance.

He explained that he had merely called—having learned that Dr. Harmon was many years ago Mr. John Lawrence's family physician — to inquire whether that gentleman was still living; and, if so, where?

"He is still living in the western part of England," replied Mrs. Harmon, who was partial to a bit of gossip. "My husband hears from him occasionally; and a few years since we visited his place, and had a very pleasant time. Pray, sir, may I ask how long it is since you have heard from Mr. Lawrence?"

"Not since he went to France, after his wife's death, madam."

"Ha! Poor gentleman—he was inconsolable on the occasion of poor Mrs. Lawrence's death. I remember the lady well. We were both married about the same time. I used to visit her frequently. Her death was very sudden and unexpected. She had but a trifling illness, and was rapidly getting better of it, when there came a relapse, with symptoms that baffled the skill of Dr. Harmon, and the other physicians that he called in. I've heard my husband say that, had he not known how devotedly fond Mr. Lawrence was of his wife, he would have insisted upon having her body opened—the symptoms were so strange: but Mr. Lawrence was horrified at the idea when, one day, he did hint something of the kind. Poor man," continued the lady — "I thought he'd died of grief. But, as you have not heard of him since he returned from France, and since you know how much he mourned over his wife's death, you'll be surprised when I tell you that he married again."

"Married again!" exclaimed Mr. Eldridge. "How long ago?"

"Let me think. Soon after his return from France. It must be twenty years ago. His eldest son is eighteen; and he has two daughters beside. And who do you think he married?"

"I have no idea," said Mr. Eldridge.

"Who but Miss Benson—his wife's cousin? A sweet girl she was; and she has made him an excellent wife. She was living with them at the time of Mrs. Lawrence's death."

"I recollect the lady," said Mr. Eldridge. "She was a very beautiful girl. So Lawrence married Miss Benson, eh? Well, madam, you have furnished me with all the information I sought. I will not trouble you by waiting for your husband. Perhaps I may bring an uncle of Mrs. Lawrence's to see him. I have the honour to wish you a good-day."

All this information was retailed to Mr. Downing, with great gusto; and he, as well as Mr. Eldridge, remarked particularly the portion that related to the singular symptoms of the disease, the sudden death, and the wish of the physicians to have the body opened.

"Lawrence never wrote me a word of this," said Mr. Downing. "And so he's married to Miss Benson, that was!"

"After having been so inconsolable after the loss of his first wife!" replied Mr. Eldridge.

"Bah!" exclaimed Mr. Downing. "We'll go and see the doctor together, to-morrow, Eldridge."

They accordingly visited Dr. Harmon together; and they learned from him, in greater detail, the particulars of Mrs. Lawrence's fatal sickness.

"Doctor," said Mr. Downing, "I'm a plain-spoken man. You've heard of this ghost story that's going round—the appearance of a young woman, with fair hair, in my deceased niece's old bedroom? Now, I believe, that's all confounded humbug. But, tell me honestly, did you, or do

you, suspect anything wrong about Lawrence during his wife's illness?"

"Knowing Mr. Lawrence's affection for his wife, and having witnessed myself his grief at her loss," replied the doctor, "I did not, and do not. But, I will candidly confess, had I not known them so well as I did, I should have suspected some mysterious poisoning."

"And you do not now?"

"How can I suspect Mr. Lawrence?"

"Humph!" exclaimed Mr. Downing.

After some further conversation, Mr. Downing and Mr. Eldridge wished the doctor good-day, and quitted the house.

"I'm satisfied there's some mystery connected with Eliza's death," said Mr. Downing, as they walked backed to the house.

"Or else the spirit of the departed would lie in her grave," answered Mr. Eldridge.

"Bother the spirit of the departed!" replied Mr. Downing. "Do you suppose I'm such a fool as to believe such old woman's stories?"

It was very evident that he did, though.

"But," he continued, "I'll tell you what I will do: I'll buy that old escretoire that's in the room, and have it searched, if I have to take it to pieces. We may find some clue there to the—"

"Object of the ghost in revisiting the chamber," suggested Mr. Eldridge.

"Nonsense! To the—the cause of—something in relation to the cause of the disease which took off my neice so mysteriously."

The escretoire was purchased, and thoroughly searched, but in vain.

At last Mr. Downing resolved to break it up, and then a secret drawer was discovered, which contained an old memorandum book, and some packages of powder, which were so mildewed by age that it was utterly impossible to analyze them, and discover of what they were compounded.

But the book concealed a terrible secret. In it were regularly entered the periods at which doses were administered to the poor suffering, deceived woman, with their effects upon her constitution, until the day upon which she swallowed the last—the day on which she died, believing that her guilty, heartless husband was watching tenderly over her to the last.

Here the entries ceased.

But Mr. Downing had read enough.

Taking a detective officer with him, he went to the village where Mr. Lawrence was living, in the western portion of the city.

Leaving the detective officer with the village constable outside the house, which was a beautiful country seat, situated in handsome and extensive grounds, he knocked at the door and requested to see Mr. Lawrence on business of importance.

Mr. and Mrs. Lawrence—the latter formerly Miss Benson—were seated in an elegantly furnished parlour, with their family around them. The elder daughter had been playing the piano; the younger was at work on some embroidery, as also was her mother; and the son, a fine-looking youth of eighteen, was reading.

Mr. Lawrence was still a fine-looking, handsome man, though his features were marked with a peculiar expression of melancholy, which appeared to be natural to them.

Mrs. Lawrence was still beautiful, and the daughters were charming girls, like their mother, and showing how lovely she must have been at their age.

"Ellen, my love, suppose you play 'The Miller's Daughter.' I heard it at Mrs. Dawson's last night. I don't know how many years have passed since I heard in before."

"No, no, Mary dear," said Mr. Lawrence—"excuse me, my love, I cannot bear to hear that tune."

"It was Eliza's favourite one," answered Mrs. Lawrence.

"Yes, for that reason I do not like to hear it."

"Dear John," replied Mrs. Lawrence, "I think you feel poor Eliza's loss the more as years pass away. I regretted her death almost as much as you; but time has left only a pleasing sorrow as I recall her to mind. We know she is an angel in heaven—perhaps now looking down lovingly upon us."

"I trust she is," said Mr. Lawrence. "I think my love, I do feel more now than I used to do. Would that I could think of Eliza as you do."

"Was papa's first wife such a nice woman?" asked the youngest daughter.

"She was an angel, my love," replied Mrs. Lawrence.

It was strange that, while (generally speaking) wives by second marriages do not like to refer to their husband's first wives, Eliza Downing was a favourite subject of discourse with Mrs. Lawrence. She was never weary of dwelling upon her beauty and goodness.

"I suppose," continued the younger daughter—"she loved papa very much.

"Everybody does," she replied.

"You'll make papa blush," said the elder girl, "so continually praising his good qualities."

"I can tell you of one ill-quality he has," said the son.

"What is that, Henry?" asked Mrs. Lawrence, with a smile.

"He won't let me learn chemistry, and I am so anxious to do so."

"My dear boy," interposed Mr. Lawrence, "chemistry is a dangerous science. The less you have to do with it the better."

"I am old enough now, papa, to keep clear of danger, and take care of myself, I think," replied the youth.

"I do not speak of physical dangers—of dangers likely to occur to yourself," answered Mr. Lawrence. "I allude to the secret power which it gives to men who sometimes make a terrible use of it,—"

At this moment the servant entered and put a check to Mr. Lawrence's speech by saying that a gentleman from Bristol wished to see her master on business of the utmost importance.

Mr. Lawrence changed colour.

"From—from Bristol—" he said.

"Yes, from Bristol," replied Mr. Downing, bursting into the parlour. "Mr. John Lawrence, I charge you with murder—with the wilful, cruel murder of my neice, Eliza Downing!"

Mr. Lawrence rose from his chair gasping for breath.

Mrs. Lawrence fancied he was going to turn the strange intruder out of the room.

She was astonished, but not the least alarmed at his manner.

"Sit down, John," she said, "or be gentle with the young man: it must be some poor creature who has escaped from the insane asylum in the next village."

But Mr. Downing advanced, followed by the officer from Bristol, and the village constables, and the former seized Mr. Lawrence by the collar, and repeated his charge.

Mrs. Lawrence and the children started to their feet; and their astonishment and horror may be better conceived than described when they heard the idolized husband and father cry in tones of piteous agony—

"Oh, spare me! spare me! I will confess all. I have felt for some time past that this was coming! Oh, my God! thy vengeance is slow, but sure. Yet spare me for the sake of my innocent wife and children."

"Villain! did you spare my niece? The wife you swore to love and cherish; who looked up to you—her murderer—as a being of superior nature. No earthly punishment can be found severe enough for such a crime as yours."

Mrs. Lawrence and the young ladies fainted. The young man stood paralyzed with horror.

The servants, who had rushed in, stood aghast with terror and amazement.

The scene was sad to witness!

We will pass over what immediately followed. Mr. Lawrence was conveyed to the assizes and tried for the murder of his wife, twenty-two years before!

He confessed his guilt!

He said that he had become desperately enamoured of Miss Benson, his present wife, from the first moment she had come to his house.

She, he said, was pure as an angel, and had not the least idea of his guilty love, neither had the devoted woman whom he had basely murdered.

He was mad, he said, and knew scarcely what he was doing.

He had, at first, no thought of committing the dreadful crime; but his wife was attacked with illness, and then the devil put it into his head to make that illness fatal, and thus accomplish his object—marry Miss Benson.

He was a proficient in chemistry, and he concocted a poison, the nature of which was a secret to all but himself, and this he had mixed with the food that his wife would, as she grew weaker and weaker daily, accept from no other hand but his own.

At length she died, blessing him with her last breath.

He had really been plunged in grief, when at last his aim was accomplished, and had some thoughts of giving up his base design of uniting the fate of another innocent woman to his, but he could not.

He went to France, but there remorse followed him; and still his passion acquired fresh strength, and he returned and married her, to possess whom he had blasted his happiness in this life and sunk his soul to perdition.

Since then he had never known a happy hour, by day or night; and he had encouraged his second victim—the victim of his base, unhallowed love—to converse of his first murdered wife, as it inflicted some penance for his crime.

He said that he was ready and willing to die, but for the sake of his poor innocent wife and children.

He was condemned on his own confession.

No pity was felt for him, but deep sympathy was expressed for the innocent beings he had brought to shame and disgrace.

He was hung opposite the jail of the county.

His wife sold the property he had possessed in England, and quitted the country, with her family, to reside, heart-broken, for the remainder of her days in a foreign land.

Whither she went few knew. Her place of voluntary exile was never made public.

The haunted house became more famous than

ever. Everybody believed that the spirit of the murdered wife had thus brought the murderer to justice.

Mr. Downing felt no remorse for the part he had played. "'The sins of the father,'" he quoted, 'are visited upon the children.' It is just that it should be so."

As to Mr. Eldridge. he was now perfectly satisfied that the spirits of the departed did visit the earth if they had met with wrong while living; and he was fond of introducing his famous ghost story on every possible occasion.

Years passed away.

One day a party of gentlemen were seated at table after dinner. Among them were Mr. Downing and Mr. Eldridge—both now very old men.

The conversation turned upon the appearance of ghosts.

Some present pretended to believe in them; others doubted; others scouted the idea as preposterous.

Mr. Eldridge, to prove the correctness of his theory, related the story of the appearance of Mrs. Lawrence, twenty-two years after her decease.

He looked around triumphantly when he had concluded the story.

"Strange!" said some. "Wonderful!" exclaimed others; while others still doubted.

"At length a middle-aged gentleman, who had not yet spoken, said:

"Mr. Eldridge, do you not recollect me?"

"I do not, sir," was the old gentleman's reply.

"Ten years ago I lodged at Mrs. Hutchins'. You lodged there too. My name is Danvers."

"Ha!" exclaimed the old gentleman—"I do recollect you well now. You have changed greatly. You were a wild young fellow in those days."

"I was a medical student," said Dr. Danvers. "One day our class was sadly in want of a subject for dissection. They were difficult to procure in those days, and the penalty for robbing graves was very severe. Nevertheless, it was often done. A very beautiful girl had died of consumption. A party of students resolved to obtain the body. You know Mrs. Hutchins' house stood near Trinity burying-ground. Taking a rope with me, I entered the house, made my way to this room, and lowered the rope from the window. My comrades fastened it round the body of the young lady. I drew it up, and laid the corpse on a bed. At that moment I heard some one approaching; and presently two women entered the room. I hid myself under the bed. I heard them strike a light. Then they went to the bed, saw the corpse, screamed fearfully, and rushed from the room. I came forth from my place of concealment. I was aware that there would be a fine piece of work if the body was found in the house. What was to be done? While I was considering, my comrades whistled —a signal that the watchmen had gone away. Immediately I refastened the corpse to the rope, lowered it from the window, lowered myself afterwards by the same rope and we carried the body to the dissecting-room. The next morning I removed the rope, which had not been discovered. We heard, also, some time after, that it had actually led to the discovery of a murder. Still we kept our council; and I don't know as I should ever have told the truth of the story had I not desired to refute the silly superstition of belief in the appearance of ghosts. The ghost of Mrs. Lawrence was the body of a young lady who died of consumption. Now, gentlemen, do you still believe in ghosts?"

Mr. Eldridge was silent; but Mr. Downing muttered:

"Humph! knew it was a humbug. Always said so. But it revenged my poor niece, and hung that scoundrel, John Lawrence."

"Now, Jack," said Ned, turning to the seaman who had so bravely exerted himself to bear the wounded captain from the slaver, "I've finished my yarn, and I reckon it's only fair that you should spin one now."

"I can't spin a yarn," replied the other.

"Avaunt there, messmate!" said Ned. "I should not like to have to haul in all the stock of yarns you can spin."

"Shouldn't you?" said the sailor. "Well, I tell you, if I spin one, it won't be of my own twisting. It's an old 'un, as was told to me a long time gone by."

"Well, let's have it then: a good thing loses nothing by keeping."

"Well, then, here goes; and, mind you, it's all true—every word on it."

JACK RIDLEY'S STORY.

On the afternoon of a bright spring day, in the latter portion of the twelfth century, a young yeoman was busily engaged with bow and round-headed arrows in a noble English forest, standing somewhat east of the river Avon.

He was shooting at a mark, made by notching a large tree, but with no very remarkable success; for his arrows shattered the bark for a considerable space around the notch, without striking the notch itself.

Time after time he adjusted his arrow, pulled the string to his ear, aimed long and carefully, and then let fly at the mark, eagerly following with his eye the course of the swift messenger, to see it knock the bark from the tree.

At length, after firing his quiver of arrows over and over again, he seemed bent upon making a last desparing trial.

Fixing the notch of his arrow with unusual care to the string, he bent the bow very slowly, and then relaxed it.

After fixing his eye intently on the mark, he again bent it, drawing the string this time nearly to his ear, and again allowed it to return.

With another fixed gaze at the mark, he drew the string until the bow threatened to pass the arrow-head, and then, after an anxious aim, he let drive the arrow with tremendous force.

It actually missed the tree itself!

At this he burst into a terrible passion, as if the poor arrows, which lay about on the ground, had been living enemies, they could not have been more fearfully execrated.

"May the infernal powers take you!" he exclaimed. "May the lightning blast you where you lie! Ye are leagued against me! Do you think to inveigle me into striving for her hand with such base tools as ye have proved yourselves to-day?"

With these words, he quickly snatched the last arrow which remained in the quiver, and with scarcely an aim, he let it fly, exclaiming—

"Go, keep company with the rest of thy miserable herd!"

And without deigning a look at the course it might take, he dashed his bow furiously to the ground.

"A most yeoman-like shot, my young friend," uttered a voice near him.

He turned, ashamed to be seen in such a foolish passion, and beheld a stranger issuing from the woods at his left.

"A most yeoman-like shot," repeated the stranger, "few can drive an arrow inside of that!"

"Who are you, sirrah, who thus obtrudes himself only to insult me?" exclaimed the young yeoman, having recovered from his surprise at the stranger's sudden appearance, but not yet recovered from his temper.

"I am your friend, Richard: let this suffice," was the answer. "Pray inform me how I have insulted you?"

"How?" returned the young archer, whose anger was considerably softened by the manner of the stranger, together with the peculiar way in which he called him by name. "How? By affecting to praise my shots, which you know to be execrable."

"Your former shots were bad enough, I'll acknowledge. Richard; but I again affirm that your last was a brave one. Come, let the mark itself testify to the truth of what I say."

With these words the stranger led Richard to the tree—and sure enough, an indentation, made by the round head of the arrow, appeared well toward the very centre of the notch.

Richard looked first at the mark, and then at the stranger in complete bewilderment.

His companion smiled and said—

"You must learn to send off all your arrows as you sent that."

"I let that fly in a fit of passion," returned the young man. "I can't make myself thus angry when my skill is most needed."

"I will teach you to do it without the aid of passion. But why so gloomy? You may win Constance yet."

The young yeoman blushed, but said nothing.

"You need not be ashamed, my young friend," continued the stranger. "She is a noble prize to win, if I judge aright from what I have heard."

"You do judge aright!"

His own eagerness, together with the smile that passed over his companion's countenance, caused Richard to blush more deeply, and to turn his head away in confusion.

"I doubt it not," was the answer. "And, moreover, my young friend, I doubt not that she would as warmly testify in your favour, if I should affirm that you were, in all respects, worthy of her. But time flies, and I must give you a lesson in archery, before the sun disappears. We will gather the arrows which were so recently the victims of your maledictions."

"I feel like asking their pardon," said Richard, with a voice of considerable humility. "I confess I was terribly provoked. When I cried out to them so, I felt as though each one was maliciously determined to rob me of—"

"Constance," added the stranger, with a smile. "Well, well, I think I understand your feelings. But how did her father come to make such a proclamation as the one which has reached my ears?" he inquired, as he went about picking up the scattered arrows.

"That sneaking cur, Hugh, because, forsooth, he is accounted the leading archer of this part of the country, thought fit to sue for Constance's hand. And, seeing she wouldn't have him—the ill-looking dog!—he has been filling the head of her stupid, stubborn, tyrannical father, who, perhaps you have heard, was accounted the best archer round about when he was younger—filling the head of her father, who is half-blind, struck with the palsy, and sometimes, I believe, half-witted, by the way he carries on matters—filling his head with the abominable notion that his daughter must be given to the best archer who is willing to try for her, because forsooth, she is the daughter of a man who has been the best archer here in past times. So out comes his proclamation, as though he was the king, declaring that whoever proves himself the best archer on the village green, on the next holiday, shall have his daughter in marriage!"

Richard was evidently returning to his former state of passionate anger, if indeed it was not already upon him.

"Then you have a fortnight to practice in," said the stranger, in a quiet voice, who had been listening quietly to the excited account of his companion.

"Well, what can a fortnight do for me against that scheming Hugh? He's the best shot in these parts, and he knew it when he worked on the old man. He's ten years older than I am; and he's handled his bow since he was old enough to stand on his feet—while circumstances have prevented me from necessary practice."

"You can do a great deal in that time, if you keep busy. Come, let us see what you can do in the half-hour before twilight."

With these words, the stranger led the way to the spot from which Richard was shooting his shafts when we were first introduced to him. Picking up the bow, he quietly adjusted an arrow, and, almost before Richard was aware of his intentions, he had sent it full into the centre of the mark.

"Now, having presented my testimonials," said he, smiling at the look of wonder fixed on Richard's countenance, "allow me to be your teacher for awhile."

To this proposition the young yeoman most willingly assented.

"You have a few bad faults, which I noticed as I watched you from yonder," said the stranger. "You draw the arrow awkwardly out of the line when you pull the string. The arrow is not guided correctly by either hand. Your eye is fixed too much on the end of the arrow; and you aim too long, and allow the arrow to hang on the string when you discharge it. Now, you are not very faulty with any one of them separately; yet, taking them all together, they make bad work with your shooting. When you were in your passion, and grasped your last arrow, you forgot to be anxious about all these things, and your natural grace and boldness obtained the mastery. In your rage you did not look at your shaft longer than two seconds; but I saw you looking straight at the mark, as though you were including it among the objects of your wrath. You see the result."

Having thus delivered himself, he proceeded to show Richard the direct manner of holding the arrow, drawing the string, and letting the notch of the arrow spring neatly and smartly from it; and, in half an hour, the latter had made remarkable progress.

At the end of that time the mark could not be seen with sufficient distinctness, on account of the twilight: so they prepared to depart.

"And, pray," said Richard, "to whom shall I return my thanks for your kindness?"

"To one to whom your father performed a service, when he was alive, which he can never forget. He had not sufficient opportunity to express his gratitude to the father, so he has come to repay the favour through the son. This is all I can say at present. Meet me here to-morrow, three hours before sunset, then we will practice again."

With these words the stranger passed into the forest, and Richard returned home, filled with wonder at the incidents of the afternoon, and with a buoyant hope that he should yet out-match Hugh, the archer, on his own grounds.

You have gathered, from the conversation carried on between Richard and the stranger, hints sufficient to suggest what I need not tell you.

The principal facts stated by the young yeoman were correct.

He, however, in his excitement, somewhat exaggerated the weaknesses of the father of Constance.

Yet the main idea conveyed by him was true: and the weaknesses he really possessed were such as could be easily worked upon by so crafty a man as was Hugh, the archer.

His daughter had begged him, with all the tearful eloquence which a daughter, under such circumstances, could command, not to sacrifice her to a whim, which originated in the mind of a hard-hearted and unprincipled man.

The old man's weak points, which in one sense were his strongest points, were utterly under the command of Hugh, who knew but too well how to make the best use of his advantage.

Under his influence, the father saw in the moans and prayers of his daughter nothing but the expressions of an obdurate and undutiful child, setting herself against his authority.

He was well aware that she looked with strong favour on Richard, whom, through the insidious influence of Hugh, he viewed with strong dislike, if not with positive hate.

Consequently, every exhibition of sorrow on the part of Constance was looked upon as an expression of love for Richard, and rather steeled the old man's heart than softened it.

On the following afternoon the young yeoman and the stranger met according to agreement, and practised until sundown.

Richard was delighted with his progress; and, when we consider the prize at stake, we may be sure that he attended most assiduously to all the hints and suggestions given him by his strange friend.

Before they parted the second time, the stranger had promised to meet him each day, until the holiday when the trial was to take place.

Each succeeding evening found Richard wonderfully improved in his archery; and when the sun went down for the last time before the long expected day should arrive, Richard felt that the prize would be his ere another twenty-four hours had passed.

As they were parting on this last evening, the stranger bid him keep his nerves steady on the morrow, and shoot home with a bold heart and prompt hand.

The long expected day came at last.

We may be sure that the novel trial for the hand (the heart no triumphant bow could win) of Constance, who was known far and wide for her goodness, had brought a great collection of people together in the village where the trial was to take place.

Some thought it was a shame to sacrifice a noble girl to such folly; while others thought there was something very romantic about it, and pronounced it but proper for the man who married the daughter of him who had been the best archer of the county, to be able to take the father's place.

And so they conversed—the conversation sometimes characterised by considerable excitement, especially when a particular friend of Constance would happen to enter into a debate with one of those who advocated the last mentioned opinion.

At length with considerable pomp and circumstance, the father, accompanied by his daughter, entered the green, followed by a selected train.

They were both supported: one trembling from the effects of a recent stroke of palsy, and the other from the effects of an almost broken heart.

The former was conducted to a sort of throne, from which he was to preside over the trial; and the latter to an elevated seat by his side.

The attendants stationed themselves according to arrangements dictated by the fancy of the old man.

Then the preparations for the trial began.

The mark was set up at a proper distance, and the order in which the competitors should follow each other was arranged.

By common consent, Hugh and Richard were to shoot last — Hugh managing to precede Richard, calculating, with subtle sagacity, that his own excellent shots (for he rarely made indifferent ones) would so excite his rival, in his anxiety to excel him, that what little skill he believed he possessed would be exerted at no inconsiderable disadvantage, for nervousness in nice archery is as bad as it is in shooting with the rifle.

Several had entered the lists: and, as one succeeded another in the trial, each firing three arrows, the spectators manifested the most intense interest.

Many fine shots were made; and, as often as one was unusually fortunate, a general shout expressed the pleasure of the people.

The arrows were pointed—for the old man said he wanted "every shaft to be its own mark;" and they were removed as fast as they too much obstructed the target, their places being properly designated.

At length came Hugh's turn.

With confidence and promptness he delivered his shots—his arrows striking well towards the centre of the target.

A loud shout went up from a great portion of the people.

The old man rubbed his trembling hands, exclaiming:

"This is the son for me!"

Constance turned pale as death.

Her own and Richard's friends gazed on the arrows with scowls and compressed lips.

Richard, in spite of all his efforts to remain calm, trembled, and the blood rushed painfully to his face.

He succeeded in somewhat composing himself, however, and stepped, with as much confidence as possible, to the spot from whence he was to shoot.

Carefully adjusting his first arrow, he pulled the string, but again relaxed it, for he found he was not in a proper state to fire.

H. ANELAY.

But as the people, as well as the old man, manifested impatience, he drew again, and let fly the
shaft.

As he had feared, it struck outside of Hugh's
three arrows by a considerable distance.

Adjusting his second arrow, he determined to
wait awhile to collect himself.

"A brave fellow for rabbits!" shouted a coarse
voice from the crowd. "How many leagues would
one run before he could get ready to shoot it?"

Stung by the taunt, Richard sent this arrow
more wildly than the other.

Many of the people laughed; his friends expressed their dissatisfaction by still deeper scowls:
Hugh rubbed his bony hands, and grimly smiled;
while Constance, poor girl, appeared as if but little
blood or strength remained to sustain her longer.

"Take courage, and remember my instructions!" uttered a calm soothing voice behind him.

Turning hastily round, he beheld the stranger,
dressed in green, and equipped with bows and
arrows.

A slight sign warned him to manifest no surprise.

Instantly the calmness of his friend of the forest
seemed to take command of his own nerves.

Waiting a few moments, in spite of the taunts of
several of Hugh's admirers, subtly encouraged by
Hugh himself, he fixed his third shaft to the
string, and pulled with a steady hand.

With a quick prompt start the arrow left the
cord, and flew inside Hugh's best, nearly piercing
the centre.

A shout now went up from the friends of

Richard and Constance, and from the great mass of the people, which echoed and re-echoed among the hills and woods.

Constance leaped to her feet with the sudden revulsion of feeling from sorrow to joy, and fell fainting into the arms of an attendant.

"He's won the prize!—he's won the prize!" arose from the spectators; and then again they thundered their applause to the hills and woods.

Hugh turned pale with rage.

"It's false—by all that's holy, it's false!" he shouted, with a hoarse, yet powerful, voice. "Ralph!" he cried, stalking up to the old man—"dost thou intend to throw away thy daughter on a slip of that base churl's bow?"

"It's a fair shot!" cried a voice from the crowd.

"He who strikes nearest the centre gains the prize!" shouted another, as the old man seemed to receive Hugh's words with favour.

"So said the proclamation!"

"This you proclaimed, old man!"

"The best shot wins! So thou hast promised!" issued from the crowd, almost simultaneously.

Hugh saw his mistake in giving way to his passion. He changed his tactics.

"But," said he, in a mild tone, "Ralph wants the best archer for his son. Does a chance shot prove a man the best archer?"

These words, and the manner of their delivery, began to affect a number of the spectators, and the old man seemed wavering.

"Allow me to enter the lists, and by the time I am finished your minds may be more clear," said the stranger, in a calm voice.

"Would you make the trial?" asked the old man, eagerly, glad for a little respite.

"I would," was the answer.

"Let him try, then!" shouted some of those who had been affected by Hugh's wily words.

"I am willing, if my friend Richard is," said Hugh, glad to regain the good-will of the people by appearing generous.

The tumultuous demonstrations of feeling in favour of Richard, which grew stronger with the great mass, who still remained unaffected by his last words, caused him to fear the results of further pressing his protestations at that time. Moreover, he hated Richard, and any other winner of the prize was better than he.

Richard also acquiesced, for he knew that he had nothing to fear, being assured both by the stranger's manner, and by certain words he had dropped in his ear.

"Thou may'st enter," uttered old Ralph, with faltering dignity.

The stranger advanced, and with scarcely an aim, rapidly discharged three arrows into the target.

"Those are for the brave young yeoman yonder;" he said, nodding towards Richard, and then disappeared in the crowd.

All were surprised at his conduct, but when the target came to be closely examined, surprise changed into wonder.

The arrows, which had been delivered with such rapidity, stood in a rude semi-circle around Richard's lucky shaft, each one being about a quarter of an inch distant from it, and yet leaving it nearest the centre.

These remarkable shots, together with the sudden memory of the green dress, caused the truth to burst on the minds of those nearest to the target.

"Robin Hood!"

This cry spread from the target to all parts of the crowd, as the sound of the approaching tempest spreads through the forest.

Each man looked quickly about him—but he saw not the object of his search.

The stranger had disappeared.

It is hardly necessary to add that Hugh was obliged to succumb to the overwhelming spirit of the multitude.

Richard was declared victor by universal acclamation, in which declaration the old man was compelled to join.

Robin Hood was a great favourite of his, as he was with the people generally, and the recent incident served to stir up his generous blood, of which he was in reality not without a goodly share.

He felt obliged to acknowledge that Richard had fairly won his daughter, according to his proclamation.

Richard offered to try again with Hugh, but the people would not have it so; and old Ralph confessed their determination was just.

And so he allowed them to lead the young man to Constance, (who had now recovered, though sitting, as if in bewilderment she was striving to comprehend the happy conclusion of the, to her, long-dreaded trial, join their hands, and conduct them to his home with as much pomp and circumstance as when the train entered the green, and with far more joy; while Hugh wandered away in an opposite direction, a lonely, disappointed, and unhappy man.

Ere long the happy couple were joined in those firm and holy bonds, which so felicitously close the trials and sorrows of anxious lovers; and the old man learned to love his new son as though he were of his own blood.

The young yeoman became established as the first archer between Sherwood and the Avon; and he ever remained a steadfast friend to the stranger of the forest.

CHAPTER CXXXVII.

WILD MADGE MADE PRISONER—HER DEFIANCE—DEPARTURE FROM THE CABIN WITH ELLEN.

THE poor, broken-hearted captive, Ellen, was seated brooding in gloomy sadness, and watched over by her dissolute keeper in the cabin of Wild Madge, when a heavy blow was struck upon the door, and the forms of Charles Lawson and his black companion strode into her prison.

With a cry of surprise not unmingled with fear, the prisoner and jailer sprang to their feet.

But how different the exclamations that escaped their lips—how contrary their feelings, as their eyes fell upon the forms of those two men who, unannounced, had thus forced their way into the cabin.

Rage and despair shone from the eyes of the besotted Madge.

Love and hope beamed from those of the beautiful Ellen.

Both spring forward at the same moment.

But the intentions and feeling of each were different.

Chafing like an enraged tigress, the fury sprang at the throat of Charles.

With a heart bounding with joy and hope Ellen flung her arms around the neck of her lover.

"Charles—Charles!" she gasped, "my own, my beloved Charles!"

"Furies! Escaped!" shrieked Madge—"but you are in the tiger's lair, and its fangs shall rend your heart!"

And her long bony fingers clutched at the throat of the youth.

"Fiend!" exclaimed Charles, grasping her wrists, and endeavouring to remove her fingers from his neck; "your course has run—your vile career is over. This ship is in my hands, and justice awaits to meet out the punishment your crimes have merited."

"Liar!" shrieked the fury, fastening her nails into his flesh—"never will Wild Madge die unavenged. She has sworn to embitter your life—make her you love a thing of scorn and loathing; and she will keep her oath spite of heaven or hell!"

With a cry of horror, Ellen strove to tear the furious woman from the throat of her lover, but Wild Madge turned her long thin fingers around the neck of Charles, who, too manly to strike her, struggled in vain to make her relax her fearful hold.

Zoolooh, the black, who had accompanied him, had less compunction of conscience, so finding that Madge, spite of all, still persisted in retaining her hold, he drew his long knife, and seizing the fury by the hair of her head, drew it back, and was about to gash her throat with the weapon when Ellen and Charles simultaneously shrieked out for him to spare her.

"For the love of heaven spare her!" exclaimed Ellen, being sick at the black's motions.

"Hold! I command you," exclaimed Charles, as, in terror, the fury let go his grasp. "Hold! Bad as she is, we must not forget that we are men, and that to slay a woman is a despicable action."

"She kill you," said the black, sullenly.

"Aye, and worse, if she could," said Charles.

"Den she die."

"No," said the young man, firmly.

The black looked upon him in surprise; but he still held the fury by the hair.

He could not understand how Charles could show mercy to one so cruel and base.

Poor fellow, civilisation was a stranger to him: he could only believe that brute force and cruelty must be met with its own weapons.

"Release her!" said Charles.

"She no die?" asked the black, in a disappointed tone of voice.

"Not by your hand."

The African offered his knife to Charles.

"Massa kill her," he said.

Charles pushed back the weapon with a shudder.

"No, no," he said—"vengeance is not for us. Bind her hands, so that she can do no further injury. Her punishment must be reserved for those who have a right to inflict it."

"Heaven will reward her wickedness, according to its merits," said Ellen, now clinging fondly to the neck of her lover—"in its own good time. Oh! Charles, I had began to despair—hope had fled my soul."

"And I," he said, straining her to his heart. "But heaven has not deserted us. The blacks have mutinied against these inhuman fiends; and, by heaven's aid, all may yet be well."

He untwined her arms gently from his neck, and, taking his handkerchief from his throat, he seized the hands of Wild Madge, who, foaming with rage and despair, was unable to articulate even a curse, and bound them tightly together—the black holding her securely all the time by her hair.

Once or twice she essayed to bite the hands of the youth; but Charles was wary, and her exertions to accomplish her fiendish wish proved useless.

When securely bound, Charles motioned to the African to let go his hold.

This the black obeyed.

Wild Madge stood glaring from one to the other, whilst a thick foam gathered round her lips.

Her look was full of fearful meaning, and she strove to burst the bond, which held her wrists, asunder.

But in vain.

Her passion at length found words.

Curses, loud and deep, issued from her lips.

Maledictions, fearful, were poured out upon them.

But Charles paid no further heed to them than by casting a look of pity and contempt upon her.

Then, turning to Ellen, and flinging his manly arm around her slender form, he said:

"Come, dear one; let us leave this woman to her own conscience. Such words are ill-fitted to your gentle ears. Come, my friend."

And he motioned to the black.

The African played nervously with his knife, and looked questioningly at Charles, and then savagely at the malicious face of Madge.

He wished to show his devotion to his new captain—to prove his loyalty—by ridding the world for ever of one so base, so degraded, so merciless, as the bloated besotted libel on woman, Wild Madge.

But Charles shook his head.

A feeling of horror stole over him at the bare idea of sanctioning such a deed.

Bad as Wild Madge was, he could not permit her to die by the hand of the African.

Fearful as had been the miseries she had caused the fair girl he once more held in his arms, he could not be an accomplice in her destruction.

"No, no," he said, fixing upon the African a forbidding look—"we are not murderers."

"God forbid!" said Ellen. "Fearful as has been the misery she has inflicted upon us, I would not see her harmed. That God who watches over the prince and the peasant, and deals out justice to both, will yet avenge the horrors we have had to encounter. To him, then, we must leave her; and may he be as merciful to her as she has been cruel to us."

"Your generous soul, Ellen, has not been warped by your sufferings," said Charles.

Then, turning to Madge, he added:

"Woman, if one spark of feeling yet remain in your breast, what must be the feelings of your heart when these words reach your ears! Bad as you are—cruel as you have been to her—can your heart be closed to every emotion when she you so deeply wronged pleads for your guilty life?"

"The heart of Wild Madge pants but for vengeance," shouted the woman—"and it will have it. I have sworn to heap misery upon misery on your souls. My oath is registered in hell; and that oath shall yet be kept. Revel in the transient pleasures you now possess. Gaze upon the beauteous face and form of her you now hold in your arms. Your joy shall be short-lived; your triumph but a fleeting vision. Fools! you triumph now; but, ere long, your victory shall be turned to a defeat; your joys to sorrow; your hopes to fears; your happiness to misery. Wild Madge fears you not; she laughs to scorn your words; defies your power; spurns your mercy. Ha, ha! —bask in the sunshine of each other's love whilst you may. Black clouds are rising, and the storm will burst over your happiness!"

"Woman, woman!" interrupted Ellen, clinging to her lover's breast in terror.

"Nay, tremble not, dear one," exclaimed Charles —"the dark hours of adversity and sorrow are clearing away!"

"Ha, ha!" laughed Wild Madge—"lay not such flattering hopes to your soul. Wild Madge lives, and—"

"Let me kill her, massa—let me kill her!" exclaimed the black, brandishing his knife.

"Oh, no, no!" gasped Ellen, springing forward, and placing herself between the black and Madge. "Spare her—spare her!"

"It must not be," said Charles.

The African drew back sullenly.

"Oh, woman, woman!" said Charles, with a look of pain upon his generous face, and pointing towards Ellen—"can your heart be so bitter that not one reproach can rise when you behold her you so deeply wronged—so bitterly pursued—shield you from death?"

"It can," said Madge.

"Then heaven have mercy on you!" said Charles, turning away in utter disgust.

"Heaven!" exclaimed Madge, bitterly—"what is heaven to me? Psha!—talk not to me of heaven! I have defied it; and defy it still. In hell I have trusted, since that alone can give me vengeance."

"Woman!" he exclaimed—"have you no hope, no fear, of an hereafter?"

"None," she replied.

"Cannot the dread of punishment in the next world lead you to—"

"No," she interrupted, passionately. "What hereafter can have pangs like those I have endured? Boy, go prate to fools—not to me. I despise your warnings, as I despise your power. You hold it but for a time. Fate has decreed that vengeance shall be mine. When satiated, then may Wild Madge know rest. But never till then; never till the child of him whom I hate with all a woman's hatred has fallen as low as I have fallen; never till she has become a thing like to me—dead to every hope—lost to every feeling, degraded, scorned, reviled, despised. Never till then will the victim of man's perfidy rest content—never, never!"

"Woman, I have never wronged you," exclaimed Ellen.

"Liar!" shouted Madge.

"No—never, never!" gasped Ellen.

"Your mother did!" exclaimed Madge, her bleared eyes lighting up with a terrible light. "She is dead, and on her child I hurl my vengeance. Girl, you cannot escape it. I will hang on you like a shadow; sleeping or waking, I will still be thy curse—thy terror!"

"Shame!" said Charles — "shame, woman! Your crimes have brought you within the pale of the law, and justice will consign you to a fearful doom. You should seek mercy now—not vengeance—for your days are numbered, and death will rob your wicked soul of its revenge."

"Ha, ha!" laughed Madge again. "Wild Madge will not die unavenged. Her time has not yet come; will not come till the lovely girl by your side can take her place—become like me. Then, then, and not till then, has the career of Wild Madge, the fish-woman's daughter, ended. Fate has decreed it; and in fate I trust."

With a sad shake of the head, Charles grasped the arm of Ellen, and drew her towards the door, as the loud shouts of the Africans, telling of the capture of Lang, came to their ears.

"Come," he said—"fear not: I am captain here."

"Heaven be praised!" gasped Ellen. "But my father—seek him—save him!"

And, clinging to his arm, they hurried from the cabin, followed by the black.

CHAPTER CXXXVIII.

FATHER AND DAUGHTER—HOPE GLEAMS THROUGH THE CLOUDS—A WOMAN'S VENGEANCE—TIMELY RESCUE.

WITH a thousand wild emotions struggling within her breast, Ellen clung to the arm of her faithful lover.

With a thrill of joy in his heart, Charles Lawson pressed the hand of the girl on whom all his fond affections were centered, and led the way to the cabin in which her father was confined.

With a dissatisfied scowl upon his ebony features, Zoolooh, the African walked behind the two lovers, ever and anon casting a by no means pleasing look at the chafing and furious woman whose throat it would have afforded him no ordinary delight to have cut.

With foaming lips and bloodshot eyes, Wild Madge glared like an enraged tigress at bay, upon the retreating forms of her captive and her rescuers.

Scarce had they left the cabin than she fastened her teeth in the handkerchief which bound her wrists, and strove in mad fury to tear it asunder, bitterly cursing those who a few moments before had borne away the girl whom she had taken such pains to secure.

Her red and bloated face had become livid with rage, and her limbs trembled with the ungovernable passion which shook her soul.

Grasping the knot of the silken bond in her teeth, she tore at it till blood mingled with the froth upon her lips.

Meantime, Charles Lawson, and his companions gained the door of the cabin in which the poor girl's father was confined.

It was locked.

All endeavour to open it without violence proved futile.

Charles beckoned to the African, who stood calmly and respectfully behind them at a short distance, and pointed to the door.

The man nodded, and moved them aside.

Both Charles and Ellen drew back from before the door, and the black, summoning all his power flung his stout body against its panels.

It shook and creaked violently.

Again the African threw his whole weight upon it.

Crash went the woodwork, and the door was stove in by the force of the blow.

Alarmed by the noise, and fearing that some danger was about to overtake him, Mr. Hanfield sprang from the cot on which he had been lying and stood before the wreck.

"Father—father!" exclaimed Ellen, rushing towards him.

"My child—my child!" gasped the old man, holding forth his arms.

Ellen sprang towards him, and the next moment her head rested upon his breast.

"You here?" exclaimed Hanfield, as Charles presented himself before him.

"Yes, father, for such, in truth, I hope now to be able to call you. "Providence has answered my prayers, and by the aid of this noble African I have escaped from the hold of this ship where I have so long been kept prisoner. The crew have revolted against their miscreant officers, and I sincerely trust that now our dangers are over.

"God grant they may be so!" said the man. "But her—what of her?"

"Of whom do you speak?" asked Charles Lawson.

"Of whom?"

"Yes."

"Of her—that woman—that fiend!" exclaimed the old man.

"Wild Madge?"

"The same."

"She is bound in her cabin," replied Charles Lawson.

"Wretched woman!" said Hanfield. "Oh, my poor child! what, indeed, must you have suffered from that fearful and wicked being."

"Oh, father, much—much," exclaimed the poor girl.

"The old man sighed as he pressed her to his heart.

"Truly, my poor child," said the old man— "yours has been a hard life of late; your young heart has been scared and crushed by the wiles of this pitiless and inhuman woman. Heaven grant that your sufferings are now at an end, and that brighter days are dawning upon you."

"In your father's arms, dear Ellen,' exclaimed the young man—"I will now leave you, and return to the deck, where I hope to tread as captain till I have conveyed you to that proud land of freedom from which the cruel hands of the Boy Rover so ruthlessly torn you. Farewell, dear one, for a short time: fear not, that inhuman woman is powerless to harm you more, and you may rest in peace, for the shouts which came to my ears assure me that the vessel is in the hands of those who will stand or fall by us."

With an affectionate wave of the hand, the young man darted from the cabin, followed by the black.

Hope had once more dawned in the breasts of the captives.

Their hearts beat with wild emotions.

Their eyes met in looks of joy and gladness.

Their pale cheeks once more glowed with pleasure.

And the arms of the fair girl encircled the neck of her parent, as he strained her to his bosom.

"My father, my dear father," she murmured, as her fair head rested on his breast—"oh! how can I express the happiness I feel at once more standing by your side. The knowledge that you, too, were submitted to all the influence of that woman's wicked passions has rendered my own captivity doubly wretched."

"And the knowledge that you, my child, were here a prisoner has shaken this aged form till death had been a merciful relief to all my sufferings.

Oh! my Ellen, how grateful I am to Providence that I can once more clasp you in these arms, feel your heart beating against my own, and know that spite of the fearful sufferings you have undergone you are still the pure innocent being."

Ellen sighed.

"Oh! heaven, father, did you know the fearful ordeal to which I have been subjected."

"I do know," he replied, hastily. "My heart told me all when I heard into whose hands you had fallen."

"Alas, alas! I have been sorely, fearfully tried," he sighed.

"But heaven never deserts the innocent and true," said Hanfield, gazing lovingly into the depths of Ellen's eyes. "It has sent us succour; and hope once more glads my heart; for I shall see my child rescued from the power of those who have so wickedly sought her ruin."

"Brave Charles!" she murmured—"how nobly has he acted—how does he deserve my love!"

"He does, indeed!" said Hanfield; "and, as his bride, days of happiness will surely repay the weeks of suffering you have borne.'

Ellen nestled her head still closer to the old man's breast.

A blush overspread her cheeks.

A tremor of joy ran through her veins.

"He is a brave youth," said the old man, "and richly deserves the happiness which, I trust, is in store for him."

"It shall ever be the aim of my life to make him happy," said Ellen, "and to repay, by true and ardent love, the struggles he has made to rescue me from the ills which have surrounded me so terribly."

"Bravely, nobly, has he won his bride," said Hanfield.

"But never shall he possess her!" exclaimed a loud and passionate voice.

Hanfield and his daughter looked towards the cabin-door.

A cry escaped the lips of both father and daughter.

A thrill of horror pervaded their frames.

Their cheeks again became pale as marble.

Their limbs trembled, as these harsh tones met their ears.

They shrank back in terror.

They glanced in despair in the direction of that hated voice.

Wild Madge stood in the door-way of the cabin.

Her bleared eyes were fixed, with a hellish gleam, upon the father and child.

Her finger was pointed derisively at their forms.

Her bloated features glowed in triumph.

She had torn the kerchief from her wrists with her teeth.

She had seized the pair of pistols which she always kept loaded in her cabin.

She had strode through the open door, panting for revenge.

Believing her secure, neither had taken the precaution to close it, so as to keep her prisoner.

Bitterly did Ellen regret the want of foresight which left her at liberty to escape from the cabin did she release herself from her bonds.

But regret was now useless.

She was before them.

The woman most dreaded alike by her father and herself.

The sight of that furious form chilled the very blood in their veins.

The glance of that bloodshot eye appalled their very souls.

Surprise held them speechless.

The cup of happiness, dashed thus rudely from their lips, held them spell-bound and powerless.

They could but gaze upon her as she stood there, gloating like a demon in the misery she inflicted.

After a pause, the furious woman stepped over the threshold into the cabin.

"Ha, ha!" she laughed, triumphantly—"I told you that the vengeance of Wild Madge must be consummated Behold me—escaped from the hands which bound me!"

"What seek you here?" gasped Hanfield, tremulously.

"That which must come sooner or latter," replied Madge, casting a meaning glance upon the poor girl, who shrank back, and hid her face in her parent's breast.

"Revenge, Joseph Hanfield!" she exclaimed. "'Tis for that, that Wild Madge, the victim of your perfidy lives. 'Tis for that, and that alone, this hated form pants. You can never escape it."

"Begone, woman!" exclaimed the old man. "Already have you inflicted suffering enough upon myself and my poor innocent child."

"Enough! Ha, ha!" laughed Madge. "No, no—my revenge will never be satiated till the beautiful face which now nestles on your breast becomes seared and bloated as mine own. That slender form which your arms support must become like mine—repulsive—the mere semblance of woman. I was once fair and beautiful—loving, kind, pure, and innocent. But a blight fell upon me. The spoiler came; and his traitor kiss robbed me of all that woman holds dear. He sipped the sweets of the pure flower, and his breath poisoned it. Its beauty withered and decayed, till it lost all resemblance of what it had once been. Joseph Hanfield, can I ever forget that I was once a woman, beautiful, lovely, as she you now hold in your arms? Think you, I can ever blot from my memory the purity and innocence of my girlhood's days — ever turn my thoughts but with feelings of vengeance upon the happy hours long since passed away? Into that home of happiness and peace the serpent crawled. Its venomed tongue wooed me to its embrace; its poisoned sting sank deep into my soul; and the well-springs of a fond woman's heart were dried up for ever! Where all was happiness and peace, misery and despair sought and found a resting place; love turned to hatred—happiness to misery—joy to despair—and revenge took possession of that heart which beat with love and joy!"

"Madge—Madge!" gasped Hanfield, "in mercy hold."

"Ha! ha!" she laughed derisively. "Do you speak of mercy—you, who denied it to me? Had you been merciful when on my knees I craved it at your hands, I had been saved body and soul: but you refused my prayers, scoffed at my misery, spurned the girl who had sacrificed peace, happiness, honour, purity! all—all for you. And now you plead to me for mercy—to me, your victim—your curse! Then that mercy you denied to me, will I deny you. Though all hell stood forward to oppose—though the portals of death were open to receive me—though by that one act I could atone for all my crimes—win back salvation, by all the powers of heaven and earth I would still have my revenge—still triumph in the misery of him who inflicted misery on me!"

"Oh, woman — woman !" exclaimed Ellen, tearing herself from her father's arms, and flinging herself upon her knees at the feet of Madge. "Be merciful; forgive, and that one good act will shine in heaven, when the recording angel shall open the book of sin. That one good deed will counterbalance your many crimes: lost and degraded as you have become, there is still hope; spurn it not. Be generous, be kind, and heaven will reward the deed."

"As I defy him," she exclaimed, pointing to the pale and trembling Hanfield, "so do I defy heaven. To me it is nought : my soul plunged into depths beyond salvation, what more need I fear—nothing. In hell alone do I look for rest, for strength to help me to revenge. Girl, you plead in vain; the word is spoken—the die cast The child of him who spurned me must and shall fall. The man who made me what I am must yet feel the vengeance of his despised and outraged victim !"

Ellen rose from her knees, and returned to the side of her father.

"Heed her not," said Hanfield. "Poor thing, her sufferings have driven her mad ; let us rather pity than censure her."

"Pity," yelled Madge—"I scorn your pity now, though on my knees I have asked it ere this."

"Leave us," said Hanfield, waving his hand to the door ; "this vessel is no longer in the hands of those inhuman wretches who so long have trod its decks, and with their fall your power to harm me or my fair daughter is gone."

A scornful look curled the lips of the fury.

"Go to your cabin," continued Hanfield, "repent of your sins, and by atonement seek mercy of him whose laws you have so grossly outraged. Wickedly disposed as you are towards myself and my child' I will do all that man can do when the time comes to lighten the punishment which your crimes will bring down upon you."

The countenance of Madge became black as midnight.

Her bleared eyes shot forth a gleam of fire.

Her teeth were clenched savagely together.

She thrust her hand into the bosom of her dress and drawing a pistol therefrom, she exclaimed, savagely—

"Wild Madge asks nor receives no pity from you. My followers may be conquered by traitors, my ship borne a prize into port, and myself arraigned in a court of justice ; but never shall the lips of him who caused my ruin and spurned my love open in my defence. I ask not intercession at his hands nor will I accept it ; and never shall he live to see my fall. Joseph Hanfield, the woman who once madly loved, but now hates you repays you thus—die ! Thus does a despised and discarded woman avenge her fall !"

She levelled the pistol at his head.

"Oh—help ! mercy, mercy !" shrieked Ellen, flinging herself wildly upon her father's bosom ; "through me alone shall the fatal ball enter your heart."

"Ha, ha !" laughed Madge, gloating in triumph at the fear her acts produced—" away girl ; you are reserved for a more terrible fate. Traitor—villain—spoiler, die !"

She pulled the trigger.

But her arm was struck upwards by a fearful blow, and a shriek of pain escaped her lips, as the weapon dropped from her hand to the floor of the cabin, and mingled with the report of the discharged pistol.

One wild piercing cry of thankfulness escaped the lips of Ellen—one deep glance of gratitude she cast upon the tall powerful Zoolah who rushed towards her; then her eyes closed. and she fell, in a stupor on to the neck of her father.

CHAPTER CXXXIX.

A CRITICAL MOMENT—THE DETERMINATION TO STAND BY CHARLES—AGONY OF MIND.

WHEN Charles Lawson left the cabin of Mr. Hanfield, he proceeded to that of Lang, where he discovered that personage bound and lying on the floor beside Snipe, the British sailor, who had been prevailed upon to join them.

A loud shout arose from the throats of the triumphant blacks as he stepped over the threshold, and they pointed to the prostrate forms of their prisoners.

Charles looked upon them for a few moments, and then said, addressing Lang:

"As a British officer I shall do my duty to my flag, and bear you to England, to answer for the crimes you and your ruthless companions have been guilty of on the high seas."

"You be d——d!" roared Lang, furiously. "You are not yet master here, my fine fellow."

"Indeed!"

"No, indeed!" roared Lang. "Or, if you are, it won't be for long. The cussed niggers will see through you in no time, and, to escape the gallows, desert and hand you over to those they now rise against."

Charles shook his head.

"You fools!' roared the pirate, addressing the blacks—"ain't you got the sense to see through his views? He will have command of this ship by your mutiny, and will carry you all to England to be hung for piracy."

The blacks looked from one to another at these words.

Lang observed the movement, and perceived the doubt upon the face of the Africans.

He was not slow to take advantage of this.

"Look you," he said: "would you rather swing by your necks, or run the chances of falling in an engagement? Here, on board this ship, and under my command, you at least have a chance of escape from death; but where he will take you there is none. You have been pirates; and a pirate's doom is the rope. Fools!—are you mad, that you can thus listen to his persuasions, when his only object is to lure you on to your destruction?"

The blacks commenced to murmur.

Their faces grew thoughtful; and a misgiving took possession of his heart.

He saw the influence that the words of Lang had made upon them, and he hastened to avert it.

"My friends," he said, in a cool calm tone of voice, "pay no heed to this man whom you've made prisoner. What I have promised I will perform. Place your faith in me, and I will have the vessel's bows put towards your native shore, and land you on the coast of Africa. I am a British sailor, and the word I have pledged I will not break. Surely you cannot deem me so base as to reward your interest in my welfare in so dishonourable a manner! I have promised you escape to your native land, and, anxious as I am to convey others on board this bark to England, I will steer no other course but that to Africa. Doubt not my intentions towards you, but place implicit faith in my honour, and you will have no cause ever to say that Charles Lawson broke his word, or forfeited the honour of a British sailor!"

"Hurrah!" exclaimed Bill Snipe, struggling into a sitting position, and looking admiringly into the face of Charles. "I'll bet a can of grog he means what he says, and will keep his word. He's a real, right-down, genuine British tar you can see by the cut of his jib, and he'll never deceive a messmate as trusts to the protection of the Union Jack."

Both Lang and Charles gazed intently upon Bill Snipe, while he gave full vent to his sentiments.

Lang, with a savage scowl, ground his teeth in rage at every word.

Charles, on the contrary, only looked upon the form of the sailor half pitifully yet half admiringly.

"You d——d turncoat of a traitor," yelled Lang, grinding his teeth; "is this the way you turn upon us."

"I ain't no traitor," retorted Bill Snipe, "I am a British tar, or at least I was once, and demme if I can forget it either. If I have struck my colours and turned pirate, that's no reason why I shouldn't respect them as can show they are true to the old flag."

Charles cast upon him a look of kindness, as he remarked—

"I did not think that a British sailor would shed so much dishonour upon the old flag, as giving way to the persuasions of the pirates; but, though I must condemn the guilty act, there is some extenuation of the crime in the words you now utter."

"He's a snivelling cur!" exclaimed Lang, savagely.

"You're a liar!" retorted Snipe; "and sink me, if my hands were free now, if I wouldn't show that all the courage of a British seaman ain't left me neither. I know I said I'd join you; an' I know I am a traitor to my flag; an' I only wish my tongue had been blistered afore I consented."

"Yes, now the tables are turned," said Lang. "Were I captain of this bark again, you'd swear you didn't care a can of grog for the Union Jack."

"It's a lie!" retorted Snipe; "and, cuss me, captain, or no captain, I tell you I'd see the plank got ready for me afore I'd turn pirate—there!"

"Look you," said Lang—"you ain't such fools, I know, as to put your lives in danger. I've been a good captain, and dealt fairly by you all. Will you desert me now, and be carried to a prison, to answer for your work under my command? Down with him, and return to your duty; and, if you have any cause of complaint, it shall be heard and altered. Obey me, and you not only make a fortune, but save your lives. Obey him, and you rush upon certain destruction. The blacks still looked questioningly into each other's face.

They hesitated how to act.

Could Charles only be going to hand them over to justice, under pretence of carrying them to their native shores?

Was this but a subterfuge?

True, they had called upon him to become cap-

captain, and take command of the ship and crew. But might they not be worse if under his rule than that of the pirate?

The youth evidently abhorred piracy.

He deemed it a crime which called for the greatest punishment.

What, then, could they think?

Their features grew gloomy.

They cast suspicious glances upon the young man whose aid they had sought to release them from the command of one whom they had learned to hate.

Charles saw all this in a moment.

A chill struck upon his heart.

"Will they desert me," he thought, "and leave me and Ellen, and her father, to their vengeance?"

This must not be.

The hopes they had engendered in his heart must not be dashed away now.

He must appeal to them.

But how?

He remembered that their dissatisfaction was caused by the murder of their countryman.

It was revenge they sought for his death.

It was not pity for his sufferings, or the wish to do an act of justice and humanity, that prompted them to set him free.

He turned to the dissatisfied blacks.

"Hear me," he said. "It was not me who sought you; it was you who sought me; and will you now basely turn and leave me, and those I hold dear, to the mercy of this man—him who slew your countryman in cold blood, and who to-morrow would not hesitate to send a bullet through your heads did you complain of any injustice or hardship? Will you trust him who has already proved that his only argument is the pistol or the sword; and who, when he is tired of the wicked life he leads, will seize all the plunder, and laugh you to scorn for the assistance you have given in procuring it? I tell you, upon the honour of a sailor and a British officer, that I will land you upon your native shores—restore you to the homes from which you have been so cruelly torn. He will not do this. When glutted with the spoils of helpless vessels, he will find a means to secure all the booty for himself and his white companions, and reward your fidelity by death. Aye, by death; for, living, you would be witnesses against him: and this he would not permit. I, who am not a pirate, have not this to fear; therefore, can have no wish to ensure your silence. I have said that my first object shall be to restore you to your native land. Trust in me—aid me to stay the career of this ruthless man, and thereby avenge the murder of your comrade. Stay by me now, and you have the word of a British sailor that no harm shall come to you; but, on the contrary, that escape from all pursuit, and restoration to your own homes, shall be the reward of you all."

"Stick to him, my hearties!" exclaimed Bill Snipe. "If you listen to any more of Lang's palaver you are greater fools than I believe you to be. The youth speaks fair; and, if your brains ain't as soft as your skull is hard, you'll hold on with him, and secure your lives and your liberties. This game can't last for ever. Old England will soon have ships enough to scour the seas in search of you; and, if you are taken under the black flag, you'll dance a hornpipe in the air at the yard-arm—you will, as sure as that's baccy!"

And, to give greater emphasis to his words, Bill Snipe spat out a used-up quid of tobacco from his mouth, at the feet of Zoolah.

"We will—we will!" shouted the blacks.

Lang tried to persuade them from their decision, but they would not listen to him, and were about to follow Charles to the deck, when Lang called out, loudly:

"Smith! Bond!"

Charles paused, and turned to the blacks.

"Where are the men on whom he calls?" he asked, hurriedly.

"Here," said Zoolah, pointing to the doors of the cabins occupied a short time previously by the pirates.

"Secure them, but harm them not," said Charles.

The blacks divided into two companies, and entered the cabins.

In an instant they rushed out with the intelligence that the men they sought were not in their berths.

"Alarmed, they have doubtless hid themselves," said Charles; "seek them out and secure them, but offer no violence."

The men nodded.

"We will ascend to the deck, and proclaim to the crew that their late captain is a prisoner, and that the vessel's bows are turned towards home."

He placed his foot upon the ladder.

He paused.

The sound of an angry voice came to his ears.

A sound which caused a shudder of fear to run through his frame.

It was the tones of Wild Madge.

But they proceeded from the cabin where he had left Ellen and her father.

In an instant the truth flashed across the young man's mind.

She had released herself from her bonds.

She had quitted the cabin in which he had left her, and sought that of old Mr. Hanfield.

He turned to make his way to the cabin, when the last words of Madge struck with terrible force upon his ears.

"Stand aside," he exclaimed hurriedly to the Africans who stood behind him.

The blacks parted to give him access, but Zoolah, who had likewise heard the voice of Madge, and who now stood behind the other blacks, made a rush towards the cabin.

With a loud cry of horror Charles heard the report of the pistol ere he could reach the door, and his heart almost ceased to beat.

But when he entered the cabin he saw Zoolah standing near the fierce woman in an attitude of anger, and perceived that Ellen lie senseless in the arms of her father.

His first impression was that the fury had killed her, and he sprang upon her with a cry like that of a wounded tiger.

But the recollection that she was a woman held his arm uplifted in the air.

"I saved her!" exclaimed Zoolah—"I saved her!"

"Thank God!" gasped Charles, and his arm fell almost powerless to his side."

CHAPTER CXL.

THE FOILED WOMAN—CHARLES AND HIS FOLLOWERS VICTORIOUS.

FOR a few moments Charles stood gazing, like one in a dream, first upon Wild Madge, and then upon Ellen and her father.

It was not until he raised the drooping head of the poor girl, and gazed into her pale face, that he could realise the truth that she had escaped the shot he fully believed to have been intended for her.

In a few moments, however, Ellen recovered; and Mr. Hanfield, after his terror had subsided, explained that the shot was intended for him, and not for his daughter; and he was profuse in his expressions of gratitude to Zoolah for his timely aid.

Wild Madge, after the first burst of passion at the ill-success of her plan, took the other weapon from her breast, where it lie concealed; but, ere she could level it, Zoolah had wrested it from her, nearly dislocating her wrist by the fearful twist he gave it in so doing.

Baulked in her evil intention, the furious woman now goaded almost to madness, sprang forward towards the old man, with the intention of inflicting her wrath upon him.

But Zoolah, handing the weapon which he had torn from her to one of his comrades, seized her roughly round the waist, and held her forcibly back.

She struggled hard to escape from him; but, violent as were her endeavour, she could not—for Zoolah held her with a grasp of iron.

Several times she strove to fix her teeth in his arms; but the black jerked up hard each time, and inflicted a blow upon her mouth.

Finding all her endeavours fruitless, she at length desisted, and stood glaring like a demon upon all assembled.

"Secure her now," said Charles, and be sure you leave her no chance to break her bonds."

In a few moments the arms of the fury were securely and not over tenderly bound behind her.

Chafing with rage, the blacks who performed this operation found it no easy operation; for she plunged and kicked at them all the time.

At length, however, she was secured, and the operators looked to Charles for orders what to do with her.

"Shall we fling her overboard?" asked one.

"Shoot her," said another.

"Cut her throat," said Zoolah.

"No, no," said Charles: "take her to the cabin from which she has escaped, and secure the door so that she will be unable to leave it.

The blacks led her away to the cabin, and made the door secure.

With a look of thankfulness, Charles turned to Ellen and her father.

"I had feared," he said, "that you were wounded, or, worse, killed."

"No," said Hanfield — "thanks to the black who struck up the arm of the would-be-murderer."

"Oh, that we were far from her!" said Ellen. "Her words—her threats—her acts appal me."

"She is powerless now to harm you, dear one," said the young man; "and I will take good care that she does not escape from her confinement again."

"Heaven grant she may not," said Ellen, with a sigh.

"Amen to that," said Hanfield. "Oh, that woman can become so base, so degraded, as to lose all semblance of woman!"

"She is indeed a monster, in the form of all that should be good and lovely," said Henry. "But do not heed her now. I will have a guard placed over her, till such time as I can place her on board some vessel, to be conveyed to justice."

Hanfield sighed, but spoke not.

He could not but feel a qualm of self-reproach for the injury he had done her in days gone by.

He could not but acknowledge that his youthful indiscretions had tended greatly to dry up the milk of human kindness in her heart; and bitterly did he feel the injury he had done her.

Waiting a few moments to soothe and console the girl, he turned once more to leave the cabin.

"I will come to you again, ere long," he said, as he passed through the door.

He mounted the stairs, followed by the blacks, and stood upon the deck.

As he did so, the voice of Bond rang through the ship.

"Mutineers," he exclaimed, "this gun is loaded to the muzzle; "and, if you do not instantly retire to your births I will blow you all to h—l."

As these words fell upon their ears, the blacks slunk back, and Charles was left standing alone.

For a moment the young man's presence of mind deserted him; but it was for a moment only, when, turning to the awed Africans, he exclaimed:

"What do you fear?"

"The gun," exclaimed several voices.

"Advance, and cut them down," he exclaimed, in a loud tone of voice: "follow me!"

"Back!" exclaimed Bond, "or I sweep the decks."

Seizing a sword from one of the blacks, Charles waved it above his head.

"Follow!" he exclaimed.

"And rush upon your death!" exclaimed Bond,

still holding the match dangerously near to the touch-hole of the fearful weapon.

Zoolah dropped noiselessly on the deck, and, crawling along beside and under the shadow of the bulwarks, made his way, like a snake, towards the centre of the deck, on which the gun was placed.

Not a sound did he make; but, drawing himself along on his belly, he gradually neared the gun.

No one perceived the action — not even Charles, who anxiously cast quick and hurried glances around all sides.

The blacks still hesitated.

The fearful weapon of destruction awed them.

They dared not move, lest they met the fearful shower of lead which they believed would issue from its gaping mouth.

Charles was in agony.

Had success attended them so far, that now all his hopes were to be dashed to the ground?

The glimmer of the match over the gun told him that to rush forward was to tempt a certain doom.

But delay was also destruction.

He hesitated.

He strove to conjure up some idea to turn the man's attention, and thereby enable him to dash upon and deprive him of the match.

But he could devise none.

As he stood thinking how best to act, he perceived that the man at the gun was not alone.

He saw another figure beside him, with its arm extended downwards.

As he strained his eyes through the darkness, he discovered that the extended arm had grasped a pistol, and that it was presented at a small cask.

In an instant the truth flashed upon him.

His heart sank again.

Though he had numbers at his back, and his opponents were but two, yet the odds against him were fearful.

Besides, the blacks had such a terror of the cannon.

They had seen it belch forth its smoke and flame, and send its messages of death with such unerring certainty upon the decks of those ill-fated vessels with which they had come in contact; and had gazed with surprise upon the terrible execution which it did.

Once more Charles strove to urge them to follow him.

"One dash forward," he said, "and the vessel is ours."

Still the blacks could not be induced to move.

In utter despair, the young man cast one look towards the gun, and exclaimed:

"Then I will go alone!"

And he sprang forward, his weapon raised above his head.

Dark as it was, Bond, whose eyes had become accustomed to the gloom, saw the movement, and he lowered the match.

But the smouldering match fell not upon the powder.

It rested upon the black head of Zoolah.

It burned into the skin; but the African uttered no cry of pain.

He had glided on till he had passed the gun, then risen to his feet, and placed his head over the touch-hole.

It was a brave deed, and well executed.

Finding that it did not instantly explode, Bond struck the match against the side of the gun, to clear away the white embers from its end; but, before he could again place it to the spot, it was torn from his grasp, and a hand clutched his throat.

So quick was the movement—so sudden the cry—that Smith turned his head.

That moment was fatal to him; for Charles, who, finding the blacks would not follow, had rushed on alone, brought his cutlass down with fearful force upon the head of the pirate.

The pistol fell from his hands to the deck, and, as the youth again raised his weapon, the pirate fell beside it.

One bound, and Charles, with his raised weapon, stood before Bond, ere he saw that the black had him securely by the throat, and that the match lay burning slowly at his feet.

But he saw it all ere he struck the intended blow, and he lowered the gleaming steel.

"I got him him tight," said Zoolah. "Just put your foot on the match."

Charles ground the match beneath his feet, as, with his disengaged hand, he seized Bond by the collar, lest he should break away from the black. Then, raising his voice, he exclaimed:

"The ship is ours!"

A loud cry of joy broke from the lips of the blacks, and they sprang forward to the side of Charles and the brave Zoolah.

CHAPTER CXLI.

HENRY'S RECEPTION AND TREATMENT ON BOARD THE 'DIAMOND'—THE CAPTAIN'S PRESCRIPTION AND ITS EFFECTS

THE fearful race for life was over, and Henry Chambers sank back, with a prayer of thankfulness on his lips, and a feeling of gratitude in his heart, into the bottom of the boat, which the strong arms of the sailors had propelled, with swift and powerful strokes, over the bosom of the waves to his rescue.

As though goaded to fury by the loss of his prey, the shark bolted the shoe which he had torn from the foot of the youth, and lashed the waters with his tail till they were encrusted with a thick white foam. Then down, down, he dived into the bosom of the sea, and was lost to the view of those who had robbed him of his almost certain repast.

Panting and breathless, the young man lay gazing first at the commiserating features of those who had rescued him from the threatened doom; and then upon the blue clouds, so calm, so serene, high up above the waste of waters on which the ark of refuge was tossed.

Not a question was asked him by the bronzed-featured seamen, save by the glances which they cast upon his haggard face.

They saw that he was too weak from the exertions he had made to escape the fangs of the shark; and they forbore to appease their curiosity by entailing on him a momentary pang, which even an answer to a question might cause him in his present exhausted and powerless state.

Once more the waters the little boat, with its crew of brave-hearted seamen, danced like a thing of life, leaping over every wave, as if in glee at the life it had saved: then bending its bows to kiss the white spray, as it careered towards it; or dived in sportive play beneath the sparkling shower whose cool refreshing drops fell upon the warm features of her devoted crew.

The vessel had reefed her sails, and put back to meet the boat; and every instant the hull loomed larger and clearer before the eyes of the rescued youth.

Little did he expect ever again to tread the deck of a ship.

The close proximity of that terrible monster had left but little room for hope.

He shuddered now that he lay powerless in the bottom of the boat, as, in his mind's eye, he reviewed the fearful chase; and could scarcely realise the truth that the dreaded monster was now powerless to harm him.

That despair which had lent him courage had now left him weak and powerless; and, though he doubtless would have struggled on had not the boat reached his side, his energies were now gone, and he lay like a helpless babe in its cradle.

A long pull, a strong pull, and a pull altogether, soon brought the boat alongside the ship.

The oars were tilted from their rollocks; and one of the seamen, catching hold of a rope flung over the side, steadied the boat whilst Henry was lifted on board the 'Diamond' by the willing hands of her crew.

A thousand questions, and as many anxious glances, were heaped upon him the instant he was lifted on the deck.

But no reply was vouchsafed by the youth, who, in truth, found it impossible to make any to the numerous inquiries.

"Avaunt there!" exclaimed a young man, waving his hand to the seamen who crowded around the rescued youth. "Sheer off, will you, and let him have air!"

The men fell back at the tones of his voice; and the alacrity with which the order was obeyed told Henry that the speaker held command on board that vessel.

It was the mate who had spoken—a tall handsome man, whose appearance denoted him every inch a sailor, and whose laughing face proclaimed him to be of a kindly disposition.

"The lubbers are like a set of old women on a washing day," he said, addressing Henry: "but I'll learn them better manners than merely to stifle a half-dead man. Here, let me take you by the arm; you are very weak and ill. A bath in the sea will strengthen a man's limbs; but an immersion such as you have had takes all the power out of them."

"It does indeed," answered Henry.

"There, don't talk—you are too weak," said the mate, throwing one arm around the youth's shoulders to support him. "Here's the captain."

At this moment a tall, firmly-built, bronzed-featured man, about fifty years of age, made his way to his side, and looking hard at Henry, who, with some difficulty saluted him.

Happy to have been the means of rescuing you from death, sir. Have you been long in the water? Shipwrecked, I suppose. I see you are an Englishman. What vessel did you sail in? Has she gone to pieces? But there—don't answer: you are too much exhausted. Mr. Hart, see that he be well cared for. Give him a good stiff glass of grog Don't mind what the surgeon says: he is a regular old woman. Nothing like a good stiff glass of grog for a case like his."

"I will see to it, sir," he replied, with a smile—"I will take him to my berth."

"Do so, Mr. Hart," said the captain. "You know I would punish drunkenness severely; but grog, sir, in a case like this, is a necessity: and I don't care what the doctors say. Physic is all very well in its way; but grog is the only thing to do a drowned man any good."

"It is certainly the most palatable medicine," said the mate.

"To be sure it is," replied the captain, who was not at all addicted to drunkenness, though it was asserted by a few on board that he would bear up against a very great quantity, and was somewhat partial to a rather extraordinary number of glasses—stiff and strong to boot. But, be that as it may, Captain Penny was never seen the worse for it.

"Let me help you down to my berth," said the mate, "and get these wet togs off you. A glass of the captain's medicine, and a quiet snooze, will soon put you all to rights, and bring back the colour to your cheeks, and the strength to your limbs."

"And don't worry him too much," said the captain.

"All right, sir," said the mate. "We will wait till he is well again before we run over the log. Can you walk, or shall I carry you down?"

"If you will allow me to lean upon you," said Henry, "I can walk."

"Hurrah!" said the mate. "Bear on as much as you like, my hearty. There—don't mind how you lay to: I can bear it."

And the generous-hearted fellow more than half-carried Henry down to his berth.

"Now let us get the wet togs off," said Hart, proceeding to undress the young man as he spoke.

In a short time the wet garments were removed.

"Now turn in," said Hart, lifting him into his own cot, "and I'll bring you the grog in an instant."

But, before the youth was snugly ensconced in the mate's berth, the cabin-boy entered, bearing in his hand a large tumbler, filled to the brim with rum-and-water.

"Captain's sent the medicine, sir," he said, while a broad grin played over his features. "It's jolly strong."

"He knows how to make grog," said the mate, taking the tumbler from the boy's hand.

"Just does, sir," replied the boy. "He puts in more rum than he does water; because water, he says, spoils the taste of the spirit."

The mate handed the tumbler to Henry; he placed it to his lips.

The first mouthful verified the boy's assertion; for the grog was so strong he could scarcely drink it; and the mate would persist in his swallowing every drop in the tumbler.

With several gasps for breath, Henry succeeded in emptying the tumbler of its contents; and, with a long sigh, he dropped back upon the pillow.

"Close the scuppers," said the mate, "and, after a good snooze, you'll be all right. Don't speak—but go to sleep; and, when you wake up, we'll run over the log, and learn all that has happened to you."

Henry did close his eyes, and in a few moments was fast asleep.

The sun rode high in the heavens on the following day when Henry awoke.

The exertions he had undergone, the utter prostration of body from which he had suffered, and the soothing qualities of the grog which the captain's own hands had mixed for him, had all tended to steep his senses in forgetfulness for no less a space than twenty-five hours.

But rest and quiet had worked wonders.

His limbs were somewhat stiff; and in one or two parts of his body, where he had bruised the flesh in struggling to get into the boat, there was a sense of pain: but otherwise his robust constitution had suffered little.

In fact, he was as well as he could possibly hope to be, and much better than anyone expected to find him.

He tumbled up, and looked about for his clothes, which he soon found lying on the chest of the mate, thoroughly dried; and he commenced to dress himself, resolving to seek the captain, and thank him.

But whilst attiring himself, the door of the cabin was softly pushed open, and the mate entered.

"Hilloa!" he exclaimed, as looking toward the cot he perceived Henry nearly dressed. "Woke up at last. I'm blest if I didn't begin to think you never meant to open your daylights any more."

"Have I slept long?" asked Henry.

"Well, only about five and twenty hours," was the reply.

Henry opened his eyes to their utmost width, and gazed incredulously into the face of the mate.

"Five and twenty hours," he said, at length.

"Quite that, if not more."

"Surely you mistake."

"No, I don't. All day yesterday—all night, right up to now. Something like that number I think," said the mate. "You look all the better for your snooze though, and a good deal more like a living man than a corpse, as you did yesterday. I declare I expected that shark you so narrowly escaped, wouldn't be disappointed of his meal after all, for I began to think you never intended to wake up any more till doomsday."

"I have indeed slept long," said Henry.

"It was the captain's medicine as caused you to do so, I reckon," said Hart, "and, upon my soul I believe you could not have had nothing better. You only wanted rest, and something to keep you from catching cold, and I hope it has done all that for you."

"I think it has, for I feel quite strong, and was about to seek the captain, and thank him both for his aid and medicine."

"Bye and bye will do for that," said Hart. "You must not exert yourself too much at present. Sit down on my chest, and I'll bring you another glass of grog, and then if you feel strong enough, I should like to hear how you came into the pickle from which our crew were fortunate to rescue you."

Henry consented, and the grog having been procured, he narrated all that had happened since the wreck of the 'Swallow,' in which he had been so kindly treated by Captain Penny.

"A sailor's life is full of danger," said the mate, after listening attentively to Henry's recital. "But Providence is kind, and if we place our faith in Him He will save us. Too well do I know the fearful sufferings you must have endured, having myself been wrecked. If it will not tire you, I will give you an account of the wreck of the 'Golden Eagle,' and the sufferings of her crew."

CHAPTER CXLII.

THE WRECK OF THE GOLDEN EAGLE, AND SUFFER-INGS OF THE CREW—A STRANGE DISCOVERY.

SAILORS always find a charm in the recital of ad-ventures, through which in the ordinary course of their pursuits many have to pass, and all are liable to.

It was the same with Henry, as with others of his profession, and he willingly sat himself down to listen to the recital of the mate's adventure, which, unlike most yarns, was a true story, and one which at the time of its occurrence, made a deep impression upon the minds of the public, who, are pretty sure to hear of the awful calami-ties which befall the wanderers of the main.

"Well, you see," commenced Hart, "I was but a young hand at the sea, it being my second voyage, when I sailed in the sloop 'Golden Eagle' from New York, bound for Fayal, one of the Azore Islands, in the Atlantic Ocean.

It was in the August of 1765, when the anchor was run up to her bows, and her white sails ex-panded to the gentle breeze, and with light hearts we bid adieu to the shores of America.

The crew consisted of a captain's mate, five seamen and myself, and the cargo was timber and beeswax, and a negro slave.

The tight little bark arrived in safety at the place of our destination, and in the latter part of October, we departed on our return to New York, with a mixed cargo, and still carrying with us the nigger, who remained unsold.

For some few days we experienced fine weather and favouring gales, and expected to make a more than usually quick passage home.

'But there is many a slip 'twixt the cup and the lip'—as that shark you doubled on could prove, and, it was not long before we discovered how fallacious were our hopes.

It began to blow a dreadful storm.

One after the other the sails were carried away by the hurricane, and the vessel was unable to make anything but little headway in the dis-mantled condition in which she soon was.

To make matters worse, the bark showed signs of having sprung a leak, and the water in the hold had to be removed by pumping.

For an entire month, until the 1st of December, the crew of the 'Golden Eagle' did their best to keep the vessel on its course; but at the end of that time they had made but little progress.

And now a new and still more dreadful cala-mity presented itself.

The time already spent on the voyage had con-sumed the stock of provisions on board, excepting bread and water, of which a small quantity only was left.

The cargo of wine and brandy also remained; but these could be of little benefit, from the want of substantial food on board.

In this distressing state of affairs we came to a daily allowance of a quarter of a pound of bread, with a quart of water and a pint of wine, for each man.

Every day from the first of December our con-dition grew worse.

The ship was now become very leaky, the waves were swelled into huge rough billows by the storm, and the thunder rolled almost inces-santly over our heads, in those loud peals which are common to hurricanes within the tropics.

In this frightful conjuncture, either of sinking with the wreck or floating on it till we perished with hunger, we fell in with two vessels; but, to our unspeakable distress, the weather was so bad that there could be no communication between the ships.

We, therefore, with sensations probably more bitter than death itself, saw the vessels that would willingly have relieved us gradually disappear on the distant and tempestuous horizon.

It was now thought necessary that the allow-ance of bread and water to each man, however scanty, should be further contracted.

All consented to a regulation of which all saw the necessity.

The allowance was lessened by degrees, till every morsel of food was exhausted, and only about two gallons of dirty water remained at the bottom of a cask.

Both from respect for the captain, and from his being in a state of severe illness, the dregs of the water were abandoned to him in his cabin, where he lay in a species of rheumatic fever.

The remainder of the persons on board, includ-ing the negro, had now no other means of suste-nance than the wine and brandy in the hold.

These were consequently seized upon; and, in desperation, the crew drank of both, till the frenzy of hunger was increased by drunkenness, and exclamations of distress were blended with impious howls and imprecations.

In the midst of these horrors—this complication of want and excess, of distraction and despair—we espied another sail.

Every eye was instantly turned towards it, and immovably fixed upon it. Every one broke out into extacies of joy and devotion.

Devotion among such people, and in such cir-cumstances, naturally deviated into superstition.

Some of the company observed that it was Christmas-day, and seemed to think that the season had an influence on their approaching de-liverance, and was appropriated to their temporal as well as spiritual salvation.

A proper signal of distress was hung out, and, about eleven o'clock in the forenoon, we had the unspeakable satisfaction of being near enough to the ship to communicate our situation.

The captain of the strange ship promised us such relief as was in his power, which he said ex-tended only to some bread, being himself con-tracted in every other article.

This bread, however, he delayed with the most unpromising insensibility to bestow, upon the pretence that he was making an observation which it was necessary to finish.

The poor famished wretches, therefore, waited an hour in the most anxious suspense, yet in per-fect confidence of supply.

Our captain, being quite exhausted with hunger, fatigue, and infirmity—finding his eyes fail him, and having a severe rheumatism in his knees—went down to rest himself in the cabin.

He expected every moment to hear that the promised biscuit was coming on board. But he had not waited a quarter of an hour before his people came running down with looks of unutter-able despair, and told him, in accents scarcely in-telligible, that the vessel was making away as fast as she could, without affording them even the little relief she had promised.

At this terrible intelligence the captain crawled upon deck, and found it was true.

The wretch who commanded the vessel had even crowded more sail than he had spread before, and in less than five hours was out of sight.

As long as the poor creatures whom he had deserted to distraction and famine could retain the least trace of him, they hung about the shrouds, and ran from one part of the ship to the other, with frantic gestures and ghastly looks, to collect more visible signs of distress.

They pierced the air with their cries while they could be heard, and implored assistance with still louder lamentations as the distance between them increased.

But the vessel, under the direction of inexorable inhumanity, pursued its course, and no further notice was taken of our distress.

The crew, once more deserted, and cut off from their last hope, were still prompted by an instinctive love of life to preserve it as long as its preservation was possible.

The only living creatures on board the vessel besides ourselves, were two pigeons and a cat.

The pigeons were killed immediately, and divided among us for our Christmas dinner.

The next day we killed our cat, and as there were eight to partake of the repast, they divided her into eight parts, of which they disposed by lot.

It would naturally be supposed by those who have suffered only such distresses as is common to man, that anxiety, terror, anguish, and indignation, all the passions that upon such a desertion could have contended in the breast, would have taken away, at least, that appetite which makes food pleasing, even while nature was sinking for want of sustenance; yet Captain Harrison declares that the head of our poor cat having fallen to his share, he never ate anything that he thought so delicious in his life.

The next day our people began to scrape the ship's bottom for barnacles, but the waves had beaten off most of those above water, and our men were too weak to hang long over the ship's side.

During all this time the poor wretches were drunk, and a sense of their condition seemed to evaporate in execration and blasphemy.

While they were continually heaving wine in the steerage, the captain subsisted on the dirty water at the bottom of the cask, half a pint of which, with a few drops of Turlington's balsam, was his whole subsistence for four-and-twenty hours.

In this condition he waited for death, the approach of which, he said, he could have contemplated without much emotion, if it had not been for the difficulties in which he should have left his wife and children.

He still flattered himself, at intervals, with some random hope that another vessel might come within sight of us, and take us on board; but the time allotted for the experiment was apparently short, as well because we had nothing to eat, as because the ship was very leaky, and the men were too feeble, and, indeed, too drunk, to keep the water under, by working the pumps.

We suffered another aggravation of their calamity.

As the men had devoured every eatable on board, we had neither candle nor oil; and, it being the depth of winter, when we had not perfect daylight eight hours in the four-and-twenty, we passed the other sixteen in total darkness, except the glimmering light of our fire.

Still, however, by the help of our only sail, we made a little way; but on the 28th of December another storm overtook us, which blew our only sail into rags, and carried us all overboard.

The vessel now lay quite like a wreck in the water, and was wholly at the mercy of winds and waves.

How we subsisted from this time till the 13th of January, sixteen days, it is hard to say.

The biscuit had been long exhausted; the last bit of meat which was tasted, was the cat, on the 26th of December; all the candle-fat and oil were devoured before the 28th; and we could procure no barnacles from the ship's side; yet on the 13th of January we were all alive; and the mate, at the head of the people, went in the evening to the captain in his cabin, half drunk, indeed, but with sufficient sensibility to express the horror of their purpose in their countenances.

They said they could hold out no longer; that their tobacco was exhausted; that they had eaten up all the leather belonging to the pump, and even the buttons from their jackets; and that now they had no means of preventing their perishing together, but casting lots which of them should die for sustenance of the rest; they therefore hoped he would concur in the measure, and desired he would favour them with his determination immediately.

The captain, perceiving they were in liquor, endeavoured to soothe them from their purpose as well as he could; desired they would endeavour to get some sleep; and said, that if Providence did not interpose in their favour, he would consult further on the subject the next morning.

This mild attempt to divert them from their design only rendered them outrageous; and they swore, with execrations of peculiar horror, that what was to be done, must be done immediately; that it was indifferent to them whether he acquiesced or dissented; and that, though they had paid him the compliment of acquainting him with their resolution, they would compel him to take his chance with the rest; for general misfortune, they said, put an end to personal distinction.

The captain not being in a condition to resist, told them they must do as they pleased, but that he would on no account give orders for the death of the person on whom the lot might fall, nor partake of so horrid a repast.

Upon this they left him abruptly, and went into the steerage; but in a few minutes came back, and told him that they had taken a chance for their lives, and that the lot had fallen on the negro, who was part of the cargo.

The little time taken to cast the lot, and the private manner taken of conducting the decision, gave the captain strong suspicions that they had not dealt fairly by the victim.

The poor fellow, however, knowing what had been determined against him, and seeing one of the crew loading a pistol to despatch him, ran to the captain, begging that he would endeavour to save his life.

But the captain could only regret his want of power to protect him; and the next moment the poor wretch was dragged into the steerage, where he was almost immediately shot through the head.

Then a large fire was made, and the crew began to cut him up almost as soon as he was dead.

One of the ringleaders, whose name was Collins, was so ravenously impatient for food, that he tore the liver out of the body, and devoured it raw, although there was a fire at his side, where it might have been cooked in a very few minutes.

The men were busy enjoying their horrid feast the best part of the night—it being nearly morning before they retired.

On the next day the mate went to the captain to ask him about pickling the body.

But this the captain considered an instance of the greatest brutality, and was so much shocked at it, that he took up a pistol, and declared, in his turn, that he would send the mate after the nigger if he did not instantly leave the cabin.

It is a great pity that he did not make the same effort to save the poor nigger's life that he did to prevent the pickling of his body.

The best thing he could have done, when he was dead, was to give such orders as might make the food, so dearly obtained, go as far as possible; so that it might be longer before hunger again urged them to the same horrid necessity to commit another murder.

The man was dead, and to pickle the body seems to me the best thing that could have been done with that view.

As the captain, however, refused to give his advice, the crew took care of their provisions without him; and, having all consulted together, they cut the body into small pieces, and pickled it after, throwing the head and fingers overboard.

How the captain managed to subsist for about three weeks has often been, and is now, a puzzle to me: but as it is certain that total abstinence would have killed him, I suppose the dirty water and drops kept him alive.

Three days after the death of the nigger, the man who had devoured the raw liver of the African, died raving mad.

This was imputed to his impatient voracity, and as the hunger of the men was now kept down, and there was still some food in store, they were more under the government of reason, and more impressed by the apprehension of danger, yet nearer than that of perishing for wan of food.

Dreading therefore the consequence of eating the madman's body, they threw it overboard, although it was with great reluctance that they did so.

On the next day as they were preparing for dinner, by frying or boiling some of the body, one of the crew wished to offer the captain some of the meat, and another was despatched to the cabin to offer him a steak.

This offer, which, though prompted by a good feeling towards him, was rejected by the captain, who shuddered as much as did myself, at the idea of dining off a human body."

"Then you did not partake of the black," said Henry.

"Ugh! no!" replied Hart, with a shudder, "though heaven knows the pangs of hunger were fast consuming me."

"How then did you survive?"

"I will tell you. Being the youngest hand on board, I often performed the duties of cabin boy, and on one occasion, the captain ordered me to throw overboard a bag of rice, which had become damaged. This I neglected to do, and when our provisions were exhausted, I thought of the rice, and hid it away in the hold, whither I repaired at intervals to satisfy the cravings of hunger."

"But how did your messmates take your refusal to eat of the body—did they not suspect—"

"I took my share with the rest," interrupted the mate, "but never ate it. I watched my opportunity, and threw it overboard, though it could but have been the horror of eating of a human body, for the rice was so damaged that it smelled awful, and was full of maggots.

Well, the negroe's carcase was husbanded with severe economy.

It lasted the crew, now consisting of six persons, nearly a fortnight, when they were again reduced to total abstinence, except their wine. This they endured for three days, and then the mate went again to the captain at the head of the people, and told him that the negro's body having been totally consumed some days, and no sail having been sighted, it had again became necessary that they should cast lots a second time.

He said that it was better to die separately than all at once; as some might possibly survive by the expedient he proposed till some passing vessel might fall in with and rescue them from their awful sufferings.

Again the captain endeavoured to reason them out of their purpose—but without avail; and, considering it more than likely, it the lot was managed without him, he might not have fair play, he consented to manage it himself.

He, therefore, called them all into his own cabin, where he was in bed; and, having with much difficulty raised himself up, he caused the lots to be drawn in the same manner that is usual with lottery tickets.

The lot fell upon a foremast man, named Flat; and the shock of the decision was so great that the whole company remained motionless and silent for some time; and, probably, would have done so much longer if the poor wretch himself, who seemed perfectly resigned, had not expressed himself ready to die.

He only asked a short time to prepare himself for the doom, and requested that the man who had shot the black should perform the same office for himself.

His request was immediately granted; for he was greatly respected by the whole of the crew; and, during the interval granted to him, they did not seem much inclined to insist on his life.

Finding no alternative but to perish with him, and having in some measure lulled their sense of horror at the approaching scene by a few draughts of the wine, they prepared for the execution, and the fire was kindled in the steerage to dress their first meal, as soon as their companion should become their food.

As the dreadful moment approached, their compunction increased.

Friendship and humanity at length became stronger than hunger and death.

They determined that the man should live at least till the next morning—hoping that Providence in the meantime would send them some relief.

Poor Flat, however, could derive little comfort from the concern all expressed, and it is not improbable that the expressions of friendship and affection increased the agitation of his mind.

Such, however, it was as he could not sustain; for, before midnight, he grew almost deaf, and by four o'clock in the morning was raving mad.

His messmates, who discovered the alteration, debated whether it would not be an act of humanity to despatch him immediately, but the first resolution of sparing him till morning prevailed.

About eight in the morning, as the captain was ruminating in his cabin on the fate of this unhappy wretch, who had but three hours to live, two of his people came hastily down with uncommon ardour in their looks, and seizing both his hands, fixed their eyes upon him without saying a syllable.

The captain, who recollected that they had thrown the body of the man who had eaten the liver overboard, notwithstanding their necessities for fear of catching his madness, now apprehended that, fearing to eat Flat for the same reason, they were come to sacrifice him in his stead; he therefore disengaged himself by a sudden effort, and snatching up a pistol, stood upon his defence.

The poor men, guessing his mistake, made shift to tell him that their behaviour was merely the effect of surprise and joy, that they had discovered a sail, and that the sight had so overcome them, they were unable to speak.

They said that the sail appeared to be a large vessel, that it was to the leeward, and stood for them in as fair a direction as could be wished.

The rest of the crew came down immediately afterwards, and confirmed the report of a sail, but said that she seemed to bear away from them upon a contrary course.

The account of the vessel's being in sight of signals, on whatever course she steered, struck the captain with such excessive and tumultuous joy, that he was very near expiring under it.

As soon as he could speak, he directed his people to make every possible signal of distress; the ship, indeed, was a signal of the most striking kind, but he was apprehensive the people at a distance might conclude there was nothing alive on board, and so stand away without coming near it.

His orders were obeyed with the utmost alacrity; and as he lay in his cabin, he had the inexpressible happiness of hearing them jumping upon deck, and crying out,—

"She nears us! she nears us! she is standing this way!"

The approach of the ship being more and more manifest every moment, the hopes of all on board naturally increased; but in the midst of this joy, we remembered our unfortunate shipmate Flat, and regretted he could not be made sensible of his approaching deliverance.

Their passions however, were still characteristic, and they proposed a can of joy to be taken immediately.

This the captain, with great prudence strenuously opposed; and at length, though with some difficulty, convinced them that their deliverance, in a great measure, depended upon the regularity of that moment's behaviour.

All but the mate, therefore, gave up the can—which would have made them all very drunk before the vessel could come up with them—and he disappeared to take the can of joy by himself.

After continuing to observe the progress of the vessel for some hours, with all the tumult and agitation of mind that such a suspense could not fail to produce, we had the mortification to find the gale totally die away, so that the vessel was becalmed at two miles distant.

We did not, however, suffer long by this accident; for, in a few minutes, we saw the boat put out from the ship's stern, and row towards us, full-manned, and with vigorous despatch.

As we had been twice before confident of deliverance, and disappointed, and as we still considered ourselves tottering on the verge of eternity, the conflict between hope and fear during the approach of the boat may be easily conceived.

At length, however, she came alongside ; but the appearance of the crew was so ghastly, that the men rested upon their oars, and, with looks of inconceivable astonishment, asked us what we were.

Being at length satisfied, they came on board, and begged us to use the utmost expedition in quitting the wreck, lest we should be overtaken by a gale of wind, that would prevent them getting back to their ship.

The captain being unable to stir, they lifted him out of his cabin, and let him down into the boat by ropes.

Our people followed him, with poor Flat still raving.

They were just pulling off when one of them observed that the mate was wanting.

He was immediately called, and the can of joy had just left him power to crawl to the gunwale, with a look of idiot astonishment, having, to all appearance, forgotten everything that had happened.

Having, with some difficulty, got the poor drunken creature on board, they rode away, and in about an hour reached the ship.

She was the 'Susannah,' of London, in the Virginia trade, commanded by Captain Thomas Evers, and was then returning from Virginia to London.

The captain received us with the greatest tenderness and humanity, promised to lie by the wreck till the next morning, that he might, if possible, save some of the captain's clothes; the wind, however, blowing very hard before night, he was obliged to quit her, and she probably with her cargo went to the bottom before morn.

The 'Susannah' proceeded on her voyage, and though she was herself in a shattered condition, and so short of provisions as to be obliged to reduce her people to short allowance, she reached the Land's End about the 2nd of March.

There we went on shore, and were hospitably received by a wealthy Cornish gentleman, named Hanfield—"

"Hanfield!" interrupted Henry; "Hanfield, did you?"

"Yes, that was his name, and never shall I forget it, or his kindness to us,' said the mate. "We made his house our home, and he sent all to our own homes, and furnished us with everything we required, at his own expense.'

"Strange," said Henry.

"Do you know him?" interrupted Hart.

"I do."

"Then you know a good man " said the mate.

"Not only do I know him," said Henry, "but have been in his company lately.'

"Where is he?" asked Hart. "The last time I was in England I sought his house, but learned that he had gone abroad."

"Where he is now, heaven only knows,' said Henry. "I last saw him borne on board a pirate vessel a prisoner."

Hart leapt to his feet, and clenching his hand, he shook it above his head.

"By all that's holy!" he exclaimed; "I would willingly sacrifice my life for that man. A pirate said you—a pirate. Hanfield a prisoner. By heaven, I would that the vessel which holds him thus, would cross our track, so that one to whom he stood a good and kind friend, could strike a blow for his rescue. But tell me the vessel whither was she bound ; for I would track her like a shark, till I could seize him from their grasp ! "

CHAPTER CXLIII.

THE AFRICANS PUT ON SHORE—THE REQUEST AND THE CONSENT.

THE pirate Bond was bound securely, and placed in the hold; and Ling was soon taken to his side.

Wild Madge had a guard placed over her cabin; and in it the furious woman howled her rage in vain.

Jack Snipe, under the promise of assisting Charles all in his power to carry the ship to the shores of Africa, was released; and, in gratitude for the kindness extended to him, the sailor used every exertion to redeem the one black trait in his character.

The love of home is strong even in the breast of the savage, and gaily did the kidnapped Africans perform the various duties assigned them.

Over the sea the vessel bounded towards the hoped for shores.

In consultation with the now happy Ellen and her father, it was resolved not to take the ship into a frequented port, lest the good intentions of the brave young seaman should be thwarted, and the black pirates demanded at his hands by the authorities.

He had promised them forgiveness for their crimes, and he was not the man to break his word.

Tracing his finger along the chart, he discovered a spot where he thought he might land his blacks without any fear of entailing danger upon them.

He had the vessel's course steered in the direction; and, as the weather continued fine, he made a quick run for the haven.

It was just as the bright sun lifted its golden head over the distant waves the speck in the horizon proclaimed their approach to land.

Charles pointed it out to the blacks, and their joy was extravagant in the extreme.

Eagerly that speck was watched by the eyes of those on board, till it took shape and form—looming larger and larger every moment, as the vessel, dipping her proud bows to kiss the spray, glided along, like a thing of life and joy, as though proud of her mission.

The sun had passed the meridian when she was brought to anchor alongside the verdant shores of the island on which the brave Martinez and his lovely bride had found a home and peace—to be broken for a time by the demon jealousy—on which the mutineer had been cast, and to where the bold Captain Wildwell had been conveyed by the heroic Jack Ridley.

When the anchor had dropped from her bows, and fixed itself in the bed of the shore, and the vessel swung around, one loud long cheer broke from the lips of the blacks.

Home had been reached; though several miles away from the spot on which they had resided, still it was home: their native shores had been reached.

Then Charles, standing on the poop, with Ellen and her father by his side, summoned the African crew around him, and said:

"Africans!—I promised you, when you chose me for captain of this ship, to bring you to your native shores. I have kept my word. I know not in what part you have existed—for Africa is large. You are free. Go—and never more lend yourselves to such crimes as you have been guilty of on board this ship. Man's villainy tore you from your homes; but your own hearts led you to sin. Go —seek your friends, and tell them then that the white man is not always the enemy of your race: 'tis few indeed who wish you ill—many who would be your friends. Go—and heaven be with you; and never forget that by the laws of nations your life is forfeit; but that there is one who, though his sufferings have been great from the wickedness of such as have followed the same career as yourselves, can forgive and aid the repentant. Farewell!"

He turned away, with Ellen hanging upon his arm; and, the boats being lowered, the blacks swarmed over the sides, and pulled for the shore.

In the course of about an hour not a single African remained on board.

Each boat had been brought back to the ship but the last, which Charles gave them; and, as the last boat's crew touched the shore, Charles, turning to Ellen, said:

"I have done my duty."

"Nobly," she replied; "and heaven grant our troubles are now ended!"

"It will be impossible," he said, "for us to work the vessel back to England; but I hope to fall in with some passing ship, and get assistance to bear us to our native clime. The sailor who has shown so much regret for having joined these men has done all in his power to compensate for his one false step; and, therefore, we must not by word or deed inculpate him should we be fortunate enough to procure a crew."

"Indeed, no," said Hanfield: "but what do you propose doing?"

"Sailing at once, and steering for some port on the coast, which the chart will enable us to find."

He turned, with the intention of going down to the cabin for this purpose, when a movement on the shore attracted his notice, and he perceived the form of a man signalling to them by waving his handkerchief above his head.

Charles took the glass; for, though the distance was short, the rays of the sun prevented him distinctly perceiving what description of form it was; and, to his surprise, he discovered that it was a young man, and an European.

"There are whites on the island," he said; "and they are now making signals to us. Evidently wishes to come on board. Jack, row to the shore, and bring him on board."

Jack Snipe dropped over the side into a boat, and rowed away to the shore.

Those on board stood watching him, and perceived that the person who had signalled them got into the boat to return with him to the ship.

In the course of ten minutes Jack, and the stranger who had taken an oar, pulled alongside, and the moment that the boat touched the ship, he seized a rope, and with the agility of a cat, sprang over the bulwarks on to the deck.

Bowing politely to Ellen, he turned to Charles, exclaiming—

"Sir, I have heard from the seamen from whom I have just parted, that you hold command."

"I do."

"Permit me then, to solicit your aid in bearing away from these shores five persons, whom the force of circumstances have compelled to make this island their home for many weary days?"

Whilst he spoke, he cast his eyes up at the rigging of the ship and along her decks with a true sailor's eye.

"By Neptune!" he exclaimed, before Charles could reply to his request—"if this is not the 'Scorpion,' I never trod a deck before!"

"True—that is the name of the vessel," said Charles—"formerly a slaver, then a pirate, now ——"

"Sir, I was a lieutenant on board of her, and her captain now lies ill and weak on shore."

"Then he escaped the fearful fate to which he was consigned?" asked Charles, who had heard from Zoolah all that had transpired.

"He did."

"Heaven be praised! but, sir, I have determined to take this vessel to England in order that persons now in confinement on board, may be handed over to the laws they have so deeply outraged."

"Captain Wildwell and myself will offer no objection to such a course," said Martinez—"for the prisoners you have on board, are a portion of those who have done him so much injury; besides, sir, the captain has resolved never more to engage in the traffic, and you will have the assistance of myself and two able seamen to work her to England."

"I shall be only too happy to see them on board," said Charles.

"If you will allow me to return to the shore with the boat, I will soon bring them back to the ship."

"Certainly. And now, sir, to whom have I the honour of speaking?"

"To Lieutenant Martinez!"

"I am Charles Lawson!"

The Spaniard bowed.

"Take this man with you," said Charles, pointing to Snipe, and tell Captain Wildwell that I shall only be too happy to welcome him on board his own vessel, but that I shall consider myself master here till such time as I shall have placed my prisoners in the hands of the authorities."

With a bow, Martinez descended to the boat and pulled for the shore.

—

CHAPTER CXLIV.

THE TRIAL—THE DISCOVERY—DEATH OF WILD MADGE.

CONTINUED attention at the hands of the surgeon soon restored to health the Boy Rover.

The suspicion as to his real character induced an inquiry to be made around the coast on which so many a gallant bark had been lured to destruction, brought forward the old sailor's daughter, Mary.

She was conveyed on board the revenue cutter, and despite the disfigurement which the explosion had caused, she had no difficulty in recognising him.

The Boy Rover was therefore sent on shore strongly guarded, and once more a prison walls enclosed his bold, bad form.

Upon the same day as that which saw him a fettered wretch lying in a dark stone cell, the 'Scorpion' reached the land and was brought to anchor.

The brave Charles Lawson and those whom he had brought off from the island, formed the whole of her crew; and no sooner did the vessel ride at her moorings than he telegraphed to the revenue cutter.

Mr. White and the young middy, together with several sailors were soon on board; and Charles consigned to their charge the guilty Madge and her two companions Lang and Bond.

In a short time these worthies became inmates of the same jail as the Boy Rover.

Surrendering the vessel to the charge of the captain of the cutter, Charles, Ellen, and her father went on shore.

The former immediately started for London, to make known to the proper authorities all that had transpired; whilst the fair girl and her now happy parent took up their abode in the very house he occupied years before.

Soon as his business could be transacted Charles returned to Cornwall, and awaited the trial of the smugglers, which was set down to take place in the course of the week.

Captain Wildwell, who had almost recovered from the fearful injuries he had received, still remained on board, together with Martinez and Inez. Ned, the mutineer, also remained, as did Jack Snipe and Ridley.

They had been informed that their evidence would be required to bring home the crimes of which the smugglers were charged.

Ned alone had any fear; but, upon the assurance that his connection with them would be pardoned did he appear to give evidence, he became more reconciled to the ordeal he was to undergo; and the recollection of the ill-treatment he had received, at the command of the Boy Rover, decided him in making no effort to escape from giving evidence at the trial.

Bitter indeed were the invectives heaped by the wild fury upon all who had any hand in her incarceration, and the cell rang with her oaths of vengeance.

Like a caged tiger she chafed; but all to no avail—too securely was she held in thraldom.

It was on the second day of her imprisonment that she was informed that the Boy Rover, who was likewise an inmate of the same jail, would take his trial by her side on the same day.

Madge heard it in silence; but there was a strange look gleaming in her eye, and a demoniac smile upon her face.

Not one word did she utter till those who bore the intelligence closed the cell door behind them.

Then she sprang from the seat on which she had been sitting, and waved her hands wildly above her head, exclaiming:

"Ha, ha!—then all my hopes of vengeance are not gone for ever. Oh, if I have not brought his girl to shame and misery, I will yet wring his heart to madness! Wild Madge shall yet be avenged—she has sworn it! Her oath is registered in hell, and her soul shall yet triumph. Joseph Hanfield—seducer, betrayer—you think you triumph! Think on—think on! But I will dash the cup of happiness from your lips! Ha, ha!—Wild Madge shall yet triumph!'

From that moment her furious ways ceased. She became calm, collected, quiet, and serene; and seemed only to await with anxiety the day of trial.

It came at last.

Side by side in the dock stood Wild Madge, the Boy Rover, Lang, and Bond.

The indictment was read, and the trial proceeded.

One by one the mutineers were called, and their evidence taken.

It was not till Mr. Hanfield appeared in the box that Wild Madge gave any indication of being at all interested in the trial.

But, when he spoke his damning evidence, her lip curled, and her bleared eye shot fire.

Ned's appearance, too, caused some surprise to the Boy Rover.

He had long since believed him dead.

His evidence was fearfully telling against the smugglers; for, being one of them, he could say more than all the rest.

The trial was ended.

The verdict of guilty was recorded against all the prisoners, and the judge proceeded to pass the dread sentence of death.

Then, and then only, did the eye of the Boy Rover fall.

Then was it that Wild Madge drew herself erect.

The veins on her forehead swelled like blue cords; the blear eye lighted up; and she stretched forth her arm towards to the grey-headed father of poor Ellen.

"Joseph Hanfield," she shrieked, loudly, "your triumph shall be of short duration! The youth whom you, and those by whom you are surrounded—the Boy Rover whom you have consigned to death, is your own son!"

A cry of surprise broke from the lips of every person in the court.

The judge, who had risen from his seat, at these words, said:

"Officers, remove that woman! Her reason is shattered. She knows not what she says."

"Hear me!" she exclaimed, moving back the officers. "This youth—for such he is indeed even now—I stole twenty years ago from its cradle. His father robbed me of all woman holds dear; then basely deserted me for another. I swore to have revenge, and waited. The woman who usurped my place gave birth to this boy; and, in the dead of night, I stole it from its cot, and trained him up in sin, that I might have vengeance on the father. See how I have kept my oath! Look upon the offspring of the woman for whom you spurned your victim! Look upon him—the smuggler—the murderer! Blood has flowed like water by his hands. Crimes black as midnight—dark as hell—has he committed at my instigation. Joseph Hanfield, who triumphs now — you, the seducer, or me, your victim?"

And she laughed loudly and ironically as she pointed to the condemned Rover.

"The sentence is passed," she exclaimed, "and he will be led forth to an ignominious doom. Ha! ha! how it gladdens my heart to feel that I have wrung your soul. How shall the jeers of the crowd as they heed his presence on the gallows salute your ears? With what feelings will you hear the hisses and groans of outraged humanity as his breath is strangled out of his body? Oh! with what agony will you see the finger pointed at you, as the words ring in your ears—behold the father of the inhuman monster, the Boy Rover!"

"Great heaven!" exclaimed Charles—"can this be true?"

"No," said Hanfield—"that a child was stolen from my house in the dead of the night I admit, but that child I found upon the sea shore, at daybreak, with the waves washing up and over it. I took it home, intending to bring it up as my own, but in the night it was carried off and I never more heard of it."

Whilst he spoke the bleared face of Wild Madge became pale as death.

"I never had a son," continued Hanfield; 'the only child to which my lamented wife gave birth stands now by my side—my daughter Ellen."

With a shriek of agony Wild Madge flung her arms above her head.

"Speak—speak!" she yelled—"in the name of heaven, man, do you speak true?"

"As heaven is my judge, said Hanfield, "what I have said is true."

One wild spasmodic gasp came from her breast, then she fell forward upon the front of the dock.

The officers lifted her up and wiped the thick white foam from her mouth.

Her head was bathed with cold water, and she slowly opened her eyes and stood erect.

But, oh! what a change had come over her. No longer was she the demoniac fury. All her energies seemed paralysed, and she looked first from the Boy Rover to Hanfield, then back to the smuggler.

"Oh, God!" she gasped—"how am I punished. I have defied thee and thy laws, and plunged my soul to hell that I might have vengeance, but it has recoiled upon myself. The child I believed to have been the offspring of her whom I hated with all a wronged woman's hate, was my own. To hide my shame I placed it on the sea shore that the wild waves might bury my disgrace for ever. Oh, how am I punished—for twenty years have I never ceased to instill into his mind the most wicked and bloody precepts—for twenty

years have I prayed for the hour to come when I might see him upon the gallows, and feel that vengeance had been mine at last—know that I had consigned him to a doom which should bow the head of him who wronged me to shame and death. But, oh, how wondrous are the workings of Providence! The misery I had plotted to inflict, has fallen on myself. Richard, behold your tutor and your murderess!—Boy, behold your mother!"

"Curse you—curse you!" exclaimed the Boy Rover, furiously.

"Aye, curse me, for it is my just reward!" she exclaimed. "Heap on cursed upon my head, for well do I deserve them. Boy, I cannot ask your forgiveness—I will not—rather curses than pity. Lead me away, let me not see him more—let me not gaze upon the face of the child I have murdered!"

She staggered back, a loud cry broke from her lips, blood oozed from her mouth, and she fell heavily to the floor.

They raised her up, but she was dead! A fit of apoplexy had ended her guilty career.

———

CHAPTER CXLV.

THE ESCAPE—THE PURSUIT—THE STRUGGLE—DEATH OF NED WILTON.

THE court was flung into the greatest confusion by this strange and fearful scene; and the eyes of all present were fixed upon the form of her who a few short hours before had entered the hall of justice with venom on her lip, and poison in her soul.

Truly, heaven is just, and works out its punishment in its own good time.

The Boy Rover cast one glance only on the form of her who had goaded him on to crimes for which he was now condemned to suffer.

Then his dark quick eye travelled over the court.

In the excitement he was forgotten.

He whom the crowded audience had come far and near to obtain a glimpse of—he whose name had become a terror and a disgrace to civilisation—was now unheeded.

All thoughts, all eyes, were centered upon the woman whom the vengeance of heaven had struck down.

The Rover saw this, and he was not slow to profit by it.

The chains which had bound his wrist had been removed when he had been placed in the dock—the strong body of officers being deemed a sufficient guarantee for his safety.

But now they had forgotten their duty in the height of the confusion, and he was not the man to neglect to profit by it.

One look only then he took at Wild Madge; one glance only he cast towards the open door of the court.

It was sufficient.

With a bound, he sprang upon the edge of the dock; with a wild plunge, he leaped over the heads of the officers.

Striking furiously right and left, he gained the door; and, drawing it to after him, he rushed into the streets of Penzance.

So quick, so sudden, so unexpected had been the bold and daring deed, that he had gained some distance from the court ere those inside could recover from the confusion into which they had been thrown.

Charles was, perhaps, the first; and, consigning Ellen to the care of her father, he rushed off in pursuit, closely followed by Ned and the officers.

They could just catch a glimpse of the Rover, as, with the speed of an antelope, he rushed past those whom the loud cries of his pursuers called upon to stop his flight.

With a giant's strength in his arm, he struck down all who opposed his passage; and, goaded to desperation, he cleared for himself a passage, and bounded on.

On, on he sped, towards the vale of Lamorna; and on to the deep hollow of Penrith Cove.

Never once stopping to draw breath, he sped on; whilst his pursuers, increasing every moment in number, yelled loudly behind, as they struggled to come up with him.

Still on he went; and still followed Charles, and Ned, and the officers.

On, towards the famed Logan Rock he bent his flight.

He cast hasty glances behind him, and smiled in derision at his pursuers.

"Never shall the Boy Rover—the Smuggler of the South Seas—furnish a holiday to a mob! Never shall his body dangle in the air, amid the howling execrations of those who would gloat on his doom! The rope is not yet spun, nor the tree grown, that shall serve to rid the world of my presence. Boldly I have lived; bravely will I die. But no felon's death shall ever be my doom!"

Still on!

He reached the base of the rock, and looked up the famed Logan stone.

He was about to hurry off in the direction of the sea, when, with a cry of rage, he perceived his pursuers had divided, and were cutting off his retreat.

"Curse them!" he yelled—"but I will foil them yet."

He commenced to ascend the rock; and nearer and nearer came his pursuers.

He had got about half-way up when they reached the base; and, for a moment, the Rover paused for breath.

"Yield!" exclaimed Charles.

"Never!" was the reply of the Rover, as he once more commenced to ascend.

"Surrender!" called out one of the officers—"or I fire."

"Fire—and be d——d!" roared out the Rover, still keeping on his way.

But the officer had no weapon, and the remark only excited the laughter of those around him.

"No matter, he cannot escape," said the jail officer.

"He will," replied Charles—"unless we succeed in seizing him before he reaches the top of the rock. Follow me! so great a criminal must not give justice the slip."

But the officers hesitated.

"Then I will go alone," said Charles.

"No, you won't," said Ned. "Lead, and I'll follow."

"Nobly spoken," replied Charles.

He commenced to ascend the rock, and Ned Wilton followed quickly at his heels.

The officers, ashamed to be seen skulking, followed somewhat slowly.

The dreaded name of the Boy Rover had struck a sort of terror to their hearts, and they feared to meet him on the rock.

On—on he went towards the top, and on followed, at no very great distance, Charles and his companion.

He gained the summit, and stood looking down fiercely upon his pursuers.

"There he will make his stand," said Charles, "and he can go no farther if we are resolved, and remain firm."

But as he spoke his foot slipped, and the young sailor fell somewhat heavily.

Ned stooped to render him some assistance, but Charles waved him on, saying—

"Heed not me—quick, and stop him!"

Ned continued on his way, and Charles struggled to his feet.

Still the Boy Rover moved not from the position he had taken.

Ned was now but a few steps from the spot on which he stood.

The mutineer looked up and hissed between his teeth—

"Now we meet on equal terms, captain."

As he spoke, he sprang forward and clutched the Boy Rover by the throat.

"Hell-hound, I have you now!" he exclaimed furiously. "My hands are free, not bound to the mast. Justice demands her due, and she must have it."

Not one word did the Rover reply.

He grasped the shoulder of Ned, and together they were locked in a deadly embrace on the summit of the rock, and beside the rock which, poised upon its axis, had for years called forth the admiration and wonder of all who had beheld it.

Exhausted as he was by his arduous struggles to escape, he was still strong, and desperation nerved his arm with a terrific power.

He set his feet firm on the gray stone, and summoning all his strength he lifted Ned bodily off his feet.

Then he swung the mutineer round with fearful violence.

Ned for a moment relaxed his hold of the Boy Rover's throat.

It was a fatal mistake; for with almost superhuman strength the Boy Rover hurled the mutineer from him, and he fell over the rock crushing his skull in the descent, and calling forth a cry of horror from those below.

A dozen hands were stretched forth to aid him, but too late; the vengeance of the Rover had been too sure—Ned Wilton was dead!

His skull fractured by the fearful fall—his neck broken, he breathed but a few moments ere he died.

He had paid the penalty of his crimes—though he had resolved to sin no more.

Loud, derisive, and mocking was the laugh of the Boy Rover as he gazed down upon the mangled remains of him he had sent to his last account.

Fierce and demoniac was the aspect with which he turned to meet the brave Charles Lawson.

The young sailor had noticed the doom of the mutineer, and for a moment his heart sickened and his courage failed him.

It was but for a moment only.

He sprang upon the summit of the rock to the side of the Boy Rover.

"Villain!" he exclaimed.

"Fool!" answered the Rover—"you rush upon your doom."

"In heaven I place my trust,' exclaimed Charles. "I fear you not."

And he sprang upon the Boy Rover, and flung his arms around him.

"Follow the fool who has gone before you!" said the Rover, striving to lift him from his feet, as he had done the mutineer.

But Charles was more wary. He shifted his position each moment as the other's power bore upon him, and they struggled further from its edge.

The officers, now perceiving that the Rover was in the grasp of Charles, hurried to assist him in effecting the smuggler's capture.

The Boy Rover redoubled his exertions—but in vain.

He began to despair of defeating the brave young sailor ere assistance arrived.

His position became desperate, and he redoubled his exertions.

Desperately struggling, he urged the youth towards the side over which Ned had fallen, and forced his body partially over the edge.

But Charles still clung tenaciously to him, and the Rover found he must go over the side of the cliff as well, did he not succeed in releasing the hold of Charles.

In an instant he bent his head, and fastened his teeth in the wrist of the young sailor.

"Cowardly villain!" exclaimed the youth.

"Release your hold!" yelled the smuggler.

"Never!" replied Charles.

"By h—l, you shall!" roared the Rover, as he cast one glance towards the officers, who were nearly at his side.

"I will drag you to the gallows, or die," exclaimed Charles, struggling to force the smuggler back to the centre of the rock.

Once more the Boy Rover fastened his teeth in the young man's wrist; and, with a cry of pain, Charles released his hold.

"Die!" said the Rover, as he summoned all his power to hurl him over the side.

Charles felt he must go; but he uttered no cry.

One thought alone pressed upon him—it was for Ellen.

He closed his eyes, with a groan, and gave himself up for lost.

CHAPTER CXLVI.

THE CAPTAIN'S STORY—A NARROW ESCAPE.

It cannot be wondered at that friendship should quickly spring up between Henry Chambers and Mr. Hart.

Of course the man who would show attention to a fellow-creature in his sufferings, and tend him with a brother's care—sacrifice rest and comfort for his sake—would be pretty sure to merit the respect of those for whom he had shown so much disinterested commiseration.

But the good feeling which Henry entertained for the mate of the vessel on which he now found himself was doubly enhanced by the knowledge that he was acquainted with the father of the beauteous Ellen Hanfield, and that his good regards were centred in one whom he himself respected deeply.

It was towards the close of the day that the worthy captain, with a smile on his face, and a proud feeling of triumph at the restorative powers of his medicine, entered the cabin where the youth was seated.

He was a true type of the old sailor—frank and generous in his manner, with a genial look always upon his bronzed countenance, and a rakish devil-may-care expression about his eyes.

He strode in unannounced, and extended his hand to the youth, who rose to receive him.

"Glad to find my medicine has worked so well," he said. "Nothing like grog for a sailor's constitution. 'Throw physic to the dogs!' say I. Grog, sir—grog—always in moderation, you know—for I do not countenance intemperance—is the best thing in the world to restore the nerves to their proper order. Lor, bless you, the surgeon would have made you up a dozen of tar and paint, or else something a great deal more nauseous; and, instead of finding you with a smile on your face, and the glow of health on your cheek, as now, I should have seen you lying like a battered hull amid the breakers. But, lor, bless me, I quite forgot. Sit down, sir—sit down. You are not quite strong enough to stand. No ceremony with me. I like to be treated with respect; but do not exact too much of that flummery. There! Well, how are you—eh?"

And he gently forced the young man back on to the chest from which he had risen as he entered the room.

"Thanks to your medicine, sir, and the kind treatment I have received at the hands of Mr. Hart, I feel quite restored now to health and strength."

"Of course you do," said the captain—"to be sure you do. You look as strong as a lion who has dined off three men and an elephant before breakfast. But there—don't exert yourself; don't do anything to throw yourself back again. Physic—bah! That's the physic, my boy, I sent you. I have tested it myself for all complaints, and have found it a never failing remedy."

"I am sure, sir," said Henry, "I cannot find words to express my gratitude for your great kindness—"

"Avaunt there, my lad!" interrupted the old sailor. "I have danced over the blue ocean too many years not to feel that danger lies in every wave, and that it is the duty of all men to succour their less fortunate fellows. I should be worse than a shark did I not do so when an opportunity offered; for heaven only knows but our own turn may come next."

"True, sir," said Henry; "and it is only those who, night and day, face the dangers of a sailor's life, that can know of the risks and perils he has to encounter."

"Quite right—quite right;" and, though I say it, I believe there is no class of men in the world more ready and willing to encounter them, or risk their lives, to serve a fellow-creature who has been drawn within their coils. Ah, sir, the landlubbers know nothing of what we have to encounter—the hurricane, the wreck, the watery grave!"

"From which your crew rescued me," said Henry—"heaven be praised!"

"Well, well," said the captain—"I hope they may none of them ever need the aid they gave to you. Though, I believe, we have on board two or three who know what it is to have been wrecked."

"Mr. Hart has been giving me an account of his sufferings when wrecked in the "Golden Eagle.""

"Has he?" said the captain. "He suffered a good deal, poor fellow, there; and I should be a little surprised if he did not feel some sympathy for you. If you feel strong enough, and will favour me with your company in the cabin, I will mix you another dose of my medicine, and give you an outline of what I myself have suffered on the briny ocean."

Henry accepted the invitation with thanks, and repaired to the captain's cabin, where they were joined by the mate, and after mixing a stiff glass of grog for each, the captain seated himself and said—

"Mr. Hart, the account of my sufferings and that of my companions on board ship, may be stale to you, but to Mr. Chambers, who has not yet heard it, it may not be uninteresting. I have invited him here to tell him the story, so as you know all about it you can keep the glasses filled while I talk and our young friend listens."

Mr. Hart smiled acquiescence, and the captain commenced:

"You must know, sir, that although a sailor, I did not form one of her crew. I had sailed out to Quebec in another vessel, but being disappointed with the treatment I received on board I left, and paid for a passage home to England in a vessel of that name.

We set sail with a pilot on board on the 9th day of November.

Nothing remarkable occurred while in the river except that once we had to come an anchor on account of a very heavy snow storm.

We lay-to about twenty-four hours, when we weighed anchor and set sail, the pilot leaving us the next day.

In the Gulf of St. Lawrence we one night saw the Aurora Borealis of a splendid red colour, and all on board remarked that they had frequently seen it of a deep yellow or orange colour, but none had seen it ever before of such blood-red hue.

We all conjectured that the appearance portended a violent storm, but the wind continued favourable and the weather fine for several days.

On the 20th, however, it began to blow fresh from the north-west, and for three days it increased till it amounted to a hurricane.

Our ship was now compelled to run before the gale under close-reefed fore-top sails. She laboured much, and two men were placed at the wheel which governs the rudder.

The sea had become tremendous, and our master was much alarmed.

Being unable to go on deck himself he was constantly calling down the mate and inquiring how matters stood.

It was proposed to heave her to, but it was the opinion of the captain that to do so in such a heavy gale would at once prove fatal; so he advised them to stand firm to the wheel and keep her scudding.

The night which closed in upon us will never be obliterated from my memory.

I was sitting by the cabin fire, occasionally going up the companion ladder to see how things looked, and the master was moving about the cabin much discomposed, when a tremendous sea broke over the stern of the vessel, carrying destruction before it.

The wheel came down with a crash through the cabin skylight in broken fragments, and in an instant we were in total darkness.

The floor of our cabin was almost immediately covered with water, and a scene of horror and confusion ensued which beggars description.

The two men who had been at the wheel came down the companion, having fortunately caught hold of something as the water dashed them forward on the deck.

In a few minutes all were down in the cabin; and having good tinder boxes, we soon struck a light again, and getting a lantern, all hands went on deck except the captain.

The state of the deck was terrible to look at: the hammocks swept overboard, with great part of the bulwarks; the water-casks broke loose, and going to pieces.

After getting the helm lashed, and keeping the ship to, the wind moderating a little, we went to the pump, and found she was leaking very considerably.

All hands at once yoked to the duty of the pump.

We worked incessantly all night, and found by doing so we could keep the water under.

We all joined in the work except the captain, who was in a bad state of health.

The one-half of the men pumped, while the other rested.

When the morning came, to our utter consternation we found our rudder had been broken, and rendered quite useless.

It only hung together, and kept flapping violently against the stern of the vessel, at every blow breaking and opening the seams of the ship.

At length the broken part detached itself leaving nothing but a small part of the stern hanging in the rudder trunk, and the planks so shattered that the water was coming in torrents.

To stop the leak was now found impossible, and we discovered that all our pumping was of no avail.

Our only comfort was, that we had a firm timber-laden ship under us, and of course were all aware of the fact, that though she filled, she would not sink.

We had, therefore, no other alternative but to prepare with the utmost dispatch for taking refuge in the rigging, seeing that the water would soon be level with the deck.

We were at this time near the outer edge of the great bank of Newfoundland.

The weather was excessively cold.

The wind blew hard, with snow and sleet.

We could only contemplate how difficult it would be for us to survive on the rigging of a ship in such a dismal situation at such an inclement season.

At the same time, the sea was breaking over the decks, every moment threatening to overwhelm us.

We began to despair; for there was a likelihood that our decks would have burst by the rocking of the water beneath, and our timber been shifted.

The melancholy catastrophe that would have ensued on this taking place can readily be imagined.

Indeed, the shifting of a single log would have been the signal of our fate.

The first night we stopped on the rigging was the second after the ship was struck; and most miserable quarters we had.

The ship, now thoroughly water-logged, was pitching and rolling, and we had to lash ourselves to the mast.

What a prospect lay before us, in such a cold latitude at such a season, in the middle of the

Western Ocean, and the long winter nights, with neither rudder nor compass, and storms and tempests to encounter!

The horrors of our situation can be imagined, but cannot be described.

Our captain was a man up in years, with a broken constitution; and, under present circumstances, he became so ill, that he could take no command.

Fortunately, the mate and carpenter were active, and they immediately took charge, which was a fortunate circumstance.

As may be supposed, we immediately had to go upon an allowance of bread and water.

These were divided to us in a most just and impartial manner during the whole period of our sufferings.

For the first four days we had a moderate allowance of about one biscuit and a half, a small slice of beef or pork, and nearly two pints of water.

We suffered dreadfully from cold and wet; and, if we had not frequently shifted our position, would have become quite benumbed.

I had the misfortune, the third night after I had gone to the main-top, to lose both greatcoat and blankets.

I happened to have on two shirts, drawers, a pair of good stockings and shoes, with a black vest, a pair of good Canadian cloth trousers, and a blue cloth jacket: and this was my all—everything else was gone.

I regretted the loss much; for, although the blankets frequently got soaked with water, they still did something towards preserving the heat of the body.

This unfortunate accident took place while I was asleep.

Being overcome with cold and fatigue, I had fastened my great-coat on the rigging to dry, and rolled myself in the blankets.

It happened to come on to blow, and, on turning myself, the wind caught the loose clothes, and swept them overboard.

When I looked for my greatcoat, the rope-yarn that made it fast was there, but the coat was gone.

This would have been a fatal circumstance to me if we had drifted to the northward, or continued much longer in this cold climate.

The sleep we enjoyed in our rigging was neither sound nor refreshing; but we were thankful for it. It passed the time, and, no doubt, was of some benefit to us.

It was a kind of dog-sleep, and only lasted from fifteen minutes to half an hour at a time, and was generally disturbed with dreams about our friends and far-distant homes, which we had little or no expectation of ever again seeing.

Sometimes we awoke in a dreadful fright, dreaming we were pitched overboard, and some of the monsters of the deep ready to snatch us in their terrible maws.

When we opened our eyes, it was, alas! to perceive signs of famine or a watery grave.

Most fortunately, the wind began to prevail from the north-west, and we were drifted fast to the southward.

It was, therefore, a considerable alleviation to our sufferings to think that we were fast approaching a warmer and more genial climate.

We then thought that, had we enough of bread and water, we might survive a long time under our present circumstances.

The only immediate cause of alarm was the ship breaking up during some of the frequent and heavy squalls we had to encounter.

For the purpose of standing it out as long as possible, on the sixth day after the ship had been damaged, we put ourselves upon just so much provisions as would preserve the spark of life.

This was scarcely three ounces of bread, in a very wet and mouldy condition, a small slice of beef or pork, and not more than two or three gills of water.

We were so scarce of this last article, that we had to take every opportunity of securing as much as possible from the sails every time it happened to rain.

This water drank very sweet; although tarry tasted, it was to us most refreshing.

I am certain that the most voluptuous gourmand never enjoyed his most favourite beverage with better gusto that we did a drink of water squeezed from the dirty canvas.

We had soon the satisfaction of getting into a milder atmosphere.

However, till towards the end of December, we occasionally had very heavy weather, with a great number of thunder storms.

Having saved a quadrant, we found ourselves in the latitude of the Azores; but whether to the east or west we could not tell, having drifted so many ways, and keeping no log.

On Christmas-day, which happened to be fine, we proposed to make a feast as well as we were able.

We dared not venture on the bread, but we got an extra slice of pork, which some of us ate raw, others roasted.

When the weather was fine we could remain on deck, where we kindled a fire for cooking.

The sea frequently broke over the deck with so much fury, that we were generally glad to remain on the rigging.

Having by this time suffered nearly five weeks, some of us were excessively weak, and very much emaciated: so much so, that we could scarcely go up and down the shrouds.

Hunger had brought on us a kind of burning fever, and if water had been in our power we would have drunk incessantly.

Instead of heaving overboard the rats which we caught, as we did at first, we now flayed, roasted, and ate them, and found them delicious.

On every favourable opportunity we assembled together for the purpose of devotion, praying to Him, with heartfelt earnestness, who can make the storm a calm, and still the raging of the mighty deep.

We were constantly on the look-out for ships, and, when we saw any, hoisted signals of distress.

They were, however, always at such a distance, that they certainly could not have seen us. At any rate, none approached us.

We also cut pieces off our cable, and made burning torches, which we hoisted in the dark nights at the mizen-top, in case of any vessel passing in the night.

This was frequently done; but all of no avail.

We determined, therefore, that the first vessel we saw, if she was on such a tact as there might be any probability of getting to her, we would launch the jolly boat and chase her.

In a day or two we saw a vessel on what we thought a good tact, and immediately launching our little boat six brave fellows jumped into it, and took to the oars, with the carpenter, who steered them.

We could afford them but a small allowance of bread and water.

They gave us assurances, that should they get up with the ship, they would use all their endeavours to get its master to come after us; we, on the other hand, promised that, in the event of their missing her, we would keep large torches burning all night, so that they might find their way back again.

It was about one o'clock in the afternoon when they left us, and we kept our eyes on them and the ship in breathless expectation till the shades of the evening shut them from our view.

About two o'clock in the morning, they all returned, poor fellows, much fatigued, led by the torch-lights which we had kept blazing. They had approached within two miles of the vessel about nightfall, when to their grief and mortification, they saw her men squaring the yards, and setting off before the wind, leaving them far behind. Whether they had observed the boat, and suspected her to have piratical intentions, we could not tell. The men were all so much exhausted, that they said they would never leave the ship again under such circumstances.

The first day of the new year was approaching, and we could not but revert with melancholy to the scenes of festivity and social enjoyment in which we had often participated during that happy season. Our dismal situation suggested the propriety of attending to the incoming of the new year befitting our prospects.

On the evening of the 31st of December, which chanced to be more than ordinary placid, at a quarter to twelve o'clock we lighted up the lantern, and having two or three Bibles, we proceeded to the quarter-deck, sang part of the 107th Psalm, read a portion of Scripture, and offered up an humble prayer, which although not adorned in language like the homilies of the learned, was the sincere and fervent language of the heart, and derived an imposing sublimity from the situation in which we were placed. When our devotions were over it was New-yearss Day morning; and after shaking hands and wishing each other a good year, we retired to try if we could get a little sleep : and the weather being now fine, we did enjoy some refreshing repose.

On Saturday the 2nd, a vessel hove in sight. Not waiting to try signals, having so long tried them in vain, we launched our little boat with a mast and sail; some of the former crew volunteering, and some offering to go who had not gone before, there were seven ready, among whom were our first and second mates.

Provided the same day as formerly, and making the same engagements to each other, they set sail, assisting the boat with their oars.

There was no cheering this time when we parted; we were in too melancholy and uncertain a state for this expression of joy and triumph, so pleasing and natural to seamen.

We spent that night keeping up torchlights, expecting in the morning to see the vessel approaching us, or at least the boat in view; but alas! there was not a speck seen in the horizon—both vessel and boat were out of sight.

This was a painful result to our expectations, and our sole hope was, that the men had been rescued, though we could not well see how; and we had the consolatory prospect of being able to stand it out a little longer, by keeping ourselves still on the same allowance.

Another day passed, and no immediate prospect of relief. There was now an accurate examination into the state of the provisions which were left, and we ascertained that we could divide something for ten or twelve days longer. Our case grew more appalling. Day after day passed, and our stock of provisions was wearing to a close.

Horrible feelings now took possession of us. No one gave utterance to his thought, but it was evident that we must either perish of famine, or that one of us must be slaughtered to furnish food for the remainder.

Thus we stood upon the crisis of our fate.

While in this desperate physical and moral condition, we were again visited by a ray of hope.

On Thursday the 7th of January, towards evening, and while trying to gather water, it being rainy, the carpenter went to the foretop, and immediately descried a brig to leeward; he watched her attentively, and observed that she put about.

He now cried to us, and told us that she was standing towards us, for there was sufficient light for her to see us.

No one can picture the joy we now felt for this prospect of deliverance; it can be but faintly imagined.

At twelve o'clock, midnight, the vessel was longside of us, and we were soon taken aboard.

The ship was the Blucher, of Boston, commanded by Captain Lourie; she was bound with a cargo of flour, &c., from New York to Monte Video and Buenos Ayres.

Our happiness was increased by finding our fellow sufferers with whom we had parted a few days ago, and who were ready to welcome us on deck.

I will briefly go over the circumstances that led to this extraordinary deliverance.

As I have already mentioned, it was on the Saturday when our companions left us.

That night they rowed till they lost sight of the vessel which they were chasing; and at the same time, all attempts to regain a sight of the wreck had proved unavailing, notwithstanding that we had kept up torchlights all night, as on the former occasion.

It appears that we had drifted from each other, and the poor fellows found themselves, with a small boat on the trackless waves of the Atlantic, almost without food or water; a more helpless situation cannot well be conceived. They could do nothing for themselves, and drifted in their tiny vessel at the mercy of the winds and waves.

On Monday morning, their slender supply of bread was exhausted; and of the remaining small quantity of fresh water, they got a little served out by the second mate in his watchcase.

In the course of Monday when the fog cleared away, to their inexpressible joy they saw a brig at no great distance.

She immediately bore down towards them, by which they saw they were observed; and in about an hour and a half from their first sight of each other, they were on board the Blucher, which vessel was nearly a thousand miles out of her course, driven by adverse winds, being then only from three hundred to four hundred miles in the South-west of Fayal, the nearest of the Azore Islands.

Our mate, an able sailor from South Shields, told the captain of our miserable situation, and the latitude they had left us in, and found that their boat had drifted, from Saturday till Monday, the extraordinary distance of one hundred and forty miles.

With the utmost alacrity, the good American went in search of us, and at length had the satisfaction to fall in with us, as I have described.

Thus after suffering for a period of forty-five days, we were again in the midst of comforts and safety.

Captain Lourie afforded us all the humane attentions which our situation required, giving us our food in very sparing quantities at first, but afterwards abundance of nourishing diet; and we begun to recruit under his care.

Resolving to land on the Azores, he proceeded towards these lonely islands; and in four days' sailing, we stood off the Island of Fayal.

The wind proved unfavourable for landing there, and Captain Lourie being anxious to proceed on his voyage, in which he had been so much retarded by his exertions in our behalf, he desired us, the weather being fair, to get our boats launched, and go ashore at St. John's, a small village on the Island of Pico, where there was a landing place for fishing boats among the rocks.

We bade our deliverers farewell, wishing them every blessing, and in about an hour we were landed at the foot of the Peak of Pico, a very lofty extinct volcanic mountain, covered nearly two-thirds of the way up with vines, orange, lemon, and fig tree, while the top or crater is crowned with eternal snow.

We were received at Pico by a great concourse of islanders, who belong to the Portuguese nation.

We had the good fortune to meet a Portuguese gentleman here who spoke English fluently, and who immediately told our situation to the vicar, who was likewise in attendance on the beach.

We were under very great obligations to this gentleman, as he acted as interpreter.

We were treated here with much kindness; bread, cheese, wine, and fruit being brought to us in abundance, and a place of shelter provided.

The inhabitants, in general, are very poor in this island; nevertheless, they are extremely hospitable, and we recovered very fast.

The vicar, who took the charge of us after we got some refreshment, sent our captain's dispatch over to the British vice-consul at Fayal.

In two days our messenger returned with a reply, thanking the vicar for his attentions to us, and at the same time stating the British government allowance of one shilling and sixpence per day for each individual in such cases.

We remained here about a fortnight, the people all along treating us with much kindness, and we were given to understand that the vicar, after our arrival, had assembled his flock, and publicly returned thanks to Almighty God, who had so wonderfully saved us from a miserable death.

We were so much refreshed and invigorated here, that in a fortnight we considered ourselves able to proceed on our way homeward.

For this purpose a large boat and a Portuguese crew were provided to take us over to Fayal, a distance of about thirty miles, where we saw the British vice-consul, and received every attention from him.

From Fayal we were carried to St. Michael's in a coasting schooner, and thence passages homeward were provided by the British consul-general, for the whole in different vessels, which were here lading with fruit for England.

"Now Mr. Chambers," said the captain after a long pull at the tumbler, which the mate had just concluded in mixing, "you perceive that I have had my sufferings as well as yourself, and Mr. Hunt, but that thank heaven, Providence kept watch and ward over me, and I never see the slightest indications of a storm but I recollect what I have myself endured, and always keep a sharp look out for any vessel in distress, and see the scan with my glass in search of any shipwrecked mariner who with anxious eyes and throbing heart seeks aid and safety. Take a pull at the medicine, my lad, it will do you more good than all the physic in the doctor's chest."

CHAPTER CXLVII.

THE PIRATE BARK.—THE YOUTHFUL STEERMAN—DEATH OF THE CAPTAIN.

THE bright full moon rode high up in the clear blue sky, lighting up the undulating waves, whose seemed tops in its golden rays, filled with sparkling diamonds, as a small schooner glided like a phantom-ship amid the numerous islands which abound in the South Seas, and which is better known as the Low Archipelago.

Her white sails glistened in the moon's rays, and her shadow dived low beneath the surface, whilst every rope stood out in bold relief, as dripping her boom to kiss the sparkling spray which like a cocquet leaped up to woo the embrace, then bashfully fell back, ere it was received with a laughing murmur.

Silence deep and almost oppressive reigned on board, and all around.

The air was still. Scarce a breath bellied her sails, and the flag on her masthead flapped idly, or partially unfurling its folds sank, like a tired man, lazily down to rest.

The watch stood silently gazing at the shadow of the ship, as they lent over the toprail and bulwarks, and peered with half closed eyes into the blue and almost transparent sea beneath them.

The man at the wheel or rather youth for man he was not scarcely yet, alone seemed watchful.

His eagle-eye scanned the distant islands, as his strong arm brought the rudder to whatsoever position he required it. As he guided the small bark between the rocks, which here and there scarce showed their tops above the surface of the waves.

But if the vessel was small, her build was perfection and strength, and she carried an armament which was quite unnecessary for the protection of a simple trader, and when he whole ports were unveiled, the muzzles of twenty guns would have been counted, beside a long swivel piece on deck, which could be raised or lowered or turned right or left at will.

The colours under which she now sailed were Spanish, but she changed them as often as does the Camelian change its hue.

One flag alone was honoured, and respected by her crew, and that flag was blood-red in colour.

She was a pirate!

Piracy was the work in which she was engaged, and that blood-red flag floated over as sanguinary a set of ruffians as ever sailed the salt seas.

She was named the "Poisoned Cress," and never did Malay dog with such perseverance his foes, as did the vessel of which we write pursue the unhappy trader which evil fortune brought across her path.

She was commanded by one Pedri di Salti, an Italian, a man whose love of gold could on y be equalled by his love of vengeance.

The gold he had betrayed his country came whilst captain of a sloop of war.

He had been arrested, tried, and condemned, but he had escaped, and now roved the seas a terror to his own land and that of every other civilized country in Europe.

The speed of his vessel, her heavy armament and the desperate characters of his demon crew, made him as much an object of fear as it did of abhorrence and the manner in which he had so often succeeded in eluding, those sent to destroy him at the very moment when defeat seemed certain, gained for his vessel the title of the "Phantom of the Wave."

Brave as a lion, wily as a fox, cruel as a panther, and deceitful as the serpent, he was respected, feared, and detested by those who sailed under him, but not one on board liked him.

There was something which, though it held in awe and reverence, still excited the desire to destroy the man who swayed an iron will, and wielded an iron sceptre on board that terrible bark.

Pedro di Salti was also a man much addicted to drink, and when his blood was heated and his passions inflamed by the fiery liquid, he'd perform the most unheard atrocities on his own men.

Openly the crew professed to respect him, but secretly they longed for his death.

It may seem strange that such a desperate set of ruffians should have hesitated any length of time to rid themselves of him, but the fact was his desperate bravery and foresight had carried them through so many dangers, that they doubted whether there was another on board, who could command so well and successfully as he did.

His lieutenant, too, was much disliked by the crew, and if the captain fell he would be installed in his post, and it would be but jumping from the pan into the fire.

What was required by the crew was that some one well fitted for the post should stand forward as a candidate.

It was thus that matters stood on board the Phantom of the Wave or the night in question.

During the day the captain had been morose and insulting, and in the fore-part of the evening blind with drink and rage, he had buried his sword in the breast of one of the men who had answered a question somewhat hastily.

This had incensed the crew very much, but still they had gone no further than to murmur their dislike to his command behind his back, not entertaining the idea of avenging their comrade's death and ridding themselves for ever of the command of one whose cruelty and oppression now become unbearable.

Not one did we say.

That is an error for there was one. The youth who stood so silent, yet so watchful, at the wheel.

He was a new hand on board the pirate. He had only gone on board and taken the oath a few days previous, declining to give any account of where he came from or his motives in joining the crew.

But the quick eye of Di Salti soon discerned that he possessed all the qualities necessary for the life he would be lead, and that besides he was a thorough sailor, and well knowing that it was generally to escape the penalties of some crime that persons were willing to ship on board his craft, he asked no more questions than were absolutely necessary and the youth was duly entered the ship's company.

Though he would say nothing of himself, he showed much inclination to learn the feelings of his fellows, their motives and passions, and he was not slow to perceive that the captain was disliked and that any one, save the lieutenant, who would run the chance of death by seeking the pirate's life, would be hailed as captain of their own band.

It was the subject which engrossed his thoughts, or his hand steered the pirate bark along the narrow channel, and his eagle eye searched the horizon.

Fixing his glance upon the cordage, and the flag as it flapped lainly in the almost unfelt breeze, he placed his right hand, in the bosom of his shirt and murmured, as his fingers entwined around the handle of a long Spanish knife,—

"And this would make me captain of as fine a craft and as brave a crew as the "Venomed Snake." Why should I hesitate when one blow could give me back the power I have lost. I must command and not be commanded. 'Tis but one blow—one, and how many have I struck ere now! What have I to fear, nothing! What to gain, position's station. It must be done. The crew are dissatisfied and would hail me as a liberator rather than an assassin. I will watch and wait, and then to the very hilt in his heart my steel shall find a sheath, and I shall tread the deck of this bark, a captain!"

The piercing eye sparkled, and the nostrils were dilated as he spoke.

"I will watch my opportunity," he continued after a pause. "My hand shall not tremble, but with unerring aim it shall find his heart. One blow and its pulsation ceases for ever. One blow and I rise to the eminence from which fate has hurled me. Sleep on, Captain Salti, soon shall the sleep of death close thine eyes for ever."

A grim smile played around, is beardless face as he grasped the spokes of the wheel, and steered the little schooner clear of a low lying rock on whose head the wave broke white with foam, and spent their power in vain.

Still on through the narrow channel, guided by a skilful hand, sped the pirate bark.

She now cleared the rocks and was shaking the spray from her bows, when the tall dark form of a man issued from the companion-way, and casting one glance up at the blue canopy of heaven, permitted his eye to wander over the deck of the vessel·

So silently had he appeared on deck, that three men who formed the watch, being unaware of his presence, moved not from their position at the toprail and bulwarks, but continued to gaze down into the blue depths of the sea, on which the glorious orb of night had cast a sheet of sparkling gold.

Di Salti's glance, for he it was who had so silently left his cabin and so unexpectedly appeared on deck, settled on the forms of the seamen as they watched the sparkling waters rise and fall in fantastic shapes.

His dark heavy brows knitted as he ground his teeth, and clenched his hand, fiercely, as with a quick bound he sprang across the deck to the side of one who, lost in admiration of the sparkling waters, had allowed his thoughts to drift far over the boundling ocean to the once happy place of his childhood and innocence.

"Curse you!" he yelled furiously, and at the time striking the unsuspecting man a heavy blow on the side of the head which sent him staggering across the deck, "is this how you keep the watch?"

"Captain!" exclaimed the man, as soon as he could recover himself from the effects of the surprise and the blow—"I—"

"Don't speak to me," yelled di Salti, advancing furiously upon him, "I'll—oh, God! I am stabbed!"

He reeled backwards and fell heavily to the deck, as the bright moon's rays glaned upon the long blood-stained knife, which the youth at the wheel held at full arm's length above his prostrate body.

Di Salti clutched nervously at the air for a few seconds, then became still.

His carier was ended; he was dead.

And over his still warm corpse strode the youth, with the bloody knife in his hand, as the ship drifted on at the will of the wind and the waves.

CHAPTER CXLVIII.

THE ASSASSIN REVEALS HIMSELF—A STRUGGLE FOR COMMAND — ANOTHER VICTIM—THE BOY ROVER ONCE MORE IN POWER.

SURPRISE for a time held powerless to move or speak, the dark-bearded ruffians who had sailed so long under the Italian Captain.

All was hushed.

There was a dead silence.

They gazed as if in doubt of the evidence of their senses alternately upon the youthful assassin and his prostrate victim.

At length the man who had been struck by di Salti exclaimed—

"What have you done!"

"Freed you from the tyranny of one whom you alike feared and destested," was the cool reply.

"Fool!" exclaimed the other, "that blow has sealed your doom."

"How so?"

"You have murdered him and must die," said another of the men, drawing a pistol from his belt, and cocking it.

He advanced towards the youthful steersman.

With a bound the youth was upon him and bore the weapon from his grasp.

But the man closed with him and endeavoured to hurl him to the deck.

This however he found no easy matter, on the contrary he discovered that though the assassin of the captain was but slight in build, hs possessed a muscular power equal to his own.

Freeing his arm, the youth placed the muzzle of the weapon against the pirate's brow, and pulled the trigger.

The loud report had not died away ere the man's hold relaxed and he fell without even uttering a groan at the feet of the murderer.

Startled and awestruck by this second deed the others, who upon the impulse of the moment had rushed forward to assist their comrade, fell back and as they did so the slumbering pirates, alarmed by the report, hurried upon deck.

Lieutenant Grades, a swarthy Spaniard was one of the first.

Attired only in his shirt and drawers, but with a cutlass gleaming in his hand, he sprung to the spot on which the captain and the pirate lie.

With the fumes of the liquor he had been deeply imbibing ere he turned into his berth still muddling his brain, he exclaimed,—

"What does this mean?"

The men who had formed the watch spoke not a word but silently pointed to the two prostrate and bleeding bodies.

Grades looked in the direction indicated, and as by the bright moon's rays he discovered the features of di Salti, a grin smile of satisfaction lit up his swarthy countenance.

"Ah," he muttered after a briefly pause, "dead!"

"Yes," was the reply.

"Who has done this?" he asked.

The man pointed to the youth, who unflinchingly glanced from one to the others.

Raising his heavy cutlass above his head, he took a step forward, then pausing, with the blade still suspended in the air, he looked fixedly into the face of the defiant youth, and said,—

"No, I wil not strike, for you have made me captain of as fine a bark as ever chased a trader. I leave it to the crew to avenge his death."

And he lowered the point of the weapon and rested it upon the deck.

"Death to the traitor!" exclaimed several voices.

"Just as you please," said Grades, looking round upon the whole ship's company now assembled. "Although I am captain now, my first act shall be to allow you to have your own way."

"Death death!" exclaimed every voice in the ship.

And the glancing blades of several knives flashed before the eyes of the still calm youth and glistered in the refulgent rays of the bright chaste moon.

"Hold!" exclaimed the youth, in a loud and commanding tone, drawing himself proudly up, and looking defiantly around upon the swarthy face of the crew "hold! and hearw me."

The tones in which these words were uttered caused the crew to fall back.

"Pirates!" he exclaimed, "though I have been but a few days among you, I have learned that he whom this knife has struck to the earth was a tyrant that his rule was distastefully to you all, and that his death would prove the greatest boon to the whole ship's crew. You desired his death yet lacked the courage to strike the fatal blow. I resolved to rid you of a tyrant and I have done so, but I resolved also to benefit by the act. His death leaves you without a captain—"

"Avast, there you lie!" roared Grades, "for I am captain now."

"The men detest you as much as they did him!" exclaimed the youth pointing to the prostrate body of di Salti, "I say that this bark has no captain till the voices of the crew proclaim one. I struck not the fatal blow for revenge but for agrandisement. I murdered di Salti that I might take his place. Pirates, I will be your captain, and lead you to fortune."

"You," roared Grades scarcely believing that he had heard aright. "You—who the devil are you?"

"One whose fame has resouned from east to west and north to south, and whose name is a terror on every shore; one who has strode the deck of as daring a vessel and commanded as brave a crew as ever sailed the boundless ocean.

"The Boy Rover the dreaded smuggler of the South Seas!"

At the mention of this name the pirates fell back in surprise, even including the swarthy Spanish lieutenant, who dropped his cutlass from his grasp and stood glaring upon the youth before him as though fascinated and spell-bound by some magnetic agency.

The Boy Rover coolly folded his arms across his breast, and calmly and silently watched the effect of his words.

And that effect was great, indeed!

The knives that a moment before gleamed threateningly before his eyes were sheathed, the fierce attitudes of the men had given place to looks of surprise and admiration, and their malicious glances had changed to looks of perplexity.

The features of the lieutenant, however, lowered till they were black as midnight, and at length he gasped forth, rather than spoke—

"The Boy Rover—you—you—"

"Yes, me," replied the youth. "I am he, the Smuggler of the South Seas, and the Captain of the Phantom of the Wave. How say you, comrades?"

"Yes, yes," roared twenty voices, "the Boy Rover for Captain."

"No," roared Grades.

"Yes, yes," exclaimed the crew.

"What?" exclaimed Grades, stooping and raising the cutlass, which had fallen from his hands to the deck, "Dogs, do you mutiny—do you—"

"The Boy Rover for Captain," exclaimed a stalwart pirate behind him.

"Damn you for a traitor," roared the Spaniard, and with a howl of rage he swung the heavy weapon round, and clove the head of the man who had spoken almost in twain.

The wretch fell at his feet with a fearful howl, and striding over his body, Graders flourished the weapon, exclaiming—

"Who says I am not Captain here? Let him speak, that he may die. Dr. Salti is dead, and I, as next in command, take his place, and by hell I'll stretch him dead at my feet who disputes my authority."

Awed by the desperate bearing of the Spaniard, and his menacing attitude, the pirates fell back out of reach of his glaring cutlass.

"What," he roared. "A boy captain of this ship—a boy to command this vessel, whose very name strikes terror and dismay to the heart of every sailor who has crossed the main—a boy captain of the Phantom Wave—never!"

And he strode towards the Rover with a threatening mien.

"One step nearer and you die," exclaimed the youth, raising the pistol which he had discharged at the head of the lieutenant.

The man hesitated.

He thought not of the fact that the weapon was unloaded.

He saw only the levelled barrel and the resolute look of the Rover.

But his savage nature was cowed, and he paused ere he struck the threatened blow.

Without taking his gaze for a moment, or taking his weapon from its aim, the Boy Rover exclaimed—

"Pirates, your voices have proclaimed me Smuggler of the South Seas, Captain of the Phantom of the Wave. You alone have a right to decide who shall command and who obey. Your late captain was a tyrant, his lieutenant would prove himself the same. You know me to my fame. I ask your suffrage. Once more, am I captain, or is he?"

"You, you," exclaimed the pirates. "The Boy Rover for Captain, and down with the lieutenant."

"By hell, it will not be without a struggle," roared Grades, springing upon the Rover, who never for a moment allowing his glance to wander, perceived the movement, and quickly stepping aside, avoided the blow aimed.

The furious onslaught of the lieutenant proved fatal to him, for striking at the air, he lost his balance, and fell heavily to the deck.

In an instant the Rover was upon him, and his fingers clutched the throat of the pirate, and his knee pressed heavily on his chest.

"Surrender!" exclaimed the Rover.

"Never, to a boy and a traitor," yelled Grades, making a desperate effort to fling off his assailant.

"Then take the reward of your obstinacy," exclaimed the youth.

And raising the pistol, which he now grasped by the muzzle, above his head, he brought down its butt upon the forehead of Grades with all his force.

The blow stunned the lieutenant, and his head fell back, as a fearful oath escaped his lips.

Once more the Boy Rover raised the weapon. Once more it descended upon the temples of the Spaniard.

No groan escaped his lips now, but the sound of the cracking bone, as the butt-end of the weapon crushed in and fractured the *ox frontis* of the pirate, fell upon the ears of the assembled pirates.

Not one word did they utter.

Not one look of sympathy did they cast towards the murdered man.

He was detested by the crew as much as was Dr. Salti, and the name of the Boy Rover struck terror to their souls and filled their hearts with admiration.

A few minutes before they would have slain him for killing the Captain.

Now they worshipped him, for his fame had gone before him, and the knowledge of who he was had changed their feelings towards him in an instant.

Releasing the throat of the pirate, he rose to his feet.

Glancing round upon the assembled crew, he pointed to the form of Grades.

"Through the bodies overboard," he said. "You are rid of the tyrants. What they possess shall be shared amongst you, and I claim no portion of their wealth. Obey me, and I will soon give you a chance of making sufficient to leave the seas, and live in wealth and peace. I will lead you to victory and fortune."

A loud hurrah broke from the lips of the pirates, and as it died away in the distance, the sound of the bodies, as they fell with a loud plash into the sea, mingled with it and proclaimed the Boy Rover Captain of the Phantom of the Wave.

CHAPTER CXLIX.

THE RETURN TO THE TOWN. — THE GRIEF OF ELLEN.—THE DAY OF EXECUTION. — JUSTICE DEFEATED.

AT the foot of the cliff on which the famed Logan Stone was poised, on its axis lay the form of the brave young sailor, whose life and adventures we have followed so long.

The strong arm of the Boy Rover aided by his own fearful position had hurled him over the rock, and he had fallen within a few feet of the Mutineers, who, panting for vengeance, had rushed upon his doom and into the presence of his Maker whilst the glow of youth was still upon his cheek, and the sins of years upon his soul.

Loud was the cry of horror which escaped the mouths of the officers and those who had joined in the pursuit of the fugitive when they perceived the body of Charles Lawson descending down the steep sides of the granite rock.

Strong men felt the pulsation of their hearts cease as they closed their eyes to shut out the fearful sight.

The officers stood palsied as it were by this second deed, and the horrible fate of Charles and the mutineer forced the last spark of courage from their breasts—they turned to fly where they had pursued.

The panic however lasted but a few seconds. Again they turned and with starting eyes, dilated nostrils, and clenched teeth, they cheered each other on to the capture of the smuggler, and vengence for the doom of the two brave men who lie bleeding in the valley beneath.

But their previous visitation had defeated the object of their desires.

Quick as thought the men spring along the rocks. One glance only he cast around him.

One defiant cry he raised loud and clear.

One bound and out from the rock he sprang and dropped over its side.

With a howl of disappointment the officer sprang to the spot on which he had last stood and looked over.

He was now nowwhere to be seen.

The waters leaped and danced in the bright sunlight many yards beneath them, but not a speck floated on the surface — not a trace of the Boy Rover could they discern.

He was gone.

Where?

The officers pointed to the waters beneath them, shook their heads and muttered

"Drowned!"

To this decision one and all came—they believed having struck his head in the descent he had been stunned and instantly sank to rise no more.

They turned their thoughts now to the two men whom the rovers arm had hurled over the rock, and they commenced to descend to render what assistance lie in their power.

Alas, for Ned the mutineer all their kind offers were unavailing.

Death now set its seal upon his brow, and stamped in ghastly wounds its fearful mandate. Silently they raised him from the hard rock on which he lay and bore his boots to the place from which a short time before he had started full of life and health.

Charles still breathes.

Pale and insensible he lay, but unlike Ned his handsome features had not been lacerated in the fearful descent.

No blood stained his flesh — no ghastly wound showed where the cruel granite had lacerated the form.

But when they raised him up a deep groan escaped his lips,—and his eyes open for a moment only to close again in insensibility.

Heaven was still merciful to him, and under the veil of stupor assuaged his sufferings.

Back with saddened brows and aching hearts. they bore him to the town, sad evidence of the ill success of their errand.

Medical aid was procured as quickly as possible, and all that science and skill could do was done to assuage his sufferings.

The doctors shook their heads ominously, and d blank   y carefully examined the body.

Two ribs were broken and his right arm shattered by the fall.

Intense, indeed, was the grief of the fair Ellen, and their friends.

It was a sad blow to the happiness of the poor girl, for happiness indeed she had fondly believed had begun to dawn upon her.

It was the black cloud sweeping over the light horizon.

Fondly had she imagined that her sufferings were at an end.

But, alas, too acutely did she feel that all her miseries were not yet ended.

The Rover captured and condemned to death had implanted in her breast hope, where despair had so long reigned.

It was but an evanescent gleam.

The breaking through of the sunbeams in a lowering sky, only to be obscured by clouds darker and heavier than before.

Her grief, too deep for tears or utterance, found no relief but in the deep sigh which shook her bosom as she flung herself upon the body of him she so fondly loved.

The wounded youth was carried to the house of her father.

Unceasing were the offices Ellen performed for him.

Ever by his side to bathe the fevered brow and smooth the pillow of the suffering man, to kiss the pale cheek and press the almost pulseless hand.

And there he lie, suffering the acutest agony where he had fondly hoped to enjoy the brightest happiness, tended by a weeping nurse he believed he should have clasped to his breast a bride.

And thus days and weeks wore on, and the death of Wild Madge and the escape of the Boy Rover was remembered only by these so deeply interested.

The Scorpion had been given up to Captain Wildwell, and he sold her to an English merchant, and together with Mortimer and Tray had taken passage for America.

Ridley and Sharks had entered on board the revenue cutter, after receiving a substantial acknowledgement of their services from Wildwell and the father of Ellen.

Thus things stood a month after the fearful adventure on the rock.

Lang and Brand, whose execution had been delayed in the hope that they would reveal where the booty they were supposed to possess had been hidden, had been finally condemned to suffer the penalty of the laws they had outraged, and the dark gibbett raised its dismal head to the sky and awaited its victims.

On the morning assigned for the execution, one of those mobs which are a disgrace to civilisation and humanity had congregated around the scaffold to learn the great lesson which the murder of a fellow creature by strangulation was to teach.

From far and near hundreds of men, women, and boys came to gloat over the death of two made after God's image,—came to howl forth their ribald jests and howling execrations in the ears of those about to die.

Screeching, singing, fighting, and swearing was the order of the hour, and women with babes sucking at their breasts muttered imprecations upon the tardiness of time as they waited and watched for the horrible scene.

Ennobling, indeed, to the soul must be the lesson learned at an execution, when it calls forth all the baseness of nature, turns men to fiends and women to furies, calls forth the oath and fist instead of the tear and prayer, and ushers the soul to eternity amid the shrieks of trampled women and suffocating babes.

Out upon the foul blot whose black stain still disgraces the most civilised country in the world.

Murder will not turn the evil doer into paths of rectitude and honour, but mercy can and does.

It has been tried and proved, and yet the gallows still rears its head, and those who are paid to bring the strayed lamb back to the flock are among its upholders.

Ministers of religion, who alone should preach mercy, defend the scaffold—whose mission should be to save souls, uphold the murder of the body.

Shame upon them, if shame can creep beneath the sacerdotal robe.

The cloak of religion covers a multitude of sins, and hides a black heart and sanguinary nature from the contempt of mankind.

From before the altar he impresses upon his hearers the commandment "Thou shalt do no murder," yet holds that the strangling of a fellow-creature is acceptable in the eyes of Him who gave him being.

Mercy comes from their lips but not from their hearts, the oily tongue can spit forth venom, the minister of salvation can uphold murder.

But we deviate from our path.

The hour approached for the execution of the pirates, and the howling of the mob, eager for their sanguinary treat, became more loud and discordant.

Inside the prison the excitement was not less intense.

The executioner had arrived prepared to fulfil his fearful duty.

The chaplain stood ready to administer the sacrament and lead them to salvation.

But a loud cry is echoed through the long passages and thick walls.

The officers have entered the cell to demand their victims.

The cell is empty !

The doomed men are gone !

"Escaped ! escaped !" is shouted from a dozen throats.

The prison bell is rung loudly.

The officials speed hither and thither in frantic haste.

The governor looks black and furious, the chaplain wears an air of disappointment, and the executioner with his hands dived deep into the pockets of his breeches, mutters an oath at the loss of his fee.

The prison is searched—not a cell or passage but is examined with the greatest care.

Still no trace is discovered.

The pirates have escaped, and none know how or whither.

CHAPTER CL.

THE ESCAPED PRISONERS. — THE FALSE GAOLOR, AND HIS UNLOOKED FOR REWARD.

DAY was fast breaking through the clouds, and chasing the sable gloom of night from earth's canopy, throwing a fitful and spectral light upon the tops of the tall trees, yet deigning not to penetrate the thick foliage of their massive beneath, which all was dark and damp as midnight.

Beneath the dense foliage of a cluster of great elms stood three men.

Two of them appeared to have suffered much, as their features were wan and pale, and deep furrows, ploughed by other hands than time, for they were still young, wrinkled their foreheads and mouths.

Each held in his hand a chain, which passed down the leg, and adhered to a ring that encircled the ankle.

The third personage was a man of about forty years of age, with hard and repulsive features, tall and stout, apparently possessing much muscular power, but withal, a reckless nervousness in his demeanour which betokened a mind ill at ease.

His glance wandered quickly and frequently from the two men at his side out from the trees towards the town, the buildings of which seem as if through a veil loomed up in the early morning light, spectral and gloomy.

"When the devil will you come to the spot where the money is buried," he asked, looking anxiously into the faces of his two companions. "We are more than four miles from the town, and you said it wasn't three. How much further have we got to go ? It's getting light, and you will be missed, and then ther'll be the devil to pay, and a pretty hullabaloo into the bargain. I must be off before they can get any clue of me, or I shall pay dearly for aiding your escape. Come, where's the money hidden ?"

"Not far from here," said Lang, for he it was. "Not far, is it Brand ? only a short distance now."

"Then why do you stop here," asked the man, suspiciously.

"Because it would be dangerous in the daylight to proceed further with these cursed chains clanking at our sides. You say you have the means to take these from our limbs, why don't you do it ?"

"When you have pointed out the spot where the money is buried," replied the man. "Not before. Do you think I am such a fool as to run the risk I have and then allow myself to be done. No, no." I have cleared you of the prison and the gallows, and laid myself open to a heavy penalty, on the promise that you should show me the spot where you have buried the wages of your crimes, and I must see it before I release your limbs."

"You are a fool," said Lang, "to imagine that we have ideas of deceiving you."

"I don't know that," replied the man coldly."

"But I do !"

"Do you ?"

"Yes."

"Well I don't see it."—retorted the man, " fair's fair, and right's right—I've done what I promised, and you aint—when you show me the gold, then I'll run this file over the ring and release you from your chains."

"Not before," said Lang.

"No ?"

And the man returned the file to his pocket as he gave the emphatic answer.

"Then look here," said Lang. "You'll do yourself much injury and us no good. The ring has caused my ankle to swell so greatly that I cannot walk another step. Don't be obstinate. You will find no better place than this to file off our iron besides I shall then be able to walk, and you will see your reward much sooner."

"I've run enough risk, I tell you, to run any more, without seeing the money," said the man, sullenly.

"I am thinking you won't see it at all if you don't alter your mind," said Brand. "Our escape will

M. ANELAY.   C.H.W.

be discovered before we can get clear off from the town, and if we are taken through your obstinacy, by hell we will split upon you, and then what will you get by it."

"He'll have his reward and gain a terrible punishment," said Lang.

The man looked anxiously out from the shadow of the trees down the road they had been pursuing.

"It won't take them long to catch us," said Lang, "once they discover we have gone, the whole town will be up and in pursuit. File these cursed rings ere it is too late and our trail is discovered."

The man hesitated.

"Do you want to be in our company," asked Brand.

"No," replied the man, surlily.

"Then, you will for I can go no further with these irons on my limbs," said Lang.

"Nor I," said Brand.

Still the man hesitated.

His eyes restlessly wandered up the road.

"Come on," he said.

"I can't," said Lang.

"I am not able to move, my legs are swollen so," said Brand.

And to illustrate his words he limped painfully a few steps.

"Don't be a fool to your own interest," said Lang in a vexed tone. "See how light it is getting and mark how the time flies. If we go on like this we are sure to be detected, whilst if our limbs are free there will be something to excite the suspicion of any one we may chance to meet."

"You'll meet nobody," said the man.

"It's more than likely we shall though," said Brand, "there's sure to be some one going to see us hung."

"I fear you will deceive me," said the man, "if I release your ankles from the rings."

"We won't," replied Brand.

"Upon my honour—no," remarked Lang.

"You mean it."

"To be sure we do," said Lang, a gleam of hope beaming in his eye.

"Swear it," said Brand, "yes, a thousand times."

"You will show the place where I may find the gold," said the man.

"Yes."

The man looked searchingly into their faces, but the pirate's features remained calm and immoveable as if chiselled in marble.

Apparently satisfied they had no intentions of playing him false, the man drew the file from his pocket and stooping down grasped the foot of Lang.

"Quick," said the pirate captain "bear heavily upon the file, don't fear to make a noise. I will look down the road and give you notice of any ones approach."

The man commenced to labour away at the iron, and the file which was a new one, cut deep into the iron band.

The eyes of the escaped pirates glistened with every movement of the man's arm, and their hearts beat quicker and quicker, as the file cut deeper, and deeper into the ring.

Every movement of the instrument was one step nearer to liberty—and from death.

Lang did as he had promised, kept his eye fixed upon the road.

And eagerly did he watch for the approach of any one, yet dread it lest they should be discovered, and carried back to the gaol, around which a yelping crowd were gathering to see them die.

The man plied the file quickly and hard, he was anxious to receive the reward of his perfidy.

Placed in the cell to see that the doomed men made no attempt to deprive the gazing crowd of the entertainment which the laws of this great and civilised country had prepared for their amusement and instruction, by laying violent hands upon themselves and attempting to rush into the presence of their maker, before the time the merciful agents of justice set down that they should die. He had leant a fascinating and greedy ear to their tale of wealth which they had hidden a short distance from the town, and soon fell into the trap laid to catch him.

On the condition that he should possess that wealth he consented to forfeit honour, sully his reputation, be guilty of a breach of trust, turn traitor, and assist in the escape of those he was placed to guard.

He nibbled at the golden bait, and the willing anglers had him at their mercy.

True, he fancied that he would be well rewarded for the work, and endeavoured to force himself to believe that he was doing an act of mercy, in rescuing the two rascals from the gallows.

He would as unhesitatingly have sold them to the hangman as to liberty.

The man who will accept a bribe will betray a friend, he who would sell himself would sell another.

The reward goaded him on; but he dreamed not of the nature of the reward he would receive.

He looked for gold and gold alone, never for a moment did he think how strongly it was allied to death.

The iron band was at length cut through, and grasping it on either side of the part brightened by the action of the file, he wrenched it asunder.

With a loud cry of joy Lang swung the chair around his head.

"Free, free!" he exclaimed.

"Aye, free," said the man looking up in the face of the pirate as he still knelt upon the ground, and was about to commence operation on Brand's irons. "Freedom is a blessed thing and deserves to be considered such. I have trusted you. Be true to your words for I have earned my reward."

"You have!" exclaimed Brand "nobly earned it."

"And shall expect it," said the man, "before long."

"Take it now," said Lang, swinging the heavy chain round in both hands and bringing the iron band which so lately wrenched his ankle, down with fearful force upon the temples of the half prostrate jailor. "There is your reward. You have fully earned it."

With a shriek of pain the man struggled upon his feet, but another blow upon the forehead with the iron chain dropped him instantly to the earth.

And as he lay the villain rained blows fierce and fast upon the temples of the false jailor, till not one spark of life remained in that heart a few short minutes before elated in hope.

CHAPTER CLI.

THE PIRATES DISPOSE OF THE BODY OF THE MURDERED GAOLOR—THE SUDDEN SHOT.

THE false servant had had his reward.

To do evil and believe that good will come of it is indeed a vain hope.

The guilty never thrive, no matter how fair may seem the prospect. Vice must have its punishment. Justice claims her due, and sooner or later receives it.

Satisfying himself that the gaolor was dead, Lang hauled the chain from him and possessed himself of the file with which he stepped towards his companion.

"The fool is silenced for ever," he said.

"Dead men tell no tales," remarked Brand, "and it was about the best way to get rid of him, though the poor devil scarcely deserved it, after getting us out of limbo, and just at the last moment to."

"It was a narrow squeak," said Brand, "I could hear the howlings of the mob outside. Lord won't they be disappointed in their treat. I hope they will pull the gaol down when they find we have given them the slip."

"We are not free yet," said Lang, beginning to file the ring around the ankle of his companion, "but we must not holloa till we are out of the wood. There's many a slip 'twixt the cup and the lip, my old mother used to say, and it's a precious narrow escape we've had, but we ain't quite safe yet. I must get these cursed chains free from your limbs and then we must hide them and the body of that chap out of sight.

It won't do to leave anything by which to give a clue to the direction we have taken. What a fool he must have been to believe we had any money buried."

"Rather green," said Brand.

"He's like all the rest of us," said Lang, as he continued fileing away at the iron band. "Sell his soul for money."

"Gold is the talisman to open the hearts of all of us," remarked Brand. "I think the devil must have invented it."

"They do say its found next to the gates of hell," said Lang with a grin. "I only wonder the old gentleman when he gets them so near don't take them inside."

"What old gentleman?"

"The devil."

"But take who inside?"

"The gold diggers to be sure," said Lang. "But there you see, he leaves them to fight over it and murder each other for it, and by making it a means of exciting the evil motives of mankind, he makes a haul of thousands where he could only get one."

"And us among the number," said Brand, "for gold has been our god, and we have sinned enough to obtain it."

"And shall again I hope old boy," said Lang, "now that those cussed chains no longer hold our limbs in confinment. There, you are free again Hurrah!"

"Hurrah!" exclaimed Brand, as Lang snapped the band asunder and the chain fell with a ratling noise to the earth.

"Now to conceal them and the body of the gaoler," said Lang, "your leg is not swollen now is it."

"Swollen, no," replied the other, capering about, "why I could do the double shuffle, and Spanish twist with any man afloat."

"Ha! ha!" laughed Lang, "but there is no time for that now. Quick or you may yet dance a hornpipe in the air at the end of a string."

"Yes, we must away from here, and seek the coast," said Brand. "For look, the sun is rising and to escape detection will be no easy matter."

"True," said Lang, "where can we hide the body?"

"Drag it up and lay it under the trunk of this tree," said Brand.

"It is more than likely it will be discovered too soon," said Brand.

"It's the only chance I see," said his companion.

"We can't bury it, for we have no means to turn up the scent."

"It's damned awkward," said Lang musingly. "If we leave it here it may be discovered immediately and be certain to put our enemies on the secret."

"What can we do with it then?" asked Brand.

"I don't know."

"Nor I."

They both paused thoughtfully for a few moments.

"I have it," said Lang at length, striking his hand upon his thigh, "I have it."

"What?"

"We will conceal the body where none are likely to come," said Lang, his face brightening up at the project he had formed.

"Where?" asked Brand.

"Why, up among the branches of that large tree yonder," he said, pointing to the tall elm, through whose luxuriant foliage the sun had scarce power to penetrate.

"What!" said Brand in surprise "up there."

"Yes, the thickly-leaved branches will hide it from the passers by, and as no one is likely to suspect of it's being there, it may remain undiscovered till the flesh rots and the bones fall to the ground."

"Or the cold weather sets in and the leaves fall off and expose it to view," said Brand.

"Well either way it will give us a good three months' start," said Lang, "and if we get that I reckon we may defy them pretty safely."

"Stop," said Brand, "we must not be too sure that it will remain there. The weight will bend the boughs and the body fall, so all our trouble would be in vain."

"We will secure it."

"How?"

"Fasten it to the boughs," said Lang.

"With what?"

"The chains that manacled our limbs," replied Lang.

"A good thought," said Brand, "but a novel idea."

"Not so novel after all," said Lang, "it will only be giving him an Indian's funeral."

"What in a tree?"

"Yes," said Lang. "I have seen the body of many a red man resting amid the branches of the tree, after his soul had flown to the hunting grounds."

"Well, I gave you credit for the idea," said Brand.

"I'll infringe no man's patent," said Lang, "for it is not mine. So bear a hand, mate, for time flies, and the rope still dangles from the gallows beam."

The two hardened wretches lifted the still warm body of the murdered man, and bore him to the branch of the tree in which Lang designed placing the body.

Throwing it down beside the trunk, they possessed themselves of the chains which had adorned their limbs and returned to its side.

"Now, how are we to get it up," said Brand.

"I will climb up to the first branch, whilst you fasten one of the chains round his neck, and then if you raise the body in an upright position I can grasp the chain and draw him up."

"Good," said Brand, with a smile of satisfaction, "up you go."

Lang was not slow to obey this order, and springing up the trunk, he clasped the lower, and consequently thickest branches, and drew himself up amid the thickly leaved boughs.

Meantime Brand adjusted one of the chains around the neck of the murdered man, and fastening the other to it, he lifted the body into an upright position and leaned it against the trunk.

Steadying it with one hand he raised the end of the chain as far as he could reach with the other.

"Here you are, Lang," he said.

Lang leant over a thick bow as far as he safely could do so, and still keep his balance, and stretching out his hand, grasped at the chain.

"All right!" he exclaimed, as he drew it tight, "he can't fall now, so come up and bear a hand."

Brand commenced to ascend the tree on the other side.

"Avast, mate," said Lang, "afore you come aloft, just cast your peepers up and down the road, and see if you can discover any craft sailing on this course."

Brand descended, and stepping out from the shadow of the trees, glanced up and down the road.

There was no one in sight, as far as the eye could reach.

He returned to the tree.

"Not a sail in sight," he said in answer to an inquiring look from his companion.

"All right," said Lang, "catch hold of the rigging, and pull yourself up."

In a few seconds Brand was by his companion's side.

"Now, mate, up with the anchor," said Lang "a long pull, and a strong pull, and a pull together will send the battered hulk among the rocks—branches I mean. Have you got a fair hold?"

"Yes," replied Brand, grasping at the chain.

"Pull then," said Lang, "yea—a—ho!—yea—ho—ho!"

Up went the battered and bleeding form into the branches of the tree, and pitching the chains over a thick bough, Lang held it firmly and kept the body of the wretched gaolor suspended by his neck whilst Brand, climbed higher up amid the interstices of the immense elm.

Brand now held the chain which was handed up to him by his companion, till Lang could reach his side, and then the same course was pursued, and the body drawn higher, and higher till it was shut out from view from the road by the luxuriant foliage.

Laying it across the branches so as to give as equal a weight to each as possible, the chain was made fast to the stern, and with a look of satisfaction they commenced to descend to the ground.

"All trace of our whereabouts is destroyed," said Lang, "and we can deceive them all."

The last words had scarce left his lips, than a loud report echoed around, and a ball whistled amid the branches in which they stood.

CHAPTER CLII.

THE STORM—THE CAPTAIN'S FEARS REALISED.

UNDER the kind treatment of the captain and mate of the "Diamond," Henry Chambers speedily recovered the effects of his long immersion in the water and the illness consequent upon the sufferings he had endured since the night of the storm, when the brave Captain Perry met his untimely end.

Whether it was that there was a greater virtue in the captain's medicine than is to be found in the most noxious drugs which the surgeon would of a surity prescribed we cannot say, but certain it is that Henry was soon restored to health and strength, and was enabled to take his turn at the various duties as any man of the crew.

The shades of night were closing around the ship as she neared the Isle of Conception, and the weather, which had been excessively hot, gave indication of a storm.

Large black clouds loomed up thick and heaving, and the air came like the blast of a furnace to the cheeks of the broad mariner as, with anxious eye, they scanned the surface of the horizon.

Henry stood looking thoughtfully up at the huge heavy clouds, as they drifted about the blue heavens, when Hart approaching his side, said,—

"How do you like appearances yonder, Mr. Chambers."

Henry shook his head dubiously.

"We shall have a storm or I am much deceived," he said.

"Yes, and a stiff one too," replied Hunt. "I don't much like the look of things out yonder for we shall have to scud along under bare poles before day-break."

"Whew?" whistled Henry, as a bright flash, darting from the sable cloud on which they had been gazing lighted up the heavens. "Here it comes."

A loud peal of thunder rolled heavily over the vessel, and then down came the storm in perfect torrents.

The captain now came on deck, and commenced giving orders to furl the sails, and place the vessel in such trim as the better to bear her safely through the storm.

The sails were braced tight to the yards, awnings taken down, and the hatches put on, and all made right and snug, in a few minutes by the orderly crew.

"Ease her off a point or too," called out the captain to the man at the helm, "and another man go to the wheel, for here comes the wind. Lay her to it. Whew!"

And the captain brought his arm hard down with great force upon the top of his cap, which at that moment was lifted a few inches from his head by the gale of wind which passed over the vessel.

"You will have wet skins to night, Mr. Chambers," he said turning to the young lieutenant.

"I trust, sir, that will be the only hardship we may have to encounter," replied the young man with a smile.

"Oh, that's nothing," remarked Hunt, "Mr. Chambers has got use to that by this time."

"Yes, and the prevention from catching cold too," said the captain with a chuckle. "We shall doubtless have a rough night, and a dose of my medicine will do you no harm. So if you will drop down into the cabin, I will see that it is properly prepared."

"Willingly, sir," replied the youth.

"See that everything is made straight, Mr. Hunt," said the captain turning to descend to the cabin, "and then join us below, a dose will do you as much good as our young friend here."

And beckoning to Henry he descended the companion ladder.

The young man followed him to the cabin, where the captain immediately set himself to work to mix the favourite grog, or medicine as he always himself termed it, and by the time it was prepared the mate joined them.

"Well, sir," said the captain.

"All's made snug, and she stands before the gale like a swallow," replied the mate.

"Are there any signs of the gale abating?" asked the captain.

"I am glad to say there is," was the reply.

"And so am I, sir," said the captain looking over the steaming glass at his mate, "so am I, sir, I should be sorry to have the ship crippled in this latitude."

"Or any other, sir," remarked Henry.

"Yes or any other sir," was the reply, " but in this more especially."

"And why, may I ask ? " inquired the young man.

"Because the course we are now on is a dangerous one," replied the captain."

"True, the number of islands in this part of the Pacific,—"

"Not that sir—not that," interrupted the captain. "The rocks and channels are nothing to cause me to fear, but—"

"What sir ? "

"What !" exclaimed the captain bringing his glass down with a thump upon the table. "The pirates."

"The pirates," echoed Henry.

"Yes, the pirates. This sea is infested with the thieving villains !" exclaimed the captain. "The numerous islands afford them shelter, and they pounce on a poor defenceless trader before she can spread her sails to the wind and seek safety in flight."

"I trust sir, we may be so fortunate as to steer clear of the sharks," said Henry.

"And so do I," replied the other, "but this storm may drive us from our course, and right into the hornet's nest."

"Then we must fight for it," said Hunt.

The captain shook his head.

"I will never strike my flag to a pirate," said the captain, "but as to fighting if we should have the ill-luck to fall across the "Phantom of the Wave" we might just attempt to fight the devil."

Hunt shrugged his shoulders.

"Well, I don't suppose we should have much chance against the schooner," he said, "armed so heavily as she is, and manned by so numerous and desperate a crew."

"Not the shadow of one," replied the captain, "but there, we will take another dose and trust in Providence. If the worst comes to the worst, and the red flag floats beside us, we will not forget that we are British sailors."

The subject dropped here, and another glass of the captain's medicine was soon steaming on the cabin table.

But though nothing further was said upon the subject, it was evident that it still retained a prominent place in their minds, for there was a thoughtful air about them, and their ears seemed alive to every sound.

The thunder as it rolled over the vessel caused them to listen intently lest they should be deceived in its sound.

Still the storm continued, and the vessel pitched and rolled before the gale for the space of two hours, during which time the captain, mate, and Henry, sat in the cabin of the former.

The motion of the vessel now gave evidence that the storm was abating, and Hunt had risen from his seat to go on deck, when a loud knock at the cabin door, and the cry of a sail on the larboard bow caused the captain to leap hastily to his feet.

At the same moment the roar of a gun echoed over the waves, and reached the ears of the trio.

Another gun, and the face of the captain paled, as he exclaimed,—

"The pirates, by God !"

CHAPTER CLIII.

THE JOURNEY HOME—THE TALE OF THE MERMAID.

THE return to America by Captain Wildwell, Mortimer, and Tray in the same vessel, completely obliterated all those feelings which had at one time taken possession of the breast of the slaver lieutenant, and happiness alone reigned where misery had held away.

The voyage was a pleasant one, and much enlivened by the company of five other passengers, three of the men who had travelled much, and two ladies who had likewise seen a great deal of life in various forms and phases.

As is usual on a sea voyage, with little to break the monotony, a strong friendship was soon found, and the party congregated together on deck during the fine weather, or in the state cabin, when the clouds lowered, or the gale rendered exposure unpleasant, and opened the portfolios of their minds.

And thus it was by relating the various adventures through which they had passed, and incidents which had come to their knowledge, the time was passed pleasantly enough, and tended to enliven the hours which always seem to crawl so lazily along when we are anxious to reach the end of a journey.

Perhaps there is nothing tends more surely to give a clear insight into a person's nature than by hearing him speak of his dealings with the world and its struggles and vicissitudes, and such was the opinion entertained by our travellers, who seated in a circle around the state cabin table, or on the clean swabbed decks of the vessel told the story they believed most interesting to their companions.

Whilst Charles Lawson lies sick, watched by the loving Ellen, and the Boy Rover ploughs the sea in search of plunder, we will turn for a short time to the deck of the ship on which the slaver and his companions were seated and hope that the reader may feel the same interest in the stories which enliven their voyage as did their willing listeners.

One of their fellow passengers, a tall wiry formed man, the lines on whose face showed that he had taken life at the roughest and by sheer hard labour had built for himself a comfortable independence, on being asked to relate some story to wile away the time said,—

With regard to myself there is little I can say but perhaps an affair which nearly ended serious to a friend of mine at home may not be uninteresting. Well you see, the person of whom I am speaking as true a man as ever lived, Peter Winton, was one of the earliest settlers in Arkansas whither I myself repaired when quite a boy in search of independence.

He was a bold, hardy man, made of just such stuff as is necessary to the conquering and subduing of a new and wild country.

His cabin was close by the White River, and ere many years he had a broad piece of land smiling under the influence of successful cultivation. His time was about equally divided between the field and the forest, though he had more liking for the latter than for the former, the rifle being a more agreeable companion than the plough.

His family consisted of his wife and two children. Susan Winter was not yet thirty-five, and though living in the wild woods, yet she was fair and modest, and possessed a fund of sound sense that would have done credit to a better education. Andrew, a bright, apt boy, was s x years of age, while little Lucy, the laughing, romping girl, was only four.

One evening as Peter and his family were at supper, the door was opened, and a large, powerfully built man entered.

"Ah, John, is this you?" said Peter, as he recognised his visitor.

"Yes," answered the new-comer, in thick tones, at the same time reeling towards the fire-place.

"What! drunk again, John?" resumed the hunter, in a reproachful tone.

"Been drunk a fortnight, Pete," grumbled the man, looking up with a vacant leer, evidently unable to see distinctly. "Give me a bed, old feller."

"Certainly, you shall have a bed, John. But won't you have something to eat first, John," asked Susan.

"Eh, Suke Winter? Egad I will eat."

He sat up to the table, but his appetite proved treacherous, and he moved back again without tasting food. As he gained the chimney-corner, he drew a bottle from his pocket, but it was empty."

"Drunk the last drop just afore I come in," he said, his utterance becoming more thick. "Give us a tip of yer own bottle, Pete."

"Haven't got a drop for you, John."

"Not a drop of whiskey."

"Not a drop."

"Singe a painter, old boy! What are ye comin' to."

Peter made some careless reply, and then urged the poor fellow to go and lie down. He saw that he was growing more stupid every moment, and that he would soon fall from his chair. After a while the man consented to go, and his host led him to a place in one corner, where a buffalo skin was hung up for a screen, and behind which was a bed of bear-skins. John was soon asleep, and Peter returned and finished his supper.

John Armstrong was a good hunter; a firm friend, ready to help in times of need; and "death on Injuns."

He lived nowhere particular, but found a home anywhere. A week or two would be spent in hunting; then he would carry his skins to the nearest settlement and purchase rum; and then came a spree which lasted while he could get fuel for the fatal flame.

When Peter got ready to go to bed, he went in and looked at his guest, whom he found just as he had left him.

"It's too bad," he said as he came out. "What a noble fellow he is when he's himself. How a man can do so is more than I can understand."

"Poor John," murmured Susan.

Armstrong had ever been a warm friend to both herself and husband, and had, on two occasions, saved them from the Indian tomahawk and scalping-knife. So they loved him even now.

The hunter arose at scarce dawn of day, and and ere he dressed himself he went to see how his guest fared.

John was still sleeping soundly, though the scattered skins told that he had been very uneasy during the night.

"I must go out and look at my traps," said Peter, after he had dressed, "and if John wakes up before I get back, you'd better fix him up some warm drink, and get him to eat if he can. If he wants whiskey, tell him he must wait until I come. I shall not be gone over an hour; so you may have breakfast ready by then."

The husband took his rifle and went out, and shortly afterwards the wife called up her two children and dressed them, and then proceeded to build her fire.

After this she cut some steak from a quarter of venison which hung near the door, and then began to think what she should fix up for her unfortunate guest.

At the expiration of about half an hour, John Armstrong got up and came out.

Susan was on the point of speaking to him, but when she looked at his face she started back in affright.

She had never before seen a face look so pale and deathly—she had never seen eyes glare and sparkle so, nor look so wild and panther-like—nor she had never heard a man's teeth grind and grate as his did then.

"John!" she finally said "what is the matter?"

He glared at her, and then at the children, but spoke not a word.

"Don't you want something to eat, John?"

He glared again at her, and then at the little ones, and then turned to the door and went out.

"Dont be afraid, Andy," the mother said, as the children clung to her dress. "John is a good man, he won't hurt you. He's only sick now."

"But he looked at me so, mother. Oh, how sick he must be."

Before Susan could make any reply to her boy, the door opened, and Armstrong re-entered the cabin.

He had a long hunting-knife in his right hand, while in his left he carried a piece of rope, or halter cord.

He stopped near the threshold, and glared around the room—there was but one room in the place.

His eyes were wild and burning, his lips bloodless and compressed, and his hair standing up like quill over his huge head.

"You are afraid of me, eh?" he whispered in a shuddering tone, at the same time throwing the cord upon the floor, and grasping his knife more firmly.

"No, no, John," uttered Susan as plain as she could speak, with her heart thumping and leaping as though it would burst its bonds. "I am not afraid, for I know you would not harm me. You love me too well for that, don't you, good John?"

"Love ye?" he echoed, with a sharp, grating hiss. "If I loved ye less I might let ye stay in this cursed world. But I am going to send you out of it, Susan Winter, you and your children. I've got to do it. Ye must die!"

There where spects of white froth upon the madman's bloodless lips, and his whole face had assumed a look perfectly Satanic.

Susan Winter had hitherto been mortal powerless, but when she first realised that she little ones were in mortal danger her mother's love begot a mothers fortitude.

The terrible truth burst upon her that Armstrong was labouring under a fit of *mania a potu!* She had heard of the thing, and she knew how dangerous it was. She knew that the rum-maniac would turn his direst upon those whom he had loved best when sober.

She clasped her children to her side, and shrank away into the extreme corner of the room.

"Ye must die!" the madman growled. "I've been commanded to kill ye!"

"No, no, John. Oh, you would not kill us!"

"Not kill ye! Why, what a cursed shame to see such varmints as you a living! You'd kill me quick enough wildcat! Don't I know how you've plotted against me? Don't I know how you've held a knife at my throat for years? Get out, you she devil! Give me the whelps! I'll take their heads off first, and then off comes your'n."

As he ceased speaking he advanced towards the frightened group.

"Mercy!" shrieked the mother.

In a moment the maniac was by the open door, with Lucy crushed tight between his huge knees, while the boy was held by the long, tangled curls of the head. The little fellow, in his struggles had raised his hands, and Armstrong had them both firmly clutched with the hair. The boy's head was bent back, the white throat upturned, and the gleaming knife raised for the fatal blow.

"John," cried Susan in a tone of such agony that even the madman stayed his hand and looked up. "You cannot do it so. Let me hold the boy and then you can cut his head off. Wouldn't that be the best way?"

"Egad it would," returned the man.

"Oh, don't kill me, mother," shrieked the poor boy.

The girl was so crushed that she was unable to utter a word.

"You must die, Andrew," the mother replied with a cold look, but with a pang at heart that gave her pain for many long months.

"Now hold him tight," said the man pressing the two little purple hands out for Susan to take.

"Never fear," she replied.

She said no more.

Armstrong stood with his back to the open door, and as he released his hold upon the boy's hand, she gathered all her reserved strength for the effort, and leaped against him like a bounding panther.

With her head lowered, and with her clenched hands she struck him full in the pit of the stomach, and he fell backwards upon the hard stepping-stone like a log.

In an instant Susan shut the door, and in another moment she had pushed the stout oaken bar in its place.

The mother gathered her children to her bosom, and bare them to her bed.

The boy was almost senseless from fright, while the girl was totally overcome by the cruel pressure she had been subjected to.

But ere Susan could bestow further care upon them the madman had revived, and commenced to kick at the door.

He cursed and swore, and kicked with all his

might, but the stout bar withstood all his violent efforts.

The trembling woman dared not speak—nay, she could not.

At length, Armstrong gave up the effort, and went away.

The poor woman ran to one of the windows, and she saw him go into the shed.

When he came out he had an axe in his hand. And now the maniac violently swore that every head should be split open if the door was not instantly unbarred.

Susan Winter spoke not.

She only prayed to God in her agony that her husband might return.

Soon the blows of the sharp axe began to fall quick and hard upon the stout door.

The mother shrunk away to the side of her children, and listened and prayed.

At length huge splinters fell upon the floor of the cabin.

Another blow.

Another—and another—and the bar was cut in twain.

With one wild, piercing, frantic shriek, the poor woman shrank down upon the bed, and gathered her children beneath her bosom.

But hark—hark!

What sound was that?

The heavy tread of the maniac.

Another!

A tread light and bounding.

Then a dull sound as of a heavy blow, and then a quaking of the cabin, as a body fell to the floor.

With a wild cry the poor woman started up.

Her husband stood before her.

She stretched forth her arms, and pale and cold—without power—without life, she sank upon his bosom.

He laid her gently upon the bed, and then with the cord, which was still upon the floor, he securely bound the arms and ankles of the inanimate maniac.

When little Andrew could speak, he told his father all he could remember, but ere long his wife revived sufficiently to relate all that had transpired.

At first Peter Winter resolved to ride Armstrong off to gaol, but upon second thought he concluded to watch him till he had recovered.

And he did so.

On the third day the poor inebriate was sober and able to walk, and having told him all he had done, Peter opened the door and let him pass out.

John spoke not a word, but with his head lowered and his brow clasped in his hands he walked away.

Just one year from that time, as Peter Winter and his family sat at supper the cabin door was pushed open, and a hunter entered.

The children cried out in terror, the boy clinging to his father, while the little girl sought the protection of her mother.

"John Armstrong!" uttered Peter, gazing up with a bold, frank manly face.

"Yes, Peter," the new comer returned, while a convulsive shudder shook his heavy frame.

"It is old John, but if you can ever love me again tell your children not to fear me. Tell 'em John Armstrong has not put liquor to his lips since the day they saw him last. And tell them too that he never will again while he has life and sense, tell them that, Peter, tell them that."

And the next night John Armstrong sat by the blazing fire and the children were upon his knees.

Their mother had told them how uncle John twice saved their own, and their father's lives and they forgot the terrible hour of his madness in gratitude for his former goodness, and the confidence which his present manhood inspired.

CHAPTER CLIV.

A THRILLING ADVENTURE—A LEAP IN THE DARK. —THE TRAPPER'S STORY.

THE speaker having concluded the narrative of the maniac and excited by his revelation the sympathy, more especially of the female passengers, turned to one of his lady companions and begged of her to acquaint the others with the thrilling details of her captivity and the sufferings she had endured at the hands of the Apaches several years before whilst residing with her husband in a rude cabin at the mouth of the Santa Rita mountains.

It was not without a shudder, however, that the lady recalled the sufferings she had endured and the tremulous emotion with which she related her story told but too plainly the incidents of that fearful time were engraven deeply in her heart.

"I had not been long married," she commenced "and our family consisted of myself and husband, and a young Mexican girl about eleven years of age, and two men, who were engaged with my husband in the hunting business.

One morning in the month of March, after an early breakfast, my husband left us at camp for the purpose of setting some other Mexicans to work, and one of the men started out to kill a deer, leaving me and the other, named John Williams, alone.

As it was washing-day, I had started to procure some water, when the child screamed and said the Apaches were on us.

They came up on a run.

Having a six revolver in my hand, I turned to fire at them, but they were already so close that before I could pull the trigger they had rushed upon me and secured the weapon.

They then proceeded to plunder, seizing on everything they could carry off—flour, blankets, clothing, &c., and, not satisfied with this, they destroyed the balance,

We hallooed and screamed for assistance, but the Indians struck me with their lances and told us to keep quiet, or they would kill us.

They packed up what they could take, and marched us off hand in hand in a hurried and barbarous manner.

After proceeding thus for a quarter of a mile, they separated us in order to prevent our talking together, the girl being a little in advance of me.

We travelled thus all day, over a very rocky, mountainous, road, and finally almost reached the summit.

Having suffered much from recent attacks of fever and ague, I was in a very enfeebled condition, totally inadequate for the fatigues of such a journey, and my inability to travel at the speed which they desired was the cause of my receiving the most brutal treatment at their hands.

They several times pointed a revolver at my head, as much as to say that my fate was already decided upon, and that I was to be made the victim of savage barbarity.

The little girl who was ahead, would occasionally fall back, crying and telling me that the Indians were going to kill me.

They spoke but little Spanish, yet enough was understood to awaken my fears, and fill me with apprehension.

I knew that my strength, which was rapidly failing, would admit of my proceeding but little further, and unless my husband and other parties were following to rescue me, I must fall a victim as soon as my strength entirely failed.

We had proceeded thus about sixteen miles, as nearly as my limited ideas of distance will enable me to judge, and I now lagged behind so much, that my savage captors grew impatient, and resolved to kill me.

They stripped me of my clothing, including my shoes, and left me but a single garment.

They then thrust their lances at me, inflicting eleven wounds in my body, threw me over a ledge of rocks, or precipice, some sixteen or eighteen feet high, and hurled large stones after me, to make sure of their victim, and left me, supposing that I must die, and too barbarous to my misery by entirely extinguishing the spark of life.

This occurred near sunset.

I had nine lance wounds in my back, and two in my arm, and my head was cut in several places by the rocks which were thrown after me, but most of the latter glanced without striking me.

I had alighted on a bank of snow, almost in a state of nudity, and in a senseless condition.

In counting up my camping places before reaching home, I think I must have laid there in a state of unconsciousness for near three days.

I recollected the direction travelled, and the position of the sun from camp at sunset, and with these guides started for home.

My feet gave out the first day, and I was compelled to crawl most of the distance.

I did not dare go down to the foot of the mountain, for fear I should find water, and was therefore obliged to keep on the steep and rocky mountain.

Sometimes, after crawling up a steep ledge, labouring hard for half-a-day, I would lose my footing, and slide down lower than the place from which I started.

As I had no fire and no clothing, I suffered very much from the cold. I was at a point said to be six thousand feet above the sea, and only wonder that I did not freeze.

I scratched holes in the sand at night in which to sleep, and before I could travel I was obliged every day to wait for the sun to warm up.

I travelled what I could every day, and in the meantime had to subsist on grass alone.

One day as I looked down into the valley I perceived a Mexican girl curbing in a splendid horse which she sat with a grace and ease truly surprising.

I called aloud thinking that a woman's sympathy would be extended to a woman's suffering but she heard me not, and in an agony of mind which you can better imagine than I describe, I saw the graceful Amazon give the rein to her no less graceful steed, and pass in a mere gallop from my view.

In utter despair, I struggled on.

"On the fourteenth day I reached the camp of some workmen in the pinery, which was untenanted.

There I found a little food, and some flour which had been spilt upon the ground.

The fire was not quite out, and I kindled it up, scraped up some flour and made me a little cake, the first food I had tasted since I left home.

I was now near the workmen in the pinery, and within two miles of my home, but was too week to go on.

I could hear the men at work, and sometimes saw them, but could not attract their attention.

At length I crawled along to the road over which they must pass, and was found there and carried home, after having been out sixteen days."

"And the Apaches, and the little Mexican girl," asked Inez, "do you know what became of them?"

"Heaven only knows," said the lady, "I never saw them more. But the recollections of my sufferings after, haunts me in my dreams, and I awake with a start and a cry of horror, as in imagination I feel myself being sent over the precipice by the inhuman Indians."

"There are events in the lives of us all," remarked another of the passengers, "which fix themselves in our mind—tales which we hear in youth, that are recalled with all their freshness, to the memory; aye, and one has just now shot athwart my mind, though I learned the incidents many a long day since."

"Let us hear it," said Martinez.

"Well, first I must give you to understand how it came to my knowledge. It was one of those fine, bright, sun shiny days, in the latter end of the month of October, which autumn seems to have borrowed from summer to bestow upon earth as the last genial tribute of the year, that I set forth with thoughts intent upon the slaughter of as many grouse as I could carry home.

The scene of my intended exploits was a track of mountains near the sea-coast of Conemara, the mildest and most romantic district in the west of Ireland. I had not met with the spot I anticipated in the early part of the day, and I was induced to extend my line of operations by the extreme fineness of the weather, and by the information of a half-savage looking peasant, who was tending a flock of small sheep, almost as wild looking as himself, and who assured me there was an *illegant* pack of birds feeding on a particular part of the mountain which he pointed out.

Those who have travelled in mountainous countries must know that the eye of an unpractised person is frequently deceived with respect to the apparent distance of objects, and that in the thin atmosphere of those elevated regions, a point, which seems to the eye scarcely half-a-mile off, may possibly be three or four miles from the spectator.

Without knowing, or indeed caring much for the difficulty, when there was a chance of a bag full of game in perspective, I pushed forward, and succeeded after a toilsome march, in gaining the shoulder of the lofty mountain to which I had been directed by the shepherd, just as the sun was setting.

From the situation where I stood, I could see spread beneath me, like a map, the undulating hills and the green valleys, each one with its little lake, like a crystal set in a bowl of emerald, and the bright streams wandering like threads of silver through a rich tissue; and beyond these, the vast Atlantic, upon whose smooth waves the last sunbeams had thrown that line of light which Moore so poetically calls "A golden path of rays, to some bright isle of rest."

But I had little time for dwelling upon the beauties of this sublime scene, for the gathering mists, that began slowly to roll up the mountain sides, made me aware of the necessity of retracing my steps as quickly as possible.

This, however, was not so easy a task as I imagined, and, as the light began to fail, I found myself, at every step, floundering in some unperceived quagmire, or in danger of breaking my neck over a sudden precipice.

For two hours I continued to descend, every instant increasing the dangers of my path—"if path it might be called where path was none;" until at length utterly bewildered and overcome by fatigue, I sank down upon a fragment of rock, unable to proceed a step farther.

I was revolving in my mind the probability of my being frozen to death on the mountain during the night, when my dismal reflections were agreeably dispelled by the flickering of a light at no great distance.

My pointers, who perceived it at the same moment as myself, began to yelp with delight, and bounded off in the direction in which it appeared.

I followed cautiously; my heart throbbing between hope and fear, and in a few minutes found myself, to my infinite delight, at the door of a poor hovel, whose low walls of rough stones, and whose heath-covered roof, assimilated so closely in appearance to the surrounding objects

that even in day-light it would have been difficult for the keenest eye to have distinguished it, at a little distance from the surface of the mountain.

The noise made by the dogs brought to the door a middle-aged man, of wild, but not unpleasing exterior, who, by the light of a blazing torch of splintered bog-wood, which he held, perceived at once my situation, and without allowing me time to make my request for a night's shelter, led me with frank courtesy into his cabin, and placed me in the best seat, opposite to a cheerful fire of turf and bog-wood.

A few words in Irish from my new host to his wife, a pretty, quiet-looking woman, who was knitting on a low seat near the hearth, caused her to lay aside her work, and to busy herself in making preparations for my entertainment.

The well smoked flitch of bacon was taken from its sooty nook in the chimney-corner.

Half-a-dozen rashers were fizzing and sputtering, in company with as many fresh eggs, in a very short time.

These, with oatmeal cakes, potatoes and a bottle of poteen completed my repast, to which, I can conscientiously affirm, I did all the justice that a man who had been nearly famished on a bleak mountain could be expected to do.

My hospitable entertainer was, according to his own account, a sort of sportsman himself, earning a scanty subsistence by trapping hares and rabbits in the winter, and in summer by catching sea-fowl, and collecting their eggs from the holes and ledges of the rocks where they had been deposited.

"Yours," said I, "must be a dangerous employment."

"Yes, sir," he replied, "but what can a poor man do? He must earn food for his family, at any rate. I've had some narrow escapes in my time; and if you're not too tired to listen to me, I'll tell you about one of them."

I replied, that the recital would give me the utmost pleasure, and he then related to me the following singular adventure:—

"One pleasant afternoon in summer, Frank Costello jumped into his little boat, and pulling her out of the narrow creek where she laid moored, crept along the iron-bound shore until he reached the entrance of one of those deep sea-caves, so common upon the western coast of Ireland.

In the gloomy recesses of these caverns, millions of sea-fowl resort during the breeding season; and it was among the feathered tribes then congregated in the 'Puffin Cave,' that Frank meant, on that evening, to deal death and destruction.

Gliding, with lightly-dipping oars, into the yawning chasm, he stepped lightly from his boat, and making the painter fast to a projecting rock, he lighted a torch, and armed only with a stout cudgel, penetrated into the inmost recesses of the cavern.

"There he found a vast quantity of birds and eggs, and soon became so engrossed with his sport that he paid no attention to the lapse of time, until the hollow sound of rushing waters behind him made him aware that the tide, which was ebbing when he entered the cave, had turned, and was now rising rapidly.

His first impulse was to return to the spot where he had made his boat fast; but how was he horrified on perceiving that the rock to which it had been secured was now completely covered by water.

He might, however, still have reached it by swimming; but, unfortunately, the painter by which it was attached to the rock not having sufficient scope, the boat, on the rising of the tide, was drawn, stern down, to a level with the water; and Frank, as he beheld her slowly fill and disappear beneath the waves, felt as if the last link between the living world and himself had been broken.

"To go forward was impossible; and he well knew that there was no way of retreating from the cave, which, in a few hours, would be filled by the advancing tide.

"His heart died within him, as the thought of the horrid fate which awaited him flashed across his mind.

"He was not a man who feared to face death; by flood or field—on the stormy sea and the dizzy cliff—he had dared it a thousand times with perfect unconcern; but to meet the grim tyrant there, alone—to struggle hopelessly with him for life in that dreary tomb—was more than his fortitude could bear.

"He shrieked aloud in the agony of despair; the torch fell from his trembling hand into the dark waters that gurgled at his feet, and flashing for a moment upon their inky surface, expired with a hissing sound, that fell like his death-warning upon his ear.

"The wind which had been scarcely felt during the day, began to rise with the flowing of the tide, and drove the tumultuous waves with hoarse and hideous clamour into the tavern.

"Every moment increased the violence of the gale that howled and bellowed as it swept around the echoing roof of the rock-ribbed prison, while the hoarse dash of the approaching waves, and the shrill screams or the sea-birds that filled the cavern, formed a concert of terrible disonance, well suited for the requiem of the hapless wretch who had been inclosed in that living grave.

"But the love of life, which makes us cling to it in the most hopeless extremity, was strong in Frank Costello's breast; his firmness and presence of mind gradually returned, and he resolved not to perish without a struggle.

"He remembered that it at the farther extremity of the cavern the rock rose like a flight of rude stairs, sloping from the floor to the roof; he had often clambered up these rugged steps, and he knew that, by means of them he could place himself ot an elevation above the reach of the highest tide.

"But the hope thus suggested was quickly damped when he reflected that a deep fissure, which ran perpendicularly through the rock, formed a chasm ten feet in width, in the form of the cavern, between him and his place of refuge.

"The tide, however, which was now rising rapidly, compelled him to retire every instant farther into the cavern, and he felt that the only chance he had left him for life was to endeavour of cross the chasm.

"He was young, active, and possessed of uncommon courage, and he had frequently, by torchlight, leaped across the abyss in the presence of his companions, few of whom dared to follow his example.

"But now, alone, and in utter darkness, how was he to to attempt such a perilous feat?

"The conviction that death was inevitable if he remained where he was, decided him.

"Collecting a handful of loose pebbles from one of the numerous channels in the floor, he proceeded cautiously over the slippery rocks, throwing at every step a pebble before him, to ascertain the security of his footing.

"At length he heard the stone, as it fell from his fingers, descend with a hollow clattering noise, that continued for several seconds.

"He knew he was standing on the brink of the chasm.

"One quick and earnest prayer he breathed to the Invisible Power whose hand could protect him in that dread moment—then retiring a single pace,, and screwing every nerve and muscle in his body to it's utmost tension, he made a step in advance, and threw himself forward into the dark and fearful void.

"Who can tell the whirlwind of thought that rushed through the brain in the brief moments that he hung above that yawning gulf? Should he have miscalculated his distance—or chosen a place where the clift was widest; should his footing fail—or his strength be unequal to carry him over—what a death were his? Dashed down that horrible abyss—crashing from rock to rock, untill he lay at the bottom a muttlated corpse.

"The agony of three years were crowded into a moment—in the next, his feet struck against the firm rock on the opposite side of the chasm, and he was saved.

"At least, he felt that he had for the moment escaped the imminent peril in which he was placed, and as he clambered joyfully up the rugged slope at the end of the cave, he thought little of the danger he had still to encounter.

"All through that long night he sat on the narrow ledge of a rock, while the angry waves thundered beneath, and cast their cold spray every instant over him.

"With the ebbing of the tide the sea receded from the cabin, but Frank hesitated to attempt crossing the chasm again; his limbs had become stiff and benumbed, and his long abstinence had so weakened his powers that he shrank from the dangerous enterprise.

"While giving way to the most desponding reflections, a Stentorian 'hilloa' rang and echoed through the cavern, but never had the human voice sounded so sweetly in his ear.

"He replied to it with a thrilling shout of joy, and in a few minutes several persons with torches appeared advancing.

"A plank was quickly thrust across the fissure, and Frank Costello once more found himself amidst a group of his fridnds, who were warmly congratulating him upon his miraculous escape.

They told him that his not having returned home the preceding, night, it was generally concluded that he had been drowned, and a party of his neighbours proceeded in a boat early in the morning in search of his body.

"On reaching 'Puffin Hole' they discovered his boat fastened to a rock, and full of water, as she had remained on the ebbing of the tide. This circumstance induced them to examine the cavern narrowly, and the happy result of their search is already known."

"The fascination of sport often leads the hunter into danger," said his fellow traveller, who had not yet spoken, "and many a wonderfully narrow escape they have at times. Your story puts me in mind of one I heard from an old trapper in America, and if it will not tire you I will give it you as nearly as I can in his own words."

Of course his companions were only too glad to hear it, and he commenced—

"At Independence, Missouri, that grand rendezvous for traders, trappers, travellers, emigrants, Indians, and, in short, for all going to, or returning from, the Far West—I once met an old mountaineer by the name of Glass—John Glass—though he looked as little like glass as any substance I can think of. In fact, John clearly showed, in his weather-beaten, scar-disfigured face, that his had been "a hard road to travel." Indeed, on second thought, I hardly know as I am justified in saying that John Glass had any face at all; but he had a head, and the front part of that head much resembled one side of an overgrown badly-whitewashed gourd—a portion of the nose and original skin having been removed, leaving in place a kind of cicatrized surface, which a great amount of weather, and a total absence of soap and water, had turned to a colour that I find comparable with nothing but the aforesaid vegetable.

"I was not at that time acquainted with John personally; but being somewhat fascinated by his appearance, I begged an introduction, which was readily accorded by one having the honour of some familiarity with this nondescript specimen of the wilderness.

"'I say, old hoss, hyer's a settlement chap as wants to know you a few,' were the words which brought the attention of John Glass fully upon myself, and was my only form of presentation to the sacrificed mountaineer.

"'Wal, stranger, you kin know me a heap, ef you're civil,' was the reply of my new acquaintance, spoken in a tone that sounded not unlike the gurgling of waters from a jug.

"'Chaw hoss?' he added, inquiringly, having, like many another individual I wot of, an eye to the profit which might accrue from my acquaintance

"I instantly took the hint, and a plug of tobacco from my pocket, and handing the latter to my new friend, I observed that he had better keep the whole of it, as I had a sufficiency left.

"'Hurraw!' cried out the old trapper, 'You're a trump, you ar, and I'd play you agin any amount of dandified jimcracks I ever seed. You're a hoss as has bottom, or else I'm a wolf—hurraw!'

"I saw I had made a good impression on my native friend of the wilderness, and I naturally argued, that if a plug of tobacco could do that much, a little whiskey would do more. So, after a few exchanges of civilities, in which I endeavoured to compliment John as much as he had me, I mildly suggested that we might as well take a drink.

"'Hurraw!' he cried, in his broadly-accented dialect, ''you're one on 'em, stranger, and old peeled Jack is one as likes to know you. Drink? In course I will—and ef you kin jest find the fellow as says John Glass ever was knowed to refuse to drink when ax'd, you'll see a fight.'

"Accordingly, we adjourned to one of that kind of institutions in which these rough borderers most do congregate; and, having called together a few of John's friends, we chartered a corner of the shanty for that especial occasion.

"The whiskey having been brought forward, in due proportion to the number and quality of the guests, who at once paid their respects to it, pipes were next in order; and each man having loaded, prepared to fire—and did fire—and such a volume of smoke I never before beheld except at the discharge of a regular battery.

"My sole object in this operation was to hear from the lips of John Glass himself how it had happened that his figure-head had become so seriously damaged; and so, seizing the first favourable opportunity, I broached the subject in a quiet way.

"'Wal, stranger,' said John, 'that was one of the scrapes, hey, Bill,' he added, turning to one of his companions, ''you remember that there, I reckon.'

"'Wal, I does,' returned the other; "and if I did'nt think you war dead at that time, may I never see the backey agin.'

"'Yes, Bill,' pursued Glass, "you thought as how I war dead, and its like you warn't glad to find it different, for you'd got my hoss and gun and all sure enough. But you see, when John Glass goes under, thar's gwine to be an arthquake, and thar warn't nary 'arthquake then, stranger,' he added, filling his glass, and turning to me. "I'll just tell you how it war, for you're right decent for a settlement fellow, and decency ought to be encouraged. You see, stranger, it war a good many years ago; I don't 'xactly remember how many, that me and a party were gwine out to the mountains. Wal, we'd fixed up for a regular trapping expedition, and had our horses and mules, and all the rest of our kit ready for a regular three months' hunt. We got over into the Black Hills, and pitched our camp in one o' the purtiest places I ever seed, whar we kind a' spread ourselves to make beaver come. Me and Bill here—the old hoss—paired off kind a' partner like, and did business in our own way, and that thar way war some, I can tell yer.

One day, as we war off that thar way together, setting our traps along a stream, whar the beaver rayther seemed to like the fun, for they allers keep smelling round, looking pleased and curious, we got kind of tangled up in a thicket of wild cherry, which growed along the stream. I war pushing along a little ahead of Bill, when all at once, as I kim to a kind of opening, I seed a big grizzly, as quiet as a kitten, turning up the arth with his nose for the roots as laid below.

"Hurrah, Bill," says I, "Here's fun, and thar's meat."

"What's the muss, Jack?' says Bill, hurrying up to me.

"I showed him the b'ar about twenty yards off, and we agreed as how we'd draw his blood."

"Now, stranger," continued the old trapper.

"In a bear fight," I quietly suggested.

"Exactly—haw! haw! haw?" laughed the mountaineer. "They're some in a b'ar fight—just so; and you're some punks, any whar. Wal, as I was a saying, we fetched our rifles to an aim, and both spoke together. We both hit old grizzly plum centre; but them is critters as don't mind hitting, and our shots didn't seem to do no more nor jest kind o' rile up his dander. He kind o' started up and looked round, as savage as Old Nick; and then, seeing our smoke curling up from the thicket, he know'd thar was some'at for him thar, and broke for us like a streak o' greased lightning.

"'Hurraw, Bill!' says I, 'we're in for't, now. We'll be made meat on, sure as shooting.'

"'Wal, we will, old hoss,' says Bill, 'onless our legs is longer nor the b'ar's.'

"'It's run now, any way,' says I, as we both on us made a break through the thicket.

Bill was behind me afore, but he was ahead of me now; and ef he didn't do some tall walking then, I never seed snakes. Hey Bill?"

"Wal, I did Jack," grinned Bill, who was himself nearly a pretty specimen of the wilderness as the narrator,

"We both on us tore through the bushes like mad," resumed the old mountaineer; "but they was awful thick together, I tell you, and we didn't git along not nigh so fast as I has afore now, tumbling down hill; and we didn't get along not nigh so fast as the cussed old b'ar, who kim plunging arter us like a mad bull, gaining on us at every jump. Maybe as how I didn't swar some at them thar old bushes, which stuck into me at everp leap, and kind o' kept me from getting any whar, with old grizzly puffing up close behind.

"At last we got to t'other side o' the thicket, whar thar was a batch o' prairie, and a big steep bluff on t'other side on't, about a hundred yards off.

"'Hurraw, Bill!' says I, 'it's bluff' or die for old grizzly has got kantankerous, and ain't so fur behind but what he mought hear us holler.

'Leg it Bill!' says I; let your pegs do their duty.'

"And Bill, here, he did leg it, for he'd got the legs as could leg it; and I didn't keep a great ways behind. But the old varmint he gained on us all through them thar bushes, and when I struck that thar prairie I hadn't more'n twenty feet the start o' him. I'd hev cleared old Bruin, though, easy enough, but jest as I got half way to the bluff I struck my infernal foot agin a stone, and kim down headlong.

"I got up agin right sudden, but it was too late for running now, fer jest as I got up the old scamp stood straight up alongside o' me, and reached out his paws for a hug, like some o' the old Frenchmen I've seen out thar.

"I know'd old grizzly's hug warn't for any good, though; but seeing as thar warn't no help for it, I kindo' made up my mind to it, and gin him the contents o' the only pistol I had, at the same time yelling to Bill to load up and settle him.

"I'd jest got the words out, when old grizzly got his paws onto me, and with one infernal rake downwards, tore off skin enough for a leather apron. I drawed my knife, said some-'at o' prayers, and pitched into him with all my might, and we went rolling over and over on the grass, sometimes the b'ar topmost, and sometimes me.

"That thar, boys, is purty much all I know about the fight," pursued Glass; "but some time next day I opened my peepers agin, wiped off the blood, and found I war the wust-looking human you ever seed. My old scalp hung clean over my face—the skin o' my face, and the most c' this here nose, war spread out all around me; I'd been dug into clean down to the ribs, which looked as ef they'd been peeled,

and more'n all that, some thieving scamp—(Bill Bere, kin tell you who that war)—had stripped off the most o' my clothing, and tuk my pistol, and rifle, and everything away."

"Yes," said Bill, "I'll jest tell you how it war, boys—I jest thought as how Glass war dead, I run down to camp and told 'em so and old Sublette told me and Rube to go back and bury him. We went back, and tuk his things; but concluded thar warn't no use o' setting him into the turf, we put back and told the boys as how we'd done it; but we hadn't, and Jack warn't dead, he warn't.

"No, sir-ee!" chimed in Glass—"nor I didn't want to die nuther. Wal, I kind o' looked around like, and seed as how old grizzly had not rubbed out, and that thar was some satisfaction, anyhow."

Here Glass took still another glass, smacked his lips, and continued.

"Ef I war to tell all that happened arter that, I'd keep you here till morning—so I won't.

"The short on't is, I jest tore up my shirt, and did up my wounds as well as I could, and then lay down thar, feeding on old grizzly for a good many days, till I got strength to crawl away.

"The boys I reckoned had changed their camp, and so I set out for a fort as I know'd was about ninety miles off; and I tell you what it is, that thar war one o' the wust tramps as ever this hyer old beaver leed; for I war all cut up, almost skinned, and had to feed on roots and berries all the way.

"At last I got to the fort, and some jimcrack of a doctor set to work on me; and, stranger, I kim out as good as new, as you kin see for yourself.

"I managed to git another hoss, and then started for another fort whar I know'd the boys would be coming in to winter.

"We both got thar about the same time; and a skeeder-looksn set o' white niggers nor them war, when they seed me as they know'd war dead and buried, coming up astraddle o' that thar old hoss, this dyer child tever puts his eyes on.

"'Hurraw, Bill,' says I, as I seed him quaking, and trying to get out o' sight—for the scamp know'd as he war guilty, and I guessed it—'I'll jest kindo' trouble you for that thar hoss, and gun, and the rest o' my fixings.'

"Bill handed 'em over, and I tuk my place among the boys, ready for the next thing as mought turn up.

"Thar, stranger," concluded the old mountaineer. "You knows now how I looks so purty; and so now let's liquor agin, afore we spile."

I subsequently ascertained that this story of John Glass was true in every particular; and I give it as a specimen of what human nature—and especially such human nature as is found in the wilderness of the Far West—can endure and survive.

———

CHAPTER CLV.

THE CAPTAIN'S STORY OF HOW HE SERVED THE TAILOR.

THE stories of the little party had once or twice found eager listeners in the captain and mate of the vessel in which Martinez and his friends were proceeding to America, and Captain Wildwell requested their company in the cabin, as the weather gave some indications of becoming rough.

The invitation was accepted, and after some preliminary conversation, Martinez nudged the fair Inez to ask the captain if he would not amuse them by a story.

It is always hard to refuse a lady, even if she ask of you a favour with which you are unwilling to comply, but when the favour asked is one which meets with your own wishes, it is sure to be quickly complied with, and so, without any beating about the bush, the captain emptied a tumbler of grog and commenced.

"Well, you must know that I was born in Deadman's Ness, and my father owned a few fishing smacks, and was likewise the landlord of a tavern there.

The life he led himself he thought too dull for his son, so he sent me off when very young to the West Indies.

After two or three voyages the old man died, and I took possession of the inn and smacks, and resolved to settle down at home.

So with this decision I took to myself a wife, and invested some of the old man's money in a venture of dry goods and tobacco—mind that must go no further—for though now I have given over that kind of trading I should not like it to be raked up against me.

Well, you see, I had been settled at the "Fishing Boat," the sign of the inn, about two years, when I became rather uneasy in my mind about the non-arrival of the vessel in which I had placed my venture.

Now there are some people who can sit down and take things easy, but I must confess that I can't, and doubts and suspense soon worked me up to a sort of fever heat.

I was all in a fidget, very irritable and disposed to quarrel with my wife and my best customers.

My pipe would not burn pleasantly, and my grog had a peculiar smatch about it which made it taste more like physic or poison than pure Nantz.

I could not sit still in my chair, and instead of listening to the stories and songs of my company in the tap-room, I was straining my ears to catch the sound of a boat's bottom grating on the hard shingle, or the shouts of her merry crew.

At last I could sit still no longer, so I left the house, and having mounted the sea-wall which protects our little island from the attacks of the broad ocean, I wandered slowly down from whence you get a view round the spot of the open sea, and a good way up the river.

I applied my telescope to my eye, and swept the surface of the water, but neither lugger or cutter was in sight.

I strolled up and down for some time, using the glass at intervals, and just as it was growing dusk I fancied I could see on a bright red spot, caused by the last rays of the setting sun, a small boat with her sail set, steering for the Ness.

It had been rather a rough day, and had blown half a gale of wind until the tide had ebbed, when the wind sunk and the rain left off.

"Now, as the tide was setting in, and the water fast rising, the wind was rising with it, and the dense black clouds, just above where the sun was setting, portended a storm, if not a tempest.

When the sun went down, it grew suddenly too dark for me to see any object distinctly, much less the small boat, which must have been more than three miles distant.

The wind began to howl, and the rain to dash in my face in large warm drops—a sligh flash of lightning gleamed in the west, and the distant roar of thunder made itself heard.

Presently the wind howled louder and louder, the rain fell in heavier plashes, the lightning gleamed more vividly, and the thunder proclaimed by its increased distinctness that the storm was approaching nearer.

I began to feel nervous and agitated about the fate of that little boat, for somehow or another I felt that she was steering for the Ness, to announce to me good or evil tidings of the fate of my venture.

For some time I stood straining my eyes in hopes of catching sight of her during thee momentary gleam of lightning, but all in vain.

She was a mere speck upon the ruffled surface of the water that lay before me, and had it been broad daylight I could only have got a glimpse at her now and then, as she pitched over the top of the waves, which were now bristling under the powerful influence of a nor'wester, and presenting the appearance of what we call white horses.

When I was wet to the skin, I began to think that it would be as well, if I remained on watch, to put on my Flushing coat, large boots, and oil skin weather cap. So I hurried in doors, and when I had provided against the storm and the effects of the cold, by waterproof clothing and a dram of spirits, I lighted my ship lantern unknown to anybody, descended the wall again, and took my station on the head—the little storm jetty or pier, or whatever you like to term it.

I held my light as high above my head as I could, so that those in the boat might see where to make for by its rays, and that I might see beneath them any object that approached.

How it did rain, blow, and thunder. It would have frightened any landsman to see the lightning flash and play about him, and have driven him indoors for shelter, even if he had known his whole fortune—aye, life itself, had depended upon the little boat about which I was so very anxious.

I cared, however, nothing for the pelting of the rain, or the blowing of the wind.

I was too much used to rough weather to mind it, when I had, as I thought, so much at stake, besides, I felt that common humanity demanded of me to do my best to succour those, whoever they were, were in so perilous a position as the crew of that little cockle-shell of a boat.

I knew that if they missed the spot, and failed to round it into our creek, they must be driven ashore, and compelled to spend the night upon such a portion of the lowland as would not be covered by a high spring tide.

I watched and watched until I was tired of watching, and my feet and hands were benumbed with cold.

I had lost almost all power of seeing or hearing, for the briskness of the continual flashes, the howling of the wind, the dashing of the waters, and the booming of the thunder, well nigh deprived me of the senses of hearing or seeing.

Still I kept my station manfully, although I began to feel a little nervous, and to fancy all manner of strange sights and sounds—scenes occurred to my mind that I had witnessed years gone by.

The faces of tempest-tossed messmates appeared below me, struggling in the waves and shouting for help.

The sound seemed to be peopled with the cries of well-remembered voices, half smothered in the roar of the waters; and the din of the thunder-clap sounded like the booming of the cannon the signals of distress and danger.

I began to think of those invisible beings, those unearthly creatures, that we sailors know hover about us in storms and tempests, when death is about to perform his cruel work.

I did as we all do when we are driven to it by fear—even the very worst of us—I began to pray.

And, let me tell you, that at such a time a man does not stand to pick any particular form of prayer.

He prays from his heart.

A few inward prayers for help seemed to calm me.

Then I knew that the cries I had heard, and the white faces that I fancied I had seen, were no more than the screams and white forms of the sea mews, as they dashed over the waves, seeking shelter inland from the storm.

I laughed aloud to think what a coward and fool I had made of myself.

In the midst of my laughter I felt a hand laid upon my shoulder, and, I do not mind if I confess it, I was frightened.

A voice, however, which I knew belonged to Will Murdoch, the doctor, composed me, and just then I heard a shout between the peals of thunder that convinced me I had not watched in vain.

In a few seconds I could see the boat rowed by two men, with a third sitting in the stern, and in a few seconds more she was alongside the jetty and made fast by a rope.

To my question a voice unknown to me replied by another,—

"Is this Deadman's Ness?"

"Aye, aye," I replied.

"Are you Nessmen?" asked another voice, also a stranger to me.

"We are," I replied. "Both of us are Nessmen, and have watched you anxiously for some time.

"Then just lend us a hand to get this long-legged landsman ashore; he is in some scrape or other, and hired us to land him here, to play at hide and seek a bit."

"Come, sir—now then,—here you are,—step ashore,—look lively," exclaimed Murdoch and I, by turns.

"Lord love you," said one of the boatmen, "you might just as well ask a porpoise to come ashore and take a glass of grog with you. He's been as good as dead ever since the gale came on."

"Just show a light," said the other boatman.

I did so, and by its glare I saw him unfold a long, thin, pale person, from amidst the folds of a large blue cloak, having his hat, which was crushed by the experiment and the rain, tied tightly over his head and under his chin, with a red pocket handkerchief, which made his pale face look ghostlier than it otherwise might have done.

"Lend a hand, all of you," said I, as I set my lantern on the head, and sprang into the boat.

I lifted the gentleman in difficulties in my arms, and passing him from one to the other, we got him ashore, and carried him as though he were a dead man, by his head and his legs into the Fish by the back door, and up stairs at once to the top of the house.

There is a room where we stow away all sorts of things besides people in trouble, for it has its conveniences.

I was glad Will Murdoch happened to be at our house, for I really thought the chap in the crushed hat was either dead or dying, but Murdoch only smiled when I hinted at such, and gave me a wink which I knew meant get rid of the strangers, and bring the brandy bottle.

I obeyed, and showing the boatmen into the tap-room, returned to the lookout room with a basket of provisions, and the materials for a fire.

When I arrived, I found Murdoch had succeeded in stripping off some of my guest's upper clothing, untied his neck-cloth, and seated him in a large arm-chair.

Murdoch winked, and I put the neck of the brandy bottle into the stranger's mouth.

He took it very kindly, and I jerked about half a pint down his throat.

It set him coughing and swearing, and in a few minutes. after another gulp or two, he opened his goosberry eyes and, staring at me and Murdoch alternately, said—

"Am I safe?"

"I have saved you," said Murdock, fervently; "I am a surgeon, and I expect to meet with a due reward."

"Virtue is its own reward," said the stranger, in a snuffling, school-boy tone, and before the doctor could explain that that was not exactly his meaning, he added—

"Where am I?"

"In Deadman's Ness—where you wished to be," said I.

"And who are you?"

"Jem Tospeck, landlord of the Fish."

"And am I safe?—will you protect me?—hide me from—"

"Anybody and everybody," said I, "provided you have not murdered, fired a house or corn stack, or injured a female."

An additional paleness came over the pale man's features.

"*I* am—I am the injured party. I'll do anything, pay anything, only do not let them take me up before the bench."

"The old story," whispered Murdoch; "I never knew a guilty person take refuge here in my life."

"You'll be quite safe here, sir, said I, "if you only comply with my usual conditions."

"And what are they?"

"Pay ready money for everything, and ask no questions."

"I'll comply—I'll comply," said the stranger, pulling out an apparently well-filled purse from his pocket. "How much is the brandy?"

"Never mind that now," said I; "you'll want something more before you go to bed, and you can settle with me in the morning."

"Oh, yes, we shall want something for supper," answered the doctor. "What have you got in the house?"

"I have an excellent cold goose."

The stranger turned pale; then putting on an emciicy look, shuddered and shook his head.

"Stomach won't stand goose," said the doctor. "I'm for something hot, so are you, I suppose, landlord? What say you to a rump steak for three, with onions and potatoes?—two very excellent esculents."

"That will do for me," said the stranger; "you can order what you please."

"I do not want to impose upon you, sir," said I, "but I do think a bit of grub and a glass of something warm is not too much to bestow upon two men who have been out in such a storm for some time to save you from drowning. But as you please—the doctor and I can leave."

"Oh, dear no—no—pray don't—I shall be most happy to see you and—pay for anything. What do you charge for supper?—how much a head, including beer, with bread and cheese?—what's the lowest figure—eh?"

I looked at the brute, and said to myself—

"Is this the fellow for whom I stood two hours in the storm, got drenched with rain, and almost frightened to death with fancied spectres?"

"I felt inclined to turn him out of doors, and perhaps might have done so, had not the notion came across me that he must have perished in the storm which was still raging, and that I should be guilty of murder.

As I turned to leave the room, and order supper my guest called after me saying that he should like some vegetables.

"Cabbage, I presume," said I.

"Curse cabbage!" shouted the man looking paler than ever.

"That or a potato is all you are likely to get to-night," said Murdoch. "We are not celebrated for a variety of esculents in the Ness," continued Murdoch, between the puffs he was bestowing on the fire to make it burn.

"Well, curse cabbage—let it be potatoes," said the stranger; and I msut say, the heartiness with which he cursed cabbage somewhat surprised me.

While I was below getting the tray in readiness, and waiting for the steak, for I never allow anybody but myself to wait upon any one who is in trouble and up in the lookout room, I contrived to put a few questions to the boatmen who had brought over the chap that was too delicate to eat goose, and vented curses on cabbage.

All I could learn from them, however, was, that another chap, much of the same rig and build, had driven my guest in a sort of chaise cart to a fishing village on the opposite side of the river, and inquired if anybody would take one of them across.

"We offered our services for a guinea a piece," said one of the men, "and he tried to lower our terms to half a guinea a piece, and when he saw that would not do, he said if we'd take off five per cent. and say pounds instead of guineas he'd go with us, but we'd a-changed our minds then, and could not go under two guineas each, and while he was hesitating, we heard t'other chap say, 'you know you must go,' and so we asked five pounds between us, and of course we got it."

"Did you know he was coming here?" asked I.

"Not till we had put off, and it was too late to make a better bargain," remarked the man. "Nevertheless, we took it out of him in full, for when the storm began you never saw a chap so frightened in your life. He sat down cross-legged, as if he had been used to the attitude, bottom of the boat, and cried, and laughed, and was ill, and prayed and cursed at the same time, till at last he grew so bad, that we rolled him up in his cloak, and tied his hat over his head, with his handkerchief, just as when you found him."

"And you don't know his name, or what he is," I asked.

"All he let out was, that if he was catched, and carried before the beaks, he should be exposed and ruined for life. We drew the passage money before we started, in course, but after such a voyage we think he ought to stand grog and tobacco."

"He won't," said I; "he's not of the right sort."

"Try him, and if he's shy, just hint that we cross again as soon as the wind lulls, and have a month apiece, with a tongue inside of it."

"Well, I carried up the supper things and the boatmen's message. You never saw a chap in such a passion, or heerd one go on so about imposition, cheating, and so on. He swore he'd be I don't know what berore he'd give them another shilling; so I tried the hint given me, and I had no sooner done so than he turned pale again, and handed over a shilling for each of them, which, by my advice was enlarged to half-a-crown, much to his annoyance.

"His appetite, however, did not appear to be greatly injured, for he ate almost as much as Will Murdock and I did; nor was he backward in attempting the tankard. As he ate and drank, his tember began to improve, and he seemed inclined to make himself agreeable, until I was removing the tray, and asked him how many bottles of grog, and of what sort I should bring up?

"He turned sulky at first, but the thought of his being at our mercy seemed to come over him, and in a despairing tone, he said—

"Just as many and of what sort you please."

"So I brought up three bottles of the best brandy, and a box of the best cigars, for I was determined to punish him for his meanness.

"Before you begin your grog sir," said Murdoch, when I had set my cargo down

"just try a little neat—come, just one thimble-ful."

"Curse me—do you want to insult me," said the stranger.

"Ah, no," said Murdoch, "take a tumbler-full if you like, only I thought a thimble-full would suit you best."

"Thimble suit! I'll—but no I won't—it's no matter. Ah! ah! ah! how very odd!"

"A lunatic," whispered Murdoch to me.

"I took no notice, however, but made my grog and lighted my cigar. Murdoch and the stranger did the same, and after a few glasses we got quite chatty and agreeable until I put him out by telling him that he would be safe enough here if he could only produce enough parchments, and a bit of tape or two, and pretend to be here on business, and that these were the best measures to take to stop people's mouths. How he did stare, and muttered so

many curses that I was obliged to check him, and tell him that I never allowed such language in my house.

After this we smoked and drank quietly, and then we sung and told our stories. I was puzzling myself all the while to make out who my guest was.

I was certain that he was not a gentleman, although he wished us to believe him one, and talked loudly of high figures in his banker's book, and the respectability of his connections, which he said were very extensive, and particularly among the army and navy.

"Do you happen to know Admiral Hardress," said I.

"Know him," replied he, "I should think I did, from the collar of his coat to the button of his drabs."

"A fine large man," said I.

"Stands six feet and an inch, and measures

exactly a yard and ten nails round the waist," was the reply.

"Any fine women in your parts?" enquired the doctor.

"Superfine—all superfine—all of the first mark; and I do flatter myself that young dandy Jem, as the dear little loves call me, though my name is Jemmy Capper—is a page in their books."

"You are not married then, I presume," said the doctor.

"I should think not; I am not going to cut myself to waste," he replied. "But if you know of any nice little pattern of a wife, with a little embroidery about her, real gold and silver, no tinsel mind, that would fancy my cut, why, Jemmy's the man that won't be ungrateful, that's all."

The grog was evidently getting the mastery of the chap's brains, and he rattled away about Lady This and Lady That, winking his gooseberry eyes all the time, as if he thought to impose upon us the notion that they bestowed their bright looks upon him.

Then he launched about his property and the immense sums owing to him, if he could only get his debts paid, until I really believe the doctor began to think him somebody.

I did not.

I had been thinking while they were talking. "Goose, cabbage, thimble, parchment, tapes, patterns, said I to myself, "those are the words that offended him, and now he talks about cutting to waste, and knows the exact measure of of Admiral Hardress—hang me if he is not a tailor.

I was confirmed in my suspicions when I heard his reply to the doctor's recommendation of a wife.

I did not communicate my discovery to the doctor, but sent the bottle round merrily.

I told him that I knew of a quiet little woman that would suit him to a T.

"To an ell you mean," he hiccupped.

And that I would introduce him in the morning if he would retire quietly to bed.

What my plan was, and how it succeeded, you shall hear.

Some of you may have remarked that the islanders of the Ness are by no means diminutive in stature, and although our women are not generally above the height of women who are born elsewhere, we had a few among us who might have earned something by allowing themselves to be shown about as giantesses.

Among those remarkable for their height and size, one bore away the belt from her neighbours by some three inches in height, and some foot and a half in girth.

She was as strong as many of our men, and though she led a life of single blessedness, she never stood in need of a protector.

She occupied and tilled a few acres of her own landed property, and had two boats, in which she often put to sea in the roughest weather.

Neither the men she employed on her farm, or the crews of her boats, dared to impose upon or be rude to her, for she would not have hesitated to have seized a brace of them, one in each hand, and knock their heads together.

Indeed, to give you an idea of her strength, she once punished a burly captain of a coal brig who had insulted her, so severely that he was obliged to take to his bed for a week.

She had had several offers of marriage, for she was supposed to have saved some money, but she only snapped her fingers at the proposals when they were made, and it has been asserted that she turned the would-be bridegrooms somewhat roughly out of the house.

She was known among us as Broadstykes, that being the name of her little farm.

Well, to cut a long story short, I made a confidant of the doctor, and begged him to come down as soon as he had seen his patients, and aid my plan.

He got back to me soon after breakfast, and went up stairs to a room that I called the lookout, as it commanded not only the approach of the sea, but also the road around the Island by which the house could be reached.

Mr. Dandy Capper was not very well after his voyage, the beef-steak supper, and what followed it.

He was so low spirited too, and so fearful of having betrayed the cause of his being in concealment over his cups, that he scarcely ate any breakfast.

I supplied him with his account, he looked over the items, and paid the amount without grumbling.

"Sir," said I, "you talked of wishing to be introduced to a nice little girl with a little money, for I know of one whom I think is likely to suit you. You can call upon her. We don't stand upon ceremony here. If she likes you she will tell you so, and if she don't she won't mind telling you that also.

"I'd much rather see the article before I propose to become a bidder," said Jemmy, with a comical wink of the eye.

"Certainly, sir," said the doctor, chuckling at the idea of a bit of fun, which, by the bye, none enjoyed more than did myself. "Quite right, and it is possible you may see her pass here in the course of the day."

"By jingo," I exclaimed, "odly enough, here she comes, taking her usual walk along the sea wall."

Up jumped young Capper, and after pulling his waistcoat down, and his shirt collar up, and adjusting his locks with his fingers, rushed to the window and intently examined a girl who used to assist my wife about the place—a neat, comely wench, whom I had induced my wife to rig out for the purpose, and ordered to walk up and down before the window.

"That will do—just the thing," exclaimed Jemmy, rubbing his hands together. "Small waist, taper ankle, well-developed bust—But what's the figure—eh?"

"A nice snug freehold, a couple of serviceable fishing-smacks, besides a considerable stock of ready money," said the doctor. "Now at her at once."

Jemmy looked queer, and hesitated.

"Perhaps the gentleman would rather wait till it grows dusk," said I, before he ventures out; not that there is any fear, only I know folks in trouble grow more courageous after dark."

A sickly look spread over the face of the man, and he tried to smile.

"That's it—aint it," I asked.

He hesitated a moment before he replied, but evidently conquering his qualmishness, he said,

"You've hit it. I'd rather wait till dark. Do you two promise to show me to her house this evening, and I will stand a sumptuous dinner and wine.

This was agreed on, and I got up a nice neat little spread, and decanted some of my best port and sherry. Jemmy ate voraciously, and drank so freely, that I was obliged to check him, lest he should be too far gone, and spoil the fun.

He talked fast, too, and principally about his plans after he should have got Broaddykes, as he called the lady.

We had a cigar or two after coffee, and before it began to grow dusk, Jemmy, at my suggestion, then began to prepare himself for the visit.

I then led him down stairs, followed by the doctor, and conducted him through the private door, and my garden, to the public road.

A narrow plank over a wide gaping ditch, led out of the main road on to a sort of sheep common, across which was the footpath leading to Broad-dyke's farm.

He did not speak a word as we crossed the field towards the house, and from the way in which he kept looking behind him, I thought he was almost disposed to return.

When, however, we got to the front door, which was seldom used, our knock was not answered for some time.

This period of suspense the lover employed in rubbing his knees, pulling his collar up, and combing his long locks with his fingers.

At length a window near the door was opened and a voice, deep and sonorous as a man's, inquired—

"Who be you, and what's your wool at this late hour, and me a lone woman?"

Jemmy started back, and laid hold of the doctor's arm, who merely said—

"All right—speak to her, man."

I stepped up to the window, and told the lady that I had walked over with a gentleman who wished to speak to her upon particular business.

"Oh, if it's you, it's all well; but come into the back house—the bolts are so rusty at the front, I'll not be able to move them," said the same voice, as the window closed with a violent jerk.

"Come along, Jemmy, round this way," said the doctor.

"Stop—pray stop! Who—eh?—whose voice was that? There's a man in the house—I won't go in," said Jemmy.

"Pooh, nonsense, be a man—that was the voice of love—listen to it."

"If I do, may I be—"

"Nonsense, be a man—; what's in a voice? Think of the freehold, and the money in the stocks," said Murdoch.

And he whirled the poor tailor round the corner of the house, and into the back door, where the lady, with a candle in her hand, was waiting to receive us.

"Who the devil have you got here? But come in. Mind the step, stranger, or you'll chance to find your head where your heels ought to be," said the woman, in her deepest tones, followed by a laugh which sounded as if it had come from a saw pit.

Jemmy hung back, but the doctor put his shoulder behind him, and forced him forward.

"Allow me, Broad-dykes," said I, shaking her large hand heartily, "to name to you Mr. Jemmy Capper, a perfect gentleman, and a man of property on his own account. He has some

business to talk to you about, of so particular a nature—"

"Nothing 'erable, I hope," said Judith, placing her arms akimbo, and looking murderous.

"Of so particular a nature, that I and the doctor will go into the kitchen and draw a pint of your excellent ale while he makes it known to you."

"Don't, pray don't," said Jemmy; it's all a mistake—I never can be left alone with her."

He clung to us, but we shook him off, and pushed him into a chair, where we left him alone, looking more like a dead man than a living impostor. I took care not to close the door behind us, but left it ajar, so that we might hear all that passed.

"Well, sir, what's your wool with me?" said the loud voice.

"Judith—that is, Miss Judith Hailstorm," said Jemmy.

"Why, you pale-faced, lanky-haired——But never mind now. What might you please to want with Broad-dykes? Come, speak up!"

"Nothing, ma'm—I never heard of her in my born days—never was introduced to the connection—don't know the party," said Jemmy.

"Here's a mystery—but I'll have it out of you," said Judith. "Here, Tospeck (meaning me, of course), just step here and tell this young impudence who I am."

That was, however, no part of my plan, for I did not wish to face Broad-dykes after Mr. Jem had explained the trick I had put upon him at her expense; so I gave Murdoch a nudge, and we slipped out through the wash-house, round by the garden, and waited under the shade of the hedge to see the result.

At last we heard, "Turn out, you villain! I'll teach you to come courting! gentleman, forsooth!—want my little freehold! there—there; take that, and that, and that!"

And, by the light through the window, we could see the lady dragging the poor tailor by the hair of the head, and inflicting a series of blows about his face and body.

When he managed to escape, by leaving a tuft of his lanky hair in her hand, she caught up a birch broom, that stood near, and ran after him, but not being able to overtake him, for he ran like an antelope—she hurled the broom at him. It lodged between his legs and caused him to roll over and over in the mud. He was up again as soon as possible, and out of sight in an instant over the first plank—the voice of Miss Juliette urging him on the faster.

As soon as Broad-dykes had vented her rage and returned to her house, Murdoch and I set out home. We found Jemmy arrived at the first plank, but not daring to cross it, he had seated himself on the bank by the side. It was too dark to see him distinctly, but it was clear he had lost his hat, and had his coat nearly torn off his back.

"Mr. Jemmy Capper," said Murdoch, "is this the conduct of an independent gentleman, a man of large figures in his banker's books—to run away from two friends who put him in the way of marrying an heiress and settling for life?"

"Curse you both," said Jemmy, springing to his feet. I am unsettled for life; but I'll be revenged. I'll appeal to the law. I'll institute a suit in—"

"You'd better make a new one for yourself, Mr. Tailor," said I.

"Tailor, sir? Curse you! I'm not a common tailor, sir. I—I am an army and navy uniform maker."

"Oh, that's it. Chatham, eh?" said Murdoch. I twig; but come along, don't stand here all night. Give me your hand and I'll take care of you—you'll have to walk the plank another way some day."

For some minutes Jemmy refused to move, but seeing us about to leave him he put his hand in Murdoch's, and saying, "I forgive you all," suffered himself to be led upon the plank.

When they got to the middle of it, Jemmy gave a high spring, up flew the plank, and a fearful plash proclaimed that Jemmy was in the mud. We fished him out, and led him half smothered to the house, and introduced him into the tap-room, where we found the two boatmen who had brought him over, and a third man who proved to be the beadle of Chatham; this individual put into his hand a bit of paper, which proved to be a magistrate's warrant for his arrest, for embezzling certain moneys of his employers, army and navy tailors.

"Then your suspicions as to his character were correct," said Martinez with a laugh. But how about your venture?"

"The ship came in a few days after, all safe and sound, and I made a good hit by the speculation; but shortly after, my wife died, and I sold the smack and the inn, and took up to my old calling; and here I have remained ever since."

CHAPTER CLVI.

THE MATE'S STORY.—GETTING UNDER WAY.

"JUST take a turn on deck, Mr. Stephens," said the captain, after he had moistened his mouth and lighted a cigar, "and see how it looks overhead; and then, if all is still fair, you'll do us the honour of joining us again, and letting us have a story from you before we turn in."

The mate, thus addressed, darted out of the cabin to obey the order, and in a few moments returned, saying that all looked right at present, but that he doubted if it wouldn't blow a gale by morning.

"Then let's be happy while we can," said Wildnell; "so take a pull at the tumbler, and then let us hear one of your adventures."

"Have you ever crossed the Indian Ocean?" asked Stephens, looking around the assembly.

"No," was the general reply.

"Haven't you, now? Well, I have, and so I'll tell you about it.

It was morning; the sun was hidden under a cloud.

A triple band of vapour encircled the proud head of "Piter-Boot," whose summit, in the form of an inverted cone, haughtily domineered over the fertile plains of the Isle of France.

The sky, which ordinarily had the appearance of a splendid azure dome over the vast Indian Ocean, was obtaining little by little a sombre tint.

The wind blew fresh.

The gigantic clouds, chased violently by a strong north-west breeze, coursed with rapidity across the atmosphere and came together, clashing, intermingling, confounding, gathering in the horizon, and projected their menacing shadows in the quarter of the Grand-Port and towards the Pamplemousses.

Here and there, the powerful rays of the sun, piercing unawares through a large gap in the opacity of the mist, inundated like a stream of flame the jagged crest of the Tamarin, or the arid flanks of the mountain of the Trois Mamelles.

At other times, it was the cascade of the Savane, whose large sheet of water thrown into the air in myriads of particles, and irritated by the continued action of the silvery jet, took successively the rich and varied tints of a rainbow.

Then the clouds, rising from the sea, the waters of which the sun's rays were evaporating, mounted into the air by reason of their elasticity, there condensing rapidly they interposed their greyish masses between the earth and the luminous gleams.

Then all re-entered into a half obscurity, and the white houses of Port Louis had their roofs and sharp angles clearly defined upon the black sky and the neighbouring country.

Suddenly, effected by a change so frequent in the latitudes of the equator, the wind chopped round to the sou'-sou'-east.

The squalls, after sweeping the Isle along its whole length, beat violently upon the road and whistled amid the rigging of the vessels which were riding at anchor.

This was near the middle of the year 1796.

The second watch had been passed on board the vessels of all nations which encumbered the port. In the gusts of wind they careened, pressing the one against the others, when they would suddenly right themselves and rise above the neighbouring craft and the moveable forest of intermingled masts.

An extraordinary activity reigned above all.

The evident approach of wind accompanied by rain was clearly the source of the inquietude which was to be seen in the sailors.

Modulations of the boatswain's calls were to be heard on all sides.

On all the ships the mariners were moving; they carefully visited the cables and hawsers, they took many precautions against the vessels running foul, and sought to be prepared for the moment when the tempest should augment its fury.

The road was almost deserted.

We say almost deserted, because within an hour, all the craft, which were there moored, left their anchorage, seeking a refuge against the storm, and successfully entered the port with the exception of a ship of light burthen, a sort of lugger of small dimensions.

This diminutive vessel, moored stontly by her anchors, seemed to defy all the efforts of the storm which, at that instant, increased its strength.

And also, this foolish temerity made her the subject of conversation to a numerous body of spectators, who, grouped upon the wharves, manifested loudly their great astonishment at the spectacle.

"Can there be no person on board?" cried some.

"The captain is mad?" repeated the others.

"At the first wave it will be upset despite its anchors."

"The crew will make a heavy drain on the rum-casks if they have to stay there all night."

"But in less than ten minutes it will be too late to re-enter the port."

"It is a lost ship!" cried the principal person in one group.

Finally the clouds, more terrible minute after minute, spread over the road with its wide expanse.

The sea grew visibly before one's eyes.

The surging billows, rapidly and furiously dashed against each other, and the foaming waves gushed and frothed about the lugger, which was covered by their spray.

Now and then, the waves precipitated themselves upon the fragile bark, which pitched backwards and forwards in sudden starts.

The little vessel would disappear at intervals from the eyes of the astonished spectators; then it would suddenly reappear, pitching violently, tightening its anchor-cables till they were taut as iron bars, then would be observed below her hull a portion of her keel, which was shown by a movement not unlike that of a horse rearing upon his haunches.

The entire crowd trembled with affright, while the lugger, now for some seconds immoveable, appeared to regard with carefulness the new billow which menaced it.

Attracted by this interesting spectacle, the people were carried little by little to the extremity of the piers, and, crowded at the entrance to the port, concentrated all their faculties upon the vessel threatened by a speedy destruction.

In the meantime, all were lost in conjecture.

At this moment, three men, arm-in-arm, descended the street which, running from the upper town, led to the fountain of the Leaden Dog.

They were three sailors, true sons of the ocean, with square shoulders, bronze countenances, their pantaloons wide and large, woollen shirts, shoes decked with ribbons, wearing earrings which hung upon their loose and flowing cravats.

Cheeks swelled by the action of the traditional chew of tobacco, a red cap fixed upon the top of the head, nose in the air, large mouth and eyes open like the hawse-holes of a vessel.

And what a gait!

Like that of the two arms forming the grapple! As if the members were dislocated from the true line! It appeared as if the legs, wide apart, were rounded and bent by the rolling of the ship.

Reckless of the breeze which whistled by their ears, all three sang as they advanced to the harbour.

And what voices! what sounds, hoarse, rough, unearthly!

Each one of the three struck up a different air to these old couplets, a *chef-d'œuvre* of the helmsman :—

The captain and the mate,
  Are standing by the guns ;
The bo'-swain by the anchor,
  And he gets a friendly jog
From our right jolly steward
  As he serves out the grog.

By the galley stands the cook
  With his fork and his spoon ;
To the hissing of his coppers
  He hums a merry tune.

While the breeze, both fresh and free,
  Drives us shorewards with glee.

Whilst the singers were thus executing the above symphony to the great delight of the negroes, whose woolly heads appeared here and there, some at the sills of the doors, others at the windows of the houses which stood upon the street, a small boat, making its way through the midst of the vessels, came abreast of that part of the harbour which faced the fountain of the Leaden Dog.

This yawl contained two persons.

One was an old mariner, who, without doubt, had made at least twenty-five or thirty voyages in his adventurous life ; the other was a child of ten or twelve years of age arrayed in the costume of a cabin boy.

On an imperious gesture from his master, the little boy leaped lightly to the land, and, passing an end of the painter within a ring clamped to the wharf, prepared everything for embarkation.

During this time, the old sailor, having tranquilly filled his pipe, lit it with a small bit of tinder which he placed finally in the bowl of the pipe.

The three singers were proceeding upon the pier, shouting as loud as they could bawl the third couplet of their interesting ballad :—

"For our miserable luck
  The calker was to blame ;
When the pumps didn't suck,
  The fo'-castle——"

At this moment the little boy was perceived running to meet them.

"Oh, ho! you are here, Cartahu!" cried one of the trio, addressing the child. "What has brought you on shore, my lad?"

"The yawl is ready, M. Gatifet," responded the cabin-boy, carrying his hand to his cap.

"That's right! Where is your boat?"

"Here, right ahead, with M. Malentrain."

"See," said the mariner, addressing his comrades, "that is a signal of sailing! Adieu to the mulatoes, my friends."

"Yes," said another, "but to return also. Here, we've been at the *grand cafe* for six months, without any pleasure."

"And only to adorn the creoles' head, and fill their skins with plenty," said the third.

"Cut short," brusquely replied Gatifet; "see, there is father Malentrain, with his face to the light breeze which we hail with joy. Embark—and quickly !"

The three men bounded into the boat, in front of which they had arrived.

The boy cast off the painter and shoved off.

The boat, recommencing to glide betwixt the shipping by which it was surrounded, began to take its way towards the road.

Once within the last basin, and more at liberty than before, the three sailors and the boy unshipped each one an oar, and, while father Malentrain remained at the tiller, the little skiff began rapidly to bound over the water.

The wind was blowing right upon the lugger.

At the moment when abreast of Point-aux-Anes, a violent blast of wind seemed as if it would capsize her.

But, by the skill and knowledge of the old sailor, the wave which threatened to swamp them was avoided, and it passed before the yawl, which bounded upon its foaming crest and shot forward defiantly.

"Thunder of Brest!" murmured father Malentrain. "There is always the devil in these voyages commenced on Friday!"

"Well, then, master. Is that what you think of those there," responded Gatifet, tightening his grasp upon the oar.

"I think that which I think, sailor. The week which is come is not passed. Everlasting night-watches! That's not what I said."

"Well!—what? When it does blow very strong, what harm?"

"And you like to pull on the gaskets, do you?"

"Why not? Is it not better than walking around with the handspikes——there is nothing to do after, is there?"

"Eh?—you will have that to do with the end of a boat-hook. Don't fail now, or you'll get more than a glass of salt water. Take care, you others, and watch when we come alongside!"

At this double command, the mariners raised their oars and arranged them along the bottom of the yawl, while two of them, seizing their gaffs, got ready to prevent the little boat dashing violently against the sides of the lugger which it approached.

One man, leaning over the side of the little craft, threw to the boat a coil of rope, which was fastened to the seat, and the sailors leaped upon the deck.

Five minutes after, the yawl swung upon its tackle, sheltered from the waves.

The madmen—as they were thought—were viewed with great astonishment during the course of their embarkation.

'Ah!' said they, 'the lugger will now enter the port. Will they try to come without aid?'

'Yes, it seems so; but it will need great skill to contend against that wind.'

'Oh, there! see that! They are heaving up the port anchor—they are perpendicular above the other.'

'I see the men who are heaving at the capstan,' said a young creole, who, telescope in hand, inspected for some instants the deck of the lugger.

'Is the crew numerous?' demanded one of his neighbours.

'Nearly twenty or thirty men.'

'Ah! it is the starboard anchor that they are tripping up! But does the other one remain now?'

'But look! how it holds against the wind! It is marvellous.'

'See, they are loosening the jib and mainsail. See!' cried a fisherman, standing near the young creole. 'She is only held by the larboard anchor, and that cable so taut. Thunder! they are a rough set of lads on board that craft.'

'It must be very rough on board now,' said the creole. 'It is so stormy out there.'

'Well, well!' said the fisherman, with a gesture of astonishment. 'Her foresail is now loosened! It catches the wind! Thunder! she is getting under weigh quickly.'

'She is sailing!' cried the entire crowd, now freed from the danger to which they thought the lugger was exposed, and seeing that, instead of entering the port, she was standing out to sea.

In fact, the vessel, liberated from her anchors, coquettishly inclined under the wind, and heav-

ing over as if it would overset, bounded lightly over the foaming sea.

During some moments a man could have been seen in the group in which the young creole figured so prominently, watching the movements of the lugger.

This man, with pale face, anxious look, and clenched hand, lost not with his eyes a single motion of the vessel.

As the bark glided over the billows, and departed out of sight of land, he uttered a sigh.

'Ah!' said the creole, as he turned round; 'is that you, Zacharie? Know you the name of that vessel?'

'Yes; that lugger is called the Hazard.'

'The Hazard? Well, she justifies her name by taking to sea at such a time. Is she from the Isle of France?'

'Yes.'

'Bah! who is her owner?'

'I.'

'You, Zacharie?'

'I, myself.'

'But what devil incarnate have you commander of your craft?'

'A lad who arrived from France some months back, and who was anything but coldly recommended by an old friend, in whom I place all confidence.'

'And you call this lad——'

'Robert.'

'What cargo have you on board of her?'

'A lading of powder, bullets, swords, and boarding-pikes.'

'You mock me!' cried the creole, with a burst of laughter.

'Oh, no.'

'What, seriously!—that little lugger?'

'Is in pursuit of the English.'

The interlocutor of Zacharie now reversed the conversation.

'Ah! that is too good,' said he; 'it has only twenty-five men for crew, and possesses but two cannons; your corsair-lugger! The first convoy of the India Company will swallow it whole as a tit-bit, always admitting it escapes the tempest. Go, then! go, then! my poor Zacharie, you are almost as foolish as your adventurous captain. I suppose you think sacks of piastres are strewn over the sea. Happy we, if our plantations are bountiful this year; that is our compensation.'

And the creole, taking the arm of the proprietor of the letter-of-marque, which commenced to vanish in the horizon, turned round and re-entered the town.

The wind blew a little feebler.

The sails of the Hazard, white like the pinions of a sea-gull, were faintly to be discerned upon the border of the sombre sky.

All at once a ray of the sun pierced through an aperture in the cloud, and seemed to fall upon the little bark.

'Ah, ha!' said the fisherman, who had not quitted his post of observation. Ah, ha! The commander of that craft is a roistering tar, that I say; and they're jolly sea-dogs who are embarked on that craft! I'd not pay dear for the first Englishman who comes within her clutch!'

Zacharie, always entertained by the jests which his friend threw out upon his brilliant speculation of which he was the owner, Zacharie, we say, had arrived in front of the *Grand Cafe*, the ordinary resort of the privateer captains and rich creoles who inhabited the city. The young man, without leaving the arm of his companion, passed through the door of the establishment, and entered, followed by Zacharie, into the room.

"Gentlemen," cried he in a railing voice, and addressing a group of smokers, who were seated around a table, "gentlemen, for the future you must acknowledge Zacharie as the master of us all.

He is the only one who has fitted out and armed a letter-of-marque, and we shall see him rolling in the enormous wealth which will be brought in by his superb vessel!"

'What vessel?' asked one of the smokers, with astonishment.

'What one?' said the creole, 'the renowned one which was laying so slugglishly at that point, and you not apprised? Did you not assist for an hour in the excitement attending a certain vestel——'

'The coaster which was out at sea?' interrupted a second interlocutor.

'Herself.'

'And is that one the vessel in question?'

'Just so.'

'Impossible!'

'Ask Zacharie. A nutshell, first-class, captain unknown; there look at that for the present. Fortune, honour, and happiness—all those for the future! Is not that so, Zacharie?'

The owner of the Hazard had but to pronounce a word to cause innumerable bursts of merriment, mixed with mocking laughter from the company.

'I will buy the profits,' cried one.

'I will purchase the cargo on the return,' said another.

'A louis for the whole!' said a third, 'and I demand an association to divide the same.'

'Listen,' said the young creole, making a gesture for a moment of silence. 'I propose a wager. Twenty louis that Zacharie sees not the lugger's return.'

'*Done!*' responded a sonorous voice.

All turned instantly.

A stalwart man of about forty years of age was standing upright before a neighbouring table.

This new personage, whose costume and manners had something about them that it made it easy to declare him a mariner, was tall, with a very powerful figure, and possessed one of those frank and open countenances which command sympathy at the first sight.

He stood still for several seconds, and then approached slowly the laughing group.

'Marcof!' cried the creoles.

And all tendered their open hands with alacrity to the intrepid Breton corsair, who had achieved an universal reputation, and who, supposed to be for some months upon the route to the Indies, they now found returned to the Isle of France.

'My good friends,' replied Marcof, addressing especially the mocking comrade of Zacharie, 'my good friends, you have laid a wager; I will propose another; you are ten and I am one; I bet two hundred louis for the Hazard, and for the captain whom I recommended to Zacharie. Take you against me?'

There was a moment of hesitation; the cou-

rage and experience of Marcof acted upon the laughers with a dampening effect.

Finally, self-love prompted upon the thoughts of those who recovered their natural mood.

'We will take it!' responded the creoles, with the natural exception of the fitter-out of the lugger.

'Then a glass to seal the engagements and prepare your purses, my very dear friends; within six months, perhaps earlier, you will count out my silver. It is Marcof who predicts it.'

CHAPTER CLVII.

ROBERT, THE BRETON.

NOTWITHSTANDING the observations of the young creole, the little bark, which M. Zacharie had confided to the command of an unknown sailor, had not a very terrible appearance.

But if her model was delicate, in requital she was well formed for pursuit or flight.

Her mizen mast inclined coquettishly.

Her deck, large, level, well-arranged, presented the appearance of a man-of-war.

Her two carronades, poised upon their carriages, bent downwards by their tackles, passed their menacing mouths through the open portholes.

Leaping lightly over the waves, her cutwater dashing away a froth of snowy scum, her stern leaving a small valley in her wake, the lugger rapidly coursed towards the African coast.

The wind had slackened a little, but still the sea ran high.

The trim of the lugger was truly fearful, and it seemed as if the man at the helm must need an active eye, a sure hand, and great presence of mind to avoid all danger.

In the meantime the little craft had given to the breeze a great portion of her sails.

She was under her jib, her mainsail, her mizen, and her topsails.

The fourth watch was upon deck.

These men, careless of the peril by which they were menaced, were, the ones stretched at the foot of the mainmast, the others leaning against the bulwarks, laughing, talking, spinning yarns, yet were ready to obey the first order of their chief.

Malentrain, his whistle suspended upon his breast—an inevitable accompaniment of a boatswain—leant on his elbows at the forward extremity of the bulwarks, and regarded philosophically the waves as they burst into foam on the starboard.

Catifet, placed a few paces from the old seaman, was in conversation with one of his companions, embarked in quality of novice, to whom he was imparting and explaining, by the aid of his highly-coloured language, all the joys which attended a crew engaged in an enterprise such as was the lugger.

'When we get to the Indies,' said he, 'it will all be well. The captain has engaged that. Ah, the Indies, then you will speak! That's the country fot pleasure. It is a paradise, that! Always battles and gold. The women pretty like true loves, and yellow as that old topman; and the fruits and liquors! all that; and the beasts there—the serpents, boas, tigers in profusion, alligators enough to satisfy all; all that, and more. Ah! what a country! Is that not so, master?'

This last phrase of his discourse was addressed directly to Malentrain.

The old tar made an affirmative gesture, and then said, in a voice very intelligible,

'Don't forget! Friday carries bad luck. I have said it.'

'Aloft, there, topmen!' cried a voice, vibrating and clear as a bell. 'Let go the flying-jib and staysails!'

'Ah! that is the manager of all,' murmured Gatifot, as he sprang up the rigging.

The order being at once obeyed, the sailors resumed their former indolent attitude.

One man stood by the mainmast, and attentively regarded the horizon.

This person was the commander of the lugger. His name was Robert.

His costume differed but little from that of the rest of the crew. He wore pantaloons of grey stuff, a shirt of blue wool, a red sash, and a vest of grey cloth. A cap surrounded by a thin stripe of gold lace was the sole sign by which he was distinguished.

Robert was a man of twenty-five or thirty years.

He was tall, supple, alert, robust, and vigorously formed.

His face, covered with freckles, was large and broad; it was surrounded by a forest of rude and coarse hair.

His eyebrows were thick, his nose flat, his eyes like a deer, small but brilliant. His lips moved without cessation.

After what we have said, Robert was not handsome. But when any emotion, enthusiasm, hate, love, or anger, was reflected upon that vulgar physiognomy, it suddenly transformed its whole aspect.

Thus was Robert himself.

His head was proudly raised, the pupil of his eye darted about with rapidity, his brow irradiated, his mouth well cut, above which his nostrils were strongly dilated, and with that general expression of the visage, which denoted nobleness of heart, the vigorous disposition of spirit, audacity, courage, intelligence, and perhaps of genius.

His was an image of physical force allied to moral power.

One comprehended the irresistible ascendance which this man would have upon the masses, and one would not be astonished at the devotion without bound and confidence without limit, which inspired those who were under his order.

What had conducted Robert to the port of Saint Malo, and caused him, an humble person, but lately coasting along the shores of Bretagne and Normandy, to solicit, of a ship owner of the Isle of France, the command of a microscopic corsair, and given him the boldness to finally cause the merchant to deliver to him the sole command of the venture?

Which sentiment had made him abandon the bays and inlets of La Manche for the vast majestic fleets of the Indian Ocean.

This passion, which had caused ambition to develop in the heart of Robert, was another sentiment more powerful than all the others—by the love of a pretty young girl, lately, like him, upon the Breton earth.

Well—yes—Robert was loved, and loved Mademoiselle Louise Marcy, the very rich inheritess of Saint Malo.

He, a poor sailor, more than obscure, to aspire to the love of a child of Madame Marcy, the opulent widow!—certainly that was folly.

The difference of conditions was enough to lead the most sanguine to despair of annihilating it; but Robert was of an age when hopelessness rarely enters into the heart of man.

What means could he employ to forget Louise, or the distance which separated them.

How can love be divided?

This was of course only conjecture: but that in some measure confirmed it was that, upon a fine evening in autumn and sheltered from all indiscreet regards, Louise, leaning over the window-sill, answered in reply to the deep voice of her adorer—

'My mother will grant my hand to none but a rich man,' said she.

'Well, I will be so,' responded Robert. 'If you will but wait eighteen months, I will return richer than you are yourself.'

And the young girl ejaculated mentally—

'Or I shall die!'

Then, fixing his clear gaze upon Mademoiselle Marcy—

'You promise me, Louise?' continued he in a low voice.

'I swear to you, Robert!'

'Well! give me your hand, that I may touch it lightly to my lips, and have the kiss as a pledge of our mutual feeling.'

Louise tendered her two little hands, which Robert pressed tenderly to his mouth.

Robert passed that night without sleep.

Of all the means by which one could obtain a rapid fortune, that which seemed the most simple and the most pleasing to Mademoiselle Marcy, was to enrich himself from the enemies of France.

To be a privateer's-man came thus the dominant idea of the young man.

But the grave, insurmountable difficulties were presented at once to his view.

To engage upon a vessel making a cruise was easy enough; yet Robert was not desirous to do so. The result was too distant—the prizemoney could not be enormous for a common seaman.

Then the reputation which would be acquired would give his name honour enough to espouse the daughter of the rich Madame Marcy.

On the other side, Robert an obscure sailor, could not hope to obtain the confidence of a wealthy ship-owner.

A corsair captain was not a vain title at that epoch. To obtain it they must give long and energetic proofs and skill, audacity and maritime experience.

A vessel was much too precious to be lost at the first venture.

Many of the ports of Brittany abounded with men seeking the honours and advantages of commanding, and having eligible antecedants.

Then, within La Manche there was assembled more vessels of war than merchantmen.

Robert depressed by these series of reflections, little consolatory, was, despite of his ordinary strength of mind, thrown down by despair and encouragement, suddenly had a brilliant idea which he determined to act upon directly.

'If I quit Europe?' said he. 'If I go from the Isle of France, and solicit a position. There a double advantage! the privateer captains are

few, and the fleets of the India Company have immense fortunes in their holds.'

And, without further reflection, the young man resolved to put his project in execution.

Alone—without any one to aid him in his enterprise; because who would believe his words about creole merchants, who had but a poor navy at their disposal.

As for the travelling thither, although Robert had a valiant soul, he was inquieted a little.

To pay his passage, he engaged as a sailor.

And there a protector was found.

Robert discovered a friend of his father's, a mariner like himself, and one of the bravest corsairs of Brittany; this friend was named Marcof, and was like Robert.

By some happy hazard, Marcof was at Saint Malo for five days. His vessel moored in the roadstead was on the point of putting to sea, Robert on board.

He experienced much emotion when presented face to face with the terrible Breton who had achieved such a universal reputation.

On giving his name, Robert was received with encouraging favour.

At the same time, by a freedom provoked by the corsair, he recounted simply his love and his plans.

He told him for what he was to apply.

Marcof heard him without interruption, and attentively contemplated the ardent expression which was shown upon the young man's features.

'I like ambition,' said he, finally, 'when that ambition has such a noble object. Thy father was my friend; I wish to be thine. I am going myself to the Isle of France; bring your bag, and install yourself on board my vessel. Once there, I will promise to you a position in the service of a fitter-out of these privateers, and thus put you at the first step of your fortune.

The rest depends upon yourself.

You are brave and determined; if the bullets do not send you to the other world, you will succeed.'

Marcof rose as he spoke, and prepared to take leave of his interlocutor.

The latter opened his mouth to express his thankfulness, but he could not find a word to paint the tumultuous feelings which agitated his heart.

A tear coursed down his already bronzed cheek.

Marcof placed his hand on the shoulder of the young sailor, and plunged a profound glance into his eyes.

'I invite myself to the wedding,' said he, gravely; 'because if all is true before me, you merit the union and success. God loves and protects valiant souls. Remain true to that saying.'

That same evening, Robert was installed on board the letter-of-marque, which the day after fired its parting gun.

At the dawning of day, and as the tide rose, the vessel, hoisting its white sails, launched out upon the immensity of the ocean.

Robert, at the stern, cast a long look towards the land upon which was left all that was loved by his heart.

Children played upon the strand; the sky was clear and cloudless, the waves but slight.

At a distance a pretty young girl, leaning from the window, contemplated the horizon.

The young sailor was in that situation so decisive to a man who leaves to Destiny his future existence.

His heart was pure; he hoped.

A few months after, Robert arrived without accident upon the shore of the Isle of France.

Then Marcof, holding religiously to his promise, called upon the ship-owner, Zacharie, to whom he recommended Robert.

Zacharie had not a vessel at his disposal, he said, but he would do his best, and Robert waited some time.

During this time, Marcof travelled the sea, and finally reached Port Louis.

Robert always attended him.

Marcof again sought Zacharie, and so influenced him by his description of the gifts of fortune which would undoubtedly befall his his *protege* that the creole decided to sacrifice anything to oblige the corsair.

Thus it was that he came to announce his determination to confer a little vessel upon the young sailor.

Robert was in all haste to profit by this hardy good will.

At the moment of sailing, Zacharie regretted bitterly his having put a portion of his maritime property in the hands of a man so foolish and mad, and deplored the hasty confidence expressed to Marcof.

This having been said, the poor merchant, gazing at his lugger, an hour after its leaving the roads, pitching under the effect of the breeze with a force which threatened its entire destruction in the sea.

As for the young commander, his countenance impassive, and his eye ever watching, he stood by the mainmast.

It was now seven months since Robert had quitted Louise, and, true to his word, he was, with two cannons and twenty-five men for crew, engaged, in less than a year, to gain a fortune equal to that of Mademoiselle Marcy.

CHAPTER CLVIII.

THE TRITONS.

To the east of the almost island of India, since the road of Balasore almost joins the Strait of Manaar, is the terrible Coromandel coast, so well known for shipwrecks, storms, and perils of all sorts.

Deprived of harbours and ports, beaten by an incessant surge, it presents jagged rocks to the furious billows which form a triple line of foam between the shore and vessels at large.

The sea breaks with a tumultuous rage upon the rampart of granite which forms the neighbouring coast, and debarking is rendered impossible for all European means, which would be annihilated in less than an instant.

To gain the shore, one is compelled to call upon the services of *katemarans*, indigenous barks, primitive boats, made of a hide, in the formation of which there enters neither nails nor pegs, and the portions are joined, the ones to the others by the aid of a great seam, formed of the flax stripped from the cocoa-nuts.

This sort of pirogue dances upon the waves, and moves with a marvellous rapidity under one slightest impulse given by its vigorous rowers.

A native sailor at the helm—performing at the same time the functions of pilot and chief director—governed the bark, and gave the diapason to the crew, who were singing a most lamentable chant, medley of all the *patios* of the coast, the most monotonous notes, and the most discordant tones of the octave.

This was one of those frail skiffs, manned by the stupid Indians, who, from three hundred leagues of coast, transported from time immemorial the Europeans brought from the Indies, and the prodigious treasures of the East departing to the West.

Two months had now passed since the Hazard had quitted the Isle of France.

It was now the last hours of the day, and the beams of light irradiated from a sky without clouds, dazzled the eye, and were reflected upon the arid rocks.

The heat was grievously oppressive.

Madras displayed, under the glistening rays, the sumptuousness of its edifices, half oriental and half European. Like ancient Carthage with its elegant constructions and its wealthy population whose treasures gleamed beneath the ardour of the sun.

One perceived, relieved upon the azure horizon, the governor's house, the Cathedral of Saint George, the pinnacles of a mosque, or a pagoda, the nodding tufts of the cocoa-nut trees and the clusters of the sacred fig-trees, waving their variegated limbs or their shadowy branches, the coolness and the rest of a bronzed multitude who murmured, fumed, laboured, and performed their ablutions in the open air with all the carelessness of a world without shame.

The white population, carefully enclosed within their charming houses with terraced roofs, defied all the endeavours of a burning sun to penetrate within.

At sea, two vessels solely were at anchor.

One was a little craft, having the appearance of the numerous pilot-boats which throng the Gulf of Bengal, and whose duty it is to show to shipping, desiring their aid, a way of penetrating within the waters of the Ganges.

The other was a magnificent East-Indiaman, arrived from Bombay, and touching at Balasore previous to sailing finally to Calcutta.

This vessel was embarking, from Madras, a numerous freight of merchandize which the traders of the Coromandel Coast were thus despatching to the merchants of the Ganges.

Moored some leagues from the town, she majestically elevated her large hull, and balanced easily upon the gentle waves.

Twenty-four guns broadside, as many upon her deck, two hundred men as crew, responded sufficiently to the shippers as surety for the wealth which was confided to her hold.

This ship, one of the strongest that appertained to the East India Company, was named the Triton.

During the day a continued communication was kept up between the Triton and the town.

The katemarans—rude crafts conducted by the blacks of the Makona tribe—transported boxes, cases, bundles, and packages of all sizes, which the sailors arranged within the hold.

An extreme agitation reigned upon the deck.

Officers, midshipmen, mates, boatswains and fore-hands, remained strictly to their duties, the one commanding, the others obeying and working.

A skiff, within hail from the larboard, threatened to be sunk under the weight of the enormous cases by which it was encumbered.

A man of tall stature, dressed in the costume of a passably wealthy trader, half-bent over the ship's sides, regarded with anxious solicitude particularly the operation of disembarcation.

Once the boxes were placed upon the deck, having been raised by means of a stay-tackle, they were removed by a half-dozen of workmen.

The man, of whom we have spoken, did not for a moment allow his eyes to pass from his cases, and gazing into the depths of the hold, he checked not his recommendations all of kinds, having apparently no thought but for the preservation of his goods.

'Takee care—takee care!' cried he, in bad English, 'or you will breakee my boxes. Ah! if they only go safely. My friends, they are all my fortune. Takee great care, I implore you. There, that more than the others,' and the man designated an enormous coffer formed of solid oak—'that above all. Look out, at the bottom of the hold—there—carry the others here. Thank you, my friends, my good friends, my good English. And my casks of rum—and such rum!—it is the most exquisite!—take care you don't break them. Ah! it is my fortune I confide to you."

The sailors smiled and shrugged their shoulders, without appearing to notice the entreaties of the worthy merchant, who elevated his hands to heaven, seeming to be a prey to the utmost inquietude.

'This M. Michael is very tiresome,' said a young officer, turning towards the second mate of the vessel, who cast an indifferent glance upon the anxious trader.

'Tiresome is the word. Since he has been here, we are wearied by the questions, 'Is the ship strong? Is the wind favorable? Is the Triton perfectly prepared in case of an attack?' and a hundred others of a like nature. Instead of five miserable cases that he has embarked, one would think he had confided to the Triton the mines of Peru.'

'But he is French, is he not?'

'Of course!—that is easily known by his accent.'

'Well, then,' said the young officer, continuing, 'if this merchandise is captured it will be a lucky thing.'

'Not so. The rogue has put them under the protection of the English flag for the continuance of his trade. He abandons Pondicherry, and is to re-establish himself in Calcutta.'

'Has he been a long while in the town?'

'Five days nearly, so they tell me. He waited for the first vessel of the company which touched at Madras.'

At this moment, M. Michael interrupted the conversation of the two officers.

'My dear sir,' said he, addressing himself to the mate, 'I wish to speak to the commander.'

'The commander is not on board.'

'Where then is he?'

'On shore.'

'Then I would ask you—'

'Oh, sir,' interrupted the other, 'I have something else to do besides answering. So, it is useless for you to annoy me with your foolish questions. If you wish to speak to the commander, go on shore. As for me, I do not like the French sufficiently to submit to their company.'

M. Michael bent his head at these plain-spoken words, muttered some excuses, and moved backwards.

The officer turned his back upon him.

The poor trader, thus abashed, ceased to watch the removal of his goods, and sought to re-embark upon the boat which had brought them; but, doubtless, little habituated to maritime travelling, he caught in the rigging, narrowly escaping being thrown overboard at the slightest motion of the ship, and approached the bulwarks, where, clinging to the bottom of a mast, he seemed totally to have lost his senses.

Sailors and master's-mates laughed without stint, and hurled upon M. Michael all the mockeries and gibes which his double character of a Frenchman and an inexperienced navigator called forth.

The unlucky man, without a word, without appearing to understand the insults which fell upon him, descended into the skiff with an awkwardness which augmented the gaiety of the crew.

The boat shoved off, and was directed to the land under the efforts of the native seamen, howling their startling chant.

M. Michael was stretched upon a seat in the stern.

When the bark had moved some distance from the Triton, the merchant's countenance was changed to a singular aspect.

His figure, rising gradually, quitted the half-bent position which he affected some instants before.

The frail craft bore the pitching of the sea, to and fro, backwards and forwards, as it glided between the crests of two waves.

The man who had been so mocked at by the

English seamen for at least an hour—this man who walked upon the deck of the Triton with such difficulty—suffered with quiet carelessness the frightful shocks which menaced the destruction of the frail bark.

The expression of his countenance was not the same; the humility, the deference, the stupidity, the inquietude which he wore before the crew of the East-Indiaman, had become by degrees dark, terrible, and menacing.

The light of intelligence brightened up the looks which M. Michael cast upon the Triton.

'Forty-eight guns,' murmured he; 'two hundred men—plenty of arms—thunder!—but more than four millions!—two months with nothing to do. Yes! if I had only ten guns and a crew of fifty men.'

And, in saying the above, the eye of M. Michael was directed from the English vessel to the little craft moored at a distance, and which had been taken for a pilot-boat of the Ganges.

The merchant gave vent to a sigh.

Finally the skiff grated upon the strand. Two men, leaping into the water, which mounted to their girdle, presented their shoulders to M. Michael.

The features of the latter resumed their former timid expression.

Clinging to his bearers, he was conducted almost upon the quay, whe he was deposited in the gentlest possible manner.

Once upon land, he threw some money to the Indians, and directed his way to the white city. Madras is divided into two distinct parties, the white and the black; that is Europe and Asia separated by an esplanade.

Scarcely had M. Michael advanced some paces within one of the umbrageous avenues of trees which serve as streets to the European town, than a man who had been crouching at the foot of an old wall raised himself quickly and followed him.

This man, even to his copper-coloured skin, had all the appearance of a native.

M. Michael made him a sign, and the person, who had stopped some steps from the trader, approached close to him.

M. Michael threw around him a rapid glance, This part of the avenue was deserted.

'Master!' said he quickly, addressing the Indian, 'are all on board?'

'Yes, captain,' responded the new comer; 'all is ready.'

'The carronades in the hold?'

'Yes.'

'Few of the men upon deck?'

'They are but five only. The others are in the orlop-deck, and there they can't see the nose on their faces.'

'Right. You will return on board.'

'Yes, captain.'

'You will have all ready to get under weigh to-night without fail.'

'Yes, sir.'

'Have the crew the appearance of pilots of the Ganges?'

'Their skin is as yellow as mine, which they say is like a porpoise skin.'

'That is all they say on board?'

'They say—saving your presence, commander—they say nothing; they do nothing but chew their cuds. Damme! that they well know, I would cram them down their throats with a marlinspike if they gabbled.'

'Well, treat them to a glass of rum; this evening we go on the chase.'

'Not possible.'

'Take care. You bray like an ass.'

'Pardon me, captain, that is the effect of joy. They will all say a word to the English?'

'Yes.'

'Thunder of Brest! to them they will not be straws of iron.'

'Silence! and go forward. In an hour I will be aboard.'

The pretended Indian respectfully bowed, and as he glanced in the direction of the sea, he murmured, in a bass voice—

'Thunder of Brest! all would be well if we had not sailed on Friday.'

M. Michael had by this time gained the white portion of the town.

The merchant soon quitted the avenue, and proceeded along a street which ran around at the rear of the Church of St. George.

It was after six o'clock, and the heat was too furious for the most venturesome of the inhabitants to dare to encounter.

M. Michael, passing through the deserted streets of Madras, thought it a town completely uninhabited.

At the moment of turning an angle of a house of rich appearance, he heard the murmur of a voice which seemed almost upon him.

The merchant stopped, and, measuring his paces, he cautiously advanced.

On the other side of the mansion was a straight alley, little frequented at any hour of the day.

A curious and discreet regard on the part of M. Michael caused him at once to comprehend the source of the voice which had struck upon his ears.

One of the low windows was open, and at its base stood a young man of eighteen or twenty summers, wearing the elegant uniform of a midshipman.

Above the blonde head of young Englishman appeared another head, with superb blue eyes and long curls dressed *en diademe*.

The latter appertained to a young girl of the same age, or younger than the sailor, and who, her hands clasped within those of her interlocutor, fixed upon him long and tender glances.

M. Michael had evidently interrupted the conversation of the lovers.

The worthy man stopped anew, fearful of disarranging this charming *tete-a-tete*.

The young people were speaking of love, of projects of union, of their happy future, and thinking of better times than at present, and the to-be of that adorable word love, which has an equivalent in all languages.

In listening to the dialogue, broken now and then by sighs or tender pressing or the hands, M. Michael wept, and, in spite of his grey beard, his countenance took a strange expression of youth.

But though the sight of the lovers had caused him to lose his character for one of gaiety and spirit, yet his features again became sad and serious.

The poor children voyaged since one hour upon the ocean of tumultuous billows, of winds always prosperous, of a sky always pure, which the future presents to the foolish and too ardent imaginations of youth, to accomplish the voyage called life—and they cast but a look upon Time

BOARDING OF THE TRITON.

which would thereafter show all as a present reality.

The midshipman raised his thoughtful face, and a tear obscured the limpid and diamond-like pupils of his pretty companion.

The words of departure, of separation, and of eternal farewell, were received also by the ear of the indiscreet listener.

'Oh!' said the young sailor, with flaming eyes, fixing an ardent expression upon the delicate countenance of his interlocutor; 'oh, my Cecily, if I were but rich, if I possessed only five hundred pounds, our happiness would be completely assured.'

'What would you do then, George?' demanded the girl.

'What could I not do, Cecily? I but repeat for the hundredth time that that would quiet your uncle whom you detest.'

'Alas! it is too true.'

'Well, if I had this money, we could, as is not likely we will, depart this evening for Calcutta or Bombay, to another residence, in short. There, we are one; you are my wife, and we would embark upon the first vessel which leaves for England.'

'But that would be deserting your post, George. The ship to which you belong also departs this evening.'

'Yes; but it will return in two months or more. Oh, my God! my God! how distressing to be poor!'

'You must leave me, my friend, and accept some other's hand.'

'I give you up? Oh, no! I love too much. Cecily, before renouncing you, I would suffer a thousand deaths!'

A white hand, tapping the cheeks of the young man, cut short the articulation of the last word. M. Michael still listened; but the sounds were so low, that nothing distinct reached his ear. He murmured, in a deep bass, the soft name of woman, and suffered a sigh to escape from his chest.

This sigh, echoing in the midst of such profound calmness, disturbed the security of the lovers.

The young girl retired precipitately, and the window, which for more than an hour had encased her graceful form, closed sharply.

The midshipman, on his part, turned and found himself face to face with M. Michael.

The figure of the latter had regained its former mask of humility.

'Pardon, sir,' said he, bowing with an exaggerated obsequiousness; 'a thousand pardons. Have I not the honour of speaking to an officer of the Triton?'

'Yes, sir,' said the sailor, politely.

'Could you inform me where I will find Captain Williams at this moment?'

'The captain? He is most likely at this hour in the mansion of his cousin, Sir Berkely.'

'And Sir Berkely's house is situated——'

'But two steps from here—there, to the right, at the end of this street.'

'Thank you, sir; I thank you most sincerely.'

And M. Michael, bowing still lower than the first time, quitted the midshipman, and directed his way towards the indicated spot.

Five minutes after, the captain received the French trader in his ante-chamber.

Captain Williams was a man of forty years of age, straight, spare, angular, with an impassible physiognomy, red hair, and imbued as much as possible with English rudeness and prejudices.

Cordially detesting the French, whom he profoundly scorned, he thought it but his duty to humble the Pondichery trader by a long attendance.

Finally he decided to have M. Michael introduced to him.

The latter entered, half bent, his countenance submissive; whilst the English officer, with raised head and lighted cigar in his lips, designated only by a slight motion the chair upon which he wished him to be seated.

'What do you wish?' demanded the captain, throwing a look of contumely upon poor M. Michael, who seemed too fearful to move.

'But, commander, I wish—I demand——'

'What?'

'That is, to propose that my goods——'

'Well, they are safe on board.'

'I would recommend to you——'

'To the deuce with your recommendations. You appear to think that, instead of your paltry ware which is to be delivered at Bombay, you had confided a throw of the pearl-fishery. My word! these French are so stupid.'

'Ah! you have pearls of the Persian Gulf!' said M. Michael, his eye for a moment flashing at the insult to his countrymen; though like lightning the flash disappeared.

'Eh! I have many more valuable, by ——! Think you that a ship of the East India Company is charged with such insignificant merchandise as lie in the hold of the miserable canoes of your nation? I tell you,' continued the naval officer, desirous of finding a new means of humiliating the French trader, by enlarging upon the wealth which was contained in his vessel, 'I tell you there are more than twelve millions of francs within the hold of the Triton!'

'Twelve millions!' cried the trader. 'They said but four.'

'You speak of your miserable bales!' exclaimed the officer, without taking the least notice of the response of his interlocutor. 'One grain of dust in a vase of gold!'

'Twelve millions!' again repeated M. Michael, and he replied with an expression of inquietude— 'All this is then in surety on your vessel with my valuables?'

Captain Williams shrugged his shoulders.

'The Triton is strong,' said he.

'That is much needed upon these coasts; the French privateers——'

'The French privateers!' replied the commander, with a gesture of scorn. 'If the knaves venture within these seas, think you they will have the audacity to attack a vessel of the Company with their cockle-shells? Ah, by my faith! I wish so. I would feel great pleasure in hanging some of the rascals at the yard-arm; but enough—I but lose time in addressing you. Only remember this well: I consent to take your merchandise under English protection and the British flag; but as to your person, I positively refuse to allow you with them. Almost a Frenchman, you stand not upon the vessel's decks or take passage.'

'Captain!'

'Enough!' said the Englishman, rising. 'Take care, or I will revoke my decision.'

And with a motion, the naval officer indicated the door to his interlocutor.

The latter bowed humbly, but before he regained an upright position, the Englishman turned on his heel, and passed into an adjoining room.

The merchant, taking his hat in his hand, quitted the residence and re-took his way towards the wharves of the town.

Arrived at its northern extremity, he stopped some instants upon a mass of rocks, and contemplated philosophically the magnificent spectacle which was then passing under his dazzled eyes.

The sun, setting in the west, extended its rays horizontally upon the surface of the ocean, which reflected all the tints of the opal and the mother-of-pearl, while from it floated cold vapours whose white forms floated phantom-like over the sparkling crests of the waves, and amidst the rigging of the Triton and upon the low masts of the pilot-boat.

Only the dark zone of the forests which cover the low grounds to the west of Madras, and behind which moved visibly the orb of day, intervened its dark shadow, from which were detached the monuments of the city, its villas and its palms.

A southern breeze was blowing.

The Triton, which had finished embarking her cargo, was ready to start.

In less than a quarter of an hour from the time when we saw M. Michael absorbed in the contemplation of this scene, Captain Williams appeared upon the quay.

He was accompanied by some friends, whom he shook cordially by the hand before entering the skiff which was ready.

Then the bark shot forward into the river, gained the ship, and the English officer mounted gravely upon the deck.

At this moment, the solar disc disappeared below the horizon, and an immense jet of transparent green, thrown from the invisible prism, now occupied the place, and marked almost exactly the route which the vessel pursued.

Neither pen nor pencil could depict the variety of forms and movements which this flame showed in all the mystic undulations of its fading light; a net-work of gold and fire, it was a spectacle to which nothing could be compared.

Then the interval was but short between the disappearance of the sun, and the falling of the shades of night, and soon the celestial dome was studded with diadems of brilliant stars.

The Triton seemed but a shapeless black mass upon the silvered crest of the waves.

Sometimes, when a ray of the moon fell upon her port-holes, one could perceive the muzzle of her guns, and distinguish the numerous sailors of the watch, who were keeping their vigil upon her deck.

CHAPTER CLVIX.

THE PILOT-BOAT.

THE darkness was complete, and during the two hours which had passed since M. Michael had taken his position at the extremity of the wharf, it had not been disturbed by a single incident.

M. Michael's eyes, ardently fixed on the East Indiamen, indicated the profound attention which the merchant had given to all the evolutions of the vessel on leaving land.

Often an energetic resolution fired his glances, but this flame disappeared as quickly as it had come.

Evidently the interior thoughts of M. Michael were of a violent cast.

At the moment when the form of the Triton commenced to be lost in the darkness, the French trader seemed suddenly to have taken a resolution.

Rising quickly, he struck his feet to the earth, and uttered an energetic oath.

Then, directing his steps towards a boat whose crew were busily engaged in taking a light repast ere they embarked, he leaped into the boat, and gave the order for the Indians to row him on board the pilot boat moored at a quarter of a league from the strand, where since a few instants, her rigging had appeared singularly to elongate.

Was this an optical effect, an aberration of the sense of view? So some affirm; but true it was that the vessel had taken a new aspect.

One would have sworn that the mainmast and mizzen-mast had increased from the deck to the top, add from thence to the top-gallant mast, and that the bowsprit itself prolonged its horizontal line, as also the jib-booms.

As the distance decreased suppositions varied, and when within hail they changed to certitude.

The pilot-boat, more than an hour firmly moored, was held by but one anchor, whose cable, passing through a hawse-hole, fell perpendicularly into the waves, and indicated by its position that it could be a trip in a few seconds.

In fact, some men were standing, their arms resting upon the capstan-bars.

The topmen, suspended on the yards, were all ready to set sail.

At a call from the boatswain's whistle the vessel took its flight.

The skiff rapidly approached.

M. Michael was prepared for the time when they should range side by side with the little craft. At the expected moment, he seized an end of rope, and lightly sprang upon the deck.

The Indian boat shoved off.

Scarcely had the trader set foot upon the planks than an instantaneous transformation took place.

By a turn of his hand he cast off the grey hair that covered his brow, and, tearing from him his clothing, donned instead a sailor'r vest which was presented by a boy.

M. Michael, the timid trader, the humble Frenchman bowing before the officers of the British vessel, was replaced by Robert, the hardy corsair, the daring adventurer.

With the eye of a master he inspected the deck of the lugger, late the Pilot-boat, for it also had abandoned its disguise for war-like attire.

The carronades, remounted upon their carriages, were trailed in the rear.

Every one stood at his post.

Malentrain approached his chief.

'Well?' demanded the latter.

'All is ready,' replied the old master.

'Heave away, then! Hearty—alert—and vigorous!'

The seamen, by a few turns of the bars, caused the anchor to hang dripping at its place.